Praise for *A PRINCE'S ERRAND*

"Absolutely fantastic! [In *A Prince's Errand*] you get those hints of the *Wheel of Time*—that huge epic scale Robert Jordan really tried to produce. You get that sense of majesty with the books that Brandon Sanderson writes. There is a gritty realism to it with something like Robert E. Howard, with threads of David Eddings... [*A Prince's Errand*] is a beautiful, beautiful piece of passion. If you're looking to pick up a book that will keep you hooked for a long, long time, make sure to get this book."

—Cameron Day, Comics, Clerics, & Controllers

"*A Prince's Errand* is an intricately crafted tale of high fantasy that is as rich in detail as it is in entertainment."

—Michael Cole, Design Wizard Blog: Top 50 Wattpad Books of 2018

DAN ZANGARI & ROBERT ZANGARI

A PRINCE'S ERRAND

Book One of
TALES OF THE AMULET

A LOK PUBLISHING BOOK • SALT LAKE CITY

LEGENDS OF KALDA®

Tales of the Amulet

A PRINCE'S ERRAND

Paperback Edition

Copyright ©2018 Dan Zangari & Robert Zangari
All rights reserved.

Made in the U.S.A.

Cover Art by Kerem Beyit
Chapter Heading Illustrations by Suleyman Temiz
Cartography by Robert Zangari

Edited by Linda Branam

First Printing: December 3rd, 2019
First Paperback Edition: June 16th, 2019

ISBN 10-digit: 1-947673-02-5

ISBN 13- digit: 978-1-947673-02-1

Visit our web site at www.legendsofkalda.com

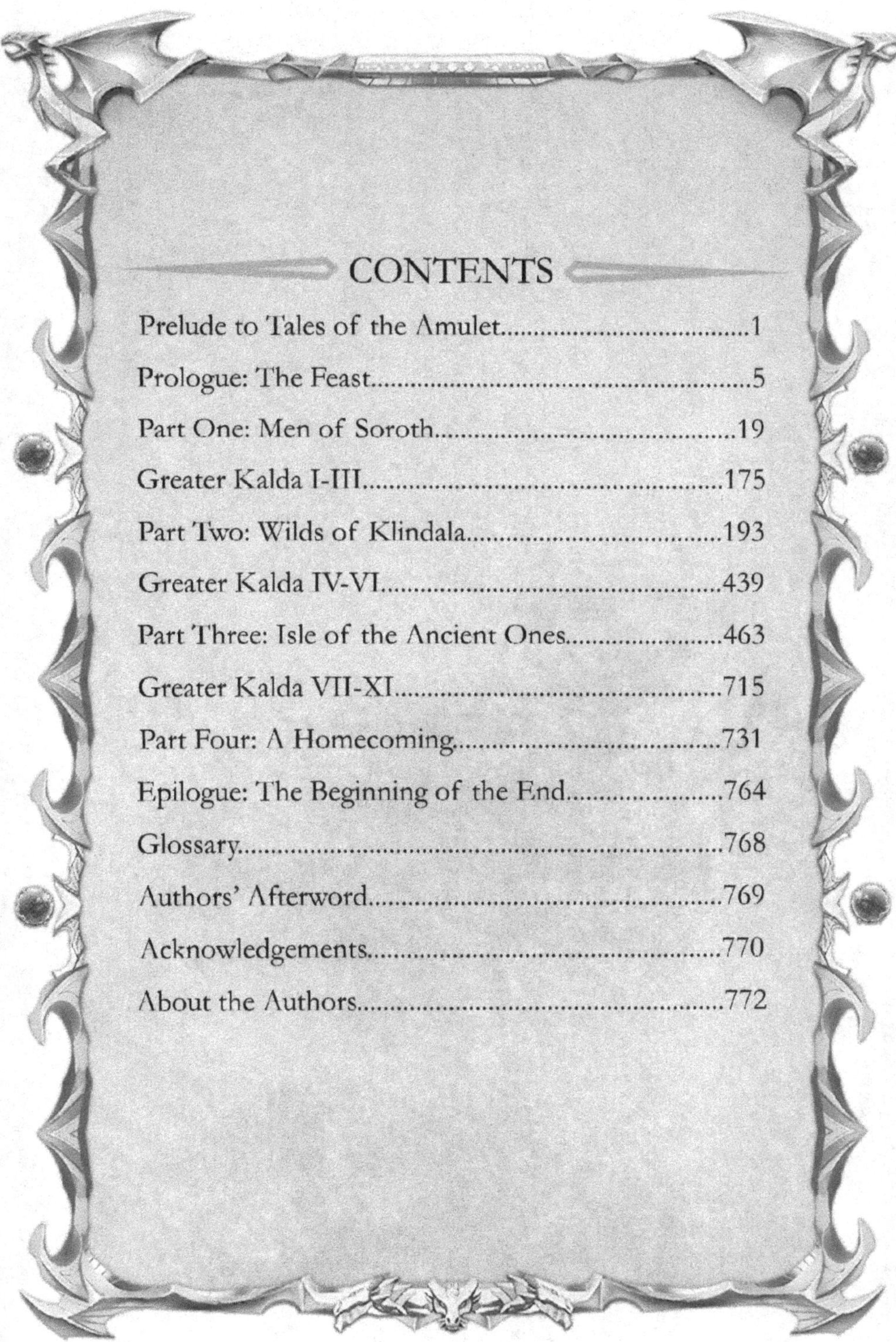

CONTENTS

For Tamila,

Who thought this story was

"Actually good."

Without you this story

Wouldn't have become what it is today.

You've truly been

An inspiration.

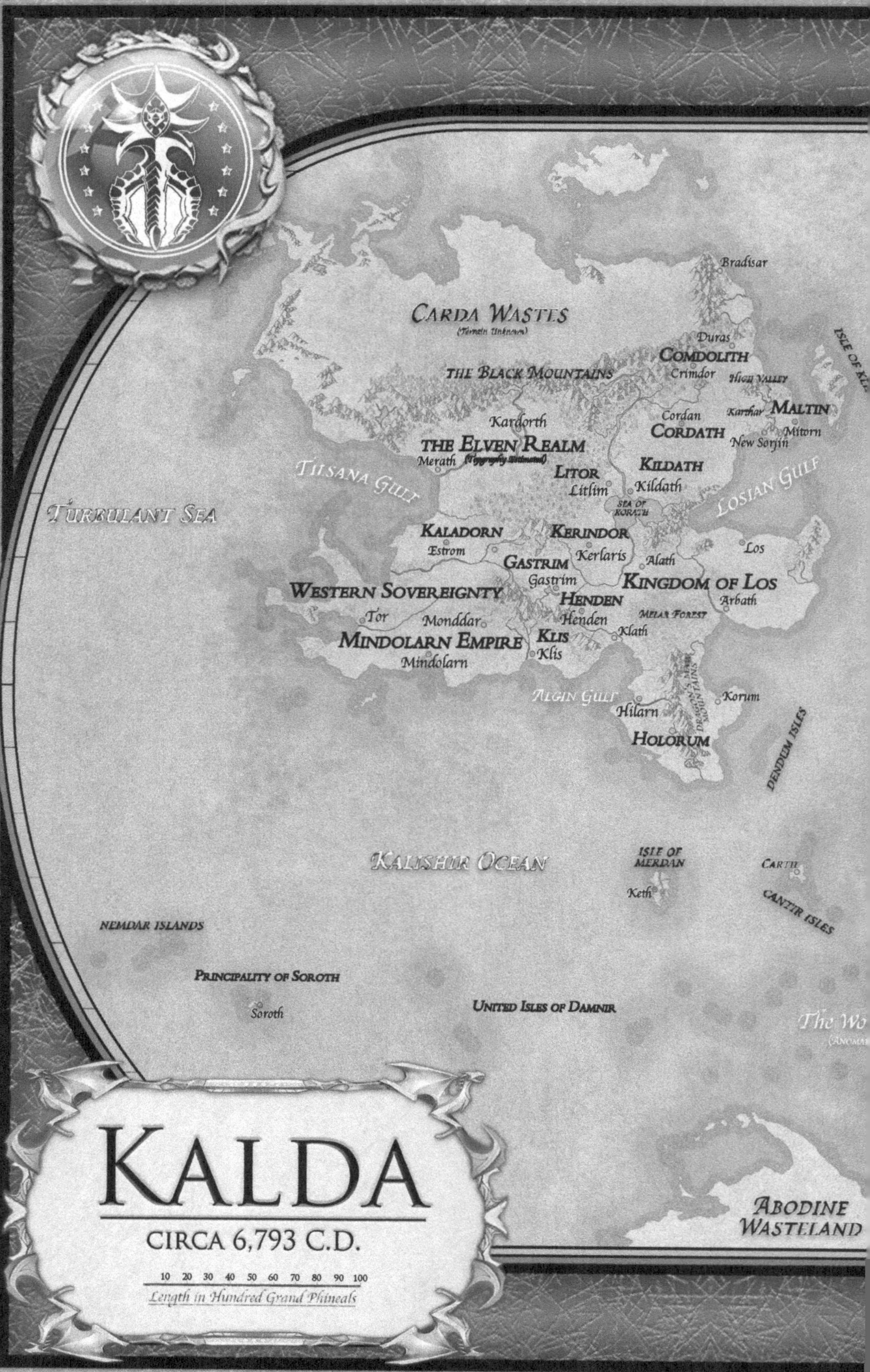

Carda Wastes
(Terrain Unknown)
Bradisar
Duras
Comdolith
Crimdor
High Valley
The Black Mountains
Kardorth
Cordan
Karthar
Maltin
Mitorn
Cordath
New Sorjin
The Elven Realm
Merath
(Topography Estimated)
Tilsana Gulf
Litor
Litlim
Kildath
Kildath
Losian Gulf
Sea of Korath
Turbulant Sea
Kaladorn
Estrom
Kerindor
Kerlaris
Alath
Los
Gastrim
Gastrim
Kingdom of Los
Western Sovereignty
Henden
Arbath
Tor
Monddar
Henden
Melas Forest
Klath
Mindolarn Empire
Klis
Klis
Mindolarn
Algin Gulf
Hilarn
Korum
Holorum
Dendum Isles
Kalishir Ocean
Isle of Merdan
Keth
Carth
Cantir Isles
Nemdar Islands
Principality of Soroth
Soroth
United Isles of Damnir
Abodine Wasteland
KALDA
CIRCA 6,793 C.D.
10 20 30 40 50 60 70 80 90 100
Length in Hundred Grand Phineals

Nyesil
THE FORSAKEN LANDS OF
AZRIN'IL
Xilarim
Osivir
DESERT OF
ASH
DALISIN
CONFEDERACY
Dalistim
SILRLAIN OCEAN
OCEAN OF TEMPESTS
Veir
Bithar
ACHEYLON
Arithan
IGEACEAN SEA
RUINED KINGDOMS OF
KRESH'DAL
THE FORBIDDEN LANDS
DESOLATE LANDS
SEA OF SAND
Remllari Peninsula
PEGALIC SEA
N

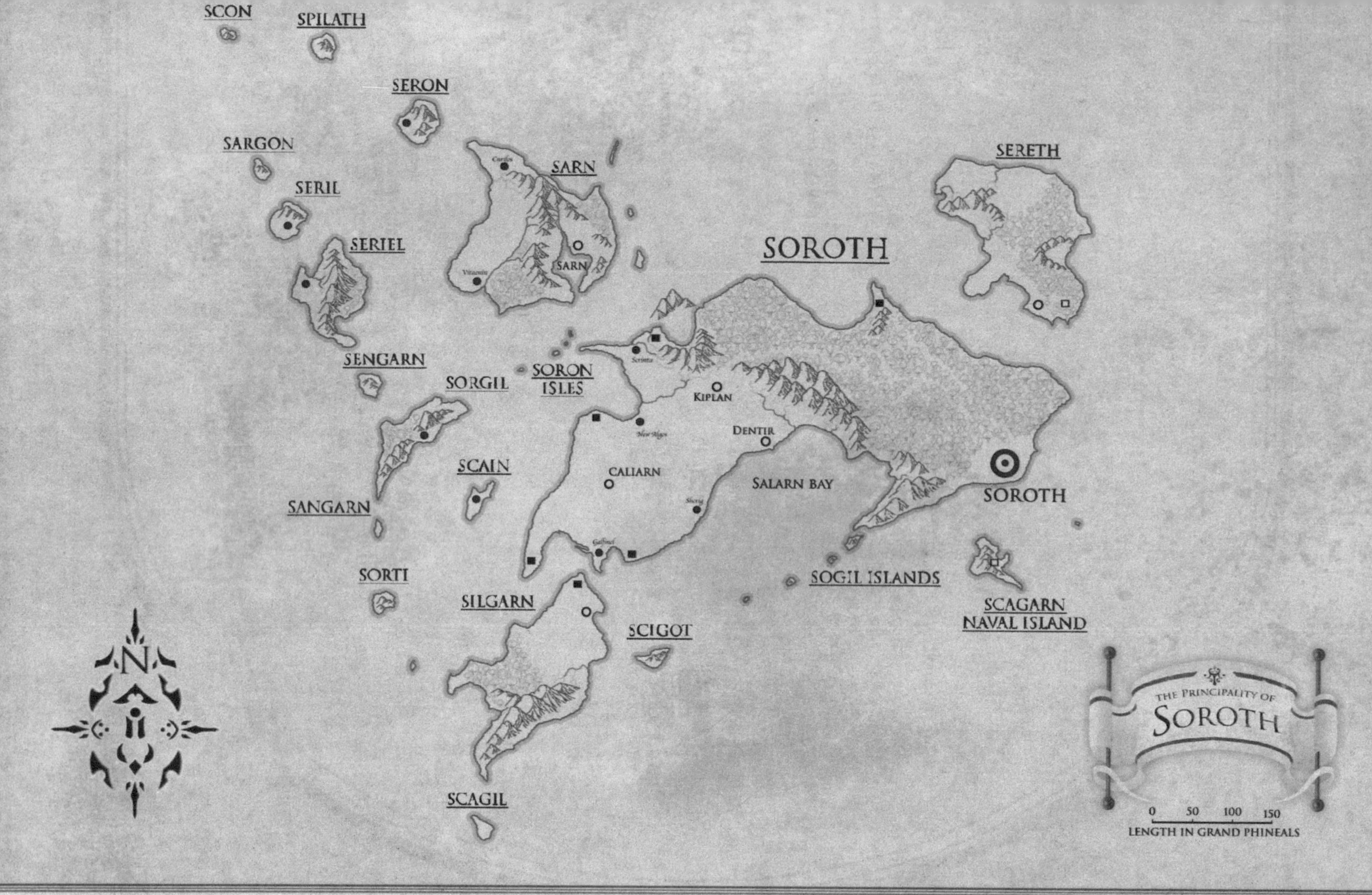

N
SCON
SPILATH
SERON
SARGON
SERIL
SERIEL
SARN
SOROTH
SERETH
SENGARN
SORGIL
SORON ISLES
KIPLAN
DENTIR
SANGARN
SCAIN
CALIARN
SALARN BAY
SOROTH
SORTI
SILGARN
SCIGOT
SOGIL ISLANDS
SCAGARN NAVAL ISLAND
SCAGIL
THE PRINCIPALITY OF
SOROTH
0   50   100   150
LENGTH IN GRAND PHINEALS

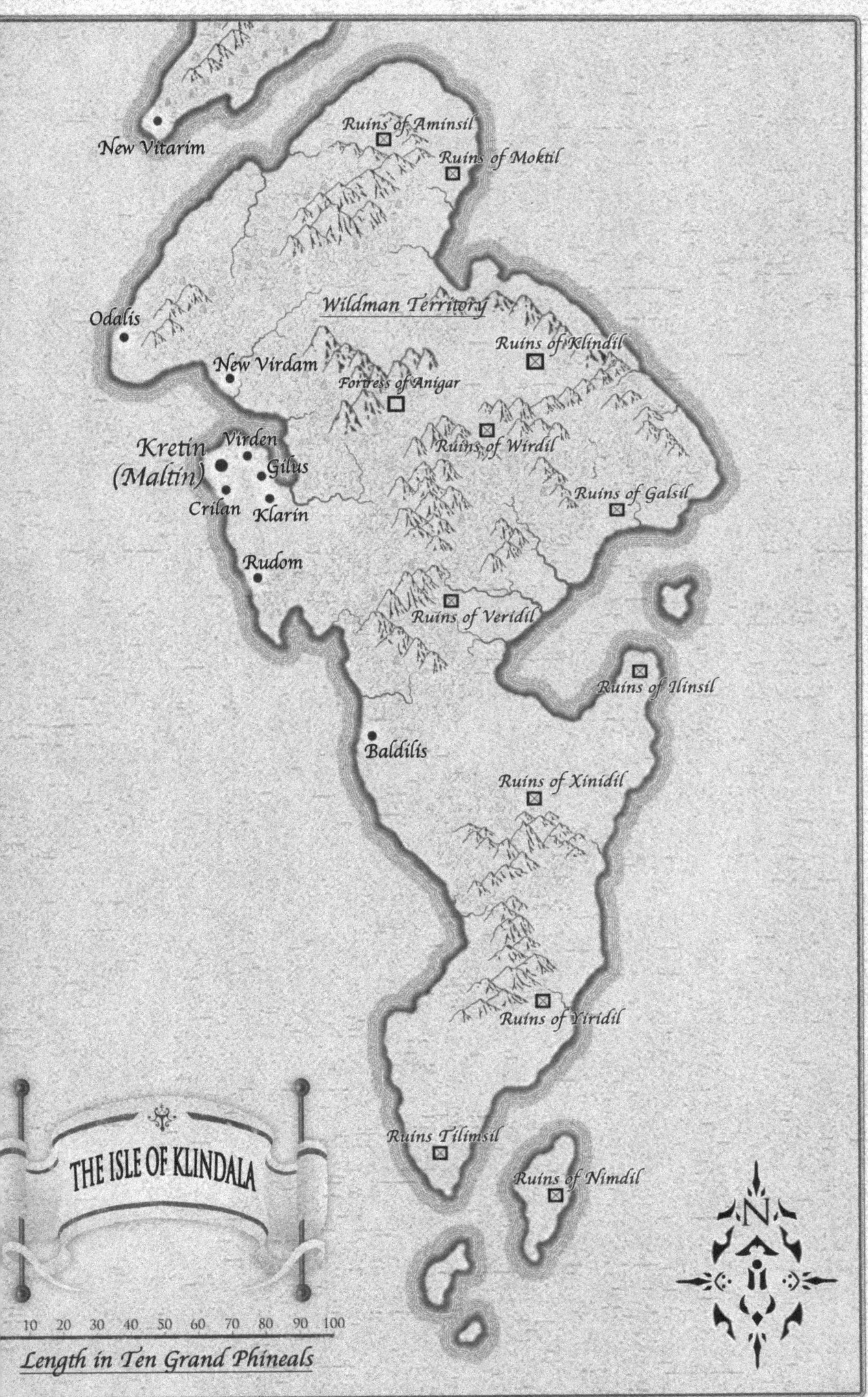

New Vitarim
Ruins of Aminsil
Ruins of Moktil
Odalis
Wildman Territory
New Virdam
Ruins of Klindil
Fortress of Anigar
Kretin
(Maltin)
Virden
Gilus
Ruins of Wirdil
Crilan
Klarin
Ruins of Galsil
Rudom
Ruins of Veridil
Ruins of Ilinsil
Baldilis
Ruins of Xinidil
Ruins of Yiridil
Ruins Tilimsil
Ruins of Nimdil
N
THE ISLE OF KLINDALA
10 20 30 40 50 60 70 80 90 100
Length in Ten Grand Phineals

TALES OF THE AMULET

Dusel rose from the bloodied sand and stumbled to his feet, staring about him. Thousands of armored soldiers—clad from head to toe in thin-plate armor—littered the arid plain, their blood staining the sand crimson. Like him, Dusel's comrades wore white plate armor with golden gilding, the various pieces arrayed with diamond-shaped plates that shielded the more vital areas. Flexible metal sheets covered their joints, crafted with metallurgy that involved imbuing the metal with transmutative properties. With their helmets on, Dusel couldn't tell if they were men like him, or elves.

His gaze shifted to the fallen enemy ranks mingled with his dead allies. The men of the Cheserithean Empire wore a variety of armor-types dyed in various colors, accenting the bloodied sand. The qui'sha, however, wore identical armor. Each qui'sha had an elongated helmet at the front, allowing room for their snouts. Their armor was scaled with sharp points and spikes. Qui'sha looked wicked in that armor, although they also looked wicked without it.

Weapons littered the battlefield, their sharp metal gleaming with a deadly light—energy called magic.

A sudden pang of sorrow struck Dusel's heart. Despite his years of battle, he found the corpse-littered plain a horrific sight.

This was not the first time Dusel had walked away the sole survivor. It was becoming commonplace, and not because he was a coward. Dusel fought valiantly, and died often.

But death never lasted long with him.

He turned from the dead armies, searching the crimson sand for his fanisar. The staff-like weapon lay nearby, next to where he was slain. The fanisar was as long as he was tall and a dull-platinum color. It was much like the channeling staff used by mages, with a groove all along one side. Of course, the weapon could be wielded as such, but it was capable of so much more.

Grabbing the fanisar, Dusel pressed on two oval indentations near the staff's center. Crimson light formed along the ends of the weapon, becoming glistening blades of razor-sharp metal. Both blades gleamed red, surrounded by an aura of annihilation particles.

With fanisar in hand, Dusel picked his way across the battlefield. Other parts of the plain were a mismatched mess of grass and sand, the result of Alliance Transmuters. It was their plan to leave this place desolate after the battle, a warning to all who defied the Kaldean Alliance and the Lords of Metal.

Across the horizon, a beam of light sped skyward. It pierced the multi-hued sky above a rising ridge, but soon disappeared into the void beyond the stars.

They did it! he cheered, grinning beneath his helmet. *Finally, Cheserith is banished. Without their* god *this war can end and Kalda can be at peace.* Hope filled Dusel, and he hastened toward the ridge.

He soon descended into a level basin, finding more blood-soaked battlefields. Unlike where he had fallen, not all here were dead. Groans and pained cries filled the air in a dreadful cacophony. Explosions of magic echoed in the distance. Those eruptions were accompanied by shrilling roars, undoubtedly the cries of gangolins or tarrasques. Those beasts were commonplace in this theater of war. They were devastating creatures, especially when enthralled by draconic mages. The Lords of Metal were said to be the only ones who could coerce such creatures, though some claimed that the elven conjurer, Hasernal, could control a gangolin.

Beyond the last battlefield lay a city of considerable size and partly in ruin—the capital of the Cheserithean Empire. It was where the light had beamed skyward. Though the city was vast, Dusel knew the place where the beam originated: Cheserith's Palace at the capital's eastern edge.

Luckily, it wasn't too far away.

It took Dusel an hour to reach the palace, at least what remained of it. Cheserith's Palace had sat on a mound, surrounded by beautiful gardens and hemmed by elegant crimson stone walls. But now, the palace grounds were desolate. Spires of rock replaced trees and grass was now sand. The palace walls were toppled, strewn across the ground in pieces. The mound was also destroyed, and in its place was an enormous crater.

Faint pale-blue light shone from the bottom of the crater. Soon, Shem'rinal appeared from a misty cloud, standing in the air and looking down.

"What is he doing—" Dusel flinched. A glint of red shone beneath Shem'rinal. *Impossible! It couldn't be the* Amulet, *could it?* Scrambling, he dashed into the crater, skidding down its sides.

As Dusel neared the crater's bottom, his fear was realized. His eyes widened as he gazed upon a white-metal amulet on the crater's floor. The upper half of the amulet consisted of seven curved petals surrounding an eye-shaped slit that held a large, faceted ruby as the iris. In the lower half of the amulet, three draconic talons extended downward, gripping a polished black sphere. Within the polished sphere, tiny bright flecks gleamed from seven spirals. It was the weapon that had turned the tide of this millennium-long war—the Amulet of Draconic Control.

"It can't be," Dusel groaned, dropping to his knees beside Shem'rinal. He reached shaking hands toward the amulet, but before Dusel could grab it, Shem'rinal spoke.

"Unfortunately, the Amulet of Draconic Control still remains. But our *Enemy* has been exiled. The Irum'mak'sha succeeded."

Still kneeling, Dusel braced one hand on the ground and turned toward Shem'rinal. "But this… this will bring folly to us all." His voice shook with horror.

Shem'rinal gazed skyward. He looked young, as if in the prime of his life. His face was thin and his chin narrow. Pointed ears peaked from his blond hair. Though he looked like an elf, Shem'rinal wasn't elven. He was unique, the only one of his kind—a being composed of pure magic and life, inseparably connected.

"You undoubtedly speak the truth, Dusel," Shem'rinal said in a calm tone. His words were tender, a reflection of his kind, paternal nature. "I am glad you made it here first."

"What?" Dusel cocked his head. Did Shem'rinal not want the other leaders of the Alliance to know about the amulet? This wasn't what they had planned. It was meant to be sealed away with Cheserith, lost to all of Kalda, forever.

"You know the division among the leaders of the Kaldean Alliance, Dusel. Sealing the Amulet with our *Enemy* was the only compromise. But now…" Shem'rinal said with a sigh, finally turning from the sky.

Dusel felt overwhelmed. One war was over, but would another conflict begin? Could the Amulet of Draconic Control sunder the Kaldean Alliance?

"The elves fear its power," Shem'rinal said, shaking his head. "They don't trust that humanity won't turn it against the other dragons. If Ilvina got her hands on it, she would destroy it. That act, however, would enrage Esil'ha and the other golden dragons. They see it as a symbol of victory, something to be revered."

"What are you suggesting?" Dusel asked, wary of the answer.

Shem'rinal sucked in a deep breath, although he didn't need to breathe. The gesture was an emotional reflex. "You might not like what I have to say, Dusel. I've come to a decision by myself. Any attempt to decide its fate by democracy will only lead to division. And, this world has seen enough war…" He paused, and then sternly stared at Dusel. "You must take the Amulet."

A sudden pang of horror struck Dusel. That notion was traitorous. Why trust one man with such a thing? Oh, the peril…

"I sense your trepidation," Shem'rinal said with a grin. "You know all too well how power can corrupt one's soul. But a virtue resides within you, one that tames greed and lust. Some would call it righteousness."

Dusel turned away, but was drawn to the amulet's gleaming. What would he do with such a powerful thing? And how would the others react? The weight of that responsibility became heavier. He almost couldn't bear it.

"You are a Guardian of Kalda, Dusel," Shem'rinal urged. "A keeper of truth and might. You've been tried in the fields of battle and have proven tenacious. I trust whatever you decide is right. Now, you must hurry, before the others arrive. I sense a cessation."

Dusel's hands shook again as he reached for the amulet. He grabbed its woven chain and donned the powerful jewelry. It hung heavy around his neck, but the emotional weight of his charge made it feel like a millstone.

He turned back to Shem'rinal, who was now standing at eye level with him. "What will you tell the others?"

"I'll think of something." Shem'rinal said, chuckling and clasping his hands behind his back. "Just disappear for now. We can talk once our world settles."

Dusel cocked his head. "That could be centuries."

"Perhaps," Shem'rinal said, "but you'll still be around. That ring of yours does more than just revive you on the battlefield. It will prolong your life."

Another pang struck Dusel. He had tried to ignore ideas like that. When his ring was first bestowed upon him he wondered if it could do such a thing. He had feared that everyone he loved would vanish. Shem'rinal had just verified they would. The world would change and fade, but he would remain.

"Do not fear, Dusel. You will adapt. It may not seem so now, but immortality can be a sweet thing."

Dusel doubted that, and turned from Shem'rinal, climbing up the crater. He wanted to run, like a little child frightened by something he didn't understand. Yet he understood all too well the burden placed upon him.

He paused at the crater's rim. The desolation of war spread across the horizon. Smoke rose in patches across the vast battlefield, accented by the occasional eruption of magic.

My sacrifice could stave off more carnage like this, Dusel thought. He took courage and brought a hand to his chest, touching the Amulet of Draconic Control.

What would he do with such a powerful thing? He couldn't destroy it. That would be foolish. Yes, the Amulet of Draconic Control could strip the most precious gift of mortality, moral choice. But it was a necessary evil to win this war and finally bring peace to Kalda. Such a thing shouldn't be destroyed, nor should it be kept intact.

That left only one option.

Dusel uttered an incantation and focused his mind, mustering white-blue particles of concealing magic. The magic surrounded him and he vanished, as did the amulet's glow.

Now invisible, Dusel stealthily left the decimated palace. He turned, walking away from the battlefields. The burden Shem'rinal had placed upon him became lighter with each step as he reluctantly accepted the perilous charge of safeguarding the Amulet of Draconic Control.

When the weight of responsibility finally lifted, he stopped and turned, looking back to the land from which he'd come. To his surprise, he couldn't see the bloodied battlefields, or the ruined capital of the Cheserithean Empire.

He was alone. Forsaken. A vagabond.

And yet, he was empowered. His weighty responsibility had refined his soul. He was purified. Renewed.

Dusel glanced toward the invisible amulet around his neck. "I am your Guardian now," he said, touching his gauntleted hand to the jewelry's sharp points. "I will insure your safety."

With that, Dusel continued across the ravaged wasteland.

He will come in a time of sorrow.
Man will be primitive.
He will manifest the Ko'delish without word.
He will usher in my return.

- Prophecy of the Unspoken One

6,500 YEARS LATER

Kaescis Midivar, seventh in line to the Mindolarn throne, strolled through the gardens outside his uncle's grand palace. He was late, but that was usual.

Tardiness would attract attention, and he needed to stand out. This Mindolarn prince needed to be seen today. There would be others not of the empire dining at the feast tonight. If he stood out, people would remember him.

Important people.

Kaescis and the other princes of the empire looked very much alike—they were brothers and cousins after all. He and his brothers each had wavy golden-blond hair, except for Negaris. The brothers shared the same sharp nose and long forehead, a trait common to their grandfather, who Kaescis had never met. There were variations in their features, though. Of all his brothers, Kaescis's eyes were the palest violet, while his brothers' were darker. Kaescis also had the thinnest lips, the most chiseled face, and the roundest ears.

Besides their similarity in features, Kaescis was dressed like the other members of the Royal Family. He wore a fanciful crimson coat with tails hanging partway down the backs of his thighs. The coat was adorned with gold-and-white tassels and embroidered with patterns all paired in groups of seven. Seven was an important number in Mindolarn. He wore a ruffled beige shirt and charcoal-colored pants with matching boots. Kaescis couldn't change what he looked like, so the tardiness was needed if he were to stand out against the backdrop of Mindolarn aristocracy.

The harmonious sounds of music reached Kaescis's ears. The royal orchestra was playing its third movement, heralding the next part of the momentous feast. He had missed little. The first course was already served, but he didn't care for much of what it offered.

As he rounded a corner, Practil approached. The brown-haired man wore a lavender coat with silver tassels. Beneath it, he wore a white formal tunic and matching pants. His black boots echoed as he hastened along the stone pathway.

"Your Imperial Highness!" Practil called, stopping a few paces from Kaescis and bowing. "I was worried. When you didn't show, I—"

"Calm yourself, Practil. You've been my servant for how many years, and you still don't understand my methods?"

"Thirty, Your Imperial Highness," Practil bowed once again. "Forgive me, but there is someone here in the palace who wishes to speak with you."

Kaescis raised his brow, confused. The Feast of Sorrows was not a time to hold conversation. Partakers were to observe reverence and solemnity. If one needed to speak, it was to be in a whisper. Nothing more.

"Who is this person?" Kaescis asked, continuing through the garden path. Practil followed beside him.

"He wouldn't say," the servant said, ashamed he didn't have the answers his master desired. "The man was shrouded, in a black cowl. But... he spoke the *Words*. And uttered the *vow*."

Disturbing, Kaescis thought. Anyone who knew such things wouldn't dare hold conversation during the Feast of Sorrows.

Troubled, Kaescis wound his way through the gardens with Practil in tow. The music grew louder as they arrived at the banquet yard where the feast was held. The grassy space behind the palace was vast, with a view of the grand city of Mindolarn. Dozens of tables filled the palace green, occupied by hundreds of men and women dressed in formal garb.

Kaescis, however, ignored the banquet yard, searching for the stranger mentioned by Practil.

A hulking man lurked behind a pillar, not far from the palace. He was shrouded in black robes, his head buried inside a cowl. The stranger's hands, however, were covered in thick plate gauntlets. *Curious,* Kaescis thought. Who would wear robes and plate? Especially to the Feast of Sorrows.

The orchestra's third movement quieted as Kaescis and Practil approached the stranger.

Standing resolute beside the pillar, the hulking man said in a rasping whisper, "Cho'k, su'zak, Cho'k."

So he does know the token, Kaescis thought. Of course, Practil was not one to lie, but hearing the sacred Words spoken by this stranger caught Kaescis off guard. It was bizarre. If the fellow knew those words, he would be a Devout and therefore required to adhere to the rules of the feast.

"Cho'k, su'zak, Cho'k," Kaescis whispered. "May the Crimson Eye remain hidden for all time."

"Yes." The deep voice oozed from inside the cowl, and the word sounded muffled somehow, as if spoken from behind a helmet. Or a mask. "You are, Kaescis Midivar, heir to the Mindolarn throne?" he asked.

"I am," Kaescis said, cautious. "And who are you?" He peered into the cowl, but only saw blackness.

"A benefactor," the hulking man said. "I wish to see your empire reformed. You are a blessed people, highly favored of Cheserith and his Chosen."

"You dare speak that sacred name, on this day?" Kaescis asked, anger boiling. It was sacrilege for anyone other than the Presider to speak that divine name during the Feast of Sorrows. No, this stranger couldn't be a Devout.

The stranger chuckled, folding his arms. "A pious one, huh? That will do well. Well indeed. Perhaps your piety will serve you for the tasks that lay ahead."

Kaescis cocked his head, growing tired of this stranger. He glanced to Practil, who simply shrugged.

"Are you perturbed?" the stranger asked, amused. "Then I'll be succinct. I'm calling on you to restore your people's greatness."

Kaescis grunted, shaking his head. He was already doing that. That's why he wanted to stand out tonight. Stronger ties needed to be forged with those outside the empire. It was the only way to rebuild Mindolarn to its former greatness. Kaescis put his hands on his hips, listening skeptically as the stranger continued.

"Mindolarn cannot be rebuilt by diplomacy. Only by force. You must take back what your father and his brothers lost."

"You want us to start a war, then?" Kaescis scowled, displeased. "War is what fractured our empire."

"You didn't have the right tools," the stranger said. Kaescis could have sworn the stranger was smiling. "There is a place where I believe you can find such things. Men have called it the Isle of the Ancient Ones."

Kaescis fought back laughter, but he couldn't contain it. He brought a hand to his lips, muffling his mirth. This man was speaking ridiculousness. He obviously was referring to tevisrals. Didn't he know that such objects were rare? Tevisrals were even outlawed in many kingdoms and nations across Kalda.

Kaescis quelled his laughter and eyed the stranger. "So you want me to find a hidden cache, a treasure trove of tevisrals? I suppose you've never heard of the Edicts of the Mage-King?" Kaescis asked, snorting. This whole conversation was turning preposterous.

The stranger was not amused. He folded his arms and straightened up in a distant posture. "I've come to you, Kaescis Midivar, because of all the princes of Mindolarn you have the strongest desire to expand your borders." He paused, looking back to the palace. "Seek Dalgilur's Isle. I'm sure you'll find what you need there. It's the only place that those rebellious citizens of Karthar could have hidden them…"

Still chuckling, Kaescis asked, "Why can't *you* do this?"

The stranger began to walk away, but stopped, looking directly at Kaescis.

"Oh, I've tried. Something prevents me from entering the island."

The warm scent of lavish foods danced through the air. Kaescis glanced from the stranger to the palace, drawn by the savory foods.

Dozens of servants descended wide stairs, carrying steaming platters. They walked toward Kaescis and Practil but ignored them, their demeanors solemn and reverent, much like the participants of the Feast of Sorrows. Their gaits were somber and deliberate.

Kaescis turned back toward the stranger, but to his surprise he was nowhere to be found. A fading black mist dissipated within the garden where the stranger had walked.

Where is he? Kaescis wondered. He hadn't heard an incantation, or words to activate a teleporting tevisral. Soon, the mist was gone. Had it really been there? Or was it something he had imagined?

"Come, Your Imperial Highness," Practil urged gently. "We should get ahead of the servers."

Kaescis stared at the area where the stranger had stood, disturbed by his swift disappearance. But he turned and followed Practil to the banquet yard.

What was this Dalgilur's Isle? Kaescis had never heard of such an island. All of Kalda's seas were charted. Every island had been discovered and explored. After all, men had sailed the seas of Kalda for thousands of years.

The orchestra's fourth movement began as Kaescis and Practil picked their way past the tables of the banquet yard. Many of the men and women there—the Partakers of the Feast—were from other parts of the world. Some were renowned, others notorious. These people were all devout followers of the One True God, bound together by their religion.

Hardly anyone paid attention to Kaescis. The Partakers of the Feast were drawn to the smells coming from the palace. That foolish stranger had spoiled his plans. If Kaescis hadn't stopped to speak he would have been the center of attention. Now he was lost amid the servants bearing food.

Two middle-aged men whispered to each other, seated at a nearby table. Both were dressed in the formal garb of Losians. It was odd to see people like them here. Losians weren't typically fond of religion, nor the Mindolarn Empire. Did they even believe in a higher power?

His eyes were drawn to a ring on one of them. The ring bore the emblem of an organization in the Losian government, the League of Surveilors. *We have Devouts there?* Kaescis was surprised. *We really are spreading everywhere as Father predicted.*

Kaescis and Practil continued across the banquet yard to the far end where the Mindolarn Royals sat. There were, however, foreigners seated among his family. He recognized two of them: an aristocrat from a backwater chain of islands and a mage from that same nation: a pitiful place called Soroth. The latter was the grandmaster of an Order of mages.

This foreign aristocrat was a burly man, with wavy blond hair. His complexion was fair and his face clean-shaven. He wore a formal crimson garb—a stiff tunic and pants with black embroidery. He could have passed as a Mindolarnian. Kaescis couldn't remember his name but knew he was a baron and the sovereign ruler of an island.

The mage, however, wore a black robe. Kaescis barely saw the woven symbols on the robe, but he knew what they represented—the mystical art of necromancy. Unlike the aristocrat, he had dark-olive skin, a long, thick white beard, and white hair hanging past his shoulders. The necromancer's hazel-blue eyes coldly studied Kaescis.

These two had attended the Feast of Sorrows many times. But why weren't they sitting with the rest of their people? The other Sorothians sat closer to the palace.

Kaescis shrugged off the thought and sat in the only empty seat between his cousins. Kaescis was fond of one and tolerated the other. Raedina was the favored of the two. She was a tall woman, slender and elegant. Her long black hair was braided, hanging over her shoulder past her chest. She had vibrant green eyes that could send a chill up your spine. But, she was a kind woman, at least to Kaescis. Like many of the other regal women, she wore a blood-red gown.

Kaescis waved off Practil, and the servant departed. He carefully picked his way through the crowd of servers bringing the food, moving to the rear of the banquet yard where other servants of the royal house sat.

Raedina leaned toward her cousin, tapping a finger to the back of his hand. "You are dreadfully late," she whispered. "I thought you were planning to arrive at the last stanza of the third movement?"

"I was delayed," Kaescis answered, matching his whisper to hers in volume. "Some crazed fool wanted to speak with me."

"During the Feast of Sorrows?" Raedina asked, incredulous.

"It was nonsense," Kaescis said.

"Well this *nonsense* has disrupted our plan," Raedina said with a sigh.

She turned away, twisting her lips in a crooked frown. Her neck seemed to pull away at one side, thus causing the odd frown. Raedina always made that strange frown when she was upset.

Kaescis turned his attention to the servers. The servers all gathered along a series of tables running the entire length of the banquet yard. The savory aromas caused a sudden pang of hunger. It was tradition to forgo food for a day before the feast, although some Partakers went longer. Kaescis had gone without longer than most, due to his tardiness. His short delay would have been worthwhile, but now it seemed a worthless sacrifice.

A server unknown to him caught his eye. Was he new? Kaescis wasn't aware of a staff change. He didn't know all of the palace servants personally, but he made it a point to recognize all of them. A Mindolarn prince couldn't be too cautious. The empire had many enemies. Not paying attention to servants could be fatal.

Kaescis cocked his head, staring at the server. Something was off about him. Many of the other servers plated the food uniformly, but this man was a little off. Perhaps he *was* new. There was ritual when plating food for those partaking in the feast, and this man was doing it wrong.

All the other servers—totaling seventy-two—put together plates for the

Partakers. Once they had two plates in hand, they marched across the banquet yard and served Kaescis and the others.

Kaescis continued eyeing the unknown server, who gave plates to both the Sorothians seated with the Royals.

The servers returned to the steamy platters, dishing out more food. They took two plates each to the rest of the Partakers. Two runs were enough to serve everyone. Nearly three hundred people were present at this feast.

The orchestra's fourth movement faded. Silence hung over the banquet yard, and everyone patiently waited for the Presider of the Feast to speak. It was customary after each plate was delivered to hear from the Presider, or someone elected by him, on the purpose of the feast. By tradition, the emperor fulfilled the role as Presider, but that observance was not practiced in this day and age.

Vikanin rose from a nearby table. He was the Steward of the Empire. Kaescis's uncle—Emperor Monddar—wasn't present at the Feast of Sorrows. His absence was not unusual. Kaescis couldn't remember the last time the emperor had attended such an event.

Uncle Monddar often kept to himself, secretly moving around the empire, always guarded by the Crimson Praetorians. It seemed paranoid, but with the assassinations of the other emperors it was expected.

But today, Uncle Monddar was sequestered inside his palace. No one knew it, though, besides Kaescis and a few others. The emperor only made it known to those with whom he wished to speak. Kaescis planned to meet with him after the feast to discuss his plans for a stronger Mindolarn.

Vikanin walked to a raised stand at the far end of the banquet yard. He stood against the backdrop of the grand capital. The Steward of the Empire was a short man, but had a strong build. He had been a general in the wars to defend against eastern aggression. Now he was a politician, taking the public place of Kaescis's uncle. And, today he acted as Presider.

"My brethren and sisters," Vikanin declared loudly, addressing the Partakers of the Feast. "Once again, we come in remembrance of our God and Father. As we eat and drink, reflect upon His absence. But cling to the hope of His advent. Recall the signs that herald—"

A beam of violet light struck Vikanin in the chest. It was disintegrating magic. The beam burned a hole through him, and Vikanin fell, collapsing lifelessly.

That servant, Kaescis thought, turning violently. He looked to the servers. The man unknown to Kaescis looked horrified, gazing at another near the center of the banquet yard. The newcomer wasn't the attacker. Surprising! Kaescis followed his gaze, seeing the attacker, a man he had known for many years, Ascrol.

Ascrol held his hand outstretched, pointed toward the dead Vikanin. But it couldn't be Ascrol. Ascrol didn't know how to cast spells. Did he? Fifteen other servers around Ascrol mustered magic. Each uttered incantations, gathering destructive energies.

Sharp words resounded from behind Kaescis, coming from Raedina's lips.

Her hand reached over his shoulder. She wore a silvery bracelet with gems inlaid all around it that gleamed a blue hue and hummed. The bracelet was a tevisral. Soon after, a wave of blue light rippled from Raedina's hand, veiling her and Kaescis. The light was a type of magic called barsion. It was a protective magic and could prevent anything, both physical and magical in nature, from passing through it. The bracelet encased both of them in an ovoid shield of barsion.

They were safe, but others were not.

Kaescis watched as the traitorous servers flung deadly bolts into the crowd of Partakers. Many of them fled, frantic. Some others, however, began mustering their own magics.

One such man hurled an off-white mass of dispelling magic at the attacking servers.

The servers' faces contorted, then washed away, revealing imposters dressed in the servers' clothes. They all looked aggressive, hostile, and determined to kill.

"We need to get to Uncle," Raedina almost shouted, sounding frazzled.

Kaescis glanced to her calmly. Hostility didn't bother him. He was accustomed to it—

Sounds of battle erupted from the palace. That worried him. No one before had ever dared attack the seat of the empire. Their enemies had never come this far into their domain.

Angered, Kaescis uttered a sharp string of words, the words to a magical incantation. Blackness seeped from the pores of his hands, gathering like a mist. It coalesced into a shaft. Within seconds, it became a sword composed entirely of blackness. It was a destructive power called Ko'delish by his ancestors. The black sword glowed a deathly light, faintly misting black particles.

"Where is your wand?" Kaescis asked Raedina coldly.

"My chambers, of course!" she shrieked. "Why would I bring it to the Feast?"

She had a point.

Kaescis grabbed Raedina by the waist with his freehand, guiding her across the banquet yard. His grip was protective and firm. Empty chairs in their path flew out of their way, repulsed by the barsion of Raedina's bracelet.

Those who hadn't fled were now engaged in a deadly duel with the imposters. The necromancer from Soroth was fighting two of them, keeping both at bay. He was protecting the baron and another member of the Mindolarn Royal Family. He seemed skilled in the art of combat, a deadly opponent.

Arcane bolts struck the barsion protecting Kaescis and Raedina, flung by one of the imposters. Kaescis glanced at the man but continued onward to the palace.

Nearly two hundred of the Partakers of the Feast were fleeing through the gardens. Royals. Foreigners. Servants. Where was Practil?

Kaescis and Raedina pushed their way toward the grand steps leading to the palace. Two men, clothed like Alathians and dressed in foreign mage's robes, exited one of the palace doors.

How dare they attack us? Kaescis growled. When had the easterners' aggression grown to the point of besieging the heart of the empire?

The Alathian mages hurled deadly magic at the fleeing men and women in the gardens.

Kaescis wouldn't stand for this. His people had to be protected.

"Raedina, let me free."

She complied, touching the gems on her bracelet. The bubble of barsion magic that had encased them became a wall between them and the palace.

Kaescis darted to his left, casting another spell with a sharp-sounding incantation. Dark-blue particles of barsion magic appeared around his regal clothing. It enveloped his body, veiling him with armor-like protection. At the same time, Raedina reversed the power of her bracelet. The ovoid barrier encased her once again.

"I am a Mindolarn prince!" Kaescis shouted to the two Alathians, intending to draw their attention.

His hopes were realized.

The two mages stopped flinging their magic at the fleeing crowd, then focused on Kaescis, who was bounding up the stairs. They were obviously here to attack the members of the Royal Family. Alathians had a tendency to focus their hostility on the leaders of the empire.

Kaescis charged at the mages, raising his black sword high into the air.

Both mages stepped aside, mustering more magic. Like Kaescis, thin barriers of barsion magic rose around them.

Kaescis bounded toward the mage on his left, who was gathering fiery energies in his hands. Streams of red and orange flame swirled around the mage.

As Kaescis came within weapon's reach, the mage stretched out his hand. A beam of fire struck Kaescis's barsion barrier. His protection flickered, but Kaescis pushed through the flame. He sliced his black sword diagonally, striking the mage's shoulder.

The mage's barsion eroded once struck by the Ko'delish. That magic devoured all it touched. Kaescis pressed harder, and within seconds, he cut through the barsion.

Black particles of the Ko'delish wisped beneath the rest of the mage's protective spell, spreading across his body. It consumed his flesh, turning it to gray dust.

Kaescis gritted his teeth, mentally focusing more of his sword's devouring mist to seep into his foe.

The consuming magic dropped the mage to his knees. He was dying.

Kaescis turned, casting another spell. Gray telekinetic particles gathered beyond the barsion of his freehand. The prince's eyes focused on the other mage who was hurling magic at Raedina.

She, however, was awkwardly dodging the spells. Raedina hadn't seen much combat.

Kaescis's telekinetic magic formed as he finished the incantation. It shot toward the mage, striking him and hurling him diagonally through the air. The mage hit the stone walls of the palace and then fell into the gardens.

"Come on!" Kaescis shouted to Raedina, motioning with his freehand to the palace door.

Side by side, they bolted into the palace, where more fearful sounds of pandemonium greeted them.

———◊•◊———

Kaescis hurried through the upper halls of the palace. The fighting hadn't reached beyond the grand foyers. It was fairly quiet until he reached the fourth floor.

Eruptions of magic resounded.

More blasts echoed from a hallway leading to the chambers where the emperor had sequestered himself.

"Those filthy Alathians," Kaescis spat, bolting into the hall.

He passed several dead Crimson Praetorians—they were the empire's elite guard. Many were trained in each school of magic and skilled with a variety of weapons. Each Crimson Praetorian wore blood-red plate armor that was enhanced by magic. The emblem of the empire was emblazoned across their breastplates: a silvery version of the seven-headed red hydra. It took much to fell a Praetorian.

Anxious, Kaescis wound through a series of corridors. The halls were built to slow intruders or would-be assassins, intended to give the emperor—or whoever was hiding in the chambers—ample time to escape.

More Praetorians lay lifeless, their armor scorched by various types of magics.

How many Alathians had infiltrated the heart of the palace? And where were their dead? Kaescis only saw Praetorians.

Soon, he arrived at the chambers where his uncle had been hiding. More Praetorians lay in the doorway. That was twelve. More eruptions reached his ears.

Hurrying inside, Kaescis gasped in horror, his eyes widening.

His uncle, the emperor, struggled to defend himself with a shield made of the Ko'delish. The black misting particles flowed from Uncle Monddar's arm, emitted from a tevisral. It repurposed the Ko'delish in a manner similar to barsion magic, creating a black shield that devoured assailing spells. But the black shield was flickering. Uncle Monddar also wore armor that looked as if it were dyed in blood. It was scaled, with thick scallops along his upper arms and back.

Across the chamber, a lone man assailed the emperor. He wore a mage's battle garb; thin sheets of armor melded into a thick robe. His hawk-like face was wrinkled, his nose sharp, his chin long. A gray beard shrouded his face. Vibrant sapphire eyes glared at Uncle Monddar. This mage looked familiar, but it couldn't be who Kaescis remembered.

That man was dead.

Several layers of barsion magic encircled the intruder, his barrier infused with a myriad of colors representing various types of magics, a rare sight. He wielded dozens of orbs of various destructive powers: arcane, fire, disintegration, telekinetic, lightning, and acid. He masterfully hurled them at the emperor while gracefully keeping a safe distance.

Was this intruder the only one who assaulted these chambers? There were no other dead Alathians. *He must be the only one*, Kaescis thought. Alathian mages were notorious combatants. Some of their Order had mastered all the Channels of Magic. Grand mages, they were called. Was this intruder such a mage? He had to be.

Enraged, Kaescis bounded across the chamber toward the grand mage, swinging his black blade.

The intruder noticed Kaescis, flinging orbs at him. He threw his arms at the elbows in sweeping motions. Such techniques were common among true masters of the magical arts as a means to prevent fatigue. It also allowed a mage to hurl mustered magic at a much faster rate.

Seven deadly orbs flew at Kaescis, and he sliced across two. Both orbs exploded against his blade, causing him to stumble. The other five hit his barsion, weakening it.

The grand mage uttered an incantation, mustering more of his deadly orbs. Hundreds appeared around him, dancing above his layers of barsion. He steadied himself, glancing at both of his foes. Settling into a wide stance, the grand mage hurled magic at both Kaescis and his uncle.

Kaescis pressed forward, swatting and evading the bolts thrown at him. But this intruder was too skilled. The evaded magic simply whizzed through the air, striking Kaescis in the back. Magic struck him from all sides, pinning him a leap and bound away.

Kaescis couldn't get any closer. All he could do was defend himself while watching his uncle succumb to the vile mage.

After several more hits, Kaescis's barsion shattered.

The grand mage seemed to sense this and shifted his focus, hurling all of his magic at the emperor. The bolts tore through the misting shield, striking Uncle Monddar's crimson breastplate.

A violent explosion of light filled the room, blinding Kaescis and knocking him to the ground. A horrified wail resounded behind him while a pained scream shot through the blinding light.

The light faded as Kaescis recovered from the repulsion. His vision blurred as he strained to focus on a figure looming over another. He blinked. The intruder extended his barsion-encased hand toward the fallen emperor. Uncle Monddar lay on his back, a hole marring his breastplate.

"Today you die, Monddar!" the intruder shouted. "Your reign of terror ends now!"

"Uncle!" Kaescis screamed, rising to his feet with fury.

"Kaescis, no!" he heard Raedina shrieking behind him. She must have been the one who wailed amid the explosion.

The grand mage turned, noticing Kaescis's advance. He stepped backward, uttering an incantation. Green magic swirled in his hands.

Once near the mage, Kaescis swung his black sword with fury. It left a trailing mist as it sang through the air, striking the mage's barsion. The magical blade and the mist devoured the outermost layer of the mage's protective sphere.

At that moment, the mage finished his spell. Ensnaring tentacles burst from his palms toward Kaescis.

The tentacles wrapped around Kaescis, forcing him upward. They splayed his arms wide while slamming his head against the stone ceiling. One of them raced for his mouth, forcing its way inside and past his tongue. It stopped short of suffocating him. Kaescis could breathe through his nose, but he couldn't speak, and that meant he couldn't cast a spell either.

Totally debilitated, Kaescis dropped his sword. The blade's faint mist eroded the surrounding floor.

"You are not my foe today, young prince," the intruder said. His tone was tranquil. How could he be so calm while committing murder? Kaescis had never been that calm.

A bolt of magic sped toward the mage, but he deflected it and hurried away. Kaescis couldn't see him, but he heard the mage's footsteps heading toward the far side of the room. They soon faded.

He can't know where the secret passage is, can he? Kaescis wondered, noticing Raedina moving beneath him.

She was still encased in her ovoid of barsion. But now, she wielded her wand.

"Dispel." She said the word in the ancient Keadal tongue, aiming the wand toward Kaescis. The Keadal language was spoken among their ancestors, used to activate certain tevisrals.

Off-white light formed at the wand's tip—dispelling magic. The magic shot within a second, striking the ensnaring tentacles. They vanished, and Kaescis fell to the floor.

"Are you hurt?" Raedina asked, helping him upright.

"No," he replied, grabbing his sword. Kaescis looked across the room, toward an opening in the wall: the secret passage. Who was this mage? He had intimate knowledge of the palace. But no one knew of that passageway beside the Royal Family. Could one of their kin have betrayed the empire? Perhaps it was those Losians he saw—

Uncle, Kaescis snapped back to reality, hurrying across the room.

The emperor lay on his side, a hole burned through his torso. Blood dripped from his breastplate to the floor. The wound looked fatal. Uncle Monddar groaned, scraping his bloodied gauntlet across the floor and smearing blood.

If I only had an arpran tevisral… Kaescis grumbled. Then, he could pursue that villainous mage without worry for his uncle. He uttered an incantation, mustering arpran magic. As the green light swirled around his hands, Kaescis glanced to Raedina and her wand. Why did that wand have to be limited to arcane magics?

While green arpran magic coalesced, Raedina hurried out of the chambers and through the secret passage.

You fool, Raedina, Kaescis thought, finishing his incantation. The mage had been enhanced. There was no way she could catch up to him. Kaescis focused on his uncle, surging the arpran magic toward the gaping wound.

Uncle Monddar gasped as the green light penetrated him. The light surged, but he fell limp, his gauntleted hand collapsing against the stone floor.

No…

Eyes widening, Kaescis started with horror. He *knew* he was too late.

The arpran light filled the emperor but soon faded. Uncle Monddar remained limp and lifeless.

"No…" Kaescis moaned sorrowfully, but then his emotions culminated in an enraged cry. It echoed through the room, ringing even after Kaescis ceased screaming.

After a moment Kaescis regained his composure, though he was still enraged. "I promise you, Uncle," he vowed with wrath, "I will kill this assassin!"

Fueled with fury, Kaescis bolted out of the chamber and into the secret passageway. He darted through the winding passage until reaching a hole in one of its walls. The breech led to a room for palace guests, currently unoccupied. A door was wide open, undoubtedly where the villainous mage had fled next.

Kaescis continued with haste, following the path he assumed his uncle's killer had taken. Eventually, he found Raedina at a broken window overlooking the entrance to the palace. She aimed her wand, screaming as she fired bolt after bolt through the shattered pane.

On the steps below, hundreds of Alathian mages retreated, clustering together. They flung magic at the palace guard, holding the Mindolarnian soldiers at bay. *Filthy Alathians!* Enraged, Kaescis searched for his uncle's killer. The lone mage was dashing down the palace steps, the only one not among the cluster of Alathian mages.

"You won't get away that easily, murderer!" Kaescis shouted, and hurled his Ko'delish blade like a javelin. Black mist trailed from the weapon as it sped through the air. Raedina's bolts whizzed beside the blade. Both magics were aimed at the crowd, meant to intercept the murderous mage.

A ripple of brilliant blue light washed from the cluster of mages just as Uncle Monddar's murderer reached his fellow Alathians. The magic washed through the air like a roaring tide, forming a towering multi-layered domed barrier. Kaescis's black blade struck the reformed barsion, tearing through several layers before dissipating. Raedina's bolts erupted against the outer layer, causing the barsion to flicker.

Amid the explosions, golden light shone from the enemy ranks, the beginnings of a conjuration portal.

"No!" Kaescis yelled, watching his uncle's killer disappear within the crowd.

Raedina continued screaming, firing bolts in furious desperation.

Golden light rippled across the Alathian ranks, veiling them from sight. "I'll find you…" Kaescis vowed through clenched teeth. "And when I do, I'll carve out your heart with my blade." Suddenly, the golden light pulled back toward the center of the crowd, and the mages disappeared, teleporting away through the conjuration magic.

Raedina stopped firing at the enemy intruders and wailed in despair. Her cries echoed through the hall and out the broken window. Her hand trembled, and she dropped her wand. Raedina opened her mouth to speak, but no words left her lips.

Kaescis exhaled, shaking his head. This was just like the assassinations of his other uncles, the previous emperors of Mindolarn. He wasn't present for those deaths, but he'd heard the tales. Remembering those stories stoked his rage.

Raedina dismissed the effect of her bracelet and staggered toward Kaescis. Gripping his arms tightly, she said, "He's dead, isn't he?" Kaescis nodded, and she collapsed against his chest, sobbing softly as her tears stained his coat.

"Come on," he urged, and they left the broken window.

Together, Kaescis and Raedina returned to the once hidden chambers. Their uncle lay lifeless, his gauntleted hand outstretched. Blood spread across the floor in an arc.

Raedina's sobs turned to wailing, and she fell to the stone floor. Her despair was infectious.

How could Kaescis strengthen the empire now? His uncle had reigned for nearly thirty years, ruling the longest of all the seven brothers, beside the eldest—Kaescis's father. During Uncle Monddar's reign he rebuilt their cities, advanced their abilities to create tevisrals, and enlisted more foreigners to their cause. Now, the empire would be in disarray, as it had when the other emperors died. It was hopeless—

The blood on the ground wasn't smearing or random spatter as Kaescis had first supposed. His uncle had written something with his own blood. It was a scribbled mess, but Kaescis could read it.

"*Seek the Isle. Heed Lord Ca*—" the name was incomplete.

The isle? He couldn't be referring to the same thing that crazed fool spoke of, could he?

"*Mindolarn cannot be rebuilt by diplomacy. Only by force…*" The words rang in his mind. Kaescis saw truth in that notion. Their enemies attacked with brute force, never striking through diplomacy, but starting a war now would be suicide for the empire. They needed a sure means to victory. Tools of war that would tip the balance of power against mages like the wicked one he and his uncle fought.

"Perhaps I was naïve…" Kaescis said, standing above his uncle's corpse. "I will do whatever I must to expand our empire's borders. I will reclaim our lands and push our domain to the seat of Losian power. Then, all the men of Kalda will bow in reverence to the Mindolarn Empire."

With a surge of glorious purpose filling his soul, Kaescis Midivar, now sixth in line to the Mindolarn throne, embraced his uncle's dying wish.

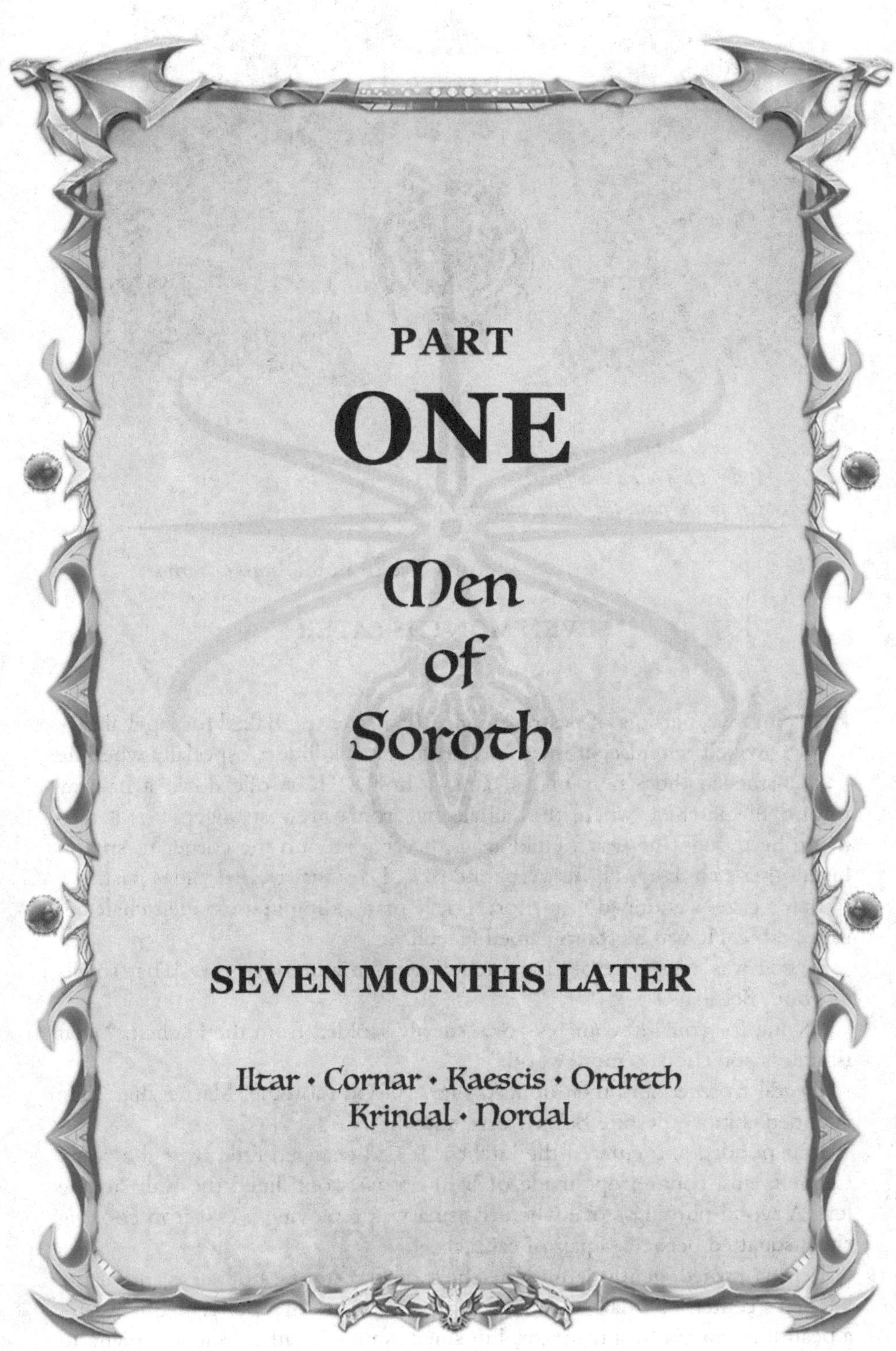

PART

ONE

Men of Soroth

SEVEN MONTHS LATER

Iltar · Cornar · Kaescis · Ordreth
Krindal · Nordal

1

HOMESTEAD

- 7th Verse from the *Feast of Sorrows*

SEVEN MONTHS LATER

The sweet aroma of pastries tingled Iltar's senses. Baked furnapel always evoked reminiscent memories from his childhood, especially when he smelled them here in his family's home. He strode down a hallway toward the kitchen, where the tantalizing aroma grew stronger. For a moment, he thought he was a child again, peering around the corner to spy on his mother's cooking. Those were fond days. Days that were decades past.

Iltar's gaze was drawn to a short, portly man sitting in a wooden chair beside a table. He was a groom named Hegdil.

Hegdil was staring across the kitchen with an admiring grin. "That smells so good, Belsina!"

"None for you!" a woman's voice sternly scolded from the kitchen. "That is, unless you chop so'more wood."

Hegdil frowned and then noticed Iltar. "Good morning, Master Iltar." He sounded chipper, despite Belsina's sternness.

Iltar nodded and entered the kitchen. It had changed little over the years. Cabinets and countertops made of light-brown wood lined the walls to the left. A wood-burning stove where Belsina was removing a cast-iron cooking sheet squatted between a pair of cabinets.

Belsina turned, gently setting the sheet on flat stones atop an island at the kitchen's center. Her hair was a dull brown, tied back in a ponytail. She wasn't a beautiful woman by any means, but she wasn't ugly either. She was plain, to say the least. Belsina never wore makeup. Iltar didn't know why. He paid her enough to afford such things.

She smiled at Iltar, and the wrinkles around her eyes became more pronounced. "This is the first batch." Belsina motioned to the cooking sheet. "I can also make some tangrils. Delrin brought brandleberries from Cornar's orchard last night. So, I can make a batch of those if you'd like."

Iltar raised his brow. Brandleberries for children? How absurd.

"You can make a batch," he said, reluctantly. "But the brandleberries will be for us." Iltar shot a glance to Hegdil, who rubbed his hands giddily. Though the man was in his forties, he acted childish when it involved food. Especially good food.

"As you wish." Belsina rolled her eyes. She moved to another part of the kitchen, grabbing uncooked pastries and placing them on another cast-iron cooking sheet. "Are they here yet?"

Iltar shook his head, putting his hands on his hips. "They're late. Hopefully, Pagus didn't get distracted."

"The boy's got a mind of his own," Hegdil said frankly. "He's a bit of a rebel. I can see why his family wanted *you* to teach him."

Iltar shrugged. Hegdil had a point. Pagus was a spoiled brat, although he was improving. But what else would one expect from a Sarn Royal?

A faint whinny reached Iltar's ears. Both he and Hegdil turned their attention toward the hall. Trotting noises echoed from the home's side door.

"That sounds like them," Hegdil said, grunting as he rose from his chair. "I better tend to Filly. Poor guy has probably been worked hard today." The groom passed Iltar, disappearing down the hall.

"When do you want me to serve these, Master Iltar?" Belsina asked, putting the uncooked pastries inside the stove.

"When those are ready," Iltar replied. "The boys will need some energy for this morning's exercises. And we'll break for lunch at the usual time."

"Very well," she said, wiping her hands on her apron. "What grueling things are you making those boys do today?"

"Defend against armed men, of course."

"Iltar!" Belsina chided. She rarely called him by only his first name. Hardly anyone ever did.

"They'll be fine," he said with a chuckle. "They are *my* pupils, after all. Now, if these were students of Alacor or Jalel, then we'd be using sticks instead of swords."

Belsina bit her lip and rolled her eyes. "Why can't you respect Grandmaster Alacor? When will you ever let go of your resentment?"

Iltar's face twisted in a grimace. Belsina had dredged up distasteful memories. Gwenyth. Balden. His heart sank, and he fought back tears, but they still came. He hurried down the hall where Hegdil had gone. Iltar didn't want to be seen. Not now.

His and Alacor's intertwined pasts brought back bitter memories that he wished to forget. Iltar often suppressed them. Being here in his family's home often squashed those memories, unless he thought of Alacor's long-dead master, Cordis. Then, being here in his family's home only made it worse.

The fire!

He could smell it as if it was freshly burning.

Grass aflame.

His mother's horrific screams.

The sounds of magical eruptions.

Seared flesh.

No!

Iltar stopped, throwing himself against the wall. He rested his head on the polished wood paneling. It was cold to the touch. That helped pull him from his nightmarish reverie.

"I am in the present," he whispered. "There is no fire. There is no death. There are no monsters here."

Iltar swallowed hard, taking a deep breath. He opened his eyes, and tears streamed down his cheeks, lingering in his gray-haired goatee. As he straightened, he caught a glimpse of himself in a nearby mirror.

His vibrant sapphire eyes were reddened. Wrinkles surrounded those eyes, channeling tears before they trickled down his slender cheeks. Though he was aging, his face was still slim, a trait that accentuated his hawk-like features. His once-blond hair was gray, though the short-cropped style had remained the same over the last four decades. Iltar had been a young man when he decided upon that look.

After taking in his aged visage, Iltar wiped the tears from his gray goatee.

An old man like you shouldn't be crying, he told himself, regaining his composure.

Movement caught his eye, and Belsina peeled from the kitchen's entrance. She had seen him, hadn't she? This wasn't the first time she'd caught him in one of his fits. Belsina never said anything about the fits, never once. He appreciated that. Those fits of his were a detestable weakness.

Shaking off his woes, Iltar regained his composure and continued through the hall, arriving at the home's side entrance. He stepped onto a covered porch that emptied onto a stone path between the home and the stables.

A small wagon sat on the path, filled with a dozen boys between the ages of ten and fourteen—Iltar's acolytes. They wore black robes, attire common to the wielders of the necrotic magical arts. The boys whispered to each other but abruptly stopped as they saw Iltar. They straightened up attentively.

Iltar, however, paid them little attention and looked about, raising an eyebrow. *Where's Pagus?* he wondered.

Hegdil emerged from the stables with another young man. The youth wasn't Pagus.

Iltar pursed his lips and stepped from the porch. "Agen, where is Pagus?" he asked.

Agen, who was barely fourteen, timidly approached Iltar. He averted his gaze to the ground, muttering an answer. "He… he said he had things to do, back in Soroth."

"Did he say what?" Iltar asked sternly, putting his hands on his hips. Iltar had a stern reputation, and the boy knew it, though he was not like Alacor or the others. Barbaric fools.

"Uh…" Agen glanced to the boys and sighed. "No. He just took us to the city's northern gates, then told us how to get here. That's why we're late. I… I got lost… Took a wrong turn."

"All right," Iltar grumbled, rubbing his eyebrow. He took one more look at the acolytes, who all seemed frightened. He hated seeing that look on young boys. It was all too familiar. "I'm not going to punish you," he said, shaking his head. His mood lightened, and he smiled at the boys. "Go inside. My maid has prepared some snacks for you."

The acolytes cheered, leaping out of the wagon. They hurried to the house's side entrance, filing inside one by one. Agen, however, remained outside with Iltar and Hegdil.

"I'm sorry, Master Iltar," Agen apologized. "I, I should have stopped him. He… he just gets so pushy, and I just give in."

"It's not your fault, Agen," Iltar said, motioning for the boy to come closer.

Agen reluctantly complied, head still hung low.

"It's because I'm not as harsh as the other masters," Iltar continued. "Pagus thinks he can go about without being punished like his peers. It's his royal blood." He gently grabbed Agen's shoulder. "Go get a pastry, then meet me out front."

The boy finally looked up and nodded once, but didn't speak. He hurried past Iltar, following his peers.

Iltar called to his groom. "Hegdil, I want you to watch the gate while Delrin and Jalim are helping me."

"As you wish, Master Iltar."

"Now go snag a pastry." Iltar slapped the man's arm playfully.

Hegdil grinned widely, clapping his hands. If Iltar had "ordered" him to get a pastry, Belsina couldn't stop him.

Iltar turned partway, walking to a walled area behind his family's home; the wall was made of gray galstra, a stone similar to granite. He strode toward a wrought-iron gate housed within the galstra walls. The walls hemmed in nearly half of the property, with a five-story tower at its center. A neatly manicured lawn was spread all throughout the walled area.

The tower and the walls were newer additions, not native to Iltar's youth. He had them constructed after inheriting the family homestead. His family's land sat on a large enough plot after all. The entire homestead was precisely five phedans. A phedan was the basic unit for measuring plots of land on Kalda. Most city blocks were four phedans, arranged in a square.

"Delrin, Jalim!" Iltar shouted, looking toward the tower. "They're here."

Iltar waited patiently as two men clad in brown chain mail marched to the gate. Delrin walked with a limp. He and Jalim opened the gate and joined Iltar on the stone path.

"Hegdil will watch the gate," Iltar said. "The boys are eating some of Belsina's pastries."

"Fruit-filled ones, I hope?" asked Delrin, cocking his head. Delrin was slightly shorter than Iltar and had a stocky build. His face was covered in thick auburn bristles. Part of his matted auburn hair hung beneath his helmet. "Belsina made some for us, didn't she?"

Iltar grinned. "She'll make brandleberry ones."

Delrin closed his eyes, joyfully taking in a long whiff.

Jalim chuckled at Delrin. "It's no wonder you're fat," he said. In contrast to his counterpart, Jalim was tall. He would have been lanky if it wasn't for his rigorous training.

"I'm not fat, I'm sturdy!" Delrin retorted. "And a person always puts on a little weight when they age…"

Jalim snorted. "Speak for yourself."

Delrin and Jalim were hearty warriors. In their youth, they had embarked on many adventures with Iltar. Now in their late forties, they were retained as guards for Iltar's homestead. He trusted both of them, having been through many perilous times with them.

"Look at Master Iltar and myself," Jalim continued. "We're both in good shape. And then, there's Cor…"

"Yeah, but Cor has always been fit." Delrin said with a sigh, looking back to the house. Iltar knew he longed for a pastry.

❦

Not long after, the acolytes gathered in the lawn in front of their master's home. They practiced spells Iltar intended them to use for their training exercise. Many of the boys fared well in manifesting the magic, but a couple were slower than Iltar hoped.

After an hour of drilling the incantations over and over, Iltar decided they were ready.

"Everyone, listen up!" Iltar shouted, walking in front of the young acolytes. He paced back and forth as he continued. "You've learned two new spells today: The Acidic Barsion and the Ensnaring Tentacle. Some of you might have already guessed this, but we'll be using these two spells in action today."

Several boys muttered to each other, intrigued.

"My guards here"—he pointed to Delrin and Jalim—"will be attacking you. With real weapons." He let the idea sink in for a moment. Iltar wanted to simulate a sense of fear, fear that they could really get hurt. He would never allow it, nor would his guards.

"I'll demonstrate the exercise, and then all of you will try it."

Iltar walked a few paces away from the acolytes. Delrin and Jalim both hurried across the yard. The area in front of the house was vast and grassy, hemmed in by the leafy trees of the forest.

"Don't give me warning," Iltar shouted. He closed his eyes, taking a deep breath.

He could hear the wind rustling through the trees. A few of the boys whispered, wondering why he closed his eyes. All else was silent.

Clanking armor echoed across the yard, accompanied by hurried footfalls.

Iltar kept his eyes closed.

His guards' dash grew louder, and the acolytes gasped.

That should do… Iltar thought, opening his eyes and focusing on his pretended aggressors. They were only several paces away and would reach him in seconds.

Iltar swiftly uttered an incantation, extending his right hand, palm open. Yellow-green magic gathered at his fingertips as Delrin approached. Jalim had maneuvered around the yard, running to flank Iltar. The magic erupted as both guards came within weapon's reach. The acidic magic surged, flowing around Iltar, encasing him like a bubble.

As the acidic barsion formed, Iltar uttered another incantation and pulled his left hand back. Both guards halted, careful not to crash into the corrosive barrier.

Dark green particles swirled in Iltar's left hand, forming a mess of balled strands. He threw his hand like a punch, hurling the ensnaring magic at Delrin; all the while, the guard retreated.

The dark green mass expanded as it flew through the air, the strands becoming thick tentacles. Several reached out, gripping Delrin's arms and legs. They pulled Delrin to the lawn, pinning him there.

Too easy… Iltar smiled inwardly, turning to Jalim.

He cast another spell, leaping backward.

Jalim swung at Iltar, his sword glowing a white hue. Before the demonstration, Iltar had imbued both guards' weapons with dispelling magic—another incentive for the acolytes to succeed in their exercises. If the weapons struck the barsion, they could pierce through it. And, if they struck repeatedly, they could shatter it.

The blade sung through the air, narrowly missing Iltar's acidic barsion. Undaunted, Iltar continued retreating while finishing his spell.

Another mass of ensnaring tentacles formed, and he hurled the green mass at Jalim.

Jalim dodged, throwing himself sideways. He rolled back onto his feet, ready to attack once again.

Iltar, however, waved his hand in the direction of Jalim, and the magic whipped through the air. Several tentacles spread from the speeding ball and gripped Jalim, pinning him to the grass like Delrin.

The young acolytes clapped their hands, whooping and cheering for Iltar. Several hollered excited remarks about their master's demonstration.

That was nothing, Iltar smiled arrogantly, looking at Jalim. Iltar loved proving his skill. It invigorated him. But, these men were no real challenge. Yes, they were hearty warriors, but he had fared far worse in the past.

"Now it's your turn," he said, facing the acolytes. "Don't close your eyes. I only did that to put myself in a precarious situation that will undoubtedly befall you—attackers bearing down on you."

Iltar dismissed the magic and both of his guards stood up, moving back across the yard.

"Agen, you're first," he said, walking beside the acolytes. "When they start running, defend yourself. Remember, barsion first, then subdue them. That's an important lesson. Always follow that order. You can sometimes deter an aggressor simply by mustering a barsion barrier, especially if infused with a destructive magic."

Agen stepped forward, taking a deep breath. He steadied himself into a wide stance, anxiously watching Delrin and Jalim.

The guards bolted, drawing their weapons.

The young acolyte froze, but soon regained his composure. He uttered the incantation to muster the acidic barsion. It formed as the guards were partway across the yard.

Delrin and Jalim continued their dash.

Agen uneasily cast his next spell. The green tentacles formed slower than the barsion. He completed the spell as both guards reached him. They sliced their weapons through the barsion, causing it to flicker.

Agen screamed, panicked, but threw the magic at Jalim.

The ensnaring tentacles grabbed Jalim, pinning his arms to his sides. Agen squeezed the tentacles and Jalim dropped his sword.

Agen hastily turned and ran from Delrin, casting a second spell as he fled.

Delrin, however, picked up Jalim's weapon. He bolted after the young acolyte, swinging both of the weapons at the youth's barsion.

The protective magic flickered.

Agen finished the spell and hurled it at Delrin. He missed, the magic grazing the guard's arm. Yelling, Agen swept his arms across his chest, redirecting the magic. It latched to Delrin's arm, then pulled him sideways, pinning him to the ground.

One of the boys gasped.

"Seems harder than it looks," another groaned.

Iltar raised his brow at the comment, then called to Agen. "Not bad, but you could have cast your spells quicker. Dismiss the magic so they can reset."

Agen complied, joining the others.

Another boy stood, readying himself. He whispered the words to each of the spells as a means to prepare himself.

Delrin and Jalim reset, then resumed the drill.

One by one, each of the boys practiced Iltar's scenario. Like Agen, they were sloppy at first. Several had their barsions dispelled before they could disable both guards. But, they got better after each time.

While on their fifth round, Belsina emerged from the house. She quietly approached Iltar. "Lunch is ready," she said.

Iltar nodded. "After this one we'll be in," he whispered, returning his focus to the drill.

The acolyte dropped Jalim, pinning his sword to the ground. The boys learned from Agen's first run that they needed to trap the swords. That was a lesson Iltar didn't intend to cover, but he was pleased they had figured it out. He liked that about these acolytes; they were always adapting and improvising.

The boy cast his second ensnaring spell just as Delrin reached him. He pinned the guard before he could swing his sword.

It was the best drill yet. Each of the acolytes cheered, shouting the boy's name.

Belsina whooped and clapped loudly. "I'm impressed, Master Iltar," she said.

Iltar grinned a devious expression, glancing at her out of the corner of his eye. "And that's why you use real weapons."

The acolyte dismissed his magic, and another stood up, ready to take his turn.

"Wait," Iltar called. "Lunch is ready. Let's eat before we resume practicing."

The boys hurriedly filed past Iltar and entered his family's home. Belsina chased after them, but Iltar lingered outside.

"You know, they're not too bad, Master Iltar," Jalim called as he approached.

"Ya, not bad at all," Delrin added. "Now for some brandleberry tangrils!"

"You'll spoil your lunch," Jalim teased. "And those sweets will just slow you down."

"Well, I gotta give them an advantage with you running circles around 'em." Delrin waved his hands, exaggerating the sweeping motions.

Jalim laughed, and both men entered the home, leaving Iltar alone.

Smiling, Iltar turned back toward the yard, gazing into the trees as if peering beyond the forest. His amused expression, however, was fleeting. *Where are you, Pagus?* Iltar thought, the muscles in his face tensing. It had been nearly three hours. What was that boy up to?

2

THE STORM

The sun set in the east as the acolytes continued drilling with Iltar's
guards. Each of the boys had progressed since lunch. Many of the acolytes stopped both Delrin and Jalim before they reached them. Their
progress pleased Iltar. He stood watching his acolytes, hands clasped behind
his back.

"Master Iltar," one of the boys called, "How long are we going to keep at
this?"

"Tired, Bilda?" Iltar asked without looking at the boy. Bilda was one of the
youngest acolytes.

"Well… I'm kinda bored, y'know?"

"It takes much discipline to become a powerful mage," Iltar said.

"What if I wanna be an average mage, y'know? A regular ol' necromancer."

Iltar grunted. He knew that's not how Bilda really felt. The boy was tired
and trying to make excuses to get out of running the drills again.

"There's more to the magical arts than necromancy."

"But you're a necromancer, Master Iltar," the boy retorted.

That struck Iltar as funny. "I'm more than just a necromancer," he said,
looking down at Bilda. The boy sat cross-legged, leaning forward and propping up his chin with his hands. "I started off as an illusionist."

"Really?" Bilda turned toward Iltar with wide eyes. "You didn't have to become a necromancer first?"

Iltar shook his head. "I first wanted to become a grand mage, but my father
said I wasn't skilled enough. When I was twelve, he said he'd test me further.
But that never happened."

"So, why didn't he?" Bilda asked.

"Something came up," Iltar said calmly, though he choked back the real answer. His father had left after Iltar's grandfather died. His father never told Iltar why. He left him and his mother alone here on their homestead. And the next time he saw him—

No!

Iltar sucked in a deep breath and walked away. He was having another fit. He couldn't let the boys see it. These fits had never occurred this often. What was happening to him?

Iltar hurried around the house, the sounds of the acolytes and guards barely reaching his ears. He continued around the walls of a chimney and tucked himself beside it. Iltar leaned against the house, tears trickling from his eyes.

Tears? The tears turned to soft sobs, and he wept, slumping against the chimney. This had not happened in years. Iltar struggled to bring himself to the present. He was lost, overcome by sorrow. Iltar closed his eyes, trying to think of something else, but he couldn't shake those baleful memories of his parents.

No!

His mother's horrified screams echoed.

No!

Eruptions of magic rang loud.

No!

Iltar opened his eyes, but saw a dreadful sight. His mother lay on the grass before him. *No, she's not here!* Her elegant form was still, her eyes glazed over, looking skyward.

"This is not real," he told himself, clenching his teeth. "You've been gone a long time," he said to the corpse.

Burned leaves filled the air. Iltar looked around. The forest was on fire. Men in black robes and crimson armor hurled deadly orbs of magic through the yard.

No!

"This isn't real." He closed his eyes, but the sounds of battle raged around him. They resounded, growing louder and louder. "This isn't real!" he shouted. He focused on the grass, but he could see the battle raging around him.

"Master Iltar," a soft voice said from behind him.

All became silent.

His mother's body was gone. The forest wasn't on fire. The errant magic vanished. All was normal.

Eyes reddened and tear-soaked, Iltar turned around. All the acolytes stood nearby, watching him. Some were confused, others concerned. Delrin and Jalim jogged up behind the boys. They both saw Iltar's woeful demeanor.

"Come now, boys," Delrin said, grabbing the nearest by the shoulder. "I think we can use a break. Let's go inside." Both guards ushered the acolytes away, leaving Iltar alone.

They saw him. They *all* saw him. A moment of weakness, and now they knew. Overcome, Iltar slumped against the chimney. A wind rustled through the trees, breaking against Iltar and the house. Dark storm clouds loomed over the northern horizon. The clouds were traveling fast.

"YOUR TIME FOR VENGEANCE IS COMING, ILTAR," a voice whispered on the wind. It sounded familiar, almost like it was his own.

Startled, Iltar stood up, frantically scanning the lawn. "Who's there?!" he snarled, stretching out his hand, poised to cast a spell. Faint laughter reached his ears, but soon faded.

What was happening? Was he going mad? It seemed like it. Seeing things that weren't really there. Hearing strange voices. The inability to control his emotions. *Oh, I'm going senile...*

Thunder clapped in the distance.

The storm!

Iltar came to his senses and hurried around his home. None of the acolytes were in the yard. Iltar darted to a covered porch, to the home's main entrance. The door was open, slightly ajar. He hurried inside and closed the door behind him. More lightning crackled, muffled.

He took a deep breath and searched the home's foyer. No one was present. Faint conversation echoed from his left. Iltar turned, walking to a staircase leading to the upper floors. It rose along the foyer. Belsina's voice faintly sounded from one of the upper hallways. Soon after, the maid walked onto the landing atop the stairs and descended the steps.

"I was showing them to some rooms," she said, looking earnestly at Iltar. "Those clouds look thick, and I don't want those boys traveling back to Soroth in the storm."

Iltar simply nodded, stepping aside so Belsina could pass him. Belsina stopped beside him, gently placing her hand on his arm. Her gaze was concerned. She knew. Belsina had to know. "Why don't you have some tea?" she suggested and walked down the foyer.

"That sounds fine." Iltar nodded and followed her. "I'll take some messel." They moved down the foyer, passing several rooms on either side. They eventually came to the rear corridor that led to the kitchen.

"Twice in one day," Belsina said in a hushed voice. She didn't look at Iltar, but glided across the kitchen to fetch a large, black stockpot. Iltar silently watched her fill the stockpot from a spigot near the stove. Belsina stoked the fire and set the stockpot on a rack inside, placing a lid with a whistle atop it. They had an apparatus that could hold magical flame, but it was only good for something as small as a teapot.

"I know of what's happening to you, Master Iltar." She turned around, looking him square in the eyes. "It's this place. I know you love this home, but there's a lot of sorrow here."

Iltar folded his arms, averting his gaze to the kitchen island. Belsina had never brought this up. Why now? But, she was right. He was fond of this place. It was home. Iltar had warm memories from his youth, and even after his parents' death, there were good memories then too.

He opened his mouth to speak, but footsteps echoed into the kitchen. Soon, Hegdil and all the boys were present. The acolytes eyed their master in the magical arts, concerned. Young Bilda, however, approached him.

"Master Iltar?" the boy asked. "Are you okay?"

Iltar narrowed his eyes and raised his brow, attempting a hard look. "Why wouldn't I be?"

"You looked like you were going crazy," said one of the boys with a grin. "Like that old conjurer out in the woods."

That lightened Iltar's mood, and he chuckled. The thought of him becoming like old Amendal seemed humorous. Amendal was a crazed man, but he'd been that way since the dreadful expedition to the Abodine Wasteland. Amendal was the sole survivor. And, he had the strangest delusions about his survival. Amendal *was* mad. But Iltar couldn't imagine him otherwise.

"You were screaming like a lunatic," Agen said, looking worried.

"Don't worry, Master Iltar, if you go crazy we'll take care of you," another boy chimed in.

"Take care of me?" Iltar asked, grunting. "It'll take a lot more than a few acolytes to put me down."

The boys laughed.

"No!" the same boy retorted. "Take care of you, like a grandparent."

"Are you calling me old?" Iltar asked with humor in his voice.

Everyone laughed

After the laughter died down, Bilda stepped forward and hugged Iltar. He was small; his head barely reached Iltar's stomach. Although, Iltar was quite tall. Taken aback, Iltar raised an eyebrow. None of his apprentices or the acolytes in his charge had ever showed this type of empathy. Except Balden.

All the other boys gathered around Iltar and Bilda, embracing their master. A tear trickled down Iltar's cheek. These boys were unique. There was something about them that made them different from the other acolytes of Iltar's Order. Perhaps it was the way he treated them? He wasn't harsh and cold like Alacor and the other necromancers. But then again, they were nothing like Iltar.

"Wow…" Hegdil muttered, glancing back and forth between the crowd of boys and Belsina.

Lightning flashed through the windows, followed by thunder.

"Well, I think this is enough of *this*," Iltar said, and another tear trickled down his cheek, catching in his goatee. The boys stepped back, smiling at Iltar.

"It seems this storm has evoked some strange things, in all of us," Iltar said. "As we won't be practicing any longer today, why don't we retire to the parlor? I can tell you all a story."

⇒•⇐

The storm waxed throughout the evening. As Iltar had suggested, he and all the others gathered in his parlor, including Hegdil. The guards, however, returned to their posts at Iltar's tower.

Iltar sat in a large high-backed chair beside the fireplace, reading aloud from a book called *The Myth of Morgrid*. It was a mythical tale about a young boy and his journey to reclaim the realm of Aletstyr. It originated from long ago, perhaps a thousand years. This particular tome was a reproduction of the tale, penned a hundred and fifty-two years ago.

The acolytes were scattered across the parlor. Some sat on the sofa in front of a window with a view to the front yard of the homestead. Three boys sat on the other chairs while the youngest sat on pillows in front of Iltar. The tale intrigued the acolytes. They leaned forward, intently listening to the story.

Hegdil, however, listened from the far end of the room, eating one of the brandleberry tangrils Belsina had made earlier that day.

"*And so,*" Iltar read from the book, "*Dorith and his friends reached the pinnacle of Mount Ulinar. They found, atop the peak, a flat spot of ground hemmed by forty-two pillars. Legends said councils were once held here that decided the fate of all Aletstyr.*

"*Dorith strode boldly to the center of this council area. He twirled his staff and slammed it into the ground. He then removed a black sphere from his pouch. It glowed with tiny lights, arrayed like the stars of the night sky.*

"*Holding his staff in one hand, and the black ball in the other, Dorith spoke the ancient words of the Irumsebsil. The ball glowed. It shone exceedingly, beyond the luster of the sun at noon. A hum rippled through the air, then a violent screech.*

"*The light faded, and a gigantic sphere hovered before Dorith. It was a portal to another realm. The sky was a blood-red. The landscape looked like char, with rivers of orange. There were no trees. Only spires of rock.*

"*Taking courage, Dorith stepped forward. His friends joined him. Together they reached for the portal—*"

"Dinner is ready," Belsina's voice carried from a dining room next to the parlor. A wide archway connected both rooms.

Iltar paused, glancing to his right, where Belsina was putting out place settings. The dining room was large enough to hold a table that seated sixteen. "We'll resume reading after dinner," Iltar said, placing a velvet strand on the page he was reading. He shut the book, placing it on the mantle.

The younger boys groaned. Enthralled by the tale, they pestered Iltar to keep reading. The older boys, however, got up from their seats and filed into the dining hall. Iltar was the last to take his seat at the table. He sat at the far end, looking back at the parlor and watching the raging storm. The trees of the forest danced wildly. A broken tree branch bounced across the yard then flew through the air. It struck the parlor's window with a resounding clatter.

"Dreadful storm," Belsina muttered. "It's a good thing you boys are staying the night."

She had a point. This was a dangerous storm. But even if it had let up, Iltar wouldn't have wanted them traveling back to Soroth. The roads through this part of the forest would have been washed out. Hopefully the storm would end soon, or they'd have to stay another day. Well, that would afford more training.

Belsina dished out the food for each of the boys first, then Iltar and Hegdil. Their evening meal consisted of a stewed beef, with cooked vegetables native to Soroth. They were served over boiled potatoes.

They ate and conversed about different things: the exercises of the day, current events, and aspects of the tale read by Iltar. The storm, however, continued raging.

After they finished their meal Belsina rose from the table. "Hegdil, come with me," she said. "I need help with dessert." The groom nodded, and wiped his face, leaving his napkin on his plate.

"Master Iltar," one of the boys said, "Do you think there's any truth to *The Myth of Morgrid?*"

"Truth?" Iltar asked with a chuckle, leaning back in his chair. He glanced to the ceiling, eyeing the chandelier hanging over the table. It had small clear stones encased in decorative gold, each emitting light. The stones were mostly gray, except for a couple which were blue. They were gems imbued with magic. Most people called them lightstones. "You can always find truth in tales," he continued, still staring at the chandelier.

"I mean, do you think any of it really happened?"

That struck Iltar as funny. He found himself laughing. *The Myth of Morgrid* was just a fanciful tale used to inspire young boys to become great men. In fact, the main hero's name had changed throughout several editions. Iltar had even heard people tailoring it to their own children when they told a verbal reiteration.

"Well, he's laughing," Agen said. "So to answer your question, I'd say no."

Iltar quelled his laughter, and Belsina reentered the room, carrying ramekins filled with dark-blue pudding. Hegdil was not too far behind her. "Are we talking about real tales now?" the groom asked, excited.

Each of the acolytes turned toward him, and one spoke up. "Do you know of any, grooms-master?" That title seemed a little inflated. The boy was obviously stroking Hegdil's ego.

"Well, everyone knows the Dragon Wars were real," Hegdil said, setting down the ramekins.

Iltar rolled his eyes. Yes, the fabled Dragon Wars. Everyone had heard that story. There were as many versions and iterations as there were stars in the sky. In fact, that was one of the first stories that Iltar's father ever told him. At least, the first one that he remembered.

"Dragon Wars?" Bilda asked. "I've never heard of them."

"But, dragons aren't real," Agen said. "No one's ever seen one."

"Just because you haven't seen it, doesn't mean it doesn't exist," Hegdil retorted, following Belsina back out of the dining hall. They still had to dish out more pudding.

"Doesn't that crazy old conjurer think dragons are real?" one of the boys asked, the same who had called Iltar crazy earlier in the kitchen.

"Yes, he does." Iltar nodded with a sigh. "Amendal claimed to have fought one in the Abodine Wasteland."

Several of the boys snorted, attempting to quell their laughter. Iltar shared their opinion. Yet, he wasn't as vocal.

"Can you tell us the story, Master Iltar?" Bilda asked. The boy seemed to be the only one who didn't know about the Dragon Wars. Very odd that no one had ever told him the tale. It was a foundational story for all Kaldeans, or so he thought.

"Certainly," Iltar said, grabbing a spoon. He tapped it on the table, waiting for his pudding. "A long time ago, it was said that dragons ruled Kalda. Various breeds composed a council. They ruled for centuries until one of their own turned against them. He slew those who opposed him, taking control of this council. From there, he waged a war that spread across Kalda, engulfing the human and elven realms—"

"Like Morgrid!" Bilda interrupted, but flinched.

Iltar chuckled, but continued relating the tale. "The war was said to have lasted for a thousand years. Both worlds of elf and man were split, and brother fought against brother."

Belsina and Hegdil returned, carrying the last of the ramekins. Iltar paused and began eating his pudding. Hegdil, however, chimed in excitedly. "They say that the leader of the evil dragons, he who killed the others who ruled with him, could grant immortality. He was a living god! People worshiped him all across the world. That's why everyone fought. Some didn't believe that a deity could walk among them."

The boys sat intrigued, not even touching their pudding. They watched Hegdil emphatically tell the tale.

"Then, one day, the hatchling of one of the slain dragon leaders started a rebellion. He rallied both men and elves and waged a war to avenge his father. He was a platinum dragon. The greatest of his kind! The three races— dragons, elves, and men—banded together to fight against tyranny. They were valiant soldiers, gifted in the magical arts. The good dragons, which were of the platinum and golden breeds, forged armor and weapons for their allies. They say that those weapons could absorb magic."

Hegdil continued, telling of heroic battles and fables of intrigue. He vividly described the fictional war. He told how evil dragons were slain, or imprisoned. But some were banished—where, he didn't say. He also spoke of inventions, describing many tevisrals—both fictional and real—as products of the war. That was a common tale. Many men believed that tevisrals were ancient. In this day and age, no one knew how to recreate such things, not even experienced mages. Even methods of repairing them were unknown.

Iltar sat back, listening. His groom was entertaining.

"The platinum dragon had finally turned the tide of the war. It had been hundreds of years. He marched at the head of an army built on hope. They laid siege to the enemy capital. The battle was bloody. Many died. But, they won. The enemy was finally defeated. But," Hegdil gestured, holding up a finger, "one day the enemy will return and the men of Kalda will have to fight for what's right once again."

"Well, I've never heard that ending," Agen said. Neither had Iltar.

Hegdil finally took his seat. He had been standing the entire time. Everyone else had since finished their pudding. "Well, it's true," Hegdil said in a matter-of-fact tone. He sat in his chair, eating his pudding.

"Wow…" Belsina said with a playful tone. "I can't believe you abstained from your pudding this long."

She had a point. Hegdil loved food. But he was equally engrossed in telling the tale of the Dragon Wars. Usually, it would have been a boring tale. Iltar had heard it so many times, so many ways. But today, the way Hegdil told it conjured a sense of curiosity. *Weapons that could absorb magic,* Iltar thought. That was something he had never heard attributed to dragons or their war. He knew of such weapons. Worked with them, even.

"Food isn't the only thing I love," Hegdil said with a sullen tone. "There're horses and… stories!"

"Hegdil the Fabulist," Belsina said, chuckling. "Breeder of Horses, Connoisseur of Desserts. In that order?" She smiled playfully.

She always teased him. Never hurtful, though. They had a sweet tension between them. Iltar wondered why they hadn't gotten together as a couple. Perhaps they had, and he didn't know it. After all, Iltar lived primarily in the tower behind the home.

Hegdil squinted, thinking. "No…" he said slowly, shaking his head, "flip the last two." He winked at Belsina, scooping up a last spoonful of pudding.

Belsina grinned widely, holding back laughter. Soon after, she stood and gathered the empty plates. Hegdil joined her, carrying what he could.

"Why don't you help them out?" Iltar said to the acolytes. The boys complied, taking the plates, ramekins, utensils, and other dishes used to serve the evening meal.

Everyone filed out of the dining hall, except Iltar. He strode to the parlor and stopped at the fireplace. The wind still beat against the window, and the rain continued pouring. It was springtime, after all. Storms like these weren't uncommon. But, by all that was magical, this was an awful one.

Lightning streaked across the sky, thunder faint.

Iltar grabbed the tome atop the mantel and opened it. He took his seat and looked over the last page he had read. It told how the hero and his friends opened the portal to the realm of Desnong. *Wouldn't that be something?* he thought. *Traveling to other worlds.* That idea seemed so absurd, but it was fun to imagine. Just the thought of it made him feel like a boy again, filled with wonder. He hadn't felt like that in a long time.

One by one, the boys reentered the parlor, eager for their master to resume reading the tale.

Iltar took a deep breath and eased into his seat. "*Together, they reached for the portal,*" he continued reading. "*Upon touching it they found themselves on that distant world of Desnong. The Ancient One had told them it was a location for one of the Shards of Aulnak. Now, where would they begin their search?*"

⟞•⟝

Iltar opened his eyes, finding himself in his parlor. Sunlight shone through the window, and there was no sign of the raging storm. Odd, since it had been pouring when he retired to bed. Not even the remnants of rainfall were on the grass. But why was he here in the parlor? Iltar had retired to one of the bedrooms upstairs.

He wasn't sleepwalking now, was he? Shaking off the thought, Iltar entered the foyer. "Belsina," he called. He moved through the foyer, to the rear of the home. The kitchen was empty.

"Agen!" Iltar shouted, moving back to the foyer. "Bilda, Tigan!" He expected to hear a pitter-patter of footfalls from the second floor, but there was nothing. Iltar hurried up the stairs, rounding the landing and arriving at the first bedroom. It had been his when he was a child. The door was wide open; the bed was made up neatly. It didn't look like anyone had ever slept there. His eyes were drawn to the window, to a yellow sky with blood-red clouds.

That's not normal… he thought, hurrying to another room. It was just like the first. Tidy.

"Where are they?" he whispered warily, thinking of his acolytes. Iltar hurried back down the stairs, darting outside. He ran around the home to the roadway leading to the stables and his tower.

"Hegdil!" Iltar shouted, nearing the stables. The wagon and the horse, Filly, were gone. "Delrin, Jalim!" he shouted toward the tower. Usually, the guards would have been standing at the tower's entrance, but they weren't there.

"Where is everyone?" Iltar grumbled with annoyance. Nothing seemed right. Then there was that odd sky.

Puzzled, Iltar hurried down the path leading to the forest. It turned from stone to dirt shortly after the tree line. Surprisingly, the ground was dry. No trace of mud. He ran for what seemed hours. Usually there was traffic on the forest roads, but all was quiet. Too quiet. Iltar passed no one. Where had everyone gone?

Iltar eventually broke from the forest, entering the vast coastal plain containing the city of Soroth. However, what lay ahead of him wasn't Soroth. At least the Soroth he knew.

The forest highway which led to the northern gates of the city was destroyed. Large craters marred its face. Walls which lined the city were toppled. Buildings which would have been standing were demolished. Soroth was in ruin.

How…? He gawked, dumbfounded. "What happened?"

Iltar regained his composure and ran to the ruins. Many of the roads were destroyed like the forest highway. Remnants of buildings were strewn across many of the roads, making them impassable.

Eventually, he neared the southern piers. Soroth was a major port city on the various trade routes of the world. Surely, there would be vessels moored. Perhaps the survivors were there. But, Iltar hadn't seen anyone as he hurried through Soroth. Not even corpses. With all that destruction there would have been dead about, wouldn't there?

Iltar rounded a corner, seeing the city's southernmost piers. To his dismay, they were like the rest of Soroth. Wharves were crushed. Vessels were capsized. Some ships were snapped in two, their broken hulls rising above the water… water that was purple! What was wrong with this place?

"This can't be real…" Iltar muttered, raising an eyebrow. Was he dreaming?

He hurried down the road, nearing the coast. An undamaged pier caught his attention. It was the only thing intact. Iltar hurried toward it, running faster than he ever had. Seeing that intact pier sparked a hope within him. He darted onto the wooden planks, his footsteps resounding.

A masculine figure stood at the end of the pier, clothed in a red robe.

Finally, another living soul! he thought. Perhaps he could find answers. That was silly. Wasn't this a dream? It didn't feel like one though. He was lucid, totally and completely.

The robed man stared out into the ocean. Iltar couldn't see his expression although he thought it full of resolve. He was imagining it, wasn't he?

The man's red robe was finely detailed, with embroidered symbols unknown to Iltar. The embroidery was mostly red, with accents of gold. The symbols had a symmetrical pattern to them, mirrored along an invisible line along the back of the robe.

A wind picked up, rustling the stranger's robe.

Iltar stopped his hasty dash only a few paces away. "You there!" he shouted. "What happened here?" The robed stranger glanced over his shoulder. His white hair was long, hanging partway down his chest. His face was covered in a thick white beard. Brilliant sapphire eyes peeked at Iltar. But he didn't turn. His expression was grim, not stoic as Iltar had imagined.

"Who are you?!" Iltar shouted. The stranger continued glancing over his shoulder, but he didn't speak.

Iltar tilted his head, raised an eyebrow, and set his jaw. He had to be dreaming, but he found himself speaking, anyway.

"Tell me what's going on here? Where is everyone? Why is Soroth in ruin?"

The robed stranger finally turned around, holding two dark-red tomes in his hands. Their covers were embossed with a strange design. Iltar couldn't quite tell what it was, but it looked like seven spikes above a ball. But there was more to them. Claws around the ball?

Still confused, Iltar stared at the stranger. It was like looking into a mirror. He looked exactly like Iltar, except for the beard and hair. But his face... it was exactly like his, how he was now. That hawk-like face and that sharp nose! They were his. Every wrinkle. Every blemish. He was a perfect reflection.

"Why do you look like me?!" Iltar found himself shouting. The stranger's identical appearance angered him, though he knew not why. The robed man blinked, but said not a word.

A resounding knock echoed across the ruined pier. Iltar looked around, frantic. Where was that sound coming from?

The knock sounded again, and again.

"Iltar," a feminine voice boomed from across the ocean. "Master Iltar." Iltar looked around, but was drawn to the stranger once more. The man looked sternly at Iltar, his gaze exuding determination.

Suddenly, everything changed.

He was no longer on the pier over that strange ocean.

"Master Iltar,"—Belsina's voice was muffled through a door—"breakfast will be ready shortly."

Iltar sat up on his bed. It was the same room where he had retired after reading to the boys. His childhood bedroom. The sheets were tossed on the floor, and so was the pillow.

He darted from the bed to a nearby window. It wasn't storming outside, but it was partly cloudy. The blue sky peaked through the clouds. Gray clouds. "What a nightmare," he muttered.

Iltar pulled himself from the window, walking to a dresser. Neatly folded on top of it were the black tunic and pants he often wore under his black robes.

I need to go into Soroth today, he thought. *I have to find Pagus. That boy better not have gotten into trouble.*

"Eventually, I came to the shores of those desolate lands. I fashioned a boat by use of transmutative magic. Luckily, I had some solidifiers with me. Or that would have been a short trip."

- From *Origins and Oaths of the Keepers*, preface

Cornar dodged a shimmering claymore. It swung past his face, just barely. He was still spry for his age, only fifty-three. But he was in good shape. Tall. Toned.

Evading another swing, Cornar twirled his serrated dagger—a favored weapon. The dagger's blade was as long as his forearm, almost the length of a short-sword. But his father always referred to it as a dagger, so Cornar did too.

Cornar shuffled through the tall grass, weapons ready. In his other hand he wielded a double-bladed short-sword. The short-sword was longer than the serrated dagger, but not by much.

Kalder—a large, burly man wearing brown chain mail—charged at him. Kalder was a little taller than Cornar.

Gripping both weapons, Cornar blocked another blow from the claymore, catching the larger weapon between the dagger's serrated edges while reinforcing the block with his short-sword. Pushing the claymore away, Cornar lunged forward, kicking the burly Kalder in the stomach.

Kalder staggered backward, but he didn't fall. Kalder was too skilled for that. He'd better be.

"Ha!" Cornar said with a grunt and smiled. "Not bad, Kalder," he shouted as his opponent rebounded for another assault.

Kalder wasn't the only one advancing on him. Gregan, clad in dark-brown plate armor, was approaching. His breastplate bore the emblem of a sword rising out of the water, with a snake wrapped around it. That emblem signified the Soroth City Watch, the organization that policed the isle's capital. Gregan, however, was no watchman. At least, not any longer.

Gregan wielded a fanisar—a staffed weapon, much like a halberd. It had a curved blade on one end and a metal ball on the other.

Cornar didn't care much for those weapons. He knew how to use them, but they weren't preferable.

At that moment, Kalder came close, swinging his claymore. Cornar parried the blow, directing the large weapon toward Gregan. The parry forced the second fellow to shuffle sideways, slightly slowing his advance. But Gregan continued, swinging his fanisar in a downward strike.

Cornar crossed his blades, catching the fanisar in front of his face. Kalder swung again. Noting the rebounding swing from Kalder, Cornar redirected the fanisar to the side. He ducked under the claymore, and it sailed over his head. Cornar spun, kicking Kalder's knee while throwing his elbow at Gregan's plate gorget. Cornar recoiled from the unison strikes, spinning as he landed behind both his foes.

"C'mon boys!" Cornar shouted. "You can do better than that!" Kalder and Gregan spun, settling into defensive postures, waiting. *Clever.* They wanted him to come to them. Neither had landed a blow the entire sparring session. They had been on the offensive, and Cornar simply reacted to them.

"What's wrong, Cor?" Gregan asked from beneath his helmet, his voice muffled. "Tired already?"

Cornar grinned with exhilaration. "Not yet." No, he was not tiring. Cornar was invigorated! Though this was just a sparring match, it simulated what he yearned for most.

Twirling both weapons, Cornar lunged forward and let out a battle cry. He meant to distract his opponents, but they didn't react. Instead, both Kalder and Gregan eyed him carefully, weapons at the ready. Their stances mirrored each other, their leading arms side by side, so that Cornar couldn't pass between them, like he had before. This was a common tactic Cornar had developed. If one were to fight side by side with another they could easily watch each other's backs.

Cornar pulled his feigning strikes, shifting in front of the armored Gregan. He moved sideways, jabbing at the joints of Gregan's armor. Gregan, however, twirled his fanisar across his chest, forcing away Cornar's weapons.

Cornar danced back around them, but both men shifted their stances. They blocked and parried Cornar's swings, defending each other when possible. Cornar landed fewer blows, but he sneaked in an occasional one here and there.

They continued sparring for a while longer until a feminine voice shouted across the field, "Cor, Ordreth and your sister are here!" His wife Karenna's voice came from Cornar's nearby home, undoubtedly from one of the windows overlooking the field.

The men stopped, breathing heavily. Cornar swiftly sheathed his weapons and took in a calming breath.

"Well, that was fun," Kalder said, dropping the point of his claymore into the grass.

"As always," Gregan exclaimed, lifting the visor on his helmet. Sweat dripped down his freckled face, his bright red beard wet.

"I'm going to get cleaned up," Cornar said, running his hand through his brown hair, still thick and free of gray. Cornar didn't have many wrinkles either, and his round face was clean-shaven, making him look younger. He cast his emerald eyes westward, noting the sun rising over the horizon. Last night's storm was nowhere to be found. The winds had torn up part of the brandleberry vineyard. It was a good thing they had harvested a few days before.

"Yeah, I'm sweaty," Gregan said with a chuckle as he removed his helmet. "I doubt anyone will want to be in the same room with me."

"Uh-huh," Kalder groaned. "Please, clean up."

The three of them laughed and turned to walk across the field. They all looked about the same age, though Cornar was the eldest, twelve years Kalder's senior. Gregan was a year younger. They laughed and bantered as they crossed the field. They were close, like family. The three of them had been through a lot together. Their sparring and training wasn't the only thing that bound them.

Once out of the field, the two younger men continued bantering as they approached a small guesthouse. It was one of several buildings on Cornar's countryside property. Besides the guesthouse, there was a stable, a winery, and the main house. Kalder and Gregan often stayed at the guesthouse, even though they had homes of their own in the city, Soroth. Many of Cornar's former pupils often stayed there when visiting.

Cornar, however, continued to his home. It was the largest building on the sprawling property. He'd raised three children here with Karenna. They had settled on this plot of land nearly thirty-five years ago. *My, time flies,* Cornar thought. This wasn't the same house they had started with.

When Cornar had bought the land, they lived in a tiny shack. That humble home had now grown into the manor house standing before him. It hadn't taken long. Cornar was an adventurer, and a good one. He had amassed a fair amount of wealth before he was twenty-five, about the same time his oldest daughter was born. She was the middle child.

Cornar hurried up to a side door, which led to a mudroom. He quickly slipped off his chain mail; it was much like what Kalder was wearing. Cornar dumped the armor into a large trunk and then hurried into the house carrying his weapon belt. He wouldn't leave that there.

Cornar wound his way through a hallway, coming to the rear staircase leading to the upper floors. He climbed the steps two at a time, a habit he had picked up as a child. Cornar rounded another hallway and came to his bedroom, where the door was cracked open.

"Honey," he called as he entered, looking around for his wife. But Karenna wasn't there.

Locking the door, Cornar hurried to an oversize bed. It was a little too luxurious, but that's what Karenna wanted. It was carved from dark-brown wood with speckles of gold, with tall posts on each corner.

Cornar knelt beside the bed, pulling out a lockbox from underneath it.

Now, this was a safe place for the weapons. He unlocked it with a key, and then gently secured both the serrated dagger and short-sword. Cornar couldn't bear losing them. Those weapons were precious.

Once the weapons were secured, Cornar walked across the room to a doorway leading to the bathing chamber. It was time to clean up. He had gotten sweaty too, but not as bad as Gregan in his plate armor. Cornar didn't like wearing plate. Yes, plate armor afforded greater protection than chain mail, but so did barsion magic. Most plate wearers wore chain mail beneath the clunky armor. But why do that when you could have barsion covering you? It seemed a silly thought. If there weren't mages around, he saw the logic behind wearing plate. But who traveled into hostile territories without a mage? That was foolish.

⟤•⟥

Cornar walked back through his bedroom, wearing a semi-formal tunic and pants, both made of green silk. He briskly exited the bedroom and descended to the first floor, this time traveling down the circular main staircase that led to a vaulted foyer.

At the foot of the stairs a double doorway on the right led to a private study. Both doors were wide open as usual. Cornar used the room mostly for reading.

He trotted across the foyer, toward a parlor opposite the stairs. It was a large room with a hearth at the far end. Beautiful furniture—crafted with flowery designs—was arranged in a square throughout the parlor. The furniture was from Arbath, a faraway city in the Kingdom of Los. Each of the pieces was like the bed upstairs, opulent.

"Uncle!" a voice called from behind him. Cornar spun. His nephew was in his study, standing beside a thick desk. Ordreth was youthful, in his mid-twenties. His face was round, like Cornar's. Ordreth wasn't as tall as Cornar, but he was built like his uncle, a hearty young man.

"Ordreth," Cornar said with a smile, hastening into the study. He hugged his nephew and then placed his hands on Ordreth's shoulders. "You seem excited," he observed.

Ordreth blushed. "I'm gonna do it, Uncle." He sounded determined. "Here, let me show you." Ordreth dug into his pocket and pulled out a small black-velvet pouch. "It was finished three nights ago. I had Nath help me with the design, and it's perfect!"

Cornar laughed, shaking his head. Oh, what would it be like to be young again… *I do hope he took* her *wishes into consideration.* He motioned to the pouch. "Well, let's see it."

Still grinning giddily, Ordreth reached inside the pouch, removing a feminine cobalt ring inlaid with a golden sapphire. A betrothal band.

"It's beautiful," Cornar said.

"Tomorrow night," Ordreth said, "I'm going to ask her. I found the perfect place, overlooking the southern shores of the island."

Cornar smiled. The last time he'd seen Ordreth this excited was when he'd finally allowed his nephew to join him on one of his adventures. In fact, that's when he'd met *her.*

"I'm sure Sharon will like it," Cornar said.

"I'm certain, too," Ordreth said, slipping the ring back into the pouch. "She had drawings of what she wanted, or so Nath said. Nath saw her one night, and she was looking at the pictures longingly. When I told him and Tilthan about my plans, Nath said he'd swipe them from her diary. So, he did."

Cornar cocked his head. That was daring.

"I know what you're thinking," Ordreth said. "Yes, she'll probably be upset, but in the long run, she'll get what she wanted."

Shaking his head, Cornar turned aside. Ordreth was young. But Sharon did love him… No matter. "Let's see if your aunt has breakfast ready," Cornar said.

Uncle and nephew walked side by side through the large house. They wound through a couple of hallways until they reached the keeping room overlooking Cornar's vineyard. The keeping room was divided into a sitting room and a dining area. Chairs and sofas were arranged near the windows. A table ran the width of the room on the opposite side.

Faint chatter echoed in from another doorway. Then Cornar's wife entered the room carrying a covered plate. Karenna was petite and elegant. Her light-brown hair hung just past her shoulders. She had a long slender nose that came to a perfect point. Her thin lips always seemed to smile. Her voice… Oh, it was tender! Always loving. She set the plate down, gazing at Cornar with love in her hazel eyes. That stare seemed to last forever. It exuded kindness, devotion and undying love.

"Well, aren't you going to say hello to your sister?" Karenna asked Cornar. He hadn't even noticed his sister standing beside his wife. Karenna had always been enthralling. She could completely and totally distract him. He needed that, especially in the coming days. Cornar glanced beyond his wife to where his sister, Galana, stood with folded arms.

Galana cocked her head at her brother. Sometimes people thought them twins, but Cornar was a year and a half older. Like him, and their father, Galana was tall, with brown hair and vibrant emerald eyes.

"Good morning," Galana said with a sarcastic tone.

"Sorry, Galana," Cornar said, rounding the table. He hugged her and held her for a moment.

"You're fine," she said, patting his back. "Did Ordreth tell you the news?"

"He did."

"This is so exciting!" Karenna exclaimed. She grabbed her husband's hand with both of her small ones. "Another marriage in the family! This is going to be the last one… until the grandchildren begin to marry," she said with a contemplative tone. Karenna was always thrilled with the thought of expanding their family. She was one of nine, the eldest daughter. Ordreth was the only nephew on Cornar's side, and the thought of having a new niece excited her.

Especially one she knew and adored.

"Come help me," Karenna urged, tugging on Cornar's arm. Soon, they were out of the keeping room and on their way to the kitchen.

Kalder entered a moment after them, stern and alert. People often joked that he was like a stone statue, but Kalder had a good heart. He was a kind man and a fierce warrior, but he was disinclined to talk unless he found it necessary.. Kalder was dressed in casual attire. His light brown hair neatly combed over. "Do you need any help, Karenna?" he asked.

"You can wash the brandleberries," she said, motioning across the kitchen. Karenna handed a covered plate to Cornar. "There," she said, smiling. Karenna leaned forward, stood on her tiptoes, and pursed her lips for a kiss. Cornar complied gladly.

Karenna could make him forget about everything. All his cares. All his worries. Cornar needed that.

She's perfect.

After their embrace, Cornar returned to the keeping room. He set the covered plate beside the other and resumed talking to his sister. Kalder and Karenna returned shortly thereafter with the rest of the morning meal. Then Gregan finally arrived.

The tall, burly, auburn-haired man stood like a tower, hands to his hips. He sniffed the air with a smile. "You know, Cor," he said, "I really come here for Karenna's cooking. Yes, we're friends, and I do enjoy the sparring, but… I'm drawn to the food."

The men laughed.

Everyone took their seats around the table. They ate and conversed about Ordreth's news. Karenna was the most excited of them. She spoke giddily about the forthcoming wedding. One might have thought it was her own.

Cornar found Karenna's excitement even more intoxicating than the thrill of the battlefield. That's why Cornar loved her. That's why he *needed* her. He was getting old. Cornar couldn't always be out in the world adventuring.

After breakfast, Cornar and the men moved to the sitting area of the keeping room. They stared out the windows to the vineyard, where a couple of workers were surveying the vines. Cornar and Karenna were perfectly capable of taking care of the vineyard themselves, but Karenna wanted to share their wealth. So, they hired help.

"Anything new happening?" Gregan asked. He sat back with his legs crossed, picking at his teeth with a metal toothpick.

Kalder shook his head. "Not that I've heard."

"Cor?" Gregan cocked his head. "It's been a year and a half, and we haven't gone anywhere. I'm getting bored."

Cornar chuckled and leaned forward. He glanced to Ordreth, who listened intently. "I'm not the person to ask," Cornar said.

"Huh?" Ordreth piped up, surprised. Gregan had a similar expression smeared across his face.

"I was going to tell everyone next week," Cornar said reluctantly. "But I suppose I'll tell you two now." He glanced to Ordreth and Gregan. "I'm retiring. I promised Karenna that after this last trip I would be done. She wants us to do more things together, and I'm getting old. I realized that when we were escaping that fortress…" He trailed off, thinking of how he had almost died because he was too slow, even while enhanced with magic. Enhancing magic only amplified your capacities; it couldn't restore your physical prowess to what it was, not if it was waning.

"You're joking!" Gregan blurted. "What about this morning? You were landing blows like a wild man."

Cornar laughed. He wasn't feeble yet, but he didn't want to grow old while out adventuring. That would get him killed. *Then I'd never see her again…* "No, I'm not joking." Cornar quelled his laughter. "I'm leaving Kalder in charge of our little band."

Kalder quietly nodded. The weighty responsibility heightened his stoic demeanor.

Cornar had trained hundreds of men and women over the years. Many of them joined him on his adventures with mages of Soroth. Some had died on those adventures while others had left his band for various reasons. But, about fifty remained.

"It's not going to be the same," Ordreth muttered. He looked sad, his excitement over his engagement deflated.

"You'll all go on without me," Cornar said with a grin. "I've trained you well."

"Nearly all of us go on these adventures because of *you*," Gregan said, his tone almost angry. "We trust you. We know you'll protect us. We're loyal to a fault."

"Don't you trust Kalder?" Cornar asked, gesturing to the burly man.

"I do, but *you* bind us together," Gregan retorted. "You're the man who brought us all together. You keep us together. You can't just leave."

"I can't?" Cornar laughed and leaned back. "I'm not immortal. I can't go on, charging at the head of our small army. I'm getting old, Gregan."

"Cor deserves a life without danger," Kalder finally spoke up. "I don't like it either, but we'll all get used to it."

Gregan grunted, looking at Kalder. "You don't really mean that. I can tell it in your voice, Kalder. You don't believe it." Kalder simply stared at Gregan.

"Just keep this to yourselves," Cornar looked at the three of them. "I'll tell everyone next week."

Gregan sighed and folded his arms, his mood foul. Ordreth nodded solemnly. Would the others react this way?

Kalder had been somber when Cornar told him. But that was typical of Kalder. That was often how he reacted to ill news. Kalder had been a sober child. Perhaps it was his upbringing as an orphan. Cornar and Galana were orphans as well, yet they had known their parents. Kalder didn't have that luxury.

They all sat quietly, watching the workers in the vineyard. This was not how Cornar had envisioned their day. He could feel an actual divide in the room. Would that division creep into his little band? Cornar had worked so hard over the years to cultivate camaraderie. Would his decision to walk away shatter it?

Cornar hoped not.

4

MISCHIEF

- 10th verse from the Feast of Sorrows

As Iltar's wagon emerged from the forest, the morning sun warmed his face, contrasting with the cool spring breeze blowing from the eastern shores of the island. Hegdil sat beside him and drove the wagon. Filly, the black horse, trotted, his horseshoes clanking against the stone highway. Chatter from behind reached Iltar's ears; the acolytes were teasing each other. Iltar, however, contemplated the ride through the forest.

That dream was still fresh in his mind. Though the forest, the various dirt roads, and the highway were fine, the destruction he had witnessed still haunted him.

Why would I dream of such things? he thought. And that man who looked like him. There was something eerie about that *reflection*. Iltar shook the thoughts aside, turning his attention back to the road.

The wagon moved toward Soroth, amid riders on horseback and horse-drawn carriages. A merchant caravan was up ahead, probably from the western side of the island. Farmers there sold their produce here in the capital city, a more profitable market than any other city in the west.

After a short while, Iltar's wagon neared the city gates. Soroth was a modest city compared to those Iltar had seen in other parts of the world. But Soroth was home and held a special place in his heart. Iltar didn't remember much of Tor, the city of his birth, except for the hustle and bustle of its citizens. Soroth was much quieter. Although the city was a major port, the docking district was mostly on the southern side of the city. There were piers and wharves along the northeastern edge, but not many.

The location of the docks caused a divide among the citizens. The northern half of Soroth consisted of neighborhoods and shops. It was the more attractive part of the city. The wealthy lived there. The farther south one went, the less affluent the city became. The southwest side was the worst.

Soroth enveloped most of the southeastern corner of the island that shared the city's name. With a population of nearly two hundred and fifty thousand, the city was the largest in the nation, which consisted of sixteen other, smaller islands. The islands of Sarn, Silgarn, and Sereth—each half the size of Soroth—had one large city and several smaller towns scattered along their coasts.

Pagus was from Sarn. The rebellious youth was a member of one of their Royal Families. *That boy,* Iltar thought. What was he up to? Pagus had been mingling with the older acolytes recently, the apprentices of several council members of Iltar's Order.

Iltar's wagon slowed, and he braced himself as it came to a halt.

The merchant caravan up ahead had arrived at the northern gate. City watchmen in brown plate armor inspected the various wagons. After the guards finished their search, they waved the caravan through. Each of the other riders or carriages stopped briefly, but the traffic behind them continued without coming to a complete stop.

"Purpose in the city?" a guard asked, studying Hegdil and Iltar. "Oh— Master Iltar! A pleasure to see you." The guard bowed, then raised his face-guard. He looked familiar, but Iltar couldn't remember his name.

"We're just dropping my pupils off at the Order," Iltar answered, and the guard waved them on.

Hegdil flicked Filly's reins, and the horse trotted through the gate. "Did you boys eat all the tangrils?" Hegdil asked over his shoulder.

"Uh… yeah," one of them replied sheepishly. Hegdil sighed and flicked Filly's reins again.

After a short while they reached the gates of Iltar's society of mages, the Soroth Necrotic Order. The wrought-iron gates within the pale-gray galstra walls were drawn shut.

"Agen, go open the gate," Iltar called as the wagon came to a halt. The young acolyte complied, leaping out of the wagon and pushing first one side open, then the other. Hegdil flicked Filly's reins, and the horse pulled the wagon inside.

The Soroth Necrotic Order's compound covered four city blocks, arranged two by two. Buildings made from pale-gray galstra dotted much of the compound. Some of the buildings were vacant. At one time they had housed classrooms for students of the various magical arts, but not since the Order had changed. One of the buildings had been converted to a dormitory for the current acolytes. In Iltar's youth, there had been no dormitories.

Iltar's wagon rolled down a short road that wound around a statue. Hegdil stopped the wagon along the roundabout in front of a pathway leading to the Order's Main Hall. The boys all jumped out of the wagon and hurried across the grassy lawn. They waved goodbye to Iltar, hollering thanks to him.

"Are you sure you don't want me to wait?" Hegdil asked Iltar.

"I'm sure," Iltar said, climbing down from the wagon. "Go to Pagus's estate home. See if he's there. If not, maybe one of his servants knows his whereabouts." Hegdil nodded somberly. The groom had obviously been looking forward to another pastry. Iltar should have kept some up front. "Here," Iltar said, reaching into the pocket of his tunic. He pulled out several small coins and handed them to Hegdil. "Go find yourself a snack."

"You're kind, Master Iltar," Hegdil said.

Iltar nodded with a grunt. "I'll be here most of the day. If there isn't another storm, I'll borrow a horse and ride home. Whatever you find out, come back and tell me."

"Yes sir!" Hegdil said, flicking the reins. He rode off, leaving the grounds of the Necrotic Order.

Where should I start my search? Iltar wondered, scanning the grassy grounds. He eyed the Order's stable, down a road which ran along the wall, but shook his head. Pagus wouldn't be there.

All was quiet around him. The acolytes had dispersed, either entering the Main Hall or making their way to their dormitories.

Iltar's gaze fell upon the Main Hall. The entrance to the four-story rectangular building was guarded by two men wearing leather armor and holding fanisars. He could ask one of them, but they'd report it to their captain. That would eventually get back to Alacor, and Iltar didn't want that. He'd search for Pagus on his own.

Iltar strolled across the grass toward the eastern side of the campus. The lawn was neatly kept, but there weren't many trees. Mages needed room to practice, and trees would just be in the way. Iltar continued around the Main Hall, nonchalantly peering into the windows but not seeing anyone. That wasn't uncommon. Most of the rooms weren't used here at the Order, not since necromancy had reigned as the dominant magical art.

He continued to the center of the grounds. Shallow steps led down from the Main Hall toward a courtyard with smooth stone paths leading to the various buildings. All was quiet, except for the occasional patrol of guardsmen who moved along the walls.

Iltar took in a deep breath and clasped his hands behind his back. He blinked, and then everything changed. The buildings of the Order were in ruin, just as in his dream. Walls were toppled. A crater marred the place where the fountain should be. The sky turned yellow, the clouds crimson.

"What's going on...?" Iltar muttered. *Not this strange place again.* It was like a mirror, a twisted reflection. Some dark and demented reality. But why was he seeing it? Were his fits of anxiety morphing? That didn't make any sense.

"Iltar," a stern voice called from behind him, where the shallow stair should be.

Iltar spun, and the desolate vista vanished. All was normal.

Alacor, Grandmaster of the Soroth Necrotic Order, stood atop the staircase with arms folded, staring at Iltar with his hazel-blue eyes. His gaze was cold and condescending. A long sharp nose jutted from a gaunt face accented by high cheekbones. The grandmaster was a tall and slender man, dressed in a black robe more elaborate than the one Iltar wore. Alacor's dark-olive skin was wrinkled, his face covered in a long white beard. White hair hung past his shoulders, wispy and thin. Though he and Iltar were not too far apart in age, Alacor looked much older.

"I didn't expect to see you today," Alacor said, descending the shallow stairs.

"Alacor." Iltar bowed his head, purposely omitting the title. "I was dropping my students off and decided to come into the city."

"Oh?" Alacor asked, chuckling. He stopped beside Iltar, frowning with disapproval. "That's a task for apprentices."

"I had things I wished to discuss with the acolytes on the way back to Soroth," Iltar lied. He didn't want Alacor finding out about Pagus.

"I see," Alacor said with a sigh of disappointment. "And here I thought young Pagus was being rebellious."

"Pagus needed a break," Iltar lied again. He wondered if Alacor had any idea that Pagus hadn't shown up for yesterday's exercises. Though, Pagus would have gathered all of Iltar's acolytes here at the Order. Alacor would have had to be watching them depart at the northern gate to know what really happened. Unless Pagus got himself into trouble—

"He seems to need a lot of those," Alacor said, grunting and stepping around Iltar. The grandmaster stood beside the fountain. "Perhaps he needs a master who can hone his discipline properly."

Iltar grunted, not trying to hide his opinion.

"You don't agree?" Alacor cocked his head.

"Pagus isn't just a necromancer in training," Iltar retorted. He had to conjure an excuse that seemed plausible. "He's heir to his father's dukedom. The boy has other responsibilities besides learning."

Alacor laughed, shaking his head. He obviously didn't believe Iltar. "You need to rein him in, Iltar," Alacor snapped. "If you don't, the rest of us on the council will act. You don't want what happened to Balden to happen to Pagus, do you?"

Iltar's hate for Alacor flared, almost boiling beyond control. *Not now…* he told himself. He couldn't lose his temper here.

Alacor raised an eyebrow, studying Iltar. He grinned, seeming pleased that he had struck a nerve. *Arrogant bastard.* "Still that timid boy, aren't you, Iltar?" he asked, snickering and stepping away from Iltar. "Enjoy your time in the gardens."

The grandmaster ascended the stairs, walking toward the three-story windows lining the rear side of the Main Hall.

Timid? No, restrained. Now was not the right time to release all that suppressed anger. One day, when the time was right, Iltar would put Alacor in his place. Just not here. Not in the Order's gardens where there would be witnesses…

Taking a calming breath, Iltar strode from the fountain, following the path toward the Order's Record Hall.

Could he be there? Pagus had expressed an interest in studying the forbidden knowledge kept there. But the Record Hall was well guarded. Old tomes were locked away in the deepest floors, tomes containing spells meant to be wielded by only the masters of the magical arts. Pagus wouldn't be able to access them without incapacitating the guards.

The Record Hall was made of the same pale-gray galstra. It was only two stories tall and L-shaped. Windows lined both floors, accented with chiseled patterns of bricks along their edges. A small portico led to the only entrance, with two of the Order's guards standing at attention.

"Good afternoon, Master Iltar," the guards said in unison. "Back so soon?"

Iltar squinted, confused. What did he mean by that? He hadn't visited the Record Hall in months. Unless… oh, Pagus! "Ah, yes," Iltar said, and cleared his throat. "I believe I forgot something."

"That's twice in one day." The other guard laughed, but then flinched. "Sorry."

"Well, I am getting old…" Iltar played along with what he thought the guard implied. "I can't even remember when I left this morning."

"Actually, we didn't see you leave," the first guard said. "I guess the stories *are* true. There *is* a secret passageway beneath the Record Hall."

There was no such thing.

Found you now, boy, Iltar thought. He was glad he had, before someone else discovered this reckless ruse.

The guards opened the doors for Iltar, and he entered, shaking his head. Iltar made his way through the building, descending a flight of stairs. He picked his way across the basement, eventually reaching a darkened hallway barred by a wrought-iron gate. Another guard stood there.

"Master Iltar…" The guard gawked at him. "How did you—"

Iltar raised a finger, his demeanor stern. He eyed the man with a raised brow. "Don't say a word." The guard hastily nodded.

Mood now dour, Iltar opened the gate and stepped through the darkened hallway. It soon curved toward a steep stairwell. Faint chatter reached his ears, but he couldn't discern words. Careful to not make a noise, Iltar crept down the steps. One had to be stealthy while exploring ruins or dangerous hideouts.

Once down the stairs, he ducked behind a nearby bookshelf. Iltar still couldn't understand the faint conversation, but there were three voices. Iltar slipped along the bookshelf, weaving his way closer to the sounds.

"… I think it's supposed to be pronounced, ah-vel-knee-nah," a young masculine voice said. Was that Kreely? It sounded like him. But Iltar didn't spend enough time around the young necromancer to know for certain.

"No," another said. This voice he knew. It was Pagus! "It's avilnena. aa-vil-neh-naa."

"Let me read it," a third voice said. That was definitely Odinal. The first had to be Kreely. What a name… it sounded feminine.

Those three boys: Pagus, Odinal, and Kreely. Put them together, and you had trouble. As students they were bad for each other. But, they had a bond. If they ever became full-fledged necromancers, they'd be assets to the Order. They could become a powerful triad.

Pagus was Iltar's apprentice, studying how to mesh the illusionary and necrotic arts. The rebellious youth was obviously putting his skills to the test by infiltrating the Record Hall. Odinal was Melnor's apprentice, learning how to blend the arts of conjuration and necromancy. He was quite good. And Kreely; he was Alacor's apprentice.

The three of them continued arguing about the pronunciation as Iltar moved around the bookcase. They had their backs to him.

All three—each in their late teens—were shorter than Iltar. Pagus had light-brown hair. He was slender, unlike Odinal. Melnor's apprentice was a little on the chubby side. Kreely, however, was not as slim as Pagus and had dishwater-blond hair.

"It's pronounced ah-velk-na-nal," Iltar said, correcting the conspiring boys.

Pagus spun, smiling as he saw his master. He held an old spell book, its contents the source of their debate. The other two started: Odinal backed away, stepping into a bookshelf. Kreely, however, tripped and fell on the stone floor.

"The K-sound is derived from the sequence of the other words in the incantation," Iltar continued, his expression stern. "And the script you are reading uses the character sound for 'E' as a misnomer to deter curious students from doing exactly what you three are doing."

"Thank you!" Pagus exclaimed, still grinning.

"Pagus…" Iltar grumbled, stomping toward the youth.

Pagus arched his eyebrows innocently. "What?"

"You know *what*," Iltar said sternly. He stopped within arm's reach of Pagus. "You abandoned Agen and the others yesterday. And then, there's this!" He gestured to this forbidden part of the Record Hall.

"Oh," Pagus smiled smugly. "So, you don't mind that I impersonated you?"

Iltar frowned, his eyes alight with impatience. Kreely began to sob, sputtering pleas. Odinal, however, knelt on the ground, fearfully gazing at Iltar. "Please, Master Iltar," Kreely begged, "make it swift!"

Pagus laughed, shaking his head. He closed the book and looked to his friends. "Really? What's wrong with you two?"

"We'll be beaten!" Kreely screamed. "Not the acid. Not again! Please!"

"Silence!" Iltar snarled through clenched teeth. He didn't want the guard to hear.

"I will submit," Odinal said shakily. He began to tremble and leaned forward.

The boys' pleading darkened Iltar's mood. *Alacor and Melnor are decrepit fools,* he thought. *Their "discipline" only breeds weakness.*

"Wow…" Pagus turned back to Iltar. "I'm sure glad I'm *your* apprentice."

"Stop your sniveling," Iltar snapped at Odinal and Kreely. "Get on your feet!"

The terrified apprentices stood, unsure of what Iltar would do next. They didn't know him, really. Their masters rarely allowed them to interact with other masters in the Order.

"Iltar isn't going to do anything." Pagus chuckled. "Well, besides talk your ear off."

"Where do your masters think you are?" Iltar asked.

"At home…" Odinal answered timidly.

"And you?" Iltar asked Kreely.

"Same." The boy squeaked the reply.

That would make things easier. *Thank all that's magical.*

"Good," Iltar nodded. "*This*"—he gestured between himself and the boys—"never happened. You were not here. You have not seen this book." He pointed to the tome in Pagus's hand, then took a deep breath. "Now, tell me why you're here." He looked at Pagus.

Pagus sighed, hanging his head low. "We wanted to learn some new spells. I was getting bored, and so were these two. We're ready for such things."

"You're ready when we decide you're ready," Iltar retorted.

Pagus pouted, averting his gaze to the ceiling. "Uh-huh…"

"Pagus,"—Iltar spoke slowly—"I am not trying to hold you back. You might have the skill—the mental focus—needed to perform the spells. But there's much more to advancing in the magical arts."

"Really?" Pagus said, still looking at the ceiling. "That's not how Grandmaster Alacor put it to Kreely."

"Alacor is a fool," Iltar spat. Kreely gasped. "He's only the grandmaster because he inherited the position, not because he was the best suited."

"Then you should do something about that," Pagus said, finally meeting Iltar's gaze. "Where is the great Iltar that I've heard of? The one in the daring tales whispered among mercenaries, in the fantastic legends sung in taverns?"

Iltar clenched his teeth. Pagus was acting stubborn. The boy stood like a prince, arrogant and defiant. If Pagus continued at this rate, he'd be endangering more than himself. This was the first time Pagus had enlisted others in his disobedience. Something had to be done.

Narrowing his eyes, Iltar swiftly uttered the words to muster his ensnaring tentacles. Dark green magic swirled in his palm, tiny strands weaving together.

Pagus's eyes widened. He dropped the tome, stunned for a moment. He probably thought Iltar wouldn't act in such a way. But Pagus soon regained his composure, uttering his own incantation. Off-white dispelling particles began swirling around the youth's hands, but it was too late.

Iltar thrust his hand forward. Ensnaring tentacles burst from his outstretched palm, striking Pagus. They knocked him into a nearby bookshelf, binding him against it. Pagus nearly completed his dispel, but one of the tentacles flew into his mouth.

Unable to speak, Pagus couldn't finish the incantation, and the dispelling particles vanished.

"You need to stop this flagrant disrespect," Iltar said with restrained anger. "You're putting your friends in danger. If you care about them, you will listen to me and be obedient." He stopped and looked at the two boys, who gawked at him. "Some might think I've been lenient with you. Perhaps some consider me a coward, assuming I fear your family and wouldn't dare 'discipline' you because of their power. That's far from the truth." Iltar stepped closer, his face close to Pagus. "I don't fear them."

Then he stepped back, returning to where he had stood when he cast the spell. "What you see as boring and tedious cultivates discipline. Punishment doesn't cultivate discipline, only fear. You cannot breed greatness through fear. If you want to be a powerful mage, you'll do what I say. Not because I'm a pompous fool, but because I've walked the path and know what must be done." He waved his hand, dismissing the magic.

Pagus stumbled from the bookshelf and swallowed hard. He looked at Iltar with a gaze his master had never beheld. Respect.

"Now the three of you need to get out of here," Iltar said. "Follow me." He bent down, picking up the book Pagus had held. "You"—Iltar looked to Pagus—"go up to my office and wait there."

One by one, the three apprentices followed Iltar. He gestured for them to wait before they turned the corner leading to the gate. Iltar continued forward, and the guard stationed there opened it for him.

"All done?" he asked.

"Not quite," Iltar said. "Go tell the guards at the doors to send word to those stationed at the Main Hall. Relay a message to my groom that I've resolved the matter. I'll wait here by the doors while you're gone." He waved, dismissing the guard. "No one will get through."

Puzzled by the request, the guard shook his head and hurried off. Once he was gone, Iltar went back around the corner. "The guard is gone," Iltar said. "Go." He gestured the apprentices forward, and they complied.

As they reached the gate, Iltar suggested, "You should probably be invisible." The boys passed through the gate, and Iltar closed it behind them. They each turned, looking at Iltar. Kreely's and Odinal's faces were twisted in confusion mingled with gratitude. Pagus, however, was somber.

"My office," Iltar reminded the youth.

The three of them hurried off, and Iltar couldn't tell if they did as he suggested.

Soon after, the guard returned. "Your orders were relayed," he said.

"Good, I'll be up in a little while."

Back in the forbidden area, Iltar examined the book, *Praxion Velon's Repository*. Hefty read. Some odd spells were contained within it, complex but ultimately useless. Praxion failed to grasp important ideas about the ebb and flow of magics. There were much better tomes to learn powerful spells from.

This is why one needs a master, Iltar thought.

He made his way toward the place where the book belonged. Iltar replaced it near another volume hanging partway off the shelf. *That looks like Rovin's journal,* he thought. Why would it be here? Pagus and the others must have moved it around.

Iltar hefted it. He remembered seeing the journal years ago as a young boy studying the necrotic arts. Rovin had never let Iltar see its contents, claiming it was private. Even after Rovin's death and the journal's inclusion in this forbidden library, Iltar had never perused it. Not that he wasn't privileged to do so. After all, Iltar was one of the members of the Necrotic Order's council. He occupied the fifth seat. So, any of these tomes were his to read.

Curious, Iltar opened the journal, finding a page bookmarked with a folded piece of parchment.

He scanned the page as he walked to where the journal should be placed within this library. The entry was just one of the many recollections of a mission undertaken for the Mindolarn Empire by Rovin and his brother. It told of a battle in the nation which was now Litor. It was a boastful entry. Iltar grunted. He'd never cared for Rovin's exaggerations.

Iltar unfolded the parchment. "Now what does this say?" he mused aloud.

It was a letter addressed to Rovin, from his father. Iltar read past an introduction and cut to the heart of the letter. "*The seat of this empire is glorious! They have so many kinds of tevisrals, things I'd never imagined. But, before I carry on, I'm writing this to tell you that we're relocating here. One of the princes told me I'd be welcome to stay as long as I wished, and that I could send for you and your brother. I'm sure your mother would have wanted this. It's a good opportunity for you two. I even have a private tutor arranged for both of you, and then after you're tested you can attend the Hilinard. Their knowledge far exceeds what the others are teaching at the Sorothian Magical Order.*

"*I also sent a letter to your uncle, explaining everything. The two of you will love it here! But most importantly, we can worship freely. No longer will we have to slink in the shadows. This is where our family needs to be. Hopefully you will be here within a month. I've heard rumors that one of the Chosen is coming to the Feast of Sorrows. I'll see if I can get us in. Your brother will probably be too young to attend, but you're just the right age. Oh, Rovin. This is such an exciting time!*

"*I love you so much. May the Crimson Eye remain hidden for all time!*"

Crimson Eye? What was that? That seemed odd way to end a letter.

Iltar folded the letter and stuck it back in the journal. He closed the journal, then moved to put it back in its place on the shelf, but hesitated.

Why? There wasn't anything he wanted to learn about Rovin. Iltar hated the man, almost as much as he hated his brother. His brother…

Images of a forest aflame filled Iltar's mind. His mother's horrified screams. Eruptions of magic. The smell of smoke.

No! Iltar growled, shoving the journal onto the bookshelf.

The fit began to fade, and Iltar walked away. "I won't entertain such rubbish."

He continued through the forbidden library, climbing the stairs. But, that phrase lingered in his mind. *May the Crimson Eye remain hidden for all time.* Iltar tried thinking of other things, of Pagus, his acolytes.

But the phrase kept repeating in his head.

5

A PLEA

"After days of wandering on the ocean I came to the shores of an unin-habited island. That was strange. It seemed untouched from the war. How could such a place exist? It was a paradise, and I claimed it mine."

- From *Origins and Oaths of the Keepers*, preface

Krindal Heyardin paced at the bow of the *Executor's Breath*, moving between the forward cannons atop the raised forecastle.

I hope they listen, Krindal thought, worried, glancing back across the ship. The *Executor's Breath* was a large vessel, like the Sarin-class warships used by the Sorothian Navy, six decks and five masts. The ship required nearly fifty crewmen to sail, but there weren't that many manning the rigging. Soldiers had to fill in for the dead crewmen. Each looked pitiful, but who wouldn't after surviving the ordeal they had endured?

"We were lucky," Krindal whispered. "That gives me hope. Perhaps I will succeed…"

Turning back toward the bowsprit, Krindal looked across the ocean horizon, to his island homeland in the distance. *You can't ignore me now!* Krindal's internal voice was furious. This was not some foolish errand he had undertaken. This quest was the culmination of years of research, planning, and exploring. And now, he had proof. No longer would they ridicule him. Krindal had seen—with his very eyes—that the peoples of Kalda had once been more than they were now. Not only that, he had tangible evidence! Finally, Krindal could prove his theory of Cultural Regression.

Krindal could certainly compel his fellows, couldn't he?

"Master Krindal," a stern voice called.

Krindal spun, eyes wide. "Your Imperial Highness," he said with a bow, "I thought you were resting."

Prince Kaescis Midivar strode toward the ship's bow, his gait measured. He gazed at Krindal with his pale-violet eyes. "I was," the prince said, his stern, blond-bearded face marked by pain. Not physical pain—the prince's wounds were healed. No, this was a deep mental anguish. "But I heard reports of land, so I decided to search for you."

"I see," Krindal nodded. The prince came to rest beside Krindal, standing regally. That pose was *so* natural, but he was royalty after all.

"Are you sure you want me with you?" Prince Kaescis asked, eyes focused across the bowsprit.

"Yes," Krindal nodded. "You will lend credibility to my work. They will listen if you're present. I'm sure of it!"

"The tevisrals you found are not enough?" the prince asked.

Krindal looked at him frankly. "Many of my brethren are childish. It will take more than one witness to change their stubborn minds."

The prince cracked a smile. Krindal hadn't seen him grin since they'd fled to the ship. That was good; this young prince shouldn't be so somber. But whatever drove Prince Kaescis cursed him with seriousness.

"You can corroborate what we found, what we couldn't bring back. And, as our goals are aligned, your interest in the matter should be more than enough to persuade them. Too long have they ridiculed me for the knowledge I've sought."

The prince nodded in agreement.

"Fate brought us together," Krindal continued. "Our mutual discoveries couldn't be happenstance."

"We are guided," the prince said, looking to Krindal. "Inspired by the *Will*."

Krindal remained silent. He did not agree with the prince. They were not guided by a supernatural *Will* of some unknown deity, but arguing the point was useless. The prince was *too* devout.

Something had brought them together, but it wasn't a divine force. There were no gods. Krindal had seen enough of the world to know that. There was, however, something that pulled things together, a force of sorts. This new alliance wasn't just a happy coincidence. The Lost World had yearned to be discovered.

The times of darkness were coming to an end. He could feel it. Truth couldn't stay hidden for long, no matter how hard one tried.

"We should moor soon," the prince said, sighing. "I will rest some more. I suppose you will go to the Necrotic Order immediately after landing?"

"Yes," Krindal said, his succinct answer ringing with determination. "I'll call for an emergency council meeting. It could take several hours to gather each of them if they're not all in the city."

"That'll give us time to clear the unscheduled mooring with your people's port authority," the prince said, walking away.

"Thank you again," Krindal said, glancing over his shoulder. "I appreciate your faith in me and in what I seek, Prince Kaescis." The prince stopped briefly, but only gave a nod before crossing the main deck. Then he ascended the quarterdeck and disappeared within the aft portions of the towering ship.

Alone again, Krindal turned around, gripping the railing near the forward starboard cannon. His island homeland grew in the distance, spreading across the horizon.

"I will no longer be the old fool of the Order," Krindal whispered. "I will be remembered for these discoveries. I *will* change Kalda."

Kaescis entered his cabin atop the highest deck of the *Executor's Breath*. He continued his regal gait across the cabin though he was alone. He could relax, but why be different in private? Narrowing his eyes, he stopped behind a lounge chair and leaned against its back. He stared out the windows lining the cabin, into an ocean view behind the vessel.

"Are you sure about this?" a familiar feminine voice asked.

I thought I was alone, Kaescis thought, but didn't turn. He knew his visitor. "Why do you always sneak about, Laeyit?"

A soft chuckle echoed from behind Kaescis. Laeyit enjoyed theatrics, both on and off the battlefield. "Was that rhetorical, Kaescis?" Laeyit asked, stepping across the cabin. She stopped beside Kaescis, eyeing him briefly. "We don't need this old necromancer."

"He's been to everywhere else besides Klindala," Kaescis said. "It'll take months to retrace his steps. We don't have time for that."

Laeyit grunted. "I don't see why you're so worried. If the Alathians strike again that'll only put you closer to the throne."

Did she see him as an opportunist? No… he was far from that! Kaescis could not let his last uncle fall to another Alathian assassin.

"Besides," she continued, "involving another organization only puts our discoveries at risk. We're already in competition with that damned Aristocracy."

"The Sorothians are our allies, Laeyit," Kaescis reminded her, his tone firm.

Laeyit sighed. "If you go, don't you think it'll arouse suspicion? Krindal is not one of us. He speaks no token, nor promises a vow." Her tone was hostile, even resentful. "The one he seeks aid from is one of us."

"Do you doubt the Devouts of Cheserith?" Kaescis asked, finally turning to face Laeyit.

She was dressed in her typical tan outfit: free-flowing clothing with a plain sash tied around her waist. Laeyit carried an empty metallic-gray sheath upon her back. Her dark-blond hair was pulled back in a simple braid, her hair ornamented with enhancing tevisrals. The tevisrals looked like simple jewelry, a good disguise for such things.

As always, her face was free of makeup. Her eyelashes were short, giving her eyes a masculine appearance for a woman. Those yellow irises didn't help either. Though Laeyit was not ugly, she was definitely not the ideal specimen of a fetching lady.

"I don't trust him," Laeyit retorted, teeth clenched. "I saw him during the Feast of Sorrows. He fought those who beleaguered the palace alone. He's self-centered. Men like that seek to forward only their ambitions."

Kaescis grinned, amused by her observations. She could always discern one's true character by watching them on the battlefield. Strange gift. But it had proved useful.

"I know you've made up your mind, Kaescis, but I will still try to persuade you."

Grunting, Kaescis turned back to the windows. "I am only obeying the *Will*, Laeyit." He had to agree with Krindal. Kaescis was commanded to do so. That was not an excuse, though. Cooperating with Krindal made strategic sense. "Our enemies were stronger this last encounter. If we can round up even a handful of Sorothians, then this venture will be fruitful. Krindal thinks he can amass a small army, all in the name of scholarship. Whoever we enlist here will only add to our forces. Besides, there's no telling what we will find on Dalgilur."

"We could have killed them, you know," Laeyit said, her tone sullen.

"When we encounter them again," Kaescis said, clasping his hands behind his back. *We'll unleash the fury of truth.*

⬥•⬥

The *Executor's Breath* moored several hours later. Krindal left the vessel in haste. He was a citizen of Soroth, so entering the city was swift for him. The Mindolarnians, however, were not as fortunate. Though Kaescis was a prince, sixth in line to the Mindolarn Empire's throne, he still had to be cleared by the city's port authority.

Dusk had settled when Krindal arrived at the gates of the Soroth Necrotic Order. He strode boldly toward the Main Hall, speaking to the guards who stood outside as sentinels, conveying urgency in his voice and his words. That earned him an expedited meeting. Luckily for him, the masters who occupied the seats of the council were all present, a stroke of luck Krindal hadn't expected.

Fate was on his side.

Krindal's boots echoed off the stone atop the fourth floor of the Order's Main Hall. He had walked this way many times. Traversing these halls reminded him of his childhood, every time. Since he had no family, this was home. Krindal stopped at a pair of double doors, pulled shut.

Clutching his pack, Krindal paced back and forth near the doors. He was nervous, but who wouldn't be in his situation? Many of his Order laughed him to scorn. Some called him a crazed fool. Several of those ignorant men occupied seats on the council. But Krindal only needed a majority vote. Just four. If four of them would believe him, it would be enough.

One by one, each of the council members filed past Krindal and entered the council chambers through the double doors. Several ignored him. But, a few gave him a brief greeting. Their words were cordial yet cold.

Eventually, the last council member ascended a nearby stairwell. He was younger than Krindal, probably by twenty years. Krindal never knew his exact age. But of all the men who occupied a seat on the Necrotic Order's council, this man was probably the most trustworthy.

"Good evening, Master Krindal."

Krindal bowed but didn't speak.

"Are you all right?" the younger man asked, taking him by the arm. He leaned in then whispered, "You look worried."

"I am," Krindal said with a sigh.

"You'll be fine. I'll put a stop to any snickering."

"Thank you, Master Iltar." Iltar grinned, patting Krindal on the shoulder, then entered the council chambers. *He's not like the others,* Krindal thought. Why wasn't he grandmaster? Krindal could follow a man like that. Many would.

Hushed whispers came from the council room, but Krindal couldn't discern anything in particular. Then the doors were shut.

After what seemed an eternity, the doors opened and a guard emerged, waving for Krindal to enter. "They're ready for you, Master Krindal."

Krindal nodded, a knot forming in his stomach. He would not be the old fool tonight. He would not! Still holding his pack, Krindal stepped across the large room. He approached the seven council members, each sitting around an ornate wooden table painted to look like polished stone. The grandmaster was seated across from Krindal, at the head of the table, in a pretentious chair resembling a throne.

Does he think himself something divine sitting there? Krindal wondered, stilling his nerves. Alacor had ignored Krindal while entering the council chambers.

Krindal looked to each of the others. On Alacor's left were Toroth, Melnor, and Jalel—he was the grandmaster's younger brother. *When had he ascended to the council?* Krindal wondered. No doubt Jalel's ascension was a by-product of nepotism. Jalel looked similar to his brother, with dark-olive skin and that same pointed nose. His hair, however, was dark-brown, almost black. Opposite those three were Kallan, Iltar, and Velkor.

Alacor spoke up, drawing Krindal's attention. "Would you like to sit, Master Krindal?" Krindal nodded, and another guard brought a low-backed chair, placing it behind him. Krindal muttered a thank-you, and then sat, looking at each of the other necromancers.

"Your message seemed urgent," Alacor said, relaxing in his would-be throne. "What discoveries have you for our Order?"

"Time is of the utmost importance," Krindal said, resting his pack on his lap. "I've relied upon the mercies of a Mindolarn prince these last few months, but I come to you seeking aid." He let the idea sink in before continuing. Jalel gasped in surprise, he obviously wondered how Krindal could have royal connections. Several of the others displayed similar emotions.

"Many of you know what I've been doing the last few years," Krindal continued. "I've been searching for what I call the Lost World. I believe in Cultural Regression."

Kallan and Jalel had always snickered at the name for Krindal's theory. But this wasn't a wild theory. Many stories currently circulating through Kalda told of wondrous times and grand civilizations of the past, but there was no solid evidence, only random and isolated accounts from those who claimed they saw grandeur in the ruins of the past. Nothing more.

Simply put, the Lost World was a term used by scholars like Krindal to describe the long-forgotten greatness of Kalda: a world built and run on tevisrals, far more complex than what existed today; grand cities powered by magic and the absence of illness; the otherwise perfected humanity. Of course, the Lost World was older than the oldest recorded histories of the last several centuries. Many people claimed the Lost World concept a product of forced futurism, twisted to reflect on the past. There were many arguments against it, chiefly the lack of historical evidence.

Cultural Regression was a theory that explained the absence of the fantastical civilization painted by Lost World ideals. The general idea was that ancient cities were lost or destroyed during the fall of the Karthar Empire, which was nearly a thousand years in the past. Some scholars blamed the first monarch of Los. Others attributed the decline to a general ignorance that befell humanity.

Historically, not much was recorded after the fall of the Karthar Empire. Much of the information held by scholars today was secondhand.

"I finally have proof," Krindal said. "I've found the remnants of a highly advanced culture far predating the Karthar Empire."

"That's impossible!" Jalel spat, looking at the other council members with wide-eyed disbelief. His brother, Alacor, waved dismissively at him.

Toroth cleared his throat, then put forth a hand signaling that he would like to make a comment, so Krindal paused. "Would you mind giving us details, Master Krindal? I think we are well aware of your work this last decade."

"Very well." Krindal sighed and then took in a deep breath. "Three years ago I received a journal from a colleague of mine who was following a lead in Karbenath. It wasn't his journal, mind you, but something he found there in the city. The journal had a family tale in it about a great-grandmother—many generations removed—who guarded a mountaintop fortress, a place of wonder. She was called a 'Keeper,' but of what it didn't say. There was not much else. But there was another mention about this grandmother and her daughter. It spoke of the daughter making a pilgrimage to become like her mother. This discovery is what started me on my current quest."

Krindal continued explaining the particular details. He and several others had searched for similar stories about mountaintop Keepers and sojourns. To their surprise, they did find more information in several cities. But none of the accounts were firsthand. Some even seemed fraudulent.

"Eventually I was able to cross-reference the same mountain peak in not two, but four accounts. I set out with a few hirelings and trekked to the mountain, which was along the borders of Comdolith and Maltin. It was one of the peaks north of the supposed ruins of Karthar."

The council members sat silently, intrigued by Krindal's story. Usually Krindal didn't produce such tales. That's because he came back empty-handed.

"After days of searching, we discovered a cave near the peak. At first it seemed natural, but as we got closer, we could tell it was man-made. Weathered architecture was built into the mountain." Krindal paused, wanting to get this next part right. "Doors were cut from the mountain matching the strata of the nearby stone. They were hard to open, but we eventually entered this Keepers' Temple.

"A foyer led to a circular room, lit by skylights. There were sconces on the walls, but there were no lightstones in them. Seven rooms branched off from the circular one. Most of the rooms were empty, except for one, the one aligned with the entrance. There I found this." Krindal reached into his pack, removing a silvery oval disk, domed on one side. He placed it on the table—domed side up—and continued. "There was a raised dais in that room, with an altar of sorts. The altar had markings on it, arranged in three pairs: symbols in a strange dialect of the Kaldean Common Tongue, another that appeared Elvish, and a third pair that none of us could decipher."

Krindal pulled a necklace from his neck, setting it beside the silvery disk. "I started examining the altar and touched it in several places. Light shone from the altar, and then this materialized." He pointed to a white gemstone within the necklace. It was seven-sided, though the necromancers wouldn't be able to see that while it was in its setting. Krindal had placed the gemstone within the necklace so as to not lose it

"You won't believe what happened next," Krindal said, grinning widely. "We heard a hum in the room, coming from this disk. It shot through the door, zipping into the circular chamber. A beam of light then burst from this gemstone, through me and toward the disk. My hirelings thought I had died from some deadly beam of magic," Krindal said with a laugh. "But that wasn't the case."

He eyed each of the council members. Each was intrigued. *Astonishing!*

"Then this happened." Krindal removed the seven-sided gem from the necklace and placed it atop the silvery disk.

The gem rose from the disk, hovering in the air, and then a white light beamed from the disk to the gem. The light erupted, filling the council chamber with a blinding flash. The guards gasped in surprise and ran toward the table; their footfalls the only sign of their hasty attempt to rescue their employers.

The guards gripped Krindal's arms, pulling him from his seat. They stopped, however, as the light faded.

The guards gasped, along with the others in the room.

A map of the world hovered above the table, created by magic emitted from the silvery disk and projected through the gem. The disk was a tevisral, an ancient one. This mapping tevisral—as Krindal had come to call it—created a topographical representation of Kalda. All of Kalda. The map, however, was not a globe but lay flat.

The guard's grips relaxed and Krindal leaned forward, hands on the table.

"That's an illusion!" Velkor gasped.

"How complex!" Kallan exclaimed. Krindal would have thought him the most skeptical of the group but he was just as intrigued as the others.

"At first I thought this just a complex map, a wonder left over from the Lost World. But I was wrong. We camped there in the temple for nearly a week. We copied every inscription, drew an accurate floor plan, and searched for hidden rooms. We didn't discover any hidden rooms or secret messages, but kept finding various references to the number nineteen all over the temple. It was on the doors, across the walls, and covering the altar. So I wondered, what was the significances of nineteen? I didn't understand that until I studied this map." Krindal pointed to a mountain range on the large western continent. It was in the region between Comdolith and Maltin.

A glint of golden light shone in the mountains. Krindal waited until all of them were looking at it. Then he inserted his fingers into the particles comprising the mountains and spread his fingers.

The gesture magnified the map, zooming into a finely refined topographic view. One of the peaks glowed with golden light while the symbol for nineteen hovered above it.

"This temple was number nineteen," Alacor observed with a gasp.

"Exactly," Krindal said then pinched his fingers. The map returned to its original appearance. "Notice any more of those lights?"

Each of the necromancers leaned in, eagerly studying the map.

"Yes!" Jalel laughed. "There's more of them!"

"Twenty?" Melnor asked.

"Twenty-one," Krindal said, sliding a finger across the map and adjusting it so the large island of Klindala was centered above the mapping tevisral. "It's the last one. That one in Klindala didn't appear on the map until I visited all the other temples."

"And you want help to locate this last temple?" Alacor asked. The grandmaster's question wasn't too far from the truth.

"I can find it all right with this." Krindal gestured to the silvery tevisral. "My initial group of hirelings were either lost or died while helping me find all twenty of these temples. And I dare not continue this alone."

Of course, Krindal was not alone. Prince Kaescis was with him. But where was Kaescis?

"I've used all my coin to fund these excursions," Krindal continued. "At this moment, I am completely destitute." That was the truth. Krindal had spent everything, sold everything he had to come this far. But progress couldn't be made without sacrifices.

"I've had to rely on—"

A knock at the council room doors interrupted Krindal.

Perhaps I didn't *need you after all, Your Imperial Highness,* Krindal thought, glancing over his shoulder.

One of the guards opened the doors, revealing Prince Kaescis with several Crimson Praetorians acting as escorts. The Praetorians' blood-red armor glistened from lightstones in the hall. Kaescis whispered to the guard, who then crossed the room to the council. Krindal waited to explain further. He had to play this right, now that the prince had arrived.

"His Imperial Highness, Prince Kaescis Midivar, wishes to join this meeting," the guard said to the council.

"Let him enter!" Alacor gestured toward the door. Kaescis strode toward the council table, leaving his Praetorians in the hall. His gait was regal, bold, and purposeful.

"Master Krindal," Prince Kaescis said, "I apologize for my tardiness. We had trouble finding a permanent wharf." The prince stepped up beside Krindal's seat and clasped his hands behind his back.

"No need for apologies, Your Imperial Highness," Krindal said, bowing his head. "I was just explaining our request."

"Our?" Jalel demanded, cocking his head. He glanced to Alacor, confused, but Alacor made no reply to his younger brother.

"We have been seeking the same thing, Master Krindal and I," Prince Kaescis said. "Our paths crossed three months ago. It was a wonder we found each other at all."

"It was quite fortuitous," Krindal interjected. "His Imperial Grace has kindly taken me in, but I hardly think it his responsibility to champion my cause. Hence the reason I've come to this council. I am a necromancer of the Order after all. I would ask for supplies, able-bodied mages, and any others that can be spared to help me complete my quest."

Krindal eyed the necromancers, each considering his request.

Prince Kaescis cleared his throat. "Might I add, the Mindolarn Empire will act as a supplementary force. This is Master Krindal's discovery, and he should be credited with it."

"And why is your empire involved?" Iltar spoke up, raising an eyebrow at the prince.

Iltar hadn't said anything throughout Krindal's entire presentation. Krindal thought that was strange. Of all of the council members, Iltar should have been the most interested. Iltar was, by far, the most scholarly of the seven, and the most adventurous. Iltar had an explorer's reputation that was well known in Soroth.

"We want to see this truth come to light," Prince Kaescis said, calmly. "It can change the world for the better. Kalda needs it."

Iltar simply nodded and turned away. Did he not believe the prince?

"Any discoveries would be Sorothian claim," Prince Kaescis added. "And if any discovery would prove beneficial to the empire, then that's something for our governments to work through. Mindolarn and Soroth are allies after all."

"You are a benevolent prince," Alacor nodded. "We appreciate your respect and the aid you've given to Master Krindal."

Krindal watched the room, waiting.

Finally, Alacor spoke. "We will deliberate for a moment. If you two would excuse us?" The grandmaster gestured to the doors.

"As you wish." Prince Kaescis bowed and then strode from the council chamber.

"I thank you for your time," Krindal said, placing the seven-sided gemstone back in the necklace. The gem's separation from the mapping tevisral caused the magic to dissipate.

Krindal slipped the silvery disk back into his pack. He followed Kaescis outside and the guards closed the doors. Only Krindal and the Mindolarnians were in the hall.

"They were awestruck," Krindal whispered cheerily to the prince.

"I told you that you didn't need me." Prince Kaescis chuckled.

"And I said nothing of what befell us on the last island," Krindal whispered.

The prince nodded aloofly as if he were ignoring Krindal.

Perhaps I shouldn't have said it, Krindal thought.

After a quarter of an hour, the guards opened the doors, letting Krindal and Prince Kaescis back inside the council chamber. Both stopped at the edge of the table, waiting to hear the council's verdict.

"Master Krindal," Alacor said, his tone pompous. "We have voted unanimously to grant you aid."

Unanimous? Krindal wasn't the old fool tonight!

Alacor continued, "We will pull a stipend from the Order's treasury for you and those of the Order accompanying you. We expect a detailed report upon your return from Klindala. Any relics or tevisrals found by you or any mage under your charge will be considered property of the Soroth Necrotic Order. The discoverer will receive proper credit and a payment after a thorough appraisal. Do you accept these terms?"

Krindal glanced to Prince Kaescis, who nodded once.

"We do, grandmaster."

"Very well," Alacor said with a nod. "Brethren, those in agreement signify it."

In unison, each of the seven council members extended their right hands over the table, acknowledging their approval for ratifying the agreement.

"It is decided," Alacor said. "Master Krindal, you will be contacted tomorrow to finalize the details with the treasury and to receive your stipend."

The council members all rose from their seats. Many of them filed out of the room without further acknowledging Krindal or Kaescis. Iltar, however, stepped up to Krindal.

"I know of someone else who can help you," Iltar whispered, waiting for the other council members to leave before continuing. "I didn't want to bring this up around *them*. It'd just cause contention."

Krindal's eyes widened with excitement. Was Iltar really volunteering *them?* Surely, the Lost World yearned to be discovered! How fortuitous!

"I'll need more details from you, but I'm sure Cornar will commit."

Iltar *was* volunteering them! *By all that's magical!*

"Who is this Cornar?" Prince Kaescis asked.

Krindal grinned like a child seeing overflowing bags of candy. "Who is Cornar?" He laughed. "Why, one of the most notorious adventurers in all Soroth. A legend! He and Iltar built a band of explorers that are rivaled by no other! They've searched the world over for decades, amassing wealth and increasing their fame!"

The prince nodded, but didn't speak. He exited the council chambers and joined his Praetorians.

"Have you eaten, Krindal?" Iltar asked.

"Just rations aboard the *Breath*," he answered.

"Then let's eat and discuss the details," Iltar said, wrapping his arm around the older necromancer. His embrace was gentle, kind almost.

Iltar really should be grandmaster, Krindal thought.

"Let's go to the Sea Vistonia," Iltar continued. "It'll be my treat."

6

CLARION

Cornar skidded across the grass of his country estate and rose to his feet, eyeing Kalder. Kalder speedily approached with his claymore pulled to the side, tip pointed skyward.

Nice, Cornar thought, lunging forward. He swung his weapons but Kalder intercepted both the serrated dagger and the short-sword with the claymore.

They danced about, striking and parrying each other's blows.

"You already started?!" Gregan shouted, agitated.

As the red-haired warrior donned his helmet at the edge of the field, Cornar turned back to Kalder just in time to dodge a sweeping swing by rolling sideways. He stole another glance at the plate-covered warrior; Gregan ran, gripping his fanisar horizontally, his dash showing his eagerness to join the sparring match.

Evading another blow, Cornar rebounded, coming close enough to swiftly strike Kalder's belly with the sole of his boot. Kalder tumbled backward, rolling over his shoulder, but Gregan replaced him.

"You're not too old for this!" Gregan shouted, swinging his fanisar at Cornar. Gregan's words were true. Cornar *wasn't* too old for this... But there was that promise to Karenna.

Cornar ducked beneath Gregan's next attack, twirling his dagger so its smooth edge rested against his forearm. He slid forward, hitting Gregan's armored belly with a forearm strike. But that didn't jar the once–City Watch-man. Gregan continued swinging his fanisar while Cornar dodged the blows, striking plate-armored forearms. Soon, Kalder joined the fray. Cornar gracefully evaded both warriors' attacks.

Suddenly, white light zipped past Cornar's head. The light struck Kalder, surging through his armor and spreading across his body. Kalder glowed faintly.

"Magic?!" Cornar blurted. He wanted to look over his shoulder but he didn't dare.

A second later, Gregan was surrounded by a similar white aura.

Both warriors moved at speeds faster than normal. Enhancing magic did that sort of thing. Cornar struggled to defend himself, and *something* swept out his legs. Was that Gregan? Cornar hadn't seen the kick. But they were moving fast, faster than normal.

The hard ground met Cornar's back, and a sharp rock tried to pierce his chain mail. All the while, something slithered beneath him. *That was no kick!* The slithering thing was an ensnaring tentacle, wasn't it?

Gregan swiftly lowered his fanisar, but Cornar deflected it away. The fanisar struck the ground near Cornar's head, kicking up dirt that sprayed across his face. Through the dirt, Cornar saw Kalder slashing downward with his sword. The bladed end came crashing down toward his chest, tip near his neck. Cornar tried to block the claymore but was too slow.

Kalder abruptly stopped his blade just before it touched Cornar's armor. The burly warrior had amazing control, and his ability to pull the slice was a perfect example of his skill—especially since Kalder was enhanced with magic. If one weren't familiar with how one's body worked while enhanced, pulling such a blow would be difficult. This was not the case for Kalder.

"Match over," Gregan gloated. Cornar couldn't see his face, but he knew Gregan was grinning widely beneath his helmet.

Slow deliberate clapping echoed across the hemmed pasture, drawing his and the others' attention. Cornar craned his neck, looking around the fanisar still stuck in the dirt. A tall black-robed man stood near the half-fence, looking pleased with himself. He was obviously the source of the magics.

"I should have figured," Cornar said, rolling over on his side with a grunt. He flipped to his feet, standing beside his two subordinates. "That's cheating!" Cornar shouted, shaking his head. "Not fair, Iltar!"

"Oh, really?" Iltar said with a laugh, still clapping. "And when has battle ever been fair? You should know such things."

Cornar laughed and hurried across the pasture, Kalder and Gregan in tow. They soon reached the newcomer.

Iltar leaned against the half-fence, hands resting against one of the posts. He had bags under his eyes, but he smiled with anticipating glee. Cornar knew that smile. It meant only one thing. An adventure… *Blast!*

"You're here early," Gregan observed.

"And you look tired," Kalder said.

"I rode all night," Iltar said with excitement. "There's no time to waste."

Cornar could feel both Kalder and Gregan's eyes boring into the back of his head. They undoubtedly guessed at the purpose of Iltar's visit. Though Iltar often visited, he rarely did so this early in the morning. After all, the three of them hadn't had breakfast, and the ride from Iltar's home would have been a half day's journey.

"We need to talk," Iltar said, glancing to both Kalder and Gregan but settling his gaze upon Cornar. His expression asked, *Do they know that you're retiring?*"

"Do you want to sit?" Cornar asked, climbing the fence. On the other side, he and Iltar stood face-to-face. They were similar in height, tall men—though Iltar was of a more slender build. Iltar was only a year Cornar's senior, but he looked a lot older, his hair gray, his face wrinkled.

"It doesn't matter," Iltar said, glancing again to the two younger warriors. "You decide. Pagus is escorting the horses to your stables. I told him to go see your wife after he finished. The boy is hungry. He kept complaining on the ride here."

Gregan laughed and climbed over the fence, followed by Kalder.

"Then we can talk out here," Cornar said, sheathing his weapons. "What's got you so excited that you rode here all night? You're obviously not here for Karenna's cooking."

"But she's such a good cook," Iltar retorted with a wink. "To answer your question, I've come on behalf of Krindal Heyardin—"

Gregan grunted. "That old fool? Uh, Master Iltar, his wild gosset chases aren't something to be excited about."

Iltar raised an eyebrow at Gregan but continued talking to Cornar. "Krindal's stumbled across something big. This will probably be one of the greatest expeditions of our century."

All three warriors remained silent, but they knew that Iltar wasn't one to exaggerate. And he *was* excited. Riding all night? Yeah, this was important.

"And what is he looking for?" Cornar asked.

"Krindal has been sailing the entire world, chasing after the remnants of an ancient Order called the Keepers of Truth and Might. He's found temples of theirs all across Kalda, twenty to be exact."

"Has he found any relics or artifacts?" Kalder asked with interest. He obviously was interested in where this could lead. If this was all true, working with Krindal would prove profitable. Very profitable.

"Or things we could make *appear* as relics and artifacts," Gregan said with a smirk, glancing at Kalder.

"Something even better." Iltar paused, grinning widely. "Tevisrals. Ancient tevisrals."

"What?!" Gregan blurted, dropping his fanisar. He threw off his helmet, eyes staring widely at Iltar. Gregan probably saw piles of coin.

"You heard me," Iltar said, chuckling, then focused once again on Cornar. "Krindal came to us last night, asking the Order for aid. He has lost everyone who was assisting him, and he's spent every coin to his name. Krindal had to sell his home last year. The man's destitute."

"So he needs help to do what?" Kalder asked. "Looking for more of these temples?"

"Sort of," Iltar said, and then paced back and forth. "There's only one left.

At least he's pretty sure there's just one. It only appeared on his map a few weeks ago, once he left the one in the Igeacean Sea."

"The Igeacean Sea?" Gregan asked, looking confused.

"It's in the Desolate Lands. Northern side," Cornar replied. "And what do you mean it *appeared* on his map?"

"One of the tevisrals in his possession maps the world," Iltar said. "It's quite impressive. Anyway, another location appeared after he left the last temple. Krindal suspected there was another temple concealed, based on what he learned within the other temples."

"So, he's *not* on some wild gosset chase?" Gregan asked, raising a brow to both Kalder and Cornar.

It was true, Cornar thought. Krindal had a reputation, and not a good one. His insistence on his beliefs was akin to religious fanaticism. What a strange trait for a scholar.

"No, this is real," Iltar reassured them. "And from what he described about the temples, they're pre–Karthar Empire. One that he found in the northwest regions of the Black Mountains was even heated somehow. The weather was frigid, but they had to take off their winter gear while inside the temple, because it was so hot in there." Iltar chuckled. "The first temple he found was the most weathered. The others, however, were constructed of polished stone so refined that it glistened like metal. Doesn't that sound familiar?" Iltar grinned at Cornar.

Iltar was referring to several ruins both he and Cornar had explored years ago.

"Too bad you won't get to see it." Iltar sighed, still looking at Cornar. "I assume you told them, since you let them stay for this conversation?"

Cornar nodded. It *would* be a pity. Seeing this temple sounded intriguing, but there was Karenna and his promise. He *couldn't* break that promise.

"He did," Gregan said, grunting, "and we've been trying to convince him that he's not too old to keep adventuring."

"It's not working," Kalder said, his voice matter-of-fact.

"Of course it's not," Iltar said, laughing and shaking his head. "When does Cornar Dol'shir *ever* break promises?" The necromancer eyed Cornar, smiling. "You should respect his wishes. Kalder is fully capable."

"Thank you, Master Iltar." Kalder bowed. "That means a lot coming from you."

"Though I will miss him," Iltar said, his expression turning solemn. Cornar thought he could even see a glint of a tear in the necromancer's eyes. By Heleron's Trident! Cornar wasn't dying! *They're all making a fuss about my retiring.* How would the rest of his band react? This adventure would force Cornar to confront them sooner rather than later.

"How long do we have to prepare?" Cornar asked, changing the course of the conversation.

"They cast off in four days," Iltar replied. "Krindal should be receiving the funds as we speak. Last night when I took him to dinner, we bumped into Captain Salisar of the *Promised Maiden*. Krindal has sailed with her a few times.

That old scholar seized the opportunity and got her to commit to charter him and this expedition. Salisar was eager to comply after she heard his tale."

"He didn't have a ship before?" Kalder asked.

"No, Krindal returned to Soroth with some Mindolarnians. A prince had been helping him."

"Mindolarnians?" Gregan asked with disgust. "I'm glad he found someone else to carry this expedition. I'd hate to be stuck with a bunch of pompous self-righteous bastards on the high seas. Good riddance!"

Kalder cocked his head at Gregan and so did Iltar.

Cornar, however, shared Gregan's opinion. He didn't care for them, but that was probably prejudice inherited from his father. Cornar's father, Melthas, had experienced Mindolarn oppression firsthand during the empire's occupation of Tor and the Western Sovereignty. Melthas was a member of a resistance that eventually overthrew Mindolarn rule. That was a little over fifty years ago.

"They're still accompanying him…" the necromancer said, raising his brow. "Both Krindal and the prince are looking for the same thing."

"Great…" Gregan grumbled, kicking the dirt.

"But Prince Kaescis needs to return to Mindolarn before he can continue with Krindal. They lost some deckhands in a storm, and he wants more scholars to join them. Both Kaescis and Krindal are anticipating a huge find. Krindal intends to travel as a fleet until he reaches the Mainland, then the *Promised Maiden* will break off and head to Klindala."

"So I take it you'll be leading our band, under Krindal?" Cornar asked Iltar.

"Nope," the necromancer shook his head. "The council put a stipulation on Krindal's request. He could enlist anyone who didn't have a current apprentice. We can't sacrifice our pupils' progress for the sake of some expedition, no matter how grand or groundbreaking it might be. Besides, I need to be here for my students."

Iltar paused, looking at Cornar's country home. "Pagus has been causing problems. Yesterday, I caught him and two other apprentices pilfering spells from the restricted area of the Record Hall. If I leave, he'll run amok. An unchecked Pagus will most likely end up dead. I promised his family I'd watch over him, and I've not been doing a good job of that. Hence the reason I brought him with me."

"What's wrong with these Sarn Royals?" Gregan asked. "They think they can do whatever they want. Royals are not above law or order."

"Pagus is spoiled," Iltar said flatly. "He thinks he knows what's best. The boy is just like any other teenage boy his age. The royal blood only compounds his rebellious nature."

"So, this is going to be a strange adventure without either of you," Kalder remarked, folding his arms.

"Yeah," Gregan said. "Not the same. Not at all."

Iltar sighed and then continued. "Unfortunately, many of our usual mages won't be joining you either. The council's stipulation also applies to those teaching outside the Order's halls."

"That doesn't leave many options." Cornar frowned. Perhaps it was a good thing he wasn't going on this trip. It *would* be strange without their entire band. "That leaves only Igan and Vargos."

"I volunteered Clodin," Iltar said, "but I haven't spoken with him yet. I wrote a letter and had one of my acolytes deliver it."

"What about those two young wizards?" Kalder asked. "The ones Hex and Igan taught? They seemed okay on the last trip."

"Tinal and Renal?" Iltar asked. "Possibly. Neither has taken on apprentices. Then there's Hem. Hem has been helping Hagen with his pupils but he hasn't taken on an apprentice yet."

"So three wizards, an illusionist, a necromancer and a barsionist," Cornar said. "That's a little disappointing." A barsionist would be handy. An expedition the likes of what Krindal was amassing would always need a mage to cast protection spells.

"Yeah," Gregan said with a sigh.

"Plus any other mages that Krindal enlists," Iltar continued with a reassuring tone. "You'll probably encounter little danger. I doubt there will be a need for the wizards or Clodin. But we don't want to exclude them from any discoveries. This will be a historic venture."

"What about Amendal?" Cornar asked. "He doesn't have an apprentice."

"He's not around," Iltar said. "Amendal left with Dith last month, and is waiting for him to complete his *trials*." The necromancer shook his head. "Lorith went with them as well."

"I see," Cornar said. "Trekking those damned woods?" Iltar simply nodded.

Amendal had some strange ideas for advancing his apprentices. In fact, Dith wasn't even his apprentice anymore. The young mage was twenty-five and hadn't been a true apprentice since he was seventeen. Amendal, however, didn't treat him as a full-fledged conjurer. Dith was required to complete what Amendal called the Aramien Test of Valor. It was foolhardy.

The test, or *trial*, as Iltar put it, required Dith to travel through a dense forest on the eastern end of the Mainland—the main continent in the western hemisphere of Kalda. This forest, called Melar, was a prohibited land as decreed by the Kingdom of Los. Amendal's trial was technically illegal by Losian law. But the old conjurer didn't care. He and his brother had participated in such a trial when they were young, encouraged by their father. The trial was a family tradition of sorts.

Old Amendal decided to keep up the tradition and had Lorith—his first apprentice—undergo the trial. Lorith almost didn't make it out alive. Now it was Dith's turn. *Poor kid.*

"I sent word to Igan and Vargos that we should meet here," Iltar said. "I hope that's fine?"

"Of course," Cornar said. They always planned their adventures here at his country estate. Cornar just had to give his wife warning. Karenna would love the opportunity to play hostess. Besides, if Iltar hadn't said they'd be gathering here it would arouse suspicion.

"Good, I set for us to meet tomorrow night," Iltar said. "That should give us enough time to gather everyone."

Cornar nodded. That still would be pushing it. They'd only have one day to prepare.

"Do we need to contact Tilthan and his troupe?" Kalder asked.

"No. Kaescis has some people skilled in the art of thievery and stealth," Iltar said. "Is Tilthan even around? I haven't heard from him in months."

"I don't know." Cornar shrugged. "They can't be on a job, because Ordreth is proposing to Sharon tonight. I suppose we'll have to round those two up early in the morning."

"We can leave them a note," Gregan said. "I know where he's taking her."

"That sounds smart," Iltar said sarcastically, rolling his eyes.

"Wait till the morning," Cornar insisted. He didn't want to ruin his nephew's special evening. A couple shouldn't share the eve of their engagement with a call to adventure, no matter how monumental the trip. But they were adventurers… Who knows, it might make the proposal even more special.

"So no thieves, limited mages," Gregan reviewed their roster. "And neither of our leaders." He frowned as he spoke.

"We'll be fine," Kalder said, patting Gregan on the shoulder. "Now let's put our gear away and start contacting everyone."

"Just have everyone make their way here," Cornar said. Both warriors nodded and hurried off, leaving Iltar and Cornar alone.

"Do you want to go inside and rest?" Cornar asked as Iltar stepped forward. Iltar looked tired. His excitement was fading. Iltar nodded, but stopped abruptly, frantically glancing over his shoulder.

What was that about?

"Are you okay?" Cornar whispered. He knew the others were still within earshot and didn't want to reveal anything Iltar might want to keep private.

"I just heard something…" Iltar mumbled, shaking his head.

"One of your fits?" Cornar whispered as Iltar came beside him, and they slowly walked toward Cornar's home. Iltar shook his head but said nothing. He looked troubled, but his uneasiness didn't seem to be anxiety or trauma. Cornar could remember a time when Iltar would wake from reliving the nightmare of his parent's death.

Cornar knew what that was like, to an extent. He hadn't seen his mother struck down, nor had he heard it. But Cornar could remember his father's words as if he were speaking at this very moment. A year after his mother's death, Kandish, the man who raised Cornar's father, relayed Melthas's fate. That's how a child should learn of his parent's passing. No one should be a firsthand witness.

Those memories brought a tear to Cornar's eye, and he wrapped his arm around Iltar. The necromancer grunted humorously, but reciprocated the gesture. They were kindred orphans. Brothers bound by shared experiences and similar pasts. Iltar was as much family as Galana and Ordreth.

Arms still wrapped around each other, Cornar and Iltar entered the large home. They moved apart while Cornar removed his armor but kept his weapons belted around his waist.

"Let's get you something to eat," Cornar said. "I'm sure you're hungry."

"Yes," Iltar said, and chuckled. "I can feel the creature comforts calling."

When they reached the kitchen, they found Karenna, wearing a simple green dress and a full length apron, slicing fruit and placing the chopped pieces into a bowl. Karenna turned to look at Cornar. She didn't seem to notice Iltar.

Oh my, was she breathtaking! Even after years of marriage, he still found her a wonder to behold.

"Aren't you supposed to be exercising?" Karenna asked, wryly pursing her lips. She returned to her cutting as Cornar approached her.

"We have some guests," Cornar said.

"We *always* have guests," she said playfully. Glancing up from her cutting board, she finally noticed Iltar. "Aren't you here a tad early?"

"I couldn't wait till later," Iltar said. "We have an adventure coming fast upon us."

"Well not *us*," Cornar corrected him. "More like our little band."

"When should I expect everyone?" she asked without skipping a beat. Karenna was an amazing woman, always putting up with these adventures and the meetings that came before and after such trips.

"I told everyone to arrive tomorrow night," Iltar said. "I didn't want to spring it on you today."

"That's very thoughtful of you, Iltar," Karenna said, glancing over her shoulder to the necromancer. "But still, it's short notice."

"The expedition is leaving in a few days," Cornar said, leaning on the counter. "We're pressed on time. I told Kalder and Gregan to get everyone here as soon as possible. The weather is nice, so we can put everyone out in the field."

"Oh, don't be barbaric, Cornar!" Karenna sighed and playfully slapped her husband. "We'll have no such thing. We have plenty of beds." She paused then pointed at Cornar, poking his chest. "But you'll have to get them ready."

Iltar laughed, but soon made a whipping sound with his mouth. Cornar raised his brow at his friend. He was not some subservient man strapped down by marriage.

"And you," Karenna spun, waggling her knife at Iltar, "make sure the house is in order."

"Me?" Iltar asked coyly. "I don't even live here…"

"Well, you could have had me fooled… You certainly spend enough time here eating my food," Karenna retorted. "You're practically my brother-in-law. And that comes with responsibilities."

Karenna did run a tight household, especially when surprise guests were sprung upon her at a moment's notice. She was orderly and neat. Both traits made her perfect for Cornar.

Karenna returned to her cutting after giving her orders. "So, what's this adventure about?"

"The revival of ancient civilization," Iltar said. He always had a flair for the dramatic when being succinct. "Our band will undoubtedly discover ancient tevisrals, things beyond your wildest imaginations. We believe it will be one of the greatest quests to beset the human realm."

Karenna glanced up to Cornar. Her gaze asked, *Is he telling the truth?* Cornar simply nodded, getting lost in her eyes. Those eyes were captivating. Beautiful. Sensual.

Coming to himself a bit, Cornar thought he glimpsed Karenna looking at him with disbelief, not at Iltar's statements, but at his own love-struck demeanor. Was she dumbfounded by him? Her eyes seemed to scream, *Have you lost your senses?! This is an adventure of a lifetime!*

No, he was not senseless, just a man who intended to keep his promise to his wife. Cornar had accepted that he would never again set foot on unexplored land. Having confronted Gregan and Ordreth only strengthened that reality. He was not an adventurer anymore. Cornar was going to keep his promise to Karenna. They would have their life together, uninterrupted. No more danger. No more battles. It would be just him and Karenna.

It would be a happy life.

THE GATHERING

"Life was peaceful on this island. The animals were kind. The weather was temperate. I made myself a home beside a river which ran along a plateau. I had everything I needed. I soon realized the Au'misha'k could remain here out of the reach of men or elves, forever forgotten."

- From *Origins and Oaths of the Keepers*, preface

Many would consider the air inside Orchin's Tavern disgusting. The air *was* musky: a mix of smoked lavin root, alcohol, and body odor. But those smells didn't bother Nordal, he had smelled much worse. One could expect the vilest of smells while exploring the world.

A puff of smoke with the scent of lavin wisped in front of Nordal, clouding his view of the cards in his hand. The cards were a perfect pair of *Drake* and *Fairy*. Nordal would probably win with that hand. There were still several dozen cards stacked on the table.

Nordal casually glanced to his right at Midar. Midar had a blank expression on his clean-shaven face, his brown eyes staring at his cards. He methodically ran his freehand through his thick brown hair, scratching his scalp, but did nothing else. Midar was good at bluffing. Nordal could never tell when Midar was winning or losing.

Beyond Midar, Hemrin sat with a smile on his face, his brown eyes gleaming. Hemrin was always smiling. Hemrin's cards lay facedown on the table, his hands clasped over them.

That boy is always in a good mood, Nordal thought.

In addition to Hemrin's jovial attitude, he had a reputation for luck. And his luck was infectious. Bring him along on an adventure with dismal prospects of discovery, and you'd stumble across a treasure trove. Take him into battle against a force stronger than your own and come out nearly unscathed. Hemrin was the personification of luck.

The scent of lavin dissipated, and Nordal looked about the card table. Besides his two friends, four other men held cards. They were random strangers from the tavern who had agreed to play a few rounds of Sharzen.

Sharzen was an old card game. *Did it originate in Kildath?* Nordal wondered. *Or was it Los?* The game had seven suits with twelve cards in each. Drake and Fairy were only two of the suits. Each of the other suits was named after a mythological creature.

"Well?" barked the man sitting across the table from Nordal. He glared menacingly. The scar across his left eye didn't help.

"Are you that eager to lose?" Nordal said with a smirk. Another man grunted, shaking his head.

Nordal had won each of the previous rounds. Little glass marbles sat in a pile in front of him; the marbles were the markers used at Orchin's Tavern. Each of the marbles had colored flecks inside them, denoting denominations of coin: single digits, tens, hundreds, thousands. People usually didn't gamble more than that at Orchin's.

"You shouldn't act so smug," the scar-faced man said. "I'll get my coin back."

Nordal sat back, grinning. He looked to his friends and then set his four cards upright.

"What?!" blurted one of the men, staring wide-eyed at Nordal's cards.

"No!" Another slammed his fist on the table, shaking the marbles in front of Nordal.

Marbles elsewhere on the table shifted. *Whoever thought marbles would be good markers?* Nordal wondered. He'd been to other places that used clear cubes with colored flecks. Now that seemed smarter than balls that could roll all over the table.

The scar-faced man, however, simply glared at Nordal. There was an unmistakable hatred in his eye. Mister Scar-face had gambled and lost all his markers. Nordal, however, ignored the disdained look and grabbed the marbles near the stack of cards at the table's center: the bets for that round. The number of marbles represented enough money for a small family to live on for three months. That was pocket change for Nordal.

"You cheated," one of the men said, glowering.

"Nah," Hemrin piped up, waving his hand, "he's just lucky tonight."

"Uh-huh," Midar nodded.

Feeling smug, Nordal looked at each of the men playing with him and his friends. "Thanks for playing. Maybe you'll do better next time." Scar-face just continued glaring, but the others muttered complaints.

With the game concluded, Nordal pulled out a wrapped bag that he kept in the pocket of his pants and put the marbles inside it. Midar and Hemrin did the same, taking the marbles that remained from their bets.

Without a word, Nordal left the table and sauntered across the tavern. Several other friends of his sat at a nearby bar: Cordel and Shen. Both of them were talking to several women, undoubtedly trying to find some pleasure tonight.

Nordal eventually stopped at a barred window and counter where the tavern's clerk sat in a chair reading a book. "I need to cash these in," he said, placing his sack on the counter.

"Us too," Hemrin said. Both he and Midar set their bags on the counter beside Nordal's sack.

The clerk looked up, took the bags and counted each of the marbles. He then replaced them with Sorothian gold coins. One by one, he handed the bags back to the men.

"It's a good thing we decided to pool our money," Midar said.

"Yeah," Hemrin said, "or I'd be walking away with all your money!" The three of them laughed. It was probably true.

"Are we doing anything else here?" Midar asked, putting a hand in his pocket.

Nordal looked about the tavern, searching for a pretty face, but he didn't see any that weren't already engaged with other fellows. "Nah." Nordal shook his head. "I'm getting tired."

"All right," Midar said, motioning with his bag to Nordal, "shall we head back to your place and split this?" Nordal nodded. He turned around, noticing their fellow card players moving throughout the tavern. They were whispering to several other men. Scar-face tried gesturing discreetly to Nordal, but his gesture didn't go unnoticed by others. That didn't bode well. Well, perhaps for a normal person. But Nordal enjoyed a good brawl.

"Let's go," he said, jerking his head toward the door.

The three of them nonchalantly crossed the tavern, but as they reached the doors, one of the men they had played with called to them. He was a squat man.

"You three," the squat man said. "Stop."

Nordal turned, raising an eyebrow.

"Wanna play another game?" the squat man asked.

"I'm done with Sharzen," Nordal said, grabbing the doorknob.

The squat man laughed. "Nah, we got something better."

"Sure, why not?" Hemrin chimed.

"Okay," the squat man said. "But not here. We'll meet you outside." He hurried off, moving through the tavern to Scar-face. Both Scar-face and Squat-man talked to several others, about twelve in all. They all looked like tough men. *Soldiers?* Nordal thought. *No, probably mercenaries.* Those were common here in Soroth. They—

A firm hand gripped Nordal's shoulder, belonging to one of the tavern's bouncers. He stood taller than Nordal, which was surprising. Not many people were. But this man was a bouncer after all. "No trouble, you hear?" the bouncer said firmly, his tone matching his grip.

"Do I *ever* cause trouble at Orchin's?" Nordal asked innocently, tying his sack of coins around his belt.

The bouncer sighed and then stepped back. He folded his arms and looked at the crowd of men gathering around Scar-face. Squat-man, however, moved across the tavern.

Midar opened the door, and both he and Hemrin stepped outside. Nordal, however, lingered for a moment and looked once again at Cordel and Shen.

Should he grab them? *Nah, we'll be fine,* he thought as he joined Midar and Hemrin outside.

A cool breeze wafted across Nordal's face. It felt nice. Dusk had fallen upon the street, but oil-burning lampposts lit the area.

"We're going to the right," Squat-man said as he passed Nordal. Scar-face and another man were beside him. The three of them continued but the rest of their fellows stood behind Nordal and his two friends.

Nordal looked at the others, twelve of them. *So, fifteen total?* he thought, glancing to Midar with an anticipating grin. Midar, however, rolled his eyes. Nordal hurried to follow Squat-man and Scar-face. They turned down an alley two buildings away from Orchin's Tavern.

"We can cut across here," Squat-man said. He had done all the speaking so far. Scar-face was probably too infuriated.

Once they were partway down the alley Nordal slowed his gait. "So what's this game we're gonna play?" he asked, feigning ignorance.

Scar-face stopped, turning to Nordal. Squat-man and the other man stopped as well. So did all of their buddies behind Nordal.

"Well," Scar-face finally spoke, "It's called, *Beat the cheater—*"

Nordal heard his name shouted over Scar-face's answer. It came from behind him. *That wasn't Shen or Cordel,* Nordal thought, turning around. A large and burly man stood at the alley's entrance, but Nordal couldn't make out his face. It was too dark—

"That was all my coin for the month, and I'm gonna get it back!" Scar-face shouted.

Nordal turned back around just as Scar-face swung his fist at his nose. A thrilling sensation surged through Nordal, and he dodged the blow, moving along Scar-face's arm. Scar-face tried to recoil, but Nordal grabbed his wrist. In one swift motion, Nordal pulled Scar-face's arm and slammed an open palm into his elbow, throwing his entire weight into the blow.

Now off balance, Scar-face screamed, falling to the ground with his elbow inverted.

A cacophony of grunts, shouts, cracking bones and jingling coins echoed through the alley at that same moment. It was beautiful!

Nordal spun, arcing a kick to Squat-man's head. The blow landed before Squat-man could defend himself, and it sent him stumbling into the wall. The other man in the lead leapt forward, drawing a concealed dagger from his tunic. With lightning reflexes, Nordal launched a kick into the man's stomach, knocking him backward.

Scar-face whimpered beneath Nordal. "W-wh…"

"You obviously didn't know what you were getting into," Nordal said, looking back across the alley. Midar and Hemrin were relentless. Their opponents were pretty sloppy and easily fell unconscious. But Midar and Hemrin were quite skilled. They had been trained by the best, after all. Two to twelve wasn't a fair match. Scar-face should have brought more friends.

Nordal glanced over his shoulder where the dagger-wielding man was advancing again. "Haven't had enough, huh?" Nordal asked, evading a piercing blow. He grabbed the wrist of the hand holding the weapon and raised it high, then followed up with a flurry of blows to the man's ribs. "You shouldn't play with sharp things," Nordal scolded, disarming the man. The dagger fell to the ground, and then its wielder followed.

Nordal turned once again. He clearly saw the burly man who had called his name. His wavy brown hair rustled from the breeze blowing through the alley, and his hazel eyes stared sternly at Nordal.

"Not going to join the fun, Kalder?" Nordal asked, putting his hands on his hips.

"No," Kalder answered.

Several of the men who had been brawling with Midar and Hemrin ran past Kalder, hurrying out of the alley.

"If you're done playing, we need to go," Kalder continued. "Cor has called a meeting."

"Oh?" Nordal perked up.

"Did he say what about?" Hemrin asked.

"Yes, but that's not something I should mention here," Kalder said, looking at the beaten men groaning in the alley. "Eighty-seven hounds dancing in the moonlight."

Nordal's eyes widened in surprise, *Oh boy!* The phrase was one of many codes used by Nordal's mentor, Cornar Dol'shir, to relay information when calling upon those of his adventuring band. They were a way to conceal jobs from other mercenaries or treasure seekers. People were always trying to find grand discoveries and sell them to achieve unrivaled fortunes.

This code spoken by Kalder, however, was one Nordal had rarely heard. *Moonlight* conveyed urgency, *hounds* represented artifacts—*dancing* was code for magical artifacts, tevisrals—and the number signified the grandeur of the job or adventure. Nordal had never heard anything higher than forty-five.

Tilthan is going to hate missing this, Nordal thought. Tilthan had left two days ago on a job for a snooty man named Chernil. A gem heist. Nordal had wanted to join them, but Chernil insisted on only Tilthan, Nath, and Nemral. *Well, now I'm glad I didn't go,* Nordal thought, smiling.

"I better grab Cordel and Shen," Midar said, picking his way through the alley. Kalder nodded and then moved back through the alley. Hemrin and Nordal followed. The younger man was excited. Hemrin looked like he couldn't contain it. Nordal felt the same.

Once in the street Kalder looked around. "I think we've notified everyone else here in Soroth."

"Are we meeting at Cor's estate here in the city?" Hemrin asked.

"No, out in the country," Kalder said. "The meeting is tomorrow night, but he wants everyone gathered as soon as possible. I'm going back tonight. I'll need to go to Sarn in the morning."

"We'll ride with you," Nordal said, and turned to walk away, but stopped when Kalder called to him.

"Let's meet at the city's northern gate."

"Fine by me!" Nordal shouted, jogging down the street.

Moonlight reflected off the calm waters of Alarn's Cove within Salarn Bay. There hadn't been any vessels moving for hours, and so the water looked like a sprawling mirror. It was the perfect setting, ideal for Ordreth's plans tonight.

He sat quietly at a dining table for two on a private balcony. Ordreth wore a formal tunic and pants, both made of blue silk, with white paneling along the pant legs and chest. Flowery embroidery adorned the white areas, woven with dark-blue threads. Tonight was a special occasion after all. Why spare on the clothing when he was spending an extravagant amount on this place? The Andelbree Inn was one of the classiest places on the entire island, probably even in this quarter of the ocean.

This will be a night to remember, Ordreth thought. He looked skyward, staring at Kistern, one of Kalda's moons. The moon was full and shone white, unlike Kaelyrn which shone a mismatch of colors: blue, green, brown, yellow, white, and sometimes red. What a strange moon that was. *Good thing Kaelyrn isn't out tonight,* he thought.

A pattern of clicking and clanking echoed from behind Ordreth. *That's her,* he thought. *Don't screw this up…* Ordreth took in a deep breath, imagining his lovely Sharon made up and dressed fancifully. Intoxicating! *But why imagine it? Just turn around!*

Ordreth slowly let out his breath, turning in his chair. His eyes widened in surprise as he gazed upon Sharon.

Sharon walked toward him, her heels clicking against the floor. She wore a pale-blue, knee-length gown, one shoulder bare. The other arm was exposed, toned yet feminine. Her tanned olive skin looked soft and silky next to the dress. She smiled at Ordreth. Oh, those dimples! And those deep-set green eyes… breathtaking!

"You can stop gawking," Sharon said, her tone roguish. She grinned, raising the left side of her lip, something she did when being playful.

"But you're just so tantalizing," Ordreth said, watching Sharon take her seat across the table. She smiled but rolled her eyes. She always did that when he commented on her beauty.

"The food should be here soon," Ordreth said, tightening his lips. He was getting nervous. But who wouldn't be when asking the most gorgeous woman in the world for her hand in marriage?

Sharon nodded, looking out over the cove. Ordreth followed her gaze. The Andelbree Inn was far enough away from the city of Dentir that there wasn't much commotion. The shores on this side of the Isle of Soroth were often quiet. Shipping vessels didn't come this far west. They'd stop in Soroth, and then native ships would carry their goods to the other islands of the Principality. Those ships rarely passed through Salarn Bay. Sailing to the other cities or towns on the western side of the Isle of Soroth would take just as long as traveling by horseback or caravan. Beside the occasional leisure boat, Salarn

Bay was empty—

Boats?! Ordreth chided himself. *You're thinking of boats and shipping routes?* He shook his head slowly. No, this was the perfect moment. He couldn't let it be ruined.

Ordreth glided his hand from the table, checking the pocket of his pants. He felt the tiny envelope holding Sharon's betrothal band. *Just like you practiced,* he thought. *You can do this…* Ordreth took in another breath, finding courage. Who would believe that this would be more nerve-wracking than charging across a battlefield? "Sharon," Ordreth said, his voice calm. He waited for her to turn toward him. She raised her brow, batting her eyelashes.

"Sharon," he continued, "you have been an inspiration to me ever since we met seven years ago. The way you walk, the confidence that you exude… It's really incredible." Ordreth paused, taking in a breath. Sharon said nothing, but she kept looking at him with her raised brow. "And your skills with a blade are…" Oh, no! That wasn't part of what he rehearsed. "I mean, you're very good at what you do for a living."

"Thievery?" Sharon laughed. She squinted her eyes and smiled at him. "Okay…"

"You're incredible," Ordreth blurted. "That's what I'm trying to say. You're amazing. I'd dare say, perfect." He let that sink in for a moment. Her expression softened. "You're perfect for me," he added. Yes, that was better! "I don't think any woman could rival you."

Sharon opened her mouth. That expression said, "That's the sweetest compliment you've given me." Ordreth savored that look, but heard footsteps approaching. He'd better hurry before the waiter arrived—

"Ordreth, Sharon!" a man called out. The footfalls hastened. Sharon jumped, bracing one hand against the tabletop. Ordreth, however, turned sharply. That didn't sound like the waiter… Within seconds, a man of average height stumbled onto the private balcony. It was the illusionist, Hem. His dark-brown hair was disheveled, and sweat beaded his forehead.

"You guys won't believe it!" Hem exclaimed. "Eighty-seven hounds dancing in the moonlight! Eighty-seven hounds dancing in the moonlight!" He nearly shouted it the second time.

Sharon blinked several times and then shook her head in disbelief. Ordreth, however, cocked his head, confused. Surely Uncle Cor knew what Ordreth had planned for tonight. By Heleron's Trident, Ordreth had shown him the ring!

"Are you sure, Hem?" Sharon asked.

"Oh yeah!" Hem nodded, smiling broadly. "This is going to be amazing!" he cried again, clapping his hands.

"Wow…" Sharon said with a gasp. She looked wide-eyed at Ordreth, but then studied him quizzically.

Ordreth didn't share the enthusiasm. Sure, he could get excited about an adventure, especially one that sounded as intriguing as this. It obviously was big if Uncle Cor was using eighty-seven. And the code for tevisrals, well that was always good. But none of that mattered when compared to tonight. He was proposing to the most important woman in his life! That was worth far more than any hidden treasure.

"Did you not hear him?" Sharon asked Ordreth. "Or are you just dumbfounded?" That last remark lightened Ordreth's mood.

"Come on," Hem said. "We've got to hurry! Tinal said that Cornar wants everyone gathered at his estate as soon as possible. I ran across Demsal, and he said you two were the only ones that hadn't been told yet. Demsal said we'd send word in the morning. Ridiculous! But the meeting is tomorrow night, and I couldn't let you guys miss out! We have to set sail in four days, so that doesn't give us much time, you know. Anyway, Demsal said he didn't know where you were, so I found Markin. Markin said that he thought you were out in the country, but he wouldn't say any more, even when I pressed him! Then I crossed paths with Grensil, and he said he overheard Kalder saying you were staying here for a few nights. So, I enhanced my horse and galloped all the way here. Poor guy is tired, but that's okay, because now you guys know!"

Ordreth stared blankly at Hem. The man could be so dense sometimes… Obviously, Demsal knew not to bother Ordreth. Ordreth deduced that Uncle Cor was probably waiting until the morning to send word *after* the proposal. Ordreth supposed he couldn't be upset with his uncle. Uncle Cor had obviously tried to keep tonight special. But then Hem got into the mix… *Oh well.*

"We should have them wrap up the food," Sharon said, tapping Ordreth's arm. Did she think he wasn't paying attention? Well, he was looking absent-mindedly across the balcony, thinking over Hem's convoluted outburst. "We can eat it at your uncle's," she added and rose from her seat. "You go talk to the chef or waiter, or whoever. I'm going to change. I can't ride like this!" She rushed past Hem, disappearing down the hall.

After a moment, the interrupter approached the table. "What's wrong, Ordreth?" Hem asked. He raised an eyebrow and rubbed his bald chin. Ordreth slowly turned to Hem. He let his blank expression fade and his displeasure show.

"Hem, tonight was supposed to be *special…*"

"Oh, it is!" Hem cried. "This is a night to be remembered! Ordreth, this is going to be huge!"

"No, Hem." Ordreth shook his head, his voice becoming stern. "Tonight was supposed to be special for just *me* and *Sharon.*"

"Huh?" Hem scratched his head. "Why? It's not like an anniversary or anything. You two have only been seeing each other for a year and a half…"

"Hem." Ordreth growled the name. He couldn't find the words to speak, so he reached into his pocket and removed the envelope holding the betrothal band. The ring's outline protruded enough so that one could discern what it was.

Hem's eyes widened, finally enlightened after seeing the ring's outline. "Oh!" he cried. "Oh! Oh…" He looked back over his shoulder, searching for Sharon. But she was already long gone. Hem leaned close to Ordreth and whispered. "You're finally asking her?"

"Well… I was," Ordreth said, perturbed.

"Oh…" Hem sighed. The illusionist looked like he was replaying events in his mind. Sadness and embarrassment contorted his face. He must have realized what he'd just done. "I'm sorry, Ordreth." He slumped down into Sharon's chair. The two of them sat silently for a moment, and then another pair of footsteps echoed onto the balcony.

Ordreth turned to see the waiter carrying a platter with a domed bronze cover. His and Sharon's dinner… The waiter halted abruptly upon seeing Hem. He looked to Ordreth, confused, and then studied Hem. The waiter continued looking back and forth between the two men until Ordreth finally spoke. "Can you have our food wrapped up?" Ordreth asked, his face wreathed in disappointment. "We need to be going…"

"Of course," the waiter said, and then hurried back down the hall, leaving Ordreth and Hem to sit in silence once again.

What a disaster…

— ·· —

The following evening, Cornar paced the foyer of his country home. He hardly ever paced when waiting. But this was an unusual night, putting together an expedition without actually intending to be a part of it. It was strange, perhaps even sad.

Chattering noises reached Cornar's ears from the parlor. Dozens of men filled the room. Some occupied the parlor furniture, but others sat on chairs from the dining room, stools from the kitchen, or chairs from other places in the house. There were at least thirty in that room, and people were still missing.

A knock resonated from the home's main entrance, and Cornar opened the door. A thick-set man and a short woman stood in the portico—Igan and his wife Baekal, both masterful wizards. *Why was Baekal here?* Cornar wondered. Didn't she have several students under her tutelage? Perhaps she was curious. Cornar's message had been quite unusual.

"Good evening, Cor," Igan said, smiling reminiscently. He extended an arm toward Cornar and the two of them embraced. Igan stood almost a head shorter than Cornar. His brown hair was neatly combed back, and his brown eyes had the eagerness many of the others' had shown. "This is exciting!" he said.

"It sure sounds like it," Baekal said, folding her arms. She always acted aloof, even when she was interested. What a strange woman. But Baekal was a great elementalist—a type of wizard who focused on harnessing the destructive powers of nature.

Unlike her husband, Baekal was slender, her face thin, with high cheekbones and a sharp, pointed chin. Her long brown locks cascaded over her shoulders, almost touching her breasts. She had been a good-looking woman in her youth, but now her face bore some wrinkles and prominent lines, particularly between her sharp nose and her thin lips. Baekal hadn't aged well, not like Karenna. But no woman could rival Karenna.

"So, tevisrals?" Baekal asked. "Iltar said something about a magical map, shrines of an ancient Order?" So Iltar told them about Krindal and the meeting with the council. *Interesting…*

Cornar nodded.

"Fun," Baekal said, stepping past Igan. She moved down the foyer, leaving her husband with Cornar.

"We're gonna be famous, Cor," Igan said, grinning. "And rich beyond measure!"

"I'm already too famous, and I have sufficient for my needs."

"You're no fun," Igan grumbled and stepped past Cornar. "So, does that mean I can have your share of the loot?"

Cornar simply grinned. *Igan doesn't know my intentions,* he thought. *That's good.* And Cornar wasn't worried that Iltar would say anything. Cornar could trust that man with his darkest secret. Of course, Iltar would do the same. In fact, he had.

Igan and Baekal mingled with the others. They found the younger mages sitting at the back of the parlor. Tinal, Igan's former apprentice, stood and offered Igan his seat. Igan declined, but Baekal took the offer. She was an imposing woman. Cornar was glad Karenna wasn't as pushy.

With the door still open, Cornar poked his head out into the portico. A horse-drawn wagon was coming down the path bearing three with familiar faces and a fourth one he didn't recognize.

That must be Krindal, Cornar thought. Iltar was talking to the stranger. The other two men, Jalim and Delrin, sat at the front of the wagon beside the driver, Iltar's groom.

Delrin and Jalim came? That was surprising. They hadn't been on an adventure with Cornar in at least ten years. Besides, they were supposed to guard Iltar's tower. If they weren't there then who was watching the tower? His maid, Belsina, would be the only one at the homestead… Strange that Iltar would bring them. Were they that eager to join the adventure? Or did Iltar want them to hear Cornar's announcement tonight? Cornar would be joining them in retirement; perhaps Iltar thought he'd want some support from men who had done what he intended to do.

The carriage stopped upon nearing the home, and the four men disembarked. Jalim hurried to the open door with Delrin hobbling close behind.

"Evenin', Cor!" Jalim said with a smile, and patted him on the shoulder. "Doing well?"

Cornar nodded. "As well as expected."

"Cor!" Delrin shouted. He hobbled over and hugged Cornar. He was a good man with a cheerful disposition, despite the limp. Why hadn't he hired an arpranist to heal that limp? Iltar paid him generously enough.

The sound of more horses drew both Cornar and Delrin's attention. Farther down the path leading to the large home, three men approached. Kalder was at the head, followed by Aron and Brendar. The latter two men were natives of Sarn. Kalder must have had to take the ferry from Serinta—a village on the northwestern side of the Isle of Soroth—to fetch them.

"This is like the old days," Delrin chimed, a huge smile on his face. "Isn't this great, Cor?!"

"C'mon, Delrin," Jalim urged. "We're gonna need to grab some chairs."

Cornar pulled back from the doorway, looking into the parlor. They needed at least five more seats. By Heleron's Scales, when had their party grown so large? And they still didn't have their entire arsenal of mages.

"Go find Karenna," Cornar said. "She'll help you find some more chairs. We need five more."

As Delrin and Jalim hurried down the foyer, Iltar and Krindal entered the portico. "I believe some introductions are in order," Iltar said to Krindal. "This is my friend Cornar."

Krindal stepped into the home, his wrinkles becoming more pronounced as he smiled at Cornar. "It is a pleasure to meet a man of such esteem," the old scholar said. "With you and your men at my side we will surely triumph!"

"My men will be at your disposal, Master Krindal," Cornar said, gesturing for the necromancers to enter his home. "Everyone is gathered in my parlor. We've run out of seats, but I've sent Delrin and Jalim to get more."

"Oh, I can stand," Krindal said, maneuvering his pack to rest against his stomach. The old scholar reached inside, removing a domed disk.

Is that the tevisral? Cornar wondered.

Krindal held the domed object close and looked to Iltar. "We'll be over there." Iltar pointed to the parlor. "I'd have a word with Cor for a moment." Krindal nodded and walked toward the crowd, picking his way, careful not to step on anyone's feet.

Once Krindal had moved to the center of the parlor, Iltar gestured with his head toward the door, and the two men stepped out onto the portico. They watched as the three horsemen rode down the path.

"How has Pagus been?" Iltar whispered.

"He's fine," Cornar said. "I did what you asked. He seemed eager to go head-to-head with me in the drills you suggested. He's a good mage, Iltar. He has the potential to rival even Balden." Iltar winced at the mention of his former apprentice. Cornar regretted mentioning Balden, but he couldn't just forget about him completely. "I miss that boy," Cornar said, his tone melancholy.

"As do I," Iltar said, frowning.

The three horsemen disappeared around the home, heading for the stables.

"When do you want to make your announcement?" Iltar asked.

"At the end," Cornar replied. "I don't want to dampen this meeting." Iltar nodded. They stood silently until Kalder rounded the home, Aron and Brendar close behind. Kalder nodded to the two leaders of their band.

Aron stopped at the steps leading to the portico and raised his brow at Cornar. He glanced to Iltar then back to Cornar. "You're serious?" Aron asked. "Really serious?"

Brendar groaned. "I've been telling you since we left Sarn. When does Cor ever joke about an adventure? It's not like he's using deceit to lure us here."

No, Cornar wouldn't resort to lying to his men. They were loyal to him, fiercely loyal. But when they heard his announcement, would some of them see this meeting as deceitful?

Both Aron and Brendar pushed past Cornar and Iltar, still debating the matter. Their voices lingered as they entered the parlor.

"That's everyone but Vargos," Cornar said.

"He'll be here," Iltar said, turning around. He was about to enter the home but stopped at the threshold. "Don't you remember he's always late?"

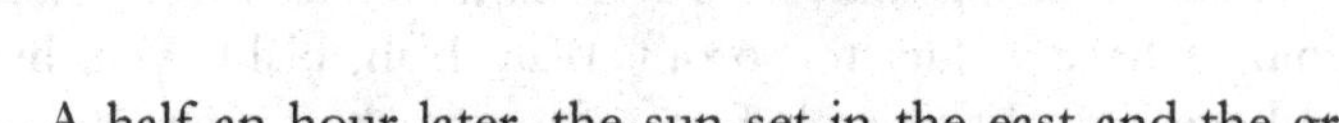

A half an hour later, the sun set in the east and the grounds of Cornar's country estate had darkened. Cornar had stayed outside the whole time, waiting for Vargos. He didn't want to be around his men, not when his announcement was weighing on his mind. Cornar was sure it was visible on his face. It was best not to show that to his men.

A glimmer of light caught his eye over the hill at the front of his property. It was bright enough to illuminate a lone figure on horseback. Although Cornar couldn't discern who it was, he knew it was Vargos. Like Iltar said, the man was always late.

It took Vargos awhile to ride from the hill. He cantered his horse past the home, and Cornar heard a brief exchange between Vargos and Iltar's groom. Hegdil was reassuring the late-comer that he'd take care of the animal.

Soon after, Vargos arrived at the portico. He was a rugged man, with salt-and-pepper hair encircling his bald pate. His grizzled beard matched. The man's gray-violet eyes studied Cornar for a moment. Vargos often looked wild. One might expect old Amendal to look like this, but that codger was neatly kept. Vargos, however, looked downright uncivilized. His dark-blue robe was almost always dirty. Even when it was washed, it had faint stain marks. It wasn't that Vargos was barbaric; he was just so engrossed in his magic that he tended to neglect things. That was actually the chief reason behind his frequent tardiness.

"Been waiting long?" Vargos asked, still standing at the bottom of the steps.

"About half an hour," Cornar said.

Vargos bobbed his head and made a contemplating face. "Not the worst, but not the greatest," he said, climbing one step. "How many people are here?"

"Nearly forty," Cornar said. "There would be more if we had all our mages."

"Ah, yes." Vargos said with a grunt, climbing one more step. "That stupid stipulation. Let me guess, Alacor made it, right?" He studied Cornar with a hard look.

"He, Jalel, and Melnor."

"Well, glad I don't have to worry about that," Vargos said. "I haven't had an apprentice in nearly thirty-five years, I think? Something like that. Had to dismiss—oh, I forget what his name was—when the Order changed." Vargos climbed another step. "Did I ever tell you that Alacor asked me to train some youngster three years ago?" Cornar shook his head.

"Yeah," Vargos said, grinning, "he came groveling. Saying I was the last hope for the barsionist discipline here on Soroth."

"What did you do?" Cornar asked, his brow raised.

"I spat in his face!" That struck a jovial chord. Vargos kept laughing as he continued, "The pompous bastard just wiped the spittle from his cheek and asked again. If you'd seen him, you'd have thought him some diplomat or something. Alacor kept droning on and on that I shouldn't let the barsion discipline die. Claiming I have a duty to Soroth. Blah, blah, blah! Well, his predecessors should have thought twice before reforming the Order. By all that's magical, I would have left the island too if it weren't for my family. And good friends too." He gestured to Cornar.

"Thank you?" Cornar muttered quizzically, his brow still raised.

Vargos laughed again, then patted Cornar on the shoulder. "You know," he continued, "I'd take another apprentice if Iltar was in charge. Things would be much different with him running the Order."

"It *would* be different," Cornar said.

"If I were Iltar, I'd just put Alacor and the others away privily," Vargos said, waving his hand. "Iltar could do it. He could make murder look like a disappearance." Vargos stopped, looking squarely at Cornar. After studying him for a moment, Vargos spoke again in a much lower voice. "I've wondered if that's what happened all those years ago with Cordis, Rovin, and all their cohorts. One by one, they all just disappeared, never to be heard of again." Vargos stopped, gazing at Cornar with a probing stare that seemed to ask, *Is that what happened? Did Iltar kill them out of vengeance for his parents' demise?*

Cornar ignored that unspoken question. He smiled and patted Vargos on the shoulder. Shaking his head, Vargos shuffled past Cornar and entered the home.

Finally, everyone was gathered. They could have their meeting and Cornar could make his announcement. Then life would be peaceful.

8

THE MEETING

Silence hung in the parlor as the men and women turned in their seats to look at Cornar. He stood in the entryway, behind a row of chairs that spilled into the foyer. Usually, Cornar stood at the front of the room beside Iltar when announcing adventures to the far reaches of the world. But not today. Perhaps that was fitting? Or even foreshadowing.

Cornar looked to Iltar and simply nodded. It was an indication for him to start the meeting. He often deferred to Iltar in such matters. Both of them were natural leaders, yet they didn't clash. They complimented each other well. It was a strange dynamic that many noticed.

"I'm sure all of you are anxious," Iltar said, and cleared his throat. That drew the attention of most but several eyed Cornar with suspicion. "This is an amazing opportunity for us, after all."

Iltar continued prefacing the meeting with notions of fame and fortune; it was a common rhetoric of his that often inspired those who heard it.

As Iltar spoke, Karenna tiptoed through the foyer toward Cornar, listening as she approached her husband. Karenna glanced to Iltar and all the others, counting each of them, mouthing the numbers as she counted. Her eyes widened in surprise. Perhaps Karenna hadn't thought that they could muster this many of Iltar and Cornar's band on such short notice.

After counting the men and women, Karenna nestled next to Cornar. She wrapped her arm around his waist and leaned her head against his chest. There was a bittersweetness to her embrace tonight. He could have her like this whenever he wanted… but it would mean sacrificing what was unfolding before him in the parlor.

For the first time, his retirement struck him with resounding realization. *This is it; it's all over,* he thought. Cornar sucked in his breath and tried to hide his emotions, but his brow furrowed. Karenna tugged at him, and Cornar looked at his wife. She stared up at him in concern. Her gaze asked, *This is painful for you, isn't it? You can't hide that from me, dear husband.*

Cornar forced a smile and leaned down to kiss the top of her head. Karenna's scent tingled his nostrils. That sweet aroma was always comforting, except now… now, it evoked a sad realization. Cornar would never embark on another adventure. And that pained him.

He had to focus elsewhere.

"… Hold your questions until after Krindal is finished," Iltar was saying, "and try not to be surprised."

Iltar took a step back, and Krindal stepped forward. The old necromancer-scholar moved the domed disk in his hands to the table at the parlor's center.

"What you are about to see might startle you," Krindal said, resting the disk—obviously the mapping tevisral Iltar had mentioned—on the tabletop. Krindal removed something from a necklace and placed it on the tevisral's domed top. It looked like a small gem.

Suddenly, a burst of light erupted in the parlor, but soon faded. A map of the world hovered above the small table and spread throughout the room. It was about chest-level with those sitting and wrapped around many of them. They were literally sitting in the map. Of course, the map was made of magic, probably illusionary magic.

Many of the men and women whispered admiring comments. Some were silent, particularly Kalder, Iltar, and Vargos. Vargos was a hard man to impress, so his reaction wasn't a surprise. Kalder customarily took almost everything straight-faced. And, obviously, Iltar had seen this before, so he wasn't as impressed as the others.

"It's beautiful," Karenna whispered. She stepped away from Cornar and reached her hand to the edge of the map which spread just beyond the doorway bridging the parlor to the foyer. Her fingers didn't disrupt the map at all. Karenna looked back to Cornar, eyes wide. They seemed to ask, *You're not having a part of this?! Are you mad?*

Cornar smiled at her, but Karenna shook her head and rolled her eyes.

"Well, I'm surprised at your lack of surprise," Krindal said with a grunt.

"I think we all expected magnificence," Nordal chimed. "Don't be offended if we don't seem awestruck."

"Yeah," Gregan said with a chuckle, "we're used to this sort of thing."

Krindal nodded. "As you can see, there are dots scattered all throughout the world. But this one is not like the others," he said, pointing to the island chain of Klindala. Klindala lay to the northeast of the large continent known as the Mainland. "Whatever is here on Klindala is important. It didn't show up on this map until I visited all other twenty locations."

"That looks like it's in the ruins of Klindil," Igan observed, raising an eyebrow and folding his arms. "Hasn't that place been picked clean of everything? Relics and tevisrals alike?"

"Yes," Krindal said, "Klindil is well documented in the annals of history. Plenty of people have studied that place, but look at this…" His words trailed off as he inserted his thumb and forefinger into the map, near the island of Klindala. Krindal spread his fingers apart, then removed his hand and repeated the gesture several times. Each time the map magnified; its actual size, however, didn't change. It filled the same amount of space in the parlor, no matter how much it was magnified. This projection seemed a fixed rectangle.

Soon, the map was a three-dimensional and topographical representation of the island. The speck Krindal referred to as the last location was actually below ground, beneath the ruins of the city of Klindil.

"It's underground," Baekal said.

Several others muttered similar reactions.

"This isn't a surprise," Krindal said. "All the other temples were in remote locations. One other was subterranean, inside an island on Asurir Lake, at the base of the Dragon's Maw Mountains."

"Are we going to dig?" Aron asked, leaning against the wall beside the parlor's window.

"No," Krindal shook his head, and then enlarged the map several more times. The map showed the terrain around the ruins. Well, they didn't look like ruins. The ruins looked like a city, a city with towering buildings that reached almost as high as the mountains.

Cornar looked at the projecting magic with wide eyes. *Impossible! How can those buildings stand?* Those buildings defied logic. One might build a structure six or even seven stories tall, as was common in the human realm. But those comprising ancient Klindil rose dozens, if not a hundred, stories.

"There look to be caves beneath the city," Krindal said, pointing at lines beneath the logic-defying structures. "Perhaps at one time people lived in the caves before the city was ever established. That's my theory at least. This last temple is beneath the caves, which leads me to believe a secluded group of Keepers of Truth and Might lived in the caves and guarded this sacred place." He cleared his throat before continuing. "The city of Klindil was most likely built to cover up the caves and the temple."

"So we search the ruins to find a cave network," Gregan speculated. "Should be easy enough."

Krindal nodded. "Whatever is in this temple is of great worth. The caves alone will be enough proof to validate my theories about our ancestors. But the temple is the real find. Hopefully, there will not be any cave-ins during our trip. Klindala is prone to earthquakes throughout the year. And we do face the potential of experiencing an earthquake underground while we're exploring."

Ordreth raised a hand, patiently waiting to ask a question. Krindal nodded, and the young warrior voiced his concern. "Is there anything else that's dangerous on Klindala?"

"There are some creatures native to Klindala," Iltar spoke up, "but nothing that isn't manageable."

"What about the natives?" Vargos asked dispassionately.

"The Maltins?" Nordal asked, raising a brow.

"No, the Wildmen in the deeper parts of the island," Vargos said. "They're the remnants of the Klindala Dynasty. The Maltins haven't colonized the entire island, only Kretin and a few smaller cities on the western shores. So, Krindal, have you taken them into consideration?"

"Yes, we have," Krindal said. "I was planning to unfold this part once we were on our way. Prince Kaescis intends to barter with them to allow us safe passage. Our journey across the island should be uneventful, as the various tribes keep close together near the ruins."

"And what does he intend to barter with?" Vargos asked, still doubtful. One might think Vargos a pessimist, but he was simply overly cautious.

"I don't know," Krindal admitted, sounding a little ashamed.

"So we might have to fight the Wildmen," Vargos said, grunting.

"We'll be fine," Gregan said, gesturing to everyone in the room. "With all of us we should be okay."

""So," Nordal spoke up, his tone sarcastic, "we're going to encroach on their land, take their stuff, probably kill them, and then go on our merry way?" He grinned and shook his head, not amused.

Neither was Cornar.

Krindal continued explaining the details of the trip. The old scholar explained that they would be sailing on a vessel he had chartered, the *Promised Maiden*. One of the men asked why they weren't using Captain Kenard's ship, the *White Duchess*. Nordal smirked and said Kenard's ship would definitely prove Krindal's theories true.

Cornar and the others often chartered Kenard's ship for adventures. It was a favored vessel of theirs. Beautiful ship. The *White Duchess* was also one of the fastest ships in the Kalishir Ocean, and perhaps even in the entire world. Why didn't Iltar push Krindal to charter it? That seemed odd. Surely, Kenard would be in port this time of year.

Krindal then went on to explain his past discoveries in the other temples, telling of various finds that Iltar had already conveyed to Cornar. But the tales were interesting to hear again.

Many of the warriors asked questions about those visits, trying to get as much information as possible so they wouldn't walk blindly into this adventure. That was a trait Cornar had drilled into most of them, and their behavior tonight pleased him. Cornar could comfortably leave his band, knowing that he had trained them well.

Krindal answered their questions, all while keeping the map of Klindala active. The tevisral and its effects blended into the meeting like a common object. That was probably a by-product of the many adventures these men and women had experienced throughout the years. They were familiar with tevisrals, probably more so than most of Kalda's inhabitants.

After all the questions were answered, Krindal dismissed the magic of his mapping tevisral. He replaced the gem in his necklace while securing the tevisral in his pack. "We leave in three days," Krindal said. "The *Promised Maiden* is currently docked on Pier Eight, Wharf Twenty. You can make your way there any time; Captain Salisar is expecting us. The vessel is currently empty, and you can take up lodging in your proposed quarters for this trip." Many of the men nodded, eager to begin the journey.

"I believe I am finished," Krindal said, looking back to Iltar.

Cornar, however, picked his way through the parlor, finally joining Krindal. He looked at the old necromancer-scholar, then to Iltar. "We have one more thing," Iltar said. "I am not accompanying you on this trip. Due to my responsibilities at the Necrotic Order, I cannot come along." Several of the warriors let out sighs of disappointment, but Cornar chimed in before they could voice any of their concerns.

"Iltar isn't the only one not going with you," Cornar said, taking a deep breath. His heart was pounding. Was he really nervous? Cornar could face the dangers of the unknown, but he couldn't say a simple phrase to his own men? Men he trusted with his life. Cornar exhaled, looking at each of the warriors, yet his gaze fell upon Ordreth. The sight of his nephew brought him a sense of comfort. "I am not going with you either."

The room erupted with gasps of dismay. The warriors frowned. Several of them looked at each other with disbelief. Many were confused. Cornar had expected this reaction. At least they weren't treating it like a funeral. He glimpsed Gregan, who shook his head and folded his arms.

"I made a promise," Cornar said. He turned to the foyer. Karenna stood at the back of the crowd, sadden. Were those tears in her eyes? Cornar turned from her, looking back to Ordreth. "And you know me and promises. As of today, I am officially retired. But that doesn't mean I won't help organize any future adventures or trips. I'm sure Iltar will go with you on the next one." Cornar glanced back to Iltar, hopeful that he'd back him up. Cornar rarely put Iltar on the spot like this, but he knew Iltar would support him. Iltar only nodded. Well, that was enough. Who knew if Iltar really would go on the next adventure? The situation with his acolytes might not change by then.

"I hope none of you back out because of this news. I wanted to wait until we were finished so as to not dampen the excitement. It truly is one of the greatest trips you'll embark on." Many of the men nodded in agreement, but they were still saddened by Cornar's news of retirement.

Cornar eyed all of them for a moment. "Now, to satisfy my curiosity, and probably Krindal's, how many of you still want to join this quest?"

Everyone besides Baekal, Delrin, and Jalim stood, affirming their interest in the voyage to Klindala. That was a good sign, for the trip at least. Cornar felt a knot in his stomach. He had feared that some might back out. Those three who didn't stand weren't going anyway… In that moment, he felt lonely.

Gregan stepped forward, standing on one end of the table opposite of Cornar, eyeing his mentor. "Does our unanimous vote sway your decision at all?" Gregan asked. He was determined not to let Cornar retire.

Many of the warriors smiled at Cornar, but they had sadness in their eyes. They knew he wouldn't reconsider. He had explained himself adequately. Cornar felt a hand on his shoulder and looked to see Iltar standing beside him. The necromancer was smiling at the others.

"You know," Nordal spoke up, "if Cor comes along that means there's less loot for the rest of us." Some of the men laughed, particularly Markin, Shen, and Cordel.

"It won't be the same without you, Cornar," Igan said solemnly.

"Thanks, Igan," Cornar said, then nodded to them all. "I suppose we're done. Karenna has some food prepared back in the dining room. Stay as long as you wish. We have plenty of beds for anyone who wants to leave tomorrow."

With the meeting finished, many of the warriors shuffled out of the parlor, emptying into the foyer or through the side door at the back of the room. Some of them, however, stayed and moved toward Cornar. Aron and Cordel were the first to reach Cornar. They hugged their mentor, each whispering how they would miss him. Several others did the same, and then Igan and Baekal approached.

"When we get back, you and I need to spend some time together," Igan said, looking somber. A moment later, a frown appeared on Igan's face.

He's probably thinking how different this adventure will be, Cornar thought. There wasn't a single trip or adventure that both had not joined.

"Perhaps the four of us should do dinner," Baekal suggested, her tone aloof. "We haven't done that in ages."

Cornar nodded. "Let's do that," he said.

Baekal rested her hand on her husband's shoulder. "I'll help Karenna," she said. "These boys will probably overwhelm her with their stomachs."

After she left, only Igan, Iltar, Krindal, and Vargos remained with Cornar.

"I am disappointed that you won't be joining me," Krindal said, clutching his pack. "I hoped that one day I'd work with the magnificent Cornar."

"It sounds like someone has been giving Cor here a little too much credit," Vargos said with a grunt. Krindal shook his head then stared at Cornar, studying him.

"Well, I think you're being a fool," Vargos said frankly, raising an eyebrow at Cornar. "This is probably the greatest adventure of your life. And I say the same to you, Iltar. You should just spit in Alacor's face and come with us."

"Promises, Vargos." Igan shrugged. "You know Cor and his promises."

"Yeah…" Vargos turned from them. "It still doesn't mean he's not being foolish. He'll come to his senses. Just watch. Cornar will be chasing after the *Promised Maiden* as it leaves port, swimming through the wharves to get aboard." The old barsionist grunted and shook his head, following the path the others had taken to the kitchen.

Change my mind? Cornar thought. *Never.* He *was* keeping his promise, no matter what. Nothing could stop him, not even this ache growing inside him. No matter how much of a hole he felt in his soul. That would change, wouldn't it? It had to.

"We have three days before we leave," Krindal said, patting Cornar on the shoulder. "I would hope you change your mind."

Cornar feigned a smile, and Krindal walked off, heading for the doors. Was he not staying? Cornar looked to Iltar for an answer.

"Hegdil will escort him back to Soroth," Iltar said. "Krindal has more things to attend to before he sets sail."

"Are you staying?" Cornar asked Iltar, and the necromancer nodded.

"So are we," Igan said. "Baekal won't want to ride back this late at night." He looked to Iltar. "You didn't seem surprised about Cor's announcement. How long have you known?"

"A year and a half," Iltar answered flatly. Igan looked stunned.

"After our last trip, Karenna and I had a talk," Cornar said. "There were things she wanted us to do that we hadn't had time for, between the children and our exploits. She didn't want to reach the end of her life regretting that we had not spent as much time together as she thought we should. Karenna didn't have to convince me. I came to this on my own."

"As expected," Igan said. Cornar nodded. He wasn't one to be pushed or maneuvered into making a decision.

"She's made me happy ever since she walked into my life. The least I could do would be to honor her wishes and dreams. So I made her a promise. Karenna could have me all to herself, for the rest of our days. No matter how long or how little that would be."

Cornar smiled, thinking over the last year and a half. He and Karenna had spent every day together. Of course, he had trained regularly with his men, but he hadn't left on an adventure. He and Karenna were free to pursue whatever they desired. It was like an indefinite vacation. And now, he'd have that, for the rest of his days…

"Well," Igan said, sighing and gripping Cornar's arm. "I hope you're happy. Remember, marriage is about a proper balance of give and take." Igan stepped away, leaving Iltar and Cornar alone in the parlor.

The two men looked at each other without a word. They were both solemn. It felt like the end of an era, an era of adventure for the both of them. From now on, they'd live solitary and peaceful lives.

⎯⎯◆⎯⎯

Iltar sat up in his bed in one of Cornar's guest bedchamber. The room looked *too* neat. The clothes he had strewn across the floor before falling asleep weren't there. In fact, the clothes weren't even in the room. Iltar had started messing up the rooms where he intended to sleep. This way he could know if he was back in that place with the weird yellow sky.

Wary, Iltar climbed out of bed and exited the bedroom. He hurried down the hallway leading to the stairs in the foyer.

All was silent.

That wasn't a good sign. There had been nearly forty people staying in the home throughout the night. Someone should be stirring, or snoring.

Iltar was probably in that place again. He needed to find a window. Why hadn't he just checked the bedroom window? It was the simple mistakes that cued he was probably in the yellow-sky dreamscape. No matter, he was close to the two-story foyer.

Iltar turned the corner, walking along the balcony overlooking the foyer. The window above the door allowed a view to the lawn in front of the grand country home, but not the sky. He'd have to descend the stairs to see if the sky was yellow.

Iltar kept his eyes on the window, watching for the sky to peak out from the portico's eaves.

"What are you looking for?" a voice asked. It sounded like his own.

Iltar jumped, stumbling down the stairs, but caught himself before tripping completely. *Where had that voice come from?* Now in the foyer, Iltar looked around, but stole a glance at the window. There was dark red beyond the eaves—those strange clouds. Yup, he was there again in that strange dreamscape.

"I asked what you were looking for…" the voice said, coming from the parlor. There was a sense of curiosity to those words as well as an underlying tone of tension.

"The sky," Iltar said without thinking. He'd done it again! It was like he was compelled to do certain things here. He couldn't completely control his actions. Iltar soon found himself walking toward the parlor.

That same reflection of himself, clothed in the red robe, stood in front of the parlor's fireplace. The reflection had his back to the foyer, his hands clasped behind his back. Two red books, like the ones he had carried before, sat on the table.

"You've not sought me the last few times you've come to Vabenack," the stranger said. He turned, looking at Iltar with a solemn gaze. "Why?" That seemed strange coming from a delusion of the mind. Was he really questioning Iltar's motives in a *dream?* Absurd!

Every night Iltar had found himself *waking* in his parent's home or in his tower, then stepping out into the world with the yellow sky. Each time, he went to Soroth, and each time, it lay in ruin. Subsequently, Iltar found that same strange reflection of himself standing on the only intact pier in the southern docks. But the reflection never spoke. Why was he doing so now?

"I need to wake up," Iltar muttered, turning to the windows beside the home's main entrance. "I don't need to be wasting my time in this stupid dream world."

Suddenly, everything changed.

Iltar found himself sitting up in the bedroom where he had retired the night before. As expected, the clothes were strewn across the floor. All was as it had been when he fell asleep.

Iltar yawned and moved to the curtains. They were pulled shut. He opened them, finding a starry sky.

How long had he slept? Did he just barely doze off? It felt like it… No matter. It was still dark and that meant he could go back to sleep, so he did.

⎯⊃●⊂⎯

Cornar sat quietly in his study, bent over, his hands clasped. *This is really it,* he thought sorrowfully. His face twisted into a pained frown. Why was he feeling like *this?* Cornar had been happy about retiring when he first spoke with Kalder. That was nearly a year ago. He was truly happy since their last adventure. Cornar cherished every moment he had spent with Karenna. It was wonderful! And she was so beautiful.

Footsteps echoed from the foyer, a faint pitter-patter entering the study. Who would be up at this late an hour? Everyone had retired to bed quite some time ago. The door to the study opened, and then Cornar heard his wife's voice. "Why aren't you coming to bed?"

Cornar sat up straight, turning toward Karenna. She was wearing a pale-pink nightgown made of lace and silk; it was modest, but showed off her curves. He sucked in a breath, regaining a stoic composure. "I couldn't sleep."

"You never even came up to bed," she retorted flatly. "Baekal helped me with the kitchen, and we only finished a few minutes ago. I thought you were talking to Iltar, but his door is closed."

Cornar shook his head.

"Have you been sitting here since the meeting ended?" Karenna asked, concerned.

Cornar nodded and pursed his lips.

"Are you regretting that promise you made?" Karenna asked, her face stern.

Was he? Not consciously at least. The thought of breaking the promise never crossed his mind. How could he do that? Cornar had never broken a promise in his life. It was a trait he was proud to possess.

"Cor, I understand if you want to go," Karenna said. "From what Krindal showed us, you'd be a fool not to go."

"No." Cornar shook his head. "I'm just tired, and this was an eventful night." Those words felt hollow. But he *was* tired, and the evening *had* been an active one.

"If you say so," Karenna said doubtingly. "Just don't stay like this. And come to bed."

"I will in a bit," Cornar said, forcing a smile.

Karenna cocked her head, narrowing her gaze at Cornar. "I love you, Cor, more than anything. I hope you know that." How could he not know?

"I love you too," Cornar said.

Karenna slipped back through the foyer, her footsteps echoing into the study. Soon, her footfalls faded, and Cornar was alone once again. He did love Karenna, and that's why he *had* to keep his promise. Yes, Krindal's quest was the most intriguing venture ever proposed to him, but intrigue was not enough to break his resolve.

9

BEHEST

"Elynia was not what I expected. She stayed for almost fifteen years but didn't seem to age one bit. That oddity worried me, as she didn't have a ring such as mine. But she wasn't malicious or devious."

- From *Origins and Oaths of the Keepers*, preface

Iltar was back in that strange place again, Vabenack, as Reflection called it. He had decided that if he was to continue experiencing these strange dreams, he should give a name to the only other occupant, although what he came up with was more of a title.

As usual, Iltar found himself where he had drifted off: the couch in the living room of his parent's home. No one was around, which was typical. He expected to be alone when he came here.

He stepped outside, seeing the yellow sky, as he expected. This strange place was becoming natural to him. There weren't many of the blood-red clouds in the sky. A denizen of this weird realm might have called it a sunny day, yet the sun here was a dark blue. The sun almost looked like a hole in the sky, as if that round blue spot was the real sky and the yellow was a transparent tapestry veiling the world.

Iltar had been here twice since the dream-encounter at Cornar's home in the country, where Reflection finally spoke to him. Both times Iltar just waited until he awoke. That decision made the dream drag on for what seemed an eternity.

"So, should I seek this Reflection?" he asked himself. Maybe the dreams would stop if he saw them through? Each of the dreams Iltar had before the encounter in Cornar's home ended much like the first. Something woke him before he reached the docks. Perhaps he needed to have an actual conversation with Reflection.

"To Soroth it is," Iltar said reluctantly. He sauntered down the path, but heard a whinny. A horse? Iltar turned back around and hurried to the stables near his home. He looked inside, finding his black stallion.

"Well, this will make things faster," Iltar said, hurrying to the horse. Once mounted, he galloped out of the stables, bolting down the path into the woodland. The horse didn't tire, which wasn't too strange for the dream realm of Vabenack. Real world rules didn't seem to apply here. Iltar galloped his horse all the way through the forest, reaching Soroth in a matter of minutes.

To Iltar's surprise, Soroth stood intact. Buildings were not ruined, city walls weren't crumbled, and roads weren't spotted with craters. Another oddity that contrasted the other dreams.

Iltar hummed thoughtfully, riding his horse into the city. Soroth looked deserted. Carts full of wares dotted the streets, vacant and unattended. It was as if the citizens had been plucked from their daily activities and taken elsewhere.

Iltar eventually rode to the docking district, where he found all the wharves occupied by tall trading vessels, lavish yachts, and warships. *Which pier was Reflection standing on?* In the other dreams it was the only intact pier, everything else was in ruin, so it was easy to spot.

But why the change of scenery? Did his subconscious not want him to have this conversation? But no, he refused to be doomed to a lifetime of reoccurring dreams. "One pier at a time, I suppose," Iltar said. "It was eastward, I know that."

Iltar guided his horse along the piers, searching with his eyes before moving on to the next one. He read the signs as he passed. A large font identified the pier number, and a smaller script identified the various wharves.

After several minutes Iltar stopped at one of the piers, noticing a red spot at the far end. In the other dreams, only part of the pier was intact, so he saw Reflection clearly. This time, Reflection stood at the end of the pier nearly a grand phineal away.

Iltar looked to the sign, taking note of the pier number in case he had to come here again. It'd be faster if he knew where he was going—

"What…?" Iltar gasped, his expression turning ghastly. The sign read, "*Pier Eight. Wharves One through Thirty-Eight.*"

"It can't be…" he mumbled. Pier Eight was the pier where the *Promised Maiden* was moored in reality. Was this dream some twisted manifestation of Iltar's desires to go on that adventure with Krindal and the others?

Shaking off the thought, Iltar guided his horse down the pier. He reached the end within minutes and dismounted.

Clothed in that same red robe, Reflection stood at the pier's edge, staring at the purple ocean. The waves rippled across the purple water, moving *away* from Soroth, despite the lack of wind.

Iltar's boots didn't make a sound against the wood as he approached Reflection. It was just one of many oddities here.

"Tides ebb and flow," Reflection said in Iltar's voice. "Just like civilizations." He didn't turn around.

"Who are you?" Iltar asked. It was the first of many questions he had. But he would be asking himself, wouldn't he?

"Men are like water," Reflection continued. "They move every which way, aimlessly."

"Are you saying humankind is fickle?" Iltar asked, stepping up beside Reflection. He looked the old man up and down. Reflection was just as before, looking exactly like Iltar, but with long white hair. Iltar took a moment to study the emblems on the crimson robe. He committed them to memory; hopefully those symbols would stay with him when he awoke.

"You can divert water with a dam," Reflection continued. "You can do the same to men. Some use religion. Others use civil laws. And there are some who devise their own rules, codes they adhere to… Those men, they are the great ones—the first droplets at the head of newly formed streams. But in a way, they're just following the course of the environment around them. So, still like water."

Reflection kept on about this strange philosophy. Iltar's questions hadn't diverted him into a conversation. Reflection was like an orator on a stage. You couldn't interrupt such men; they just kept on with their rhetoric until they were finished. Perhaps a different approach was needed.

"Why did you want to speak with me?" Iltar asked.

"… When a civilization becomes stagnant, its people become filthy, like a stilled pond. Moss builds in the water, vile insects swarm the shore, and disease festers in the pond. The only way to eradicate the filth is to flush the pond, and to do that it must be drained and replaced with fresh water." Reflection stopped and turned to Iltar, looking directly at him. "That's why I've wanted to speak with you, Iltar—to remove the vileness caused by stagnation."

"What?" Iltar asked, bewildered. Reflection had finally spoken to him, but what did he mean? Was that speech about water all for him?

"You're not deaf," Reflection retorted. His eyes were stern. "Nor stupid."

Of course he was not. *Bah, crazy dream-thing,* Iltar thought, gritting his teeth.

Reflection raised an eyebrow and then blinked several times before speaking. "Why did you decide to seek me?" he asked.

"I'm tired of these dreams," Iltar said frankly. "You can't imagine how tedious it is reliving the same thing over and over." Reflection smiled. He seemed amused by Iltar's comment, his expression almost patronizing. "I just want to rectify whatever it is that's happening to me," Iltar continued. "You're obviously a manifestation of my subconscious mind. That's why you look like me."

"You think of me as someone to direct you? Guide you?" Reflection asked, nodding. "So be it. I will *play* the guide."

"Good." Iltar was pleased by the cooperation. Perhaps he could be rid of this nightmare once and for all. "So, why were you talking about stagnant water?"

"Parables are poignant methods to convey ideas to those open to hearing the truth," Reflection said. "Did you see truth in my tale?"

"I can see some truths," Iltar said. "But men are masters of their own wills. We forge our own destinies." The last bit he nearly yelled. It was a sore spot for him. Rovin and Cordis had tried to manipulate Iltar's life so that it would benefit them, while being detrimental to him and those he cared for. They had almost succeeded.

"Some is better than none," Reflection said with a chuckle. "Perhaps, in time, your eyes will be opened. You will see the stagnation firsthand."

"Whose stagnation?" Iltar asked. "Soroth's?"

"The Chosen have faltered," Reflection said. "They no longer guide my children. Things must be rectified, and that's where you come into play." He looked at Iltar, studying him up and down. "But you're not ready, not yet."

"In what ways?" Iltar asked.

"Many ways."

Iltar groaned. "So I'm dreaming about an internal growth, growing myself into something greater."

"You could say that," Reflection smiled. "But it will take a great deal of effort and sacrifice."

Iltar eyed the strange mental-reflection for a moment. Reflection was cryptic, speaking answers that only had a half-substance to them. *I shouldn't be surprised.* Whatever his mind was working through, he didn't know the answers, so why would he expect more from a dream?

"You know," Reflection spoke up, "there are things in this world far greater than what Krindal seeks."

"Oh, pray tell," Iltar said, his tone mocking.

Reflection frowned. "A doubtful tone," he said. "What a pity. No matter. I will prove myself to you, Iltar. Kalda was far grander than the picturesque past Krindal has painted with these theories of Cultural Regression and the Lost World. Indeed, Kalda has fallen from its grace. The things you call tevisrals were more sophisticated than you could ever imagine. They were machines that shaped civilizations and changed humanity itself. It was grand, I tell you, grand! No people were ever as fortunate as the ancient Kaldeans. They had cities that scraped the sky. They could travel halfway around the world in an instant. Disease was eradicated, and they lived in perfect health. The tevisrals you own personally were child's playthings compared to the wonders of ancient Kalda. And Kalda was peaceful... until a rebellion occurred. That changed everything." He paused, looking Iltar up and down, as if gauging his interest.

"The architects of this rebellion formed a proverbial dam, forcing the men of Kalda out of their divinely appointed course. War ensued, then abated for a time, but eventually resumed, crumbling that beautiful civilization..." There was a sorrow in Reflection's voice.

"This river of men flowed for some time, like the swells of this ocean." Reflection pointed across the horizon. "They advanced in some areas while becoming primitive in others. There were some who remained faithful to the ancient ways, but even they have turned out of their course, pooling in dirty ponds."

Reflection paused, looking at Iltar once again. "A new channel must be carved for the river of men."

Iltar narrowed his eyes. Wasn't this a delusion of grandeur? Iltar had always wanted to be great—a renowned mage, specifically. This ambition had been seeded by his father, who had hoped for him to join the ranks of his brethren, to follow in the footsteps of Iltar's older half-brother. But never had Iltar's father spoken of becoming a man who could change the world.

"You are special, Iltar," Reflection said with a smile that seemed almost devious. "You are destined to form this new channel." Iltar grunted dismissively.

"As I said before," Reflection said calmly, "your eyes will be opened. You will *see* what you must accomplish."

Iltar shook his head and turned back to his horse, but the black stallion was gone. He walked back down the pier, and after a moment he heard Reflection speaking to him, as if he were standing right next to him.

"You cannot deny your destiny, Iltar," Reflection said.

Iltar turned around, finding himself on the edge of the pier, only a pace away from Reflection. He had been walking for a while, hadn't he? Why wasn't he farther down the pier? Iltar turned around, quickening his pace.

Again, Iltar heard Reflection; the voice spoke from beside him. "You will reshape this world."

Iltar was standing right where he had been a moment before, at the edge of the pier. How was that possible? Well, this was a dream, after all. Iltar quickened his gait again, jogging down the pier.

"Why are you running, Iltar?" Reflection asked, his voice in the same spot over Iltar's shoulder. Iltar didn't dare look back. He'd find himself at the edge of the pier again. He was certain of it! Although Iltar kept running, the streets of Soroth never seemed to get any closer. After a moment, Iltar stopped. He turned hesitantly, finding himself on the edge of the pier, right beside Reflection.

Reflection had finally turned around, facing Soroth. He looked sternly at Iltar. "In time you will realize who you truly are, Iltar," Reflection said. "Now, go. Find your way."

The yellow sky vanished, the purple ocean dispersed, violet droplets flying everywhere. The ground shook and broke apart. The pier ripped in half, separating Iltar and Reflection.

Iltar stumbled and then felt himself falling. The strange colors which made up this dream world faded, like streaking lines of light zipping away from him. Soon, only blackness remained, and Iltar stopped falling. He hadn't hit the ground, had he? Well, there was no ground. He was floating, suspended in the abyss.

"MAY THE CRIMSON EYE REMAIN HIDDEN FOR ALL TIME," a voice boomed through the blackness. "ONLY MY FAITHFUL SPEAK THIS VOW."

Iltar turned in the abyss, searching for the source of the voice, but it came from every direction.

"SEEK MY FAITHFUL, UNSPOKEN ONE, AND FULFILL YOUR DESTINY."

The booming voice faded and brilliant light flashed in front of Iltar, blinding him. He blinked several times, and when his vision returned, he found himself in the living room of his family's home, still on the couch. He sat up, breathing deeply.

Rain beat against the window. It was dark outside. The lightstone lamp on the porch was all that illuminated the yard.

"That phrase…" Iltar mumbled, "It was in the letter from Rovin's father." But why would that be a part of his dream? And what was the Crimson Eye? He pondered those questions for a moment and then saw a flash of memory in his mind's eye; the patterns on Reflection's robe. The emblems were still fresh in his mind. He hadn't forgotten!

Tossing aside a blanket, Iltar sprang off the couch. He stumbled through the room, tripping over furniture, heading for the dining room. The dining room was mostly dark. The chandelier was shrouded in a thick velvet drapery tied to its chain hanging from the ceiling. Iltar pulled on the drawstrings of the drapery, and the velvet covering fell to the tabletop, brightly illuminating the dining room.

"Parchment," Iltar whispered, frantically searching the room. There had to be parchment nearby. He *had* to transcribe these symbols before they faded from his mind. Iltar hastily opened and closed the drawers on the nearby cabinet, but found only utensils and place settings. Nothing here was useful.

The den! he thought, hurrying out of the dining room and into the hall leading from the home's foyer. Iltar turned a corner, running down an intersecting corridor. The light from the dining room barely reached this new hallway. Iltar passed a couple of doors, then stopped at the last one, squarely positioned at the end of the hall. He threw the door open, squinting his eyes. He could barely see the outline of a desk to his left. His grandfather had used this as a small library. But the room had not been used since Iltar inherited the place.

Moving carefully but quickly, Iltar picked his way through the study and searched the desk with his hands, feeling for parchment and an ink vial. He soon found them and then hurried back to the dining room.

Now sitting, Iltar spread out the sheets and pulled the quill from the vial. He could still see the emblems in his mind, but some details were fading. Putting quill to parchment, he meticulously drew the first symbol. Iltar was a decent artist, but he excelled in copying documents. At one time he had almost considered forgery as a trade, but then his and Cornar's adventure's paid off handsomely.

After a moment, Iltar finished drawing the first symbol. The center part looked like the blade of a sword with a jagged fuller. Six spikes curved from the bottom, arcing upward. Eight-sided stars rested at the tips of each spike. There were other details to this symbol, but they had since fled from Iltar's memory.

"Now for the other six," he whispered, urgently setting his quill to another parchment.

"I decided to confront Elynia but I needed to be prepared for the worst. So I dusted off my old armor and weapon and began practicing. After several sessions I approached her, feigning fatigue. As expected, she asked questions about my armor and weapon. She said they looked like the stuff of legend. Had I been gone that long?"

\- From *Origins and Oaths of the Keepers*, preface

Cornar sat quietly in his dining room, staring aimlessly out the windows to the vineyard. Morning sunlight shone upon the workers tending to the brandleberry vines. Another batch was ready to harvest.

He looked down at the open book in his hands, *Towers of Comdolith*. It was historical fiction, the tale of a civil war which spread among the nations on the northeast part of the Mainland, taking place several hundred years ago. The author, a low-ranking soldier in the Losian army, had written the book fifty years ago. He used plenty of source materials from Losian military records, memoirs of past generals—great and small alike—and historical events. Of course, those events were twisted and dramatized, but it was done in a way that made the war come alive.

Cornar's father had owned a first edition of the book. Melthas raved about the book, and so left quite an impression on his son. When Cornar was an adult, he bought a copy from a merchant who trafficked foreign novels in Soroth. *Towers of Comdolith* soon became one of Cornar's favorites. But today he couldn't even keep his eyes on its pages.

Three days had passed since he'd told his men and his friends-in-adventure about his retirement. Things hadn't been the same since then. The sorrow Cornar had felt while sequestered in his study still lingered.

The *Promised Maiden* would be setting sail sometime today. Cornar furrowed his brow, looking past the book and to the table, although he wasn't focused on it. His mind was elsewhere. In his mind's eye, he saw his men jovially carrying supplies to the ship. The warriors bantered with each other as they climbed a gangway. The mages conversed with each other, seriously speculating about the venture. The boat had an air of excited anticipation.

Oh, he longed to be there and—

"Are you going blind?" Karenna asked from behind him. "You've been stuck on that page nearly all morning." She loved teasing him, and Cornar loved it when she did.

"No." Cornar cracked a smile.

Karenna set a plate in front of Cornar. It held one of his favorite morning meals. Three biscuits were arranged around browned ground beef, garnished with sautéed mushrooms and yalvinen, a squash-like vegetable native to Soroth. Yalvinen grew in other locales, mostly islands in the southern oceans. It didn't seem to grow well on the Mainland, though, so yalvinen was a major export.

The meal did smell good, but its aroma seemed hollow. *Towers of Comdolith* read the same way. Hollow. But perhaps the hollowness didn't come from those things. Perhaps *he* was the source?

"Cor," Karenna said firmly, placing her hand on his shoulder. "What's going on with you?"

"Nothing," he said.

Karenna groaned. "Of course, nothing!" she said in exasperation. "That's the problem. The last three days you've just sat around the house, trying to do things, but never actually *doing* them."

She was right. Everything was empty to him. It was as if life itself had lost meaning. That was frightening. *Was this what it was like to retire?* Cornar wondered. Had Delrin and Jalim felt this way? But they were still doing what they loved. They were just not as active as they had been in their youth.

"I…" Cornar started to speak. He wanted to get the words right. "I think I'm just adjusting, coming to terms with reality."

"Cornar," Karenna said firmly. She grabbed his clean-shaven chin and turned his head toward her. Karenna's eyes were fierce, her lips drawn to a line. Her expression was stern. "In the last three days your life hasn't changed from what it has been this last year and a half. Really, it hasn't. The only thing that *has* changed is that the decision you made is no longer private."

She was right again. Cornar *had* been retired. He had been living the peaceful life he had fantasized about when first speaking to Gregan and Ordreth about his retirement. This life was exactly what he wanted. Helping Karenna tend to the horses, visiting family, cultivating their land, attending plays in Soroth and Sarn, and long nights of reading together. The longest trip Cornar had taken was to Tor to accompany Karenna to the annual Equestrian Exhibit of the West. Otherwise, they were island-bound.

If this is what he wanted, then why, oh why, was he feeling hollow? Was he not truly committed to this life? That terrified him. "Perhaps I need to talk to someone," Cornar suggested. "I should have spoken to Delrin…"

"No, Cor," Karenna said flatly.

"No?" Cornar asked, looking confused.

"You heard me," Karenna said. "I was foolish to think this would work."

She sighed, averting her gaze to the windows.

"No," Cornar said, clasping her hands. "We can make this work. This is just the first time everyone is going away. It'll get better."

"Cornar, I don't think it will. Your retirement will tear you apart. You won't be the man I fell in love with, the man I married. For Kalda's sake, you're not even that man now! Where is my jovial husband that would sweep me off my feet every time he came home?"

"He's sitting here getting old," he quipped, but Karenna didn't find it funny. She stepped back and folded her arms.

"And you can't tell me you're not the least bit intrigued about Krindal's quest." Karenna shook her head. "Of all the men at the meeting, you were the most impressed by that map, even though you were trying to hide it. And you didn't even do a good job at that." She rolled her eyes.

"Of course I'm intrigued," Cornar said. "It's probably the most important adventure any of us have ever undertaken."

Karenna nodded. "Exactly!"

"But," Cornar continued, "I made a promise to you. And you know I won't break it, no matter what."

"Well, you are loyal…" Karenna sighed. "I just wish you weren't so sulky about it."

"Sulky?" Cornar furrowed his brow and rose from his seat.

"Yeah." Karenna made a flabbergasted face. "Look in the mirror." She gestured to her side. "There's Sulking Cornar, right there. You can see it in his eyes."

His hollowness was that obvious, wasn't it? *Blast it!*

"If this is going to be what it's like to have you retired, I want no part of it."

Those words stung, like an arrow piercing his heart. What did she mean? Karenna wouldn't leave, would she? She had remained faithful to him all these years, even when he and Iltar were thought dead some twenty-seven years ago. Perhaps it was easier to love a dead man… A hollow man, though… was that even a man at all?

"I'll fix this," Cornar said, his voice shaking. Karenna raised an eyebrow. "I'll be that man again, the man you fell in love with."

Karenna sighed. Tears brimmed in her eyes. "There's only one way to fix this, Cor," she said, and a tear trickled down her cheek. "You need to go." *Go?* Go where? Was she trying to kick him out? Karenna wasn't through with their marriage, was she?

Another tear trickled down Karenna's cheek, followed by another. She extended her hands toward him, but Cornar didn't respond. What was she doing? "Take my hand," she said, reaching out with one hand and wiping her tears with the other.

"I…" Cornar looked at her hands, her beautiful hands. A tear trickle down his cheek. *By Heleron's Trident, what was happening?*

"Take my hand, Cor!" Karenna said through clenched teeth. He complied reluctantly. Karenna's hands were cool and smooth. Her touch was bittersweet. "Look at me," she said.

Once their eyes locked, Karenna spoke again, her voice and her hands trembling. "Cornar Dol'shir, you're going to promise me that you'll never allow anything to stop you from being the man I fell in love with all those years ago. The man who was always excited for life. You'll follow your passions, no matter what tries to defy you. You'll live your life to its fullest, both on and off the battlefield. And when you come home, I will be your entire world, cherishing every moment."

Tears streamed down both their faces.

Cornar couldn't speak. He couldn't find the words. Was she really making him promise to never stop being who he was, an adventurer, a warrior?

"I don't want you missing the greatest opportunity of your life," Karenna said. "I know you were conflicted because you weren't going with the others. I could *feel* the yearning radiating from you. The promise you made me was selfish. I should never have asked that of you."

"You didn't ask," Cornar said, fighting back more tears. "I made that promise of my own volition."

"You underestimate the power of a woman," she smiled and sniffled, blinking away more tears. "You made that promise because *I* wanted you to."

No, she was mistaken. Cornar was not one to be manipulated. "I can't break my word, Karenna. You know I've never broken a promise."

"Now you're being selfish," Karenna said. She was right, yet again. By Heleron's Scales, what was he doing? Karenna was telling him to go with the others, and he just declined. Was he really using his own pride as an excuse?

"Promise me now," she urged. "Promise you'll do those things I said."

You must always keep your word, Cornar heard his father's voice. *And be faithful to those loyal to you, especially your future wife. Do whatever you can to make her happy.*

Those words echoed in his mind.

"Cor, I'm not happy with you like this," Karenna said, another tear falling from her chin. "Not like I was throughout our marriage."

Do whatever you can to make her happy, Melthas's words rang again.

"You always know what's right, Cor," Karenna said. "Those feelings of yours—those promptings that you get—they never lead you amiss. I know you weren't following them when you made your promise. You know you weren't." As always, she was right.

Cornar remembered the feeling he had when he'd made that promise to stop adventuring. It didn't feel wrong, but it felt different. *Off* would be a way to describe it. At the time, he thought that feeling was because the promise seemed like such a radical change. Cornar eventually dismissed it. Well, consciously at least. *Always follow your feelings, son.* Melthas's voice sounded in Cornar's mind.

"Cornar," Karenna said again. "What say you?"

Cornar rubbed at the middle of his forehead, his eyes closed. He had always been able to keep his wife happy while also keeping his promises. But at this moment he couldn't do both. It was one or the other. If he kept his promise, she'd stay sad for who knows how long; until he came to terms with never going on an adventure? When would that happen? If he made this new promise, Karenna supposed he'd become the man she once fell in love with. She'd have her husband back, but not here with her.

Karenna would have her old life. She didn't hate that life, but it wasn't perfect. "Cornar," she said, her voice still trembling, "I know you want to give me everything I desire. You want me to have my ideal world. But I don't think my ideal world will make me truly happy. Because it won't make *you* truly happy."

By Heleron's Trident, she was selfless.

"Your promise was rash, Cor," she continued. "When you're ready to stay home with me, you'll come back. But you're not ready." Again, Karenna was right. Her wisdom vanquished his doubts. Cornar had married a woman far better than he. No hidden treasure of any worth could be as valuable as Karenna.

"I promise," Cornar said, his voice soft, "that I'll never allow anything to stop me being the man you fell in love with. I will be excited for life. I'll follow my passions, no matter what attempts to defy me. I'll live my life to its fullest, both on and off the battlefield. And when I come home, I will cherish every moment, making you my entire world."

The tears stopped, and a fire lit inside him, a burning fervor. This was right! He knew it, felt it in every fiber of his being.

Karenna pulled away, sniffling and wiping her cheeks. "Where are your chain mail and weapons?"

Cornar grinned. He was happy, truly happy! The thought of exploring the ruins of Klindil invigorated him. Finding tevisrals, ancient relics, and learning more about this ancient Order from Kalda's past. It was tantalizing!

"The weapons are in the chest at the foot of our bed," he replied. "I'll get my armor."

"Wipe that smile off your face," Karenna said. "We need to hurry."

"We?" Cornar asked, confused.

"You're going to need to ride Heinseil to the docks, practically up to the gangway. Someone needs to bring him home." Cornar hadn't thought about that. "I'll pick up Nilia," Karenna continued. "She'll ride him back to the manor." Nilia was a young woman who tended to Cornar and Karenna's manor home in the city. He and Karenna often wintered there.

"Did Krindal say when they were leaving port?" Karenna asked, moving to a hallway leading to the foyer.

"No."

Karenna hurried out of the dining room. "Let's hope you don't miss them!" she hollered.

Cornar darted through the kitchen and toward the home's side entrance. Hopefully he wouldn't miss the *Promised Maiden*. Then what would he do?

※

Cornar rode through the docking district of Soroth, girded in his brown chain mail, with a sack strapped to his back. His serrated dagger and short-sword bounced against his thighs as Heinseil struggled to canter down the busy road. The trip to Soroth had taken most of the day and poor Heinseil was tired. Karenna had since parted ways to fetch Nilia.

Pier Eight, wasn't it? Cornar thought, maneuvering his horse around a slow cart. *Wharf Twenty.*

Chatter, bells on ships, and the regular hustle and bustle of a port filled the air. But Cornar wasn't distracted by the noises. Within a few minutes, he neared a large sign above one of the nearby piers: Pier Eight.

Cornar kicked Heinseil's sides, spurring him into a gallop. His hoofs echoed against the wooden pier, where carts and wagons traveled easily on either side as well as a pedestrian or two. Cornar weaved his horse around the sparse traffic on the pier. Some people shouted at him, calling him a madman. But that didn't matter. He had to board that ship! Cornar passed wharf after wharf. Some were empty, but others were occupied. Eventually, Cornar came to Wharf Twenty.

The wharf was empty.

Blast!

Ships were moving in and out of the nearby wharves. Others were in the waters beyond the piers. But he didn't know what the *Promised Maiden* looked like, so he couldn't tell if those tall ships were the vessel he wanted.

"Now what?" Cornar asked. He looked down to Heinseil, who cocked his head and then whinnied. "Looks like I worked you for nothing," he said with a sigh, patting the horse's mane. "I'm sorry."

Cornar sat in the saddle for a moment, gazing at the tall ships sailing into open waters. His men were probably on one of those ships—or perhaps not, if they had set sail earlier today. Krindal was in a hurry after all. If Cornar wanted to join them he'd have to charter another ship and—

"You there!" a harsh voice shouted from behind Cornar. "On the horse!" Cornar tugged gently on the reins, turning Heinseil. A man wearing a gray uniform with a yellow stripe approached Cornar—a City Watchman.

"I've heard you've caused a ruckus, galloping your horse through the pier. What are you doing here?" the watchman demanded.

"I was trying to catch a vessel before it left," Cornar said. "But I was late."

Flashes of gray caught his eye farther down the pier, two more watchmen. *Great.* Both watchmen came to a halt behind the first man. One was quite rugged, and the other—*By Heleron's Fins! Yeldric!* He was one of the men Cornar had trained nearly twenty years ago. Not all the men he had instructed over the years had become adventurers. In fact, plenty of them had been part of other civil organizations, or went off to join those organizations after they were finished with Cornar's tutelage.

Yeldric was one such man. He'd been a boy when he came to Cornar, learning all he could until his early twenties. Then Yeldric went off to join the City Watch.

"Cor?!" Yeldric blurted. Cornar smiled. It was good Yeldric recognized him. That would probably help the situation.

"Do you know this man?" the first watchman asked.

"Yes," Yeldric replied. "This is my mentor, Cornar Dol'shir."

The other watchmen perked up, intrigued by the name. Though they had probably never met Cornar, they knew him by reputation.

"He said he was trying to catch a ship before it weighed anchor," the first watchman said.

"Going on an adventure, Cor?" Yeldric asked. Cornar nodded. "Not like you to be late," Yeldric said, and chuckled. "Wasn't that old barso-what's-it supposed to be the late one?"

"Yeah," Cornar said, smiling, "it's a long story, but I was hurrying from my home out west."

"What ship was it?" Yeldric asked. "We can see when it departed."

The watchmen snapped surprised glares at Yeldric, as if *he* were a madman. Their gazes said, "*You're an officer of the law, and you're helping someone who just caused a disturbance?!*" It seemed the loyalty of those Cornar trained lingered no matter the distance.

"The *Promised Maiden*," Cornar said, "but I know where they're going. I just need to find a certain captain. He'll get me to them." The watchmen looked uneasily at Cornar.

"You're not going anywhere," the first watchman said. "At the very least, we need to cite you for the disturbance you caused." Cornar gripped the reins and sucked in a deep breath, about to speak. But the watchmen looked behind Cornar with wary gazes.

"Excuse me," a stern masculine voice said. "You said you were looking for the *Promised Maiden?*" Cornar glanced over his shoulder, resting a hand on the back of Heinseil's saddle.

Standing several paces away was a blond-haired man wearing an elegant red coat adorned with gold-and-white tassels. The red coat was embroidered with patterns clustered together. The coat had tails, which hung behind his thighs. Beneath the coat was a ruffled cream-colored shirt. The man's pants were charcoal colored, and he wore matching boots. The newcomer was obviously royalty, but he was not some Sarn Royal or any other island aristocrat of the Principality of Soroth. He looked more sophisticated than that.

"Yes, I'd hope to sail on the *Promised Maiden*," Cornar answered, his gaze fixed on the newcomer's face. He started upon seeing the man's pale-violet eyes. *Violet eyes?*

"You're one of the men hired?" the stranger asked, his brow raised. "I thought Krindal said they were all aboard."

"My men were hired, yes," Cornar said. "I wasn't planning to come along, but I had a change of heart."

The stranger smiled at that. "Couldn't ignore the allure of ancient tevisrals, huh?" he asked.

"Something like that," Cornar said flatly. "Are you the Mindolarnian prince?"

"I am," the stranger said with a bow. "Prince Kaescis Midivar, at your service." Kaescis then looked at the watchmen. "This man is part of my retinue.

If you detain him, you'll delay an important mission of the empire."

The watchmen looked at each other, but Yeldric stepped forward. "Master Cor is free to go with you."

"Yeldric, you don't have that authority!" the first watchman barked. Yeldric snickered, then gestured to Kaescis. "If you want to argue with the prince, go right ahead. I'm sure he'll escalate this beyond our superiors."

The watchman hesitated.

"Good," Kaescis said, nodding, and then turned to Cornar. "We were about to cast off, but I was prompted by the *Will* to wait. Now I see why."

What was the *Will?* And this prince had a prompting to wait? *I wonder if it's anything like my feelings,* Cornar wondered, but shook the thoughts aside.

"Yeldric," Cornar said, dismounting from his horse, "Karenna is coming to fetch Heinseil here. Could you see that she finds him?"

"Of course, Cor," Yeldric said with a nod, hurrying around his fellow watchmen.

"Yeldric!" the first watchman shouted.

"We're to serve and protect, right?" Yeldric said. "That's what I'm doing." The two watchmen grumbled, then turned around and hurried back down the pier. They weren't going to cite Cornar with the Mindolarnian prince around.

"Good luck," Yeldric said, his tone chipper. "Maybe one of these days I'll quit my job and join you."

"You'd like it, Yeldric," Cornar said, clasping his hand on the man's shoulder. "Thank you."

"Always."

Cornar walked away from his horse, coming alongside Kaescis. The prince turned to him and gestured farther down the pier. "My ship is moored at the very end," he said. "I decided to walk the pier, hoping to gain further instructions from the *Will.* Then I saw you galloping and was intrigued. I hurried over and heard you say the name of that ship Krindal chartered. Then I *knew.* You were the reason I was to wait."

Cornar nodded. He was curious about this *Will* Kaescis kept mentioning.

"So, you're the man who retired?" Kaescis asked, his tone probing.

"Yes, my name is Cornar Dol'shir."

Upon hearing the name, Kaescis stopped abruptly. The prince looked him up and down, carefully studying him. Kaescis's gaze, however, was drawn to Cornar's weapons. The prince's eyes widened.

What was this prince thinking? Kaescis looked like he recognized the weapons, but that was impossible. This prince looked no more than thirty, and both the dagger and short-sword had been in Cornar's possession since he was thirteen, some forty years ago.

Kaescis stared at the serrated dagger for a moment longer, then resumed walking, but said no more. They walked in silence until they neared the end of the pier where a large vessel was moored.

The ship was grand looking, with metal plating adorning much of its hull. The plating was practical but also decorative. A vessel fit for a prince—a Mindolarn prince, no less.

"We have a banquet planned for tonight," Kaescis finally said as he climbed the gangway. "Those of Krindal's ship were to come aboard the *Executor's Breath*. We'll be slightly behind, but after the banquet you'll be able to join your men."

"I appreciate your help. How would you like me to address you?" He didn't know what would be proper for a Mindolarn Royal.

"Kaescis is fine," the prince said. "People call me Your Imperial Highness or My Liege. But I tire of that, especially these last few months."

Wow, not pompous at all, Cornar thought. Kaescis didn't seem like a typical Mindolarn Royal. They were often the most arrogant kind of aristocracy. But Sarn Royals were almost as bad.

Once they were aboard, Kaescis shouted for the crew to pull up the gangway, then gave further orders to prepare to weigh anchor.

"You can wait where you wish," Kaescis said, then walked across the main deck to the vessel's raised quarterdeck.

Cornar walked to the nearby rail. He dropped his sack and waited for the impending backward jolt. Cornar was going out into the world once more, ready to unearth a colossal secret, the likes of which no man had ever brought to light.

"After I answered Elynia's questions, I put forth my own. Why didn't she age? Why did she look the same as the day I first saw her? She smiled wryly, like a child anxious to tell a secret. But Elynia didn't speak. Instead, glowing faintly, she erupted with brilliant white light. I should have known…"

- From *Origins and Oaths of the Keepers*, preface

The sea breeze brushed along Cornar's face as he leaned against the starboard rail. It was good to be on the open seas again. Soldiers and sailors moved behind him, attending to their duties on the ship. Cornar thought it odd to see so few sailors for such a large vessel. No wonder the soldiers had to help.

Cornar had never been aboard a Mindolarn vessel. But the *Executor's Breath* wasn't much different from the larger ships of the Sorothian Navy, Sarin-class warships.

He turned away from the rail, looking to the raised quarterdeck. That part of the *Executor's Breath* was almost identical to a Sarin-class warship, with an open-air bridge two decks above the main deck. The similarity in design intrigued Cornar. Did the Mindolarnians copy the Sorothians, or the other way around?

A short man in a charcoal uniform accented with golden buttons and embroidery gave orders to various soldiers, who in turn relayed the orders to the rest of the ship. *That must be the captain,* Cornar thought, glancing about. Crewmen and soldiers grudgingly performed their duties. *I should probably help.*

Cornar wasn't the kind of man to stand idly while others toiled. So he hurried across the main deck and climbed the starboard stairs leading to the open-air bridge. As Cornar neared the bridge the captain shouted more orders. "… Gresym, check on the galley. I need to know when they'll be ready. Alestyrn, get the current distance of the *Promised Maiden,* and—"

The captain cut himself short upon noticing Cornar, obviously not expecting a passenger on his bridge.

"What can I help you with, citizen?" the captain asked, standing stiff-backed, chin raised.

"I was just coming up to ask you that very same thing," Cornar said, grinning. "Well, I would have said *captain* instead of *citizen*."

The captain cracked a smile at Cornar. "So you want to help?"

"Yes, your crew looks a little ragtag. No offense intended."

"None taken," the captain said. "Perhaps you can run to the galley for me. Gresym, check on the officers' mess deck. His Imperial Grace said we should be expecting sixty-two guests."

Sixty-two, huh? Cornar thought. Who else had Krindal conscripted? Cornar didn't think Alacor would commit many of their Order for this journey. Cornar's men and the few mages with them totaled forty-three. So Krindal had recruited at least sixteen—if only Captain Salisar and her first mate were attending the meal tonight.

"You! Citizen!" the captain called to Cornar. "Do you know where the galley is located?"

"If the ship is like a Sarin warship," Cornar shouted back.

"Aye, it is," the captain said.

"I'll be back in a moment, Captain…?" Cornar fished for a name.

"Admiral. And the name is Kaetet."

An admiral captaining a ship? That surprised Cornar—in the Sorothian Navy, that normally didn't happen unless the captain died.

"Right away, admiral," Cornar said, hurrying back down the stairs to the galley, located on the first deck below the main.

⟶•⟵

Cornar continued helping the crew of the *Executor's Breath*. He relayed messages back and forth from the galley to Admiral Kaetet. After that, he helped Gresym—a Mindolarn soldier—prepare the officers' mess deck for the coming dinner. It typically seated only twenty-five, so they had to bring tables from the general mess deck, one deck below the main.

The officers' mess deck was fairly large, with a vaulted ceiling that rose two decks, but the extra tables and chairs made for a tight fit. Four rows of tables were set up, each with eighteen chairs. A smaller table was positioned along the aft bulkhead, with five seats, centered along floor-to-ceiling windows. This was obviously for Prince Kaescis and the others in charge of the expedition to Klindala. Cornar meticulously put out place settings for the head table while Gresym and a servant from the galley tended to the other tables.

"They're coming aboard!" a man shouted as he entered the officers' mess deck. Cornar glanced over his shoulder, seeing the messenger run to a stairwell at the opposite side of the room. The stairs emptied onto a balcony overlooking the mess deck. He glimpsed the messenger disappearing down a hallway on that upper deck. Cornar, however, resumed placing the table settings.

After he finished, Cornar looked to his left, out the portside windows near the stern of the *Executor's Breath*. Cornar could see the stern of a smaller ship, the *Promised Maiden*. The smaller vessel drifted close to the *Executor's Breath*, but settled a gangway's distance away.

Cornar stepped to the windows to get a better view. Two gangways were extended from the *Promised Maiden*'s rail, lowered by ropes and pulleys rigged to the nearest mast. Crewmen from the *Executor's Breath* were extending metal poles with large clamps on either end, used to maintain a safe distance between vessels when they traveled side by side.

The process was complicated and required synchronization with both crews. Without proper synchronization, the vessels could be driven off course or suffer structural damage. Most captains wouldn't risk such maneuvers. They'd rather slow their ships and ferry passengers back and forth with long-boats.

Cornar stared at the process for a moment but was drawn away by several pairs of footsteps from the balcony overlooking the mess deck. The messenger was ahead of Kaescis and another man—was that a man? This other person was dressed in tan, free-flowing clothing. It looked like some type of battle garb. He, or she, had dark-blond hair pulled back in a braid. This person was slim, but neither feminine nor masculine.

A moment later, the messenger rounded the stairs and headed back toward the open-air bridge, but Kaescis and his companion remained.

"Your Imperial Highness," both Gresym and the servant said in unison, bowing together.

Kaescis waved his hand, dismissing their civility. "What else needs to be done?"

"Just the dessert bowls," the servant answered timidly.

Kaescis nodded and then looked around the room. The prince noticed Cornar and waved him over. "Mister Dol'shir," Kaescis said. His tone was serious, but Cornar thought he could hear contempt in the prince's voice. "This is one of my advisors, Laeyit."

Cornar was taken aback upon seeing Laeyit's yellow eyes. He had never seen anyone with yellow eyes. Mindolarnians were said to have strange eye color, but he had not expected anything as bizarre as this. Laeyit's face was smooth, lacking stubble. That led Cornar to believe Laeyit was probably a woman.

"A pleasure to meet you," Laeyit said coldly. The voice was feminine.

What an unfortunate-looking woman, Cornar thought. Laeyit lacked the typical feminine form, and the absence of makeup only added to her unattractive appearance.

"Likewise," Cornar said with a bow.

Laeyit, however, continued studying him with her cold gaze. Was she trying to gauge him? Laeyit looked more a bodyguard than an advisor. That role would be a good disguise—protecting the prince while pretending to be his advisor.

"Laeyit has been a member of my retinue for some time," Kaescis said. "She can be callous at times, but don't let that bother you," the prince said, as he moved to a serving table that held stacks of bowls. He picked up one of the stacks, walked to the far portside table, and began placing the bowls one by one.

Was Kaescis actually doing the work of servants? Most members of aristocratic castes wouldn't dare tend to duties of the lower classes. Cornar had never considered humility as an attribute Mindolarnians possessed. Perhaps he had misjudged these people.

"Laeyit, tend to the other table," Kaescis commanded, his tone firm and authoritative. Laeyit complied but continued eyeing Cornar. There was a sense of hostility in her gaze. Cornar knew not to ignore such things, so he kept her in his periphery while finishing his duties.

Once they were done, Kaescis strode aft, to the table for five. "Would you care to join us at the head, Mister Dol'shir?"

"It would be an honor," Cornar said.

"Good. You will sit on the far starboard seat, beside Master Krindal." Kaescis took a seat at the center of the table. Laeyit stood beside him, but didn't sit. What a strange woman.

Cornar cast a sweeping glance over the mess deck. Everything was in order. Elegant. Cornar took his seat at the table beside Kaescis, waiting for the others to arrive.

Soon, a clatter of footfalls echoed into the officers' mess deck. One of the Mindolarn soldiers walked at the head of the visitors from the *Promised Maiden*. A woman walked right behind him. She was of average height, her brown hair tucked into a simple bun. She had attractive features but wore no makeup. *Captain Salisar*, Cornar thought.

Krindal walked beside the captain, followed by Kalder and Gregan. Many of the other warriors and mages were mingled together, walking two by two.

"This is the officers' mess deck," the soldier said, stepping aside so Krindal and Salisar could pass him. "Sit wherever you wish."

Krindal nodded and stepped around the soldier, picking his way across the banquet hall. Then he stopped abruptly, his jaw dropping as he noticed Cornar. "It can't be…" Krindal muttered with a gasp.

Salisar simply cocked her head and moved around the old necromancer as he continued to stare, dumbfounded, at Cornar.

Both Kalder and Gregan heard Krindal, turning their attention to Cornar. Their eyes widened, and Gregan grinned so widely his mouth almost tore apart. "Cor!" Kalder shouted. The name drew the attention of everyone else. The warriors and mages scrambled into the dining hall, gasping and muttering surprised phrases about their leader's appearance.

Cornar rose from his seat, maneuvering in front of the table so he could greet his men properly.

"I knew it!" Vargos shouted from the middle of the men, pointing at Cornar. "You couldn't stay away!"

"Oh, Cor!" Gregan shouted, hurrying across the mess deck, bumping chairs as he darted. The warrior hugged Cornar and grabbed him by the shoulders. "You're here! You're really *here!*"

Nordal laughed, pushing his way to Kalder. "Did you think him an illusion, Gregan?" Several of the warriors chuckled.

"Uncle!" Ordreth's voice rang above the crowd. He picked his way between the tables. When he reached Cornar, he grabbed his uncle's arm. "You came! But, I thought…" Ordreth's eyes saddened. He knew what his uncle had sacrificed. Cornar simply nodded. He'd speak with Ordreth about the matter of Karenna in private.

"So, did you swim aboard like I predicted?" Vargos said, chuckling as he took a seat near the rear of the room.

"No," Cornar said, grinning. Being here with his men felt good. It felt right! This was where he was meant to be.

Several others voiced similar questions—each curious about how Cornar had gotten aboard the *Executor's Breath*.

"I'll go into greater detail later," Cornar called to them, his simple promise satisfying their curiosity. "But Prince Kaescis found me on the pier and kindly allowed me to board his ship." That was a good enough answer for many of the warriors, and they took their seats.

Several of the others, including Kalder, Nordal, Midar, and Aron approached Cornar to express gratitude that he had reconsidered.

"I'm glad you decided to come," Kalder said, clasping Cornar's shoulder.

"You're not upset?" Cornar asked. "I'm stealing your job, so to speak."

Kalder shook his head. "You're our leader, Cor. It's *your* job to lead us." Those words rang true.

Igan stood at the back of the mess deck, his arms folded. The wizard smiled at Cornar, nodding to him. Cornar nodded back. Igan took his seat beside Vargos, but continued looking fondly at Cornar.

Several more men filed into the mess deck, all dressed in black robes—the other necromancers recruited by Krindal. Cornar didn't know them. Two of them were older, probably about Krindal's age. The others were graying but not as wrinkled. Those scholars were probably Iltar's cohorts during his training at the Necrotic Order. They looked to be about that age.

All in all, there were fifteen. Cornar hadn't expected that many.

Cornar thought he recognized one of the necromancers. Was his name Bredaryn? Yes, that was it. Bredaryn had studied the conjuration arts under old Amendal's brother, Arintil Aramien. Bredaryn was a dual-disciplined mage. It was a common practice among the members of the Necrotic Order to take upon themselves the study of necromancy when the Order had changed some forty years ago. Iltar was an illusionist-necromancer, at least in formal training, although he was more than either of those two disciplines.

Krindal stepped up to the table, still staring at Cornar. The old scholar hadn't said any more.

"Master Krindal," Kaescis said, gesturing to the seat between his and Cornar's. "Please sit here."

Krindal didn't respond, but looked Cornar up and down. He seemed shaken by Cornar's presence. "How?" Krindal muttered. "Master Iltar said it would be impossible for you to come. He told me of a promise you made to your wife."

Cornar nodded. "Karenna wanted me to come along," he said. "She said it was one of the greatest adventures of my life, and that I shouldn't miss it."

"A wise woman," Kaescis interjected.

"Yes, she is." Cornar smiled. He always took pride when others complimented his wife. What other woman would sacrifice her desires for his happiness? Cornar was a lucky man.

"I see," Krindal said, walking around Cornar and taking his seat. Cornar followed the old necromancer-scholar, then sat and watched the others shuffle about the room.

"Captain Salisar," Kaescis said, his voice ringing across the mess deck. "Your seat is here." Salisar turned in her chair. She sat by several of Cornar's warriors and another woman dressed in a sailor's garb; probably her first mate. "Unless you desire to sit there," Kaescis added.

"I'm fine here, Your Imperial Highness," the captain said, and resumed talking to the woman beside her.

"Perhaps Kalder would like this seat?" Krindal asked. "I will move over." The old necromancer rose and sat on the other side of Kaescis.

"I appreciate that," Cornar said, waving Kalder over. The brawny warrior nodded and sat between Cornar and Kaescis. Only one chair remained unoccupied at the head table. Was Laeyit going to sit there?

Each of the other tables was filled with the visitors from the *Promised Maiden*. It seemed Kaescis and Laeyit were the only Mindolarnians in the room.

A moment later, Admiral Kaetet entered the mess deck. He strode to the head table and took the empty seat. The admiral didn't speak at all; Kaetet just sat there, surveying everyone in the room.

Kaescis took in a deep breath and stood. "Welcome to the *Executor's Breath*," the prince said, clasping his hands behind his back. "I am Prince Kaescis Midivar, sixth in line to the Mindolarn throne. At this time, I wish to convey the pleasure of working with each of you. Master Krindal has spoken briefly about you, but tonight I wish to get to know each of you. We are, after all, embarking on a momentous quest, and I think it wise for us"—he gestured to the Mindolarnians and Krindal—"to become acquainted with you."

Kaescis looked at each of them before continuing. "Many of you are adventurers, so you know that trust is vital when exploring the wilds of Kalda. We do live in a dangerous world."

The prince's words had truth to them, but the ruins of Klindala couldn't be *that* dangerous, could they? Cornar had never set foot on that island, only heard stories about the Wildmen who inhabited the remote parts of Klindala. The Wildmen were savages, but they weren't dangerous, at least not to his band. Cornar and his men could handle primitive people.

"As we feast tonight, I would like for each of you to stand and speak about yourselves," Kaescis said. "Tell us about your past, some of your strengths, and any interests you have outside your careers. Practil, please notify Chef Gesin that everyone is seated." The prince said the last bit to a man dressed in a black uniform who stood at the base of the stairs.

Where had he come from? Cornar hadn't noticed this Practil enter the mess deck.

"While my servant fetches the chefs, I'll begin," Kaescis said, relaxing from his regal stance. "I've lived in the capital most of my life. I have rooms in the palace, but I have my own home on the western side of the city. I was married, but my wife died some time ago." The prince paused. Kaescis looked like he was steadying his composure.

That must be awful, Cornar thought. He couldn't bear the idea of losing Karenna. That would be devastating.

"I have no children, but perhaps one day I'll have an heir."

Practil returned, followed by several chefs carrying platters of food. They distributed the platters while Kaescis continued talking. "Throughout my life I have enjoyed the study of history," Kaescis continued. "That hobby is one of the reasons I'm on this quest. I want to unlock the secrets of Kalda's past and share it with the world," his tone was bold and determined "Our people need not be shackled by archaic laws founded by delusional men." *Delusional men?* Was he referring to the kings of Los and their supreme law?

"I also enjoy the study of tevisrals. My cousin, Raedina, has founded an organization devoted to the replication of current tevisrals and the development of those told of in stories. So, I often dabble in that with her."

Some of the mages in the room were surprised. Even Cornar was intrigued. People didn't *make* tevisrals. There were a handful of magical objects in the world. The only way to obtain them was to inherit them or discover them in the remote reaches of Kalda. Of course, if one had plenty of coin they might be able to buy a tevisral. But people *making* tevisrals? Was that even possible?

Kaescis continued talking about himself as the chefs returned to the galley. They soon came back with another course of food. What a grand meal! How many courses were they eating tonight? Cornar was used to eating at upperclass establishments where meals were served in multiple courses. But this was hospitality at its finest.

Now, the chefs were placing bottles of liquor on the tables. The various contents were red, pale blue, orange, and green. What was the green one?

The red was obviously wine, same with the orange. The pale-blue liquor—called keav—was distilled from a fermented vegetable with a blue leaf and flesh, kealor. It was a strong liquor, bitter and sour.

"Feel free to drink as much as you want," Kaescis said. "But I suggest you save room for the other courses.

"Now, Laeyit," he said, looking over his shoulder, "I believe it's your turn." Laeyit didn't look amused. She set her jaw and then sighed. The woman wasn't very eloquent with her words. Laeyit gave a brief history about herself and claimed she didn't have any interests outside her duties to Kaescis— which she didn't disclose. Strange woman.

Kalder turned to Cornar and raised his brow. His expression asked, *"She's a dull one, isn't she?"*

As Krindal stood to speak, the chefs picked their way across the room, pouring drinks for everyone. Krindal explained his past and how he became a necromancer. He was descended from the man who established the first mage's guild—the Sorothian Magical Order—on their island home. That had been nearly four hundred years ago. Krindal's choice to become a necromancer was also family related, as each man in his family line, dating back over a dozen generations, had studied the art of necromancy. He—like most necromancers—focused more on wielding acidic magics and life-draining energies rather than reanimating the dead.

Amid Krindal's autobiographical discourse, a chef approached Cornar with the bottles.

"What's the green one?" Cornar asked in a whisper.

"Colvin brandy," the chef replied, his voice low. "This batch is from Bradisar. It's a darker green than other types, because the barrels they use to age them are made from trees with green inner barks. The bark adds an extra kick to it." The chef smiled with a wink.

"I'll try it," Cornar nodded, folding his arms. The chef poured the liquor as Krindal finished.

The old scholar sat, and Admiral Kaetet stood, clasping his hands behind his back, a commanding presence. The admiral was brief with his past. As for interests, he said he enjoyed working in a vineyard, but nothing else. Cornar could relate to that. The admiral sat as the chefs finished with the drinks.

"We'll go around the room," Kaescis said, motioning to the table on the far portside of the room, opposite Cornar. "Wind back and forth along the tables," Kaescis said, gesturing with his hands. "Then you can go." He pointed to Kalder. "And, we'll end with you, Mister Dol'shir."

One by one, the men and women introduced themselves. They didn't spend as much time talking as Krindal, but they weren't short like Laeyit. Cornar knew them, so what they said wasn't anything new. Most of them were from Soroth, except for Nordal.

Nordal was actually very talkative about his background. He proudly declared his Losian nativity, undoubtedly to see if he could strike a nerve with the Mindolarnians. At the age of nineteen, Nordal had left Klath—the Kingdom of Los's southwestern port—and come to Soroth. He was following his childhood friends, Tilthan and Nath, who had taken apprenticeship under the notorious thief, Cedath. Cedath and his troupe were freelancers and had worked with old Amendal several times. When Nordal arrived in Soroth, Cedath was a frequent addition to Iltar and Cornar's band of adventurers. That was how Nordal met Cornar. One thing led to another, and Nordal became one of Cornar's students. Nordal hadn't returned home since then.

Sharon was another non-native Sorothian. She too was from Klath and was the granddaughter of Cedath's associate, Vilarin. Sharon was several years younger than Tilthan, Nath, and Nordal. She followed them about six years after they left Klath—about the same time her grandfather retired. Sharon was twenty-two then. That's when Ordreth first laid eyes on her.

Cornar still remembered his nephew gawking at Sharon. Ordreth was barely eighteen at the time. It wasn't until several years later that Ordreth and Sharon began seeing each other romantically.

Cornar continued nursing his glass of brandy until it came time for the necromancers to speak. He was interested in hearing about them. Cornar had heard of several of them by name, cohorts that Iltar had mentioned years ago. Many of them had taken up positions as scholars at the Order of Histories, a government-sponsored organization in Soroth dedicated to the study of the past. No wonder Alacor permitted them to join the expedition.

The Order of Histories managed several libraries throughout the various islands of the Principality as well as museums on Sarn and Soroth. Several of the men were from the Sarn Museum. They came along to study the supposed temple Krindal sought, intending to build a replica of it at the museum.

These necromancers, however, were more like archeologists. Yes, they were trained magic-wielders, but they had other interests. Magic was more or less a hobby to them. Amid the necromancers' introductions, the chefs plated the first appetizer, fish cakes made with red filets.

Eventually Captain Salisar spoke. She was Sorothian by citizenship only. Salisar was born, raised, and lived on the seas. The captain had inherited the *Promised Maiden* from her father, who had passed away six years ago. Her mother, however, was still around and tended to the ship's galley. Salisar's mother had no interest in furthering her late husband's business, so their only child took over the shipping routes.

The captain's first mate, Emila, was next. She too was a woman of the sea; Emila's father was Salisar's father's first mate. Emila simply inherited the position after her father retired.

The chefs returned again, serving a dark green soup. It tasted bitter, with a tart aftertaste. Cornar was not impressed, but then he didn't care for bitter things. The only tart foods Cornar enjoyed were desserts.

Igan and Vargos introduced themselves next, followed by the younger mages.

As the chefs served the first entrée—a meal with potatoes, leafy greens, and crab legs—the last of Cornar's band finished. Kalder was next.

The brawny warrior stood, eyeing the plate just placed in front of him. "My name is Kalder Galistrn. I'm an orphan. My parents were killed in a border dispute with rogue soldiers from the Mindolarn Empire." Kalder paused, but continued speaking after a moment. "I don't harbor any resentment for their deaths. I was a baby at the time. If it hadn't happened, I don't know if I'd be the man I am today. And I like who I am. Besides, I probably wouldn't be as close to Cornar if my parents had survived. And I cherish that friendship." He glanced to Cornar, smiling. Kalder was like a younger brother to Cornar, and Cornar loved him, probably more than any of the others that had trained and adventured with him over the years.

"I'm sorry," Kaescis said, speaking up before Kalder could continue. The prince looked pained by Kalder's words. "On behalf of my people, I wish to extend an apology to you."

"It's fine," Kalder shrugged. "You weren't around. It's not like you had a hand in it." Kaescis averted his gaze. "I am an adventurer and a warrior. There's not much else to my life, and I like it that way." With that, Kalder sat.

"You and Laeyit would probably get along," Kaescis whispered. Kalder simply raised his brow.

Cornar laughed inwardly. Laeyit was not Kalder's type of woman. Kalder was straight to the point, not aloof as Laeyit seemed. He was the quiet type unless you were alone with him. Then Kalder opened up. Though he had never married, Kalder had had several long-term relationships. Was he seeing anyone now? Cornar didn't know.

Pushing the thought aside, Cornar stood, holding the glass of his Colvin brandy. "I'm Cornar Dol'shir, son of Melthas Dol'shir, a general who lived during the reformation of the Western Sovereignty. You know, I stand here amused at all of this." He gestured with his half-empty wine glass to the assembly. "We come from a variety of backgrounds. We have some Losians, Westerners, Sorothians, and Mindolarnians. Our nations have not always been friendly to each other, but here we are, feasting together." He sounded a tad drunk. This brandy was quite potent. "My parents were also killed by Mindolarn forces. My mother died at the same time as Kalder's parents. My father died later, during a battle.

"My father taught me everything I know about war and combat," Cornar continued, his tone solemn. "That knowledge has carried me throughout my life. I too am a warrior and an adventurer. That's why I couldn't stay away," he admitted. "Well, and my wife said I was sulking and that she'd leave me if I didn't shape up." Many of the men laughed at that statement. It was an exaggeration made up by his own fears… and drunkenness.

"I love my wife," Cornar said. He *was* drunk. "Karenna means so much to me. I wish I could pluck out the warrior and adventurer in me, and just be with her… But I don't think that's a fate meant for me." Cornar paused, thinking about what else he should say. He was oversharing. "I enjoy horses—raising them, particularly. My wife does all the hard work. I just stand around ready to help move the heavy stuff and clean up the dung." Many of his closest subordinates laughed. They could probably tell he was drunk. Nordal was looking at him, shaking his head and rolling his eyes.

"I like vineyards too." Cornar glanced to the admiral. Kaetet simply nodded in reply. "I raise brandleberries. But my friend often steals them, and his maid makes pastries out of them." More laughter filled the mess deck. "I like reading," Cornar continued, taking another sip of his brandy. My, it was strong! "That's about it."

Cornar sat down, taking another sip. This stuff was good. Why hadn't he drunk Colvin brandy before? He looked down at his plate. The crab looked good, crab was *always* good. *Yum!*

Kalder tapped Cornar's shoulder, leaning toward him. "Is your liquor a little too hard?" he asked, smiling good-humoredly.

Cornar winked at the brawny man, then held up his fingers in a pinching gesture. "*Just a little bit,*" that gesture said.

With the introductions concluded, the men and women began conversing with each other and eating their meals.

Kaescis stood, tapping his fork against his empty wine glass. Had he not drunk anything? Or maybe he'd drunk it all. "Feel free to mingle as long as you like," Kaescis said. "We have several more courses for our meal tonight, but after that I'd encourage you to get to know Admiral Kaetet's soldiers and crew. We have enough bunks, so if you'd like to stay the night, you can."

The prince sat down and resumed eating his entrée. Cornar did the same. By Heleron's Tail, it was good!

If his count was correct, there were seven courses. Seven! Cornar knew the Mindolarn Empire was obsessed with that number, but he hadn't thought they'd incorporate it into their meals. It seemed excessive. Many of his men probably thought the same. They weren't lowly commoners, but they weren't fashionable aristocrats either, so feasts like this were foreign to them. But Kaescis was royalty. Did Cornar really expect anything less, even on a ship?

⟞•⟝

"He looks like his father," Laeyit said, a scowl forming on her face. Kaescis nodded, pacing back and forth. Both he and Laeyit had since retired to his cabin. The guests from the *Promised Maiden* were still mingling with the rest of the crew. Kaescis had learned what he wanted and slipped away during the last course of the meal.

"You're worried, aren't you?" Laeyit asked.

"I'm not worried." Kaescis stopped pacing and looked at the woman. Laeyit gazed at him warily. "He was a mere boy when *it* happened."

"Children can remember much," she said. "I can make it look like an accident, you know." Laeyit was being foolish. Kaescis wasn't a cold-blooded killer, not anymore. Those days were behind him.

"I can do it while we're in Klindala," she continued. Laeyit made a fist and slapped it against her other hand. Kaescis shook his head and waved his hand in a dismissal. "Don't be a fool, Kaescis! I know you sense that he'll come for you in vengeance."

That was true. It was a concern of his; that's why he was pacing, why he'd retired to his cabin early. "I must seek the *Will*," Kaescis said nervously.

"The *Will* commanded you to wait," Laeyit said, "doubtless to have him delivered into your hands. Lord Cheserith has granted you this opportunity to slay him."

Was that it? Laeyit's opinion was one possibility. One often didn't know the reasons for promptings when the *Will* was not specific. Kaescis had to either wait, or seek further instruction.

"Well, Kaescis?"

He didn't like being rushed, but Kaescis gave her an answer to sate her bloodlust. "Let me think this over, Laeyit. We can discuss this further on our way to Klindala."

⟞•⟝

The following day, Cornar leaned against the portside rail of the *Executor's*

Breath. He watched as the *Promised Maiden* moved into position to transport his band back to their ship. They had all stayed aboard the *Executor's Breath* for the night, taking advantage of Kaescis's hospitality.

"You know, I don't think I've ever seen you *that* drunk," Nordal said from beside Cornar.

"Me either," Ordreth said with a chuckle.

Cornar grinned. He didn't make it a habit to get drunk in front of his men, but he would enjoy a drink now and again, usually if they were at home in Soroth. Being intoxicated anywhere else was just plain foolish. Cornar hadn't expected that brandy to be so potent.

"Did Aunt Karenna really threaten to leave you if you didn't quit sulking?" Ordreth asked.

"Did I say that?" Cornar asked, hoping to avoid the topic. He didn't want to trouble his nephew with his personal problems.

"I'm sure it was just a drunken inference," Kalder said, slapping his hand on Ordreth's shoulder. "You know Karenna loves Cor. She'd never leave him." Cornar hoped Kalder's words would settle his nephew's fears.

The officers of the *Executor's Breath* called orders to start the process of transferring their guests. The metal poles were lowered and their clamps secured to both ships' hulls. Soon, the gangways were extended from the *Promised Maiden*.

Captain Salisar pushed through the men and was the first to return to her ship. She was followed by Krindal and the necromancers he had conscripted. Then, one by one, each of the others filed onto the gangways. Cornar waited for his men to go ahead. Igan, however, stayed with him.

"I'm glad you're here," Igan said, smiling. "It wouldn't have been the same without you." Cornar clasped Igan's shoulder in agreement.

They walked across the gangway and stopped at the crowded main deck of the *Promised Maiden*. The crew was busy pulling up the gangways and releasing the clamps on the metal poles from the *Executor's Breath*.

"I wish Iltar was here," Igan said. He walked over to the starboard rail and leaned against it.

"Me too," Cornar said, grabbing the rail beside Igan.

"Do you think we'll ever have an adventure with all of us?" Igan asked, sounding melancholy.

"Perhaps someday," Cornar said, watching as the *Executor's Breath* pulled away to a safe distance for the voyage. "Who knows, maybe this trip to Klindala will spark another adventure."

12

MORE MISCHIEF

"A majestic creature stood before me, towering above my small home. Elynia was not as grand as others of her kind, but she was still exceptional. Sunlight reflected off her glistening white-metal scales. It was a beautiful sight."

- From *Origins and Oaths of the Keepers*, preface

Pagus stood with Iltar on the Necrotic Order's grounds, mustering magic. They were in a grassy corner, not far from the dorms. The boy's spell coalesced in front of Iltar. It was a swirling mass of orange life-draining magic, half the height of a man.

"Good," Iltar said in approval. "Now lash it to the ground and expand it in three directions at once."

Pagus grunted and pursed his lips, focusing on the ground ahead of him. *Come on, boy,* Iltar thought, *you can do this.*

The orange magic settled on the grass, and then three tiny spikes protruded from the mass, wiggling into the air. They stretched outward, becoming arm length strands.

"In order for the spell to be effective it has to reach farther than that," Iltar said.

"I'm trying," Pagus gritted his teeth. "It's harder than it looks!"

Iltar folded his arms, watching Pagus concentrate. Then a movement at the corner of his eye caught his attention. He turned as young Bilda was approaching.

The youth looked at Pagus and then hurried to Iltar. "Master Iltar," Bilda whispered, "you're not having us practice these two weeks, are you?"

Iltar shook his head. It was the time of year for the semi-annual break for students of the Necrotic Order. They had two weeks to go visit their families, or whatever else they chose.

"No, and you're free to leave whenever you choose," Iltar said.

"I am?" Pagus asked, chuckling. The magic hadn't moved any farther.

"Not you, boy," Iltar sneered. "Once I'm satisfied with your mastery of this spell, *then* you can go home." Bilda smiled and stood with Iltar for a moment. They both watched Pagus struggle to extend the magic farther.

"This is impossible," Pagus said, "moving it three directions at once. A human mind can't think like that!"

"That's why you need to practice," Iltar said sternly. He closed his eyes and rubbed his forehead.

"Does this work like the ensnaring tentacle spell?" Bilda asked innocently.

"In theory, yes," Iltar replied, glancing to the young acolyte. "But moving a spell three directions at once isn't like moving three tentacles at once. Most of the time you're focused on a single target. Pagus is trying to hit three targets at once."

"Oh," Bilda said, and nodded.

Pagus grunted, forcing the strands of the life-draining magic a little farther than before, but it wasn't far. "I give up!" Pagus yelled, throwing his hands into the air. The spell dissipated within seconds, orange particles rising into the air and disappearing.

Iltar sighed, shaking his head with disappointment. For all of Pagus's ambition, he couldn't even finish the exercise. *What am I going to do with this boy?* Iltar frowned.

"I want to learn new spells!" Pagus shouted. "Not rehash old ones over and over in stupid variations."

"Most new spells are going to be variations of what you already know," Iltar retorted. "Channels of magic are like the individual streams of a reverse delta. They branch from the most basic of spells. That's why we teach you to master the basics."

Pagus sighed and averted his gaze. He didn't look happy. Of course, he rarely did when he failed. The boy didn't cope well with failure.

"You can keep practicing or you can go home," Iltar said. "I'm sure your father will want to see your progress. I've already sent him a letter with spells he should request you perform."

Pagus bit his lip. Anger was swelling within him.

"Master Iltar knows best," Bilda chimed. Though he sounded timid, he was trying to be brave.

"Oh, quit sucking up, Bilda!" Pagus shouted. The young acolyte flinched.

"Just go, Pagus," Iltar said, waving his hand in a dismissal. "You need a break." Pagus glared at Iltar, contempt oozing from his eyes. He stared at his master for a moment and then stomped off.

"He doesn't like to listen, does he?" Bilda asked, looking up at Iltar. Iltar shook his head and rolled his eyes.

"It can't be that hard, can it?" Bilda asked.

"It can," Iltar said, and started walking the opposite direction as Pagus. Bilda trailed behind him. The boy seemed eager to learn something new from Iltar. "You're trying to split your focus three ways at once. It's not like firing one way, then another and another. Some mages think a 'simultaneous' spell can be cast by firing each direction in rapid succession. It might look like simultaneous, but it's not."

"I see," Bilda said, now alongside Iltar.

"The current requirements of the Order only involve learning how to split a spell in three directions. But, in my opinion, three is just a stepping stone toward becoming a full-fledged mage." Iltar continued walking towards the center of the Necrotic Order without sharing any further insight.

"What are you going to do, Master Iltar?" Bilda asked. "For this break, I mean."

Iltar took a deep breath as they reached the fountain at the central courtyard. He stared at the water for a moment before answering his pupil.

"Rest and relax."

Rest and relaxation were exactly what Iltar had intended. After the students of the Necrotic Order vacated the grounds, Iltar left his private office on the second floor of the Main Hall. It was late in the evening, and he was eager to get home.

Iltar walked the corridor where the other council members had their chambers. Their doors were all shut, except Alacor's. The grandmaster's office was at a bend in the hallway. Both double doors were ajar, allowing the faint chatter inside to be heard.

"… can't believe it! This is foolish!" Jalel snapped.

Intrigued, Iltar stepped up to the doors, but stopped alongside them. He didn't make a habit of eavesdropping, but when it came to Alacor and Jalel, he couldn't help but be interested in what they were scheming. Both of them were snakes. Sneaky. Conniving.

"He knows what he's doing," Alacor retorted. "The plan has been set into motion." Jalel grumbled under his breath. "I am eager to discover the truth. And this is the best way to go about it."

"Fine," Jalel said, and sighed. "I just wish you had trusted me with the matter. Can we really trust Jahevial to report everything?"

"Mm-hmm." Alacor was probably nodding in the affirmative.

Jahevial? Iltar wondered. *Where have I heard that name before?*

"We'll know what's happening when," Alacor said. "I picked up a new tevisral during my sabbatical seven months ago. One can relay a message instantaneously across any distance."

"Like an Ul'thirl?" Jalel asked. What was that? Iltar had never heard of such a thing. And that name sounded strange.

"No. It's less complicated. I don't think our brethren at the Hilinard have reached sufficient skill to duplicate such wonders. They have, however, made magnificent strides in crafting tevisrals in the last decade."

People crafting tevisrals? Iltar thought that knowledge was all but lost. And the Hilinard… wasn't that the place mentioned in the letter to Rovin—

Footsteps echoed out into the hall.

They must be leaving, Iltar thought, and then strode past the doorway, as if he were casually passing by the office.

"Iltar," Jalel barked. Iltar stopped, looking over his shoulder. Alacor and his younger brother entered the hallway. Alacor locked his doors while Jalel eyed Iltar.

"Yes, Master Jalel?" Iltar asked, his tone was mocking to say the least. He considered Jalel far from deserving of that title.

Jalel scowled at his tone. "What are you doing here so late?"

"Finishing some reports," Iltar said flatly. It was the truth. He had written several letters to his students' parents informing them of their progeny's progress the past several months. Iltar made a point to send them out, unlike the others who only sent word if there was trouble with their pupils.

"Not eavesdropping, were you?" Jalel narrowed his eyes.

Iltar raised his brow, feigning exasperation. He really didn't have to feign that emotion, as he often felt exasperated when dealing with Jalel. The bastard was as arrogant as he was annoying.

"I always walk this way," Iltar said. "And I think if Alacor didn't want his conversations overheard he would close his doors." Iltar turned around and continued down the hall. The curve straightened out, and the hall emptied into a grand three-story welcoming room, made of polished gray galstra. The hallway turned into a balcony that ran along the floor-to-ceiling windows overlooking the central courtyard of the Order's grounds.

While stepping onto the balcony, Iltar glanced out the windows. His eyes were drawn to movement near the Record Hall. He stopped and squinted. A man wearing a black robe walked away from the guards. The guards saluted him and then resumed their post.

Who is that? Iltar wondered, still narrowing his eyes at the man. As the man drew nearer to the Main Hall Iltar could see his features clearly. It was none other than himself! His hawk-like features were unmistakable.

Pagus! Iltar growled inwardly. *You fool—*

Footsteps echoed from the hall behind him. It was probably Alacor and Jalel. Iltar couldn't let them onto the stairs. They'd undoubtedly see Pagus dressed in Iltar's illusion.

That would be disastrous.

Iltar spun, hurrying back into the hall. He almost ran right into Jalel. Alacor wasn't around. The grandmaster had probably gone the other way.

"Forget something?" Jalel grunted.

"Actually, I wish to speak to you for a moment," Iltar said, gesturing back down the hall. "But not here. Your office? Or mine?" Jalel raised an eyebrow.

"Well?" Iltar asked.

"I suppose," Jalel said reluctantly. He slowly turned, sauntering back down the hall.

Iltar sucked in his breath and glanced over his shoulder. He could see the illusion of himself crossing the courtyard near the fountain. *What on Kalda was that boy thinking?*

"Are you coming?" Jalel asked.

"Of course," Iltar said, returning to the hall.

They passed Alacor's chambers, and Jalel stopped at the doors next to his brother's office. Jalel fumbled for a key and opened the door. The office wasn't extravagant by any means, but it was still splendid. Jalel was a pain at times, but he did have good taste in furniture. Yet, that was not enough of a redeeming quality to make him likeable.

Iltar stopped at the doors and Jalel took a seat on a velvet couch.

"You know," Iltar started, "I didn't get to hear your opinion on Master Krindal's venture." Jalel looked at Iltar with cold eyes. "I know your brother's stance," Iltar continued. "But what is yours?" Jalel didn't respond.

Iltar sighed. "Nothing to say, Jalel?"

"My opinions are my own," Jalel said contemptuously.

"All right," Iltar said, and shrugged. "Have a good break." He bowed and exited the office. He hurried back down the hall but didn't see his illusion through the windows.

That bought Pagus enough time, he thought. But he couldn't leave just yet, not without exposing Pagus.

Iltar took one look at the grand welcoming room. No one was present. Not even the guards. That gave Iltar an idea. He retreated back down the hall toward Jalel's office. Jalel had locked it and was walking away from Iltar.

Good, Iltar thought. Taking note that no one else was around, he whispered an invisibility spell. White-blue particles wisped about him, and within seconds Iltar vanished from sight.

Now invisible, Iltar sneaked back into the grand welcoming room and quietly strode toward the foyer leading to the entrance of the Main Hall. Once near the entrance, Alacor approached from an adjoining hall. The grandmaster reached the doors ahead of Iltar and opened them. *Perfect,* Iltar thought and slipped through the opening before the doors closed.

"Good evening, grandmaster," the sentries outside said in unison. Alacor simply nodded and walked down the path to the gates.

The illusion crossed the grounds to Iltar's right, walking with a haughty gait. Pagus would undoubtedly reach the gates at the same time as Alacor. After everything he'd tried to do, it was still not enough! *The things I do for this kid...* Iltar grumbled inwardly.

Alacor glanced to his right, noticing the illusion of Iltar walking across the grounds.

"Are you making rounds now, Iltar?" Alacor said with a chuckle. "That's why we have guards."

The illusion of Iltar shrugged then said, "I thought I saw something. But it was nothing." Pagus was quite skilled. Iltar couldn't even tell the difference in the voice. Perhaps he wouldn't have to intervene. The illusion of Iltar continued walking to the gate, ignoring Alacor.

"Not riding your horse?" Alacor called out, gesturing to the stables.

"I'll fetch him later," the illusion said. His tone was hurried, nervous. Pagus probably thought Iltar had already left the Necrotic Order for the day. But Alacor's words inferred that Iltar hadn't left yet.

The illusion hurried out the gates and disappeared down the road.

Well, that was close. Iltar shook his head. He'd better follow Pagus.

❖

Iltar trailed the illusion of himself for nearly an hour. He was still invisible and was careful not to bump into anyone in the busy Sorothian streets. This furtive tailing was actually fun.

Eventually, the illusion entered an alley, cautiously looking about. Where was Pagus going?

Iltar crept into the alley as the illusionary particles wisped from Pagus. The rebellious youth took a deep breath and then pulled at his satchel. It too had an illusion upon it, making it look exactly like the one Iltar carried. Pagus opened the pack, took one look inside, and then closed it.

What did he take? Iltar wondered.

Pagus then looked farther down the alley and headed that direction. Iltar crept close behind, but was careful not to draw any attention.

Pagus stepped out onto another road and hurried through the street. He wound his way toward a neighborhood on the northwest side of Soroth. This particular neighborhood consisted of modest homes, where the average citizens of Soroth lived. The houses were situated on small lots, with tiny yards between the homes.

What was he doing here? Pagus had a home not far from the Necrotic Order. His father had purchased it for him, so Pagus wouldn't have to stay in the dormitories with the other students. It was actually not too far from Cornar's home here in the city.

Pagus went to one of the three-story homes and knocked several times in a pattern. The door opened and Odinal—the apprentice of Melnor—ushered Pagus inside.

"Those sneaky boys," Iltar whispered.

A raindrop fell onto his cheek. He looked up. The sky was darkening. *Well, that's not good.* The rain would show his outline if it came down too heavily. Iltar had to get into Odinal's home and see what they were up to before he lost his ruse.

Iltar crept across the street and stepped onto the porch just as the door opened again. Pagus, Odinal, and another youth named Tindil exited the home. Tindil was Jalel's apprentice, and one of the oldest of the current acolyte ranks, barely older than Pagus.

"I wish you had brought your carriage, Pagus," Tindil complained, scowling at the sky.

Pagus grunted. "If I had gone straight home, I would have been noticed. A little rain won't kill you."

"I'm not worried about us," Tindil snapped. "I just hope that bag of yours doesn't have any holes. Those tomes are priceless."

Odinal simply locked the door.

"You don't think I know that." Pagus sighed, raising his brow.

The three youths walked down the porch, passing the invisible Iltar. They continued into the street and exited the neighborhood; all the while, Iltar followed them. The apprenticing necromancers continued together for a time but eventually split up. Iltar heard something about a gathering and decided to stay with Pagus, following the boy up to another home in a more affluent neighborhood.

Pagus knocked on the door in that same pattern, and then another familiar young man exited the home. The boy pulled a cloak over himself and donned a cowl. Iltar couldn't remember his name, but he knew the boy was a student at the Necrotic Order. This new boy joined Pagus for a time but eventually went off on his own. Iltar watched as he knocked on another door, fetching another acolyte of the Order.

What are these acolytes up to? Iltar wondered and caught back up to Pagus. Iltar followed the boy up to another home, one he recognized. It belonged to the parents of Agen.

Agen soon emerged after Pagus knocked, and they both walked together. Was Agen part of this mischief too? What was Pagus dragging these children into?

Not long after, the storm was upon the city in full force. It was raining hard and Iltar's disguise wasn't a disguise anymore.

Pagus was still gathering more students of the Order but Iltar had to stay with him. So, Iltar decided upon a new plan. While Pagus fetched another student, Iltar quickly ducked between two homes and relinquished his invisibility spell. Then he cast his own illusion about himself, taking the guise of a plump man with a scrawny beard.

Now clothed in an illusion, Iltar stepped out onto the street, watching the boys. He had to keep his distance now. Hopefully none of them were paranoid enough to be watching for someone following them.

They weren't.

Pagus led the small band to his home not far from the Necrotic Order. Darkness had fallen, but the rain continued pouring. Pagus's Sorothian abode sat on a nice fenced lot. It was a third of a phedan, quite large for a city estate. A wrought-iron gate in the fence opened to a wide path leading to the three-story home. The home was charming, with a black roof and a beige stone façade. Its large porch was flanked by a small garden and a two-story turret with ascending windows. At the rear of the property sat a detached carriage house that doubled as a stable for Pagus's horses.

Iltar watched as the boys filed into the home. They looked soaked, and so was he.

Soon, Odinal and Kreely ran down the street with a handful of acolytes. They hurried through the gate and entered Pagus's large home. That left only Tindil and whoever he picked up along the way, unless he was already inside.

Iltar looked around the street. It was empty, except for the occasional carriage parked on the street. That gave him an idea. He strolled nonchalantly to the nearest carriage and dismissed his illusion.

Looking about to see that no one was around, Iltar whispered another spell. Pale-green particles gathered in his hand, weaving together like fibers.

The magical strands twisted, coiling beneath his feet. Within seconds, a rope formed, made of pure magic. Ropes such as these could adhere to any surface and were nearly impossible to break. Of course, one could sever them with destructive magics or a dispel.

With his magical cord formed, Iltar wound it around his arm and recast his invisibility. The gate to Pagus's property was still open, so Iltar slipped inside. He scanned the yard. It was empty. *Perfect!* Iltar crept up to the nearest windows and peered inside. The boys were all gathered in a parlor, thirteen total. Tindil, however, wasn't present.

Iltar had to sneak inside. He was familiar with this home and knew all of its secrets. It had once belonged to his former master, Rovin, after all.

Never thought I'd sneak into this house again, Iltar mused as he crept around the backside of the home. He looked upward, eyeing a dormer with shutters above the third floor.

With rope in hand, Iltar threw it as high as he could. Though it was invisible, Iltar could feel it adhere to the roof. Careful to not make any noise, Iltar scaled the side of the home. Thunder rumbled in the distance as he climbed. *Good, something to mask my ascent.*

Soon, Iltar was on the roof. He opened the shutters to the dormer and braced his hands on the glass, wiggling it back and forth. This window had a loose lock. At least it had when he was younger. Hopefully none of the other owners had changed it. A click reached his ears, and the lock gave way. Iltar slowly slid the window open.

Thunder rumbled again, this time closer.

Pleased with himself, Iltar coiled his invisible rope and slipped inside the attic. He closed the shutters and then the window. The attic was dark, but Iltar knew his way around it. He crept through the space, carefully avoiding the creaking floorboards. A familiar musk tingled his nostrils. It reminded him of his past, but Iltar pushed those memories aside.

The door to the attic wasn't locked, and Iltar opened it without a sound. Faint, unintelligible chatter rose from the home's lower floors. An anteroom lay beyond the door to the attic, lit by a single lightstone sconce. The walls were a simple dark beige, painted to resemble stone. A narrow set of stairs led to the third floor, covered in dark wood.

Iltar crept down the stairs and into a loft overlooking the first floor foyer. The foyer was the main hub for the house. The living room, parlor, and dining room were all open to it. Here, Iltar could hear the conversation.

"… yes, when Tindil gets here, we'll start," Pagus said.

"Can we at least see them?" an acolyte asked.

"I don't see any harm in that," Pagus said. The sounds of rummaging through a pack reached Iltar's ears. "Here it is, *Praxion Velon's Repository*. While we're studying these two weeks I'm going to make copies of the tome."

Iltar groaned to himself. *You're an obstinate one, Pagus.*

"And what's the other one?" another boy asked.

"This one, well, Tindil was saying this book has some of the greatest secrets of all time. He heard Master Jalel speaking of it to a friend of his just last month."

So they're having their own study time, Iltar mused. He rolled his eyes and made his way down to the first floor, still invisible.

The doors to the home opened as Iltar left the base of the stairs. Tindil entered with four others. They removed their cowls one by one, and Iltar didn't recognize anyone until he saw the last… It was little Bilda! *Oh no.* Now three of his students were mixed up with this mischief Pagus had caused.

"It took you long enough," Pagus called from the parlor.

"Sorry," one of the new arrivals shouted. "My little brother wanted to come along." Bilda looked sheepish at the remark. He glanced to the boy who had spoken but said not a word.

Tindil marched through the foyer and into the parlor. He acted as if he was the leader. "Well, this is a good turnout," Tindil said, eyeing the boys in the parlor. Counting those who had just arrived, there were nineteen. Tindil glanced at a low table in the parlor where two old tomes were resting. Iltar recognized one as *Praxion Velon's Repository.*

"What were you doing, Pagus?" Tindil asked.

"Showing them the tomes," Pagus replied flatly.

Tindil placed his hands on his hips. "Did you collect their dues?"

"Dues?" one of the boys asked. He and some of the others looked confused.

"They don't need to pay us," Pagus retorted.

"That wasn't the deal," Tindil said, exasperated. "We said they'd pay us."

"No, that's what *you* wanted to do."

Tindil sighed and paced back and forth. "Look, we're going to be teaching them. It's only right that they pay us."

"No one ever said anything about paying," one of the acolytes spoke up.

"I brought my money," said one of the boys who had arrived with Tindil. He handed over a small sack to Tindil.

"Well, I had definitely spread that word around," Tindil said, taking the coin. "If you don't have your coin, you'll need to leave." Some of the boys looked astonished, others disappointed.

"This is my home," Pagus retorted.

"Actually it's your daddy's home," Tindil said with a snicker. Two of the boys who had come with him laughed.

I hate children like that, Iltar groaned inwardly. They weren't really boys, but Iltar considered them as such. Each of these acolytes was between fourteen and eighteen.

"Maybe you'll just cover their costs," Tindil suggested. "How does that sound?"

Pagus's brow furrowed. He was angry at the suggestion. Did Pagus believe he was helping these boys? Tindil was obviously trying to exploit them. But what would motivate Pagus to help them?

"This is all I've got." Agen pulled some coins from his pocket. He set them on the table beside the tomes.

"We'll take a deposit," Tindil said, picking up the coins. "You can pay us the rest later."

Many of the other boys dug into their pockets, removing various sizes of Sorothian coins. Tindil didn't even count how much they were paying him.

What an opportunist.

Pagus, however, folded his arms. He eyed Tindil angrily.

"Well, that should do," Tindil smiled wryly. "For now. Did your servants prepare anything to eat, Pagus?"

Pagus didn't reply, but walked out of the parlor. He headed straight for the invisible Iltar but walked past him, disappearing into the rear parts of the home while Tindil took charge.

"I think it's too late to start any training tonight, but let's have a read, shall we?" Tindil picked up the other tome. It was bound in off-white leather, but Iltar couldn't read the title on the binding or the front cover.

"What's that book, Tindil?" an acolyte asked.

"*The Codices of Soron Thahan.* It holds the secrets to the past and prophecies of the future, written by one of Soroth's founding fathers. It's his retelling of the world's history. I heard Master Jalel speaking of the truths contained within it." Tindil moved to a corner of the parlor and stood in front of a chair occupied by one of the younger acolytes.

"Why don't you move?" Tindil said with a snide tone. "I need a place to sit." The acolyte moved begrudgingly and sat on the floor. *What a bully*, Iltar thought. *Just like his master.*

Pagus walked back into the foyer, grumbling under his breath. Again, he walked right past Iltar. "Food is coming," Pagus said as he entered the parlor.

Tindil smiled. "Good." He opened the *Codices* tome and began reading from it. "*Preface. Words cannot describe how magnificent ancient Kalda was. That world was perfect, filled with tevisrals. If our enemies have their way, my posterity might not know that term. But these tevisrals were grander than anything you could imagine…*"

That sounds oddly familiar, Iltar thought. This preface sounded like Reflection's words in his last dream. Iltar hadn't dreamed of him since that last encounter. The nights had been quiet.

Tindil continued reading. "*… that was until the Crimson Eye shadowed the world. It came, ever searching, and caused a devastation the likes of which our world had never seen. The Eye plucked our gods from us, and we were left alone, doomed without their divine influence.*"

There's that phrase again! Iltar thought. *The Crimson Eye.* What was it? The letter from Rovin's father mentioned it, then the dreams, and now *The Codices of Soron Thahan.*

Tindil continued reading from the preface, speaking about survivors of a cataclysmic war. The survivors banded together, taking shelter beneath the world. They had taken upon themselves a vow to never allow such devastation to strike again. "*As long as our blood runs true,*" Tindil read, "*and a remnant of our posterity roams Kalda, we will ensure that the old ways live on. We will not fear our Foe. We will stand fast. We will ensure that the Crimson Eye remains hidden for all time.*"

Iltar was taken aback. Hadn't that booming voice said something about his followers speaking a vow like that? Perhaps those dreams weren't dreams at all. But that would imply they were of divine origin. Krindal mentioned that the Mindolarn prince claimed divine guidance, led by something called the *Will.* Could Iltar's dreams be somehow tied to Krindal's quest? That was a disturbing thought. *I'm not some hero,* Iltar mused. *I'm far from it. Not with what I've done.*

Tindil kept reading, but Iltar was lost in his own thoughts. "*… and now it falls to you, who read this. I implore you. Seek the Ca'trusin, and take upon yourselves the vow, 'May the Crimson Eye remain hidden for all time.*'"

A bell rang from deep within the home, heralding the food prepared by Pagus's servants. Tindil paused, bookmarking the page with a velvet strand.

I need to find out more about this book, Iltar thought. He strode to the parlor, dismissing his invisibility.

Several of the acolytes saw Iltar's approach, including Tindil. Tindil paled in fear, dropping the *Codices* tome. "Oh no…" he said with a gasp. The tome hit the ground amid the frantic cries from the acolytes. Some were screaming phrases in an attempt to ward off torturous punishment. Their participation in Pagus's rebellious actions was enough for them to be *disciplined* by Alacor and the others. How barbaric!

Chaos ensued. Some of the acolytes ran past him, headed for the home's entrance. Others huddled in corners, screaming or crying.

Iltar's students, however, remained in the parlor, looking at their master with uneasy gazes. Though they didn't fear him—as the others feared their masters—they were unsure of what he would do. Agen and Bilda hadn't been caught doing something out of line. Pagus, however, was his typical defiant self.

Odinal and Kreely remained as well, but they were leery. Their encounter with Iltar in the basement of the Record Hall was still fresh in their minds. They knew Iltar wouldn't hurt them, but they were unsure of what would happen next.

"Silence!" Iltar shouted, his voice ringing through the foyer and the other adjoining rooms. "And cease your flight!" The fleeing boys froze, stopping short of the home's entrance.

"Master Iltar," Bilda spoke up timidly, "What are you doing here?" He stepped toward Iltar, unafraid of punishment. Several of the frightened acolytes stared at Bilda in bewilderment. Iltar ignored the boy and glared at Pagus. He raised his brow in disappointment but Pagus didn't seem the least bit ashamed.

"I was following your ringleader," Iltar said mockingly. "I noticed him sneaking out of the Record Hall wearing my illusion." Pagus started, eyes widening. "Don't worry"—Iltar waved his hand—"No one else discovered him. I saw to that myself." He took a deep breath and paced for a moment. Some of the boys looked at each other nervously.

"You obviously realize the seriousness of what you've done," Iltar said, "else you wouldn't be so frightened." He let that sink in for a moment.

"What are you going to do to us?" Tindil asked, pressing himself against the chair.

"He won't do anything," Pagus said, his tone full of contempt. "He's too *soft*."

"Don't test me, boy." Iltar cocked his head toward Pagus and eyed his apprentice. He needed to be more forceful with Pagus. Perhaps some discipline in front of his peers would do him good. It had worked for a time after catching him in the Record Hall.

Iltar grinned, uttering an incantation. Orange magic coalesced in his right hand. Pagus flinched and began casting his own spell to retaliate. Green magic wove through the air. He was trying to do what Iltar had done in the Record Hall: use an ensnaring tentacle spell to shut his master up.

But such a tactic wouldn't incapacitate Iltar.

An orange ball of life-draining magic formed in Iltar's hand before Pagus could finish his spell. Iltar flicked his wrist, and an orange cord flew from his hand. The cord wrapped around Pagus's neck like a snake, dropping the rebellious youth to the floor and interrupting his spell. The cord pulsed once, and Pagus gasped for breath.

"He's going to kill him!" one of the boys cried.

Young Bilda was looking up at Iltar. The boy looked confused but thoughtfully studied what was happening. His eyes widened with enlightenment, and he smiled.

"Pagus," Bilda spoke up, "you really should treat Master Iltar with more respect."

"Please stop!" another acolyte shouted.

Soon, footfalls echoed into the foyer from the rear of the home. Two of Pagus's servants dashed into the foyer, a maid and a chef. They had obviously heard the commotion.

"What's going on here?" the chef demanded. He was a burly man who wielded a kitchen knife.

"That's life-draining magic!" the maid cried, her face pale. "You'll kill the royal heir!"

The chef readied his knife, edging forward.

"He won't kill him," Bilda retorted. "Master Iltar is just holding the bond in place. He only siphoned a smidgen. Isn't that right, Master Iltar?" Iltar nodded.

The chef stopped his advance, but maid remained frantic. "We must alert the City Watch!" the maid blurted and ran for the door. "This is treason against Sarn!"

"You'll do no such thing!" Iltar bellowed. The maid didn't stop. She hurried to the door and turned the knob. *What a fool*, Iltar thought, and then cast another spell, mustering his own ensnaring magic. He couldn't let this woman leave. She'd only cause more harm.

The maid dashed outside as Iltar finished his spell. A burst of green magic slithered after her, speeding from Iltar's other hand. The tentacle whizzed around the corner and grabbed the maid, pulling her back into the foyer.

"Bilda, the doors," Iltar commanded. The young boy complied quickly.

"Let me go!" the maid screamed, Iltar's magic pulling her back into the foyer. "You necromancers are all alike, corrupt and evil! How dare you torture your pupils!" She continued ranting, but Iltar ignored her. The woman was ignorant.

"Master Iltar"—Pagus's voice was raspy—"I am sorry. I yield."

Iltar raised his brow, intrigued. Pagus had never apologized for his behavior. *Finally, he's learned his lesson.* Iltar relinquished his life-draining magic, a stern expression on his face. Pagus coughed and rubbed his throat. The other acolytes were dumbfounded. They had obviously never seen one of their masters forgo punishment.

Iltar returned his attention to the maid. "If you go to the City Watch, you'll only bring down wrath upon these boys. You obviously don't know what they've done."

"What have they done?" the chef asked, relaxing his knife-hand.

"Stolen forbidden tomes from the Necrotic Order," Iltar said. "Mandatory punishment for such acts is expulsion from the Order. Although, Alacor would add something more violent and sinister to that punishment." He let the thought sink in for a moment. "I can forgive such things, but my brethren will not."

Iltar smiled. He held all the power here. He could just take the tomes, but the boys would probably steal them again. He had a better plan. "Well," Iltar said, sighing, "these boys are determined. They want to learn things beyond their current curriculum. And I am interested in one of the tomes they've stolen. Seeing as 'I' have already checked it out, there's no need for me to return them in haste." The older acolytes looked at each other with uneasiness.

"I probably should hang onto them for a few days, so as not to arouse suspicion from the guards." Iltar studied the acolytes, who seemed to relax a little. "Now, I was planning on resting and relaxing. But I suppose I can rest while studying that tome."

"What about our training?" an acolyte asked.

"From *Praxion Velon's Repository?*" Iltar asked. "That's not happening. None of you are ready for those incantations."

Some of the boys groaned, and several of them grumbled in frustration. They had apparently hoped to learn something new and hear a few grand tales. The miscreants seemed to have taken this rebellious act as an exciting excursion for knowledge. Disappointment showed on every face.

That made Iltar think. He was going to study *The Codices of Soron Thahan*. And though Iltar couldn't let the acolytes learn from the *Repository*, he could come to a compromise. But there would be no rest and relaxation for him. *Oh well…*

Iltar cleared his throat. "I'll make you all a deal," he said. "I'll read the contents of the *Codices* tome to you, and I'll give you some special lessons to improve your magical prowess."

The boys perked up. Although it wasn't what they had initially wanted, it was better than nothing. And it was certainly better than being punished.

"But"—Iltar extended his forefinger—"you'll have to be discreet about it.

We'll train here, at Pagus's home. And every night, we'll read from *The Codices of Soron Thahan*. How does that sound?"

Agen and Bilda yipped and cheered. Several of the other boys smiled and nodded in agreement. The older ones, particularly Tindil, weren't amused.

"Do you have a problem?" Iltar asked the older boys.

"You're going to take our coin," Tindil grumbled.

"Actually, no." Iltar grinned. "You're going to give that back." Tindil scowled at Iltar but the boy quickly quelled his emotions. *Did he forget who he was dealing with?* Iltar thought, but averted his gaze and continued talking to the others. "Why don't you all eat, and then we can read this tome."

The acolytes filed out of the parlor and moved past the chef. The maid was still bound, but she wasn't shouting anymore. That was progress. "Pagus," Iltar said, "you should have a word with her."

Pagus nodded. He was actually obeying! The rebellious youth walked over to his maid and explained the situation in further detail. Pagus told her the ramifications of involving the City Watch and went into detail about the consequences he'd face from Alacor. Her patriotic nature seemed to kick in; she was not going to allow her liege to face a fate far worse than a minuscule siphon from a life-draining spell.

Once everyone dispersed, Iltar picked up the off-white tome written by Soron Thahan. Its craftsmanship was exquisite. Iltar had never seen such a tome. He flipped it open and found pages made of a semi-glossy substance, but there was no glare when reading the pages. *How odd…* And it looked pristine! It was as if it had been crafted yesterday. And what were these pages made of? They didn't feel like any tome or book he'd handled. Bizarre…

Iltar flipped through the pages once again. He paused to read several passages. A couple of them sounded like riddles. Still curious, Iltar turned to the beginning of the tome. There was a date written beneath the title page. *"The Year of Our Lord, Seven Thousand Three Hundred and Thirty-Three."*

Seventy-three hundred years? Iltar's eyes widened. If this was written by one of Soroth's founders, it should be dated nearly nine hundred years ago. The date should be closer to fifty-five hundred Coridai Delnasium, often abbreviated as C.D. on written dates. Scholars weren't certain what Coridai Delnasium meant, but the name dated back well beyond a thousand years and was the only known calendar system on Kalda.

The date only made the tome more intriguing. Iltar gently closed it and then exited the parlor. His stomach was growling. He'd best get some food.

13

THAHAN'S SECRETS

"Elynia had some strange views. She preferred the company of humans over her own kind. When she ran away, she was a child, but for a human that would have been well into adulthood. She wanted to see the world, all of it. She didn't want to be like the others, wasting away in Ul'goth'sinsa'uminar, absorbed in scholarship. She yearned to explore Kalda."

- From *Origins and Oaths of the Keepers*, preface

While the acolytes ate their dinner, Iltar and Pagus stood in a nearby hallway, conversing.

"You realize I can have you expelled for this, don't you?" Iltar asked, his tone stern.

"Would you?" Pagus asked, wrinkling his brow.

"Yes." Iltar's answer was sincere. Pagus had violated a code of conduct he had vowed to obey. "I would if it was just you," Iltar continued, "but with the others involved, I'm hesitant. Perhaps if we had different leadership... But Alacor is too brutal, too barbaric. He'll destroy the Order if he's not careful."

"So what are you going to do?" Pagus asked. The boy seemed genuinely interested in Iltar's decision.

"I don't know yet," Iltar narrowed his gaze at the boys. They were all crowded around the long dining table, talking cheerfully. He remembered days like this with his friends when they'd gather at the old Aramien Estate in the forest. Those were the days before the adventures. Iltar's adventuring band could be traced back to then. Those were good times.

"Why are you smiling?" Pagus asked.

"Just reminiscing," Iltar answered.

Amid his strolling through rosy memories, Iltar remembered his horse. "Why don't you return to the Necrotic Order," he said, looking Pagus squarely in the eyes. "I need my horse."

"In this weather?" Pagus asked. "I'm just barely dry now."

Iltar smiled. "Yeah."

"Can I just send a servant?"

Iltar shrugged. "Just make sure my horse is in your stables before we retire tonight." Pagus nodded and disappeared down the hall.

Iltar remained near the dining room, eyeing the boys. He had eaten quickly and then taken the opportunity to speak with his rebellious apprentice. Iltar watched the boys finish their meal. The chef served them a cake for dessert, and they devoured their slices quickly.

"Let's retire to the hearth room," Iltar suggested. "We need to warm ourselves, since we all got wet."

The boys followed him down the hall to a keeping room at the rear of the home. It had a large fireplace and several couches. Outside the windows, lightning streaked across the sky.

"Get comfortable," Iltar said, and walked to a plump chair on the wall beside the hearth. There weren't many lamps in the room, and he needed the light of the fire to illuminate the pages to *The Codices of Soron Thahan*.

As the boys settled into their spots around the keeping room, Pagus's maid arrived with blankets. The younger boys grasped them. Bilda and his brother shared a blanket, but everyone else had their own, except Odinal, Kreely, and Tindil. There weren't enough blankets for them.

"Where's Pagus?" one of the boys asked.

"Fetching my horse," Iltar said, opening the off-white tome. "We'll start without him. I intend to have him transcribe this tome for me while I teach the lot of you. He won't be missing anything."

Iltar flipped past the title page and the preface. He glanced at the table of contents. The chapters had interesting titles: *Nature of the Chosen, The Role of Tevisrals, Signs of Our Lord's Advent*, to name a few. Some of them were prophetic sounding; others had a philosophical tone to them. All in all, the contents of the tome were intriguing.

Iltar flipped to the first chapter and began reading. "*Before I tell you of the past, I must direct your mind forward. There will be a time when our ancient world will be restored. The glorious ways of old will return, and so will our gods. But the Harbinger must prepare the way for Our Lord's Advent.*

"*I must needs suppose that at some future time, our people will become lost, foreigners to the truth. They will forsake the Chosen and the Grand Oracle. I fear that day. I bemoan it! Oh that I could prevent it, but alas I cannot. It was foretold and so must occur.*

"*The Harbinger, however, will rectify all of that. He will be led by the Messenger of the Promise. The Messenger will come to the Harbinger, clothed in red. He will light his mind like a flame, showing him the past, the present, and the future. With his assistance, Our Lord's Harbinger will gather the remnants of the Chosen and return the gods.*"

Iltar paused after reading the passage. It sounded an awful lot like Reflection's behest.

"Wow," one of the boys muttered, "do you think that'll really happen?"

"Master Jalel seems to think so," Tindil replied.

The boys debated the subject while Iltar retreated into his mind. Soron Thahan's words were a lot like Reflection's rhetoric. They both spoke of restoring Kalda to its ancient ways, whatever that meant. Iltar hadn't the slightest idea.

"Are you going to keep reading, Master Iltar?" Agen asked. He leaned forward, studying his master. Iltar nodded. He continued reading for a while but paused again when Pagus entered the hearth room.

The boy was wet. He actually had fetched the horse himself. That surprised Iltar. Was Pagus genuinely repentant? Or was this a ruse to satisfy him? Either way, Iltar wasn't going to let his guard down. He'd be watching Pagus closely from now on.

"*I implore you to watch for the Harbinger's coming,*" Iltar continued. "*I will explain more of the signs as I recount the important events of the past. It is key to understand the past in order to have a keen eye for the future.*"

The rest of the chapter consisted of vague or cryptic descriptions of the ancient past. It was as if Soron Thahan was referencing things that they should know. It read like a commentary and companion volume to a vast library of forgotten knowledge.

After Iltar finished reading the chapter, he relaxed in his chair. The fire was dying, and the boys were yawning.

"Wasn't I right?" Bilda asked generally. "Master Iltar is quite pleasant. And he's a good storyteller."

Agen nodded with a smile.

"He's not like the others," one of the boys said, looking at Iltar. "Maybe I could transfer under your tutelage?" Iltar asked, chuckling.

"I think everyone would want to study under Master Iltar," Pagus said. He was sitting on the raised hearth, rubbing his arms.

"You should rub your chest, Pagus," Iltar suggested. "You'll warm quicker." Pagus cocked his head, but heeded the suggestion.

"Why aren't you like the others?" Tindil asked. He was leaning back, arms over his head. "You don't seem harsh, like Master Jalel and his brother."

"Because I had a better teacher than they did," Iltar answered frankly. "They had poor examples."

"Are you saying Grandmaster Cordis was inferior to his brother?" Tindil asked.

Iltar laughed and shook his head. "I don't credit Rovin for my demeanor or my high standards in the arts. That's my father's doing."

"Who was your father?" Agen asked. "I've never heard you speak of him." Sorrow flooded Iltar. That question dredged up unwanted memories. He felt a fit coming on.

No!

Not here!

The scent of flame tingled his nostrils.

An eruption of magic sounded in the distance.

His mother's screams followed.

Iltar shut his eyes, taking in a deep breath.

No!

A small hand touched his knee, snapping him back to reality. Little Bilda knelt in front of him, smiling. "What was his name? Your dad…"

"Adrin," Iltar said in a whisper. He hadn't spoken his father's name in ages, and it felt odd to say it aloud.

"Like the Hero of the West?" one of the boys asked. "Wasn't he that grand mage who liberated the Western Sovereignty from the Mindolarn Empire?"

The acolytes discussed the matter, repeating facts they had learned about the history of the last fifty years.

"My father had a high standard for wielding magic," Iltar spoke up, interrupting the boys. They quieted, intently listening to Iltar. "That's why I'm so hard on you, Pagus." He glanced to his apprentice, who was no longer shivering. "My father was hard on me, always pushing me to do more, be greater than I was."

If Adrin were training Pagus, he'd be pushing him to hurl spells in more than three directions. The boy wouldn't last long as his father's pupil.

"I don't remember that name in the annals of the Order," Odinal said. "What type of mage was he?"

"A grand mage," Iltar answered. The boys gasped, looking at each other.

"Aren't those Alathian mages?" an acolyte asked. "They're supposed to be the most powerful, I've heard."

"I heard a grand mage slew the Mindolarn emperor last year," another chimed. "During some celebration. My parents were whispering about it."

That piqued Iltar's interest. He hadn't heard much of the emperor's death, only that it had occurred seven months ago.

Agen raised his brow, then looked at Iltar. "So, why aren't you a grand mage, Master Iltar?" he asked.

"My father said I wasn't gifted enough," Iltar said, averting his eyes to the ceiling. "Since my childhood, my mother had trained me as an illusionist. I begged him to test me again. He did. But the results were the same. When we relocated to Soroth, I joined the illusionist sect at the Order."

"We had an illusionist sect?" one of the boys asked.

"The Necrotic Order was not always the Necrotic Order," Iltar said. "At one time they welcomed all the arts."

"Where'd they teach all of them?" another boy asked.

Iltar chuckled. "Your dorms weren't always dorms. The Order was quite packed back then. We had thousands of students when I attended."

"Thousands?!" the younger boys blurted in unison. Less than a hundred students were currently studying at the Soroth Necrotic Order. That didn't include any private students, like those currently studying under his friends. But even those didn't raise the student body beyond two hundred.

"So you graduated as an illusionist?" Agen asked.

"No, he graduated a necromancer-illusionist," Kreely said. "I looked up Master Iltar's records the other day. After our… uh, encounter."

"When did you become a necromancer, then?" Tindil asked.

"When I was eleven," Iltar said, his tone saddened. Those were dark times. Lying to his mother. Sneaking out in the middle of the night. Agreeing to study the necrotic arts was like signing his parents' death warrant.

"And Rovin was your only teacher?" an acolyte asked.

"In the necrotic arts, yes," Iltar answered. "He taught me outside the Order."

"Do you ever wonder what happened to him?" Tindil asked. "Master Rovin disappeared about the same time as Grandmaster Cordis, didn't he?"

"Does anyone know what happened to them?" Agen asked.

"They just disappeared," Tindil said. "A lot of mages went missing back then. Master Jalel said it almost crippled the Order. It was a trying time. A lot of other mages left Soroth too, non-necromancers. Eventually, the entire council disappeared. But Grandmaster Alacor rose to the occasion, or so Master Jalel said. He and several others banded together and took upon themselves the burden of leading our guild."

It wasn't quite that way, Iltar thought. *The others were using Alacor as bait.* The boys continued discussing the disappearances. Iltar declined answering any questions, simply shrugging or shaking his head whenever they asked him about details they were unsure about. Iltar didn't want to remember those times. That was his past. He was not that man anymore.

"We should get to bed," Iltar said as the fired died. "You'll have an early day tomorrow. And I have just the right exercises for the lot of you."

He rose from his chair and exited the hearth room. Iltar glanced back, and the boys stirred. They gathered their blankets but continued discussing the disappearances of long-lost mages.

⸺◦⸺

Iltar found himself standing in the hearth room of Pagus's home, sunlight struggling to shine through the draped windows. It looked different from when he retired to bed. There were different chairs by the hearth. He knew those chairs, had sat in them as a boy on cold evenings. This is how the room had looked when it belonged to Rovin.

"Why?" Iltar said with a groan. "Why am I dreaming of that time?"

"You know who you are, don't you?" a familiar voice asked from behind him.

Iltar spun about, seeing Reflection standing in the hallway.

"The Unspoken One," Reflection said. "The Harbinger of Hemran'na."

"What am I doing here?" Iltar demanded, frazzled.

Reflection smiled wryly.

Iltar stomped across the hearth room, coming to stand squarely in front of Reflection. The oddity was dressed in his same crimson robe. "I want you to leave me alone," Iltar said, his voice shaking.

"Afraid of your destiny?" Reflection said, chuckling, and then snapped his fingers. Iltar started, then saw movement out of the corner of his eye.

Another familiar voice spoke. "Iltar, my boy, what brings you here?"

It was Rovin! Iltar turned, looking at the hearth where his former master liked to stand.

Rovin was dressed in a casual tunic and pants. He was a little taller than average height with a pot belly. His black hair had large streaks of gray and his clean-shaven face was wrinkled. Rovin's brown eyes weren't looking at him, though.

Reflection snap his fingers again, and another person appeared in the hearth room, directly in front of Rovin's gaze.

It was Iltar! But his hair was blond, and he looked younger, *much* younger.

"I heard you went off with that crazed conjurer," Rovin said. "Were you actually able to enter the Karthar Valley?"

"We sure did." The younger Iltar grinned.

"Spinning tales, eh?" Rovin asked, chuckling. "You should learn that lying gets you nowhere, Iltar."

Oh no… Why was he experiencing this? It had to be because he was back in this home, spending all that time in the hearth room reading to the acolytes. Worried, Iltar peered around Reflection. A darkened silhouette of a large man holding two weapons stood farther down the hall. A youth was right behind him, clutching a large two-handed sword. Iltar could faintly see a black light around each weapon.

Iltar glanced back to Reflection. "Why are you showing me this?"

"To remind you of who you are," Reflection said, gesturing with his head toward the exchange between Rovin and the younger Iltar.

But Iltar couldn't look.

"Your actions that day weren't evil, Iltar," Reflection said. "Rovin was a parasite, corrupting the pond. His filth only added to the damming effects that others had put in place."

Iltar turned away, looking down the hall at the man and the youth, but he still heard the exchange between Rovin and his younger self. He couldn't bear to watch.

"I actually have something to show you, master," the younger Iltar said.

"Oh?" Rovin asked. There was tension in his voice, something Iltar hadn't noticed all those years ago. Had Rovin an intimation of what Iltar had planned?

Iltar heard Rovin gasp, "It can't be!"

"Oh, it is!" younger Iltar cackled.

"B-bu-but, how?!"

"That's a very good question," younger Iltar said. "I haven't quite figured it out myself."

Rovin rattled off an incantation, but screamed in pain. Rapid footfalls rushed from the hallway, accompanied by a leap, a landing, and swinging metal. Still pained, Rovin continued his incantation.

"This is impossible!" Rovin yelled, panicked.

Iltar couldn't be here anymore. He opened his eyes, briefly seeing four figures in the hearth room, two of whom were clothed in a black aura, before hurrying down the hall. Iltar dashed past where the man and the youth had been concealed, but kept going.

Soon, Iltar darted into the home's large foyer. Blood-red clouds covered the sky, visible from the windows surrounding the home's main entrance. A pained scream howled behind him, but he kept running toward the doors. He grabbed the knobs, but they wouldn't turn.

"Don't you remember all the precautions you took?" Reflection asked. "You planned this perfectly. No one could come in or out." Another scream wailed from the rear of the home.

"Get me out of here, now!" Iltar shouted.

Reflection sighed and shook his head. *"The Harbinger will betray his master, slaying him in his very home."* Reflection's tone was like Iltar's when quoting something. *"The master's passing will go unnoticed. His death will be dismissed without consequence."*

Wailing sobs echoed from the hearth room, followed by younger Iltar's shouting, "This is for my mother!"

That cry pained him. The memory of his mother evoked tears, and Iltar slumped against the door, covering his ears. But he could still hear the screaming.

A moment later he heard his younger self shout again. "This is for my father!" More sounds of agony resounded through the home.

"Stop this!" Iltar shouted. "Stop this, now!"

"You were already doing it, Iltar," Reflection said, "fulfilling Soron Thahan's prophecies."

The wailing died out, but Iltar knew it wasn't over.

"Embrace who you are," Reflection said. "Don't fight it."

Silence lingered for a moment, but was soon broken by younger Iltar. "And this is for me!"

One last resounding wail echoed through the home, and then all fell silent. Rovin was dead.

"Keep searching that tome," Reflection urged. "It'll be a guide to you when you're lost, or in times that I cannot speak to you. Something approaches that bars me from Kalda. But it will pass."

Then Reflection stepped aside.

Soon, footfalls echoed from the hallway, and Iltar looked up. His younger self entered the foyer with a younger version of Cornar. The teenage Kalder was right behind them, carrying a pail. The black aura that had surrounded each of them had since faded.

"You have *it?*" younger Iltar asked the youthful Cornar. The young warrior grinned, removing a blue rock from beneath his armor, a rogulin crystal.

"Let's go to the attic," younger Iltar suggested, waving his hand toward the doors. He was dismissing a spell placed upon them. "No one should see us teleport in there. And that dank stench will mask the crystal's smell."

Without any further exchange, the three conspirators climbed the stairs, leaving Iltar alone with Reflection.

"Get me out of here," Iltar complained. "Get me out of this stupid dream!"

Reflection snapped his fingers. The foyer vanished.

Iltar felt himself falling, as he had in the other dream. He fell through a mass of darkness, but heard the words in the distance, "HEED THE WORDS OF THE MESSENGER OF THE PROMISE AND FULFILL YOUR DESTINY."

The words faded, and Iltar gripped silky sheets beneath him. He was lying on a bed inside the chef's chambers, and he was alone. The chef had vacated the room to allow Iltar a place of privacy. Iltar was grateful for that. He didn't want to wake from one of those nightmares with the acolytes nearby. That would be embarrassing.

Sitting up, Iltar took in a deep breath. These dreams were becoming tiresome. Would they ever stop?

14

THE HIGH SEAS

A wave of heat washed over Cornar. He looked about frantically. The sky was covered in smoke, and homes were burning all around him. Homes? But he was aboard the *Promised Maiden*, sailing through the Kalishir Ocean toward the Mainland. They had left Soroth seven days ago.

He must be dreaming. Steeling himself, Cornar took a deep breath and surveyed the burning buildings. Cornar stood at the edge of a village, upon a cobblestone road. Dying screams wailed through the air.

He ran toward those sounds. Most men would run away, but not Cornar. Those screams were like a clarion call, beckoning him to provide aid. Cornar ran through the streets for several minutes. This place looked familiar. He knew this road—

A burning lamppost fell before him, and Cornar leapt over the burning pole and into a billow of smoke. Coughing, Cornar could see the outlines of two small figures moving through the street. Soft sobs came from their direction. Cornar remembered hearing cries like that long ago.

The smoke cleared briefly and a young boy and a girl ran toward Cornar. Both were dirty, covered in soot. The boy clutched a baby in his arms, wrapped in a filthy beige blanket. They stopped upon seeing Cornar. Both looked familiar. In fact, they looked exactly like—

"Galana, run!" the boy cried, handing her the baby. With tears in his eyes, the boy stood ready to fight Cornar.

Galana? Cornar wondered. That was his sister's name. *Am I reliving that frightful night?* He took another look at the boy. The boy looked exactly like Cornar when he was that age. The boy lunged at him, fist poised to strike.

"Wait, Cor!" Cornar shouted to the boy, dodging his advance. "I'm here to help."

"How do you know my name?" the boy demanded as he recovered, dropping back into a fighting stance.

"I'm a friend," Cornar said. "Keep going down this street. Don't take the alley to the market."

"Why?" the boy demanded, edging forward. "The market is the fastest route out of town!" He was slowly closing the gap between him and Cornar.

"Trust me," Cornar said in a slow deliberate tone. "Bandits are ransacking the market. This path is clear. I just came that way." The young boy looked at him with distrust.

"You've got to save baby Kalder," Cornar said urgently. His tone exuded paternal protection. "You can't let him get hurt. It's your job to protect him now!" The young boy dropped his guard, studying Cornar quizzically.

"He's probably a friend of Father's," the girl said to her brother. "Like the other man."

The other man? Cornar had remembered his sister mentioning another man on this night, all those years ago. But after the initial attack, Cornar had run straight to the cradle where baby Kalder was sleeping. After that, Cornar had heard his father's command for him to run, and so he had, with his sister Galana in tow.

This *was* a frightful night. Why was he dreaming about it?

"If you're lying, I'll hunt you down," the boy threatened.

That sounds like something I'd say at that age, Cornar mused.

"Just go," Cornar said, and then hurried down the street, leaving the younger version of himself.

Cornar knew where he needed to go; the heart of the town. It had been years since he'd been in his hometown of Tergol, but he knew it like the back of his hand. Tergol was about halfway between Tor and Tilim, about a thousand grand phineals from either city. Tergol was north of the river which divided the Western Sovereignty and the Mindolarn Empire. It wouldn't have been an easy target for disgruntled soldiers, but somehow they had found a way to attack.

Soon, Cornar arrived at the heart of Tergol. A manor home sat atop a mound, burning. His family's home. The sounds of battle rang from beyond it. Soldiers—both Sovereign and Mindolarn alike—lay upon the mound, mingled with citizens. Cornar eyed several swords lying about.

"I'm going to need one of these," Cornar said, picking the sword up from near a slain soldier. It was too long to dual-wield comfortably, so he decided to grab only one.

With weapon in hand, Cornar hurried up the mound. He rounded the burning home, passing corpses. Cornar didn't want to look. His mother would be among them, and Cornar couldn't bear to see her like that. He hadn't seen her fall when living this night all those years ago. Cornar only knew of her death because his father told him.

The sounds of battle grew louder. Eruptions of magic resounded in the air.

Magic? But there hadn't been any mages in Tergol when the rogue soldiers attacked. And the enemy consisted of only disgruntled footmen and bandits, right? Cornar rounded the manor home, approaching the southern parts of the village. Nearly a hundred soldiers were clustered around a small group of men. The soldiers weren't trying to push into the city. They were all focused on that group.

As Cornar drew near, he realized the group was actually only two men. Both glowed with brilliant blue light. Was that barsion magic? They moved wildly, slaying the enemy soldiers. One of the men was dual-wielding two short weapons coated in flaming magic. His movements were familiar to Cornar. Was that his father?

The other was mustering magic and moving with acrobatic finesse. He flung a variety of destructive bolts into the enemy ranks, felling them quickly. Cornar hurried down the mound, ready to reinforce them. He hurried beside the mage and clashed with one of the Mindolarn soldiers.

"What are you doing here?" the mage shouted to Cornar. "You need to flee with the rest of the soldiers and citizens! We can hold them back ourselves!"

Cornar ignored the cry, piercing his foe between his armored plates. The soldier groaned and backed away; Cornar hadn't delivered a mortal wound. As his foe retreated, Cornar glanced to the mage beside him.

The mage stood tall, his face hawk-like with piercing sapphire eyes. By Heleron's Trident, he looked like Iltar! The mage even had the same goatee, but his beard and his hair were brown.

"To your right!" the mage shouted to Cornar. Cornar spun, seeing another soldier advancing.

"Melthas!" the mage shouted between spells. "One of your men is being insubordinate!" Melthas? So, the other man *was* his father.

Cornar dueled with the soldier and struck several blows, one to the leg and another to his sword arm.

The battle raged for several minutes. Cornar and the others eventually felled all the soldiers. Not all the Mindolarn soldiers were dead. Some were severely wounded. Cornar, however, hadn't walked away unscathed. His left arm was bleeding. The pain felt real. This dream was *too* lucid.

Cornar carefully hoisted his sword in his belt and put pressure on his bleeding arm. He watched as the mage knelt beside one of the dying soldiers, whispering an incantation. As gray enthralling magic coalesced, the mage removed the soldier's helmet.

"Good sir," Cornar heard his father's familiar voice. Oh, it was good to hear it! "I thank you for your assistance, but it wasn't necessary."

Cornar turned around, seeing his father walking toward him. Cornar wanted to run and embrace him, but doing such things would seem strange. But this was a dream, wasn't it?

Melthas stopped a pace away from Cornar, eyeing his wound. Cornar's father looked unscathed, even though he was wearing only simple clothing. Melthas was, however, glowing with a pale-blue hue. He was encased in barsion magic.

"Let me see the wound," Melthas said, reaching toward Cornar, who nodded.

"It doesn't look too bad," his father said, and then looked to the mage. "Adrin can heal this right up."

Adrin? Cornar's eyes widened. *Iltar's father!*

Faint garbled words reached Cornar's ears, and both he and Melthas looked to the sounds. Adrin had finished his incantation, and the soldier was speaking, "… scout will relay your location. Our master planned this well. You will not survive…" The soldier suddenly fell limp, eyes glazed.

"What else did he say, Adrin?" Melthas asked, his tone stern. Cornar had rarely seen his father that serious. It seemed odd to him.

"The Mindolarnians have a larger force outside the town, cloaked in invisibility," Adrin said. "They knew we'd send the rest of the village away. They're planning to come in full force to kill us."

"I'd better get my armor," Melthas said, and hastily climbed the mound back to the manor home. The blue magic surrounding him vanished.

"You'd better go," Adrin said to Cornar. "We can handle this ourselves."

"Are you sure?" Cornar asked. "A hundred soldiers is one thing, but the two of you against an army? I don't like those odds." Cornar and Iltar had faced those odds before, and though they hadn't fallen, they were not victorious either.

"We'll be fine," Adrin said with a smile. Cornar thought those words cocky, but there was a quiet confidence in Adrin's face as he looked across the ruined town. "We'll take them by surprise." He paused, then noticed Cornar's wound. "Here, let me heal that." Adrin cast his spell, and green arpran magic wisped into Cornar's arm. The healing magic stopped the bleeding and vanquished the pain. Within seconds, Cornar felt whole.

A moment later, Melthas hurried down the mound toward them. Cornar could see his father's grim expression through his helmet. "Elana didn't make it out," Melthas said.

"I'm sorry," Adrin rested a hand on Melthas's armored shoulder.

"We're going to make those bastards pay, Adrin!" Melthas growled.

Adrin nodded, looking solemn. "Your wife will be avenged, my old friend."

My old friend? Cornar wondered. Were his and Iltar's fathers friends? Cornar never remembered hearing his father talk about a mage he was friends with. Perhaps they fought alongside each other when his father helped liberate Tor. Surely, Kandish would have made mention of the friendship. How ironic that their sons would become like brothers.

"I think your insubordinate soldier is determined to stay and fight," Adrin said, gesturing to Cornar.

"He's not one of mine," Melthas said. "But I welcome the help."

Adrin grunted, raising an eyebrow at Cornar. "Well, let's get invisible and head out there. That scout should be there any moment." As Adrin cast enhancing magic upon the three of them, a familiar quickening surged through Cornar. He often commanded the mages of his band to enhance him and his warriors in such a manner.

Adrin cast a few more spells on both Cornar's and his father's weapons. Lightning, fire, and disintegrating energies surged along the weapons. Melthas's weapons, a serrated dagger and a short-sword—the same weapons Cornar favored—absorbed the magic. The blades exuded those magical properties. Imbuing magic would float around normal weapons, but the serrated dagger and the short-sword *held* the magic. The blades could maintain a spell where a normal weapon could have its enhancements dispelled.

Adrin cast barsion magic on all three of them and then concealed them.

"They're on the south, by the entrance near Dalgiri's Tavern," Adrin said, his voice trailing. He was obviously running.

"Try not to get yourself killed," Melthas said to Cornar.

Cornar hurried after them as they ran through the ruined town. The fires were dying, but smoke still filled the air. It should have been hard to breathe, but the barsion magic seemed to filter the smoke. That was something Cornar had never experienced. Odd to have new experiences in a dream...

Soon they reached the edge of the city. The field beyond the burning walls was empty.

"I'll cast a mass-dispel," Adrin whispered. "I'll run up the middle, you two should flank the other side."

"I'm good with that," Melthas whispered back.

"As am I," Cornar replied. There was something invigorating about fighting alongside his father. At first this dream was frightening, but now it was thrilling.

Adrin's light footfalls hurried away. An off-white light gathered quickly, moving away from the town, and then a massive wave of dispelling magic washed across the field. Hundreds of soldiers clad in silver armor appeared from out of nowhere. They wielded fanisars, swords with shields, hammers, maces, and other deadly weapons. Mages dressed in crimson robes stood amid their ranks. Horsemen wore blood-red armor, wielding glowing shields and black swords—swords that looked as if they were composed of magic.

"By Heleron's Scales!" Cornar swore with a gasp. He wasn't astounded by the size of the army, but rather the odds it represented for him, his father, and Adrin.

"This is no time to be cursing the names of false gods," Melthas said. "I'm going right. You take the left flank." Cornar heard his father hurrying away. It was time for him to move too.

He, Adrin, and Melthas were still invisible. Commands resounded from the enemy ranks and the mages amid the army began casting their own dispels.

Must advance, Cornar thought, darting from the ruined town. He bounded across the field, moving faster than normal. Cornar needed to get to the soldiers before the mages finished casting their dispels. He came within a dash of the enemy line as a wave of white magic washed past him. The dispel tore apart the invisibility particles but not the barsion shielding him.

The soldiers lunged toward Cornar, weapons flailing. Amid their advance, they and the rest of the army shouted in unison, "May the Crimson Eye remain hidden for all time!" It was like a battle cry. The soldiers shouted another phrase, but Cornar ignored it. He had more important things to focus on.

Cornar dodged a blow from a fanisar, tumbling sideways. He sprang up, striking the fanisar's shaft, his blow cleaving the weapon in half; Adrin's imbuing magic was devastating. Cornar swept his sword, piercing the soldier in the gut. His enhanced blade tore through the plate like wet parchment.

The thrill of battle surged through him. Oh, it was invigorating! Cornar moved swiftly, felling another foe. Another fell, and another. Out of the corner of his eye, Cornar saw Adrin and Melthas pushing through the enemy ranks. They were killing faster than he was! They really could hold back this entire army by themselves…

One of the crimson-armored horsemen dismounted, pushing his way through the crowd of soldiers. The other soldiers shied away from him, careful not to touch his weapon. Those fighting Cornar backed away, clearing a spot for the dismounted horsemen. Was he some kind of commander? The soldiers seemed to regard him as such.

"Foolish man," the commander said, his tone mocking. "You cannot stand against the might of Mindolarn!" Cornar lunged forward, sweeping his sword toward his foe's legs. The commander blocked the blow with his sword. Both weapons clashed, and the commander's magically composed sword ripped through Cornar's blade, severing it.

Surprised, Cornar darted sideways, avoiding a swing from the commander. The weapon moved just beyond his face, trailing a black mist. *It does look like Iltar's magic,* he thought. Cornar continued evading and tumbled backward, putting distance between him and the commander. How was he going to defeat this—

A sharp whistling noise whizzed past Cornar—like an arrow cutting through the air. He felt something pass by, and then a flash of black and white struck the ground. Cornar had expected to see an arrow, but it was a curved sword in a charcoal scabbard with a white hilt.

The commander stared at the weapon, muttering something strange. The words weren't Common. In fact, they sounded like gibberish. Seizing the opportunity, Cornar dropped his broken weapon and grabbed this new sword. It had a strange oblong guard, which looked like scaled wings. The guard curved downward, providing some protection. Scaled patterns adorned the handle.

Cornar drew the sword. Its curved blade had only one sharp edge. The blade had a remarkable reflection, like a mirror. Cornar had never seen such craftsmanship. He quickly pulled the scabbard from the ground, wielding it with his other hand.

Cornar squared off with the commander, but the commander backed away, looking to the skies. *Why was—*A brilliant flash of light erupted behind Cornar, near the town. He didn't turn. He didn't dare, not with that deadly weapon a mere leap away. A thunderous crash resounded behind him, accompanied by tremors shaking the ground.

The enemy ranks in front of Cornar backed away, completely ignoring him. Some of the soldiers looked frightened. Perhaps he should look. So he did.

A masculine figure stood within a ball of light upon a small crater in the field. The light soon faded, revealing an armor-clad figure in white formfitting armor. The armor looked melded to the man, without seams or joints. Cornar heard shouting from the enemy ranks in that same gibberish. Although he couldn't understand the words, he heard one repeated several times, "Ulk'sha." The soldiers spoke that word with tones of fear and anger.

The man in white armor bolted forward, moving faster than even a man enhanced with magic. He drew a sword from the sheath upon his back; it looked like the one Cornar was holding. Once near, the man leapt into the air, soaring above Cornar and crashing into the enemy ranks, weapon swinging with beautiful finesse.

The commander turned away from Cornar completely, focusing on the man relentlessly slaying the soldiers. Cornar could see the detail in the newcomer's armor. It was scaled and seamless. The armor flexed with the man's muscles as he moved, like skin.

Soon, the commander and the newcomer clashed. The commander's black sword struck the newcomer's blade, but it didn't have the same effect as with Cornar's first sword. How was that possible? That black magic should have ripped through that sword… They dueled fiercely, but the commander fell to the man in white armor.

The soldiers around Cornar fled. The man in white armor steadied himself, sword gripped with both hands. He glanced toward Adrin and Melthas, now deep within the heart of the army. But before moving, the man turned to Cornar.

"Do you know how to use that thing?" he asked, voice muffled beneath his armor. His voice sounded familiar.

"Yeah," Cornar said, nodding.

"Good," the man said, "follow my lead." The man in white armor darted toward the soldiers fighting Adrin. Cornar followed, struggling to keep up. How was the white-armored figure moving so fast? Cornar had been enhanced by Adrin's magic. But enhancing magic could only bolster one's abilities so far. A slow runner would still be slower than an athletic sprinter if both were enhanced by the same spell.

The enemy soldiers fell swiftly to the man in white armor. His blade cut through the Mindolarnians as if they weren't wearing armor at all. Cornar followed along the edge of the man's wake of devastation. He struck soldiers as he passed, and they fell easily. Cornar couldn't even feel the resistance in the blade as it struck his foes. How was that possible?

The man in white armor neared Adrin, fighting side by side with him.

"Zatryn!" Cornar heard Adrin exclaim. Was that the man's name?

Cornar joined them, and the three cut through the enemy ranks. They had felled hundreds. How many were in this army? It had to be thousands.

A horn resounded amid the ranks of the army, calling for a retreat.

Cornar kept killing the soldiers as they fled, but Adrin and the man in white armor stopped. Cornar noticed Melthas out of the corner of his eye, also standing still. His weapons were lowered.

Extracting his blade from his foe, Cornar turned around. The last stragglers fled past him. He ignored them and surveyed the field. It was littered with fallen soldiers. What a massacre! The four of them had done this?

Melthas picked his way through the corpse-filled field and joined Adrin and the other man. "I thought you were investigating that lead in Marden," Melthas said, looking at the man in white.

"I was. That's where I learned of this attempt on your life."

"Then you know who's behind this?" Melthas asked with fury. Cornar had rarely seen his father angry, and definitely not like this.

The man in white nodded. "An aspiring prince. One of Mindolarn's sons. He wishes to prove himself to the new emperor."

"We should get back to the town," Adrin suggested. "And find your children." Melthas grunted and nodded.

"I'll track the Mindolarnians," the man in white said.

"Keep us informed," Melthas said. "But don't kill any of them. I want to exact vengeance myself."

"Be careful, Melthas," the man in white warned. "Seeking vengeance is not always the right answer." He then walked toward Cornar. "My blade," he said, extending his gauntleted hand. Cornar nodded, sheathing the weapon. He handed it to the man in white, who then hoisted it over his left hip.

"Cor." A voice echoed across the horizon. Cornar spun, searching for the source of the sound, but didn't see anything.

"Cor! He glanced at the others, who didn't seem to hear the voice. They continued discussing their next course of action.

"Cor!" Cornar felt a kick against his boot, but looking down saw nothing.

Then everything changed.

A sea breeze brushed across Cornar's face. The sky was blue, not smoky. He felt a sack of grain beneath his head, a makeshift pillow. Was he lying on his back? *A dream*, he realized.

"Are you all right, Cor?" Nordal asked. He stood a pace away from Cornar. "There's blood on your arm."

Confused, Cornar glanced down to his arm; his sleeve was covered in blood, and still damp. There were no tears in the sleeve. Cornar felt at his arm, but there wasn't a wound.

"How'd that happen?" Nordal asked, kneeling down and examining the area where Cornar had slept.

"I don't know," Cornar said, propping himself up.

"Krindal wants to meet with you and Captain Salisar," Nordal said, standing. "The *Executor's Breath* is veering off."

"All right," Cornar said and rose to his feet with a grunt. He looked over the rail to the large Mindolarn vessel. The *Executor's Breath* was heading north.

What a strange dream, he thought, watching the ship move away. The man in white had said the attack was an attempt on Melthas's life. That's not what his father had told him about that night. The men who attacked Tergol were supposed to have been disgruntled footmen who had lived in that area before the Western Sovereignty won their independence from the Mindolarn Empire. They were attacking out of spite.

"Are you okay, Uncle?" Ordreth asked.

Cornar turned, seeing his nephew behind Nordal.

"I'm fine."

"And the blood?" Ordreth asked, sounding worried.

"It's nothing. Probably nicked my arm sleeping." Cornar shrugged. "I was having a vivid dream about my past. Fighting Mindolarnians alongside my father."

Nordal cocked his head and grunted. "When did that happen?"

Cornar grinned. "It didn't. I was reliving the night of my mother's death, but I was like another participant. So I saw my younger self, interacted with him, and then found my father. I helped him fend off the soldiers. Those Mindolarnians were quite cunning…" He couldn't help but think of the plot the man in white had mentioned.

"Do you not trust them, Uncle?" Ordreth asked.

"Well, they seem trustworthy," Cornar said, shaking the thoughts aside. "Kaescis doesn't act like typical Mindolarn Royalty. Nothing seems amiss."

Cornar walked across the main deck of the *Promised Maiden*. He found Krindal and Captain Salisar on the open-air bridge, talking beside a table which held a logbook and various maps of Kalda.

"Good morning!" Krindal called. "I hope we haven't wakened you too early? Lying on that sack of grain couldn't have been comfortable…" He trailed off, looking at the blood on Cornar's sleeve.

"Just nicked myself," Cornar replied with a smile, "and I slept just fine." He actually preferred sleeping out in the open when on a ship. Being cramped in a small cabin was actually more uncomfortable than using provisions as bedding. Krindal shrugged and uneasily eyed the stain.

"What did you want to talk about?" Cornar asked, stepping up to the table.

"We'll be traveling on our own until we reach Klindala," Krindal said. "I wanted to discuss the particulars with you and the good captain here. Prince Kaescis is mooring in Keliur's naval yards to resupply. He's bringing two more vessels with him, with five hundred soldiers."

Five hundred soldiers? Why would they need more men? Kaescis hadn't mentioned recruiting more help. "Why so many?" Cornar asked. Krindal shrank at the question. He was hiding something.

"I'd like to know that answer as well," Salisar said. "I thought this was a simple expedition of discovery."

"Well, in case the Wildmen refuse to barter with us," Krindal replied, sounding nervous. "There are thousands of those tribesmen. And we wouldn't want to risk our lives."

"I thought the Mindolarnians were certain the Wildmen would accept." Cornar asked.

"Well, they are," Krindal said. "This is just a precautionary measure."

Cornar folded his arms. He didn't like last-minute surprises.

"I didn't want to tell the Order," Krindal continued. "I thought if I came to them saying that the Mindolarnians were helping me and that we'd have a sizeable force, they wouldn't lend any aid."

That seemed sound, but Cornar felt there was more to Krindal's reasoning than he claimed. What was he trying to hide?

"We're going on ahead to make preparations," Krindal said. "We'll wait in Kretin for Prince Kaescis and his fleet. The trip to the ruins will take nearly twelve days." The old scholar looked to the captain. "I'm planning on being ashore for a month and a half. Would you and your crew care to join us on the trek?"

"I will think about it," Salisar said. "It would be a grand discovery, but I need to ensure that nothing happens to the *Promised Maiden*."

"I understand," Krindal nodded.

"I assume you want me and my men to help with gathering the provisions?" Cornar asked.

"Yes," Krindal said. "We will need enough food to feed six hundred and a means to transport those provisions across the island." This was going to be a big expedition; probably the largest in which Cornar had ever participated.

Krindal and Salisar continued talking. The *Promised Maiden* would continue traveling along the Coastal Current, through the Kalishir Ocean. They would pass between the Isle of Merdan and the Dragon's Maw, the large peninsula of the Mainland which consisted of the nation of Holorum. Depending on the weather, it would take them roughly thirty more days to reach Klindala.

15

ORDER OF HISTORIES

"Elynia was giddy at the idea. She had explored for years, but only out of her own curiosity. Now, she would pursue the secrets of the world for a purpose greater than her own self-indulgence. In a way, I consider her the first of the Keepers of Truth and Might, although we didn't organize that Order until several hundred years later."

- From *Origins and Oaths of the Keepers*, preface

Nearly a week and a half had passed since Iltar began training the acolytes at Pagus's home. The training had been grueling for them. Only Pagus, Agen, and Bilda were prepared for Iltar's all-day exercises. Most of the boys were average in their skill, and Iltar felt he needed to improve their forms and techniques rather than teach new spells.

In that time, Iltar had studied the entire *Codices of Soron Thahan*. It was as intriguing as it was cryptic. Soron Thahan claimed predictions of the future, having seen visions manifested by the so-called Messenger of the Promise. Iltar deduced that he and Soron were probably experiencing something similar.

That bothered him.

Iltar could easily dismiss the dreams as the result of an overactive imagination. At first he had. But now there was written evidence that his dreams were more than what they seemed. Iltar didn't want to believe it.

Soron spoke often of the person called the Unspoken One. *The Harbinger.* This prophesied person was also the one to usher in the return of a god. Reflection had called Iltar that in the last dream. Iltar wondered if it was a by-product of his mind processing what he had read. But then he came across that passage Reflection had quoted.

"The Harbinger will betray his master, slaying him in his very home. The master's passing will go unnoticed. His death will be dismissed without consequence."

Rovin's death *did* go unnoticed. No one ever suspected that he had been killed, at least not right away. Theories floated around the Necrotic Order, especially when other masters had disappeared several months later. But no one ever questioned Iltar's involvement, not even the City Watch. Iltar had thought himself lucky. Soron Thahan, however, claimed otherwise.

Supposedly, the Harbinger had divine protection. This was manifest in later writings about the prophesied hero. One such passage claimed he would stand alone against the *Beast*, defeating the monster single-handedly. Soron didn't explain who or what the *Beast* was, but he did reference him several other times. The Harbinger would also stand alone against an army and survive.

Soron's predictions, however, weren't only about the Unspoken One. He wrote cryptic foretelling about certain nations. He claimed Kildath, one of the greatest powers on Kalda, would fall. Soron had, however, accurately predicted a civil war in the Kingdom of Los. Though that prediction was accurate, Soron claimed the war was incited by a great evil, an evil the Unspoken One would face. That seemed improbable to Iltar since Los's civil war had happened over three hundred and fifty years ago.

All in all, the book felt a little too religious for Iltar. He didn't subscribe to any of the religions of Kalda. They all seemed a farce. The fact that Soron Thahan was religious surprised Iltar. Most Sorothians didn't follow any religion. The most common patronage was among sailors, but that was more of a reverence than anything else. They revered the pagan god of the ocean, Heleron, often praying to him before a voyage or pleading his aid during a storm. The latter never seemed to help.

After finishing the *Codices*, Iltar was both frightened and intrigued. He had many questions. Soron Thahan wrote with such fervor that he almost persuaded Iltar that this foretold world *would* occur. But didn't men forge their own destinies?

Yes. They did. Iltar *had* forged his own destiny. He was not the puppet that Rovin and Cordis had tried to mold.

⊷•⊶

There were still three days left before classes resumed at the Necrotic Order. Iltar's questions couldn't wait till then. So, he decided to leave for the Order of Histories. Perchance, their tomes might be able to clarify references in *The Codices of Soron Thahan*.

Before departing, Iltar gave the acolytes, except for Pagus, a list of exercises to perform. He didn't trust Pagus enough to leave him alone, so Iltar took him with him. To his surprise, Pagus didn't even complain. Compliance wasn't a trait Pagus possessed. What was that boy up to?

Near midmorning, both master and apprentice neared the center of the city. They rode their horses through the crowded Sorothian streets toward the bastion of scholarship.

The Order of Histories was a large building, rising four stories. It covered an entire city block, with several wings branching off from a central structure. Twisting columns lined much of the exterior walls, with rows of windows between them.

Iltar and Pagus struggled to find a place to leave their horses. The Order of Histories was a popular place today.

Pagus groaned. "We should have just walked."

"We'll find a spot," Iltar reassured him. He searched the streets for empty posts where they could tie their reins, but all the places were occupied.

"Let's try the next street over," Iltar suggested, guiding his horse across the way. Pagus followed silently.

Soon they found several empty posts. They dismounted, tied their reins, and paid a nearby post-keeper the fee to watch their horses. Post-keepers were typically local residents—young boys or girls—who would watch a person's carriage or horse on busy streets. Thievery was common in the denser parts of Soroth.

Within minutes, Iltar and Pagus returned to the Order of Histories. They entered one of the side doors and made their way to the heart of the building, toward the lobby. It made sense to have the lobby at the center.

"Whoa…" Pagus gasped from behind Iltar.

"You've never been here?" he asked the youth.

"No."

Iltar smiled. The lobby was quite grand—a giant rotunda, four stories high, with a dome for its ceiling. Curved stairwells lined the walls, leading to various floors. Each of the floors had hallways leading to the separate wings. Each wing except one was devoted to a different aspect of history. The remaining wing was an enormous library. The lobby was an impressive sight, especially the murals on the rotunda. There were four of them, each between coffered ornamentation. Much of the room was covered by elaborately crafted stonework.

While Pagus admired the lobby's architecture, Iltar headed to the reception area at its heart. Nearly twenty receptionists were gathered behind a circular area large enough that each could have their own desk.

One of them—an older man with white hair—noticed Iltar's approach and stood. He bowed his head in a gesture of greeting. "What may I help you with?"

"I need to speak with some associates of mine," Iltar said. "Kilan and Midal. Are they here?"

The old receptionist hummed. He raised a finger for Iltar to wait and then moved to the center of the reception area, toward a chest-high cabinet. The receptionist shuffled meticulously through the drawers. Scholars at the Order of Histories would leave notes here for anyone who was calling on them. The notes would also include their availability if anyone were looking to hire them.

After a moment, the old receptionist returned. "It looks like Kilan is in, though he has unavailability starting tomorrow for several months. Midal is currently out."

Iltar sighed. *Well, at least one of them is here.* "Thank you," he said, nodded to the receptionist, and walked away.

"Do you need directions?" the receptionist asked.

"No," Iltar said without turning back. "I know their office."

Iltar and Pagus made their way to the Historical Sociology Wing of the Order of Histories, where Kilan and Midal shared an office on the third floor.

Iltar had known Kilan and Midal for a long time. He trusted them almost as much as he trusted the men of his adventuring band. Iltar had known the two scholars since his youth. In fact, they had studied at the Sorothian Magical Order with him, before its change. Kilan was studying to be an illusionist and Midal an arpranist. They, however, didn't graduate. Both of them dropped out of the Order when Rovin and Cordis took over.

Iltar wound his way through several corridors and then stopped at one of the many doors in the hallway. He knocked once, then opened the door.

To his surprise, *both* Kilan and Midal were inside. Why was Midal here? Both scholars loomed over a table piled with opened tomes and neat piles of scroll cases.

"Iltar!" Kilan smiled and hurried across the room. Four years Iltar's senior, he was shorter than Iltar—only average height—with graying black hair and olive skin a bit darker than most Sorothians. His wrinkled face was clean-shaven. His dull blue eyes studied Iltar for a moment and then glanced to Pagus. "What are you doing here, my friend?"

"Conducting some research." Iltar patted his pack. "May we come in?"

"Yes, yes," Kilan said, nodding. "Come in."

Iltar stepped inside. "Good day, Midal."

Midal simply nodded. He was a quiet man who spent much of his time contemplating, but when he spoke, one knew to listen. Not only was Midal distinguished by his quiet demeanor, but by his unique mustache. It was long, curving below his chin. Both ends were bound together by a leather clasp. It was an odd look. Most men would have kept their mustaches free.

"That's a weird mustache," Pagus said.

Midal raised an eyebrow, studying Pagus with his green eyes.

"Try to be respectful, Pagus," Iltar said, then set his pack on the table.

"Is he an apprentice of yours?" Kilan asked.

"I am," Pagus answered.

Kilan chuckled. "I didn't think you'd take on another after Balden."

Midal narrowed his eyes at Kilan and then glanced to Iltar. He knew Iltar was sensitive about hearing that name.

Iltar sighed and reached into his pack, removing *The Codices of Soron Thahan*. "Do you have time for some questions?" he asked.

"I always have time for questions," Kilan said, smiling. "The correct question would have been, 'Do I have time for answers?'"

Iltar rolled his eyes and set the tome on the table.

Midal's eyes widened. He leaned over the table, intently studying the volume.

"What is that?" Kilan asked.

"Something my apprentice found in the basement of the Order's Record Hall."

"Huh?" Kilan cocked his head. "But that's forbidden to anyone but the council, isn't it?" The scholar looked to Pagus with amazement.

"*Codices of Soron Thahan?*" Midal asked. "Is this genuine?"

"I would assume so," Iltar said.

"But it looks so pristine," Midal observed. "May I?" He gestured to the tome. Iltar nodded.

"Hmm. Soron Thahan, you say?" Kilan said. "But I don't recognize it. We have all of his writings here in the library. I have never seen anything like *that*. Are you sure it's not a fake?"

"Why would we keep a fraudulent tome at the Necrotic Order?"

"Because it's the Necrotic Order?" Kilan said with a chuckle. "Because that's something Cordis and Rovin would have done to deceive those who would come after them." The Necrotic Order seemed to be a sore spot for Kilan. Did he still resent the Order's change?

"I didn't come here to debate its authenticity," Iltar said. "I have some questions about things that it references."

"So you believe, without any corroborating evidence, that this tome is authentic?" Kilan asked skeptically. "What happened to your sense of scholarship, Iltar?"

He *did* have corroborating evidence: the dreams, Reflection. But Iltar couldn't share that with these men. They were even more atheistic than he was. Kilan would laugh him to scorn, and Midal would frown disapprovingly.

"The verbiage is consistent," Midal said.

"What?" Kilan darted a glance to his scholarly associate.

"It sounds like Soron," Midal explained. "But what is this date? It's implies a calendar starting over eight thousand years ago."

"That's impossible!" Kilan blurted, almost shouting. The man could be quite excitable when it came to scholarship.

"Soron claims the year seven thousand three hundred and thirty-three," Midal said calmly. "And he would have written it over nine hundred years ago."

Kilan sucked in a breath, eyeing Iltar. "You look confident, Iltar," he said warily.

"I told you I'm not here to discuss authenticity," Iltar retorted. He reached into his pack and removed several pieces of parchment; the drawings he had penned after the dream where he studied Reflection's robe. "I also want to know if either of you have seen these elsewhere in the world."

Kilan took the sheets, carefully examining them.

Midal, however, looked up from the tome. "What questions did you have, Iltar?"

"Well, have you heard of a title called 'the Unspoken One' or 'the Harbinger' in any religious contexts?"

"We're not theologians, Iltar," Kilan quipped. Iltar raised his brow at Kilan, but the man was studying the drawings.

"No," Midal answered. "But if this is related to Thahan, you'd best research his religious background. Hmm." He thought for a moment. "I believe Soron was born during the reign of the Karthar Empire. There was a unified religion during that time, called Cherisium. A lot of religions have splintered from it since then. Cherisium's influences have been prevalent in most of the societies that developed over the last thousand years. The most—"

"I know this symbol," Kilan interrupted, pointing to the sheet he held. "A triangle with a wide base, seven dots on the inside, and three lines beneath. I saw it at the Hilinard in Mindolarn—the capital, I mean, not the nation."

The Hilinard? Iltar mused. That was thrice he'd heard the name. *Mindolarn, huh? Perhaps this is tied to Krindal's quest. Symbols from Mindolarn, and a Mindolarn prince. Interesting…*

"Are those symbols from the book?" Midal asked.

Iltar shook his head. "I transcribed them from elsewhere."

"Well," Kilan said, and sighed. "It looks much like the symbol. There are some minor differences." He cocked his head at Iltar. "It's a little sloppy. If I could see the source, I could say for sure."

Well, sure, Kilan, let me invite you into my dream realm to study the robe of the person who looks exactly like me. Oh, and don't mind the yellow sky. Damnation!

"May I see those?" Midal asked. Kilan handed them over, but took the tome.

Seeing the scholars engrossed, Iltar waited to ask his next question. He glanced to Pagus, who patiently waited, leaning against the doorframe with his arms folded. The boy looked amused by the exchange between his master and the scholars.

"I agree with Kilan," Midal said. "It looks like one of the glyphs etched into the floor of the Hilinard."

"These others I don't recognize, but we have a colleague who specializes in symbols of ancient cultures. I can show them to her if you'd like." Iltar shook his head. He didn't trust anyone besides his friends with such information. Someone else would ask too many questions, pry into his motives. These men wouldn't.

"I also wanted to know if you've heard of something called 'the Crimson Eye' or a group called 'the Chosen,'" Iltar said.

"Like what was referenced in the preface?" Midal gestured to the tome in Kilan's hands.

"Yes," Iltar said. "This Crimson Eye must be an object—maybe even a tevisral. And a powerful one at that, from what I could discern. Although, it could be some kind of force."

"Hmm," Kilan said, flipping through the pages.

Midal frowned. "I've not heard of either of those."

"I have other questions," Iltar said. "I know Kilan's marked as unavailable starting tomorrow, but are you available, Midal?"

"Unfortunately, I am not." The scholar sighed. "I'm here only because I needed to find some reference material. I've been working for the Duke of Seriel the last few months. The research is… *ongoing,*" he said in a perturbed tone. Since Midal wasn't one to become annoyed by research, his tasks under the duke must be absurd.

"Do you know when you'll be finished?" Iltar asked. Midal simply shrugged.

"Well, that was interesting," Kilan chimed in, closing the tome. "Too bad I'm busy; otherwise I'd be more than willing to help. The book itself is intriguing enough, and I'm not talking about the contents. Its craftsmanship is… unusual, to say the least."

"How long are you going to be gone?" Iltar asked.

"Six months. The Order of Histories would like to verify some records in Kildath, and I've been assigned to return with copies." Kilan didn't sound excited.

Midal's tasks could take who knew how long, so Iltar would need to wait six months for Kilan. Six months wouldn't be too bad. Unless Reflection plagued his mind at night, urging him to fulfill his destiny. Iltar hadn't had any more dreams since that first night at Pagus's home, but he knew they'd come.

"YOU CANNOT WAIT," a voice echoed faintly, but none of the others seemed to hear it.

Iltar raised an eyebrow, looking toward the ceiling. What was he supposed to do? He wasn't going to trust his questions to anyone else here at the Order of Histories. Was he to drop everything and go seek the answers himself? Iltar couldn't do that, not with Pagus's behavior. Then there was the council. How would he explain his absence to them? They'd surely question his motives. He could attempt to do research here at the Order of Histories, but that would require him staying in the city. Perhaps he could rent a place temporarily…

"YOU MUST FULFILL YOUR DESTINY, UNSPOKEN ONE," the voice said, this time fainter than the first. "SEEK MY FAITHFUL. THEY WILL ENLIGHTEN YOU."

You ask the impossible, Iltar groaned inwardly.

"Is everything all right, Iltar?" Midal asked. The question shook Iltar from the unnatural communion with that unknown being.

"Yes," Iltar said, nodding. "I'll take my leave of you." He gathered up his things and headed for the door.

"Shall we resume this in six months?" Kilan asked.

Iltar stopped at the door, reaching for the handle. He glanced back to Kilan. "Hopefully by then I'll have this entire thing figured out."

As he and Pagus wound their way toward the center of the enormous building, Iltar thought over his dilemma.

They were near the junction to the central lobby when Pagus grabbed Iltar's arm, urging him to stop. "Master Iltar, I have an idea."

"About?" Iltar asked, not amused. His dilemma irked him.

"Finding the answers to your questions," Pagus said. "I can tell you're impatient to discover the truth." Impatience was the wrong word. Iltar could be patient. He had been. Plotting Rovin's death took patience. No, this was something else. It was frustration, a frustration that burned his very soul.

"We can go ourselves to Mindolarn. That's where you'd want to go, right?"

Go to Mindolarn? Iltar hadn't jumped to that conclusion. He'd need to conduct research, but that could be done here, until he exhausted the tomes.

"I'm sure they'd have bigger libraries, more texts," Pagus added. "And maybe those other symbols will be there too."

"We can't go to Mindolarn." Iltar sighed. "And I don't want—"

Footsteps echoed into the corridor from the central lobby. Iltar paused, watching two scholars approach, engrossed in conversation with each other. They paid little attention to Iltar and Pagus, passing them and disappearing down an adjoining hall.

"I don't want the council to find out what I'm doing."

"Trying to protect us?" Pagus asked with a smile.

It was not just that. Iltar didn't know how Alacor and the others would react to his visions. Damnation, *he* didn't know how to react to the blasted things.

"Well, that's okay, because I have a plan," Pagus said cheerily. "My father owns a ship, and we can take it. It won't be on any charter. Your name won't be tied to it in the slightest. Alacor won't even know you're gone."

Iltar raised his brow, confused but intrigued. "Are you planning to impersonate me?"

Pagus laughed. "No! I'm going with you. You're going to teach me some new spells in exchange for my services."

Well, there it was… Pagus was being his same old self. The offer was tempting, but Iltar could get a ship, no problem. Money wasn't an issue. And he could do it discreetly. He just didn't have a good enough reason to slip away.

"Come here," Pagus said, gesturing to a nearby door. He opened it, stepped inside, then poked his head back out. "It's empty."

Iltar reluctantly followed his apprentice and closed the door. The room was a small study available to the public. If one were studying or conducting research here at the Order of Histories, one could simply occupy one of these rooms.

"You need an excuse to get out of Soroth," Pagus said. "I can be that excuse."

"How?" Iltar asked flatly.

"Well, you see, while I was home during the sabbatical, there was a distressing incident at my family's home. I *had* to stay, but I couldn't drop my training as a necromancer. So, I'm going to request that my teacher be sent to Sarn for private study."

Iltar raised his brow thoughtfully. That was a cunning ploy. But it would be verified by the Order. Could it work?

"It'd be several months before I could return to Soroth. Enough time for us to sail to Mindolarn, find what we need, and return to Soroth."

A tempting offer, but Iltar couldn't abandon the other acolytes.

"What about my other students?" Iltar asked. "Is the council supposed to divide them up among themselves to teach?"

"Nah," Pagus waved his hand. "They'll come too. My family can supply rooms for them. Well, you know what I mean. You could probably use them to help with the research. That's a lot of little footmen to run errands for you."

"That sounds too complicated, Pagus."

"It's not like they're going back and forth to their homes between lessons," Pagus said. "Most of them live at the Necrotic Order. And their parents have resigned them to the Order's care."

"Except for Bilda and Agen," Iltar said. "They live at home." Pagus shrugged. Iltar continued, "If their parents decided to make a trip to Sarn to visit them, we'd be found out. Or if their parents wanted them to come home."

"I find that unlikely," Pagus folded his arms. "Trust me, this is going to work."

"I don't know…" Iltar sighed.

"Look," Pagus said sternly, "you failed to 'properly' discipline us not once, but twice. If the council found that out, then you'd have some problems. Big problems." He grunted. "I bet Alacor would turn on you so fast!"

"So you have a knife to your throat *and* mine?" Iltar asked, shaking his head. "What kind of blackmail is that?"

Pagus grinned. "The best kind. Shows that I'm as invested as you in not getting caught." That was strange teenage logic.

"Or we could just go about our lives," Iltar said. *But then there was that behest…*

"Iltar," Pagus said frankly, "I know you don't want to wait."

Did the boy just call me by my first name? Iltar blinked. What audacity!

"Just trust me," Pagus insisted.

Iltar narrowed his eyes at the youth. Pagus was determined to follow this through. But Pagus *had* concealed his activities from Alacor and the others. Perhaps this could work. And if the boys were with him, Iltar could protect them.

Silence passed between them for several minutes, as Iltar mulled Pagus's proposal. The more he thought about it the more he warmed to the idea.

"Well?" Pagus broke the silence.

"Let's do it," Iltar agreed reluctantly.

"Yes!" Pagus cheered, triumphantly punching his hand skyward. "I'll sneak off to Sarn at once. Be ready for my letter. Well, my father's letter."

16

AUDIENCE

*"After a decade, the Keepers had spread across the world. They were my
eyes and my ears. We vowed to protect the inhabitants of Kalda. Each
Keeper was stalwart in their charge."*

- From *Origins and Oaths of the Keepers*, preface

The *Executor's Breath* neared the naval yards of Keliur, nearly a week and
a half after parting ways with the *Promised Maiden*. Kaescis Midivar had
grown uneasy during that time. He stood in the observation room
atop the highest deck, hands clasped behind his back. The top buttons of his
uniform were undone.

What am I to do? Kaescis thought, staring at the port across the horizon.
Laeyit thought they should kill Cornar Dol'shir before it was too late. But was
that the answer? He had sought the *Will*, but hadn't received an answer.

That bothered him. Had he done something to provoke the displeasure of
Cheserith?

Kaescis remembered the stories of the ancients claiming their God had forsaken them, abandoning them in times of need. They had sought the *Will*, but
received no answer. Kaescis feared the same was happening to him.

"What have I done, Lord Cheserith?" Kaescis whispered in despair. "What
must I do to regain your favor?"

A faint breeze rustled past him. But he was indoors! How was that—

"KAESCIS, YOU ARE NOT FORSAKEN," a voice whispered along the breeze.
Kaescis started at the words, looking about frantically. He heard *words!* But
only the Chosen and the Grand Oracle were said to be able to hear the Voice
of God. Kaescis had only experienced flashes of visions and distinct impres-
sions, but never words.

"FEAR NOT THE MAN," the voice whispered again. "HE DOES NOT KNOW
YOU."

"Aunok'sha!" Kaescis implored, using the ancient word for Divine Father.
"What must I do?"

There was no answer. All was silent.

Kaescis relaxed, taking in a deep breath. He wasn't forsaken after all. Perhaps he was not ready for the answer. That thought gave him courage. Kaescis buttoned up his uniform and resumed watching the *Executor's Breath* near the Keliur naval yards.

After a quarter of an hour they moored at the edge of a large pier not far from the construction yards. Several ships were under repair. Others were under construction, looking like the ribcages of enormous beasts.

"Your Imperial Highness," Practil said behind him. "A messenger at the docks delivered this for you." Kaescis turned. Practil held out a scroll with a wax seal bearing the emblem of the empire, a seven-headed hydra.

"The messenger didn't say any more," Practil continued, "even though I probed."

Kaescis took the scroll, carefully broke the seal, and cocked his head as he unfurled the scroll. It was a summons to the command fortress at the heart of the naval yards. He was to report to the admiral in charge of Keliur.

"What is it, Your Imperial Highness?" Practil asked.

"A summons," Kaescis said flatly, rerolling the scroll. He handed it back to Practil, gazing once more out the windows of the observation room. The crewmen were busily securing the vessel. Kaescis looked past them to the island, staring at a structure that rose into the sky.

"Is it about your requisition?"

"That I don't know," Kaescis said. Before reaching Soroth, Kaescis had sent the request for additional forces by a unique tevisral created by his cousin, Raedina. She had given it to him not long after the Feast of Sorrows, knowing that he might need to stay in contact. The tevisral, however, was damaged and had stopped working the day before mooring in Soroth.

"Come with me, Practil," Kaescis said. Practil straightened, and they strode together from the observation room.

⤙⬦⤚

Kaescis and Practil soon arrived at the command fortress of Keliur, accompanied by Admiral Kaetet, who was interested in knowing why Kaescis had been summoned.

The command fortress was an elevated castle with towers reaching what seemed unfathomable heights—at least for the average man of Kalda. This type of construction was not foreign to those of the Mindolarn Empire. Kaescis's father and uncles were privy to the secrets of the past. They had access to ancient tevisrals that made such construction possible. But they were cautious with that knowledge, creating structures like the command fortress of Keliur only where they would remain unseen by commoners' eyes.

Kaescis presented the summons to the soldiers stationed outside, and they allowed the three to enter. They made their way through the wards to the central building of the fortress—its main keep, so to speak. The towering doors opened to reveal Admiral Vedigar, the fortress commander, and a small company of soldiers and officers. A battle-hardened man, Vedigar's rugged face bore many scars, and he wore a patch over one of his violet eyes. On the left side of his head, a white streak ran through his light-brown hair.

"Prince Kaescis," Vedigar said with a salute, touching his left fist to his right breast, and bowed. "Welcome to Keliur."

Kaescis returned the salute and simply nodded.

"The emperor and the Supreme Council wish to speak with you," Vedigar said, gesturing inside. "There is also a contingent of the Crimson Praetorian Guard waiting to accompany you on your voyage."

Kaescis raised an eyebrow, intrigued. Vedigar turned to one of the soldiers and whispered a command. The soldier hurried off, disappearing into the depths of the main keep.

"Please, follow me," Vedigar said, turning to the doors. The company of soldiers parted in unison, their boots echoing through the castle's entrance. Kaescis and his companions followed Vedigar into a towering five-story foyer. Elaborate stonework ornamented the walls and ceilings, crafted by tevisrals that could make the most precise and minuscule cuts. Massive columns lined the room, bearing exquisite designs. Kaescis longed for the day when architecture like this would be common. *Would that it be soon.*

"Admiral Kaetet, I heard of your tragedy," Vedigar said softly. "I offer my condolences for your losses."

"Much appreciated," Kaetet said. "We wouldn't have survived if it wasn't for the prince."

"Mm-hmm," Vedigar said. "That's what I heard. Who knew the Sapphire Guard could be so skilled."

"This is the first time we've ever clashed with them," Kaescis said. "I don't think anyone knew the extent of their abilities. They were undaunted by the Ko'delish. Most foes would flee at its presence."

"That is disturbing," Vedigar said, leading Kaescis and his companions down a corridor at the end of the grand foyer. "And here I thought they were just a ragtag bunch of mercenaries and treasure hunters."

They continued through the castle, discussing the details of their experience in Soroth. Vedigar was politely interested, but didn't seem to care about what happened with the Necrotic Order or that Krindal had conscripted a band of adventurers. After all, Soroth was a backwater chain of islands. An insignificant place... but, *he* was there.

Soon, they reached a war room often used for councils. It was quite large, with a long table that spanned most of the room's length. Fifty people could sit around it. A black sphere the size of a man's head—an Ul'thirl—sat at the center of the table. The room was empty except for Kaescis, his servant, and the admirals. Was the Ul'thirl active?

Kaescis edged around the table, nearing its center.

"The messenger I sent ahead informed the man on the other side," Vedigar said.

Kaescis nodded. *So, it is active.*

Soon, several members of the empire's Supreme Council entered the war room, taking their seats at the opposite end of the table from Kaescis and the others. Well, they were not actually in the same room, of course. These men were thousands of grand phineals away from Keliur, communicating with him via the Ul'thirl.

Ul'thirls were quite remarkable. Whoever had thought of crafting such tevisrals was brilliant. They used various forms of magic to capture the area around them and project that area elsewhere in the world.

Raedina had spent years studying them. She hoped to be able to replicate such wonders, but it was nigh impossible. Her labors, however, were not fruitless. Raedina and her associates had devised a means to send audible messages, and it was that kind of tevisral Kaescis had used to relay his request.

Kaescis marveled at the sight projected by the Ul'thirl, but his eyes were drawn to the stone along the walls of those who had taken their seats. He could see the slight difference in color from the war room here in Keliur.

The war room and the room where the Supreme Council was seated were just two of many identical chambers scattered throughout the empire. It was more pleasant to have conversations via Ul'thirl if the places looked the same, otherwise you would have a mismatched amalgamation of a room. Identical rooms also made it easier to conceal the true nature of the Ul'thirls from anyone who might accidently stumble across a meeting, although Praetorians or other soldiers often guarded both places. Kaescis's uncles had also used them to ward off would-be assassins attempting to strike during an audience with the emperor.

Such an assassination had been attempted once. Kaescis remembered the man charging through the room, ready to strike but being surprised upon discovering that the emperor was a cluster of magic. The assassin was perplexed until his beheading. The whole thing was actually quite humorous.

Footsteps echoed from behind Kaescis, and he turned to see another man entering the war room. "Bratan!" Kaescis exclaimed with a smile. He hurried back across the room to meet the burly man.

A smirk spread across Bratan's broad face. He stood taller than Kaescis, with a larger build. Bratan wore a fanciful garb. Though he wasn't a noble, Bratan often dressed like one—at least when he wasn't wearing his crimson armor as a Crimson Praetorian.

"Kaescis, my friend!" Bratan stretched out his arms, gripping Kaescis in a tight hug. His yellow-green eyes beamed with excitement, then narrowed as he studied Kaescis.

Could Bratan sense the conflict within him?

"What's wrong?" Bratan asked calmly.

Kaescis averted his gaze, remembering his confusion while traveling from Soroth. As he opened his mouth to speak, he heard a declaration from behind him.

"Presenting the Emperor of Mindolarn," exclaimed a servant in a crimson coat, "Marden, son of Madars and descendant of the Almighty Karath'nos, the ruler of our sublunary dominion beneath the watchful gaze of our God and Father, Cheserith." Kaescis sucked in his breath as everyone in the war room snapped to attention.

A moment later, the emperor entered the room. Uncle Marden wasn't wearing his royal robes, which surprised Kaescis. Instead, the emperor wore a simple black garb with a black cape and cowl over his shoulders. His hands were shrouded in leather gloves. Marden didn't carry himself like the past emperors. He was a casual man who often slouched. The emperor eyed Kaescis with a probing gaze before taking his seat at the head of the table.

"What is this meeting about?" Kaescis asked, stepping away from the others. He moved to the right side of the table, stopping near the Ul'thirl. He didn't like crossing through the magic; doing so tingled his senses.

"You shouldn't address His Imperial Majesty in such a casual way," chided the man beside the emperor.

"He's fine," Marden waved his hand. "Kaescis *is* my nephew. I don't expect him to use formality around me." Kaescis nodded to his uncle.

"I've called this meeting," the emperor said, "to ascertain why you requested additional forces. Why were your two hundred not enough for such a simple task?" Did Uncle Marden not know? But Kaescis had sent word weeks ago. Had the news not made it to him? He found that unlikely.

"You don't know, Uncle?" Marden shook his head.

How could such news not reach the emperor? And wouldn't he have had to authorize dispatching the Crimson Praetorians? None of this was making sense.

Kaescis eased his mind and answered his uncle's question. "While accessing the Keeper's Shrine in the Igeacean Sea, we were attacked by the Sapphire Guard."

"The mercenaries from Merdan?" a council member asked.

"Yes," Kaescis said. "They were relentless. They slew all of my associate's fellows. They nearly killed him too, but I was able to save him. But we suffered great losses. Nearly all of my soldiers died trying to escort Krindal back to the *Executor's Breath.*"

"You sacrificed Mindolarn soldiers for a petty scholar?" demanded another council member. He seemed angered at the idea.

"He's not just a scholar," Kaescis said. "Krindal is the key to accessing the Isle of the Ancient Ones. If he had died, we'd have lost progress. Of course, we could always start over, but it would take years to traverse all the shrines in order to attune another man. And to make matters worse, we're already in competition with the Sapphire Guard. They would have a head start and would most likely plunder the Isle before we could reach it."

The council members looked grim at his report. It was the truth, though. The lives of a few hundred soldiers were well worth the sacrifice to ensure the safety of millions. Their deaths would secure the might of the empire.

"Are you sure the Sapphire Guard was after the Keepers' Shrine?" another asked.

"Yes," Kaescis said incredulously. "I heard their leader shouting for some of his followers to secure it while we fled. The Sapphire Guard knew where to find it. There is no doubt they are attuning someone." Many of the council members sighed with disappointment.

"I only had two hundred with me," Kaescis said. "The additional forces should be enough. We were evenly matched in numbers, but the members of the Sapphire Guard were quite skilled. Five hundred of our most skilled soldiers should be enough. Krindal also recruited a notorious band of adventurers, led by the son of Melthas Dol'shir."

Hearing the name of one of the greatest enemies to the empire, several council members gasped, as did the emperor.

"The son of the Butcher of Tor?" muttered a council member. "Are you sure it is wise to work with him?"

"Mister Dol'shir does not know who I am," Kaescis said confidently. His most recent experience with the *Will* bolstered him.

"You should be wary, nephew," Marden said.

"He seemed a decent man," Kaescis said, "and doesn't harbor any resentment. He admitted to that."

"I warn you again," Marden said firmly. "Be wary of the sons of our enemies. Do not forget what the son of Adrin did to my brother just eight months ago."

How could he forget? Kaescis had watched helplessly as that vile Alathian fatally struck his beloved uncle. Kaescis would have revenge upon that man, sooner or later.

"Now I have more questions," Marden said. "I would like to know, in detail, everything that you have discovered since leaving the seat of the empire."

⎯⎯⎯◆⎯⎯⎯

The sun had long since set when Kaescis finished his report to his uncle and the empire's Supreme Council. They seemed intrigued by the discoveries he and Krindal had made. Those who had been apprehensive about his protection of the old scholar were consoled after hearing about the various shrines and the ordeals it had taken to reach them. Kaescis also spoke of his plans concerning the Wildmen of Klindala. The Supreme Council seemed pleased that he intended to barter an alliance with those tribesmen. An alliance would prove fruitful now *and* in the future.

Stepping into the night, Kaescis found Laeyit outside the command fortress's main keep. She looked sullen at her lack of involvement. Kaescis hadn't wanted her at the meeting, and so had left her behind.

"You left without me," Laeyit scolded him. Kaescis stopped on the steps leading to the main keep while Kaetet and Practil walked past Laeyit. They paid little attention to her.

"It was best you weren't present," Kaescis said.

Laeyit's expression turned from sullen to furious, but changed again upon noticing Bratan. Laeyit bolted up the stairs and leapt into Bratan's arms. They too had a bond of camaraderie. She stepped back, grinning, and then punched his arm playfully. "When did you get here, you big buffoon?"

"I've been here for weeks," Bratan said. "I and several other Praetorians were sent by Raedina after she learned of your dilemma at that last shrine." Laeyit smiled broadly, looking like a giddy child.

Kaescis, however, cocked his head. *So Raedina sent the Praetorians,* he mused. But she hadn't the authority for that. And, Uncle Marden wasn't surprised in the least at Bratan's presence during the meeting. Perhaps the emperor had altered some things…

"That reminds me," Bratan added. "I have another communication rod for you, Kaescis. And Raedina says you need to be more careful with this one."

Kaescis opened his mouth to retort, but Laeyit chimed in, laughing as she spoke. "This, this is great!" she exclaimed. "Like old times, Kaescis!" Kaescis nodded. It *did* feel good to have the three of them together again. How long had it been?

"Did he tell you everything?" Laeyit gestured with her head to Kaescis, but was speaking to Bratan.

"I think so," Bratan said.

Kaescis continued down the stairs and his two friends followed, chatting along the way.

"Did he tell you who Lord Cheserith delivered into his hands?" Laeyit asked. There was a sense of bloodlust to her words.

Bratan hummed with confusion. "Are you talking about the child of Dol'shir?"

"Yes!" Laeyit exclaimed. "I told Kaescis we should get rid of him before it's too late, but he didn't listen. Maybe he'll listen to you."

Bratan chuckled.

"What?!" Laeyit blurted. "You don't agree?"

"No, if he's not a threat," Bratan said.

Laeyit grumbled.

Why was she so eager to kill the man? It's not like Cornar knew the truth. She feared he did, or would—how, Kaescis couldn't fathom. Laeyit wanted to be rid of the man because of his lineage, not because of anything he had done, simply because he was the son of the Butcher of Tor. That was enough in her mind to warrant an ignominious death.

Bantering with each other, the three continued down to the shipyards. Their reminiscing felt like old times. They had been a force to be reckoned with, and they would be again. Together, they would topple that accursed Sapphire Guard.

Soon, they reached the *Executor's Breath.* It was filled with a proper crew and a full complement of elite soldiers. Two other ships were moored nearby, the *Helidar* and the *Ulicin,* named for fallen generals who died during the war with the Kingdom of Los. They were warships identical to the *Executor's Breath,* provided as promised by Admiral Vedigar. The men on the ships were some of the most accomplished soldiers and sailors in the entire Mindolarn navy.

Surely, his enemies couldn't defeat him this time. With this force, he would be victorious, especially with the addition of Bratan and his fellow Praetorians.

Kaescis and his compatriots boarded the *Executor's Breath*. To their surprise, they were welcomed aboard by the captains of the reinforcing vessels.

"Your Imperial Highness," the captains said, bowing in unison.

Kaescis shook his head. He was getting tired of formality. But why? Eight months ago he would have been content to be called lavish titles and showered with praise. Now, all he wanted was to bring glory to the empire and avenge his uncle. Was that the cause of all this informality? "You can just call me Kaescis," he said.

"As you wish, Your—" A captain cut himself short. "Um, Kaescis."

"Are your ships ready?" Kaescis asked.

"They are," the other captain replied. "We can set sail at once."

"Then once Admiral Kaetet says the *Executor's Breath* is ready, we'll be off," Kaescis said.

"And where are we going?" the first captain asked.

"To the Isle of Klindala—more specifically, the ruins of Klindil."

"I see," the captain said with a nod. The other studied Kaescis with a raised eyebrow, awaiting further explanation.

"This will be one of the greatest voyages you and your crew will ever undertake," Kaescis proclaimed. "For the glory of Mindolarn—no! For the glory of Kalda! Tonight marks the dawn of a new day for our empire. After we are through, the world will know the might of Mindolarn once again!"

THE END OF

Part One

GREATER KALDA

I-III

Griffith · Ercanin · Krigi

A pprehending criminals was not something Griffith had imagined doing when he agreed to become an Agent of the Order, although he seemed to do it more often than not. Griffith had thought he might be undertaking tasks much like the ones his mentor had done during his days as an agent: infiltrating enemy strongholds, assassinating generals, gathering intelligence. The typical espionage stuff.

But times were different. The world was no longer at war.

Griffith rode toward the town of Dorin-Shrela upon his transmogrified steed—it was an amalgamation of earthen substances, bound together into the form of a horse. The cohesive bond was generated by a baelnarn under Griffith's control. Some people said the baelnarns were the souls of dead creatures and that the ones used by the Alathian mages were the essences of deceased horses. They weren't wrong. Most Alathian mages rode such creatures. Transmogrified steeds were far superior to ordinary horses. They never tired, and they galloped at speeds many times greater than their living counterparts.

Griffith eyed the small town. It really should have been considered a village, but Dorin-Shrela was a major port on the eastern coast of the Kingdom of Los. He was getting close to the town, so Griffith dismounted, waving his hand in a form of dismissal. He didn't want to ride into town atop the transmogrified steed. That'd just give him away.

The steed lost cohesion, becoming a pile of dirt, grass, and rock bits. A white speck hovered where the horse had stood, then wisped to Griffith, disappearing beneath his clothing, where he felt it penetrate his skin.

Griffith then strode onward, continuing on foot. He fought the urge to move faster, as one had to do when enhanced with quickening magic. Your legs would want to burst into a run.

Soon, he reached the home mentioned in the letter from the local authorities. From an alley nearby, a tall fellow stood watching him. The man wore a broad hat and chewed on a straw.

Is that you, Bredan?

Griffith didn't give him an acknowledgment, but continued onto the house.

The man in question, Gildin Von, had been accused of using an unsanctioned tevisral. A couple witnesses saw him injure himself while working on his home. Gildin had gone inside and returned unscathed, continuing the job as before. It sounded like the effects of an Arpran Cube. Griffith had never seen one, but the device was said to heal whoever touched it. Such tevisrals were kept under tight lock and key.

Once at the door, Griffith took a deep breath. He hated this part. Most of the time they'd run. Only once had he apprehended a willing suspect.

Griffith knocked on the door and tried to act as casual as he could, but he felt a stiffness growing inside him. *Just relax...* No answer came, so he knocked again. Griffith took a step back, glancing at a nearby window. A flash of movement sped across the room, moving away from the door.

Griffith groaned, grabbing the doorknob. *Here we go...* The door was unlocked, and he threw it open. "Gildin Von!" he shouted, "Are you here?" Of course, the man wouldn't answer. If Gildin was running, he'd already figured out who was at his door.

A crash echoed from the rear of the home. Griffith hurried through the entry and through a sitting room, the same room where he'd seen the movement. He swiftly bounded over the furniture and darted into a kitchen. A table was tipped over, blocking a hallway.

He's got guts. Griffith shook his head and leapt over the table. It was an easy feat when enhanced with quickening magic. Griffith hurried through the hall, finding a door swaying on its hinges. He bolted through it and scanned the yard. Faint footsteps trailed off to his left.

There, he thought, looking beyond a wooden fence to a space between two other homes. Griffith leapt the fence with ease and ran through another yard, leaping over another fence. He hurried onto another road as a dark-haired man ran into a nearby alley. *Gildin Von!* The street was mostly empty and Griffith ran at unnatural speed to the alleyway. A thud echoed between the buildings as he entered.

Gildin Von lay on the ground, groaning and reeling on his back. Looming over him was the man with the broad hat. The tall fellow lowered a fist and shook his head, glancing to Griffith with a smirk.

"That worked out well," the tall fellow said, laughing and grabbing Gildin by his shirt. Griffith knew that voice. It was Bredan's, although Bredan didn't look like himself. He was definitely under an illusion.

"I wondered if that was you," Griffith said. "How did you get to the alley so fast?"

"I've been back here the whole time," Bredan said, pulling Gildin to his feet. "That was my illusion you saw out in front of his home."

"No, no, no!" Gildin shouted, trying to break free.

"Calm down," Griffith urged, then uttered the words of a transmutative spell. Brown magic wisped into the ground, breaking apart the cobblestones. The now–raw matter rose into the air and wrapped around Gildin's wrists, forming handcuffs. The chain between them was long, but it shortened at Griffith's mental command, bringing Gildin's hands together.

"Gildin Von," Bredan said, "you are under arrest for possession of an unsanctioned tevisral."

"No!" Gildin cried. "It's not mine, I swear it!"

"We have proof," Bredan said flatly. "And witnesses."

"No!"

"This can go smoothly if you cooperate with us," Griffith said. He stepped forward and put a hand on Gildin's shoulder, attempting to calm him. "We need to know some details. How did you come into possession of it, what do you intend to use it for, and why did you decide to take possession of it?"

"It's not mine!" Gildin shouted. "I was only transporting it."

"Trafficking tevisrals too?" Bredan grunted, grabbing the chain on the transmuted handcuffs.

"No!" Gildin cried, "I'm not selling it! Someone asked me to hold it for him for a few days. That's all."

"But you used it," Bredan said. "That's punishable in and of itself."

"I was hurt, okay?" Gildin squirmed. "I didn't have time to find an arpranist. We only have one here in town, and he's quite busy. Sometimes he's even gone to neighboring villages."

Griffith looked to Bredan, but the other agent had no pity for the man.

"Who asked you for help?" Griffith asked.

"He's a merchant," Gildin said. "I've only seen him a few times. Goes by the name of Dreyen. That's all I know. Dreyen comes into port on different ships."

"Did this Dreyen say why he had the tevisral?" Bredan asked.

"He was selling it to a man," Gildin said. "Rumors said that the poor in the capital weren't being healed by arpranists because they couldn't pay them."

"That's absurd!" Bredan shouted. "That goes against the Alathian Code. No arpranist here in the Kingdom would dare *charge* for their services."

Gildin shied away at Bredan's outburst. Bredan's words were true. Not only was it a violation of the mages' code of conduct, but it was illegal under the Edicts of the Mage-King. A mage could be stripped of his rank and banished for doing such things. No one would dare risk it. Besides, the Edicts granted unalienable rights to the Kingdom's citizens, such as the right to be healed by an arpranist.

"What I want to know is how you smuggled it past the Frontier Guard," Bredan said.

Gildin sighed, ashamed. "Dreyen told me about the atrocities several months ago. Last month, when he was leaving port, he told me he was going to deliver something that would stop them. I agreed to help. Dreyen said he'd drop the tevisral overboard. I watched for his return, and when he arrived, I took my fishing boat out to where he said he'd drop it. I fished it out of the water and hid it beneath one of my loose planks. A few days later I brought it home. Dreyen said it'd be an easy job, that I'd never get found. He was wrong…"

Bredan grunted, "Well, that was forthcoming."

"I thought if I'd cooperate you'd let me off…" Gildin winced.

"Let you off?" Bredan burst into laughter. "Justice cannot be denied!" Gildin winced again.

"I'm sorry," Griffith said, feeling a knot form in his stomach. "But from what you've told us, we cannot just let you go."

"B-bu-but!" Gildin stammered. "I was deceived by Dreyen!"

"Your ignorance cannot negate the consequences of your actions," Bredan said firmly.

"But it wasn't malicious!" Gildin cried, a tear trickling from his eye. "Please, I have a daughter. I'm all she has left. Her mother died last winter!" Pain struck Griffith's heart.

"You should have thought about her before you acted," Bredan said, shoving Gildin through the alleyway. "Come on, to the City Watch with you!"

"Can't you make an exception?!" Gildin cried, tears flowing from his eyes.

"Unfortunately we can't," Griffith groaned, following Bredan and Gildin. "You should be prepared for what's coming. You'll be tried here in Dorin-Shrela and then sentenced to Ahzeald. You'll most likely receive five years."

"No!" Gildin cried, tears still flowing. "No!"

The man's pleading stung Griffith. He felt a conflict growing within him.

"Not Ahzeald!" Gildin screamed, "Please! Not Ahzeald!"

Bredan hauled the poor man away, dragging him through the street. He was making a spectacle for others to witness. Bredan was crude in that way. Gildin tried to break free, but Bredan, enhanced with magic, pulled him with ease.

Griffith trailed after them. *Gildin, you poor fool,* he thought. *You really thought you were helping people.* What kind of man would trick someone into breaking the law? No, not a man. A monster.

People now edged into the street, watching the two Agents of the Order haul Gildin away. The poor man was screaming for his daughter, calling her name, begging to see her one last time. Gildin cursed at Bredan, calling him a filthy Alathian Mage.

This part always felt gruesome to Griffith. He hated when people spewed insults, attempting to tarnish the Order's reputation. He was an Agent of the Order, a Grand Mage of Alath. Wasn't he destined to do greater things than hunt men and women who broke the law? Griffith yearned for the day that he could save people, protect the weak against the forces of evil.

Candles were wondrous things. They had such a variety to them. Different colors, shapes, and scents. Ercanin loved that about candles. Each one could be tailored to suit a wide range of moods.

Being a chandler was like being a god. You were the master of the wax or tallow, molding it to your will, crafting it in a manner that pleased you. Chandlery was a metaphor for godhood. And, like a god, a chandler loved each of his creations equally. At least, that's how Ercanin thought a god would treat his creations. That was how he treated his candles.

Ercanin's shop was a meticulous place. Every candle was grouped with others of its kind, like nations or tribes. Shelves were like grand continents, harboring various types of candles, all neatly rowed. It was a quaint place, his own little world—the world of chandlery.

Many people came from across the world to visit his shop here in the city of Karbenath. Well, perhaps not to see him in particular. Most people who passed through his shop were tourists basking in the leisure of Karbenath.

Karbenath was known for its white sandy beaches. The city became a resort town after the Great War, nearly sixty years ago. Well, at least that's when the fighting stopped in this part of Kalda. The war continued for several more decades, but not here. Not in Karbenath. The city was in a peaceful spot on the northeast side of the Isle of Korath, within the landlocked sea sharing the same name. Towering cliffs lined most of this side of the island, and so the city grew up along the edges of the cliffs. Streets wound back and forth from the beaches to the cliff tops.

People came to Karbenath to see those cliffs—which rose hundreds of phineals high—and to enjoy the crystal clear water. It always seemed odd that the water was so clear since the sea was landlocked. You'd think the water would be dirty, but tourists swore it was the clearest they'd ever seen. Well, everyone except visitors from Mindolarn. Mindolarnians claimed the waters of Laelin Lake, on the shores of the city of Monddar, were the clearest in the world. Supposedly, the lake was made by tevisrals.

How preposterous! Crafting a lake with tevisrals? Bah! But those Mindolarnians were fellow Devouts, so perhaps they weren't exaggerating.

A bell rang through Ercanin's shop, signaling a customer. Wearing a dirty apron, Ercanin stepped out of the back room, where he made his candles. The apron was stained from dyes he'd used over the years. Some hadn't come out of the fabric. But that was okay. The apron showed that Ercanin wasn't just a merchant peddling someone else's work.

A portly man stepped through the rows of shelves, eyeing the multitudes of Ercanin's creations. He seemed mesmerized.

"Can I help you?" Ercanin asked, untying the apron as he approached the customer.

"Uh, yes," the man said, smirking. He picked up a nearby candle, taking in a whiff of the scent. "I hear you make the best candles in town." Flattered, Ercanin nodded. "I wonder, do you ever craft ones of Aldrery?"

Aldrery? That stuff was expensive! It would cost him more than the price to craft ten candles in order to make one from Aldrery.

"Not really," Ercanin replied. "But maybe on special order. I'd have to charge you seventy chilgins."

"Seventy chilgins?!" the customer blurted. "By the Crimson Eye, man, that's expensive!"

Crimson Eye? Ercanin's eyes widened. How dare he swear by that vile thing? They were in public!

"That's something you shouldn't swear by," Ercanin whispered. "Why I—"

The shop's bell rang again.

"Really?" the portly man asked, raising his brow. "May the Crimson Eye remain hidden for all time."

Ercanin flushed with rage. How dare he speak the vow in public?! Who did this man think he was?

Enraged, Ercanin bolted forward, grabbing the man by his tunic. "You shouldn't say such things in public!" Ercanin whispered threateningly.

The portly man rolled his eyes. "You know, nearly half the world ascribes to Cherisium. It's not like it's a secret—"

"Excuse me," another voice interrupted.

Ercanin didn't look at the newcomer. He was too frustrated with the irreverent customer.

The portly man, however, turned around. "What do you—" The man froze. He was completely motionless.

Confused, Ercanin turned toward his second customer. He was a tall man with a chiseled build. He was the kind of man you'd see parading himself on the beach, drawing the lustful eyes of women and queer men. The tall man stood still, gazing into the eyes of the portly customer.

Suddenly, the tall fellow uttered a sharp phrase. It sounded like the forbidden tongue! Green magic erupted from his hand, instantly forming a sword-like shaft.

Oh no! It couldn't be! Not one of *them!* Not here, not in Karbenath! This was no man. It was... a *beast!*

In a flash of movement, the green shaft pierced through the portly man's chest. He fell lifeless to the shop floor without as much as a groan. Ercanin gasped, but shielded his eyes. *Not the eyes. Do not look at his eyes!*

Ercanin slammed into the nearby shelf, knocking it over. His candles spilled across the floor, rolling around the customer-turned-beast. Ercanin hit several other shelves as he bolted for the door. Ercanin could hear the beast kicking the candles.

He had to run!

Now in the street, Ercanin bolted southward, up the rising road. He heard a sharp word coming from his shop, but couldn't tell what it was. Ercanin didn't dare look back for fear of being caught by the beast's unholy eyes.

Ercanin neared a merchant cart, its owner calling for people to try his wares. Bolting straight for the cart, Ercanin grabbed its handle and pulled it to the ground. The wares spilled across the street, tumbling down.

"Thief!" the cart owner shouted. "Thief!"

I hope that slows him, Ercanin thought, quickening his stride. Ercanin neared another cart full of fruit and toppled it like the first. This cart's owner yelled after Ercanin, shouting incessant curses. *Maybe the commotion will scare him off?* he thought, continuing up the switch-back road.

Ercanin didn't pass any more carts, but there were barrels along the street. He tipped a few over, hoping they'd roll down the street and hit that monster. But what good could a barrel do against a *beast?*

Soon, Ercanin reached the top of the cliffs. Had he really outrun the beast? That surprised him. But what could he do? Ercanin couldn't defend himself against the likes of such a monster.

His family came to his mind; his beloved wife, his darling daughter. Ercanin would never see them again. If he did, it would only spell their doom.

There was only one answer.

Ercanin bolted straight for the cliffs. He darted across lush grass to the edge of the precipice. For a moment, he saw a beautiful contrast between the grass, the sandy beach and the crystal clear ocean.

Oh, it was a beautiful sight! A fitting last sight…

Ercanin leapt through the air, fearless of the fatal fall. It was a fairer fate than what would have awaited him in his shop, his beloved shop! His candles… He would never see them again. That pained him. But Ercanin had lived a good life.

As Ercanin felt himself falling, he flailed his arms instinctively. Something slithered around his waist, and Ercanin stopped falling.

Oh no….

He was rising backward through the air. Dark green light caught his eye, and he looked to his right, seeing a vine composed of magic. An ensnaring spell.

No!

The grass of the cliff top came into sight as his limbs stiffened. He struggled to break free, but neither his arms nor his legs could move. He screamed in terror. "I couldn't save them! My beloved wife, my darling daughter!

They're doomed…"

"Your family will remain unharmed," said a voice from behind him. It was the same Ercanin had heard within his shop. The beast. "As long as they are not defiled by your evil ways."

No, the beast was lying. He'd massacre them if given the chance!

Ercanin turned in the air, though not of his own volition. He glimpsed the vile monster standing with a hand outstretched. The beast *looked* like a man, but he was no man. The other hand clutched that shimmering shaft of deadly magic.

If that fool had only kept his mouth shut, Ercanin thought angrily.

"Just spare my daughter!" Ercanin clenched his teeth. "She's only six years old!" The beast said nothing, and simply lowered Ercanin, bringing him eye level. Ercanin, however, closed his eyes. *Not the eyes…*

"Your feeble attempts only postpone the inevitable," the beast said with a sigh, then uttered a sharp phrase in the forbidden tongue.

A surging force penetrated Ercanin, and he lost control of himself. Ercanin felt his eyes open. He tried to scream, but he couldn't. Ercanin was at the mercy of this monstrous horror. While Ercanin's eyes were forced open, the beast's blue irises shifted in shape, swirling in a pattern around his pupils. Flecks of red and black appeared within the curving lines.

Then it happened.

Ercanin's life flashed before him, from his earliest memories to his most recent experience in his shop speaking with the portly customer. He relived things he had forgotten, locked away deep within his mind. Ercanin re-experienced the first time he met his wife, reliving their first kiss. It tantalized him as it had back then. Images flashed of his daughter's birth, and he felt the pride of parenthood flood through him. It was as if he relived his entire life in just moments. How bittersweet! Ercanin felt all the joy and all the pain. A blessing and a curse!

"You are not an evil man, Ercanin," the beast said. "It is a pity, but I must fulfill my mandate."

The surging force left him, and Ercanin regained control over himself, although he was still bound by the monster's magic.

"I will not harm your daughter," the beast said. "As long as she is not defiled by the time I reach her. Your wife, however, will not be as fortunate." A tear trickled down Ercanin's cheek. "I will ensure that your daughter does not see her mother's execution," the beast said. "A child doesn't need to be scarred in such a manner."

That did not console Ercanin. "What will you do to her?" Ercanin sobbed. "To my daughter."

"She will be looked after," the beast said calmly.

Ercanin struggled to break free, but the magic binding him didn't give way. It never would.

"Don't struggle, Ercanin. Death will be swift for you. You won't feel a thing."

"I don't want to die!" Ercanin cried and more tears streamed down his face. Then he felt the magic turning him around.

"A man deserves to gaze upon beauty as he dies," the beast said. Ercanin couldn't see him anymore.

"My shop," Ercanin sobbed. "My family."

"I will see that your world of chandlery lives on," the beast said. "Your posterity will flourish, untainted by your evil ways, cherishing your love for candles. That's the least I can do for you."

Ercanin's sobbing grew more intense as the beast continued. "And as for you, Ercanin, though you will die, you will live on in my memory. Now quell your heartache. A man should not go out of this world without dignity."

Time flowed forever as the raging ocean of emotions inside Ercanin calmed. The beautiful vista before him soothed his soul, and he felt a growing resolve welling inside him.

"Oh, Lord Cheserith, receive my soul!"

And then, it all went black.

Krigi grunted as he dragged the large sloglien down the slope of the High Peaks. Why did slogliens have to be so big? It was bad enough that they were hard to catch and irksome to slay. *Such wild beasts!* Why couldn't the tribe use other animals for the festivities? The tenets of the Celebration of the Desolates were so strict it made him nauseous. *Yuck!*

The dead sloglien caught on a rock, its claw wedged inside a crevasse.

"Stupid beast!" Krigi shouted, tugging on the ropes. The beast wouldn't budge. Grumbling, Krigi tried to pull the claw free, but it was stuck. "Au Mala!" he cursed, and stepped away.

A fresh breeze blew past him. It was the only good thing that had happened on his hunt. First, his bow string snapped. Then an arrowhead fell off. And then a bird scared the sloglien just as he let loose his arrow. That made the hunt even longer. Krigi almost lost the beast, but luckily it ran into a snow patch. The sloglien rightly stood out against that backdrop. One couldn't miss its brown fur. So perhaps it could have been worse…

Krigi threw off his percala—foreigners wore something similar that they called coats, but percalas were better. A percala covered everything! It was good for the cold months, but it wasn't that cold yet. Fall was barely upon the High Peaks, but one wore a percala anyway especially when out hunting.

The breeze rustled through the rest of his clothing; they were thin layers. It was common attire for those of his tribe. One didn't need to wear a percala when at home in the High Valley. It was warm there.

The cold began to sting, but not before Krigi felt invigorated. "Praise Vau Kalen!" he shouted, his voice echoing down the mountainside. Now refreshed, Krigi donned his percala once again. He worked at the sloglien's claw and managed to free it.

I should have brought more rope, he thought. *I could have tied its limbs back. Au Mala curse me!*

Krigi wished he could flip the sloglien over, but the beast was too heavy. One had to drag the things from their nests in the High Peaks and hope they came down the way you wanted them.

Soon, Krigi reached a small valley cradled between the mountaintops, his beloved home, the High Valley. Most everything was '*High*' here. But it was a fitting preface. They were on top of the world after all. One could stand at the edge of the High Valley and see everything! It was splendid!

Sometimes foreigners came to the High Valley, eager to see the view. His people, the Yelinail, permitted such things, as long as strangers stayed within certain bounds. If foreigners ventured too far down the canyon known as the Path to Sorrow they would have to be killed.

It was the law.

Krigi looked at the Path to Sorrow, shaking his head. Why did people want to poke their noses into places they shouldn't? Didn't they see the crosses and the dead hanging upon them? Maybe they didn't have warnings like that elsewhere in the world. That was the only explanation that came to him.

Movement caught his eye, and Takali hurried up the mountainside, huffing and puffing. He must be getting old if a climb from the village was wearing him such. Krigi hoped that wouldn't be him in several years. But Takali wasn't much older than Krigi.

"Krigi!" Takali shouted, cupping his hands around his mouth. "*They* are here!"

Krigi grunted. "As expected." The sloglien caught again, this time on a branch. Krigi sighed and turned around to free the felled beast, and Takali hurried up beside him.

"Good hunt today?" Takali asked, helping pull the branch away.

"Terrible," Krigi said, grunting.

"But you have it," Takali chimed. "And so you retain your right as Gatekeeper."

The sloglien came free, and they pulled it together. It was always better to hunt with two people. Everyone knew that! But going into the High Peaks alone to hunt a sloglien? What stupidity! Why did they have that foolish tradition for the Gatekeeper? Krigi wished he could find the fool who decreed it and throw him off the High Peaks. *Au Mala curse him…*

The air warmed as Krigi and Takali dragged the beast into the High Valley. Krigi had to remove his percala and sling it over his shoulder. No one knew where the warmth came from. It never got cold in the High Valley, even in the winter. Snow would cover the peaks but never the valley. When winter storms came, snow would fall on the mountainside, but rain would shower the valley. Foreigners thought it unnatural, but this was normal.

They now were out of the foothills and into the valley. Both Krigi and Takali were careful not to drag the beast through the fields lining the path. Their people grew their crops up to the foothills, and sometimes the crops encroached on the various paths to the peaks.

Grunting, Krigi and Takali pulled the beast toward Yelinailmaki. Yelinailmaki was the only home either of them had known. It was a peaceful village. No one ever made a fuss. Life was perfect here in the center of the High Valley.

The sun was setting when they finally made it home. They dropped the beast off at the center of the village, where their tribal leaders awaited: Tebal, Leina, and Chorksiv. The festival's dancers were also present.

"You have done it once again," Tebal said, smiling. "You are Gatekeeper for the twenty-fourth time."

Every year Krigi had to do this stupid ritual. Go to the peaks, slay a sloglien and drag it back home. He didn't have any say in the matter. Well, he could renounce it, but no Gatekeeper ever gave up the responsibility. Perhaps it was because the title enabled them to walk anywhere, see anything. A Gatekeeper could go as far as they wanted into the Path to Sorrow.

The dancers started chanting, moving slowly around the slain sloglien, and Tebal continued talking. He said the same things he had said the last several years, the same as all tribal leaders had said before him. Krigi listened only half-heartedly.

Had it really been twenty-four years since the lot fell upon him? He was unlucky. But being the Gatekeeper wasn't his only problem.

After Tebal quieted, he heard a woman calling after him. "Oh, Krigi!"

Au Mala… Not now, not today. Couldn't she wait? Sometimes Krigi wished he could just disappear. But the village couldn't be without a Gatekeeper. That'd send the village into turmoil. Well, for a short time, until another unlucky fellow had the lot fall upon him.

"Oh, Krigi!" she called again. Krigi didn't dare acknowledge her.

"Oh, Krigi!"

"Will you not answer Baheyla?" Takali asked. His tone was probing.

Krigi raised an eyebrow at Takali. No. He wouldn't. That woman had chased him since childhood. People in the village had tried to get them to pair. Their parents were the first. Then it spread. Now *everyone* in the village wanted them to pair.

"You know it's getting late for her," Takali said with a frown. "She wants a child."

"I know that," Krigi grumbled. He wouldn't mind having a child either.

"Tell me, Krigi, why do you ignore her?" Takali asked.

Krigi just sighed. He didn't ignore her because she was ugly. Baheyla was said to be the most beautiful woman in the entire tribe. Foreigners who came to the High Valley often tried to take her away with them. Some even tried to pay her to spend the night with them. How blasphemous!

Baheyla was not the problem. He was. Krigi had heard of others experiencing passions in their youth, a thrilling excitement that drove both men and women wild. But Krigi never experienced such things. As a child he hadn't minded the idea of pairing with Baheyla, but after he learned of his friends experiencing the passions, Krigi became ashamed. As the years went on, Krigi still hadn't felt the passions. Baheyla made her advances, and she certainly was overtaken by those strange emotions. But Krigi could never reciprocate.

The last time was the worst. She cried then, cried like he had never beheld. It left him pained and so ashamed. He couldn't do that to her again.

"Krigi!" Baheyla yelled again.

"You are being a fool," Takali said. "If you don't go to her soon, they'll pair her with a boy."

"Then he'll be a lucky lad," Krigi said.

"She'll be more than twice his age," Takali said, snorting.

Krigi ignored him. He had other things to do to prepare for the Celebration of the Desolates. He heard Baheyla calling him again, and this time Krigi glanced to her. *I can't make you happy,* he groaned with a frown. Krigi wished he could please her. She deserved it.

Overtaken with sadness, Krigi slunk through the village. Others were busy preparing for the festival. It would be upon them tonight. Krigi exited Yelinailmaki a different way. He walked down a wider path, carrying his percala. This way was traversed more often.

Not far from the village he heard groans and cries of passion. A pair had been made that morning. The boy barely turned fifteen today. The girl was a little older. Krigi had overheard her complaining that she had to wait half a year for the pairing. That was nothing to what poor Baheyla had to endure.

Krigi always thought it a strange tradition that pairs came out to the fields to embrace their passions. It was to show the others of the tribe that they were a faithful pair. They were to continue this practice for a year. Occasionally, pairs would come for no reason at all. Some claimed that the fields helped conceive a child.

It all just seemed silly.

Krigi continued to the canyon that lay south of Yelinailmaki where the Path to Sorrow lay. Being the Gatekeeper meant he was the only person permitted to enter the canyon. Well, he and the Two who always came.

As usual they waited for him at the crosses with the dead tied to them. Krigi called one Mask and the other Hood. He didn't know their real names; they never spoke them. But Krigi had to name them. Several years ago he'd accidently called them by the names he had given them. They both were amused. Hood laughed quite loudly.

A third man stood with Mask and Hood near the canyon wall, staring at the crosses and the dead. *Au Mala!* Krigi moaned, quickening his stride. Why? Why, why, why? He had never shed blood on the eve of the Celebration. Krigi reached for his knife but Hood spoke up quickly.

"Don't mind him, Krigi," Hood said. "He's my grandson, so to speak."

"Many times removed," Mask said, laughing. Mask was named Mask because of the metal mask that covered his head. It had openings for his eyes, nose, and mouth, but nothing else. Krigi had never seen Mask without his mask.

Hood grinned and rolled his eyes. He wore a cream-colored robe with lots of little patterns. It was too frivolous. Hood had caught Krigi staring at the patterns once and told him that they were symbols of power. They represented the *Words.* *Words* were forbidden among the Yelinail. Not even Krigi could hear *Words.*

"Shall we make our way to the gate?" Hood asked, looking to his grandson. The third man barely looked like a man at all. He was young, between being a boy and a man.

"Nice to meet ya," the grandson of Hood said. "My name's Saprin." He bowed in that weird way foreigners liked to greet people. It was stupid, taking your eyes off someone you had just met. What if they tried to attack you?

"Sap?" Krigi asked, scratching his head. "Like the sticky stuff you find on trees?"

Mask chuckled and Hood laughed. But Sap-boy didn't seem amused. That's what Krigi would call him. Sap-boy. Saprin was probably not his real name, so why should he call them by a made-up name? Krigi's names were always better.

"Let's get going," Hood said, gesturing down the Path to Sorrow.

They walked together, the four of them, and both Hood and Mask asked their usual questions. How many people tried to traverse the Path to Sorrow? Who actually made it to the bottom? Did anybody slip away? But most importantly, they wanted to know about the Gate.

Krigi answered each of their questions. Only three people had ventured into the Path to Sorrow since the last Celebration of the Desolates. Unfortunately, Krigi had to bind them and bring them before the tribe. Each was strung up and left on the crosses. That's normally how they handled violators, but one year Krigi had to chase a man down. The man fled out of the High Valley. It took Krigi a day and a half before he felled the man with an arrow in the back; he was almost as bad to hunt as a sloglien. Slogliens, however, were *always* more irksome than man.

After several hours of walking, they reached the Gate. It was a towering structure, taller than anything Krigi had ever seen. The Gate was as wide as the canyon and maybe twice as tall. A hundred men could walk side by side through it. Krigi remembered the first time that he had come here with the last Gatekeeper. Krigi was astounded at its size. He wondered how someone could make such a thing. Hood had explained it to him once, but Krigi didn't understand. His answers were gibberish.

"So, is this normal, Grandpa?" Sap-boy asked Hood. "Why is it red?"

The boy-not-man was referring to the stuff within the gate. Krigi didn't know what it was, but it made it impossible for anyone to go through the Gate when it was there. People disappeared if they ran into it.

"The barsion the gate emits is mixed with annihilation particles," Hood answered. What did that even mean?

More gibberish, Krigi thought.

Sap-boy's eyes widened, looking intrigued.

"I'm going to deactivate it, Krigi," Hood said watching him.

That was the cue. Krigi placed his hands over his ears and began yelling as loud as he could. This was to ensure he didn't hear the *Words* Hood used when taking the red stuff away.

Soon the red stuff disappeared.

Krigi relaxed and took a deep breath. One of his responsibilities as the Gatekeeper was to ensure that no one, besides Hood and Mask, learn the *Words* that dismissed the red stuff. If those *Words* became known, it could doom the entire world—or so Hood had told him.

"Why do you do that?" Sap-boy asked.

"It's what must be done," Krigi said. "No one must hear the *Words*. And if a Gatekeeper hears them, they must leave the High Valley, and wander there," he pointed to the wasteland beyond the Gate. It was a desolate place out there. This was as close as Krigi wanted to get to it.

"You mean, you exile yourselves into the Karthar Valley if you hear the phrase to deactivate the gate?" Sap-boy asked.

Krigi raised his brow. "Is that what I said?" He really didn't know. Sap-boy was speaking more gibberish. *Au Mala!*

Sap-boy joined Hood and Mask when he realized Krigi wouldn't pay attention to him. They were busily inspecting the Gate. They did that every time they came. Krigi often heard them talking about strange words, "decay" and "structural integrity." They were telling Sap-boy all about the Gate. Mask was worried that the Gate wouldn't hold for more than a century. What was a century? Hadn't the Gate always been here? The songs his people sang said the Gate existed even before the Yelinail. That meant it had to have existed before creation, didn't it?

Eventually, Hood and Mask were finished. Krigi watched them, and Hood nodded.

A horrid thought crossed his mind. What if he didn't clasp his ears? That could solve a lot of problems. Krigi would have to flee into the Desolate plain. With him gone, Baheyla could be paired with someone else. He wouldn't have to go hunt slogliens by himself anymore—

Au Mala! Krigi shook his head. What was he thinking? He'd be alone! Until he got eaten. He couldn't survive out there!

"Krigi?" Hood asked, stepping away from the Gate. He looked concerned.

Au Mala curse me! Krigi lamented. Hood stepped close. He seemed a kind man. Hood wasn't very tall. He looked average, actually.

"What's wrong?" Hood asked, gently placing a hand on Krigi's shoulder. Krigi frowned. He was taught to not hold back from Hood and Mask. The songs called them the Ancient Keepers. Were they from the ancestral world? They seemed too insightful to be men.

"I am… ashamed," Krigi said. "I thought if I heard you speak the *Words*, I could banish myself."

"Why would you want to do that?" Hood asked. He spoke like a father talking to his son.

"Because of stupid things," Krigi complained. "But mostly Baheyla."

"Is she the other half of your pair?" Hood asked.

"No…" Krigi said, sighing. "She's *supposed* to be. But I have no passions." Mask and Sap-boy approached. They had probably heard what he had said.

"What's the passions?" Sap-boy asked.

"Sexual urges," Mask said. *Sexual?* How dare he say that word! They were *passions!*

"How long have you been without passions?" Hood asked. Hood was more like a Yelinail than the other two. He spoke like a Yelinail, understood them. One time, Hood stayed for the entire Celebration of the Desolates. He joined in the festivities, like a dweller of the High Valley. No foreigner had ever done that.

"As long as I can remember," Krigi whispered. He didn't want Mask or Sap-boy to hear. Hood sighed with disappointment. He rubbed his hairless chin. Why didn't he grow any hair on his face? Sap-boy didn't have any either. After a moment, Hood pointed to the side of the canyon, but gestured for Mask and Sap-boy to stay back. What was he doing?

"What I am going to ask you might sound odd," Hood said. "But have you ever looked at a woman and become lost in her beauty?"

"No."

"Never felt anything grow within your clothes?" Hood asked, gesturing to his waist.

"No."

"Mm-hmm." Hood nodded. Silence passed for a moment.

"You should stop your ears, Krigi," Hood said, looking determined. "Shout as loud as you can. I'll do my best to whisper."

A knot formed in Krigi's stomach. "What are you going to do?"

"Give you your passions." *Vau Kalen!* Was that even possible?

"Your ears, Krigi," Hood insisted.

Krigi complied. He shouted as loud as he could, watching Hood's lips move. Krigi could tell he was saying *Words*. Green light appeared around Hood. It happened so fast, not like those other foreigners who claimed to know *Words*. They would drone on and on before they could make light appear. But not Hood. He knew *Words*.

The green light struck Krigi, washing through him. It tingled! Hood nodded, and Krigi let go of his ears and ceased shouting.

"That should do," Hood said with a smile.

That should—whoa! What was that feeling surging through him? Was that… the passions? Krigi's mind turned to Baheyla. She consumed his thoughts. He felt something inside him, something burning, something that he couldn't sate. The passions!

"Why don't you close the gate," Hood said to Mask.

Krigi barely cupped his ears in time. His mind was so consumed by the thoughts of Baheyla that he forgot to shout. It didn't matter though. He was too focused on Baheyla to hear the *Words*. All Krigi wanted to do was take her into the field outside the village.

Soon, the four of them were on their way back into the High Valley. Hood, Mask, and Sap-boy talked amongst themselves, but Krigi didn't pay attention. He yearned for Baheyla.

"It was good to see you again," Hood said as they neared the area of the canyon with the crosses. "From now on you'll be seeing my grandson," he pointed to Sap-boy. "He'll come once a year, just like I have."

"And why aren't you coming anymore?" Krigi asked, suppressing the passions. It was harder than he thought.

"I'm getting old," Hood grinned. "It's time another take my responsibilities here." Hood getting old? But Hood always looked old. He hadn't changed at all since Krigi first saw him. That was a long time ago. Why hadn't he changed?

"Take care of yourself, Krigi," Hood said, then looked to his grandson. "Take us home, Saprin."

Sap-boy held out a hand and began saying *Words*. Krigi frantically clasped his ears. Golden light shone from Sap-boy's hand and reached out, swallowing him, Mask, and Hood. Krigi couldn't see them anymore. They were just a ball of light!

The light faded, and they were gone. They were gone! Krigi had never seen such a sight!

Thoughts of Baheyla returned, and Krigi darted back to Yelinailmaki. The festivities for the Celebration had already begun. But he had to find Baheyla. He found her in the crowd gathered at the village's heart. Oh, she was beautiful! He saw it now! What every other man had seen!

Krigi hurried over to her, pushing his way past his fellow tribesmen. Baheyla noticed the commotion he made and studied him. She looked confused.

"Oh, Baheyla!" Krigi called. A smile formed upon her face. Krigi had never called to her in such a manner. Usually, one only called that way when consumed by the passions. Baheyla made her way over to him. Those nearby gasped at the sight.

"Baheyla," Krigi whispered, feeling a surge of passion within him. "Come with me to the field." Baheyla flushed as red as niglur fruit.

"But, Krigi, we aren't even paired," she said with a gasp, breathing fast. Krigi could see it in her eyes. Her passion was swelling.

Grinning, Krigi said, "We can fix that."

PART

TWO

Wilds
of
Klindala

Cornar · Iltar · Kaescis · Solidin · Krindal · Igan
Kalder · Nordal · Ordreth

17

THE LETTER

A week had passed since Pagus had returned to Sarn. Iltar hadn't received any word from the boy. He was beginning to wonder if Pagus's letter would ever come. Perhaps Pagus couldn't convince his father to lend him that vessel. No matter, it wouldn't be any loss to Iltar. He could still conduct some research here in Soroth.

On the last day of the Order's semiannual break—five days after Pagus departed for Sarn—Iltar had set out to city's central market to peruse the local listings of vacant dwellings for rent. He had no desire to stay at Pagus's home once he finished training the acolytes. That place dredged up too many unwanted memories. He considered sleeping in his office at the Necrotic Order, but an extended stay would arouse suspicion from Alacor and the others.

While at the central market, Iltar had run into Cornar's wife, Karenna and their maid, Nilia. He was shocked to hear that Cornar had left to join Krindal's expedition at the last minute. Cornar breaking promises? How odd…

When Karenna learned that Iltar was at the market looking for a place to rent near the Order of Histories, she scolded him for not asking to stay in her home and insisted that he stay as long as he needed. Iltar found it difficult to argue, although it wasn't an ideal arrangement. It would do.

Karenna was actually surprised that Iltar hadn't sneaked away on the adventure, as Cornar had. It was the most intriguing adventure of their lives. She joked with him that he should have concocted a story to get him out of Alacor's stipulation. Little did she know, that was his intention, but only if Pagus could succeed.

How ironic. Both he and Cornar were not having anything to do with the quiet life. They were men of adventure after all. Asking them to stay put was like asking the sun not to rise.

⟶◗•◖⟵

Iltar stood in the gardens of the Necrotic Order, watching Melnor instruct his acolytes. There was something clumsy about his methods. Melnor wasn't a bad mage, but he wasn't a good instructor.

Iltar shook his head as several of Melnor's students bungled a spell. Magic appeared but soon vanished. The acolytes were obviously doing something wrong.

"Uh, excuse me!" a voice called from behind Iltar. "Master Iltar."

Iltar turned to see one of the Order's guardsmen holding a rolled parchment sealed with dark-blue wax. He couldn't see the engraving on the wax, but only inhabitants of Sarn used blue wax to seal documents.

"You have a summons, sir," the guard said. "It came with another, addressed to the council."

Good, Iltar thought, fighting back a smile. He raised an eyebrow instead and made a show of reluctantly taking the scroll. He broke the seal and carefully unfurled the summons.

"*Master Iltar, it has come to my attention that my son is in need of tutorship here on Sarn. I regretfully inform you that my sister and her husband have passed, and my son must take upon himself his uncle's responsibilities for some while. Pagus has expressed interest in furthering his studies as a necromancer and doesn't want to lose precious time.*" Iltar paused and glanced to the guard as if studying him, but he was really wondering about the ruse Pagus had created. *You went too far, Pagus. What a serious implication… It will be investigated.*

Iltar sighed and resumed reading the summons. "*Pagus has informed me that your Order permits one such as yourself to teach outside the grounds of your magical society. So, I cordially invite you to come to my sister's mountain villa and resume my son's tutelage.*" Iltar skipped past certain details about the nature of the accommodations available to him.

"*My son has also informed me of your acolyte ranks and your responsibility to them. He fears that this request will be denied because it will hinder their progress. Therefore, I also invite them to my sister's mountain villa. While my son sees to his other responsibilities, you can see to your acolytes' instruction in the magical arts.*"

Iltar grunted, feigning irritation over the letter. *He actually did it!*

"Master Iltar?" the guard asked with hesitation.

"What did the other letter say?" Iltar asked.

"I'm not sure," the guard said. "I—"

"Iltar!" Alacor shouted from near the fountain. The grandmaster was approaching quickly.

"Iltar, did you receive a summons?" Alacor asked.

"I did," Iltar said flatly.

"And?" Alacor demanded, his eyes aflame with impatience.

"That I go to Sarn," Iltar said. "For Pagus's sake."

"I can't believe this," Alacor said, grumbling. He stopped in front of Iltar and glanced to Melnor. "Melnor! Melnor, get over here!"

Melnor ceased his instructions, and all his students turned toward the grandmaster. Melnor cocked his head and gave Alacor a disgruntled look that demanded, "What do you want?"

Alacor waved urgently. "Melnor!"

Finally Melnor complied. He strode across the grass and stopped beside Iltar. All the while, his students looked on with curiosity.

"This better be important," Melnor grumbled. "Those bumbling buffoons were just getting the hang of the—"

"Oh, shut your mouth, Melnor!" Alacor spat.

Melnor blinked once then glanced to Iltar. "What's his problem?" he asked.

"We need to meet as a council," Alacor sneered. "Go get Kallan."

Melnor pursed his lips and walked off.

Iltar, however, remained. "Do you want me to fetch your brother?" he asked. "I saw him over by the Record Hall."

"Fine," Alacor said, sounding flustered. He stomped off, leaving Iltar with the guard. Once Alacor was out of earshot, Iltar turned to the guardsmen. "Go fetch Jalel. Tell him to come to the council chambers."

The guard complied. In fact, Alacor himself should have asked the guardsmen to go find Kallan. That was why the Order employed them. The grandmaster was obviously losing his control. Had Pagus's letter infuriated him that much?

◆◦◆

Not long after, all the council members—except for Jalel—were gathered in the Order's council chambers. They sat around the table, Alacor at its head. Iltar sat in his usual seat, at the left side of the table, between Velkor and Kallan. Toroth sat opposite Velkor, to Alacor's right. Melnor sat lazily across from Iltar; he was still not amused by Alacor's outburst.

Soon, Jalel entered and took his seat beside Melnor. He looked confused.

"This is absurd!" Alacor growled, slapping a letter on the table. "I cannot believe this audacity!"

"What, brother?" Jalel asked.

"A summons, for Iltar!"

Velkor leaned back and raised an eyebrow. Melnor rolled his eyes.

"It is legitimate," Toroth said.

"I don't care if it's legitimate!" Alacor shouted. "It's still absurd!"

Iltar fought back laughter. What had Pagus written?

"You should read it to us," Kallan said, folding his arms.

"I'm not reading it," Alacor said, and shoved the letter across the table. "Have Iltar read it."

Iltar forced a blank expression and reached for the letter.

"*Dear council members of the Soroth Necrotic Order, I hereby inform you of an intent to summon Master Iltar, the most prestigious necromancer of your Order, to my domain on Sarn.*" Iltar paused. The most prestigious necromancer? Pagus, you sly bastard... He sucked in a deep breath and continued reading. *"As you have un-doubtedly heard, my dearly beloved sister and her husband have passed away. I assume you have received this news in Soroth, as they were a couple of great importance.*

"You should be aware that my son, Pagus Aliteran, was in line to inherit my sister's lands, as she and her husband had no heirs. Their passing requires Pagus to remain on Sarn and be trained in the proper methods of overseeing these lands. I am determined that Pagus shall continue his training. Since I paid your guild handsomely to instruct him, I refuse to have my coin wasted. I therefore summon Master Iltar to continue my son's tutelage.

"My son has informed me that Master Iltar has other students that require his attention. I am willing to board them here in my domain while Master Iltar continues instructing my son.

"This summons is to be effective immediately upon your council's receipt of it. I am aware that such summons are out of the ordinary, but not forbidden by your Order. If, however, you deny this summons I will deliver a case against you to the Senate of the Principality." Iltar paused again. That was a bold move, probably too bold. *Pagus, what are you thinking?*

"See?!" Alacor cried, slamming his hand on the table.

"Well," Toroth said, "we are dealing with a Sarn Royal. The high duke is used to getting what he wants."

"I don't think his threat is malicious," Velkor said flatly. "The high duke is a little enthusiastic to have his son trained, that's all."

Alacor growled, looking flushed. This letter had gotten beneath his skin. It was wonderful! Why hadn't Iltar thought of doing something like this earlier?

Iltar took a deep breath. "There's more," he said, looking to his brethren.

Melnor nodded and gestured with his hand for Iltar to continue.

"I only bring up the Senate because of my son's fears. Pagus doesn't believe that you will grant this summons, as it will remove some of your students from your watchful eyes." Iltar paused again. That line was another attack on Alacor and his controlling behavior as grandmaster. *"However, I have faith that you will grant this request.*

"I have sent my private yacht, the Yaelinum, *to retrieve Master Iltar and his students. It will be waiting for him upon delivery of this summons.*

"I regret that I couldn't have delivered this request in person, but I am a very busy man." Iltar stopped reading. "It's signed High Duke Finlar Aliteran."

"Of course it's signed that!" Alacor snapped. "What other bastard would be arrogant enough to make such demands of us?"

Melnor pursed his lips and raised an eyebrow at Alacor. "I say we honor it. Let Iltar go with his students."

"I second that," Kallan said.

"What?" Alacor blurted, anger contorting his face. "Without even a discussion?"

"Do you want this matter dragged through the courts?" Melnor asked frankly. "Aliteran will slander us and the Order. We can't afford such a disaster."

"Melnor is right, brother," Jalel said. "But I think we can add a simple stipulation to his summons."

Iltar cocked his head suddenly. What was Jalel proposing? Hopefully it wasn't that one of them come along with him. This whole plan would be for naught if that were the case.

"I propose that we amend the high duke's request. Iltar is to report back once a week, in person, before our council." Alacor sucked in a deep breath.

"That is wise," Toroth said, waggling his finger. "This shows High Duke Finlar we are not dogs that will roll over at his every command." Iltar pursed his lips in disapproval.

"Don't like that plan, Iltar?" Jalel asked contemptuously.

No, he didn't. How was he going to comply with such an amendment?

"I think that's a tad tedious," Kallan retorted.

"I second that," Melnor said, slapping the table. He rolled his eyes again. "I say we just let Iltar go."

Iltar looked around the table. Jalel, Alacor, and Toroth were obviously in agreement to have the stipulation in place. Velkor's decision would determine the council's course of action.

Everyone silently studied Velkor, awaiting his opinion on the matter.

"Your eyes are a little much," Velkor said, leaning back. Several of them backed away, but Alacor, Jalel, and Iltar continued eyeing him.

"I have to side with Melnor," Velkor said. "We cannot afford a confrontation with the high duke." Iltar cheered inwardly. This plan was going to work!

"Capitulation is not a sign of unquestioning submission," Velkor continued. "As Toroth implied." Jalel gasped and shook his head.

"Well, it looks like we know where your loyalties lie," Toroth spat, looking at Velkor.

"I pledge allegiance to Soroth," Velkor said. "Yes, my mother was Sarnian, but I don't consider myself a subject to that aristocracy."

"You lying snake," Toroth said, shaking his head. Melnor rolled his eyes again. He was fond of that gesture today.

"I move for a formality," Iltar said, urging the meeting along. He wasn't going to wait for someone else to call for the next step toward ratifying the council's decision.

Melnor, Kallan, and Velkor joined Iltar in signifying the ratification of the formality. They extended their right hands forward, palms down and fingers close together.

"It is done, then," Alacor said, sighing with annoyance. "Iltar will go to Sarn with his acolytes. Get them ready. Meeting adjourned." The grandmaster rose from his seat and stomped across the council room, followed by Jalel. The brothers were the first to leave, followed by Melnor.

"You're a fool, you know that," Toroth said to Velkor.

"There was nothing wrong with the request," Velkor said, standing.

"Everything was *wrong* with that summons," Toroth retorted, leaning across the table. His eyes met Velkor's with fierce anger. Iltar stood as tension increased between the two necromancers.

"I sense a duel coming on," Kallan said with a sly smile.

"Someone needs to be beaten back into *correct* submission," Toroth snarled.

"Do not forget where your loyalties *should* lie."

Iltar hurried out of the room. He didn't want to be part of Toroth's and Velkor's bickering. Velkor was next in line as grandmaster and Toroth envied the position. This outburst was just one of many that had arisen over the years.

Iltar was partway down the hall when he heard a pair of familiar words among indistinguishable jargon—"Crimson Eye."

What? Iltar stopped abruptly. Was he hearing things? Or had he actually heard the words *Crimson Eye?* Iltar couldn't tell who had said it.

Footsteps echoed from the council room, and Iltar continued on his way, heading down a spiral staircase leading to the main floor. It was possible that his brethren knew the term since it was mentioned in two texts within the Record Hall. But in what context were they using that title? Iltar pondered that question until he reached the foyer, where two guards stood at attention, ready to open the doors for him.

"Go assemble my acolytes," Iltar said to the guardsmen. "I have some news to deliver."

❖

Twilight had settled on Soroth by the time Iltar and his acolytes arrived at the pier where the *Yaelinum* was moored. That particular pier was along the eastern shores of the city, a few grand phineals from the city's northern border. Each of the boys carried sacks of clothing for their long stay away from the Necrotic Order. Iltar had his own satchel, filled with a few belongings and *The Codices of Soron Thahan*.

The boys eagerly talked about visiting the lavish Isle of Sarn. Little did they know they wouldn't be going to that isle. Iltar planned to keep that part of the voyage a secret, at least until they were safely in open waters.

High Duke Finlar Aliteran's private yacht, the *Yaelinum*—named after a type of rare metal found on the eastern continents of Kalda—was moored near several other tall ships. The *Yaelinum* didn't look like any other vessel of the current era. Every part of the ship was enclosed, except for the highest deck. Three masts rose from that open-air deck, with three sets of sails. Each bore the emblem of the Aliteran Royal Family—the silhouette of a great cephalopod with wreathed vines and leaves wrapped around it.

A gangway protruded from the starboard side of the vessel, about halfway between the waterline and the top of the ship. Judging by its position, the gangway was on the fourth deck from the ship's bottom. Two other decks were above that one, not including the open-air deck.

Two men stood at the bottom of the gangway, wearing fanciful clothing indicating that they were bodyguards for the Royal Family. Their stiff tunics bore the same emblem as the ship's sails.

"Welcome," the man on the right said, gesturing to the gangway. "You boys may go aboard."

Young Bilda pushed past the others and was the first up the gangway, followed by Tigan. The others filed in behind them and Agen was the last to board. Once they were safely inside the *Yaelinum*, Iltar preceded up the gangway.

"Did you like my letter?" one of the bodyguards asked. Iltar spun upon the gangway, darting a glance to the man. "Pagus?" he asked, narrowing his eyes.

"At your service." The bodyguard bowed. Either Pagus was under an illusion, or he was using one as a puppet. Iltar couldn't tell. The bodyguard's movements were flawless. "I wish I could have been there. Oh, to see the look on Alacor's face—"

"*Grandmaster* Alacor," Iltar corrected him. He didn't care to refer to Alacor by that title, but he wanted to instill a sense of respect within the boy.

"Yeah, whatever." The bodyguard waved his hand. "Now don't bump into the other guy. He's an illusion too." Iltar raised an eyebrow then walked up the gangway.

Several servants were waiting inside. The nearest servant clapped his hands as Iltar and the two illusionary bodyguards came aboard. The illusions moved perfectly. Pagus's training was paying off.

A couple of crewmen hurried down the hall toward the opening, then raised the gangway. The entire thing lay vertical against the hull. The crewmen yelled to their fellows on the open-air deck once the gangway was raised. The crewmen topside secured it, and then those beside Iltar closed the opening with an interior door. They released some kind of mechanism and the cracks between the opening and the door were sealed, becoming watertight.

Quite impressive.

"This way," the bodyguard said, pointing aft. He moved through Iltar.

Iltar glanced at the servants, who didn't seem surprised. They obviously knew that the bodyguards were illusions. The second bodyguard—who remained quiet—turned into a puff of smoke. The illusionary particles making up its body vanished into nothingness.

"Come on!" the illusionary bodyguard yelled.

Iltar wound his way to the back of the ship, passing several lavish rooms designed to entertain guests. He followed the illusion to the last room. It was a large sitting room as wide as the vessel's berth, a length of twenty-six phineals. Windows lined the aft bulkhead, allowing a view to the eastern ocean.

"So, what do you think?" Pagus's voice echoed from both the illusion and a chair near the windows.

"I think your claims were a little reckless," Iltar answered.

"I'm talking about the illusions," Pagus said, his voice in two places. He stood from his chair. The roguish Royal was wearing a black button-up uniform with tassels.

"Those were good," Iltar said with a nod. "You've definitely improved, my apprentice." Pagus grinned slyly. "Now back to the letter," Iltar said. "You really overdid yourself. And making claims about deceased relatives. The council will surely look into that."

Pagus waved his hand playfully. "I got that taken care of," he winked.

Iltar's eyes widened. "You didn't kill them, did you?"

"Aunty Elsia?" Pagus asked, laughing. "She's my favorite aunt. I couldn't kill her!" The *Yaelinum* lurched backward, and Iltar stumbled into a wide stance.

"So what did you do?" Iltar demanded.

"Pagus enlisted my help," said an alluring feminine voice, coming from the other side of the cabin.

Iltar darted a surprised glance to a regal-looking woman standing at another doorway near the vessel's port side. She stood about average height, with curvy hips and a full bust. She looked to be in her mid-forties. Her light-brown hair was braided and hung over her left shoulder.

"This is my aunt," Pagus said, gesturing to the woman. "Countess Elsia Scurn, my father's sister."

"It is a pleasure to meet you," Elsia said, crossing the room. Her gait was natural, even with the movement of the ship. She extended her hand for Iltar to kiss. Iltar had never understood the need for Sarn women to greet men in such a way. As he bent to comply, he couldn't help but notice the intricate ring on her middle finger. The ring was made of gold, with two birds holding up a black sapphire wrapped in golden casing. Ten white gems were inlaid within the casing, spaced equally around the black sapphire. Iltar reluctantly took the countess's hand and kissed it. It was hard to not get scratched by the wings on that darned ring. They were practically rustling his goatee.

"I have heard so much of the notorious Iltar and his band of adventurers," Elsia said, smiling.

"She's going to help with the research," Pagus said, sounding proud. "Aunty Elsia is very scholarly."

That didn't please Iltar. He raised his brow disapprovingly as he let go of Elsia's hand. Iltar wanted to keep his research a secret, but now Pagus had indiscriminately involved someone else. Iltar didn't know this woman. How could he trust her?

"I am intrigued," Elsia said. "I spent several years of my youth studying Soron Thahan, but I've never heard of him making prophecies. Nor that he wrote a book about it. My nephew insists that these texts of yours are authentic."

"They are," Iltar said, not amused. He scowled at Pagus.

"I would like to read them," Elsia said, then hurriedly added, "with your supervision, of course."

The *Yaelinum* slowed and turned. The view out the aft windows shifted from the eastern ocean to the southern horizon. Some of Soroth's piers were visible out the starboard windows.

"Pagus has told me of your lack of trust with others," Elsia said with a sigh. She was obviously trying to pick her words carefully. "And I'm willing to do whatever you wish in order to gain your trust."

Whatever he wished? That piqued Iltar's interest. He eyed the woman for a moment, then glanced to Pagus. "Anything?" Iltar asked, narrowing his eyes at Elsia.

"Anything," Elsia said, leaving her mouth partway open. She eyed Iltar with a longing gaze. Was she trying to seduce him? No one had ever looked at him like that, except Anela…

"So, what shall it be?" Elsia asked, stepping close to Iltar. She put her long fingers on his shoulder.

"This," Iltar said, then quickly but precisely uttered the words to an incantation. Gray particles appeared within his right hand, the manifestation of enthralling magic. There was only one way to learn of her sincerity—a mind-control spell.

Elsia's eyes widened, but she didn't flinch. Iltar half-expected her to step away, or run. But she did neither. Elsia just stood there, waiting. Surprisingly, Pagus stood still, watching the magic coalesce.

Within seconds the magic formed and Iltar reached for Elsia's face. The enthralling magic wisped into her mouth, nose, and ears. Elsia's expression turned blank as Iltar took over her mind, and the woman became totally subservient.

"What are your true intentions with me?" Iltar asked. Pagus stood beside him, completely silent. *How out of character for the boy…*

"I crave truth," Elsia said in a mindless monotone. "I want to know the secrets of Kalda. Secrets that only you know."

"Why?" Iltar demanded.

"Because knowledge is power, and I crave power just as much as I crave truth."

"Will you betray me?"

"Only if you harm me or my kin," Elsia admitted. That was expected. "But no. I know your reputation. You're not a person one should double-cross." A good answer, but that still wasn't enough to win Iltar's trust. "Who else knows about this trip?" Iltar asked.

"My husband and my brother," Elsia answered.

"Will you keep the truth of this entire trip a secret?"

"I will," Elsia said.

Iltar nodded. He was pleased with the answers thus far. "Now, how do you plan to rectify the lie Pagus has set into motion, about your death?"

"It is simple," Elsia said, still speaking in a monotone. "Our passing was orchestrated to thwart assassins. When we return to society, we'll declare this as truth."

"And how are you going to explain the trip to Mindolarn?" Iltar didn't want to leave any loose ends.

"We had a lead that the assassins were headquartered there. I used the protocol of our land inheritance to lure you aboard. You were to protect me while we drew out the assassins. And then, you'd kill them. You're good at that sort of thing."

Iltar was impressed. Elsia and Pagus had thought this through. A lie within a lie. Quite good. That satisfied Iltar, but he still wanted to know the answer to one more question. "If I asked you to sleep with me to prove your loyalty, would you?"

"Yes," Elsia said, "if that is what you needed to gain my trust."

Iltar grunted in amusement. Sarn women weren't that different from Sorothian women: willing to sleep with a man in order to get what they wanted. Iltar waved his hand, dismissing the mesmerizing spell.

Elsia sucked in a deep breath and wobbled backward. "Whoa… I've… never experienced that." Elsia sounded unnerved.

"You have my trust," Iltar said.

Elsia smiled. "Thank you, Master Iltar."

"I'm glad that's out of the way," Pagus said with a sigh of relief.

The *Yaelinum* was now moving northward, making its way along the eastern shores of the Isle of Soroth.

"Pagus, gather the boys," Iltar said. "It's time to tell them what we're really doing."

18

KRETIN

> *"A band of twenty-four descend into the pit, led by abominable creatures. They go to their deaths."*
>
> - *Prophecy of Soron Thahan*

Cornar knew he was dreaming again. The *Promised Maiden* was still in open waters, but he stood in the darkened streets of a city. Cornar couldn't tell which city, but it was quite busy.

"Breyen!" a voice called from across the street. Cornar glimpsed a man waving at the door to a tavern; light from inside spilled into the street, faintly illuminating passersby.

"Breyen!" the man shouted and then stalked across the street toward Cornar. Was that man trying to talk to him?

"Breyen, what are you doing just standing there?" the man demanded, slapping Cornar's arm. "The other generals are waiting."

Cornar simply raised an eyebrow. A general named Breyen? *Breyen Haliurclast?* he wondered. Breyen Haliurclast was one of the men who had liberated Tor. When Cornar was a child, his father told him stories of General Haliurclast's exploits. The man was a brilliant tactician. But Cornar couldn't be that man, could he? "I think you have me mistaken for someone else," Cornar said.

"Really?" the man asked, laughing. "Who else has a scar across their left eye in the shape of a fishing hook?" Cornar just looked at the man. The scar was a trait General Haliurclast was said to possess. Perhaps he should play along? This was a dream after all, wasn't it? What harm could it do?

Sighing, Cornar reluctantly nodded and pointed to the tavern. "Are they in there?"

"Uh-huh," the man pursed his lips.

They crossed the street and entered the tavern. Smells of alcohol washed from the common room, enveloping Cornar. The dream was so vivid, it was as if he were *in* the tavern.

"This way," the man said, heading down a hallway beside the entrance.

Cornar lingered for a moment, taking in the intense nature of the dream. He had experienced nothing like this besides reliving those horrific events of Tergol's sacking. Was there something important to these dreams?

"Are you coming?"

Shaking off the thought, Cornar hurried down the hall. Both he and the man climbed the stairs and entered a private dining chamber, the upper room of the tavern. Seven others—including his father, Melthas Dol'shir—sat around a table. Adrin was there as well, looming over a map. Both looked the same as they had in his other dream.

Cornar eyed the other five, starting at the sight of Kandish Loush. "Kandish…" he whispered, eyeing the familiar man. Kandish sat at the table, rubbing his bald chin. The merchant's brown eyes stared at the map Adrin was studying. Sighing, Kandish ran his freehand through his wavy dark-brown hair. Kandish was a merchant, not a fighter. Cornar hadn't thought him heavyset as a child, but seeing Kandish now changed his opinion.

"You're late, Breyen," Melthas said with a strict tone. Cornar had only heard his father speak that way once. Cornar had done something to evoke his father's displeasure—what, he couldn't remember—but the tone stung in such a way that Cornar decided he never wanted to hear it again.

"I'm sorry," Cornar said.

"I suppose we can begin?" Kandish asked, raising his thick eyebrows at Melthas.

Melthas nodded.

"So *he* was last spotted on the shores of Laelin Lake," Adrin said, pointing at a map. Cornar took a step closer. It was a map of the Mindolarn Empire. "He has been holed up in the castle between the forest and the river."

"How do you know this, Adrin?" one of the men asked.

"Adrin has a reliable source," Melthas said in a monotone.

"Agents of the Order?" another asked.

Adrin didn't reply.

"It doesn't matter," Melthas said. "All you need to know is that the source is reliable."

The other men, the generals of Tor, grumbled. They seemed displeased by accepting facts blindly. But who wouldn't? Cornar hated lacking all the facts for a battle scenario.

"We don't have much time to strike," Adrin said. "His movements have been sporadic. *He* doesn't stay in one place for long."

"The Castle of Laelin Lake isn't an easy target," one of the men spoke up. "It'll be hard to breech its walls. And the castle has a garrison of a thousand."

"You'll need at least a brigade to lay siege sufficiently," another general said. "How are you going to get that many men across the border?"

The other generals debated with Adrin and Melthas about their strategy. Two of them wanted to wait. Their target, a Mindolarn prince named Alegar—the same who had ordered the attack on Tergol—would undoubtedly move to another location. The generals suggested ambushing Alegar once he left Laelin Lake. Melthas was not fond of that suggestion. In fact, the suggestion evoked a rage Cornar had never seen in his father.

They debated the subject for a while until Kandish spoke, quelling the rising hostilities. "I say attack the castle," Kandish said. "It can be infiltrated. A siege will only cost lives. A surgical strike is best."

"Your suggestion seems too idyllic, Kandish," one of the generals said. "No offense, but you should stick to what you're good at. Commerce. Let us deal with the strategy."

Adrin sucked in his breath, looking flustered. "No, Za-Kandish has a point. We can stealthily breech the castle. We'd only need a small strike force of Tor's Elites. Eighty or so should do."

"That's foolhardy," one of the generals said. He stood and walked to the door. "I'm getting a drink. Hopefully you'll be onto serious matters when I return."

Melthas glared at the man as he left, then studied the others, his hostile expression meant for each of them.

"Do you even have to go at all?" Cornar asked, but immediately regretted the question.

Melthas stared straight at Cornar. "I cannot believe you just proposed that, Breyen. And here I thought you were in support of this attack?"

Cornar flinched, but spoke up boldly. "Think of your children, Melthas. You put yourself in danger by seeking this prince. Shouldn't you set your vengeance aside?"

The others looked dumbfounded, except Kandish.

"I thought we already established that Melthas wasn't backing down," Kandish said, turning toward Cornar.

"Perhaps we should revisit that option," Cornar said. "What if you don't come back? Then your children will be orphans."

Melthas shook his head. "Breyen, you're my strongest supporter. Why have you suddenly decided to flip your opinion?"

Because I am your son, and I don't want you to die. No, he couldn't say that.

"Prince Alegar deserves a painful death," Melthas scowled. "By my hand!"

Melthas sighed and stalked out of the room.

"Perhaps we need to break," Kandish suggested, clearing his throat.

The other generals nodded and left the room. Soon, only Cornar and Kandish remained.

Cornar sat beside the aging merchant, pleased to see Kandish again. Cornar regretted walking out on the man all those years ago after Melthas's passing. Kandish had offered to take Cornar, Galana, and baby Kalder in as his own. Kandish didn't have any children. He wasn't even married. But he was like a grandfather to Cornar.

Cornar had promised to return, and he did visit the merchant once after he married Karenna. He intended to see Kandish again, but by the time he made it back to Tor, Kandish had died. That was twenty years ago. Cornar had regretted his lack of interest in visiting the old merchant.

"You struck a sore spot," Kandish said, glancing to Cornar. "He's made up his mind. None of us can sway him."

"You don't agree with him?" Cornar asked.

"No," Kandish said. "Vengeance will only lead him down a dark path. I'd hoped that Adrin would deter Melthas's rage, but Adrin is encouraging it. Adrin also despises the Mindolarn Empire and would see them destroyed. I fear for both of them, actually…" Kandish trailed off, staring at the wall. He looked like a parent dismayed over wayward children.

It seemed odd to Cornar that his dreams captured the essence of someone he hadn't seen in over three decades. It was as if Cornar were sitting beside the actual Kandish Loush. But this couldn't be Kandish. He was dead. Perhaps this dream was his mind's effort to alleviate regret.

"I'm sorry," Cornar said. "I've felt for years that I disappointed you, Kandish." Kandish simply looked at Cornar, setting his jaw. "I wish I had returned to visit more often," Cornar confessed. "You were so kind to take Galana, Kalder, and me in after my father died. Our disappearance was like spitting in your face."

Kandish grinned with half his mouth. He always did that when amused.

"Don't worry about that, Cor," Kandish said.

Cornar jumped. Was the dream actually talking back to him? *Him*, not Breyen. But why this sudden change? Why did Kandish call him by his real name and not Breyen?

"I don't have any resentment for your decisions," Kandish continued. "You were young and distraught."

Tears welled in Cornar's eyes. "Can you forgive me?"

"Of course," Kandish said with a comforting smile. "You were forgiven years ago. Besides, if you hadn't left you wouldn't be the man you are today. You *need* to be that man for what is to come." Cornar felt a weight lifting from his shoulders. But what did Kandish mean? "Might I give you some counsel, Cor?" Kandish asked, though he wasn't seeking permission. He would speak his mind, regardless. "Heed these dreams. Your experiences in Vabenack will prove fortuitous if you play along."

Play along? What did that mean?

"Many answers for the future can be found in the past," Kandish continued. "You may just find something of importance that will change the course of this expedition."

"The expedition?" Cornar muttered. Was this some kind of external introspection he was experiencing?

"Yes," Kandish said, still smiling. "To Klindil and beyond. Let your dreams guide you. You'll need the insight if you don't want to end up dead."

Cornar blinked and studied Kandish. Kandish wasn't talking like himself anymore. Something seemed odd about the way Kandish sat, and his expression was unsettling. Kandish's brown eyes evoked an eerie sensation.

Unnerved, Cornar stood and backed to the door.

"Afraid, Cor?" Kandish asked with feigned concern. "And here I thought you'd enjoy this breaking of the fourth wall. You know I've made these experiences just for you."

A surge of fear shot through Cornar. There were no windows in the room, only the door. The door! Cornar burst out of the upper room and darted into the hallway. He hurried down the stairs and back into the main part of the tavern. The common room lacked the scents of alcohol he had smelled when first entering. And it was empty! Where were all the people?

Must get out! Cornar's heart pumped wildly. Cornar threw the tavern door open and dashed into the street. Rain pelted him and pooled in the cracks between cobblestones. A bolt of lightning streaked across the sky, illuminating dark-red clouds. Red clouds?

Where in Heleron's name was he?

"I have to wake up," Cornar said, looking about. The street was empty. The previous hustle and bustle was just gone. He took off, bolting down the street.

More lightning streaked across the sky.

Cornar ran for what seemed hours. He didn't tire. He just ran. The city was endless. If Cornar was in Tor, he was in some twisted version of it. Streets wound back and forth but never seemed to end.

More lightning surged across the sky, striking the road in front of Cornar. The lightning lingered, growing in intensity. More bolts struck from the clouds, widening the persistent lightning. Then, a silhouette appeared within the ever-present lightning strike. It looked like a tall man in a robe.

"Calm yourself, Cor," a voice boomed from the silhouette in the lightning.

"What in Heleron's name are you?!" Cornar shouted. A surge of panic pumped through his veins.

"Heleron?" the voice boomed with laughter. "You shouldn't swear by the name of such a petty creature."

Cornar instinctively reached for his serrated dagger and short-sword, but neither weapon was there.

"As I said before," the voice boomed. "I have crafted these experiences for your profit and learning. They are to guide you on this quest you have undertaken. I could give you the answers, but it is better that you learn firsthand."

More lightning surged across the sky, striking the persistent bolt. Dozens more struck, then hundreds. Thunder resounded in a culminating explosion, blinding Cornar's vision.

He felt himself falling.

"Heed these experiences," the same voice boomed. "Or you'll die. Beware the evil behind the eyes of allies."

An abysmal blackness engulfed Cornar, and he continued falling. Cornar fell for what seemed thousands of grand phineals before he snapped awake. He gasped for breath and sat up, frantically studying his surroundings.

A thick fog blanketed the main deck of the *Promised Maiden*. Cornar reached beside him, fumbling for his sheathed weapons. Their presence brought him comfort. Cornar felt naked without them, especially after what he had just experienced.

That was no ordinary dream. It was more than a nightmare… It was fear incarnate!

Rubbing his head, Cornar shook off the horror and hoisted his weapons upon his belt. As usual, he had fallen asleep in his clothing.

"Are you okay?" a crewman asked.

Cornar glanced at the man and nodded, then stalked across the main deck. He descended the stairs to the first deck below the main where the quarters and the galley were located. Cornar made his way to the galley and found Captain Salisar and Krindal talking over steaming mugs of tea.

"Good morning, Cornar," Krindal said with a smile. "Care to join us?"

"Certainly," Cornar said. Normally he would have wanted a moment to himself. Cornar wasn't much of a morning person, but after his strange dream he wanted to be around other people. The immediate disappearance of everyone in his dream was unnerving. It was as if he were the only man in the world.

"Still foggy?" Salisar asked.

"Yes," Cornar said. "Can't even see over the rails."

"That doesn't bode well," the captain said, and sighed.

Soon, the ship's chef came over. She was an older woman with braided gray hair. The chef looked a lot like the captain; she was her mother after all. "Your usual?" the chef asked Cornar.

Cornar nodded.

"And do you want more?" the chef looked to Salisar. "An extra cup will fight back the chill."

"Yes, mother," the captain said.

The chef hurried across the galley, and after she disappeared Krindal cleared his throat. "The good captain here thinks we'll be mooring today."

"As long as the fog doesn't deter us," Salisar said with a chuckle. "Hopefully it will clear soon."

⊃•⊂

The fog did clear by noon. The *Promised Maiden* had gone off course, but only slightly. By evening the port of Kretin was visible on the horizon. The city was smaller than Soroth, or so it seemed from this distance. According to maps, Kretin was the largest settlement on the Isle of Klindala. Other towns and villages lined the coast, but most were insignificant to foreigners.

Cornar stood at the bow with Igan and Vargos. As they eyed the city, the three men discussed plans to start outfitting the expedition. None of them had ever been to Kretin.

"I say we wait a few days," Vargos said.

"Krindal wants to be ready to leave when Kaescis arrives," Cornar said. "He seems antsy."

"Did he say why?" Igan asked. The wizard always asked questions that cut to the heart of people's motives. Igan liked to understand the reasoning behind a man's actions. That trait made him quite valuable.

"No," Cornar said. "Krindal was close-lipped about it."

"He's hiding something," Vargos whispered. "There's something he's not telling us."

"Maybe we can get it out of Kaescis when he arrives," Igan said, glancing over his shoulder.

"Why would you need five hundred soldiers for a simple scholarly expedition?" Vargos asked.

That was a good question. Cornar had wondered that very thing these last few weeks. There was no need for that many soldiers, at least from what Cornar understood of Krindal's quest. Then there was that dream… the strange voice said his dreams would unfold answers concerning this expedition. Could his dreams really tell him what was going to happen? Neither had shown him anything. At least nothing he translated as useful. And what of that warning, "*Beware the evil behind the eyes of allies.*" What did that mean?

"Cor?" Igan asked. The wizard nudged Cornar, drawing him from his reverie. Cornar snapped a glance to Igan. Both mages looked warily at Cornar.

"Are you okay, boy?" Vargos asked. "You looked like you were somewhere else. And it didn't look pleasant."

"I'm fine," Cornar lied.

"You don't look fine," Igan said. "Something is bothering you. You can tell us…"

Cornar studied Igan and Vargos. They were genuinely concerned. He could tell them what had happened. They wouldn't dismiss him as mad. But Cornar didn't want to bring up what might be a onetime thing. It was just a dream. A very vivid dream, but still a dream.

"I didn't sleep well," Cornar admitted and turned his attention back to the port before them.

"It's all that sleeping on wooden planks and sacks of beans," Vargos said. "You need to sleep in a bed."

"We should get an inn," Igan said. "I'm sure we could all use more space. I know I could."

❧

The *Promised Maiden* moored an hour later as the sun was setting in the east. Kretin was situated along the northern banks of a wide peninsula, so the sun hung to their left. The sunset was pretty, accented by the turning leaves. A colorful sight, really. Unlike Soroth—which was in the southern hemisphere of the world—Kretin was experiencing the cooler seasons. Fall was upon the island.

Cornar stood at the starboard rail with his more senior warriors: Kalder, Gregan, Nordal, and Midar. Captain Salisar was yelling orders to her crew while the warriors conversed.

"So we're staying in one place?" Midar asked.

"Why not?" Nordal asked. "It's not like we're trying to hide our expedition."

"Well, I'd like to stay somewhere nice," Gregan said.

"If they have anything nice," Nordal said. "This is a remote part of the world."

"We do have a budget," Cornar said. "The Necrotic Order only allotted so much for the entire expedition, and we'll have to use most of it to reserve horses and wagons."

"I'll make up the difference," Nordal said, patting a satchel hanging at his waist. Coins jingled within it.

"That's generous of you," Midar said, a surprised expression on his face.

"Don't give me all the credit," Nordal said, grinning. "If it wasn't for Hemrin, I wouldn't have the coin to spend." He was referring to his most recent gambling spree. Nordal had told Cornar the story. He was proud to beat the men not only at Sharzen but in a fistfight as well. Nordal could be brutish sometimes. He loved confrontation, thrived on it. That was a good trait on the battlefield, but it could turn a pleasant social experience sour.

"I was looking at the map," Kalder finally spoke up. "There's a smaller town outside Kretin, along the path we want to take to Klindil. We should stay there." Gregan sighed; he obviously didn't like the suggestion.

Kalder's words were wise. The rates would be cheaper, though they would have to come into Kretin to supply the expedition.

"What are you all whispering about?" Ordreth asked as he approached.

"Debating where to stay," Gregan said. "Ol' frugal here wants to stay in the sticks." Ordreth raised an eyebrow.

"Why don't we just split up?" Midar asked. "Those who want nicer accommodations could stay in Kretin and gather the supplies while those of us who don't care can wait in that village."

"Are you trying to get out of work, Midar?" Gregan grunted, raising an eyebrow. Midar simply smiled.

"Splitting up doesn't seem like a bad idea," Cornar said with a nod. It would make things easier and cheaper. Cornar was one for saving coin, here and there. Once they gathered the supplies, they could send them to those outside the city. "Let's have ten of us stay in Kretin, the rest will go to that village."

"I'm in Kretin," Gregan said quickly.

"Same," Nordal affirmed.

"I'll stay too," Cornar said. "That leaves seven more. I think we can share three rooms, or get one suite. What do you two think of that?"

Nordal nodded.

"I can live with that," Gregan said.

"I'll round up everyone else for that town," Kalder said. "It'll probably be late once we get there."

"Do you have cabin fever, Kalder?" Nordal quipped.

Kalder hummed a sigh. That made Nordal and Gregan laugh. They loved giving Kalder a hard time. Nordal had once said he did it to see if Kalder would ever react with anything more than a simple reply. It was hard to get a rise out of that man. Kalder's even-keeled temperament was one of his best qualities, making him reliable in the toughest of situations.

The warriors continued bantering with each other as Krindal approached. Two of the necromancer-scholars from the Order of Histories, Jahevial and Deglin, accompanied him. Both men were average height with white hair. They looked like the typical Sorothian, with olive skin and brown eyes.

"Are we ready to disembark?" Krindal asked, stepping close to the warriors.

"We are," Cornar said. "We've decided to split up part of my band. Ten of us will stay in the city to purchase supplies, and the rest will go to a village outside Kretin. It's along the path you showed me that we'll take to Klindil."

Krindal clapped his hands. "Perfect. We'll accompany you." He gestured to Jahevial and Deglin. "We can send the other scholars with your men."

"That sounds fine," Cornar said, then gestured to the gangway. "Shall we?"

Krindal was the first to disembark, followed by Gregan. Jahevial and Deglin were next, and then Nordal hurried after them.

"Kalder," Cornar called, "see who wants to stay in Kretin, then gather the others and head to that village."

As Cornar stepped to the gangway, Ordreth called, "Uncle, mind if I come with you?"

Cornar glanced over his shoulder. "Of course not," he said. "Come along."

The two familial warriors followed the others, who were already partway down the pier. Krindal seemed awfully hurried. He kept looking at the various ships moored nearby. What was he looking for?

"Uncle," Ordreth whispered. "I overheard Igan and Vargos before I came topside. They sounded worried about you." Cornar raised a brow at his nephew, attempting to feign ignorance.

"I woke up early today and came on the main deck to see if you were awake, but you were thrashing about. It looked like you were having a night terror."

Cornar frowned and took in a deep breath. "It was just a bad dream, Ordreth."

Ordreth looked at his uncle with disbelief. Was it that difficult to hide his emotions? His nephew kept looking at him, expecting a better answer.

"It was another dream about my father," Cornar whispered. "It was… disturbing."

"What happened?"

"They were having a meeting, plotting revenge against a prince named Alegar. But that wasn't the disturbing part."

"And that was…?" Ordreth asked, prying for more information.

That was not something Cornar was ready to speak about. He wanted to forget that last part. Kandish not being Kandish. That booming voice. And those strange blood-red clouds. Those clouds were probably the most disturbing part of that dream. There was something evil about them, something unholy.

Ordreth put his hand on Cornar's shoulder. "If you want to talk about it, you can," he said. "If not, that's okay. I'm here for you, Uncle."

That brought a smile to Cornar's face. Ordreth could always sooth his worries.

"It was just a dream," Cornar said. He wrapped his arm around his nephew, and they continued into the city.

——◦•◦——

Not far from the *Promised Maiden*'s wharf, Cornar and the others arrived at an inn, Heldergan's Flower. The inn was a decent place, but probably not something Gregan or Nordal were expecting. But it was *nice*. Probably the nicest place in Kretin. They filed inside and waited in a cramped welcoming room. There was a window to a clerk's office opposite the doors. A hallway lay to their right, leading to the other parts of the inn.

"Anyone here?" Krindal asked, stepping up to the clerk's window.

"Hold on," a cranky voice shouted, sounding old and husky. Soon, the top of a head bobbed beneath the window, and then a very short woman climbed atop a stool. She stood no taller than a child.

"Yes?" she asked.

"We'd like a suite," Krindal said. "For ten."

"Sorry," the woman said, "those darned elves took the last one."

"Elves?!" Krindal asked in a panic, backing away to the doors.

"Yeah," the midget woman said, "the people with pointed ears who speak that weird language."

"I know what they are," Krindal said, frantically grabbing the doorknob. "We'll find other accommodations."

The midget woman grunted. "Don't have to be a bigot. Not everyone can be normal-looking like you." Krindal ignored her and hurried out of the inn, Jahevial and Deglin close behind him. Cornar and his men, however, remained.

"Fine!" the midget woman shouted after Krindal. "We don't want to serve intolerant riff-raff like you anyway!"

Gregan glanced to Cornar and sighed. "This seems like the nicest place. The other inns we passed didn't seem suitable." Cornar shrugged.

"They're not!" the midget woman shouted. "You won't find a better inn in all Kretin!"

"Get a room or two," Cornar said. "I'll reimburse you. I'm going after Krindal."

Gregan stepped to the counter and apologized to the woman. Nordal was right beside him, being very cordial. Ordreth, however, stayed with Cornar, and they hurried into the street.

Krindal had darted off in such a hurry that Cornar couldn't see where he went.

"Let's split up," he suggested to Ordreth. "If you find him, stay with him until he settles on an inn, then come back here. I'll do the same if I find him."

Ordreth nodded and headed westward. Cornar went the opposite direction. He couldn't see Krindal nor Jahevial or Deglin. Where had they gone to? No other streets branched off from this one. There were alleyways, but they were dead ends. The roads to the south were on a higher tier of land.

Had Krindal made himself invisible? But why would he do that? Did the mention of elves scare him so much that he wanted to be completely unseen? What could have caused that?

19

DARKNESS

Cornar searched for hours, until well beyond nightfall. Much of Kretin was retiring for the night. Even some of the taverns were closing. Despite all his searching, Cornar found no sign of Krindal. Cornar had checked every inn, asking after the three necromancers, but none of the innkeepers had seen them. If Krindal had indeed made himself invisible, no amount of searching would unearth the old scholar. Krindal could be anywhere.

Finally, Cornar returned to Heldergan's Flower. He plodded into the inn's foyer where Ordreth waited patiently. His nephew looked tired.

"Any luck?" Cornar asked. Ordreth shook his head. "Where did he go?" Cornar wondered aloud.

Footsteps echoed into the inn's foyer, and Gregan appeared, holding a half-empty stein. "Where've *you* been?" Gregan asked, slurring his words.

"I was chasing Krindal," Cornar said. How long had he been gone?

"It's a three hours past midnight," Gregan groaned woozily.

"And you're still drinking?" Cornar asked.

"Yeah!" Gregan yelled, raising his stein. "I'm a proving that elves don't hold their liquor well. Three of them already backed out. I just got-got to get the last one…"

Elves, huh? Cornar mused. Well, as long as they were around, Krindal wouldn't be showing his face here. Cornar could resume the search in the morning.

Gregan peeled away and Ordreth followed.

"I need some sleep," Ordreth groaned. "Sharon is already upstairs. Nordal said she and a few others arrived while we were searching."

The mention of the thief piqued Cornar's interests. *Yes!* he thought. Sharon could help him search for Krindal. If Cornar had had her lenses, he would have easily found that Heleron-forsaken man. Those lenses were a type of tevisral, with the ability to see through invisibility spells and other magics.

Soon, Cornar was alone. He hurried down the hallway and entered the inn's tavern and dining area. It was a quaint place, only able to accommodate twenty or so patrons. Only one table was occupied. Gregan sat there with several elves.

The elves were tall and lanky, as most elves were. They had smooth faces and sharp features. Their ears were pointed at slight angles, reaching only a thumb's width higher than a man's ear. They all looked the same, not that all elves were indistinguishable, but these elves looked like they could have been brothers, or cousins at the very least.

Gregan aggressively gulped the rest of his stein and then slammed it on the table, taking a deep breath. The elves all laughed and clapped their hands approvingly, apparently amused by Gregan's ambition to best them.

"Can you handle another?" Gregan slurred, looking at the elf across from him.

The elf raised an eyebrow and smiled. "Of course!" He waggled his finger in Gregan's face. "You cannot hold another, I wager." The elf spoke with an accent and his words sounded sharp, choppy, and oddly formal. That was common with Mainland elves, because they didn't use contractions. Iltar had once told Cornar that it was because the elven tongue had none.

"You want to make a bet?" Gregan slurred.

The elf laughed. "A tingarn," he said, pulling the Losian iron coin from a satchel.

"A tingarn?" Gregan asked disappointedly. "That'll barely buy me another drink!"

"Drink another one of those, and it is yours," the elf said, pointing at the stein.

"Deal!" Gregan laughed and waved his hand high in the air, signaling for another drink.

A tired barkeep sauntered to the table, grabbed the stein, and disappeared behind the bar, where she refilled Gregan's drink. As Gregan and the elves continued bantering with each other, Cornar scanned the room. His eyes were drawn to a tall figure leaning against another doorway.

The stranger quietly watched Gregan and the elves, the expression on his chiseled face solemn. The stranger had wavy brown hair, eyes that matched his hair in color, and a neatly trimmed goatee and mustache. His thin lips were drawn to a line and he rarely blinked while studying the jovial drinking match. There was something about the man's gaze that Cornar disliked. Cornar could sense when there was something *wrong* about a person. That uneasiness drove his next action.

Cornar strode across the tavern to the man—no the elf… Cornar hadn't seen his pointed ears. How had he missed them? And an elf with a goatee? Cornar had never seen an elf with facial hair.

The dark-haired elf eyed Cornar, completely focused on him. The elf's brown eyes quickly scanned him, probably sizing him up as a potential threat. Was he like Cornar—an adventurer, a warrior?

Cornar thought it wise to lighten the mood. Two men—or rather an elf and a man—sizing each other up in a bar never led to anything good.

"So, how many did you have?" Cornar asked, and leaned against the wall beside the door.

"None," the elf said. His voice was deep and that single word didn't show signs of an elven accent.

"Just like to watch, huh?" Cornar asked.

The elf didn't respond. He seemed to keep one eye on the others and one on Cornar. Who was this elf? Cornar studied the mysterious elf for a moment, but then returned his gaze to Gregan. The drunken warrior struggled to finish his stein. The elf who had challenged him, however, steadily guzzled his drink.

"Ah…" the elf said, taking in a deep breath. "That was good. I will do another." He smiled wryly, watching Gregan.

Come on, Gregan, Cornar thought. *You got this…*

Gregan kept drinking, slowing each passing moment. Eventually he set his empty stein on the table. Gregan shook his head, breathing slowly. The elves applauded and cheered.

"I suppose this is yours," the challenger said, sliding the coin to Gregan.

Gregan nodded and took the coin, but didn't speak. He looked pale. Gregan's eyes widened, and he leaned forward, vomiting all over the floor.

The elves laughed again, more hysterically than before.

Poor Gregan, Cornar thought, walking toward the man. The dark-haired elf peeled away from the door, disappearing down a lantern-lit hallway. *Where are you going?*

Still wondering about the elf, Cornar reached Gregan and grabbed his shoulder, attempting to steady the drunken warrior. Gregan vomited again.

"You're done," Cornar said, urging Gregan from his seat.

"B-b-bu-but…" Gregan complained.

"No, you're done," Cornar said. "To bed with you." He bent down, pulling Gregan's arm over his shoulder.

Gregan stood at Cornar's behest but dropped the tingarn. Cornar didn't care to pick up the coin. The elves continued laughing as Cornar pulled Gregan across the tavern. *Damned pointed ears, can't they see he's helpless?* Cornar had dealt little with elves, but most of them were civil. This group, however, was downright despicable.

Soon, Cornar and Gregan were out of the dining room. "What room are we in?" Cornar asked. Gregan groaned something incoherent and gestured to his tunic. Cornar felt the spot, and his hand slid along the jagged outline of a key. *That works,* he thought, and reached into Gregan's tunic. The key had their room's number etched upon its wide end—twelve.

Cornar awoke late the next day and resumed his search for Krindal, but the man was nowhere to be found. Krindal's satchel with all his coin, however, was back on the *Promised Maiden*. The satchel had somehow appeared in Captain Salisar's cabin. Cornar deduced that Krindal had returned it after his hasty flight from the inn. But there was no note. None of the crew had seen Krindal either.

Cornar decided to gather the supplies himself, since he knew what they needed. Before lunch Cornar met with those who had stayed in Kretin; they had all returned to the *Promised Maiden* at his request. Cornar didn't trust meeting elsewhere. Krindal's disappearance made him leery.

Five other men stayed behind besides Ordreth, Sharon, Nordal, and Gregan: Cordel, Shen, Markin, Brendar, and Hem the illusionist. It was sometimes confusing having a man named Hemrin and Hem among their band. Luckily, Hemrin never went by a shorter nickname.

"We have some work cut out for us," Cornar said, setting the satchel of coin on a table in the mess deck. "We need to rent some wagons and horses first. Then we can round up supplies."

"How many are we going to need?" Cordel asked.

"We need to outfit an expedition of roughly six hundred," Cornar said.

Shen gasped. "Six hundred!" His green eyes widened with surprise. Shen was excitable, especially when it came to large things. The size of the expedition was no exception.

"So, how many wagons will that require?" Brendar asked.

"I'm thinking twelve to fifteen for the food," Cornar said. "But that depends on the size of the wagon beds. There's a river along the path we intend to take to Klindil, so we should be fine with water. But I wouldn't mind getting a few wagons to carry some barrels. We will get a few today, and reserve the rest to pick up later in the week. I think we should have everything prepared before the Mindolarnians arrive."

"We're going to need more people to drive the wagons," Brendar said, pursing his lips.

"We'll see," Cornar said. "Hopefully Krindal will show up with Jahevial and Deglin."

"Where did they go?" Shen asked.

Cornar shrugged and spread his hands. "Hopefully, he'll turn up."

"He was unnerved by those elves," Nordal said. "What was so frightening about them? They seemed fine. Not the best drinking partners, but not the worst either."

"Krindal acted like he'd seen a monster," Ordreth said. "I'm betting he went invisible with the other two. Uncle Cor and I looked everywhere. We couldn't find them."

"That's… odd," Shen said.

"Who were those elves, anyway?" Brendar asked.

"Mainland elves," Nordal said. "From someplace outside Merath. I don't remember the name. They seemed like decent folk."

"Really?" Shen asked. "Why would Krindal run away from that?"

That was an answer Cornar wished he knew. Krindal obviously intended to hide. The warriors debated what they should do about the matter. Cornar worried that searching for Krindal was not the correct course of action. But why? Krindal wasn't hiding from *those* elves, was he? What reasons would he have for that? It didn't make any sense. But every time Cornar thought of sending Sharon out with her lenses, he got a bad feeling in the pit of his stomach. Cornar knew to trust those instincts.

"We'll wait for him to show," Cornar said. "Krindal wouldn't abandon this quest now. I say we get what we need and meet up with the others. Three of you should go reserve supplies, the usual things we take with us on adventures. Gregan, are you up for doing that?"

Gregan nodded. He looked hung over, and rightly so. He had drunk like a lunatic last night.

"Good," Cornar said. "Markin, Cordel, and Shen, help Gregan. Pair up so you can cover more merchants. Ordreth and Sharon, join me in fetching the wagons. Hem, Brendar, and Nordal, the three of you go figure out where the others settled."

Everyone nodded in compliance.

"We'll meet at Heldergan's Flower tonight."

⟞ ⬥ ⟝

Kaescis settled into a battle stance within the observation room of the *Executor's Breath*. The ocean view was clear, and the horizon sprawled in every direction. His left leg slid forward, his torso angled in a line between his feet. Kaescis flung his right hand aside, uttering an incantation as fast as he could.

The black particles of the Ko'delish misted from his palm, forming a blade composed of the dissolving particles. The blade was shaped like a thick doubled-sided claymore, patterned after the weapons from that millennium-long war between the gods, the sha'kalda. The weapon was nearly as long as he was tall.

This weapon was not what he was used to summoning. His other weapons composed of the Ko'delish were barely two phineals long. This one was almost five.

"Practicing, Kaescis?" Bratan asked, his footsteps echoing into the observation room.

Kaescis turned, still clutching the newly formed blade.

"That blade seems a tad long," Bratan observed. "It's a good thing that such weapons are not inhibited by weight."

"That's why I'm practicing with it," Kaescis said, sweeping his sword. He lunged, executing a flurry of slices. His moves were precise. Kaescis was an expert at this method of swordsmanship.

Bratan leaned against the wall, arms folded.

Kaescis executed another succession of sweeping strokes. The blade came close to cutting the glass on the floor-to-ceiling windows. He pulled the last swing perfectly; the misting particles of the Ko'delish almost touched the windows.

"Impressive," Bratan said, clapping. "Very impressive!"

Kaescis reoriented himself, facing the opposite direction. He executed several more stroke combinations, each different from the ones he had performed earlier. Kaescis moved partway across the room, swinging his blade, and then reoriented himself again. He continued drilling techniques with the large blade. His arms didn't tire since there was no weight behind his swings. He swung magic, not metal.

Wielding a weapon composed of magic was harder than it looked. When swinging an actual sword one could *feel* the course it would take. There was a resistance to each movement. Yes, one could encounter resistance with a magically composed blade, but it was only against other forms of magic. That was a different sensation than striking a solid object with a metal sword. For one, there was no reverberation. Magic clashing against magic was like being stopped mid-motion.

Kaescis continued drilling his sword techniques, increasing the speed of his swings each time. More footsteps echoed into the observation room, but he didn't turn to see who was there. Kaescis was focused on more important things.

"He's still practicing, huh?" Laeyit asked, directing her question to Bratan.

"Yes," Bratan said, "Kaescis is doing quite well with that large blade."

"Of course he is!" Laeyit exclaimed, laughing. "He's not some simpleminded footman."

Laeyit and Bratan continued talking while Kaescis resumed his drills. Sweat beaded on his forehead and soon trickled down his face.

"Kaescis," Laeyit urged. "Why don't you take a break?"

A break? Why? Why on Kalda would he want to rest and relax? Did she not realize what awaited them on Klindala?

"You don't look pleased," Laeyit said.

Kaescis glimpsed Laeyit pouting. "No," Kaescis said, stopping mid-motion, then recoiling to unleash a flurry of blows while standing still.

"I think you're obsessed," Laeyit said.

Obsessed? No… he wasn't obsessed. He was enraged. The closer they got to Klindala the more anger he felt toward the enemies of the empire, particularly the Sapphire Guard.

Kaescis resumed swinging his black blade as his anger boiled. He imagined the ranks of that accursed band falling to his every stroke. It was like he was back at the last shrine. Kaescis stood alone, surrounded by armor-clad foes. He would kill them all before he let them take what rightfully belonged to the empire. The Isle of the Ancient Ones was his to claim and none else. Kaescis would heed the words of that stranger at the Feast of Sorrows. For the glory of Mindolarn, he would seize those tevisrals and bring order and servility to the world. Only the might of Mindolarn could bring peace and vanquish their ancient enemies once and for all.

"Kaescis!" Laeyit shouted, jarring him back to reality.

Surprised, Kaescis pulled his swing just before slicing through a pillar near Bratan and Laeyit. He was back in the observation room… Had he lost his focus while dwelling on his enemies? His technique had been perfect, but had his rage made him lose a sense of his surroundings? That had never happened in all his years.

Kaescis looked from his blade to the pillar. The black mist had eroded the polished finish and was now dissolving the wood, turning it to gray ash.

What was that sensation? he wondered. It was like an uncontrollable bloodlust.

Death… the word hissed in Kaescis's ears. *Destruction.*

Where was it coming from?

Kill. The word sounded like an echo.

Kaescis looked around, searching for the source of that strange voice.

Give us death… the words hissed again, this time sounding like several voices speaking in unison.

"What's wrong?" Bratan asked, sounding concerned. He only spoke like that during dire circumstances.

"Do you hear that?" Kaescis asked, scanning the room.

"Hear what?" Laeyit asked, sounding perturbed.

"The voices…" Kaescis slowly crossed the observation room.

"See," Laeyit said with exasperation, "his obsession is driving him mad!"

Bratan sighed. "Calm yourself, Laeyit."

"They want death," Kaescis said. "Could it be…?"

"Are you referring to the prophecy?" Bratan asked. "When the souls of the forgotten would speak to the Harbinger?"

Laeyit grunted. "That's a crude translation. Why would you consider a hiss'thrak to be a soul when every legend describes them as insect-like creatures? There's even a children's story about them."

"Because those forms are only metaphors," Bratan retorted.

Laeyit and Bratan argued about the nature of the hiss'thraks, the beings responsible for manifesting the Ko'delish. Hiss'thraks produced those black particles of magic—how, Kaescis didn't know.

Kaescis ignored the argument and looked at his weapon, which was still misting. There was an otherworldly pull drawing him toward the blackness. Kaescis heard voices coming from the mist, like faint echoes bouncing off a cavern's walls. The words were not clear, but he sensed a commonality.

Death.

✦

"This is madness, Krindal," Jahevial groaned.

Cloaked in an invisibility spell, Krindal ignored the man and peered around the corner of the alleyway. He had to be careful to remain unseen with *them* around. If not, he was doomed.

"We can just settle into a place," Jahevial said. "There's no point moving every hour." The damned fool didn't know what he was talking about. Of course they had to keep moving. It was the only way to stay ahead of *them.*

"Are you even sure they're part of the Sapphire Guard?" Deglin asked.

"Why else would elves be here?" Krindal whispered.

"Plenty of reasons," Jahevial said.

What do they know? Krindal thought. *They aren't adventurers.* Of all the people to get stuck with, Krindal had to be stranded with these idiots. Did they not know of the Sapphire Guard's reputation? Had they not listened to his tale of the encounter at the last Keepers' Temple? Krindal had told them yesterday. What were they, senile?

"It's clear," Krindal whispered.

"Wait," Jahevial said, agitated. Krindal paused and crept back into the alley. "How long are we going to keep doing this?" Jahevial demanded.

"Until the prince arrives," Krindal said. "Then we can join the others in that village outside Kretin."

"That's asinine!" Deglin almost shouted.

"Quiet!" Krindal chided through clenched teeth.

"*You* can keep on hiding," Jahevial said, and dismissed his invisibility. They had each cast their own concealing spells. "I'm going to find a place to rest."

Krindal panicked. "But—"

"No," Jahevial interrupted, "they don't know me. For Kalda's sake, I doubt they even saw you! You really are paranoid, Krindal."

Jahevial wouldn't have said that if he only lived through the horror of what had transpired in the Igeacean Sea.

"I agree," Deglin said. "I appreciate your concern for us, but I don't think we're in any danger. We'll help Cornar gather those supplies."

"Fine," Krindal whispered. *Perhaps it is better this way…* He could more easily sneak about Kretin alone. But if he got tired… *No!* He couldn't sleep, not until Prince Kaescis arrived.

Jahevial and Deglin exited the alley without any further acknowledgment of Krindal. They mingled with the sparse traffic, making their way back to the docking district.

Perhaps I should find an attic or cellar in which to squat, Krindal thought. He could sleep there. He needed sleep. It was getting late after all. Dusk had already settled and nightfall would soon be upon Kretin.

20

THE STICKS

> *"The Grand Oracle and the Unspoken One shall meet. Their encounter will herald the beginning of Cheserith's return."*
>
> *- Prophecy of Soron Thahan*

Everything was peaceful in the village of Klarin, the settlement where Igan and the band had decided to stay. Klarin was one of four villages on the outskirts of Kretin, the farthest away from the city. Kalder had thought it a wise position, and Igan agreed with the warrior. Kalder was a wise man—he had been raised by Cornar, after all. Cornar's wisdom rubbed off on anyone who spent a great deal of time with him. Even Igan felt wiser for being Cornar's friend.

The place Kalder chose to take up lodging looked more like a farmstead than an inn. Igan had learned that the inheritors of the farmstead had turned it into an inn about forty years ago. They made some additions and turned the barn into another wing to accommodate more guests. The inn wasn't large by any means. It wouldn't accommodate everyone from the *Promised Maiden,* so some of Cornar's men pitched tents in the pasture behind the inn. There was one more place that they could stay, but Kalder didn't want them spread across the village.

The past few days had been uneventful. Each day, Igan had sat in a rocking chair on the inn's side porch. It allowed a view to the pasture and the nearby forest. This was a particularly good spot for quiet contemplation, despite the warriors practicing in the pasture.

Igan let out a sigh and rocked his chair, watching the warriors. The men were sparring or drilling forms with their weapons. It was a comforting sight to see them practice. Mages needed a strong wall of defense during a battle, and these men were just that.

"Aren't you getting anxious?" Vargos asked.

No, he wasn't. Igan was a patient man. In fact, this entire part of their quest was quite relaxing. Igan glanced to Vargos. "Are you?" he asked.

The rugged barsionist stopped beside the rocking chair, his hair disheveled as if he'd barely awoken from a nap. "Ha!" Vargos grunted. "Don't twist things around on me, boy."

"Boy?" Igan smiled. Well, Vargos was several years his senior. The barsionist was in his thirties when Igan and the others first accompanied him on an adventure. Igan was eighteen. He was a boy back then. *My, that was a long time ago...*

"Yeah," Vargos said. "Don't you think they should be saving their strength?" He pointed to the warriors.

"We're leaving today," Igan said matter-of-factly.

Vargos grunted, sauntering to another rocking chair. "So what do you make of ole Krindal disappearing?"

"I don't know," Igan said, narrowing his gaze at the warriors. He rested his elbows on the chair and brought his hands together, clasping them beneath his chin. "I've been wondering why he disappeared, but haven't come up with anything reasonable."

"Krindal better turn up." Vargos fidgeted in his chair, trying to get comfortable, but the chairs weren't made with the best of craftsmanship. "Otherwise, we're without a map. Then what are we supposed to do? Go unearth all those ruins?"

"It's only been four days."

"And why would Jahevial and Deglin disappear?" Vargos grunted again. "I hate this chair!"

Igan grinned at the outburst, then said, "The other scholars found it odd. They were just as perplexed as we are about the disappearances."

Another pair of footsteps echoed into the porch. Igan turned in his chair. "Cor!" he blurted, eyeing the burly man as he approached, his gait confident and determined. The warrior always carried himself in a way that commanded respect. He always looked sure of himself, even when he was unsure. That's why so many men followed him. He was the type of man that would run into a burning house to save those inside and somehow manage to inspire a bunch of others to follow him. How Cornar did it Igan didn't know.

Cornar stopped beside the rocking chair, putting his hands on his hips.

"Do you have the *stuff*?" Vargos asked.

"Nearly all of it. Fifteen wagons. Five of them are back in town. We'll do another run in the morning."

"Any word from Krindal?" Igan asked.

"Well, Jahevial and Deglin returned to our inn the evening I sent Nordal to find you," Cornar said, scratching his beard. It had grown to what Igan was accustomed to seeing. Cornar could grow a good beard, but he only did it while away from home. "They said Krindal was raving about danger. He flew into a panic upon hearing that elves were staying at our inn. Jahevial was tired of Krindal's paranoid behavior and left him. Krindal's wandering somewhere around Kretin."

"Did they say what kind of danger?" Igan asked. He couldn't think of many connections between elves and danger. Most elves were peaceful. In fact, no elf had ever participated in any of the recent wars. Not to mention, they rarely ventured out of their realm in the west. What would elves be doing all the way out here?

"No," Cornar said with a sigh. "I tried to pry it from them, but Jahevial said it wasn't worth his time explaining."

"Pompous bastard," Vargos grumbled.

Cornar nodded. "The elves left port yesterday. I checked with the harbormaster, and he said their ship had come from Bradisar and was bound for Merath. I've sent Sharon and Ordreth to do some digging. See if there are any other elves around the city. Those I met were rude, but ultimately harmless."

Vargos went on a rant, but Igan ignored it, racking his brain trying to figure out a connection between the elves and Krindal's flight. Elves weren't typically explorers. Well, not Mainland elves—which were undoubtedly what Cornar and the others had encountered.

But… elves from Merdan got around the world. What were they called? They had an odd name for themselves, not very elven-sounding—

"Igan," Cornar said, "do you want to join me in the morning?"

Igan blinked, staring at Cornar for a moment. What was that name?

"He's daydreamin'…" Vargos grumbled.

"Yes," Igan said.

"Good." Cornar stretched his arms. "I'm going to join my men, let off some steam. We'll leave at sunrise." Cornar continued across the porch to a short flight of stairs and hurried into the pasture.

"I can't believe you were daydreamin'," Vargos said, shifting in his chair.

"I was thinking," Igan corrected the old barsionist. He was not daydreaming.

"Same thing," Vargos said, flicking his wrist as he sighed. "These chairs are horrible…" The old barsionist rose from his seat and stalked away, grumbling annoyances about the inn's poor accommodations.

Igan chuckled, but watched Cornar join the ranks of his men, where he fell in line and began drilling forms with his weapons.

Oh! Igan thought. *The Elven Aristocracy of Merdan!* That was their name. Those elves were a strange bunch. Igan had never met any of them, but from what he understood, the Elven Aristocracy of Merdan acted more like men than elves, most definitely *not* like Mainland elves. Igan had only ever met one elf from Merdan—well really, a half-elf. Iltar's apprentice, Balden. Balden was definitely more man than elf in many ways.

Igan narrowed his eyes in concentration, watching Cornar with his men. *But why would Krindal be afraid of them?* The Elven Aristocracy of Merdan was a merchant coalition. Why would a necromancer be afraid of wealthy merchants?

Krindal sneaked behind a caravan of five wagons driven by Cornar, three of his men, and the wizard Igan. The warrior didn't know he was following them, of course. Krindal had stumbled upon them and overheard their plans to deliver the rest of the carts to the others in a village named Klarin. He couldn't just make his presence known. That would be foolhardy. Anyone could be watching.

A cool afternoon breeze wisped past Krindal, and he pulled his invisible robe tight around him. Just because he wasn't discernible to one's eyes didn't mean he wasn't detectable by one's ears.

Someone could hear him rustling! He couldn't have that…

The wagons turned a corner, rounding a grove of trees with turning leaves, and then a cluster of buildings appeared. Was that Klarin? It looked so small. *Village* was probably the wrong term for such a tiny place.

Krindal continued creeping behind the wagons as they moved through the only street in the village. Watchful eyes stared at the wagons as they passed.

For magic's sake, he gasped inwardly, *I can't appear here.*

The wagons turned onto a dirt path near the southern part of the village. The path was the only thing that diverged from the road.

Krindal peered around the caravan. A large farmhouse stood at the edge of a sprawling field.

Why would they be staying here? Krindal thought. *We don't have enough money to rent a farmhouse!*

The caravan neared a wooden sign with faded paint. It read, *"Thurgar's Farmhouse, the only place for travelers to stay in Klarin."*

Oh. Krindal felt slightly ashamed. He took another look at the field, and it looked barren, besides the wild grass.

The caravan pulled up beside ten other wagons, each full of supplies. Cornar dismounted and gave orders to his men, then walked to the farm-house with Igan.

Krindal followed.

"I hope he shows," Igan said as he and Cornar stepped into a covered porch. "It's a pity she couldn't find him."

Who was he talking about?

"Kretin is a fairly large city," Cornar said. "Sharon's still looking. I told her and Ordreth to stay in town for another day."

Oh, that thieving woman. Krindal had heard of her and her troupe using some kind of tevisral to see through invisibility. He felt some relief that she couldn't find him. If she couldn't, perhaps those elves couldn't either. But he wasn't safe yet.

Krindal had to hide.

Igan took a seat in one of two rocking chairs, but Cornar remained standing, talking about his plans until Prince Kaescis arrived.

Ignoring the conversation, Krindal scanned the area around the farmhouse. It was a good five hundred phineals away from the road. He could appear… but what if *they* were watching him? He'd be seen, and they'd come in their wrath upon Cornar and his band. *They* would slaughter them. No, Krindal couldn't have that! It was best he remained hidden. Perhaps the farmhouse had an empty attic…

Footsteps reached Krindal's ears, and Cornar walked away from Igan. *I better stay close,* he thought as he crept toward the warrior.

Cornar went straight for the farmhouse's side entrance, opened the door, and called for Kalder as he entered. Krindal slipped inside right behind him.

The warrior continued calling for the man, but Krindal didn't care to listen. He had to find some stairs.

Careful not to make any noise, Krindal crept through the farmhouse. He tiptoed into a kitchen where a middle-aged couple—probably the owners of the place—were cooking a stew and talking about their guests.

Krindal stopped to listen. They couldn't be spying on them, could they? He had to be sure.

No, it was just casual chatter. *That's a relief.* Satisfied, Krindal crept through a butler's pantry and into a dining room. Cornar and another man were talking nearby. It wasn't Kalder.

Where were those darned stairs? He crept toward the sound and found the warriors in a hallway. No stairs there…

This place is confusing, he thought, and continued down the hall. It turned a corner, opening to another part of the home that didn't seem part of the original construction.

Soon, he found a staircase, with windows all along it. *Too many windows,* he thought and climbed the steps. A floorboard squeaked, and Krindal froze, sucking in his breath. He looked around, panicked.

No one was nearby.

Relieved, he continued up the stairs, ever careful.

Faint chatter echoed from behind the closed door of the second-story room. Krindal recognized one of the voices, but not the others. No other guests were staying here besides Cornar's band, were they?

He definitely couldn't appear! Steeling himself, Krindal crept through the upper floor of the farmhouse-turned-inn. He searched the entire floor but didn't see an entrance to an attic.

What was he going to do now?

He couldn't just appear, not without arousing suspicion. And if he did appear, Cornar would probably recall those two who were looking for him, and what if *they* overheard that recall, or saw it and wondered why the thief-woman stopped looking?

No, it was best to stay hidden. But Krindal couldn't stay in this hallway. What to do? What to do? It was times like this he wished he knew how to conjure something or make an illusion. He could find that attic with either of those.

Do I start checking doors? he wondered.

Footsteps echoed from the hallway, accompanied by a faint voice.

"… up here," the voice said. It sounded like the man in the kitchen. "We haven't used them since the farm shut down."

"I appreciate you lending them to me," Cornar said.

The footsteps grew louder and Cornar rounded the corner with the farmhouse's owner. They were walking straight toward Krindal.

Krindal froze. His heartbeat quickened. He could feel it thumping in his chest. *By all that's magical, calm yourself!*

"This door," the owner said, grabbing the handle of the door beside Krindal. "Just bring the tools back when you're done."

The farmhouse's owner opened the door, revealing a dusty anteroom and some stairs. *Stairs!*

Yes! Krindal cheered.

Cornar followed the owner, and they climbed the rickety stairs. Their footsteps were loud and sounded like they could echo throughout the entire farmhouse.

Krindal better be careful on that staircase.

After they were well inside the attic, Krindal crept to the anteroom. He climbed the stairs, taking one step at a time. There was some creaking, but it was muffled by the clatter of things moving and the conversation between Cornar and the owner.

The noises ceased as Krindal left the top step.

Phew… just in time, he thought. He stepped aside and surveyed the space. Sunlight shone through a pair of dormers to his left. Those dormers would be facing the village if he correctly remembered the course he had traveled thus far. He'd have to be careful moving around those. But piles of things—old furniture, children's toys, clothes, paintings, and farm equipment—were scattered all over, so Krindal could easily evade the sight of any prying eyes.

Footsteps echoed through the attic and Cornar returned with the owner, carrying a metal box. They talked while descending the staircase and then shut the door.

I should look around, Krindal thought. *But I can't get comfy until Cornar returns those tools. Can't let him find me here.*

"He will suffer in the depths of the void for a season. No light shines there, nor can it be made manifest."

- Prophecy of Soron Thahan

The sea looked calm to Iltar. The *Yaelinum* had left Soroth two-and-a-half weeks ago and would moor in Mindolarn any day now. Iltar stood at the bow, gazing at the waters. The fresh sea breeze was a welcome change from the stuffy cabins. Iltar had spent countless hours these last few days rereading *The Codices of Soron Thahan* with Countess Elsia. She was an inquisitive woman with a keen mind. At first, Iltar had considered Elsia an annoyance and a burden, but after a few days she began to grow on him.

Elsia had cross-referenced much of the information in the tome. She took particular interest in the group called the Chosen. From what Iltar and Elsia deduced, the Chosen were a select group of humanity that was entrusted to see that the world stayed aligned with the ideals of the ancient Kaldeans. The Chosen were to watch over the inhabitants of Kalda and make corrections to their civilization. Iltar couldn't help but think of these Chosen as individuals who ensured that the river of men—as spoken in parable by Reflection—stayed on the right course.

But Reflection claimed that the Chosen had faltered. The Chosen obviously weren't doing what they were supposed to do. Soron didn't come right out and say it, but Iltar deduced that at some time after writing the *Codices* tome, the Chosen would stop performing their duties.

Elsia also made meticulous notes on the various foretold acts of the person called the Unspoken One. Iltar made a copy of that list for himself. If he truly was this Unspoken One, he'd best understand the things he must do… or had done.

"Master Iltar," Bilda said behind him. Iltar turned as the boy approached, holding fast to the rail. Bilda looked a little scared.

"What is it, Bilda?"

"Well… uh, we're just wondering if we're going to be there today."

Iltar grinned and returned his gaze to the horizon. "I don't know."

"Can't you use some magic to see how far away we are?"

What? Iltar grinned. He turned back to Bilda, who looked sheepish. "I have no means to measure nautical distance," Iltar said.

"Oh…" Bilda sighed and turned around, tightly gripping the rail. The boy acted as if he were about to be tossed into the ocean.

Iltar watched Bilda creep across the high deck and descend the stairs to the enclosed parts of the ship. Once Bilda was gone, Iltar returned his gaze to the horizon. He stared at the line between ocean and sky until a sailor from the crow's nest shouted down a report.

"Fleet spotted off the starboard bow!"

Intrigued, Iltar turned and watched as another sailor ran across the high deck to the mast where the crow's nest sat. The sailor up top yelled down the specifics. It sounded like a merchant convoy.

We should be there soon, Iltar thought.

Another hour passed, and more ships were spotted off the port and starboard rails. The *Yaelinum* was definitely nearing Mindolarn.

Iltar strode across the high deck, following the path Bilda had taken. The boys wanted to be told when the ship neared Mindolarn so they could see the grand city across the horizon. It was a sight that intrigued Iltar as well, since he had never been to Mindolarn.

Once below deck, Iltar approached one of the ship's parlors, where his acolytes were enjoying the pleasures inherent to the vessel. The *Yaelinum* was meant to host lavish parties and entertain the most sophisticated of minds. Luxurious was an understatement. Iltar didn't see any harm in permitting them to enjoy themselves, since they would have their work cut out for them in Mindolarn.

The twelve acolytes were spread throughout the room. A few were reading while others played games. Bilda was sitting with Tigan at one of the tables, playing a strategy game called Tambrino. The game was played atop a fourteen-by-twelve grid, with the objective to capture your opponent's pieces using your own. Each piece had a predetermined set of movements to advance and capture. Tambrino had various rule sets, but the game typically ended when one player lost their last piece.

Iltar had once witnessed a Tambrino tournament in Comdolith. The tournament used a modified rule set that awarded points based on the capture of certain pieces by other pieces. One could theoretically lose the match but win based on overall points. That exact thing happened to the man who won the final match. He had won each of his matches, but lost the tournament because his opponent had a better overall point score.

Several boys noticed Iltar, and each turned toward him. "We're getting close," Iltar said, passing the parlor. "But no land has been sighted."

Sighs reached Iltar's ears as he continued toward Elsia's cabin. Soft chatter sounded through the ajar door, the voices of Pagus and Elsia.

"… conclusion that they might be the same," the countess said, sounding excited. Iltar stopped and listened. What was she talking about?

"That's intriguing!" Pagus blurted.

"Makes me wish I had gone with them," Elsia said, sighing.

"I'm sure you can go visit it later," Pagus reassured her. "And this way you won't have to go through any of the grueling dangers of exploration."

Elsia chuckled. "Oh, Pagus…"

Once the conversation ceased, Iltar knocked twice and then strode inside. Pagus sat in an oversized chair beside his aunt, who lounged in her own throne-like seat turned partway from her desk.

Elsia smiled at him as he entered. Iltar found it odd to have a woman smile at him like that. Sure, Belsina smiled at him, but he was her employer. Belsina was obligated to smile.

"Had enough fresh air?" Elsia asked, putting her elbow on the desk.

"One can never have *enough* fresh air," Iltar said, pacing the cabin. It was quite large, about the size of the parlor were all the acolytes were relaxing. "Some ships were sighted nearby, all heading north."

"We should be close then," Elsia said, running her fingers through her hair. "I was just telling my nephew here about a theory I have been musing upon."

"Oh?"

Elsia looked at Iltar with a wry grin, pursing her lips. Iltar learned that expression meant she was not pleased with him. It was not quite exasperation, but it was close to it. Damnation, what would it have been like to be married to this woman? No wonder the count was willing to let her come along.

"You said that Krindal was searching for an ancient Order," Elsia said. "I think the Chosen *are* that Order."

That connection had crossed his mind, but Iltar had dismissed it. Reflection hadn't mentioned them being one and the same.

"Nothing to say?" Elsia asked.

"It makes sense," Pagus chimed in. "The Keepers title conveys the same responsibility as the Chosen. A select group of men, meant to make sure everything stays right. I bet that's why our world has regressed, as Krindal put it—"

"*Master* Krindal," Iltar interrupted. He would ensure Pagus used proper titles.

Pagus rolled his eyes, "Yeah… Uh, where was I? Oh! Without any Keepers or Chosen to maintain things, society crumbled. That would explain why the prince is so interested."

What an interesting theory. Although, it probably wasn't correct. Pagus was jumping to conclusions without all the facts.

"You're not convinced," Elsia turned back to her desk. "That's okay…" Was she sulking now? *Women,* Iltar groaned.

"I have everything prepared for your acolytes," Elsia said, rising from her chair with a stack of sheets in her hand. "I included your questions, as well as detailed breakdowns of what we have discovered." She handed the papers to Iltar.

He took them, perusing their contents: twelve sets, one for each of his acolytes.

"I already gave my nephew his copy," Elsia said. "Now if you'll excuse me, I'd like to rest before we moor."

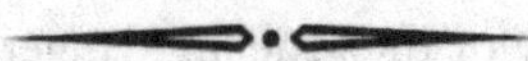

That afternoon, Iltar stood at the bow with the boys. The acolytes gazed eagerly toward the horizon at the majestic city of Mindolarn. Towers rose into the sky all around the city, higher than Iltar had ever seen in the human realm. They were probably lookout towers. Two of the towers were in the ocean, on either end of the port. Walls connected the towers to the land, hemming the port.

Much of the city's terrain was hilly, which raised Mindolarn considerably above the ocean. Except for the towers, the city's skyline didn't look too different from other cities across the world.

"Amazing!" one of the boys exclaimed.

"Look, is that the palace?" another cried, pointing.

Iltar followed the acolyte's gesture. A shallow, red-brown, domed structure stood atop the highest point in the city; it was surrounded by several towers like those around Mindolarn.

"Probably," Iltar said.

"Do you think we can visit it?" Bilda asked. The boy held tight to the rail, just as he had done earlier that day.

"I doubt they'll let us tour it," Pagus said, folding his arms. Bilda frowned. Several of the other boys murmured about Pagus's answer.

"This place sure is busy," Agen said, noting the vessels that were moving toward the port. The *Yaelinum* had been joined by dozens of other ships sailing for Mindolarn.

Distinct footsteps—from a woman's boot—clicked across the high deck behind him and the boys. Iltar glanced over his shoulder as Countess Elsia approached. She was dressed in a pair of women's trousers and a plain blouse. Her light-brown hair was pulled back in a simple ponytail and her face bore hardly any makeup. Elsia didn't look aristocratic in the slightest.

"Enjoying the view?" she asked the boys.

"Yes, ma'am," several replied in unison. Others just nodded, still gazing across the bow. The acolytes continued staring at the city as the *Yaelinum* veered westward, following the other ships. An acolyte shouted to one of the sailors, asking where they were going. The sailor replied that all ships coming into Mindolarn from the sea flowed into port from the west while all departing vessels left along the east.

The *Yaelinum* drifted close to the western tower in the ocean. At this distance Iltar had a better view. It rose to what he guessed to be twenty stories. The wall that connected it to the city was eye level with the *Yaelinum's* high deck—which was four decks above the waterline.

"So where are we staying?" Agen asked.

"I have a friend that will give us lodging," Elsia said while eyeing the bridging wall. "She has a guesthouse that is big enough for all of us."

The young acolytes gasped; probably surprised at the implication that the guesthouse could fit them all. They undoubtedly expected that each would have their own room. Iltar knew better. The acolytes would probably be squished into a couple of bedrooms. Iltar and the countess would be the only ones not sharing a room.

Iltar raised an eyebrow at her. "I was planning on renting some rooms near the Hilinard."

"She's not too far from there," Elsia said, not looking at Iltar. Was she still upset about his reaction earlier? *Women…*

After an hour of sailing through the port, the *Yaelinum* moored at the end of a long stone pier far more extravagant than the wooden piers in Soroth. Lightstones imbedded into ornate stonework lined the pier, with gold-plated reliefs of a seven-headed hydra between berths. Deckhands scurried about the high deck, furling the sails and securing the lines.

"We should get moving," Elsia said, then gestured for Iltar to follow. "I suggest we leave the boys here," she said, waiting for Iltar. Once he was near, Elsia intertwined her arm with his.

"Why?" Iltar glanced to her arm, not amused.

"It'll be easier to get a carriage for two," she said, guiding him across the deck. "We can send for them in the morning."

Leaving Pagus alone overnight? That struck Iltar as worrisome.

"My nephew will be fine," Elsia said, gesturing with her freehand to the boys still at the bow. The acolytes were watching the sailors lower the gang-way. "I'll instruct the servants to keep everyone aboard. They'll see to it."

Elsia obviously didn't know her nephew as well as she thought she did. Iltar could easily imagine Pagus slipping away, using his abilities to make an illusion of himself to stay aboard while invisibly sneaking off the boat.

"You don't approve?" Elsia asked as they descended the stairs.

"I think you underestimate Pagus's sense of curiosity."

"Do you mean mischief?" She grinned. "I'm not naïve, Iltar. And you don't need to hold back with me." They descended another flight of stairs and wound their way through the ship's corridors. "The servants packed your things," Elsia said. "I hope you don't mind. I didn't want your time with the boys interrupted."

Iltar drew his lips to a line. He didn't like anyone touching his things.

Elsia laughed, patting his shoulder. "Iltar, Iltar… you're going to need to accept others doing things for you. You are—by association—a member of the higher echelons of society. I had heard of your grandmaster's need to control every facet of his life, but I didn't expect you to be as bad as he is."

How dare she compare me to—

"Your Excellency." A servant stepped up, drawing Iltar's attention. The man bowed to Elsia. "I have ordered a dockhand to fetch a carriage. Yours and Master Iltar's trunks are waiting on the pier."

"Thank you," Elsia said, bowing her head. She looked to Iltar and asked, "Shall we wait outside?"

22

HIGH DUCHESS ALANYA TASIVIR

"Kildath shall fall in one day. The Tower shall vanish before the glorious power of the Chosen."

- Prophecy of Soron Thahan

The ride through Mindolarn was quite interesting. It wasn't laid out in a grid like Soroth. Many of the roads followed the terrain, weaving around hills. Most buildings they passed were made of stone, of what stone Iltar couldn't tell. The buildings looked like they might have been transmuted, but most transmuted structures would collapse after the mage who formed it lost his concentration.

Each road they traveled was more affluent than the last. They hadn't passed through any of the poor parts of the city, of course. The coachman driving the carriage knew his passengers were important people, even though they were dressed simply.

Darkness settled upon the city as the carriage came to a halt.

"We're here," Elsia said, gazing out the window. She had since put on more makeup and braided her hair since leaving the docking district. Elsia looked like herself; at least the self Iltar was accustomed to seeing. Even throughout their long nights of research, Elsia had looked her best.

The door opened, and the coachman stood nearby, hand on the door. Elsia exited first, carrying a small bag, then Iltar stepped down to join her. The carriage door shut behind Iltar as he eyed the home belonging to Elsia's friend, the High Duchess Alanya Tasivir. It was massive. This wasn't a home… it was a mansion!

A fence made of dark-orange stone and wrought iron surrounded the property, spanning several city blocks. The *mansion*—which was set back from the fence—was made of the same orange stone and rose five stories in some spots. Another building, about the size of Cornar's country home, was off to the left—most likely the guesthouse.

The coachman removed Elsia and Iltar's trunks and set them before a pair of guards standing at a gate in the wall. Each guard wore an elaborate red coat adorned with fanciful patterns over red-and-brown leather armor. Side swords hung at their waists, sheathed in black scabbards.

"I am Countess Elsia Scurn of Sarn," Elsia said, approaching the guards. The guards bowed and then opened the gate. They must have been expecting her. How, Iltar didn't know.

One of the guards entered the grounds while the other stooped to grab Iltar's trunk.

"I've got it," Iltar said, extending his hand. Wordlessly, the man turned to the countess's belongings.

Elsia sighed and put her hands on her hips. "Iltar, I thought I told you that—"

Iltar held up a finger, then began an incantation. White-gray light gathered in his hand, and then shot to the trunk, lifting it into the air. It hovered at waist height.

With his spell finished, Iltar grabbed a handle and dragged the trunk through the air. Elsia's eyes widened, and she looked impressed. "You were saying?" Iltar asked smugly. Elsia shook her head, fighting a smile.

Soon, more guards joined them at the gate. They had undoubtedly been fetched to help with the luggage. Each started upon seeing Iltar dragging his trunk through the air.

"Come with me, Your Excellency," one of the guards said. He led them down a wide stone walkway toward the mansion. They entered a towering portico, held up by off-white pillars. Colorful stone vines wound up each of the pillars. At first glance they looked to be real, but once Iltar was closer, he could see the vines' stone texture.

Another man stood near the mansion's two-story doors. He was of average height and wore a fancy dark-orange coat with white tassels. "Welcome, welcome!" the man said. "I am Hazais, the high duchess's butler. You are Countess Elsia Scurn of Sarn, I presume?"

"I am," Elsia said as she curtsied.

"And this is your bodyguard?" Hazais asked, pointing to Iltar.

"Yes."

Oh right. The whole lie. Iltar had nearly forgotten about the ruse. Elsia hadn't mentioned it since their first meeting.

Hazais studied Iltar for a moment with pursed lips and a raised brow. Iltar didn't look like a bodyguard. *Cor would have been more believable,* he thought. Cornar's physique was more imposing than Iltar's. *Perhaps I should have worn an illusion,* he thought, chuckling inwardly.

The butler abruptly shot a glance beyond Iltar, where his trunk floated. "Ah... a mage," Hazais said, nodding. "A wise choice for protection, Your Excellency. Please, come in."

Guards opened the two-story doors, and Hazais ushered Iltar and Elsia into the mansion. They entered a foyer that was at least double the size of Iltar's living and dining room combined. Suits of armor lined the walls between archways and hallways.

"Follow me," Hazais said, walking to the right. "I will inform the high duchess of your arrival." The butler stopped at an archway leading to a parlor that could seat thirty. The parlor was lit by extravagant lightstone sconces and a chandelier that looked like it belonged in a palace.

Elsia entered the room briskly, and Iltar trailed behind her, leaving his trunk hovering within the archway. The butler instructed the guard to set Elsia's trunk near the parlor's entrance.

A thud echoed between the rooms, followed by fading footsteps. Iltar and Elsia were alone in the parlor. The countess walked to one of many couches and sat primly upon it. Iltar, however, roamed the parlor.

"Are you playing the part?" she asked, fighting back laughter. Iltar looked to Elsia. She had her hand to her lips, smiling deviously. Was she mocking him?

"No," Iltar answered, and continued walking around the room. He was simply admiring the room's detail: deep coffered ceilings, walls with colorful scrollwork. Paintings hung on the walls as well, and those intrigued him. Most were beautiful landscapes, except one. Iltar started upon seeing that *remarkable* scene, then picked his way across the parlor toward the peculiar painting.

"Impossible…" he muttered.

"What are you whispering about?" Elsia asked, sounding playful.

Iltar ignored her and focused on the painting. Seven figures lay prostrate upon a glassy ground before a slender man in a red robe. The man in red stood with his hands outstretched, looking up at a yellow sky and surrounded by a black aura. An elaborate crown with seven curved points, ornamented with crimson jewels, hovered above him. Above the crown hung a blue sun, its pale-blue light beaming through the crown and highlighting the centermost prostrate man.

"Reflection…" Iltar whispered. "In Vabenack…" *But who are these seven?* Curious, Iltar stepped closer to the painting, searching the red robe for any symbols. But there weren't any. Iltar examined each of the prostrate men, but he couldn't see any detail on their faces. Their hair color was their only distinguishable feature. The center one had blond hair. The others were varying shades of brown and black.

"Iltar…" A hand pressed on his shoulder. Turning around, Iltar found Elsia staring worriedly at him.

"What?"

"You weren't answering me," she said, removing her hand from his shoulder.

"Sorry," Iltar said dispassionately and returned his attention to the painting.

"Do you suppose that's the Messenger of the Promise?" Elsia asked, pointing to the man in red. Iltar didn't answer. He continued to marvel at the painting. *Those details are too perfect to be a coincidence,* Iltar thought, looking for anything else that might prove enlightening.

"Elsia!" A woman's voice rang from the foyer. The unmistakable clicking of Elsia's boots filled the parlor as she spun and crossed the room. Both women exchanged greetings, sounding like excited girls sharing a secret.

Women… Iltar rolled his eyes, still studying the painting.

"Iltar, come here," Elsia urged.

Sighing, Iltar turned around and started upon seeing the high duchess. *By all that's magical,* he gasped. Alanya Tasivir was tall and slender, with a mature but lovely face. Olive skin accented her braided brown hair. Golden jewelry contrasted with her striking emerald eyes. The gown she wore would make most women's dresses look like rags. Despite the elegant attire, she looked Sorothian. She was… she was breathtaking! Iltar couldn't help but stare at her.

Alanya grinned playfully at Elsia, then looked Iltar up and down. She turned away from him and focused on Elsia.

"Don't worry, he's harmless," Elsia said, waving her hand in a placating gesture.

"That's a horrible trait for a bodyguard," the high duchess said with a chuckle.

Elsia laughed, clapping her hand over her mouth to muffle her laughter, and then ran her hand through her hair. "I mean, in *other* ways." What did she mean by that?

The women moved to the couches and resumed their conversation. Iltar stared at Alanya as she seated herself with perfect poise. *She's tantalizing.*

While the women conversed, Alanya glanced to Iltar several times, but always redirected her focus to Elsia.

Got to stop staring. Iltar gritted his teeth and spun around. *Focus on the painting.*

"Do you like that painting, Master Iltar?" the high duchess asked.

Iltar turned slowly. "It is interesting," he said. "Does it have a name?"

"The Calling of an Emperor," Alanya said. "It's supposed to be Emperor Mindolarn's divine appointment by… I don't remember who." She chuckled and waved her hand negligently over her shoulder. "Some important figure in Cherisium."

Alanya resumed talking to Elsia but Iltar interrupted them. "Do you know where this scene is supposed to have taken place?" Elsia turned to him, surprised at his intrusion.

"I'm sorry, I don't," Alanya said, then waited for Elsia to turn around.

Elsia mouthed something to Iltar, which looked like, *"Come over here."* After a moment Iltar decided to act upon that instruction and came to stand behind Elsia. He might as well *act* like a bodyguard.

Once Iltar joined her, Elsia turned back to the high duchess. "As I was saying, we're splitting up. My husband is in hiding. We thought it best if I come here." She paused, sucking in her breath. "We're using research into some ancient texts as a cover for my stay here." Elsia gestured to Iltar, touching his arm. "It's a legitimate reason, as Master Iltar here is a well-versed scholar and explorer."

"Oh," Alanya nodded, pursing her lips. "A good choice for a bodyguard. But will he be enough to fend off your would-be assassin?"

"Of course," Elsia said reassuringly. "Master Iltar is accomplished. He has survived far more dangerous things than assassins."

Pagus must have been telling stories, Iltar mused.

Elsia boasted about Iltar's abilities, though she had never seen him in action. It sounded as if she were describing a magnificent hero that could face an army. He *had* faced a sizeable force once… it hadn't turned out well for him and Cornar.

"As I mentioned in my message, we have my nephew and some of his peers—all of whom are studying under Master Iltar. They'll be helping with gathering information for the research while Master Iltar stays close to me."

The high duchess started, her eyes widening in surprise. "You brought *boys* along?" Alanya studied Iltar condescendingly. "Amid the dangers of assassination?"

Elsia sat back and grinned. "They too are very capable," she said. "Iltar is a grueling teacher. Any one of his acolytes could subdue any one of your guards. Their youth adds another layer of protection to me. Like you, many people wouldn't think a teenage boy would pose a threat. An assassin would let his guard down around them, thus giving them an advantage that grown men wouldn't have."

What a sly one Elsia was…

Alanya squinted thoughtfully, pondering Elsia's words.

"I suppose that makes sense," the high duchess said. "But I still think it foolish."

The women continued talking, and Iltar didn't pay too much attention until Elsia asked about the high duke, Scovis Tasivir.

That question shook Alanya. Her poised demeanor faded, and tears welled in her eyes. Her face contorted in pain and sorrow. "He…" she choked out, biting her lower lip. "He's dead."

"Alanya!" Elsia exclaimed, putting a hand to her mouth. "How?"

"Eight months ago," Alanya said, "during that attack on the palace when the emperor was assassinated." Her voice trembled. "He was trying to protect the Partakers of the Feast. He… he sacrificed himself. Damned Losians!" Alanya wept, burying her face in her hands.

Elsia rose from her seat and sat beside the mourning high duchess, wrapping her arm around Alanya and looking at Iltar as if asking him to say or do something. When he didn't react, the countess glared at him.

What was he supposed to do? *Women…*

Once the high duchess calmed herself, she wiped away her tears. The makeup around her eyes had smeared across her cheeks. Even so, Alanya was alluring.

"Thank you for letting us stay," Elsia said, gently rubbing the high duchess's back.

"You're welcome," Alanya sniffled. "Now if you'll excuse me, I must prepare for bed." The high duchess turned to Iltar and curtsied. "It was a pleasure meeting you, Master Iltar." Iltar lowered his head in acknowledgment.

Elsia hugged the woman tightly. Alanya returned the gesture and left the parlor.

Elsia sprang up from the couch, her face furious. "Why didn't you say anything?"

"What would I say?" Iltar asked, folding his arms and assuming a distant posture. He was going to get scolded, he just knew it.

"Anything to console her!" Elsia said through clenched teeth. "You couldn't think of one polite thing to say?"

Iltar shrugged. What would he say to a grieving widow? *I'm sorry your husband is dead?* What good would that do? Nothing he could say would make a difference. The man was gone.

"I can't believe your audacity…" Elsia sighed. "So you can gawk at her, but you can't say anything."

"I wasn't gawking," Iltar retorted.

"Oh, you were gawking." Elsia waggled her finger and stalked to the foyer.

"No, I wasn't…" Iltar grumbled, following after her.

"Stop trying to deny it—and make my trunk levitate. I don't want to carry it."

Who did she think he was? Some errand boy?

"Well?" Elsia put her hands to her hips.

Damned Sarn Royals… Elsia was just as bad as Pagus.

"You can be so demanding," Iltar said with a sigh and uttered the incantation to lift the trunks. It was a form of telekinetic magic, just one of the many spells in Iltar's repository of incantations.

"Oh," Elsia said with a chuckle, "you haven't *seen* demanding." She grabbed the trunk's handle and dragged it to the door. "Come on, we're in the guest-house."

"A rogue monarch will steal the power of the ancients. His actions will cost the lives of many and he will thwart the Harbinger's plans for a time."

- Prophecy of Soron Thahan

Cornar was dreaming again. He stood on a manicured lawn, gazing up at that strange sky… Unlike the other dreams, Cornar could clearly see those blood-red clouds. They stood out against the backdrop of the bright yellow sky. What was this place? Was it even a place at all? This *was* all in his mind, wasn't it? But it felt so real. Every sensation was so vivid. Cornar felt in control of himself, unlike in normal dreams. He was lucid, in a way.

A horse's whinny carried through the air to Cornar's right, accompanied by trotting footsteps on a cobblestone path. "I know this place…" Cornar whispered, turning about. There was a large building behind him, made of polished white stone. Its ornate craftsmanship was undeniable. He was standing on the lawn of Tor's capitol building.

"Kandish!" Melthas's voice rang from the cobblestone path.

Kandish? Cornar thought, turning around. In the first of these odd dreams, he had been himself. But in each subsequent dream he was reliving events from another person's point of view. First General Breyen and now Kandish Loush. But why?

Melthas dismounted. He wore a uniform made from thick cloth and brown chain mail. His weapons bounced at his hips as he approached Cornar.

Unsettled by the nature of these dreams, Cornar gave his father a questioning glance.

"Why the unfriendly demeanor?" Melthas asked, gesturing with his hands.

I crafted these experiences for your benefit. Cornar remembered the words of that booming voice. *My benefit?* Cornar narrowed his eyes. Was he to learn from the past?

Still unsettled, Cornar glanced about, studying his surroundings. He recalled an exchange he'd witnessed between his father and Kandish Loush here at the capital, the last time Cornar saw his father alive.

"Well?" Melthas prodded, putting his hands on his hips. He brushed against the hilts of his weapons, causing them to sway.

"Nothing," Cornar shook his head.

"Where are the children?" Melthas asked, looking past Cornar.

Cornar hadn't seen the younger version of himself or his sister, Galana. "Around," he answered and searched the lawn. "Are you sure you want to do this?" Cornar asked. "Go off to Laelin Lake?"

"I can't believe you're still bringing this up," Melthas groaned. "I thought you wanted us to strike at the Order of the Red whenever we had the chance."

The Order of the Red? Cornar had never heard of that organization. Wasn't Melthas after a Mindolarn prince?

"This is a prime time to strike. We'll deliver a devastating blow and then vanish. The plan is perfect, Kandish! We'll show them that the Western Sovereignty will not suffer their wickedness."

"You'll die," Cornar blurted.

Melthas furrowed his brow, eyeing Cornar.

"Your children will be orphans…"

"Then come along if you're so worried," Melthas said. "Having you by our side will ensure victory. Those half-breeds are no match for you."

Kandish, a warrior? Cornar almost laughed at the thought, but he held his composure, studying his father. Melthas had a fiery look in his eyes. "I know you said it goes against your *Oaths*, but that hasn't stopped you in the past," Melthas said. "I remember you told me you wished your kind could act more overtly, actively change the world."

Act overtly? Kandish wasn't some sort of spy, was he? *I wonder what would happen if I played dumb… could I get answers?*

"What do you mean?" Cornar asked.

Melthas grinned. "I see… Well, we are in public, after all. I suppose I can't blame you."

What did he mean by that?

"Father!" a boy cried, followed by a girl, shouting.

Cornar turned as the younger version of himself ran toward them. The boy darted right past Cornar and tackled Melthas, nearly knocking him to the ground. "Cor!" Melthas shouted with glee. He wrapped his arms around his son and hugged him tightly.

Heartache struck Cornar as he watched the scene, and a tear trickled down his cheek.

"What's wrong, Kandish?" little Galana asked, grabbing Cornar's hand. She looked up at him with innocent eyes. Cornar couldn't bring himself to answer her.

"Galana!" Melthas shouted the name in a melodic tone. He swept his daughter up and carried her in his arms, kissing her on the cheek.

"I'm glad you two could meet me here," Melthas said, setting Galana down. He wrapped his arms around both of his children, smiling. "Oh, I love you both!"

"We love you too, Papa," Galana said, resting her head against Melthas's arm.

"How long are you going to be gone this time?" young Cor asked.

"A few months," Melthas said. Cornar was replaying the conversation in his mind, hearing his father's words before Melthas spoke them. "But I'll be back. I always come back."

"Where are you going this time?"

"That's a secret," Melthas said. He tapped young Cor's nose, as he always did when keeping a secret from his children. "I'll be back in a month. You'll be staying with Kandish until then."

Young Cor wasn't happy. Cornar remembered feeling left out of all the action. At the time, Cornar thought he was old enough, strong enough, to go out with his father.

"Don't be sulky, Cor," Melthas said. "One day, you'll be on the battlefield. You'll be valiant."

"But if you keep going out to battle there won't be any bad guys left," young Cor lamented.

Melthas laughed. "Evil is always lurking in this world, Cor. The world needs good men like you to lead those willing to defend what is right. One day, you'll lead your own company of men. And you'll be a good leader. I see it in you, son. Kandish sees it in you." Melthas pointed to Cornar.

Young Cor frowned. Cornar wished he hadn't frowned, nor said what he was about to say…

"It's always *later* with you, Father," young Cor said, sighing and pulling away. He stomped off across the lawn. Sorrow erupted within Cornar. Why did he have to relive this? If there was one thing Cornar could do over in his past, it would be this very moment. Ever since his youth Cornar had regretted treating his father harshly.

Melthas sighed and hugged his daughter tightly. "Be good, little one. I love you."

"I love you too, Papa," little Galana said. She gave him a kiss on the cheek. Was that the last gesture of affection Melthas had experienced?

Little Galana ran after young Cor, leaving Melthas alone with Cornar.

"You can still come along," Melthas said.

That beckoning felt so surreal…

"We should be at Laelin Lake in three weeks," Melthas said, and returned to his horse. He mounted and looked to Cornar. "Just don't *swoop* in at the last moment and take all the credit," Melthas said, grinning, as if those words were to mean something.

"Don't go yet," Cornar urged. "Don't part with your son like this."

Melthas pulled on the reins, turning the horse. He glanced across the lawn to where young Cor sat, looking at the sky. "He'll be fine."

Melthas kicked the sides of his horse and trotted back the way he had come.

"Melthas!" Cornar shouted. "Melthas!" But his father didn't answer.

Overcome with anguish, Cornar dropped to the ground. "What am I supposed to learn from this?!" Cornar shouted as tears began flowing from his eyes. "There was nothing here!" He cried, heartbroken at reliving the pain of never seeing his father again. Tears clouded his vision as Cornar watched Melthas disappear. He wished he had Karenna to hold.

"Cor…" That was Karenna's voice.

Heart beating wildly, Cornar rose and spun, steadying into a battle stance. Karenna stood before him, hands clasped at her waist. This was not his wife, it couldn't be…

"Oh, Cor," the not-Karenna said, giggling. She cupped a hand to her mouth, exactly how Karenna behaved when acting playful…

"You're not my wife," Cornar said.

The not-Karenna shrugged playfully.

"What am I supposed to learn from this?" Cornar demanded, still poised to strike.

"Well, there was quite a bit of information here," she said. "And if I told you outright it would ruin the fun. Not to mention that you probably won't do certain things, things that you *need* to do." The not-Karenna squinted. "But, I'll give you one hint. No, I take that back." She waggled her finger.

Cornar gritted his teeth. Who was this person infecting his dreams? It was no coincidence that this *being* appeared in the form of the one from whom he most sought comfort.

"Who are you?" Cornar demanded.

The not-Karenna smiled and shook her head. "That, you are not supposed to know… yet. Time to wake up, Cor. Kaescis has arrived."

The world flew away. Colors whizzed past Cornar in a dazzling display that made him woozy. Everything went black, and he snapped awake.

Cornar found himself in a tent outside the farmhouse inn, the same place where he'd retired the previous night. The sound of horses echoed across the pasture.

Are the Mindolarnians really here? he wondered, grabbing some clothing. Cornar dressed in a hurry, secured a belt around his waist and hoisted his weapons.

He exited his tent and stood at the door, dumbfounded. Hundreds of soldiers were crowded between the village and the farmhouse. They were dressed in silvery armor, their breastplates emblazoned with the seven-headed hydra of Mindolarn. Some carried flags ornamented with that symbol.

Others were on horseback, clad in blood-red armor, with wicked-looking fanisars hoisted upon their backs. There was something ominous about *those* soldiers in red.

A black horse caught Cornar's eye. Its rider was armored unlike the rest of the soldiers. He wore golden-red plate armor that looked formfitting. Like the others, the symbol of the Mindolarn Empire was on his breastplate. Parts of the armor glistened, as if they were gemstones shining in sunlight. Bright red rivets lined pieces of the armor.

Cornar couldn't tell who was under the armor, but he assumed it was Kaescis. The helmet covered his face but didn't have any slits for his eyes. How could the prince see in that thing?

Curious, Cornar picked his way across the field. The man in the golden-red armor dismounted and gave orders to the soldiers concerning the wagons procured by Cornar and his men.

"Kaescis," Cornar called, hoping to draw out the prince from the crowd.

The man in golden-red armor turned. He flipped up the helmet's faceplate, revealing himself to be the prince.

"Mister Dol'shir," Kaescis smiled, his violet eyes staring at Cornar. "It is good to see you again."

"Likewise," Cornar said, coming within arm's reach of the prince. "We look like we're preparing for war."

Kaescis smiled wryly. There was something sinister about that grin. A bloodlust. Cornar hadn't seen Kaescis in such a manner.

"If our enemies attack us, we will be prepared," Kaescis said. "Where is Master Krindal?"

Cornar shrugged. "He disappeared shortly after we moored in Kretin. I sent some of my people to look for him, but they couldn't find him. I supposed he was invisible, so Sharon was looking for him with her lenses."

"Invisible?" Kaescis cocked his head.

"He fled after hearing about elves staying at the inn where we chose to lodge," Cornar said. The prince narrowed his eyes, and Cornar felt that bloodlust intensify. "Why would he be afraid of elves?" Cornar asked. "Do you know anything about that?"

"Krindal had a hostile encounter with them," Kaescis said. "It was frightening for him." Cornar could sense the prince was holding back. What was he hiding? "We will need to find Krindal before we leave for Klindil," Kaescis said. "I will scour the city—"

"Your Imperial Highness!" a voice shouted from the farmhouse. It sounded like Krindal… Cornar spun, gazing at the porch. *By Heleron's Scales!* When did *he* get here?

Krindal stood boldly on the porch, looking like a wild man. His robe was wrinkled, his hair disheveled, and his beard scraggly. Krindal swiftly descended the stairs and hurried toward Cornar and the prince.

"Master Krindal," Kaescis said, bowing respectfully.

"How long have you been here?" Cornar asked Krindal with confusion.

"A few days," said the necromancer-scholar, giving Cornar a curt glance. What was his problem? Why was Krindal acting terse…?

"Now that we're all here, there's no need to delay our trip," Kaescis said. "Ready your men, Mister Dol'shir. We will get the wagons moving. Once your men are roused, come to the head of the convoy. I have a horse waiting for you. There's one for you as well, Master Krindal."

Kaescis lowered his faceplate and strode back to his horse. *How can he see in that thing?* The prince swiftly mounted, shouting more orders to his soldiers.

Cornar turned to Krindal. "Is everything all right?" he asked in a whisper.

The old necromancer-scholar nodded, then said, "If you'll excuse me, I must round up the scholars." Krindal hurried off to the farmhouse.

Cornar stood where he was, thinking. Krindal must have been sneaking about in order to know that the men from the Order of Histories were inside the inn. Nordal had mentioned hearing a noise above him two nights ago. But the attic was locked. Cornar couldn't investigate it properly and had dismissed the noise as a wild animal.

Cornar returned to the tents, but glanced back to the small Mindolarn army. He felt that Krindal and Kaescis were keeping something from him and his men. Nothing could bother him more.

The dream… he thought. Melthas had shielded Cornar from the truth all those years ago. Cornar felt left out because of it, just as he was feeling now with Krindal and Kaescis. That couldn't be a coincidence, could it? If Cornar had known his father was facing the possibility of death, he would have treated him differently. Cornar would have hugged his father, telling him how much he loved him. Cornar would have overcome his resentment.

After the exchange between the scholar and the prince, all Cornar wanted to do was to remain aloof at the back of the convoy. He wanted to ride with his men, taking comfort in their camaraderie. But perhaps that was not the right thing to do.

Actions, he thought, remembering the not-Karenna's words. He needed to do *certain* things. Was being at the expedition's head one of them? Perhaps he *needed* to be there.

This was obviously not a simple expedition of discovery as he'd been told… But what motive would Krindal have to lie?

Cornar dismissed the thoughts and called for his men. "Kalder, Midar, Hemrin. Let's break camp. We're leaving."

—⟫•⟪—

It was midmorning before the expedition was ready to leave Klarin. The army filled the street which ran through the middle of the village. It seemed that almost all of Klarin's citizens stood along the street, gawking at the soldiers. Their expressions said they had never seen such a gathering of troops.

After seeing to his men, Cornar pushed his way to the head of the expedition. As Kaescis had said, a white horse was waiting for Cornar.

Some riders with familiar faces were on horseback near Kaescis: Admiral Kaetet, Laeyit, and the servant Practil. There were a few others Cornar didn't recognize, men dressed like Admiral Kaetet—undoubtedly other captains from the ships Kaescis had conscripted for the journey—a couple of commanders in plate armor, and one of those crimson-armored soldiers. Cornar had overheard a soldier calling them the Crimson Praetorians. Cornar knew of them, the elite guard of the Mindolarn Empire.

"Mister Dol'shir," Kaescis said, gesturing to those around him. "I wish to introduce you to the rest of our leadership." He pointed to one of the captains. "This is Captain Hetarin, commander of the *Ulicin*. And this is Captain Regader, commander of the *Helidar*."

"Captains," Cornar said, bowing, and then mounted his horse.

"These two are Grand Marshals Hezidex and Galiur." Kaescis gestured to the men in plate armor. Their helmet's visors were lowered, so Cornar couldn't see their faces.

Grand marshals, huh? Cornar mused. *The highest ranking officers in the Mindolarn army.* What would Kaescis be doing with two grand marshals? Usually a grand marshal oversaw an entire theater of war. But two grand marshals for an expedition? Odd… There was something more to this trip to Klindil than either Kaescis or Krindal was telling him.

"And lastly, my friend Bratan." Kaescis pointed to the Crimson Praetorian.

Bratan's horse was standing close to Laeyit and her steed. Cornar glimpsed her eyeing him while whispering to Bratan. She had a glint of hostility in her yellow eyes. Cornar didn't trust the woman.

"It's a pleasure to meet all of you," Cornar said, gripping his horse's reins.

"Mister Dol'shir will be protecting Master Krindal and his associates," Kaescis said. "And he's a renowned adventurer, so I say we heed his suggestions as we explore Klindil."

That was a backhanded compliment.… *If you think so highly of me, let me know what's* really *going on,* Cornar thought. He would discover the truth about this trip, one way or another, even if he had to figure it out on his own.

I'll use those dreams if I must, Cornar told himself. *Perhaps in the next one I'll learn something pertinent to this quest.* He would have to pay attention to the details, but for now he could replay the first three in his mind. There would be time, since it would take nearly two weeks to reach the ruins of Klindil.

Kaescis said a few words to the small army, and then kicked his horse, urging him into a trot. The other riders did the same.

A roar of clanking armor, the beating of hoofs, and marching soldiers echoed behind him. Cornar glanced over his shoulder, watching the procession leave the village. The villagers were still watching with wide-eyed amazement. Their innocence reminded him of little Galana from his dream. That soothed him.

Now calmed, Cornar resumed his focus forward. A thrill surged through him. Somewhere out there, one of the greatest secrets of Kalda lay awaiting discovery.

24

THE HILINARD

A knock awoke Iltar from his slumber. He propped himself up on one arm and gazed at the floor beside the bed. The clothes he had scattered before sleeping were still there. Sunlight shone through the sheers from a nearby window,. Iltar hadn't drawn the drapes so he could easily tell whether he was on Kalda or Vabenack. The sky was a clear blue.

"Master Iltar," Hazais said in a cheery tone, "the ladies are waiting for you in the solarium."

Iltar threw back the covers and crawled out of bed, picking up the clothes.

"Mast—"

"I'm coming!" Iltar yelled. "Let me get presentable, and I'll join them."

"Ah, yes," Hazais said, and Iltar thought he heard the butler sighing in exasperation.

Here I thought Mindolarn servants weren't supposed to show emotion, he thought, folding his clothes. Iltar made his bed, then turned to an extravagant dresser. It was longer than he was tall, and he was quite a tall man. A couple of small mirrors on stands were arranged at one end beside a tray full of combs and brushes. It looked very feminine.

Iltar dressed quickly, putting on a clean black tunic and matching pants—his favored outfit. Then he grabbed a small, curved dagger and put it on his belt. It was more ornamental than anything else, but Iltar thought he'd better brandish a weapon if he were to play the part of a bodyguard.

"Master Iltar—"

"Hold on!" Iltar said through clenched teeth, grabbing a brush. He ran it through his hair while Hazais continued encouraging him to hurry. The butler made some comments that implied Iltar was a poor bodyguard.

"Your mistress could be in danger!" the butler almost shouted.

Iltar sighed and continued stroking the brush through his gray hair. After dealing with the cowlicks Iltar used a comb to straighten his hair and then his goatee.

Hazais was still droning on as Iltar put the comb back in its place. *What an annoying man.* Iltar rolled his eyes and took one last look in the mirror. He looked good, if he did say so himself.

"I must insist that this behavior of neglect is—" Iltar swung the door open, finding the butler and two women dressed like maids standing in the hall. Hazais straightened up with a *harrumph* and adjusted his fancy orange coat. "Please follow me," he said, then turned from the door and started down the hall.

Iltar looked at the women, and they bowed in response to his glance. He forced a smile, then turned and followed Hazais. Behind him, he heard the women enter his room then utter surprised exclamations about the chamber's tidiness. The maids had probably expected to find it in disarray.

"Do not take offense at this," Hazais said, glancing back to Iltar, "but you really must do better at waking before your mistress rises."

"I'm no servant," Iltar said with a grunt, coming alongside the butler. They wound through a couple of halls before arriving at a staircase leading to the lower levels of the guesthouse.

"But you have a sacred responsibility to the countess," Hazais said, sounding frustrated as they descended the stairs. "You are to protect her. If an attempt on her life were to happen here, I would have to claim some responsibility."

"So are you saying that I should never sleep?" Iltar asked, deliberately acting terse. This butler seemed easily excitable, and thus a source of entertainment.

"No!" Hazais almost spat the word. "That's why we have guards. I am saying that when she is awake and moving about, you must be too."

"Well, I don't see any harm in letting the men continue their duties before I'm ready."

Hazais was taken aback by that statement. The butler stopped at the bottom of the staircase and looked directly into Iltar's eyes. His gaze had a fiery indignation that made Iltar want to laugh. Hazais obviously didn't know who he was dealing with.

The butler's nostrils flared. "You, sir, are an arrogant, self-centered social climber!" Iltar fought back a smile. *Oh, this is simply too much fun.* He chuckled. "Do you think this is funny?" Hazais demanded.

"Assassinations? No. You, on the other hand…" Iltar trailed off, grinning. The butler turned his nose up as he spun and walked down an adjoining hall. Iltar followed him, reveling in his goading of the butler.

Soon they reached the solarium, a seven-sided room that extended from the guesthouse, positioned near the mansion. The high ladies were sitting at a glass table set for three. They were sipping on an orange liquid and enjoying a cheery conversation.

Hazais stepped inside, stood to attention, addressed the women by their titles, then *presented* Iltar with a perturbed tone. Once Iltar entered the solarium, Hazais stalked off, disappearing down the hall.

Elsia laughed and cupped the top of her glass, preventing her drink from spilling. "What was that all about?" she asked.

"I didn't take kindly to his berating," Iltar said, sitting in the only empty seat. He looked out the glass walls of the solarium and examined the gardens. They were far more beautiful in the sunlight. There was even a large patch of grass where he could hold training sessions with the acolytes. *This is better than what I had planned. The boys can be training out there while I catch up on my research. Training in the morning, studying in the afternoon and evening.* It was perfect—

"Iltar?" Elsia asked. Had she said something?

"What?" Iltar looked at the countess.

"You weren't paying attention again," Elsia said with a grin, taking a sip of her drink. Alanya was also smiling at him.

"Were you admiring the view of the palace?" Alanya asked. "Many of my guests get lost in that view."

Iltar started, then looked back out the window. He hadn't noticed, but the palace was sitting on a hill not too far away. It stood out among the leafy trees, its red-brown coloring stark against the greenery. The palace gave the scene a sense of magnificence, making the entire view from the solarium quite amazing. From this vantage, Iltar could see that seven extremely high towers surrounded the palace, guarding it like sentinels.

"Hadn't noticed it."

Elsia laughed. "Then what were you staring at?"

"The grass." Iltar pointed to the spot where he intended to train the acolytes. "It looks big enough for the boys to conduct their training."

"I've never seen mages train," Alanya said. "Perhaps I can watch?"

"Certainly," Iltar said with a shrug and then raised his glass to his lips. He took a sip and his mouth puckered from the tart, citrusy taste of the drink. *What is this?*

"Do you not like it?" Alanya asked. "I can have something else brought."

"It's fine," Iltar said, taking another sip. This time it didn't seem as tart.

"So, what did he say?" Elsia asked.

"Who?"

Elsia fought back laughter and rolled her eyes. "Hazais."

"He pretty much called me a poor bodyguard. Kept nagging me while I was trying to get ready." He took another sip. There was a hint of sweetness to the drink.

"Please accept my apology for any offensive remarks he made," Alanya said cordially. "I will have a word with Hazais." Iltar grinned.

"I already sent word to the *Yaelinum*," Elsia said, clearing her throat. "The boys should be here in the late afternoon."

"Good," Iltar said, nodding.

"Do you want to go to the Hilinard today?" the countess asked. Iltar nodded, taking another sip. The drink was growing on him.

"What ancient texts are you researching, Master Iltar?" Alanya asked. "Or are you feigning research?" Iltar sat his glass on the table but didn't answer.

"Oh, it's legitimate," Elsia chimed, and then glanced to Iltar as if seeking approval to say more.

Iltar didn't react to her glance. Did he dare include another person in his affairs? They were staying with this woman. Alanya would undoubtedly stumble across notes lying about or an open text.

"But I'll let Iltar explain it," Elsia said, sitting back in her chair.

Are you really putting me on the spot...? he thought. Iltar hated when that happened.

Alanya was staring at him, awaiting an answer. She looked even more stunning than when he had met her last night. Her gaze was tantalizing. His stomach fluttered, and he suddenly felt nervous. Iltar hadn't felt like this since... since meeting Gwenyth—a fellow illusionist he adored who shared his mother's name—all those years ago.

"You're gawking again," Elsia said. Iltar snapped a glance to the countess. Elsia's arms were folded, and she smirked at him.

Cool fingers touched his hand, and Iltar jumped, seeing the high duchess's long and elegant fingers resting atop his own. "Don't worry, Iltar," Alanya said, still smiling. "You're not the first man I've caught staring at me. And I don't mind."

Iltar looked at her fingers, not knowing what he should say. Should he mention the *Codices* tome? Vabenack? Nightmares with a strange Reflection who thinks he's some harbinger?

"I'm looking into prophecies," Iltar said, still gazing at the high duchess's fingers.

"Whose?" she asked. Iltar glance to Elsia, who had her hand across her lips. Was she mocking him again? Elsia was just like her nephew.

"Soron Thahan," Iltar said, redirecting his gaze at the high duchess's face. Alanya's smile was disarming. "They were written in a book Elsia's nephew found within the Master's section of the Necrotic Order's Record Hall."

The high duchess studied Iltar with a puzzled gaze. "But he's an acolyte still, isn't he?"

"An apprentice," Elsia said. "It's a rank higher than acolyte."

"It sounds like he was snooping someplace he shouldn't," Alanya said, glancing to her friend.

"He was," Iltar said flatly. Alanya returned her focus to Iltar. Her attention was more compelling than an enthralling spell... "Pagus is a bit of a rogue. I blame it on his Royal Sarn blood."

The women grunted disapprovingly.

"I was a Sarn Royal, once," Alanya said. "Do you think me roguish?"

Iltar bumbled through his thoughts. What was he supposed to say to that? "Uh... no," was all he could mutter.

Alanya grinned and patted his hand. Iltar had expected her to pull away, but she hadn't. At that moment, footsteps echoed into the solarium.

You never know what to say... he lamented. Iltar did his best to regain his composure as servants filed into the room. They carried covered plates and set them before Iltar and the women.

He just stared at the shiny covering, looking at his reflection in the metal with Alanya's hand still atop his.

"You're smitten!" Elsia said, smiling. She slapped Iltar on the arm as they climbed into the carriage the high duchess had prepared for them. Alanya had temporarily loaned it to them for their stay in Mindolarn. The carriage was like the rest of Alanya's possessions: lavish and extravagant.

"No, I'm not," Iltar said, taking his seat on the bench facing the rear of the carriage.

"You are!" Elsia said, smiling as she sat across from him.

Iltar rolled his eyes and studied his surroundings. Hopefully, his distracted manner would cause her to stop badgering him. The interior of the carriage was covered in red velvet with golden scrollwork adorning the ceiling. The scrollwork was arranged in a seven-sided pattern, and golden trim lined the four corners of the carriage, becoming a framework for the lush velvet seats.

"Quit denying it." She kicked his foot.

The driver shut the carriage door, leaving them to argue.

Iltar drew his lips to a line and furrowed his brow. Elsia was being very familiar with him. Too familiar. They hadn't become *that* acquainted with each other, had they? He could understand Karenna teasing him like this, perhaps even Baekal... but Iltar had known those women for years, and they were married to his closest friends. Cornar and Igan were practically brothers to him, making their wives pseudo-sisters-in-law.

"There's nothing wrong with it, Iltar," Elsia said as the carriage lurched forward. "She's a beautiful and *available* woman." Iltar ignored her and gazed out the carriage window. Elsia went on a little more about the matter, then gave up once she figured out he wasn't listening.

There is no point pursuing something that isn't going to happen. No woman as beautiful and wealthy as High Duchess Alanya Tasivir would ever show any genuine interest in him. No woman would... besides Anela. Anela was the only woman who had wanted him... but even she left. Granted, Anela thought he was dead.

Iltar dwelt in his reverie until the carriage came to a halt.

Elsia exited first, speaking with the driver about their intentions for their visit here at the Hilinard. They would be staying until the boys arrived, and then he was to return and retrieve them. High Duchess Alanya's mansion was only a short ride from the Hilinard. Iltar thought it to be two or three grand phineals away.

Iltar grabbed a small pack full of notes and *The Codices of Soron Thahan*. He stepped out of the carriage and was taken aback by the grandeur of the Hilinard. Was everything here in Mindolarn so fantastically massive?

A building shaped much like the palace rose before him: round, with a shallow dome for a rooftop. Red-brown stone covered the exterior. White galstra columns lined part of the building; they looked decorative. Statues of men in robes—carved from the same white stone—lined a walkway leading to the building.

Elsia hurried down the walkway, not waiting for him.

Iltar followed her, but glanced about the grounds. More buildings were nearby, each with similar architecture. The Hilinard and the other buildings were atop a wide hill and overlooked the city. Iltar could see the bay in the distance. The moored ships looked like tiny specks.

Several steps led up to the Hilinard's entrance, a three-story doorway with the doors opened. They looked heavy and were probably moved by mages.

Elsia strode ahead of Iltar, swaying her hips as she entered. Sunlight spilled into the rectangular foyer from windows on either side of the opened doors.

Iltar slowed as he entered, eyeing the floor. His scholar-friends had mentioned that one of the symbols on Reflection's robe was in the floor. But there was nothing here. The floor consisted of squares of sparkling gray galstra. He finally reached Elsia, who was speaking with an attendant dressed in a white robe.

"… Royalty from Sarn. That should afford me some leniency."

"I'm sorry, m'lady," the balding attendant said. He was a short man with a large mole on his cheek. "But the tribute is the same for all people. Not even the aristocracy of the empire can negotiate the price."

Elsia sighed and stepped aside, letting Iltar join the conversation. "He'll be paying." She folded her arms and ignored the man. *Snooty woman.*

"As I was telling her," the attendant gestured to Elsia, "you will need to pay tribute to access the records held here in the Hilinard."

"That's fine," Iltar said, opening his pack. He had exchanged some of his Sorothian coin with Alanya's treasure keeper. Normally, Iltar would have stopped at the docks to exchange his money, but Elsia insisted they head straight for the high duchess's mansion after leaving the *Yaelinum*. That proved fortunate, as the treasure keeper didn't charge him any fees.

"It will be five schigarins," the man said.

How much was that? Iltar raised an eyebrow at the man. He should have paid more attention to their currency system.

"Do you expect me to know how much that is in your currency?" the attended asked.

"I have your coin," Iltar said, removing five round coins. They were made of gold, with a side-profile depiction of a man on one side and the empire's seven-headed hydra symbol on the other.

"Thank you," the attendant said, handing him a green token. It was about the size of his palm, with a triangular symbol on one side. "Return this to one of us when you leave. At least one attendant is always at an entrance."

Iltar took the token without a word and walked with Elsia through the foyer, passing other patrons and attendants in white robes.

"Alanya thinks we should rent an alcove," Elsia said. "Do you want to spend the money?"

"How much is it?" Iltar asked as they stepped up to a black monolith with a map of the Hilinard etched in stone. The lines of the map were glowing a pale-blue hue.

Taken aback, Iltar raised an eyebrow at the map. He thought at first that the stone surface was a slab with holes, lit by lightstones placed within a cavity behind the slab to illuminate the map, but that wasn't the case. This wasn't light from a lightstone. It was too uniform, not to mention that the lines were shallow grooves in the stone, not holes. Was this some kind of tevisral?

Iltar studied the map, which consisted of seven floor plans, one for each of the floors of the Hilinard. Tiny text was inscribed within many of the floor plans, denoting topics of study.

"I suppose I should learn to wait to speak until you're facing me," Elsia said. Had he missed something again? Probably the price of the alcove.

The countess stepped around the monolith. She opened her mouth to speak but gawked at the monolith's other side.

"Iltar, there's more to the Hilinard than this building," she said, gesturing for him to come close. He complied. Another map was on the rear side of the monolith. On it several outlines denoted the various buildings Iltar had seen from outside. Six other buildings were connected to the one where they stood, each about the same size. There were also a dozen more scattered around the enormous compound. Descriptions within each of the outlines detailed the topics of study.

Elsia slid her finger across the stone and came to a menu etched beside the map of the complex. It had general subtopics listed below the names of each of the buildings. "I think you'll want this wing in the center," Elsia said. "Religion and Philosophy."

Iltar read each of the subtopics: History of the empire and Sociology, Battle Records and War Strategy—*They have an entire building devoted to war?* That surprised him. Other wings included various sciences—mathematics, biology, physics, and chemistry—and their applications, various topics of magic, and lastly literary fiction.

He felt a poke against his arm and turned to see Elsia's finger wrinkling his sleeve. "That got your attention!" she exclaimed, sounding like she had just made some great discovery. "I'll do that when I need to talk to you. We should make our way to the center wing, the one called Religion—"

"I heard you the first time," Iltar said. He took one look at the map, then walked around to the front of the monolith. Three lines protruded from the floor plans. Small script beside each indicated to which wing the hall led.

Looks like we take that corridor. He looked to a circular hallway not far from the monolith. According to the map, it wrapped all the way around the building. *A well planned layout,* he mused. Iltar hated buildings with deliberately elongated paths. Those were all too common in Soroth.

"This way," he said, pointing to the curved hall lit by white lightstones.

⟐•⟐

Iltar decided to rent an alcove in the Religion and Philosophy wing of the

Hilinard. The alcoves were arranged around the edges of all the floors but the first. Those on the second floor were the most expensive, with those on the seventh being the cheapest. Being a frugal man, Iltar decided to rent a spot on the seventh floor. He and his acolytes would be running to other wings, so Iltar didn't think the distance between the second and seventh floors would make too much of a difference.

His alcove was nestled partway into the dome ceiling. It was large enough to fit two chairs and a table. Shelves lined the upper parts of the alcove, undoubtedly meant for books and scroll cases. Two empty sconces meant to hold lightstones or candles were aligned with the chairs. One of the attendants said that they would have to provide their own lightstones; too many people had walked off with them in the past.

A wrought-iron gate was folded along the right side of the alcove. When closed, the gate signified that the patron did not want to be disturbed. Iltar and Elsia had passed several alcoves with their gates shut and their tables full of books and loose pages.

Iltar stepped up to the wrought-iron gate and examined a lock with its key stuck in it. He took the key and slipped it into his pants pocket.

"What do you want to search for first?" Elsia asked. She leaned back against the table, her hands gripping the edge.

"I want to start with something called the *Will*," Iltar said. He turned from the alcove, moving to the nearby railing. This hall containing the alcoves wrapped all around the seventh floor, like a balcony looking down into the rest of this wing of the Hilinard. There weren't many books up here. A few platforms with bookshelves stood in the center of the space, accessed from bridges connected to this circular hall.

Sunlight shone from a ceiling made mostly of glass secured within red-gold framing. That allowed ample sunlight to fill the wing during the day. It was quite intriguing to see a glass ceiling. There were seven tiers to the ceiling's framework. *Mindolarnians and their obsession with seven.*

And then, he saw it.

One of the symbols—the same which Kilan claimed seeing here in the Hilinard—was at the top of the glass dome in the form of golden trim. The trim looked fused into the glass. It had a jagged triangle with two points wider than the third. Seven eight-sided stars were arrayed within its interior, with six around a central one. It was, however, lacking the three lines beneath the triangle.

"Are you okay?" Elsia asked, poking his shoulder.

"Yeah…" Iltar muttered.

Elsia sighed. "Well, we'd better start grabbing books. I doubt we'll be able to do much reading before the boys arrive."

25

TREK

Nearly eight days had passed since Cornar and the others had left the village of Klarin. The trek had been uneventful thus far. They had traveled southeast for a time, following the course of a river that emptied into a bay near Kretin. Now, the expedition was traveling along the central mountain range, moving northeast between a river and a forest.

The path they were traveling was made mostly of dirt, but occasional protrusions of stone marked the path's edge. Krindal and several scholars thought them to be ancient markers for a road buried beneath the path. A few scholars wanted to dig to see if they could find such a road, but they hadn't had the opportunity.

All in all, the trek was leisurely. The Isle of Klindala was quite beautiful this time of year, not to mention the fall temperature was perfect for traveling long distances. The forest was quite colorful, unlike those in Soroth which had mostly trees with yellow and orange leaves. Cornar took note of a few trees with purple and pink leaves. He had not seen many trees like that.

As evening drew near, Kaescis called for the expedition to halt. The prince had spotted a grove beside the path where he wanted to set up camp.

The six hundred or so Mindolarnian men and women erected their campsite swiftly. The Mindolarn encampment was like a tiny war camp, set up in three ringed tiers: the soldiers' ring, the officers and servants' ring, and the Royal ring.

A few-dozen paces from the Mindolarn camp, Cornar directed his band to set up their tents. From the outside, it would look like two different groups camped together. Cornar's was a tenth the size of the Mindolarn encampment.

Years ago, Cornar had established a standard layout for his band's camp: a fire pit in the center, with two rings of tents facing the fire, staggered so that each tent door could easily access the central part. They had fifteen tents set up, eight on the inner ring and seven on the outer. Each tent could comfortably hold three men, although it could accommodate four in cramped fashion.

Cornar had a tent to himself. Usually, he shared the tent with Iltar. Camping without him felt odd the first few nights, but Cornar was now getting used to sleeping alone.

He hadn't had any more dreams since Kaescis's arrival in Klarin. Since that first night on the road Cornar actually wanted to go back to that strange dreamland. If the dreams could tell him about this quest, he needed to experience more of them.

After everyone was settled, Cornar surveyed his campsite. Ordreth and Sharon were cooking a stew over the campfire. His nephew loved to cook, and he had quite a talent for it. Cornar wondered if Ordreth would have chosen the life of a chef if he hadn't gotten into adventuring. Sharon constantly teased him that the only reason they were still together was because of that talent. Of course, there was more to their relationship than that, but it was a running joke between them. Ordreth kissed Sharon as he stirred the pot. She smiled coyly and stepped away to get more ingredients.

Many of the other warriors were seated around the campfire, talking about the trek or gazing at the evening sky. The sun had already passed the mountains beside them, but they could still see the effects of the sunset over the peaks. It was a beautiful sight.

Cornar rounded the common area of the campsite and went straight for the opening that led to the Mindolarn encampment.

"Where are you going, Cor?" Nordal called.

Cornar stopped and glanced back at the man, who was playing Sharzen with a few other warriors. "To meet with Kaescis. They're looking over maps tonight."

Nordal nodded and returned to playing. Several others heard Cornar's reply and watched as he exited the camp.

The Mindolarn camp had two entrances, one leading to the road and another to Cornar's band. Soldiers guarded both entrances at all times, taking shifts so everyone could be rested for the next day's march. Cornar nodded to them as he entered, but the soldiers didn't reply.

Once inside the camp, Cornar passed a tent barrack that could hold fifty men. This particular barrack was beside the spot where they had gathered all the wagons beneath a cloth pavilion. Another barrack flanked the wagon pavilion on the other side. There were other clusters like this set up across the camp. Even the horses had their own tent-like stable with barracks beside them. Cornar wondered why they didn't use picket lines… it seemed a waste to erect covering for the horses.

Several servants rushed past Cornar and into the wagon pavilion, grabbing foodstuffs. He glanced at them but continued through the camp along the outer ring. He finally came to the entrance to the second ring where the officers were lodged. The chefs' station was also in this middle ring.

A sweet aroma of cooked meat tingled Cornar's nostrils. Several soldiers had spotted a pack of wild animals at the forest's edge earlier in the day. He knew they had ventured off but didn't know if their hunt had been successful. The aroma answered that question. The creatures—called deer by the Mindolarnians—were a little gamey for Cornar's liking, but the meat wasn't bad. They kind of looked like horses, but the males had wicked, vicious-looking horns. Cornar imagined squaring off with such a creature, head-to-head. One would have to be good at dodging to evade the beast's attacks.

"Excuse us!" a voice yelled behind Cornar.

He turned, noticing the same servants who had passed him. They ran by again, carrying bags of supplies, hurrying off the opposite way Cornar was headed.

Soon, Cornar passed an open tent door and glimpsed the scholars from the Order of Histories. The Mindolarnians hadn't accounted for the scholars when planning the encampment, so the scholars were lumped together with the various servants. The tents were brimming to capacity.

Cornar heard a few of the scholars complaining, and Jahevial stalked out of the tent, noticing Cornar as he passed.

"There's still room in our camp," Cornar said, slowing his walk.

"I might consider that," Jahevial said, clutching his robe. It looked like he was holding something under it. Cornar narrowed his eyes to get a better look, but Jahevial hurried off, moving toward the entrance to the war camp's outer ring.

Soon, Cornar came to the entrance of the innermost ring, where two Crimson Praetorians stood as sentinels. They looked to Cornar but didn't speak. The Praetorians knew they were to allow him entrance, but both kept a watchful eye, vigilantly searching the war camp, although there was no sign of danger. But even if there were, the soldiers at the outer ring would sound an alarm.

Cornar strode through this third opening and entered the center of the encampment, where the Royal retinue was lodged. Several more Crimson Praetorians marched past him, circling an enormous tent with various parts: the Imperial Tent. Cornar had watched them set up this place on the first night. It consisted of a central tent and three smaller tents, all joined together. Each of the smaller tents had their own purpose. One was a war room, another a chapel, and the third was a common room. Kaescis's chambers were in the central section, at the cluster's heart. Cornar hadn't been inside, since a pair of Crimson Praetorians always stood watch. They allowed entrance to only Kaescis and his two friends, Laeyit and Bratan.

Other tents composed the Royal ring: a few mid-sized tents for five, used to lodge the Crimson Praetorians, the tents for the grand marshals, and some for Admiral Kaetet and the other ship captains.

Once Cornar arrived at the entrance to the Imperial Tent, a Crimson Praetorian lifted the tent flap, and Cornar slipped inside.

As one would expect, the Imperial Tent's interior was a bit ostentatious.

From what Cornar could tell, the tent had three layers to its walls: an outer layer made of water-resistant material, another layer of a thicker sturdier cloth, and the inner layer made to look like fine tapestries. The inner layers looked like the walls of a palace. Some parts had picturesque scenes woven to look like paintings hanging on a wall. It was a little much…

Cornar hurried through the tent's foyer and turned a corner, walking along the tent's outer hallway. A faint conversation reached his ears, but Cornar couldn't tell what was being said. He didn't walk far before reaching the war room. Two more Crimson Praetorians stood watch while another pair marched through the tent's hallway.

Thus far, Cornar had passed a third of the Crimson Praetorians assigned to the expedition. These men were ever vigilant to protect their prince. More were probably stationed throughout the camp. That meant half of the Praetorians were on duty. *They must switch off during the night,* he thought. That didn't give much time for sleep. But this part of the camp was always struck the last. Perhaps Kaescis let them sleep up to the moment of disassembling their tents.

"… they could be," Bratan said.

"Are we sure this map is accurate?" Laeyit asked. She sounded agitated, but then again, she always seemed that way.

Cornar strode to a table at the center of the war room where all the other leaders were gathered.

"I'm positive," Kaetet said, pointing at a topographical map of Klindala. "There is a set of ruins in the mountains, here. The Fortress of Anigar." He tapped on the map, at a spot not far from where they were currently camped. Cornar had studied the map the first night after leaving Klarin and committed it to memory. Every time they moved camp he knew exactly where it was on the map. Cornar's extraordinary sense of direction was a peculiar gift, but it came in handy.

Kaescis stood silently at the opposite end of the table, folding his arms and eyeing the map.

"I agree with the admiral," Krindal said. "The Wildmen are most likely there, or at least a group of them."

"And what if they're not friendly?" Laeyit argued. "This particular spot is farther away from the ruins. The Wildmen are tribesmen. These here might not be part of the main tribe."

Hezidex cleared his throat. "Even if they aren't part of the tribe, it doesn't mean they're not allied with the main group, Laeyit." The grand marshal sounded cold. Laeyit shook her head and rolled her eyes. Bratan put a hand on Laeyit's shoulder to calm her, but she just gave him a sullen glare.

"I say we proceed to this Fortress of Anigar," Hezidex continued. "We have enough men to subdue a hostile force of Wildmen. We can take them prisoner if need be."

"If they are rogues, we could offer them as tribute to the others," Grand Marshal Galiur said, humming thoughtfully. "In addition to what you've already prepared, Your Imperial Grace."

Kaescis nodded.

What had Kaescis prepared to barter? Cornar had not heard the plan. He figured he would hear about it at some point. Cornar was used to getting information at the last moment, since Iltar had a nasty habit of doing that. The man could get so wrapped up in the adventure that he would forget to tell you something important until it was almost too late. Luckily, no one had ever died from it.

The men continued expressing their opinions about the fortress and its possible Wildmen inhabitants. Cornar, however, studied the map. The ruins of Klindil were still five days away, across a mountain range. The ruined city was cradled by other mountains at the far end of another valley. The Fortress of Anigar, however, was only a day's journey. They could probably set up camp there tomorrow night. Cornar preferred such a spot as opposed to camping out in the open. It was easier to defend. But if the Wildmen called it home, they might see the expedition's camp in the ruins as an invasion. Either way, caution was warranted.

"What say you, Your Imperial Grace?" Hezidex asked.

Kaescis studied the map, his arms still folded. The prince then looked at Cornar.

"What do you think, Mister Dol'shir? Have you ever encountered a wild tribe?"

Yes, he had… but that encounter hadn't turned out well. *What a nightmare.* Memories flashed of him and Iltar fleeing from a ferocious tribe who turned out to be savage werewolves.

"I have," Cornar said. "We should be ready for a fight."

"Finally!" Laeyit shouted, throwing her hand in the air. "Someone shares my opinion."

"Uncivilized men are unpredictable," Cornar continued. "We should be ready to defend ourselves, but not go in as a hostile force intending to invade. It looks like those ruins are only a day's journey away. We should make camp at the base of the mountains, then send an emissary party into the ruins."

Krindal nodded approvingly.

"That's the best suggestion I've heard," Admiral Kaetet said.

"Yes, it is." Kaescis relaxed, putting his hands on the table. The prince bent over the map, studying the terrain. "Hezidex, send a scouting party ahead before we break camp. Have them find a suitable spot that is near the path but also convenient to the fortress ruins." The grand marshal nodded. "Now on to reports," Kaescis said.

One by one, each of the leaders reported on their divisions. Everyone's reports were mundane except for Krindal's. Krindal said the scholars were excavating the path tonight, searching for a buried road. They had borrowed some lightstones and tied them to posts so they could dig past nightfall. None of the Mindolarnians seemed to care in the slightest. Cornar found that odd.

The meeting was over after half an hour. Most of the others lingered in the Imperial Tent. Kaescis's servants had wines prepared in the common room, but Cornar didn't care to stay. He found it unwise to drink while out in the wild. Only a fool did that. These men, however, were surrounded by soldiers, so Cornar could understand their choices.

The sun had already set when Cornar exited the Imperial Tent and headed back toward his camp, walking alone. He passed the guards stationed at the edge of the Mindolarn encampment but paused before continuing to his campsite. Cornar looked across the grove to where the scholars were digging. He could barely see the heads of some. How deep had they dug? Most of them were there, digging or taking notes. Cornar took a count of the men, but Jahevial wasn't among them. Jahevial was the only scholar missing.

Odd, Cornar thought. Perhaps Jahevial had taken him up on his offer to move campsites.

Cornar turned back to his camp, but glimpsed movement in the forest. A sharp-looking face recoiled behind a tree. Were those pointed ears?

Intrigued, Cornar approached the forest, his gait cautious. A silhouette darted from a tree. It looked humanoid. Quiet footfalls faded into the forest. Cornar felt at his side for his weapons. He began drawing them from their sheathes as Gregan called to him.

"What did you see, Cor?" Singing metal accompanied the question. "An intruder," Cornar said, glancing to Gregan. "Get Sharon."

Cornar darted into the trees. He could still hear the faint footfalls. Someone was running away. Behind him, a cry of alarm resounded from the Mindolarn encampment. Soldiers shouted commands, but their words were fading as Cornar wove around the trees, chasing the faint footfalls. Some of the leaves had fallen, allowing moonlight to illuminate the forest floor.

A lanky figure dashed around the trees ahead of Cornar. *A spy?* he wondered, leaping over exposed roots.

More footfalls echoed behind him. Cornar heard another pair coming beside him that soon got ahead of him. That was undoubtedly Sharon, a fast sprinter. Cornar couldn't see her; Sharon was obviously wearing her cloak. Clanking armor and shouted commands echoed through the trees. The Mindolarn soldiers were behind Cornar, too far behind to overtake him.

Cornar soon lost sight of the figure ahead of him, but could hear Sharon's footfalls. She whistled every few seconds, helping guide him and the others in their pursuit.

The trees thickened, and then Cornar heard Sharon shouting, "Cliff!"

The ground disappeared a moment later, and Cornar fell. He threw himself forward as he hit the ground, rolling over his shoulder. A sharp rock scraped his back, and Cornar staggered onto his feet. Pain shot through him. "Argh!" Cornar gritted his teeth but kept running.

He could see the figure ahead of him, running toward a foggy veil. Why was there fog? That shouldn't be there this time of day… The figure dashed into the fog, disappearing.

Cornar reached the fog but didn't stop. It was so thick! Where had this come from? Cornar could barely see his weapons. Disconcerted, he came to a halt and called for Sharon.

"I lost him!" Sharon said. "It's like he just vanished…"

"Let's get out of this fog," Cornar said. He carefully backed out the way he had come. "Did you get a good look?"

"No," Sharon answered. She was still veiled beneath her cloak.

"Did he look like a man, or an elf?" Cornar asked, exiting the fog.

"Don't know. Couldn't tell."

Cornar hummed with disappointment. It could have been a Wildmen scout. Whoever it was did know the terrain well enough to stay ahead of Sharon.

They soon reached the cliff where the Mindolarn soldiers were standing. None of them dared to make the jump. It was nearly two stories tall.

"We lost him," Cornar shouted up to the soldiers. "Disappeared in some fog."

"We sent some others back for rope," a soldier said. "We'll pull you up."

One of the soldiers shouted commands for some of them to start patrolling the cliff. Soon, a few soldiers returned with a rope, accompanied by some of Cornar's men. Kalder and Nordal helped pull him and the still-invisible Sharon up the cliff.

"What happened?" Nordal asked.

Cornar pointed back to their camp, a gesture meant to command his comrades to return. "We lost him in some fog."

"Was it a Wildman?" Kalder asked.

"No," Cornar whispered. "I think it was an elf."

"An elf?" Nordal asked warily.

"I couldn't tell," Sharon interjected. She appeared from a veil of magic, removing a shimmering cloak, a type of tevisral that caused instantaneous invisibility. Cornar had used one several times in the past. They had two clasps on them, one to latch the cloak and another to activate the tevisral.

"Maybe Krindal's fears weren't unfounded," Kalder said.

Perhaps, Cornar thought. But what kind of elf would strike that kind of fear into a man?

They continued in silence until they reached the edge of the forest. A crowd had gathered between the camps. The scholars had stopped digging and had joined the crowd.

Several of the expedition's leaders were near the Mindolarn encampment, including Kaescis. The prince pushed his way through the soldiers and scholars, carrying a wine glass in his hand.

"What happened, Mister Dol'shir?" the prince asked.

"I saw someone in the trees," Cornar said. "When I went to investigate, they ran off. We chased him off a cliff and into some fog. It was too thick to go through, so we came back."

"Him?" Kaescis asked. "What did he look like?"

Others murmured questions about fog appearing at this time of day. It wasn't natural. They sounded just as perplexed as Cornar when he saw it.

"I don't know," Cornar said, deliberately omitting his speculation that the spy was an elf. "He was too far ahead by the time we started chasing him." He gestured to Sharon.

Kaescis frowned, then the grand marshals started shouting orders to the soldiers to go search the forest. The scholars talked among themselves, then headed back to the hole they had dug. Jahevial was still not among them. Where had he gone?

The rest of the crowd dispersed, and Cornar returned to his campsite with his companions. Sharon joined Ordreth back at the pot while Nordal returned to his card game.

Igan and Vargos stood near the fire, eyeing Cornar as he approached. "What was all that about?" Igan asked.

"Someone spying on the camp," Cornar replied. He glanced over his shoulder, but too many people were still within earshot. Cornar didn't want to speculate on the spy's identity with them around. "We chased him until he reached some fog and lost him. It was so thick I could barely see my weapons."

"Fog?" Igan raised his brow.

"That's not natural," Vargos said. "Someone must have cast it." The fog the result of a spell? Cornar hadn't thought of that.

"Was it blowing with the wind?" Igan asked.

Cornar couldn't recall. Which way had the fog been billowing? Was there even a breeze tonight? He couldn't feel one now.

The younger mages approached Igan, asking about the nightly commotion. Hem looked shocked and glanced about the camp in a paranoid manner. The wizards, Tinal and Renal, were disconcerted at the news and eyed the trees.

Everyone will be on edge tonight, Cornar thought and pushed his way to the fire. He sat on the ground and leaned forward to warm his hands.

"Food is ready!" Ordreth shouted.

⬥•⬥

"Do you suspect the Wildmen?" Hezidex asked. The grand marshal stood at one end of the common room in the Imperial Tent, holding a wineglass.

Kaescis sighed, feeling worried. A Wildman *would* know the terrain, but a member of the Sapphire Guard would be just as agile. However, Mister Dol'shir didn't mention the oddities associated with the Wildmen. Kaescis recalled the man not knowing much about them.

"No," Krindal said, his tone panicked. "It has to be *them*. The Sapphire Guard is sizing us up, seeing when they can strike."

"You're a paranoid old fool." Laeyit laughed, taking a sip of her wine. Kaescis frowned. Laeyit was being too lax. Had she forgotten the battle? Krindal had every right to be worried. For Lord Cheserith's sake, Kaescis was nervous too!

"And you don't think it is them?" Krindal demanded.

"No," Laeyit said. "Their ship wasn't in port."

"They could have moored elsewhere," Krindal insisted. "There are coves on the eastern side of Klindala."

"Not feasible for mooring," Laeyit retorted. "And we checked the other ports before we landed in Kretin. They're not on the island. Besides, we don't even know if they've traversed the other shrines."

"They don't need to have found the temples," Krindal said with a shake of his head. "They could be following us! The Sapphire Guard *is* here—we need to be careful! The fog is proof enough."

"My men found no fog," Hezidex said.

"See!" Krindal shouted, spilling his drink. "They must have cast a spell to make the fog. Use it as a ruse to make us think—if anyone chased them—that they were just Wildmen using the advantage of the terrain."

"Or Dol'shir was lying," Hezidex said coldly.

"Cornar isn't one to lie," Krindal said sharply. "He has no reason to lie."

"Unless he suspects that we're withholding information from him," Bratan chimed in. Bratan had stayed quiet since they returned to the tent. "I think you should have told him about our enemy."

"No," Krindal shook his head.

"You should tell him sooner rather than later." Bratan sighed. He folded his arms and leaned against a pole holding up the tent. The pole was fastened to the ground by a tevisral; it was practically immoveable.

Bratan and Krindal continued to argue while Kaescis took another sip of his wine. *Death.* The word echoed faintly in Kaescis's mind. A surge of bloodlust shot through him, sparking hope that this spy was a member of the Sapphire Guard. Then, he could have vengeance.

⟫•⟪

Cornar awoke the following morning to find that the hole in the path had grown. The scholars had made a discovery—a road *was* buried underground. It was made of solid stone. Some were saying it was like the highways in the Kingdom of Los. Cornar didn't linger too long at the discovery, but it was interesting. The road looked like it had been laid yesterday, and minus the dirt, the road looked in good condition. Krindal claimed it was more proof for his theories.

Perhaps it had magic flowing through it, Cornar thought. He dismissed his speculations and helped his men disassemble their campsite. It took nearly an hour to take down the camps. Cornar's men were finished well before the Mindolarnians. So, the warriors and mages helped disassemble the war camp.

A short while later they were on their way northward. The excitement of the previous night hadn't unnerved the members of the expedition. Cornar, however, kept a watchful eye as he traveled along the path to Klindil.

The path now narrowed between two sets of mountains, to the east and northwest. The river still ran along the path's eastern edge, at the base of the eastern mountains, while the forest continued westward to the nearing mountain range.

Around mid-afternoon the scouts sent by Grand Marshal Hezidex returned. From their calculation, the Fortress of Anigar was only two hours away. The scouts had found a large field at the edge of the forest, near the base of a path leading to the fortress ruins.

Cornar looked to the northwest mountain range. Something protruded from the mountainside. It was wedged within a narrow canyon. He couldn't see any details, but the shape didn't look like a natural rock formation.

That must be the fortress, he thought. It looked imposing even from this distance.

Another hour and a half had passed when the expedition climbed a rise. The forests grew along the northwest side of the path, preventing any view of the mountains and the fortress ruins. Weathered statues lined the other side of the path—towering depictions of men and women wearing free-flowing clothing and wielding shields and fanisars. Many of the statues wore helmets, but those without helmets were missing their faces. Beside the human statues stood statues of strange beasts that looked like a cross between a reptile and a wolf. Most of those statues were intact though they were weathered with age.

A mound of misshapen rocks, covered with dirt and trees, lay beyond the statues. Cornar thought the rocks looked like the toppled remains of a much larger statue. A large scaled finger protruded from the mound, looking like the end of a claw, though unlike any claw Cornar had ever seen. A curving wall of rock rose along part of the mound. It looked like a wing. Farther away, a large chunk of chiseled rock protruded from the mound, looking like an elongated snout.

Scaled claws? Long snouts? Wings? Those were traits attributed to creatures of myth and legend: dragons. Intrigued, Cornar turned his horse to get a better look. *Interesting…*

"We're almost there," Kaescis shouted and pointed beyond the trees. "The fortress is to our left."

Cornar was about to look in the direction the prince had mentioned, but a glint of light sparkled along that broken wing. It looked like the distorting effect of an invisibility spell; that only happened at the moment when the magic completely enveloped the person or object.

Curious, Cornar pulled on his reins, directing his horse to the misshapen mound. He stopped beside the claw, straining to hear any noises around the rubble. All he could hear were the sounds of the expedition moving behind him.

Blast, he thought, looking to the caravan's rear, toward his band. *Whoever was hiding here will be long gone before I can fetch Sharon.*

Sighing with disappointment, Cornar redirected his horse and galloped back to the head of the expedition.

"This is a good spot," Kaescis said, guiding his horse off the path, down the hill alongside the tree line.

Cornar followed after him but gazed at the mountains to the northwest. That strange outcropping was now visible, and it was an astounding sight. The Fortress of Anigar looked like a grand palace. Towers rose as high as the peaks, their bases halfway up the mountainside. The architecture was unlike anything Cornar had ever beheld, looking like a castle straight out of a myth. There was exquisite detail to these ruins. It was spectacular!

"So that's the Fortress of Anigar," Krindal said. "It looks imposing."

"As it should," Hezidex said. "It was the first line of defense for Klindala against the rebels of the Karthar War. The defenders held this valley for decades from that fortress."

Cornar passed the other leaders and stopped beside Kaescis. The prince was surveying the proposed campsite. The field was quite large. They could set up their camp in the center and still have a clearing of nearly a grand phineal.

"Will you incorporate your men into our encampment tonight, Mister Dol'shir?" Kaescis asked, sounding concerned.

Cornar raised his brow. "Do you really think the Wildmen are that much of a danger?"

"No," Kaescis said, "but I think it'd be best if we were all close together."

Cornar didn't reply. He could tell the prince was worried about something else. Though Kaescis hadn't said it, the spy from last night bothered him.

"Your men will be in the Royal ring," Kaescis said. "Have them set up their tents beside those of the Praetorians."

"As you wish," Cornar said. He guided his horse across the field, passing the bulk of the expedition. Soon Cornar reached his band, which was at the hill's crest near the broken draconic statue.

"What's going on, Cor?" Gregan asked, shielding his eyes from the sun as he gazed at Cornar.

"Kaescis wants us close to him tonight. We're going to set up our tents inside the war camp, near the Imperial Tent."

Several of the men muttered worriedly.

"Are they expecting a battle?" Kalder asked.

"Not that was said." Cornar sighed. He scanned the misshapen mound before continuing. "But we should be prepared. After we set up camp they are sending scouts into that castle."

Sharon pushed her way toward Cornar. "Want me to go with them?"

She would have an advantage. And, this way Cornar could find out any details that might not be shared with the other leaders, as the scouts would report directly to Grand Marshal Hezidex.

"Yes," Cornar said with a nod. "Now, let's go set up our tents."

"A boy shall endure unimaginable pain. His anguish will unleash the Harbinger's fury. It will catalyze the Unspoken One's journey to usher in the divine advent."

- Prophecy of Soron Thahan

I t's been four hours," Ordreth said, pacing back and forth between the tents in the Royal ring of the Mindolarn war camp. He looked nervous. Cornar couldn't blame him. How else should a man feel when letting the love of his life dash off into an unexplored and potentially dangerous place, alone? By Heleron's Scales, Cornar would be just as worried if it were Karenna out there. Would he dare let Karenna go? That thought stung him.

"I doubt the Wildmen can see through her cloak," Nordal said. "She'll be fine." Ordreth sucked in a deep breath and stared at Nordal for a moment. Cornar could see a restrained panic growing behind his nephew's eyes.

A hustle of commotion echoed into the Royal ring from the camp's middle tier. Cornar turned, as did Ordreth and Nordal. Several of the mages and other warriors emerged from their tents, curious about the disturbance. Cornar could feel the tension mounting.

"I don't hear an alarm," Nordal said. "Perhaps—"

The scouts sent by Grand Marshal Hezidex dashed into the Royal ring, heading straight for the Imperial Tent. The Crimson Praetorians let them pass without argument.

"I told you." Nordal glanced to Ordreth, who looked anxiously to the entrance of the war camp's heart.

A faint whistle echoed from behind Cornar and the others, changing tones in a familiar pattern. It started out mid-range, then rose in pitch, dropped to a low tone, and rose back to the mid-range sound.

The stress melted from Ordreth, and he grinned widely, responding with an identical whistle. That whistle—established by Cornar years ago—was to signal a party member's return. Often on adventures, the party would be holed up in dangerous places. The whistle was used to forestall an ambush by the main group.

"The place was empty," Sharon whispered. She was still concealed beneath her mystical cloak.

"Deserted?" Cornar asked.

"No, people were there recently," the thief said, sounding worried. "Several fire pits were lit less than a day ago."

Igan, Vargos, Kalder, Midar, and Hemrin gathered around Cornar. They had undoubtedly heard the signal. No one else in the Royal ring seemed to notice it, and the Crimson Praetorians didn't react.

"Perhaps the Wildmen fled upon seeing the caravan?" Midar asked. Cornar nodded. That seemed likely. This was an imposing force.

"I also found some odd seams in many of the walls. They looked like hidden doors and were all over that castle. I didn't want to pry at them, in case the Wildmen were tucked away in a hidden room."

A wise choice.

Sharon continued whispering her report. "The scouts found clothing, cooking tools, and children's things. They think the Wildmen fled upon seeing us set up camp in the valley."

"Or they're hiding and waiting for reinforcements," Nordal said.

"That's what I think," Sharon said. "They would have taken more things if they were retreating."

"An ambush?" Igan asked, stroking his chin thoughtfully.

"I bet those seams led to hidden rooms," Vargos said. "It's smart. Lure your enemy inside and then pick them off in small groups."

The men continued voicing their opinions on the matter until a Crimson Praetorian approached the group.

"Mister Dol'shir," the Praetorian said. Everyone quieted, looking to the armored man. "His Imperial Grace wishes you to join them for the scout's report."

Cornar nodded and glanced back to where he heard Sharon's voice. He was faced with a decision: inform the other leaders about Sharon's observations or keep it to himself. *What should I do?* Cornar thought, looking skyward. He hoped for an answer, but nothing came.

The Praetorian returned to his post, and the men resumed chatting. Ordreth moved to one of the tents and deliberately held it open for a while. Sharon could remove her cloak inside the tent without arousing suspicion.

Perhaps telling them would win their trust, Cornar thought as he crossed the grounds to the Imperial Tent. He made his way to the war room where light chatter reached his ears.

Cornar strode into the room. All the other leaders were there, looming over the table. The scouts—a woman and two men—stood beside Grand Marshal Hezidex. Cornar stopped at the table as Kaescis spoke.

"That's everyone," the prince said. "Now, Crenai, please give us your report." That was odd. She wasn't reporting to the grand marshal first?

"We encountered no resistance," the scout said. "The Wildmen are not in the ruins."

"What do you mean?" Krindal blurted worriedly. "Were they attacked? Were there signs of a struggle?" The scout, Crenai shook her head slowly, unsure of what to make of Krindal's hasty questions. "It looks like they just disappeared amid their daily activities," she continued. "We found recently used fire pits. Clothing was hanging out to dry."

"We scared them," said Grand Marshal Galiur, sighing and shaking his head.

"Are you sure they weren't attacked?" Krindal asked, sounding paranoid.

Another scout spoke up, his words ringing with agitation. "There was no sign of battle."

The scouts continued their reports, elaborating on the brief tale Sharon had given Cornar and the others. They spoke about the ruins' layout. None of the scouts mentioned the seams. They wouldn't have noticed that detail, despite this time of day. Sharon's lenses could detect such things, even in pitch blackness.

How will they react? Cornar thought. Would they be angry? Would they feel betrayed? The more Cornar heard about the ruins, the more he believed the Wildmen were hiding inside hidden parts of that forlorn castle.

"Another party should go up there," Kaescis said. "We need more information. Perhaps we can find a trail or another path coming out the other side."

They didn't go anywhere, Cornar thought.

The prince continued laying out his plans as Cornar struggled with the decision to relay Sharon's report. Kaescis intended to chase after the Wildmen and find another encampment. The prince didn't want to march on Klindil without the acceptance of the Wildmen.

The other leaders began giving their input when Cornar interrupted them. "The Wildmen are still in the ruins." Everyone stopped and studied him. "My thief followed the scouts," he continued. The scouts didn't look pleased, nor did their commander. Kaescis, however, remained calm and regal. "She found hidden doors throughout that castle," Cornar added. "I think the Wildmen are hiding inside. They're probably waiting for us to pass by before they come out of hiding."

Laeyit glared at Cornar. What was her problem? "I say we go into the ruins," Cornar said. "And seek their leaders."

"They could be waiting in ambush," Laeyit retorted, raising her upper lip in a wicked-looking scowl. Bratan nodded in agreement.

"So, you think it's a trap, Mister Dol'shir?" Kaescis asked.

"No," Cornar shook his head. "These people are primitive. They're just trying to protect themselves. Trust me. I've run across enough primitives to understand how they react to outsiders. As long as we don't go in there with weapons or hostile intent, we should be able to open a peaceful negotiation."

"You want us to walk into a trap, unarmed?" Laeyit growled. *That woman has problems…* Cornar thought, fighting the urge to roll his eyes. Kaescis stared at Cornar blankly.

"That's foolish," Hezidex said.

"They could be off seeking reinforcements," Galiur said. "We should be fortifying the war camp. Have the transmuters erect barricades."

"No we need to chase after them," a scout chimed in.

A heated debate started. Everyone had their own opinions about the matter.

"You're thinking like civilized men," Cornar shouted, but no one was listening.

The meeting became chaotic. Cornar sighed. Kaescis, however, was still staring at him. The prince was the only one not speaking. Chaos ensued for a moment until Kaescis shouted, "Silence!" Everyone obeyed. "We go into the ruins. Unarmed—"

"Kaescis!" Laeyit chided. "Don't be fool—"

"Shut up, Laeyit," Kaescis rebuked the woman, then continued. "We'll take the scouts, Mister Dol'shir's thief, and us leaders except Hezidex. Bring your best men, Mister Dol'shir, but keep their number to a minimum." Cornar nodded.

"We leave now," Kaescis said, walking away from the table. None of the leaders made a complaint, except for Krindal, who muttered to himself.

Did he say something about elves? Cornar wondered.

With the meeting concluded, the men and women reluctantly turned from the table. Cornar, however, hurried out of the room before any of them could leave. He dashed through the Imperial Tent and ran across the grass to where his men were gathered.

"Kalder, Nordal!" Cornar shouted. "Ordreth, Midar, Gregan!" Nordal was still where Cornar had left him, talking with Igan and Vargos. "Vargos, you too."

"What's going on, Cor?" Igan asked. "We heard some ruckus coming from the tent." He gestured back to the protrusion where the war room was located.

"Just a heated debate," Cornar answered. "We're going into the ruins to draw out the Wildmen." Igan raised his brow. The wizard obviously thought that course of action unwise.

"So you want a barsionist, huh?" Vargos asked. "It's a good thing I'm still around. Don't know what you guys would do without me."

"Die?" Nordal asked. But no one laughed at a morbid joke.

"Sharon!" Cornar called.

Soon, everyone Cornar had called was gathered around him. He relayed the discussion in the war room. None of them even flinched at the idea of walking into an ambush, unarmed and unarmored. Of course, they had a barsionist with them. Barsionists always vanquished the fear of death.

The Fortress of Anigar was more impressive up close, even at night. The ramp leading up the mountainside, wide enough for ten men to walk abreast, was astounding in itself. Much of the ramp was suspended above the ground—in one spot the mountainside was a good one-hundred-phineal drop. Cornar felt woozy looking over the edge. What was that sensation? Not everyone experienced it, only he and Krindal. Perhaps it was the onset of old age…

His men were eager to see the steepness, and they took turns looking over the ramp's edge. They had been on mountaintops before, but this was totally different. It was like looking off a cliff, but one where you could clearly see the bottom. Both of Kalda's moons were so bright that Cornar and his men could easily see the forest below them.

The Mindolarnians didn't seem to even notice the staggering height. They walked right by Cornar and the other warriors. Perhaps they were simply consumed with springing this trap the Wildmen had set. The massive ramp led straight to a towering gateway, rising at least five stories high. There was no sign of a gate, only an empty opening. Cornar had expected to see the remains of tarnished metal, but there was nothing. Perhaps the gate had rusted long ago.

Kaescis led the party through the gateway, carrying a lightstone-powered lantern. The prince was the first to reach a bridge—no longer than a dozen paces—and waited for everyone to catch up to him.

From this vantage, Cornar could easily make out the various parts of the fortress, despite the lack of light. The Fortress of Anigar was in fact a compound of buildings interconnected by covered walkways. There was no central keep as one might expect, just a random layout of large buildings and towers that conformed to the topography of the mountain. Walls branched off from the structure that housed the gate, completely enclosing the compound.

There was an exquisite beauty to the ruins that had survived the test of time. Some of the buildings, the towers in particular, had bulbous-shaped rooftops. Many of the buildings had columns lining their walls. The columns looked decorative, but Cornar couldn't make out details. Perhaps if he got closer, he could use his lantern to illuminate the columns.

All was quiet as they moved off the bridge and into the first set of wards. There were raised sections of ground that had plants growing in them. The plants looked… cultivated. They weren't arrayed neatly, but Cornar could swear it looked like these plants were being farmed. The party passed a few towering buildings, which looked mostly intact. Many of the windows, however, were broken or completely missing their panes. The glass had probably decayed years ago.

The prince hurried through another courtyard. This one seemed larger than the first. It had more of those raised spots of ground with plants growing in them; the plants bore some kind of fruit. Cornar departed from the others and went over to investigate, holding his lantern to the plants. One of the plants had radish-looking bulbs growing from its stems. They even had tails growing on one end. Why would something on a branch grow like that?

"Hey," Vargos called out in a hoarse voice, "stop gawking at that. It's not safe to eat." Cornar chuckled and turned back to the others. Vargos was standing at the base of a wide staircase leading to the largest building in the fortress. The others were already at the top of the stairs, heading for a towering doorway.

"How do you know it's not safe to eat?" Cornar asked, nearing the old barsionist.

"Because I don't know what it is," Vargos retorted. "Just listen to your elders."

Cornar shook his head and rolled his eyes. He jogged up the stairs, leaving Vargos behind. Cornar caught up to everyone just as they reached the towering doors.

"… here, we can go down the left branch," Sharon said, gesturing with her lantern. She stopped inside a towering foyer. It was rectangular, and wider than it was deep. Two broken humanoid statues stood along the far wall, poised with their arms in the air. Much of their identifying features were broken off, but the pieces were nowhere to be found. "There's a large room there that had the largest concentration of things."

"We can get there faster going to the right," Crenai said, pointing in that direction.

"But there are more of those seams in the hallways to the left," Sharon retorted. She hurried off down the left side of the foyer with Ordreth close behind her. Cornar paused and raised his lantern, studying the statues for a moment. *Odd that they'd be weathered,* he thought. *Especially when the architecture outside is in good cond—*

Vargos bumped his shoulder, causing the lantern to sway. Light bounced all over the room. The old barsionist grinned. He had collided with Cornar on purpose. "So when should I cast my spells?" Vargos asked, looking around cautiously.

"Not yet, master barsionist," Kaescis said.

Vargos grunted, looking to Cornar. "We should all be lined by a thin layer of barsion," Vargos said. "Who knows, maybe we could palm ourselves off as divine beings. Glowing a brilliant luster. Invulnerable to attack." The old barsionist grinned at his remarks, thinking he made a joke.

Vargos… Cornar shook his head.

The party wound their way through a maze of corridors, passing rooms without doors.

Cornar admired the architecture in the halls. The halls were completely illuminated with their lightstone lanterns. It was just as grand and intricate as the architecture outside. There were even sconces on the walls that were intact. They most likely held lightstones at one time, but now they were empty.

"Here," Sharon said, stopping beside the wall to their right. The place where she stood looked smooth. Not even the light could show the seam in the wall. "I don't see a mechanism…" The scouts began searching for something to activate the hidden door. Soon, everyone was searching. "There's another one here," Sharon said. She was about thirty phineals away from the first hidden door. "I don't see anything between them."

"Perhaps they're activated by words," Kaescis speculated.

"Like a spell?" Vargos asked.

"No," Kaescis shook his head. "Some tevisrals are sound-activated. A lot of ancient tevisrals were made in such a manner, especially ones fused into architecture."

"Fused into architecture?" Krindal spoke up. "Are you saying there's tevisrals in these ruins?"

"Most likely," Kaescis said, sliding his hand across the wall. "It could be touch activated… or coded to biological indicators." The prince nodded as if coming to a conclusion. "That'd provide an additional layer of defense." What was Kaescis talking about?

"Biological indicators?" Krindal asked. "What is that, Your Imperial Highness?"

"You wouldn't understand," Kaescis said, pulling away from the wall. "I'd have to explain theories and laws of nature that would be unfathomable to you." Now that was arrogant… Was Kaescis claiming—in a roundabout manner—that the Mindolarn Empire had a better understanding of the world than anyone else? Krindal pursed his lips and glanced to Cornar.

"Maybe there's something in the big room," Sharon suggested and continued down the hall. Everyone hurried after her. Cornar took up the rear.

Soon, they entered a huge room with a barrel ceiling. It was at least four stories high. Moonlight spilled into the space from openings lining the base of the ceiling. Beds were organized throughout the room. A fire pit was near the hallway, and another near the far wall. The nearest pit had ashes in it. Clothing hung on lines, stretched between more broken statues lining the walls.

"There's more of those doors in here," Sharon said, pointing to a spot between two statues. "One there, another at the far end." The party broke up and began searching the space, but Cornar surveyed the room. A knot formed in his stomach, accompanied by an ominous presence. *Danger!* The hidden doors in the walls flew open. Footfalls echoed from the hallway Cornar and the others had traversed, as well as from another corridor.

Darkened figures of the Wildmen burst from the hidden doors and the hallways, carrying crude weapons. Sharon jumped. Ordreth ran in front of Sharon to protect her. Laeyit dropped into a battle stance as well as Bratan. Krindal reached for Kaescis, grabbing the prince's arm. Kaescis, however, stood still. The scouts froze. The warriors began moving but stopped; they glanced to Cornar, awaiting orders.

Crenai screamed and dropped her lantern. She hurriedly backed away, but tripped and fell. Vargos groaned with disgust.

Why had he—

Cornar finally focused on the Wildmen surrounding them. He had only seen darkened figures and was too busy accounting for everyone's positions before really noticing *who* was surrounding them.

Their faces… they… they were deformed and covered in strange fur. They looked humanoid, but… they weren't men! By Heleron's Trident, what were they?

WILDMEN

"Worlds will be bridged, kingdoms will collapse, and a star will fall from the heavens."

- Prophecy of Soron Thahan

Cornar steadied into a wide stance, gazing at the Wildmen surrounding him and his men. Cornar could clearly see their features, now that they were illuminated by the lightstone lanterns.

The Wildmen's faces looked like someone had stretched their noses and their mouths to mimic the snout of a beast. Protruding brows stood out above their eyes, like a strange cranial feature. Their hands were large, with thick fingers. The Wildmen wore ragged clothes but their arms, neck, and faces were covered in thick brown hair. Everything else, however, looked human.

The Wildmen edged closer, weapons ready. They eyed Cornar with fierce hostility. He was obviously perceived as an invader. *Don't fight,* Cornar thought, breathing calmly. Laeyit and Bratan were ready for battle. Kaescis, however, remained calm.

The prince shook Krindal's arm free and walked in a circle, looking at the Wildmen. *What is he doing?* Cornar thought.

Vargos caught Cornar's eye, and the barsionist mouthed, "Should I cast a spell?" Cornar shook his head. Although the Wildmen looked hostile, they didn't seem bloodthirsty.

"Ahrond uhm ahp!" one of the Wildmen shouted. *Was that Common?* Cornar wondered. It sounded like he commanded the others to—

The Wildmen rushed toward the perceived invaders, swinging their weapons. A cacophony of battle resonated throughout the hall. Amid the noises he heard several spells being cast, by Krindal and Vargos… and was that Kaescis too?

Cornar glimpsed a Wildman approaching from the left and another from the right. They wielded crude cudgels.

Left is holding his weapon sloppily, Cornar thought and dashed to the Wildman on the left. The Wildman looked young. He was probably inexperienced.

Cornar evaded a swing, dodging under the cudgel. He grabbed the Wildman's wrist as the weapon passed, yanking his foe's arm. The jolt threw the Wildman off balance, and Cornar kicked out his nearest leg. Cornar circled around, still holding the Wildman's wrist, and hammered the bottom of his fist to the base of his foe's neck. Stunned, the Wildman let go of his weapon, but before it fell Cornar snatched it.

By this time, the other Wildman had reached him. Cornar leapt forward as the second Wildman swung his cudgel. The blow was too low to duck but also too high to jump over. Cornar spun, blocking the blow. He came about, elbowing the Wildman in the head. The first Wildman grunted while struggling to stand.

Cornar backed away, putting both of his opponents in front of him. He glimpsed his men effectively defending against the Wildmen. Kalder and Gregan were covered in Vargos's shielding magic; the warriors glowed with bright blue light. Everyone was moving, except for Kaescis.

The prince was just standing there, holding a—no! It couldn't be, could it? A black vapor misted from Kaescis's outstretched hand, and then a black blade coalesced, composed of magic.

Like those knights, Cornar thought, remembering the first dream he had experienced, the one with his father and Adrin.

Movement caught his eye, and the two Wildmen advanced. The armed one swung his weapon while the other leapt to tackle Cornar. Their movement was telegraphed sloppily, and Cornar easily evaded them.

Amid the melee, Kaescis shouted a sharp-sounding phrase, and all the Wildmen froze. The two beside Cornar began talking to each other in that broken form of Common. It sounded like they were confused.

"Put down your weapons," Kaescis shouted. "We mean you no harm." One of the Wildmen stepped forward, the same who had given the order to attack. The Wildman approached the prince, eyeing him up and down, and then asked a question Cornar couldn't understand.

"Are you the leader?" Kaescis asked, dismissing his black blade. The weapon broke down to mist, then wisped away.

So he can use that magic too, Cornar mused. *But Kaescis used an incantation to muster it…* Intrigued, Cornar thought of Iltar and how he could muster those same black corrosive particles—without incantation.

The Wildman nodded while speaking a reply. The two words weren't intelligible, but Cornar thought he might have said, "I am."

"We must speak," Kaescis said. "Alone."

The armed Wildman beside Cornar shouted, sounding worried. He repeated a word, "Gevistra," using it like a name. Cornar eyed the Wildman with a curious glance. *What's wrong with these people?* Cornar thought. They talked like children learning to speak for the first time.

There was a short exchange between the Wildmen and their leader. Amid the conversation, the armed Wildman beside Cornar spoke, his tone commanding. "Euw," the Wildman said. "Go." He repeated it, nudging Cornar with his cudgel.

Euw? Cornar wondered as the Wildman pointed across the room. *Could that be 'you'?*

The Wildman nudged Cornar again, more forcefully this time, and resumed pointing. He gestured to the statues along the wall. Several other Wildmen were urging the others in the same direction.

"Everyone stay calm," Kaescis said. "Do as they say." The prince was the only one not being urged to the wall. Cornar took a step forward. The Wildman spoke another unintelligible word while holding out his freehand. "Ehpin!" he repeated.

Confused, Cornar raised his brow, then glanced to the stolen cudgel. *Oh,* he grinned, *he wants this weapon…* Still grinning, Cornar handed his stolen cudgel back to the Wildman and joined the others. They huddled together between the two maimed statues. His warriors looked at him with disappointment. They were itching for a good fight.

The scouts chattered to each other while the Mindolarn leaders stayed quiet.

"Well, that was fun," Nordal said. "While it lasted…"

"You're always looking for a fight," Ordreth observed.

"Yeah?" Nordal said, hoping to provoke more from Ordreth. Ordreth, however, just glanced at him.

The Wildman leader shouted a command, and several Wildmen grabbed some rope. They bound the prince and then moved for those against the wall.

"Let them bind you," Kaescis shouted.

The Wildmen tied everyone up with a long rope, keeping them close together.

"This is ridiculous," Gregan said with a grunt.

"We need to be compliant," Kalder said calmly.

The warriors and scouts complained about the cords, but Cornar ignored them. Cornar watched the Wildman leader, as he supposed, walk away with Kaescis and a few armed Wildmen. They went deeper into the large room, their footsteps fading. It sounded like they went down another corridor. Cornar hadn't seen a hallway at the other end. Then again, he hadn't had much time to examine the room before they were jumped by the Wildmen.

"What are those things?" Crenai asked, sounding terrified.

"They're the Wildmen," Laeyit said. She leaned against a statue, clasping her tied hands. Her face showed her utter disgust.

"But they're not human…" Crenai muttered.

Were they not human? Cornar didn't know much about the Wildmen of Klindala, only that they were primitive tribes that inhabited most of the island and were descendants of the Klindala Dynasty. But that dynasty had crumbled at the end of the Karthar War, an event that occurred nearly a thousand years ago.

If the Wildmen were cut off from the outside world, it would explain the corruption of their language and their primitive nature, but not their strange features.

The people of the Klindala Dynasty were human, weren't they? Humans and elves were the only kind of *people* that inhabited Kalda, as far as Cornar knew.

So what were these Wildmen?

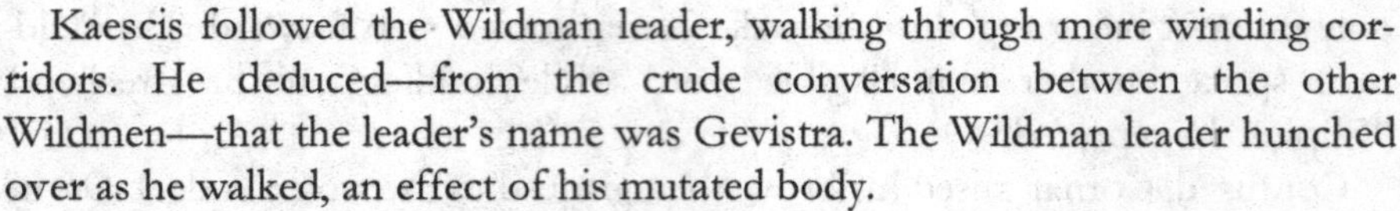

Kaescis followed the Wildman leader, walking through more winding corridors. He deduced—from the crude conversation between the other Wildmen—that the leader's name was Gevistra. The Wildman leader hunched over as he walked, an effect of his mutated body.

These poor fools, Kaescis thought. *They don't even know what they're missing.* That fueled a burning anger inside him. His hatred toward the Karthar rebels grew, igniting a bloodlust.

Death. The word lingered at the back of his mind, like a distant whisper. Kaescis sighed. *I'm becoming my old self,* he mused. It had to be the more frequent use of the Ko'delish, and that blade. *Yes, the blade.* Whenever his father and his uncles wielded those massive blades they were filled with fury. *That must be the answer.*

They neared an open door, and Gevistra gestured to it. He spoke, but was hard to understand. Gevistra repeated himself, obviously wanting Kaescis to enter before him.

"In there," Kaescis guessed. *"You first."* The accent was so thick, almost like another language. The Wildman spoke as if his tongue was swollen.

Gevistra opened his mouth again, but Kaescis complied and entered the room. The Wildmen remained at the door, eyeing him. By the way they stood it seemed they were trying to bar him from escaping. Well, at least they thought they were barring him. Kaescis could easily cut through them and slay the entire population of the fortress. Their corpses would—

Focus, he told himself. The Ko'delish's effects were becoming nigh uncontrollable. It was like his mind ran amok with thoughts of death.

Death.

Gevistra finally entered the room, standing as straight-backed as possible. He asked a question, then another. They both started with the word *Wae.* *Probably "why,"* Kaescis thought, parsing the corrupted language. "Why you here," was the first question. The second was harder to understand.

"Your language is corrupt," Kaescis said, "It is hard for me to understand you. Please, be patient."

Gevistra nodded, seeming agitated, and slowly repeated the questions. The second question ended with the word, "took-kin."

Token? Kaescis wondered. Was Gevistra asking about the Token spoken by the Devouts when reverencing Lord Cheserith? Kaescis had spoken it amid the assault. "The Token is the sign of true discipleship," he answered. "I knew that if I were to speak it to you, that you'd forgo attacking us."

The Wildmen looked at each other in confusion.

"I am Prince Kaescis Midivar, sixth in line to the Mindolarn throne. I am the son of Mindolarn the first emperor, who was the son of Madars, the son of Karath'nos, begotten through the lineage of Ku'tharn."

Upon hearing the names the Wildmen's eyes widened. They gasped and trembled. Gevistra fell to his knees and huddled before Kaescis, repeating a word in a shaky tone. It sounded like "forgive," although certain sounds were emphasized and neglected. The others also repeated the word and knelt.

Kaescis smiled, pleased at their piety. It would make this next part that much easier. "Now to answer your question. I have come to your home to seek safe passage for me and my people as we venture to the ruins of Klindil."

Gevistra looked up to Kaescis, blinking several times. He commanded the others to cut Kaescis loose. They obeyed, and the rope fell to the ground.

"Thank you," Kaescis said, rubbing his wrists.

Gevistra furrowed his thick brow, then asked another question in his corrupted Common. "Why you go to Klindil?" He pronounced the name "khil-en-dil." He then said another phrase Kaescis couldn't understand.

Was that, "it is dangerous"? Kaescis thought, then answered the question. "I must uncover a great secret hidden there, something that will enable me to bring lasting peace to our world."

Gevistra didn't look convinced.

"There is a temple, a shrine, hidden beneath your ancient city," Kaescis said. "We need to visit it. My people will not take anything. We only need information from it."

Gevistra said something else about Klindil and spoke of something called *fareenars.*

"We're not here to steal from you," Kaescis extended his hand to placate the Wildman. "And, I will give you and your people something valuable in exchange for allowing us safe passage to Klindil. Do you speak for all the tribes?"

Gevistra shook his head. He said something else, including what Kaescis determined was a name, Bhrane.

"High Chieftain Bhrane?" Kaescis asked. "He leads the tribes?" The Wildman's impediment was growing tiresome. Gevistra nodded.

"Can you take me to him?" Kaescis asked. Gevistra nodded again, then asked another question. It included the word *geev,* and Kaescis deduced Gevistra was asking what he would give them.

Kaescis grinned. "I will return your people to your former glory. Here, I'll demonstrate on one of your men."

Gevistra motioned for one of the Wildmen to approach. The man knelt before Kaescis in reverence.

Kaescis uttered an incantation—not in the tongue used among the men of Kalda. That was a pitiful imitation of the true Words of Power. "Si'nak ma'nal senda." Green arpran particles gathered in his hands. "Ulak'xin ma'ril kusaz."

The arpran magic wisped into the Wildman's nostrils, and his elongated faced glowed and began to shrink. The Wildman gasped in horror, splaying his mouth wide. The Wildman's tongue was shrinking.

Now it'll be easier to understand them, he thought. *Well, this one at least.*

Some of the hair around the Wildman's neck fell out while his hands shrank. He was starting to look human. Gevistra paled and scurried away, pressing himself against the wall beside the door. The other Wildmen darted through the hall, running away from the room.

"Gevistra," the changing Wildman groaned, "what happen to me?" He screamed in pain, collapsing on the ground.

His speech isn't perfect, but it's better than before. Kaescis grinned, pleased with his deed.

The arpran light faded, and the Wildman curled up on the floor. His mouth and nose were not as pronounced as before, and only some of his hair had shed. Kaescis couldn't have gone any further with him, or the other tribes would not believe that this man was kin.

"What you do?" Gevistra asked, still trembling, his words barely understandable.

"I am undoing an atrocious act," Kaescis said. "Your people have been deprived for generations, stricken by our ancient enemies. Cursed to live in this… state." He gestured to Gevistra with disgust. "You and your kind are a fragment of what you could be."

"What you mean?" Gevistra asked, *mean* sounding like *mein.*

"To put it simply, your ancestors were cursed because they sided with the true rulers of our world. A thousand years ago, the people of Klindala were turned savage. Your conquerors didn't want to subjugate you, they thought that barbaric… but they couldn't allow a chance of you rising in rebellion against them. So they cursed you. They crippled your bodies so you would be clumsy. They twisted your tongues so you couldn't utter incantations to muster power. They dulled your minds so you couldn't maintain your cities or operate tevisrals—"

Kaescis's anger boiled amid his rhetoric, but he tamed his fury.

Destruction, the voice whispered.

"They hurled you into a dark age… but I will undo that curse, restoring you and your people. You will become powerful once again, powerful enough to drive out the invaders that have claimed parts of your land." That piqued Gevistra's interests. He moved from the wall and knelt before Kaescis, asking another question.

"Am I a god?" Kaescis grinned. "No… the gods have been gone for a long time, but their blood runs through my veins." Gevistra looked confused. No matter, he was too primitive to understand.

"Gevistra," the changed Wildman groaned, "I feel… different." Concerned, Gevistra turned to the changed Wildman and asked another question. This time, none of the words were understandable.

"No," the changed Wildman said. "No hurt now."

"You will feel some pain, Gevistra," Kaescis said. "But this is arpran magic I am using. It will simply restore you to your true form."

Gevistra nodded uneasily. The changed Wildman's cries had frightened him, and rightly so. The lifting of the curse was painful, but the pain would subside once the transformation stopped.

"Now, do we have a deal, Gevistra? Will you take me to Chief Bhrane and advocate for us to search Klindil unmolested?"

Gevistra nodded.

"Good," Kaescis grinned. He knew this plan would work. If the other tribal leaders were like Gevistra, things would be easy. Surely they'd see this restoration as more valuable than what Kaescis was receiving. Then he would enlist them.

The Sapphire Guard won't stop us this time, he thought. *Not with an army of Wildmen at my command.*

And then Kaescis uttered another incantation.

⸻◦⸻

"I don't like this," Laeyit grumbled. That woman didn't seem to like anything. She was more of an annoyance than anything else. Why did Kaescis tolerate her?

"Kaescis knows what he's doing," Bratan said.

"What *is* His Imperial Grace doing?" a scout asked.

"Bartering," Grand Marshal Galiur said curtly.

"I know that," the same scout said timidly. He was trying to hide his exasperation. "But with what?"

Bratan eyed the man for a moment. "I suppose I can tell you," he said, sighing. "Kaescis is—"

Footsteps echoed into the large room, and Bratan abruptly withheld his explanation.

Had the prince returned? Intrigued, Cornar leaned forward, as much as he could with the rope holding him back.

Kaescis strode into the room unbound. The prince walked with two Wildmen—no… those weren't the same Wildmen, were they? They looked different. More human… Their faces didn't protrude as much, and their cranial feature had receded. They had less hair too.

By Heleron's Trident, Cornar thought. *What's going on?*

"Cut them free," commanded the Wildman on Kaescis's left. The Wildmen who had guarded Cornar, and the others gasped.

"Do not fear," the same Wildman said. "It is I, Gevistra." One of the guarding Wildmen blurted an incoherent phrase, looking confused. Was he asking why this Gevistra looked different?

"I know," Gevistra said. "Cut the prince's people free."

The Wildmen didn't obey. They looked at each other with growing fear.

"Calm yourselves," the other changed Wildman said. "We are the same, but better. You can be too. It will not hurt."

What had happened to those two? They looked different and spoke without that strange Wildman accent.

Kaescis stood with his arms folded, looking like he was in charge. Had he cast a spell on the Wildmen? Used some sort of enthralling magic to make their speech more understandable? Those were obviously illusions he had put on those two. Well, that's what Iltar would do if he were here.

Another Wildman shouted at Gevistra, sounding worried. That shout seemed like a plea. "*We... can... not*"? Cornar wondered. The words sounded distorted, emphasized in the wrong places.

"Obey," the one called Gevistra commanded, his tone harsh. The Wildmen looked to each other, unsure of what to do, but one turned to Cornar and cut him free.

Cornar watched with intrigue as the Wildman complied with Gevistra's orders.

"Well done, Tutil," Gevistra said, gesturing for him to come near. "You will be the first of our tribe to be restored. Kneel before the prince." Restored? Perhaps Kaescis wasn't controlling these two.

"In due time," Kaescis said, glancing to Gevistra. "I will relay some orders, and then I will restore your people." The Wildmen nodded and Kaescis addressed the others.

"Bratan, Laeyit. You're coming with me. We're leaving tonight to speak with the Wildmen high chieftain." The prince looked to Galiur. "We'll need our things. Send part of the Crimson Praetorians with our armor, horses, and packs of supplies."

Galiur nodded and saluted the prince. "Yes, Your Imperial Grace!"

Kaescis then turned to Krindal. "You'll lead the rest of the expedition to Klindala. We'll meet you on the outskirts of the ruins."

"But, Your Imperial Highness," Krindal spoke up, sounding frazzled. "What about the—"

"Krindal," Kaescis interrupted, "there's no need to fear our enemies. They have not come this way. We are the only outlanders Gevistra's tribe has encountered in several years."

Cornar eyed Krindal, intrigued. Had Krindal been about to say the name of the group that frightened him?

Grand Marshal Galiur called for everyone to follow him, marching back the way they had come. Krindal hurried after him, and then the scouts fell in line, followed by the warriors and Sharon. Laeyit and Bratan, however, joined the prince.

Cornar stood between the statues for a moment, eyeing the Wildmen. He noted the difference between those who guarded him and those who spoke with Kaescis.

"Are you coming?" Vargos asked. He was the only other member of the emissary party—besides the prince and his friends—that was still in the large room.

"Yeah..." Cornar said, stepping away from the statue.

"They're strange looking, aren't they?" Vargos asked.

"The changed ones?" Cornar asked.

"All of them!" Vargos blurted, glancing over his shoulder. "I knew Wildmen were primitive, but I didn't think they were *not* human. They're like animals…"

Cornar took one last look at the Wildmen before leaving the room. The one who had cut him free was kneeling before Kaescis. The leader was saying something but Cornar couldn't hear what.

"I wonder what he meant by *restored*," Cornar said as they entered the hallway.

"Beats me…" Vargos said with a shrug.

"What do you know of Klindala?" Cornar asked the old barsionist.

"Obviously not enough." Vargos shook his head. "I've never heard of people like *that*. The Wildmen have always been shrugged off as primitives. There aren't many stories about them. The Maltins tend to keep away from this part of the island, and no one has made an exploratory venture out here in decades. If someone did encounter the Wildmen, they probably didn't record their findings."

That seemed odd to Cornar. Wouldn't someone have made mention of these people?

"Makes me wonder, though," Vargos continued. "How those two looked more human than the others." Cornar nodded, mulling the entire matter over in his mind.

They continued in silence until they reached the foyer. Cornar walked over to the marred statues. They looked human. One's face was worn off, and the other's head was missing completely. Neither statue portrayed the appearance of the Wildmen. They didn't even come close. The Wildmen didn't walk upright; they hunched as they stood or walked. Their demeanor was completely different from these statues.

Restore them, Cornar thought.

The Wildmen were said to be the descendants of the Klindala Dynasty. These ruins belonged to that dynasty…

"They defaced them," Cornar muttered.

"What?" Vargos yelled from the door.

"They couldn't stand what they had become, so they destroyed the statues."

Vargos put a hand on Cornar's shoulder. "What are you talking about, boy?"

"The leader said Kaescis would 'restore' them," Cornar said, pointing to the nearest statue. "Look, that statue is of a man. These ruins belonged to the Klindala Dynasty. The Wildmen are their descendants. If you think about it logically, the Wildmen were once human and somehow became *that*…" He gestured back whence they had come.

"Or maybe they were born that way," Vargos said. Why was he always the cynic? "Sometimes children are born with odd traits."

A whole society sharing the same physical deformities? That didn't seem likely.

"So you think they're all cursed?" Vargos balked. "And the prince is going to restore their humanity… False hope. That's always a good bargaining chip."

"Curse?" Cornar asked, not amused.

"Wouldn't you call it that?" Vargos raised his brow. "If you're thinking logically? Lycanthropy is passed on from parents to children."

No, this couldn't be a curse. Kaescis had done something to the Wildmen. Changed them. Magic couldn't lift curses. Arpran magic couldn't reverse lycanthropy any more than it could ease Amendal's madness. That old conjurer was definitely cursed.

"Look." Cornar pointed to the nearest statue. "The statues prove my point. The Wildmen were once men. Those statues have damage on them, unlike the exteriors of the buildings we passed. If the statues' damage was due to weathering, then both the buildings and the statues would share similar erosion."

"If they were made of the same stuff…" Vargos said skeptically.

Cornar shook his head. There was no use trying to convince Vargos. *That's what Kaescis is using to barter. He's going to turn the Wildmen back into men.* How was he going to do it, though? Did Kaescis have some type of tevisral that could do it? But Cornar hadn't seen the prince carrying anything when they left the war camp. Perhaps the prince was more adept at wielding magic than he led others to believe.

Shaking the thought aside, Cornar walked to the entrance of the building with Vargos. The grand marshal and the others were partway across the large courtyard. "We better catch—"

The ground shook beneath Cornar, and a rumble echoed from the mountainside. A violent tremor surged throughout the fortress. Both he and Vargos stumbled, falling to the floor. A chunk of stone fell from the building's exterior, striking the stairs leading to the entrance.

Cornar glimpsed Galiur and the others on the ground. None looked harmed.

An earthquake.

"Looks like your curiosity saved us." Vargos grunted, pushing himself up from the floor.

"That's the first earthquake we've experienced since mooring," Cornar said, still on the ground.

An aftershock surged through the mountain, and Vargos stumbled. Cornar continued waiting on the floor. Another aftershock shook the ruins, less violent than the first.

"We should be fine," Cornar said, standing briskly. "Now, let's catch up to the others."

"He will wander for a time, crossing the land of the gods, though he shall not know it."

- Prophecy of Soron Thahan

The *Will* had been a readily accessible subject within many volumes at the Hilinard. It was a central focus of the Cherisium religion, after all. The *Will* embodied a communion with the Cherisium god, Cheserith. He was esteemed as the Creator of the world, the Great Deliverer from eternal bondage. Through Cheserith, his followers would be granted an eternal splendor that was incomprehensible.

Iltar found that to be ridiculous religious drivel.

The *Will*, on the other hand, was quite intriguing. There were many ways to receive the *Will*. Some people claimed a feeling that compelled them to action. Others said the *Will* could be heard, like an audible voice. Those were things ordinary people experienced, or so the text claimed.

The leaders of the Cherisium religion, the Prophets of the Trifica, were granted greater manifestations of the *Will*: chiefly, visitations of a man in red who delivered the *Will*. This man—who Iltar assumed was the Messenger of the Promise—sometimes granted visions. A verse from an annual feast cited a description of what such experiences would entail: *"I come, clothed in red. I light the mind like flame. I show the past, the future, and the present."* That sounded a lot like a passage from Soron Thahan's introduction when referring to the Harbinger and how he would understand his predestined path.

One book told an account from a man who had lived seven hundred years ago, claiming that he experienced a vision in the realm of the gods—a realm called Vabenack. Neither Iltar, Elsia, nor the acolytes found any other references to Vabenack or a place with a yellow sky.

Other texts spoke of the realm of the gods, claiming all the devoted followers of the religion would end up there after dying. It was a place of paradise and eternal joy.

That was quite contrary to Iltar's experience in Vabenack.

Elsia had found references to the Chosen and the *Will*. The Chosen were said to have direct access to their God, walking between the realms of the living and the gods. As far as Iltar could tell, they were the only ones who could initiate the *Will*. All other instances were imposed upon the individual.

While Elsia and the acolytes focused on the *Will*, Iltar went off on a tangent, researching the Chosen. After some digging, Iltar discovered a little more about their nature. The Chosen were immortal beings, blessed with divine power that only Cheserith possessed. The Chosens' power permitted them to withstand the burning splendor of their deity, unlike mere mortals.

According to a few modern scriptural passages, written in the last few centuries, the Chosen had led humanity in ancient times. They were the Stewards of Kalda. One of the passages spoke of them being the caretakers of tevisrals belonging to a utopian civilization. It sounded a lot like Krindal's theories of Cultural Regression and the Lost World.

Iltar came to a dead end on the subject, finding material that was a rehashing of other passages. Minor details were different, but nothing monumental.

⸺◆⸺

Eleven days had passed since Iltar began his research at the Hilinard. He had made some progress. But he was no closer to finding answers about the Unspoken One. Iltar had left that subject to Pagus. The boy hadn't given him a report yet.

Yawning, Iltar set his borrowed books and notes on the shelves within his rented alcove. He was tired, and rightly so. It was quite late. He then grabbed the lightstones from the sconces and secured all but one in his pack.

Much of the seventh floor of the religious wing of the Hilinard was dark. In addition to the illumination from his lightstone, moonlight poured through the glass ceiling as well as starlight. Constellations filled the night sky, many visible through the glassy dome.

Sighing tiredly, Iltar pulled the alcove's gate shut and locked it. *I probably stayed later than I should have,* he thought. But when it came to research, Iltar always had a tendency to push himself into the wee hours of the night.

With lightstone in hand, Iltar made his way through the darkened religion-philosophy wing. Each of the other floors was just as dark as the seventh, except the first. Iltar passed a dozing attendant and entered a brightly lit hall.

He blinked several times, adjusting to the light in the hall. Each of the Hilinard's halls was brightly lit by lightstone sconces. The sconces were positioned higher than a man could reach, to prevent theft.

Iltar wound through the corridors, making his way toward the Hilinard's main entrance. He passed no one in the halls. Most, if not all, of the patrons had probably left. Iltar had sent Elsia and the acolytes back to the high duchess's mansion hours ago. The carriage probably hadn't returned.

I'll have to walk, he thought. That was fine. Alanya's mansion was only a short walk from the Hilinard. He could use the exercise. Most of his day had consisted of sitting and reading.

Iltar soon reached the foyer, the same room which held the map etched into that black monolith. He'd had one of his acolytes investigate the thing, but the boy hadn't come up with any answers. It had to be a tevisral.

The Hilinard's foyer was empty, except for two attendants dressed in white robes who stood beside the closed three-story doors. This was the first time Iltar had seen them shut.

One of the attendants held out his hand, expecting Iltar to return his green token. Iltar removed it from his bag and handed it to the man without a word.

"Have a pleasant night," the other attendant said, gesturing to the doors.

Iltar raised his brow in confusion. "Do you expect me to push this open?" He gestured to the towering slab. The door was at least half a phineal thick and probably weighed as much as twenty men.

"Do you not see the door within the door?" the attendant asked.

Iltar took a closer look at the patterns in the large slab. A slight gap was between a few of the lines. A hidden door?

"Just push it open," the attendant urged him.

Iltar pushed the area within the gaps, and an arched doorway, barely taller than he was, opened outward. *Well, that was clever,* he mused and exited the Hilinard. The door closed behind him.

The Hilinard's grounds were empty. It was a little eerie, like being in Vabenack. Iltar made his way along the path with the statues and down a road leading to a large metal gate. The Hilinard's guards—clad in silver plate armor—opened it for him, and Iltar stepped out onto the empty streets of Mindolarn.

Looking both ways, Iltar cautiously crossed the street.

He wasn't afraid of what could happen on a street that was dark and quiet; he could easily take care of himself. In fact, he wouldn't mind an encounter with a bandit or a gang of thugs. It had been quite some time since he had seen any *real* action. Of course, Iltar had trained with Cornar frequently after their last adventure, but that wasn't the same.

Cor, what are you up to? Cornar's decision still boggled Iltar's mind. *We really are men of adventure, aren't we? Drawn to action like moths to a flame.*

Iltar envied Cornar in that moment, longing to explore the Isle of Klindala. What secrets were Cor and the others unearthing?

Thoughts of adventure flooded Iltar's mind as he passed several large estates, each guarded by several men. The guards eyed Iltar as he passed, unnerved by his presence. It was quite late, after all. Iltar didn't pay much attention to them. He was caught up in the memories of past adventures and the imagined doings of his friends half a world away.

Marching footfalls reached Iltar's ears, and he turned around to see a patrol of Mindolarn soldiers approaching him. Iltar moved aside, but didn't slow his pace. They hadn't called out to him, so he probably wasn't in danger of being stopped. Was there a curfew in Mindolarn? Soroth had one, but it was rarely enforced.

After walking for a quarter of an hour, Iltar reached the gates of High

Duchess Alanya Tasivir's mansion. Her guards recognized him and opened the gates, eyeing the patrol as it passed. Iltar said nothing to Alanya's guards, and they didn't talk to him either. He continued in silence, walking down the private road leading to the mansion. Iltar rounded the fountain in front of the mansion's entrance and took the side path leading to the guesthouse.

More guards stood outside the guesthouse's main entrance, but Iltar didn't walk that way. He sauntered across the grass toward the guesthouse's back door, but stopped upon seeing warm light shining from a window on the mansion's second story.

Was someone awake at this hour? he wondered. Perhaps one of the servants forgot to cover the lightstones.

Iltar stared at the window for a moment and was about to turn around when he saw movement. Someone *was* awake. Iltar moved to the grassy area where he trained the acolytes, which gave him a better view of the window.

A shadow danced across the grass, then High Duchess Alanya Tasivir stepped up to the window. She intently read from an open book in her hands.

Alanya's hair was down, and she wore no makeup. She still looked stunning. Iltar couldn't help but stare at her. He was tired, but gazing at her invigorated him. The high duchess lowered the tome and gazed out the window. She stared across the city, then shot a glance down to Iltar.

Oh no…

Alanya cocked her head at him, then smiled, motioning for him to come to her.

Did he dare? It was late… The guards might not even let him in. Alanya tapped on the window, then pointed down at an angle to her right. Iltar shrugged, not knowing what she was trying to convey. The high duchess pointed again, then made a gesture like she was opening a door. She pointed two fingers down and made them walk upward at an angle. After that, Alanya traced a few lines on the window. Was she giving directions to her chambers?

Iltar didn't move. Why was she inviting him in at this time of night? Had Alanya found something in that book she was reading? The high duchess had expressed some interest in his research the past few days and said she would peruse her library.

That must be it, he thought, *but why meet at this hour?* Iltar sighed and walked across the lawn to a door at the mansion's rear. The door was locked, but a guard on the inside opened it.

"Uh, I need to see the high duchess," Iltar said.

"I'm sorry, she is sleeping," the guard said, looking a little confused. "Is this a matter that concerns the Countess Scurn?"

"No," Iltar said. "May I enter?" The guard reluctantly nodded and stepped aside.

Iltar could see an L-shaped staircase across the hall; two steps led to a landing and then the staircase turned another direction.

What were those directions again? he wondered upon reaching the stairs. Once on the second floor, Iltar wound his way through several hallways. The walls were covered in decorative wooden paneling and dotted with an occasional painting.

Iltar turned a corner and came to a small hall that ended at a beautifully carved door. It was unlike any of the others he had seen in this mansion, or the guesthouse. Light peaked beneath the door, spilling across the floor.

After knocking once, Iltar heard the high duchess bid him enter.

He stepped into a two-story bedchamber with ornate décor. An oversized bed sat against the left wall, hemmed by beautifully carved nightstands. The bed looked like it could fit three or four people. Recessed bookcases flanked the window where Alanya was standing.

The high duchess wore a pale-pink robe made from shimmering silk, embroidered with flowery designs. The robe went only partway down Alanya's shins, leaving her bare feet exposed.

"Shut the door," she said, "and turn the lock, please." Iltar complied. But why would she want it locked? He felt a spike of worry.

"I take it you just returned from the Hilinard?" Alanya asked, settling into a high-backed chair near the window. Iltar nodded, and she gestured to an identical chair beside her, separated only by a small round table.

Iltar took that as a suggestion for him to sit. But as he walked toward her, she gasped. "Oh! Take off your boots."

He halted and complied again. *Odd request,* he thought, returning to the door and dropping his boots.

"Thank you," Alanya said. "I'm sorry... I have a *thing.*" She scrunched up her face.

Iltar nodded, but didn't speak as he crossed the room. What could he say to that? He settled into the high-backed chair, and Alanya handed him the book. "I found something about the Chosen within my late husband's library," she said. "I don't know whether it is a redundant find, but I figured I should show it to you."

"All right," Iltar said, reading the passage. It began by explaining how the Chosen initiated manifestations of the *Will of Cheserith.* Iltar hadn't seen this particular passage. The writer claimed they did this through a special bond between them and their God. They shared something unique that others of the Cherisium religion didn't. The Chosen could also allow others to experience this manifestation. They could even craft visions for those of the faithful they deemed worthy. That was a detail Iltar hadn't seen. *Crafting visions?* It seemed a lot like what Reflection had done.

"Is it helpful?" Alanya asked, sounding a little worried. Where was her regal demeanor?

"Uh, yes," Iltar said. "It has a lot of similar information to other passages we've come across, but there are details in there that make it... uh, unique." He handed the book back to Alanya.

"You know," the high duchess said as she took the book, "I've never subscribed to the Cherisium religion. My late husband was a devotee... always attending the Feast of Sorrows, praying daily, seeking the *Will.* At times he seemed so desperate to commune with his God." Alanya averted her gaze to the floor. "I always thought it superstitious. You're from Soroth. You know what it's like on our islands. Religion is… trivial."

Iltar hummed and nodded.

Alanya talked for a while about the differences between the Mindolarn Empire and the Principality of Soroth. Was she missing her homeland? From what Iltar could tell, life here in Mindolarn was far better than in Soroth.

The high duchess sighed and looked at him. Was that longing he saw in her eyes? She was probably missing her husband. The dead man had undoubtedly sat in this chair during conversations like this.

"Tell me about your day," she said, resting her elbow on the armrest. Alanya settled her slender chin into her palm, still eying him with that odd gaze. She wasn't interested in *him*, was she? No. A woman like her wouldn't find him attractive…

"Well, we didn't find anything new," Iltar said. "I'm still waiting for Pagus's report. I have him searching for information on someone called, the Unspoken One. He—"

"He's the man who can muster magic without incantation," Alanya said.

How did she know that?

"It's in this book." She tapped the tome she had handed Iltar. "Algas Marn mentions him. The Unspoken One is the one who will usher in the return of the Cherisium god. There's even a verse that he quotes from some ancient texts." She flipped through the pages. "Here." Alanya handed the book back to Iltar.

"*To* him *will I grant the authority to wield my power without the use of tongue. Thought will yield the manifestation of destruction. He shall pave the way for a triumphant return, ushering in my final reign. Nations shall know him as* the Unspoken One, *the Harbinger of Hemran'na, the Destroyer of the Wicked. Through him I, the God of this world, will rise once again, never to be vanquished by mine enemies. For only then will the Crimson Eye remain hidden for all time.*"

Iltar leaned back in his chair, surprised to see so many details in that quoted verse.

"I take it you haven't read this?" Alanya asked, her face betraying her anticipation.

"No…"

Alanya smiled and reached her hand to his. What was she doing?

"I think that's a good note on which to end your research for the night," she said as she glided her fingers against his. Her touch was cool, as it had been that first time in the solarium. "You remind me of my late husband, Scovis. Determined. Dedicated."

Iltar stared at her fingers for a moment, then slowly looked to her face. Alanya bit her lower lip, still gazing at him. He hadn't seen a woman look at him that way since his last night with Anela.

"I like those traits in a man…" Iltar's stomach tensed with nervous anticipation.

Alanya continued gazing at him. Her breath quickened. The pupils of her eyes dilated. The high duchess looked like a woman *yearning* for affection.

All Iltar could do was stare at her. *This isn't happening, is it?* Iltar glanced to the window, afraid that Reflection was playing a cruel trick. But the sky was dark.

Alanya raised her hand to Iltar's chin, forcing him to look at her. "If you won't start it, I will," she said, her words ravenous. "I know you want me. I've seen you staring at me." Alanya gripped his hand, then came close, leaning forward and pressing her lips against his. Her kiss was cool, but her lips warmed as they lingered against his.

She pulled back and straightened, still holding his hand. "I didn't call you here *just* to discuss research," she said, loosening the knot in the silky belt around her waist.

Iltar's eyes widened. It *was* happening. But… but he hadn't been with a woman in years. Decades, even.

Alanya tugged at his hand.

Got to stand up, Iltar told himself and lurched out of the chair.

The high duchess grinned at him, guiding him to her lavish bed.

> *"The hiss'thraks shall reawaken, taking upon themselves forms long forgotten."*

> *- Prophecy of Soron Thahan*

Three days had passed since the encounter with Gevistra and his people within the Fortress of Anigar. Since then, the Wildman had led Kaescis and his friends down the mountains through a pass behind the ruined fortress. The Wildmen had beaten a path through the forest that they used to travel to the other tribes. Thus far, the trip had been uneventful.

"The high chieftain live over that hill," Gevistra pointed to a rise in the forest path. The Wildman rode atop a valerin, an animal that resembled a bear but was more docile; it had white fur with pale-gray spots. Valerins usually had fangs, but Gevistra and his people had defanged this one when domesticating it. The creature's claws had also been removed. Valerins were common in the mountains of Klindala, so Gevistra and his tribe would capture the babies and raise them. Gevistra said the animals were useful for hauling things between his tribe and the other Wildmen. They rarely rode a valerin not laden.

"We be there before sun fall," Gevistra said. "I—"

A tremor surged beneath them, causing the horses to panic. The valerin, however, didn't react.

"Whoa!" Kaescis pulled on his reins and patted his black horse, which started to buck. "Calm down, boy." The horse whinnied and shook with fright.

A loud thud resonated from behind Kaescis. He glanced toward the sound, seeing Bratan on the ground. Bratan's horse was running, packs of supplies bouncing as the horse galloped away.

Laeyit's horse turned and bolted, nearly throwing her from the saddle. Her horse galloped away as she yelled an incantation, mustering enthralling magic. The gray particles wisped into the horse's nostrils, abruptly stilling it.

"Damned beast!" Laeyit shouted. "Come back!"

"Why they run?" Gevistra asked, his valerin undaunted.

Kaescis held tight to his reins, and the shaking ceased. "They're scared," Kaescis said, watching Bratan's horse flee into the trees. "Stay here, Gevistra."

"Where you go?" the Wildman asked.

Kaescis didn't reply. He had to get Bratan's horse. Kaescis kicked his horse into a gallop and uttered an incantation, mustering enhancing magic. White particles gathered in his hands and surged across the reins, seeping into his horse. Some of the magic, however, wisped into the gems on his armor.

The magic quickened the horse's gallop. His steed moved fast, as if he were not laden by Kaescis and his armor. The armor, however, wasn't heavy by any means. His plate was crafted by a metallurgical technique—using tevisrals—to form an alloy called Triaindium. With impact strength greater than any naturally occurring metals, the plate's toughness was equivalent to a suit that, if crafted by natural metals, would weigh eight times Kaescis's weight. The suit was inlaid with tevisrals that drew in certain magics—barsion, enhancing, and illusionary, to name a few. The armor would draw in those magics through the gemstones if present, hence the reason some of the enhancing particles meant for his horse wisped to his armor.

Kaescis's horse wove through the trees and caught up to Bratan's steed within seconds. But, before he could overtake the horse, the brown steed bolted into a clearing.

You're not getting away, Kaescis thought, uttering an enthralling incantation. He hunched forward and stretched out his hand, aiming at Bratan's horse. Kaescis broke the tree line as the gray particles shot from his hand.

The magic zipped through the air, surrounding the horse as it leapt over a ledge and onto a lower part of the clearing.

Kaescis lost sight of Bratan's horse, but felt his magic taking effect. He could hear, smell, and see everything the horse was experiencing. Kaescis slowed his horse to a canter, stopping near the ledge. He forced Bratan's horse to trot toward a nearby slope. Kaescis, however, glimpsed a cave through the horse's eyes. Something moved.

What was that?

Kaescis turned the horse's head while guiding it toward the slope. The cave was quite large, and something moved inside it.

From what Kaescis had learned from Gevistra, the Wildmen didn't inhabit caves. Like Gevistra and his people, some inhabited ruins, while others lived in tents. The leader of all the tribes—the high chieftain—was nomadic and had a traveling tent city that moved between the various tribes. Whatever was in this cave was not a Wildman.

The movement was clearer. A giant silhouette neared the cave's mouth.

That horse, Kaescis shook his head with annoyance, quickening the enthralled horse's trot to a canter. Bratan's horse ascended the rise, moving straight for Kaescis.

Lumbering movement reached his ears, and Kaescis looked to the ledge. He whispered another enthralling incantation, guiding the new spell into his own horse. Whatever was coming out of the cave was surely going to spook his steed. It was bad enough chasing one horse.

The second spell took hold as a massive hand-like appendage peeked over the ledge, gripping the rock. It was tipped with six sharp gray talons and covered in dark green scales.

Six fingers? Kaescis wondered, dismounting. He grabbed his helmet before commanding his steed to move. *A troll?* Why would one of *those* be here? Yes, they were near mountains, but Kaescis had never heard of such creatures living this far from any mountain peak.

Six more talons peeked over the ledge, followed by a reptilian head. Yes, it was a troll. The creature's snout was long, with loose gray skin hanging from its sides. That flabby skin was nearly as long as Kaescis's arm. Four nostrils twitched, obviously smelling Kaescis and the horses. The creature's eyes were drawn to the horses now near the tree line. The troll's six-sided pupils grew wide, and it opened its snout, revealing an abhorrent maw without tongue or tooth. Finger-long feelers lined the entire orifice, the opening large enough to fit a man. Kaescis had seen a troll devour a soldier whole. The beast had snatched him up with its massive claws and dropped him inside, swallowing the soldier in a single gulp.

The troll straightened, its snake-like neck peering over the ledge. Its neck and underbelly were lined with gray-green skin, moist and slick, that reflected the sunlight with a disturbing sheen. It stretched during feeding, as the beasts were accustomed to consuming live meals. Their prey would die slowly within their innards. Sometimes trolls would pound their chests if their prey was too violent.

Kaescis eyed the towering creature and donned his helmet stoically. Everything went black for a moment, and then Kaescis could see as clearly as if he weren't wearing his helmet at all. During the failed attempts to recreate the Ul'thirls, the scholars at the Hilinard had inadvertently developed a tevisral that could visually perceive. They began further development on the mistake, which resulted in Kaescis's helmet. Besides the prototype, this helmet was currently the only one in existence.

The troll climbed the ledge, standing much taller than Kaescis. He barely reached the monster's knee. Trolls were around three times the size of a man, but this one looked larger.

With its mouth still open, the troll glanced to Kaescis.

"Come at me, beast," Kaescis shouted with anticipating glee. *A perfect opportunity to test my weapon.* He uttered an incantation, mustering his long Ko'delish blade. Black mist seethed from Kaescis's hands, forming a shaft that became the deadly blade. Once the weapon formed, it continued to mist the black particles.

The troll lumbered toward Kaescis, swinging its massive six-fingered hand.

Kaescis lunged, poised to strike. He sliced his gigantic sword through that sweeping hand, severing it halfway through the palm. *Wonderful reach!* The troll wailed, but still struck Kaescis, tossing him backward.

Recovering from the blow, Kaescis rolled onto his feet, still clutching his magically composed weapon. Kaescis heard his name shouted from within the trees, but he ignored the call. He had a beast to slay.

Kaescis bolted forward, and the troll came at him again, swinging its maimed hand. He slid beneath the arm, dashing straight for the creature's knee. The troll tried to back away, but it only took one step before Kaescis reached its leg. He leapt, slicing his black sword down the troll's knee.

The troll wailed and lost its footing. Kaescis backed up, careful to not be crushed by the behemoth.

Soon, Laeyit rode into the clearing and leapt from her horse. Her steed was still enthralled, and she forced the horse back to Kaescis's and Bratan's horses. Laeyit regained her footing with ease.

"You idiot," Laeyit chided him, reaching for the empty sheath upon her back. "Why did you awake a troll?"

"Blame Bratan for not holding on to his horse," Kaescis said, watching the troll stagger backward. The creature wobbled.

"I heard that!" Bratan's voice carried through the trees.

Laeyit murmured as transmutative particles gathered within her sheath, forming a single-sided straight sword: a haviklur. That type of sword was used mostly for close range. The haviklur's blade length was between that of a short-sword and a traditional blade. Haviklurs also lacked guards.

Laeyit drew the weapon and the blade burst with shimmering purple light—disintegrating magic. "I'll flank its right," she said, bolting toward the troll. Kaescis went the other way.

They evaded clumsy swings and struck the troll's legs. Their blows were swift and precise, striking at the same time.

The troll screamed and fell backward, tumbling off the ledge. It landed in front of its cave.

Kaescis and Laeyit stood together, watching the troll writhe. Footfalls echoed behind them and Bratan leapt past them, his crimson armor a flash of red.

"Free my horse, beast!" Bratan shouted, twirling his double-bladed fanisar as he fell. He struck the troll's belly, the weapon's sharp edge pointing toward its head.

Kaescis raised his brow. *Had Bratan not noticed the horses?*

Orange blood spewed from the wound, splashing against Bratan's armor. The Crimson Praetorian yelled a battle cry, furiously dragging his fanisar across the troll's belly to its neck.

The troll let out dying wails, flailing its arms and legs. It soon fell limp, twitching every few seconds.

Bratan pulled his fanisar from the creature and pushed aside its stretching skin. "Where's my horse?!" he shouted, then looked back to Kaescis.

Kaescis dismissed his blade and removed his helmet. "Back by the trees," he said, pointing to the horses. Bratan let out a sigh and leapt off the twitching troll.

Laeyit burst into laughter, sheathing her transmuted weapon. The disintegrating particles faded, and the haviklur vanished. She didn't dismiss it like Kaescis. Her weapon was actually generated and maintained by the sheath.

The sheath was a tevisral, after all.

"Oh, Bratan," Laeyit continued laughing. "You never cease to entertain me!" Bratan trotted up the slope, shaking his head.

Kaescis grinned at his friend. Bratan could be overzealous at times. But that trait made him a great asset on the battlefield. Bratan's zeal had turned the tide of several battles.

"I amaze," Gevistra said. Kaescis turned around as the Wildman approached on his valerin. "You slay a throll!"

"It's pronounced *troll*," Laeyit corrected him.

"Oh…" Gevistra said, looking sullen. He was a tribal leader and probably hated being corrected. "You must bring," Gevistra pointed to the corpse.

"You want us to drag a troll?" Bratan asked. "That thing is too heavy for our horses."

"You know sacred tongue," Gevistra said. "You drag troll with power."

Laeyit sighed. "Why drag it when we can just reanimate it?" she asked.

"Reahmin…aeight?" Gevistra asked, trying to pronounce the word.

"Reanimate," Laeyit said. "I can make him walk again."

"No," Gevistra shook his head. "Troll wild. Will hurt many."

"I'll be controlling it." Laeyit rolled her eyes.

"I don't think that's wise, Laeyit," Kaescis said. "We might scare the Wildmen."

"Exactly," Laeyit said, looking sharply at Kaescis. "They *need* to reverence us. Their tales tell of men who wielded necromancy."

Kaescis studied her for a moment. A reanimated troll would be a wondrous sight to behold. Besides, Gevistra wanted them to bring it.

"Fine," Kaescis said with a wave of his hand. "But if anything goes awry, you're dismissing the spell."

Laeyit nodded and returned to the ledge. Kaescis commanded the horses he enthralled to come near.

"What she do?" Gevistra demanded, his tone furious.

"Don't worry," Kaescis said, extending his hand in a placating manner. "Laeyit is in complete control. The troll is dead. She is moving it, like a puppet."

"Puupit?" Gevistra asked.

"It's a toy, used to entertain people," Kaescis said. "A puppeteer moves the puppet, and it looks like the puppet is moving on its own."

"Strange," Gevistra shook his head. "Very strange. Why do this?"

"Use puppets?" Kaescis chuckled. "It's fun."

"That not fun," Gevistra pointed past Kaescis. "That scary."

Bratan shook his head and mounted his horse.

Kaescis smiled at the Wildman. He had an innocent quality that was endearing. *Perhaps I'll take him with me*, he mused. *The empire will need an emissary to these tribes.* Kaescis would see to an alliance between his people and these Wildmen, once he restored them. That was his ultimate goal for the Wildmen. The empire would need allies in this war they were to wage.

"Let's go," Laeyit said, mounting her horse. She gestured to the trees with her hand, commanding the reanimated corpse to move.

Kaescis walked toward his horse, but another tremor shot through the ground. He fell and waited for the shaking to stop before standing.

Two so close together, he thought. There had been tremors every day since encountering the Wildmen, but not this frequent. That worried him.

Kaescis mounted his black steed and Gevistra guided them back to the path. They would arrive at the Wildmen tent city before sunset.

—⊃•⊂—

Cornar steadied himself against the tremor. It was the fourth one today. The second had been so violent that many of the horses bucked off their riders and fled. A third struck shortly thereafter, but not as intense as the others. It took them awhile to round up the horses. Hem and some of the Mindolarn mages had to use their magic to coerce them back to the expedition. By the time everyone was back together, it was time to make camp.

Sensing that the tremors were finished, Cornar continued through the war camp. He passed several Wildmen who were escorted by some of Galiur's men.

The Wildmen tribe from the fortress had come with them as escorts. Half of them had undergone some kind of transformation at the hand of Kaescis, looking like a hybrid of human and Wildman. The leaders of the expedition knew where they were going, but the Wildmen were there in case they ran across others of their kind.

Cornar headed to the mess tent within the war camp's outer ring. His men had decided to mingle with the soldiers. Cornar was not one to elevate himself above his men, so he intended to join them in the mess tent.

He passed one of the war camp's entrances, glancing through it. Cornar had a habit of checking entrances to camps. Sometimes he didn't notice he was doing it. A robed masculine figure caught his eye, approaching from the trees.

Who is that? he wondered.

The guards didn't flinch at the stranger's approach.

Cornar took a few more steps, edging away from the war camp's entrance.

He warily watched the robe figure approach—it was Jahevial. The scholar was clutching his robe, much like the night Cornar saw him exiting the servants' tent.

Where had he gone? The expedition hadn't passed anything of archeological importance on the way here.

Jahevial passed the guards and entered the camp, walking the way Cornar had come. The scholar didn't even notice Cornar. Jahevial hurried through the camp, disappearing around the bend.

Cornar furrowed his brow, contemplating the possible reasons behind Jahevial's actions. That was twice he had seen Jahevial sneaking out of the war camp.

I'm going to follow him next time, Cornar vowed. Tomorrow he would keep a close eye on Jahevial until they set up camp. If Jahevial left again Cornar would follow him.

Perhaps I can borrow Sharon's—

The ground shook, and Cornar stumbled. Some of the soldiers around him fell.

"That's five," he whispered. How many more were going to strike today?

❖

The tremor faded as Kaescis rode toward the sprawl of tents in a vast plain. He and Laeyit hadn't dismissed their enthralling spells. It was a good thing, else their horses would have run again.

Five tremors in a day, Kaescis thought. Were they foreshadowing a devastating earthquake? That didn't bode well for the expedition, since the temple was underground.

"They will marvel," Gevistra said. "You give High Chieftain Bhrane… troll,"—he seemed to want to get the word right—"to hang head."

"Like a trophy?" Bratan asked.

"I know not what that is…" Gevistra shrugged.

"Hang the heads of your fallen prey," Bratan said. "Hunters do it as a token of bravery."

"Ah," Gevistra nodded. "Is same thing. He show all tribes as he travel. Make him look strong to them."

Laeyit laughed. "So we're going to help him with his image," she mused.

Kaescis nodded. *Another bargaining chip.*

They continued onward. Laeyit and Bratan talked with Gevistra while Kaescis mulled over the coming meeting. He considered how to phrase his offer to the high chieftain.

Twilight was upon the island as Kaescis's small band reached the camp. A wall of Wildmen, armed with clubs, stood at the edge of the tents. They wore green-dyed clothing. Each eyed Kaescis warily, looking at Laeyit's reanimated troll with trepidation.

As Kaescis and the others neared the Wildmen, Gevistra broke into song. He had told Kaescis that it was how the tribal leaders announced themselves. This particular song was about Gevistra and his people. Kaescis couldn't understand what Gevistra was singing about, as it all seemed gibberish.

The Wildmen relaxed and several stepped forward.

"I greet you," Gevistra said, bowing his head. The approaching Wildmen gasped. They looked to each other, then one continued toward Gevistra.

Confused, the foremost Wildman threw several questions at Gevistra.

"What is this?" Kaescis parsed the first question, raising an eyebrow. And… The other questions weren't intelligible. Kaescis thought one of them might be, "Why you sound odd?" but the words were too distorted for him to be sure.

"I restored!" Gevistra exclaimed raising his hands to the air. "Touch by god son." The Wildmen muttered panicked phrases, apparently unsure what to think of Gevistra's declaration.

"We must see High Chieftain Bhrane."

"Why?" the Wildman asked, the word sounding like *way*.

"He must speak," Gevistra pointed to Kaescis, then to the troll. "He slay troll. He know Words of Power."

Kaescis dismounted from his horse, looking at the Wildmen. "Do not fear me. I come in peace." He let that sink in before continuing. "I have come to bargain with your chieftain, and present him with a gift." Kaescis gestured to the reanimated troll. "A prize for him."

"Take us to High Chieftain Bhrane," Gevistra said.

The Wildmen cleared a path, allowing Kaescis's band to enter the tent city.

Laeyit, Bratan, and Gevistra remained on their beasts of burden, but Kaescis walked. He wanted to show a sense of humility to these Wildmen, to gain their trust, so to speak.

The foremost Wildman uttered a word and then gestured for Kaescis and the others to follow.

They walked through the tent city for a while, passing rows and rows of simple tents made from animal skins and wood. The Wildmen really were primitive. They watched the procession from their tents, whispering to each other. They probably had never seen foreigners welcomed in such a manner, especially in their capital. If one could call this tent city a capital. That thought amused Kaescis, and he fought back laughter.

Most everything looked the same until they reached what seemed to be the middle of the mobile city. A wide path ringed a unique set of tents, much larger than the others.

These tents had an emblem painted on their sides; a half circle with a narrow triangle on its top.

A Wildman woman exited one of the tents, hurrying over to Gevistra. She shook her head, looking frightened. The Wildman woman asked Gevistra a question while fear spread across her face.

Why you odd looking? Kaescis parsed the question. The last two words were barely comprehensible. *Odd* sounded like *oud*, while *looking* sounded like *louken*.

"I restored, Fenia!" he exclaimed, raising his hands in a gesture of praise. He quickly dismounted from his valerin and hurried to her.

Fenia, the Wildman woman, looked at him with horror. She stepped away from Gevistra, shaking her head. She shrilled a statement in a tone of denial, ending with a word that sounded like *brother*.

Gevistra looked pained at that remark. "I am brother, Fenia."

Her brother? Kaescis thought. This could be beneficial.

"We must speak to High Chieftain Bhrane," Gevistra said, gesturing to the center of the unique tents. "Come." He waved for Kaescis. "Leave troll here."

A resounding thud echoed from behind Kaescis, and he glanced back to see Laeyit waving her hand in an exaggerated fashion.

Kaescis followed Gevistra and his sister through the compound and entered the high chieftain's tent. It was quite large, held upright by long poles carved from trees with a red inner bark.

Gevistra began singing again, drawing everyone's attention. The Wildmen gawked at him with disbelief.

Soon, they all stood at the foot of a wooden throne where a burly man—obviously High Chieftain Bhrane—sat, gazing at Gevistra. The skulls of wild animals hung behind the throne. Even some human skulls were among the collection.

"I kneel before you, High Chieftain Bhrane," Gevistra said, dropping to his knees. "I bring you prince." He stood and pointed to Kaescis.

That must be the cue for him to speak.

Kaescis stepped forward and clasped his hands behind his back. Laeyit and Bratan stepped up behind him.

"High Chieftain Bhrane, I am Prince Kaescis Midivar, sixth in line to the Mindolarn throne. I am the son of Mindolarn the first emperor, who was the son of Madars, the son of Karath'nos, begotten through the lineage of Ku'tharn."

Bhrane's dark-brown eyes widened and his snout-like face twisted in fear. The others in the room gasped, and some wailed in terror.

"You… god?" Bhrane asked.

Kaescis barely understood the simple question, but didn't answer. He wanted to let the high chieftain stew in his perplexity. That would give Kaescis the upper hand.

"He god son," Gevistra said. "He know word of power. He speak token."

That disturbed Bhrane even further.

Good. Kaescis grinned. "I have come to strike a bargain with you, good chieftain, and I also present a gift. You will find the corpse of a great beast outside your tents. I'm sure it'll look nice with your collection." Kaescis gestured to the skulls.

Bhrane demanded another question, one Gevistra had asked in the Fortress of Anigar.

Why you here? Kaescis parsed the question, then grinned. "I seek a great secret hidden within the ruins of Klindil. I merely want safe passage."

Bhrane frowned, spreading his hands wide. He spoke of Klindil, repeating what Kaescis thought was the word *sacred.* The Wildman pronounced it *sahkreed.* Bhrane continued, proclaiming choppy declarations that Kaescis must not go to Klindil.

"I must go," Kaescis said, "for the good of all Kalda. Our world depends on it." Bhrane looked troubled. He sighed, averting his gaze from Kaescis.

"In exchange for your permission, I will restore you and those of your choosing. You and those of your choosing will be returned to the glory of your ancestors. No longer will you be shackled by the fate forced upon you by our enemies."

Kaescis couldn't help but think of the Karthar rebels, which sparked a glimmer of anger.

Death…

Shaking the word from his mind, Kaescis continued. "I restored Gevistra here, partially," Kaescis said. "Allow me to demonstrate further. His sister, Fenia, perhaps?" he suggested, turning to the Wildman woman. Fenia gasped, bringing her hairy hand to her protruding lips. Her eyes flashed with terror.

"It fine, Fenia," Gevistra said, grabbing his sister. "You safe. No hurt."

"Gevistra!" she cried.

Kaescis glanced back to High Chieftain Bhrane, awaiting an answer.

The high chieftain nodded, sucking in his breath. He probably didn't know what to expect.

Kaescis uttered that same arpran incantation, "Si'nak ma'nal senda." Green particles gathered in his hands. "Ulak'xin ma'ril kusaz." The light beamed from his palm, striking Fenia. She glowed a green hue, her elongated face shrinking.

Fenia screamed, touching her hands to her face. The hair on her fingers shed, then more fell from the back of her hands and her arms. Her neck shed as well, and then her disproportionate extremities shrank.

Kaescis wasn't going to spare anything this time. Fenia would no longer be a Wildman when he was done with her.

Fenia collapsed, shaking from the transformation. The cranial feature completely flattened, and her face looked... human. She remained on the floor, shaking.

Gevistra knelt beside her, stroking her back. "You restored," he said calmly. "You whole."

Fenia sobbed, feeling at her face.

Kaescis turned from the siblings and studied the high chieftain. Bhrane was in utter shock. He looked terrified by the entire occurrence.

"As you can see, your people have been deprived of their true natures. Atrocious acts were committed against your ancestors, and I intend to see them righted."

Bhrane didn't reply.

Gevistra helped Fenia to her feet. Fenia had an exquisite face. She would draw the eyes of many Mindolarnians, especially if she were properly dressed. Fenia's figure had slimmed from that thick Wildman build to that of a petite woman.

Many of the Wildmen in the room gasped, muttering dismayed phrases.

Fenia eyed her brother, taking comfort in his gaze. They embraced, and Kaescis focused on the high chieftain.

"Well, High Chieftain Bhrane? What do you have to say concerning my offer?"

Bhrane leaned back in his throne, apprehensive. He blurted a perplexed statement, using the word *fareenar.*

You think I made her a foreigner, Kaescis mused. What a primitive fool. *He doesn't understand.* Well, there was a way to fix that...

Kaescis uttered the sharp incantation again, extending his hand to the high chieftain.

Bhrane froze as the arpran magic shot from Kaescis's palm. The green light surged across Bhrane's body, and he fell from his throne.

The Wildman gasped but didn't dare approach Kaescis. He was wielding Words of Power, as they put it. Besides, Gevistra had deified him.

Bhrane screamed as his body transformed; his hair shed and his limbs shrank. He was soon like Fenia, a man. The high chieftain pushed himself up, staggering to his feet.

Laeyit burst into laughter. She sounded diabolical. It was good to hear her that way.

"That's one way to ensure the bargain," Bratan said, sounding amused.

"Wha… what you do to me?" Bhrane asked, his eyes widened upon hearing his own voice. "My voice! It different…"

"Now you know what I can do firsthand," Kaescis said. "Do we have a deal?"

Bhrane looked at his audience. The Wildmen gazed at their leader with disbelief. The high chieftain moved his fingers, looking surprised. They obviously had greater dexterity to them. Bhrane took several steps, his face beaming with intrigue.

"I move better!" Bhrane exclaimed. He danced about, acting out various movements that were part of some rehearsed combat exercise. "I fast!"

The high chieftain furrowed his brow, looking off into the distance. "I think better… idea come fast!" His eyes darted back and forth, as if recalling thoughts.

"What say you, High Chieftain Bhrane?" Kaescis asked.

The high chieftain considered Kaescis's proposal for several minutes. What Kaescis had done could be detrimental to Bhrane. His people could riot against him. They might not consider him a Wildman since he looked like a foreigner. But the high chieftain had proclaimed the benefits of the transformation. Bhrane couldn't ignore that. These were the proper motivations Kaescis wanted to instill in the man. Bhrane *had* to agree.

"You change all my people?" Bhrane asked. "Make better?"

"In due time," Kaescis said. "I would that our peoples, the Mindolarn Empire and the Wildmen of Klindala, become allies. Our world will soon change, and I will see that your people prosper."

That piqued Bhrane's interests.

"Do we have a deal?"

Bhrane stepped away from his throne, approaching Kaescis. The high chieftain eyed him before bowing. "By word of my father, I agree."

Gevistra whooped triumphantly. The others in the room muttered about the implications of the deal between Kaescis and Bhrane. They sounded worried. No matter. Kaescis would ensure that any dissension be dealt with privily. He could have Laeyit see to that. She would relish such a task.

30

DREAMWALKER

"The rulers of the world shall be humbled before him."

- Prophecy of Soron Thahan

Waking beside a beautiful woman was something Iltar wasn't accustomed to doing. He shielded his eyes against the sunlight pouring into the bedroom from the same window where he had spotted Alanya. How late had they slept? It had been quite late when he returned from the Hilinard.

Worried that he might be in Vabenack, Iltar sat up and gazed out the window. The sky was blue. *Good,* he sighed, settling back on his pillow. *So this really did happen.*

Iltar turned to Alanya, who stirred within the sheets, exposing her bare back to him. Her olive skin was darker than most Sorothian women, and looked tanned, though she lacked any tan lines. Iltar found that oddly attractive. He couldn't help but stroke her back. Her skin was so smooth. That had surprised him when he first touched her. She was only a few years younger than he was—in her late forties—and Iltar expected to find a less than youthful feel. But that wasn't the case.

Alanya shifted at his touch, groaning. Iltar pulled away and took a deep breath, watching as she awoke. Alanya yawned and stretched her arms, noticing him. "You're awake," she said, glancing over her shoulder. "How late is it?"

"I don't know," Iltar replied, admiring her beauty.

She turned toward him, becoming entangled in the sheets. "You should stay here today. You can ransack my private collection." She playfully touched his nose. Was that supposed to be some odd innuendo? If so, he didn't understand it. Iltar looked at her blankly.

Alanya rolled her eyes. "My library… where I keep my books. Perhaps you'll find something else you hadn't come across. There are a lot of books in there that are unique."

Iltar had been so wrapped up with searching the Hilinard that he hadn't thought to ask if she had her own library. He should have figured Alanya owned an extensive collection, as this mansion wouldn't be complete without one.

"All right," Iltar nodded. "How big is it?"

"The library? Umm, it is three stories, and a little bigger than this room."

His eyes widened. *That could take some time to search.*

"I'm hungry," she said, kissing his cheek. "We should eat. I'll have Hazais send for your acolytes. You can focus your research here. And when you get tired, we can sneak back here for our own *research.*"

Now *that* was an innuendo…

With that, Alanya rolled back across the bed and crawled out of it.

<hr>

"You sly, sly, man." Elsia grinned at Iltar, playfully nudging him with her elbow. "I can't believe it. And here I thought you were totally incapable of romance." Elsia laughed, cupping her hand to her mouth. The countess seemed awfully amused.

Iltar just looked at her blankly as they walked the halls of Alanya's mansion. They turned a corner and came to the entrance of the private library.

The library's double doors were open, revealing a space as grand as the rest of the mansion. As Alanya had said, the library was three stories tall. Dark-brown bookshelves lined the walls, all filled with books. Two rows of bookshelves, rising to the ceiling, divided the room into thirds. Wrought-iron balconies lined the second and third floors of the library; they were accessed by a tight spiral staircase to the left of the doors. A floor-to-ceiling window aligned with the library's double doors drew Iltar's eye.

Elsia continued teasing him, but Iltar ignored her, passing between the bookshelves. That towering window provided a grand view of the city. Iltar moved around a large desk and stood before the window. The Mindolarn Palace rose above the city's skyline to his left. The red-brown structure looked imposing upon that hill.

"You like to ignore me, don't you?" Elsia said, poking his shoulder.

"Only when you don't have something important to say," Iltar said aloofly, still gazing at the magnificent view. The countess grumbled and thumbed through a book on the desk.

Footfalls echoed into the library, and Iltar turned to see his acolytes approaching. Bilda and some of the younger boys gawked at the library. They had probably never seen a library like this in a home. But then again, this wasn't a typical residence.

Pagus strode at their head, holding a small stack of pages. "Here's what I found on the Unspoken One," he said, handing the pages to Iltar.

"Thank you," Iltar said, taking the pages but not looking at them. "We're going to suspend our research at the Hilinard until we've found all we can here. You're still assigned to the same subjects. Get to work."

The acolytes broke up and dispersed throughout the library. Pagus, however, remained.

"Yes, Pagus?" Iltar asked.

"Aren't you going to read it?" He gestured to the pages.

"I will," Iltar said, glancing at the first sheet.

"Well, talk to me when you get to page four," Pagus said, then walked off.

Page four, huh? Iltar flipped through the pages. Page four was filled with several quoted passages and references to the books from which they were taken.

"He shall be able to travel to Cheserith's Realm, seeking divine guidance whenever he chooses. He shall be like the Chosen, able to walk between worlds."

Iltar shook his head and his eyes widened, then looked at Pagus's speculation. *"I think 'Cheserith's Realm' is the dream realm Iltar has mentioned. If that's true, then this Unspoken One can access that place at will."*

Iltar read the other passages, which cited more connections between Vabenack and the Unspoken One. One passage said he could manipulate that place, making it manifest whatever he wished. Those passages referenced another book, something called *Dreamwalker*. He flipped through the other pages, looking for references from *Dreamwalker* but didn't see any.

Iltar hurried over to Pagus, who was perusing the shelves along the wall. "That was fast," Pagus said, sounding snarky.

"I just skipped to page four," Iltar said. "What did you want to say to me?"

Pagus pulled a book from the shelf and looked at his master. "I couldn't find *Dreamwalker* anywhere in the Hilinard. I asked some of the attendants about it, and they couldn't find any record of a book called *Dreamwalker*." The youth opened the book he had pulled from the shelf and continued talking. "I did, however, find out about a secret section of the Hilinard that only Mindolarn Royals can access. I made an illusion of Aunty Elsia and, uh… *persuaded* a few attendants for information."

Iltar raised an eyebrow at Pagus, not amused at what he had done.

"Nothing to say?" Pagus asked. "Not a 'good job, Pagus,' or 'I'm impressed at your skill, Pagus'?"

"Well, what did you find out?"

Pagus sighed. "Unlisted texts are kept in there, things that the emperor has declared *sacred knowledge*. *Dreamwalker* must be a pretty important text if it's locked away."

More footsteps approached the library. Iltar turned, watching Alanya enter. She wore a frilly peach-colored gown. Her hair was done up in a braid held together by a spike with a pale-green gem inlaid at one end.

"So, shall I go get it?" Pagus asked.

"You're not a Mindolarn Royal," Iltar said, then turned back to Alanya. She stopped at the desk and removed a few books from a drawer.

"Uh, yeah…" Pagus said, sounding sly. "But I can get around restrictions like that." The thought of Pagus stealing from one of the most powerful nations on Kalda bothered Iltar. What kind of wrath would that unleash upon him and his acolytes? There would be no escaping punishment for such an act. Perhaps there was another way…

"Well, do you want me to steal it or not?" Pagus asked.

Iltar held out a finger to silence the boy and then walked away. He approached Alanya, who greeted him with a smile.

"You look especially determined," she grinned, a flare of passion in her gaze.

"Are you considered a Mindolarn Royal?" Iltar asked.

"No…" Alanya shook her head and pouted, looking confused. "To be considered a Royal, one must be a descendant of Mindolarn or one of his brothers, or married into the Royal Family."

It was worth a shot, Iltar thought, turning away and rubbing his goatee. What to do now? He didn't dare risk Pagus stealing the book.

"Why do you ask?" Alanya prodded him.

"Pagus found a book I was interested in reading," Iltar turned back to the high duchess. "But it's inside some forbidden part of the Hilinard."

Alanya cocked her head at him. She obviously didn't know about that place deemed sacred by the emperor.

"What is the book?" Alanya asked.

"*Dreamwalker.*"

"I know that book," Alanya said. "Scovis mentioned it in his last journal entry. He had been reading it to prepare for the Feast of Sorrows." She turned back to the desk and opened a drawer, removing a dark-blue tome. "It's right here."

⟨•⟩

Iltar spent most of the day reading *Dreamwalker.* It wasn't long, only a little over two hundred pages. Alanya's late husband had been studying the book, according to his journal. The high duke was seeking a way to further prove himself to his deity. Somehow he had learned about Vabenack and yearned to walk upon its "Translucent Fields."

Partway through the book, Iltar dismissed his acolytes from their research. Elsia stayed in the study, conducting further research while Iltar, Alanya, and the boys retired to the gardens outside the mansion. Iltar gave his acolytes a training exercise to perform and sat with Alanya.

Most of the book explained the nature of Vabenack, which to mortals appeared to be a dream world. This was because men were only able to enter Vabenack while sleeping. Cheserith created it to mirror reality, and provided a place of security for Him and his followers, the Chosen. The book claimed Cheserith and the Chosen could access the realm at will.

"*Vabenack is not like other worlds, like the realms where the gods were exiled,*" Iltar read from *Dreamwalker.* He found that line confusing. *Other worlds?* Like what was mentioned in *The Myth of Morgrid?* But that tale was fictional.

"*It has a literal tie to Kalda. One exists both on Kalda and Vabenack, and not in a non-physical sense. When one appears in Vabenack, they receive a new body. Their mind and soul are transported from Kalda into their body on Vabenack. If one were observing you on Kalda it would appear that you were sleeping. And there is a connection between both of your bodies.*

"To put it simply, if you are injured in Vabenack, it is reflected on your body on Kalda, and vice versa. But your body in Vabenack has no lasting substance. It disappears once you return to Kalda, becoming renewed upon your next visit. This was wisdom on our God's part, as leaving your body in Vabenack would be a devastating vulnerability."

Iltar looked up from the book, watching as Tigan dodged a blow from one of Alanya's guards. Tigan threw himself sideways, rolling away.

The boys' training exercise for the day involved them attacking the guard with acidic bolts until his barsion shattered. Pagus protected the guard, using a simple barsion barrier. It was common for mages to learn a basic protection spell. Most disciplines had their own versions, such as the Acidic Barsion for necromancers and the Flaming Barsion for elemental wizards.

Iltar intended the exercise to help the boys understand how to deal with close-range foes who couldn't be subdued by the other methods he had taught them. One couldn't trap a man shielded with barsion, as he had the boys ensnare Delrin and Jalim. The enemy's barsion would have to be shattered before any subjugating measure would take hold. Iltar couldn't count the number of times he had encountered foes shielded by barsion while adventuring.

Tigan stumbled to his feet and threw one of his acidic bolts. It surged across the man's barsion, causing it to flicker.

"A few more hits," Iltar shouted.

That didn't bode well for the boy. Tigan only had one bolt left. He would have to muster more magic.

Iltar turned from the bout and resumed reading.

The sun was setting when Iltar arrived at the last chapter of *Dreamwalker:* "Accessing the Realm of the Gods." That piqued Iltar's interest, as this and other texts claimed only the Chosen could enter Vabenack.

"I said earlier that accessing Vabenack was for God and his Chosen. That is in part true. They can access it at will. But I have walked the Translucent Fields myself and beheld the wonders of that realm. I have taught others my discoveries, and they have joined me in that supernal world. Here, in this final chapter, I will show you what you must do."

<hr>

Alanya leaned over Iltar's shoulder, watching as he closed *Dreamwalker.* "So, what did you find?" she asked.

Iltar took in a deep breath, watching as the last of his acolytes broke the guard's barsion. The boy swiftly uttered an incantation and mustered an ensnaring spell to stop the guard.

"Well, it says I need to concoct an elixir to *prepare* my mind," Iltar said, shaking his head. Was this all just some psychedelic hoax? The author of *Dreamwalker* claimed it wasn't. He spent several pages using refuting language to counter the reader's skepticism about the matter, but that didn't stop Iltar from questioning its authenticity.

"There's an ingredient list here"—he tapped the book—"as well as instructions."

Alanya fell silent, looking lost in thought. Was she as skeptical as he? Iltar had heard of potions used to *expand* one's mind. Each turned out to be a farce, used by its peddlers to entrap addicts.

"What is on the list?" Alanya asked.

"Some basic things," Iltar said. "A few herbs: halisym, ganiard, wevid, and colisry. It also calls for freshly juiced brandleberries, sugar, and water. The last ingredient was probably the oddest: powdered rogulin." None of those ingredients on their own would cause a psychedelic experience. But Iltar didn't know what they would do when combined, especially the powdered rogulin. Was rogulin even edible?

"Halisym is quite rare," Alanya said. "I think I might have the others. We'll have to go shopping for the rogulin, though. We can go in the morning."

Iltar raised an eyebrow at her. He hadn't even said he would go through with it.

Pagus jogged across the grass and stopped in front of Iltar. "So you finished it?" he asked. "Find anything useful?"

"Maybe," Iltar said, shrugging. He leaned back in his chair and gazed at the palace towering above the horizon.

"That's all you're going to give me?" Pagus demanded.

Alanya glanced to Pagus, then stared at Iltar. "What else does it say you have to do?"

Iltar didn't answer her right away. Most everything else the author had said seemed sound. "There is a whole list of things," Iltar said. "Several meditation techniques, even a hypnosis method. Not all of those things are necessary, though. It all comes down to training your sleeping mind to recognize a certain object while dreaming. An object with a symbol, really. The symbol brings you into a state of awareness. Once that happens, you have to manifest a doorway. You then say a strange-sounding incantation—'Alza Cho'k sa'maz nira'—and open the door. Then you'll be in Vabenack. The whole thing sounds simple enough, but it could take months or years to get your mind prepared for such awareness while sleeping."

"And the elixir is to…?" Alanya asked, sounding confused.

"Accelerate your progress in becoming *aware*," Iltar said. In theory, he wouldn't need the elixir if his mind was focused enough.

"There is alchemy involved?" Pagus sounded intrigued.

"Yes," Iltar said flatly as Elsia approached.

"I'm done for the day," Elsia said, putting her hands on her hips. "How did you fare?" She nodded at *Dreamwalker*.

"That is yet to be determined," Iltar said. "I have some new information, but I don't know how much of it is valid."

Alanya turned to Elsia, looking serious. "We need to go shopping in the morning." She recited the list of ingredients, noting which they needed.

"Ground rogulin?" Elsia asked, contemplating the strangeness of the ingredient.

"I didn't even know you could eat that stuff…" Pagus muttered.

"We will have to go to Desirin's Market," Alanya said. "Otherwise, we will have to find a conjurer willing to sell us their rogulin crystals." She turned to Iltar. "I don't suppose you have any?"

Iltar just looked at her blankly. Alanya sighed with disappointment and then resumed chatting with Elsia about gathering the ingredients. Iltar was amused that she intended to gather everything for the elixir even though he hadn't committed to making it.

Amid the women's chatting, the acolytes crowded around Iltar and the women. Each looked intrigued, and several gazed at *Dreamwalker*, still in Iltar's hands.

"Did you find what you were looking for, Master Iltar?" asked Kaelar, one of the younger boys. Iltar nodded and rose from his seat. That drew the women's attention.

"Are you finished with that?" Elsia asked, gesturing to *Dreamwalker*.

"Reading it, yes," Iltar said, glancing to the book. "I was going to copy the last chapter."

"That part has the instructions?" Elsia asked.

Iltar nodded.

"I'll do it," she said, stepping across the grass to Iltar. Elsia held out her hand. He reluctantly handed the book to her, and she continued, "Besides, I'm not going to let you have all the fun and go off to some strange dream world on your own."

Alanya chuckled and crossed her legs, resting her hand on her neck. She looked amused by Elsia's familiarity with Iltar.

"We want to go, too!" little Bilda exclaimed. The boy looked at the other acolytes, seeking an affirmation from them. Several of the boys nodded. Iltar studied his acolytes. *Dreamwalker* claimed that not everyone could mold their minds to enter Vabenack. There was no guarantee that Elsia could join him. Perhaps he should let them try.

"It's a dangerous place," Iltar said. "Whatever happens to you there, happens to you here."

That didn't dissuade the boys. They still looked eager.

"All right," Iltar said with a nod. "You can study Elsia's notes. There's a list of meditation techniques you can practice. But"—he waggled a finger at the boys—"no making concoctions. I will handle the elixir."

The boys whooped and Bilda danced excitedly.

Elsia stepped past Iltar, holding *Dreamwalker*. "Why don't you all get cleaned up, and we can read this together," she said. "Pagus, you can transcribe for me."

Pagus nodded respectfully to his aunt while the other acolytes dashed across the lawn. They soon disappeared inside the guesthouse.

Turning to Iltar, Elsia asked, "Are you coming?"

Was he? Iltar hadn't thought about where he would spend the night. Would Alanya invite him back?

Iltar glanced back to the high duchess, who stared at him with a devious grin. Was that an invitation?

"I take that as a no," Elsia said, and Pagus whistled. Iltar gave the boy a sharp glance. "Good night, Iltar," Elsia said, and walked back to the guest-house with her nephew, leaving Iltar with Alanya.

Cool fingers wrapped around Iltar's hand. "Let's go," Alanya whispered in his ear.

It was happening again. Perhaps he *would* become accustomed to waking beside a beautiful woman.

*"The Harbinger will be a vagabond, cast out from his own country.
None shall receive him."*

- Prophecy of Soron Thahan

Cornar rode with his men at the back of the expedition. He wanted to keep an eye on Jahevial, and he couldn't do that from the front. Much of the day's journey had been through thick forests, and Cornar couldn't see much of what lay ahead, though he knew they were close to Klindil. The day before, they had set up camp in a field near the forest. Beyond the trees rose mountains and the vague shapes of towering ruins. That view had disappeared once they resumed their trek.

Excited chatter from the expedition's head reached Cornar and the others.

"I think we're there," Gregan observed. He was driving one of the wagons.

The expedition turned, following the path, and Cornar could see the tree line.

Soon, they were out of the trees and on the plain where Klindil's tent stood. The ruined metropolis sprawled across a valley, nestled between two mountain ranges. The ruins looked bigger than Soroth, *much* bigger. Stone buildings were toppled, but some were intact. The buildings didn't reach as high as those depicted in Krindal's magical map, but they were still towering. *Perhaps the map is a representation of what the city used to look like.*

"Wow!" Ordreth shouted. "It's magnificent!" Some of the other warriors muttered similar accolades of excitement. Cornar, however, just stared at the ruins. He had seen a similar sight years ago.

"Looks like Karthar, doesn't it?" Igan asked, guiding his horse up beside Cornar.

"It does," Cornar nodded. Had Karthar looked like Klindil? Karthar's ruins were tall, but Cornar had thought them rising no more than a dozen stories.

"Karthar?" Ordreth asked. "I didn't think it was possible for anyone to reach Karthar. Isn't it protected by magic, or something?"

"It is," Igan replied. "But old Amendal found a way to sneak our band past the twisted barsion."

"When did that happen?"

"Before you were born," Cornar answered, focusing on the scholars near the middle of the expedition. He could marvel at the ruins another time. He had to keep an eye on Jahevial. Cornar had to know what that man was up to…

Igan related some of the details about the adventure. He told Ordreth that the only known way to enter Karthar was through a gate in the mountains. No one had ever successfully breached it, because a tribe called the Yelinail killed anyone who attempted to reach the gate. They called the canyon where the gate resided the Path to Sorrow, and for good reason.

In addition to the murderous mountain men, the entire region of Karthar was surrounded by cliffs, wide rivers, and mountains. People said to have braved the natural barriers found walls of deadly magic that could destroy a man in an instant. But all this didn't stop old Amendal. He possessed a tevisral that enabled them to bypass the magic, using a conjuration portal to teleport into the Karthar region.

Ordreth was awestruck at the tale. Cornar didn't know why. Hadn't he told his nephew about all his adventures? Perhaps Ordreth had forgotten.

The leaders of the expedition called for the camp to be set up between the ruins and the forest, a distance of about three grand phineals. The Mindolarnians erected their war camp exactly halfway between both.

Many of the members of his band helped, setting up their own tents near the Imperial Tent. Cornar, however, wandered through the camp shrouded in Sharon's cloak. He kept a close eye on Jahevial.

After erecting the tents with the other scholars and Mindolarn servants, Jahevial sneaked out of his tent. He hurried through the outer ring of the war camp, which was partially constructed. No one paid attention to him.

Where are you going? Cornar wondered, keeping his distance from the scholar.

Jahevial went straightway toward the forest, clutching his robe the entire way. Cornar was careful not to get too close once Jahevial got into the trees, but he was still close enough to see and hear everything that Jahevial was doing.

Once Jahevial was well within the trees, he reached beneath his robe, removing a forearm-length rod with a gem on one end and a porous sphere on the other. He brushed his finger over the gem in a clockwise pattern and then touched some protrusions along the rod. The gem pulsed a pale blue, glowing with what looked like magic. Was that a tevisral? Cornar had never seen anything like it.

Jahevial cleared his throat and brought the porous end toward his face. "We've reached the edge of the ruins," the scholar said, speaking into the porous sphere. "It is grander than I imagined! The prince still hasn't returned, but the Wildmen we found in Anigar escorted us. We didn't encounter any resistance." He tapped the gemstone, and the light faded. Jahevial just stood there.

Was he waiting for something?

The gemstone pulsed a dark-orange hue, and then Jahevial touched the gem in a counter-clockwise pattern. A voice came from the porous end. It sounded familiar.

"We're glad to hear that. When will you be searching the ruins?"

Jahevial twirled the rod and tapped the gem, then swept across it in a clockwise pattern. "Hopefully tonight, Krindal wants to start examining the nearby buildings. But I doubt we'll find anything. Once Kaescis arrives, we'll be moving to the city's heart. Cornar Dol'shir noticed a place to access to the tunnel network, so we're going to try there."

Who was Jahevial talking to? The voice was distorted, sounding odd.

"Do you still suspect him watching you?" asked the voice in the tevisral.

"I didn't notice him yesterday," Jahevial said. "And today I haven't seen him. He was riding with his band and not up front, so I lost track of him as we were setting up camp."

"Be wary, Jahevial. Cornar is not a man to be trifled with."

"I know, Grandmaster Alacor, I'll be careful."

Alacor? Why was Jahevial talking with him? And how did he get this tevisral? Cornar wasn't aware of the Necrotic Order possessing tevisrals like this…

Jahevial jumped, looking farther into the trees. Cornar followed his gaze. There was someone lurking nearby. Careful to not make any noise, Cornar crept through the trees to get a better look.

"I have to go…" Jahevial whispered. "I'm being watched." He tapped on the tevisral's gem and tucked it beneath his robe. Jahevial tiptoed backward, still gazing into the woods.

As the scholar retreated, a tall figure moved behind one of the trees. *It can't be*. It was that same sharp face he'd seen the night the scholars excavated the path. This time, Cornar could clearly see the spy's features. Those pointed ears were unmistakable. He *was* an elf.

So, Krindal's fears weren't unfounded, Cornar thought, watching the elf ease away from the tree. *I should follow him.*

This time, the elf calmly retreated. Cornar was not about to lose him. He needed to find out what this elf was up to, and why he was spying on the expedition. He crept behind the elf for a time, and then the ground shook. *Another tremor?* The tremor grew into violent shaking. No. It was an earthquake!

Cornar fell, and so did the elf. Trees cracked, tumbling around them. The elf scurried away from a falling trunk, but the felled tree pinned his leg. The elf cried out, but forced an incantation through clenched teeth. Gray magic wisped into the tree, lifting it into the air.

Who is this elf? Cornar wondered, dodging another tree as it fell. The ground continued shaking, and he dropped to his knees. Was this an actual earthquake? A resounding crack echoed from the ground. What was that?

The grass and dirt shook, and then it all collapsed, swallowing up the elf.

Cornar felt himself falling; he hit something hard and slid. Sunlight disappeared as he fell into an abyss. His head bounced against another hard surface but he kept sliding. That last hit made him dizzy. It was hard to keep his eyes open… and everything was so dark.

━━━◆•◆━━━

Krindal braced himself under the table in the war room of the Imperial Tent. Polished stones, used to hold down the maps of Klindala, fell from the table.

"This is a big one!" Hezidex shouted. He was huddled beside Crenai near the table's other legs.

The ground shook, and Krindal jolted upward, hitting his head against the table. He blinked several times, spots clouding his vision as he tried to focus. Crenai groaned.

The earthquake continued for a little while longer, then subsided.

My head, Krindal moaned to himself, rubbing the spot that hit the table.

"We need to check the camp," Hezidex shouted, moving out from under the table.

Krindal crawled behind the grand marshal. The tent had remained standing through the entire earthquake, probably because of the tevisrals holding it in place. He stumbled past some Crimson Praetorians and entered the Royal ring of the camp. The ground felt… uneven. It was like he was on a slope. Some of Cornar's men were helping each other up and checking their collapsed tents.

The whole war camp looked to be in shambles. He could see parts of the outer ring from here. That wasn't possible when everything was set up correctly. That part of the outer ring looked lower than the rest…

A horse bolted through the war camp, crying a panicked whinny.

A rumbling crash resounded to the north, toward the ruins. That worried him. Krindal looked toward the sound but couldn't see much beyond the tents, even though most were toppled. The ground to the north looked like it was tilted.

He hurried through the war camp, picking his way across the collapsed tents. The ground *was* uneven, the east higher than the west. He made it to the camp's edge to behold a frightful sight.

That part of the plain where the war camp sat was higher than the city, tipping at an angle. Though the war camp was raised, Krindal could still see the ruins of Klindil.

One of the buildings had already collapsed, and another was sliding. The walls broke apart and then fell in a resounding crash. Other buildings were falling in the distance. Some of the tallest buildings—which were previously unseen from their old vantage point—were tilting. The buildings looked to be in the spot where they had planned to search for the entrance to the tunnels.

"No…" he groaned, dropping to his knees. *Please, do not block my path. I must reach the temple.* Krindal watched in horror as one of the tall buildings faltered and crashed against another. Both buildings fell, burying other structures beneath them.

Horrified by the sight, Krindal remained on his knees while the expedition scurried about behind him.

—❍•❍—

"Did Cor make it back?" Gregan demanded. Kalder stood warily. Was the earthquake finished? Mindolarn soldiers were frantically moving about the camp.

"Kalder!" Gregan shouted.

"I don't know," Kalder answered. "We need to check on everyone first, then we can look for Cor."

Kalder and Gregan searched through the camp for their companions in adventure. Luckily, everyone was accounted for; not one soul had been lost. There were a few bumps and bruises but nothing that wouldn't mend with time.

"Where's my uncle?" Ordreth asked.

"I didn't see him in the camp," Nordal said. "Did anyone see the scholar?"

"Jahevial?" Igan asked. "I haven't."

"We should start looking," Kalder said. "Break up into your usual groups of three. I'm going back toward the forest. Gregan, bring your group. We'll search together."

The warriors and mages divided into their groups and hurried through the camp, searching for Jahevial. Kalder and Igan walked together, followed by Gregan, Vargos, and Aron. They exited the camp and marveled at the now-plateau that the war camp sat upon.

"By all that's magical…" Vargos muttered, gasping.

Kalder could see the ruins of Klindil breaking apart from the earthquake. *It's a good thing we're not in there,* he thought. *Or below ground.* He thought of the entire expedition buried under a collapsing city, trapped. The idea sickened him.

"Look!" Gregan shouted, pointing down the slope in the plateau toward the trees.

Kalder spun about, seeing a robed figure approaching. *Jahevial…* Kalder hurried toward the man. Jahevial noticed their hasty approach and shied away, acting as if he were simply moving out of their path.

"Did you see Cornar?" Kalder demanded.

"Why would I have seen him?" Jahevial asked, climbing the slope back to the shambles of the war camp.

Kalder narrowed his eyes at the scholar. Cornar had told Kalder that he intended to discover what Jahevial was doing.

Shouts of Cornar's name roused Kalder from his reverie. Everyone else had hurried down the slope, calling to the warrior. They shouted his name as they headed to the trees. Kalder and the others searched for hours, to no avail. The sun had set, and darkness was falling. Igan had cast a spell, mustering a ball of light that hovered nearby. That spell was more useful when indoors. Out in the open it only illuminated a small area.

"We should get back," Kalder said to Igan, "grab some lightstones, and resume searching for Cor."

Igan nodded and looked at his illuminating globe with disappointment. It wasn't lighting much.

"Kalder!" Aron shouted. "Over here!"

Kalder and Igan exchanged worried glances, then hurried toward Aron. Aron was standing at the precipice of a gaping hole in the ground. How had that happened? Earthquakes didn't tear random holes in the ground. This hole was so big you could fit several estate homes inside it.

Igan guided his light into the enormous hole.

"Is that stone?" Gregan asked, pointing to the far side of the hole.

The wizard guided his illuminating globe across the hole, and the light shone upon a dirty slab as large as a ship. The massive slab had a curve to it.

"That stone looks at least fifty phineals wide," Gregan said.

"Do you think this is part of those tunnels?" Aron asked.

Vargos hummed. "It could be… I didn't get a good look at the map, but I thought all the tunnels were beneath the ruins."

Kalder stepped closer to the hole. It seemed to go on a way, several hundred phineals. Had Cor fallen down there? *That would have been fatal…* He quelled his fears, resuming the mantle of leadership. "We need to grab more lightstones and some rope."

"We'll need magic cords," Vargos said, his tone matter-of-fact. "I don't think the Mindolarnians have any rope that's more than fifty phineals long."

Kalder nodded. "One of you grab Hem. He can weave us some."

They continued back through the trees—Aron leading the way. The ground began to shake again.

"Another tremor?" Gregan blurted.

Vargos's eyes widened, and he began casting a spell, mustering barsion magic. There was panic in the old man's face. Did he think the ground was going to collapse? The barsion magic surged beneath Vargos's feet, spreading in an area around him wide enough to enclose the search party.

"To Vargos!" Kalder shouted the command and bolted to the barsionist.

Tree trunks cracked amid the spell, and several trees fell around them.

Igan and Gregan darted to Vargos, grabbing his robe. As Aron neared, a tree fell, barring his path. The warrior backed up and leapt over the trunk, but before he could reach Kalder and the others, the ground gave way.

Kalder felt himself falling. Aron struggled in the air, trying to reach them. Vargos's spell finished and the four of them were surrounded by a bubble of barsion magic.

Kalder watched in horror as Aron fell, unprotected. The warrior hit something and vanished.

The barsion bubble hit something as well, and the four of them tumbled about, bouncing off the magic. They collided with each other, then fell against the barsion again. Falling against barsion was like falling on a pillow—well, many pillows. They fell for quite some time, then came to a halt. The bubble settled on a cavern floor, made of… stone?

Igan's illuminating globe shone through Vargos's protective barrier, lighting the unnatural cave. Were these the tunnels Krindal and Cornar had mentioned?

Kalder looked behind them, where a steep face of curved stone led back up to the surface.

"Where's Aron?" Gregan asked, his tone panicked.

A faint cry reached Kalder's ears, coming from the opposite direction of the curved stone.

"There!" Igan pointed toward the sound.

Vargos dismissed his magic, and they all bolted toward the noise, calling for Aron.

"Here-ahh!" Aron's voice echoed off the stone.

Kalder rounded some debris and found Aron wedged between piles of stone along a towering wall.

"M-my leg!" Aron shouted, his face reflecting his excruciating pain. His leg had probably been crushed.

Kalder hurried to Aron, while Vargos knelt beside the younger warrior. The barsionist began casting another spell, pointing his hand to Aron.

The sound of cracking stone reached Kalder's ears. It was coming from that wall beside Aron. Kalder looked around. The cavern was at least two hundred phineals tall. Its ceiling—which was probably that curved slab leading to the surface—was gone. Kalder could see the night sky through a gaping hole, like the first they had seen. More cracking sounded from beside him, near Aron.

"You hear that?" Gregan asked, looking frightened.

Kalder gave him a hollow glance, then returned his attention to Vargos and Aron. Barsion magic shrouded the wounded warrior.

"Pull him!" Vargos shouted, frantically turning to Kalder.

Kalder quickly grabbed Aron, and Igan helped him pull the wounded warrior. As they got Aron free, the nearby wall fell toward them, covering the sky.

A spike of adrenaline shot through Kalder, and he ran, dragging Aron. Frantic footfalls echoed around Kalder—the others were also running. A resounding crash echoed behind Kalder and reverberated throughout the cavern. The cavern seemed to get darker. How was that possible?

"Kalder…" Gregan began. Kalder turned around and started. The entire wall barred the way to that slanting slab leading to the surface. Igan was guiding his illuminating globe all along the collapsed wall, looking for any way around it. Unfortunately, the areas that weren't covered in stone were packed with dirt.

"We're trapped," Vargos growled.

"Can't you disintegrate that?" Gregan pointed to the stone, his question aimed at Igan.

"And risk further collapse?" the wizard said. "I don't want to chance it."

"Put him down," Vargos said, gesturing to Aron. "I should set his leg."

"How are you going to do that?" Kalder asked, gently guiding Aron to the cavern floor.

"A concentrated cast of barsion magic. It should stop the bleeding too."

Aron groaned. The procedure sounded like it was going to hurt.

Barsion faded around Aron, and Vargos cast another spell, concentrating on Aron's left leg. The limb was bent unnaturally below the knee. Had that happened when he was dragging Aron? Or was it a result of the fall?

"You're going to be all right, Aron," Kalder said, kneeling beside the wounded warrior. "Once we out of here we'll find one of those Mindolarn arpranists. You'll soon be in tip-top shape."

Aron looked at him with pained disbelief and then screamed as Vargos set the bone. Kalder stayed beside Aron until he stopped screaming. *You poor man*, he thought.

Kalder gazed at the wall barring their way. *The earthquake must have weakened this structure.* That explained the hole they found. Cornar must have fallen. But he was unprotected… Had what happened to Aron happened to Cornar? Was he mangled in some part of this godforsaken hole?

"We're stuck," Igan said, coming beside Vargos. "And there's no telling how much of the ground and or whatever this structure is"—he gestured to the broken stone—"is on top of us."

"We should go farther into the cave," Vargos said, resting beside Aron.

"Into the cave?" Gregan asked, bewildered. "We don't even know what's down there."

"The temple is down there," Vargos said in a matter-of-fact voice. "If we keep going, we have a chance of running into the others."

That logic seemed sound.

"We might find Cor," Igan said. "He could be hurt like Aron."

"But he was back that way," Gregan pointed to the collapse.

Igan shrugged. "Maybe, maybe not."

"I don't think we should wait for a rescue," Kalder said, frowning. He hoped no one would be foolish enough to try to come after them. Some of them might try, Ordreth in particular. With himself, Cornar, and Gregan gone, Nordal would be in charge. For now, Kalder was leading this ragtag bunch.

"Let's move deeper into the cave," Kalder said. "Gregan, help me carry Aron."

Gregan complied without any complaint, and they hoisted Aron between them. Aron was shorter than the two of them, so carrying him with his arms around their shoulders made it easier to avoid dragging his leg on the ground. The tip of his foot barely touched the stone floor.

Igan took the lead, guiding them with his illuminating globe. The light barely reached the cavern's walls and ceiling. This tunnel was massive. What use had it among the ancient Klindala people?

I hope you're okay, Cor, Kalder thought. *Please, don't die on us.* The thought of losing Cornar tore at Kalder's heart, and a tear trickled down his cheek.

"We're going to find him," Gregan said, his tone stern.

Kalder nodded. They had to find Cornar, even if it was the last thing they would do.

32

AN UNEXPECTED COMPANION

"Naedar, are you all right?" Cornar heard his father's voice. He was dreaming again… Was his father talking to him?

Cornar sucked in a breath, taking in his surroundings. He was lying on his back within a forest. Tall trees covered most of the area, their leaves high above a ledge not too far away. What was this place? Cornar didn't recognize it. And there was a sickly whine nearby. Was that a horse crying?

"Naedar!"

Cornar glanced toward the call, seeing Melthas hastily approaching atop a horse. Melthas was wearing simple clothing. His father dismounted and knelt beside him. There were dozens of others behind Melthas, all dressed the same. Adrin was there too. They looked like a band of travelers. Where was their armor?

"Naedar?" Melthas asked, cocking his head in a way that awaited a reply. "Are you hurt?"

"What?" Cornar asked. Was Melthas talking about that fall Cornar had taken during the earthquake? How could his father know about that?

"The ledge you were on gave way," Melthas said, checking Cornar for wounds. "Can you move?"

Cornar started by wiggling his fingers. They were fine. Cornar raised his wrists but a sharp pain surged up his right forearm. He gritted his teeth against the pain.

"Adrin!" Melthas called. Within seconds, Adrin was kneeling beside Cornar, casting an arpran spell. Green magic coalesced within his hands. "What about your legs?" Melthas asked. Cornar strained to move his legs, but couldn't. He didn't even feel them.

Melthas sighed, clasping a hand to Cornar's shoulder. "At least you're alive," he said. "You didn't see it coming, did you?"

His father's question was eerie… The last thing Cornar remembered was falling and sliding into that dark abyss. Had he been knocked unconscious?

"Kalric," Melthas shouted, "see to Naedar's horse."

"Yes, sir," a man from the company replied and hurried through the ranks. Cornar heard the man—Kalric—casting an arpran spell.

"We're going to resume scouting ahead," Melthas said. "Take your time getting up." He patted Cornar's shoulder and returned to his horse. The others rode away, but Adrin remained, healing Cornar's—or rather Naedar's— wounds.

"That was a nasty fall," Adrin said, guiding the healing magic to Cornar's legs. "You're lucky to be alive."

Was he? How far had he fallen in the real world?

"Two hundred and seventy-three phineals, give or take a few fractions," Adrin said, as if answering Cornar's question. "Trans-lines of that era had a standard diameter of two hundred and fifty-three phineals. Then take into account the thickness of the tube, then the dirt between it and the surface. You're looking at about a thirty phineal difference."

Cornar looked at Adrin, confused. Was this that strange being that had haunted his other dreams?

"You were lucky." Adrin smiled, finishing with Cornar's legs. Cornar could feel them again. "That elf, on the other hand… well, he's just a blob of mush."

"You're not Adrin," Cornar said, pushing himself up.

Adrin put a finger to his lips and smiled wryly. "Don't tell anyone." Cornar gave the not-Adrin a hard look.

"You're wondering why you're here, aren't you? I put you into this Naedar character because he suffered a similar fate during your father's journey to Laelin Lake. It was the only way to keep you alive."

"What?" Cornar asked.

"Your horse is ready, Naedar," Kalric said, walking back to his own horse.

Soon, Cornar and the not-Adrin character were alone.

"I can't reach out and heal you," the not-Adrin said. "So, I pulled you into this situation here in Vabenack. When you awake, you'll be fine." He stood and offered a hand to Cornar.

Who was this being? And why was he helping? He had told Cornar that these dreams were for his benefit. Cornar had yearned to experience another, but had not been granted an opportunity. Cornar looked skyward, seeing that strange yellow sky with sparse red clouds. It had been days since he had been in this dreamland.

"So what am I supposed to learn today?" Cornar asked the not-Adrin.

"Not much," the not-Adrin hummed. "I brought you here to heal you. You're not ready to see what happens next." He smiled. At that moment, this visage of Adrin looked exactly like Iltar. It was like Iltar was standing right in front of him, smug expression and all.

"Are we near Laelin Lake?" Cornar asked.

The not-Adrin nodded and gestured for his horse to come near. Cornar hadn't noticed before, but Adrin's horse wasn't like the others. It looked transmuted, formed from dirt, grass, leaves, and rock. The horse's eyes glowed a white hue. He recognized the features of the horse as an Alathian Thoroughbred. Cornar had become accustomed to the various breeds because he had participated in horse shows with Karenna.

"I suggest you stop with the questions and play along," the not-Adrin said, trotting his horse toward the others. "Naedar is part of your father's Elites; he's a vicious and skilled soldier. There's still an evening's ride to the incursion point. You won't dream longer than that."

Cornar sighed, turning toward his horse. It was of the Custerwin breed. Custerwins were common in the region of the Western Sovereignty, native to the western plains of the Mainland. The horse let him on without a fuss, and Cornar hurried after the others.

Soon, Melthas's party was at the edge of a lake, a purple lake. What was wrong with this place? Why did some things look so different?

"The castle should be over there," Melthas said, pointing to the left side of the lake. "We could probably be at our planned incursion point after nightfall."

Melthas guided the others into the trees along the shore. Cornar went to follow but felt a nudge against his shoulder. He turned in the direction of the nudge but didn't see anyone. Another nudge swayed him in his saddle.

What was happening?

"Are you alive?" a voice boomed across the sky, followed by a third nudge.

Someone is trying to wake me, Cornar thought. He glanced to Adrin, who didn't pay attention. *You better pull me back here soon.* Laelin Lake, the place his father would die—or died. Cornar had to know how this was related to his quest to find the Keepers' Temple of Klindil.

Suddenly, everything dimmed. A faint light shone behind a masculine figure huddling over Cornar.

"Good, you're breathing," the stranger said. His voice sounded like that one in the dream, except not as booming. "Can you move?"

Cornar coughed and raised his hand, shielding his eyes against the light. Was that a lightstone? It wasn't flame. A musky smell assailed his nostrils, the kind that only lingered in places that hadn't seen the light of day in centuries.

"Nothing looks broken," the stranger said. His voice was deep, masculine, and stern. It wasn't one of his men. Was it one of the Mindolarnians?

"Who, who are you?" Cornar asked, pushing himself upright.

"So you can speak," the stranger said, standing. He towered above Cornar, extending a hand toward him. Cornar grabbed the hand and pulled himself onto his feet. He stood almost equal in height with the stranger, whose face was still hidden behind the shadows cast by the light. The light was coming from a simple lightstone.

"Where are we?" Cornar asked. The lightstone didn't illuminate much.

"Buried," the stranger said. He walked toward the lightstone, kneeling to pick it up. He turned toward Cornar, exposing his face to the light.

Cornar started. *Impossible!* It was that elf from the tavern, the one with the goatee. But hadn't those elves left port?

"Who are you?" Cornar asked, his tone wary.

The elf stood, eyeing Cornar with an equally cautious gaze. "My name is Solidin," the elf said. "And you?"

"Cornar."

"Pleasure to meet you," Solidin said, looking about. Cornar nodded. Who was this elf? He wasn't the same one spying on Jahevial. "How did you get down here?" Solidin asked.

Cornar remembered sneaking through the trees, wearing—*Sharon's cloak!* he thought aghast, ignoring the question. The cloak wasn't on him. Cornar spun back to where he'd fallen.

"I'm missing something," he said. He scanned the floor but didn't see the cloak. *Where was it?*

"Your cloak?" Solidin asked, glancing to a pack slung over his shoulder. The elf opened it and pulled out the shimmering shroud.

"Yes," Cornar said, extending a hand. "It's mine."

Solidin nodded and handed the cloak back to Cornar.

"It was wrapped around your neck," Solidin said. "Looked like it was choking you, so I took it off."

Cornar nodded and latched the cloak but didn't fasten the clasp to make him invisible.

"You know, those things are rare." Solidin gestured to the cloak. "I've only heard tales about them."

"It's not for sale," Cornar said.

"I wouldn't have assumed it was." Solidin smiled.

He doesn't talk like an elf, Cornar thought. There weren't many places in the world where elves talked like men. And using contractions… this elf must not have spoken his ancestral tongue as a first language.

"We should get moving if we want to escape this place," Solidin said, turning around. He held out his lightstone, studying the ground before taking a step.

Cornar stood still. Should he follow this elf? Krindal's fears nagged at the back of his mind. Where there were two elves there were probably more. Was this Solidin part of a larger group, the group Krindal was so terrified of encountering again? Cornar felt to his sides. His weapons were still girded around his belt.

Solidin continued forward, cautiously studying the ground as he moved.

He has a lightstone, and I don't, Cornar thought, frowning. If he were to navigate his way through this abysmal maze he'd have to ally with this elf.

"So, do you know where to go?" Cornar asked, hurrying after Solidin.

"Not that way," the elf gestured behind them. "I barely made it through before everything collapsed."

Cornar glanced over his shoulder. The lightstone barely illuminated an angled wall of curved stone. *Curved stone?* Was this part of those tunnels under Klindil? It looked like it might have been a ceiling, judging by the angle by which it fell. Cornar remembered seeing several tunnels that spread from the ruins to the plains. Krindal had shown the leaders of the expedition a close-up view of Klindil on his mapping tevisral. Cornar had taken the time to memorize the map. Which tunnel was this? It was northwest of the path. There were two tunnels in that direction; they ran alongside each other until they reached the ruins.

Cornar looked ahead, noting the angle of his fall and the direction he was walking during the earthquake. His and Solidin's current heading would take them toward Klindil.

"So what brought you down here?" Cornar asked.

"I was looking for my friend," Solidin said. "He wasn't as lucky as you."

So the not-creature was right, Cornar thought. What else had that strange being been right about? Cornar wondered if he had been wounded. Did he really receive some type of healing through that dream?

"Your friend was another elf?" Cornar asked.

"Yeah," Solidin said, focusing ahead.

"I'm sorry he didn't make it," Cornar said with half-hearted sympathy, and his thoughts turned to his men. Hopefully none of them had come looking for him. Would they have been as lucky as he or Solidin?

"It's one of the dangers of being in the wilds," Solidin said flatly. Did he not care about his friend? The elf seemed callous. "Our group's leader sent him to watch another party, a large one brandishing the flags of the Mindolarn Empire. When he didn't return, I went looking for him. I found his corpse under stone, but another tremor shook the debris around me, and I had to flee. And now, here I am."

Cornar studied the elf. Solidin carried no weapons, unless they were hidden in his pack. The elf wore simple clothing, nothing extravagant. The other elf—the dead spy—wore something similar.

"So why are you here?" Cornar asked.

"Besides the obvious?" Solidin chuckled.

"Yeah," Cornar nodded. "Why are you on Klindala?"

"Exploring," Solidin answered. "It's what I get paid to do."

"You're a mercenary, or a hireling?"

Solidin raised an eyebrow at Cornar. "You're full of questions."

"Well, we're both trapped down here," Cornar said. "If we're going to make it out of here alive, we need to trust each other. What better way by getting to know each other?"

Solidin grinned. Did he see truth in Cornar's words?

"My employers sent us here," Solidin said, "to explore the ruins."

"So you *are* a hireling," Cornar said.

Solidin nodded grimly. That made Cornar's mind churn. An elf without an accent, begrudgingly working as a hireling. There was only one place Solidin could be from… the Isle of Merdan, more specifically the city of Keth.

Was Solidin forced into this life? Cornar knew of Merdan elves who sold themselves as cheap labor. Life was hard for Keth elves. They were the dregs of that city. Some had been taken in by bands of adventurers. Cornar had run across one such group several years ago. Those elves were treated like pack animals. Despicable… Solidin was probably an expendable scout, just like his crushed friend back there.

"You're from Merdan, aren't you?" Cornar asked.

Solidin started, leaning away from Cornar. "How do you figure that?"

"By your accent, or lack thereof," Cornar grinned. "And by everything else you've told me. You weren't working with those elves back in the tavern, were you?" The question was more rhetorical than inquisitive. "They were Mainland elves. One of my men learned they were from Merath."

"No," Solidin said, laughing. "And you're right. I am from Merdan."

"Half-elf?" Cornar asked. "That'd explain the goatee."

"My goatee?" Solidin smiled. "I take it you've never seen a full-blooded elf with a goatee?"

"I didn't think elves could grow facial hair." Cornar had never seen one with a beard. Their faces looked so smooth, like that of a child.

"It's possible," Solidin said. "It takes conscious effort. I prefer the goatee. Allows me to blend in better. People tend to forget the pointed ears when they see the goatee. Puts people at ease."

"So you're around men, mostly?" Cornar asked.

Solidin gave Cornar a sidelong glance. "How about I take a turn at the questions?"

That seemed a fair request. Cornar had just badgered Solidin for a great deal of information. He wasn't here to interrogate the elf—well, he didn't want to make it seem that way. But Cornar did want to know more about him.

"Go ahead," Cornar said. "What do you want to know?"

"Are you part of that Mindolarn envoy? Or another group?"

"I'm with them," Cornar answered. "But I have my own band. We're tagging along for support."

"Support?" Solidin burst into laughter. "Since when has the *Mighty* Mindolarn Empire needed *support?*" His tone was mocking.

Solidin's sarcastic quip made Cornar think. Kaescis didn't need him and his men. That had been demonstrated thus far. The scholars from the Order of Histories were just as superfluous as Cornar and his men.

"What does that empire want with Klindala, anyway?" Solidin asked. "There isn't anything of military importance here."

"It's scholarly," Cornar answered. Did he dare tell him more? Cornar doubted this elf could get back to his band faster than Kaescis and the others could secure the Keepers' Temple. He could probably tell him the truth.

"We have a scholar among us that is seeking to validate some old truths."

"Really?" Solidin said, sounding intrigued. "What kind of *truths?*"

"About the ancient world. We're following the footsteps of an ancient Order of men. The Keepers of Truth and Might."

"Never heard of them," Solidin said quickly.

"Well, there's a temple of theirs hidden somewhere in Klindil," Cornar said, not wanting to say more. He didn't want to give away too much to the elf, but just enough to gain his trust.

Solidin grunted and shook his head. "And here I thought you Mindolarnians were all about weapons and tevisrals."

"I'm not Mindolarnian," Cornar spat with contempt.

"Really?" Solidin asked, surprised. "Well then, where are you from?"

"Soroth." Solidin eyed Cornar up and down. The elf turned away, looking like he had seen a ghost.

"What's wrong?"

"I know who you are," Solidin said. "Cornar Dol'shir, one of the greatest adventurers in the Kalishir Ocean. Those are *his* weapons, aren't they?"

"Are you referring to my father?" Cornar asked. "They were his, but they've been mine longer." Well, now that this elf knew who Cornar was, perhaps he could get more information out of him.

Cornar's stomach grumbled.

"I doubt there's anything edible down here," Solidin said.

"There could be creatures lurking about," Cornar said, sounding hopeful. People didn't often hope for creatures lurking in dark confines, but Cornar was hungry. He just didn't have a way to cook it…

"Wow…" Solidin shook his head. "You're hoping there's *something* down here for you to kill and eat? I knew you were fierce, but I didn't take you for a ferocious savage."

"Well, when you've been through things that I've endured, you learn to eat whatever you can get. Even if it's some disgusting creature."

Solidin laughed. "Tell me, what's the most disgusting monster you've ever eaten?"

Disgusting? There were a few… Cornar remembered the time he and Iltar were stranded halfway across the world, wandering the Desolate Lands for months. They ate the strangest things.

"A mages' parasite," Cornar answered. Mages' parasites were vile creatures. Old Amendal was fond of summoning them, as they could absorb magic and reflect it back to the mage. As conjurations, they were quite useful, but they were far from a tasty meal. Just the thought of eating one again almost made Cornar puke.

That rubbery flesh. The putrid taste. And the smell… Oh, that was the worst of it. Cornar gagged. *Disgusting!* Solidin narrowed his eyes and raised his upper lip.

"If we find one of those down here," Cornar said, "I'll pass. We'll eat the next monster."

"I'll take your word for it."

They continued onward for a while, not talking. The thoughts of the mages' parasite had sullied the conversation. Finally, Cornar spoke up.

"Are you good with magic?"

Solidin shook his head. "What makes you think a Keth elf would be trained in magic?"

"Well, aren't all your kind adept?"

"Those that try." Solidin shrugged off the question. Silence lingered between them again.

"Are you getting tired yet?" Solidin asked. It was probably late, but this tunnel didn't look a safe spot to rest.

"Yeah, but we should keep going."

<hr>

Nordal looked down into that abysmal pit. It had swallowed his friends, his comrades… He wanted to stab it until it bled. But this was not some beast he could slay, and that infuriated him.

"The other hole is just like this," Ordreth shouted. He marched toward Nordal with Sharon, Demsal, and Hem. They each carried lightstone lanterns. Demsal and Hem also held a glowing green rope, woven from the illusionist's magic. "And it was deep, a couple hundred phineals to the bottom."

Sharon looked troubled, as if she were about to cry.

Buck up, woman, Nordal thought. *This is no time for tears.*

"Didn't find anything?" Nordal asked.

"A crushed corpse," Ordreth said. "Smashed between huge slabs of stone. It wasn't Uncle, though. His skin was too pale, and he wore the wrong clothes."

Nordal narrowed his eyes. Was there someone else out here during the earthquake? He wondered if it could be the spy from the other night. They hadn't encountered anyone else spying on them, although Cor had thought he saw someone by the statues outside that fortress. It was probably just his imagination.

"Nordal!" Midar's voice rang through the trees. "Nordal!"

Nordal turned, his fury for the pit still boiling within him. "What is it?" Nordal asked, seething.

"Krindal has called a meeting," Midar said, looking concerned as he approached. "Any… luck?"

Luck? Perhaps they should have brought Hemrin on the search…

"No," Ordreth spoke up. "The pits don't lead anywhere."

Midar looked confused. "So… where are the others?"

Nordal ignored the question and stomped through the forest. He climbed the unnatural slope made by the earthquake to the tilted war camp. Tilters… that's what he would call these blasted fools. Damned Tilters. Why couldn't they have gotten lost in those pits?

Nordal hurried through the wreckage of the war camp. That bastard, Jahevial, stood in a tent with the other scholars, each babbling and marveling at the destruction in the ruins.

How dare they? Cor and the others were missing, probably dead or dying, and these pompous, ass-kissing scholars were more concerned with decrepit heaps of stone rather than men in perilous circumstances.

That only fueled his rage.

It's your fault, Nordal thought, his anger boiling. He lowered a hand to his waist, palm hovering over the hilt of his sword. If it wasn't for this bastard, Cor wouldn't have gone off alone, and then Kalder wouldn't have chased after him.

Jahevial *buried* six of his comrades as surely as pushing them off into those pits himself. If Nordal couldn't make the pits bleed perhaps he could—

"Sir!" a Crimson Praetorian called, stepping in front of Nordal. "You are wanted in the Imperial Tent."

"You can piss on the Imperial Tent!" Nordal shouted. The Praetorian started, leaning back in surprise. He glanced to Nordal's weapon and his hand hovering over the hilt.

"Come with me," the Praetorian insisted, his tone firm. "We don't want trouble."

Of course the fool didn't want trouble... The Praetorian didn't want a sword shoved through his throat. And Nordal would do it. But... that wouldn't bring Cor or the others back. Nordal took in a deep breath, glanced to Jahevial one last time, then stalked off toward the Royal ring.

He went straightway toward the Imperial Tent. The Praetorians moved to block his path with their fanisars but remembered he was now in command of Cornar's band.

He was now in command? *Oh no.* Nordal sighed inwardly, passing the guards. Nordal couldn't lead them. He was too hotheaded!

Why couldn't you be here, Master Iltar? Nordal wondered as he stomped into the war room.

Krindal stood at one end of the tilted table, his tevisral map covering most of it. The two grand marshals stood on the other sides of the table, studying the map. What frivolous titles... They should have just stuck with *general.* Stupid Tilter Mindolarnians and their damned pompous titles.

"Nordal," Krindal said, "did you find them?"

"No," he spat the word and leaned over the table. "We did find a corpse, but it wasn't one of ours."

"Whose was it?" Grand Marshal Hezidex asked. What a name. *Who in their right mind names their kid Hezidex? You get nicknames like Dexy and Hezy.* Such a name would only condemn the kid to a life of wimpiness.

"Nordal?" Krindal asked.

Guess I should answer. Nordal thought. "Sorry... It wasn't Cor or any of the others. He was wearing the wrong clothing."

"The spy," Galiur said, nodding his head.

"Cornar must have been chasing the spy when the earthquake struck," Hezidex speculated.

"The pits we found were massive," Nordal said. He wasn't about to tell them that their assumptions were wrong. "At least twenty stories deep."

"Twenty stories?!" Galiur gasped.

"That must be these tunnels." Krindal pointed to the map.

Nordal leaned close. The mapping tevisral showed a few lines leading to the ruins. With his eyes, he followed the supposed tunnels into Klindil, where they met another mess of lines. It was like a maze down there.

"His Imperial Grace will be another day?" Krindal asked warily, looking at the pompous-titled generals.

"Yes," Galiur said. "Are you worried about this spy?"

Krindal nodded.

What a coward. Nordal stared through the map, eyeing the mapping tevisral. All the while, the sissy generals and the cowardly scholar talked about the spy and the group they thought he belonged to. Nordal could use that tevisral to get to those tunnels… He wasn't as good with maps as Cor, but he could follow directions. This was his missing comrades' only chance. He had to go find them.

"I'm taking your tevisral," Nordal interrupted the conversation and leaned across the table. Galiur grabbed his wrist, stopping him a fraction of a phineal from the tevisral.

"Let go of me," Nordal demanded. "I'm taking that tevisral and finding my friends."

"You're assuming they're alive," Hezy said. That very sentence made Nordal boil. Was this sissy general too afraid to go down there and look?

"This is Cornar Dol'shir we're talking about." Krindal shrugged. At least there was one man who had hope in Cor's survival. *Stupid Mindolarn Tilters.*

"If there's a chance that they're alive, I'm going to take it," Nordal said, a scowl forming upon his face. He wasn't good at negotiating, unless it involved a little hostility.

The generals looked at each other, then to Krindal.

"We need this tevisral to get to the temple," Galiur said, still holding tightly onto Nordal's wrist.

Nordal resisted the urge to break free of the grapple and beat the man to the ground. That'd probably bring down the wrath of the entire war camp… *Not a good idea, Nord,* he thought.

"We can't permit you to take the tevisral," Hezy said.

"I'm not going to die down there," Nordal said with a grunt. "I'll be taking the rest of my band with me. If we use the map, we can get back here by tomorrow evening."

The craven generals said nothing.

"If it were you trapped down there, Cor would be looking for you," Nordal said. He hoped a different approach might work. "Or any of your men. Cor wouldn't forsake the lowliest soldier or servant. You should afford him the same consideration."

Galiur let go of Nordal, turning away from the table. Nordal continued for the tevisral.

As he picked it up, Hezy blurted, "You can't take it!"

"Try to stop me," Nordal said. "And I'm taking one of your arpranists."

"I can't condone that," Hezy said, his face flaring with frustration.

My fist can condone it, Nordal thought, eyeing the sissy general with hostility. He yearned for an excuse to punch the sissy in the throat. *Make a move.* Nordal grinned. *I dare you…*

"Uh… Nordal," Krindal said timidly.

"Yeah?"

"That's *my* tevisral," Krindal said. "I…" he hesitated.

"You don't think I know that?" Nordal said, leaning away from the table. He held the tevisral in his hand, tilting the map sideways through the war room.

Krindal sighed. "I… I just."

Spit it out, man! Nordal raised an eyebrow, annoyed.

"I can't let it leave my sight," the scholar said, taking a deep breath.

"Then come with me," Nordal said frankly. "It's not like my band can't handle a few elves. You'll be safe with us."

Galiur chuckled and shook his head.

"Got a problem?" Nordal asked.

"You're an arrogant fool," Hezy said.

"There's a fine line between arrogance and confidence," Nordal said. "Only a coward would mistake the latter for the former. C'mon, Krindal. We're leaving."

Nordal spun around, he dashed out of the war room, and ran through the Imperial Tent. Nordal would find Cor and the others, no matter how long it took.

⎯⎯◗•◖⎯⎯

Aron groaned, "I need a break." Kalder looked to Gregan. The other warrior nodded.

"Okay," Kalder said.

Igan knelt before them, gently raising Aron's legs. The three of them set the wounded warrior on the ground.

"You know, we can't stay down here forever," Gregan said, folding his arms. "We'll die of thirst and starvation."

"We can last a few days," Kalder said.

"Aron won't," Gregan grumbled. "We need to find a way to break the surface."

"Not here," Vargos said. "It's too unstable."

"Well, it's better than what we passed back there," Gregan thumbed in the direction from which they'd come.

Gregan was right. They'd had to squeeze through a tight spot where the tunnel was crushed to one side. Igan thought it about the same area as the war camp, and that the sideways collapse was a result of the fault line pushing upward.

Gregan and Vargos began arguing about a plan of action. Gregan was adamant that Igan could disintegrate a hole to the surface and launch bolts of magic into the sky as a type of flare to alert the others. Vargos thought it foolish, as any type of disturbance could bring the tunnels down on top of them. Gregan rebutted by saying Vargos could use his barsion to protect them.

True, Vargos could shield them in such a way… but if another collapse happened, they'd risk becoming stuck.

Kalder didn't want to risk it. Gregan's ideas were reckless. But they needed food, and they needed water. And they needed it fast.

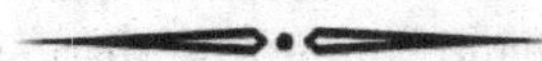

Several hours had passed since Solidin had awakened Cornar. In that time they had learned a great deal about each other.

Solidin claimed he was currently from the nation of Gastrim, though born in Keth. He, along with his deceased friend and a couple of other elves from Merdan worked as scouts for a group of adventurers who called themselves the Sanguine Blades.

Cornar had never heard of them and wondered if they were brutal or optimistic. Perhaps both, as Solidin didn't seem the least bit worried about being trapped beneath a long-forgotten city. But this group didn't sound like anything that would have frightened Krindal. The Sanguine Blades wouldn't have been a match for Cornar's band. So, Cornar found it unlikely that Solidin was part of the group Krindal feared.

The Sanguine Blades worked out of the city of Rystra. Rystra was on the shores of the Hidegarn River. The river bordered the Kingdom of Kerindor and flowed into the Sea of Korath.

Cornar had never traveled to Rystra. He had only been to the southern parts of Gastrim, exploring ruins in his youth. In fact, it was his first adventure. If it hadn't been for Iltar, he wouldn't have gone at all. That was a bittersweet trip, as there were plenty of broken promises and betrayals. But, it was the start to this incredible life of adventure.

While searching for a place to rest, Solidin showed some stoic resolve. He seemed a natural-born leader. Cornar wondered if the elf had persuaded his friends to join him. All in all, Solidin was a good fellow. He was the kind of person Cornar wanted by his side on an adventure.

Finally, Cornar and Solidin found a niche in the wall. The opening was as wide as they were tall, but only rose partway to their chests.

"This looks as good a spot as any," Cornar said, bending down.

Solidin angled his lightstone, illuminating the niche. It was not very deep, barely enough room for one man to lie comfortably. *A stone alcove?* Cornar wondered what it had been used for in the past. The niche's purpose baffled him, like most of this place.

"Do you want to take turns resting?" Solidin asked.

"That would be best," Cornar nodded.

"You go first," the elf suggested. "You need it more than I."

"Thank you," Cornar nodded, tucking himself into the cubby. He unlatched Sharon's cloak and rolled it up into a makeshift pillow. It would do, for now—

"Here," Solidin interrupted Cornar's thoughts, dangling his pack. "You can lie on this; use the cloak to cover up."

Reluctantly, Cornar grabbed the pack, feeling it and its contents. It was soft. Definitely, no weapons were concealed within it.

"Thank you," Cornar said, placing the pack where he had laid Sharon's cloak.

"Take this," Cornar removed his short-sword from his belt. "In case anything comes."

"You're trusting me with this?" Solidin's eyes widened.

Cornar nodded. "You gave me your pack. It's a fair trade."

The elf grinned and drew the blade. Solidin held the lightstone up to the weapon's sharp edge, admiring the craftsmanship. "This is unlike any blade I've ever seen... exquisite!"

That made Cornar smile.

"Where was it forged?" Solidin asked.

"I don't know. Both the sword and the dagger are identical, like they were made by the same person. My father had them for as long as I could remember. I think his friend found them? I'm not really sure, though." Cornar drew the dagger and handed it to Solidin.

The elf put the short-sword down gently and took the serrated dagger. He handled them with reverence, his adoration akin to that of a masterful swordsman.

"These weren't forged by men," Solidin said. "The hilts look like they have tevisrals inside them."

Cornar raised his brow. He had never thought of his weapons as tevisrals. Yes, they could hold on to magic, retain whatever spell had been cast on them even amid a dispel. Cornar had wondered how it was done, but never found an answer. He had accepted their nature and never prodded any further.

"These weapons look like they were forged yesterday. The purity of their metal... and their edges are so fine. They could cut through anything. Especially if imbued with the proper magic."

Solidin seemed too knowledgeable about weapons for a scout. Those details were not something a common man—or elf—would perceive.

"Beautiful!" Solidin exclaimed, returning the dagger.

Cornar sheathed the weapon and Solidin picked up the short-sword, holding it at the ready.

"Sleep as long as you need," the elf said.

Cornar nodded and covered up with Sharon's cloak. It shimmered, faintly illuminating the ceiling of the cubby. That reminded him of how he and Karenna would tuck lightstones under blankets in their children's rooms at night. It was a practice of theirs to help ease their children's fears about the dark.

The faint light brought a smile to Cornar's face. *Oddly comforting,* he thought and nestled against Solidin's pack, getting as comfortable as possible on the hard stone floor.

Take me back to that dreamland, Cornar thought. Or was it a prayer? He wanted that strange being to hear his plea, didn't he? *I need answers. You promised me answers. Please, take me back to that place, to Laelin Lake.*

33

THE TUNNELS

"She shall awaken with a fury, unaware of the signs of His coming."

- *Prophecy of Soron Thahan*

The night in the stone alcove was uneventful. Cornar hadn't dreamed of his father's incursion into the castle on Laelin Lake. In fact, he hadn't dreamed at all. Cornar crawled out to find Solidin leaning against the wall, eyes gazing across the dark cavern with the short-sword across his lap.

"Feel refreshed?" the elf asked.

Cornar shrugged. His stomach was grumbling. But this wasn't the first time he'd been stranded in some forsaken place without food.

"Let's get moving then," Solidin said, standing and handing the sword back to Cornar.

"You don't want to rest?" Cornar asked.

"I'm fine," Solidin said, stepping deeper into that abysmal tunnel. Looking into it was like staring into a pit that stretched into infinity.

Did he fall asleep too? Cornar wondered, coming beside Solidin. The elf didn't look one bit tired.

A faint sound—like someone breathing—reached Cornar's ears. "Do you hear that?" he grabbed Solidin's arm. The elf halted and listened for a moment before shaking his head.

Cornar pointed to their right, and Solidin shone his lightstone in that direction. Nothing was there.

"Maybe you're hearing things?" Solidin asked. "No offense intended… but my ears *are* better than yours." That eased the tension and Cornar cracked a smile.

They continued for a way, nearing an opening to their right. Cornar walked toward it, drawing Solidin's attention.

"I thought you said we needed to keep following this tunnel," the elf said.

Cornar poked his head into the opening; it was the size of a large hallway. This probably led to the other tunnel, the one that paralleled this one.

"WAIT…" a voice whispered through the dank air, sounding like the not-creature from his dreams.

Peeling away from the opening, Cornar warily glanced to Solidin. "Did you hear *that?*"

"Hear what?" The elf cracked an amused grin. Did he think Cornar mad? First the breathing, now the voice…

"A voice," Cornar said curtly.

Solidin steeled himself but approached the opening. He turned an ear into the hallway.

Both Cornar and Solidin held their breath.

"I don't—" Solidin cut himself off and strained toward the opening. "Wait, I hear them."

Them? Cornar hadn't heard anything besides that whisper. Was there something there? The voice *had* told him to wait… but for what? Cornar recalled Kaescis claiming a similar experience back on Pier Eight in Soroth.

Faint inaudible sounds wisped through the hallway, finally reaching Cornar's ears. It sounded like conversation.

Perhaps there *was* some supernatural force guiding this quest.

"There are three," Solidin whispered. "One sounds agitated."

Cornar felt the need to seek the source of the noises. He was compelled. Someone was hurt… he just knew it! Cornar darted into the hallway, fueled with protective passion.

"Cornar!" Solidin called through clenched teeth.

Light faded as Cornar dashed through the tunnel. He ran right into a solid wall, then felt along it, searching for a corner. Soon, light spilled into the area behind him. Solidin ran with his lightstone outstretched. With the hallway lit, Cornar easily saw he was in a corridor that ran perpendicular to the first hall.

"The voices are coming from there," Solidin pointed to their right, at an opening leading to another hallway.

Cornar dashed to the opening. He could hear them. Was that Kalder speaking?

A pained cry resounded through the hallway, and Cornar quickened his dash. One of his men *was* hurt. Light shown at the end of the hallway. Was that a lightstone? Between heavy breaths, Cornar whistled his party's signal. At that moment, Solidin caught up to Cornar.

The chatter stopped and Cornar whistled again. Their hurried footfalls and heavy breathing were the only sounds in the hallway. The light at the other end didn't move. Cornar and Solidin soon neared the end of the hall where another massive tunnel awaited them, partially illuminated. But Cornar's men weren't visible.

Why aren't they answering? Cornar wondered.

Solidin's light reached the end of the hallway, further illuminating the massive tunnel.

A replying whistle sounded just as Cornar dashed out of the hallway. He came to an abrupt halt a few paces from Igan, Vargos, Kalder, and Gregan. Aron was held up between the two warriors, with brilliantly lit barsion wrapped around his leg.

"Cor!" Gregan blurted.

"You're alive!" Igan gasped, smiling. The wizard ran to Cornar, hugging him tightly. "How… how did you survive that fall?"

"I don't know," Cornar said with a shrug, then turned to the warriors. He examined Aron's leg. It looked bad. Aron's face was pale. He forced a smile, but his pain shone in his eyes. He wasn't going to survive this…

Cornar looked to the tunnel's ceiling, *Can't you heal him?* he pleaded. *Like you did with me?*

There was no reply.

"Here, take this," Solidin said, stepping beside Cornar. The elf proffered a green leaf with bright yellow veins. The leaf's tips were a dark violet. "It was meant for my friend…" Solidin looked somber as he moved the leaf to Aron's mouth.

"It's Taegish leaf. They grow in the elven realm and are used to accelerate regrowth," the elf explained. "You'll be starving in a moment, as it forces your body to repair itself quicker than it is used to."

Aron hesitated and looked to Cornar.

"Take it," Cornar urged, and the wounded warrior complied.

"Your friend?" Igan asked incredulously. "You mean that corpse in the pit?" Solidin nodded.

"Who are you?" Vargos demanded, folding his arms. "And don't say an elf. That's obvious."

Solidin grinned, amused by the old barsionist. "A fellow adventurer. A scout. We're exploring the ruins to see if there are any valuable artifacts. My employer is a bit of a con artist."

Vargos raised an eyebrow and looked at Cornar with a questioning expression. Was he doubting Cornar's judgment?

"Who are *we?*" Gregan asked. "And… you look familiar."

"I should," Solidin said, grunting. "I watched you plaster the floor of Heldergan's Flower with your vomit."

Kalder narrowed his eyes, warily studying Solidin. "I thought you and your fellows left Kretin," he said. "I saw the ship leave port."

"They weren't my friends," Solidin said flatly.

"He doesn't sound like an elf," Vargos observed.

"No," Solidin grinned.

"He sounds like a Merdan elf," Igan said warily.

"He is," Cornar chimed. His friends were being defensive, and rightly so. But Cornar trusted Solidin. "Solidin is part of a small band from Gastrim that is exploring the ruins. He's only one of four elves." Cornar said the last bit to placate them, as each knew of Krindal's fears. "Now, was anyone else looking for me?"

"We all were," Kalder said.

Gregan grunted. "We were just unlucky and got caught in another collapse."

Those answers worried Cornar. Were there any others of his party that had succumbed to the earthquake? Were others injured, like Aron? Cornar had to find them, ensure that everyone was safe and—

"GO TO THE TEMPLE," that same voice whispered, like a beckoning on the wind.

Cornar looked around, searching for the source but also checking if anyone else had heard it. They didn't react.

"It doesn't hurt!" Aron exclaimed, drawing everyone's attention. The wounded warrior pushed himself away from Kalder and Gregan. He stepped on his once-injured leg and beamed with excitement.

"Whoa…" Igan shook his head, taken aback at the quickness of Aron's recovery.

Vargos dismissed the magic binding Aron's leg, and the warrior pulled up his pant to reveal a perfect limb.

"Thank you!" Aron exclaimed, smiling at Solidin.

"Yes," Cornar said, putting a hand on the elf's shoulder. "Thank you."

Solidin nodded, aloof. Aron wobbled, suddenly succumbing to the effects of the leaf. He looked exhausted.

"Are you all right?" Igan asked, stepping toward the warrior.

"Exhausted… and tired," Aron answered.

"We should keep going and find you some monster to eat." Solidin grinned and continued down the tunnel. The warriors and mages looked confused.

"I'll explain later," Cornar said, chuckling. "Let's get on our way."

They caught up to Solidin and walked in a line down the massive tunnel. Igan was on one side with his sphere of light while Solidin was on the other edge. Their combined light illuminated most of the cavernous space.

"If I recall correctly," Cornar said. "This tunnel will take us to the heart of Klindil, about where the others were planning to enter these depths."

"What do you think, Cor?" Igan asked. "Do we wait there, or try to get back to the war camp?"

"Neither." Cornar shook his head. "We'll head straight to the Keepers' Temple."

Everyone looked surprised except Solidin. The elf looked pleased, as if he had won some victory. But Solidin hadn't expressed much interest in Cornar's search. The elf had shrugged off the whole idea.

"Are you sure that's wise, Cor?" Gregan said. "We need food and water. Aren't you starving?" He looked to Aron.

"Uh, yeah…" Aron replied. "I could eat an entire cow."

"Yeah, I do think it's wise," Cornar said. "I doubt the Mindolarnians will use all their resources to search for us. If we meet them at the temple, they can send word back to any search parties."

Gregan frowned. He obviously didn't agree with Cornar's decision. But Cornar had to follow that whisper. It *felt* right.

Wildmen horns blew beside Kaescis. They sounded primitive, not like a fancy trumpet or any other fine instrument. The Wildmen blew the horns to notify any nearby tribes when approaching the ruins of Klindil.

Kaescis could see the faint outline of the once majestic city. The ruins stood out against the morning twilight.

That must have been a grand city, he mused, tiredly gripping the reins. They had ridden from the Wildmen tent capital nonstop since last morning. There was no time to waste when it came to the Sapphire Guard. Kaescis would ensure that his army would reach the Keepers' Temple before them.

"God of our fathers..." Bratan said with a gasp.

"What is it?!" Kaescis demanded.

"The ground..." Bratan muttered, pointing to the right of the city. "An earthquake must have struck."

Kaescis followed his gesture. A plateau of upheaved rock rose above the plain surrounding the ruined city; its height reached nearly as tall as the ruined buildings. And... the war camp was atop it.

"You're just now noticing that, Bratan?" Laeyit remarked with a sly grin. Bratan sighed and then grumbled.

Wildmen chattered about Bratan's observation. Their words about the upheaved plateau were garbled. Some said that it was done by those that slept within the ruins. Kaescis had briefly heard of such beings after striking a deal with High Chieftain Bhrane.

Turning to the high chieftain—who rode a valerin beside him—Kaescis asked, "Remind me, what sleeps in the ruins?"

"Oh," Bhrane shook his head. "The Sleepers are mighty. They are fierce. They live in the dark, do not like light. I see them only once. Purple skin, like night sky. Red eyes, and they know words. They burn..."

Purple skin? What kind of mutation would have caused that? Bhrane explained again about the Wildmen who lived in Klindil. He had told Kaescis before their departure from the tent city but thought it prudent to explain it again. They were a tribe consisting of members from each of the other tribes. It sounded like a monastery, as the tribesmen were very devout and trained to kill trespassers and Sleepers. Wildmen joined this tribe to fight. The tribe lived above, while these Sleepers lived beneath. Bhrane had said it was all symbolic. What strange ideas...

Kaescis looked back at the army of Wildmen that had followed him and the high chieftain out of the tent city. Nearly two thousand restored Wildmen, all human again, marched behind Kaescis. He had spent most of that first evening restoring those that High Chieftain Bhrane had selected. Others, Kaescis restored in a manner like Gevistra and his tribe.

Gevistra, however, had been turned human, like his sister, Fenia. He and Fenia rode behind Kaescis as part of his retinue. Kaescis would see to their integration into the Mindolarn Empire as ambassadors.

"The Sleepers do this?" Gevistra pointed to the plateau.

Kaescis glanced at him. Gevistra probably wouldn't understand the concept of an earthquake, but it was worth trying. "No, Gevistra. The ground moves."

"Because the Sleepers move it?" Gevistra asked.

"No, the ground moves itself. Imagine the ground as large planks where you place your food." Kaescis let go of his reins and demonstrated the earthquake with his hands. "The pieces of land push against each other. Sometimes they hit and part of the land gets pushed upward."

Gevistra looked troubled. He sighed and his sister patted his shoulder to comfort him.

"You say Sleepers do not do this?" Bhrane asked, not sounding pleased. Kaescis was challenging everything these men believed. First their very natures, now the nature of their lands.

"That's right," Laeyit chimed. "Your Sleepers are just a bunch of silly creatures with sensitivity to light."

"No!" Bhrane shook his head with disgust. "Sleepers are powerful. They speak and the ground shakes. The Galanchum hear them and moves the world."

"Galanchum?" Laeyit asked, snickering.

"The biggest Sleeper," Gevistra said. "He moves the world, living in the pools of fire."

Oh that's right. Kaescis recalled some of the details about the tribe in Klindil. They were to prepare for a conflict with the leader of the Sleepers, a gigantic beast made of magma that spewed fire.

Gevistra and Bhrane reiterated the lore behind the Sleepers and their feud with them while Kaescis focused on the war camp.

"Laeyit, send a signal," Kaescis said. Laeyit complied by casting a spell. Illusionary magic gathered in her hand and shot into the sky, exploding in a ball of red and white. The red particles wove together in seven strands, resembling the seven-headed hydra on the empire's flag.

Kaescis trotted ahead of the army, guiding them to a slope that led to the war camp. Everything was tilted at an angle that made it feel like the war camp was going to slide off the plateau.

Soldiers hurried down the slope, accompanying the grand marshals. Where were Krindal and Mister Dol'shir? Surely the soldiers would have roused them from their slumber.

"Your Imperial Grace," Hezidex said, saluting Kaescis. "We have ill news."

Kaescis pulled on his reins, stopping his horse. "What?"

"As you can undoubtedly see, we experienced an earthquake," Galiur said.

"As did we," Kaescis said.

"We lost some Sorothians," Hezidex said solemnly. "Mister Dol'shir is missing, presumed buried. We think he spotted a spy and gave chase. We found a corpse, half of it. But it wasn't Dol'shir."

"The Sapphire Guard?" Kaescis asked.

"We think so," Galiur said. "It looked elven."

"We also lost a few others," Hezidex said. "Nordal took Krindal and the Sorothian adventurers to Klindil—"

"Into the ruins…?" Kaescis demanded.

"The places where Dol'shir and the others disappeared," Hezidex said, pointing to the forest behind Kaescis. "There were pits there, caused by the earthquake. Nordal and his band went into the ruins to access the tunnels so they could get to the collapsed parts. To check for survivors, Your Imperial Grace."

"And you didn't stop him?!" Kaescis shouted.

"No… Your Imperial Grace," Hezidex muttered. "Nordal was… determined."

Kaescis growled and dismounted, grabbing his helmet. He waved for a soldier to take the steed, who was undoubtedly exhausted from the ride. Kaescis glared at the grand marshals for a moment.

"You're telling me," Kaescis said, "that the Sapphire Guard has been here for a day, and you let the one man they're after go into a potential trap without Imperial escort?"

Hezidex sucked in his breath. The grand marshal briefly averted his eyes and opened his mouth to speak but Galiur chimed an explanation. "We thought the Sapphire Guard behind us. With their scout dead they would have needed to send another. We set some of the mages about, casting dispels. They've seen nothing. We had—have time, Your Imperial Grace."

Kaescis shook his head, disgusted. What had happened in his absence? The Wildmen horns sounded again, from the base of the slope.

"Mobilize the camp," Kaescis said, turning around and taking his helmet in both hands. "Move everyone into that entrance to the tunnels Mister Dol'shir noted on the map."

"And where are you going, Your Imperial Grace?" Galiur called after him.

Kaescis stopped mid-stride, glancing to the grand marshal. "I'm going to retrieve Krindal. He's too valuable to lose now." With that, Kaescis donned his helmet.

An hour or two had passed since Cornar's rendezvous with the others. They chatted about their plight, and how they fell into the pit. Vargos was awestruck that Cornar hadn't sustained any wounds. So was Cornar. He would have fallen the equivalent of twenty stories. It was like jumping off a towering cliff. How was he still alive?

Eventually, they came to a fork in the tunnel. One side veered to the left while the other made an abrupt curve to the right.

"Which way?" Solidin asked.

"The left side," Cornar said.

They continued in that direction for what seemed half an hour. Then the tunnel opened into a massive space. Ledges lined both sides of the tunnel, a third of the way from the ground to the ceiling. It looked maybe four stories off the ground.

"What is this place?" Gregan wondered aloud.

"Why would the ancient Klindala people need such big tunnels under their city?" Igan posed the question. "What were they even used for?"

Solidin eyed the men, but didn't offer any speculation. The elf had been unusually quiet since Cornar met up with the others.

"Who knows," Vargos said. "Now they're just death traps and—"

Solidin stopped and held out his hand, signaling for everyone to halt. Cornar hovered his hands above his weapons and strained to hear anything through the eerie silence. Finally, faint scratching reached his ears. It sounded like claws scraping against stone. The noise grew louder.

"From the left," Solidin whispered, guiding his lightstone in that direction. He aimed it toward the ledge. The light barely illuminated the edge, and the scratching noises stopped.

"Is that our breakfast?" Gregan asked, snickering. He glanced to Cornar with a smile. Cornar had recounted his conversation with Solidin about eating a mages' parasite.

"Vargos, cast some barsion," Cornar ordered and stepped ahead of the others.

The barsionist complied and soon everyone was veiled with a thin layer of protective blue magic. They lit the surrounding area, shining from the glow of the barsion.

Cornar eyed the ledge uneasily. "Let's continue," he said, stepping farther into the tunnel.

They continued for a moment. Then the scratching resumed. This time the sounds were on both sides. Igan and Solidin directed their light to the ledges, but saw nothing.

The wizard took his probing a step farther and guided his glowing orb to the ledge.

A shrill resounded shortly thereafter, and then a ball of flame flew toward the orb, passing through it, and crashing into the opposite ledge.

"Here we go…" Gregan said, sighing as everyone drew their weapons.

The warriors' blades sang as they left their scabbards. The weapons' song was accompanied by howls and whooping.

Cornar looked at both of his blades. He only needed one… "Solidin, catch!" Cornar cried, tossing the short-sword to the elf. Solidin caught it gracefully. He twirled the blade instinctively and settled into a battle stance, leading with his freehand.

Igan began uttering an incantation, and so did Vargos.

A cacophony echoed in the tunnel and crouching figures crowded around the edge of the ledge. They weren't more Wildmen, were they? No, these looked different.

Finally, one stepped into the light of Igan's sphere, which was still atop the ledge. That was no Wildman up there… not a man at all. The thing was humanoid, but it had dark-purple skin. Ivory horns adorned the crown of its head. It shielded its eyes, but Cornar could see a bright red glow coming from beneath the creature's twisted hand. Another horn protruded from the creature's elbow. The thing edged through the light, showing its horned silhouette. More horns protruded from its joints.

"Damovians," Solidin whispered with disgust.

"What?" Gregan asked. "That doesn't sound Common."

"It's Elvish," Solidin said. "I don't know what you call them in the Common tongue. Creatures twisted by dark magic."

"Like goblins?" Igan asked.

"Worse…"

The damovian leapt from the ledge, tumbling through the air. It was followed by dozens of others, leaping from both ledges and diving into the tunnel. Sounds of seething anger resounded as the damovians hit the ground. Then the entire tunnel lit up as flame appeared, blazing within the hands of the creatures. Each of the damovians clutched fireballs formed out of thin air.

"They didn't speak an incantation," Aron muttered.

"Attack!" Cornar commanded through clenched teeth. He leaned forward, ready to charge, but before Cornar could move, the creatures hurled their fireballs at him and his men.

Cornar dodged and the fiery magic raced past him. He lunged, evading another flaming projectile. Cornar dodged another, and another, until one struck him. It erupted against his barsion, obscuring his vision in fire. Though he couldn't see, Cornar continued forward. He could hear the others charging behind him, as well as a crackling of magic.

The flames subsided as Cornar tackled one of the damovians. The creature swung an elbow at his face, but the horn at the end was stopped by Vargos's barsion. The horn looked like a protrusion of sharp bone; like part of the elbow had grown out of the creature's skin.

Cornar stabbed his serrated dagger into the damovian's ribs, angled toward its chest. He hoped that was where the heart was lodged. The damovian screamed and thrashed, trying to push itself away from Cornar, but it soon fell limp. Cornar withdrew his weapon and pale-pink blood dripped from the creature's wound.

Battle cries resounded nearby, and Cornar turned to see Kalder and Gregan slicing their foes in half. Kalder's claymore afforded him great reach, as did Gregan's fanisar. They mercilessly leveled their foes.

Solidin danced awkwardly with one of the damovians, clumsily poking his borrowed short-sword at it. That struck Cornar as odd. Solidin had caught the weapon so gracefully…

Movement caught his eye, and a damovian leaped through the air. It arced above Cornar, falling toward him with its claws outstretched; the claws looked like the horns.

Cornar dashed forward, evading the damovian by sliding beneath it. He threw himself sideways; the jolt turning him toward his foe.

In the distance, Igan hurled bright pink orbs at the damovians: arcane energy. As the word would otherwise imply, arcane magic was neither mysterious nor old. It happened to be the name for a type of destructive magic. The arcane orbs struck the damovians not engaged with him or his men and exploded upon impact.

Cornar and the damovian who lunged at him both rebounded. They clashed once more, and Cornar stabbed the creature in the chest. It let out a shrill, and Cornar pushed the creature off his dagger.

More fire erupted around him, striking Aron and Kalder. The warriors were unharmed, as the barsion protected them.

Dagger ready, Cornar turned to engage another of the vile creatures, but the one in front of him darted away, scurrying across the tunnel. It yelped in a pattern of calls and climbed up the far wall. Others followed after the one who had called for a retreat, and they scaled the tunnel's walls, disappearing into the darkness.

Cornar and the other warriors relaxed. Igan, however, remained tense. The wizard was maintaining several of the pink-red orbs; they hovered about him.

"What were those things?" Gregan asked, shifting his fanisar back and forth between his hands.

Cornar looked at the corpse beneath him and was drawn to the creature's pointed ears… they looked elven. The damovian's face looked sharp, with angular features. The rest of its body was disproportionate, with arms almost as long as its legs.

Creatures twisted by magic. Cornar thought on Solidin's brief explanation. Weren't the Wildmen twisted in a similar fashion? Cornar studied the corpse for a moment but was roused by an outburst from Aron.

"I'm so hungry I could eat one of these raw!"

"They don't look tasty…" Gregan said, sounding disgusted.

Cornar stepped toward his men but eyed Solidin. The elf had a blank expression across his face. Solidin regarded the corpses with indifference.

"Dare we eat these, Cor?" Kalder asked. Cornar didn't know the answer to that question. If these things were twisted by magic, could they pass that on to him and his men?

"They should be fine to eat," Solidin said, approaching Cornar. He handled the short-sword with its hilt pointed toward Cornar. "Thank you." Cornar nodded and took his weapon. The blade had some blood on its edge, but he flicked the pale-pink liquid off before sheathing the sword.

"There's probably water nearby," Solidin said. "Shall we go look?" He gestured to Cornar and pointed to Sharon's cloak. That speculation seemed sound. Where there was life there was bound to be water.

"Kalder, Igan, start cooking up one of those corpses. Vargos, come with me. We don't have anything to carry water, so your magic will have to do."

"That's clever," Solidin said, coming beside Cornar, "using barsion magic as a barrel."

⸺ ▪ ⸺

The damned tunnels were dark. Too dark.

Where are you, Cor? Nordal wondered, shaking his head. Nordal and the others had searched nonstop for the missing members of their band. Eight hours had passed, or so Nordal thought. It had taken them three hours to reach the entrance to the tunnels.

"I think we're under the plain now," Krindal said, holding the tevisral that made the illusionary map. Many of the other party members kept their distance from the necromancer-scholar, to keep the map undisturbed. Krindal stood in the center of it, so some parts weren't discernible.

"Ordreth, Midar, take your groups ahead," Nordal commanded. "We'll break here for a bit." The others removed their packs and sat on the stony ground. Nordal, however, paced around the party.

I hope we're not lost, he thought, watching as Ordreth, Demsal, and Hem took off down the main tunnel. Midar led Cordel and Tinal another way, a side tunnel smaller than the main one. *This place is like a maze…*

"We're several hundred phineals away from a junction, I think," Krindal said, humming with curiosity. "That leads to the southern tunnel—"

Scratching sounds echoed into the tunnel. Many of the men stirred. They stood and drew their weapons. Krindal started, panicked at the noise.

The scratching grew louder.

What was that sound? Nordal thought, he turned toward the noise, which was in the direction from where they'd come. It sounded like claws scurrying across stone.

"Are there creatures living down here?" asked a warrior named Sharn.

They hadn't passed anything thus far. The tunnels were empty and quiet.

"Wildmen tales," Krindal said warily. "No scholar has ever seen anything, though."

The men held up lightstone lanterns, aiming the light into every darkened hole or crevice in the tunnel.

Nordal looked about, but was drawn by Grensil shouting, "There!" He turned, following the direction of Grensil's outstretched arm. A hunched figure crept along a ledge and then stopped. The scraping sounds became faint as whatever was on the ledge came to a halt.

Two of the warriors shone their light toward the ledge, illuminating the thing that perched there. It had purple skin that shimmered, like a moist layer. It took one look at the men then hurried off.

"What was that thing?" Sharon asked, stepping beside Nordal.

"Beats me…"

Midar's group returned shortly thereafter. They had nothing to report. Nordal sat for a moment and waited for Ordreth to return.

He soon appeared with news. "We found a junction," Ordreth said. "It leads to another tunnel." He looked at the map surrounding Krindal. "I think we should search it. Kalder and the others might be there."

"Let's split up," Midar suggested. "We haven't encountered anything dangerous thus far. We can meet back at the junction when we can't go any farther." Several of the other warriors agreed with Midar. Nordal didn't like the idea of splitting up further… but they could cover more ground, and that meant finding the wounded quicker. Yet, they only had one arpranist with them…

Nordal looked to the Mindolarn mage, who seemed nervous to be down in these cavernous tunnels. Did he know something that Nordal didn't?

"Midar," Nordal spoke up, "take Brendar, Markin, Grensil, and Shen's groups. The rest of you will be with me."

34

MYSTERIES

"The Unspoken One will ascend from the void, fueled with eternal splendor."

- Prophecy of Soron Thahan

The damovian meat wasn't the worst thing Cornar had ever tasted. It was filling, but so were most distasteful things when one hungered. He walked over to a half-sphere of barsion magic holding water. Igan had used a basic fire spell to boil the water, and it had finally cooled to a decent temperature. Though Igan was a wizard who specialized in nonelemental magics, he knew a few elemental spells—taught to him by his wife, Baekal.

"This stuff is gross," Gregan complained, chewing the meat.

Igan had also cooked the meat Kalder had butchered. The wizard had roasted muscles of the creature on Kalder's claymore.

"Don't complain about my cooking," Igan said, shaking his head. He looked at Gregan with a serious gaze.

"At least he's not Amendal," Vargos said, "conjuring something for you to eat."

"When did he do that?" Igan asked, appalled at the idea.

Vargos laughed and told a tale from his youth. It ended with him, old Amendal, and some others eating a bird that Amendal had conjured.

Amid the tale, Cornar cupped the water in his hands and drank. The water wasn't any better than the meat…

"We should get moving," Solidin suggested. "Which way should we go, Cornar?"

Cornar pointed at the large tunnel. "Down that way. We need to get to the center of Klindil before we can descend farther." He studied the others. Kalder had just finished eating, and so had Solidin. The mages were talking and chewing on the meat while Aron lay on the ground; he had passed out after devouring half of what Igan had cooked.

"We'll let Aron rest for a little longer," Cornar said, settling down on the ground.

A short while passed before they moved again. Their trek through the rest of the enormous tunnel was uneventful. The tunnel was mostly straight, from what Cornar could tell. Perhaps there was a curve, but it wasn't discernible. They walked for several hours until arriving at a sudden drop. The tunnel ended at the edge of a pit. It looked to be a massive room, but for what Cornar didn't know. A set of descending stairs lined the wall to their right.

That's convenient, Cornar mused. He warily approached the steps, which had no railing. *Don't look down,* he thought, remembering that odd sensation when ascending to the Fortress of Anigar. Cornar descended the stairs but soon stopped at a break between several steps. They would have to jump across it.

"Great," Gregan grumbled behind Cornar.

"Uh, Vargos," Cornar called as he reached the break in the staircase, "why don't you put up some barsion as we jump across."

The old barsionist hummed and cast a spell. Blue light zipped past Cornar, forming a bridge across the gap.

"Or I could just do that so we don't have to jump," Vargos said, sounding pleased with himself.

"That was clever," Solidin observed.

"That's what happens when you get old, son," Vargos said.

Cornar glanced over his shoulder to glimpse Solidin raising an eyebrow at Vargos. The elf's expression said, "I'm probably older than you." Intrigued, Cornar wondered about Solidin's age. How old was the elf? Most elves stopped aging after thirty—that was, until they were around four or five hundred years old.

The stairs continued on for what seemed forever. They descended at least the equivalent of ten flights of stairs, but it was so dark in that massive room that Cornar couldn't tell for certain. Eventually they reached a level spot that stretched beyond the party's sources of light.

"Two hundred and three steps," Gregan said, "not including those missing ones we had to bypass."

"Wow, that's deep," Kalder said, sounding impressed.

Cornar looked around for something that he could use to keep their bearings while crossing the room. "Any of you still have a compass?" he asked. Cornar wasn't hopeful. They all answered in the negative, except Solidin. The elf removed a pointed oval compass from his pack. It was domed, with a flowery design beveled upon its surface.

That's fancy, Cornar thought as Solidin handed him the compass. It had strange letters for the four cardinal directions, undoubtedly Elvish characters. The letters and the spindle were glowing a pale-blue hue. Was this compass some sort of tevisral?

"That one is north," Solidin said, pointing to the top letter. It was a curved letter, arcing outward to the left.

"Thank you," Cornar said, and took the proper heading for the direction he intended to travel. It was roughly a north-by-northeast heading. "Let's go."

As they crossed the enormous room, their sources of light lit the occasional pillar, but nothing else. That was, until they came across a skeleton.

The remains looked humanoid, but the joints had extra lengths of bone on them. Damovian remains? They approached the skeleton only to find more lying beyond the first. Other bones looked human, except that their fingers were thicker and their skulls had thick ridges and protruding snouts.

Cornar knelt beside the first skeleton, examining the skull. It had horns protruding from its crown, like the damovians they had encountered earlier. There was no doubt that these were the remains of one of those creatures.

"This looks like a Wildman," Kalder called out, kneeling beside the other type of skeleton. The warrior grabbed a broken sword beside the remains. The blade was cut in half but it otherwise looked in good condition.

"It looks like a battlefield," Igan said, picking his way through the skeletons.

"Let's keep moving," Cornar said, and followed Igan.

The two of them led the party across the boneyard. From what Cornar could tell, the deceased Wildman forces had pressed their way toward where he intended to travel. Did they know about the temple? Or was this room home to a congregation of damovians? Solidin had briefly explained a legend about a conflict between the Wildmen and the damovians.

"Whoa," Igan paused, holding out a hand. His glowing ball illuminated a massive rock barring their way. Well… not quite. It looked humanoid, like a towering statue strewn across the ground.

"Is that… an elemental?" Gregan asked.

Cornar stepped to the side, attempting a better view at the stone heap before them.

"It looks like cooled magma," Igan said, following Cornar. "Do you think it's a magma elemental?"

Possibly… But Cornar had never seen an elemental without it having first been summoned by a conjurer. Were the damovians able to summon such a creature? He suddenly wished old Amendal were here. Amendal would probably have some insight about this, though his theories might be a tad crazy.

"Where's that crazy old codger when you need him," Gregan said.

"Look." Solidin pointed to their right. "There's another."

The second elemental lay on its back and was missing an arm. The creatures were obviously used in the battle. When had it happened? The bones of the Wildmen weren't brittle, but there wasn't much airflow down here. If Iltar had been with them, he could have guessed when this battle had taken place.

They continued across the boneyard in silence. Cornar wondered about the battle and why it occurred here, of all places—deep beneath the city.

Soon, they were across the massive room. A hole marred the wall, leading to a roughly hewn cave. Cornar hadn't remembered a cavern on the map at this point. There were caverns between the tunnels and the temple, but it was too soon to be encountering anything like that.

"Something wrong, Cor?" Aron asked.

"We need to find another tunnel," Cornar answered, squinting his eyes. "And I don't remember a cave like this on the map."

"Maybe those things made it?" Gregan speculated, thumbing back to the boneyard. That was probably the truth.

"Igan, Kalder, come with me," Cornar said. "The rest of you check that direction." He pointed to their left. "We'll meet back here after we search the wall. We're looking for a small tunnel. Like a hallway."

The others dispersed while Cornar lingered at the gaping hole. Igan guided his light to hover within the opening, illuminating part of the earthen cavern.

"Are you thinking this might be a shortcut?" Igan asked.

"Yeah," Cornar said, "but we need to go down more. We're definitely near the center of the ruins. Move your light farther into the cave." Igan complied and the hovering ball drifted.

"There." Cornar pointed to a rectangular opening along the right. "I think the tunnel we needed was here. That's the hallway we need to take."

"I wish I had your memory." Igan grinned at Cornar. "I'm glad I'm not stuck down here with anyone other than you, Cor." The compliment made Cornar smile.

"I'll get the others," Kalder said, and hurried away.

Cornar stepped into the earthen cavern, picking his way around boulders and stalagmites. The air was humid in here, as opposed to that massive room. He approached the hallway-tunnel just as the others neared the cave's mouth.

"This way," Cornar said, looking back to the others. "We should be beneath the city soon."

"Beneath the city?" Solidin asked.

"The temple is within a cavern below the ruins," Cornar said. "It's deep below the surface of Kalda."

⊷•⊶

Ordreth worried for his uncle. The longer they went without encountering someone, the worse he felt. Had Uncle Cor really perished in that earthquake? Oh, it hurt to think that...

"Don't be gloomy, Ordreth," Hem said cheerily. "We'll find him. He'll be sitting against some dirt pile, smiling. 'You finally found me, boys'—that's what he'll say." Hem imitated Cornar's voice, trying to sound husky and firm.

"Cor doesn't sound like that." Demsal shook his head.

Ordreth said nothing. He thought of the others. Kalder. Gregan. Aron. Igan. Vargos. Were they... No, Ordreth couldn't think that. They were still alive. They had to be...

Ordreth and the others continued down the tunnel until their lightstone lanterns shone against a slope of dirt—and something on the ground.

"No..." Demsal said, gasping.

Ordreth hesitated, but then moved his lantern toward that shape on the ground. It... it looked like a man. The brown armor. That scabbard. Oh, that pommel was unmistakable. His uncle lying there, face down in the dirt.

"Uncle..." Ordreth dropped to his knees, tears clouding his vision. He thought he glimpsed Demsal hurrying to the body, but Ordreth buried his face in his hands and sobbed.

"I was wrong," Hem groaned.

"Hem, help me!" Demsal shouted. Shuffling sounds and grunts followed the command. Ordreth couldn't bear to look.

"Damn it!" Demsal cursed. "It's him."

Those words struck Ordreth's heart like a thousand daggers. Their pierce was agonizing. All he could do was cry. An eternity filled with tears seemed to pass until Ordreth felt the familiar touch of his lover. Sharon's long fingers glided across his shoulders, interlocking across his chest. She felt warm, and that warmth was comforting.

"I'm sorry," she whispered shakily. Then, Sharon sobbed too.

"Arpranist!" Nordal shouted. "Heal him now!"

"I-I can't," the Mindolarn mage stammered. "He… he's dead. No magic can bring life back from beyond the grave."

"Just cast the spell!" Nordal screamed, his words frothed with fury.

Sharon continued sobbing with Ordreth as the arpranist cast his spell. Ordreth heard the incantation, but didn't dare open his eyes.

"I told you," the arpranist said. "He's gone."

"Again!" Nordal screamed.

"Master Nordal, please," Krindal said timidly, "we have to—"

"Have to what?!" Nordal blurted. "Get out of here because you're such a coward?!"

A coward… *Is that what I am?* Ordreth wondered. *Am I a coward because I have my eyes shut?* He feared losing his uncle. Uncle Cor had been like a father to Ordreth after his father passed away. Ordreth hadn't known his father well, but Uncle Cor spoke fondly of him. Now, both his father and his uncle were gone. What would he do?

He had to do something.

Nordal continued shouting at Krindal and the arpranist. Others bemoaned the discovery. They had never dared to imagine such a loss. But now it stared them in the face.

Be brave, Ordreth, he heard his uncle's voice say. Was that the whisper of his ghost? Ordreth slowly opened his eyes and touched Sharon's hands. He had to stand and face his loss. He had to *see* his uncle. Ordreth recalled his uncle's words about overcoming wounds on the battlefield. *Embrace the pain. Don't let it stop you. Make it fuel you, drive you to greatness.*

"Sharon," Ordreth said, turning to his lover. Tears stained her cheeks. She let go of him, allowing him to rise.

Ordreth stood and walked to the corpse, now turned face up. The others were gathered around, all somber and angry. His uncle's face was frozen in a moment of agony.

Everything seemed to fade at that moment. Nordal's shouts, Sharon's sobbing, the frustrated sentiments of his fellow warriors. All that remained was Ordreth, and his uncle's corpse.

"I'm sorry, Uncle," Ordreth said, kneeling beside Cornar's body. "I… I will miss you." He paused. Everything felt empty. Ordreth had lost friends during past adventures, but this was his uncle, the man who survived *everything*. Now he was gone.

Ordreth looked at his uncle's emerald eyes one last time and gently closed them.

"Things won't be the same," he said with a frown. "But, I'll carry on. I'll make sure Aunty Karenna is okay—" Aunty Karenna, how was he going to tell her? This was such a cruel thing for her to bear… She couldn't realize her dreams with him. They would all be shattered. *If you only had stayed,* Ordreth lamented.

"Move!" A gauntleted hand grabbed Ordreth, yanking him from his reverie. Noise flooded over him. Nordal had stopped shouting, but everyone was in an uproar.

Ordreth turned to see the Mindolarn prince moving toward his uncle's body. Where had he come from? Wasn't Prince Kaescis out with the Wildmen tribal leaders? The prince was clad in his unique armor. Those thin plates were astonishing.

"What are you saying?" Nordal demanded. "That this was a trap?"

"Precisely," Prince Kaescis said, his voice muffled beneath his helmet. "It's exactly what *they* would do." Ordreth was confused, who was the prince talking about?

"The Sapphire Guard is notorious for antics like this," the prince said, running his hands over Uncle Cor's corpse.

"So that's who you're afraid of." Nordal looked to Krindal. The necromancer-scholar nodded timidly and looked over his shoulder, gazing down the darkened tunnel.

The Sapphire Guard… Ordreth had heard that name before, but he didn't know what it meant or represented. "Who are they?" he asked.

"The deadliest elves in all the Kalishir Ocean," the prince said, continuing to examine the body. That explained the Mindolarn army that Kaescis had brought.

"They're from Keth," Nordal said. "They work for the Elven Aristocracy of Merdan. The Sapphire Guard are their henchmen."

"And they're looking for the Keepers' Temple as well," Kaescis said.

Everything came together for Ordreth. Uncle Cor had told him that the Mindolarnians were holding back something of import, especially after the incident on the road. They were being secretive because they didn't want Uncle Cor to know about the Sapphire Guard… but why?

Prince Kaescis ripped the short-sword from its sheath and held up the blade. He uttered an incantation, mustering a black mist. How did he know how to use that magic? Ordreth thought only Iltar could muster that power. The Darkness magic, he called it. And the prince was using an incantation… Iltar never did that when manifesting the Darkness.

The prince guided the mist to the blade. His spell cankered the sharp edge and soon eroded the entire shaft.

Everyone gasped.

That's impossible, Ordreth thought. Uncle Cor's weapons were able to hold onto magic—even the most corrosive—without succumbing to their effects. *Then, was this not—*

"This is not Mister Dol'shir," the prince said, tossing the blade aside. "Leave the corpse." He spun around, grabbing Krindal by the arm. "Your leader is still alive, albeit I don't know for how much longer. This is the Sapphire Guard, after all. Now we must hurry; the rest of the camp is mobilizing at the entrance to these catacombs."

Kaescis turned and hurried off, leaving everyone awestruck.

The warriors and mages marveled at what the prince had done and said. They looked unsure of what to make of the entire ordeal.

So you're not dead, Uncle, Ordreth sighed, feeling relieved. Seeing the short-sword succumb to the dissolving magic cemented a realization that his uncle was alive. Ordreth wouldn't have to face Aunty Karenna or his mother. His mother… The thought of evading his mother's wrath was enough to lighten any weight.

But where was Uncle Cor? Anyone who could perfectly replicate a corpse was dangerous. Uncle Cor was skilled, but he couldn't escape the clutches of the likes of this Sapphire Guard. Ordreth *had* to find his uncle.

"Let's go," Nordal said. "Someone needs to fetch Midar and the others." He chased after Kaescis, Krindal, and the Mindolarn arpranist. The prince was practically jogging down the tunnel.

No time to waste then, Ordreth thought, feeling determined. He dashed after Nordal. "The prince is in a hurry," Ordreth remarked, coming beside Nordal.

"Kaescis practically ran to us," Nordal said. "I guess he has one of those mapping tevisrals, too. You didn't see him bolt through the tunnel?" Ordreth shook his head. Sharon came beside him and took his hand, still sniffling.

"He was running, clutching a giant black sword," Nordal said. "It looked like Iltar's magic."

"The prince was holding a sword made of magic?" Ordreth asked, intrigued. He had heard tales of mages wielding such things, but had never seen it.

"Yeah, but Kaescis dismissed it upon finding us," Nordal replied. "Didn't you see or hear any of this?"

"No," Ordreth admitted, partly ashamed.

Nordal grunted. "Well, he was cursing at us, saying we were fools for coming down here when the Sapphire Guard was near. I can't believe I didn't put two and two together. They're the only group of elves that could frighten Krindal."

Ordreth turned his thoughts to his uncle. He was even more worried than before. What was Uncle Cor up against with these elves? And what did they want with him? The Sapphire Guard obviously wanted something from Uncle Cor. Else, why fake his death?

⇒•⇐

"This is it, I think…" Cornar said. He stood in front of a blank wall.

"Really?" Vargos asked, chuckling. "Wouldn't there be a door of sorts?"

"You'd think," Gregan smiled, sliding his hand across the stone. "Are you sure we didn't take a wrong turn, Cor?" Cornar raised an eyebrow at the man, not amused. Gregan was obviously joking.

"I thought you were confident in his skill?" Solidin asked, looking confused.

"Oh, I am," Gregan smiled. "Just giving him a hard time."

"Ah," the elf said, nodding.

"Do you think the wall reacts to Krindal's gem?" Igan asked. "Like his mapping tevisral?"

Cornar hoped not… else they would have come all this way for naught. He sighed and pleaded to that voice. *I followed the map. Nothing is here. What must I do?*

Nothing came. No voice. No prompting. No instruction.

Cornar sucked in a deep breath and looked around. The room wasn't large. It was mostly empty, except for a shoulder high pillar in the center of the space. Odd pipes of various sizes descended from the ceiling and into the top of the pillar.

"Maybe we check all the walls again?" Kalder asked. "Perhaps there is a mechanism."

"You know," Igan said, frowning as he looked to Cornar. "I hate to say it… but it's times like this that I wish Tilthan were around."

Cornar laughed. That was really saying something, as Igan didn't get along with the conniving thief. Cornar didn't care too much for Tilthan either. But he tolerated Tilthan more than Igan.

"Well, it can't be those walls," Gregan said, pointing to the left and right. "There is a room to the left, and that dead-end hallway to the right."

"It must be this direction," Cornar said, tapping on the wall in front of him. "The caves are there."

"Are you sure we can't go any deeper?" Vargos asked. "We didn't miss anything, did we?" No, they couldn't go any deeper. By Heleron's Scales, how far down into the ground had they gone already? There was that fall, then another two hundred phineals. After that they had descended at least another ten stories.

Cornar ran through the map again in his mind, retracing all the steps he had taken. Yes, they were in the right spot.

"I have an idea," Igan said, rolling up the sleeves of his robe. "Everyone stand back." The wizard had a determined expression upon his face. Cornar took that as a cue to heed Igan's words. The others also obeyed.

Igan uttered a laborious incantation. Purple light flickered around his hands, then gathered into a ball between his fingers. It was disintegrating magic.

Genius, Igan! Cornar cheered inwardly.

The magic coalesced and then beamed forward, striking the wall. The disintegrating magic bored through the stone. Igan sucked in a deep breath and closed his eyes, concentrating on forcing his magic through the wall. After a moment, the wizard lurched forward.

"Let's check it," Igan said tiredly, pulling the beam of violet light into a ball between his palms.

Cornar stepped up to the newly formed hole, feeling a wave of heat. The warmth washed through the perfect circle cut clean into the wall. The hole was no bigger than Cornar's head. Light spilled through the hole, but soon faded.

"Solidin," Cornar called. The elf quickly came beside Cornar, sticking his lightstone into the hole.

The hole went on for nearly three phineals before opening into what looked like a natural cave. It was not at all like the tunnels Cornar and the others had traversed. The cave was wide enough for the six of them to walk abreast.

"Yes!" Cornar cheered, triumphant. "Igan, keep going." He and Solidin stepped away while Igan resumed his spell. The wizard bored another hole into the wall along the bottom right of the opening.

"Well, that's the scholarly thing to do," Vargos said. "When you can't find the switch, you just burn a hole in the damned thing."

"We're adventurers, Vargos," Gregan chimed. "Not scholars."

Vargos hummed with disappointment.

They all watched as Igan bored multiple holes in the wall, all arrayed around the first. After drilling the seventh hole, Igan disintegrated the chunks that remained, making the seven holes one.

Once Igan dismissed his magic, Vargos stepped up to the wizard. "You took a perfectly good door and made it crude. Well done," the barsionist said, patting Igan on the shoulder.

Igan rolled his eyes.

"It's warm in there," Gregan said, leaning into the hole. He scowled at the heat then glanced back to the others.

"Let's get going," Cornar said. He crawled through the hole, which lacked any dust or debris. Igan's magic had literally evaporated the stone. Cornar didn't understand how it worked, as it should have left behind some residue. But magic often defied the laws of nature.

Soon, Cornar was within that earthen cave. The warmth was enveloping. It actually felt good, as opposed to the cool weather on the surface.

"I hope it's not too hot in here," Vargos griped, fanning himself.

"And here I thought old people liked warmth," Gregan grinned. The old barsionist shot Gregan an annoyed glance.

Cornar smiled. It was good to be adventuring with these men. He loved the excitement of seeing something new, but he *craved* the interaction between his fellows. The bantering was what made trips like this fun.

Solidin and Igan stepped ahead, lighting the cave. It went on for a way, twisting and turning. It also descended. The party followed the tunnel for quite some time. Cornar was starting to tire. Was it nighttime up above? He wished there was a way he could tell. Cornar had once read a story that featured a tevisral that told the time of day. Oh, he wished it were real and that he possessed one.

A wave of heat washed across them as they turned a corner, and then Cornar caught sight of orange light shining around another bend. Light this deep beneath the surface? What could be doing that?

Cornar pushed ahead of Igan and Solidin, hurrying to the illuminated part of the earthen tunnel. The heat grew more intense with each step. The cave opened into a massive space, lit from below. Cornar stepped out onto a wide ledge overlooking an enormous lake of lava. Stalactites were suspended over a hundred phineals above the lake. This was a magma chamber...

Had the Keepers actually built their temple inside such a dangerous place? *It does make for a good hiding spot,* Cornar thought.

"Whoa..." Gregan muttered, stepping past Cornar. He neared the edge and looked down. "That's a long drop."

"Don't trip," Vargos said. "Where to now, Cornar?"

Cornar looked around, taking in his surroundings. The ledge continued to their right, wrapping around the enormous magma chamber. The chamber, however, curved away from the ledge, its entirety obscured from view.

"I think we need to get around that bend," Cornar said. But how long was it? He couldn't recall the exact scaling on the map. It would probably take them several hours.

"I'm sorry." Solidin sighed, hunched forward with his hands on his knees. "Do you mind if we rest for a while? Fatigue is starting to hit me."

Cornar was feeling tired too. He glanced at the others, who showed similar signs of fatigue.

"I think it's a safe bet to say that we're ahead of Kaescis and the others," Igan said, walking back through the cave. "Why don't we go back a bit and nap. It's too hot in this chamber."

"Agreed," Vargos said, and stomped away. The old mage was grumpy, and rightly so.

"I'll take first watch," Gregan said.

They wound their way back through the cave, stopping when they felt a difference in temperature.

"Don't let us sleep for too long," Cornar said, lying on the floor. He wrapped Sharon's cloak to make a pillow, then nestled against it, trying to get as comfortable as possible. After a short while, Cornar felt sleep overtaking him.

⎯⎯◆⎯⎯

Solidin lay quietly, watching Gregan keep watch. The other men were fast asleep, exhausted from the ordeals of the last two days. Cornar and Aron were the first to drift into slumber, followed by the mages. The brawny man, Kalder, was the last to fall asleep, since he'd spoken with Gregan before retiring. Solidin hadn't clearly heard their conversation, but he thought he heard them mention the Mindolarnians.

Solidin fought the urge to sleep as he laid his head against his pack. It and the ground were quite uncomfortable. Solidin missed the luxury of his own camp. But he couldn't entrust this task to just anyone. Solidin was the only one who could ensure the success of this venture.

Stay awake, he thought. The debilitating heat from the lava lake—coupled with the lack of sleep—made remaining conscious nigh impossible.

Gregan stirred, shaking himself awake. At least Solidin wasn't the only one succumbing to the heat.

The warrior started dozing again, but he soon snapped upright, cursing. Gregan was the most uncouth of the bunch. He was a likeable man, and so were the others. Cornar… well, he was everything the stories claimed. His sense of direction was better than the nose of a bloodhound. That amazed Solidin. Stories whispered in taverns were often exaggerations, but Cornar lived up to his reputation in every regard. Solidin liked him, a lot.

That was dangerous.

A moment later, gray and violet particles of light danced through the air, moving across the sleeping men and straight for Gregan. Solidin watched as the magic wisped into the man's ears. Gregan wobbled and then slumped against the cavern wall, succumbing to the sleep-inducing spell.

Solidin watched as more of the magic wisped to the others, insuring their slumber. It was an extra precaution he had ordered. After all, he had done the same to Cornar as he slept that first night.

With everyone asleep, Solidin was free to move. He dusted himself and ascended the winding cave. He found it interesting that the Keepers had kept this path natural. *I wonder if the Klindala Dynasty ever discovered these caves?* Solidin wondered, rounding one of the bends in the earthen tunnel.

"Solidin, esul daekali manil?" The whispered question was in his native tongue. He didn't recognize the voice. It probably belonged to one of his newer recruits.

I really should take the time to get to know these new fellows, Solidin thought, rounding the corner. There, standing in front of him, was an elf wearing white armor with blue accent trim. It was the standard uniform for everyone that belonged to his elite force, the Sapphire Guard.

"I'm fine," Solidin said in answer to the question.

Several more elves stood behind the first. Solidin recognized many, as they were some of his most trusted soldiers.

"Are you hungry, Solidin?" Gladis asked in Elvish. He pushed past the others, also wearing white armor. Gladis's breastplate was a little different, as it had the emblem of the Guard emblazoned across it. The emblem depicted the immortal tree blooming beneath the crescent of order. The crescent was upheld by the pillars of justice and topped with the five stars of the Guard's founders.

"Not really," Solidin shrugged. "We cooked the meat of those damovians we encountered. It left me… not wanting."

"Disgusting!" Fingas made a puking face.

Gladis rolled his eyes. "You know, Solidin, that is akin to cannibalism."

"How could you stand to eat them?" Tergos asked, looking bewildered.

Solidin shrugged as Kaldarin approached. "How's everyone?" Solidin asked, still speaking Common, though his fellows spoke Elvish.

"The troops are fine, commander," Kaldarin said, saluting Solidin. "And we sealed up the hole in the last Klindil chamber."

"Good." Solidin grinned. "That should stall the Mindolarnians for a bit. Hopefully, they won't suspect that we're ahead of them." He looked to Gladis. "Did you transmute a new wall?"

Gladis nodded. "It looks the same. I used a mimicry line in the incantation."

"Are we close to the temple?" Kaldarin asked.

"I think so," Solidin said. "I vaguely recall a chasm on the map. It's a massive magma chamber."

"A moat of magma?" another elf mused. "Genius!"

"Are we moving ahead?" Kaldarin asked.

Solidin shook his head.

"Why not?" Fingas demanded. "We do not need the man anymore. He got us through the under-depths of Klindil. He's served his purpose."

"Are you going soft, Solidin?" Gladis asked, raising an eyebrow with disapproval. Gladis looked stern when he made that expression.

"They're decent people," Solidin said. "I don't want to deprive them of the discovery. I'll continue with Cornar until we reach the temple."

"But, Solidin!" Tergos shouted. "The Mindolarnians could be close behind. We cannot waste the time!"

"This is unwise, commander," Kaldarin said with a sigh.

"I appreciate the concern," Solidin said, clenching his teeth. "But *I* lead the Sapphire Guard. We do as *I* say… Understood?"

The elves shied away. They knew not to anger Solidin.

"Does Cornar suspect anything?" Gladis asked. He was the only one who wasn't afraid of Solidin. After all, they were friends, and their friendship spanned more than two centuries, since childhood.

"No, he doesn't," Solidin said. "His friends were leery, but once they saw his trust in me their worries faded."

"The mark of a good leader," Gladis nodded. He stepped away from the crowd. "I will tell the others of your intent."

"Thank you, old friend," Solidin grinned.

The other elves looked nervous, especially Tergos. The death of his brother during the battle in the Igeacean Sea probably haunted him still.

"Keep patrols active as we move," Solidin said. "And if the Mindolarnians encroach on your rear, sound the klaxon. Keep someone with my gear ready. I'll abandon the humans and come to your aid."

That seemed to ease the elves.

Turning away, Solidin bade them farewell. "I'm going to sleep for a bit. And Fingas, dismiss your spells once I get settled."

> *"A man will brave unspeakable odds and unearth a secret that will change the world. Together, he and the Unspoken One shall seek a forgotten power. I cannot see where or when this will happen, but it will be pivotal to the Harbinger's mandate."*
>
> *- Prophecy of Soron Thahan*

Yes!" Cornar cheered, gazing to the sky. Though it was twilight, Cornar could see a yellow tint and several blood-red clouds. He was back in the dreamland. Cornar rode in the middle of his father's company of elite soldiers, eighty-four in all. They were moving through the trees, but Cornar could see the shores of a lake, Laelin Lake.

"And what are you excited about, Naedar?" one of the soldiers asked Cornar. So he was playing the part of Naedar again. He could handle that.

Melthas held up a fist, calling for the party to halt. "Mages, cast your invisibility." In perfect unison, the mages cast their concealing magic on the party, and everyone vanished. Adrin uttered another spell, and pale-yellow particles alighted on the invisible party. Then everyone appeared again, sort of…

Cornar squinted. He could see the others, but they had a strange film covering them. That film had to be the invisibility spell. Cornar glanced to his hands, which were also covered in that strange film. *Like the thieves' lenses,* he mused. He never knew such a spell existed. When Cornar and the others traveled invisibly, they always held onto a rope.

The party was moving once again. They traveled through the trees for a while until Melthas called for a halt. A cave was nestled within a hill, about a hundred phineals away. A moment later, a patrol exited the cave, marching toward the lake. The patrol consisted of fourteen soldiers, the equivalent of two squads in the Mindolarn army.

This must be the incursion point, Cornar thought, eyeing the cave. A path led from it down to the shore. Cornar hadn't noticed the path when the soldiers were marching.

Melthas and the others watched the patrol move along the shore. The soldiers marched toward the castle, unaware of the invisible men.

The Castle of Laelin Lake was a towering off-white structure atop a rocky hill. It was grand looking, with towers rising high into the sky. At its highest point it looked to be over twenty stories tall. How was that even possible? Cornar knew of towering structures—the Fortress of Anigar and the ruins of Klindil rose that high or higher—but he thought no one in Kalda's current era had the skill to construct such wonders. A stone bridge spanned the distance from the rocky hill to the foothills of nearby mountains. That bridge looked to be the only way into the castle.

Cornar caught a glimpse of his father giving a signal, gesturing with two of his fingers. The party continued, two by two, until they reached the cave.

Melthas gave signals with his hands, but Cornar didn't know what the signals meant. The other members of the elite band dismounted and broke up into several groups. Then they filed into the cave, guiding their horses.

Unsure of what to do, Cornar got behind one of the groups. The cavern was roughly hewn but was lit by lightstones recessed into cracks in the ceiling.

Partway through the cave, Melthas noticed him and signed something that Cornar didn't understand. He knew a little about hand-signing languages, but what Melthas was using was completely foreign.

Shaking his head, Melthas broke from his group. He handed his reins to Adrin and crept to Cornar. "What are you doing, Naedar?" Melthas demanded. "You're out of formation."

"Sorry…" Cornar frowned. "My head is still fuzzy from that fall." Would that work?

"You're with Vedin," Melthas whispered. "First group on the left." Cornar looked farther down the cave to the group mentioned by his father. They were turning down a side tunnel. Cornar quickened his pace and caught up to them.

"Are you okay, Naedar?" one of the men asked. Was this Vedin?

"My head is still fuzzy," Cornar said, feigning embarrassment. *Perhaps I can get some answers about specifics.*

"He's a liability," said one of the men.

"Perhaps he should head back," another suggested tersely.

"No," the first said. He gave Cornar a refresher of their plan. They were to ambush patrols as they passed through the caves. Patrols came through a hidden path from the castle, through these caves, and down to the lake. Melthas and his Elites, however, couldn't infiltrate the castle that way, as patrols marched one direction through these caves. They would have to pick off several patrols and finish their rounds in order to get inside. Adrin's source had given them a specific patrol route to follow, as well as other routes they could use inside the castle.

After a while, footfalls echoed down the cave's main vein. Within seconds, another patrol of fourteen soldiers passed. Vedin led the others back into the main vein, blocking a possible escape for the patrol. Two other groups would be doing the same at the cave's mouth.

Gasps and startled sounds filled the cave as Melthas and some of his Elites attacked the patrol. The Mindolarnians were dead within seconds.

The group that had gone ahead on the right—led by a man named Jamar—appeared from their invisibility and undressed the soldiers. Soon, they were all clad in Mindolarn armor. One of the men cast a spell, washing away the blood on some of their armor with magical water.

Jamar's group continued down the cave, marching like the Mindolarnians.

Once they were gone, Adrin moved to the bodies, casting a spell. Purple magic gathered in his hands and persisted around his fingers. He touched each of the bodies, completely disintegrating them. There was nothing left of the Mindolarn soldiers when he was done. The men around Cornar sneaked back into the side tunnel, waiting for another patrol.

Another patrol came and was dispatched like the first. One of the groups in the rear, by the cave's mouth, took the armor and continued the dead men's patrol.

Three more patrols were felled in like manner.

Cornar's group donned the armor of the last patrol as Adrin approached. The grand mage stopped before touching the dead. "Naedar, you should come with us," Adrin said.

"Good," one of the men grumbled. "Don't want him messing up our formation."

Vedin chided the soldier for his rude remark, but the man just sulked. Soon, Vedin's group was marching out of the cave, having taken someone from Melthas's group to replace Cornar.

Adrin went about destroying the bodies and Cornar lingered beside him. Cornar glimpsed his father tossing something on the ground, but he couldn't tell what; the light from the ceiling wasn't bright enough.

All the soldiers with Melthas rounded up the horses. They moved back toward the cave entrance with Adrin, each gripping several reins.

Cornar watched Adrin cast a spell, mustering golden light. *A conjuration spell?* he wondered. Cornar stopped beside his father, watching as a wave of golden light washed from Adrin and enveloped the soldiers and the horses. The golden light pulled back toward Adrin, but when it faded, they were all gone. All that remained was a lingering odor, like rotten eggs mixed with citrus juice. It was an unmistakable scent that screamed, "Someone just cast a teleportation spell."

Not a minute had passed when more golden light appeared, coalescing above a black dome on the ground. Cornar started upon seeing it. How was his father in possession of *that?*

Several silhouettes stood out within the light. As the light faded it revealed Adrin and the other Elites who had taken the horses.

"We need to move ahead," Adrin said. "The next patrol will undoubtedly smell the effect of my crystals."

Melthas guided everyone farther into the tunnel. Somehow, everyone managed to stay invisible. Adrin must have cast his invisibility on those who teleported away with him. That impressed Cornar. His father's band of Elites was highly organized. It made him wonder how this mission would fail.

Soon, another patrol came. Melthas and the others slew them quickly. Once the Mindolarn soldiers were dead, Melthas and the others removed their armor. Adrin disintegrated the dead Mindolarnians, and then the last group of Elites marched out of the cave.

It had taken nearly an hour to reach the bridge leading to the castle. The Castle of Laelin Lake was even more impressive up close. The decorative stonework on the outside was exquisite. Much of the architectural detail consisted of sharp curves, like a talon or claw. Each of the towers looked like a cone cupped by a clawed creature. They looked… wicked.

Cornar and the others passed another patrol crossing the bridge. Melthas marched at their head, with Adrin right behind him.

They approached the castle's main gateway and waited for it to open. Another gate was behind the first. When both gates were closed, this space became a kill box. Cornar was careful not to take in sweeping glances as he studied his surroundings. Arrow slits lined the walls of the gateway, occupied by archers and what looked to be mages.

A wave of white magic fell upon him and the others, but did nothing. It was probably a dispel.

"You're clear," a man said from beyond the second gate, making a gesture—undoubtedly a signal to raise the gate.

Once the second gate was open, Melthas led Cornar and the others into the castle wards, passing several buildings. They continued their patrol toward the towering main keep. Cornar swore it looked taller up close. Instead of moving to the entrance, Melthas took them to the right. They filed into an alleyway where more of Melthas's Elites waited.

"Jamar's group is making rounds on the ramparts," Kaemar said. He was one of the men who had led a group back at the cave's entrance. "Vedin is making a round in the main keep. Someone overheard a banquet being held on the eighteenth floor."

Eighteenth floor? Cornar fought the urge to widen his eyes. How tall was this place?

"Alegar is most likely there," Adrin said.

"I agree," Melthas nodded. He surveyed his troops and then turned. "We make a round up there, then find a quiet place to gather everyone."

Melthas led his group back toward the entrance of the main keep. They entered the castle's grand foyer without any resistance. After all, they looked like a typical patrol.

Grand was too modest a word for the grand foyer. It was downright ostentatious. The room was three stories of gaudy décor, all colored in red and gold. It was made of off-white stone—what kind Cornar didn't know—although it didn't look like anything natural.

Melthas guided them to the left of the grand foyer, toward a hallway. It was only one story tall, but it was decorated in the same fashion as the foyer. Melthas led them through the hall, turning a corner.

A wave of heat washed over Cornar as they turned.

"Cor," Igan's voice boomed through the hallway.

No! Cornar wailed. *Not now, can't I sleep longer?* He looked to Adrin. *Can't you keep me here?*

Adrin glanced back to Cornar and shook his head.

Suddenly, myriad colors raced away from Cornar, like shooting stars. Everything went black for a moment, and he glimpsed a gigantic figure before him. It was not human.

Cornar blinked, finding himself back in the tunnels below Klindil. *Damn it!* he cursed inwardly.

"I think I passed out," Gregan groaned. "I'm sorry."

"It's fine," Cornar said, steeling his composure. "It was probably the heat." He wished he were back in that yellow-sky realm. Then his stomach growled, and he recalled that he never felt hungry or fatigued in that dreamland. "Let's get moving."

Soon, they were all back in the magma chamber. Cornar strode at the head of the band, carefully descending the sloping ramp. He shielded his face from the heat, squinting. It got hotter the farther they went.

After an hour they rounded the bend at the far end of the chamber. To Cornar's surprise, nothing was there—besides more lava. The ridge along the cavern's edge stopped about three hundred phineals away, descending into the lava.

"Well, that was a short trip," Vargos said, sighing.

Cornar looked about the cavern, searching for anything that might look out of the ordinary.

"Perhaps it's buried under the magma," Kalder speculated. He paced ahead of Cornar, peering into the boiling magma.

This couldn't be a dead end, could it? Cornar struggled to remember the rest of the cave's layout. He sighed, feeling defeated. The magma chamber curved again, sprawling around another bend to the right.

"Uh, Cor," Igan said.

Cornar turned, seeing the wizard standing beside the cavern's wall. Igan was touching what looked to be handholds. The handholds, however, weren't just random notches in the wall. There was a pattern to them. With his eyes, Cornar followed their path, which rose two stories and stopped at a narrow ledge.

"Up there?" Solidin asked, pointing to the ledge. "Shall I scout ahead?" The elf stepped toward the handholds but Cornar grabbed him.

"If you fall—"

"I won't fall." Solidin grinned. The elf swiftly scaled the wall and pulled himself onto the ledge. There was barely enough room for him to stand.

"There's a cave up here," Solidin shouted. He hugged the wall, edging away from the party. He was dangerously close to where the ramp descended into the lava.

Don't fall… Cornar sucked in his breath. "Vargos." He glanced to the barsionist, but Vargos was already doing what Cornar had intended to command.

Vargos finished his spell and the barsion magic wisped along the ledge, creating a temporary footing for Solidin.

"Thanks!" Solidin shouted down to them. The elf soon disappeared beyond the narrow ledge.

As Cornar anxiously awaited Solidin's return, Gregan said, "We should follow him." Cornar nodded in agreement.

"I'll make a ramp," Vargos said, waving to the area behind him. "Go over there."

The men complied, and Vargos cast another spell. More barsion magic formed a brilliant blue ramp that merged with the barrier extending the ledge.

From this vantage point, Cornar could see the cave. How had he missed it before? The six men quickly crossed the magic. Once they got to the cave, Solidin reappeared.

"It's there!" the elf said with excitement. "Oh, and it is a grand sight!"

Solidin led Cornar and the others through the cave. It turned a few times, but soon emptied onto a ledge within an enormous U-shaped cavernous chamber. This second chamber, however, didn't have a pool of magma for its floor. In fact, Cornar couldn't see anything beneath them. And the entire space was lit… jagged veins shone pale-purple light along the cavern's walls and ceiling.

"Now where?" Igan asked, looking about the cavern.

Cornar quietly surveyed the cavern with a panoramic gaze. Huge stalactites hung from the ceiling, glistening much like the walls. At their bases, they were about the size of a building.

While the others studied the space, Cornar's eyes were drawn across the cavern, to the protruding curve in the wall. About a couple of stories below them was a wide niche, hollowed like a gigantic alcove. The glowing veins lit the alcove brightly, showing the exterior of a building chiseled out of the stone.

"There." Solidin pointed to the alcove. "The temple is in that stalactite."

Stalactite? Cornar set his jaw. Wasn't that the cavern's wall? *That wasn't a stalactite—no…* He gasped, seeing the cavern's wall narrow the farther it descended into that bottomless pit.

It *was* a stalactite… but how was it hanging? And… it was massive!

Solidin and the men debated how they would cross the chasm.

Footsteps reached Cornar's ears, coming from the magma chamber. He furrowed his brow, listening. There were dozens of footfalls.

"Everyone, quiet!" Cornar commanded. He took one step back toward the magma chamber.

Men in white armor appeared, startling Cornar. He didn't recognize them. He jumped, reaching for his weapons. As Cornar grabbed the hilts, he realized the men were not men at all—they were elves!

By Heleron's Trident! he gasped, glancing back to Solidin, who didn't look surprised.

Cornar returned his focus to the elves. Some of them had a blue emblem emblazoned across their breastplates. He recognized that symbol… it was used by elves from Merdan—notorious soldiers of the Elven Aristocracy of Merdan.

"It's them!" Igan shouted. "The Merdan elves… but—"

"The Sapphire Guard," Cornar said, and gritted his teeth. These, these were the elves that frightened Krindal. And rightly so. The Sapphire Guard was a relentless bunch with an odd sense of morality. They would commit atrocities but see men like Krindal and Iltar—wielders of the necrotic arts—as the true evil in the world. They were chaotically zealous and would do anything to impose their standards upon all Kalda.

Had they killed all of Krindal's men? Is that why Krindal had come to the Necrotic Order, to receive aid against *these* elves?

"Solidin, esul tigil mairali naidial," one of the elves said in Elvish, holding out a necklace with a gem inlaid at its center. The gem looked like the stone Krindal used to activate the mapping tevisral.

That bastard! Cornar growled, spinning to face Solidin, his anger boiling. Without restraint, Cornar drew his weapons, but he was seized upon before the blades left their scabbards.

Solidin grinned as he stepped to the elves. He grabbed the necklace and put it around his neck.

Other elves moved past Solidin, gauntleted hands outstretched. They squared off with Cornar's men but didn't advance.

Words of an incantation echoed from behind Cornar, cast by one of the elves. Vargos began casting his own spell, as did Igan.

"You're outnumbered," Solidin said sternly, "Forty to one. Just surrender."

The elven mage finished his spell faster than Igan and Vargos. Gray particles zipped through the air. The magic struck the mages and warriors, abruptly stilling them with a mind-control spell.

Once Cornar's men were stilled, elves rushed forward, pulling Kalder and the others back into the cave. A couple of elves unraveled scarves glowing a lime-green hue. They wrapped those around Igan and Vargos's mouths.

Elven scarves, Cornar thought with a groan. They had a different name, but Cornar couldn't remember what it was. Merchants sometimes peddled them on Soroth's black market. Iltar had considered buying one a few years back. The necromancer claimed the fibers were made with a type of dust that had nullifying properties. Such scarves would inhibit anyone from mustering magic. Some governments used them to capture criminal mages.

"Calm yourself, Cornar," Solidin said. The elf holding Cornar turned him to face Solidin. "I want you to know that this was not personal," Solidin said. "I actually like you, a lot."

"Why…?" Cornar demanded.

"To put it simply, I lost my tevisral that creates the map to the Keepers' Temples," he said, and sighed. "Those collapses outside Klindil weren't the first, you know," the traitorous elf said, setting his jaw. "The night before the earthquake, our camp experienced a tremor. We must have been sitting on top of a weakened part of the trans-tube line. When the tremor struck, half of our camp collapsed, including my tent.

"Luckily, we only lost a couple of the Guard, but my tevisral was crushed beneath the rubble, sheered in half. Needless to say, it wasn't working after that." Solidin paused, stepping closer to Cornar.

"I didn't know how we were going to find the temple. I thought we might try following the Mindolarnians. But they have such a sizeable force, we would risk a battle. With their current numbers, I don't know if we could slay them like last time. We were evenly matched in number then, but my company had the better skill." His words rang with arrogance. "We could have slain them all, if it hadn't been for that abominable prince."

Solidin looked sternly at Cornar. "You shouldn't trust him. Kaescis is not what he claims to be."

Cornar wanted to spit in Solidin's face. *What a hypocrite!* How dare Solidin lecture him about trust?

"Anyway," Solidin continued, "I ordered my scouts to follow the Mindolarnians. That's when the earthquake struck. We went looking for our scout—the friend I said was crushed—and found you in that pit." The elf beamed with excitement. "I recognized you from the tavern in Kretin. Cornar Dol'shir, the most renowned adventurer of Soroth. The man with the impeccable sense of direction. At first I thought that finding you in that pit was some cruel trick of fate, as no one could survive such a fall. But to our surprise, you were alive and unharmed. How, I don't know…

"But I didn't want to find fault with this gift I had received," Solidin grinned. "I knew you could lead me here. Thank you." The elf put a hand to Cornar's shoulder, gripping him tightly.

"You used me," Cornar growled.

Solidin shrugged. "I wouldn't call it that. We helped each other."

Cornar reflected on that moment when he'd met Solidin in the cave. Those faint noises he heard were these elves watching him. He had been so gullible—trusting Solidin, seeing him as another stranded adventurer. *Blast!*

A few elves stepped through the crowd and handed some armor to Solidin. It was white plate armor with the emblem of the Sapphire Guard emblazoned in blue across the breastplate. Another elf handed him a belt with two sheathed daggers strapped on either side.

"What are you going to do with us?" Cornar demanded.

Solidin didn't answer until he was fully armored. "Ask for you to join me," the elf said frankly. "There's no point in wasting talent such as yours. You shouldn't be working with the Mindolarnians. They are as much my enemy as they are yours."

Solidin stepped to the edge of the ledge. Light surged down along the veins in the cavern, descending into that abysmal pit. Cornar watched as a beam of light shot from the darkness, striking the gigantic stalactite that housed the temple. White light arced across the chasm toward Solidin, transforming into a glistening bridge.

Once the bridge was formed, Solidin strode across it. The elf holding Cornar urged him forward, and they followed after Solidin.

Cornar wondered if he could shake himself free of the elf, but every scenario he ran through his mind resulted in him falling off the bridge. He'd have to wait…

They were across the bridge within minutes. Cornar hadn't noticed a waist-high wall hemming part of the alcove. The bridge emptied into a stone courtyard, shaped like a rounded triangle. The courtyard looked like it could hold a few hundred men.

Solidin walked straightway toward the temple's towering double doorway. Twenty symbols adorned the doors, ten on each slab. A strange-looking emblem marked the top of the door: seven sharp points protruded from a hendecagon, all arrayed above three claws clutching a circle.

Light shone from beneath Solidin's breastplate. The elf removed the necklace, letting it dangle against his armor. A beam of light shot from the gemstone and struck the strange symbol, causing it to glow.

The symbols upon the doors also glowed, and then the doors swung open on their own. Words echoed from within the temple. They sounded Elvish. Previously unlit sconces burst with light, further illuminating the alcove-courtyard.

Cornar glanced over his shoulder, seeing his men herded across the bridge. Kalder and the others were surrounded by two hundred members of the Sapphire Guard.

"Kaldarin, let go of Cornar," Solidin said.

Cornar jolted forward, shoved by the elf. He staggered, but dropped into a battle stance. Cornar instinctively grabbed his weapons, drawing them with lightning finesse.

"I wondered if you'd do that," Solidin mused, eyeing Cornar warily. Kaldarin glowered.

Out of the corner of his eye, Cornar glimpsed the elf approaching. Cornar spun, kicking the elf in the gut. That sent Kaldarin tumbling backward. Rebounding from the kick, Cornar landed and squared off with Solidin.

Was he really attacking? What madness… Solidin grinned. "That's why I like you, Cornar," he said, extending his hand in a placating gesture. "Come with me. Let's discover the secrets of this temple together, and perhaps we can leave as allies."

Cornar held tight to his weapons. He expected that elf, Kaldarin, to attack again, but Kaldarin didn't advance. He just stood there. Cornar glanced back at the elven army, worried for his men. He couldn't face the elves all on his own. He had two choices, accept Solidin's offer or succumb to defeat. If he fought, that battle would end in captivity or death. The latter seemed less likely.

But Cornar had to protect his men. Perhaps he could bargain for their release.

In one swift motion, Cornar twirled his weapons, sheathing them in a showy display. He stepped up to Solidin, and they entered the Keepers' Temple together.

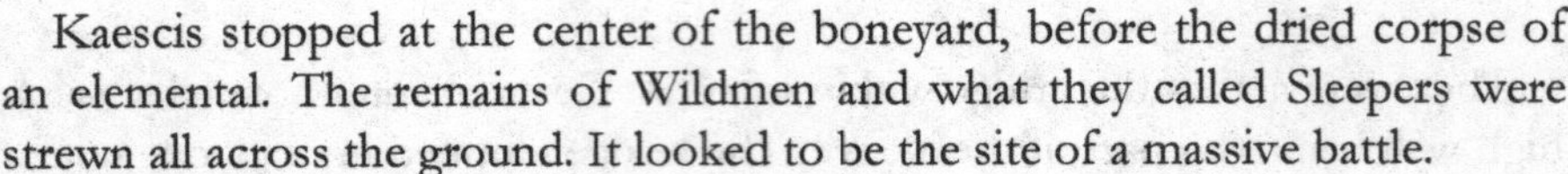

Kaescis stopped at the center of the boneyard, before the dried corpse of an elemental. The remains of Wildmen and what they called Sleepers were strewn all across the ground. It looked to be the site of a massive battle.

"Oh," Gevistra said with a gasp. "This… this can't be."

The Wildmen who had come with Kaescis muttered woeful sentiments. They were all in disbelief.

"The Time of Doom is not yet come," Bhrane muttered. "Why, why do these lie here?" The high chieftain was referring to the apocalyptic battle mentioned in their whimsical tales about the future.

Krindal stepped up to Kaescis amid the Wildmen's discord. The scholar held his tevisral, projecting the map of Klindil's under-depths. "We need to keep going that way." Krindal pointed at the elemental husk in front of them. "There is a tunnel there, an access to the lower parts of this labyrinth."

Labyrinth was a good term for it. The underground workings of ancient cities were always a mess to navigate.

"Let me see," Kaescis said, extending his hand to Krindal. He grabbed the tevisral and studied the map. They still had a long way to travel. Beyond this massive chamber they'd have to move in threes. That would delay them further, as they had nearly a thousand men. Most of the Wildmen were on the surface, guarding the entrance to this labyrinth, as Krindal put it.

"Where do you think *they* are, Your Imperial Highness?" Krindal asked.

"Don't know," Kaescis said. He hoped the Sapphire Guard was behind them. He didn't dare think of what would happen *if* those accursed elves were ahead of them. If they were at the temple—

Death… The word lingered at the back of his mind. *Destruction…*

Kaescis handed the tevisral back to Krindal and picked his way across the boneyard. Nordal—the temporary leader of Mister Dol'shir's band—was right behind Kaescis. The man had stuck close after their encounter at the collapse. That was not the reaction Kaescis expected, especially after brandishing his Ko'delish blade. Most men feared that magic, but Mister Dol'shir's band didn't even bat an eye at it.

Troubling, Kaescis thought, passing another elemental husk.

"Excuse me, Your Majesty," Nordal said, his tone mocking. "Why don't you send us ahead? We're good at exploring this type of terrain."

Kaescis looked at the man. He was Losian, wasn't he? Losians… vile Losians. Murderers. Butchers.

Death…

Nordal simply raised a brow, confused.

Had Kaescis shown his reaction to that voice in his head? Nordal looked at Kaescis as if receiving a scowl.

"That's fine," Kaescis said. "Study Krindal's tevisral before you leave."

Nordal nodded and hurried back to the rest of his band. Kaescis, however, returned his attention to the voices. They were growing stronger and appearing more frequently. He felt a familiar drive every time he heard those words of annihilation. A surge of fury ignited within him each time his thoughts were turned to his enemies.

I can use this to my advantage, Kaescis thought. *The Sapphire Guard will feel the fiery indignation of Mindolarn. When I see them, I will strike with the fury of a thousand suns.*

"A traitor will guide the Harbinger to the truth."

- Prophecy of Soron Thahan

The Keepers' Temple wasn't like anything Cornar had ever explored. Its architecture was totally foreign. The walls were so sleek, made of polished stone that reflected light shining from lines in the walls and ceiling. Cornar walked with Solidin across a hendecagon-shaped room, probably a foyer of sorts. Seven of the walls held alcoves, each with a statue within it. The statues were almost lifelike depictions of men, women, and elves. Each statue stood twice the height of an average man. Though they were made of stone, they were crafted with exquisite detail.

Two hallways branched off from the foyer, three sides away from the main doors. If one were to connect the entrance with these hallways by lines, it would look like a shallow Y-shape.

Solidin led Cornar toward the right hall, stopping beside the statue next to the opening. "You know, we're the first people to step on this hallowed ground in over a thousand years."

Cornar said nothing; Solidin's deception still upset him. He also felt a growing anger towards Krindal and the others. If they had only told him the truth, he wouldn't be in this predicament.

Solidin shouted something in Elvish. The members of the Sapphire Guard poured into the foyer, hurrying down the other hall.

"They listen to you," Cornar said coldly, referring to the elves. "Are you their commander?"

Solidin nodded. "I've led the Sapphire Guard for the last ninety-six years," he said. "I am well respected. My father was one of the Guard's founders—he taught me everything I know about the arts of fighting and leadership. He was a Protector of Merda when our people were driven from our ancestral home." Solidin looked solemn, falling into a reverie.

Cornar didn't know much about the ancient elven city of Merda. It lay on the eastern side of the Isle of Merdan, the same island which was home to the city of Keth; Solidin's hometown. Many people attributed a variety of horror stories to the forlorn city of Merda. No one ever ventured to it and returned. Merda was taboo among adventurers.

"These," Solidin said, pointing to the statues, "were the first Keepers of Truth and Might. That one"—he waved to the center statue opposite the entrance—"was their founder, Dusel Nadim."

Intrigued, Cornar stepped closer to the statue. It depicted a man wearing an odd-looking long-sleeve shirt and equally strange pants. The statue's hands were clasped over his waist. The expression chiseled into his face was kind and confident, with soul-piercing eyes.

"Come," Solidin said.

Cornar complied, and the elf led him down the hallway which soon flowed into a four-way intersection. They turned left, ascending a short flight of stairs. They soon entered a large circular room. Six other hallways branched off, totaling seven ways to access the room.

"This is the central chamber," Solidin said. "Each of the other temples had similar hub-rooms like this, although they weren't as grand." The elf smiled. He was being so cordial, undoubtedly trying to win Cornar's trust.

Cornar remained silent. He studied the circular room, which looked to be about seventy or eighty phineals in diameter. It was also vaulted, rising seven stories. The higher three floors tapered toward the center. A stained glass–looking window adorned the center of the ceiling like a skylight. The window was primarily made up of that same symbol, seven sharp points around a hendecagon. Being so far beneath the surface, the window was obviously lit by a tevisral or lightstones.

A group of elves filed into the central chamber from another hallway. Soon, Kalder and the others were hauled inside. They were no longer under the mind-controlling spell, but Igan and Vargos were still gagged with the magic-inhibiting scarves.

"This way," Solidin urged, stepping past Cornar. He walked across an elaborate circular painting on the ground. It looked like a diagram, annotated with sharp-looking symbols.

Cornar remembered seeing a diagram similar in shape and pattern within one of Iltar's books. It was a depiction of all the Channels of Magic, showing how various spells were connected to each other.

Solidin was already halfway across the room before Cornar followed him. Cornar glanced at his men, and Kalder gave him a nod that said everything was okay. The elves seemed to be treating them fairly. Cornar caught up to Solidin, who stood waiting for him at the entrance to another hallway. If Cornar recalled the layout correctly, this hall was aligned with the foyer and the temple's entrance.

"The room I need is this way, I think," Solidin said, turning down the hall. "At least the other attunement chambers were arranged similarly."

Attunement chamber? Cornar wondered. Was that the room in Krindal's tale where he discovered the gem and the mapping tevisral?

"How much do you know about this temple?" Solidin asked. They reached a set of stairs leading to the second floor.

"Not much," Cornar said. "Just that it's the twenty-first location of a series of shrines across the world."

"Ah, *shrines* is a good word to describe the other temples," Solidin said.

They reached a triangular landing, shaped much like the courtyard outside. Two flights of stairs branched off from either side of the first staircase. Solidin once again took the path to the right.

Cornar, however, paused, eyeing the landing. An oval stained glass window curved along the landing's outer wall. The window had the same symbols as the main doors, all arrayed around that symbol with the seven sharp points .

"Admiring the architecture?" Solidin asked, partway up the stairs.

"Just looking at the symbols…" Cornar said, and stepped away, joining the elf on the steps.

Solidin hummed with amusement. "Do you know what those are?"

"No."

The elf grinned wryly. "They represent the ancient Orders of the Kaldean Alliance."

The Kaldean Alliance? Was that some ancient coalition?

"Never heard of them, I take it?" Solidin pursed his lips. "That saddens me, Cor."

Cor? How dare Solidin call him that? Especially after his deceit.

"Too familiar?" Solidin chuckled. "Well, no matter." He continued up the stairs. "Twenty Orders were organized during the last couple hundred years of the Thousand Years War, when the Kaldean Alliance was pushed back to Kardorth. They were called the Guardians of Kalda, founded by elven generals. Each Order was dedicated to certain disciplines of war. Some say the first classes of mages were birthed with the Orders."

Cornar listened as Solidin continued his history lesson. "The generals, known now by the title The Twenty, perfected the disciplines over the course of a hundred years. They selected men and elves to join their Orders' ranks. The Guardians of Kalda were partly responsible for turning the tide of that war."

"And what war is this?" Cornar asked. None of the terms or titles were familiar to him.

"You might know it by another name," Solidin said as they turned a corner, walking down another hallway. "The Dragon Wars."

The Dragon Wars? Cornar fought back mocking laughter. That war was just a fable, with thousands upon thousands of varied iterations, some contradicting. Everyone had heard of the fabled Dragon Wars, but no one believed the events had *actually* occurred. Besides, no one had ever seen a dragon, or draconic remains. Sure, people claimed seeing drakes and wyverns in the Black Mountains, but those were *not* dragons. Cornar had been around enough of the world—seen plenty of dig sites—to know that dragons were a myth. Old Amendal claimed otherwise, but his encounter was probably a hallucination, a result of his accident in the Abodine Wasteland.

"You don't believe me?" Solidin asked, sounding amused. "And here I thought you'd be more open to truth than other men." The elf sighed and rounded another corner, ascending another flight of stairs.

"There's no proof of the Dragon Wars," Cornar said incredulously.

"This temple is proof," Solidin said, gesturing in a wide arc. "Tevisrals are proof."

"Don't elves claim to be the creators of tevisrals?" Cornar asked. He was referring to arguments made by Mainland elves.

"Not all of them," Solidin shook his head. "I know dragons are real, Cornar." There was conviction in his words. "That's why I'm here, to discover where they and the Keepers disappeared…"

They climbed the stairs in silence and walked through another maze of corridors. This temple was massive.

"Dragons were common in Kalda until the rise of the Karthar Empire," Solidin said. "And so were the Keepers of Truth and Might. But one day they all disappeared. Our world has suffered in their absence."

Cornar listened as Solidin went on about the follies Kalda had experienced since the reign of the Karthar Empire. The elf believed these atrocities would not have occurred if the Guardians—the Keepers of Truth and Might—were still among the inhabitants of the world.

Solidin gave a brief history, saying that several years after the end of the Dragon Wars a man named Dusel re-founded the Twenty Orders. This Dusel called them the Keepers of Truth and Might. This time, dragons were included among their ranks. The Keepers watched over Kalda, ensuring peace. They were the reason no conflicts had occurred after the Dragon Wars. That was until the rise of the Karthar Empire. A war of conquest was waged across the world, and Kalda became subject to Emperor Karath the First.

The Keepers, according to Solidin, were supposed to stop such things from ever occurring. Solidin was determined to discover why they'd failed, and if possible, re-found their Orders.

After hearing the tale, Cornar felt a little more respect for Solidin. The elf didn't seem maniacal, so why would Krindal fear him?

Cornar stopped and took a deep breath. He glanced to his right, to an opening allowing a view down to the central chamber. The elves were giving Kalder and Gregan something to eat. Several surrounded Igan and were removing the scarf around his mouth. A couple held their weapons pointed at the wizard, undoubtedly threatening him before removing his debilitating gag. Kalder and Gregan watched Igan while eating.

"Aren't you coming?" Solidin asked. Cornar reluctantly stepped forward. "Watching your men…" the elf mused. "Don't worry. As long as your mage friends don't make a scene, they'll be fine."

Solidin continued through the hall once Cornar was beside him. "From what I've learned, this temple held the final step of initiation for potential Keepers. One text says that the process was quite arduous. You see, the trek to the twenty shrines—as you put it—was to expose potentials to the various disciplines. To see where they were best suited. One would spend time with the members of that shrine's Order, learning the basics of their discipline.

"This," he lifted up his necklace and tapped the gem, "was given to a potential Keeper upon visiting their first shrine. Once the gem was attuned, the potential Keeper would begin their training and stay until they achieved a certain level of mastery. Then they would move on. One account claims the process could take up to a decade. It definitely wasn't for the fainthearted," the elf grinned.

"Here at this temple one would receive their calling to one of the Twenty Orders, and be granted access to Dalgilur's Isle, the Keepers' headquarters."

Yet another name Cornar was unfamiliar with.

Solidin turned another corner, coming to a straight hallway. Grand doors marked the end of the hall; they looked like the ones at the temple's entrance. Thick stonework surrounded the doors, with glowing words etched upon its surface. They were in Common, Elvish, and another language with sharp-looking characters.

"That's Draconic," Solidin said, pointing to the unknown set of symbols. "More proof." That wasn't really proof. Those scribbles could be anything. Cornar focused on the Common words. It looked like a code of ethics. *"Preserver of Innocents. Shield to the Defenseless. Honorable in all things."*

As Solidin neared the doors they opened outward, revealing a darkened room. "And this is the Chamber of Attunement," the elf said, stepping into the darkness.

"That wall is giving off some strange light," Sharon remarked. She squinted, straining to see through her thieving lenses. Ordreth stepped beside her. He couldn't see anything, of course. Whatever Sharon was studying was hidden from the natural eye.

"Do you think it's a hidden door?" Nordal asked. He was holding Krindal's mapping tevisral. It currently showed an upside-down-looking structure. They had followed the map to the very bottom of the catacombs of Klindil. From what they had guessed, they were in a room that connected to a series of caves.

"No…" Sharon shook her head. "It looks like magic… umm, that kind that reforms stuff."

"Transmutative?" Hem asked. The illusionist stepped forward, rolling up his sleeves. "Want me to try a dispel?"

"Go for it," Nordal said.

Hem uttered the words to cast the dispel. Off-white magic flowed around his hands, then shot to the wall. Parts of the wall turned to dirt and a large section fell into the room, almost crushing Sharon's toes.

"Whoa!" Hem exclaimed, eyes wide.

"Someone must have passed through here recently," Midar speculated. "Do you think it was Cor?"

"Master Igan probably dissolved those parts of the wall," Tinal said, he spoke fondly of his teacher in the magical arts. "Look at the holes. It looks like disintegrating magic bored through the wall."

"But we don't have a transmuter among us," Cordel said, sounding worried.

That Sapphire Guard, Ordreth thought. They probably had transmuters.

"I'll inform the prince," Nordal said, and turned to exit the room. "Ordreth, take a group ahead and start looking."

"Yes, sir," Ordreth said, stepping close to the hole in the wall. He extended his lightstone lantern into the opening, finding an earthen cavern. "Hem, why don't you conceal us?"

"Why?" Hem asked. The illusionist was always so oblivious.

"You weren't paying attention, were you?" Demsal asked, coming beside Ordreth.

"Oh…" Hem nodded. He quickly cast a spell, veiling himself, Ordreth, Demsal, and Sharon.

Now invisible, Ordreth crept through the opening. Ordreth *would* find his uncle.

⟐•⟐

The Chamber of Attunement became lit once Solidin was inside. Cornar followed close behind the elf, intrigued by the room's instantaneous illumination. Light shone from circles in the ceiling, each bearing a symbol for one of the Twenty Orders. They were arranged around a larger circle in the ceiling's center, which bore the symbol with the seven sharp points. What was the significance of that symbol? It was all over the temple.

Solidin sauntered to the center of the chamber while Cornar stayed near the doors. Cornar was wary of what would happen next and kept his hands over his weapons' hilts.

There were no other entrances or exits in this room. Columns lined the walls, with twenty-one lavish thrones placed between them. Why was there an extra one? Weren't there supposed to be twenty Orders? Cornar wondered if these thrones were for the heads of the Orders.

Solidin reached the center of the room, and a voice speaking Elvish boomed within the chamber. Cornar didn't understand any of it. A beam of white light shot from a gem inlaid above the central throne, striking Solidin in the chest. The elf gasped, falling backward. He struggled for breath, his limbs twitching.

Cornar started to lunge forward but hesitated. Solidin had tricked him, used him for his own purposes. The elf and his people were holding Cornar and the others hostage. Yet, something compelled Cornar, a surge of conviction within him. Cornar dashed to the elf, sliding and then settling upon his knees beside Solidin.

The elf's gem was glowing a brilliant hue, giving off faint heat. Solidin gazed at the ceiling without blinking, his mouth open.

"Solidin!" Cornar grabbed the elf, but Solidin didn't move. He wasn't even breathing. *Blast!*

"Help!" Cornar yelled toward the door. "We need an arpranist!"

He turned back to Solidin, still motionless. Cornar leaned to Solidin's mouth, but felt no breath.

What should I do? he wondered, then a flash of memory struck him. Cornar remembered a technique his father had taught him. Cornar put his lips to Solidin's and blew into the elf's mouth. Nothing happened. *The nose.* He pinched Solidin's nose shut and blew again. Still, nothing happened.

"What was next?" he grumbled. *Press on the chest…* Cornar groaned. Solidin's armor was in the way. He reached to unfasten it.

Then a voice spoke from beside him. "Well done!"

Startled, Cornar turned to see a stranger standing near the throne aligned with the door. The stranger smiled and looked down to Solidin, pleased. Where had he come from?

The stranger was of average height, wearing odd-looking clothing, like the statues in the temple's foyer… In fact, he looked identical to the statue in the foyer. *How was that—*

Solidin gasped, sitting upright. He blinked several times, then glanced to Cornar. "I know …" the elf said, wide-eyed. "I *know!*" Cornar shook his head, confused. What was Solidin babbling about?

Footsteps echoed into the chamber, undoubtedly those coming in response to Cornar's cry for an arpranist.

Solidin pushed himself up, grinning. "I am a Bladesinger."

"A worthy Order," the stranger said, nodding. He stepped in an arc, circling Solidin and Cornar.

"Bladesinger?" Cornar muttered.

"The Guardian Order devoted to the mastery of bladed weapons, particularly dual-wielding," the stranger said. "Entalin founded the Bladesingers on the principles of tenacity and finesse. They were often the second wave of troops after Wardwalkers or Shieldriders broke through enemy lines."

What odd names, Cornar thought.

A clatter of armored footfalls echoed into the chamber, followed by shouts in Elvish. Cornar turned to see ten members of the Sapphire Guard, all converging toward Solidin.

"I'm fine," Solidin said, waving off his soldiers.

"There are many elves here," the stranger said, eyeing the members of the Sapphire Guard.

"And who are you?" one of the elves demanded.

The stranger stopped pacing, placed his hands behind his back and raised his brow. He raised his chin before answering. "I am Dusel Nadim," he said, "the first and last Guardian of Kalda."

"The Unspoken One will fight against his brother. This will fuel his fervor."

- *Prophecy of Soron Thahan*

Dusel Nadim? Solidin said that was the man who founded the Keepers... But how was he standing before them? Shouldn't he be dead? Cornar shook his head in disbelief.

"You are now a Keeper of Truth and Might," Dusel said to Solidin, stepping up to the elf, "a Guardian of Kalda. Welcome to our ranks."

"How is this possible?" blurted one of the elves. "Is he not dead?"

Solidin narrowed his eyes. What was he thinking?

"Dead?" Dusel cocked his head toward the elves.

Solidin stepped forward, stretching out his hand to Dusel. His gauntleted fingers touched Dusel's clothing, then moved *through* him.

By Heleron's Trident! Cornar's eyes widened. Was this an apparition? Cornar had heard of ghost tales, but he had never seen a ghost. Most ghost stories were not actually ghost stories at all. Creatures in the remote parts of Kalda—called phantasmal essences—could mimic a person, but in order to do so it had to kill them. Comrades of the slain would often find corpses and then see their dead friend walking nearby. Those 'ghosts' never said anything, nor acted in a way that resembled the minds of the fallen.

Dusel simply looked down at Solidin's hand, now partway through his chest. "You should stop doing that," the man said.

"You're not really Dusel, are you?" Cornar ventured the question.

The man smiled and paced back to the central throne, the one where Cornar had first spotted him. "I am Dusel as much as Dusel is Dusel."

Another elf stepped between Cornar and Solidin. He said something in Elvish that Cornar didn't understand.

Solidin shook his head. "He's not a magical essence."

"Gholirisulem?" the elf asked, proffering another unknown term. Solidin cocked his head, looking unsure.

"I am neither," Dusel said.

"And neither are we," two other voices said in unison.

Cornar and the elves spun, looking to the right and left. Now, a woman and an elf stood on either side of the chamber. They wore identical clothing, odd shirts and equally strange pants. They approached Cornar and the elves.

Where did they come from? One second they weren't there and the next they were.

The woman's thick brown hair bounced as she walked around Cornar. Her lime-green eyes studied him and the elves. *Lime-green irises?* He had never seen someone with *that* eye color. And their shape… dark lines *swirled* toward her pupils. That was not natural. Sure, people had different-colored irises, but the dark lines in their eyes always pointed straight to the pupil, not *swirled*.

"I am Elynia," the woman said, pursing her full lips into a amused expression. She had high cheekbones and olive skin.

"And I am Arceylain," the elf said. Arceylain looked much like the other elves beside Cornar—tall, blond-haired, and fair-skinned. His eyes were a pale sea-gray color.

"The three of us," Dusel said, "represent the three races of the Kaldean Alliance."

Arceylain and Elynia stepped away from Cornar and the elves and joined Dusel. They all clasped their hands behind their backs.

"Three races," Solidin said, looking to Cornar. "Human." He pointed to Dusel. "Elf." He pointed to Arceylain. "And dragon." He pointed to Elynia.

A dragon? But she looked human, except for her strange-looking eyes.

"You are correct," Elynia said with a chuckle.

Cornar shook his head. "Impossible," he muttered. The three Keepers glanced to Cornar with confusion, but returned their focused to Solidin.

"We congratulate you on completing your pilgrimage," Dusel said. "We know you are in need of rest, so you are welcome to stay here before proceeding to Dalgilur."

"There is lodging in the southeast wing," Elynia said, gesturing to her left. "The other Keepers there will tend to your needs."

Other Keepers? But there was no one else here; surely she should know that…

"Ah… kolphigrym," an elf said, nodding. "That makes sense."

"What is that?" Cornar asked.

"A projection of illusionary particles that are acting on a predetermined set of instructions and reactions," Solidin said. "These three aren't real. They're a manifestation of some tevisral."

"I beg to differ," Arceylain said, pursing his thin elven lips.

Footsteps hurried into the attunement chamber, and several more elves marched to Solidin.

"Solidin," the lead elf said. "We found a transportium."

"Is it working, Tregal?" Solidin asked, turning away from the three projection-things.

"We don't know," Tregal replied. "Gladis and some of the others are checking it. But it doesn't look damaged, like the others we found."

"This transportium network is only to be used by full-fledged Keepers," Dusel said.

The elves seemed to ignore him. They talked among themselves in Elvish, then hurried out of the room, leaving Cornar with the three projection-things.

All three of them eyed Cornar thoughtfully.

"Who are you?" Elynia asked.

"I could ask you the same thing," Cornar said.

She giggled, then looked to his weapons. "You are an odd man. You deny the existence of my kind, but you wield weapons forged by us."

Weapons forged by us? He squinted an eye thoughtfully.

"Those blades of yours were not forged by men," Elynia continued. "They were made by draconic hands… probably inside Mount Ul'goth. Draw them for me, will you?"

That seemed a reasonable request; after all she was just a cluster of magic, right? Cornar drew both of his blades, extending the serrated dagger toward Elynia.

"Fine craftsmanship," Dusel said, nodding.

Elynia extended her fingers and touched the serrated dagger. "Absorption," she muttered with intrigue. "*And* reflection… my, whoever crafted this knew what they were doing."

Her observations surprised Cornar. Wasn't she just a simple projection of magic? Yes, his weapons could absorb magic. And on a rare occasion he had deflected an arcane bolt. It was a tricky stunt, but it sent the bolt back into the caster's face.

"Odd shape, though," Arceylain said. "Like an oversized bread knife."

Dusel chuckled and grinned at the elf-projection.

"But deadly…" Elynia observed, gliding her fingers across the serrated edge. Tiny particles of light trailed from her fingers and wisped into the blade. If she was real, the blade would have cut her. "These are weapons worthy of a Keeper."

"They probably belonged to a Keeper." Arceylain frowned. "Where did you get them? Did you steal them?"

Taken aback at the accusation Cornar replied, "They were my father's."

"So *he* stole them," the elf-projection said. That thing definitely acted like an elf. Pompous. Self-righteous.

"They were a gift to him," Cornar said, and gritted his teeth.

"So someone else stole them."

"Why is that your answer for everything?" Elynia spun, glaring at the elf-projection.

"Because when a Keeper falls in battle their weapons and armor are rescued, taken by others of their Order and housed within their armories," Arceylain retorted. "Unless the Order is overrun on the battlefield."

"Nonsense," Elynia said. "Besides, the blade doesn't have any seals indicating to which Order it belongs." She turned back to Cornar. "The other one?"

She pointed to the short-sword..

Cornar held out his other weapon.

Elynia hummed and squinted. "The same properties..." Another trail of light followed her fingers, seeping into the blade.

Solidin descended one of the many stairs inside the Keepers' Temple, following Tregal. They were in the northeast wing of the temple, now on the third floor. Another group of elves entered the hallway, waving for Solidin.

"Sir," a newcomer said, and saluted Solidin, speaking in Elvish. "We have not found anything else. There are no weapons or tevisrals in any of the chambers we have searched."

"Then this is all for naught," Fingas said. He was one of the elves who had responded to Cornar's call for aid.

"We still have Dalgilur to search," Solidin said. This place was not the Keepers' headquarters. It wouldn't make sense for them to hide a weapon cache here.

The elf continued with his report, but Solidin didn't care to listen. He had come to this temple with one purpose only—finish the attunement process. They could find other trinkets that the Aristocracy's High Lords could sell elsewhere. Besides, diagrams and depictions of this temple would fetch a fortune if sold to the right people. They could fulfill the High Lords' goals for this arduous quest just by writing it all in a tome.

They turned a corner and walked down a long corridor that opened into a large circular room. Solidin could see several members of the Sapphire Guard kneeling around a raised dais in the center of the room. Others were inspecting pillars with floating globes atop them; they were the size of a man's torso. Gladis was across the room, standing behind a chest-high pedestal.

"Gladis," Solidin called. "What is the status of this thing?" he pointed to the dais. Gladis looked up and gestured for Solidin to come close.

That didn't bode well.

Solidin crossed the chamber in silence. He looked up, searching for the ceiling, but it was nowhere to be found. The walls rose as far as he could see. That was expected for a transportium chamber this far below ground.

"I don't think it is working," Gladis whispered in Common. "One of the globes is cracked."

Solidin glanced around the room, eyeing each of the pillars until he saw the one with the cracked globe atop it. It had a large gash the length of a sword.

"And this is stuck," Gladis said, tapping on the pedestal. "It's like someone deliberately sabotaged the transportium."

Solidin nodded. "Like the others."

"Why would they do that?" Gladis asked. "It seems so wasteful..."

From a mages' perspective, yes... but from a strategist's, it was brilliant.

"Think of it this way, Gladis," Solidin said. "If your enemy threatens access to the heart of your stronghold, are you going to let him have at it?"

"I see your point," Gladis replied, "but it's still wasteful. So, how are we going to get to Dalgilur?" He was doubtful, and rightly so. They had hoped to find a way to teleport to the island from this temple, since Solidin had lost his mapping tevisral. After all, one of the texts High Lord Medrayn had purchased spoke of walking to Dalgilur. One couldn't *walk* to an island. The text was obviously referring to the transportium.

"We'll just have to sail there," Solidin said, looking up once again.

"You are crazy, my friend," Gladis said with a chuckle. "No ship has ever found Dalgilur. It is as if the isle were invisible."

"Not to me," Solidin said. "We came here to get me attuned. Now that I have received my election as a Bladesinger I can see Dalgilur. The isle calls to me…"

Gladis paused, raising his left eyebrow. He always did that when thinking deeply.

"We will find Dalgilur," Solidin insisted, "despite the loss of my mapping tevisral. I *know* I can find it. I have seen the isle as clearly as if I were there. Even now I can feel the vision persisting in the back of my mind." That didn't convince Gladis. He was still thinking.

"Trust me," Solidin firmly gripped Gladis's shoulder. "But first, we need to get out of here."

Gladis sighed, rubbing his forehead. Their plan—after encountering Cornar—was to get ahead of the Mindolarnians and use the transportium to leave the temple before they arrived. Solidin intended to leave a mage behind to destroy the transportium, to prevent the Mindolarnians from following them. Tregal had volunteered, knowing very well it was suicide.

Solidin looked up once again. *Transportiums need a clear path between them*, he thought. So this chamber went all the way to the surface, however many hundreds of phineals that was… That gave him an idea.

"Separate that dais from the floor," Solidin said thoughtfully, stepping up to the dais.

"What are you suggesting?" Gladis asked, following Solidin.

Solidin didn't answer immediately. He measured the dais's diameter by stepping toe to heel all the way across it. They could fit fifty atop the dais.

"We use this"—Solidin pointed to the dais—"and escape that way." He pointed upward.

"No…" Gladis shook his head. Several other elves gathered around, drawn by the conversation.

This would work! Solidin grinned confidently. "Use barsion to reinforce the dais," he said to Gladis. "We'll have to use it five times."

"Do you know how many kineticists it will take to lift that thing?" Gladis asked, cocking his head at Solidin.

"Yeah, all of them. Now get to work."

•

Kaescis didn't feel the heat the others mentioned. The warmth couldn't penetrate his armor, not with his helmet donned. He walked at the head of the Sorothian adventurers. The rest of the army wasn't far behind them. Several of his mages further opened that hole in the last of the Klindil underdepths, allowing the army to enter the caves in groups of three.

Nordal—the Losian—still held onto Krindal's tevisral. He was eager to lend a hand, but Kaescis couldn't help but hate him.

Death… The voice inside Kaescis pleaded for him to kill the Losian. Not because of anything he had done, but because of his nativity. He was Losian. That was enough.

"There is a big cavern up ahead," Nordal said. "It looks like we can walk along a ledge. It leads to a cave adjoining another cavern where the temple should be located. Ordreth's group is ahead of us, checking on it."

Kaescis nodded. "Good."

They rounded a corner and entered an enormous magma chamber. *Clever hiding spot,* Kaescis thought. *No one would expect to find the temple this far below ground.*

Nordal stopped and the other Sorothians did the same. Kaescis, however, continued forward.

"Don't you want to wait for a report, Your Majesty?" Nordal asked.

Kaescis glanced over his shoulder. "No," he said, hurrying down the ledge. Mister Dol'shir's nephew and three others were approaching. They were yellow outlines in his visor, indicating that they were veiled beneath invisibility magic.

"Your Imperial Highness," Ordreth said, stopping in front of Kaescis. "It's not clear. We found elves guarding a tunnel—"

"Good," Kaescis interrupted the report and bolted down the earthen ramp. A bloodlust welled inside him. He yearned for a battle, to see corpses strewn before him.

Give us death… the voices said. *Give us destruction!*

◆◦◆

Cornar made his way back to the central chamber after talking with the three projections. They had told Cornar the purpose of the Keepers of Truth and Might. The Keepers safeguarded one of the greatest secrets of Kalda; what, the three did not say. They also snuffed out evil when it appeared in the world, to ensure that another Thousand Years War never occurred. The Keepers were judges, jurors, and executioners. That frightened Cornar. No one should have that much power.

Cornar voiced his objection—such ideals and practices were unjust. Arceylain fought against his point, saying that if certain principles and ethics were strictly adhered to, then one *could* be all three. That just seemed to Cornar as a convenient excuse for committing murder.

Sure, Cornar had killed many people. But it was either in self-defense or in situations where the person deserved that fate. Arceylain argued over the last point, claiming that was exactly what the Keepers did. Cornar left shortly thereafter, as the conversation became a debate. He didn't want to argue with clusters of magic.

Cornar descended the last set of stairs and entered the hallway leading back to the central chamber. Kalder, Aron, and Gregan stood along one of the walls holding their weapons and talking with Igan and Vargos. To Cornar's surprise, neither mage was gagged.

"Cor," Igan called, waving for Cornar to come close. Once he was near, the wizard asked, "What happened?"

Cornar glanced about at the nearby elves. None of them were paying attention to the humans. The elves were all busy writing or drawing sketches of the towering room. They weren't wearing armor and were probably scholars associated with the Elven Aristocracy of Merdan.

"Cor?" Gregan prodded.

That brought Cornar back to reality. "Solidin was looking for an attunement chamber," Cornar said. "He has one of those gems that Krindal has… I think it grants access to the Keepers' headquarters."

"I thought *this* was the Keepers' headquarters," Igan said.

"No, this is just a way station," Cornar said. "It—"

An elf burst through one of the corridors leading to the foyer, running to another hall on what would be the northern side of the central chamber. The men watched for a moment and then Cornar relayed the rest of his and Solidin's conversation and experience on the temple's seventh floor. Amid Cornar's retelling of the tale, Solidin entered the central chamber with more elves.

Solidin spoke in Elvish and looked like he was rounding up the elves. Were they finished here?

"What do you think that's all about?" Kalder asked.

"I don't know…" Cornar said, and hurried after Solidin. The elf strode into another corridor, one that led to the foyer.

With his men in tow, Cornar passed elves packing up their belongings. Soon, Cornar and the others were in a four-way intersection and followed the branch back to the temple's foyer. More scholars were packing up their things. One had drawn a depiction of Dusel Nadim's statue; it was quite good.

"Move!" a stern voice shouted from behind Cornar and the others. A group of ten members of the Sapphire Guard ran past Cornar and his men, darting toward the towering main doors.

Worried, Cornar eyed his companions. Their faces all asked the same thing, "Are the Mindolarnians here?"

Another group of the Sapphire Guard hurried past them, and Cornar led his small band back into the courtyard recessed within the enormous stalactite.

Solidin was hurriedly giving orders in Elvish, pointing to the bridge and the walls surrounding the courtyard.

"They're preparing for battle," Gregan whispered.

Several of the Sapphire Guard mages cast spells at Solidin's command, forcing brown-gray transmutative magic into the walls of the niche. Stone broke apart, reforming into metal barriers where Solidin had pointed.

"Vargos." Cornar turned to the barsionist, but Vargos was already doing what Cornar was about to ask; mustering his protective magic. Igan uttered an incantation as well.

The elves were too busy preparing the courtyard to notice Cornar and the others making their own preparations.

Amid the casting of spells, Cornar noticed movement near the cave leading to the magma chamber. An elf clad in white armor flew from the ledge, screaming as he plummeted into the pit surrounding the temple. A flash of black struck another elf, and he too tumbled over the side.

Solidin shouted an order in Elvish and backed up to the center of the courtyard, drawing his daggers. Some of the mages finished casting their spells. White enhancing magic washed across the courtyard; it bolstered Cornar and the others, as Vargos's barsion had not yet formed. The enhancing magic was followed by a wave of brilliant blue barsion, surrounding each member of the Sapphire Guard. More magic flew from other Sapphire Guard mages, imbuing the elves' weapons.

Vargos and Igan finished their spells, shielding all five of them and imbuing Cornar and the other warriors' weapons with purple disintegrating magic. Then, Cornar saw *him*…

Prince Kaescis emerged from the cave, clad in his golden-red armor. He held that black sword high above his head. The blade was massive, and it misted blackness. It actually looked bigger than those the horsemen wielded from his first dream with his father.

"That's Master Iltar's magic!" Aron exclaimed, gasping.

"I didn't think anyone besides Iltar and Balden could muster the *Darkness* magic," Igan said warily, then uttered another incantation.

The prince dashed across the bridge, leaping into the air. He soared unnaturally, bypassing the barricade the Sapphire Guard mages had erected.

"Death has come for you!" Kaescis shouted, his voice muffled beneath his helmet. He plummeted into the courtyard, impaling a member of the Sapphire Guard as he landed. Kaescis's blade pierced the elf as if the barsion and armor weren't there.

Impossible…

38

ASSAULT

"The Brethren will be purified, cleansed by the Holy power of Hemran'na."

- Prophecy of Soron Thahan

Rising from his unnatural leap, Kaescis violently removed his misting Ko'delish blade. The mist eroded the vile elf's armor and repulsed the barsion still persistent around the corpse. His other blade had not cut through barsion as easily; it could take seconds to breech barsion barriers, depending on the density of the spell. This weapon's effectiveness pleased him. *That's one,* Kaescis mused, dashing to the nearest elf, his weapon trailing a devouring mist behind him.

The elf lunged away, preemptively evading Kaescis's swing. All the while, the rest of the Sapphire Guard readied to attack. There were only forty of them. They all wore the same armor, and the only way to tell mages apart from foot soldiers was by their weapons.

Incantations sounded from several directions. A disintegrating beam, a fiery blast, and a summoning spell. Were those acidic bolts, too? *Had they a corusilist among them?*

Kaescis took note of the elves casting the magic. The conjurer was his most pressing foe. Kaescis would aim to kill him first. The portal forming in front of the elven conjurer was three times his height. The rest of the Sapphire Guard, however, moved to bar his way to the mages. Each of their weapons glowed with various destructive magics—a combination of flame, lightning, and acid—all intertwined with a disintegrating aura.

Well prepared, Kaescis thought. Their weapons were imbued with a deadly combination. His armor could absorb much of it, becoming a thin damaging veil of repurposed magic. The suit would emit the repurposed magic, hurting any he touched or who touched him. But enough hits from those weapons, and they would breech his armor. Those who crafted his extraordinary Triaindium Suit said it would take hundreds of blows, though.

I hope I don't have to test that, he worried.

Death… That internal voice rang within his mind, replacing worry with rage.

Invigorated, Kaescis charged through the enemy ranks. He rammed his shoulder into the nearest elf, knocking him off balance, but that didn't stop the elf from swinging his sword. The imbued metal clanged against Kaescis's armor, magic dissipating and flowing to his armor's gemstones.

Not bad. Kaescis threw a forearm into the next elf's face. That dazed the elf briefly, allowing an opening.

Kaescis spun, slicing his blade through another foe. It cut through the barsion so easily. What raw power. It was glorious! *That's two,* he thought as the Ko'delish blade sheared straight through the armor as if it were wet parchment. The elf fell in pieces, torso going one way while his legs and forearm went elsewhere. The fanisar dropped with a resounding clang.

This blade is wonderful! He rebounded, kicking another elf away. *What awesome power!*

More elves surrounded Kaescis—twelve, it seemed. Nothing he couldn't handle. They all came at him, swinging their weapons in varied directions. Kaescis tried to dodge, but was struck by four of the weapons—fanisars mostly, as they had the greatest reach. A bolt of lightning surged across his armor, erupting in a flash.

Temporarily blinded, Kaescis felt more hits from the elves. He staggered and dropped to one knee. Clanging reverberated through his armor and rang in his helmet.

Loud thuds echoed behind him, and Kaescis spun to his feet, his vision returning.

Laeyit and Bratan rebounded from the ground, dashing to the nearest members of the Sapphire Guard. They had undoubtedly leapt over the barricades. They drew away part of Kaescis's opponents, engaging three foes each.

Like old times, Kaescis thought with a smile. The three of them had led assaults together like this in the past. They were a deadly trio.

Kaescis spun back around, swinging his blade at another elf. Mister Dol'shir and the other missing Sorothians stood at the far side of the courtyard. They were protected by a thin layer of barsion magic, and their weapons were imbued by their arcanist. But they were just standing there. What were they waiting for?

Kaescis dodged his foe's flaming fanisar, and the fiery magic wisped toward his armor; his left gauntlet began to glow with flame. Kaescis punched the elf, propelling him away with a fiery eruption.

The reprieve didn't last long. His foe was replaced by another elf wielding an imbued fanisar. Kaescis swung at the newcomer, slicing through the weapon. The fanisar's bladed end dropped to the ground, sparking the courtyard floor while also eroding it from the acid and the arcane energy.

The elf didn't skip a beat and swiftly used his broken fanisar as a short spear. He struck beneath Kaescis's helmet, attempting to jar it loose.

"Nice try!" Kaescis shouted, slicing his Ko'delish blade down on the elf's nearest shoulder. The black magic tore right through his barsion, slicing down to the elf's waist. *That's three.*

The elf fell and Kaescis dashed past him but was tugged backward. Something held his leg.

Kaescis spun, seeing the felled elf gripping his sabaton with his remaining arm. "What ambition," Kaescis said, snickering as he rammed his Ko'delish blade into the elf's face. ***Now***, *that's three.*

Invigorated with a growing thrill, Kaescis pushed through more of the elves, wounding three. He dashed into the open courtyard where the elven mages had gathered. The conjurer hadn't finished, but the portal was nearing completion.

A beam of disintegration shot from the elven mage to his left. Kaescis tried to dodge, but was caught in the magic. His armor began glowing a purple hue, gemstones absorbing the deadly blast. His vision became tinted in purple, which was a cue that his armor had absorbed all it could. He had to be careful now.

Kaescis struggled to throw himself out of the way. Once free, the beam raced behind him. He glanced at the elves who had already steered clear of the magic's path. The disintegrating beam struck one of the barricades, completely destroying it. Laeyit was nearby, dueling one of the elves.

Push him into the beam—

She did exactly that, knocking the elf into the beam's tail. The elf shrieked, and dropped to the ground, a curved opening carved across his back.

"Half-breed prince!"

Kaescis turned, seeing the accursed leader of the Sapphire Guard, Solidin the Swift-Dagger. The elf stood smug in his armor, his daggers glowing, surrounded by barsion and destructive magics.

Clever... But Solidin's daggers couldn't stand up to the Ko'delish blade.

"You're too late," the Swift-Dagger boasted. He twirled his weapons and sauntered toward Kaescis.

"You shouldn't be so arrogant," Kaescis growled.

"Arrogance implies that I lack a surety. And I don't." Solidin lunged at Kaescis, weapons ready.

Kaescis slashed his blade before the elf was within dagger's reach, but Solidin tumbled forward, evading. Kaescis recovered as Solidin rolled up within close-quarters, too close to attack with the massive Ko'delish blade. Well, there was one disadvantage to it.

Kaescis leapt backward but Solidin lunged. The elf struck repeatedly at the joint between Kaescis's breastplate and pauldron. The dagger nicked the joint of the armor; it wasn't as thick as the other pieces, so it had less impact strength.

Damn him... Kaescis growled, dropping his Ko'delish blade. It misted into smoke at his mental command. He deliberately fell backward, grabbing Solidin. Kaescis trapped one of the elf's arms, preventing further attacks from one of the daggers. His disintegrating damage shield pricked Solidin's barsion at each point of contact. Kaescis grabbed the vile elf's head, attempting to break through the barsion. Solidin, however, continued striking with his free dagger. How many hits was that? At least twenty. *Damn, this elf is fast!*

Kaescis threw himself and Solidin sideways, trapping the elf's other dagger. Solidin tried to break free, but it was a futile attempt. Kaescis had him pinned.

A sharp incantation left Kaescis's lips, re-summoning his blade. It would appear in his hand gripping the elf's head. The Ko'delish blade would materialize, bursting through the barsion and then piercing the Swift-Dagger's head. He would—

Kaescis jolted upward, lifted from the ground. Thick magma-coated fingers separated him from Solidin, and then Kaescis felt himself flying. He soon crashed into something hard that gave way before him. He tumbled, sliding across a smooth floor and crashed into a wall. Kaescis kept sliding until the purple hue around his armor faded.

Damned conjurer... he cursed, looking about. He was in some kind of niche... *My armor must have carved a hole in the wall.* Kaescis had slid uncontrollably, but stopped once all the disintegrating magic was expended.

"I was too slow," he said, crawling through the niche and back into a room. It looked like those he had encountered at the other Keepers' shrines throughout the world. There was another hole across from the niche his armor had carved. This hole, however, was a good seven phineals above the ground; even part of the ceiling was demolished. Battle sounds echoed into the room from that hole. That must have been where he was thrown. He could leap back through it, or...

"Laeyit and Bratan can push the line," he mused, then quickly uttered the incantation to re-summon his Ko'delish blade. It formed from mist, seething from his gauntleted hand.

⬥◦⬥

"What do we do, Cor?" Aron asked. He looked eager to fight, but the elves hadn't been hostile with them. In fact, this was probably the most pleasant kidnapping Cornar had ever experienced. Granted, he didn't make a habit of allowing such things to occur. The elves were not as evil as Krindal had implied. That gave him pause.

Cornar relaxed. The elves were focused on the two remaining Mindolarnians. Solidin had since recovered from Kaescis's debilitating grapple and joined the battle against Laeyit. The prince, however, had been thrown into the wall behind Cornar and the others. Kaescis hadn't returned to the battle.

A clattering charge resounded from across the cavern. Cornar's men, led by Nordal, ran from the tunnel and across the bridge. Crimson Praetorians were mingled among their ranks. Once they were all on the bridge, Mindolarn soldiers poured through the cave.

This courtyard will become a bloodbath, he thought.

"Vargos, the men," Cornar said, pointing to Nordal and the others, but barsion already surrounded them. They must have been enhanced by the

Mindolarn mages.

"Are we going to attack, Cor?" Igan asked.

He didn't know if they should. This was obviously a heated feud between the Sapphire Guard and the Mindolarn Empire. Yes, they were Mindolarn's allies, but something nagged at him not to get directly involved. Then there was that warning from Solidin about the prince.

"I'm perfectly fine sitting out," Vargos said.

"We should get inside the temple," Kalder suggested. "This courtyard will be overrun shortly."

That was a sound suggestion. The conjured magma elemental had already taken up a lot of space. It stood fifteen phineals tall and had a stocky build, as most of those creatures did. They were humanoid in appearance, but they lacked a lot of human-like features. They didn't have noses, eyes, or ears. Cornar always wondered how they could sense things—but that didn't matter, as the conjurer was in complete control of their actions.

"Pull back," Cornar said, "to the central chamber." Gregan and Vargos were the first inside the temple, followed by Kalder and Aron. Igan, however, remained with Cornar.

"What are you doing, Cor?" the wizard asked.

Nordal and the others reached the barricade. The Crimson Praetorians, however, dashed along the bridge's rails. How dangerous… They leapt unnaturally in the air, vaulting over the barricades and into the fray. Nordal's head peeked above the barricade and he climbed over it.

Several more members of the Sapphire Guard burst into the courtyard. One of them uttered an incantation, mustering pale-gray magic; it looked like a telekinetic spell.

Not at Nordal, Cornar sucked in a deep breath. *Not at my men.* If that magic struck any of his men he'd attack that elf. He would deluge this courtyard in blood.

Cornar dashed to the elf, but the elven mage finished his spell. A cloud of trailing gray shot across the courtyard, zipping around the members of the Sapphire Guard.

Settling into a wide stance beside the elf, Cornar watched as the telekinetic magic went straight for Laeyit. The woman dodged Solidin's rapid strikes— that elf was incredibly fast—and she tumbled out of the magic's way.

The gray cloud circled about and struck Laeyit in the back. She screamed in shock as she was pushed diagonally through the air, toward the chasm. Laeyit yelled what Cornar thought to be an incantation, but he saw no magic manifest. The telekinetic magic redirected her, and she went straight through the opening and was hurled into the pit.

By Heleron's Fin, he gasped. He didn't care much for the woman, but he didn't wish her dead. She was an ally… well, a fellow member of the expedition. He didn't think of that as strictly an alliance. That would imply a certain level of trust. Unfortunately for Laeyit, she would never have the chance to earn it.

She was gone…

The same Sapphire Guard mage began casting another telekinetic spell.

Do I dare attack? Cornar wondered. The other elves didn't seem to pay attention, or care, that Cornar and his men were in their territory.

Light shone near the bridge, magic mustered by the young mages of Cornar's band. An orb of lime-green acid hovered above Clodin. A freezing mist gathered above Tinal, forming an icy shard. Several swarming orbs formed above Renal, becoming a dozen arcane bolts.

⎯⎯•◦•⎯⎯

"You're next, Ordreth," Midar said. He was crouched beside the barricade on the bridge; it looked like metal fused with stone.

Transmutative magic, huh? Ordreth thought.

Shen and Cordel were beside Midar, shoving their magically imbued blades into the metal. They needed to cut down the wall.

Ordreth climbed atop Midar and was pushed upward to the top of the barricade. The battle was intense. The Praetorians and the elves were wildly going at it, totally unrestrained.

Nordal clashed with one of the elves battling a Praetorian. The elf parried his blow, eyeing him up and down. After one look the elf said something to Nordal and returned his focus to the Praetorian. Nordal didn't seem to react, though. He just kept on attacking. How typical of Nordal.

Ordreth dropped to the floor of this strange courtyard, seeing his uncle and Igan standing at the far end by some massive doors. *Uncle Cor was still alive!* What a wonderful relief it was to see his uncle alive and well. Well, as well as he could be in this situation. Why was Uncle Cor just standing there?

Markin and Demsal dropped beside Ordreth, dashing into the fray. They were eager for a battle, as were all the others. The entire band was ready to save Uncle Cor from his captors.

Ordreth moved to engage the elves, but a shower of arcane bolts rained down upon his opponents. The magic struck the elves' barsion in a violent explosion. Their barsion flickered but didn't dissipate.

Should be another wave, Ordreth thought, edging toward the elves. They, however, ignored him and focused on the Crimson Praetorians.

Why? Did they not see him and his comrades as a threat?

⎯⎯•◦•⎯⎯

Solidin rapidly struck the Crimson Praetorian dueling him, evading arcane bolts as they plummeted. His daggers pierced the man's barsion—was this Praetorian a man? One could never tell with these Mindolarnians. Solidin executed a beautiful flurry of strikes, precisely hitting the Praetorian in the same spot. The blows cracked his armor. The Praetorian staggered backward.

Perfect! Solidin backed up, grinning.

The Praetorian cocked his helmet and spun. Solidin watched as Religas's conjuration scooped up the man, tossing him across the courtyard. The Praetorian sailed over the barricades and into the pit. *Poor fool.*

Spinning around, Solidin surveyed the rest of the battle. Cornar's men had joined with the Mindolarnians in the assault. Solidin's soldiers were doing the best to evade the Sorothians. They weren't their enemies, although necromancers were among them. What a despicable corruption of the magical arts…

That acidic orb—cast by one of Cornar's necromancers—flew from the ledge, flying straight for Solidin.

Too slow, Solidin grumbled and dashed toward the bridge. He slid, using the barricades as a shield against the coming acid. Solidin spun back onto his feet, nearly colliding with another member of the Sapphire Guard. He watched the magic erupt in a splash against both elf and Mindolarnian alike.

A whistle echoed throughout the cavern, and then an icy shard flew above Solidin and the clashing armies. The freezing magic struck the conjuration in the chest, causing steam to fill the air.

Good shot, Solidin thought, dashing to another Praetorian. Magic shot from near the doors of the temple, raining down on those on the ledge and the bridge.

Solidin unleashed a flurry of blows and evaded a swing from the Praetorian's fanisar. The Praetorian soon fell wounded, blood dripping from a gash in his ribcage.

A crash resounded from the bridge. The barricade had fallen. Cornar's men flooded into the courtyard. More Mindolarn soldiers were behind them.

Have to finish this one, Solidin thought, kicking away his foe's weapon. He jammed his dagger into the wound, twisting the blade. Solidin forced the Praetorian into submission, using his legs to wrestle him to the ground. One of his foe's arms was pinned against the floor and another tucked against his chest. Solidin violently stabbed the Praetorian's neck, breaking his barsion. Three more jabs and the dagger rammed through the armor, piercing the man's jugular.

Blood spewed from the wound, painting the barsion red in front of Solidin's face. Swiftly removing his blades, Solidin rolled off the dying Praetorian, blood pooling beneath him.

As Solidin stood he heard a shout in Elvish, "The last group is away!"

Solidin turned to the temple's doors, then back to the bridge. They'd be overrun shortly. Only twenty-seven members of the Sapphire Guard were alive, including the six mages. The mages had already fled upon hearing the report.

"All retreat!" Solidin shouted in Elvish. He dashed to the temple's entrance, passing Cornar and Igan. They were just standing there. *You couldn't decide, could you, Cornar?* Solidin thought, darting into the foyer. Perhaps there was hope for the man.

Solidin made his way to the northern side of the temple, running to his left. He glimpsed a wall of barsion barring the other hall which led to the area where the half-breed prince was thrown.

That should buy us enough time, Solidin thought. He ran through the halls and entered the temple's central chamber. The other Sorothians were standing there.

"Aren't you coming with us?" Solidin demanded as he bolted toward the corridor leading to the transportium chamber.

"You're joking, right?" Gregan said hostilely. That man was fiery. But he was a redhead, after all.

Kalder raised an eyebrow at him, and the other two just stared.

That was obviously a *no*.

"Suit yourselves," Solidin said and dashed into the hall, passing Gahebrial, one of the Sapphire Guard's barsionists.

"Twenty-one," Solidin shouted to the elf.

Gahebrial nodded and began casting an incantation, mustering blue light.

⸻◆⸻

The magma elemental squatted in front of the temple's entrance as elves retreated through the doors. It didn't regard Cornar or Igan. They might as well have been statues.

More soldiers flooded into the courtyard behind Cornar's men. There was barely enough room for them to stand. Shouted commands resounded from the bridge, coming from what sounded like Grand Marshal Hezidex. The soldiers fell into formation, with Crimson Praetorians in front.

One of the Praetorians stepped ahead, wielding a wicked-looking fanisar. *That looks like Bratan's weapon,* Cornar thought.

The grand marshal shouted another command, calling for the mages to attack.

"We need to move, Cor!" Igan exclaimed, dashing to the Mindolarn soldiers.

The wizard was right. Cornar followed Igan as a variety of destructive magics shot from the ledge leading to the cave.

A disintegrating beam struck the magma elemental's chest, followed by icy shards and arcane orbs. More spells shot across the cavern and struck the conjuration. It stepped back, crouching in front of the doors. The mage in control of the magma creature was probably trying to block their entrance. Brilliant strategy.

Bratan rushed forward, swinging his fanisar. Was he trying to bait the magma elemental away from the door? Bratan came within weapon's reach and struck a blow against the creature's knee.

The conjuration didn't move. Bratan had probably hoped it would swat at him, giving the mages a chance to blow off its arm.

More magic struck the conjuration, and it cracked. Soon, it fell in pieces, crumbling in front of the door.

Hezidex shouted an order for the debris to be cleared and soldiers flooded around Cornar and Igan.

Amid the clanking of armor in the courtyard, Cornar heard his name. He spun, seeing Nordal and Midar weaving around the soldiers advancing on the temple.

"You're alive!" Midar exclaimed. He was the first to reach Cornar and embraced him in a tight hug. Nordal smirked and shook his head. Soon, the rest of Cornar's band was gathered. They gave their heartfelt welcomes, expressing their relief at his safety.

Ordreth was in the rear, just staring at him. Cornar smiled at his nephew and a tear trickled down Ordreth's cheek. Ordreth pushed through the others and ran toward him, nearly tackling Cornar with a hug.

"You're all right!" Ordreth exclaimed through tears of joy. He pulled back and looked at Cornar, studying his face. "I… I…" His face contorted in sorrow and he glanced away.

Oh, Ordreth, Cornar thought, patting his nephew on the shoulder.

"It's clear!" Bratan shouted and yelled a battle cry. Cornar glimpsed him charging into the temple.

"We should go!" Nordal shouted.

"No!" Cornar barked. "Let them handle this."

Nordal looked confused. He reluctantly lowered his sword, a frown forming upon his face. Nordal was itching for more fighting, but Cornar didn't want his men tangled up in this feud with the Sapphire Guard.

⎯⎯⎯◗•◖⎯⎯⎯

Solidin dashed into the corridor leading to the transportium, several mages stood ready, including Gladis. He passed the mages but slowed upon nearing his friend.

"I have checked the surrounding area and there are no rooms on either side of this hall," Gladis said in Elvish, gesturing to his left and right. "I will make barricades to slow their pursuit."

Solidin nodded. It was a good plan. "There should be twenty-one behind me," he said, "and our barsionists."

"I thought you took forty with you?" Gladis asked warily.

"That prince has a new blade," Solidin said. "It can cut straight through barsion like it was not even there."

"Disturbing…"

Several seconds later, Kaldarin dashed into the corridor with several others. Where were the rest? Kaldarin must have sensed the unspoken question. "They are protecting Gahebrial," he said.

"Go," Solidin said, and gestured to the transportium chamber. The elves hurried past Solidin while he eagerly awaited the others' arrival.

Gladis began casting his transmutative spell; brown magic flowed from his hands and seeped into the wall. It liquefied the stone in four places along either side. Gladis slowed his incantation, slowly exhaling the sound of one of the words. This was a necessary technique to keep a spell from completely forming.

In the case of transmutative magic, the transformation caused by the spell would persist after the incantation was finished. But, in order to keep it in this liquefied state a mage would have to hold the spell mid-incantation. Otherwise, the matter would be turned to mush, and the spell would have to be recast.

Gladis's spell remained in this fluctuating state until the rest of the Sapphire Guard dashed into the hall.

Gladis created the first barricade, then one of the barsionists cast a spell behind it. They repeated this pattern three more times, and then retreated into the transportium chamber, with Solidin trailing behind them.

Solidin was the last to step onto the dais. It floated above the floor, surrounded by barsion magic. Six of his mages knelt around the dais, hands nearly touching it. White-gray magic persisted around their hands and spilled over the sides—telekinetic magic. They were humming a part of their incantation, as Gladis had done.

The mechanics of this telekinetic spell was similar to Gladis's transmutation. The kineticists were simply holding their magic in place. Telekinetic spells pushed an object one way or another. In this case, three of the mages were pushing down, and the others were pushing up, thus creating the hovering effect. The spell they were using was a multi-directional one, at least ten directions.

All the elves gathered at the center, except for those levitating the dais.

The elves maintaining the telekinetic spells resumed their incantations, and the dais steadily climbed into the air. It was slow at first, but increased in speed as it rose.

Thirteen, Solidin thought in despair, *thirteen of you. I will ensure your deaths were not in vain.* He took in a deep breath, staring at the circular walls of the chamber. Detailed stonework flashed before his eyes. They were climbing quickly now. It would be only a matter of seconds before they reached the surface.

39

A SCHOLAR'S CLAIM

"Only one of the Three shall remain. He will deal justly with his adversary."

- Prophecy of Soron Thahan

Kaescis stalked through the halls of the Keepers' Temple. It was empty. *Where were those accursed elves?* Surely the Swift-Dagger had brought his entire company with him. At least two hundred of those vile elves were in their last encounter.

He turned a corner and was met by a wall of barsion. Angered, Kaescis sliced his blade through the magic; it broke like glass.

"This must be the right way," he said beneath his breath. Several more barsion barriers blocked his path, but Kaescis destroyed them as easily as the first. Soon, he entered a round chamber that rose seven stories.

"Prince Kaescis!"

He knew that voice… one of the Sorothians, Kalder. Kaescis turned to see three of the Sorothian warriors with their barsionist. Anger boiled within him. Had he made the—no! *They're not my enemy.* Kaescis shook off the hostility.

Another wall of barsion blocked another hallway; there were seven connected to this chamber. A good number. Kaescis dashed straight for the barsion, slicing his sword through it. He heard the others chasing after him. Kaescis led them through the halls, breaking barrier after barrier of barsion magic. Did the Sapphire Guard deliberately want him to follow?

Soon, they came to a corridor blocked by a wall of rock. It looked raw, like the caverns outside the temple.

"Where to now?" Gregan asked.

"There's no other barsion," Aron remarked.

The Sorothians debated which way to go next. Kaescis heard them say that this didn't look like any other hall they had seen in the temple. That gave him an idea.

Kaescis shoved his Ko'delish blade into the rock, carving a circular opening. He slammed his fist into the rock and spread his gauntleted fingers, pulling the chunk he had cut from the rest of the wall. His armor afforded him greater strength, as did the enhancing spell he had cast upon himself before donning the suit.

The hewn rock fell to the ground and revealed more of the corridor, but it was barred by another earthen wall. *A transmutative spell?*

Kaescis cast a dispel. Off-white dispelling magic formed beyond his freehand and he slammed it into the stone. The rock turned to sand, spilling across the corridors.

"What kind of incantation was that?" the old mage demanded. "It was too short and choppy to be a *real* incantation… Do you know some kind of ancient magical tongue?"

Kaescis ignored him and continued to the next wall. He cast the same spell, turning the rock to sand. A barsion barrier was behind this one, and Kaescis sliced through it, shattering the magic. He destroyed two more barriers and found a doorway leading to a circular chamber.

Cautious, Kaescis stepped inside. He wondered if it was a trap, that perhaps—

Seven pillars caught his eye, each with transparent globes sitting atop them.

A transportium? Kaescis wondered, entering the chamber. A chest-high pedestal stood at the far end of the room. Yes, this was a transportium chamber. But where was the platform? He searched the ground, but was drawn to a noise coming from above, like something falling from the sky.

Kaescis looked up along the towering room. It rose hundreds, if not thousands, of phineals. Its ceiling looked like it was descending… No. *The platform!* It was falling toward him.

Kaescis leapt backwards, narrowly evading the massive stone platform as it crashed into the floor. The platform shattered, making a shallow crater on impact.

"By all that's magical!" the old mage shouted, stepping beside Kaescis. "You could have been crushed."

Idiot, Kaescis thought and pushed himself up. He dismissed his blade, and it turned to mist and evaporated.

Had the Sapphire Guard escaped through the transportium? They would have had to leave a mage behind to hurl the platform through the chamber. Granted, the mage could be up top.

Kaescis sauntered through the chamber, eyeing every detail. One of the globes was damaged. *Why damage a globe and the platform?* It didn't make any sense. He made his way to the pedestal. The words upon its angled top weren't glowing. That could mean a variety of things. Perhaps this transportium wasn't functioning like the others he had discovered. But then why flee to this room?

"Odd room," Aron remarked.

The other Sorothians picked their way through the transportium chamber, stepping over the broken platform.

That's it! Kaescis thought, watching the Sorothians gather atop the platform. *Accursed elves used it like a lift… clever bastards.*

"Where did they all go?" Kalder asked.

"I don't smell the after effects of a teleportation spell," Gregan said.

Kaescis ignored them and stalked to the transportium chamber's entrance.

"Your Imperial Highness?" Aron asked.

Kaescis stopped at the doorway. "The temple is ours. The Sapphire Guard has fled." That statement made his blood boil. He yearned for their deaths. His bloodlust smothered him. The Sorothians were asking something, but Kaescis couldn't hear them. The voices drowned them out, demanding death and destruction.

Taking a deep breath, Kaescis stalked back through the sand covering the corridor, attempting to quell the voices in his mind.

⟶•⟵

Solidin stood upon a mountain peak along the ruins of Klindil, looking down the long shaft belonging to the transportium chamber of the Keepers' Temple. It was a long drop, probably several hundred stories. The last couple hundred phineals of the shaft lacked any of the stonework present in the temple and looked like a roughly hewn hole.

"Do you suppose that hit *him?*" Kaldarin asked.

"I doubt it," Solidin said with a sigh and walked away from the hole. Gladis and the barsionist who had erected the barricades to the transportium chamber had told Solidin that their spells had been destroyed. Solidin figured it was that half-breed prince, so he ordered the kineticists to drop the dais.

Solidin shielded his eyes from the sun, climbing a short ridge where the other members of the Sapphire Guard were gathered. They wore their packs upon their backs, stuffed with provisions and tents.

"Solidin," said an elf approaching hastily. He was one of the scouts. "The terrain is steep. We spotted—"

"Transmute a path," Solidin interrupted, pushing past the scout. "Gladis!"

Gladis stepped around several elves, stopping in front of Solidin as he approached. "What is it?"

"Make a ramp down the mountain."

Gladis studied Solidin, then nodded to the scout. What was his problem?

"Uh, sir," the scout cleared his throat. "As I was about to say, there is a Wildmen village below us."

"So?" Solidin looked blankly at the scout. What did it matter if a bunch of primitives lived along the mountains?

"They have a sizeable number, about four thousand according to a rough count."

"Then we go down another side," Solidin said briskly.

"The village wraps around the entire mountain, sir," the scout said, sounding flustered.

That didn't bode well. Solidin sighed. The only way to get off this mountain was to cut through that village. They'd be facing odds of twenty to one.

Solidin didn't like those odds.

Kaldarin and some of the others began talking strategy. The scouts argued with them. The nearby mages, including Gladis, turned up their noses at the idea of invading the village. One of them said it was foolish.

It *was* foolish. *There has to be another way,* Solidin thought.

The debate continued and Solidin did his best to ignore it. Then it hit him. "I have it!" Solidin said, snapping his fingers. "Gather all of our illusionists, Kaldarin."

"But, sir, I—"

"What crazy scheme are you concocting now, Solidin?" Gladis asked.

Solidin smiled wryly. "Those Mindolarnians have Wildmen among them, do they not?" He let that sink in for a moment before continuing. "We simply become our enemy."

Kaldarin hurried off. He probably understood the plan just by those two sentences. Kaldarin returned shortly with a couple of the Sapphire Guard's illusionists.

"Make the troops look like the Mindolarnians," Solidin told the mages. "Be sure to make a few of those Crimson Praetorians." He turned to one of the illusionists and sternly asked, "Can you recall the details of the prince's armor?" The elf nodded. "Good, make me look like him. By nightfall we will be off this mountain without subjecting our forces to heavy casualties."

❦

Krindal approached the bridge leading to the Temple of Truth and Might. The chasm housing the temple was beautiful. It was ingenious that this place was built beneath the world.

He walked with the rest of the scholars from the Order of Histories. They had all stayed behind after the rest of the expedition charged after the prince. Kaescis had gone running off, ready to avenge the men he had lost in the Igeacean Sea. The prince was a brave man, facing all those elves…

Krindal hadn't dared venture forth to the temple until it was clear. Kaescis had sent a runner back to Krindal and the other scholars, informing them that the temple was theirs. Chatter reached his ears as Krindal neared the end of the bridge, but he couldn't tell who was speaking. Those barricades were obstructing the voices. He stepped into a courtyard with the dead strewn across it, Mindolarnian and elf alike. Now that Krindal was in the courtyard the voices were clearer.

"Well, we're glad you're safe," Nordal said.

Krindal turned to see Cornar surrounded by his men. *He's alive!* Krindal blinked several times in disbelief. The Sapphire Guard hadn't killed him. But they were so vicious, so violent. They had had no mercy for the men and women of Krindal's first party. If he hadn't escaped, they would have killed him too. *Such relentless butchers…*

Cornar turned toward Krindal, a scowl forming upon his face. The warrior pushed through the crowd, glaring furiously.

Oh no… Krindal groaned, side-stepping toward the temple. The other scholars were already partway to the temple's massive doors.

"Krindal," Cornar called, his tone firm.

Krindal sucked in a deep breath. Perhaps he should have told Cornar of the Sapphire Guard earlier. He felt a strong hand on his shoulder. Heart thumping in his chest, Krindal turned, facing the notorious warrior. "Cornar…" he said, forcing a smile, "it's good you're—"

"Save the pleasantries," Cornar growled, and Krindal shied away. "Tell me, why didn't you tell us about the Sapphire Guard?"

Krindal didn't know what to say… he couldn't tell Cornar the truth. That would be disastrous. "There was no good time," Krindal lied. Would that satisfy him?

Cornar sighed. "You endangered my life and the lives of my men," the warrior said.

"I'm sorry," Krindal spat the apology, spinning away from Cornar. "But you're all alive and unharmed, right?" He glanced over his shoulder. Krindal hadn't seen the other missing warriors or Vargos.

"Yes."

"Uh, good." Krindal hurried across the courtyard. He stepped around the remains of an adolescent-sized magma elemental while eyeing the temple's towering doors. The symbols of each of the Keeper Orders were on its surface, as well as a foreign one. The unfamiliar symbol had seven sharp points protruding from a ten-sided mark, all arrayed above three claws clutching a circle. He hadn't come across that symbol in any of the temples, or his research. Hopefully one of the scholars would sketch it.

Krindal hurried into the ten-sided foyer, some of the scholars were examining the statues.

"Krindal," Jahevial called, standing beside the left hallway. There was another corridor to the right. "Where do you think the tevisrals will be located?"

How should I know? Krindal wondered. It wasn't like he knew the layout of this place. It was already different from the other Keeper temples he visited across Kalda.

"I don't know, Jahevial," Krindal said with a shrug. "Why don't you take some of Cornar's men and start looking?" Jahevial raised a brow at the suggestion. "Now if you'll excuse me, I must find something," Krindal said, stepping past the scholar.

Krindal caught a glimpse of Jahevial scowling at him. Nordal had mentioned that Cornar had been following Jahevial when the earthquake hit. For some reason, Cornar didn't trust Jahevial.

Well, Cornar probably doesn't trust me either, he sighed.

Krindal stopped at a four-way intersection, but heard voices coming from the right. He walked down that branch, up a short flight of stairs and entered an enormous chamber. It was seven stories tall, and that same strange symbol was on the ceiling within a stained glass window.

That isn't a Keepers' symbol, is it? he wondered, gawking at the ceiling while crossing the room. He bumped into a soldier and quickly apologized, but returned his gaze to the unfamiliar symbol. *Why seven points? And what is the significance of the claw? Is that circle the world?*

More questions filled his mind, but Krindal shook them off, glancing to the other scholars in the room. His associates had set up portable desks throughout this big room. They were taking notes or sketching.

Krindal noted balconies all along the upper levels of the room. *Where is the attunement chamber?* he wondered. It had always been in the room opposite the entrance. Well, there was a hallway in that direction, and Krindal could see a flight of stairs at its end.

"Master Krindal!" Krindal turned, seeing Prince Kaescis striding toward him, helmet under one arm. He looked furious. "Yes, Your Imperial Highness?" Krindal asked.

"Have you seen Mister Dol'shir?"

"He's in the courtyard, Your Imperial Highness."

Prince Kaescis set his jaw, walking the way Krindal had come. Was the prince angry at Cornar? Well, that was his problem.

A sense of triumph swelled within Krindal. He was free to explore the temple. He could prove once and for all that his theories of Cultural Regression and the Lost World *were* true. Hopefully they'd find tevisrals capable of doing things beyond their wildest dreams.

———◆•◆———

"So they faked my death, huh?" Cornar sighed. Solidin had been so deceptive. *Heleron damn that elf!*

"The body looked just like you," Nordal said. "We thought we'd lost you. At least, until Kaescis arrived and used his magic to dissolve your shortsword. He was using Master Iltar's magic."

My short-sword? Cornar thought. One of Solidin's mages must have created a likeness of it after he let Solidin borrow the blade. The fact that it dissolved upon Kaescis mustering the Darkness magic was a testament that Cornar's weapons were not something one could duplicate. That made him wonder about what the projections had said concerning his weapons.

"Cor," Grensil said, drawing Cornar from his thoughts, "what's the plan now?"

Cornar hadn't considered their next course of action. He'd been so wrapped up in the battle that he hadn't thought of planning ahead. "We should search this place," Cornar said. "See if there are any tevisrals or other artifacts." After all, the Sapphire Guard hadn't stayed long enough to plunder the temple.

"Should we make camp?" Cordel asked.

"I don't know," he said. "We should check with Kaescis and the other leaders. If we do end up staying, find us a place away from the others. I'd like some peace and quiet for a change."

"We'll find a spot," Cordel said with a nod, heading toward the temple with Markin and Brendar.

"Mister Dol'shir!" That could only be Kaescis. Cornar turned to see the prince approaching, helmet under one arm.

"Yes, Your Imperial Highness?"

Kaescis narrowed his eyes at Cornar. He looked displeased. Well, so was Cornar. The prince could have mentioned Solidin. Why hadn't he?

"I want to know what happened," the prince demanded.

"What do you mean?" Cornar asked.

Kaescis sighed. "How did you encounter the Sapphire Guard? Why were you with them?"

Was this an interrogation?

"Why didn't you join the fight against those vile elves when we assaulted the courtyard? You were just standing there."

Had Kaescis just accused him of collusion with Solidin? That made Cornar's blood boil. Some of the men shifted uneasily. Nordal hovered his hand above his weapon's hilt.

"Solidin found me," Cornar said. "I didn't know who he was when we met." Kaescis scowled disapprovingly. He obviously didn't believe Cornar. "You think I wanted to help them?" Cornar asked preemptively.

"I don't know," Kaescis shrugged. "The Elven Aristocracy is wealthy. They could have promised you anything to aid them."

Who do you think I am? he wondered, biting his tongue.

"Did they promise you something?"

"No!"

"Cor isn't a traitor," Nordal said firmly. "He's the most honest man I know."

Kaescis glanced to Nordal. There seemed to be a fire in the prince's eyes, a seething bloodlust. It was a look that said he wanted to kill Nordal. Solidin's warning about Kaescis rang in Cornar's mind.

"Kaescis," Cornar said the prince's name harshly, hoping to draw his attention. The prince turned, glowering at Cornar. *It's the Darkness magic, isn't it?* He had seen this driving bloodlust before, when he and Iltar slaughtered those responsible for the demise of Iltar's parents.

"If I had known who he was, I wouldn't have brought him here."

"Brought them here?" The prince cocked his head in confusion.

"They lost their mapping tevisral," Cornar said. "Solidin used me to lead him and the Sapphire Guard to this temple."

Kaescis looked conflicted, pleased but angry.

Igan stepped close, putting a hand on Cornar's shoulder. "Solidin was clever. But if we had had all the information at our disposal, this wouldn't have happened."

Kaescis glared at Igan.

"You obviously knew about the Sapphire Guard," the wizard said accusingly. "If Cornar had been told about them, he probably would have led Solidin in circles. They would have never found the temple."

"Are you sure they don't have the tevisral anymore?" Kaescis asked.

"Yes," Cornar said.

Kaescis smiled sinisterly. "Then they'll have no way to locate Dalgilur…"

He knows about Dalgilur? Cornar thought. Well, of course he would. Kaescis seemed to know a lot more than he let on.

"What is Dalgilur?" Nordal asked. "Is there more to this quest than finding this temple?"

Kaescis didn't reply. He stepped back, nodding. The news about Solidin's tevisral seemed to placate him.

"Kaescis!" Bratan yelled from the temple's entrance. "Kaescis! I can't find Laeyit."

That's right, she was gone. Kaescis turned, raising his brow.

"No one has seen her since we assaulted the courtyard," Bratan said.

"She's dead," Cornar said, pointing to the missing barricade. "Thrown off over there."

Bratan's face flared with fury.

"One of the mages did it," Igan said. "He used a telekinetic spell to hurl her into the chasm."

"Laeyit!" Bratan called, dashing to the opening between the barricades. The prince, however, didn't seem to care. Was Kaescis that callous?

"Laeyit!" Bratan shouted into the chasm. "Laeyit!"

"Bratan, don't bother," Kaescis said, crossing the courtyard.

"But, Kaescis!"

The prince turned, staring coldly at Bratan. "She's fine."

How was she fine? No. No one could survive a fall from such a height. Besides, that hole probably stretched to the center of the world.

"I apologize for my behavior," Kaescis said to Cornar. "Now if you'll excuse me we have a temple to search."

◆━━━◗●◖━━━◆

Jahevial stuck his head into another room on the sixth floor of the Keepers' Temple. It was empty, like most others he had encountered. He had searched a few rooms containing books, all of a strange craftsmanship. They had shiny pages and looked like they had been bound yesterday. Other than that, there was nothing extraordinary about this place.

Where are the tevisrals? he wondered. The other scholars had broken up into teams and searched the seven levels of this place. No one had mentioned finding any weapons or tevisrals.

"I thought this place was a treasure trove," he grumbled, peeling away from the room.

Jahevial opened another door, finding a bedchamber. He slipped inside, careful to close the door behind him. Bookshelves lined a squared niche to his left, with a chair and nightstand. A bed and wardrobe of a sleek design were on the opposite side of the space.

Cautious, Jahevial tiptoed to the bookcase, then perused the spines. He didn't know what half the titles meant. There wasn't much else on the shelves, so he went to the bed. Jahevial rummaged through the blanket and sheets, but found nothing. There wasn't even a speck of dust upon the fabric. *How odd…* He opened the wardrobe, but it was empty. *Perhaps all the clothes had unraveled and turned to dust?* That seemed a likely explanation… but why would the bedding remain intact? Pouting, he checked under the bed and found nothing.

"This place is empty," Jahevial groaned. "What a waste…" Grandmaster Alacor would not be pleased. Unfortunately, this was another of Krindal's wild gosset chases.

Jahevial pulled up his robe and removed his communication tevisral. He swiped his forefinger across the gem, and it pulsed a pale-blue hue—signifying that he was able to send a message. He flipped the tevisral's receiving end to his lips and spoke.

"We've reached the temple, but there isn't anything here. Krindal's and Kaescis's speculations were correct, in that the Sapphire Guard beat us to the temple. But I haven't been able to find anything of significance here. I will send another message once I can confirm any discoveries made by the others." Jahevial twirled the tevisral and tapped the gemstone, sending his message. The light faded, and he tucked the tevisral back beneath his robes.

⸺⊃•⊂⸺

"Maybe it's up here," Krindal speculated aloud, climbing the stairs to the temple's seventh floor. He wound his way through several corridors. An opened door led to a room with thrones.

In there first, he thought.

Krindal entered the room, finding an unfamiliar man beside one of the thrones. He wore odd clothing. Maybe it was a Mindolarnian style unfamiliar to Krindal. "Find anything?" Krindal asked.

The man focused on Krindal. "To what are you referring?"

"Uh… Any tevisrals?" Krindal asked, chuckling.

"There are no tevisrals here," the man said flatly.

That struck Krindal as odd. "Okay… well, did you find anything else in here? Maybe some artifacts that prove my theories true?"

The man raised his brow at Krindal, then stared at the necklace. Krindal had placed it above his robe, in case he encountered anything that might require the gem to activate.

"Another potential…" the man said, humming thoughtfully.

"Huh?" Krindal stepped forward. He crossed the room, passing through its center. Light shone from a gemstone above the far throne, near where the man was standing.

Krindal stopped and gazed at the light. "Is this—"

A beam shot from the throne, striking Krindal in the chest. Everything went white, and he felt himself falling. Images of his life flashed before him, particularly his training in the magical arts.

"YOU DO NOT FIT AMONGST ANY OF THE ORDERS," a booming voice said. It sounded like three voices in one. Where was it coming from?

"YOU ARE AN ODDITY, A CORRUPTION."

"What?" Krindal demanded. He was no longer in that room with the thrones. He was in some white void.

"YOU ARE CLOSEST TO THE DEATHBRINGERS, BUT YOU CANNOT BE AL-LOWED TO JOIN THEIR RANKS."

Join their ranks? The Deathbringers? That was one of the Orders among the Keepers of Truth and Might...

"What are you talking about?" Krindal demanded, searching for the voice. But there was no one around.

"BEGONE," the voice said.

The light faded and Krindal found himself back in that room with the thrones, still on his back. Hadn't he gotten on his feet? Why was he still lying down? A sharp pain surged through his head, growing into a blaring head-ache.

"An oddity," the man said, sighing. Krindal glimpsed him still standing by the throne.

"An oddity," a woman said, coming from Krindal's left. It was hard for him to keep his eyes open, but he glimpsed her walking toward the man. And there was someone else... Who were these people? And where had they come from? He strained to see the third person and glimpsed pointed ears—

"Elf!" Krindal shouted with terror. He struggled to his feet, trying to es-cape, but fell. The headache was debilitating

"An oddity," another masculine voice said. It was probably that elf. "You are a corrupt mage."

"Perhaps he seeks to reform his ways," the woman said.

"Ha!" the supposed elf laughed.

The sensation of a thousand daggers pierced Krindal's head, and he screamed.

"He seeks truth," the man said. "To prove himself..." those words had a certain sadness to them.

"What's wrong, Dusel?" the woman asked.

Dusel? Krindal knew that name... it was associated with myth.

"He wishes to prove the world has fallen from grace," the man—named as Dusel—said in a solemn tone. "That men didn't always live in a dark age."

The pain began to subside. An image flashed in Krindal's mind of a small crescent-shaped island in the middle of the ocean. At the island's heart, tow-ering buildings reached to the sky. Each structure was majestic beyond meas-ure, similar but unique. They stood at the base of a mountain range that stretched across the island.

Dalgilur.

What was Dalgilur?

Another image flashed, and Krindal stood at the heart of those buildings, gazing at the mountainside. White statues stood all around him, guarding a path to a majestic structure carved out of the mountain, larger than anything he had ever seen.

Krindal blinked, and more pain shot through his head.

Those three people kept talking while Krindal recovered. He took a deep breath and rose to his feet. "Who are you?" he asked with a groan. The pain lingered, though it wasn't debilitating.

"We are the founders of the Keepers of Truth and Might," Dusel said.

"That's impossible," Krindal said. "You should all be dead!"

The elf shook his head and rolled his eyes.

"So, what do we do with him?" the woman pursed her lips, glancing to the man and elf. "To which Order does he belong?"

"He cannot belong to any Order," the elf retorted. "He is an oddity, a corruption."

"You always want to go to the extremes," the woman said, sighing. "Surely, he can fit somewhere."

"He must be cast out!" the elf shouted.

"He is one of us, now," Dusel said, drawing his lips to a line. "A Keeper of Truth and Might."

"I thought there were safeguards against this?" the elf asked. "How could the Orders miss him being a necromancer?"

"We weren't as careful as we thought," the woman said. She had brilliant lime-green eyes… how odd. Could she be an ancestor of the Mindolarnians? They all had strange eye color. Footsteps echoed from the hall and Krindal turned, seeing Prince Kaescis.

"What do we have here? the prince asked.

"I don't know, Your Imperial Highness…" Krindal said. The three strangers were glaring at the prince.

"Abomination!" the elf shouted.

"What is a lish qui'sha doing here?!" the woman demanded.

Upon hearing those words, Kaescis's eyes flared with surprise.

"You are not welcome in this temple," Dusel said sternly. "Depart!"

"You cannot banish me," Kaescis growled, steadying into a wide stance. He uttered an incantation, like the ones he had spoken when fighting the Sapphire Guard in the Igeacean Sea. Its words were sharp and rigid.

Black mist appeared around Kaescis's right hand, forming that gigantic black blade of his. It was like an oversized claymore, though it didn't seem to weigh anything.

"The Ko'delish!" the woman said with a gasp… "How, how can this be?"

Raising his blade in the air, Kaescis dashed across the room. Was he going to kill them?

"Your Imperial Highness, wait!" Krindal shouted, but it was too late.

Kaescis sliced diagonally across the elf.

The elf shattered… like glass. Was this some kind of illusion?

With the elf vanquished, Kaescis dashed toward Dusel. Dusel glared vehemently at the prince as the black dissolving blade crashed down upon him. Dusel shattered and disappeared just like the elf.

"Your kind will never triumph!" the woman scowled. "The—" She shattered as Kaescis sliced through her.

The prince dismissed his blade, and it puffed into mist.

"Why…?" Krindal asked, "why would you do such a thing?"

"They weren't alive, Krindal."

"Were they a manifestation of a tevisral?"

Kaescis chuckled. "Something like that. Have you found the attunement chamber?"

"I think this was it…" Krindal said hesitantly. He removed his mapping tevisral from his pack and handed it to the prince. Kaescis held it while Krindal removed the gem from his necklace. Krindal placed it upon the tevisral and it activated in an explosive manner.

The map spanned the space between Krindal and the prince. Kaescis's eyes frantically searched the seas.

"Where is it?" the prince demanded, his tone impatient. This was a side of Kaescis Krindal had never seen. Had entering this temple stripped the prince of all dignity?

Krindal's eyes fell upon a glowing white speck in the southern hemisphere. *Dalgilur…*

That speck of light called to him. He felt an urge, an insatiable pull. He *had* to go there. *No!* Krindal felt horrified, realizing where the island lay—in the treacherous waters known as the World's Frown. Dozens of islands formed the "frown" on the atlas of Kalda. Those islands lay between the Abodine Wasteland and the continent nicknamed the Forbidden Lands—though its rightful name was Meyitevar.

"I… I see… it," Krindal said fearfully.

"Where?" Kaescis demanded.

"There," Krindal said, pointing a trembling finger to the southeastern sea and the World's Frown.

The glowing speck denoting Dalgilur's location was in the center of the World's Frown, about the same latitude as Soroth. In fact, when looking at the map—which included the various temples—Dalgilur and the temple at Klindil were mirrored, if flipped along the equator and meridian.

"I don't see the marker…" Kaescis said, anger boiling. Why was the prince acting like this? He had been so peaceful before.

"Perhaps only I can see it," Krindal speculated, frightened.

Kaescis nodded, though he didn't look pleased. "Magnify it," the prince commanded.

Krindal obeyed, revealing an island on the map identical to what he had seen in vision.

"We need to go there," the prince said. "Your proof will be on that island."

"B-bu-but," Krindal said, stammering, "there's plenty of proof here!" His voice shook with trepidation. He feared venturing into the World's Frown. Those dreadful seas were rumored to swallow up any ship that dared sail their waters. But then that insatiable pull swelled within him.

No! Krindal fought the urge. He *had* to quell it and dissuade the prince.

"Take this room for instance," Krindal said. "This shows that our ancestors were capable of mimicking life by use of advanced tevisrals. Nothing in the known world can create something so lifelike. We need to stay and uncover all we can about—"

"We don't have that luxury," Kaescis said, walking to the door.

What did he mean? They had driven off the Sapphire Guard and laid their claim. The temple was theirs, as were its secrets.

"The Sapphire Guard will plunder the greater treasures on the Isle of the Ancient Ones," the prince added. "We must beat them there."

The Isle of the Ancient Ones? Krindal wondered. Surely, that wasn't the same place as Dalgilur… Not in the World's Frown.

A sudden pang of horror struck Krindal. The urge swelled within him as he considered the prince's words. The Isle of the Ancient Ones was an island of myth and legend, the supposed birthplace of humanity. No scholar accepted the Isle of the Ancient Ones as a real place. There was no validity to its existence. But if the Isle of the Ancient Ones *was* in the World's Frown that would explain the lack of evidence concerning it.

"Plunder the temple," Kaescis said, "but I don't think you'll find what you're looking for, Master Krindal."

"Death will have no hold upon him, for he shall rise from the grave."

- Prophecy of Soron Thahan

Cornar sat with some of his men inside the Keepers' Temple. He didn't want to be around the Mindolarnians, so he had sequestered himself in one of the many side rooms. This room was nothing spectacular. It had a bed and some bookshelves. Kalder said they had found other rooms like it. Those clusters of magic had said that Solidin could rest before making his trek; these rooms were probably guest quarters for the Ancient Keepers.

"It's not looking profitable." Midar sighed with disappointment and sat down beside Cornar. "Just a bunch of books. No tevisrals or artifacts."

"It's a shame," Gregan said through a mouthful of food. He sat against a wall with a bowl of beans in his hands. "I guess this *was* another of Krindal's wild gosset chases."

This temple wasn't the end goal, Cornar thought. It never was, if what Solidin claimed was true. Dalgilur's Isle was the real prize. Whatever was there was probably worth kingdoms. Solidin would get to it first, though. *Perhaps I should have agreed to join him.*

"What are you thinking, Cor?" Shen asked.

"That I made a mistake," Cornar answered frankly, gazing at the ceiling. One of the twenty symbols—which he deduced was for one of the Orders—adorned the center of the ceiling with a bunch of other symbols around it, creating a beautiful pattern.

"What do you mean, Uncle?" Ordreth asked.

Cornar squinted at the ceiling. How was he going to tell his men?

"Don't hold back, Cor," Midar said. "We can take it."

Cornar took in a deep breath before speaking. "Solidin offered me a chance to side with him."

"The elf?!" Ordreth blurted.

"Is that why they avoided attacking us?" Nordal asked. "Every time I tried engaging them they backed off and focused on the Mindolarnians."

How much more should Cornar say to them? Dare he say that Kaescis was not what they thought he was? But what *was* he? Cornar didn't know…

The door to the chamber opened and Kalder entered with Igan.

"Cor," Igan said, "they want the things from this room." The wizard just stood there. He was waiting for Cornar to respond. Igan had undoubtedly figured that this venture wasn't going to be as profitable as they first thought.

"We said that we'd fetch them," Kalder said.

Both warrior and wizard stepped inside and closed the door.

"What do you want us to hand over to them?" Igan asked.

"You choose," Cornar said, waving to the bookshelves. The tomes were the only things of value in the room. They probably weren't worth much, though. The tomes were odd. Their covers were strange and their pages were oddly glossy. Each looked *too* pristine.

Igan nodded and stepped across the room. He began reading the names on the spines. "*Science of Tevisral Manufacturing. The Art of Galvin Weapons.* Uh, I don't know what that says." He skipped past a few books, then continued reading. "*Words of Power. The City of Ithil. Strategies of the Thousand Years War—*"

"What?" Cornar asked, interrupting Igan.

"Does that one sound interesting, Cor?" Igan asked, pulling a dark-blue tome from the shelf. Its title was embossed with a glossy tint.

Thousand Years War… that's what Solidin had called the fabled Dragon Wars.

"Keep that one," Cornar said.

Igan handed *Strategies of the Thousand Years War* to Demsal, who put it into one of the party's sloglien sacks. The wizard kept reading but none of the other books stood out to Cornar. They had some strange titles. Some sounded like they could be fiction. Igan handed several books to Demsal, telling him to put them in the sack. Others he left on the shelves.

"We saw a few duplicates of these," Igan said, gesturing to the sack with the books. "The rest we'll hand over to the scholars. I'm sure Iltar will be interested in the one about making tevisrals." He grinned, looking to Cornar as if expecting a reply.

Iltar would *find that interesting.* Cornar raised an eyebrow. Why hadn't he thought of that when Igan read the title? Was he *that* bothered by both Krindal and Kaescis?

Someone snickered and Igan continued talking. "Perhaps I should snag two copies," the wizard said. "One for him, and one for me." He grabbed a few of the books on the shelves, and then headed to the door.

"We could use a hand," Kalder said, taking several books from the shelves.

Ordreth, Demsal, Shen, and Grensil each gathered a stack of books. But the shelves still had books on them.

Those still in the room with Cornar relaxed, and Gregan returned to his beans, shoveling more into his mouth. "And here I thought this was going to be more exciting," Gregan said between mouthfuls.

"You don't think discovering this temple is exciting?" Hem asked. He sounded dumbfounded.

"Umm, no," Gregan said, chewing his beans. "There's no way to profit off it. What am I supposed to do? Set up a booth in the courtyard and charge people to come tour it? I don't think tourists will make it past the purple imps."

Vargos laughed, shaking his head.

"I'm serious!" Gregan said, his mouth full.

"But you could sell your experience!" Hem exclaimed. "Write the tale, or tell it in taverns."

"You're suggesting I become a bard?" Gregan asked, not amused.

"Why not?" Hem asked innocently. Gregan shook his head and rolled his eyes.

They continued bantering but Cornar ignored them, closing his eyes. He was feeling tired. *Perhaps I can go back to that dreamland,* Cornar thought. He yearned to find out how Melthas's fate intertwined with the latest turn of events. *Take me back to Laelin Lake,* he pleaded.

Cornar lay down and got comfortable, using his pack as a pillow. He often did that while exploring the world. He tried to sleep, but couldn't. His men had come and gone, but their traffic didn't bother him. Cornar could fall asleep in such conditions.

Hours passed, but he couldn't sleep.

Cornar felt a kick against his boot. He immediately opened his eyes, finding Nordal standing nearby.

"I thought you were sleeping," Nordal said.

"I was trying to sleep…"

"Well, we're leaving," the warrior said. "Kaescis has called a meeting in that center room."

Cornar sighed and slung his pack over his shoulder. It held a couple of the books they had swiped from the shelves. He followed Nordal back to the temple's central chamber. The room was crowded, with men standing in the adjoining hallways. It wasn't big enough to fit everyone inside.

Nordal and Cornar stood at the back of one of the halls, behind the other warriors. Some of Cornar's men noticed him and invited him to stand at their head.

I probably should be up there, he thought, pushing his way into the central chamber.

Kaescis stood on the second-story balcony, beneath the area where the attunement chamber was located. Krindal was with the prince, as were the other Mindolarnian leaders. Two other men were with Kaescis, neither of whom Cornar recognized. Ordreth had told him about the Wildmen Kaescis had brought from the plains. Some had become human. Those two must have been them.

Who are you, really? Cornar focused on the prince. Perhaps when he was done dreaming of his father and his Elites, Cornar could enter the role of Kaescis's servant. He might learn something observing him in private.

"I hope everyone can hear me!" Kaescis shouted. "There is something that must be said about this quest. It has been quite an ordeal. Some of you have whispered rumors of finding tevisrals and artifacts. Unfortunately, those things are not here in Klindil." The prince paused.

"So he knew we weren't going to find anything the whole time," Igan groaned.

"I'm sorry, Master Igan," Tinal said, patting Igan on the shoulder.

"Not your fault, kid," Igan said. "I just don't like being deceived."

Cornar sympathized completely with the wizard. Krindal and the Mindolarnians had dug a trench of distrust between Cornar and his band. That trench felt like it was slowly widening into a chasm every passing moment.

"This place was only a stepping stone," Kaescis continued. "What we are truly after lies on an island that has been lost for centuries. But this temple holds its location. There we will find tevisrals of legend. Weapons more powerful than any of you can imagine."

Dalgilur, Cornar thought.

"Some of you know this place as the Isle of the Ancient Ones, the fabled birthplace of humanity."

A few of the men muttered in confusion. Kaescis relayed details about this hidden leg of the adventure, but Cornar didn't pay attention. Reaching Dalgilur was a race they were bound to lose. The Sapphire Guard had enough of a head start that they would most assuredly claim the island first.

"… Grand Marshal Galiur will stay behind to assist the Wildmen" —What was that? Cornar had missed everything Kaescis said before that announcement—"as well as a small contingent of our soldiers."

The prince went on to talk about the relationship between the Mindolarn Empire and the Wildmen of Klindala. It was a speech full of political rhetoric. The tribal leader they had encountered in the Fortress of Anigar—Gevistra—was accompanying them to Dalgilur. Several hundred Wildmen soldiers were also accompanying the expedition, offsetting the Mindolarnians staying on Klindala. Kaescis announced Gevistra's position as the future ambassador between his people and the Mindolarnians.

"Those not staying will proceed to the courtyard," the prince commanded.

Back in the temple's courtyard, Cornar stood beside the doors, waiting. He sighed, not looking forward to the trek through the tunnels. Reaching the surface would take longer this time with such a large group.

"They should just have us go ahead," Nordal complained.

"But we've got to move in formation," Midar said in a mocking tone. "We're part of an army."

It didn't take long for most everyone to gather. The courtyard was actually quite crowded, with no room to move. This was a bad spot for accommodating two hundred men, let alone the thousand who were to make the trek back to Kretin. Cornar couldn't tell how many were in the courtyard, but plenty of people were still inside the temple—Mindolarnian and Wildman alike.

Of those still inside, only about fifty Mindolarnians were to stay behind to secure the temple. The Wildmen not joining the army were staying to help, as the temple was technically in their territory.

After a while, the prince entered the courtyard, carrying a large blue sphere the size of a man's head. Was that rogulin? It had the same blue tint and golden flecks. Cornar had never seen a rogulin crystal so large or so refined.

Rogulin was a type of substance used to catalyze teleportation spells. In Cornar's most recent dream, Adrin would have needed rogulin in order to cast the teleportation spell to evacuate the horses. In fact, Adrin probably had two rogulin crystals; one to teleport to where they stored the horses and another to return to Melthas and the others.

In order for that type of portal transportation to work, conjurers would bind rogulin to themselves. Whoever used the conjurer's crystal would teleport back to the conjurer. It was the only known method of instantaneous travel… unless one possessed a conjuration anchor—a type of tevisral which bound rogulin. Cornar had only ever known of two such tevisrals. One was in Iltar's possession, and the other was held by old Amendal. However, Cornar had noticed one in the dream with his father—that black dome he glimpsed in the tunnel.

Kaescis pushed his way to the center of the courtyard. "We will all need to be touching in order for this to work," the prince said.

Commotion sounded throughout the courtyard as everyone gripped someone else.

That's why you weren't in a hurry, Cornar thought. Kaescis intended to teleport somewhere. *Back to the ships, perhaps?* No, there wasn't enough room on any of the vessels' decks.

"Make sure whoever you're touching is touching someone else that eventually touches me," Kaescis said. "If you don't have a connection to me, you won't be teleported. If you are left behind, there will be one more teleportation. And you will probably be disoriented. Be ready to remove any helmets or headgear."

Everyone took a moment to check if they were connected to the prince. Some people had to shuffle around, but after a short while everyone in the courtyard was connected.

Kaescis uttered an incantation, and golden light shone from his rogulin sphere. It grew into an aura that surrounded him, and then erupted in a wave, washing over everyone. Cornar couldn't see anything but golden light.

The light faded after a moment. Some of the men wobbled away from each other, disoriented by the teleportation. Many vomited; that was common with people who had never traveled by teleportation.

Cornar held his breath and walked away from the stench. He looked skyward, noting the time of day. Twilight was upon wherever they were. It was obviously night time, as the sun was setting in the east.

"It took you long enough!" Cornar knew that voice… it belonged to that woman. Laeyit.

The bizarre woman sat upon a large rock, chewing on a half-eaten piece of fruit. "I've been sitting here all day," Laeyit said, not amused.

How had she survived?

"Laeyit!" Bratan shouted, dashing to the woman. He barreled past soldiers recovering from the teleportation. Bratan scooped her up and spun her around, laughing. "They said you were dead!"

"Probably would have been if that chasm wasn't so deep," she said. "Now put me down, you big brute."

Cornar turned away from the reunion, searching for any clues to their whereabouts. A farmhouse was nearby... It looked like that place where they had stayed in Klarin. There was a forest nearby, and the sound of running water. *There was a stream by the farmhouse,* he remembered, looking to the south. Faint lights stood out among short buildings; a village.

There was no mistaking it. They *were* in Klarin.

Kaescis pushed his way through the soldiers recovering from the teleportation. The prince had since handed the rogulin sphere to someone else and was clutching a black disk.

It can't be... Cornar thought, bemused. The prince was holding a conjuration anchor.

"You see, I told you she was fine," Kaescis said to Bratan. The prince sounded jovial. The three of them bantered for a bit and Cornar listened until someone put a hand to his shoulder.

It was Vargos. "Whatcha staring at, boy?" he asked.

"He's got a conjuration anchor," Cornar whispered.

Vargos hummed and squinted at Kaescis. "Interesting..." The prince noticed them staring at him and cocked his head questioningly. "Whatcha got there?" Vargos called.

Subtle, Vargos... Cornar groaned inwardly.

"This?" Kaescis asked, holding up the conjuration anchor. It was a palm-sized disk with a shallow dome. "It's a tevisral. It essentially replaces a conjurer when using rogulin crystals. Handy device." He handed it to Laeyit, who slipped it into her tunic, probably placing it within a hidden pocket. "Why don't you move that off a bit, Laeyit," Kaescis said, gesturing to the vacant parts of the field. "We have another group coming."

Laeyit nodded and darted away from the army.

The last of the vomiting ceased, and then Kaescis addressed everyone. "We have just teleported back to the town of Klarin. Take a moment to ready yourselves, as we will be marching back to Kretin at once."

That'll take at least six hours, Cornar thought. He looked eastward, in the direction of Klindil. They would be a few days ahead of Solidin, if the Sapphire Guard were coming westward. But Kaescis said they hadn't spotted their vessel moored in Kretin or any of the nearby ports. They could have disguised it. Solidin had mages that could do that sort of thing. Or they could have moored along another part of the shore.

Grand Marshal Hezidex shouted a few commands, and the Mindolarn forces fell into formation. The Sorothian scholars busily gathered their things, their packs full of plunder from the temple. Several squads of soldiers began their march before the scholars were ready.

A burst of golden light erupted a short distance away. The rest of the army appeared, as well as many of the conscripted Wildmen. Wails and vomiting echoed across the field, undoubtedly coming from the isle's natives.

Amid the sounds of disoriented anguish, the scholars began their march.

Cornar gestured for his men to wait. He wanted to keep some distance between his band and the scholars. Once the scholars were out of earshot, Cornar motioned for his men to begin their march. As his band began to move, Cornar's eyes fell upon Jahevial. The secretive scholar walked to the side of his cohorts. Cornar had nearly forgotten about Jahevial and his secret plot with Alacor, what with all the commotion with Solidin.

I can't trust anyone here besides my men, Cornar thought. Though Cornar was a member of this expedition, he didn't feel part of it anymore. Cornar and his band were simply tagging along. That wouldn't be the case on Dalgilur. Whatever he found would be theirs. He wouldn't share any discoveries with Krindal or Kaescis.

Resolving upon this roguish attitude, Cornar led his men through Klarin. Soon, they'd be back in Kretin and aboard the *Promised Maiden*.

❖

Solidin ran at the head of the Sapphire Guard, swiftly winding through a colorful forest along the eastern coast of Klindala. Their ruse with the Wildmen had worked. The illusionist who made Solidin look like Kaescis had even crafted a replica of the prince's gigantic demonic sword.

The light of a campfire shone through the trees and Solidin called for a halt.. He cautiously stepped through the trees, entering a clearing.

Twenty or so elves sat around the fire, speaking in Elvish: the crew of the *Vigilance*. Captain Teviz noticed Solidin and stood with a salute.

"Ah, Solidin!" the captain said, cheerily approaching. He was slightly overweight, with neatly cut blond hair. Teviz was the son of High Lord Helius and would eventually inherit the position once his father passed. "It is good you have returned." Teviz counted the members of the Sapphire Guard. "Any casualties?" Teviz asked.

"Fourteen," Solidin said, and turned from the camp, walking to the shore. The captain trailed behind him. "We have no time to waste, Teviz."

Captain Teviz frowned. "What tevisrals did you find?"

"None," Solidin said dispassionately. *Damn merchants.*

"None?!" Teviz blurted. "The High Lords won't be pleased."

Of course they wouldn't.

"We recorded much about the temple," Solidin said. "I'm sure someone can compile it into a book worth selling."

"Surely you do not think a book will be of great value to the Aristocracy…"

Solidin shot a glance of annoyance at Teviz. "I'm sure we'll find what you're looking for on Dalgilur."

"Ah… so it does exist," the captain said, sounding pleased. They stopped at the rocky shore, and Teviz clapped his hands twice, then shouted, "Eka'sila asilum!"

The *Vigilance* appeared in the water, shedding its veil of invisibility. It was a grand ship, although it didn't appear to be much different from other trading vessels. The High Lords of the Aristocracy wanted to make it *look* humble. It had the appearance of a wooden vessel, though the hull was created from valistine, a material that neither rusted nor rotted.

Solidin climbed the gangway with the captain close behind him. "I need a map of Kalda," he said.

"I have charts on the bridge," Teviz said. "But why not use your tevisral?"

"Because it was destroyed," Solidin said. He knew he would get chided for allowing that to occur. Damn High Lords probably wanted to sell it. Teviz sighed, exasperated.

Solidin crossed the main deck, passing two of the four masts. He and the captain went to a doorway leading to the aft interior parts of the ship, where ladders led to the other decks.

The bridge was on the third deck above the main, completely enclosed. Windows lined the forward hull, allowing a view when the sails were furled. Solidin could see many of his soldiers filing aboard the *Vigilance.* Some dropped their gear near the forecastle while others filed below deck.

"Over here," Teviz said, moving to a table along the portside bulkhead.

Solidin stepped up beside the captain, eyeing a map of Kalda. *Where are you? On the run back to the ship, Solidin could feel a yearning that pulled him southward. Solidin could see the Isle of Dalgilur in his mind. A vision had been burned into his soul.

Is this how the Ancient Keepers found their way? he wondered, remembering a passage from one of the books discovered by the Aristocracy. It claimed that a Keeper could always navigate back to their Order.

Solidin stared at the map, visualizing a three-dimensional version of it. In his mind, he soared across Kalda, searching for the island. He veered away from the Mainland, following that internal pull. *Not Acheylon,* he thought, shaking his head, referring to the smallest continent located near the center of the map. Dalgilur was farther south; he could feel it. The ocean sprawled in his mind's eye. Solidin passed island upon island, but they were not Dalgilur. Soon, he came upon an island partway between the icy continent of Abodal— known by men as the Abodine Wasteland—and the continent of Kresh'dal, a forbidden land.

The yearning subsided as Solidin visualized the island. This *was* Dalgilur.

"There…" Solidin pointed to the ocean between the two continents. It was one of the few uncharted parts of Kalda's vast oceans.

Teviz gasped. "But that is the Anomalous Corridor!"

"Solidin," Gladis called, his footsteps echoing across the bridge.

"It's there," Solidin said in Common, tapping the map. "Prepare the ship. We leave at once."

Solidin stepped away from the map and turned to Gladis, who stood with his arms folded and a stern look across his sharp face.

"Have you so soon forgotten?" Solidin asked, grinning. Gladis shrugged.

"This is madness, Solidin!" Teviz shouted. "An endless storm assails those waters. We will not survive such a voyage."

Solidin turned from his friend, gazing at the captain. "When I was called to be a Bladesinger, I saw Dalgilur. Its location was imbedded within my mind. I can see it!"

Teviz was stunned. Gladis stepped forward, eying both of them thoughtfully.

"We don't need the tevisral anymore, because now *I* am the tevisral." Teviz laughed at Solidin's declaration. "You think me mad," Solidin declared stoically, "but I will prove we can reach Dalgilur."

VABENACK

"He shall be broken, but shall find an undaunted resolve that drives him to his purpose."

- Prophecy of Soron Thahan

Accessing Vabenack had not been as easy as Iltar assumed. His attempts were fruitless, despite using all the techniques found in *Dreamwalker*. He even resorted to subjecting himself to the hypnosis method, but not even that worked. Alanya had only found a limited supply of ingredients, so Iltar could only use the elixir on the second night.

Not even that worked. Iltar did, however, find himself in a lucid state. That wasn't a problem to achieve. The doorway, on the other hand, proved more difficult. One couldn't manifest any old doorway. It had to be specific. There was an illustration within *Dreamwalker* that gave detailed information about the doorway's specifications. It was supposed to be round, with seven keystones. Sharp-looking symbols were to be engraved on the keystones in a specific order. The author of *Dreamwalker* said they were the characters in their god's divine tongue that spelled Vabenack.

Iltar awoke with frustration, throwing aside his sheets. Luckily, his outburst hadn't wakened Alanya. The room smelled of calming incense. Alanya claimed it helped her experience pleasant dreams, and so she assumed it might help her achieve a lucid state. Iltar just found it smelly.

He hurriedly put on his clothes and sought out Elsia. The countess had been trying the last three nights to access Vabenack, and so had the acolytes. None of them had succeeded. Iltar found Elsia in the guesthouse's solarium, eating breakfast with Pagus.

"Good morning," Elsia said before eating a spoonful of sweet porridge. Her bowl was filled with oats and sliced fruit dipped in a caramel glaze. "Were you successful?" she asked between bites.

"No." Iltar sat in one of the chairs.

"What a pity," Pagus said, and took a bite of a pastry, and then continued with a full mouth. "We didn't either."

"Pagus!" Elsia chided the boy. "Where are your manners?"

Pagus raised an eyebrow at his aunt. "I'm not in public. Besides, Master Iltar does it all the time."

Iltar grunted. Sure, sometimes Iltar would talk while his mouth was full, but only when discussing something important that he didn't want slipping from his mind. Besides, Iltar only did that when around his closest friends.

"Well, it's a bad habit," Elsia said primly. She glared at Iltar with displeasure but soon returned to her food.

A servant entered the solarium and asked Iltar if he wanted anything to eat. He discovered that he was hungry. He pointed to Pagus's half-eaten plate. "Eggs and a couple of those pastries."

"Alanya wants to try another market today," Elsia said, resting her spoon in her bowl. "And she might know someone who can help with the elixir. I think we did something wrong with mixing it." Iltar nodded. "The boys finished with the library last night," Elsia continued. "We found nothing else related to the Chosen or the other things."

"That's fine," Iltar said. "They can continue at the Hilinard. Pagus, see that they resume their research today."

"Aww," Pagus said with a full mouth. Elsia shot him a sharp scolding glare. Pagus met her gaze, swallowed, then continued complaining. "And here I was hoping I'd get to go with you to the market."

Iltar gave the boy a hard look, and Pagus sighed.

"Another time," Elsia said, patting her nephew on the shoulder. "Was Alanya awake?" she asked Iltar.

"No."

"Okay," Elsia said, rising from the table. "I'll get ready to leave, then have Hazais fetch her. Will you be ready to leave after you eat?"

"Yes."

❖

The streets of Gilganar's market were crowded. But that didn't matter, as Alanya's guards cleared enough room for Iltar and the women to walk freely. Not long after arriving at the market they entered the herbalist's shop—a one-story building that lacked any windows. A bell rigged to the door rang as Alanya's guards entered.

"Be with ya in a moment!" a raspy voice called from the back of the shop.

Was that a man or a woman? Iltar wondered. He fell in beside the guards and shivered at the sudden change in temperature. How was this shop colder than the market?

Shelves full of bottles lined the walls. Tables occupied most of the floor with groupings of jars and bottles atop them. Iltar wandered through the shop as the women entered. He ignored their chatter and perused the shelves. There were herbs here that he had never seen. The herbs were all organized by their uses and purposes.

A small section titled "Regrowth" caught Iltar's eye. It had only a few bottles, one of which was labeled Taegish Leaf.

That sounds Elvish, he thought, grabbing the bottle. Iltar was familiar with the language, though he wasn't fluent. He was more proficient at reading Elven texts than holding a conversation in Elvish. Iltar expected to find something else on the bottle, but there were no other markings on it.

"Put that down!" the raspy voice shouted. Was that aimed at him?

A short person—Iltar couldn't tell if they were male or female—hobbled toward him. This was obviously the herbalist.

"That is *very* expensive!" the herbalist snapped, stepping up to Iltar. The he-she took the bottle right out of his hands and cradled it like a baby.

Odd person…

The herbalist muttered complaints and put the bottle back on the shelf. "Don't touch anything!"

Iltar stepped back and rolled his eyes. He wasn't some clumsy child. The herbalist hobbled away, attention focused on the guards. He-she assumed that whoever was with them was obviously more important than Iltar. "What can I help you with?" the herbalist asked. That raspy voice was annoying.

"I'm looking for these ingredients," Alanya said, stepping forward and holding out a sheet of paper with the herbs required to make the dream elixir, as Iltar had come to call it.

"How much do ya want?" the herbalist asked, swiping the paper from the high duchess and humming as he-she read it.

"As much as you have," Alanya said.

The herbalist snorted. "Why do you want all this stuff?" the herbalist asked. "Havin' trouble sleeping, are ya?"

Alanya didn't know what to say. She sucked in her breath and looked to Iltar.

The herbalist glanced back to Iltar, grimacing at him. "Maybe it isn't as innocent as that… planning to drug people?"

"I take it you know what those things combined will do?" Iltar asked.

"Of course I do!" the herbalist said, snorting. "Were you expecting an idiot?"

"No," Iltar said defiantly.

"Then what are ya doing with it?" the herbalist demanded, hobbling over to Iltar. The herbalist didn't stand very tall, but he-she looked fierce.

"That's our business," Iltar said.

"Your business?" the herbalist shook his-her head. "Well, it's *my* business to see these things aren't used improperly!"

"Will you sell to us or not?" Elsia demanded.

The herbalist spun around. "Only if you tell me what ya intend to do with it! There will be no drugging of any kind coming from my shop! No nefarious acts will be traced back to me!" He-she shot a glance back to Iltar, but settled a probing gaze on the women.

What's this person's problem? Iltar wondered.

"As he said"—Elsia gestured to Iltar—"it is our business. But I can promise you that what we are doing is in the pursuit of scholarship. Nothing nefarious will come of our activity." She sounded cordial, perhaps *too* cordial.

The herbalist grumbled in disbelief. "If you can't tell me what you're up to, it must be nefarious!" he-she retorted and spun around, facing Iltar.

What an insolent little git… He fought back a scowl as the herbalist glared at him. His-her dull blue eyes were fierce. Iltar exchanged a short stare-down with the herbalist, and then the herbalist's eyes changed… *What on Kalda?* The irises were *swirling* around his-her pupils.

Iltar started and went to step back but *froze*. He couldn't move. It was like he was under an enthralling spell… But he hadn't felt any magic penetrate him. What was happening? All he could do was stare at the odd herbalist.

Vivid images flashed within Iltar's mind, like a waking vision. Iltar relived the research he had done at the Hilinard. Every bit of information flooded back to him in an instant. The scene suddenly changed, and he was reading on the lawn of Alanya's mansion. Every page of *Dreamwalker* flashed before him. Iltar saw what he had been doing wrong; he missed a sliver of detail about awakening the mind. He needed a specific object to manifest in his dream before becoming lucid—

The odd vision abruptly ended. Was this something sent by Reflection?

Iltar blinked. The herbalist glared at him with fiery indignation. It was as if the herbalist were his most bitter enemy. A scowl formed upon his-her face and the herbalist spun around, grabbing a bottle.

"Get out!" the herbalist shouted, throwing the bottle at Iltar.

What fury…

Iltar threw himself sideways, barely dodging the bottle; it shattered against the bookshelf behind him, and Iltar felt shards of the glass bounce off his skin.

"Get out now!" the herbalist shouted, grabbing two more bottles. He-she yelled like a growling beast.

Iltar instinctively stretched out a hand—*No,* he stopped himself from mustering his most deadly magic, the same that he had used to kill Rovin. *Not here… Too many witnesses.*

The herbalist continued hurling bottles, and Iltar barely had time to shield his face with his outstretched hand. The bottles exploded against his forearm. Shards of glass flew in every direction. Some caught in his hair, another scraped his cheek.

"I said get out!" the herbalist yelled.

Iltar glimpsed him-her spinning to the guards and the women while grabbing two more bottles. He crunched on glass as he got up, watching as the herbalist hurled the bottles across the shop. Alanya and Elsia ran for the door. They made it outside just as the bottles shattered against the guards' armor.

What kind of madness was this?

The herbalist grabbed two more bottles as the guards hurried to the door. They were out before Iltar could reach them.

"Never come back!" the herbalist shouted with his-her raspy voice as Iltar dashed into the street.

The women had disappeared into the crowd, and the guards chased after them. Iltar turned to see the herbalist at the door, glaring at him one last time before slamming it shut. He stood in the street, bewildered. What had caused the herbalist to become so adversarial?

Iltar heard his named carrying above the hustle and bustle of the market, shouted by Alanya and Elsia. They were standing beside a lavish carriage bearing the symbol of the Mindolarn Empire; the seven-headed hydra. They were talking to someone inside the carriage.

"… woman just went ballistic," Alanya said, talking into the carriage. "She just started chucking things at us."

"I thought it was an old man," said one of Alanya's guards.

"Definitely a woman," Elsia said, nodding.

Iltar wasn't so sure of that assumption… But who were they talking to?

"I'll have someone look into it," a woman's voice said from within the carriage.

"Thank you, Your Imperial Highness," Alanya said.

"Oh, please, Alanya. How many times have I told you to drop the formalities? We're friends."

"It's a habit," Alanya said, then gestured to Iltar. "I want to introduce you to someone, my friend's bodyguard."

Iltar stepped up to the carriage's window, seeing a regal-looking woman inside. She wore a blood-red gown that looked like it belonged to a princess. She looked tall—although she was sitting—and her figure was slender. Her long black hair was braided and hung partway down her chest. Vibrant green eyes settled upon him with a look of intrigue that soon turned to shocked surprise.

"This is Iltar, a powerful mage from Soroth," Alanya said, then gestured to the carriage. "And this is Her Highness, Princess Raedina Midivar, eighth in line to the Mindolarn throne."

Raedina's expression became fierce as she saw Iltar. What was with people looking at him hostilely today? It was as if they perceived him as some kind of monster.

Alanya started, noticing Raedina's hostility. She looked to Iltar, then back to the princess. "Is there something wrong, Raedina?" she asked warily.

The princess relaxed her gaze and sucked in a deep breath. Iltar had never seen this woman, so why would she react angrily at his presence?

"My apologies," Princess Raedina said, sounding like she was forcing a tone of cordiality. "I thought you were someone else…"

Thought I was someone else? Iltar wondered, raising an eyebrow. He stepped away from the carriage, contemplating the possibilities of the princess encountering someone that looked like him. *That attack on the Mindolarn Palace nine months ago… could it have been—*

"Iltar," Elsia said, pulling Iltar from his contemplation. "Why don't you and I check one of the other markets for the herbs? Alanya can go get the rogulin powder."

"Fine," he said, glancing back to the high duchess, who was still talking with the princess.

◆━━●◆●━━◆

It was late when Iltar finished brewing the elixir. The sun had already gone down in the east. He, Elsia, and Alanya's head chef had used the main kitchen in the mansion. The room reeked of the potent concoction. The heat used to boil the elixir had caused the rogulin powder to give off its putrid odor. That hadn't happened the first time they made the elixir. Iltar thought it might be because of the length of time between purchasing the crystal and grinding it into a powder. Earlier that day, Alanya had met with an acquaintance, and the man had made the powder shortly thereafter. Iltar didn't know how long the other powder had been lying around. Perhaps freshness would make a difference.

The chef portioned out goblets of elixir for Iltar, Elsia, Alanya, and Pagus.

"Why don't you get some more served for the other servants," Iltar said. "Hazais and a few of the guards." The chef started and looked to Elsia, seeking permission from her.

"Do as he says," she said, and shrugged. "I'm sure your mistress will be fine with it."

Wary, the chef grabbed some more goblets as Pagus and some of the acolytes entered, including Agen and Bilda.

"We're ready," Bilda said, putting his hands on his hips.

"I'm not letting you drink this," Iltar said, gesturing to the pot of elixir. "You're too young."

"And us?" Agen asked, gesturing to the other acolytes. Iltar raised his brow at the question. A stern gaze was his only answer.

"C'mon, Master Iltar," Kaelar said with a frown. "It's not like there's anything harmful in that drink."

"Yeah!" Bilda chimed. Several of the other boys agreed with him, pestering their master to grant them permission.

"It's too dangerous," Iltar said. "Perhaps after I can successfully access that realm. But I can't let one of you go tromping into that place without me there."

"You just want the discovery all to yourself, huh?" Tigan griped. Iltar shot the youth a perturbed glance. That wasn't the case. He was genuinely worried for the boys. If the information in *Dreamwalker* was true, then the boys could die in Vabenack. Iltar couldn't allow that.

Soft pitter-patter echoed into the kitchen and Alanya entered. She was wearing a silky robe that showed off her elegant figure. Iltar caught several of the boys gawking at her. He cleared his throat, jarring some, but Agen and Kaelar continued staring with lustful eyes.

"This stinks," Alanya said, walking to the counter where the goblets were waiting. She made a face and raised the goblet to her lips. "Did you do something different?" she asked.

"It's the rogulin," Elsia said. "Iltar said it smells like its aftereffects."

Alanya made a face as she drank the elixir. She stepped away from the counter, but moved back to steady herself. Alanya abruptly set the goblet down, bracing herself against the counter.

Hazais and one of the maids entered at that moment and noticed their mistress. "Your Excellency!" Hazais shouted, dashing across the kitchen.

"I'm fine…" Alanya said. "I-just-need-to-sit." She slurred the words and grabbed the goblet, taking another sip. Alanya made another face, looking like she was about to vomit.

Elsia looked at Iltar warily. Her gaze seemed to ask, "What did we do wrong?" Iltar wondered the same thing. They had followed the recipe exactly, so nothing should be different.

Alanya stumbled, splashing some of the elixir from the goblet. Hazais grabbed her, but she staggered past the boys, and then fell forward out of Hazais's grasp. Iltar went toward her, but he was too far away. The high duchess hit the floor face-first, spilling the goblet across the floor.

"Your Excellency!" Hazais and the maid screamed in unison.

Iltar was the first to reach Alanya, and he knelt beside her. He touched her neck and felt her pulse. It was slow and rhythmic. He glanced to the boys. "This is why I don't want you drinking it," he said sharply.

"Is she dead?" Bilda asked with a gasp.

"No," Iltar said as Hazais knelt across from him.

"Your Excellency!" the butler cried as he shook Alanya's shoulder. "Your Excellency."

"I think the elixir must have knocked her out," Elsia said. "The last apothecary we visited said her halisym was extremely potent."

"We must make her comfortable," Hazais said, pulling Alanya's arm over his shoulder. Iltar helped, and they lifted the limp woman to her feet. Alanya's head hung as they carried her through the kitchen and down a hall. Everyone followed.

They carried Alanya into a sitting room and gently sat her down on a long couch. The butler swung Alanya's legs up, propping them atop a pillow.

Soon, everyone was in the sitting room. Elsia came up beside Iltar, holding one of the goblets. Was she going to drink it despite seeing what it had done to Alanya?

"Did you pass out that quickly?" the countess asked, holding her goblet at eye level.

"No," Iltar said. "But I don't succumb quickly to things like that." He was the only one who had drunk the elixir the first time.

"I see…" Elsia sighed and moved to one of the chairs with an ottoman. She looked quiet and determined.

A tight grip pulled at Iltar's arm. Hazais stared at Iltar with a menacing gaze. "Did you know *it* would do this?"

Iltar glanced at the butler's grip. "No," he said coldly. Hazais scrunched his forehead, then a crash resounded beside them, and Iltar spun.

Elsia was unconscious in the chair. Her hand hung over the chair's arm, dangling above the shattered goblet.

"Aunt Elsia!" Pagus shouted, dashing to the unconscious countess.

"What have you done?" Hazais demanded, sounding furious.

Iltar ignored him and stalked back to the kitchen, with all his acolytes but Pagus in tow.

"This could kill them!" Hazais shouted after Iltar. "What kind of man do you think you are, endangering the ladies?"

Iltar simply raised his brow at the butler, and Hazais continued railing at him. He ignored the opinionated butler and found Petral—one of Alanya's guards—standing in the kitchen.

"This is the concoction, Master Iltar?" Petral asked.

"Yes, but sit down before you drink it," Iltar said.

The guard nodded and grabbed a goblet before exiting the kitchen. Petral had been selected due to his ability to recall the vivid details of his dreams. Alanya thought he would be a perfect test subject.

"I won't have any part of this!" Hazais shouted.

Iltar continued through the kitchen and glanced at the butler. "Your mistress ordered you to participate." He stopped at the goblets and grabbed two of them. Iltar rounded the corner, holding a goblet toward Hazais.

The butler, however, refused to take it. Iltar and Hazais exchanged fierce gazes until Pagus entered the kitchen.

"Uh… Master Iltar?" Pagus asked.

"Here." Iltar handed the goblet to his apprentice.

Pagus carefully held the goblet and strode out of the kitchen. He looked eager. Hazais spun, sighing in exasperation. The butler exited the kitchen, shouting for more of the servants to come help him carry Alanya to her bed. It seemed an indecency to him that she was sleeping on the couch.

Ignoring the butler, Iltar turned to his acolytes. "If we're not awake by midmorning, use enthralling spells to wake us." Then he hurried out of the kitchen and toward Alanya's bedchamber.

❖

Iltar was sound asleep within seconds of drinking the elixir. Greens and browns whirled around him, and he found himself wandering through a familiar forest. He *knew* those trees; they led to his family's homestead on Soroth.

Soon, Iltar stumbled into the clearing. Streaks of yellow and pink light whizzed around him, like arcane and acidic bolts. It was as if they were trying to hit him.

Must focus, Iltar told himself, struggling to move toward his grandparents' home. His muscles felt heavy.

To become lucid these past few times, he had imagined a man with a white tunic and used that anchor to take control of the dream. But that wouldn't do this time, not if he wanted to reach Vabenack. The author of *Dreamwalker* had missed a particular detail in his instructions that he had included in a prior part of the book: The object that draws one into lucidity must have the First

Emblem—a diagram in the Cherisium religion—somewhere upon its surface.

Strong winds blew against Iltar as he crawled toward his home. A boulder flew from the sky, crashing before him and obscuring his view.

"Damn it!" he shouted and fought against the wind. Why was there so much resistance? In none of his other dreams had it been this difficult to take control. Deep down, was he fearful of accessing Vabenack? Or was this a by-product of the elixir?

Iltar rounded the boulder, and the grass became spotted with red, accompanied by intense heat.

Magma.

Iltar swiftly picked his way across the grass, but almost fell into one of the pits from the wind. Magma bubbled and burst behind him. The winds raged. Another boulder crashed, followed by another, and another. Amid the chaos, Iltar hurried to the porch and stopped at the door.

There it is.

The First Emblem was carved into the door. It was a sword with a jagged fuller, pointing skyward. Six spikes curved below the pommel, arcing upward, with eight-sided stars resting at the tip of each spike.

The commotion ceased behind him and Iltar felt in control of the dream.

I need a clear space, he thought and opened the door. It led to a white landscape with a white sky. Once through the door, Iltar closed it, and it vanished. Only he remained in this place.

Focusing his mind, Iltar manifested a circular doorway, forming seven keystones out of polished galstra. It hovered in the air before him, as if held up by a spell. He quickly constructed the rest of the doorway, then spoke the incantation from *Dreamwalker,* "Alza Cho'k sa'maz nira."

Iltar felt no magic manifest upon speaking those words, and he supposed if they would open the doorway they were more like phrases to activate a tevisral. He had heard of magical objects that required words to activate them, but had never encountered any.

Yellow light surged from the keystones—that hadn't happened before. The light surged to the center of the doorway and expanded, erupting in a brilliant flash. Iltar shielded his eyes, but not quickly enough. The flash blinded him. Spots formed in his vision, but eventually faded.

"I've done it!" Iltar cheered. "Finally!"

The circular doorway he had formed was like a window looking into that strange yellow-sky realm. Triumphant, Iltar laughed with a twinge of hysteria and stepped through the doorway to Vabenack. His feet landed on sleek glass, and he expected to slide upon it, but there was traction. *How odd...*

"Amazing," Iltar muttered. Glassy ground spread as far as he could see, and the sky was devoid of the blood-red clouds. He looked down and saw a shifting landscape of a hillside beneath the glass. It was like standing in the sky and looking at the ground. The grass grew, became dormant, and then greened; all within a second. Buildings suddenly sprang up, then crumbled. The ground beneath kept cycling through these changes, which happened every few seconds. It was the oddest experience, like he was watching the world age and renew.

Dreamwalker claimed that one could see any part of Kalda's past here in Vabenack. One must only focus on the place where they wished to be and then guide that area to the proper time using words and thoughts.

Iltar walked a short distance, and then turned. He expected his portal from his dream to vanish, but it was still there.

"Alanya!" Iltar shouted. "Elsia!" He spun, searching for the women, but the glassy landscape was empty. He was alone.

"Pagus!" Iltar shouted, but the boy didn't answer. "Petral!"

Perhaps no one else made it... Iltar had told them of his revelation in the herbalist's shop. They all knew they must focus on manifesting an object with the First Emblem somewhere on it. Perhaps they had trouble getting their subconscious minds to register that change.

Iltar continued wandering across the glassy landscape for what seemed to be hours. "There has to be a better way to traverse this place," he said with a sigh. "I need a landmark or something."

Iltar kept walking. A dark spot loomed over the horizon. He continued toward that spot for a long time, and it soon grew. The tips of mountains rose from the glass, meeting the darkened spot in the sky. The darkness seemed to extend for quite a way.

Does magic work here? he wondered, then uttered an incantation to quicken his pace. White magic surged from his hands and enhanced his legs. Iltar felt an urge to run, and he dashed across the glass. He felt youthful as he sprinted. Though he had kept in good shape even after his last adventure, Iltar hadn't run this fast for so long.

The skies darkened and the peaks he had seen became towering mountains cradling a valley filled with trees. After an hour of running, Iltar dashed into the valley, a dark-purple lake at its heart. Across the lake and along the foothills of the mountains was a towering castle unlike anything he had ever seen. It scraped the sky, rising at least thirty stories.

"By all that's magical!" Iltar gasped, still running.

What was this oasis in the desert of glass? Who put it here? He hadn't manifested it, had he? So many questions, and Iltar was determined to answer them all.

*"A beast shall stay his hand against the Unspoken One. He shall not
have a mind to slay him."*

- Prophecy of Soron Thahan

The Castle of Laelin Lake had a peculiar smell within its halls. It somehow reminded Cornar of the Keepers' Temple, though he didn't know why. Cornar had reentered the dream walking down another gaudy corridor behind Melthas. Was he Naedar again? Cornar studied each of the men, none of whom looked unfamiliar.

"Naedar," Adrin whispered, "come with me." The grand mage slipped out of formation and hurried to an intersecting hall. There wasn't anyone around besides their infiltrating band.

Cornar quickly caught up to Adrin, who was climbing a stairwell. They seemed to be quite high up in the castle. Beautiful windows rose to the next floor, allowing a view to the lake and the surrounding area. The view didn't look so odd at this time of night. Cornar couldn't even tell that the lake was purple.

"We need to find an empty room," Adrin said, "some place where we can gather everyone."

They arrived on the next floor—Cornar didn't know which it was—and quietly moved toward a door. Adrin pressed his ear against it then nodded to Cornar as he opened it.

The room was a large suite, with a sitting room and bedchamber. It was just as ostentatious as the rest of the castle.

Adrin hurried across the room and carefully rummaged through a desk. He read through several letters and then opened a book filled with handwriting. "I think we're safe to gather in here," he said. "This suite belongs to the Countess of Yaenarez. She's probably at the banquet." He turned to Cornar. "Tell Melthas."

Cornar hurried out of the room and back down the staircase. His father and his group of Elites were still where he had left them. "We found a spot," Cornar said. Melthas nodded and guided the group down the hall.

Cornar, however, lingered for a moment, gazing at the castle's gaudy detail. *What am I going to learn here?* he wondered, musing on the supposed purpose of the dream. Prior to sleeping, Cornar had instructed his men not to wake him. He had retired to his cabin on the *Promised Maiden* and locked the door. Cornar was determined to discover all he could.

On the march back to Kretin, Cornar had recorded all the details of the previous dreams. He wrote them all down, usually immediately after he awoke. The phrase he heard in the second dream when falling—*Beware the evil behind the eyes of allies*—lingered with him. Initially, Cornar interpreted that as evil intentions among those of the expedition, particularly Jahevial. But now he couldn't trust any of them; that much had been made clear throughout his experiences beneath Klindil.

"Soldier!" a firm voice called. It sounded familiar. Cornar turned, fighting the urge to jump as he saw the source of the voice. Prince Kaescis Midivar strode smugly toward Cornar, dressed in a royal garb. Two others trailed behind him—

Impossible, Cornar gasped inwardly. Bratan and Laeyit hurried after Kaescis, each looking fierce. How…? how were they here? They looked the same, as if they had walked into his dream.

Kaescis blinked several times, looking at Cornar with annoyance. "Do you not know who I am, soldier?" the prince demanded.

"Perhaps he's just awestruck," Laeyit said, snickering. "It's not often that average soldiers get to stand in the presence of a hero."

Kaescis a hero? In this time period? But he shouldn't even exist… the prince was younger than Cornar, wasn't he? Yet, Kaescis had never disclosed his age. Cornar had assumed Kaescis was younger, due to his youthful looks.

The prince sighed haughtily. "Will you show us to the banquet hall?" Kaescis asked. "The last group of soldiers we passed ignored us."

"Yeah," Bratan said with a grunt. "They wouldn't even look at me."

"Probably scared of you, Bratan." Laeyit smiled, flicking her wrist at Bratan's chest. "Most people piss themselves when you stride into a room."

Kaescis laughed and then returned his attention to Cornar. "You're not going to piss yourself, are you, soldier?"

"Uh, no, Your Imperial Highness," Cornar said, feigning the role.

"Oh good, you can speak." Kaescis chuckled. "The banquet hall?"

The banquet hall… where had his father said it was located? Cornar couldn't remember.

"Eighteenth floor," Cornar muttered.

"I think he's fighting the urge," Laeyit said mockingly, and Bratan laughed.

"So two more floors," Kaescis said, sighing. "C'mon," he waved for his friends to follow and he walked back down the hall. "I'm not climbing any more steps."

Bratan and Laeyit looked at each other, and then Bratan lunged toward Cornar. "Boo!" the Praetorian shouted.

Cornar stood his ground, glaring at the towering man. He wouldn't be intimidated. Bratan studied Cornar with his yellow-green eyes, then slowly leaned back. He was obviously contemplating Cornar's reaction.

"I can't tell," Laeyit said, narrowing her eyes. "Did he piss himself?"

Bratan threw a final smirk at Cornar, then stalked off after Kaescis. Laeyit paused and glanced at Cornar. She was as plain as she had been the moment he met her. Laeyit sighed and spun around, following the prince.

"Naedar…" The name whispered from the adjoining corridor housing the stairs. Cornar turned to see his father beckoning him. He glanced back to Laeyit, who was rounding a corner. Once she disappeared Cornar joined his father on the stairs.

"Are you all right?" Melthas asked as he and Cornar climbed the stairs.

"Yeah," Cornar replied, but he was still wondering about Kaescis.

"Were you talking to someone?" Melthas asked as they reached the top of the stairs.

Cornar didn't answer until they entered the guest quarters. "I just ran into a prince."

Melthas stopped abruptly. "Alegar?" he demanded, grabbing Cornar's arm.

"No, Kaescis…" Cornar answered, closing the door.

"The Decimator of Angolith?" asked one of the Elites.

Melthas extended a hand to calm the man. "What happened, Naedar?"

"They were looking for the banquet hall," Cornar said.

"They?" Adrin asked, stepping close. He looked worried.

"Bratan and Laeyit were with him," Cornar didn't think it unusual if he used their names casually.

"Who?" asked another Elite.

"The other two who helped Kaescis hold the battlefront at Angolith," Adrin said with a sigh. "The three of them bought time for their forces to retreat into the Litor Woods."

"We can kill both of them," Melthas said. "Kaescis and Alegar will die today."

A knot formed in Cornar's stomach. Was Kaescis somehow tied to Melthas's death? But how was that possible? The battle Adrin spoke of had taken place sixty-four years ago, when Mindolarn, the emperor, was slain. If Kaescis had participated in that battle he would be at least ninety years old.

"We need to scout the banquet hall," Adrin said warily. "Haedin, go find Jamar and Vedin. Have them bring their groups here."

Haedin, a stocky man, nodded and hurried out of the room.

Melthas and Adrin were right behind him, but Melthas turned back to Cornar. "Are you coming, Naedar?"

Might as well, Cornar thought. Perhaps he would recognize someone else from the expedition.

◄═►•◄═►

Cornar crept behind his father and Adrin, moving down a narrow hall on the nineteenth floor. They had passed several doors, all guarded by Mindolarn soldiers. None of the guards regarded Cornar and the others; the soldiers probably thought the three of them were a small patrol. They had passed others in groups of three and four, but never two. That was probably why Melthas had called for Cornar to join them.

"There should be a service staircase around here," Adrin said. They turned a corner and found an unguarded door. Adrin hurried to it. "In here." He opened the door, beckoning to Melthas and Cornar.

The room was quite small, with a tiny spiral staircase. They climbed the staircase one by one and entered a simple-looking space. Though it was large, its décor was quite stark when compared to the rest of the castle. Part of the far wall curved away, looking like the unseen part of an arched ceiling.

"Over here," Adrin said. "The servants use these accesses here to clean the chandeliers." He moved to a square wooden panel along the curving wall and slowly opened it. Melthas stepped up right beside Adrin, barely allowing Cornar a glimpse through the opening.

"By all that's magical…" Adrin said with a gasp.

"They're all there!" Melthas restrained his voice. He sounded excited.

"Who?" Cornar asked.

"Take a look," Melthas said, and moved away, grinning. "We can strike a devastating blow against the Mindolarn Empire tonight. We might even be able to crush this reign of tyranny once and for all!"

Melthas's stoic resolve worried Cornar. Mindolarn tyranny *had not* been crushed this night. Cornar stepped up to the hole, swallowing hard.

The banquet hall sprawled below him. It was filled with tables of men and women dressed in aristocratic clothing.

"Over there." Adrin nudged him, pointing to a long table that spanned the length of the far wall. Nearly two dozen men and women sat at the table, but the center five were distinguished by lavish thrones. They all looked similar, like brothers. Cornar didn't know who they were. Adrin must have sensed this.

"You don't recognize them?" the grand mage asked.

"No…"

"For goodness' sake, Naedar," Melthas said through clenched teeth. "Those are Mindolarn's brothers! The one in the center is Emperor Medis."

The emperor of the Mindolarn Empire?

"We can kill them all, Naedar!" Melthas sounded crazed with a bloodlust. "Medis, Mendal, Magdolin, Monddar, and Marden."

"There are bound to be countless Praetorians here," Adrin said warily. "We might have to call off this attack."

"But they're not armored," Melthas said. "They're just there, feasting. If you had a channeling staff, you could kill all five of them right here." He sounded overzealous.

"I don't know…" Adrin shook his head. His resolve about the attack seemed to be waning.

"Adrin, when in the history of this accursed empire have all the brothers been in the same room?" Adrin didn't answer. "We will strike a devastating blow tonight," Melthas said.

"I wish Zatryn were here," Adrin said with a sigh.

"I doubt Kandish will swoop in, like at Tergol," Melthas said.

Kandish at Tergol? Cornar wondered with bewilderment. The only person who had *swooped in* was that man in the white armor. And hadn't Adrin called him Zatryn?

"We need to reevaluate our plan," Melthas said, hurrying to the spiral staircase. Adrin moved to close the access panel, but Cornar held it open. The mage took one look at him but followed after Melthas.

Cornar studied the banquet hall, searching for anyone he might recognize. It was quite large. Windows behind the table with the emperor allowed a view to the mountains. The windows rose three stories and followed the arch of the ceiling. The whole room was gaudy, like the rest of the castle.

Kaescis sat at one end of the long table, to the right of the emperor. A woman sat beside the prince, her hand intertwined with his. Kaescis leaned toward her, whispering in her ear. She turned, giving him a flirtatious grin. Kaescis leaned in and kissed her.

His wife? Cornar remembered Kaescis mentioning her death that first day on the *Executor's Breath*. Kaescis gazed at her like only a man in love would. The woman leaned back in her chair, placing a hand on Kaescis's arm and revealing her pregnant belly.

But Kaescis said he didn't have any children—

Cornar suddenly felt sick to his stomach, and sadness washed over him. He pushed those feelings aside and surveyed the rest of the room. At least two hundred feasted in the banquet hall. Soldiers wearing red armor stood along the walls: Crimson Praetorians. A balcony lined the second story, filled with more Crimson Praetorians. His father's band was definitely outnumbered, though the odds were not as bad as when the three of them faced that army outside Tergol.

"Naedar!" Melthas's voice whispered from the stairs. "Aren't you coming?" Cornar took one last sweeping glance at the banquet hall and closed the access panel.

They marched back through the narrow corridor and made their way to the guest chambers where the others were gathered. The room was cramped with eighty-four of them in there.

"We have a new target," Melthas said, grinning. "The emperor is here, along with his brothers. All of them."

Some of the Elites let out surprised gasps. They seemed as eager as he was. Granted, most of his father's Elites were men that had suffered under the tyranny of the Mindolarn Empire.

"Alegar is still mine to kill," Melthas said. "But Medis and his brothers are fair game."

Melthas elaborated on the plan to break into the banquet hall. They would slay the guards in unison and then charge inside. Melthas planned to enter through the access area and strike Alegar from above while Adrin led the charge. Cornar learned that Alegar was the man sitting on the other side of Kaescis at the table.

Once the plan was reviewed, the mages began enhancing everyone. Those wielding destructive magics imbued all the weapons: side swords and fanisars. The last mages to cast spells were the barsionists.

Cornar felt quickened by the enhancing magic, and slightly stronger. One of the support mages had cast a spell that seemed to bolster everyone's abilities. Heartbeats fluttered around him, like a cacophony of drums.

"Jamar, Vedin, with me," Melthas said, and stepped to the door. He listened for a moment and then exited the guest chamber.

"Six of you need to be invisible," Adrin said. Several Elites moved to the door and Adrin made them disappear with his magic. "Kill in unison." He turned and exited the guest chambers, leading the army to the banquet hall.

By the time Cornar and the others arrived, the guards at the banquet hall's entrance were already dead, their lifeless bodies propped up beside the double doors.

Adrin went straight for the center set of doors, uttering an incantation. The grand mage threw the doors open, drawing the attention of all inside while glowing a lavender hue. The people feasting started upon seeing Adrin and his coalescing magic. Many gasped.

Disintegrating bolts swarmed around Adrin as he finished the incantation, drawing screams from the crowd. Crimson Praetorians bolted from along the walls while Melthas's Elites charged in, mercilessly cutting down those trying to flee.

Some of the people feasting moved to block Adrin's advance, but he dashed to one of the tables and leapt up onto it. Then he jumped to an unnatural height, ready to unleash his magic.

"Your time is at an end, Medis!" Adrin shouted, hurling dozens of disintegrating bolts at the emperor.

One of the men on the thrones—Monddar perhaps—grabbed Emperor Medis and brought his other forearm in front of his brother. A ripple of blackness erupted from a band on his forearm, forming a shield.

Adrin's bolts struck the black shield, which misted devouring particles. *A tevisral that could harness the Darkness magic?* Cornar wondered with wide eyes. The mist consumed the disintegrating orbs. *Just like Iltar's Necrotic Sphere of Protection.*

At that same moment, Melthas dropped from the vaulted ceiling, falling with his weapons drawn. None of the Royals at the long table noticed him. Melthas fell straight for Alegar. He collided with the prince, knocking him to the ground. Cornar couldn't quite tell, but he thought he saw his father's serrated dagger make contact with Alegar's face.

Pandemonium erupted in the banquet hall as Elites and Praetorians clashed. Some of the people fled out of the now opened doors but were cut down by the invisible soldiers. Melthas's men ensured that no one escaped. Praetorians on the balconies leapt over the railings, joining the fray. Adrin continued his advance, mustering more deadly magic.

Cornar stood still, surveying the battle. *I don't have to fight here,* he thought. Jamar and Vedin leap from the ceiling, dropping onto Praetorians engaged with other Elites.

Adrin's advance was stopped as Bratan rose from a nearby table, tackling the grand mage. The brutish man yelled a battle cry and picked up Adrin, pushing him across the banquet hall, ramming him into table after table.

"You shall face the fury of Cheserith!" the emperor shouted. Cornar looked across the banquet hall, seeing Emperor Medis raising his hand into the air. He shouted sharp-sounding words, and blackness oozed from his out-stretched hand. It formed a long shaft that shaped into a thick claymore-like blade. *That weapon...* It was a lot like the one Kaescis had used against the Sapphire Guard.

Once the weapon formed, Medis leapt atop the table, blade held high. He gazed at Adrin, who had just kicked Bratan away.

"You!" the emperor growled, pointing the massive Darkness sword at Adrin. "You slew our brothers! We will have—"

Melthas rose from behind the table, weapons glowing with deadly magic. Medis turned, but Melthas tackled the emperor, knocking him off the table.

Father! Cornar clenched his teeth. Melthas was so close to that deadly blade. One hit and it would tear through Melthas's barsion.

Those behind the table, including Kaescis, began casting their own spells. The prince stretched a hand to the woman behind him, covering her pregnant belly. Blue light shone from his hand, then veiled the woman in a layer of barsion. In Kaescis's other hand, a simple shaft of blackness appeared. It looked to be the length of a side sword. Why hadn't Kaescis summoned that massive blade?

Adrin made his way toward Melthas, leaping over Praetorians that tried to intercept him. The grand mage's armor made it harder for him to be as acrobatic as he had been during the battle outside Tergol.

"Naedar!" an Elite shouted. "Fight!" The Elite was dueling with a Praetori-an. "Fight!"

"I knew we should have sent him back!" another complained, stabbing a Praetorian between his breastplate and helmet.

A nearby Praetorian broke through an Elite's barsion, driving his purple-hued fanisar through the Elite's breastplate. The Praetorian withdrew his weapon, blood disintegrating and evaporating along the blade. With his foe dead, the Praetorian turned and dashed straight for Cornar.

Guess I can't just observe, Cornar thought and lunged to intercept the Praeto-rian. Cornar dodged a blow and wildly swung at his foe with his side sword. He had a fanisar in his other hand, but it was too clunky to dual-wield.

Cornar put some distance between him and the Praetorian, throwing his fanisar like a javelin. The destructive magic around the fanisar's blade pierced the barsion surrounding the Praetorian, gouging his breastplate.

The side sword, he thought, glancing to the fallen Elite.

The Praetorian lunged, attacking again. Cornar dropped to the ground, roll-ing sideways over some bodies while claiming the dead Elite's side sword. He could do some real damage like this… Gripping two short weapons invigorated him.

Cornar spun to his feet as the Praetorian lunged again, but so did Cornar. He got close enough to be out of effective range for the fanisar. Cornar rapidly sliced along his foe's breastplate, then struck the gouge in the armor. It cracked, and the Praetorian backed away.

Cornar grinned and continued his advance. He threw a piercing blow, but the Praetorian pushed the weapon aside with his gauntlet. Cornar had expected that and followed up with his other side sword. The movement was so fast that by the time the Praetorian reacted Cornar had already pierced his chest.

The Praetorian slumped, falling backward.

Cornar spun, surveying the rest of the battle. Melthas was holding his own against Medis, blocking blows from that massive misting blade with his serrated dagger. Both of his father's weapons had a persistent mist of blackness around them. They must have absorbed part of the emperor's weapon.

Adrin had since engaged the emperor's brothers. The grand mage wielded a telekinetic spell and hurled it at one of the Royals—not the one who had shielded Medis. The magic hurled the man through the windows, shattering them completely. He plummeted out of view, shouting what sounded like a spell.

That left only three of Adrin's opponents.

Cornar glimpsed Kaescis guiding the woman along the far wall. The prince was obviously trying to get her out of the banquet hall, but the raging battle blocked their way.

One of the Praetorians near Kaescis fell before Jamar, and then the Elite turned to the prince. Jamar dashed with his weapon outstretched, clashing with Kaescis. Another Elite was right behind Jamar.

Kaescis shouted for the woman to run, calling her by what Cornar assumed to be her name, Helgara. Kaescis engaged both Elites, but Jamar repulsed the prince. Panicked, Helgara ran, darting along the wall. She was halfway to the doors when one of Melthas's Elites spotted her.

The man dashed toward Helgara, tackling her to the ground. Cornar watched with horror as the Elite repeatedly struck the barsion protecting her. Helgara screamed and thrashed, breaking free of the Elite as the barsion surrounding her shattered.

Defenseless, Helgara staggered, falling against the wall. The Elite, however, rebounded, mercilessly slamming his side sword into Helgara's face. She screamed, but fell silent quickly.

So, that's how it happened, Cornar mused, and then started.

The Elite then did the unthinkable… he drew his weapon from Helgara's face and—Cornar couldn't watch. He turned away, but heard Kaescis's cries of anguish and rage ringing above the pandemonium of the battle.

43

THE UNNERVING TRUTH

Eruptions of magic resounded through the banquet hall as Cornar regained his composure. He had never supposed his father's troops were so ruthless. It sickened him. Cornar had killed in the past, but never innocents.

"FIGHT WITH HIM," a voice boomed throughout the banquet hall, but no one seemed to pay attention to it.

Cornar looked to the ceiling, searching for the source of that voice. "Why?" he demanded. Then everything quieted. Cornar turned, seeing that everyone in the banquet hall was frozen. Some were suspended mid-air.

"BECAUSE NAEDAR FOUGHT ALONGSIDE YOUR FATHER. IN ORDER FOR THIS SEQUENCE TO BE PLAYED OUT CORRECTLY YOU MUST ENGAGE THE FAITHFUL."

Cornar furrowed his brow, confused. *The Faithful?* he wondered.

"YOU ARE READY TO BEHOLD WHAT I PROMISED YOU," the voice boomed. "BUT YOU MUST FIGHT."

Cornar took a deep breath. He hated being compelled. Shaking his head, Cornar paced around the room. With the battle paused in this odd manner, Cornar thought he could glean some insight—what, he didn't know.

Curious, Cornar examined the dead around some of the tables. Many had been run through, but their wounds weren't bloody. The imbued magic on the Elite's blades had cauterized the wounds. At least a dozen Elites had fallen.

A man dressed in affluent clothing caught Cornar's eye, clutching an odd coin. It was nothing like Cornar had ever seen. The coin was silver, oval-shaped, with a golden lip around its edge. Within the coin's center was a protruding figure of a winged creature. The man's fingers were covering much of the effigy, but Cornar thought it looked like a dragon—at least, the supposed depiction of one.

"WHAT ARE YOU LOOKING FOR?" the voice demanded.

"I don't know," Cornar said. "And it's not like I'm in a hurry."

An amused grunt resounded throughout the banquet hall.

Cornar picked his way around toppled tables, corpses, and frozen combatants. He shied away from Helgara's corpse and made his way to the table where the Royals had sat. He glimpsed Alegar's headless body lying beside the table, chest down, his hands covered in red. The prince's head was nowhere to be found.

"So you did it," Cornar whispered. "You avenged mother." The sight of his mother's murderer quelled a once-burning vengeance Cornar thought was all but forgotten. Although Alegar hadn't slain her directly, he was still responsible. His mother's true killer had undoubtedly died during the battle at Tergol.

Cornar began to turn away but started upon seeing the dead prince's hands. He thought Alegar's hands were covered in blood, as they were red—but no blood pooled nearby. In fact, Alegar's neck was completely cauterized.

What…? Cornar muttered, squinting at the dead prince. Alegar's hands were rough, like the scales of a reptile. Where the nails should be were dark obsidian cl—

An eruption of magic thrust Cornar sideways and the chaotic sounds of battle resumed. Cornar slid across the polished stone, straight for the broken window.

No! Cornar slammed his side swords into the ground, attempting to slow himself, but the magic coating the blades negated any resistance they once had. Cornar slid until reaching a lip of stone beneath the window, stopping abruptly, his torso hanging over the edge.

Cornar looked over his shoulder. The banquet hall was at one end of the main keep and hung over the castle's outer walls. Though the room was on the eighteenth floor, the ground was farther away. That fatal drop was most likely twenty-five or thirty stories, due to the elevated nature of the castle.

Dizziness struck Cornar, and he reeled back into the room. He watched as Jamar was hurled over the nearby table; the Elite skidded to the window, but rebounded and engaged Kaescis once again. The prince fought with wild ferocity, more vicious than his clash with the Sapphire Guard in the Keepers' Temple.

Get up, Cor! Cornar heard Iltar's voice in his mind, like a distant whisper. *And fight! If you die here, you die on Kalda.*

Iltar? Cornar wondered, rising to his feet. Why him? No matter, Cornar had more important things to worry about.

Cornar dashed to the table, bounding over it. He landed and bolted straight for his father and the emperor, striking at a veil of barsion surrounding Medis. His side swords caused the emperor's protective magic to flicker.

Medis spun, swinging his gigantic Darkness blade. Cornar dodged, but the weapon trailed a devouring mist in its wake, eroding Cornar's barsion.

"Naedar!" Melthas shouted. "Your side sword." Melthas then threw his short-sword at Cornar.

Reacting swiftly, Cornar tossed his left blade at Melthas, throwing it behind Medis. Cornar sidestepped, catching his father's short-sword. It felt good to wield this weapon. After all, this particular short-sword had become part of him, like an extension of his body.

Medis recoiled, slicing again. Cornar blocked the blow with his father's short-sword. The Darkness magic didn't dissolve the blade like it had with others. In fact, the short-sword pulled more of the devouring particles into its aura of mingled magic.

The emperor growled, and Melthas struck a blow to his back. Enraged, Medis spun, kicking Melthas away.

Yelling a battle cry, Cornar attacked with a furious flurry, blocking with his short-sword. Melthas soon rejoined the fray, and both he and Cornar engaged Emperor Medis in a flurry of identical blows. They fought in unison, mirroring each other's movements. They moved quickly, striking occasional blows against Medis that weakened his barsion. It was magnificent!

But would they slay him? Cornar didn't know when Medis had died. He hoped it was tonight.

Cornar fought with a raging fury, blocking blows from Medis and striking at the emperor's barsion. They almost had it shattered. Though Cornar knew his father's fate, he would do all he could to prevent it in this bizarre dreamland—

Cor, behind you! Iltar's voice shouted in Cornar's mind, but it was too late.

Cold metal pierced Cornar's thigh, and he screamed, dropping to one knee. What had hit him? He blocked a blow from Medis while glancing over his shoulder. Bratan retracted a fanisar from Cornar's leg. The fanisar wasn't imbued with magic, so how could it have pierced both barsion *and* armor?

"You better piss now, bastard!" Bratan shouted with frothing rage.

Bratan came in for another blow but was struck by a mass of green magic, ensnaring tentacles. The magic hurled Bratan across the room, trapping him against the wall.

Cornar twisted around and barely blocked a blow from Medis. He glimpsed more Mindolarn soldiers spilling into the banquet hall, as well as archers filing onto the balcony.

Damn it! Cornar struggled to stand, but he buckled and fell back onto his knee. The pain was so real.

Medis twirled his gigantic blade, ready to deliver a death blow. The emperor began to raise the misting blade but Melthas jumped on his back, slamming both the side sword and his serrated dagger into the emperor's shoulders. The weapons shattered the barsion and tore through Medis's clothing.

Screaming, Medis buckled beneath Melthas's weight and dropped his black blade. It tumbled, striking the ground point first.

"I'll relish killing you!" Melthas shouted, digging his weapons further into the emperor. The Darkness particles around the serrated dagger consumed Medis's flesh, turning bone and muscle to gray dust.

"Uncle!" Kaescis shouted.

The prince dashed across the room, tackling Melthas. That raging familial protection reminded Cornar of Ordreth.

The impact freed Medis from the deadly grip, and the emperor fell onto his knees, gasping. Medis struggled to speak sharp-sounding words, and once he spoke them they mustered magic. *How was that an incantation…?* Cornar wondered, perplexed. The incantation was too short, but arpran magic wisped from Medis's hands and into the wounds on his shoulders.

"No…" Cornar cried, dragging himself toward the emperor. He got within his weapons' reach and began to stab at Medis's face, but was thrown sideways by a powerful kick. He tumbled across the floor, almost losing his grip on his weapons.

One of Medis's brothers had kicked Cornar away. That left two fighting Adrin. Adrin and the other royal brothers fought in an acrobatic display of magic and hand-to-hand combat. It was awe-inspiring. Then Medis and his brother again spoke those sharp words, mustering more magic. What kind of incantations were those? One mustered barsion while the other gathered a gray mist—telekinetic magic? Once a bubble of barsion was around both of them the mist condensed, hitting the barsion and launching them out the broken windows.

What a retreat, Cornar grunted and struggled to stand. The best he could do was kneel. It would have to do.

Cowards! Iltar's voice rang in Cornar's mind. He heard the necromancer uttering a slew of curses. *Why can't I interact with anything?!*

The outburst was distracting, but Cornar returned his attention to the battle. More of Melthas's Elites fell throughout the room. Only ten were left standing, but they were being overrun by the reinforcements still pouring into the banquet hall. They wouldn't last long.

Melthas was dueling Kaescis, and the prince had already severed the side sword Melthas was using.

"Father!" Cornar shouted, but Melthas didn't acknowledge the cry. Of course he wouldn't. "Melthas!" Cornar threw the short-sword.

Both Melthas and Kaescis noticed the coming blade, but the prince kicked Melthas in the gut while swatting at the short-sword with his Darkness blade. That sent both the weapon and Cornar's father in opposite directions.

Damn it! Cornar growled, watching the short-sword hit the ground between him and the table.

Fighting against the pain, Cornar dragged himself to his father's short-sword. As Cornar reached for it, he heard Bratan yelling, "No you don't!"

Cornar turned just in time to see the hulking Praetorian dashing toward him with a fanisar aimed like a spear. All the while, Cornar heard Iltar's voice, yelling with enraged frustration.

Bratan lunged, striking at Cornar's face. Cornar moved to defend himself, but Bratan feinted, swiftly pulling back and thrusting the fanisar into Cornar's stomach. The blade pierced through the metal breastplate and drew blood. But where had the barsion gone? It just disappeared…

No! Iltar's voice rang once again in Cornar's mind, followed by grotesque curses.

"I'll make you piss through your gut, bastard!" Bratan shouted. Bratan came in for another blow, but Vedin—one of the last standing Elites—blocked the fanisar. Vedin swiftly engaged Bratan, forcing him backward.

Cornar felt light-headed. He touched the wound, his gauntlet turning red. Cornar struggled to his feet, but everything spun, and he fell, landing sideways.

Damn it, Cor! You can't die in here! Iltar's voice shouted.

Cornar looked up, which was really sideways. The short-sword was just beyond his reach. Though it was close, it felt so far away.

"GRAB IT," the booming voice commanded.

Mustering all his strength, Cornar struggled to grab the weapon. His hand shook as he gripped the sword's hilt.

"YOU HAVE FULFILLED THE ROLE," that voice boomed throughout the room. Again, no one noticed it beside Cornar. "NOW YOU MAY OBSERVE."

Bewildered shouts rang in Cornar's mind, coming from Iltar. The necromancer was railing against the booming voice. Was this some sort of delirium?

Cornar watched his father dueling Kaescis. Melthas struggled to fight with only his serrated dagger. If only Cornar could throw his father his short-sword, then Melthas would have a chance.

Vedin landed in front of Cornar, eyes glazed. Blood dripped from his breastplate and pooled on the floor. He didn't blink. Bratan charged past Cornar, yelling a battle cry. He engaged Melthas, swinging his fanisar wildly. Melthas contended with both of his opponents for a short while, dodging blows while landing an occasional strike. But it didn't seem to help.

Another figure flew into the fray, wielding a shaft of lime-green light. It looked like acidic magic. The third combatant spun, revealing her face. It was Laeyit. The three of them fought Melthas, delivering an occasional blow that weakened his barsion.

Melthas struggled, using hand-to-hand combat to try to repulse his foes, but Kaescis and his friends were relentless. Arrows sang from the balconies, striking Melthas and the other Elites that were still fighting.

Soon, only Adrin and Melthas remained. Melthas had sustained a wound on his left arm, a blow caused by Laeyit's acidic magic. Bratan delivered a blow to Melthas's left thigh, wounding him as he had Cornar.

No... Cornar groaned.

Melthas buckled, and Kaescis pierced his foe's shoulder, causing Melthas to drop his serrated dagger.

A resounding yell filled the room, and then a wave of telekinetic magic repulsed the combatants around Melthas and Adrin. Cornar watched his father drop to his knees. Adrin grabbed Melthas, casting a spell. Melthas grabbed his serrated dagger as blue magic surged around them, creating a barrier of barsion.

"HOLD IT UP," the booming voice urged Cornar. Was he referring to the sword? "They need to see you."

Struggling to heed that behest, Cornar heard Iltar's voice once again. The necromancer shouted in frustration to that booming voice, angered that he was unable to participate in the battle. But why was Cornar hearing Iltar? And why was Iltar able to hear that voice? No one else had… those questions felt fuzzy, distant, even.

Focused completely on raising the short-sword, Cornar shakily forced his hand into the air. Though he barely raised the weapon, Adrin saw it.

Arrows flew from the balcony, striking Adrin's magic; they ricocheted without damaging the barsion. Orbs of deadly magic whizzed through the room, also assailing the grand mage's protective bubble. Unlike the arrows, the orbs caused the barsion to flicker.

Adrin's magic widened, swallowing up Cornar and Vedin. Melthas groaned while Adrin stretched out his hand to reinforce the barsion. Adrin began casting another spell, and golden light shone from beneath his gauntlet.

They were teleporting away… but Melthas was still alive.

Melthas struggled to kneel but grabbed his short-sword from Cornar. A look of defiance was on his father's face, fierce and determined.

Adrin's barsion shattered. Arrows struck Adrin and Melthas, bouncing off their armor. Magic whizzed toward them, and then Kaescis threw his black sword like a javelin. The Darkness blade flew through the air, impaling Melthas through his chest.

Father! Cornar struggled to utter the word. He could barely keep his eyes open.

Melthas jolted, arcing forward but falling backward. Kaescis's sword protruded from Melthas's back. A black mist spread across Melthas's armor, devouring flesh and metal. Melthas collapsed, his head landing on Cornar's wounded thigh as Adrin finished his incantation.

Golden light washed across them. Cornar blinked once, and they were someplace else…

The smell of horses. The scent of hay. The stench of dung. *A barn?*

"No!" Adrin screamed.

"Oh, Melthas!" Kandish groaned.

Kandish?

"Look, Naedar is alive," Kandish said.

Cornar thought he saw Kandish push aside Melthas and then kneel, saying sharp things. It sounded like that too-short-incantation. What was happening?

Green light.

Cor! Iltar shouted again in Cornar's mind. Why was he shouting…? Cornar shut his eyes, his mind drifting. It was peaceful, like falling asleep—

A surge of energy shot through Cornar, and his eyes flashed open. He gasped, breathing rapidly.

Kandish knelt beside Cornar, clutching flowing arpran magic. But how? Kandish wasn't a mage. He was a merchant. The arpran magic surged across Cornar, and he felt his wounds closing. After a short while, Cornar felt normal.

Sobs filled the air, and Cornar looked about, studying his surroundings. They were in a barn, a large one.

"You should be fine now," Kandish said, grabbing Cornar by the shoulder. "Here, let me help you stand." Cornar took Kandish's hand and rose to his feet.

Adrin was kneeling over Melthas, weeping profusely.

"Oh…" Cornar gasped, bringing his hand to his mouth. A gaping hole marred Melthas's breastplate, surrounded by a festering black mist. That hole continued through his father's chest, where his heart should be.

Kandish knelt beside Adrin, wrapping his arms around the weeping man. Tears trickled down Kandish's cheeks. They cried together for a while until Adrin regained his composure.

"We should have turned back," Adrin took in a deep breath. "They were there, all of them…"

"Who?" Kandish asked, wiping away more tears from his eyes.

"The abominable qui'sha princes… all five of them."

"All of Mindolarn's surviving brothers?" Kandish demanded, his face resembling a flaming inferno of fury.

"Yes."

Kandish slammed his fists into the ground. "I should have gone!"

"They would have fled," Adrin said. He still looked overcome by the losses they had suffered.

"They're probably still there." Kandish rose, his lips turning into a scowling snarl. "I could be there in a few hours if I—"

"No," Adrin shook his head. "I can't lose you too. Not again. Don't go, Zatryn. I cannot bear you dying twice. It tore me apart, losing you all those years ago."

What was Adrin talking about? Dying twice? How was that possible?

Kandish sighed, appearing dissuaded by the brief argument. "All right…" He paced across the barn. "Those poor children… first their mother, and now their father." Kandish groaned and more tears trickled down his cheek.

Silence hung in the barn for a moment until Adrin pried Melthas's weapons from lifeless hands. He gently sheathed both of the weapons and then unlatched the scabbards from Melthas's belt.

Adrin rose and handed both of the weapons to Kandish. "I think he would like his son to have them."

Kandish took the weapons without a word.

Cornar could still remember the day that Kandish delivered the serrated dagger and short-sword. Cornar wept upon taking the weapons, regretting how he had treated his father the last time he saw him. He felt that sorrow again as he watched Kandish handle the weapons.

"I need to go," Adrin said. "They recognized me, and surely they'll retaliate soon. I need to protect my family."

"Take them to Alath," Kandish said absentmindedly.

"Gwenyth won't go," Adrin said, sighing. "But I think I know of a place where they'll be safely hidden."

Kandish just turned and looked at Adrin. "If you take them to Alath, the Guardians can keep track of them. My uncle will see to their safety."

Adrin sighed and frowned. "I'll try to talk her into it."

"Where would you take them?" Kandish asked, he sounded concerned.

"Soroth. My father-in-law has a place in the forest. They'll be hidden there."

Kandish nodded, then glanced to Cornar. "Are you okay?"

Cornar nodded but didn't speak. He was overcome by witnessing his father's demise. Now he and Iltar had something else in common.

Kandish and Adrin walked away, leaving Cornar in the barn with the corpses of Vedin and Melthas. After a moment, Cornar removed his armor and knelt beside his father's corpse. Melthas gazed at the ceiling with that fierce determination. Cornar was glad to see that was his final moment. He had always thought of his father as fierce and determined, full of zeal. Witnessing his last moments only cemented that legacy.

"I feel like I've learned much from you," Cornar said, tears welling in his eyes. "I always wanted to fight beside you, and now I can say that I have."

"Oh, Cor…"

That was Iltar's voice. But this time it wasn't in Cornar's mind.

Startled, Cornar spun, seeing Iltar—clothed in his typical black garb—standing beside a bale of hay. Anger contorted Iltar's brow and twisted his lips. Their eyes met and Iltar started.

"Can you see me?" Iltar asked, anger tainting his words.

"Yes…" Cornar replied, settling into an apprehensive posture.

Iltar squinted thoughtfully, the squint on his left eye more pronounced. That was something Iltar did when thinking deeply on a subject. But this couldn't be Iltar. It had to be that creature who mimicked everyone.

"You're not Iltar," Cornar said sternly. "I don't know what you are, but you're not him."

Iltar laughed. "I'm as much Iltar as you are Cornar. I know Reflection looks and sounds like me, but he's not me, Cor. Trust me."

Cornar furrowed his brow, confused. Who was Reflection?

"Look," Iltar said, gesturing with his hand. "I know you're not going to believe me, but I've been beside you since you almost fell out that window. I was nearing the castle when I saw the battle erupt and ran to investigate it. Had to climb the walls with my magic…"

Iltar continued relating the tale, claiming he couldn't interact with anything. His story made sense. The shouting Cornar heard in his mind was frustrated.

He smiled wryly at Cornar. "I'm glad you survived that ordeal," Iltar said with relief. "You should avenge him," he said, gesturing to Melthas. "I saw what Kaescis did. That bastard needs to pay for killing your father. You know, he's probably responsible for my parents' deaths, too."

"Are you really Iltar?" Cornar asked.

"Uh, yeah," Iltar said, rolling his eyes. Iltar did that when annoyed.

But this could be a figment of my imagination, Cornar thought.

"I've been learning things here in Mindolarn, about this place," Iltar said.

"It's called Vabenack, a realm that mimics Kalda. I don't know how else to explain it. Regardless, I've learned how to access this place at will. At least, I think I'm here. If only I could verify this experience with someone else. Neither Pagus nor the women seem to be able to reach this realm. Pagus's aunt has tried everything we found in *Dreamwalker*, but she hasn't made any progress. I have a theory that—"

A flash of red appeared in the barn door. Cornar turned, seeing a tall man in a red robe embroidered with strange patterns. The patterns looked similar to the symbols in the Keepers' Temple, but they were different.

"Reflection!" Iltar blurted.

"You're not supposed to be here," said the man in red, sounding exactly like Iltar.

Cornar started. The man in red also looked *exactly* like Iltar. Well, except the long white hair and full beard. But every other detail was identical. Was this the creature Cornar had encountered throughout these dreams? The same being that claimed to have healed Cornar from that deadly fall in Klindil? The one Iltar called Reflection?

"Why?" Iltar barked with frustration.

"Begone," the man in red said, flicking his finger at Iltar.

Iltar vanished.

The man in red studied Cornar. "Your time is up," he said, sounding displeased. He flicked his finger, as he had done to Iltar, and the world zipped away.

Soon, Cornar found himself in an abysmal pit, although he briefly saw a gigantic shape out of the corner of his eye. It had a tail and wings— The blackness abruptly disappeared, and Cornar gasped. He was lying down, and he felt wet. The sheets were wet, too. And, there was a smell... like iron. He tossed the sheets aside and rolled out of bed, stepping into a puddle. Was the *Promised Maiden* taking on water?

Light spread from beneath the door, but it wasn't enough to illuminate the cabin. Cornar staggered across the room, stepping in more of the puddles. He reached a box containing a lightstone, nailed beside the door. He opened its lid, illuminating the cabin. Cornar pulled out the stone, turned around, and started.

Blood marred the cabin. The sheets were all red, and so was the decking. It looked like a murder scene. Frightened, Cornar looked down at the places where he had been wounded in the dream, but every fiber of his clothes was drenched.

"By Heleron's Trident..." he cursed, staggering backward and falling against the door.

"Cor, are you all right?" Kalder asked from outside the cabin, his voice muffled.

A key turned in the lock and Cornar steadied himself as the door opened.

"What on Kalda?!" Kalder blurted. Cornar turned. The burly warrior looked frightened, studying Cornar with a horrified expression. "Whose...?"

"Blood?" Cornar finished the question. "I think it's mine."

"How are you still alive?" Kalder asked. "And *how* did it happen?"

"That's a long story…" Cornar sighed. "I need some air." He stepped past Kalder and strode through the corridor to the stairs leading to the main deck. It was still dark. Both of Kalda's moons—Kistern and Kaelyrn—were high in the night sky. Kistern was almost full, but Kaelyrn was halfway through its phase; its speckled light didn't do much to light the night, anyway.

Cornar was cautious as he moved from the stairs. Much of the main deck was covered with sleeping Wildmen. Kaescis had ordered them to spread across the fleet, so as to not crowd a single vessel. A couple of sailors manning the rigging noticed Cornar, probably alerted by the smell of blood. They whispered to each other, but Cornar ignored them. He carefully picked his way to the starboard rail, careful not to step on any of the sleeping Wildmen.

Once at the rail, Cornar gazed at the Mindolarn vessels sailing nearby. His eyes settled on the *Executor's Breath*.

"So, *you* killed my father, Kaescis," Cornar whispered. "And he and his men killed your brother, wife, and unborn child." Though those closest to both him and the prince had died on that fateful night there wasn't any fairness about it. Murder was never fair.

You shouldn't trust him. Kaescis is not what he claims to be. Solidin's words rang in Cornar's mind. How true had those words been…? Kaescis was not at all what Cornar thought him to be. The young aspiring prince Cornar once saw was now a man much older than he. That gave Cornar pause.

He reflected on the strange encounter with Iltar… if that was Iltar. Should he avenge his father? Cornar didn't feel a burning desire to kill the prince. Perhaps that's because he saw the circumstances of his father's demise. Kaescis was just as much a victim as Cornar. Where there should have been anger, there was only sorrow… and pity.

Perhaps the anger would come later.

Cornar stared at the *Executor's Breath* for a time, thinking about everything that had happened, starting with that moment he met Kaescis on Pier Eight. The prince had stared at Cornar's weapons as if he knew them. And he *had* known them. They'd almost taken the life of his uncle, the emperor.

Is this why they haven't trusted me? he wondered. *Because I am the son of Melthas Dol'shir? The man who invaded their homeland and slew their people?* If Cornar had encountered the son of a man like that he didn't think he could trust him either. It seemed a plausible answer. But it didn't make the situation any easier to bear.

Cornar stared at the *Executor's Breath* for a long while, then searched for his usual spot near the bow. Luckily, it wasn't occupied.

Fatigue overcame Cornar, draining his very soul. He plodded to his favored spot and nestled against the sacks of provisions.

I need to sleep, he thought. Hopefully, this time it would be dreamless.

THE END OF

Part Two

GREATER KALDA

IV–VI

Balden · Lirathay'lu · Dith

The screams of dying men haunted Balden's mind. His victims had often plagued his dreams these last nine-and-a-half years. Balden vividly relived his part in their deaths, over and over. *And only thirty more to go,* he lamented. Balden wished he could leave, but he couldn't. His contract with Baron Cilgan wouldn't be finished for another thirty years.

Balden clutched the sides of his head, trying to block out the screams. But it didn't help. Baron Cilgan's jailers and interrogators suggested he should just embrace his role. They encouraged him to revel in those abominable acts he was forced to perform. After all, that's what they themselves had done. Each of those men had become cold and callous. One man had only been in the dungeons half as long as Balden, but now he was as bloodthirsty as the rest of them.

Balden wouldn't become like that. He couldn't…

Sighing, Balden placed his head against the cold stone wall of his cell. He wasn't like the others who worked in Baron Cilgan's dungeons. Balden was as much a prisoner as the men he was forced to kill.

Years ago—when Balden was first banished to Cilgan's service at the age of sixteen—he tried to escape, not once, but five times. They tried binding him with magic-inhibiting cords, but that didn't work. To his employer's surprise, Balden could muster magic *without* incantation. But not just any magic. He could produce a mist of blackness that eroded all it touched. When bound, Balden simply *dissolved* his bonds.

Seeing the danger Balden possessed—but not willing to give up such power—Baron Cilgan locked him away deep beneath his castle, within the dungeons. Balden was permitted to leave his cell for only two things: bathing and torture.

Balden tried escaping once after his exile to the dungeons, but that was ultimately a futile attempt. He reached the wards outside the baron's main keep but was wounded before he could escape the complex—soldiers broke his legs and cut him to the bone. Balden probably would have died from the bleeding, but the baron gave him an opportunity to use his life-draining magic on a prisoner.

Regretfully, Balden seized the opportunity. He wished he had let himself die instead of siphoning that man—a man who turned out to be innocent. That man's death haunted Balden the most. From then on, Balden didn't try to escape. He kept his head low, biding the time until his release… or rescue.

At one time, Balden hoped his master in the magical arts would deliver him from this servitude. But Iltar never came. Balden was bitter for years, but recently began to understand the predicament in which Iltar had been placed. The other necromancers on the Necrotic Order's council gave him a choice: Kill Balden or hand him over to them.

I hate those bastards, Balden groaned, thinking of the council. They saw him as property and sold him like a slave, and all because of his half-elven heritage. Balden sighed and slumped against the wall, resting his head against the stone. His long blond hair hung partially across his face, obscuring his vision.

Balden sat there for a while until the door to his cell creaked open. "Hey, pointed ears," Tegaris, the jailer, said. "Silik just finished interrogating that man from Sarn. It's your turn."

Balden didn't move.

"Are you going deaf?" Tegaris demanded. "Get up!"

"Can't it wait till morning?" Balden asked. "I'm tired."

"Didn't sleep again?" the jailer asked, chuckling. "Well, it *is* morning, Balden."

Had this been another sleepless night? Hours blurred in this cell.

"Come on," Tegaris said. "Get up. You have work to do. If you don't move, I'll have to get Gilard to whip you. I think you'd require ten lashings with a vidaren."

Balden sighed, standing reluctantly. A few lashings with a vidaren would make him bleed badly. If he didn't want to succumb to the loss of blood, he'd have to use a life-draining incantation. Balden would be forced to die, or mete out torture.

"Good," Tegaris said as Balden approached the door. "I'm glad your sleepless night didn't deprive you of all your senses."

Balden remained silent as they walked the halls of the dungeon. Soft whimpering reached his ears, undoubtedly coming from the man he was to torture.

"We've learned a lot from this one," Tegaris said. "He confessed to spreading the rumors about the good baron. This man's employer, a Sarn noble, is trying to cause enough chaos here in Sereth to try to usurp the baron's domain. She assumes the title belongs to her, since she was a distant relation of the good baron's grandmother."

Tegaris continued relaying the information but Balden only half-heartedly listened. Balden thought the information was probably inflated to stoke Cilgan's paranoia. He highly doubted that this man's employer was trying to unseat the baron. But Cilgan had a way of finding his enemies even in the hardest to reach nooks and crannies.

The whimpering grew louder, and Balden turned a corner, entering the main torture room. The prisoner was stretched out on a rack, wearing only a simple cloth around his loins. Many scars marred the prisoner's body, wounds that were cauterized by heated brands.

"His name is Daegar," Tegaris said, gesturing to the tortured man. The jailer didn't need to say more. Balden knew what to do next. He uttered an incantation, mustering gray enthralling magic. It wisped through the air and into Daegar's nostrils. Balden felt the man succumb to his will. He was in complete control of poor Daegar.

"When Yisig is ready, begin verifying what I told you," Tegaris said, mentioning the female scribe who sat across the room. Yisig had been in Baron Cilgan's employ longer than Balden. She rarely spoke and only stayed long enough to copy down the information received from Balden's probing.

After a moment, Yisig nodded and Balden began asking questions to gauge the successfulness of the prior interrogation.

Daegar's answers were exactly as Tegaris had said. The man was a spy sent from Lady Ralisu Davig, a member of the Scolae family of Sarn. Lady Davig was an ambitious widow aiming to climb the political ladders of the Principality of Soroth. In order to advance her goals, she sent Daegar to Sereth to gather information about the island's citizens while also disseminating rumors to incite a rebellion against Baron Cilgan.

All of that gave Balden some relief. This man wasn't innocent. Yisig left amid Daegar's retelling of details. Balden assumed she had already heard and scribed that information. Daegar continued rambling details, and Balden felt sympathy for the man as he listened.

"You can go."

Balden started. He knew that voice, even though he hadn't heard it in years. Balden turned, seeing Baron Cilgan standing behind him. The baron stood taller than Balden and was of a thick, muscular build. Cilgan's wavy blond hair was accented with an occasional gray hair, and his chiseled face was clean-shaven. He wore a stiff tunic bearing his family's crest—a green hawk with its beak pointed upward.

"I'll handle this," Cilgan said, stepping past Balden. Daegar continued rambling, still subject to Balden's magic. "I said go, dog!" Cilgan's words frothed with wrath.

"Come on," Tegaris tugged at Balden's arm. "Back to your cell."

Balden hesitated. He had never seen Cilgan in the dungeons. The baron stopped beside the rack holding Daegar. Cilgan slapped the prisoner across his face, but the man continued spewing details like a broken faucet spewing water.

"Release your spell, dog," Cilgan growled, glaring at Balden. "I want to hear him scream."

Balden refused to move, but the jailer pulled him through the torture room. A fire of hate burned within Balden. The man who had ruined his life was standing before him, without guard or armor.

I could kill him, he thought. *End it all right now.*

Cilgan turned and struck Daegar's face, causing the man's nose to bleed. But that didn't faze Daegar. The poor fellow was still enthralled.

"You better cease your spell," Tegaris said, grabbing Balden's other arm. He hauled Balden out of the torture room and back into the hallway.

Balden didn't relinquish his spell. If he could maintain it perhaps he wouldn't hear Daegar scream.

Soon, Balden was back in his cell. Tegaris shoved him inside, and Balden fell upon the dirty floor. The door's lock clicked as Balden recovered. Sighing, he crawled across his cell, feeling exhausted. He climbed up on his bed and stared at the stone ceiling. All was quiet. Not even the voices in his head were screaming. For a moment, he felt peace.

Muffled shouts echoed through the hallway outside his cell. It sounded like Cilgan. Footsteps hurried past the cell door, moving toward the dungeon's entrance. Not long after, more footsteps hurried back through the hall.

As the footfalls faded Balden felt his mind slipping. He was drifting toward sleep.

"No!" Balden's eyes shot open. "If I sleep he will scream." He hoped the baron would lose patience and just kill Daegar. The man could die as peaceful a death as one could suffer at the hands of Baron Cilgan. That would make things—

No!

A scream echoed throughout the dungeon, and Balden no longer felt his enthralling influence on Daegar. Cilgan must have summoned one of his mages from the castle to dispel the enthralling effect.

More screams echoed into Balden's cell. Though they were faint, he heard them as clearly as if he were standing beside the poor man.

Time blurred as fatigue overtook Balden, and he fell unconscious.

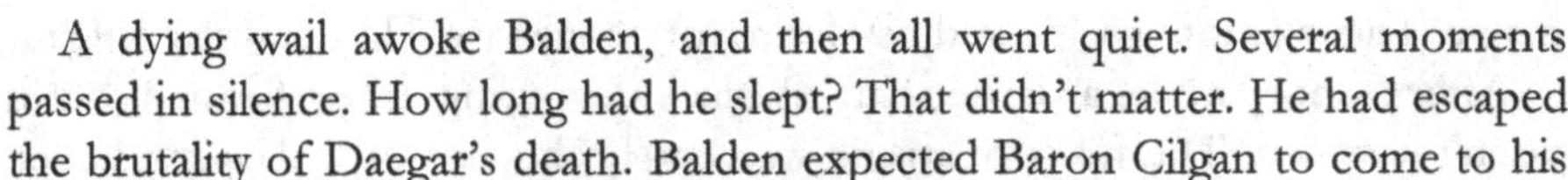

A dying wail awoke Balden, and then all went quiet. Several moments passed in silence. How long had he slept? That didn't matter. He had escaped the brutality of Daegar's death. Balden expected Baron Cilgan to come to his cell. But neither the baron nor anyone else disturbed him.

"I can't take this any longer," Balden whispered. At what point had he become so broken? Where was that youthful half-elf who yearned to be a hero? *He's dead,* Balden thought. *Long gone.*

Why don't you try escaping? a voice asked in his mind. That voice sounded like his former master, Iltar.

"Am I going mad?" Balden asked, though he knew no one would respond. Rather, he *hoped* no one would respond.

You have the means, that same voice said. *Just slaughter them all. You can make everyone disappear.*

Balden rolled over, pulling a blanket over him. He couldn't think of escaping. He would fail, like the last time, and the time before that. Six attempts with only pain and isolation to show for it.

You can kill Cilgan… the voice urged. That sparked something within him. Vengeance.

Balden sat upright. But could he really slay Cilgan? There were at least two hundred men in the castle, and Cilgan was paranoid. Balden would have a lengthy fight on his hands, not to mention the reinforcements that would pour into the castle from the city.

You just need the right weapon, the voice said.

Tossing the blanket aside, Balden crawled out of bed. *The right weapon?* That gave him pause. In each of his failed escape attempts Balden had succumbed to the soldiers who surrounded him. Balden could deal with archers and mages, using his magic to defend himself while hurling deadly projectiles. But fighting close-range was another matter entirely. It was something Iltar had not taught him.

Stories from his youth flooded into his mind, and he recalled tales of his master fighting beside a man named Cornar. Iltar would bathe Cornar's weapons in deadly magic. *I could steal a sword,* he thought. *But that'd take time to imbue… besides, they could dispel the imbuing easily.*

There had to be another answer. Balden closed his eyes, remembering a tale he'd read from a book in Iltar's library. It spoke of mages who made weapons of pure magic, using them in close quarters. Balden never saw Iltar use a spell like that, and he figured that was because Cornar and his warriors were doing all the close quarters fighting.

"That's it!" Balden exclaimed with excitement, but soon deflated. "I don't know one of those incantations…" His hope dwindled. Amid despair, he felt a distinct urge to muster his devouring mist. Could that be the answer? Balden didn't need an incantation to muster it. That magic obeyed his will.

Taking courage, Balden closed his eyes and stretched out his hand, focusing on mustering the devouring mist. Black particles appeared above his open palm, manifesting *without* incantation. They coalesced above his hand, spreading along his fingers. Hatred and a burning desire for death accompanied that magic. Those emotions spurred his desire for vengeance. He *would* slay Cilgan.

After a short while, a dense shaft of black devouring magic formed, but it wasn't a sword. The mass of magic was barely the size of a dagger. Balden gripped the magic, which didn't erode his skin. It was like his power knew not to destroy him. It took a great deal of effort to maintain the tiny weapon, and Balden felt part of it dissipate.

Balden frowned, diverting his mind from the would-be blade. The particles immediately wisped away, as if dancing on an invisible wind.

"I need better concentration," he said, pacing in his cell. He couldn't give up after one attempt. Steadying into a wide stance, Balden tried summoning the magic again. This time, the magical blade was a little longer, but it took a great deal of concentration to form. It wisped away after several seconds.

Damn it! he cursed inwardly.

Balden tried manifesting a blade for several hours, or so it seemed. Each time he was able to make the weapon a little larger and make it last a little longer. Eventually, the magic formed a shaft resembling the blade of a sword.

It lacked any of the other elements: a guard, handle, or a pommel.

He swung the black blade, and it took a great deal of effort to maintain the weapon. Balden felt part of it dissipate like all the other weapons he had mustered.

"This is going to be hard…" he muttered.

Balden focused on the blade, mentally telling it to remain in its current shape. He swung again and didn't feel as much dissipation.

Better, he thought. *But If I'm to escape, this sword can't dissipate at all.* He had to find a way to maintain its form without being too mentally absorbed in maintaining it. He would have to fight too, and that took a great deal of concentration.

I will become more proficient at this, he vowed. *Only then can I escape this nightmare.*

Balden took in a deep breath and started training with his newfound weapon.

Throwing bottles at customers wasn't something Lirathay'lu had ever done. He wasn't violent by any means, but what those fools were attempting was downright stupid. No one in their right mind should *want* to visit that accursed realm.

Lirathay'lu swept the floor of his shop, preparing it for the next day. The broken glass from the thrown bottles had been all cleared away. Lirathay'lu had since placed the flung herbs in other bottles, but had kept the shards. He would repair them when he had time. Besides, why throw out perfectly good matter?

Perfectly good matter, he laughed. That phrase amused him, as if matter could be bad. Matter was matter.

A knock beat against the door of his shop, and the door rattled on its hinges.

A burglar? he thought. No. A burglar wouldn't knock…

"Herbalist!" a harsh voice shouted through the door. "Open up at once! This is Constable Hashar."

A policeman, Lirathay'lu sighed. *No doubt in reaction to my actions today.* He leaned the broom against a nearby table and sauntered to the door. He wasn't in any hurry to open it. The constable and his accompanying watchmen weren't going anywhere.

Lirathay'lu opened the door and assumed his raspy voice. He had used that voice for forty-eight years now and he was growing tired of it. "Yes?" he asked, sounding hoarse.

A lanky man stood within the threshold. He wore a formal red tunic with golden tassels; common attire for a constable in the Mindolarnian City Watch. Six other watchmen—all clad in red-and-gold chain mail—stood behind him. Each had batons and side swords hanging from their belts.

"May we enter?" the lanky man asked. That was obviously Constable Hashar. Lirathay'lu raised an eyebrow at him. Hashar asked an ominous question. Technically, Lirathay'lu didn't have to allow them into his shop. If he was being fined or arrested, they could do it here on the doorstep. But letting them into the shop might be… fun. Besides, Lirathay'lu needed to know what they wanted, and if things went awry, he would need the enclosure of his shop to keep his actions hidden from prying eyes.

"Of course," Lirathay'lu said, and hobbled away from the door, hunching over his left side. He had become accustomed to this manner of walking. Lirathay'lu wasn't feeble by any means. In fact, he was far from it. But the hobbling helped with playing the part of an old herbalist.

"Thank you," Hashar said, leading the other watchmen into the shop.

Lirathay'lu glimpsed the watchmen eyeing the bottles. They filed into the main room and one walked to the hallway leading to the shop's rear.

"Are you herbalist Yenig Mawer?" Hashar asked.

Lirathay'lu nodded. Yenig Mawer wasn't his real name, but it was the one he had gone by in this lifetime here in Mindolarn. So, for this conversation he would be Yenig, the old herbalist with a raspy voice and a bad walk.

"We've come to investigate a matter of concern that came to our attention earlier today," the constable said, pacing between the tables. Hashar eyed Lirathay'lu with a frown. "A member of the Royal Family reported an incident here at your shop, concerning you and a member of the aristocratic caste of the city. You allegedly attacked her, her guards and her two friends. What have you to say about this?"

Royal Family, huh? Lirathay'lu eyed the watchmen. *This will undoubtedly end in an arrest… an attempted one, anyway.* It didn't look like the watchmen were holding any of those communication tevisrals—the ones recently developed at the Hilinard that relayed audible messages. *Cheap imitations,* he grunted.

The watchmen didn't seem to have any other tevisrals on them. Humanity in this day and age was dull, despite the advancements made by the Mindolarn Empire. Noting that this encounter in his shop wasn't being recorded or re-layed elsewhere, Lirathay'lu saw no harm in telling the truth. Besides, they wouldn't remember, and this would provide a great opportunity for some exercise.

"Well," he began, "they wanted to make sleeping drugs so they could access another dimension of reality—the forsaken realm of a mad god."

Hashar started and blinked several times in disbelief.

Exactly what I thought, Lirathay'lu mused, then continued talking. "They were asking for a lot, and I didn't feel comfortable selling that much halisym, ganiard, wevid, and colisry."

The men all looked at him with confusion. They probably thought him mad, driven insane by the very herbs he was citing. That was good. It would make this encounter more entertaining.

"Their intentions weren't ill," Lirathay'lu added. "A curious mind can never be accused of being malicious. But what they were doing would lead to folly. I couldn't, in good conscious, let them proceed."

The watchmen looked at each other uneasily, unsure of what to make of his words. Hashar, however, recovered from his bewilderment.

"So you refused service," Hashar said slowly. "And then what?"

"I told them to get out," Lirathay'lu said.

"And threw bottles at them?" The constable inferred Lirathay'lu's assault.

Right to the point this one is, Lirathay'lu thought. "Well, Sorothians can be persistent. It was a preemptive measure. Besides, I wasn't aiming for any vital areas. Not that these bottles are deadly." He picked up a nearby bottle of brasali leaf—a white leaf used for soothing anxieties—and handled it carefully.

"Put the bottle down," one of the watchmen said, placing his hand on his baton.

Or what…? Lirathay'lu glanced at the man, grinning wryly. He could have fun with these men.

"I seriously hope you're not contemplating resisting arrest," Hashar said, eyeing the bottle in Lirathay'lu's hand. "I would hate to harm a cripple such as yourself."

"So, you *are* here to arrest me…" Lirathay'lu nodded, letting the raspy tone slip from his voice. The watchmen started at his change of tone.

"You admitted to the crime," Hashar said, his stern voice sounding hostile. "And as I see it, there was no reason for you to assault the high duchess and her friends."

Lirathay'lu felt excited at the constable's change in demeanor. He grinned like a child eyeing a bag of candy, or a sloglien spotting its prey, or—

"Yenig Mawer, you're hereby under arrest." Constable Hashar reached for a pair of metal bindings around his belt. The constable continued reciting Mindolarnian law, and Lirathay'lu straightened up, assuming a bold posture. No longer was he the old cripple… he felt like himself. The sensation was akin to molting old scales.

Feeling renewed, Lirathay'lu's grin widened into a smile that soon turned to laughter. "Now, the fun begins!" He twirled the bottle, grabbing its cap.

The men shook their heads and moved around the tables, drawing their batons. Settling into a wide stance, Lirathay'lu swiftly uttered an incantation in the *true* magical tongue. "Rina'milista gri'lu mida!"

Brilliant blue barsion shone from his hand gripping the bottle as he thrust the container to the floor in a controlled manner. The bottle gently settled on the floor as a wave of barsion washed over it, spilling across the shop and shielding the tables, bookshelves, *and* their contents in an inverted-barrier. He didn't want to clean up another mess, so an inverted barsion spell was a necessity. Such spells were used to trap an enemy. Today they did that, but they also protected his herbs.

The barsion completely covered the room as the first watchmen approached. These men weren't slow by any means. Lirathay'lu was just *that* fast.

The first watchman swung his baton, but Lirathay'lu intercepted the weapon, prying it from the man's hands and kicking him in the chest. The poor watchman flew backward, colliding with a bookshelf.

Another watchman approached, but Lirathay'lu disarmed him like the first. Now, Lirathay'lu had two batons. He swiftly attacked the disarmed watchman with side-sweeping blows, cracking ribs.

A third watchman approached, drawing his side sword. The watchman dual-wielded both his baton and his blade, swinging them at Lirathay'lu.

Moving swiftly, Lirathay'lu twirled one of his batons and hit the blade's dull end, deflecting it away. He didn't worry about being cut—he could easily heal a wound like that. Lirathay'lu struck the man's wrist, causing him to drop the sword. The watchman moved to hit with his baton, but Lirathay'lu unleashed a furious combination of blows with his blunt weapons. Loud cracks resounded through the shop, and the watchman dropped to the floor, screaming.

Three more, Lirathay'lu thought, glancing to the constable and the others. The watchmen eyed him fearfully.

"He'll kill us…" one of them muttered.

"B-bu-but he's a cripple!" another stammered, stepping backward and bumping into one of the tables. It didn't move. The table was held in place by Lirathay'lu's inverted barsion.

Grinning, Lirathay'lu leapt onto the nearest table, stepping onto a shielded bottle and *leaping* into a sideways kick aimed at Constable Hashar's chest. The man tried to dodge, but Lirathay'lu's heel struck his shoulder, sending the man spinning over another table.

Lirathay'lu *flew*—as much as a humanoid could—and swung his batons at the next watchman before landing atop another table. He had missed the sensation of air rushing past him.

Soon I can embrace the winds! Lirathay'lu told himself, rebounding and attacking the last watchman. He broke the man's arm and inverted his knee. The watchman fell, crying like a child.

Within seconds, each of the watchmen was subdued.

"Now that felt *good!*" Lirathay'lu exclaimed, dropping the batons. "It's been centuries since I've had that much fun." The batons hit the barsion with a clatter, barely sounding above the groans and pained cries of the wounded men.

I guess that's enough exercise for now, he thought, surveying his shop. Not one bottle had been moved throughout the commotion. It was a glorious sight.

"You're… you're under—" Hashar groaned, "ar-arrest…"

Lirathay'lu spun, seeing the constable stagger onto his feet. *Bold man,* Lirathay'lu grinned. Hashar wobbled and leaned against a table to brace himself.

"You're tenacious," Lirathay'lu said, approaching Hashar. He allowed his eyes to regress to their natural state. To Constable Hashar it would look like the lines of Lirathay'lu's irises were swirling around his pupils.

Their eyes locked a gaze and Lirathay'lu *froze* the constable. Their minds melded, the process controlled totally by Lirathay'lu. *Now, what should I make you* think *happened here?* Hashar's mind was pliable under Lirathay'lu's gaze. Lirathay'lu could make the constable remember whatever he wished. He could wipe away the constable's memory if he so desired, making Hashar think he was someone else entirely. That was a little too extreme.

Lirathay'lu mulled over what he should implant in the man's mind. Hashar had mentioned a Mindolarn Royal when they first met. Lirathay'lu didn't think *they* knew his true identity, but he had to be careful. He could rework the memories of these men, but this Royal could send more men to investigate. He couldn't take the chance.

I only have one more year left in Mindolarn, Lirathay'lu thought. *I can assume another identity until I have to report to Zulsthy'l.* That gave him an idea…

Lirathay'lu manipulated Constable Hashar's mind in a way that he would remember entering an unlocked shop with a dead herbalist lying on the floor.

"Ti'ga'lis," he said, and the enthralling incantation caused a gray magic to wisp into Hashar's nostrils, stilling him.

Lirathay'lu moved on to the next watchman. He would have to implant the same memory in each of them, altering it slightly to their own perspectives—but that wasn't too hard. He would just play off what they remembered upon entering the shop. Lirathay'lu could relive their experiences, after all.

Once he finished altering their memories, Lirathay'lu cast an arpran spell. Green magic erupted throughout the room, spreading in six different directions and coalescing around each of the men he had injured. Their broken bones were mended within seconds. With each of the men still under his enthralling spell, he ordered them to their proper positions, per the false memory he had implanted. Those he had disarmed he ordered to retrieve their batons.

Lirathay'lu uttered an illusionary incantation, making a perfect image of himself on the floor. It wasn't a permanent solution to his ruse, but it would have to do. He could transmute an actual body while the watchmen were away. Doing so would require some time, and he would have to use the Sel'ndar to make it believable.

"Sium," Lirathay'lu said, casting his invisibility spell, and disappeared. Focusing on his barsion, he dismissed it and then the enthralling spell.

The men—now completely healed from the brief bout—resumed a conversation Lirathay'lu implanted within each of them.

"He's not too cold," a watchman said—he was the nearest to the fake corpse. "The death chills haven't set in completely, so I would say maybe a few hours."

"What a pity," Hashar said with a sigh. "Well, he got what he deserved. Let's inform an undertaker and get this body out of here. Gelan," he said to the watchman who had had his knee inverted, "check on this man's next of kin."

"Yes, sir." Gelan saluted and strode out of the shop, showing no signs of his previous injury.

Several others shook their heads at the fake corpse and left the shop. Hashar was the last to leave and shut the door behind him. Once they were gone, Lirathay'lu dismissed his magic. He kept his *true* demeanor, standing straight-backed. Lirathay'lu wasn't tall by any means, but he wasn't short either.

"Goodbye, Yenig Mawer," Lirathay'lu said. "You were probably one of my more intriguing roles."

Now that his alter ego was dead, Lirathay'lu could more easily gather information on this city and its inhabitants. He could freely roam the streets, spying on whomever he wished, whenever he wished. He wondered why *they* didn't do that normally. It was more effective than assuming a role and observing from a distance. But then again, he wasn't like the others. His fellows wouldn't have dared to attack the watchmen… *They're just dull*, he laughed.

Lirathay'lu hurried to the backroom. He had to transmute that body before the watchmen returned.

Wild noises filled the air of Melar Forest as Dith crept between the trees. The air was muggy and filled with all kinds of insects, but Dith didn't mind. He was used to being out in the wild, away from the creature comforts of civilization. Over the last few years he had embarked on several trips of adventure with his master, Amendal Aramien, and other renowned Sorothians. Those were exciting times, full of wonder and intrigue—not to mention magnificent pay.

This trip, however, would not be as rewarding.

Dith looked through the forest's leafy canopy, noting the sun's position in the eastern sky. Darkness would soon be upon the forest. Dith still hadn't found anything substantial to eat. He had long since run out of his rations and was relying on the forest for nourishment.

Adjusting his pack, Dith pressed westward. He had been traveling through the Melar woodland for over two months now. By his estimation he was not quite two-thirds of the way through the forest. It was more than a four-thousand-grand-phineal trek from one side of the forest to the other. Dith had entered Melar Forest west of Arbath, dodging a few patrols of kingdom guardsmen. No one was supposed to enter these woods. It had been decreed a forbidden land by one of the early monarchs of the Losian Kingdom—which one, Dith didn't know.

"I still haven't seen a gangolin," he muttered, climbing over a felled tree.

His purpose here in Melar Forest was to capture one such beast. That was the chief purpose of the Aramien Test of Valor. Master Amendal thought it prudent for him to learn to summon a gangolin. That could only be done if he encountered one and sucked it into a conjuration portal. Lorith—the only other man who had studied under Master Amendal—had traveled through the forest fifteen years ago and done the same.

Master Amendal claimed gangolins were the strongest creatures in the world, rivaling the strength of dragons. Gangolins were strong, but stupid. However, under the influence of an intelligent conjurer they were powerful tools of destruction.

Dith remembered hearing stories of how Master Amendal had escaped the perils of the Abodine Wasteland only because he knew how to conjure gangolins. The gangolins were the only conjuration that withstood the might of the dragon he faced.

Many people didn't believe Master Amendal's tale. Most thought he was mad. Master Amendal *was* a little crazy, but Dith didn't think him to be delusional.

Dith ran a hand through his sweaty dark-brown hair, glancing back to the east. Twilight had settled on the forest.

I need to find a place to camp. Stretching out his hand, Dith uttered an incantation, mustering golden conjuration magic. The golden light wisped from his hand, swirling in front of him in an oval shape about the size of his torso. The magic formed a portal to the Aldinal Plane—a nether-space that existed outside the physical realm of Kalda where magic and matter existed in their rawest forms.

Dith focused on the image of a hawk as he uttered the incantation. Soon, the bird flew from the mystical vortex and zipped through the leafy canopy, completely under Dith's control. The hawk's senses mingled with Dith's, and he felt everything the bird was experiencing. When conjured creatures passed through a conjuration portal, the portal bonded the creature to the mage who summoned it. He closed his eyes, focusing on the hawk's vision. As he guided the bird's flight, he noticed a darkened spot in the ground.

Stay, he commanded the bird through their telepathic link. Dith could *feel* the bird's location across the forest and quickly made his way through the trees. It wasn't long before he reached his conjuration, perched on a tree limb near the opening of a small cave. The hawk swooped from the tree branch and into the cave, scouting its interior for him. From what Dith could tell, nothing had occupied the space for a long time.

Pleased, Dith crouched and crawled into the cave. It wasn't that big, but it was enough for him to lie down and stretch out. Dith uttered another incantation, and a portal formed, guiding the hawk into it. The bird disappeared, returning to the Aldinal Plane.

Hunger struck Dith, and he pulled some wild fruit from his pack. A few berries and a furnapel—an orange fruit with a furry skin and crunchy flesh. Dith had stumbled across a few furnapel trees two days ago and harvested as much as he could carry. It was all that he had to eat.

After eating the fruit, Dith settled in for the night.

⟞•⟜

Vibrations in the ground awoke Dith. He sat up, hitting his head on the cave's roof. "Ouch," he griped, leaning back down and rubbing his head. The ground shook again.

An earthquake? The Kingdom of Los wasn't known for having many earthquakes, if any.

A faint pounding noise accompanied another vibration. More followed, then another, and another. The sound and the shaking was rhythmic, like giant footfalls—

"Could it be?!" Dith gasped and scurried out of the cave. The pounding grew louder, followed by a crash, like a tree being felled. *A gangolin!* He grinned with excitement. Dith hurried back into the cave and grabbed his pack. Once it was secure, he dashed into the woods. Fatigue was replaced by excited anticipation.

The noises grew louder, and Dith saw the outline of a towering creature, walking on all four of its thick muscular limbs. Master Amendal had said that gangolins resembled dragons, although wingless and with shorter necks and tails. They were also about the same size. This gangolin stood taller than a building and was a dull beige color. Though Dith couldn't see the detail, he knew the creature was covered in thick beige scales, with off-white hair protruding from the scales. A dark streak lined the creature's back, running from its stubby tail to its head; the streak was undoubtedly its maroon mane. The thick mane made it look anything but serpentine.

Dith could barely see the outline of the gangolin's wide snout. In comparison to the depictions of dragons, gangolins had a shorter muzzle—or so Master Amendal said. The old conjurer claimed their snouts were half the length of a dragon's while also being twice as wide. Dith always imagined the gangolin's snout was like the wider end of an egg, and after seeing the creature he knew that assumption was accurate.

Moonlight glistened off two white horns protruding on either side of the gangolin's mane. The horns arced backward in a circle, curving behind the creature's head and curling back to its lower jaw. Tiny tines, arrayed in a random pattern, lined the horns, also glistening moonlight. Massive paws with gleaming white talons dug into the forest floor with every step.

Yes! he cheered inwardly. The gangolin plodded toward him, knocking over trees as it tromped through the forest.

Sucking in a deep breath, Dith splayed his hands wide and uttered an incantation. Golden particles formed in his hands, then wisped in front of him, forming a portal to the Visirm Expanse. Unlike the Aldinal Plane, the Visirm Expanse was a timeless void. Conjurers placed creatures and objects inside the expanse to summon at a later time. Portals to the Visirm Expanse utilized an enthralling component, so summoned creatures wouldn't run amok. Dith continued with the incantation and the portal grew, becoming over six times his height. Dith was no small man; he stood a little taller than average height. But still, the portal wasn't large enough for the gangolin. It would have to grow two or three times larger. If not, it would crush the creature leaving it deformed or even worse. Dead.

The gangolin stopped, turning toward the formed magic. The beast sniffed the air so loudly that the noise echoed across the forest.

Soon, charcoal magic—the enthralling component used to force the gangolin through the portal—appeared, mingling with the golden vortex. The gangolin lowered its head and cautiously stepped forward. It had probably never encountered magic and was undoubtedly curious about the manifestation.

Dith's portal continued growing, and after a moment he felt it reach its apex. *It's ready!* he cheered. He was going to do it. Now he would be a full-fledged conjurer in his master's eyes, though Dith had already been awarded the title by the council of the Necrotic Order.

The gangolin edged closer, ever leery.

Come here, Dith thought, then shot the enthralling magic from the portal. The gangolin stopped abruptly, cocking its head and sniffing. The creature began to turn, glancing to its right. At that moment, Dith's magic wisped inside the gangolin. Their minds merged and the gangolin abruptly stilled.

Dith laughed triumphantly. Through his mental bond with the creature, Dith guided the gangolin toward the portal. "Yes—"

Something heavy knocked Dith sideways, forcing him to the ground. Whatever it was pinned him there. *What was it—?*

Before he could look something sharp scraped across his arm. "Ahh!" Dith screamed.

A claw?

Dith couldn't hear anything over the gangolin's loud footsteps.

Suddenly, his pack was ripped off his shoulders, followed by more scratching along his back.

Dith struggled to break free, attempting to roll over. He glimpsed his assailant's darkened figure, none other than a feline native to the forest, a yidoth. Yidoths were feral creatures that roamed the southern parts of Melar. He wasn't that far south, was he? The yidoth's dark green fur allowed it to blend into the forest. This one had brown spots, unlike most, which had stripes.

Yelling, Dith punched the yidoth, knocking it away.

The gangolin began to resist Dith's control; its gait slowed. *Damn it,* Dith cursed inwardly. He spun to his feet, and his portal flickered. The yidoth must have distracted him long enough to cause him to lose control of the portal. It wouldn't be stable enough to capture the gangolin.

The yidoth recovered and circled around him. They only did that when—

Something else knocked Dith to the ground. He rolled away, seeing a second yidoth.

This isn't going to work, he thought, slowly rising from the ground. The portal intended for the gangolin flickered again.

Dith couldn't fend off the yidoths *and* capture the gangolin. A portal the size of the one he had mustered required too much concentration. Angered, Dith whispered an incantation, mustering more golden magic. It formed a large portal to the Aldinal Plane, three times his height. The yidoths turned toward the light, careful to not make a sound. They were stealthy hunters. Master Amendal liked telling stories of yidoths pouncing on people who strolled through the woods.

Blue fingers emerged from the portal, followed by hands and arms made of ice. Soon, a towering creature stepped from the portal—an elemental giant from the Aldinal Plane.

Kill them, Dith commanded his conjuration, spinning toward the magic meant for the gangolin. The portal had almost faded. Dith would need to re-cast the spell.

A scuffle echoed behind him as the icy elemental attacked the yidoths. Dith didn't pay much attention to the fight, letting the conjuration attack on its own. Dith's hold on the gangolin was like a fraying thread as he felt his control slipping away. The gangolin stopped its approach, digging its claws into the ground. A scowl slowly formed upon that enormous snout. The very gaze struck Dith with fear, the likes of which he had never felt.

A dying yelp filled the air, and the gangolin looked as if it were trying to sniff.

Cast the spell, damn it! Dith chided himself and then uttered the incantation. Golden light formed in his hands once again.

Another yelp resounded behind him, and he could sense that both yidoths were beaten.

Stay beside me, Dith commanded his conjuration while still opening the other portal to the Visirm Expanse. The portal formed, but was only twice Dith's size. Why hadn't it been bigger? It was too small.

In that instant, the first portal vanished and the bond with the gangolin was severed.

No!

Now freed, the gangolin reared on its hind legs. It towered over the forest, rising what seemed to be over a dozen stories tall. How big was this thing? The gangolin splayed its forward limbs, bellowing a resounding honking-shrill that washed over the forest like a rippling tide. Dith started and fell backward. He had to finish the spell. He resumed the incantation in a hurry but was struck with unimaginable horror as the gangolin leapt toward him.

No!

The beast soared over the forming magic and landed between Dith and the portal, thrusting its white talons into the forest floor. The ground shook as the beast uprooted trees and made a tidal wave of dirt.

Attack it! Dith commanded as earthen debris sprayed across his face.

His conjuration obeyed, charging across the upheaved ground. The gangolin retaliated, swatting at the icy elemental, but it screamed in pain as the blow connected; gangolins, for all their might, were weak against the cold.

Dith's conjuration flew into a nearby tree, toppling it. Both the tree and the conjuration skidded across the forest floor.

Run! he told himself. *Hide!* Scrambling to his feet, Dith dashed back through the forest, running as fast as he could. His heart felt like it was going to jump out of his chest.

The gangolin yelled that horrifying honking-shrill, and the ground shook again. Dith stumbled forward. In addition to his own vision, he could see the gangolin attacking his conjuration from the icy elemental's point of view. The sight was horrifying! He kept running and saw the cave where he had been sleeping. Dith dashed toward it, hoping that it might provide some shelter. He slid inside and turned on his stomach, gazing out the cave's mouth.

As Dith watched, the gangolin grabbed his conjuration with both claws, screaming in pain. *Why would it—*

The gangolin lifted the conjuration into the air, ripping the icy elemental in half. His bond was severed, vanquished upon the conjuration's death.

By Heleron's Glistening Trident... Dith gasped.

Pieces of the icy elemental went flying, and the gangolin settled back on all fours. It sniffed the air intently, stumbled to what Dith assumed to be the yidoth corpses and gobbled them whole.

"I can't capture that thing..." he groaned shakily. What was Master Amendal thinking? It was suicide facing something like that.

The gangolin sniffed the ground for a little while longer, then tromped off, its thunderous footfalls echoing toward the east.

"I have to get out of here..." Dith muttered. He had to get out of this forest, even if he had to run all the way to the western border. Once he thought the gangolin was far enough away, Dith crawled out of the cave. He hurried to the spot where he had encountered the colossal beast and searched for his pack. But to his disappointment, the yidoths had rendered it useless. The fruit that he had gathered was crushed.

Dith salvaged what he could and made his way westward.

Dith emerged from the edge of Melar Forest a month later, haggard and starved. He hadn't run into any more of those frightful creatures, or anything else that proved too dangerous for him to handle. Fruit was scarce on the western side of the forest, and Dith resorted to eating bugs and tree leaves.

Exhausted, Dith stumbled through a field, unsure of where he was. He could be anywhere between Alath and Klath.

I should go south, he thought. Dith wandered until at sunset he came across a fence. The grass beyond the fence looked like a pasture, and Dith thought he could smell the scent of cows and pigs. *A farm?* He followed the fence westward, toward a barn with a small home beside it.

The sight of civilization—though rural as it was—gave him relief. His ordeals in that treacherous forest were over.

I'm never going back there again, Dith vowed and climbed over the fence. He got over the top but lost his grip, falling into the pasture. A pop sounded beneath him and his ankle flared with pain. Struggling with clenched teeth, Dith forced himself to stand. He put weight on the hurt ankle, but collapsed. *I hope it's not broken,* he thought and crawled through the pasture.

Dith was more than halfway to the home when a man emerged from the barn. The farmer turned and noticed Dith crawling through the grass. The man started but soon regained his composure and ran toward Dith.

"Are you all right?" the farmer yelled as he ran.

"No..." A surge of pain shot through Dith's ankle, and he stopped crawling for a moment. By the time he started moving again, the farmer was upon him.

"What happened to you?" the farmer asked. "You look ragged."

Dith looked at himself. He was in shambles. His sleeves had been torn from the yidoths. Those holes were accompanied by another gash across the back of his tunic.

"Polnia!" the farmer shouted. "We have a hurt man out here!"

Not long after the cry, a woman emerged from the house, followed by two children: a girl and a boy, each no older than five years.

"My goodness!" The woman—Polnia—shuddered and knelt beside Dith.

"Bandits I'll wager," the farmer said with a sigh. "I've heard of attacks recently while going to market."

Bandits, huh? Dith wanted to smile, but the pain didn't let him. He'd best let them assume so, as he didn't know how they'd react to hearing the truth. What he had done was a severely punishable crime. Men were imprisoned for venturing into Melar Forest. Master Amendal told him that one man—who repeated the offense several times—was sentenced to the Prison Castle of Ahzeald for the rest of his life. The man was searching for a hidden city of wonder buried in the forest, trying to prove some legend that was quite obviously fictional. The poor man's obsession had driven him mad and destroyed his life.

"You kids go back into the house," the farmer said, waving the children off. They were reluctant but eventually obeyed.

"Where are you hurt?" Polnia asked.

"My ankle," Dith said. "I can't stand on it."

"Let's get him inside," the farmer said. Then he and Polnia slung Dith under their shoulders and guided him to their home.

"Where am I?" Dith asked.

"Haldor's farm," the farmer answered, "where the best milk is made in all of Southern Los." Polnia chuckled.

"I don't know where that is…" Dith said.

"They must have really beaten you hard," the farmer said. "You're just north of Klimith."

Klimith? Wasn't that north of Klath?

"Do you know where Kinedahl is?" Dith asked.

"Oh, sure!" the farmer exclaimed. "It's about a day's ride south of here. Are you from there?"

Dith shook his head. "I need to meet my master there—" A surge of pain shot up his leg.

"Surely he can wait," Polnia said. "You're in no shape to travel."

That struck Dith as funny.

They entered the home and sat Dith on a small couch within a tiny sitting room, propping his injured leg on a few pillows. The children watched from around a nearby corner. Dith forced a smile, and the little girl waved timidly.

"You're probably hungry," Polnia said. "Children, go fetch Mister"—she turned to Dith—"What is your name?"

"Dith."

She nodded. "Fetch Mister Dith something to eat and drink."

The children scurried away, rummaging through a nearby room, probably the kitchen.

"What else is hurt, Mister Dith?" the farmer asked.

"Just the ankle," Dith said. "Everything else has healed. I look worse than I am."

The farmer frowned and then hurried out of the sitting room. Polnia, however, stayed with him.

"You don't look well," Polnia said, gently stroking his hair. It was overgrown and hung past his ears. Dith hated that. "You can stay here until you're ready to travel."

That surprised Dith. "You'd take a stranger into your home?"

"Of course," Polnia nodded. "One should always treat others kindly."

"But you don't know me," Dith said, squinting. "What if I harm you or your family? Would you dare chance that?"

Polnia shrugged as the farmer—most likely her husband—returned with bandages and splints. She stroked Dith's hair again, trying to soothe him. "Our first king taught that we should always be kind to those who are in need," Polnia said, her tone motherly, "and that we should give where we can."

"Succor those who stand in need of succor," the farmer said, kneeling beside Dith's injured leg. "And you, Mister Dith, need some succoring." He set out the bandages and examined Dith's leg.

The children entered the room a moment later, and Polnia grabbed the plate they had prepared and the glass of milk.

"Here," Polnia said, handing him the milk. "You need to eat."

Dith took a sip of the milk, expecting it to be sour, but it was actually quite good. He gulped most of it down and took the plate from Polnia. Three slices of warm bread were neatly stacked next to strangely cooked vegetables. They looked like they had been cooked in oil.

"I'm going to start wrapping," the farmer said.

Dith nodded and broke off a piece of the bread. It had a slight hint of sweetness to it, and the texture was fluffy. *Not bad,* he thought, and took a bite. *It's actually quite good.* Dith grabbed the vegetables with the bread and ate them together. He finished the plate just as the farmer finished with his leg.

"Thank you," Dith said, "for all of this."

"You're welcome," the farmer said with a smile. "Rest up. Your leg will need it. You can stay with us until you're recovered. I have to leave to go to market in Klath in two days. But Polina and the children will be here to take care of you."

"I can't," Dith protested. "I have to get to Kinedahl as soon as possible." Dith moved to stand, but pain surged up his leg. Clearly, he couldn't make the journey on foot. Defeated, Dith plopped back on the couch, and leaned his head back.

He glimpsed Polnia looking to her husband with concern. "Could you take him? Leave for the market a day early?" she asked.

The farmer sucked in his breath, looking at the floor in a contemplative gaze. After a moment he turned to his wife. "I think that's what Dorin would do," he said.

Who is Dorin?

"We can leave in the morning," the farmer said, then hurried to the door. "Children, come help me. I need to prepare the wagons. I hope you can drive, Mister Dith."

❦

The next evening, Dith arrived in the town of Kinedahl. The farmer, Haldor, and his family had taken him in one of their wagons. They were supposed to be at the market in Klath the following day and had sacrificed an extra day of milking to drive Dith to Kinedahl.

Haldor offered to take him to the inn where Master Amendal was waiting, but Dith didn't want him to sacrifice more than he already had. Besides, Amendal wouldn't take kindly to someone helping him finish his *test*.

Dith hobbled on crutches—made by Haldor—through the dirt streets of the town, looking for an inn called the *Dancing Yidoth*. Haldor said it wasn't too far from the city's entrance. He gave Dith directions, but they were wrong.

As the sun disappeared over the horizon, Dith found the inn. He hobbled inside, finding a tavern off the entry. The scents of wines and alcohols tingled his nostrils.

Rowdy commotion carried across the tavern where a crowd was gathered around a booth. The men and women were laughing at whoever was sitting there. Dith thought he heard a patron accusing someone of being a fool.

"Let him talk!" said one of the patrons. "I want to hear the rest of the story."

"Oh, where was I...?"

Dith knew that voice. *Master Amendal!* His spirits lifted.

"Ah, yes," Master Amendal said. His voice was coming from beyond the crowd. Was he telling stories?

"There I was, sliding down the icy slopes with Fench, here, fluttering beside me. We barely escaped with our lives. Everyone else had been slain, food for that abominable monster. I thought we were done for..."

Dith pushed his way through the crowd as Master Amendal continued his tale. "I looked back to see if we were being pursued, and then I saw—Dith!"

Smiling, Master Amendal jumped out of his seat and leapt toward Dith, grinning like a madman. Compared to Dith, Master Amendal was well groomed, with neatly cropped gray hair and a short beard. He was a tall man with a slim physique, despite his old age.

"You made it!" Master Amendal exclaimed, grabbing Dith by the shoulders. "You're alive!"

The crowd looked at the old mage with confusion. Some demanded that he resume his tale, but Master Amendal just ignored them.

"Oh…" Master Amendal flinched, eyeing the crutches with a raised brow. "Oh…" he muttered again, glancing at Dith's leg. Shaking his head, Master Amendal took one step back and folded his arms. "Well, I didn't expect this…" He gestured to Dith's leg.

Dith chuckled, then heard his name called from behind. He turned, seeing Lorith holding two steins of bubbling ale. Lorith was a tall middle-aged man with a thick build. His auburn hair was neatly trimmed, as was his short beard.

"You did it!" Lorith exclaimed. He handed one of the steins to Master Amendal, who drank long from it. "Was it… bad?" Lorith asked. He looked at Dith with empathy.

"A nightmare," Dith said. "I hope I never go back there again."

Lorith slapped him on the arm, nodding. They both knew the horrors of that accursed forest.

Master Amendal inhaled deeply, slamming the stein onto a nearby table. "Okay, let's go!" He rummaged through his pockets and removed a small rogulin crystal. The crowd dispersed upon hearing Master Amendal's declaration, leaving all three conjurers alone.

"B-but our things!" Lorith stammered.

"Oh yeah," Master Amendal squinted and set his jaw. "You should go get them. And take Fench."

Fench—a strange winged creature that Master Amendal had kept by his side for decades—flew through the air, zipping by Dith in a flash of blacks and grays. Some people called him a fairy, because of his small stature and his odd amalgamation of features. But Dith didn't know *what* Fench was. About the size of a toddler, Fench had a seahorse-like head, a human torso, and a snake-tail instead of legs. His wings were as tall as he was and were a transparent gray with black spots. Most of his body was that same muted color palette.

After a short while, Lorith returned with several bags. Fench fluttered behind him, struggling to carry one. He bobbed up and down through the air, trying to stay aloft with the weighty bag.

"Here, Master!" Fench said, sounding, as always, as if his nose was plugged.

"Thank you, Fench!" Master Amendal took the bag and turned to Dith. "You did well, son. You are now a full-fledged Aramien Conjurer. As your prize I will let you have Fench rub your toes tonight!" Master Amendal cocked his head, proudly turning up his chin. Actions like that gave Master Amendal his crazed reputation.

Dith couldn't help but laugh.

Master Amendal cleared his throat and held out the rogulin crystal. "Onward, to Soroth!" he exclaimed, uttering the teleporting incantation. Golden light shone from the crystal. They would be home in seconds. That realization lifted a weight from Dith's mind. The farther away from that accursed forest the better. Golden light erupted from the crystal, consuming Dith's vision.

At last, the Aramien Test of Valor was finished. Though he had failed to capture the gangolin, Dith had completed his master's grueling test. He had braved the horrid Melar Forest, a feat not many could claim. But now, he could be considered an Aramien Conjurer. And that was something he had always wanted.

PART
THREE

The Isle of
the
Ancient Ones

Iltar · Cornar · Kaescis · Raedina · Solidin

"It is uncertain when Cheserith first claimed deific status. His claim, however, wasn't insubstantial. Somehow, he became immortal and transcended the need to use the Words of Power to manifest the various Channels of Magic."

- From *The Thousand Years War, Part I*, page 7

Colors blurred, zipping past Iltar as he flew from Vabenack. Reflection had *banished* him from that barn with a simple gesture. Iltar hadn't the faintest idea how Reflection had done it. In fact, everything he had experienced in Vabenack was puzzling.

Iltar had watched helplessly as Cornar nearly died in that treacherous battle. For reasons unknown to him, Iltar couldn't interact with anything besides the landscape. He was like a ghost, moving through objects and people. Not even his magic had an effect. Iltar had tried saving Cornar from that crass man's assaults, but no matter what he did, Iltar couldn't intervene. He was forced to merely watch until his father—Adrin—and the other man left the barn. It wasn't until then that Iltar could finally interact with Cornar. But Reflection interrupted them.

That bastard, Iltar growled, still flying backward. He expected to feel wind rushing past him, as before, when he'd fallen from a great height. Now, the only indication of his repulsion was the zipping lights.

But then, everything went black.

Was he still falling sideways? He couldn't tell. Was he still in Vabenack?

Anger simmering, Iltar spat an incantation, mustering an orb of acidic magic. It coalesced in his hand, hovering above his palm. The orb was motionless, and bits of it didn't whisk away as it should when moving. It faintly lit his hand in a yellow-green hue, but nothing else.

He was in a darkened abyss. *An abyss?* A spike of worry eclipsed his anger. *Dreamwalker* mentioned nothing about an abyss—*no, a void…* That verse from *The Codices of Soron Thahan* came to his mind: "*He will suffer in the depths of the void for a season. No light shines there, nor can it be made manifest.*"

Anger returned, boiling within him. He would not be trapped in this place. He would find a way to escape. This *void* wouldn't—

"TH-THE LIGHT…" a voice boomed from behind Iltar, sounding labored. "YOU CAN MUSTER IT." It sounded like that same voice Iltar had heard the last few times he was thrown from Vabenack, but there was something different about it.

"Who's there?" Iltar demanded and tried to turn, but he wasn't sure he moved. There was no orientation in this void.

"I… AM CHESERITH." The voice came from in front of Iltar.

Iltar started. *Cheserith?* Cheserith, the god of the Mindolarnians, the deity of Cherisium. Iltar furrowed his brow skeptically. Could this be a trick from Reflection? Or was he really speaking to the so-called deity?

"Are you really Cheserith?" Iltar asked. "The god of Cherisium?"

The booming voice grumbled. "HOW IS IT THAT YOU HAVE COME TO MY PRISON?"

That question struck Iltar as odd. If this being was god, wouldn't he be all-knowing? "Reflection hurled me here," Iltar said.

"I KNOW NOT ANY BEING CALLED REFLECTION."

"Well, that's what I call him," Iltar said. "Because he looks like me. It's probably some trick, though. He thinks I'm some hero."

A rumble echoed through the void. "ARE YOU THE UNSPOKEN ONE? THE ONE I SAW IN A VISION? HE TOLD ME YOU WOULD DELIVER ME FROM MY SHACKLES."

Questions flooded through Iltar's mind. Wasn't Cheserith the one who prophesied of the Unspoken One? Who was this *He* that Cheserith referred to? And why was this so-called god shackled?

"DO YOU MANIFEST HIS POWER WITHOUT INCANTATION?" Cheserith asked, sounding desperate. "A BLACKNESS THAT DEVOURS ALL IT TOUCHES."

"Yes," Iltar said skeptically.

A booming chuckle resounded through the void. "I *WILL* BE FREE!" Cheserith declared.

Light suddenly beamed from behind Iltar, illuminating the void. Iltar glanced over his shoulder, seeing an oval opening that revealed the Translucent Fields of Vabenack.

Reflection appeared and passed through the opening, walking on the blackness as if it were solid ground. He looked at Iltar, putting his hands on his hips. "You're just in all the wrong places, Iltar." Reflection shook his head.

Iltar turned back around, hoping to get a better look at the so-called deity, Cheserith. About several hundred phineals away was the outline of a gigantic figure, standing a hundred phineals tall. Arms and legs were splayed, as if they were being pulled. Something hung between the legs, curving slightly in the air. Was that a tail?

"YOU *ARE* HIM!" Cheserith boomed. "YOU ARE THE UNSPOKEN ONE! I WILL BE DELIVERED!"

Resounding cackling echoed through the void, and Iltar felt hands on his shoulders, arms, wrists, legs, torso—dozens of hands gripped him, pulling him away.

"You're not supposed to be here," Reflection said.

Iltar struggled against those hands and tried to focus on Cheserith, but couldn't see more of the towering deity. Thirteen other figures caught his eye, all surrounding Cheserith. Their outlines looked similar, but seemed lighter in color, though Iltar couldn't distinguish what color Cheserith was exactly.

Soon, Iltar was back in Vabenack. The portal to the void shut immediately, and the myriad of hands relaxed their grip.

"You're full of surprises today, aren't you?" Reflection said.

Iltar spun, facing the oddity. Nothing was manifest on this part of the Translucent Fields, not even a cloud in the sky.

"You don't look happy," Reflection said, studying Iltar with narrowed eyes.

"I have plenty of reasons to be angry!" Iltar retorted. "Why did you almost kill Cor? He could have died in there!"

"Cor was fine," Reflection said, waving his hand negligently. "He was never in any *real* danger. I could have possessed any one of those characters at any time and healed him. Besides, he *needed* to experience Melthas's death firsthand. It will help him make the *right* choices on Dalgilur. And, now you two have something more in common." Reflection smiled wryly.

Anger boiled within Iltar, compounded by his erroneous assumptions of Soron Thahan's prophecy.

"I see you can now access this realm at will," Reflection said, pacing. "Things are unfolding differently than I remember," he hummed thoughtfully. Reflection raised an eyebrow and squinted at Iltar with his left eye. That was something Iltar would do when he thought deeply on a subject. Why was this thing copying him? The mimicry was infuriating.

Footsteps boomed across the horizon, followed by the clattering metal that sounded as if an entire city was crumbling.

"Oh good," Reflection grinned, "you're waking now. Continue your research, Iltar. You're about to stumble across something startling." Reflection's grin turned to a beaming smile, then the yellow tones of Vabenack swirled.

Iltar blinked, finding himself back in Alanya's bedchamber as his anger faded like a fleeting dream. At the foot of the bed, Hazais was organizing a tray with a morning meal for two.

"Oh, you're awake," the butler said aloofly. "Her Excellency wishes to eat here with you this morning."

Iltar sat up and looked out the window, where the sun was barely peaking over the horizon. Faint pitter-patter sounded from his right as Alanya emerged from her lavish closet, dressed in a pale-violet robe. Her hair was covered in a towel.

"Did it work?" Alanya asked eagerly.

"Yes," Iltar said. "I was able to enter Vabenack."

Alanya beamed with excitement. She hurried to the bed and crawled to Iltar, sitting beside him. "You have to tell me all about it!" she said excitedly, taking his hand.

Iltar nodded. "Is anyone else awake?"

"No, they were all passed out in the sitting room off the kitchen. Those poor boys were just lying on the floor."

Boys? Her words struck Iltar with panic and frustration. Had his acolytes drunk from the dream elixir?

Iltar tossed aside the covers and leapt out of bed. He hurried past Hazais, who was finishing preparations on Iltar and Alanya's breakfast.

"Where are you going?" Alanya asked warily.

Iltar ignored her. He bolted down the hallway and hastily descended the stairs. His acolytes might be in danger. Iltar dashed through the kitchen, to the pot containing the elixir. It was less full than when he had taken his goblet. *Stupid boys!*

He stumbled into the sitting room, seeing Elsia still passed out in the chair. Pagus was lying on the couch, and *all* the acolytes were on the floor.

"You stupid boys!" Iltar growled, hurrying to Bilda. He knelt beside the boy, shaking him.

"Bilda, wake up!" He shook the boy again, but the youth didn't respond. Iltar checked his breathing. It was normal. *Good,* he thought, moving to Tigan. The boy's breathing was normal, too. Iltar checked the others, and they all seemed fine.

With his acolytes accounted for, Iltar examined Elsia. Her lips were parted, and her breathing was heavy, even panicked.

"They're all alive..." he muttered as Alanya approached.

"What's wrong?" she asked, looking worried. "Why did you run off in a panic?"

Iltar sighed, running a hand through his messy hair. "That place is not safe for them."

Alanya chuckled. "Iltar, you train them against armed men. How much worse could that place be?"

He took in a deep breath and averted his gaze. Vabenack was dangerous, far more dangerous than his training sessions. For magic's sake, that dream he had before going into Vabenack was just as deadly.

"Lock up the elixir," Iltar said. "I don't want them touching that stuff."

Alanya sighed.

"Inform your guards that only those *we* chose are permitted access to the elixir."

"How dangerous could Vabenack be?" Alanya asked.

Iltar glanced to her for a moment and then resumed studying his acolytes. "I saw my friend nearly die, his blood pooling on the ground." Iltar imagined Cornar would have been covered in blood when he awoke; at least that's what *Dreamwalker* intimated. Poor Cor probably hadn't a clue as to what was happening to him. But why was he in Vabenack at all? Iltar knew why Reflection was communicating with him, but why Cornar? What role did he have to play in all this? And what was this Dalgilur? Cornar was headed to Klindil...

Those questions troubled Iltar. Then, there was that connection between his and Cornar's fathers. It was a connection Iltar had never considered. And Kaescis... The prince was far older than he seemed. If what *Dreamwalker* claimed was true—that one could visit any event in Kalda's past—then that battle *had* actually taken place. That realization alone was enough to give Iltar pause.

Alanya touched Iltar, drawing him from his reverie. "Let's eat," she suggested. "I'll have Hazais fetch us when Elsia and your students wake." Alanya grabbed his hand, tugging him toward the kitchen.

❦

Nearly two hours had passed when Agen, the last to wake, joined the others gathered in Alanya's grand dining hall. Iltar, his acolytes, and the ladies sat around a table large enough to seat twenty-four. The servants had prepared meals for Elsia and the boys as they awoke, serving eggs with fruit alongside slices of bread. It seemed an odd breakfast to Iltar.

"Take a seat, Agen," Iltar said. "Your breakfast should be here soon." The boy nodded and sat with some trepidation.

"Did you have nightmares too?" Bilda chimed. Agen nodded but didn't speak.

"It looks like we all did," Pagus said, looking to his aunt.

Elsia hadn't said a word since she awoke. She had come to in a frenzy, crying hysterically. Since then Elsia had sat quietly in the dining hall. The countess hadn't even touched her meal. Iltar wondered what had frightened her.

"Mine was pretty bad," Bilda said, tracing a line on the table. "Kinda like Master Iltar's. I was back home, and everything was burning. Then there was this armored man roaming the city, killing everyone with a black whip, turning them to dust."

Iltar narrowed his eyes. A black whip that turned its victims to dust? That sounded like something composed of the Darkness magic. Most of the boys shared their nightmares, horrible experiences that threatened their very lives. Only a few of them saw the door with the symbol Iltar had told them about, but none of them were able to reach it. Bilda came close, but the armored man barred him each time he neared the door.

After the last of the boys shared their experience, Elsia grabbed her fork and picked at her meal. It had since cooled beyond what Iltar would have deemed edible.

"Are you okay, Elsia?" Alanya asked, extending her hand across the table to her friend. The countess took a deep breath and poked the eggs on her plate.

"I'm sorry, Aunty," Pagus said. "But it was just a dream."

Elsia lifted some of the egg to her mouth but stared at Pagus. Finally, she spoke. "You... you stay away from Soroth, you hear?" Her voice was shaky. "Whatever you do, never go back there."

Everyone looked at each other in confusion, except Iltar. He narrowed his eyes at Elsia. What had she seen? Elsia said nothing more and resumed eating her cold food. A servant entered the dining hall soon after, delivering Agen's morning meal.

"We'll resume our research at the Hilinard today," Iltar said. "I want most of you gathering more information on the *Will* and the nature of the Cherisium god. Agen, I want you to find any references you can about something called Dalgilur. Pagus, you and I are going to look for more information on Vabenack."

"But I already exhausted those tomes," Pagus complained, leaning back in his chair. "Unless…" He perked up with a smile.

Was the boy stupid? Iltar didn't intend to send Pagus on a pilfering task. That would be foolhardy. Iltar had a better idea, one that would prove less dangerous. They would access that forbidden part of the Hilinard meant for Mindolarn Royals, but it wouldn't involve burglary.

⟩•⟨

Worry didn't often distract Raedina from her work. Most of the time, she could push extraneous matters out of her mind. But not today. The report she'd received from Constable Hashar of the City Watch nagged at her so much that she became preoccupied with it. Unnerved, Raedina paced to the window of her office at the Hilinard, clutching Hashar's letter. It told of their attempt to apprehend an herbalist named Yenig, who they found dead in his shop. They didn't know the cause. Yenig didn't have any family, and those who knew him barely associated with him. The herbalist was a loner.

Something doesn't feel right, Raedina sighed, clutching the roll of parchment. Letters on parchment seemed so primitive. Hopefully, soon, they would move past such archaic ways of communication for the empire's general populace.

"Are you finished, Raedina?" Dalkalin asked. He stood nearby, dressed in a black coat that hung to his knees.

"Yes," she said, still staring out the window. "But go on without me." Dalkalin adjusted a pair of spectacles on his face and sighed. "You'll be fine without me," she said. "You're just as skilled in tevisral construction. Besides, I've made plenty of advancements in tevisral development. You can bask in the glory for at least one project."

"Very well," Dalkalin said, sounding disappointed.

She heard him walk away, his footsteps fading as he left her office. Raedina continued gazing out the window. She was too distracted to focus on such delicate tasks. One mistaken movement or jolt could ruin the tevisral's other mechanisms, setting the project back weeks or even months. Though she wanted to be present at this particular tevisral's completion—a gauntlet-type device that could manifest various types of magics—it wouldn't kill her to sit this one out. Besides, it was one of many weapons Raedina and her cohorts at the Hilinard were constructing. She would have other chances to stamp her name on the completion of something grand. For now, this herbalist was a more pressing matter.

"His death seems too convenient," she muttered. Then there was High Duchess Alanya Tasivir's testimony of the incident. Alanya claimed that her friend Iltar—the so-called powerful mage from Soroth—froze during a stare-down with the herbalist.

Was the herbalist one of those vile metallic beasts? Raedina knew they liked to lurk about in the world, spying on humanity and searching for the Children of Cheserith. *But there are many of us here,* she thought. Had one of those beasts ever lurked in the seat of the empire? If so, they must have gone unnoticed. They were clever, just like those accursed Alathians…

That brought Raedina back to the matter of Iltar. He looked so much like the man who had slain her beloved uncle, the late Emperor Monddar. *Could he be the murderer?* Raedina wondered. Alathians were clever and full of guile. The persona of Iltar could be a ruse for her uncle's assassin. No one would suspect an Alathian masquerading as a mage from Soroth, especially one posing as a bodyguard.

If this Iltar were the murderer, and this herbalist one of those metallic beasts, were they in collusion? Had that freezing stare-down been a means to communicate a sinister plot? It wouldn't be the first time an Alathian colluded with a metallic beast…

The siege of Angolith. The decisive battle between Mindolarn and the Kingdom of Los, where her other uncle—Emperor Mindolarn—was slain. Thinking of her uncle's death filled her with rage. It reminded her of a time long ago, when the Butcher of Tor made a vicious attempt against her family at the castle on the shores of Laelin Lake. Raedina could still remember seeing them filing into the banquet hall, and that murderous man leaping into the air and hurling disintegrating magic. Those memories sickened her, especially the recollection of watching her cousin's wife fall, her unborn child murdered.

"This world needs purging," she said beneath her breath.

"That's the spirit!" her brother's voice declared. "Weapons should be crafted with such hostile attitudes. It imbues them with a hunger for death."

Raedina spun from the window, seeing Malvonican standing at the threshold of her office. He wore his typical regal garb, a red suit with golden tassels and black pants with matching boots. "But in the future, when plotting genocide, you should do it behind closed doors, dear sister."

She raised an eyebrow at him, not amused.

"What's with the fierce gaze?" Malvonican asked, closing the door behind him. He tromped across the office, weaving around a sitting area with two couches and a low table.

I don't have time for this, she thought, returning her gaze to the window.

"I'm surprised you're here, actually," Malvonican said, stepping beside her. He placed a hand on her shoulder. "Why aren't you overseeing the construction of my new blade?"

"*Your* blade?" Raedina demanded with a grunt. *What audacity.* That particular tevisral wasn't slated for completion for several months.

"Yes," Malvonican said, his tone arrogant. "It makes sense to give it to me. Uncle Marden doesn't need it. Jeridi doesn't plan on riding into battle, nor does Xalutir. Negaris is a mage, and Laedar and Kaescis prefer their Ko'delish blades. That leaves me as the next choice," he said, stepping between Raedina and the window.

"The possession of these weapons does not correspond to the order of succession to the throne," Raedina said, looking past her brother to the grounds of the Hilinard. Clouds were rolling in from the west.

"Really?" Malvonican said. "So why did Kaescis get the Triaindium Suit instead of me? The others have our uncles' armors…"

Raedina turned, looking squarely at her brother. Malvonican stood at a height equal to hers, gazing at her with his aqua-green eyes. Raedina was the only one of her siblings who did not share that eye color. Of all the Royals, she had the most vibrant emerald eyes.

"Well?" Malvonican asked, his expression demanding an answer.

"You know why," she said coldly.

Malvonican laughed. "Because some mysterious stranger came to him and told him that he would deliver our empire? That he was destined to find some weapon cache of our ancestors' enemies?" He shook his head and turned to the window. "I'm just as good a warrior as Kaescis."

Raedina grunted. Malvonican was so arrogant. But he had lived in Kaescis's shadow for decades, always trying to surpass their cousin's feats. Yes, Malvonican had led successful skirmishes against the enemies of the empire. He'd even held his front at the Battle of Angolith, though his forces suffered many casualties. But he was no Kaescis.

"You still haven't answered my question," Malvonican said. "Why aren't you working on the blade?"

"It is not scheduled for several weeks," she said, folding her arms.

"Oh?" her brother asked. "Then why aren't you finishing whatever else you've deemed more important?"

How dare he? She pursed her lips. "My work is being completed by Dalkalin. I am… distracted, and I'd rather not be working on anything at the moment."

Malvonican eyed her, then settled his gaze on the parchment.

Is he going—

Her brother swiftly snatched the parchment, unrolling it while stepping back. Raedina tried to grab the report, but she was too slow.

What a child, she fumed.

"Does this herbalist mean anything to you?" Malvonican asked, brow raised and lips pursed.

"No," Raedina said coldly, "I was helping a friend with an incident that occurred yesterday."

"With an herbalist?" he asked, laughing. "And a dead one at that." Malvonican re-rolled the parchment and handed it back to Raedina.

"I'm not so sure he's dead," Raedina said, taking the parchment and returning her focus to the window. Her eyes were drawn to a group of people, three adults and several boys, walking through the Hilinard's gardens. They were nearing the building that housed her office. A scowl instinctively formed upon Raedina's face as she got a better look at the only man in the group, Alanya's so-called friend.

"If you keep that up you'll start looking your age," Malvonican smirked.

Raedina ignored him, not amused, and continued staring out the window. "What's making you so angry, anyway?" Malvonican asked.

"I think that's Uncle Monddar's murderer…"

"Oh…?" Malvonican sounded intrigued. He leaned closer to the window, getting a better look at the so-called mage from Soroth. "Are you sure?"

"No," Raedina said. "But he looks like the Alathian that Kaescis and I encountered in the palace."

"Interesting…" Malvonican said. "You've seen him before, I take it?"

"When the matter of this herbalist came to my attention. He was with my friend when the herbalist assaulted them. He claims to be a Sorothian mage."

Malvonican hummed with amusement. "A hostile herb peddler and a backwater mage… the plot thickens." Raedina rolled her eyes, exasperated. "I'm sorry," Malvonican said half-heartedly. "But if you think he's the murderer then we should just kill him," he said in a matter-of-fact tone. "I'd need an edge against him though. My new blade, perhaps?"

You sly snake, she thought.

"We could lay a trap for him. Perhaps use Uncle Marden as bait—"

"Malvonican!"

"Well, not Uncle exactly," Malvonican said, sighing. "Do you think me heartless?" Sometimes she did.

Malvonican began to pace around the room, smiling giddily. "We make an announcement for an event at the palace. A feast—no, that's too repetitive. A ball!" He nodded, looking pleased with his idea. "Yes… we ensure that this man receives an invitation. You said he's an acquaintance of a friend of yours? A noblewoman?"

Raedina nodded.

"Perfect! We just need to ensure that she attends with him. If he is the murderer, then he'll be compelled to come. When he does, he'll undoubtedly make an attempt on the emperor—or at least who he *thinks* is the emperor."

That plan didn't sound half bad. If this Iltar was their Uncle Monddar's murderer, he would make an attempt on Uncle Marden's life. But would he suspect a decoy? Any well trained assassin would. But it was worth a shot. And if the herbalist was one of those vile beasts, this ball would draw him out as well.

"Well?" Malvonican asked, sounding eager.

Raedina opened her mouth to speak just as a knock sounded at her office door. "I like it," she said, crossing her office. "We will discuss the particulars in a moment."

She opened the door and was surprised to see Alanya Tasivir standing outside her office, with none other than that man, Iltar. "Raedina," Alanya said with a smile. "Do you have a moment? I was wondering if you could do me a favor."

Calming her demeanor, Raedina straightened up, resuming a regal pose. "Certainly. What is it that you need?"

Alanya sighed, looking a tad desperate. "We're conducting some research and hit a brick wall. My friend, Countess Elsia Scurn, overheard some attendants speaking about the Royal Archive here in the Hilinard. She's interested in perusing it, but I told her it's accessible only to the Royal Family. My late husband, Scovis, mentioned its existence once in passing," she added. "Would you be able to grant us permission to access it? It might hold the answers to my friend's research."

Raedina glanced to the so-called Iltar, then back to the high duchess. Helping them might lead to this man's letting his guard down, or at least persuade him that they weren't onto his ruse. Whatever they were researching—no matter how detrimental to the empire it might be—would cease upon this man's death.

"Of course," Raedina smiled. "Come with me."

"The first indication of war was Cheserith's seizing of the governing seat of the Ril'Sha—the highest draconic council. It was the first time that dragon blood had been spilt since the uncivilized ages, eons ago. That primordial act of passion spurred a division among the surviving Ril'Sha, eventually leading to the establishment of two separate pantheons of draconic rule."

- From *The Thousand Years War, Part I*, page 11

"A re you sure this is going to work?" Pagus whispered to Iltar. There was an exceptional amount of doubt in the boy's voice. Iltar glanced at Pagus but continued following Alanya and Raedina down the halls of the Hilinard.

Of course it would work.

They turned a corner, coming to a dead end in the hall. Raedina strode toward a reading alcove where a bald attendant was engrossed in a leather-bound volume. The princess cleared her throat, drawing the man's attention.

"Forgive me, Your Imperial Highness," the attendant apologized, standing upright. He closed the leather-bound tome, setting it on his chair.

"I need to access the Royal Archive," Raedina said. "And my *friends* here are to be granted permission to peruse its contents for the remainder of their stay in the capital."

"But, Your Imperial Highness, that cannot be allowed."

Pagus leaned close to Iltar. "See… I told you this—"

"Hush, Pagus," Iltar said between clenched teeth. The youth folded his arms and sullenly watched the exchange between Raedina and the attendant.

Raedina stared coldly at the bald man, causing him to flinch. "You will do as I say," she said. "I will discuss the matter with my uncle, personally. But in the interim you shall afford my friends the same respect that you would pay to a member of the Royal Family."

"Y-yes, Your Imperial Highness," the attendant stammered. He rose out of his seat and looked behind Iltar and the others. Satisfied that no one else was around, the attendant turned to face the alcove, muttered what sounded like a prayer, and then extended his hands wide. "Eka'lum demi nocht'mil shur'inta," he said, sweeping his hands across the stone surface.

A line of light appeared in the alcove, running from its top down to the floor. The alcove appeared to move away from Iltar and the others. Then the stone *slid* apart, revealing another corridor.

"Whoa…" Pagus muttered. "Did you see that, Master Iltar?"

"Of course I did." Iltar raised an eyebrow at his apprentice, then returned his focus to the newly opened corridor. Iltar had seen nothing like that before. The whole thing was beyond mystical.

"Follow me," Raedina said, glancing back to Iltar with a terse smile that seemed false. The princess led Iltar and his companions through the previously hidden corridor and toward a flight of stairs. As they neared the steps, Pagus tugged at Iltar's sleeve, urging him to slow his pace. "Do you think that was some sort of incantation?" the boy whispered, obviously intrigued.

"I don't know," Iltar said, glancing down to the hand gripping his sleeve. What was Pagus up to?

"You know, I was doing some reading about tevisrals that activate with words that *sound* like an incantation."

"That wasn't an incantation," Iltar said. "I'm unsure what that gibberish was…" He quickened his pace, catching up to Raedina at the base of the stairs. The princess led them from the stairs and turned a corner. They zigzagged through several hallways, passing many closed doors before stopping at an opening guarded by Crimson Praetorians. What lay beyond looked like another library.

They passed the Praetorians and entered the Royal Archive. Iltar, however, contemplated the purpose of the guards in this forbidden area. Most places would have probably thought that secret door sufficient to keep out the average robber. If that door was activated by that phrase, then any infiltrator would have to memorize those words in order to breech this area of the Hilinard. It seemed an unlikely probability.

So why the guards?

"Here we are," Raedina said, her dress rustling as she stopped. "I will inform our Praetorians to allow you entrance. And Vaegris should be around here…" She gestured with her hand, her eyes searching the archive. "Let me find him," she said, and hurried off.

Iltar looked about, studying the secluded library. The Royal Archive was fairly large, a square-looking room only one story tall. Dozens of bookshelves extended the length of the room, spanning nearly fifty phineals. Alcoves punctuated the walls, like those elsewhere in the Hilinard. Beautiful lightstone chandeliers hung within them, brightly lighting the stone tables.

Alanya approached Iltar, leaning close. "You owe me for this," she said with a flirtatious tone. Iltar caught her lustful gaze, and he fought back a smile. He had never thought a woman would look at him that way.

"Well?" she whispered, gliding her long fingers across his cheek.

"If we find anything of value," he said teasingly. Alanya pursed her lips, not amused.

Oh well, Iltar sighed. He glanced at Elsia, who had been quiet ever since leaving Alanya's home. The countess stood with her arms folded, gazing blankly at the bookshelves. Footsteps sounded from between the nearby bookshelves. Raedina returned with a short old man with wavy white hair. His striking yellow eyes were flecked with orange.

Raedina gestured to the old man. "This is Vaegris," she said. "He'll help you with your research. Now, if you'll excuse me, I must get back to my work." The princess nodded to Alanya, then hurried out of the Royal Archive.

"So, what are you looking for?" the old man asked in a grouchy tone. Vaegris didn't seem pleased to have visitors.

Elsia finally broke from her reverie and removed a roll of parchment. "We have a list," she said. "We're studying a variety of subjects."

Vaegris hummed in a way that sounded like a growl and took the parchment from Elsia. The countess folded her arms and looked briefly to Iltar. Pagus walked around his aunt, sauntering toward one of the aisles.

"Stop!" Vaegris shouted. Pagus, however, ignored him and began perusing the bookshelves. Didn't the boy know that the old librarian was speaking to him? Or was Pagus feigning ignorance?

"I said stop!" Vaegris spun toward Pagus. "You are not welcome to wander."

"Oh… I didn't know," Pagus said innocently, then meandered back to the others, eyeing the spines of the books he passed.

Iltar sighed and shook his head.

"You can wait in one of the alcoves." Vaegris gestured dismissively. "I'll fetch you books on these subjects." With a final warning glare, the old man walked down one of the aisles and disappeared.

"Come on, Pagus," Elsia said, grabbing her nephew by the arm.

"Hey!" the youth blurted as Elsia dragged him past Iltar and Alanya. The high duchess took Iltar's hand, and they followed Elsia to the far corner of the room.

"This should do," the countess said, and guided her nephew to an alcove bench. "We can discuss what we need to without worrying about prying ears." The bench looked more comfortable than those elsewhere in the Hilinard. Though the alcoves were carved from stone, they had plush cushioning on their seats and backs. The cushions were embroidered with a pattern that looked like symbols.

Once Iltar got closer to the cushions, he recognized those symbols as that strange language he found in *Dreamwalker*. The symbols were arrayed around an outline that looked like one of the emblems on Reflection's robe.

"This is one of the emblems I'm looking for," Iltar said, tapping the cushion. He looked at the back and found the same pattern. *Interesting…* Iltar squinted. "Quill, parchment," he said, extending a hand toward Pagus. "And get out the sketches of the symbols." The boy grumbled and reached into his pack, grudgingly removing the items.

Iltar shot Pagus an annoyed look as he took the things. He shuffled through the pages of emblems until he found the one that matched. Iltar held the parchment up to the fabric, noting the differences. The emblem was one of the last he had sketched and many of the details were missing or incorrect.

"Do you mind if I sit?" Alanya asked, then slipped past Iltar. She slid across the bench, sitting with her back to the alcove's wall.

"Thank you," Iltar said in a monotone and began copying the emblem. He finished before Vaegris returned.

"That's impressive," Alanya said, grabbing the freshly drawn sketch from the table. Iltar took a seat, and Alanya nestled up to him, setting the sketch back on the table.

"Now we need to find out what it is," Elsia said, reaching for the sketch, but Pagus swiped it from her. She sighed as her nephew began studying the emblem. Pagus's mind looked to be churning.

Don't do anything stupid, Pagus, Iltar thought.

Soon, Vaegris returned, carrying six thick books. Each looked to be over a thousand pages long. "You can start with these," he said, setting the books on the table with a grunt. "I will find the rest for you and hold them aside."

"We'll spread out into another alcove," Elsia said, sliding out of her seat. "We can keep the extras with us, can't we?" she asked.

Vaegris nodded with that humming growl and began to turn away. However, before the old librarian got too far away Iltar spoke. "Do you know what this symbol is?" Iltar asked, pointing at the back of the bench.

Vaegris spun partway around. His yellow eyes flicked to the bench's fabric then back to Iltar. Vaegris's only answer was a stern gaze. He grunted again and hurried off without a word.

"Rude…" Iltar grumbled through clenched teeth. He slid off the bench to give Alanya more room to spread out.

"Don't like the silent gaze for an answer, Master?" Pagus said in a flippant tone as he vacated the other side of the alcove. Iltar eyed Pagus, not amused. "Must be an age thing." Pagus winked, then slunk into the alcove where his aunt had taken up residence.

Iltar stifled a grumble. He didn't want to imitate the old librarian, but he must have had a strained look on his face, because Alanya began laughing.

"Let's start reading," Iltar said with a sigh, and grabbed one of the heavy books.

—▷•◁—

Lirathay'lu casually strolled through the gardens of the Mindolarn Palace. He wore an luxurious robe, the type commonly worn by many of the higher-ranking priests of the Cherisium religion. Walking straight-backed felt odd after playing the role of a cripple for nearly five decades. He sauntered into a secluded part of the gardens, studying the nearby palace. There weren't many guards in the gardens. From what Lirathay'lu had determined, most of the sentinels were stationed closer to the palace. Only rarely did they patrol these more secluded parts of the gardens.

"You there," a masculine voice shouted.

I missed someone? I must be getting rusty at this whole espionage business.

"Yes, you!"

Is he talking to me? Lirathay'lu slowly turned around. He stiffened in an arrogant manner while searching for the source of the voice.

"What are you doing here?" a tall lanky man asked, rounding a wall of sculpted bushes. He too wore the robes of a priest and was accompanied by two Crimson Praetorians.

How unfortunate…

Lifting his chin, Lirathay'lu raised his brow and drew his lips to a line. "It seems I am a little lost…" he said in a distracted tone.

"Oh really?" The priest halted, stopping an arm's length away. He stood almost two heads taller than Lirathay'lu. "And who exactly are you?"

Lirathay'lu hummed inquisitively. *Perhaps I should have picked a different role,* he thought, still holding his distracted demeanor.

The priest shook his head in disbelief. "You aren't one of my priests," he said with growing hostility, squinting impatiently and staring directly into Lirathay'lu's eyes.

Well, that's fortunate, Lirathay'lu mused and allowed his eyes to regress to their natural state.

The priest *froze* in reaction to the mutual gaze. Their minds melded, and Lirathay'lu picked through the man's memories like a child perusing a candy shop. This particular priest—named Regant—was the High Oracle of the Cherisium religion here in Mindolarn.

Oh. You're human… Lirathay'lu felt surprised. *Odd that the qui'sha would appoint a human to be High Oracle,* he thought. Lirathay'lu probed further, discovering that the guards had noticed him wandering through the gardens and called for the High Oracle to come identify him. If Lirathay'lu were to prove a fraud, the two Praetorians were to deal with him.

"Your Holy Eminence?" a Praetorian asked.

You remember me from the convent at Ulvilo, Lirathay'lu told Regant, then erased the brief stare-down from the priest's memory.

"But Regant, you don't remember me?" Lirathay'lu asked, relinquishing his gaze upon the High Oracle. "From Ulvilo."

Regant squinted further. "Lira?" he muttered. "Lira, is that you?" *I guess Lira will have to do.* Lirathay'lu tried to hide his disappointment amid the false reunion.

Bursting with excitement, the High Oracle wrapped his arms around Lirathay'lu in a tight embrace. "It's been some time, hasn't it?"

"Yes, it has."

The Praetorians stiffened, gripping their fanisars tightly. The High Oracle's quick turnaround obviously didn't persuade them. *This might go awry…* Lirathay'lu mused, but returned his focus to Regant.

"I didn't know they made you High Oracle," Lirathay'lu said in feigned surprise.

"Oh yes, seven years ago," Regant said, then spun to the Praetorians. "You may return to your posts. It seems I *do* know this man." The Praetorians marched off without a word.

"Tell me, what brings you to Mindolarn, my friend," Regant said. It never ceased to amaze Lirathay'lu how easy it was to alter the minds of men.

"I'm visiting the seat of the empire to observe their rituals," Lirathay'lu lied. "I'm hoping I might be granted permission to stay in the palace for a time. I won't be staying long. I must make a pilgrimage to Comdolith by the end of the year."

"I see." Regant motioned to another corridor lined with bushes, inviting Lirathay'lu to follow him that direction. Satisfied that he would go undetected, Lirathay'lu followed Regant through the gardens.

46

REALIZATIONS

"It didn't take long for Cheserith to establish his divine façade. Champions from various breeds challenged his right to rule, but all were unsuccessful. None triumphed against him, and those that came close to slaying him experienced his self-proclaimed immortality firsthand. No wound could ever be sustained against him, as the fibers of his body reknit themselves instantly. This effect was later seen in the men he twisted, the Ma'lisha."

- From *The Thousand Years War, Part I*, page 13

The Colvin brandy burned as Kaescis swallowed the green alcohol. The quartermaster of the *Executor's Breath* had purchased several barrels while moored in Keliur. This batch was stronger than what they had served the Sorothians. Exhaling heavily, Kaescis set his glass on the side table beside his chair. He had retired to his cabin soon after departing Kretin and hadn't left it in days. He wanted to let his anger simmer. But no matter what he did, Kaescis couldn't abate the hate raging within him. Not even the brandy relaxed him.

It's that blade, he thought. Kaescis had slain with it, and now it craved more destruction. But how was that possible? It wasn't an *actual* blade. Perhaps the things that produced the Ko'delish were what stoked his emotions.

Death... the word whispered from a dozen voices. *Destruction... give us death!*

"I need to calm myself," he muttered. All he wanted to do was relentlessly murder everyone who stood in his way. Kaescis sighed, gripped the arms of his chair, and closed his eyes.

"Oh, Lord Cheserith, let me focus... I can barely sleep with these voices constantly demanding destruction." He hoped his prayer would be heard. Taking a deep breath, Kaescis cleared his mind, imagining a gray void. Soon, everything faded. He no longer felt the rocking of the ship. For a moment, he felt peace. All was quiet.

And then, nothing.

⟷ ⟺ ⟷

A knock awoke Kaescis. He glanced at the side table, seeing his drink where he left it. The door to his cabin creaked open, followed by a pair of footsteps.

"You've been in here for days," Laeyit chided as she crossed the cabin. "Those Wildmen are getting anxious without you." Her hair was braided as usual, but this time she wore makeup. Why had she done that? "What's wrong with you?" she demanded.

Kaescis groaned and straightened in his chair, still groggy. Laeyit came straight for him and sat on his leg. She pursed her lips, eyeing him up and down. "This isn't becoming of you," she said.

Kaescis looked at her frankly. "I can't stop hearing the voices. They demand death."

"Then give it to them!" Laeyit said, sounding exasperated. "Slay as many as you need in order to sate them."

Was that wise? He might go on a killing spree if that were the case, slaying friend *and* foe alike.

"They want something from you, Kaescis," Laeyit said,. "And you must give it to them. The hiss'thraks guided the Chosen, and now they are guiding you. Don't you see what you're becoming?" She smiled. "No one that wields the Ko'delish has heard them as clearly as you have."

Kaescis sucked in his breath. As he pondered Laeyit's words, another pair of footsteps approached his cabin.

"About time you opened your door," Bratan said cheerily. He strolled into the cabin, carrying a keg with a spigot on one end. In his other hand he carried several steins. Bratan made his way to where Kaescis sat and set the keg on a low table. "Now we can drink," the Praetorian said, smiling broadly. "We need to celebrate our victory, after all."

Laeyit grinned, laying her hand on Kaescis's forearm for a moment before standing. "Did you bring enough, you big oaf?" she asked.

Bratan chuckled, serving himself a stein of dark-blue ale. Then, looking to Kaescis, he asked, "So how many?"

How many? Kaescis raised an eyebrow.

"Your score."

Oh...

"Three," Kaescis answered. "Maybe a few more that I wounded."

"That's it?" Bratan bellowed. "I had seven. What about you, Laeyit?"

"Two," she said tersely, grabbing Kaescis's glass of Colvin brandy. She took a sip of it and curled her lips in disgust.

Bratan carried on about the battle at the Keepers' Temple, but Kaescis paid little attention to the details. All he could think about was the voices. What would happen if he heeded their demands? Could he let himself completely embrace that bloodlust? The voices had diminished once he was on the battlefield. Pure emotion replaced their words. To his knowledge, none of the others—his uncles or cousins—had ever said anything about voices demanding destruction.

Kaescis felt a kick against his boot.

"Well?" Bratan asked.

"What?" Kaescis cocked his head.

"Do you want a drink?"

Did he? That wouldn't drown out the voices.

"Just give him one," Laeyit said. "It's better than that filth he's been sipping."

Bratan laughed, pouring a stein for Kaescis. "It was a good victory," he said, extending the full stein.

Kaescis took the stein, holding it near his lips. *Death…*

Sighing, Kaescis closed his eyes. He heard the words echoed from a dozen voices, then he saw in his mind's eye something he hadn't thought of in decades. Pandemonium flooded around him and Helgara fell, tackled by an elite soldier from the Western Sovereignty.

Kill them… the voices demanded.

But those men are already dead, Kaescis spoke to the voices.

A sense of disagreement flooded his mind. The voices inside him weren't pleased with his answer.

Who else do I kill? Kaescis asked. *Their descendants? Their families?*

A pleased sigh echoed in his mind.

Do I kill… him? Kaescis thought of Mister Dol'shir.

Slay Dol'shir! the voices chimed together.

Kaescis was taken aback. He hadn't expected this… Laeyit had been right from the start. His prompting to wait on the pier in Soroth *was* to have the son of his enemy delivered into his hands.

"Did you hear the rumors?" Bratan asked, looking at his now empty stein.

"I doubt he has," she said.

Regaining his composure, Kaescis leaned forward in his chair. "What *rumors?*" he asked.

"There's been quite a commotion over on the *Promised Maiden,*" Laeyit said. "It seems *Mister* Dol'shir awoke drenched in blood, without wounds."

What? *Bleeding without Wounds?* But that was a legend, a myth among the Devouts of Cheserith.

"It's baffled most everyone," Bratan said. "They say it happened the night after we left Kretin. The whole cabin was deluged in blood. One of the sailors says they're still trying to get the blood out of the wood."

Bleeding without Wounds…

"I was able to get something out of the sailors," Laeyit said. "Supposedly, the Sorothians were whispering about their leader dreaming of a battle that happened years ago."

"It sounds like the man was taken to Vabenack," Bratan said. "But why would a man like him be chosen to walk in such a sacred place?"

That question provoked an answer within Kaescis's mind. *Lord Cheserith is preparing him for me,* he smiled. This had to be part of his glorious errand. Not only would he recover tevisrals from Kalda's utopian past, Kaescis would become the hero needed to lead his empire to victory. To embrace the Ko'delish and defeat a man like Cornar Dol'shir—the son of the infamous Butcher of Tor—would purify him in a way that would rival the great ones who came before him. He would unite those lands his people had lost and spread the empire's borders farther than his father's domain. He would be Kaescis Midivar, Hero of the Empire, Champion of Cheserith.

Just thinking of that title filled him with glorious purpose.

"He's smiling…" Bratan grunted.

"Probably not listening." Laeyit took another sip from her stein.

Kaescis chuckled. "Oh, I'm listening, all right," he said. Laeyit and Bratan perked up, eagerly studying Kaescis. "This is a sign from our Almighty Father." Kaescis beamed with excitement. "I know what *they* want from me." He looked to Laeyit. "You were right."

Laeyit looked confused, and Kaescis continued, "The hiss'thraks are preparing me, and in order to rise to my destined station I must have a worthy adversary, and so, Dol'shir has been selected. Who better to stoke my fury than the son of my enemy, the man who slew my brother and in effect murdered Helgara and Aritese." He studied his friends for a moment.

Both nodded with approval.

"Cornar Dol'shir will die at my hand, along with anyone else who stands in my way of slaying him," Kaescis declared with fervent purpose. "Their deaths will be a fitting sacrifice."

Laeyit grinned, taking in a deep breath.

Bratan chuckled. "A fitting fate," he said, refilling his stein for the third time. "You killed his father, and now you'll kill him."

❖ ❖ ❖

Several days had passed since Alacor had received a message from Jahevial. The damned man probably hadn't the chance to send another message. The last one Jahevial had sent was right before he and the others boarded the *Promised Maiden* in Kretin. The news was disappointing. Other than odd books, the expedition to Klindil had been fruitless. No tevisrals. No artifacts from the ancient past.

Frustrated, Alacor retired to his office at the Necrotic Order after a long day of instruction. Kreely had been exceptionally stupid today. The pathetic fool still couldn't get the incantation right for the life-draining spell he was learning.

What happened to all the great ones? Alacor wondered, plodding over to a grand seat akin to a throne. *These boys are just so dull.* Nowadays only the weak came to the doorstep of the Necrotic Order. Ten years ago, droves of talented students had flocked from all the islands of the Principality. Now, barely anyone came. Most children nowadays became soldiers.

"Perhaps I can change that," he whispered. The Sorothian Navy *did* have mages in their ranks. Some of those men were getting older and would retire in the next decade or so. Although, not all those mages were necromancers.

At the next meeting of the Senate, Alacor nodded. He could put out feelers then. See if anyone would support a bill to enlist the youth of Soroth into the Necrotic Order.

Alacor—like other grandmasters before him—occupied a seat in the Senate of the Principality. Cordis had finagled the seat a year before his death. It had been retained throughout the years, although some grandmasters didn't utilize it as often as they should. None of them had been as active as Alacor. He saw his involvement as a way of fulfilling Cordis's dreams and ambitions. Perhaps one day a grandmaster would be governor of Soroth. It might not be Alacor, but he had to pave the way for future generations—just perhaps not these acolytes.

I can't even picture them running the Order, let alone a nation, Alacor grunted. These boys were a dismal bunch.

A knock at the door filled the office, and then Jalel slipped into the room.

"Any word?" his brother asked.

"No."

"How could they have been wrong?" Jalel asked, putting his hands on his hips. "They knew tevisrals were there on Klindil, didn't they?"

Alacor shrugged. "Krindal is looking for proof of his theories," he said. "That might not come in the form of ancient tevisrals. Jahevial's report about that buried temple was quite detailed. Just the architecture alone is enough to validate that trip, at least in Krindal's eyes."

Jalel groaned. "Or the Sapphire Guard took them."

That was a possibility.

"Why do you think Krindal neglected to tell us about the elves?"

"I don't know," Alacor said. "I wouldn't have committed anyone or offered aid if I'd known that Krindal was in competition with them. Besides, Krindal had the aid of the Mindolarnians. I don't see why he needed to appeal to us. They had—no *have*—a sizeable army. Cornar and his men wouldn't have made a difference either."

"Perhaps Krindal wanted to gather everyone he could to fight against the elves," Jalel speculated. "What about this island—Dalgilur? Have you found anything about it?"

"No. Not even on a map."

Jalel hummed disappointedly. "Well, what about—" Jalel abruptly shifted his gaze to Alacor's desk, drawn to the communication tevisral pulsing a dark-orange light. "There's another message!" he said, hurrying across the room.

Alacor watched as Jalel grabbed the communication tevisral. Jalel activated the receptor and waited for the message to play. Soon, Jahevial's voice came from one end of the tevisral. "I don't have any more details about this Dalgilur. The fleet has been headed south, and we've picked up a favorable tailwind. Captain Salisar believes we'll also hit a current, which should get us to the supposed island in a little over a week.

"I managed to go through all the books that were found, and a few would be of interest to the Order. One speaks of the construction of tevisrals, confirming earlier theories that tevisral manufacturing was commonplace in the ancient world. The Mindolarnians didn't seem to have any interest in these texts. Kaescis is after whatever is on this Dalgilur. I've heard a few rumors, saying that Dalgilur is the fabled Isle of the Ancient Ones."

"The birthplace of humanity?" Jalel broke in.

Alacor didn't answer. He wanted to hear all of what Jahevial had to say. Jahevial's earlier reports had been lacking.

"The prince and his retinue seem to be focused on that place. Even Krindal is looking forward to making discoveries on Dalgilur, despite all the evidence we were able to collect at the Keepers' Temple. I wish you could have seen it. The temple was a spectacular sight."

Jahevial went on for several more minutes, giving details that the other scholars had found while exploring the temple. It was the headquarters of a long-dead Order dedicated to the preservation of Kalda. Alacor had heard a little about this group, some of which had been mentioned by Cordis. These Keepers seemed to fit the description of an organization that was a threat to the Empire of Karthar.

After Jahevial's message ended, Alacor contemplated the report.

"So, these Keepers were our ancestors' enemies," Jalel mused aloud. Alacor nodded. "What do you think the prince is after?" Jalel asked.

"Anything," Alacor said. "Perhaps something to turn the tide of Mindolarn's losses… reclaim territory."

"But why wouldn't he say that when he met with us?" Jalel demanded. "This doesn't feel right, brother. I don't think Kaescis can be trusted."

"He's a pureblooded qui'sha," Alacor said, staring hard at his brother. "His very nature dictates that he *is* trustworthy."

Jalel shook his head with a sigh. "The *Codices* warn of apostates."

"Are you making accusations, brother?"

Jalel frowned. "I am only voicing possibilities. The prince *knows* you, Alacor. I don't see why he couldn't have confided in us."

"Not everyone who was present at Krindal's demonstration is part of the Ca'trusin. Krindal isn't even one of us." Jalel sighed again and Alacor gestured for him to hand him the communication tevisral.

Alacor made the appropriate actions to send a message, waiting for the tevisral's gem to pulse a pale blue before speaking to Jahevial. "I thank you for the report. If there is anything else that happens from now until you reach the island, let us know."

He handed the tevisral back to Jalel, and then the gemstone on the tevisral pulsed with a dark-orange light—indicating another message. Jalel activated the tevisral, and Jahevial's voice spoke from the device. "There is one other thing," the scholar said. "The night after we left Kretin, Cornar Dol'shir was found bloodied. It looked like he had bled out completely. His entire cabin was deluged in blood, but there wasn't a single wound on him."

Jalel turned a ghastly color, dropping the tevisral on the rug beneath him. "I-it can't be," he muttered.

Alacor set his jaw and picked up the tevisral, sending another message to Jahevial. "What else have you heard about this *incident?*"

The reply came a few seconds later. "From what I've heard from Cornar's men, he was dreaming of a battle. Cornar was wounded and healed, all within this dream."

"The prophecies…" Jalel muttered.

Alacor ignored his brother, working the tevisral to send another message. "Jahevial, gather all you can about this incident. I want to know every detail."

A brief moment passed before Jahevial replied. "I will find out all I can, grandmaster. Word has already spread through the fleet, worrying many of the Mindolarnians. It shouldn't be too hard for me to get the facts."

Alacor nodded, resting the tevisral in his lap. It spanned the entire width of his chair. It was a long device, longer than he thought necessary. But alas, it was the best tevisral-crafters were able to do.

"*Those chosen by God will bleed as though they had wounds, yet they shall be unharmed,*" Jalel quoted a line from that apocryphal tome. "*They shall herald His glorious return.*"

"You know, reading that tome is heretical," Alacor said flatly.

"Master Cordis believed in it," Jalel said, then laughed. "I never thought a man like Cornar Dol'shir would be chosen."

Chosen? Men like Cornar weren't suited for divinely appointed tasks. Besides, if anyone was to fulfill a divine role it would be a qui'sha or a member of the Ca'trusin.

"Any word from Makivan?" Jalel asked.

"Nothing this week," Alacor said. "Iltar is still missing."

Jalel shook his head. "What is that bastard up to?" Although Alacor didn't care for Iltar, Jalel downright hated the man. "I bet this was all some kind of ruse," Jalel grumbled, pacing back and forth.

"For what?" Alacor asked. "Iltar didn't even protest my stipulation on those taking part in Krindal's adventure. What could be greater than embarking on a quest that would undoubtedly change the world?"

"I don't know," Jalel said, stopping and gazing hard at Alacor. "But Iltar is up to something… I just know it."

Alacor shrugged. It very well could be a simple answer. But whatever it was, Makivan would get to the bottom of it. He was a cunning man, and a powerful necromancer. After all, Makivan had been Alacor's pupil, his first apprentice.

※

"What a tedious task," Makivan muttered. He sluggishly climbed along the winding road that ran along the northern face of Mount Setigas. It was one of the largest mountains on the Isle of Sarn. *Where could Iltar be?*

Makivan had spent nearly a month searching for Master Iltar. The sly eel was nowhere to be found. Makivan didn't know why the grandmaster and his brother wanted him to find the man, but he was not supposed to ask questions. After all, they were his superiors in both the Necrotic Order and the Ca'trusin.

Makivan grunted as the road became steep.

Iltar had hidden himself and his acolytes well. They weren't at either of the places they should have been. In fact, no one at the Aliteran Estate had seen them. Each time Makivan came to call on Master Iltar, those at Scurn Villa had said Iltar and his students were out around the island.

Makivan found that suspicious.

The road leveled, winding around a small patch of trees. Soon, a tunnel came into view. *Perhaps that's a place where I can rest,* he thought.

After his previous failures at both places, Makivan had decided to do some research on the holdings of the Scurn and Aliteran families. He found that they owned many places across the Isle of Sarn. Makivan had covertly searched most of the properties and was down to the last three.

Sighing, he reached the tunnel. It had two lightstone sconces on either side of the opening, with crude chandeliers lining the entire tunnel. A bench was recessed within the right wall, wide enough to seat three. Makivan welcomed the reprieve as he rested on the stone bench. *What is Iltar really up to?*

When Makivan first received the grandmaster's order he thought it odd. He knew the others on the council didn't completely trust Master Iltar. After all, he wasn't a member of the Ca'trusin. Makivan wondered if it had to do with his lineage, being the son of Adrin, the Hero of the West.

But now, after searching for Master Iltar, Makivan began to question the man's integrity. *What is he doing that he has to hide it?* Makivan wondered. *And using acolytes to cover his actions.* That sickened him. At that moment he understood why the grandmaster didn't care for Master Iltar.

The faint beating hoofs and squeaking wheels entered the tunnel. Makivan leaned forward, peeking around the tunnel's opening. *Was that a carriage?* he wondered. Wasn't the road too winding and dangerous to drive a carriage?

A single horse trotted past the patch of trees, drawing a covered carriage. Golden trim adorned the carriage's exterior, and a dark-blue emblem was emblazoned on the door, the silhouette of a great cephalopod with wreathed vines and leaves wrapped round it.

Who could that be? he wondered. That symbol belonged to the Aliteran family. The coachman driving the carriage didn't seem to notice Makivan. That gave him an idea.

He slipped back into the tunnel and climbed on the bench, whispering an incantation. White-blue magic wisped around Makivan, cloaking him in a veil of invisibility. Makivan waited quietly as the carriage entered the tunnel. It passed by, and he glimpsed the carriage's interior. High Duke Finlar Aliteran sat inside, reading from a ledger. *Well, isn't this interesting,* Makivan mused.

The carriage exited the tunnel and Makivan stepped down from the bench.

What is he doing all the way out here? Makivan wondered. According to the land records, this particular holding of the Aliteran–Scurn family used to be an old lookout station built seven hundred years ago. It had since been abandoned by the Principality of Soroth and replaced by a more suitable installation farther up the mountain.

Perhaps Iltar is here, Makivan thought. But why would Iltar be all the way out here? That made no sense. Regardless, whatever required the high duke's presence was obviously important.

Makivan hurried out of the tunnel, invigorated by his curiosity. He caught sight of the carriage and kept a safe distance behind it, careful not to alert the horse or the coachman to his presence. His directness in the past had bred unfavorable results. It was time to use a more circumspect method, and hopefully it would reveal something worth telling.

The winding road climbed a little higher before forking. The left branch continued around the mountain. The right, however, led to a walled compound enclosing a building of brownish-yellow stone that rose six stories. Wooden gates opened as the carriage approached but closed before Makivan could get close.

Blast, Makivan groaned. He would have to find another way inside the old lookout station.

Only a few guards were around. In fact, only one patrolled the ramparts. That gave Makivan an idea. He hurried around the walls, climbing the sloping ground behind the compound. A few trees had sprouted near the walls. He could probably climb them and jump onto the ramparts. This place obviously wasn't in active use; otherwise all the trees would have been cleared.

Makivan was on the ramparts within a minute. He glimpsed the high duke entering the main building. Makivan wasn't too far from it, and he could see into a few rooms. One of the windows was open, allowing a view into a bedchamber at the building's southwest corner.

A man sat at a table, facing another window that looked to the west. He was playing a card game by himself. He looked bored. Several loud knocks carried from the open window, and the card player turned in his chair. "Come in," he yelled.

High Duke Aliteran entered, glancing about the room. "What's this, Coralis?!" the high duke shouted, angrily gesturing to the windows.

Coralis? Not Coralis Scurn? Hadn't that man died?

"I needed some air, Finlar," the man said frankly.

"You can't keep these open. What if someone is watching?" Finlar demanded and stomped across the room to the western window. Makivan heard the window close, followed by the sound of drapes drawn violently.

"I feel like a prisoner, Finlar," Coralis said, rising to his feet and straightening his shirt. He stood in a regal manner.

"I'm sorry, but this is what we agreed upon," Finlar said, stepping to the window where Makivan was eavesdropping. "Hopefully, Master Iltar and my son will be finished soon." High Duke Finlar closed the window and drew the drapes.

Those statements, cryptic though they were, sent Makivan's mind spinning. Iltar *was* up to something. That was why he wasn't around. But what was he—?

Footsteps grew louder as the guard patrolling the ramparts approached at a slow methodical pace. Unfortunately, the ramparts weren't wide enough for both Makivan and the guard. He had to move.

Careful to keep silent, Makivan crept along the ramparts, barely staying ahead of the guard. Soon, he came to a staircase that led into the wards of the lookout station. Makivan descended the steps to get out of the guard's way, but waited to go any farther until the guard passed.

That was close, Makivan thought, making his way through the wards. The carriage sat outside the main building, its coachman yawning. No one else seemed to be around. Makivan's mind churned with ideas. The count's death must have been faked. Why, Makivan didn't know. Somehow, it had something to do with Master Iltar and whatever he was doing. But why would Iltar involve Sarn Royals?

The doors to the main building opened, and High Duke Finlar exited, shaking his head. A woman wearing a simple dress closed the door behind him.

"Let's go, Nictin," Finlar said, and climbed into the carriage. The coachman guided the horse back to the gate, and a man exited from a small building to open the wooden gates.

Three people, Makivan thought. That wasn't very many servants to attend to an aristocrat. A side door was open on the main building, and the same woman who had ushered the high duke to his carriage now exited carrying a large pot. She emptied it into a trough, then nonchalantly walked back to the side door.

Makivan crept behind her as she reentered the building leaving the door swaying on its hinges. He carefully slipped in behind her, finding himself in a kitchen. The woman grabbed a serving tray with a multi-plated dinner atop it. She carried it out of the kitchen, and Makivan followed her. The woman made her way through the building, climbing to the third floor. She rapped on a door, then carefully opened it while balancing the tray.

"I hope you're hungry, Your Excellency," the woman said, entering the same bedchamber Makivan had spied upon while on the ramparts.

Your Excellency, he thought. *So he is the count.*

"You can just set it over there," Coralis said in a preoccupied tone.

Makivan tiptoed into the bedchamber, slinking along the wall. Coralis was back in his chair, playing his card game. The woman set the tray on one corner of the table and stopped beside Coralis.

"You need to ease this tension," she said, placing a hand on Coralis's shoulder.

"What I need is to get out of here," he grumbled.

"Well, we can't have that," the woman said. "But I can relieve your stress."

Was she trying to seduce him?

Coralis sighed, glancing to the woman. He looked her up and down then returned his focus to his cards.

"I know I'm not as voluptuous as the countess, but you've enjoyed me in the past." She ran her hand down his arm. "I'll come back after you're finished." The woman studied Coralis, then left the room, closing the door behind her.

Once she was gone, Coralis grunted and shook his head. "This is ridiculous," he muttered. He looked up and stared at the window across from his table. As Coralis pushed back his chair to stand, Makivan dismissed his invisibility and began an incantation, bringing his hands in front of his chest.

Coralis jumped, staggering backward. He almost tripped over his chair, but regained his footing. His eyes widened as orange life-draining magic surrounded Makivan's hands.

"W-what is this?!" Coralis demanded, glancing to the door. He moved to escape, but Makivan sidestepped, barring the man's way as the magic coalesced

"Not a word," Makivan said, as a ball of life-draining tentacles hovered between his hands, the tiny tendrils poking through the spaces between his fingers.

"If you as much as scream you'll be dead within seconds," Makivan said.

"What do you want from me?" Coralis demanded.

"Information," Makivan said. "You're going to tell me everything I want to know, starting with what Master Iltar is doing."

47

CONFERENCE

A rowdy commotion resounded from the main deck of the *Promised Maiden* as Cornar came topside. *What are they doing up there?* he wondered, carrying a bowl of warm porridge. He ate a spoonful as he stepped onto the main deck.

Cornar had resumed sleeping in his cabin. It had taken the sailors seven days to completely clean the cabin of blood. An iron-y scent still lingered, but it was bearable.

Once on the main deck, Cornar passed a couple of sailors who eyed him warily. They whispered about him and the entire incident with the blood, arguing about whether dreaming could be fatal.

These two weren't the first to exchange hushed whispers. News of his bizarre bleeding had spread throughout the fleet like a wildfire. Cornar deduced that one of the sailors must have overheard him recounting the incident to the rest of his band. He hadn't made it a point to tell everyone about the ordeal, but it wouldn't have made much sense trying to hide it. A cabin drenched in blood couldn't be kept a secret.

Some of Cornar's men had been to the Mindolarnian warships for Captain Salisar and overheard the sailors and soldiers whispering about the incident. Cornar didn't mind the spreading of such rumors. It seemed that his experience was garnering some respect. At least, that's what Nordal claimed. Nordal boldly confronted the gossipers, demanding to know what they were saying about Cornar. To his surprise, they claimed Cornar had traveled to a mystical realm, a holy place in the Mindolarnian religion. A place called Vabenack. Cornar recalled hearing that name within his dreams. The soldiers, however, claimed that only the most faithful were thought to be able to visit that place.

Cornar shook the thoughts aside as he neared the source of the commotion. His men were gathered in a circle between the ship's masts, loudly cheering for Ordreth and Gregan. Grunts and thuds resounded from within the crowd, followed by more cheering. A few Wildmen were also watching, looking perplexed.

Sparring, huh? Cornar mused, eating another spoonful of porridge. He made his way toward the shorter warriors for a better view of the fight.

Ordreth and Gregan were wildly attacking each other with their bare fists. Ordreth ducked a hook swing aimed at his head and aimed a punch at Gregan's stomach. Gregan brought his knee up, blocking Ordreth's fist. Ordreth countered with a low kick to his opponent's other leg, but Gregan evaded swiftly, landing a punch against Ordreth's shoulder.

That sent the youth spiraling backward. Ordreth landed against the ring of men, who shoved him back toward Gregan. They engaged each other once again, blocking and evading each other's blows.

Just as they resumed hitting each other, a hand touched Cornar's shoulder. "You want in, Cor?" Nordal asked. "We're still on the first rung."

"Holding a tournament?" Cornar asked, putting another spoonful in his mouth.

"Yup!" Nordal grinned "We got nothing better to do." He moved beside Cornar, showing him a piece of parchment with brackets and names. "Midar wanted in, but we didn't have anyone to pair him with. So, what do you say?"

Cornar nodded, eating another spoonful.

"All right," Nordal said, writing Cornar and Midar's names at the bottom of the list. "Three rounds and then you're up, Cor." Nordal walked away, circling around the ring of men, undoubtedly to find Midar and tell him of his impending match with Cornar.

Gregan landed a blow against Ordreth's jaw. Ordreth reeled and fell to the decking. Gregan, however, settled back into a wide stance, bobbing on the balls of his feet.

Ordreth groaned and struggled to stand. Cornar was surprised the punch hadn't knocked him unconscious. His nephew staggered and sloppily lunged at Gregan. *Poor boy must be dazed.* Gregan evaded, landing a few blows, and then tackled Ordreth to the decking. He subdued the youth, pinning Ordreth belly down. Ordreth struggled, but couldn't break free.

After a moment, Igan entered the ring. He was undoubtedly the referee. Igan often took that role upon himself. The wizard studied the two struggling men and then began counting down from ten. The match would be over if Ordreth couldn't break free before Igan reached "one."

"Nine."

Ordreth thrashed about, getting an arm free, but Gregan still held him in place.

"Eight."

Ordreth clawed at Gregan's face, attempting to make him flinch.

"Seven."

Gregan turned his head, pressing his cheek against Ordreth's neck.

"Six."

Ordreth got a leg free and angled himself off the decking.

"Five."

Gregan swept the leg that held Ordreth's now freed limb back around the youth's ankle, causing Ordreth to buckle.

"Four."

Ordreth struggled to stay up and fell upon the decking once again.

"Three."

Gregan shoved himself over the shoulder of Ordreth's free arm, inhibiting its mobility.

"Two."

Ordreth grunted, attempting to push himself up again.

"One!"

A thunderous cheer erupted from the ring, and several of the warriors chanted Gregan's name. Everyone clapped, applauding both participants. There was a special kind of camaraderie among the members of Cornar's band. Even in competitions like this, there was no ill feeling.

The Wildmen who were watching, however, still looked confused. They obviously didn't know what to make of the match.

"And the winner is Gregan!" Igan announced.

Everyone continued cheering and the two combatants stood, then embraced each other in a brotherly hug. Gregan said something to Ordreth, but he couldn't hear what. The elder warrior patted Ordreth on the shoulder, and the youth nodded.

They cleared the ring and the next two fighters entered: Grensil and Shen.

Cornar finished his porridge partway through the match, but the sailors drew his attention. Captain Salisar's first mate was giving orders to prepare their ship to link with the *Executor's Breath*. Cornar watched as the sailors prepared the metal poles and the gangway for the maneuver. Soon, the two ships sailed closer together.

Most of the Wildmen on deck turned, awestruck at the maneuver. They gawked as if witnessing the most wondrous event in the world.

The match with Grensil and Shen continued amid the maneuver. Both warriors ignored what was happening with the ships. Some of the onlookers noticed, but quickly returned their attention to the match.

Unlike his men, Cornar's eyes wandered. He glimpsed Krindal coming topside with Jahevial and a few other scholars. The scholars moved toward the starboard rail, waiting for the gangway. As they talked among themselves, Krindal noticed Cornar studying him. After a moment, the old scholar waved Cornar over.

What does he *want?* Still holding his bowl, Cornar moved from the ring toward Krindal.

"Prince Kaescis is summoning us," Krindal said. "All the leaders of the expedition are to gather on the *Executor's Breath*."

Cornar hadn't received the summons, but perhaps Krindal was relaying that message. "Even me?" he asked incredulously. Krindal's deceit in Klindala was still fresh in his mind.

"Uh, yes," Krindal said, averting his gaze. "You may bring some of your men, if you'd like. His Imperial Grace said you should bring them."

Cornar raised an eyebrow, studying Krindal. All the while, Igan counted down.

The match was over in a few seconds, and Igan announced Grensil as the winner.

Cornar hurried away from the scholars and pushed through the ring of men. Kalder and Nordal were in the middle, getting ready to square off with each other.

"Wait!" Cornar commanded. "Kaescis has called a meeting aboard his ship." He studied each of his men before continuing. "I want some of you to come with me. Kalder, Gregan, Nordal, Igan, and Vargos."

Nordal sighed with disappointment, dropping out of his fighting stance.

"I guess that means we're putting the tourney on hold?" one of the men asked.

"Yeah…" Nordal grumbled.

Commands resounded across the main deck of the *Promised Maiden*. The crew hurried about, lowering the poles and the gangway. The *Executor's Breath* loomed over the starboard side of the ship, with its own crew preparing the vessel to receive the passengers from the *Promised Maiden*.

Cornar handed his empty bowl to one of his warriors, then pushed past his men toward the lowering gangway. Those Cornar had called to join him followed. Face stern, Cornar folded his arms, standing stoically as he watched the gangway settle onto the decking. He had decided to be cautious around the other leaders of this expedition. Yes, he would work with them, but he didn't consider his band to be subject to the prince. They were Sorothians, after all.

Once the gangway was secured, Cornar strode ahead of the others and climbed the plank to the main deck of the *Executor's Breath*.

"Welcome aboard," said the servant named Practil. Practil bowed and gestured toward the aft portions of the ship. "You will be meeting in the war room, behind the bridge. We still need to receive the other captains, so it might take some time. Do you care for anything to eat or drink?"

"No, thank you," Cornar said with stern courtesy and walked toward the stairs leading to the quarterdeck, passing several Wildmen. He heard Practil greeting the rest of the Sorothians in the same manner. Cornar didn't pay much attention to their replies.

Soon, Cornar passed through the ship's open-air bridge. Some of the Mindolarnian officers nodded or bowed to him in respect. Cornar waved but remained silent. He soon arrived at a semicircular enclosure of glass behind the bridge: the war room.

Cornar opened a pair of wood and glass doors and entered, with his men trailing behind him. The war room was quite large, larger than those found on the Sarin-class vessels of the Sorothian Navy.

A rectangular table sat in the middle of the room, large enough for twenty to twenty-five men to stand around it. The tabletop was sunken and had sea charts rolled out across its surface, held down by polished gray stones, all uniform in shape. Miniature figurines of ships were clustered along the backside of the table, undoubtedly used for planning sea battles.

Besides the table, there was nothing else in the war room. No one else had yet arrived.

"So, where is everybody?" Vargos demanded, sounding perturbed.

"Calm down, Vargos." Gregan nudged the old barsionist. "Didn't you hear that servant when we came aboard?" Vargos grumbled.

The warriors spread around the table, eyeing the sea charts. Cornar, however, stood at the side of the table nearest the entrance. He rested his hands on the table's edge, leaning over it.

The scholars entered soon after, and Krindal strode along the left side of the table. He carefully set his mapping tevisral at the table's center, activating it with that oddly shaped gem. Magic wisped from the tevisral, forming the topographical map of the world.

The other scholars entered the war room as Krindal magnified the map.

Cornar caught Jahevial eyeing him as the scholar moved throughout the room. He still hadn't discovered any more about what Jahevial was doing. Cornar had told Sharon to spy on the man, but Jahevial hadn't done anything out of the ordinary. Nor had she caught him using that odd tevisral.

Bratan entered the war room not long after the scholars arrived. The sight of him caused Cornar to flinch defensively; the encounter with Bratan in the dreamland was still fresh in Cornar's mind. The Praetorian had been brutal and crass when they fought. That left Cornar wary. Bratan, however, simply glanced at Cornar but didn't pay him any further attention.

Shouted orders echoed into the war room, pulling Cornar away from Bratan. Officers yelled for the sailors to detach the poles and gangway attached to the *Promised Maiden*. They ordered the sailors to transition the equipment to receive those from the other warships.

More of the expedition's leaders filed into the war room: Grand Marshal Hezidex, Admiral Kaetet, and a few commanders from the Mindolarnian army.

Cornar heard the equipment outside settle into place. Not long after, Captains Hetarin and Regader entered the war room with a pair of their own officers. They were followed by the Wildman ambassador, Gevistra, and one of the Wildmen women. Lastly, Laeyit and Kaescis entered.

The prince strode gallantly through the war room, eyeing everyone who was present. His violet eyes settled on Cornar, staring fiercely. There was a glint of hostility in Kaescis's eyes that grew into something menacing. The prince stopped at the opposite side of the table, his eyes still fixed on Cornar. Suddenly, Kaescis smiled. It wasn't a friendly smile, by any definition. It held a sense of malevolent anticipation.

Is that an attempt at intimidation? Cornar wondered. He didn't shy away, but boldly stared Kaescis down. News of his incident in the cabin must have reached the prince. Cornar wondered what Kaescis thought about the incident. The prince seemed to be a religious man, so would he share the same opinion of those Nordal and the others had encountered?

Kaescis finally turned his gaze to the mapping tevisral. He looked like a man obsessed.

Who are you, really? He hadn't thought about it until after his last night in the dreamland, but Kaescis couldn't be an average man. How could an average man live for as long as Kaescis had and still look youthful? Cornar had heard of arpranists using their magic to stall their aging, but he didn't know for how long exactly.

At that moment, Krindal finished magnifying the map. It showed mostly open waters, with an occasional island dotting the vast topography here and there. The scholar then took one of the markers and placed it in the southern part of the map, near Cornar.

"Thank you all for coming," Kaescis said, his eyes still fixated on the flowing magic. "Seeing as we haven't held a council since our separation at the foothills of Anigar, I thought it wise to gather us all to discuss the next leg of our expedition, the Isle of Dalgilur."

Nordal grunted. "You *are* going to share all the information about this 'next leg,' right?" he asked, sounding skeptical.

Laeyit scowled at the question, and Bratan tensed. Kaescis, however, straightened up, resuming a regal pose. Yet Cornar could see the hostility in the prince's eyes. He looked like he wanted to kill Nordal.

"That *is* why we're here, Mister Nordal," Kaescis said cordially. His face, however, belied his tone. "Since there was confusion about Klindil, I am holding this council to stop such secrecy from ruining our camaraderie."

"We appreciate that, Your Imperial Highness," Jahevial said. "My fellow scholars and I were also concerned, seeing as we didn't know the end goals for this expedition."

"I can assure you there is nothing more to hide," Kaescis said.

Nordal didn't look convinced. Neither was Cornar.

"Captains," Kaescis looked about the table, "where do we think we are positioned?"

Admiral Kaetet grabbed a thin-tipped rod and poked it through the magic. He held the tip near a set of islands at the northern section of the magnified topography. "I believe we are here," the admiral said. "We spotted three islands to our west earlier today. My calculations predicted we would be passing by them sometime this evening, so we must have had a favorable tailwind sometime during the night."

"I take it that marker Master Krindal placed denotes Dalgilur?" Captain Hetarin asked. "Smack dab in the center of the World's Frown?"

"It is," Krindal answered.

Nordal furrowed his brow and looked at Cornar as if expecting him to say something. Cornar didn't know what to say. He hadn't known where Dalgilur was located. But a location within the World's Frown did make sense. It was a section of water, scattered with dozens of islands, that was said to swallow up ships. Some sailors claimed that compasses would stop working when one entered the Frown. Ships avoided the World's Frown, and it was the subject of many farfetched sea tales. The area's name stemmed from its appearance— if one traced a line on a map from island to island, the line would form a jagged, frowning mouth.

One of the officers from Hetarin's ship leaned closer to the marker, noting the islands north of it. He grabbed one of the sea charts and lifted it off the table, moving it through the projected magic. The officer stepped back and began making calculations.

"We've already plotted a course," Admiral Kaetet said. "According to my calculations, we will arrive at the edge of the World's Frown in a little over a week and a half."

"And what happens once we get to the edge of the Frown?" asked one of Hetarin's officers.

Kaescis straightened. "Master Krindal will see us through the World's Frown," the prince said. "His *attunement* in Klindil will grant us access to Dalgilur. I don't understand the process completely, but there is some sort of magic barring Dalgilur from the outside world. Only an attuned Keeper of Truth and Might can penetrate it."

"And how exactly will this affect the ships?" Kaetet asked warily.

Krindal sucked in his breath before answering. "We… don't know."

Hubbub ensued, with many voicing their concerns. Hetarin and his officers insisted that they needed to find out more before attempting to cross the Frown.

Kaescis raised his hand in a placating manner. "Everyone, calm yourselves," he said with a sigh. "There are several possibilities. One theory is that the barrier will dissipate for a time. Another theory is that the vessel carrying Master Krindal will be transported."

"Are there any other theories, Your Imperial Highness?" Hetarin asked.

Kaescis shook his head.

"I assume you have a plan, Your Imperial Highness?" an officer asked hopefully.

"Yes," the prince answered. "We will link our vessels together, as we do when transferring personnel between ships."

Vargos snorted a laugh, drawing raised eyebrows from the Mindolarnians.

"And what do you find so funny?" Bratan bellowed, folding his arms.

"You want to *trick* magic?" Vargos snorted again. "Magic can't be fooled."

"A tevisral is obviously creating the barrier," Laeyit interjected. "It can't tell the difference between the ships if they are all linked together."

Vargos continued laughing and shook his head. The Mindolarnians ignored the old barsionist and continued discussing the matter.

"What about massing everyone on one ship?" Captain Regader asked.

"I would rather not," Kaescis waved his hand in a dismissal. "We are already pressing capacity with our allies." The prince gestured to the two Wildmen. "We link the ships."

"That sounds risky," Gregan said.

"Yeah," Nordal said. "What if we encounter a storm or turbulent seas?"

"The ships' hulls will be reinforced by barsion," Kaescis said, not looking at either warrior. "None of the vessels will be in any danger. Now, Master Krindal, show us Dalgilur."

Krindal magnified the projection further. The scholars beside him gasped in wonder as they eyed the sight now projected from the tevisral. Everyone was impressed, especially Gevistra and the female Wildman.

A crescent-shaped island filled most of the map, with a bay along its southeast side. The island wasn't large by any means. Cornar couldn't tell its size exactly. Perhaps it was as large as Soroth, the city. A mountain range rose along the north and northwest shores and tapered down to hills near the southern parts of the island. The mountains looked like they rose right out of the ocean. Most of the island's level parts were on the southern side of the mountain range.

A towering building protruded from the mountainside, oriented to the northwest. It rose nearly as tall as the mountains. A circular city lay beneath it, laid out in a pattern Cornar had never beheld. All the buildings faced the city's center, with streets spreading from the center like the spokes of a wheel. From what Cornar could tell, there were three tiers to the city's layout: a central ring that had seven buildings, a middle ring that had fourteen buildings and an outer ring with twenty-one buildings.

A road led from the city to the bay, ending at what looked like a pier. Elsewhere on the island were two other piers, on the northeast and the southwest parts of the bay.

"Behold, Dalgilur," Kaescis said. "I propose we moor along this central pier." The prince pointed to the pier aligned with the city.

"If it's still intact," Nordal remarked doubtfully. "This map showed Klindil's buildings before their ruin. I hate to say it, but your map is probably outdated."

The captains looked at the warrior with annoyance but returned their attention to Kaescis.

"These mountains pose a potential problem," the prince continued. "Grand Marshal Hezidex, I want you to send a team of scouts up the mountains to spy on the northern waters. We must be apprised when those vile elves arrive."

The grand marshal nodded.

"Captain Regader, once we moor, take your ship to the southern tip." Kaescis pointed to the shores beyond the hills. "If the Sapphire Guard attempts to moor near the piers, we will attack from both sides. Your vessel will pin them in the bay."

"Yes, Your Imperial Highness," the captain replied with a nod.

"Grand marshal, set a contingent of your archers and mages on the piers."

Kaescis continued giving orders and explained his plans once they moored on the island. The Wildmen were to reinforce the Mindolarnian army, augmenting their numbers.

"Mister Dol'shir," the prince said. "Will you and your men scout the city once we moor?"

That question shocked Cornar. Was the prince actually trusting him with a task? Or was this a means to use his band as fodder for whatever dangers existed on the island?

"Your men proved invaluable beneath Klindil," Kaescis continued. "As you are a band of explorers, I think it fitting that you lead us into the depths of Dalgilur."

Kalder looked at Cornar, awaiting an answer. Gregan folded his arms and narrowed his eyes, while Nordal chuckled.

"You're not using us as some kind of bait, are you?" Igan asked warily.

"Bait?" Kaescis asked with dismay. "Of course not."

Igan glanced to Cornar, obviously worried.

Cornar, however, felt calm about the task. "We can do that," he said.

Kaescis continued proposing his plans for the island. The prince didn't pay any more attention to Cornar or his men for the rest of the meeting.

After an hour, they were finished. Before Kaescis left, he stared at Cornar with that same anticipating gaze. The prince smiled grimly, then exited the war room with Bratan and Laeyit. The two Wildmen left soon after—they seemed wary of the voyage, and Cornar thought he heard the woman murmuring about the dooms of traveling what she called Everspanning Waters.

One by one, the other leaders of the expedition left, leaving Cornar alone with those of his band.

"I don't like the way he was looking at you," Igan whispered. "I don't trust the prince, especially after hearing about that dream of yours."

"Neither do I," Gregan said, gazing out the windows. He was undoubtedly checking to see if anyone could overhear their conversation.

"Well, he is a bit of a pompous ass," Vargos said, and Nordal chuckled.

Kalder was the last to approach Cornar, studying his mentor with a serious gaze. "What do your feelings have to say about this, Cor?" he asked.

Cornar took a deep breath, thinking about the task proposed by Kaescis. It seemed... reasonable. He couldn't say it was safe, as they were exploring someplace totally foreign. But, there wasn't a nagging feeling of danger.

"It'll be fine," Cornar nodded. "I don't think there's anything malicious at Dalgilur."

"Let's hope so," Vargos said, leaning against the table.

"We're still keeping the loot to ourselves, right?" Nordal asked.

Igan looked at him dumbfounded. "Just because they let us in on all the details doesn't mean we're going to change our minds, right, Cor?"

Cornar smiled at the wizard. "That's right."

The noise of the lowering poles and gangway reached the war room.

"C'mon," Cornar waved to his men. "Let's get off this boat and back to our tournament."

Nordal grinned, clasping Kalder's shoulder. "Yeah, are you ready for me to beat you into submission?" he asked.

Kalder glanced to Nordal with a raised brow, then a sly grin formed across his face. "Oh, you wish," he said.

Amused, Cornar shook his head at the banter as they exited the war room.

"Claiming the Ril'Sha wasn't enough for the self-proclaimed deity. He turned his eye to humankind, visiting the men of Bathiral in a form not his own."

- From *The Thousand Years War, Part I*, page 19

Since accessing the Royal Archive, Iltar had learned a great deal about Vabenack and the workings of that realm. Vaegris had delivered Iltar a copy of a tome that expounded the theories found in *Dreamwalker*. It was written by someone who shared the name of the fabled child stealer, Esmid. He was an ancient priest of a religion that was probably a parent theology to the beliefs adhered to by the Mindolarnians. The tome gave specific instructions about how to manipulate the Translucent Fields.

With proper training, one could use Vabenack to relive the past or see the future, at least the potential future. Because of people's ability to make choices, one couldn't see the *actual* future. The priest explained a principal called divergent possibilities, where the Translucent Fields could show a future event in multiple ways.

This Esmid also droned on for quite a while about how to manipulate this principle properly. If one could influence a variety of actions leading to the event—and the actions during the event—one could in essence *foresee* the future.

This priest likened the future as free-flowing water. In order to predict it accurately, one must manipulate the water into a certain course; only then could the future be predicted with effectiveness. Although, even then, it wouldn't be perfect. The whole thing sounded like the nonsense Reflection had babbled about when Iltar first spoke with him.

After several days of study, Iltar decided to venture back into Vabenack and test the things he had learned. He wanted to conjure an experience from the more recent past. A projection of the future would be too grueling a task to undertake, especially for a novice.

The whole process was similar to casting a spell, using a string of strange-sounding words, words that were sharp and guttural. They sounded very similar to the gibberish the attendants spoke to open the secret passage to the Royal Archive. Iltar had tried to get Vaegris to help him understand those words, but the crotchety librarian only glared at Iltar in annoyance. So Iltar was left to his own understanding to guess at the proper pronunciations. There were no guides in the tome he had studied, and the text was written as if whoever was reading *should* know how to enunciate such words.

It was Iltar's first time back in Vabenack since his encounter with Cornar. He expected to find Reflection waiting for him. That, however, wasn't the case. Upon entering the Translucent Fields Iltar was surprised to find Pagus standing with his arms folded.

"It's about time," Pagus said smugly. "We were wondering when you would show."

We? Iltar furrowed his brow. Was this really Pagus? Or was this some trick brought on by Reflection?

"There's that look again…" Pagus sighed, pointing behind Iltar.

Confused, Iltar spun. Three figures dashed across the field of glass. As they neared, Iltar recognized three more of his acolytes: Agen, Tigan, and Bilda.

"They actually made it?" Iltar wondered aloud.

"Uh, yeah," Pagus said mockingly. "We braved our nightmares and laid our claim to this realm."

Iltar glanced back to Pagus, but turned back around upon hearing a chorus of greetings.

"Master Iltar!" the boys chimed.

"We did it!" Agen shouted. "We really did it!"

The boys stopped a few paces from Iltar, all smiling, all looking pleased with themselves.

"Is this your first time?" Iltar asked the boys.

"No," Bilda shook his head. "This is like, uh, my sixth time, I think?"

"Third for me," Agen said.

"Me too," Tigan chimed.

"I see…" Iltar said.

Since encountering Cornar in Vabenack, Iltar had spent every day studying at the Hilinard, staying well after dark. Each morning after a night in Vabenack left him drained, worse than if he had spent the night intoxicated. So, instead of exploring the yellow-sky realm further, Iltar chose to rest.

"Well, I'm impressed," Iltar said. "You've been able to access this place without the dream elixir."

Bilda looked sheepish and the other boys averted their gazes.

Iltar drew his lips to a line. *What are they hiding?* he wondered. *They couldn't have accessed the elixir…* Iltar had ordered Alanya's guards to parcel out the rest of the elixir into bottles and put them under lock and key. There were enough bottles for Iltar, Pagus, the women, and Petral—one of Alanya's guards—to last weeks.

Each evening, when Iltar retired to bed, he checked on how much was left.

The women and the guard had drunk their shares, but Pagus hadn't touched his allotment. Iltar assumed the boys weren't trying to access Vabenack anymore. Most of his acolytes had been frightened when they met in Alanya's dining hall, and Iltar had *assumed* they wouldn't make another attempt.

Well, he was almost certainly wrong. "Did you use the elixir?" Iltar asked in a probing tone.

Bilda sighed and glanced to Pagus.

Iltar turned toward Pagus as the youth retorted, "I had the recipe." The unrepentant acolyte stood looking at him smugly. "Did you think I wouldn't just make another batch?"

Disappointment welled within Iltar, and he closed his eyes, fighting back the urge to lash out at Pagus.

"They wanted to come here," Pagus said. "I will not hold them back, like you do."

"Hold them back?" Iltar blurted. "I'm protecting them!"

"And you don't think *I* can protect them?" Pagus demanded. "Or that they can protect themselves? For magic's sake, Master Iltar, we aren't helpless children."

"You don't know the horrors of this place," Iltar said sternly, then strode past Pagus. He didn't have time to waste fighting with the boy.

Iltar knelt on a spot of ground. A shifting landscape passed through the ages beneath him. He touched his hand to the glass, focusing on putting his mind into that shifting landscape.

"It's not gonna work," Pagus said sardonically. "I tried it yesterday, and nothing."

Quiet, Pagus… Iltar groaned to himself, pushing aside the boy's remarks. He resumed his focus to manipulate this bizarre realm, reciting that long string of strange words, but nothing changed. The boys wandered off, leaving their master alone. They probably thought it best not to bother him, and they were right. However, the silence their absence afforded Iltar didn't make a difference. He remained on his knees for hours, repeating those words over and over without any change.

What am I doing wrong? Iltar growled, then slammed a fist on the translucent ground. He half-expected the glass to crack, but there wasn't as much as a blemish on the sleek surface.

"No luck, huh?" Pagus asked.

"No," Iltar shook his head. "Maybe I'm doing something wrong."

"Or you're not saying it right," Pagus grinned.

Iltar found that remark ironic. It was an obvious jab at their encounter in the master's section of the Necrotic Order's Record Hall, when Pagus and his friends were caught by Iltar. Iltar had corrected their pronunciation of a spell.

"You need a primer on that language," Pagus said, pacing back and forth beside Iltar.

Iltar chuckled. "And what language is that?"

Pagus shrugged. "Well, what do we know about it?"

He's being scholarly about this, Iltar thought. He felt impressed, but put the feeling aside.

"It's ancient," Pagus said. "It has something to do with the Mindolarnians' religion."

"The words could activate tevisrals," Iltar said. "The wall," he added.

Pagus nodded. "Do you think it could be some *secret* language of incantations?" Pagus said with awe.

"I don't know," Iltar said. "Perhaps…" Elves had their own language of incantations that was different from men. But the human and elven incantations weren't totally different. There was some resemblance.

"Could it be a forgotten tongue?" Pagus mused.

Iltar nodded. He caught sight of the acolytes practicing their incantations together. They mustered defensive spells and dueled with each other, casting destructive magics.

No! Iltar felt a surge of panic. "Stop!" he shouted to the boys, then ran after them. The acolytes, however, resumed their dueling.

"Stop, you fools!" Iltar shouted.

"They're fine!" Pagus shouted after Iltar.

The boys evaded each other's spells with a finesse that was otherworldly. It looked downright reckless.

"Don't you know that if you're wounded here you're wounded in reality?" Iltar shouted, stopping a few paces from Bilda, who dived to evade an acidic bolt from Agen.

"They're fine," Pagus said again, coming beside Iltar. "Don't you see?"

Bilda rebounded swiftly. He should have hurt himself with that dive, as it was performed recklessly.

"Watch," Pagus said, shoving Iltar sideways.

What was that fool doing? Iltar grumbled and regained his footing. "And what was that for?!" he shouted.

Pagus rolled his eyes. "Just throw yourself to the ground, clumsily."

Iltar straightened up and glanced back to the acolytes. They were *bouncing* off the glassy ground. The very act seemed to defy the laws of nature. But then again, this place was not natural.

"Well?" Pagus asked.

"Fine," Iltar threw himself backwards. He expected to land with a painful thud, but he just felt himself stop. He was obviously lying on his back, but the sensation of hitting the ground was different.

"See?" Pagus asked, smiling wide.

Intrigued, Iltar sat up and felt at his back. No pain. He recalled slamming his fist a moment ago. There was no pain from that either.

Pagus stepped closer, extending a hand to Iltar. Iltar accepted the help and rose to his feet. "I don't think this place can hurt you," he said. "At least not like this. Now if I punch you it'd hurt." He swung at Iltar.

Iltar swiftly pushed aside the punch, but felt the force of the blow as it should be in reality.

"Interesting, isn't it?" Pagus asked. Iltar nodded, then turned his attention back to the boys. Tigan's acidic barsion had just collapsed.

"That's enough playing around!" Iltar yelled. The boys stopped, and Bilda looked to Iltar.

"But no one has won yet," the little boy said sadly.

"What?" Iltar demanded.

"Since we've been coming in here, we made up this little game," Pagus said. "Last barsion standing wins. If you lose your barsion, you're out. So, Tigan's out."

"Dangerously stupid game," Iltar grumbled. "Now go back to your dreams. I want to talk with you in the morning."

Iltar turned around and opened a portal back to his dream. A chaotic storm raged across a lush woodland resembling Soroth. Bolts of lightning surged across a blackened sky. Iltar, however, remained in Vabenack. He waited for the boys to open their own doorways back to what Iltar assumed was their subconscious minds.

Traveling to and from Vabenack still boggled him. Iltar couldn't completely wrap his head around the specifics, but he knew that the process worked.

One by one, the boys departed, leaving Iltar alone.

Now to test if this was really them, he thought, stepping through the portal.

Iltar hoped that those were really his acolytes and not some trick conjured by Reflection. The only way to know for sure was to confront the boys when they awoke. He just hoped they wouldn't attempt to access Vabenack again without him.

Iltar confronted the acolytes after they awoke. The boys had indeed traveled to Vabenack.

They all went about their usual activities for the day. The acolytes spent their time in the public areas of the Hilinard while Iltar, Pagus, and the women descended to the Royal Archive.

Pagus listened intently to the attendant as the man opened the wall to the Hilinard's hidden parts.

He better not try anything stupid, Iltar thought.

Soon, the four of them were down in the Royal Archive. Vaegris watched as they entered. His cold gaze was his only greeting.

For most of the morning Iltar reread the texts on Vabenack written by the priest named Esmid. Iltar concluded that he must not have been saying the words right. A similar thing happened when one mispronounced the words of an incantation. One slur and the spell would fizzle or fail to manifest at all.

Partway through the afternoon, Alanya and Elsia left to fetch a late lunch for the four of them, leaving Iltar and Pagus to their studies. They each had their own alcove, which Iltar preferred.

Heavy-soled footfalls echoed into the library not long after the women left.

Probably forgot something, Iltar thought, still scanning the texts in front of him.

The footsteps drew closer, then stopped beside the table. Iltar could see someone wearing crimson clothing. Neither of the women were wearing such a color. Iltar cautiously turned toward his unexpected visitor, seeing the princess Raedina standing with her arms folded, clutching a pair of blood-red gloves. Her crimson clothing was a simple blouse and tightly fitting women's trousers. The princess didn't look fanciful by any means. In fact, Raedina looked rather ordinary. Even her makeup was simple.

"You look engrossed," she said, almost smiling.

"I am," Iltar said, and straightened.

"Are you finding what you're looking for?" Raedina asked, dimples appearing in her cheeks.

"Somewhat," Iltar replied. He didn't know how much he dare explain to this woman. There were already more people involved with his research than he liked.

Raedina eyed Iltar up and down, then slid into the bench across from him. Pagus peered around the corner of his alcove, but soon returned to his reading.

"I'm curious," Iltar said, flipping through the pages to the strange language used to manipulate the Translucent Fields of Vabenack. "I've never seen this language."

Raedina squinted at him, looking tense.

"And as a scholar, I would like to know the proper pronunciations of these words," he came to the long string of words written in Common. Other symbols adorned the page above the Common writing, and Iltar thought that those characters might be how the strange language was written. "Would you perchance know how to say these words?"

He turned the tome around to face Raedina.

The princess's face stiffened as she read the page. A moment of silence passed before Raedina turned the book back to Iltar.

"Anything?" he asked.

She glanced back to the page, then studied Iltar as if deciding if he was *worthy* of the information. "It's the Keadal tongue," she said. "The language of my ancestors."

"Your *ancestors?*" Iltar asked. "But the Common tongue has been the language of men for centuries, perhaps even millennia."

Raedina forced a smile. "Sixty-five hundred years to be precise," she said flatly. "The Keadal tongue is the language spoken by the true rulers of our world." Her words had a tinge of resentment to them.

True rulers of Kalda? Iltar thought. *What does that—? Never mind, focus on the words,* he chided himself.

"So, can you read it?" Iltar asked.

Raedina nodded. "Trisl miras kasilak durish manai, crilena ashiry jehvas moltak," she spoke each word with a harsh guttural inflection. "Nuri mari cheska zubrai."

Iltar was taken aback. Those weren't the words written on the page. He didn't know what she was saying, but Raedina spoke the tongue fluently, as if it was natural for her.

"Why do you want to know *these* words?" Raedina tapped the sentences used to manipulate the Translucent Fields.

Ignoring the question, Iltar wondered how he could get her to recite those words. He couldn't put her under a mind-control spell. Sure, that would get what he wanted, but the very moment that he released the spell he would be seen as a threat. He would undoubtedly be arrested for *assaulting* a member of the Mindolarn Royal Family. He couldn't have that. Perhaps there was another way…

"Alanya's late husband was studying this subject. It coincides with my own research. Merely reading the words is only half the discovery."

Raedina chuckled. "This *subject* as you put it is very sacred in our religion. It is not something to be treated lightly or mocked."

"I'm not trying to be disrespectful," Iltar said, seeking to reassure her with a tone of feigned charm.

The princess shook her head at him.

That didn't work.

"Only the most devout dare seek anything about Vabenack," Raedina said. "And those who find it wouldn't dare try to comprehend these words."

"Then why are they written?" Iltar asked, genuinely interested in the answer. Why write something only to make it forbidden?

"This is the *Royal* Archive," Raedina said. "Those words are meant to be understood by only us." Her voice was contemptuous. Though she was trying to hide it, Iltar could sense the same hostility from her as on the day they met in the market.

You're hiding something, Iltar thought. Silence lingered for a moment, and then Raedina's demeanor lightened.

"I think that is enough about serious matters for one conversation," the princess said. "I came down here looking for Alanya. We are holding a ball next week, honoring the advancements of our most recent strides in tevisral construction here at the Hilinard. As I am in charge of organizing the festivities, I thought to ask Alanya to lend a hand. Hopefully you can spare her."

Iltar sat back, folding his arms. "You just missed her," he said.

"A pity," the princess said with a frown. Raedina slid out of the alcove and looked Iltar up and down once again. "Please tell her I'd like to speak to her. Tomorrow, at the palace? We can discuss the particular details of her involvement over lunch. You are welcome to come as well," she said, and gestured to Iltar. "As are your acolytes."

"A gracious gesture," Iltar said. "I'm sure they would enjoy the opportunity."

"Well, from what I've seen, it seems like you drive them like a taskmaster spurring his slaves," the princess said, smiling wryly. "They deserve a break."

She spun around and walked haughtily across the Royal Archive. Once Raedina was gone, Pagus peeled from his alcove and slunk into the seat across from Iltar. "Whoa…" the boy muttered, chuckling. "That was a bold insult…"

"Yeah," Iltar muttered, eyeing the archive's entrance.

"So this *is* a long-lost language." Pagus tapped the still open page. "But whatever she said wasn't what's written here."

"It wasn't," Iltar said, "but now I've heard the language. Perhaps that will be enough to deduce the proper pronunciations."

Pagus shrugged. "I'm going to go ask that codger for any books on this Keadal language. Maybe now that I know the name of it, he'll actually listen to me."

Doubtful, Iltar thought, watching as Pagus crossed the archive.

Iltar decided to leave the Hilinard with the women and his acolytes. The hours following Raedina's visit had proved fruitless. Iltar had started reading another ancient tome that was religious in nature. He found that particular read dull, as the information inside it would undoubtedly prove biased.

The sun was still out when they exited the main building of the Hilinard. It loomed over the eastern horizon in a beautiful sunset.

Elsia and Alanya whispered to each other about the invitations received from Raedina. They hadn't spoken of it to the acolytes, and so they conversed quietly, giddily whispering to each other. Both women reminded Iltar of the frivolous girls who had studied the illusionary arts with him.

Turning from the women, Iltar studied Pagus. The boy had been uncharacteristically quiet since leaving the Royal Archive. Pagus walked in a stupor. The boy steered clear of the others and gave passersby a wide birth.

Odd, Iltar thought. Pagus hadn't said much after returning to his alcove. Old Vaegris had probably given Pagus a stern lecture before dismissing him.

Alanya's carriage and wagon were waiting for them outside the Hilinard's gates. The acolytes scurried into their vehicle while the women entered the lavish carriage.

Iltar was right behind them, but stopped upon noticing Pagus lingering by the gate. "Are you coming?" Iltar called to the boy.

"I'm going to walk," Pagus said sullenly.

"Is he okay?" Elsia whispered to Iltar. Iltar shrugged and stepped into the carriage, shutting the door behind him.

Soon, the carriage and wagon were back at Alanya's home. Everyone exited their vehicles, and Iltar called for the acolytes to gather in the high duchess's dining hall.

The boys hurried past Iltar and the women, running into the mansion and drawing a chiding shout from Hazais.

"I love having children here," Alanya smiled, taking Iltar's arm.

"Some children they are," Iltar said, shaking his head.

Together they walked arm in arm into the mansion. They followed the boys and entered the large dining hall. The acolytes were already seated, eagerly awaiting dinner.

"Shall we wait for Pagus?" Alanya asked.

"No," Iltar said as he guided Alanya to the head of the table.

Alanya took her seat and Iltar stood beside her, clearing his throat. "I have an announcement," he said. "Tomorrow we won't be conducting any research." The boys perked up. Bilda and the younger acolytes smiled, pleased that they wouldn't have to work. "Earlier today we received an invitation to the palace—"

Gasps echoed throughout the room.

"As I was saying," Iltar continued, his tone slightly agitated. "We received an invitation to dine at the palace. All of us." The acolytes whooped and cheered. Bilda rose from his chair and began dancing, along with Tigan. "Settle down!" Iltar barked. "Alanya has been summoned, and we are accompanying her as guests. I expect each of you to be on your best behavior."

"Shouldn't you be telling Pagus that?" Tigan asked.

Several of the boys laughed, and Iltar grinned. Yes, Pagus was the worst of the lot. But, these boys could be rascals on their own. Alanya chimed in, explaining the proper etiquette for palace visitors. She went on about Mindolarnian procedure and protocol when sharing a meal at the palace. Alanya obviously didn't want any of the acolytes making fools of themselves. Iltar assumed any misbehavior or mistake would reflect badly on her. She then added that they would require formal attire. That was something the boys lacked.

As Alanya proposed a solution for the clothing situation, Iltar glimpsed Pagus walking across the grounds, still looking sullen. He didn't come to the mansion, but walked toward the guesthouse.

I should keep an eye on that boy, Iltar thought, then said to Alanya, "Save my plate."

The high duchess paused, looking at Iltar with concern. She nodded and resumed talking to the acolytes.

⟫•⟪

Pagus waited hours for Master Iltar to stop watching him. The old man just stared. He didn't even come over to check on how his apprentice was doing. Of course, Pagus was fine. The whole sulking demeanor was just a ruse. Pagus was a little disappointed that Master Iltar hadn't even tried to call his bluff.

But, that made things less difficult. Pagus dismissed the illusion of him wandering around Alanya's mansion and opened his eyes. All was quiet down here in the secret parts of the Hilinard.

His daring feat was quite commendable. Not everyone could do what he had done. Pagus had created an illusion of himself after the futile discussion with that codger of a librarian. He then veiled himself in invisibility. The illusion of himself had returned to the alcove and "resumed" studying from the tome. Pagus let the illusion sit there until Aunty Elsia returned, and then he had to resort to a cleverer tactic. It was tricky, but Pagus had timed his own invisible turning of pages with that of his illusion. It was done so well that Aunty Elsia hadn't even noticed.

He had stayed in the Royal Archive until the others left, and then he found a secluded spot elsewhere in this hidden area of the Hilinard. Pagus had to be careful, as he would have to speak to project his words through his illusion. Luckily, he hadn't needed to do much talking.

Now, hours after hiding, Pagus crept through the underground halls of the Hilinard. They were empty, and the places where there had been Praetorians were now unguarded.

That would make things easier.

Grinning, though still invisible, Pagus sneaked into the Royal Archive. At last, he could search the bookshelves without harassment.

It was a good feeling.

Now, where to start? Pagus wondered, tiptoeing down the nearest aisle. The Keadal tongue was probably the most pressing subject, but Pagus was curious about a host of other things. He wouldn't be able to dive into everything in one night. It would probably take a while to find all the answers he yearned to uncover.

49

PATH TO
THE ANCIENTS

Krindal eagerly loomed over the projection of his mapping tevisral, his hands gripping the table's edge. A thrill of anticipation rose within him. He would actually *see* the wonders of an ancient Kaldean civilization.

We're almost there, he thought, grinning like an eager acolyte. No longer would anyone dismiss him as crazed, delusional, or mad. Dalgilur would prove his theories true. What was once a fanciful idea would become reality. Krindal would be lauded for his discoveries—the man who would restore Kalda to its ancient ways.

Krindal reveled in the grandeur of those thoughts. Smiling, he glanced at the others in the war room: Admiral Kaetet, a few of his officers, and the woman Laeyit. They were all gathered around the table, studying the map. The Admiral was reviewing the process for making all four ships appear as one.

It was an interesting strategy. Krindal and Master Vargos had similar doubts, but the prince had resolved those concerns. Prince Kaescis's explanation carried enough logic, although Krindal failed to understand certain parts.

"Admiral!" a young sailor cried, dashing into the war room. "We've passed that island." They were entering the World's Frown. Dalgilur would be only hours away.

"Good," Kaetet said. "Notify the other ships. Are the barsionists ready?" the admiral asked, turning to Laeyit.

"They've all been notified," the woman said, rounding the table. "Once the gangways are secured, they will cast their spells."

The Admiral nodded. "You will be leaving this here, Master Krindal?" Kaetet asked, gesturing to the mapping tevisral.

"Yes, sir," Krindal answered as Laeyit left the war room. "I can sense the island across the ocean."

Admiral Kaetet nodded and gave some orders to his officers, then dismissed them. He too left the war room.

Soon, Krindal was alone. *Scholar of Discovery*, he mused, grinning widely. *That's what they will call me.* He was exuberant at the thought.

Noise echoed in from the open-air decks. Krindal turned as towering poles rose along the rails of the ship. The *Helidar*—one of the Mindolarnian warships—was moving closer to the portside rail. Krindal couldn't see the *Ulicin*, but the third warship would be on the opposite side of the *Helidar*.

⟢•⟣

While the crew prepared the *Executor's Breath* to link with the other ships, Kaescis gazed out the windows of the observation room, clasping his hands behind his back. The voices plaguing his mind hadn't bothered him these last few weeks, not since Kaescis realized what he must do. The idea of slaying Mister Dol'shir seemed to satisfy them beyond measure.

Laeyit strode down the stairs to the main deck, passing huddled Wildmen. She looked confident as she shouted orders. That wasn't unusual for her. But something about her demeanor made Kaescis's eyes linger.

Laeyit had been acting strange since their return from Klindil. She wore makeup and sat on his lap to draw him from his woes. Those were things a normal woman might do to try to divert a man's attention. It was odd coming from her.

Dalgilur should be to the right, Kaescis thought, glancing over the starboard side of the ship. Dark shapes loomed over the horizon, about thirty degrees off the bow. "Is that a storm?" he whispered.

With narrowed eyes, Kaescis reached for a spyglass and glimpsed something red at the back of the observation room. It looked like a man. Kaescis spun, spyglass in hand, and then started, eyes wide with surprise.

A tall man stood in front of the door. He looked like the vile Alathian who had slain Kaescis's beloved uncle nine months ago. The man wore a crimson robe, his arms folded across his chest while a grin formed upon his hawk-like face. His eyes were a brilliant sapphire, and his hair and beard were as white as snow.

"You…" Kaescis growled, dropping the spyglass and extending his hand, ready to summon his massive Ko'delish blade. Furious, he uttered the incantation to muster his deadly weapon, and the blackness oozed from his pores.

Wait… a dozen voices echoed within his mind. *Strike not our master.*

Kaescis started again. *Our master?* Patterns in the man's robe caught Kaescis's eye as the Ko'delish blade formed. Those patterns were symbols… Kaescis recognized the symbol on the man's abdomen. It was an emblem used in the architecture of the Hilinard.

The Emblem of Knowledge. Kaescis gasped, glancing elsewhere on the robe. The six other divine glyphs were also present. This robe… Kaescis had heard tales of a man wearing this robe when appearing to the Faithful. He was called the Messenger of the Promise, the Word of Cheserith, the Herald of the Harbinger. He would speak for God when even the Chosen would forsake the world. He was the embodiment of the *Will.*

It… it can't be! Kaescis stepped back, aghast. He lost concentration and his blade flickered, parts of it misting away.

"Yes, it can." The robed man's smile turned to a wide grin. He strode across the decking, walking without the sound of footsteps. "Don't doubt, Kaescis. It's not becoming of you."

Kaescis marveled that this man—no, this divine being—knew his thoughts. "Then… you are…" Kaescis trailed off, watching as the robed man stepped closer. "The Messenger of the Promise?"

The robed man looked amused. "That's one of many names I've been called over the years," he said, stopping in front of Kaescis. "There are just so many, I could go on for hours." He glanced down to the black blade in Kaescis's hand.

"You won't need that," the Messenger said with a chuckle. "At least, not yet."

Kaescis dismissed the weapon, and the black particles misted away. "Why are you here?" Kaescis asked.

"You need some instruction before you set foot on the Isle of the Ancient Ones," the Messenger said. "These next few days are very delicate, and events must happen in a specific way. One wrong step by any critical participant will lead to folly. So, I've come to instruct you." He paced away.

Kaescis eyed the Messenger, still marveling that he was in the presence of a divine being.

"You can stop with the adoring thoughts," the Messenger said, stopping again in front of Kaescis. "Yes… you are in the presence of divinity. Now, pay attention. One wrong step and you could doom your God."

That frightened Kaescis. What did the Messenger mean by that?

"You'll understand," the Messenger said reassuringly. "Now, come with me." He tapped Kaescis's forehead.

Colors whirled past Kaescis in zipping streaks. He felt dizzy, though he knew he shouldn't. He understood all too well what was happening. His mind was traveling through the fabric of reality into the Realm of God, the Translucent Fields of Vabenack.

The streaks stilled, and Kaescis found himself within a space much like the observation room of the *Executor's Breath.* In fact, it *was* the observation room. The Messenger stood in front of him, removing his finger from Kaescis's forehead.

Kaescis spun, gazing out the windows. He smiled, inwardly praising Lord Cheserith. A yellow sky hung above a vast ocean of violet water. Red clouds dotted the sky, partially obscuring a blue sun.

"I am not forsaken!" he cried, dropping to his knees.

"Far from it, Kaescis," the Messenger said flatly.

Kaescis stared out the windows for a moment, then noticed the absence of noise within his mind. The voices which had clouded his thoughts since mustering his massive Ko'delish blade were gone.

"Only you are here," the Messenger said reassuringly. "The hiss'thraks are still within your body on Kalda."

Oh, what sweet relief! Kaescis cheered inwardly. He didn't know why he didn't say it aloud. The Messenger *knew* his thoughts.

"Pay attention, son of Cheserith, and behold your destiny."

———◦•◦———

Cornar stood at the forecastle of the *Promised Maiden*, watching the crewmen from the *Executor's Breath* lower the poles and gangway to link the ships. As usual, the Wildman watched with wonder. Cornar could see the other Mindolarnian warships beyond the *Executor's Breath*. Another set of poles and a gangway were being lowered to the *Helidar*. Many of Cornar's warriors were gathered around him, following their mentor's gaze.

Nordal sighed from beside Cornar, leaning against one of the barrels at the forecastle. "Sailing with this maneuver scares me," Nordal said. "Ships weren't designed to sail like this."

Midar laughed, shaking his head. "And here I thought nothing scared you," he said smugly. The only answer Nordal gave Midar was a perturbed glance.

"It'll be fine," Ordreth chimed. "Right, Uncle?"

Would it? Cornar hoped so. Kaescis seemed to be sure of it. There was still the possibility that whatever guarded Dalgilur would sense the individual ships and only grant passage to Krindal's vessel. That possibility worried Cornar.

"We should move everyone to the *Executor's Breath*," Cornar said in a hushed tone, careful not to draw the attention of the Wildmen. "If things don't go as expected I'd rather we be with Krindal."

Gregan squinted thoughtfully. "We don't even know how this whole *barrier* thing works, Cor. For all we know, Krindal could be pulled to that island, and we'd be doomed to face the dangers of the Frown."

Hemrin looked frightened at Gregan's remark. "You don't think that'll really happen, though. Right?" the young warrior asked warily. Gregan just looked at Hemrin blankly, the wind rustling through his auburn hair. A few other warriors chatted about the matter.

Cornar stepped away from his men, searching for the others of his band. Vargos was the only mage who was topside. The old barsionist sat on a chair the crew had fastened to the main mast. Vargos had wanted to be in a central location for his spell. He claimed it would be easier to maintain the barsion around the *Promised Maiden*'s hull.

If we move, he won't join us, Cornar thought.

Vargos turned, watching the sailors secure the poles and gangway. The old barsionist took in a deep breath as Cornar approached.

"I want to take everyone to the *Executor's Breath*," he told the barsionist. "Can you maintain the spell from the portside rail?"

Vargos frowned, studying Cornar. "So now you're cautious..." he said, grunting.

"Well, Vargos?"

The old barsionist scratched his beard thoughtfully.

"I'm going to get the others moved," Cornar said.

When he turned to step away, Vargos answered, "It'll be an inconvenience, but I can do it."

"Good," Cornar said, walking to the stairs leading below deck.

He'd almost reached the stairs when Vargos called out, "But I want my chair!"

Cornar hurried below deck, making his way to the galley. Several of the mages were there, including Igan. Kalder was also with them, as were Cordel and Shen. Cornar strode straightway for the wizard and put his hand on Igan's shoulder. "I want to move to the *Executor's Breath*," Cornar whispered, noting the captain and her first mate in the galley.

Igan slowly turned to Cornar, eyeing him with that thoughtful gaze of his. "Are you worried, Cor?" The three warriors leaned closer, eager to hear Cornar's answer.

"Cautious," he whispered. "We don't really know what we're dealing with." The wizard nodded thoughtfully. "Have you seen the other mages?" Cornar asked.

"I think Clodin and Hem were playing a game in their cabin," Igan said.

"Brendar and Drenor are with them too," Cordel said.

"Thanks." Cornar clasped Igan's shoulder, then looked to Kalder. "Go tell the others that are below deck."

"Right away, Cor," Kalder said, taking one last spoonful of his porridge.

"You want us to be discreet, right?" Shen whispered.

"If you can." Cornar shrugged, stepping back to the galley's door.

Once out of the galley, Cornar made his way through the lower decks. He came to one of the cabins occupied by the mages, but it was empty. A faint conversation filtered into the hallway from another cabin. Cornar hurried toward it and opened its door.

Brendar and Drenor were sitting on the edge of the lower bunk while the mages—Clodin and Hem—sat on chairs. Cornar's eyes settled on Clodin. The necromancer looked like the typical Sorothian: dark-olive skin and brown hair. Clodin's eyes, however, were a pale gray.

"Finish your game," Cornar said. "I want everyone aboard the *Executor's Breath*."

"Are we at the Frown yet?" Hem asked excitedly. The illusionist dropped his cards and hurried to the door. "Is there anything anomalous happening? The compasses stop working yet? Are the—"

"No," Cornar interrupted firmly. "Just quietly make your way to the *Executor's Breath*." He gestured for the illusionist to go down the hall. Hem closed his lips exaggeratedly and then walked speedily down the hall. Though he was a grown man, Hem often acted like a wide-eyed child. Sometimes it was humorous, but the behavior was mostly an annoyance.

Brendar and Drenor handed their cards to Clodin, then hurried out of the room. Their only acknowledgment of their mentor was a simple nod as they casually exited the cabin and made their way down the hall.

"Something wrong, Cor?" Clodin asked, gathering the rest of the cards. He bent down and picked up the ones Hem had dropped.

"Just being cautious, Clodin."

Clodin nodded, straightening the deck of cards. He was a somber fellow and often very quiet, the type of man who blended into a crowd. Clodin had studied the necrotic arts as Iltar's apprentice, beginning his tutelage at the age of twelve—twenty-four years ago. It had taken Clodin five years to become a full-fledged necromancer. Then, after his seventeenth birthday, Clodin joined Cornar's adventuring band. Since then Clodin had never missed an adventure. The man was fiercely loyal, especially to Iltar.

"All right," Clodin said, standing. "I'm ready now. Don't want to lose my favorite deck," he grinned, slipping the cards into his robe. Cornar chuckled and stepped aside to allow Clodin to pass. Together, they walked back to the stairs leading to the main deck.

Igan was ahead of them but stopped once he was topside. "Is everyone accounted for?" the wizard asked.

"I think so," Cornar said, scanning the main deck. All the members of his band were near the foremast. A few Wildmen were also nearby. Cornar's eyes, however, were drawn to Vargos, who was mustering his barsion magic.

Vargos and his chair were glowing a dark blue. The surrounding magic thickened, then shot across the wooden decking. It washed across the deck and spilled over the rails. Some of the magic ran along the poles and gangway connecting the two ships, where Vargos's barsion mingled with magic from one of the Mindolarnian mages.

Astounded by the magical feat, the Wildmen on the *Promised Maiden* gasped with awe. They marveled with each other in their broken language.

The old barsionist took a deep breath then glanced to Cornar. "It's done," Vargos said, then rose from his seat and strode toward Cornar. "Are we moving now?" he asked in a hushed tone.

Cornar nodded.

Vargos spun, then shouted to one of the crewmen. "I need a better vantage of the hull," he shouted. "Move this chair to the *Executor's Breath*." Several of the crew hurried to the fastened chair, and Vargos gave them further instructions.

"That's clever," Clodin whispered.

"Yeah," Igan smiled, "seeing as the main deck of the *Executor's Breath* is higher, it makes sense."

Cornar left the mages to talk, walking to the forecastle. All of his men were gathered there. The thirty-five of them filled the entire forecastle.

"Let's go," Cornar said, and gestured for his men to follow. He led them to the gangway and onto the *Executor's Breath*.

As on the *Promised Maiden*, the main deck of the *Executor's Breath* was filled with Wildmen and sailors. The Mindolarnian sailors busily adjusted the rigging, weaving around the gawking Wildmen.

Once on the main deck of the *Executor's Breath*, Cornar's band dispersed. Some of them went below deck to the mess deck. He could hear his men talking about spending the day out of the inevitable storm. The World's Frown was notorious for raging tempests.

Nearly half the men stayed topside along with all the mages, mingling with the Wildmen on the main deck. Sharon and Ordreth lingered close to Cornar, quietly conversing. Cornar couldn't tell what the couple was saying, though.

More orders were shouted from the bridge, requesting a status report across the small fleet. Runners dashed from the bridge and down the stairs to the gangways.

Once the runners were gone, Krindal somberly descended the stairs from the quarterdeck. The scholar started upon seeing Cornar, then jumped again upon noticing the rest of Cornar's band. Krindal studied them warily, then proceeded across the main deck, picking his way through the Wildmen.

Krindal didn't speak to anyone as he passed. He went straight for the raised forecastle, passing the forward-most mast and climbing the curved flight of stairs. The scholar wove around the armaments—long and short-range cannons—and stopped at the bowsprit.

The old scholar did something unexpected. He threw his arms wide and looked skyward.

"What is he doing?" Igan asked, sounding confused.

"Uh, looking like an idiot?" Nordal suggested, drawing laughter from some of the men.

"Maybe he thinks he needs to be at the front to make this work," Clodin said. "None of us really know how these tevisrals operate."

Darkness rose above the horizon. *Is that a storm?* Curious, Cornar looked to the ship's center mast where the crow's nest was located. The lookout was gazing through a spyglass across the horizon at that dark spot. He put the spyglass down and sat back, partially disappearing from sight—undoubtedly making notations in a logbook kept in the nest.

"Sailor!" Cornar shouted up to the lookout. He waited until the sailor peeked his head out. "Is that a storm?"

"Aye," the man shouted back. "There's lightning brewing in it. Looks bad."

Great, Cornar groaned.

"It's to be expected," Nordal said. "This is the World's Frown, after all."

"Find some shelter," Cornar told his men. "And corral the Wildmen below deck. I'd hate for them in their nervousness to endanger the ship." He glanced at the Wildmen all huddled together. "I'll be in the war room."

As Cornar strode to the staircase leading to the open-air bridge, the runners returned, passing him as he came onto the quarterdeck. The crewman in the crow's nest also shouted down a report. One of the officers took note of it, then strode into the war room.

A few of the warriors followed Cornar: Kalder, Gregan, Midar, and

Ordreth. Sharon followed too, holding Ordreth's hand. The six of them entered the war room, where Admiral Kaetet was taking reports from the runners. Cornar lingered by the doors while his companions arranged themselves around the large table, eyeing the projected map. The tevisral's effects were magnified to show part of the World's Frown. The islands were clearly visible, as was Dalgilur; it was smack dab in the middle of the Frown.

Once the runners relayed their reports, Admiral Kaetet turned to Cornar. "Welcome aboard," the admiral said. "I didn't think you'd be joining us here."

"Thank you," Cornar said, stepping closer.

"Are you aboard to inquire about that storm to the south?" Kaetet asked.

That wasn't the reason, but Cornar thought it as good an excuse as any. "What do you intend to do about it?" he asked.

"You need not worry," Kaetet said, extending his hand in a placating manner. "His Imperial Grace was aware of the potential encounter. We have four barsionists in reserve to protect the ships. But they might not be necessary."

What? Cornar wondered. The barsionists might not be necessary? How could he say that after hearing the reports from the runners and the crewman in the crow's nest?

"Oh, that's right," Admiral Kaetet said, shaking his head. "You weren't here. The prince believes that Krindal's attunement will grant us safe passage through the storm. He believes there are tevisrals on Dalgilur creating the storms in this area. Many reports say that the storms in the Frown are ever persistent. What better way to hide an island than a raging storm?" The admiral turned back to the table and jotted something down in his logbook.

Tevisrals creating a storm? Now that's something. He had never encountered a tevisral with that kind of capability. But Cornar knew not to doubt the existence of something improbable. If this expedition was anything to judge by, the improbable was more often the most likely circumstance. Take the Keepers' Temple, for instance. A perfectly maintained fortress buried deep in the earth, surrounded by magma chambers in a land commonly known for its earthquakes.

Cornar turned around, gazing out the curving windows of the war room. Here he could see that storm spreading all across the horizon.

⫸•⫷

An hour later, the fleet met the storm.

Winds blew harshly against the ship, and a wall of rain veiled the horizon in front of them. Dark storm clouds towered in the sky, occasionally illuminated by flashes of lightning. The storm spread as far as the eye could see. It was an unnatural sight.

Cornar removed a small compass from his tunic—one he often used on adventures. He had expected the needle to spin, but it remained true. Putting the compass back in his pocket, Cornar resumed gazing out the windows.

A temporary pavilion had been erected above the open-air bridge to shield those outside from the rain. Cornar thought the idea silly, as the officers could move all their logbooks into the war room to keep the pages dry.

A bolt of lightning shot through the clouds, then surged through the rain, striking the ocean in front of the ship. Thunder resounded, shaking the room.

"That was dangerously close," Sharon remarked. She stepped up beside Cornar, watching the storm with him.

Another bolt struck the ocean, not far from the first. Thunder resounded again. "Well, what are the chances of that?" Ordreth asked warily.

"It senses us," Gregan said. "Whatever is making that storm knows we're coming."

A third bolt hit the ocean, close to where the others had struck. "That cannot be a coincidence," Midar muttered.

"Admiral," Cornar said to Kaetet, "I think you should call for those barsionists."

Admiral Kaetet turned from the table and joined Cornar. Together, they watched a fourth lightning strike hit the ocean. Worry spread across the admiral's face, and he hurried out of the war room.

"One of you check on Vargos," Cornar commanded.

Kalder dashed from the war room, bolting across the quarterdeck. The rain hadn't yet reached the ships, but Kalder raised his forearm to shield his face. He returned a few seconds later. "Vargos is fine," Kalder said, stopping beside Cornar. "He enveloped himself in a sphere of protection."

A moment of tense silence passed as Cornar and the others eyed the coming storm. Cornar doubted the barsionists would be able to cast their spells before the storm hit.

"Uh… guys," Gregan began.

"What—oh!" Ordreth blurted.

The others let out similar startled exclaims.

Cornar spun, seeing Krindal's twenty-one sided gem rising above the table and glowing a brilliant hue.

"It just started rising from that tevisral," Gregan said.

The gem neared the ceiling, then *shot* through the bulkhead. A beam of light trailed behind it, persisting above the mapping tevisral.

⊰•⊱

Krindal remained at the bow in the face of that bitter storm. Rogue droplets of heavy rain hit him occasionally and sparsely wetted the forecastle. He stood arms wide, embracing the coming curtain of rain and lightning. A cacophony of noise filled the air.

This will not bar me, Krindal thought. He could see the individual raindrops that composed the stormy wall. They would wash over him in seconds.

And then, the storm hit. The wall of rain struck so hard that it knocked Krindal to the decking. He pushed himself upright as a bolt of lightning shot from the sky. It struck the bowsprit, then *unnaturally* lingered.

Krindal had seen many a lightning strike, but never one like this.

The lightning bolt persisted for a moment, then retreated skyward, followed by the rain. Huge droplets formed from the wet decking, then *fell* upward. It was as if the rain was being reflected. The winds ceased, and soon the decking was dry. Krindal also was no longer wet.

"By all that's magical…" Krindal said with a gasp, looking skyward.

The storm was retreating. The rain continued to fall above him, but was stopped by an invisible barrier. It was like a transparent bubble pushed the storm back, forming a tunnel of sorts. This was not the doing of those barsionists kept in reserve. No, a barrier of theirs would have a blue tint to it. Whatever this was, it was different.

Surprised shouts from the crew resounded behind Krindal. He turned. They weren't reacting to the storm. A brilliant speck of light shone atop a beam rising from the ship's stern. *What is that…?* Krindal scanned the skies, noticing that the brilliant speck was at the apex of whatever was shielding the ship from the rain.

"Could that be my gem?" he whispered, then moved to the starboard rail to get a better view of the aft portions of the *Executor's Breath*.

The beam of light looked like a spire rising above the observation room on the highest deck.

"It is," he smiled. Krindal spun back around, nearly dashing to the bowsprit. He threw his arms wide. "I have parted the rains," he shouted, "stilled the winds, repelled lightning, and forged safe passage! Dalgilur, receive us seekers of truth!"

◆━◆◇◆━◆

Strange shouting echoed into the war room, drawing Cornar's attention from the odd beam of light. He couldn't tell what was being said, but the voice sounded like it belonged to Krindal.

One of the doors swung open, and the admiral hurried into the war room. "What happened?" Kaetet demanded.

"I don't know," Gregan said. "One moment I was staring at the map, then that gem Krindal uses to activate this tevisral began to glow and hover. It shot through the bulkhead." He pointed to the ceiling.

Admiral Kaetet furrowed his brow, stomping toward the table. He stopped beside Gregan, gazing up at the hole, not amused.

"Admiral," an officer shouted, dashing into the war room, "the compasses are erratic!"

"Go fetch Krindal," Kaetet said, still eyeing the ceiling. "We'll enact our backup plan."

Cornar swiftly drew his own compass, seeing the needle spinning uncontrollably.

"Excuse me, sir." Midar cleared his throat, "but how are you going to steer the ship without a working compass?"

"Krindal can sense the island," the admiral replied. "He'll tell us which direction to steer." With a distracted look, Admiral Kaetet left the war room and returned to the bridge.

"The rain looks like it let up," Ordreth said.

"But it's still storming out there," Kalder said, pointing to the gloomy sky.

"It has to be this gem," Gregan said, hurrying out of the war room.

Everyone followed Gregan out onto the unnaturally dry quarterdeck. Cornar had seen the rain fall and rise. It was an odd sight to behold. This entire storm was *odd.*

Cornar gazed at the brilliantly glowing gem. Its light seemed to repel the storm, keeping it back like an umbrella. The forceful winds from the south had all but ceased. The waters which were once turbulent were mostly stilled, except for the wakes caused by the four ships.

"This is incredible!" Sharon said, awestruck.

"It's like that gem is creating a tunnel for us," Midar remarked. "Burrowing its way through the storm."

Perhaps Kaescis was right, Cornar thought. This storm was most likely the barrier that protected Dalgilur from the outside world.

Footsteps drew Cornar's attention, and Krindal approached the helm. The scholar paid little attention to Cornar and the others.

"Did the compasses fail?" Krindal asked.

"Yes," Kaetet replied. "Just as we entered the storm."

"That's unfortunate," Krindal said. "I suppose I will have to guide the fleet." He sounded disappointed. The old scholar had probably wanted to be at the bow to see the island before anyone else.

Krindal closed his eyes and took a deep breath. "I... I can see it," he said. "To our right. Maybe thirty degrees."

"We were driven that far off course?" an officer exclaimed. "No wonder ships are swallowed up in the Frown."

Krindal worked with the sailors for a while until they righted their course. The old scholar had to give them corrections every few minutes, as the ships drifted frequently.

⬡

Kaescis gasped awake, finding himself once again in the observation room of the *Executor's Breath.* A beam of light shone not far from his feet, passing through the decking of both floor and ceiling.

"We're in the storm," he muttered, turning to face the windows.

The sky was an inky black, lit occasionally by bursts of lightning. Heavy rain beat against an invisible barrier. It was like a dome of glass had encased the fleet, protecting them from Dalgilur's defenses.

The Messenger of the Promise claimed this storm never ceased. The ancient inhabitants of the island created the storm at the onset of that millennium-long war between the sha'kalda. It spread through the entirety of the World's Frown, except for a small area around Dalgilur. The storm's creators thought it a means to protect themselves from the rightful rulers of Kalda. Kaescis thought them fools for defying Lord Cheserith.

There was more to Dalgilur's defense than just this storm. It was only the first layer of protection. The Messenger had explained the particulars of the defenses in great detail. A veil of invisibility surrounded the waters not touched by the storm. Kaescis had been shown the storm from a great height. The storm swirled around a speck of clear blue water, like the eye of a great hurricane. There, Dalgilur remained untouched.

A third defensive measure was employed beneath the veil. It was a form of teleportation magic that encased the island and its surrounding waters like a bubble, seeping deep into the ocean. If anything touched the invisibility barrier—matter or energy—it would be transported through it, directly to the other side. That meant if something were to attempt passage through the apex of the dome, they could be sent to the bottom of the ocean, instantly crushed against the ocean floor and the island's defenses.

The only way around these defenses was to either use a transportium located at any of the Keepers' shrines or brave the storm with an attuned Keeper. Kaescis had known as much, to a degree. It was why he had gone to such great lengths to protect Krindal. Krindal's gem could repel the storm, but only Krindal could unlock the third and final defense of the island. Kaescis learned that Krindal's attunement would allow whatever he was touching to pass through those veils of magic and sail through safe waters.

There was a fourth defense, but that wouldn't affect them. It would bar the Chosen of Cheserith from entering Dalgilur. The Messenger didn't explain exactly how, but even if the other three defenses could be breeched, the Chosen could never set foot on Dalgilur.

That made Kaescis wonder about the stranger at the Feast of Sorrows. The stranger had mentioned being unable to reach Dalgilur.

Kaescis rose to his feet, still gazing out the windows. *Could that stranger be one of the Chosen?* he wondered. But the Chosen had disappeared, abandoning the world.

"If that stranger at the feast was one of the Chosen, why would he urge me to seek Dalgilur?" Kaescis muttered. That question bothered him deeply. Kaescis knew the *Will* was guiding him. But the Chosen? No…

Troubled, Kaescis clasped his hands behind his back. Those questions—along with what he had experienced in Vabenack—weighed heavily on his mind. Kaescis had seen the next three days. The Messenger had shown him the various events that would transpire and the actions he was supposed to take. Kaescis was to follow them exactly. The Messenger had warned that one wrong deviation here could doom the world and prevent Lord Cheserith's return.

That frightened him.

Death… a voice lingered at the back of his mind.

Kaescis had been so absorbed in what he experienced in Vabenack that he nearly forgot about the voices.

Kill Dol'shir… several hissed in unison.

"I have to stay my hand," Kaescis whispered. A disappointed growl rumbled in the back of his mind. Nowhere in the vision had he acted hostile to Mister Dol'shir and his band. In fact, they were to be advance scouts and were critical to securing the island. Several made significant discoveries.

The vision, however, had ended in a damaged room overlooking the ocean where Mister Dol'shir knelt before a waist-high pillar, holding a red book in his hand.

Kaescis wondered about the significance of that moment.

Kill him there! the voices cried. They chanted those words over and over as Kaescis ruminated on what he had seen. At no time had the Messenger of the Promise said he *shouldn't* kill Mister Dol'shir. It seemed to Kaescis that his actions were leading to that moment at the vision's end. Perhaps Mister Dol'shir needed to live only till then.

But what had—or would—Mister Dol'shir uncover? Was that book pertinent to Lord Cheserith's return?

Mulling the questions, Kaescis continued staring out the windows, watching the raging storm above the fleet.

"For years Cheserith walked among men, proclaiming his divine truths, performing miracles, and manifesting the powers of the Channels without incantation. Such manifestation was supposed to be impossible, as each Channel required speaking Words of Power in conjunction with mental focus. It would appear that Cheserith's very thoughts manifested the powers of each Channel."

- From *The Thousand Years War, Part I,* page 23

Thunder erupted against that invisible shield protecting the fleet. From what Cornar had overheard, they had traveled three hours in this accursed storm. He had since moved to the raised forecastle, staring up at the odd tunneling effect caused by Krindal's gemstone. Though the elements were furious, Cornar couldn't help but feel calm.

"The seas aren't as turbulent in this bubble," Ordreth observed.

"That gem probably has some calming effect," Igan noted. He had since come topside and joined Cornar and a few of the warriors. The wizard pointed to the wall of rain. "Look there," Igan said. "The waters there are a raging torrent. You can see the line where the gem's influence begins."

Igan was right. The difference between the waters in the storm was so distinct that it looked like the waves were splashing against glass.

"Visibility is pretty bad," Gregan remarked.

Cornar stared silently into the raging elements, waiting to see something different. He could barely see past the influence of Krindal's gem.

After another hour, the rains dissipated. Lightning strikes became less frequent. The clouds lightened in color. And then, the storm vanished.

Sunlight shone so brightly that Cornar and his companions shielded their eyes against its brilliance. The clearing spread far, but the walls of rain, cloud, and lightning rose above the distant horizon.

Hurried footfalls resounded from the main deck, growing louder. Cornar glimpsed Krindal dashing up the steps to the forecastle, pushing past Cornar's men. The old scholar stopped beside the bowsprit, eagerly gazing into the clearing.

"We've made it!" Krindal declared. "Now, Dalgilur, show yourself unto us!" He stretched his arms wide.

Several warriors held back laughter, looking at each other with gazes that said, "He sounds like a madman." Krindal *did* sound deranged. He kept his arms outstretched as a shimmering ripple appeared beyond the ship's bow. It looked like the same effect as when Sharon donned her cloak.

Is that a veil of invisibility? Cornar thought. *I wonder—*

The *Executor's Breath*—and the other three ships—abruptly stopped, tossing Cornar and the others forward.

Krindal yelled as he fell on top of the bowsprit. He bounced against it, struggling to grab a handhold.

"Grab him!" Cornar shouted the command, but Kalder was already moving.

The old scholar managed to wrap one arm around the bowsprit, dangling two phineals away from the forecastle. That would have been out of arm's reach for most, but Kalder's arms were unusually long. Kalder nearly threw himself over the rail as he grabbed Krindal's robe.

"Grab my arm!" he shouted.

Terrified, Krindal glanced to the water beneath him. "I—I—I—" he stammered.

"Hold on!" Gregan said, turning around to grab a long tool from the nearby cannons. With a rammer in hand, Gregan came beside Kalder, holding the wooden rammer toward Krindal. "Here!" Gregan shouted, extending the tool to Krindal. The rammer easily closed the gap between Krindal and the forecastle.

"I can't let go!" Krindal cried. "Wh-what if I fall?"

Gregan looked at Kalder, trying to hide his annoyance, but his emotions were painfully obvious. Cornar pushed his way past his men and stood on the other side of the bowsprit. Meanwhile, a commotion of hurried footfalls echoed across the main deck. The sailors were probably coming to help.

"I'm going to get on the bowsprit," Cornar said, unlatching the belt that held his weapons. "Here." He dangled the belt at Ordreth. The young warrior took the weapons and watched tensely as Cornar climbed atop the bowsprit.

The bowsprit was damp, but not enough to make it slippery. "The three of us will pull you back aboard," Cornar said, assuming a calm tone. After a few steps Cornar laid against the bowsprit, wrapping one arm around it. His face was practically beside Krindal's. The old scholar's eyes warily shot back and forth between the three warriors.

"Give me your arm," Cornar said, holding out his own hand. He could reach out and grab Krindal, but that might startle the old scholar.

"You will not drop me?" Krindal asked, his voice trembling.

"No." Cornar shook his head. "Trust me."

"How-how can you say that when I've lied to you?"

Cornar didn't reply. If he let Krindal fall that would ruin everything. Besides, Krindal's deceit didn't warrant a fate at the bottom of the ocean.

The footfalls grew louder, and the Mindolarnians were crowding the forecastle. Admiral Kaetet was shouting orders for his officers and crew. Cornar glimpsed them grabbing spare lines from the sails.

"Oh, enough of this!" a woman's voice bellowed.

That sounds like Laeyit, Cornar turned.

Laeyit pushed through the men crowding the forecastle, uttering an incantation in a magical tongue Cornar was unfamiliar with. It was sharp, staccato-like, and fast.

Green tentacles burst from nothingness, spreading wildly from her palms. They wisped around Cornar and his warriors, grabbing Krindal.

"Let go!" Laeyit barked.

Krindal looked panicked, but didn't move. After a moment, the tentacles *pried* him from the bowsprit. Cornar watched as the old scholar was lifted overhead and set abruptly on the main deck.

The sailors soon dispersed at Kaetet's orders, but the Admiral lingered on the forecastle, as did Laeyit. Cornar slid backward on the bowsprit, feeling one of his warriors grab his legs. Soon, Cornar was back on the forecastle.

"Why aren't we moving?" Laeyit demanded.

"You're asking me, madam?" the admiral blinked with disbelief.

Krindal rejoined them on the forecastle, anxiously looking about. The three of them discussed the sudden jolt and the abrupt change of their surroundings.

Cornar had been so worried about Krindal that he had failed to pay attention to what was happening beyond the ship. The air around them looked strange, like poorly made glass. Bubbles shifted in the air, with tiny reflections of the ship. The bubbles moved in all directions, up, down, sideways. There was no consistency to the bubbles' movements.

Cornar looked over the rail. That bizarre substance had also replaced the ocean. It looked like the ship—along with the other connected vessels—was hovering in this glass-like air.

The whole thing was very unsettling.

Several of the other warriors took notice of their surroundings and backed away from the rails. Ordreth nearly jumped as he laid eyes on the odd substance that had replaced the ocean. He hurried back down the stairs and across the main deck, stopping partway to the quarterdeck and looking about, completely startled. Soon, he was shouting and waving everyone over. Ordreth's words, however, were muffled and indistinguishable.

Aside from Ordreth's shouting and the conversation between the Mindolarnians, it seemed awfully quiet.

Krindal and the Mindolarnians didn't pay attention to Cornar's nephew. They lingered at the bow, debating what lay before the fleet.

Cornar and his men, however, hurried to Ordreth. Once they were past the second mast, the odd bubbles vanished, but were replaced by that shimmering in the air. Ambient noises also returned and Ordreth's words became understandable.

"… see right where it stops," Ordreth said. His expression had turned from fear to wonder.

Cornar glanced over his shoulder. Everything between the second mast and the bow was gone. It looked like the ship just ended.

"It's moving," Igan said, pointing to the decking. "Watch as the grain disappears." The warriors looked down, watching as the variations in the grain were swallowed up into nothingness. Cornar looked about, studying the other ships. Each of the vessels appeared the same as the *Executor's Breath*—only parts of them were visible and their bows were gone. The Wildmen on the *Promised Maiden* were petrified, they edged away from the disappearing deck, crowding toward the rear mast.

Laeyit soon appeared, walking near Cornar. She glanced to Cornar and his men, but continued to the open-air bridge without a word.

"I'm going back to the bow," Gregan said. A few others followed him, disappearing.

"Are you all right?" Cornar clasped his nephew's shoulder.

Ordreth nodded. "It's just strange, that's all…" he said. "I imagine I looked pretty foolish."

Cornar grinned, then followed his men back through the veil of invisibility. It felt like stepping into nothingness, as if something was muting sound. Most noises ceased around him. Even his men's footsteps were muffled, and Cornar could barely hear their conversation. But the forward parts of the ships appeared as Cornar moved through the veil.

Once on the forecastle, Cornar gripped the rail near the starboard cannon. The odd glassy substance spread as far as he could see. It was like an endless void. One of the bubbles moved past Cornar's face, reflecting him and the forecastle. He reached out to touch it, but the bubble zipped away.

What are those things? Cornar wondered.

Cornar and the others waited for something to change, but nothing happened. Eventually, one of the officers came to Admiral Kaetet, informing him that whatever was surrounding the bow had covered the entire fleet.

It appeared that the ship was standing still. They were probably still moving, though how fast Cornar didn't know. Those odd bubbles floated about—some zipping this way and that—but with no frame of reference Cornar couldn't discern the ship's speed.

Before long, the ship jolted and everyone was thrown backward. The glassy substance filling the air was gone, and the *Executor's Breath* was back in open waters.

Krindal cackled with amusement. "You've welcomed us!" he shouted. "Dalgilur is ours! And today, we restore the world to its ancient ways!"

Cornar recovered from the jolt, standing to behold an island with towering mountains. The mountains' sheer sides dropped into the ocean, making it impossible to moor there. White tips peaked above the mountains, sleek and reflecting the sun. *Those must be the buildings,* Cornar thought, remembering the towering structures on the magical map that rivaled the height of the mountains. His eye was drawn to something shiny poking out the left side of the island, looking level with the ocean. *That must be the pier,* he mused.

Commands resounded from the bridge, ordering the unlinking of the fleet.

Cornar spun, seeing that all four vessels were again sailing beside the *Executor's Breath*. He didn't know if Kaescis's theory had proven true, or if Krindal's gem had a set distance to it. Either way, the fleet had made it to Dalgilur.

"We've done it!" Krindal cheered, looking toward the ship's stern. "My gem…" he muttered, hurrying down the stairs and across the main deck.

"Crazy old man," Ordreth muttered, drawing a snicker from Sharon.

"So, where's the storm?" Gregan asked. "Shouldn't it be over the horizon?"

The warriors searched the horizon, looking back from whence they had come. To Cornar's surprise, the storm wall they had passed through was gone. In fact, no matter where he looked, Cornar couldn't see the storm.

"Perhaps it's an illusion," Igan said, speculating aloud. "If I had the capability of making that"—he gestured toward the storm—"I certainly wouldn't want to be looking at a raging tempest for my entire life. The Channelers of Aridia probably felt the same."

"The Channelers of Aridia?" Gregan asked, furrowing his brow. He pushed aside a strand of his auburn hair. "You mean the Keepers, right?"

"No. The Keepers didn't make this place," Igan said. "I was reading one of the tomes we found, and this place was abandoned thousands of years ago, during the Dragon Wars."

Ordreth snickered, then choked back disbelieving laughter. Cornar probably would have reacted the same, but his time with Solidin in the Keepers' Temple had opened his mind to other possibilities.

Igan ignored Ordreth and continued speaking. "The Channelers of Aridia made this place at the onset of the war. Many decades later, they left to join a coalition that was fighting against the Cheserithean Empire. The Keepers didn't come here until several hundred years after the war ended."

The warriors looked surprised at Igan's brief history lesson, but not Cornar. He turned back toward Dalgilur as Igan continued relating the bits of information he had gleaned from the book.

⬥◆⬥

Kaescis gazed out the windows of the observation room, his hands clasped behind his back. His vision in Vabenack had instructed him to wait here until they moored. Ahead, Kaescis could see the edges of the island beyond the sails. The sky was clear in the distance, a result of an illusion cast by the tevisrals creating Dalgilur's defenses.

I would rather gaze upon that storm, he thought. The notion of an isolated utopia sickened him. He thought the ancient inhabitants of this island were cowards. A knocked rapped on the door of the observation room. Kaescis knew it was Laeyit, come to give him a report.

"Kaescis," she said, crossing the room. "Each of the—"

"I know," he interrupted her. "Everyone made it through, and Krindal almost fell off the bowsprit."

Laeyit grunted softly, and Kaescis knew she looked incredulous. He was seeing this event in his mind as it was happening.

"How did you know about Krindal?" she asked, stepping up beside him. "You can't see the forecastle from here when the sails are unfurled."

"Because you were about to say it," Kaescis said calmly. Laeyit started. She rarely reacted so.

"I have been to the Translucent Fields, Laeyit," he said. She said nothing, as he expected. In the vision, Laeyit had given her report, and he had relayed his experience to her.

"I've lived these next few days," he said. "The Messenger of the Promise came to me. He stood right there," Kaescis pointed back to the spot where the divine being had touched him. "He showed me what I must do."

"Kaescis…" she muttered, bringing a hand to her mouth. Were those tears in her eyes? He turned, returning his gaze to the window.

"Will we find…" she trailed off, though he knew what she was asking.

"Yes, Laeyit," he said. "It is all here. All the wonders of the ancient world." Kaescis grinned, then turned to the door, glimpsing Laeyit. She looked exuberant. "Save your outburst for when Bratan arrives. He will be here in a few seconds."

Footsteps echoed through the opened doorway, and then Bratan entered the observation room as Kaescis had predicted.

"Oh, Bratan!" Laeyit cheered, then ran toward him, leaping so he would catch her. Bratan looked confused as he scooped Laeyit into his arms. She laughed, patting his chest, then pointed back to Kaescis.

"He's seen this, all of this," she waved her hand, still laughing. "He's been to Vabenack!"

Eyes wide, Bratan almost dropped Laeyit.

"The Messenger ministered to him!" she exclaimed. "We'll fulfill our mandate from the emperor. The world will bow under Mindolarnian reign forever!"

Bratan stared blankly at Kaescis. The burly Praetorian was probably unsure of what to say. Bratan stood, holding Laeyit as she laughed uncontrollably.

"How much did you see?" Bratan finally asked.

"The entirety of the island," Kaescis answered. "I was shown everything until the third day." He eyed his friends for a moment before continuing. "We must be exact in our actions. Everything we do here will have a part to play in the return of our God."

Laeyit stopped laughing. She looked serious and slid from Bratan's arms.

"The three of us must adhere to my vision. Mister Dol'shir and his band also play an important role." His friends tensed at the mention of the Sorothians.

"But…"—Laeyit squinted—"you have to kill him."

"Not immediately," Kaescis said. "He and his men must make certain discoveries. I believe the last time I saw him is the moment I must strike, but not before then. His death at the wrong time could doom us and our God."

Laeyit paled at those words. She brought a hand to her mouth and stepped around Bratan, edging to the door.

"What must we do?" Bratan asked.

"Stay with me while we moor," Kaescis said. "I will tell you our tasks." As Kaescis finished speaking, Laeyit hurried out of the room. "Laeyit!" he shouted after her,

Her footsteps echoed through the hall and down a flight of stairs.

"Bratan, fetch her," Kaescis said, concerned. "She mustn't go."

"Yes, my prince!" Bratan saluted and bolted out of the room.

Kaescis tensed as he watched Bratan bound away. This hadn't happened in the vision. Was it because he had interrupted her report? The Messenger had said each action of his was delicate. Kaescis hoped whatever Laeyit did, it wouldn't ruin what *must* transpire. Pushing down his worries, Kaescis turned back, gazing once more out the windows.

The fleet rounded the island, sailing eastward. Cornar and the others quietly watched from the bow of the *Executor's Breath*. Vargos had since joined them, and Igan had finished recounting part of the book, *Origins and Oaths of the Keepers*. It was one of the volumes they had pilfered in Klindil and was an introductory read for anyone seeking to become a Keeper of Truth and Might. Igan hadn't finished reading it, but he intended to do so on the voyage home.

They rounded the northeast tip of the island, sailing farther east to skirt the nearest pier. The entire pier glowed a faint pale blue while also reflecting the sunlight. It was sleek, like the tips of the buildings he had seen peaking over the mountains. The pier was longer than any Cornar had ever seen, and it *hovered* above the water, totally lacking any supports. He estimated fifty ships could moor along one side. That was twice the capacity of the largest pier in Soroth.

Cornar's men made awestruck remarks about what lay farther inland. It looked like a city.

Pale-blue buildings scraped the sky, reflecting the afternoon sun. As Cornar remembered from Krindal's map, the outer ring consisted of twenty-one buildings, although he couldn't distinguish each from this distance. They looked like a cluster of glistening spires.

The second ring of buildings rose higher than those in the outer, though not quite as high as the central buildings, which were white and peaked above the mountains; the central buildings looked almost twice as high as the outer ones. They all looked pristine, unlike the ruins in Klindil or the Fortress of Anigar.

The island's defenses probably shielded the buildings from the elements and therefore preserved them.

"Those are the prettiest ruins I've ever seen," Vargos remarked.

"I don't think those qualify as ruins," Ordreth said, glancing to the old barsionist.

"Don't argue with your elders, boy," Vargos said.

After a while, Krindal returned to the bow, wearing the necklace which held his gem. "Isn't it glorious?" he asked, pushing past Vargos and leaning against the bow rail.

A few more of Cornar's men came to the forecastle: Nordal, Midar, Cordel, and Hemrin. They watched with wide eyes as the fleet rounded the northeast pier.

Conversation was sparse. Most of them just admired the grand scenery. Then the *Executor's Breath* turned westward, sailing along the central pier. At this distance, Cornar could see the pier in greater detail. It was made entirely from one solid stone slab, as if it had been transmuted and reformed all at once. The glow he had seen from afar was coursing magic flowing along the entire length of the pier's surface. Cornar thought it might be a layer of barsion magic. Perhaps the barsion was stabilizing the pier above the water.

As the ships sailed inland, Dalgilur's buildings seemed to grow taller. Even the shortest buildings obscured the mountains behind them.

The *Executor's Breath* sailed as far as it could, mooring along part of the pier that spread along the shoreline, spreading as far as the cluster of buildings. Admiral Kaetet shouted orders, and the crew readied the starboard gangway.

Krindal hurried away, obviously wanting to be the first to set foot on the island. Wildmen were behind him, anxious to stand on solid ground. The storm had unsettled many of them.

Cornar looked at each of his men on the forecastle. "Kalder, round up the others below deck," he said. "The rest of you, go grab our gear from the *Promised Maiden.*"

The warriors obeyed, as did Sharon. They left Cornar alone with Vargos and Igan on the forecastle.

"That storm was incredible," Igan said. "How was it for you, holding up the barsion?" the wizard asked Vargos.

"Tiring," Vargos replied. "I could use a nap."

"You can rest if you'd like," Cornar said. "I doubt we'll be encountering trouble here. Besides, the Mindolarnians probably want to mobilize their army before we get too far away."

Vargos nodded. "I'll be in my cabin," he said, walking down the stairs and toward the now lowered gangway.

"It's spectacular," Igan said, turning back to the glistening buildings.

Cornar nodded. They stared at the magnificent vista for a moment before making their way to the gangway.

Dozens of soldiers filed down the gangway, spreading across the pier. The Wildmen were much less disciplined in their departure—they pushed their way down the gangway and scurried about the pier. One of the other warships had sailed along the pier's other side, mooring opposite the *Executor's Breath.* Soldiers from the other warship were also disembarking, with Wildmen mingled in their ranks. The soldiers piled supplies along the pier, including the tents used to erect the war camp. The Wildmen, however, knocked over supplies. It was a mess.

Cornar thought the idea of setting up the war camp silly, as they could simply retire to the ships. The island wasn't *that* big. Judging by first glance, the buildings were probably less than half an hour's walk from the pier—a good four or five grand phineals.

"Mister Dol'shir!" Cornar turned to see the prince approaching with his two friends. They looked unusually excited, especially that strange woman, Laeyit.

Kaescis grinned, his expression pleasant. The hostility Cornar had observed since the Keepers' Temple was all but gone. The prince looked like he had when they first met—an idealistic man seeking adventure and excitement.

How odd...

"Are your men ready?" the prince asked.

"We're still gathering them from the lower decks," Cornar replied. "We came aboard before the storm. Some of my men went back to the *Promised Maiden* to fetch our gear."

"Excellent!" Kaescis said, still grinning. "I would like to set up camp within Dalgilur. Find us a suitable spot to erect the war camp. Send some of your men back to us when you find it. Then, feel free to explore the wonders of this place."

"All right," Cornar said.

Kaescis turned away with Laeyit and Bratan, moving toward the gangway.

Igan looked warily at Cornar. The wizard was obviously puzzled at Kaescis's change in demeanor. Igan, however, wasn't the only one worried about the abrupt change. Cornar himself pondered Kaescis's turnabout, but he felt calm. He knew he could rely on that feeling, but he wondered why he hadn't perceived Solidin's deceit. Perhaps it was because the elf's intentions weren't malicious.

"What do you think his secret is?" Igan whispered. "That man must be at least a hundred years old."

"At least," Cornar replied. He hadn't dwelt much on Kaescis's nature since his latest experience in that dreamland. But now that they were here on Dalgilur, Cornar began wondering again. Who was Kaescis, really? And what was his true purpose here on Dalgilur?

Hoping he would soon uncover those answers, Cornar strode to the gangway with Igan. They walked side by side, traveling along the pier toward the island's heart. They—not Krindal—would be the first to behold this ancient wonder. Cornar thought it fitting, especially since he had been lied to about the Keepers' Temple and the Sapphire Guard.

51

DALGILUR

> *"With unbridled guile, Cheserith changed the societies he touched. His actions were perceived as improvement, especially his introduction of tevisrals the likes of which had never been seen, not even among the elves."*

> \- From *The Thousand Years War, Part I*, page 24

Dalgilur's towering buildings sparkled in the sunlight. *Incredible,* Cornar thought, gazing at the buildings with astonishment. *So this is what our world was like for our ancestors.* He stood with Igan near the pier, at the edge of an expansive grassy field. The field was remarkably manicured, even though this place was supposed to be abandoned.

But was it? If this place was inhabited, would the inhabitants be friendly? Or would Cornar and his men be seen as invaders? Cornar couldn't take that chance.

Many of his warriors gathered around Cornar, each gazing admiringly at the magnificent sight. They were girded in their chain mail, their weapons belted on.

Soon, all forty-three of Cornar's band was gathered. *We don't have enough mages,* Cornar thought, frowning. He wanted to place them in teams of three, one mage per two warriors. That pairing was the safest when exploring potentially dangerous territory. It was a practice he had learned from personal experience. But only a third of his band would have a mage with them.

What to do…? Then his eyes fell upon the fifteen Sorothian scholars. They were dividing their supplies beside the *Promised Maiden.*

"Kalder," Cornar said, still studying the necromancer-scholars, "grab Krindal. I want those scholars who are trained as mages to join us. This place looks peaceful enough, but I'd rather have mage support for each pair."

Kalder nodded and hurried back to the pier.

"Are you sure that's wise, Cor?" Gregan asked doubtfully, folding his arms.

"It'll be fine," Cornar said, nodding.

"I thought we were claiming finds for ourselves," Igan whispered. "That won't work if those scholars are exploring with us."

Cornar turned to Igan. The wizard looked stern. Igan too had felt betrayed by Krindal and the others. Since sailing from Klindala, the more senior members of the band had decided that whatever they found on Dalgilur would be theirs. They would smuggle their finds back to the *Promised Maiden*.

A devious thought came to Cornar. It was probably something Iltar would have done. "If they join us, it seems like we're being trustworthy," Cornar said, glancing back to Kalder. The warrior had just reached Krindal and the other scholars. "There will be six groups not with the scholars. Whatever those six find will be ours."

That satisfied Igan.

"You're sounding like Master Iltar," Gregan said. "I didn't think you had a devious streak…"

"You can't be too careful with Mindolarnians lurking about," Vargos said contemptuously, his sour tone a result of his interrupted nap.

Cornar grinned. "This isn't the first time I've claimed discoveries under the noses of scholars." Several warriors laughed, having heard the story. They hadn't been on the adventure, of course. It was a trip Cornar had undertaken several years before establishing his band.

Kalder approached and cleared his throat. "Igan will be with me and Kamdir," he said. "Kalder and Hemrin will be with Clodin. Hem, you stay with Ordreth and Demsal. Sharon, you can be with them as well."

Hem whooped, throwing a hand into the air triumphantly. Cornar knew that the four of them worked well together.

"You four will be in charge of the *deed*." Cornar referred to the act of smuggling their discoveries back to the *Promised Maiden*. "Vargos, you'll be with Gregan and Haetan. Nordal, take Tinal and Midar. And lastly, Cordel and Shen will be with Renal."

Those Cornar had organized separated themselves, standing a little way off on the grassy field. Hem's excitement carried through the air. The illusionist made wild assumptions about Dalgilur's secrets. Many of the other warriors paired off while Kamdir approached Cornar and Igan.

Kamdir was one of the youngest warriors, standing shorter than Cornar, but not by much. Kamdir, fit and sturdy, was still considered tall for most men. He knew how to fight, and sometimes proved a challenge for Cornar in sparring matches.

He had been a close friend of Cornar's youngest daughter, Elista. They had grown up together, and Kamdir had been around for many a homecoming from worthwhile adventures. Since the age of seven, Kamdir had wanted to become a member of Cornar's band. Cornar thought, perchance, that Kamdir and Elista would marry, but she followed her brother to Tor and found a husband there.

But even after Elista's departure, Kamdir continued his training with Cornar. Kamdir put every part of himself into becoming a skilled warrior. And, Kamdir was a good man. He even helped out in the vineyard. Though

Kamdir hadn't married Elista, he had become part of Cornar's family. Cornar saw him as another son-in-law, one he could *actually* spend some time with. It wasn't that Cornar didn't get along with his sons-in-law, Kamdir just shared similar interests.

"This will be fun," Kamdir grinned, clasping his hands behind his back. "Thanks for picking me to join you."

"Of course." Cornar patted the young man's shoulder, but was drawn by Kalder and the scholars.

"You want us to join you?" Krindal asked skeptically.

"Yes," Cornar said matter-of-factly. "I don't like to change what works on adventures. We're short of mages, so I thought the lot of you wouldn't mind filling in the gaps. You can be both scholars and necromancers today."

Many of the scholars looked unsure. If any had been on an expedition like this before, they had probably sat back and let men like Cornar do the initial scouting.

Jahevial, however, didn't share their uncertainty. "Where do you want me?" he asked, stepping forward.

Cornar pointed to the two men standing to his left. "You can join Aron and Vaemar."

Another scholar stepped forward—a man named Valinar. He was followed by six others. They each joined pairs of warriors. Four pairs, however, were still mageless.

That's better than before, Cornar thought, eyeing Krindal. The old scholar looked sheepish.

"Do you want to join me, Krindal?"

"Cor!" Igan whispered, gritting his teeth. Cornar glanced casually to Igan. He didn't intend to keep Krindal with them the whole time. Cornar wouldn't need the old scholar. But perhaps Krindal's initial involvement might soften the tension between them.

"You don't have to stay with us," Cornar said. "But you deserve to be one of the first to set foot into Dalgilur. I'm sure Kaescis will have other plans for you the rest of the time. But you can help us select a spot to erect the war camp."

Igan studied Cornar, then eased.

Krindal looked to his fellow scholars, those who hadn't joined the warriors. "I cannot," he said with hesitation. Cornar thought Krindal would be more enthusiastic. "The prince has something else for me to do," Krindal said, then turned around, walking back to the pier. The other scholars followed Krindal.

"Four groups aren't too bad," Kamdir said optimistically.

Once the scholars were gone, Kalder approached Cornar. "Maybe the mageless pairs can stay outside, guarding the war camp," he suggested.

Cornar nodded.

"Am I with Hemrin?" Kalder asked, glancing to those who had separated themselves. Hemrin was waving his hand high in the air.

"How did you guess?" Cornar said with a chuckle.

Kalder smiled and walked away to join his group. There was a steady chatter brewing among the men.

"Listen up!" Cornar shouted, and everyone quieted. "Our initial task is to find a suitable place to set up the Mindolarnian war camp. Once we get into those buildings, everyone will spread out. We'll scout the area for a few hours, then meet back at a central courtyard at the heart of those buildings." He pointed to Dalgilur. "Leave a marker in the center of whatever area you've scouted, that way we don't have any overlap.

"Now, let's go!"

Cornar spun around, eagerly striding toward the majestic towers piercing the sky. Many of his warriors let out triumphant cheers as they marched toward Dalgilur.

✦

The road from the pier was beautiful. It rose a little above the grass and seemed to keep the vegetation at bay. Glistening poles lined the road on both sides, probably some sort of ancient lamppost. They were bright in the daylight, and Cornar assumed the poles would be quite luminous at night.

Several of the warriors tromped across the field, moving toward the outer parts of the city. A good number, however, were still behind Cornar.

They reached the edge of Dalgilur within a quarter of an hour. All was silent. Dalgilur's silence, coupled with its pristine condition, made the city seem exceptionally eerie. Many of the warriors drew their weapons and cautiously stepped onto the road that ringed the city. The street from the pier merged into this ring-road and was lined with more ancient lampposts.

Cornar had thought it odd that there was no wall or city gate. But then he remembered the storm. That storm was essentially Dalgilur's wall.

More groups split off, and only a few remained with Cornar as he cautiously approached the nearest building. Cornar and those with him—his, Kalder, and Gregan's groups—stopped to admire the building's magnificence.

It was made of a sapphire-colored stone with indigo flecks and streaks of cobalt. The stone surface, like the road, lacked any seams. The building rose hundreds of phineals, perhaps a hundred stories tall. Its base looked to be the size of a Sorothian city block—roughly the size of four squared phedans or three hundred phineals square—but tapered every five or so stories half way up the building. The tapering effect created staggered balconies with glowing rails. Towers rose from some of the balconies, reaching partway up the building. Enormous azure windows spanned multiple floors. Cornar had seen nothing this grand.

"It's... massive," Kamdir murmured.

"And it's one of the shorter ones," Gregan remarked in awe.

"We could be here for months," Hemrin mused, awestruck with the possibility of exploring every square phineal of the city.

"Well, you're not going to catch me at the top of that!" Vargos blurted.

"Let's split up," Cornar suggested and continued forward, moving to the building's right.

Cornar crept onto a road that led between the buildings toward the middle tier of the towering structures. This road would be one of the twenty-one leading into the city.

At this distance, the uniqueness of Dalgilur's buildings was visible, although they had many common features—the towers and balconies to name a few. But each was laid out slightly different from the next.

Soon, only Igan and Kamdir were with Cornar. They cautiously stepped onto a road wrapping around the middle tier of buildings and found another road leading to the city's heart. Every building they passed was as magnificent as the first.

Cornar wondered what it would have been like to live here. Throngs of Keepers most likely had filled these streets. He wondered if they peddled goods along the roads, or did they have their own building for that?

The heart of Dalgilur wasn't as compact as the outer ring. Seven towering buildings—made of white stone—sat in a circular field of manicured grass, spaced at least a hundred phineals apart. These seven buildings differed from the others.

Their bases were oval shaped, and much of their architecture shared that trait. Towering pointed oval windows adorned the buildings' walls. The buildings tapered as they rose, but instead of forming balconies, the rooftops became the tips of pointed ovals. Their windows, however, were the same magnificent azure as the others.

Cornar thought the architecture of these seven looked elven. He hadn't seen many elven structures, but he knew the elves liked to make their buildings resemble pointed ovals, mirroring the shape of their ears.

If these are elven, were those first ones human? Cornar wondered, passing a few trees scattered around the white buildings. The trees were hemmed by a low cerulean-colored wall that rose to knee height. *And what of the supposed dragons? Solidin claimed dragons were part of that ancient coalition. And that third projection-thing in the temple beneath Klindil was supposed to be a dragon—a dragon in human form.* Cornar still wasn't convinced that dragons existed beyond myth.

Ahead of the seven white towers lay the courtyard Cornar had mentioned to his men. It wasn't what Cornar had expected.

The road they were on intersected another ring-road that circled the center of Dalgilur. Tall white-marble statues of humans and elves, both male and female, hemmed this circular road. The statues faced outward, guarding a circular platform that sat at Dalgilur's heart, elevated above the road and the grassy field.

The statues stood on squared pedestals made of the same white marble. The statues were clad in armor or robes and wielded a variety of weapons. Some weapons Cornar recognized, but others were unknown to him. Many of the mages wielded channeling staffs—a rod with a groove along its shaft that mages used to accelerate bolts of magic. Such weapons were precious— Cornar had only seen ten in his lifetime. Each of the statues had unique emblems etched upon the fronts of their robes or armor. These emblems undoubtedly represented the twenty Orders among the Keepers.

As Cornar and his companions passed, they eyed the statues; each rose two or three times higher than the men.

"Doesn't look like this will work," Igan said, climbing the deep steps to the platform. "There are too many obstacles in the way, what with the trees and statues."

"Perhaps we can set up in one of the buildings," Kamdir said thoughtfully.

They stopped at the highest step, next to one of seven pillars that surrounded the platform. A transparent globe hovered above each pillar—each globe about the size of a man's torso.

Igan moved to the platform's center, eyeing intricate designs beneath his feet. Strange symbols glowed a pale blue, while lines along the platform shifted in myriad colors grander than any rainbow.

"This looks familiar," Igan said, kneeling at the platform's center. He slid his hand over the glowing surface, eyeing the etched symbols. "I've seen this before."

"The writing?" Kamdir asked, putting his hands on his hips.

"No, this platform. There was one like it in the Keepers' Temple. But the platform was damaged."

Cornar turned around, surveying the rest of this central section. Igan was right; there was not enough level ground to set up the war camp. They could set up camp here, but the tents would be spread out.

We might have to settle for a campsite beside the city, Cornar thought. His eyes swept to the northwest. More statues guarded a street between buildings. *That's different,* he mused, stepping across the platform.

The statues lined the road on either side and led to the mountains—no, a building *carved* from the mountain. Its architecture was unlike the rest of Dalgilur, comprising sharp designs that resembled the curve of a claw. The building protruded from the mountainside and towered as high as the seven structures at Dalgilur's heart, but it was many times wider. It seamlessly blended into the mountainside.

"By Heleron's Fin…" Cornar said, his mouth agape as he gazed at the massive structure.

A towering portico was aligned with the road, rising what Cornar assumed was dozens of stories. In all truth, the portico could have been taller. Everything about the colossal structure was larger than it should have been. Was it exaggerated like that to accommodate… a dragon? But dragons weren't real.

Igan and Kamdir continued talking as Cornar stepped across the platform. Cornar was *drawn* toward the colossal structure. Something compelled him there, though he didn't know what.

"Cor?" Igan called.

Cornar replied without turning around. "Let's go in there."

❖

Krindal fought the urge to dash across those manicured fields. He paced uneasily along the pier. His cohorts who hadn't joined Cornar's warriors were busily examining the pier, debating its nature.

"It has to be barsion," Timar said.

"No," retorted Pectis, "there could be a form of kinetic stabilization."

"Don't be stupid, Pectis," Claur said, grumbling. "If there was kinetic manipulation, there would be ripples in the water."

Krindal couldn't stand the bickering any longer. He hurried away, searching for the prince. Krindal had to know why he was forbidden to go into Dalgilur. Did Prince Kaescis fear the accursed elves were lying in wait? Perhaps Cornar and his men were fodder. *Yes, that had to be it.*

Commands resounded through the air, and Krindal found the prince still aboard the *Executor's Breath.* Krindal pushed through the crowd of sailors and soldiers and climbed the gangway.

"Your Imperial Highness," he called. "Is it time yet?"

"Patience, Krindal," Prince Kaescis said. "I have received specific instructions and we *must* adhere to them."

That stupid religion, Krindal grumbled. The prince's adherence to that frivolous *Will* he followed was downright frustrating. Krindal must have been making a face because Prince Kaescis sternly raised an eyebrow at him.

"Don't say it, Kaescis," Laeyit said, putting a hand on the prince's shoulder. She gently stroked his sleeve. "He is not a believer."

Of course I'm not a believer, Krindal groaned. *I'm a damned scholar, and I deserve to be out there!* He turned, facing the towering buildings across the island.

Krindal would have taken Cornar's offer, but the threat the prince had made was more compelling than Krindal's curiosity.

"Your *Will*—or whatever you call it—better not deprive me of discoveries," Krindal groaned.

"It won't be much longer," Kaescis said. "Why don't you come dine with us? I doubt any of us have eaten since we entered the storm."

Krindal heard the prince and his small retinue walk away. Food was appealing. It was better than listening to squabbles.

⊂•⊃

Nordal decided to explore one of the outer buildings in Dalgilur. There were plenty of people looking for a spot for the damned Tilters to set up their lopsided war camp. Nordal actually hated that war camp. Its memory left a bitter taste, and that bitterness extended to everything Mindolarnian.

A little exploration would counter that distaste. Besides, the Tilters had forsaken Cor on Klindala, so they deserved a little forsaking. The other two didn't mind being disobedient. Tinal was an eager fellow, ready for adventure. The young wizard hadn't been out much and acted like a boy who had never left his homeland—well, maybe on rare occasion. And Midar, well, he was just as eager as Nordal to make a discovery for themselves.

This adventure had been quite dull. They had done little exploring in Klindil. The trek had practically been boring, except for the earthquake. Then everything after that became absurd. Not even the Keepers' Temple could be considered *exploration.*

So, Nordal decided to take things into his own hands. After separating from Cor and the others, Nordal took his trio around the right side of Dalgilur. They passed six of those towering buildings and then reached the mountainside. The road kept going, arcing in a circle. The mountainside was cut cleanly along the road's edge, forming a polished brown wall.

According to the map, there would be five other buildings tucked along the mountains. But, Nordal thought this one where the mountain was cut would be easy to remember, especially since all these buildings looked alike.

There were at least three entrances on the structure's eastern side. They approached the one in the center, and the door slid aside as Nordal and the others neared. It must have reacted to their presence.

A peculiar freshness of air washed from the opening. It was like the rooms in the Keepers' Temple. The mages thought the air was purified, but Nordal thought it stank. Fresh air was *pure*, not this nonsense.

They stepped inside, entering a narrow hallway. A narrow strip of light along the ceiling illuminated the hall. It looked like coursing magic. There was also a slight hum in the air. The interior of the building was sleek, like everything else they had encountered on the island. Nordal had expected to find flowery details, gaudy décor, and lavish furniture. But none of that was here. It was just, sleek.

"Different than I imagined," Tinal said somberly. The young wizard studied every bit of the hall.

"I wonder where this hallway goes…" Midar said, cautiously shifting his sword in his grip.

"Hopefully somewhere worthwhile," Nordal said, striding down the hallway.

"And if it doesn't?" Tinal asked.

Nordal glanced to the young wizard, raising his brow. "The one thing you must always remember about adventuring, Tinal, is that a whole lot of nothing leads to something."

"Unless it doesn't," Midar said flatly. "And then you've just wasted your time."

Nordal rolled his eyes and continued down the hallway.

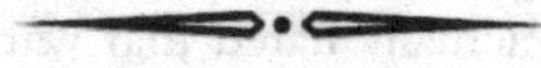

The portico was at least twenty stories tall, or so Cornar assumed. He wondered if that height had something to do with the Keeper Orders. But why would someone build a structure in such an exaggerated fashion? He kept coming back to the idea that it was constructed for a dragon… but dragons weren't real.

They couldn't be.

Colossal doors barred the way. The doors were massive stone slabs that bore glyphs for each of the Keeper Orders.

"Well, I doubt we can get in this way…" Kamdir sighed.

"Maybe there is a smaller door that opens," Igan wondered. "Or a keyword that activates the tevisrals that will move these."

Cornar continued forward, leaving his companions behind to debate the colossal slabs. As Cornar neared the doors, light shone from between the massive stone slabs; it was a brilliant white that forced Cornar to shield his eyes. Then, creaking noises resounded from the light.

The massive doors swung across the ground, arcing just in front of Cornar.

"Proximity," Igan said, striding past Cornar into the now open doorway.

The room that lay beyond could not be described as massive. *Massive* failed to describe the grandeur of this room. It rose as high as the portico and was several times wider than it was tall. The depth seemed to go on and probably was as long as Dalgilur's city was round.

Columns—that could have been buildings—held up the ceiling. Their diameter wasn't as thick as the structures outside, but the columns looked large enough to fit several large homes within them. Cornar thought he saw windows lining the massive columns. There were eight of these columns, each spaced apart farther than a city block.

Stonework the size of a road lined the ceiling, creating supports for shallow domes between each of the pillars and the outside walls. Polished coned crystals the size of buildings hung from the apexes of each of those domes, with more stonework wrapped around the crystals. The crystals' tips, however, stopped short of reaching the tops of the columns.

Wide corridors as tall as the ceiling lined the halls, aligned with the central domes.

"This place looks like it was made for a giant..." Kamdir muttered.

Igan grinned, chuckling softly. "I think we found a suitable spot," the wizard said.

They strode through the enormous chamber. Doors stood at the bases of the columns. *Perhaps those* are *buildings,* Cornar mused. That only furthered his confusion about this place. Why build something *so* colossal and then make buildings out of its pillars? It seemed a waste of space.

Unless it was for a dragon, the thought came to him. Cornar struggled with that reasoning as they walked.

"Look," Kamdir said, pointing to the towering corridors. "There are some shorter hallways beside it." The young warrior hurried away and Igan chased after him.

Cornar trailed behind them, watching Kamdir approach the *normal*-sized hallway. Kamdir and Igan stopped at the entrance, looking back and forth. They were probably as confused as Cornar.

"This is amazing, Cor!" Kamdir exclaimed, looking like an excited child. "It has exactly the same details as this huge room, just scaled down to our size."

Igan was grinning. The wizard nodded, then looked to Cornar.

"What are you smiling at?" Cornar asked, partially in jest. Igan burst into laughter.

"I wonder why they look so similar," Kamdir observed, rubbing his chin.

The wizard continued laughing for a moment, then quelled his outburst. "I think we found a dragon lair, Cor."

"No!" Kamdir exclaimed, gasping. "Really?" His eyes went wide.

Cornar folded his arms, not amused. Was this really a dragon's lair? That was one explanation for it… They could uncover this place's true nature later.

"Let's mark this room," Cornar said, turning away from the normal-sized hall, "and head back to the heart of the city. Unless anyone has found anything bigger—which I doubt they did—this will most likely become our campsite."

"It didn't take long for men to begin worshiping Cheserith and his most loyal followers. After all, he came as a benefactor."

- From *The Thousand Years War, Part I*, page 25

The Mindolarnian war camp was set up within a few hours. This place, the Hall of the Guardians as Krindal had learned, was enormous beyond comparison. The very room proved his theories true. The ancient Kaldeans had to have been magnificent craftsmen to create a space as grand as this.

Several of Krindal's fellow scholars had busily taken measurements of the place. It was seven hundred and fifty phineals wide, with a depth of almost a grand-phineal-and-a-half—exactly fourteen hundred and twenty phineals.

Krindal had discovered that each of the tower-like columns housed dwellings—three on each level to be precise. The columns were seventy-five phineals in diameter and were spaced two hundred and fifty phineals apart from each other. There wasn't the slightest deviation in distance between them. Each column was also one hundred and sixty phineals tall, the equivalent of twenty-one stories. Krindal hadn't ventured to their tops, but a few of Cornar's men had made the climb with Jahevial.

While the other scholars spread about in search of tevisrals, Krindal lingered in one of the lower-level dwellings. He made a discovery that might have seemed mundane.

But it wasn't to him.

Krindal stood in a room that resembled a kitchen, fiddling with a flat surface on the wall. He swept his hand over a glowing blue circle the size of his thumb. Suddenly, the light from the ceiling dimmed, and then winked out completely. Another swipe caused the light to return.

The light above him didn't come from a lightstone. Magic coursed through the ceiling and was the source of the illumination. Every time Krindal swiped his hand, the magic reacted. If the room was lit, the magic would retreat to where the walls and ceiling met. If it were dark, the magic would flood from that same place.

Though it was a simple thing, the entire process overwhelmed his mind with wonder. Had the ancient inhabitants of this place ever lit a candle, or burned a lantern? Such practices were foundational to him, and the very idea of *never* learning how to perform such tasks made Krindal tremble in fear.

Sliding your hand across the wall seems silly, Krindal thought, dimming the lights. *I could never get used to this.* He swiped his hand again, illuminating the room.

After a while, Krindal stepped away from the odd contraption and moved to an empty basin. *What is this?* Krindal wondered, extending his hand. Suddenly, water shot upward from behind the basin, falling in a narrow arc.

The water hit his hand and Krindal started at its appearance. Where had the water come from? Was this *actually* water? Or was it the formation of magic *into* water? He couldn't tell.

Krindal pulled his hand back, and the water flow ceased.

I wonder, he thought, extending his hand over the basin. The water resumed flowing.

Krindal tested the basin as he did the glowing circle. The stream of water turned on and off based on his hand's proximity to the basin.

Eager to make further discoveries, Krindal rummaged through the kitchen. He touched what he assumed to be a cabinet. It opened oddly; the door hovering away from the wall. A frothy breeze misted into the room, causing a sudden chill. Soon, a frozen closet lay before him. Several racks, spaced a phineal apart from one another, lined the entire length of the closet. Each rack was empty, and Krindal wondered why one would need a freezing closet.

The cold became irksome. He grabbed the door to shove it in front of the biting chill, but was met with resistance. The door began to move on its own, slower than Krindal wanted.

"What manner of tevisrals power this dwelling?" Krindal wondered aloud as the door settled back into place.

Krindal found more unique things in the kitchen, obviously tevisrals he knew nothing about. Some were small and others were large. But each looked to be used for cooking.

He wandered through the dwelling for a while, noting odd devices. His eyes, however, were drawn to a collection of books. The books were odd, like the ones found in the Keepers' Temple. The pages were smooth, with no trace of dust. Krindal wondered if the pages could repel the decaying filth… but then he saw there was no dust around.

How could a place such as this be dustless? That question gave him pause, but after a while Krindal resumed his search.

Hours later, a Mindolarnian soldier came for Krindal. "His Imperial Grace requests your presence," the soldier said. "He is holding a feast in honor of discovering this place."

Though he heard the summons, Krindal was consumed with the tevisral in his hand. It was a round disk with a shallow dome half the size of his palm. Numbers lined its circumference, with three arms sweeping across the numbers at various speeds. Krindal had seen similar devices in the world—things used to measure the passage of time. But they were all mechanical and much larger. This tiny thing seemed to be powered by magic.

"Master Krindal?" the soldier asked.

"Tell him I'll be there," Krindal said, eyeing the time-telling tevisral. The soldier stalked off, leaving Krindal alone.

"Quite extraordinary," Krindal whispered. It was the simple things that made Dalgilur's discovery worthwhile. Everything in this one dwelling had the potential to change Kaldean life forever. Krindal could alter the world drastically with these small tevisrals.

If all that was in this one dwelling were spread across the world, the next generation of children would never learn how to light a lantern, or dust a bookshelf. The thought scared him. Though humanity would lose something, it would gain so much more. Sacrifices had to be made for progress. Tucking the time-telling tevisral in his pocket, Krindal wandered through the dwelling, basking in its brilliance.

Krindal eventually made it back to the enormous chamber. A banquet hall had been erected outside the war camp. It was set up much like the officers' mess deck on the *Executor's Breath*.

Prince Kaescis—dressed in his royal garb—sat at the head table with his royal retinue, facing another table with strange objects piled on top of it. Some were glowing, and Krindal thought them to be tevisrals.

Beyond the table holding the tevisrals were seven rows of tables and chairs. Soldiers, scholars, sailors, and members of Cornar's band sat together, conversing about the wondrous discoveries they had made.

The prince beckoned with a wave, and Krindal moved around the outer edge of this makeshift banquet hall. Each of the ship captains were seated near the prince, as with the commanders of the army. The Wildmen ambassadors—Gevistra and his sister, Fenia—sat at the table's edge. They looked awestruck at their surroundings. Krindal had barely interacted with them during the voyage. He heard they had cowered in their quarters, afraid of being on the ocean.

Krindal thought it odd that they would be afraid of something so simple, so mundane—but then Krindal realized where the Wildmen had come from. They had lived in a primitive nomadic society. Their stepping onto a ship would be akin to Krindal entering Dalgilur. The Wildmen were to him as he was to the Ancient Keepers.

That notion gave Krindal pause. Amid his reverie, Krindal found an empty seat beside Cornar. Krindal still felt unsettled around the man. He admired the warrior because of his fame, but also feared him because of the deceit used to bring him along on this adventure.

"Did you find anything worthwhile?" Cornar asked in a disinterested voice. The warrior didn't look at Krindal directly. Cornar was gazing across the enormous chamber.

"I... I did," Krindal answered. "I have my proof. Our ancestors lived in ways totally alien to us." He slipped out the time-telling tevisral, setting it on the table beside Cornar's plate.

The warrior glanced down at the small device and picked it up. He handled it gently, looking intrigued.

"It tells time," Krindal said. "I've heard of things like this, but they're all mechanical and rely on gears and weights."

Cornar handled the tevisral gently, his stern expression softening. The man could look imposing, but in this instant he appeared to be something gentle.

"And here I thought *these* were just myths," Cornar said, sounding amused. "There is a tevisral like this in my favorite novel," the warrior said with a chuckle. "But the ones the characters had were strapped to their gauntlets. I wonder what that would be like," he said, placing the tevisral on the back of his wrist—

White-gold light shone from the tevisral's edges, wrapping around Cornar's wrist to form a bracelet of sorts. The light conformed to his wrist, then *became* a metallic substance. The tevisral spun, orienting itself so that the number denoting high-noon was oriented near the outer edge of his wrist.

Krindal watched with horror. This tiny thing defied the laws of magic. It formed matter out of light.

"Incredible!" Cornar jumped, laughing triumphantly. He extended his wrist, admiring the time-telling tevisral. Several others at the table heard the warrior's outburst and turned toward him. They caught sight of the tevisral on Cornar's arm and gathered around him.

Krindal felt a tinge of jealousy as the members of the royal retinue fawned over Cornar's *accidental* discovery. *Calm yourself,* Krindal thought. *Remember who you are. Just because they aren't paying you homage doesn't mean they think of you as mad.* He continued reassuring himself until he heard his name.

"… Krindal found it," Cornar said.

"What an extraordinary device!" Admiral Kaetet said.

"Imagine how useful that would be on the battlefield," Grand Marshal Hezidex said, nodding. "Like in *Towers of Comdolith*."

"Exactly," Cornar said, twisting his wrist to eye the tevisral's face.

"Your Imperial Highness," Hezidex said, "when we return to Mindolarn, will you requisition the duplication of this? We could outfit all of our officers with them. Imagine how this would improve our effectiveness."

"I will mention it, Grand Marshal," the prince said. He didn't even look at the time-telling tevisral.

Did Prince Kaescis not find the tevisral interesting? Perhaps the simpler things were *too* mundane for him. The prince was interested in far grander things… but he wasn't even surprised. Nor were Bratan and Laeyit. Those two regarded the discovery with indifference. It was almost as if the prince and his friends saw the timepiece as trivial.

How absurd.

Those at the table quieted down and returned to their seats. Cornar studied the metal wrapped around his arm, probably looking for a way to unlatch it. The warrior tugged at the metal to no avail, and it just remained there.

Serves you right for taking it, Krindal thought smugly.

Cornar tugged at the part where the numbers were located. The metal immediately became light, then flowed back into the domed disk.

"Wow…" the warrior muttered, extending the time-telling tevisral toward Krindal. Krindal, however, didn't take it.

"Don't you want it back?" Cornar asked.

"No," Krindal said, folding his arms and relaxing in his chair. "You can keep it. You were the one to unlock its secrets. I'm sure there are more around."

Cornar looked dumbfounded. That pleased Krindal, but only a little.

"Thank you," Cornar said. He set the tevisral back on his wrist, and the unfathomable transformation happened again.

Before long, the chefs brought out the evening meal. The food wasn't anything spectacular, as their supplies were reduced to rations. They had fished along the way to Dalgilur, but the fish they caught were not the tastiest of creatures.

Krindal sat quietly, picking at his food. He watched Cornar devour the meal and was amazed that the man could eat something so bland so veraciously.

After everyone at the head table finished eating, Prince Kaescis stood, assuming a regal posture. The prince always evoked a sense of royalty whenever making a speech.

"My friends and allies," Kaescis said, holding up a goblet of wine, "I wish to congratulate you on this magnificent discovery. You are the first men in over a thousand years to set foot in this great hall. In fact, you are probably the first men not vowed as Keepers of Truth and Might to set foot here, and that, my friends, is to be commended."

An uproar of cheers resounded from the Mindolarnians—sailor, soldier, and mage alike. The Wildmen clapped awkwardly. But the Sorothians were silent, and so was Krindal.

"As many of you can see"—the prince gestured to the table between his and the others—"our labors are already bearing fruit. These tevisrals that lay before you are only a fraction of those that lie hidden here on this island.

"These next few days will be monumental," he continued, speaking with a tone of finality. "Dalgilur holds ancient powers and wonders that will bolster our empire and expand our borders. The might of Mindolarn will be known once again. I hereby declare Dalgilur a new territory under the banner of the empire! Dalgilur is ours!"

More cheers erupted throughout the colossal chamber.

Cornar, however, jumped at the prince's words. The warrior looked fierce.

Krindal also started at Prince Kaescis's declaration. This was an expedition of discovery, not conquest. Besides, the prince had agreed to grant all the discoveries to the Necrotic Order. Would Prince Kaescis dare rescind his word?

Krindal felt betrayed.

Careful not to let his emotions show, Krindal slipped out of his seat and hurried into the war camp. He hoped he could make it seem like he was going to relieve himself. But Krindal couldn't listen to the prince any longer.

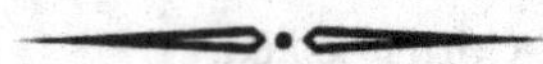

After the feast, Jahevial slipped away, clutching his communication tevisral beneath his robe. Grandmaster Alacor had to be notified of the prince's betrayal. Kaescis had gone on for nearly a quarter of an hour, expounding on the great finds they would unearth and claim for his empire. How could Kaescis know they would find such things?

Infuriated, Jahevial hurried through the normal-sized corridors of this Hall of the Guardians, as the prince had named it. Kaescis seemed to know an awful lot about this place, but he didn't explain how he had obtained that knowledge.

Jahevial turned a corner and entered another hall. After noting that no one was behind him—or anywhere else nearby—he mustered his invisibility magic and vanished.

I might get lost down here, Jahevial thought, continuing down the hall. This place was likely a massive labyrinth, although not as expansive as the tunnels beneath Klindil.

Turning another corner, Jahevial decided to mark the wall, so as to not lose his way. He drew a small knife and notched out a piece of the stone, about eye level. Jahevial wandered for a while, marking the corners as he made turns.

Satisfied that he was far enough away from the war camp, Jahevial approached one of the many doors along the hall. He touched its surface, and it *slid* open. The very act made his skin tingle with excitement. How grand must it have been to live in a place like this?

The room beyond the door was quite large, rising several stories. Odd-looking arms hung from the ceiling, metallic in nature, each arrayed above a table.

Jahevial looked around. A smaller room was to his right, with a window allowing a view to the larger space.

Over there will do, he thought. *This way I can hide if need be.*

He dismissed his magic and removed his communication tevisral. Once in the smaller room, Jahevial swiped his forefinger across the tevisral's activating gem. It pulsed a pale blue, then Jahevial flipped the receiving end to his lips.

"Grandmaster Alacor," Jahevial said, speaking into the tevisral. "We've reached Dalgilur. We passed through a treacherous storm in the World's Frown, but we all made it through safely. However, I have grave news. The prince has betrayed our Order and rescinded our right to discovery. He is claiming everything on behalf of the Mindolarn Empire."

Jahevial tapped the activating gem again, then settled onto the floor. It would be quite late back in Soroth. Grandmaster Alacor was most likely asleep by now. But Jahevial decided to wait for a reply.

Hours passed in silence until the gem pulsed, signifying it had received a message.

He tapped the gem and listened to a reply from the grandmaster. "It pains me to hear this, Jahevial. But it wasn't unexpected. Smuggle whatever you can. If this Dalgilur is indeed the isle of legend, then it must hold a bountiful yield of tevisrals. Seek what you deem would be most beneficial for the Order."

The message ended and Jahevial tapped the gemstone once again to send a reply. "I will do as you command, grandmaster. I have been working with Cornar Dol'shir's men today. They too seemed displeased about the prince's announcement. Shall I conscript them to help?"

Silence lingered in the room for a while, then Grandmaster Alacor sent a reply. "If you believe they can be trusted. You may offer them payment in return, once the value of each tevisral is determined. Be safe, Jahevial."

"Thank you, grandmaster. I will keep you apprised of our progress."

Jahevial rose to his feet, re-concealing his communication tevisral within his robe. He hurried out of the room and back through that maze of hallways. As Jahevial rounded the corner he searched for the notch, but it had vanished.

Surprised, Jahevial brushed his hand over the surface where the notch should have been. It was smooth and lacked any sign of ever being damaged.

By all that's magical... Jahevial cursed inwardly. He was both afraid and awestruck. Jahevial sucked in a deep breath, quelling his emotions. Hopefully he would remember each turn he made. Otherwise, he would be lost.

◆

Nordal and his small band hadn't returned to Dalgilur's center as Cornar had instructed. They felt a tiny amount of guilt at disobeying Cor, but they figured he would forgive them. Besides, before the appointed hour to return, Midar had spotted the Mindolarnians marching around Dalgilur's buildings. Their movement indicated that a spot for the war camp had been found.

The three of them reasoned they could continue their search because what they were sent out to do was already accomplished. Now, they could seek the hidden wonders this mysterious place had to offer.

As the sun set, Nordal and the others began their search on the eighteenth floor of this oddly pristine building. They hadn't found anything that resembled tevisrals as they knew them. Whatever devices they had run across were beyond their understanding. Nordal, however, picked up a few things along the way, hoping they might be of some value.

If Tilthan had been with Nordal, he would have called him stupid. Nordal clearly imagined his voice. "That could be a paperweight, you know." The words would have had a snarky tone to them. "Do you really think you can sell that?" The notorious thief didn't like taking such risks when it came to plunder, though he enjoyed gambling at Sharzen far more than any man should.

"This all looks the same," Tinal complained, falling behind Nordal and

Midar. The two warriors glanced to each other, then back to the young wizard.

"Well, maybe we'll run into something different," Midar said cheerily. "And if we don't, then we've had fun exploring."

Nordal grunted. "I'd like to find an upgrade to my blade." He patted the hilt hanging at his waist.

Midar laughed. "What's wrong with your current one?"

"Well, nothing," Nordal admitted. "I'd just like to find something that bursts into flame whenever I draw it."

"Just flame, huh?" Midar said, brow raised.

"You know what I mean," Nordal said, rolling his eyes.

They came to a door on their left. It slid open, revealing a large room with a circular table. Floor-to-ceiling windows lined the wall opposite the door, leading out to a balcony. Besides the table, there wasn't anything else in the room.

Still at the open door, Nordal frowned, disappointed at the dearth of tevisrals.

"I don't know about you two," Tinal said. "But I'm getting hungry."

"I could eat," Midar said, peeling away from the door.

"Let's make this the last floor," Nordal said. "Then we can go find the war camp."

53

DEVOTION

"Cheserith's divine status was elevated by his introduction of an eighth Channel: a destructive force that tore apart matter. This Channel, which became known as the Ko'delish, was the foundation for his followers' destructive arsenal. He taught man and dragon alike to harness the Ko'delish through his own unique Words of Power."

- From *The Thousand Years War, Part I*, page 28

Kaescis's announcement about claiming Dalgilur for the empire had unsettled the Sorothians. Krindal himself had fled during the speech. Mister Dol'shir had reacted with restrained fury. The others in the crowd looked distressed. Each had mentally distanced themselves in a way that showed on their faces. But none of that mattered. Kaescis was being obedient to the vision he had received in Vabenack, and that was more important than appeasing those petty men.

After the feast had concluded, Kaescis stood outside the war camp's walls, eyeing the far end of the Hall of the Guardians. The Messenger had told him that this place—hollowed out of the mountain—was home to many of his ancestors' enemies. Those pathetic Keepers lived in these towering columns when not infecting the world with erroneous beliefs.

Footsteps drew Kaescis from his reverie. Laeyit approached, alone.

"What are we to do next?" she asked.

"We must go there," Kaescis said, pointing across the hall. The other side was a good grand phineal away. "But we need Bratan."

Bratan emerged from the war camp a moment later. "The officers are gathering reports," the Praetorian said. "And someone is collating the maps."

"Good, come with us for a moment," Kaescis said, gesturing across the hall.

The three of them walked together, reaching the end of the hall within several minutes. Kaescis and his friends stopped at the foot of four white-marble statues—a dragon, an elf, and two others that *looked* human. Though they resembled the ones outside, Kaescis *knew* they didn't belong. After all, these four were not Keepers of Truth and Might.

The draconic statue was smaller than it should have been but was still tall, rising seventy phineals. The dragon sat with his wings spread around the other three, his tail curling around the front of the smaller statues. His long snout was angled down, a stern expression etched into his muzzle.

The elf—who stood on the left—was clad in armor that looked quite ancient. The armor's design consisted of congruent angles that formed diamond-shaped plating. The weapon the elf held looked like a staff—though Kaescis knew it was much more than that. The weapon's shaft was long and slender, divided into thirds by two narrow grooves a quarter of the way from each end. This weapon was a *true* fanisar. It was far superior to what was commonly wielded today. This fanisar's blades were composed of coursing annihilation particles. It also could be separated at the grooves, bound by an ever flowing chain of magic, making this weapon perfectly useable at long range.

"Who are these?" Bratan asked.

"The monsters that overthrew the Karthar Empire," Kaescis said. "This one is called Ulk'sha." He pointed to the dragon, then gestured to the elf. "There is the elf that forsook his homeland for men."

Kaescis turned toward the other statue on the right. It depicted a man in a flowing robe wearing the emblems of the Mages of Alath. In the crook of his left arm rested a weapon similar to the one wielded by the elf. That weapon was known among the Losians as The King's Scepter, wielded by Dorin, the Mage-King, the monarch who doomed the world. Dorin's Edicts outlawing tevisrals had plunged the men of Kalda into a dark age. Dorin's pronouncements neared the brink of fanaticism.

"*That's* the Mage-King?" Bratan muttered, stepping to the statue on the right.

"And that must be Lith," Laeyit snarled, gazing at the statue in the center. Positioned squarely between the two smaller statues, the statue of General Lith Luzdom stood holding a curved sword toward the ground. Lith's statue was clad in formfitting scaled armor that looked as if it was melded onto his person, lacking any seams or joints. Kaescis had seen armor like that several times throughout his life. It was always worn by one of those metallic beasts masquerading as a man.

A fitting depiction, Kaescis mused, glancing at the sword hanging from Lith's hands. The handle was forearm length, with a round guard that looked like the wings of a dragon. The blade was not in a scabbard, its tip hovering above the ground.

Kaescis had been told nightmarish tales about this weapon. It was a sword that could amplify the soul of its wielder. This weapon was something of a myth, rumored to be one of two surviving relics from a far distant past, further removed than when the gods walked Kalda. No one knew what the weapon's true form was, as its wielder could will it into whatever he desired.

"I am wary of these," Kaescis said.

"But they are just statues," Bratan said incredulously. "Or are you referring to who they represent?"

Kaescis wished he could destroy the statues right then, but he knew he couldn't. That very act might doom himself and his god.

"Do you fear they are mis'thralim?" Laeyit asked.

Bratan started furiously. "Then we should destroy them now! Before they awaken." The brash Praetorian dashed back toward the war camp.

"Bratan!" Kaescis spun, shouting to his friend. "That was not part of my vision."

Bratan stopped abruptly, looking frustrated. "Then why bring us to this spot?" he demanded.

"Perhaps to come to this realization," Kaescis said, speculating aloud, "but not act."

"At what point did your vision end?" Laeyit asked.

"Around midday, the day after tomorrow."

Laeyit smiled and walked toward Bratan. "Let's just make sure to destroy them after we fulfill our tasks."

Bratan grumbled, but Laeyit's suggestion seemed sound, though it was in no way part of his vision. This wasn't the only deviation from what Kaescis had experienced, though nothing erroneous had transpired.

Hurried footfalls filled the air. Kaescis turned as a soldier dashed toward him. "Your Imperial Highness," the soldier said, hailing Kaescis with a salute. "Everyone has gathered in the war room."

The war room in the Imperial Tent was crowded. Every officer in the Mindolarnian army was present, as well as those stationed in the navy. Several scholars were also in attendance, as were the more senior members of Mister Dol'shir's band. The only leadership not present was that of the Wildmen.

Kaescis eyed each of them, but his gaze lingered on Mister Dol'shir. The man's face was like stone, emotionless and steady. Mister Dol'shir looked like a man ready to kill indiscriminately.

The warrior's expression must have set off the voices in Kaescis's mind, as they began chanting for death. *Now's not the time,* Kaescis told the voices. *Soon, though.* The voices murmured as Kaescis passed Krindal. The scholar looked upset. Kaescis, however, didn't really care about the man's emotional state. Krindal was of little use now. They could use him to ferry more warships to the island, but it wasn't necessary.

"Thank you for coming," Kaescis said, stepping to the head of the table. Two crudely drawn maps were laid out on the table. One represented the cluster of buildings outside and the other this building—the Hall of the Guardians.

"Grand Marshal, will you start with your report?" he asked.

"We have only mapped this floor, Your Imperial Highness," Grand Marshal Hezidex reported. "It seems this structure burrows all through the mountainside." He pointed to the map. "More-detailed maps are being drawn as we speak, with exact measurements."

Crenai—the head scout—was the next to speak. "We haven't found any armories yet," Crenai said, then continued with her report of what they had found. Kaescis listened half-heartedly. He knew the armories were located three levels below the war camp, though he couldn't tell them that.

Others gave reports of their finds, and Kaescis ignored most of the details. He knew all of this, having experienced it in Vabenack. Soon, it was time for Mister Dol'shir to report. Kaescis looked to him with a pleasant grin.

"Mister Dol'shir, what have you to report?"

Cornar cleared his throat. "My last group returned a few minutes ago," he said. "Nordal's trio was exploring one of the other towers. They found many things they didn't understand, things they supposed to be tevisrals."

"Did they bring any back with them?" Hezidex asked.

"No," Cornar said, and shook his head.

Kaescis knew Mister Dol'shir was lying. In his vision, Kaescis had seen Cornar's men pilfering objects from all across the outer buildings. Kaescis felt a twinge of betrayal at hearing the lie, but then again it wouldn't matter. The man would be dead soon.

"Keep searching," Kaescis said. "And have your men bring back their discoveries."

Mister Dol'shir nodded, his expression still stone-like.

With all the reports gathered, Kaescis moved on to the next task. He would have to assign everyone to their various searches across the island. Kaescis fought the urge to jump ahead to the major discoveries, but he knew that wasn't supposed to happen.

"Mister Dol'shir, you and your band will continue searching outside. Start with the center buildings—the elven ones."

The noted adventurer nodded. "We've been working with the scholars from the Order of Histories. May I still use them?" Cornar asked.

"If that is what Master Krindal wishes," Kaescis said, deferring to the scholar, who looked irritated.

"You have full autonomy here, Master Krindal," Kaescis said warmly.

"On *your* island?" the scholar murmured.

This is no time for an argument, Kaescis groaned. "No, *our* island, Master Krindal. Just because I am claiming it for Mindolarn doesn't mean you don't have any interest in it." Kaescis hoped that would placate the scholar. "Hezidex, send your scouts to the lower levels. I would like to have as much mapped out beneath us as possible. Once they have finished there, they can move to the higher floors."

"Are we just mapping… this structure?" Crenai asked.

Kaescis nodded. "Most of those structures outside have directories within them." Mister Dol'shir raised his eyebrows inquisitively. "I overheard some of your men," Kaescis said, though he knew the detail from his vision.

That didn't seem to satisfy Mister Dol'shir or his wizard friend. The wizard, Igan, hadn't looked at Kaescis the same since departing Klindala. Igan's gazes since then had been filled with distrust and curiosity.

For the first time since hearing of Mister Dol'shir's bleeding, Kaescis wondered what the man had experienced in Vabenack. Kaescis knew it was a battle, fought long ago. If Mister Dol'shir had told his men *which* battle, they were keeping quiet about it.

And then the realization hit him, and Kaescis couldn't help but smile. While in Vabenack he had seen himself come to a realization during this meeting. He didn't know what it was, nor did the Messenger of the Promise tell him. But now Kaescis knew. He *knew exactly* which battle Mister Dol'shir had experienced.

Those around the table looked at him with questioning glances, and Kaescis regained his composure and resumed the meeting.

"Forgive me," Kaescis said, still smiling. "I'm just basking in our future discoveries." With that, Kaescis doled out the various assignments for the following day.

⸺◦·◦⸺

After the meeting, Kaescis retired to his chambers within the Imperial Tent. He couldn't help but muse on his revelation. He wasn't entirely certain that it was true, but it made sense. What better way to prepare his adversary than to stoke a fire of vengeance within him?

A tent door rustled, followed by footsteps. *Who is that?* he wondered. Kaescis had instructed Practil and the Praetorians to deny everyone entrance. He was not to be disturbed this night.

Soon, the tent door to his private room within the Imperial Tent flapped open. Laeyit stood there calmly. Her face was still made up from the feast but her braid was gone and her hair was pulled back simply.

"What is it, Laeyit?" Kaescis asked, his tone labored.

"I wanted to be here," she said, stepping forward and closing the door behind her. Kaescis frowned, and crossed the room, unbuttoning his jacket.

"What happened at the meeting?" she asked. "You look like you realized something."

"I did," Kaescis answered, hanging his jacket on a pole. He proceeded to undress further. "I know what battle Mister Dol'shir experienced…"

"And?" Laeyit asked, sounding intrigued.

Kaescis grinned and removed his ruffled shirt. "The Battle at Laelin Lake." Laeyit looked stunned.

"Here's my reasoning," Kaescis said, removing his boots. "I know we must clash. But I only know that because of the hiss'thraks and the *Will.* That man has neither of those things. So, I believe he was taken to Vabenack to behold the death of his father, so a fiery vengeance would begin to burn within him." Kaescis slid the boots under his bed, then placed a hand on his belt. "I've noticed some of his men gazing at me with curiosity, as if they're trying to determine who I am."

"That's all?" Laeyit asked incredulously. She didn't look convinced.

"Yes," Kaescis said.

"I would imagine that seeing you slay the Butcher of Tor would be unbelievable." He didn't quite understand her reasoning.

"Kaescis," Laeyit said, stepping toward him. "They don't *know* what we are. They think us to be like them. Seeing you, as you are, over forty years ago will not make any sense to him."

"Unless it was explained to him," Kaescis said.

Laeyit shook her head. "I think you are assuming too much," she said, gently resting her hand on his bare chest. Kaescis almost jumped at her touch. Laeyit had *never* touched him like that.

"Dol'shir and his men have been wary of us this entire time," she continued. "You are probably just noticing their gazes now because you've accepted your divinely appointed task. In a way, you can be blind when it comes to people. Sometimes you can't see what is right in front of you." Laeyit trailed her fingers across his chest, her touch sensual.

"What are you doing, Laeyit?" he asked cautiously.

"What I should have done years ago," she answered, then removed her hand from his chest. "I've waited too long, Kaescis. I thought that after you recovered from Helgara's passing that you would notice, but you haven't."

What was she talking about? They were *friends*. Laeyit had always been his friend, ever since childhood. She couldn't be anything more than that, could she?

Laeyit then slipped out of her boots and grabbed the bottom of her tunic, slowly pulling it up around her torso. "No female has ever stood beside you the way I have," she said. "I've stood by your side through war and peace. I've been with you to the far reaches of the world. We share something that no other pair can claim."

She pulled the tunic over her head, though she wasn't bare-chested. "You don't see it, Kaescis. But I love you, more than any other," Laeyit said, grabbing the thick band wrapped around her chest. "And I'm not going to wait any longer."

Kaescis didn't know what to say. He had never considered Laeyit as a mate. She was Laeyit. But lately, his eyes *had* lingered on her. Kaescis didn't know if that was because of the way she had acted since leaving Klindala or if it was something else.

Laeyit removed the wrap and proceeded to undress further. He had never seen her like that. She was not the most beautiful creature Kaescis had ever beheld, but she wasn't unattractive either.

"This wasn't part of the vision," Kaescis said flatly, his eyes lingering upon her.

Grinning, Laeyit moved to the bed. "You're still looking," she observed slyly. Kaescis turned away, hand still on his belt.

"You said after the meeting the three of us would retire for the night. As we are not doing anything else, I don't see the harm," she reasoned. "I will awake and go about the duties you have set for me, my prince. But tonight, be *with* me." Those words carried a weighty yearning.

A conflict stirred within Kaescis. He worried about what he had seen in his vision. *Could her presence here tonight disrupt events?* Kaescis wondered. His actions were delicate, or so he was told. But, there had been many tiny deviations in what he had seen. For instance, most of the soldiers hadn't sat where they had in the vision. The food on his plate wasn't arranged the same. And more people were at the meeting within the war room than he recalled.

But all in all, things were still moving the way they should.

"Kaescis…" Laeyit's voice drew Kaescis back to reality. "I am only asking for this one night," she pleaded. "Falling through that cavern awoke me to realization."

Kaescis hesitated, gripping the buckle on his belt.

"Just tonight…" she whispered.

With the conflict still brewing within him, Kaescis looked up, as if gazing through the tent's ceiling. He searched for the *Will*, but nothing came. Silence lingered for several minutes until Kaescis realized that his god's absence was answer enough.

"As you wish, Laeyit," he said, unlatching his belt.

"Deified by the men of Kalda, Cheserith claimed the world as his own. Millions upon millions worshiped him as their God. Eventually, most of Kalda fell under his reign. The sun never set on the Cheserithean Empire."

- From *The Thousand Years War, Part I*, page 32

Pagus had gone missing sometime that morning, or so Iltar had thought. None of Alanya's guards had noticed the boy leave. Upon further investigation, Iltar discovered that none of the acolytes had seen Pagus either. There was something foreboding about the boy's absence.

Iltar, however, didn't have much time to search for Pagus, as Alanya wanted to be early to the palace. But *early* couldn't accurately describe her intentions. Three hours before they had to leave for the palace—practically at the crack of dawn—Alanya rounded up the acolytes. Even Iltar was summoned. After dinner the previous night, Alanya had ordered each of them to bathe. She wanted the acolytes presentable—after all they were entering one of the most prestigious places in the entire world.

Once the boys were roused, Alanya led everyone into one of the upper halls of her mansion. Iltar hadn't been to this part of the mansion, but he assumed this hall housed a few of the many bedrooms. Alanya instructed the acolytes to line up in age order.

Amused at her corralling, Iltar stood by, folding his arms and patiently watching as Alanya subjected the acolytes to what they undoubtedly thought was borderline torture.

Once the boys were lined up per her instructions, Alanya began her inspection with little Bilda. The young boy stood straight-backed as the high duchess meticulously examined him. She started with his hair, ensuring that it was properly combed. Bilda's hair, however, was not up to her standards. Alanya slicked the side of the boy's head, attempting to smooth out a cowlick, but the patch of hair was stubborn.

Sighing, Alanya moved on to her next order of business—Bilda's face. Alanya gently grabbed Bilda's chin and inspected every part of the boy's face. She then sniffed the air around him. Alanya lifted the boy's left arm, wafting air. Her face tensed as she continued sniffing, then lifted Bilda's other arm. After that, she smelled the boy's hair, then patted him on the shoulder.

"Not bad, Bilda," Alanya said, then moved on to Tigan. "But have your hair washed again." Bilda, however, remained straight-backed and looked to Iltar with a wide-eyed expression of surprise. He probably hadn't expected the inspection to be so thorough.

Alanya continued inspecting each of the boys, ensuring that their hair was properly combed, their faces washed, and their body odor expunged. She gave her critiques after each inspection. None passed flawlessly. The boys seemed a little perplexed. Some glanced to Iltar with the same wide-eyed astonishment as Bilda.

After everyone was inspected, Alanya's next order of business was to have the acolytes dressed. She was disappointed that they didn't have any formal attire. So, after Iltar's announcement the previous night, Alanya had sent out Hazais and several servants to purchase matching clothing. Iltar didn't dare think about how much it had cost. He actually found the impulse to be ridiculous.

Alanya stepped past the boys, motioning for them to follow her. They came to an open door not far from where they were gathered.

"The tailors are in there," Alanya said, and gestured to the door. "They're going to fit your clothes properly."

"But we did measurements last night," Tigan complained.

"Those were crude measurements," Alanya said. "And when you wear something formal, you want it to fit just right. They'll be making alterations before we leave. Now hurry, we don't have much time."

Agen was the first to enter the room, and then the others fell in behind him.

Now alone, Alanya turned to Iltar. "Why are you looking so smug?" she demanded playfully.

Iltar chuckled. "I'm just amused at how you're mothering them."

Alanya gave him a sullen look. "You don't see me as the motherly type?" she asked sternly.

"You're too beautiful to be a mother," Iltar said.

"Oh really?" Alanya chuckled, stepping closer to him. Iltar didn't know what to say. He just looked at her and smiled.

"Sometimes you can be awkward." Alanya grinned, then stroked Iltar's face. Her expression turned pensive. "You need to shave."

"I shaved last night," Iltar objected.

"Shave again." She squinted, examining his hair.

"What?" he demanded.

"Need to comb that better…" She trailed off, running her fingers through his hair. "I'll have to fix it."

Iltar shook his head. "Now don't start mothering *me*." Alanya burst into laughter.

"I can take care of myself," he added.

"Oh good. Then I don't have to dress you."

"I'm already dressed," Iltar looked down at his usual attire—his black tunic and pants.

"You're not going like that," Alanya said with a tone of finality. Iltar stared at her blankly. She could dress up the acolytes all she liked, but he was a totally different matter.

"Now, why don't you go shave," Alanya suggested. "Then you come back here, and we'll have you fitted. In the meantime, I'll be with my *children*, thank you very much." Alanya winked at Iltar and followed the boys into the bedroom.

Women... Iltar sighed.

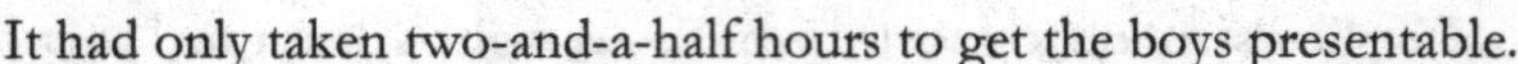

It had only taken two-and-a-half hours to get the boys presentable.

Iltar waited outside the mansion with Elsia, standing beside Alanya's carriage. They were both wearing formal attire. Iltar wore a ruffled shirt of beige and gold topped by a black-and-red jacket with tails. His pants matched the coat, with a red stripe that ran down to red-rimmed cuffs. His boots were a polished black and reflected the gleaming sunlight.

The entire outfit was a tad too much for his liking.

Unlike Iltar, Elsia embraced her gown. Her bare-shouldered dress was elegant and tastefully showed off her every curve. Embroidered red flowers were arrayed all across the dress, clustered in patterns of seven. Elsia's face was extensively made up to match the elegance of her gown. She wore heeled shoes—what kind Iltar couldn't tell—but she stood even with his chin. Normally, Elsia reached only to his shoulder.

"So you haven't seen him?" Elsia asked, raising an eyebrow. She looked fierce with the extra makeup.

Iltar shook his head.

"He's going to miss this," she said with a sigh, referring to her nephew. "I can't believe it. What could be more important than going to the palace?"

Iltar looked at Elsia with disbelief. Was she not worried that something might have happened to Pagus?

He better not have gone and done something stupid, Iltar thought.

Soon, the mansion's doors opened, and Alanya led the boys outside, beneath her lavish portico. The high duchess was dressed in a black gown with a trailing skirt that she had to hold up when walking. Its blue accents looked like swirling streams of magic. Her hair was pinned up in a braid that wrapped around the back of her head. She looked stunning.

"Don't drool on your jacket," Elsia said, chuckling. Iltar rolled his eyes at her.

Alanya approached the carriage, pleasantly smiling. "Right on schedule," she beamed. Still smiling, Alanya reached up and stroked Iltar's cheek.

"Mmm, much better."

"You did well, Alanya," Elsia said, gesturing to the boys. "I hardly recognize them."

Each of the acolytes was wearing formal clothing like Iltar. They marched straight-backed with their chins held up slightly. Alanya had undoubtedly instructed the boys on "proper walking etiquette" while in the palace.

"Did your nephew ever show?" Alanya asked.

"No…" Elsia sighed.

"What a pity," Alanya said with a frown, then moved to the carriage door.

Before long they were all in their respective vehicles and moving toward the gates of Alanya's home.

The ride toward the palace was as interesting as the ride from the docks. The roads followed the terrain. That aspect of the city confused Iltar. On the one hand, the Mindolarnians built such massive structures, but left something as simple as a road to the course of nature. He shook his head at that notion.

The women chatted the entire way, Alanya sharing her experiences in the palace and Elsia asking questions after what seemed to be every sentence. Iltar ignored them, gazing out the window.

After half an hour, the street they were on curved to the east. Iltar could now see one of the towers that surrounded the palace. The tower rose dozens of stories. Twenty or thirty? He couldn't tell. Perhaps twenty-one, since Mindolarnians were obsessed with the number seven and all its multiples. The tower's top was a glistening oval, with stone framework running along its sides to its peak. Iltar thought the tower's top looked like a claw clutching an egg—though it didn't expressly look like a claw.

Why a claw? Iltar wondered, gazing at the structure. He couldn't help but think of his encounter with Cheserith. But what did that have to do with the tower?

A wall partially obscured the tower. It ran along the road and was made of red-brown stone. The whole wall was without seams and appeared to be one solid mass. *That's impossible,* Iltar grunted, studying the wall. Surely, there had to be a seam somewhere. But there wasn't. The wall curved with the street. *It must be a transmutation.*

As the carriage continued eastward, Iltar could see the palace rising beyond the wall. It was much closer now, about half a grand phineal away. The carriage traveled along the road that wrapped around the palace, and Iltar was treated to a partial view of the southern parts of the bastion of Mindolarn Royalty.

As the road turned north, the wall diverged from the road. A manicured field spread between the road and the wall for quite a distance, hemmed in by a waist-high wrought-iron fence. The field was dotted with occasional trees. There were some stone benches beneath the trees, as well as stone paths that wound toward the north—where the carriage was headed.

Eventually, a short tower came into view across the field. It was joined to the wall that had lined the street and was one of two towers along the palace's outer gate. To Iltar's surprise, the gate looked like a solid stone door within a seven-sided arch. It reminded him of the towering doors at the Hilinard.

The carriage turned soon after, moving down a glistening red stone road leading to the gate. The carriage stopped, and Iltar heard the clanking of armor. He stuck his head out the window, seeing two soldiers approaching—both dressed in ceremonial red armor. The soldiers spoke briefly to the driver, then waved to the gate.

Iltar expected to see the gate swing open, but it *slid* apart. "By all that's magical…" he muttered.

"What's wrong?" Elsia asked.

Still stunned, Iltar glanced to the women. Alanya just smiled at him. "The doors… they're sliding open, as if they're going into the wall."

"They *do* go into the wall," Alanya said. "It's harder to breech a gate that has no hinges."

"How do they slide?" Elsia asked. It was her only intelligent question of the ride.

"Oh, I don't know." Alanya waved her hand. "There's some kind of magic involved."

The women continued talking about the gate, but Iltar ignored them. He looked back out the window as the carriage lurched forward.

A bridge lay beyond the gate, spanning a ravine. The bridge looked to be about forty phineals wide by a hundred and fifty phineals long. It had short walls on either side with posts waving the Mindolarnian banner—the seven-headed hydra—spaced every twenty phineals apart.

Iltar's eyes were drawn to the ravine that acted as the palace's dry moat. Though the ravine appeared like a natural formation—hewn by erosion—there was a man-made quality to it. The wall they had traveled along marked the edge of the ravine's sheer cliff.

Another sheer cliff stood on the opposite side of the ravine; it too was hemmed in by a similar red-brown stone wall. This wall, however, surrounded the actual palace.

The carriage passed two more towers at the other end of the bridge. The towers were full of armed men wielding bows and channeling staffs—the latter were most likely mages, though they didn't look like mages.

Not long after passing the towers, the carriage came to a halt. The driver dismounted and opened the door closest to the women. Both Elsia and Alanya stepped out, primly walking ahead of the carriage.

Iltar followed them, but was drawn by his acolytes' excited comments.

"Isn't this amazing!" one of the boys cried, leaping from the wagon. Others were following him and jumping out. A few, however, were just gazing beyond the carriage and the wagon, their mouths hanging open in astonishment.

Oh to be young again, Iltar mused, sauntering to the bridge's rail. It was carved with exquisite designs that reminded him of that place where he had helplessly watched Cornar fight for his life. Iltar peered over the rail, looking down into the ravine. Sharp stalagmites rose from the ravine bed a hundred phineals away. They were unnaturally sharp and arrayed in too fine a pattern to have been formed by nature, if indeed there was any way that they *could* have been formed.

"What a moat…" Iltar whispered, then hurried off to join Alanya and Elsia.

The women were walking toward buildings arranged in a V-shape around another gate within a two-story wall. The buildings weren't anything spectacular, and Iltar supposed they were for servants and soldiers.

The drivers of the carriage and the wagon drove their vehicles to the left. A couple of grooms dressed in Mindolarnian red rushed to the horses, unhitched them, and escorted them into a stable. Then, several men came out and pulled the horse-drawn vehicles out of sight.

A few of the boys hurriedly passed Iltar and caught up to the women. Alanya scolded the boys, firmly retelling them to behave properly. Little Bilda was among the mischievous bunch and looked back at Iltar with a sheepish grin.

Silly boy. Iltar shook his head, coming beside Alanya. Elsia had gone ahead, speaking with the guards who manned the gate. It too was like the doors of the Hilinard.

After Elsia finished speaking with the guard, the man shouted to those manning the gate. The symbols on the gate lit up, glowing a vibrant red, and then the gate split and slid open, retreating into the towers.

"How is that possible?" Iltar muttered with disbelief. The walls beyond the towers were angled toward the palace, and the towers themselves were half the width of the gate's doors. It should have been impossible for the gates to go anywhere. The stone would have had to curve or… compress.

Could that really work? Iltar wondered, raising an eyebrow. He had read once that transmutative magic was capable of compressing matter, but he had never seen nor performed that effect. This had to be the work of a tevisral.

Soon, they were all beyond the gate, inside an elongated pentagonal courtyard. White galstra covered the ground, with red veins and flecks throughout its surface. Like the walls, the courtyard's floor was seamless, as if it were one giant slab.

Iltar watched as the gate slid back into place. It looked no different than it had before, totally unaffected by what had happened to it.

A tevisral that can compress matter, Iltar thought, feeling awestruck. *These Mindolarnians really are advanced.* He spun, hurrying after Alanya and Elsia, who strode toward a fountain at the courtyard's center.

Near the fountain stood a man dressed in a white coat, matching pants, and a golden shirt. He wasn't very tall and was quite average looking. The man held a ledger and coldly studied the approaching party.

"My ladies," the white-clothed man said, and bowed, "I am Chamberlain Caedaric. Her Imperial Highness is awaiting you." The chamberlain turned crisply, walking in a proper manner around the fountain.

The women followed him, as did the acolytes. Iltar, however, took up the rear. He drank in his surroundings, but thoughts of Pagus lingered in the back of his mind. *Where are you, boy?* Iltar fought back a growl.

Caedaric was speaking, but Iltar paid him no attention. Everyone followed the chamberlain across the courtyard, toward a grand staircase that led to the imposing palace. The stairs were divided into three tiers. Fourteen deep steps—as deep as a man was tall—connected the tiers.

"… and to your left are the gardens leading to the dignitary suite," the chamberlain said. "This area, called the Lower Gardens, is exactly ten phineals above the street level outside the palace. The walls that housed the gate you just came through line this entire lower tier. That's why the wall is so high," he said, not sounding amused. "And the diameter of the Lower Gardens is roughly one grand phineal."

Caedaric continued giving bits of information about the palace as they walked. They soon came to another flight of stairs and arrived on what the chamberlain called the Middle Gardens.

"… and beyond those trees there is the Temple of Ku'tharn the Eternal, Goddess of Mindolarn. And to your right is the Chamber of the Father, another place of worship. Both buildings look similar, but are quite different on the inside."

To Iltar's right stood a domed building with a vibrant red roof. It was nestled within trees of various colors. Despite the lack of cold weather, it was fall in Mindolarn and the trees had changed colors.

A few other domed buildings were set back away from the Chamber of the Father and looked like they were in the Lower Gardens. They looked similar to the structures at the Hilinard—gaudy and ostentatious.

After walking for a short while they came to another set of stairs, exactly like the other two.

"Now we arrive at the Palace Tier," the chamberlain said as they climbed the steps.

Statues lined this last staircase, spaced one step apart. Those on the same step looked identical, their poses mirrored. In fact, each of the statues looked similar, as if depicting brothers. *These must be the emperors,* Iltar thought. *There are seven of them.*

Chamberlain Caedaric continued with his informative tour while Iltar eyed the Mindolarn Palace. The palace looked like a mushroom with a very wide base. The dome—which had been visible from the docks and Alanya's mansion—hung over part of the walls of what looked to be the first four floors. Magnificently carved pillars held up the overhanging roof. Between them were floor-to-ceiling windows framed with blood-red metal. All in all, the palace looked to be seven stories high.

A few other buildings were connected to the palace—two which Iltar could see, five others which were noted by Chamberlain Caedaric. These buildings were much smaller. Each was connected to the palace by long corridors with large windows. One of the adjoining buildings was round, and the other was oval. Their roofs were a metallic red, reminding Iltar of fresh bronze, but with a more vibrant coloring.

"… roughly three hundred phineals from one end to the other. That doesn't include the entrance," Caedaric said. He must have been talking about the palace.

They passed several Crimson Praetorians standing resolutely with their fanisars resting upright. The Praetorians guarded paths that branched off, leading to the lush gardens surrounding the palace. The paths meandered, twisting around trees and stone planters.

"Now this is an interesting tidbit," Caedaric said. "That is the window that our late emperor's assassin broke while fleeing."

Iltar followed Caedaric's pointing gesture to a window about two-thirds of the way up the palace, to the right of the palace's grand portico.

"That's high up there…" said one of the acolytes.

Caedaric nodded. "Some of the soldiers fighting here said the assassin leapt so far from the palace that it looked like he was flying."

Iltar found that unbelievable.

The chamberlain continued his lecture as they walked beneath the palace's portico. It extended from the building and rose as tall as the overhang. Four columns lined its front face, each as intricate as the others upholding the palace's overhanging roof. Windows allowed a view to the palace's foyer, as well as the open doorway, which was three stories tall.

"Where's the door?" Bilda asked as they entered the palace's foyer.

"Compressed inside the frame," Caedaric said. "Now you will please follow me. We'll be going straight to the southern dining hall." The chamberlain led them through the foyer to a hallway on their right.

Iltar, however, took in the vastness of the space before leaving. It was three stories tall and square in shape. At first glance, Iltar assumed it to be seventy phineals along each wall. Balconies along the sides allowed a view to the grand foyer. The foyer was devoid of pillars, which seemed odd to Iltar. A space of this magnitude *required* supports.

Inconceivable, Iltar muttered, gazing at the ceiling.

A magnificent mural was painted on the foyer's ceiling, depicting iconic elements from the Cherisium religion. It looked like some titanic clash. Various characters wielded magic. Mindolarn and his brothers were represented. There were three white figures near the top, each glowing with brilliant luster. Those three stood above the outline of a winged creature spanning the sky. Iltar's eye, however, was drawn to the center of the mural. A man in a crimson robe stood with his arms outstretched within a yellow oval that looked akin to a portal.

Reflection, Iltar squinted. *And the doorway to Vabenack.*

"Master Iltar?" Agen asked hesitantly. Iltar spun, seeing the boy standing in the hall where Caedaric had led the others. "I'll be right there," he said, then took one last glance at the mural. *Who are you, Reflection?*

A ROYAL MEAL

"To his most devout followers he granted unimaginable powers. He rigorously tried them in mortal combat against horrific foes. Those who survived were called his Chosen. They were exalted above mortal men, receiving a portion of their master's immortality. But in reality, they were cursed, twisted by Cheserith's vile magic. They would become the vilest of evils to walk the face of Kalda—the Ma'lisha."

- From *The Thousand Years War, Part I*, page 35

The palace's dining hall was similar to the foyer in many ways, but was not as large. Iltar still found it impressive. The hall's ceiling rose only two stories, and was rectangular shaped, roughly seventy phineals deep and thirty wide. Three lavish lightstone-lit chandeliers hung from the ceiling with clusters of tiny lightstones arrayed in groups of seven. Gaudy stonework adorned the walls, colored in reds and golds.

At the heart of the dining hall was a sprawling table with seventy seats around it—each crafted with extraordinary detail that exuded excessive affluence.

Three sets of floor-to-ceiling windows allowed a view to the gardens surrounding the palace. Iltar could see the city's skyline as well as the docks in the distance. The view was quite stunning, but then again, this was a view meant for royalty.

Princess Raedina stood in front of the windows, her arms folded. She wore a plain crimson dress that nevertheless looked oddly elegant. Her back was turned to the doors, and she didn't seem to notice that Iltar and his companions had arrived.

"Your Imperial Highness," Caedaric said while crossing the room, "your guests have arrived."

Raedina turned from the windows, looking exhausted. "Welcome," she said with a drowsy tone. "You may take your seats wherever you wish. The others will be joining us shortly."

Alanya and Elsia moved toward the head of the table, sitting on opposite sides. The acolytes filled the seats around the women, and Alanya whispered to one of the boys who tried sitting next to her. The acolyte moved to the next chair, making everyone else slide down a seat.

Iltar, however, took his time walking through the room, carefully eying the space for anything that might resemble his research. He found nothing. Besides the gaudy décor, there was nothing informational—no paintings, nor symbols, nor effigies. It was all rather disappointing.

"Iltar," Alanya said, gesturing toward the empty seat beside her. He meandered his way through the room, walking past Raedina.

The princess smiled at him, but Iltar could sense her restrained hostility. It was that glint in her eyes. Raedina looked as if she were gazing upon a man she truly hated.

Iltar simply nodded. "It's good to see you, Your Imperial Highness," he said, passing between the princess and the table.

"Likewise, Master Iltar," Raedina replied. "I hope your research is proving fruitful."

"It is, ma'am," Elsia interjected. "We truly appreciate your granting us access to the Royal Archive."

"Oh, it's my pleasure," Raedina said, smiling broadly. Iltar *knew* that smile was forced. He used to smile exactly so while hunting his parents' murderers. Kindness was a suitable façade to cover furtive actions. This lesson he had learned years ago, and it seemed Raedina had learned it as well.

I'll have to watch her, Iltar thought, taking his seat beside Alanya. *There's something wrong with these Mindolarnians.*

Elsia engaged Raedina in small talk while a few servants entered the dining hall, carrying large pitchers. The servants approached the boys first, asking which of the beverages they preferred. Iltar was careful to listen to the choices. He didn't want any of his students intoxicated. The choices were actually quite tame—water, furnapel juice, milk, and a frothy drink called tamir. Iltar hadn't heard of the last one and neither had the boys.

One of the servants explained that tamir was a drink produced by blending a variety of spices with syrup made from the root of a plant called tamiralis. He didn't explain too much of the procedure, but the result was a beer-like drink without alcoholic properties.

Several of the acolytes chose that drink. Soon, each of their glasses was filled with tamir—a dark-blue liquid that foamed with a sky-blue head.

"And what shall you have, sir?" a servant asked Iltar.

"I'll take that tamir," Iltar said, gesturing to the half-empty pitcher.

"And I'll have the same," Alanya said, leaning close to Iltar and wrapping her arm around his. Alanya beamed exuberantly. He had never seen her so happy.

"I love this," she said, eyeing him up and down. "And you look *good.*" Her words carried a tone of sensuality. Alanya's smile was enough to distract Iltar. For a moment, he forgot about Raedina's restrained hostility and the supposed nefarious nature of the Mindolarnians.

But then, *they* entered.

"Welcome, brother," Raedina said, moving to her seat at the head of the table.

Iltar turned to see the tall man, Malvonican, striding arrogantly into the room. They had met only once—in Raedina's office at the Hilinard—but Iltar could tell he was a sly man. Malvonican was wearing the same suit he'd worn when Iltar first met the prince.

"I do hope there's enough food prepared for me," Malvonican said smugly. He glanced to the acolytes and then took the seat beside little Bilda. The prince looked at the boy like a lion eyeing his prey. "If not, I might just gobble you up!"

Bilda looked at the prince with wide eyes, then flashed a wary glance to Iltar.

"I think he's kidding, Bilda," Iltar said reassuringly, though he wasn't sure if Malvonican was jesting. "But if he tries to take a bite just slap his face with an acidic orb."

Elsia put her hand to her mouth, and Alanya gasped, horrified.

"Iltar!" Alanya chided, tugging at his arm.

Iltar didn't look at her. He was focused on Malvonican's aqua-green irises. A growing tension built between them, but then Malvonican burst into laughter.

"I don't think you'd taste good," the prince said sardonically.

Bilda chuckled nervously, and some of the other acolytes snickered.

As the tension eased, Alanya tugged on Iltar's arm. "You need to mind yourself. It's not polite to be disrespectful."

Iltar just glanced at her. *She really doesn't know me,* he thought.

Soon, more footsteps approached the dining hall, then two men strode toward the table. They looked like brothers, but one had wavy blond hair and the other neatly cropped brown. The blond-haired man was dressed in a regal garb identical to Malvonican's attire. The other wore a crimson robe adorned with black symbols. Both had violet eyes and looked to be in their mid-forties.

They look like Kaescis, Iltar thought, remembering the prince who had accompanied Krindal. *I wonder if they're brothers…*

"These are princes Negaris and Laedar," Raedina said. "My cousins."

"Ilnea said you were serving lunch," said the blond newcomer.

"Do you want to help plan the ball, Laedar?" Raedina asked tersely, her eyes narrowed at her blonde cousin.

Both newcomers looked at each other for a moment, then Negaris, the robed man, shrugged.

"I guess we do," Laedar said, taking a seat.

Raedina shook her head, gesturing to the two newcomers.

"It's a pleasure to meet you all," Laedar said, nodding to Iltar and the others.

Negaris's violet eyes fixed on Iltar." Am I right in assuming you are a necromancer?"

Iltar raised an eyebrow at Prince Negaris. *How does he know who I am?* That question didn't bode well to Iltar. Why was Mindolarnian Royalty taking an interest in him?

"He is," Alanya answered for him. "Iltar is a council member of the Soroth Necrotic Order."

"Impressive," Negaris said, sitting one seat away from Laedar.

"So, you're friends with Grandmaster Alacor?" Laedar asked.

"Not really," Iltar answered.

Alanya sighed, and Iltar turned toward her. She looked at him with a gaze that said, "Is that all you can say?"

Iltar figured he should say something more… but he couldn't think of anything pleasant to say about Alacor. He despised the man. "Alacor and I have known each other for a long time," he said. "Our masters were brothers, and we often learned together."

"Then you two should be like brothers," Laedar said, gesturing toward Iltar.

"We have our differences," Iltar replied flatly.

Iltar felt a tap against his boot, then Alanya whispered to him. "Please, watch your tone."

For magic's sake, woman… Iltar groaned inwardly, briefly glancing to Alanya.

"Grandmaster Alacor is a good man," Negaris said. "I had the pleasure of his company at the last Feast of Sorrows."

Negaris's words were worthy of drawing a raised brow. *Alacor here in Mindolarn—oh, why didn't I see it before!* Iltar chided himself. While eavesdropping on Alacor, Iltar had heard him mention the Hilinard. Alacor had never said where he was going on sabbatical the last decade. Now it all made sense. He had been coming to Mindolarn. But why would Alacor attend the Feast of Sorrows? He wasn't religious.

Another pair of footsteps echoed into the dining hall. A third prince—or so Iltar assumed—sauntered around the table. He was quite plump, but looked like the others, with wavy blond hair and violet eyes.

"I was told there was food?" the plump prince said lightheartedly.

The other princes didn't seem pleased with the newcomer. Laedar tensed and sat back in his chair while Negaris regarded the plump prince coldly.

"And who invited you, Jeridi?" Malvonican said hostilely.

Jeridi—the plump prince—took a seat across from the others, right beside Agen.

"I could say the same for you," Jeridi said, leaning one arm against the tabletop.

The three other princes looked at Jeridi fiercely. There was obviously an unspoken feud between them.

Raedina cleared her throat, but the princes remained in their deadlocked stare. "And may I introduce my eldest cousin, Prince Jeridi Midivar, the first in line to the Mindolarn throne."

"So you're the next emperor?" Bilda blurted, leaning against the table with wide eyes. "I've never met an emperor before." Alanya sighed with exasperation.

"Yes, lad," Jeridi said. "As long as none of them"—he pointed to his brothers and Malvonican—"don't kill me first."

"Would they really do that?" Tigan chimed from beside Agen.

"There have been veiled threats…" Jeridi said, turning to the young acolyte. "Being a prince can be a treacherous thing and a Mindolarnian prince even more so!" He grinned slyly, then chuckled softly. "They don't like me because I talk about peace—a lot."

There was a momentary stare-down between the princes; then several women entered the dining hall and took seats around the table, greeting Raedina from a distance. More servants entered, offering drinks to the Royals. Light chatter filled the room. Then savory aromas filled the air as the servants rolled covered carts along the sides of the dining hall.

A few more people entered, taking their seats near the princes. There were twenty others besides Iltar and his party—including the four princes. Most of the others were women, all dressed in fanciful clothing. They were probably a committee Raedina had gathered to prepare for the ball.

Soon, servants were milling around the table, proffering the various foods that were available for lunch. The servants started with the Royals and worked their way around the table to Iltar and the other palace guests.

Iltar gave his order to a servant and sat back in his chair. There was still plenty of chatter in the room, but several of his acolytes were silent. The younger ones—Bilda and Tigan—were talking with Prince Jeridi. The plump prince seemed content to hold court with the two young boys. Jeridi's inner child showed as he talked. He was definitely not like the others.

Once everyone had their plates and full glasses, Raedina tapped an empty wine glass, drawing everyone's attention. The room was so quiet one could hear a pin drop.

"Thank you all for coming," Raedina said. "All those invited and *not* invited," she glanced to the princes. "You will please bow your heads." Malvonican grinned, then bowed his head. He was followed by the other princes, and soon the Royals were all reverent. Raedina looked to Iltar, and those who had accompanied him.

The boys complied immediately.

"Oh, Aunok'sha—our Divine Father," Raedina prayed, "we come together as thy children, praising thy name and awaiting thy glorious return." The princess continued her prayer, laced with religious rhetoric. She droned on for a while, and then finished her prayer with, "May the Crimson Eye remain hidden for all time."

Iltar abruptly opened his eyes, awkwardly glancing to the princess—he fought the urge to turn toward Raedina, as Alanya would obviously get upset. It was the first time Iltar had heard the phrase uttered in this world. Yes, he had read it plenty of times, but he had not *heard* anyone speak it.

The others in the room then chanted in unison, "May the Crimson Eye remain hidden for all time."

Only my faithful speak this vow, Iltar recalled those booming words from that dream months ago.

Raedina continued speaking after the prayer, relating the purpose of the gathering—they were to discuss the particulars of the ball held in honor of their advancements in tevisral construction.

Malvonican cheered, drawing accolades from the other Mindolarnians—except for Jeridi.

Princess Raedina rolled her eyes at her brother. She continued speaking about the impending ball, turning her monologue into a discussion. The women mostly talked, but the princes gave their input now and again. Iltar, however, couldn't focus on the conversation. He was too wrapped up in his assumptions about that phrase. Alanya caught him staring across the room at nothing, and she nudged him. Did she think he was bored?

After several hours of discussion, they finalized the details. Tasks were set, and a proclamation was drafted. Of course, they invited only the higher echelon of the city.

"You'll be joining us, won't you?" Raedina asked Iltar. "As Alanya's guest?" She pursed her lips in anticipation of Iltar's answer.

All eyes were on Iltar. Three of the princes—Malvonican, Laedar, and Negaris—stared at him sternly, seeming to await his answer more eagerly than Alanya. The only one not interested in his reply was Prince Jeridi.

"Of course," Iltar replied. "Why wouldn't I come?"

The Royals relaxed at his answer. *What is wrong with them?* Iltar wondered. He glanced at each of them briefly, then turned toward Elsia. Iltar looked past her, contemplating the Royals' strange behavior. Why were they taking an interest in him? Did they adhere to Soron Thahan's prophecies? If so, did they—like Reflection—believe he was something of a divine harbinger?

Chatter filled the room, but it was nothing of importance. Most everyone began to disperse, except Prince Jeridi.

"How much of the palace have you seen?" Jeridi asked the acolytes.

"Oh, not much, sir," Bilda said, then stammered, "I mean—uh—Your Grace? Or is it Your Imperialness?"

Prince Jeridi grinned. "You can call me Jeridi. I get tired of hearing Your Imperial Highness." He turned to Iltar and Alanya. "Would you all like a tour of the palace? Schedule permitting, of course."

Each of the acolytes' faces beamed with excitement.

"Please, Master Iltar!" Bilda pleaded. "Please!"

"Bilda, calm yourself!" Alanya reprimanded the boy. "Don't forget your etiquette."

"Sorry," Bilda looked down at the table, embarrassed.

"The boy is fine," Jeridi said. "After all, he's not a Royal and isn't required to adhere to our standards of stuffiness." The acolytes chuckled at that. Even Iltar thought it was amusing.

"Come with me," Jeridi said. "I'll give you a tour of the palace."

⋄•⋄

The guise of a priest didn't suit Lirathay'lu. So, he turned to gardening instead. Playing in the dirt was better than standing around stiffly or sitting primly. Mindolarnians had many odd observances. He had spent a little over a week as Lira the priest before he feigned an urgent need to embark on that pilgrimage he had mentioned to High Oracle Regant.

Unfortunately, Regant had taken a liking to Lirathay'lu and wanted him to stay and become a member of the Royal Devotary. That only made the need to leave more pressing.

Lirathay'lu wiped the sweat off his brow, relishing the ache of sore muscles. It had been years since he was able to enjoy an honest day's work.

"Oh, Sakal," a woman said from behind him. "Your lunch is ready."

"I'll be right there," Lirathay'lu said, putting down the pruning shears. Since joining the ranks of the palace servants, Lirathay'lu had been assigned to care for the Lower Gardens. He would have to make a change to that, as hardly any of the Mindolarnian Royalty ever walked these parts.

"Sure is hot today," he said, wiping his forehead again. "I might need a break."

"Aren't you used to this?" the woman asked. "You've been a gardener for a decade."

Lirathay'lu smirked and then winked at the woman. In all honesty, he wasn't used to being outside. All those years playing the part of a crippled herbalist had made him soft. He could literally count on one hand the number of times he had stepped out of his shop in the last year. After all, supplies were always delivered to him. Then, in the last few years a kind child started dropping off food. This wasn't because he was incapable—far from it. No, Lirathay'lu had to keep in line with his ruse. Denying help as a cripple would have aroused suspicion. And he couldn't have that.

"Well, some days it catches up," Lirathay'lu said. "No amount of experience will ever make you immune to the sun."

"Oh my," she rushed beside him, clapping her hand on his forehead. "Do you feel heatstroke? Are you going to faint?"

He could play off that… "You mean, there aren't ripples in the grass?"

"By the Crimson Eye, Sakal," she swore, wrapping her arm around him.

That's not something you should be cursing, he thought, then feigned a wobble.

"You are going to rest," she said. "Are you sure you've been doing this for a decade?"

Investigation and infiltration? he thought. *Why yes, and even more than that. How many decades would that be?* He wobbled again as he counted the years. *That would be roughly five hundred and—*

Lirathay'lu's eyes widened. The man, Iltar, descended the steps of the Middle Gardens with one of the princes. Those women were with him as well, the ones that had visited Lirathay'lu's shop—rather Yenig Mawer's shop. They were all dressed in formal attire… and boys trailed behind them.

What are they *doing here?* he wondered, feigning another wobble. Lirathay'lu grabbed the woman's hand and took a deep breath. *And what are they doing with a qui'sha?*

"You really don't look well," she said. "You're looking pale."

Lirathay'lu ignored her, his eyes fixed on Iltar. The necromancer, however, was focused ahead of the women, looking lost in thought.

"I need a moment," he said, taking another deep breath.

"Maybe you should sit," she said, guiding him to a bench. "I'll fetch you some water." She set Lirathay'lu down and hurried past Iltar and his companions.

Lirathay'lu, however, stared at the necromancer. He watched as Iltar descended the stairs to the palace's courtyard. Iltar hadn't even noticed him, although he wouldn't have recognized Lirathay'lu. The necromancer might have recognized Lira the priest, but Sakal wore a different face.

First you try to access the realm of a mad god and now you're carousing with qui'sha... Lirathay'lu mused. *Whatever you're seeking can only lead to folly, son of Adrin.*

It wasn't long before the woman returned with two goblets of water. "Drink this," she said, handing Lirathay'lu a goblet. She then splashed the other on his face.

"What was that for?" he demanded harshly.

"You *are* delirious," she said, taking his hand. "Let's get you inside. You'll need plenty of rest. I just received word that the Royals are planning a last-minute event in three days, and they want the gardens around the palace altered. We will have to bring in new shrubbery and flowers. I'm just glad they don't want to change the trees."

⚊⚊◗•◖⚊⚊

It was near evening when Jeridi finally joined Raedina and the other princes in one of the palace's upper rooms. Unfortunately, he had been dragged into this plot concocted by his cousins. Jeridi found the whole thing absurd.

"What took you so long?" Malvonican demanded harshly. "Perhaps you would have gotten here sooner if you didn't have that much pudge on your gut."

Negaris laughed and smirked. He always enjoyed teasing Jeridi. For the most part, Jeridi tolerated it. But today it was growing irksome.

"You're all being fools," Jeridi said, stalking over to one of the chairs. "He is not the man who slew our uncle."

"Uncles," Laedar corrected coldly. He narrowed his eyes as he gazed out the nearby window. "Don't forget Uncle Medis."

"How could he?" Negaris asked sternly. "Jeridi fled from his side like a coward," speaking as if Jeridi wasn't in the room.

Those words pained Jeridi. His brothers had never understood his actions on that dreadful day. He *had* to run. That battle changed him, and the change would be for the benefit of the empire. It was then that Jeridi realized that war was not the answer to the empire's dilemmas. Perhaps it was the carnage, or even the resolve of their enemies—they had grown strong in the last decades. Jeridi wondered if he doubted his country's cause... He had often weighed their cause against their enemies', who fought for what they deemed valiant reasons. Maybe it was the death of his uncle, Medis. What it was, Jeridi didn't know exactly, but he *knew* he walked away from that battle changed.

Eventually, Jeridi was able to convince Kaescis that there were alternatives to creating a prosperous empire. But even Kaescis was eventually dissuaded from the ideals of peace. The sons of Mindolarn craved death, and they could only be sated by deluging the world with blood. That was a path Jeridi refused to follow.

He sat quietly as his brothers and cousins conversed about Iltar, the necromancer from Soroth. They believed he was the Alathian, but Jeridi knew he wasn't. Iltar couldn't be that man. Yes, they looked alike, but didn't Adrin have two sons?

"Jeridi," Raedina said, drawing him from his reverie. "What do you have to say about the man?"

"He's not the grand mage, cousin," Jeridi insisted.

"Don't be so quick to judge, *cousin*," Malvonican retorted. "Alathians are cunning men."

"I know that particular grand mage," Jeridi said firmly. "Iltar is not that man."

"Well, I don't agree with Jeridi," Laedar said, "but I believe we should get some verification on the matter before we strike."

"And how do you propose that?" Malvonican demanded smugly.

"We simply see if there is an Iltar at the Soroth Necrotic Order," Laedar said frankly. "Their numbers have been reduced, so it shouldn't be hard to verify. And if he does exist, we should check a manifest at Soroth's Port Authority. His name would be on a charter."

"Soroth is not a carriage ride away," Jeridi said, drawing his lips into a line.

"It doesn't need to be," Laedar said, gesturing with his hands. "Surely, we have someone in Soroth with a communications rod."

"The only people outside Mindolarn with such tevisrals are spies," Jeridi retorted. "Are you implying that we've started spying on our allies? When has that become policy?"

"Since the most paranoid of our uncles became emperor?" Malvonican said sardonically. "You might be oblivious to this, but we are not beneath circumventing policies and treaties."

Jeridi gave Malvonican a cold gaze. What was happening to the empire? *Father would be enraged seeing us like this*, Jeridi thought. *We are not mighty, not anymore.*

"Whatever we do in Soroth, we must first contact Grandmaster Alacor," Negaris said. "I gleaned some details from our conversation at lunch that I wish to verify with him."

"I believe we can contact the Ambassador to Soroth," Raedina said. "We've constructed a variety of tevisrals for our foreign officials, and I believe communication rods were one of them."

Jeridi couldn't believe what was being said. He had no clue that the Hilinard was doing such things.

"I'll send a message at once," Negaris said.

Malvonican chuckled. "While you two are playing spy, I guess I'll be doing the important work—strategy." He grinned deviously.

"You're just looking for an excuse to kill someone," Laedar observed with a chuckle.

Malvonican simply grinned.

In that moment, Jeridi *knew* Malvonican couldn't be persuaded. No matter what Laedar or Negaris uncovered, Malvonican would still kill Iltar. And all because he and Raedina *assumed* Iltar was the Liberator of Klis? How preposterous.

"You're going to kill him regardless…" Jeridi muttered.

"Well, if he's not an imposter, he's a blasphemer," Malvonican said. "Did you know he is searching for information on Vabenack and our Divine Father? He's digging too deeply into matters no *man* should uncover."

"I will have no part in the murder of an innocent man," Jeridi said, disgusted.

"He's a Sorothian," Negaris said matter-of-factly. "They're never innocent."

Jeridi gave his brother a cold glare. Though he had become a pacifist, there was still some fight left in him.

"Your ideals for peace have made you soft," Malvonican spat.

Jeridi hurried to the door. He would no longer be party to this madness. As he left the room, Jeridi heard his brothers and cousins continue to plot their revenge on a man they knew nothing about.

And that sickened him.

"The Chosen became icons of Cheserith's empire. Many saw them worthy of emulation. They were esteemed beyond the draconic breeds loyal to Cheserith."

- From *The Thousand Years War, Part I*, page 35

The annexation of Dalgilur shouldn't have surprised Cornar, but the prince's speech was alarming. Cornar wondered what his father—and Iltar's—would have thought about Kaescis's bold claims. *They would undoubtedly want to stop him…* Cornar thought.

Cornar reflected on his earliest experiences in that odd dreamland, particularly his conversation with the not-creature posing as Kandish Loush. That being had claimed that Cornar would find something that would change the course of the expedition.

Am I supposed to change what's happening? Was he supposed to stop the Mindolarnians from claiming Dalgilur? Kaescis obviously intended to wage a war, one that would bring the enemies of the Mindolarnian Empire to their knees. Soroth would be safe from that tyranny—

A sense of paternal protection surged through Cornar, and he thought of his children living in the Western Sovereignty.

But they would be in danger, Cornar thought. Cornar could bring his children home, but that answer wasn't satisfying.

Unable to sleep, Cornar girded on his weapons, grabbed his timepiece tevisral, and then wound his way through the war camp, seeking solace in the open air. He glimpsed Jahevial hurriedly making his way back to the war camp, but Cornar paid little attention to the man. The secretive scholar was of little importance when compared to Kaescis.

Cornar was soon striding down the roadway lined with statues. "You would think this occupation an abomination, wouldn't you?" he whispered to the statues. Sighing, Cornar leaned against the nearest statue, gazing at Dalgilur's glistening buildings—their lights shone brighter than the stars. Cornar noted the time and then allowed his thoughts to overcome him.

One thought in particular was more prominent than others. How did Kaescis know they would unearth weapons capable of empowering Mindolarn to near global dominance? The more he thought about it, the more Cornar disliked the idea of Mindolarn subjugating Kalda. He was his father's son, after all.

A cool breeze washed through Dalgilur, drawing Cornar from his thoughts. To his surprise, several hours had passed, and the sun would be rising soon.

I'd better rest, Cornar thought with reluctance.

———▸•◂———

A few hours later, Cornar and his men were scouting the outer buildings as Kaescis had instructed them. Cornar was just as happy to be away from the Mindolarnians. He selected only seven groups to search the central buildings—the ones that looked elven. The rest of his men Cornar sent to scour the other towering structures.

Then Cornar's group searched the northernmost elven tower. Their search, however, was uneventful. This particular building consisted of homes, interspersed with strange workshops and research rooms. Cornar assumed the Ancient Keepers made wondrous tevisrals here, but neither he nor Igan understood the things they found.

They finished searching the sixty-second floor and made their way to the building's rooftop—a flat platform between four arcing walls that almost formed a curving pyramid. Each curving wall had triangular openings, resembling enormous glassless windows.

Cornar strode toward one window-like hole. They were higher than the mountains now, and Cornar could see the stormless horizon from which they'd sailed.

"Now that's a view!" Igan exclaimed, coming beside Cornar. "How long did that take us?"

Brow furrowed, Cornar looked down at his timepiece tevisral. It indicated that the time was four hours past noon. The sun was hovering across the horizon, beginning its descent into the east.

"Almost eleven hours," Cornar replied, relaxing his arm.

"We just climbed a building higher than anything else in the known world, and you're indifferent about it?" Igan asked with a furrowed brow. "What's wrong, Cor?"

Cornar looked at his friend, his expression uneasy. "I've been reflecting on those dreams..." he trailed off. "An encounter from that first dream keeps coming back to me. And I've been troubled by Kaescis's declaration—"

A snorted snore startled Cornar, and he turned, seeing Kamdir lying on the rooftop with his hands under his head. The young warrior was fast asleep.

Igan grunted. "The prince's announcement shouldn't have come as a surprise," he said. "Did you think Kaescis would *not* annex this island?"

Cornar drew his lips to a line. Igan didn't press the issue, and both of them gazed across the mountaintops toward the distant horizon. All the while, Kamdir snored lightly.

Igan eventually spoke. "You want to stop Kaescis, don't you?" the wizard asked sternly.

"How would an unstoppable Mindolarn Empire impact the world?" Cornar asked.

"There would be blood across every phedan of the Mainland," Igan said somberly. "We would probably be safe on Soroth."

"Can you really stand by and watch so many innocent people suffer?" Cornar asked, his voice pained—he thought of his children once again. "I can't let Kaescis leave this island."

"That's suicide, Cor!" Igan blurted.

The odds were not in their favor. For every one of Cornar's men there were at least ten Mindolarnian soldiers—and that didn't include the sailors or the Crimson Praetorians. And then there were the Wildmen… *Twenty to one*, Cornar thought.

"If you're going to strike, at least wait until Solidin arrives," Igan suggested warily.

"What?" Cornar glanced curiously at the wizard.

"Isn't that why you're gazing northward?"

Would Solidin and the Sapphire Guard be able to reach Dalgilur? Kaescis had mentioned their coming during their meeting on the seas. But the earthquake on Klindala had destroyed Solidin's mapping tevisral. So, how would they know where to go? Nothing in the Keepers' Temple even hinted at Dalgilur's location.

"You don't think they'll find this place, do you?" Igan asked.

"I don't see how…"

Igan's expression was thoughtful. "Krindal was able to sense the island as we passed through the storm."

That gave Cornar pause. He considered the fact that Krindal's perception had been triggered by proximity to the island. Could Solidin sense Dalgilur clear across the world?

"There was a passage in the book I was reading that claimed the Keepers always *knew* where Dalgilur was located. No matter where they were, they knew how to get home—like birds flying to their winter nests. If Solidin has been relying on that sense since leaving Klindala, he will surely know how to get here," Igan reasoned. "And as with most abilities, the more he uses it, the more proficient he will become. I have no doubt they will arrive."

If Solidin were here, it would be easier to stop Kaescis, but the prince had relentlessly cut down those of the Sapphire Guard he encountered at the Keepers' Temple. The elves had no way of resisting that blade of his…

Igan continued his reasoning, voicing what Cornar had already realized.

Cornar looked down to his weapons, remembering the words of that projection-thing in Klindil. *Absorption and reflection*… An abrupt flash of vision filled Cornar's mind of his father dueling with the long-dead Emperor Medis. Melthas had stood his ground against that enormous blade. In fact, if Cornar's father had been alone with the emperor, Medis would most likely have fallen.

"… but even with them, we're not guaranteed victory. I mean, you saw Kaescis in the courtyard," Igan said, sighing. "Oh, if only Iltar were here."

Iltar? Cornar thought.

And then it hit him. *The Darkness magic…*

"Nothing stands up to that Darkness magic," Igan said matter-of-factly.

"You're right," Cornar said, "except for these." He patted his weapons.

Igan looked at Cornar quizzically. Cornar hadn't told Igan or the others all the details about the battle he had experienced with his father. "Have you ever noticed how magic persists on my blades? Even after someone attempts a dispel."

Igan nodded, and his eyes widened with enlightenment.

"These weapons can withstand the Darkness magic," Cornar said. "My father fought Emperor Medis with these weapons, and the emperor was using a blade much like Kaescis."

Igan's intrigued faded. "But he died, Cor…"

"Not from the duel," Cornar said. "He almost slew Medis."

The wizard turned back to the horizon, pondering Cornar's words. "You're going to need a flawless plan," Igan said, thoughtfully drawing his lips into a line.

"Agreed, but we should get back and report first," Cornar said, turning from the majestic view. He walked to Kamdir and nudged the sleeping man in the ribs to wake him. "We'll hold a meeting tonight," he said, "somewhere away from Mindolarnian ears."

——◦•◦——

"This is ridiculous!" Nordal shouted, kicking over a table. He grabbed a nearby chair and hurled it across the room. It was like most of the other rooms they had encountered on this island—beautiful beyond comprehension, unnaturally pristine, and damned sturdy.

"Uh, Nordal, be careful…" Tinal warned. "That could be—"

"We don't know what half—no, any—of this is!" Nordal yelled, cursing furiously and grabbing what appeared to be a tevisral. He tossed it against the nearby window, but the glass didn't break, and the thrown tevisral just bounced back and dropped to the floor.

"Damn it!" Nordal cursed. "I can't even break anything in here!"

"Well, now we know how this place has stood the test of time," Midar smiled. "And now it's withstanding the test of Nordal."

Nordal glared at his fellow warrior. "Where are the weapons?" he demanded, stomping across the room. "Where are the tevisrals we *know?*" He grabbed his hair, growling softly.

"Why don't we start heading back," Midar suggested. "We can pick up a few of these tevisrals along the way and give them to the Mindolarnians. We'll take two of each—give them one while we take the other. Once they find out what they are, then we can keep it as our plunder."

"I like that idea," Tinal said. "We can hide a sack somewhere, then send Ordreth and the others after it."

"Good call," Midar said, nodding. "What do you think, Nordal?"

Nordal continued cursing for a while, but eventually stopped. "That's fine," he grumbled.

❮━━━━◆◗◖◆━━━━❯

Later that evening, in the war room of the Imperial Tent, Cornar gave his report to Kaescis and the rest of the expedition's council. Cornar and Nordal were the odd teams out—as the rest of their band had brought several kinds of powerful tevisrals back to the war camp.

Kalder's group had found an observatory atop one of the elven towers; it contained an enormous living map of the surrounding waters. From what Kalder reported, a topographical map—akin to Krindal's mapping tevisral—depicted a storm raging across the ocean. The Mindolarnians were quite intrigued with the find, especially Grand Marshal Hezidex.

There was plenty of speculation that what Kalder had found was controlling the ever-persistent storm in the World's Frown. That made sense to Cornar—the lightning alone was quite unnatural.

More reports were given, and Cornar learned that Crenai and her scouts had found a weapon cache. She brought several weapons to the meeting. They were unlike any weapon Cornar had ever beheld. Most looked broken—as they were only hilts of swords, or bows without strings. But when held, the weapons abruptly changed. Bowstrings and blades *materialized* out of thin air. The process looked like an instantaneous transmutation. These weapons obviously had tevisrals within them that enabled such wondrous transformations. Cornar thought the weapons looked elven, but none of the scholars or the Mindolarnians made mention of the weapons' craftsmanship.

After reports were delivered, Kaescis doled out more tasks. This time, Cornar and his band were assigned to the western section of the Hall of the Guardians. Most others were assigned to map the upper levels of the southern section.

Crenai was the first to leave the meeting. Her departure gave Cornar an idea.

After exiting the Imperial Tent, Cornar went straight to his men resting in the Royal ring. Many looked at him quizzically—undoubtedly because of the grin spread across his face.

"Well?" Igan whispered, looking tense.

"We're going to do some more exploring tonight," Cornar said cheerily, tucking a thumb under his belt. A couple of the warriors looked at each other with confusion. "Kaescis has tasked us with searching the western part of this structure." Cornar gestured his freehand in a circle over his head. "And since it's so large, I think we should get a head start."

Briskly, Cornar turned from his men and walked toward the Praetorians standing guard between the two inner rings of the war camp. The group was soon out of the war camp and headed westward through the enormous space. Cornar gave a casual order for them to break up into their groups but didn't tell them to disperse. The more senior warriors came beside him—Kalder, Gregan, Nordal, Midar and Aron. Vargos and Igan were with him as well.

"This almost feels like old times," Igan said, grinning. "Too bad we're missing the others."

Cornar nodded. Their band didn't feel complete. If everyone had been there, four other mages would be walking at the party's head. Iltar would obviously be in the lead, followed closely by old Amendal. Cornar could almost hear the speculations of the old conjurer as they crossed the hall. The other two—a lanky wizard named Hex and a short scrawny illusionist named Hagen—would be right beside Cornar. Hagen—the man who trained Hem—would undoubtedly mutter cautious, almost terrified, assumptions about what lay ahead. And all the while, Hex would make playful jabs at Hagen's wary disposition.

A startling sight abruptly drew Cornar from his nostalgic reverie.

"Amazing!" Gregan exclaimed. Several other warriors murmured in agreement. Cornar stood silent in awe.

Four white statues—akin to those outside—stood at the western end of the enormous space, and one was… a dragon. The stone behemoth stood defiantly, as if confronting Cornar's disbelief about the existence of such creatures.

"That thing is huge!" Ordreth exclaimed, pointing at the dragon. "I've never seen a statue so big…"

"You'd think the wings would break off," Vargos chortled. "Look how thin they are…"

The old barsionist had a point. Cornar had some knowledge about sculpting stone, since his son was a stonemason. The way the wings hovered above the ground seemed impossible.

"Let's keep going," Cornar said. He glanced about, noting that they were plenty far from anyone else. "We need to find a room large enough to fit us all."

The party continued past the statues. Enormous staircases—wide enough to fit thirty men abreast—led to a balcony three stories above the floor of the enormous chamber. Several oversized corridors—though not as big as the towering halls branching from the main room—were spaced along the balcony. Each rose three stories tall. Cornar led his men to the center corridor.

"I feel like we're in a mythical palace," Midar said.

Kalder nodded. "It does look that way."

"This place isn't like the other buildings, is it?" Hem asked. The men agreed that three different architects seemed to have designed the various buildings.

At the end of the corridor they came to another set of stairs. They were narrower than the others they had climbed, rising only two stories before ending at a landing. A normal-sized doorway stood opposite the stairs. It emptied into a hallway running perpendicular to the corridor they just traversed.

Closed doors, spaced at random intervals, lined the hallway.

"Now where?" Nordal asked, sounding agitated.

"Still grumpy, Nordal?" Midar asked in a mocking tone.

Nordal just glared at Midar. Cornar had heard of Nordal's tantrum during their search today.

"Let's fan out," Cornar suggested, "and see if any of these rooms are large enough to hold us."

Soon they found a sufficiently large room, a foyer adjoining a much larger council chamber. Pristine furniture lined the walls—couches and chairs with unusually angular designs. Realistic paintings hung above the furniture, depicting scenes across Kalda. There were even pictures of dragons, most of the creatures a shimmering metallic white, almost a platinum color.

Cornar stood at the entrance while the others rested on the furniture or leaned against the walls. Most were eager to hear about the latest meeting Cornar had attended in the Imperial Tent.

"I know many of you are anxious to hear what was reported," Cornar began. "I'll tell you, but that's not why I've called this meeting." Many of the warriors perked up, their expressions intrigued. "Within the northern parts of this structure, Kaescis discovered a hidden cove containing ships of ancient design. His men are currently investigating the condition of the vessels, but their initial report suggested they were seaworthy."

"Even after all this time?" blurted one of the younger warriors. "But aren't they thousands of years old?" Mutters of agreement came from the men. Cornar let them voice their speculations before continuing.

"A weapon cache was also found. Each of the weapons is the stuff of legend. Swords with their blades materializing out of thin air and bursting with magical effects—"

"Oh, I need to get me one of those!" Nordal exclaimed, his mood shifting.

Cornar grinned. "A few partially constructed tevisrals were also found in what the others assumed were workshops. But none of this," he gestured with his hand, "really matters."

Silence hung in the room as Cornar took a deep breath. "I've come to realize this expedition will bring folly upon the world. Kaescis will deluge Kalda in blood if he takes the wonders of the Keepers from Dalgilur. As you all know, I've had dreams about the past. What some of you don't know, though, is that those dreams were meant to change the course of this expedition."

The men listened attentively. None treated Cornar's experiences in that dreamland lightly. Each was familiar with Cornar's intuition, and they took these dreams as an extension of it.

"Although I don't fully comprehend the reasons why, I know that only *I* can do what must be done..."

Cornar picked his next words with care, since he knew that his men would follow him without question. "What I must do will be dangerous, perhaps even fatal. This meeting isn't to conscript you to this cause, but to warn you of it. Only I can perform this task."

"What are you getting at, Cor?" Gregan asked warily. Cornar sternly gazed at the auburn-haired man, then studied each of his men. "I'm going to kill Kaescis," he said grimly. "The prince must not be allowed to leave Dalgilur…"

A few gasps echoed within the room.

"Uncle…" Ordreth muttered, worry contorting his face.

"That's suicide!" Nordal shouted, rising to his feet. "He wields the Darkness magic, like Master Iltar."

"Sounds reckless…" Vargos grumbled, shaking his head. "Have you forgotten what the prince did to the elves?"

"You can't do this alone, Cor!" Midar shook his head.

More objections resounded throughout the room. Kalder, however, silently rose from his seat on one of the couches. He crossed to Cornar and placed a hand on his mentor's shoulder. "If you engage Kaescis, I will be right beside you."

"As will I," Ordreth declared stoically, tears in his eyes.

One by one, the warriors declared their willingness to fight beside their mentor.

"You all are a bunch of fools," Vargos said, looking at the ceiling.

"Won't you fight with us, Master Vargos?" Hem demanded.

The old barsionist chortled. "Well, of course, but I still think you are fools."

"Doesn't that make you a fool, too?" Midar asked matter-of-factly.

Vargos shrugged.

Cornar eyed each of the men. A knot formed in his stomach. There was no way to dissuade them from their zeal. They reminded him of his father's Elites.

"So tell us this plan, Cor," Nordal said. "How are we going to kill these damned Tilters?"

Tilters? Cornar didn't understand the reference, but he assumed Nordal was talking about the Mindolarnians. Nordal often came up with the oddest nicknames.

"I plan on getting Kaescis alone—how, I haven't figured out exactly."

"You're definitely going to need help with that," Gregan said. "He is rarely alone."

"Do you really think you can take him on by yourself?" Midar asked.

Cornar nodded, then related the battle of Laelin Lake to his men. He also expounded on the nature of his weapons, deducing that he could use Kaescis's magic against him.

"There's another vital component to the… assassination," Igan interjected. "We need to strike when the Sapphire Guard arrives."

The wizard's declaration drew confused glances. Igan then related his speculation about Solidin's ability to sense Dalgilur. Some of the men nodded, remembering how Krindal had guided the fleet in the storm. The arrival of the Sapphire Guard became a subject of debate. Timing the attack with the elves' undoubted assault seemed impossible. Igan suggested they wait, then turn on the Mindolarnians during the battle. That would give them the best possible chance for survival.

"Foolish…" Vargos grumbled. "Just foolish."

For the next hour they discussed ideas for executing Kaescis's demise. The consensus among the warriors was that they should deal with Kaescis's guards and hold the line against any possible reinforcements. Nordal, however, wasn't in agreement. He wanted to steal some of the weapons found by the Mindolarnians. The bloodthirsty warrior assumed those weapons could withstand Kaescis's blade.

After another hour of discussion, Cornar changed the course of the meeting. "We need to find an alluring discovery, or at least something we can *make* alluring."

"What about the scholars?" Cordel asked. "I assume they will continue searching with us."

"I don't trust any of them to not run off and tell Kaescis of our betrayal," Igan said somberly.

"Jahevial might be willing to side with us," Aron said. His words drew surprised glances. "Today he offered us a deal to help him smuggle tevisrals for the Necrotic Order."

Igan looked to Cornar with a questioning gaze.

"Did he say anything else?" Cornar asked.

"No, but he did seem incensed with the Mindolarnians—as are the other scholars."

"The more fools the better." Vargos sighed with exasperation. "Even with them, we're still outnumbered."

"Feel Jahevial out, Aron," Cornar said. "And agree to help him. But don't disclose our plans." Aron nodded.

Cornar then checked his timepiece tevisral. It was nearly two hours before midnight. "Why don't we get some exploring in for the evening. Tomorrow morning let's meet here and discuss our finds."

Solidin could *feel* the gap closing between him and Dalgilur. Since sailing from Klindala, his awareness of the isle had grown substantially. Now he could practically see it across the horizon—though they weren't near the Anomalous Corridor.

He sucked in a calming breath as he took one last look across the bow, getting the approximate heading for the *Vigilance*. The ship hadn't veered off course today.

Other elves were busy manning the rigging as Solidin crossed the main deck, making his way to the enclosed bridge.

"Well?" Captain Teviz demanded in Elvish.

"The ship is still on course," Solidin said, replying in the same tongue. He strode past Teviz toward the sea charts. After a few moments, Solidin pointed at the center of the Anomalous Corridor—the place men called the World's

Frown. "It is there, I know it."

Teviz glared with apprehension. "You could be dooming us all," the captain said warily.

Soon, more footfalls echoed into the bridge. Gladis and Kaldarin came to stand beside Solidin. Since their voyage from the north, Gladis had come to accept Solidin's ability to sense Dalgilur. Both he and Kaldarin were Solidin's strongest supporters.

"You are showing signs of cowardice, Teviz," Kaldarin said pointedly.

"Someone must be the voice of reason," Teviz retorted. "Nothing survives the Anomalous Corridor."

"If Solidin believes we will survive it, then we will," Gladis said matter-of-factly.

Their defense pleased Solidin. Grinning, he traced a route with his finger on the sea chart. "We need to sail around the island," Solidin said. "Approach it from the southwest. The Mindolarnians will undoubtedly come from the north."

Teviz was still agitated. "Why not sail directly to the island? We can move along its coast and lie in wait for the Mindolarnians to arrive."

Solidin turned a stern gaze to Teviz. "No. We must stay beyond the horizon of the island. The Mindolarnians *know* we are headed to Dalgilur. If perchance they have beaten us to the island, they will be searching the northern waters. So, approaching from the south will give us the advantage of surprise. Besides, the northern shores are too rocky for any moorings."

"But the prince is a shrewd tactician," Kaldarin interjected. "Will he not suspect such a maneuver?"

"Why not cloak the ship?" Gladis suggested. "We can move along the shores."

"Agreed," Teviz almost shouted. "The less time we spend in the Corridor the better."

"Do not let your fear cloud your judgment," Solidin chided the captain. "The Mindolarnians were cunning. They undoubtedly have a means to detect a concealed ship, not to mention the wake the *Vigilance* would leave behind—we might as well sail visibly." He shook his head. "No… we sail around the island."

"That will add several hours to our voyage," Teviz said with a scowl. "Hours that would be best spent away from danger."

Solidin gazed hard at Teviz. "Perhaps I should maroon you on one of these isles." He gestured to the islands along the edge of the Anomalous Corridor.

"How dare you!" Teviz's face flared with anger. Both Kaldarin and Gladis started with surprise. Neither of them expected that Solidin had the gall to threaten the son of a High Lord—but then again, Solidin was the commander of the Sapphire Guard.

Still steadfast, Solidin continued staring at Teviz. "I will plot a course for your crew to follow." Then Solidin waggled his finger. "No deviations. Once we circle around, moor the ship within a forested cove along the southwest. The trees will conceal the ship." Solidin intended to lie in wait for the

Mindolarnians. But if they were already on Dalgilur, mooring to the south would enable an effective sneak attack.

Cornar and several of the groups searched the level where they'd found the council chamber. He took Igan and Kamdir to the western reaches of the enormous structure while the others spread elsewhere. A few of them climbed to the higher floors. Ordreth and his group decided to discover whether this wing rose to the mountaintops.

After an hour of searching, a faint but constant whistle caught their attention.

"That sounds like wind whipping against rock," Igan noted.

"Sounds like it's coming from that way." Kamdir pointed to their right. "But what would be doing that?"

Cornar looked long where the young warrior gestured. The hallway turned to the right after nearly a hundred phineals. *Why would we be hearing wind?* he wondered.

"Come on…" Cornar trailed off, moving down the hallway.

The whistling grew louder as they turned the corner. They followed the noise, winding back and forth through the maze of corridors. The walls they passed turned from pristine to dingy. Dust and dirt soon marred the floor. Light coming from the walls and ceiling faded—whatever was illuminating this part of the structure wasn't functioning. The hallway seemed more cavern than building.

Kamdir looked to Igan and Cornar warily. Igan whispered an incantation, mustering his ball of light. The ball hovered over his shoulder, illuminating the ruined hallway. Focused ahead, Cornar turned another corner and started with surprise.

The left wall was gone, as was part of the floor. Some of the ceiling was missing, too, more so than the floor. The entire opening spread about twenty phineals, allowing a view to the ocean. Debris littered what remained of the hallway's floor.

Cornar crept to the edge, peering out the opening. The level below them was also exposed to the elements. Part of that lower level's flooring was also missing. Cornar could see two levels below them, but not much beyond that. A sheer rock face dropped into the ocean, about four floors below the last exposed level of the Hall of the Guardians.

"What on Kalda…" Kamdir muttered.

Igan stepped beside Cornar, examining the debris and the broken parts of the wall. "It looks like something blew this apart," the wizard said, running his hand along the floor's rough edge.

"What could have done that?" Kamdir demanded. "Isn't this island protected?"

Cornar narrowed his eyes. The very sight of the opening was unnerving. He braced himself against the remaining part of the wall and leaned out the opening. The floor above them also looked demolished, as was the one beyond that. *What happened here?*

What's wrong, Cor?" Igan asked.

"Take a look," Cornar said, stepping back into the hallway. Igan braced himself and poked his head out, intently studying the destruction above them.

"What is it, Cor?" Kamdir asked, adjusting his belt.

"I think something—" Faint voices carried through the broken hallway.

"Looks like someone else heard the wind," Igan said flatly.

The voices grew louder, and then Gregan appeared at the far end, with Haetan and Vargos in tow. They soon reached the demolished portion of the hallway.

"This is odd, isn't it?" Gregan asked warily, stepping over the debris and into the broken hallway. He carefully climbed over the rubble and stopped beside Igan.

"It's like something blasted the walls," Haetan said, looking up and down as he followed Gregan. Haetan too had auburn hair, long and curly. Both he and Gregan shared similar features. But that was often expected with cousins.

Vargos grunted as the two warriors joined Cornar. The old barsionist examined the broken floor and cast a spell. Brilliant blue barsion shot from his hands, stopping up the hole in the floor. "That's better," Vargos said, and finally joined the others.

"Vargos, why don't you extend this," Igan said, gesturing through the opening. "That way we can see how far this destruction has spread."

The old barsionist nodded approvingly, then cast another spell.

"Any idea what did this?" Gregan asked Cornar.

"It looks like something collided with the mountain," Cornar said. "But I don't know how that's possible..."

It wasn't long before Vargos finished his spell. His barsion ramp extended a few hundred phineals—suspended above the water like Dalgilur's unnatural piers.

As they stepped out onto the ramp, chatter from above them reached their ears.

Cornar stopped, looking to the broken ceiling. Soon, Nordal's head poked through.

"Fancy seeing you there," Nordal quipped with a grin. He examined the ruined hallway and then grunted, but turned wide-eyed when he saw the barsion ramp.

"Come join us," Cornar said, stepping out of the way.

Nordal nodded, then shouted back to Midar and Tinal. Soon, all three of them were climbing through the broken ceiling and landing upon Vargos's barsion.

Together, all three groups marched across the barsion. The moonlight from Kistern and Kaelyrn lit the night sky. Partway across the barsion ramp, Cornar glanced to the ocean now seven stories beneath them. He felt a sudden jolt of dizziness and stopped abruptly, steadying himself.

Nordal reached out instinctively and grabbed his mentor. "Are you all right?" he asked.

Cornar nodded, sucking in a deep breath. Focusing ahead, Cornar continued across the barsion ramp.

The others reached the edge of the magic and turned, gasping with surprise and wonder. The younger men, Tinal and Kamdir, gawked with slack jaws. Vargos shook his head in disbelief and Igan's eyes widened.

What's their— Cornar turned and flinched in astonishment.

A gigantic crater marred the mountainside. Unlike most craters, however, this one was sideways. The hallway they were searching was near the base of the crater. Dozens of floors were exposed all throughout the mountainside, looking like a cut-away diagram.

Tinal gasped. "By all that's magical…"

"Wha-what could have done that?" Kamdir asked.

Cornar turned, looking across the horizon. His eyes searched the ever-calm façade veiling the island from that treacherous storm. How could anything breech the magic protecting Dalgilur? Surely, a meteorite couldn't penetrate that invisible barrier—let alone make it through the storm.

The others debated the crater's nature as Cornar spun, drawn irresistibly to the center of that impossibility.

THERE, YOU MUST GO THERE, that booming voice from his dreams whispered, as if dancing on the faint ocean breeze.

"Did any of you hear that?" Cornar asked, interrupting the debate.

"Hear what, Cor?" Gregan asked.

"A voice on the wind…" Cornar said, trailing off. The warriors gave each other unsettled glances.

"What did it say?" Igan asked.

"That I must go to the center of the crater."

"Well, what are we waiting for?" Nordal asked, walking back across the barsion. Gregan and Haetan hurried behind Nordal. The three of them were almost running back to the ruined hallway.

Midar brushed past Cornar, glancing to his mentor with a look that asked, "We're going, right?" The mages came beside Cornar a moment later.

"What time is it?" Igan asked.

Cornar looked to his timepiece tevisral. "We should go back to camp," he suggested. "We can find the impact point in the morning."

"Are you going to report this to Prince Kaescis?" Tinal asked.

Vargos snorted, shaking his head.

"Not yet," Cornar said, turning back to the center of the crater. "Perhaps *that* will be our alluring discovery."

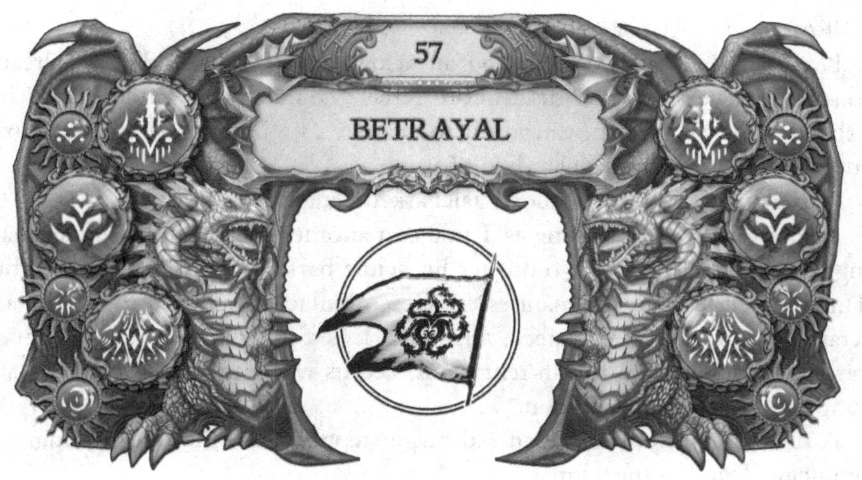

BETRAYAL

"Cheserith's true intention with the Chosen was to create an army of powerful beings that could match the strength, speed, and intellect of his draconic brethren. The minds of the Chosen were not inhibited and could use the draconic Words of Power to manifest the various Channels. And so, the Chosen could manifest the Channels faster than any man or elf, and rivaled the dragons in unimaginable ways."

- From *The Thousand Years War, Part I*, page 36

Alacor watched the duel between his and his brother's apprentices. The apprentices were but two participants in a dueling tournament the Necrotic Order hosted semiannually. It was held at the Necrotic Order in an old dueling arena sunken into the ground. Rows of benches surrounded the ring, sparsely filled with onlookers. Years ago those seats would have been full.

Only a few mages from Soroth had come to the tournament to pit their apprentices against each other. There were twenty contestants, all in all. Each of the council members had their apprentices present—except Iltar.

Iltar… The thought of Iltar made Alacor's blood boil.

Ten days ago, Makivan had returned from Sarn with news about Iltar—the necromancer's tale of the Scurn inheritance was a fraud. Count Coralis Scurn was still alive, as was his wife, Elsia. Iltar had used the ruse of their death as means to leave Soroth in the pursuit of research in Mindolarn. What type of research, the count didn't know.

Master Rovin should never have trained him, Alacor thought. Rovin's decision to teach Iltar all those years ago baffled Alacor. Iltar had always proven to be a nuisance. If Master Rovin had planned some grand scheme, it went awry years ago.

Alacor's attention was abruptly drawn back to the duel. Kreely flew backward, propelled by a blast of acid from Tindil. The fool fell awkwardly and stumbled to his feet.

What an idiot, Alacor sighed.

Kreely dashed sideways, casting an acidic javelin, but Tindil was already mustering several acidic orbs. Before Kreely could finish, Tindil hurled his orbs at Kreely's barsion, causing it to shatter. The barrier's sundering interrupted Kreely, and his javelin didn't form

"Are you jealous yet, brother?" Jalel asked haughtily

Alacor grumbled, watching as Tindil cast another spell, summoning ensnaring tentacles. Kreely tried to muster his acidic barsion barrier once again, but Tindil's spell had already manifested. Green tentacles zipped through the air, wrapping around Kreely's neck, arms, and legs. Struggling, Kreely continued casting his spell, but a fourth tentacle forced its way into Kreely's mouth, abruptly stopping his incantation.

A moment passed before an old mage stepped onto the dueling ring, announcing Tindil as the winner.

"Stupendous!" Jalel cheered, clapping for his apprentice. A few other onlookers applauded Tindil's victory; their acclaim was more polite than enthusiastic.

Alacor gave his brother a hard look. Though he wasn't on the dueling field, Alacor couldn't help but feel a sense of defeat. He hated feeling beaten. It was a loathsome experience.

"Perhaps next year, brother," Jalel said, taking his seat beside Alacor. Not amused, Alacor shook his head and grunted.

The next two contestants entered the ring—Melnor's apprentice, Odinal, and a young wizard named Danaeya. She was apprentice to an elementalist named Baekal, one of the few mages who taught in small groups outside the Order. Such tutelages were permitted, but students like Danaeya could never be officially acknowledged as full-fledged mages unless trained in the art of necromancy at the Necrotic Order.

Many mages had taken the opportunity, becoming what some called "Dualist Mages."

The match began, and both Danaeya and Odinal mustered barsion barriers. Odinal's barsion dripped acid while Danaeya's erupted into flame.

"Grandmaster Alacor!" Alacor turned. One of the Order's guards hurried down the steps. "Grandmaster," the guard said, "you have an urgent visitor from the Mindolarnian Embassy."

The Mindolarnian Embassy? Alacor raised an eyebrow. He glanced back to the match. Odinal was opening a conjuration portal, and Danaeya was casting some kind of spell—it sounded like she was trying to make a flaming blade.

"Grandmaster?"

Alacor turned to face the guard. "I can meet with them later," he said, waving off the guard.

The guard, however, didn't move. "They insist that you come, at once," he said shakily.

"What's the matter?" Jalel leaned toward Alacor, his eyes still on the match.

"Someone from the Mindolarnian Embassy wants to meet with me," Alacor replied.

Jalel's eyebrows rose in interest. "Do you suppose it has to do with that bastard, Iltar?"

Alacor didn't answer. Instead, he continued watching the match. Danaeya finished her spell. Flame burst from her hands, becoming a claymore-sized shaft of fire. She lunged toward Odinal as he finished summoning his conjuration—a cestolin.

Cestolins were large red reptilians that were as long as a man was tall. An ivory exoskeleton lined their backs and limbs, coming to razor-sharp points along their joints. Their heads were mostly covered in a thick skull-plate, adorned with sharp points.

Danaeya and the cestolin clashed, but the conjuration tackled her to the ground. Alacor could see the pain in the cestolin's eyes as the creature tried ripping through Danaeya's flaming barsion.

"Grandmaster," the guard spoke again, "I must insist. They… they were quite persistent that I fetch you." Alacor pursed his lips, not amused.

Danaeya broke free, swinging her flaming blade at the cestolin. The beast's skull-plate ignited, but the creature was ultimately undaunted.

"Fine." Alacor sighed and rose from his seat. He followed the guard up the steps of the arena and was surprised to find his brother trailing behind him.

"What are you doing?" Alacor asked, his manner brusque.

"Satisfying my curiosity."

Alacor jerked his head back toward the arena. "You'll miss Tindil's next match."

"Were you not paying attention?" Jalel asked, chuckling. "He was in the first match of this rung." Alacor turned back, disgruntled, and they followed the guard in silence.

A dozen men—ten wearing ceremonial Mindolarn plate—stood in the foyer of the Order's Main Hall. The other two men, neither of whom Alacor recognized, stood at the head of the armored men, wearing formal attire. These two were undoubtedly Mindolarnian officials.

"Greetings, Grandmaster Alacor," the man on the left said. "I am Ambassador Dumar. Please forgive our intrusion, but we come on urgent business from the Royal Family. May we speak somewhere private?"

Alacor glanced to his brother, and Jalel returned the gesture with wide eyes.

"Why, yes," Alacor answered. He eyed a trunk behind the ambassador. "We can go to my office."

"Alone, please," the ambassador insisted.

"He is my brother," Alacor gestured to Jalel. "And a fellow Devout."

Ambassador Dumar eyed Jalel for a moment, then nodded. "Lead the way."

Only the officials entered Alacor's chambers. The soldiers remained outside after delivering the trunk. The ambassador and the other man stood, while Alacor sat in his throne-like chair. Jalel, however, took a seat on the far couch.

"We appreciate your discretion," Dumar said, then gestured for the other man to open the trunk. "I received an urgent message last night from Prince

Negaris, requesting to speak with you directly."

Alacor leaned back in his chair, watching the other official open the trunk.

"Have you ever heard of or seen one of these?" Dumar said, gesturing to the trunk.

The other Mindolarnian official lifted a communication tevisral from the trunk, identical to the one Alacor had used to converse with Jahevial.

Alacor looked nervously at the tevisral, then glanced beside his desk. His own communication rod was safely tucked away. It was a good thing too. Its presence would only arouse suspicion against him. After all, Alacor had stolen the pair—his and Jahevial's—amid the confusion at the Feast of Sorrows.

"I have," Alacor answered stiffly. "One can speak across the world with one of those."

"Yes, precisely," Dumar said, grabbing the tevisral. He tapped on the bottom gem and proceeded to activate the device. "Your Imperial Grace," Dumar said, "we are here with Grandmaster Alacor."

A moment of silence passed, and then the gem on the tevisral glowed a dark orange, indicating a message had been received. Dumar activated the tevisral and held the gemless end to Alacor.

"Grandmaster Alacor, I thank you for meeting me like this," Prince Negaris's voice spoke from the tevisral. "I regret not coming in person, but this is a delicate matter that must be addressed immediately."

The tevisral's gem stopped flashing, and Dumar proceeded to activate the tevisral for transmitting, then extended the same end to Alacor.

"Of course, Your Imperial Grace. How may I be of help?"

Dumar sent the message, then the prince sent a reply.

"My brothers and I wish to verify the identity of someone who has come to the seat of the empire, a man named Iltar. He claims to be a necromancer from your Order, and a member of its council. He is here with a woman named Elsia Scurn, as well as several acolytes."

Alacor feigned perplexity. *This could be advantageous*, he thought and continued listening.

"Normally we wouldn't bother with such a matter, but my dear cousin, Princess Raedina, believes him to be the murderer of our late emperor. She was the only eyewitness to the assassination—besides my brother Kaescis— and insists this Iltar looks exactly like the murderer."

Alacor recalled the meeting with Krindal three months ago, noting that Kaescis's eyes had lingered on Iltar. The prince had sternly studied him. *So, they think Iltar is one of the Alathians who attacked during the feast,* Alacor mused. *The princes must be planning a move against Iltar; why else would they contact me?*

"… Iltar has weaseled his way into the confidence of a renowned duchess here in Mindolarn," Prince Negaris continued. "My dear cousin has encountered him several times and fears he might be here to launch an attack similar to the one we suffered during the Feast of Sorrows."

The message ended.

"Prince Negaris," Alacor spoke into the tevisral, "I can confirm that Master Iltar is indeed a member of the Necrotic Order and one of its council members. But, he is currently on the Isle of Sarn. The woman you mentioned, Countess Elsia Scurn, passed away two months ago. Iltar's apprentice, Pagus Aliteran, is her nephew and inherited her lands. Master Iltar is currently on Sarn to continue the boy's training. His acolytes accompanied him as well and they are all staying at Elsia's—rather Pagus's mountain villa."

Ambassador Dumar sent the message and silence lingered in the office.

Jalel looked at Alacor with disbelief. Alacor, however, shot his brother a fierce glance that said, "Don't give me away."

After a few minutes Prince Negaris sent a reply. "You can verify unequivocally that Iltar is on Sarn?" Prince Negaris asked.

"I visited him last week," Alacor said. "And have every week since Iltar departed for Sarn two months ago." Silence once again fell upon the room. The Mindolarnian officials were somber.

Alacor eyed each of them, feigning confusion. *This is perfect,* he thought, fighting back a smile. Alacor glanced to his brother, who sat with his hands braced against his forehead, looking as if he were praying.

Soon, the communication tevisral's gem lit, indicating another message.

"We appreciate your cooperation, Grandmaster Alacor," Prince Negaris said. "The empire owes you a great debt for your help."

"It is my pleasure," Alacor spoke into the tevisral. "Good luck in this endeavor."

There was no reply.

"Thank you for complying with our summons," Dumar bowed, handing the tevisral back to the other man. "Good day, grandmaster." The ambassador hurried out of the office, and two soldiers fetched the trunk concealing the communication tevisral.

Once they were gone, Jalel locked the door. "Are you mad, brother?!" he demanded, almost growling. "If they find out that you lied to them they—"

"Shut up, Jalel," Alacor scolded. "There is no way they can uncover the truth."

Jalel began pacing the room, as he only did when overly worried.

"The Scurns' deaths have been documented," Alacor said. "Pagus did us a favor in that regard." Jalel continued pacing, giving Alacor an exasperated glance. "If the Mindolarnians go to Sarn, they will see that both Coralis and Elsia are dead," Alacor added.

"And what if they go to the mountain villa?" Jalel demanded.

Alacor smiled reassuringly. "Then they will be met with the same dilemma that confronted Makivan," he said. Even if the Mindolarnians followed Makivan's course of investigation, they would never discover the truth. Makivan had seen to that. Even if Pagus's father—or anyone from the Aliteran or Scurn houses—admitted the truth, there was no evidence to confirm it. The linchpin to their ruse—Count Coralis Scurn—had been dealt with. No one would find the count. At least, not on Sarn.

Jalel sighed. He didn't look convinced. "You know what this implies, don't you?"

Excitement beamed across Alacor's face. "We will finally be rid of Iltar."

"But at the expense of how many lives?" Jalel asked. "How many Devouts will Iltar slay before he is killed?"

"You overestimate Iltar's abilities," Alacor sighed, rising from his chair. "But sacrifices are necessary, brother. The world will be better off without Iltar. Now, let's get back to the tournament. Hopefully, we haven't missed your apprentice's next match."

❧

Raedina nervously tapped her chin while pacing within her office. Malvonican had come to her earlier in the day, informing her that Negaris had spoken with Grandmaster Alacor. The grandmaster verified Iltar's existence, but claimed the man was on Sarn.

That did not bode well.

Ambassador Dumar was going to Sarn immediately to verify the grandmaster's claims. A predicament such as this couldn't hinge on the word of just one man, no matter how trustworthy.

This Iltar has to be that *grand mage*, Raedina thought. *Oh, I wish Kaescis were here…* She had tried contacting Kaescis, but the prince had left his communication rod on Klindala with Grand Marshal Galiur. That irritated her.

The next few hours were torturous. Raedina couldn't concentrate on anything. She had given all her projects over to Dalkalin. He was capable enough and far enough removed from the situation at hand as to not be bogged down emotionally.

After nightfall, the princes arrived. Malvonican was first, followed by Negaris. Jeridi was next—his opposition to their plan was visible on his face. *How can you still doubt us?* Raedina wondered, studying her cousin. Jeridi had undoubtedly been informed of the news from Soroth.

Finally, Laedar arrived. "What took you so long?" Malvonican asked, with his typical smug expression. Her brother sat with one leg over the arm of his chair and an arm thrown across the chair's back.

"I was waiting for Xalutir's response," Laedar said. "He's returning from wherever he's been hiding."

Jeridi sighed and rolled his eyes. The other princes looked dubiously at their eldest brother and cousin.

"You still don't believe me, Jeridi?" Raedina asked, her voice shaky. "Even after the news we received from Soroth?"

"No, I don't," the fat prince replied. "Have any of you stopped to consider that Alacor might be lying?"

Malvonican laughed.

"What's his motive to do so?" Laedar asked. Raedina couldn't tell if Laedar's tone was genuine or not.

"Don't you remember how Iltar acted when you asked him if he knew Alacor?" Jeridi asked. "Those two obviously don't get along."

Malvonican snorted with incredulity.

"Or he never met the man," Laedar retorted tersely.

"I'm sorry to disappoint you, brother," Negaris said, "but Ambassador Dumar confirmed the deaths of both Count Coralis Scurn and his wife. The woman we shared food with was not Elsia Scurn."

Jeridi looked shocked. His jaw dropped and his lips twisted with abhorrence. That dismal expression faded, and Jeridi regained his composure. "And did they find Iltar?" he asked, his tone indicating that he still clung to his erroneous beliefs.

"They received proof enough from the servants at the mountain villa where Iltar is staying," Negaris said.

Jeridi looked defeated. He sat back in his chair, averting his gaze from the other princes. Negaris went into greater detail concerning the evidence he had against this Alathian posing as Iltar of Soroth.

I knew it, Raedina thought, closing her eyes to calm herself. She recalled her encounters with this imposter, remembering his stern expressions. Those sapphire eyes of his burned with hatred. Then, Raedina thought of Alanya. Was she even Alanya? Or was she an Alathian pretending to be the high duchess? After all, those who had infiltrated the Feast of Sorrows flawlessly assumed the identities of palace servants.

"… we can bring in another battalion to replace the palace garrison, perhaps from the northern wall," Laedar suggested.

"If we replace the garrison, we reveal our hand," Malvonican retorted. "We can bring in troops, but not replace them. And the garrison *must not* know that more troops are being deployed. We mustn't change anything at the palace."

The princes continued debating strategy while Raedina focused on the ruse they must enact. In order for Malvonican to be a convincing target his disguise must be perfect. A simple illusion would not do the trick—that could be dispelled. *We need a tevisral,* she thought.

Raedina recalled reading about rings that could alter the shape of whoever wore them, though she couldn't recall their names. They were ancient, created before the fall of the great Cheserithean Empire. Those rings used illusionary and transmutative magics to create a perfect guise that was totally undetectable. The ring would adhere to the wearer, and only they could remove it.

I think I can duplicate that, Raedina thought, pacing to the window. She gazed at the moons; their light calmed her nerves. Moonlight always had that effect on her. Raedina was a creature of the night. *I have the proper materials. We could make it in a day.*

There was, however, one problem. Those rings had to be worn first by whatever they were duplicating. She needed Uncle Marden.

At that moment, the debate became heated. Malvonican began shouting, and Negaris's tone turned petulant. Raedina spun, seeing Jeridi leaving the office. The other princes were no longer seated. They stood facing each other and argued heatedly.

"Silence, all of you!" Raedina commanded sternly. The princes, however, didn't listen.

"Silence!" This time the princes stopped their bickering.

"We all have problems to overcome with this plan," Raedina said. "But in order to pull this off, we need to make Malvonican *look* like Uncle Marden. Otherwise, this is all for naught."

All eyes were on Raedina. "I think I can make a tevisral to duplicate Uncle's appearance," she continued, "but I need to put it on him in order—"

Footsteps echoed into the office, drawing everyone's attention.

Laedar cursed. "Why didn't Jeridi close the damned door?"

"Because he's a mindless coward," Negaris growled.

The footsteps grew louder, then Jeridi returned, accompanied by none other than the emperor of the Mindolarn Empire. Uncle Marden slouched in the doorway for a moment, and then nonchalantly entered the office.

"I hear you found my brothers' murderer," the emperor said, eyeing his niece and nephews inquisitively. "I do hope you weren't planning to kill him without me."

"For several years, the Chosen attacked those dragons who opposed Cheserith's reign. They hunted various breeds of dragonkind, making it a sport. One breed they eradicated completely: the Cel'sha or the Silver Dragons."

- From *The Thousand Years War, Part I,* page 42

Cornar and the others hadn't slept long once they returned from scouting the western wing. According to his timepiece tevisral, Cornar slept only five and a half hours. Instead of having their morning meal in the Mindolarn war camp, Cornar's men took their food and ate in the secluded council chamber they had discovered the previous night.

Each of the men gave their reports as Midar and Cordel prepared their breakfast. Ordreth was the last to report.

"… that was fifty-two stories," Ordreth said. "I guess that makes it fifty-eight floors, all in all." The young warrior scooped up a spoonful of his porridge.

Cornar nodded at Ordreth's report. His nephew said they had seen the crater's top while exploring the mountaintop. The crater was seven stories below a balcony overhanging the western side of the peaks.

"That puts the crater's center around the twenty-eight floor," Nordal said, stroking his chin.

Igan nodded. "Although... the point of impact might be on one of the others. I say we search from the twenty-fifth to the thirty-first floors."

"Agreed," Kalder said.

Cornar looked about, eyeing each of the groups. There were eighteen teams total. "Let's make it six floors," Cornar said. "This way we can have three groups searching each floor. Kalder, make the assignments."

Kalder nodded, then fetched each of the group leaders.

"You take the twenty-ninth, Nordal," Kalder said. "The three of us," he gestured to himself, Ordreth, and Cornar, "will take the twenty-eighth."

"I see how this is," Nordal said, dropping his spoon into his empty plate. "You want the find all to yourself."

Kalder raised an eyebrow at Nordal.

"You still have a chance," Ordreth grinned wryly.

Cornar sat back, listening as the warriors bantered.

"So what are we going to tell the prince?" Aron asked, arms folded.

Cornar rubbed his chin thoughtfully. His beard had since grown long and thick. "I think we can use the crater as an excuse to search the higher floors," he said. "The crater is enough of a phenomenon to warrant investigation."

"So… when are we going to kill him?" Ordreth asked hesitantly.

"Hopefully today," Cornar said grimly. "We'll meet after we find the impact point."

"Well," Igan said, standing, "we're going to need to hurry if we want to make this so-called *discovery* before it grows too late in the day."

Kaescis awoke from pleasant dreams, breathing deeply. He turned in his bed, seeing Laeyit lying face down. Kaescis couldn't help but muse on the last two nights. He had never thought Laeyit would be enjoyable as a lover. His mind raced ahead, to the time when they would return home to Mindolarn. To what end could they continue this newfound aspect of their relationship?

A grunt left Laeyit's lips and she stirred. She turned her head toward Kaescis, looking at him with waking eyes. "Good morning." She grinned sensually, ran her hand along the sheets, and then stroked Kaescis's bare chest.

"Good morning," he grinned. Kaescis leaned toward Laeyit, kissing her passionately.

Laeyit held tight to Kaescis's blonde hair even after their embrace. "Today your vengeance will be complete," she said in a breathy voice, her face nearly touching his.

Death… the voices whispered in Kaescis's mind.

"I wish I could be there," Laeyit groaned, her grip still firm.

"You know I cannot allow that, Laeyit," Kaescis said. "You must take the reports from the scouts."

She sighed and slumped back against her pillow. Kaescis eyed her momentarily. *Why didn't I consider her sooner?* he wondered. After a moment, Kaescis threw aside his sheets and dressed quickly. There were still more tasks for him to finish before confronting Mister Dol'shir. He adjusted his shirt while gazing at his armor, standing at the far side of the room. *At no time was I able to change into my armor,* he recounted the vision in Vabenack. If he were to kill Mister Dol'shir at the final moment of the vision, it would be without his armor.

That was not acceptable.

He recounted each of the events that must play out today, noting all the participants.

Amid his accounting, Laeyit rose from the bed and grabbed her clothing, which was strewn across the floor. Her nakedness was distracting, and Kaescis let his gaze linger upon her as she dressed. Laeyit caught him staring and gave him a flirtatious smile. Kaescis suddenly felt youthful again, as when he first met Helgara—but the memory of his deceased wife spurred the voices.

Kill Dol'shir! they chanted in his mind. *Death! Bring us death...*

Kaescis continued dressing but focused on Laeyit. Being with her these past two nights had brought an unreal serenity. He didn't know how, but Laeyit could calm the bloodlust. Staring at her caused the voices to subside.

"I've yearned for decades for you to look at me that way," she said, slipping on her boots.

"You are a determined one, Laeyit," Kaescis admitted. "If all the women of the empire were like you, we would have conquered the world years ago."

She blushed at the compliment—a reaction Kaescis had never seen from her.

After giving Laeyit a final quick embrace, Kaescis exited his private room and strode into the common area of his chambers. He opened the tent door, finding two Crimson Praetorians standing guard.

"I need you to find Practil," Kaescis said to the Praetorians. "I have an important task for him that must be discussed at once."

⊰•⊱

The rooms of the twenty-eight floor weren't all that different from elsewhere in the Hall of the Guardians.

Cornar and his group split off from the others—Kalder and his band went to the north while Ordreth and his group searched to the south. It was Cornar's plan to fan out and search all along the crater. He supposed many rooms were exposed to the elements. Each would be worth searching.

It wasn't long before they reached the first demolished room. Like the hallway they first encountered, the western wall was missing. The entire room was in ruin and lacked any indentifying features to indicate its original purpose.

"These all look more like caves than anything else," Kamdir remarked.

"I wonder how long these rooms have been exposed," Igan said, squinting thoughtfully.

Cautious, Cornar stepped into the room. The gaping hole allowed a view to other parts of the crater. He could see other rooms open to the elements. Each looked the same. From what Cornar could tell, they seemed close to the impact point.

"Let's leave a marker," Cornar said, striding to the room's entrance. He drew his serrated dagger and carved a mark in the doorframe, adorning it with his initials.

They wound their way southward. Though the rooms were beside each other, not many were close to adjoining hallways. They found hardly anything besides rubble. After a couple of hours, Cornar and his trio caught up to the mark left behind by Ordreth and his group.

"Well, that was a bust," Kamdir said, and slumped against the doorframe.

Cornar, however, strode into the room, stopping at the edge of the gaping opening. *If you want me to find this* thing *so badly, why don't you tell me* exactly *where to look?* Cornar thought, gazing across the horizon.

He waited for a moment. But why was he waiting for a reply? This creature from his dreams wasn't some deity, was he…?

A light hand rested on Cornar's shoulder, and he turned, seeing Igan. "We should get back," he suggested. "This obviously wasn't the floor we needed."

Cornar nodded with a smile. Igan's levelheaded nature always kept expeditions on track. The wizard could easily set aside his emotions, even in the most perilous circumstances.

So Cornar led his group back through the twenty-eight floor.

The wooded cove was exactly as Solidin had envisioned. He stood at the bow of the *Vigilance* with Gladis and Kaldarin, each clad in their white armor.

"The first wave is ready," Kaldarin said.

"Good," Solidin nodded, watching as the sailors readied the longboats.

The small craft were lowered, filled with members of the Sapphire Guard. Sailors rowed the boats to the surf not fifty phineals away from the *Vigilance*. Dozens of members of the Sapphire Guard hurried out of the longboats, emptying the boats within seconds.

As the longboats returned, Teviz sauntered across the main deck. "I suppose I owe you an apology," the captain said with a grunt. Solidin had heard of Teviz's surprise when the storm in the Anomalous Corridor suddenly parted and gave them safe passage. Solidin had missed the elf's shock, having slept through the entire ordeal.

"You're fine," Solidin said in Common, returning his gaze back to the longboats. Another wave of the Sapphire Guard was boarding the boats. "You had no way of knowing I spoke the truth."

Solidin returned his gaze to the beach, watching as Fingas led a group of twenty to the east. They vanished beneath a veil of invisibility as they entered the trees.

Prior to Fingas's departure, Solidin had received word from his scouts. The Mindolarnians had arrived on the island before the Sapphire Guard. They had moored three of their ships along the island's piers, but one warship now sailed to the east—undoubtedly meant to enact a pincer strategy against the *Vigilance*. The moored ships were mostly empty, with only their crew and a handful of soldiers and mages. Fingas was to engage them.

The main body of Mindolarnians, however, was nowhere to be found. Several scouts searched the area around the towering buildings, but found no trace of them.

Another group on the beach—led by Silrian—marched to the west. Silrian's forces were to eliminate any Mindolarnians keeping watch from the mountains or the towering buildings. A few of Silrian's mages wielded long channeling staffs, which would enable swift execution of anyone watching from Dalgilur's rooftops.

With the spies and lookouts eliminated, Solidin and the rest of his forces could search Dalgilur for the rest of the Mindolarnians. *Today, you die, half-breed prince,* Solidin vowed, then turned to Teviz.

"Once we are away, cloak the ship," Solidin said. "If all goes well, we'll be back sometime tonight."

⟡

Cornar and his group were near the stairs leading to the lower floors when an excited shout reached their ears. "Cor!" Nordal exclaimed, "Cor, we found it!"

Kamdir, his interest piqued, quickened his pace. He hurried past Igan and Cornar to join Nordal and Midar, eagerly asking questions about the find. Nordal answered the questions, but turned to his mentor once Cornar was near. "Tinal had to blast a hole in the wall, but we found it."

Igan frowned at Tinal. "You… what…?" he demanded. The younger wizard shied away, ashamed.

"Don't worry, it wasn't a support wall," Nordal said, waving his hand in a placating manner. "And the opening is barely the size of a door. Besides, the walls are thick!" The warrior spread his arms wide.

Igan cocked his head, staring at Nordal with a furrowed brow. The wizard wasn't amused.

"We didn't discover it until our second pass," Nordal continued, "but I *knew* we were missing something. There was just too much space between those two rooms. There had to be something else there—I mean, why would the architects of this place deliberately leave out a room?"

That intrigued Cornar. *A vault?* he wondered.

"Anyway," Nordal continued, "the room is massive, and only part of its wall was destroyed."

"What was in it?" Igan asked, his tone nearly incredulous.

"Just a plain pillar with a crack," Nordal said. Then his demeanor changed. His eyes widened with exhilaration. "We can make it seem like something grand… Surely, Kaescis will come investigate it. This will be the perfect trap, Cor!"

Cornar grinned. "Go find Kalder," he told Nordal. "Midar, take us to this room. Tinal, wait for Ordreth and any others assigned to the upper floors." Cornar then turned to Nordal. "Once you've directed Kalder, go fetch the others."

"Yes, Cor," Nordal said with a nod, then hurried off.

It didn't take long for Midar to guide Cornar and the others to the impact point.

They came to a pair of double doors leading into an anteroom. Midar said he and the others speculated that this was a usually large dwelling for one of the Keepers. It was that speculation that led Nordal to his decision.

The men passed through the anteroom and into a large sitting room. Beautiful furniture with golden trim and green velvet cushions was arranged in square configurations throughout the space. A few hallways branched off from this room, on the right and left sides. Midar mentioned that the other rooms of this dwelling were exposed to the elements—on either side of the secret room.

Cornar, however, was drawn to the circular hole marring the far wall. Chatter sounded behind him, but Cornar ignored it. He felt that irresistible pull toward the hole and the vault beyond. This *was* the place where the voice had compelled him to go.

As Cornar neared the opening, a pillar of light shone into the vault. He stepped through the hole in the wall, seeing that the wall was nearly as thick as a man was tall. The Keepers obviously meant for this room to stay hidden.

Once through the hole, Cornar cautiously surveyed the space. It was a plain gray, except for orange shards and jagged gray stone protruding from the walls—they looked to be impaled, as the walls showed signs of cracking. The vault was wider than it was deep. At first glance, Cornar supposed it was about fifty phineals wide and thirty phineals deep, rising two stories.

The hole which marred the western wall was jagged, and nearly ten phineals in diameter. Sunlight shone through that hole, beaming across the room and ending at a waist-high pillar in the center of the space. The pillar was the only thing in the vault, apart from the rubble.

What was this place? He wandered through the vault, examining the walls. The orange rock seemed unnatural and glistened.

"… was harder the farther my spell burrowed," Tinal said. "I think I spent several minutes trying to get my spell to penetrate the wall completely. It almost felt like something was dispelling my magic."

Cornar cocked his head, noting that Ordreth and his group must be in the other room. He didn't look for his nephew, though. That irresistible urge filled Cornar with an urgency to uncover what lay hidden in this vault.

Consumed with curiosity, Cornar's eyes were on the pillar. It was just as plain as the rest of the room, but was off-white—almost ivory in color. It was about a phineal wide and rose two-and-a-half phineals from the ground. Cornar rounded the pillar, finding a gash along its western side.

Intrigued, Cornar looked at the hole in the wall, then at the gash. The two points were almost perfectly aligned.

"What did you find, Cor?" Igan asked, standing with Tinal just beside the crude doorway.

"I don't know…" Cornar trailed off, kneeling beside the pillar. *This pillar is hollow,* he thought, noting darkness beyond the gash. He glanced back to the hole in the wall, perplexed. If something tore through that wall, wouldn't it have destroyed the pillar too? He looked around him, noting gray and brown rubble.

Shaking his head, Cornar slid his hand along the gash's edge. *What could have cracked this while leaving the rest of it intact?*

A soft hum resonated from the pillar, and then its western side changed. Four grooves appeared, like a transmutative shift, forming a square. Gray-green light flickered from the grooves, and another groove appeared, cutting horizontally down the square's center.

"By Heleron's Trident…" Cornar muttered, still kneeling.

The stone within the flickering lines depressed into the pillar, then split apart, violently disappearing.

Impossible…

Cornar stared at the pillar with amazement. Where had the rest of its surface gone?

Sunlight illuminated the pillar's hollow interior, revealing thick layers of dust. The dust coated several objects: two dark-red tomes standing upright and five red rectangular cases—the same width as the tomes—stacked atop each other. The seven objects barely fit in the hollow space.

"What was that?" Midar shouted, entering the vault with Kamdir. Ordreth and Sharon were right behind them, followed by Demsal and Hem.

Footsteps hurried around Cornar, but he ignored his companions. Those objects in the pillar beckoned to Cornar. How was that possible? Still kneeling, Cornar leaned forward.

"So, someone was hiding some texts?" Kamdir asked quizzically.

"Seems an odd purpose for such a large room," Midar remarked.

This is your destiny, Cornar Dol'shir, that booming voice echoed in his mind. The irresistible urge intensified, and Cornar reached his hand toward the tomes, but Ordreth quickly snatched his uncle's wrist.

"Wait, Uncle," Ordreth urged. "Let Sharon check it."

Sharon knelt beside Cornar, adjusting her thieving lenses.

"Are you okay, Cor?" Igan asked. Igan's question and Ordreth's grip awakened Cornar from that compelled stupor. Why had he reached for the opening? Normally, Cornar would have one of the thieves investigate such a find. It was all too common for ancient vaults and treasure troves to hold traps. Had that creature from his dreams caused him to throw caution to the wind? Perhaps Cornar underestimated that… *thing.*

"I… I don't see anything," Sharon said, removing her lenses.

"Odd," Igan remarked doubtfully. "This pillar is obviously a tevisral of some kind."

A brief debate of speculation sounded in the vault, but Cornar reached for one of the dark-red tomes. He could faintly make out a numeral on the spine, "Two." Cornar pulled the tome from the pillar and dusted off its cover, a thick leather-like substance. The cover lacked any signs of decay, and the pages were like those books found in the Keepers' Temple.

He continued dusting the cover, feeling an embossing on the surface. Cornar turned the tome to face him and started. That strange symbol he had seen all over the Keepers' Temple marked the center of the cover. Seven sharp points protruded from a hendecagon, all arrayed above three claws clutching a circle.

"We saw that in Klindill!" Hem exclaimed.

"That symbol was all over the temple," Demsal added.

Cornar opened the cover, wafting dust into the air. He flipped past a blank sheet, coming to the tome's title page: "*The Thousand Years War. A narrative compilation by Dusel Nadim, Volume Two.*"

Dusel Nadim? Cornar wondered. This volume was definitely not one found in the Keepers' Temple. But the title was familiar. Solidin claimed that name was the correct term for the fabled Dragon Wars.

Confused and intrigued, Cornar flipped through the pages. The text was written in the Common language, but in an old style that Cornar had only seen once before. From what Cornar gleaned from skimming the text, this tome was a chronological reckoning of a war between the Kaldean Alliance and the Cheserithean Empire. The author—Dusel Nadim—gave commentary on battles and strategies. He often referenced names that were unpronounce-able—long names that were sharp and guttural.

Throughout Cornar's survey of the tome more of his men returned. After a while, everyone was gathered in the vault.

Still holding the tome, Cornar looked at his men. They gazed at him with concern. How long had he been absorbed in the tome?

"It's that interesting a book, huh?" Gregan asked with a chuckle. "Kalder and I have come up with a strategy."

"Good," Cornar nodded, then glanced at the tome. "And we have a legiti-mate find."

"What is it, Uncle?" Ordreth asked.

A few of the other warriors asked similar questions.

Cornar was about to answer when Igan spoke. "Is this something we want to claim for ourselves?" the wizard asked.

It was the appointed time.

Finally, Kaescis thought. The voices' cries had grown louder—they too were eager.

Today, the son of my enemy dies. Kaescis envisioned a glorious battle, maiming Mister Dol'shir and forcing him to watch as the members of his band were cut down, one by one.

A thrill of bloodlust surged through Kaescis as the voices cried out in unison, *Bring us that death! Give us destruction!* Reveling in visions of his coming triumph, Kaescis spun from the war camp. He gestured for a group of Prae-torians surrounding Practil to follow him. The servant was clad in Kaescis's Triaindium Suit.

Kaescis marched westward, and the Praetorians trailed behind him. Practil, however, walked beside Kaescis. Practil had been hesitant when Kaescis ap-proached him about the task, but Practil eventually capitulated.

"I appreciate your acceptance of this task, Practil," Kaescis said graciously. "You have served me well."

"Thank you, Your Imperial Highness," Practil said, attempting a bow of his head. He looked clunky in that armor. The pieces of the Triaindium Suit were a tad oversized for him.

They continued in silence across the enormous chamber until Practil ventured a question. "Where are we going, Your Imperial Highness?"

Kaescis grinned with anticipation. "The twenty-ninth floor of the western wing," he said. "But I'll don my armor before then."

⎯⎯◆⎯⎯

It was near noon when Cornar's men finished preparing for the assault. The majority of his band would conceal themselves in the other rooms. Once Kaescis entered the vault they would attack the prince's Praetorian Guard. Cornar decided that the vault would be the best place to isolate Kaescis.

Ordreth was insistent that his group be the ones to inform Kaescis of the discovery. Cornar hated the idea of putting his nephew in danger, but Ordreth cleverly convinced Cornar that he should be the one to spring the trap.

Soon after Ordreth departed, Cornar returned to reading the tome chronicling the Thousand Years War. Cornar turned the pages, skimming their contents. Dragons were continually mentioned, as if they were commonplace. One passage claimed the dragons, elves, and humans all gathered in the elven city of Kardorth. Their coalition—the Kaldean Alliance—was repelled by their enemies and forced to fall back to the heart of the elven realm.

Cornar flipped through more pages, noting the author's prolific references to dragons and their unpronounceable names.

But they're not real... Cornar told himself, struggling with the idea of dragons roaming Kalda and mingling with men and elves. He mulled over the thoughts as his men prepared themselves in the adjoining room.

Cornar flipped another page, finding a hand-drawn illustration of exquisite detail. It depicted an amulet made of gleaming white, most likely a precious metal. The upper half of the amulet consisted of seven curved petals surrounding what looked amazingly like an eye—an oval slit holding a many-faceted gemstone as if it were an iris. Below the petals and the oval slit, the lower half of the amulet consisted of three draconic talons extending downward and gripping a large black sphere. Tiny specks within it looked like stars in the night sky.

The words at the diagram's top caught his eye: *"Au'misha'k, el Amul tila Draco Silisra, the Amulet of Draconic Control."*

More text was arrayed around the diagram, with lines pointing to different parts of the amulet. The text linked to the black sphere read: *"Shiz'nak or the Tethering Stone."* Another line went to the brilliant ruby. *"Lish'nacht'nal or the Ruby of Lish."* One of the lines pointed above the sphere: *"Til'tak'shak, or the Key of the Stars."* The last line pointed to just below the oval opening: *"Ka'nakar or the Activating Key."*

Cornar blinked in disbelief, then read the text on the page beside the diagram.

"... This was their last hope. The Kaldean Alliance was outnumbered and overpowered.

Forging the Amulet proved to be their only means of achieving victory. So, the Irum'mak'sha spent decades in the pursuit of constructing this immense tevisral. They theorized that a weapon of this magnitude would end the war. And it did. Throughout the rest of this volume I will prove to you that the Au'misha'k enabled the overthrow and utter destruction of the Cheserithean Empire. The Amulet's power laid claim to every red dragon that encountered it. None but Cheserith himself was able to defy its power…"

That passage sent Cornar's mind spinning. *An amulet to control… dragons?* he wondered, turning back to the diagram. Myriad questions filled his mind.

Startled gasps echoed into the vault. Cornar looked up as Kaescis—surrounded by Crimson Praetorians—strode toward the opening between the rooms. *It's too soon!* Cornar thought, abruptly shutting the book. Though Cornar tried stilling his composure, anxiety still twisted his face.

The prince was clad in his golden-red armor and held his helmet at his side. A devious grin spread across his face, and Cornar thought he could see a gleeful anticipation in the prince's violet eyes.

Kaescis waved his freehand, and the Praetorians took up sentinel positions throughout the sitting room.

"My, my… what do we have here?" Kaescis mused, his voice tinged with hostility. He glanced at Cornar's men and then ducked into the hole hewn by Tinal.

Cornar set down the tome, rising to his feet. Had Ordreth made it to the war camp quicker than expected? No. He couldn't have…

"I see you received my summons," Cornar said, attempting a smooth voice.

Kaescis set his jaw, sauntering through the vault. "I don't know what you're talking about."

Cornar started. Though his gaze was fixed on Kaescis, Cornar could see the Praetorians in the other room standing at attention.

The prince rounded the hollow pillar, glancing at the tome atop it. "And what is this?" Kaescis asked, picking up the tome and setting his helmet in its place.

Cornar's eyes settled on the helmet. *I could throw it out the hole…* he thought. That would give him an advantage. Cornar hadn't expected Kaescis to arrive clad in his armor. That suit of his was extraordinary, and Cornar doubted he could defeat the prince while he wore it… After all, the Sapphire Guard had failed to penetrate the armor.

Kaescis flipped through the tome's pages, then started. His violet eyes widened. "The Crimson Eye…" he muttered, staring with horror at the open tome.

The prince seemed completely unaware in that moment.

Now's my chance, Cornar thought, grabbing the helmet. "Attack!"

59

WRATH

Kaescis jerked from the tome, starting with horror. His helmet—
hurled by Mister Dol'shir—sailed through this vault of sorts and
through a crude opening, clanging against hewn stone.

"No!" Kaescis cried, dropping the tome and taking a step back. *That tome,*
he cursed. He glimpsed the depiction of the Crimson Eye on the opened
page. Had it evoked enough dismay to distract him? No matter. Kaescis had a
foe to slay. And this man *deserved* that fate.

Suddenly, Mister Dol'shir advanced with a lunge, drawing his weapons.

Kaescis threw his hand aside, uttering the incantation to muster his massive
Ko'delish blade. The black mist burst from his pores, coalescing into a shaft,
but before the blade formed it puffed into smoke. It was if the Ko'delish just
evaporated.

"Impossible—"

Dol'shir's weapon swung toward Kaescis. Perplexed and enraged, Kaescis
dodged the blows, raising his gauntleted freehand to defend himself.

Kaescis uttered the incantation once again, but the result was the same. He
dodged more blows from Mister Dol'shir and parried the man's serrated dagger. They exchanged blows—Kaescis punching and Mister Dol'shir swinging
and stabbing his weapons.

The sounds of battle resounded from the sitting room—the Crimson Praetorians and Mister Dol'shir's band clashing.

Kaescis parried both of his opponent's weapons, exposing himself while also exposing his foe. Mister Dol'shir aimed a kick at the same time that
Kaescis's foot shot toward the warrior, but Kaescis was faster, landing a blow
against the warrior's midsection that sent him tumbling.

With significant distance now between them, Kaescis threw his hand aside again, uttering the incantation a third time. As with each attempt, the Ko'delish appeared but wisped away before forming his blade.

What is wrong? he thought in confusion, watching Mister Dol'shir recover. *Why won't it manifest?* Kaescis was drawn to one of the large orange shards protruding from the wall. The shard was translucent and absorbed the surrounding light.

Mister Dol'shir made another advance. Kaescis attempted to block, but the warrior landed blows against Kaescis's armored ribs.

That rock… Kaescis blocked another blow from the dagger while parrying the short-sword. He had never seen rock like those orange shards. They seemed somehow alien—not of this world.

Dol'shir's dagger swung toward Kaescis's face. The blade grazed Kaescis's cheek, drawing blood. The wound pulled Kaescis back to the fight with a fury. He grappled Mister Dol'shir's arm wielding the serrated dagger, pulling it across the man's chest. Kaescis then charged, warding the short-sword away with his freehand while slamming Mister Dol'shir into the wall.

Kaescis repeatedly smashed his knees against his foe's groin until the warrior managed to get his short-sword free. Kaescis attempted to evade the blow, but the blade cut his ear. The pain was enraging. He grabbed Mister Dol'shir with both gauntleted hands and threw the warrior across the room. The warrior landed with a thud and skidded.

Those are no ordinary rocks, Kaescis thought. *Are they preventing my blade from forming?* He knew of objects that could nullify magic. The ancient Kaldean Alliance had possessed many of them. One of their notorious suits of armor used a ring to nullify magical effects—it enabled its wearer to pass through barsion. The ring was made of tazerin. Tazerin was not of Kalda. It fell only from the sky. Tazerin was such a rare substance that any known deposits had been mined centuries ago.

The sounds of Mister Dol'shir recovering snapped Kaescis back to reality. Kaescis couldn't remain in this room if he wanted the upper hand. Here, in this vault of sorts, they were on equal ground.

— ⊃•⊂ —

Cornar scrambled to his feet. Realization spread across the prince's face, and then Kaescis dashed out of the vault.

Are you retreating already? Cornar grunted, feeling sore from the prince's assault. He followed Kaescis into the sitting room, where the battle between the Praetorians and the other warriors was raging.

Praetorians were casting offensive spells as they dueled with Cornar's men. Barsion from Vargos shrouded the warriors, and their weapons glowed with rainbow hues from elemental and arcane imbuings from the wizards. Igan was mustering a swarm of arcane orbs—pink light almost veiled the wizard from sight as hundreds of the orbs took shape around him. The younger wizards and Clodin were hurling their own magics into the fray—lightning streaked from Renal while Tinal launched a volley of disintegrating bolts. Clodin's acidic javelin struck one of the Praetorians, weakening his foe's barsion.

Cornar was drawn back to Kaescis. The prince dashed through the room, uttering those sharp incantations. He barreled past two of the warriors and knocked them to the ground. White magic surrounded the prince and wisped into the gems of his armor. It was undoubtedly an enhancing spell.

Two more of the warriors spun to meet Kaescis—Morgad and Naelis—but the prince leapt, kicking Naelis and using the man as a stepping stone to soar through the air. Kaescis sailed over Morgad and several other warriors. Cornar hurried past his men, chasing after Kaescis.

In mid-air, Kaescis uttered that same incantation he had spoken in the vault—the one to summon his monstrous blade. Black magic clustered around Kaescis's right hand, and the blade formed. At that moment, Cornar realized the prince's intentions. Kaescis was falling toward Vargos.

"Vargos!" Cornar shouted to the barsionist. But it was too late. Old Vargos spun in time to see Kaescis falling toward him. The barsionist attempted to dodge, but Kaescis threw the newly formed Darkness blade like a javelin. That monstrous sword shattered the barsion and impaled Vargos through the stomach.

Vargos's eyes widened in shocked realization.

"No!" Cornar cried, barreling past his men.

Kaescis landed atop Vargos, crushing the barsionist's leg. An agonized wail filled the room but abruptly died as Kaescis removed his monstrous blade. The prince turned, twirling his weapon in the air as if it weighed nothing. A diabolical grin lit his face. He met Cornar's eyes for a moment, but then swept his gaze across the room.

"I," Kaescis declared, "I am the Champion of Cheserith!"

Cornar pushed past more of his men fighting the Praetorians. Others— Gregan, Haetan, Kamdir, Kalder, Nordal, and Midar—were converging on Kaescis. They yelled battle cries as they charged.

"No!" Cornar shouted, running as fast as he could. "Stop, you fools!"

But there was nowhere else for the men to go. Of course, they could move down the halls, but Kaescis would chase them. These men, as valiant as they were, charged unwaveringly toward an impossible foe. If they didn't advance, Kaescis would undoubtedly move against the other mages and those fighting the Praetorians.

"I was Chosen by his Messenger!" Kaescis shouted as Gregan neared him. The warrior swung his fanisar at Kaescis's exposed face.

Defiantly, Kaescis sliced through the fanisar, severing the shaft in half. Gregan evaded, but Kaescis's blade continued in its sweeping arc, cutting through the warrior's arm and chest.

Gregan! Cornar clenched his teeth while running through what was now a cleared path. He watched with horror as one of his dearest friends fell to the floor in pieces.

"And I will cleanse the world!" Kaescis shouted, advancing on Haetan.

Haetan lunged, screaming for his fallen cousin—but the cry was immediately halted as Kaescis's blade severed Haetan's head from his shoulders.

Within a matter of seconds, both cousins lay lifeless on the floor.

"Before *His* coming," Kaescis continued, advancing on Kamdir, "I will eliminate *His* enemies!"

Kamdir rolled sideways to avoid the blow—he obviously intended to be a distraction to allow the others a chance to strike.

"And I will purify Kalda!" Kaescis shouted, swinging his misting black blade in a wide arc that caught Kamdir by the arm and nicked his chest.

The young warrior rolled over once, losing his arm above the elbow. A gash marred his chest, and black particles festered around the wound, devouring flesh, bone, and blood.

Kamdir struggled for breath and his eyes met Cornar's for a moment. An overwhelming sense of paternal protection welled within Cornar. That young man was like another son, and Kaescis would not take Kamdir from him.

You will not take my men! Cornar vowed. *I will preserve them!* Cornar lunged toward the vile prince—weapons extended—as Kalder, Nordal, and Midar converged in a unified attack.

Kaescis raised his blade, reveling with sadistic glee while attacking Kalder. "None will stand to oppose—"

Cornar intercepted the blade. Black particles misted from the prince's weapon and wisped into Cornar's serrated dagger. The dagger *absorbed* the devouring particles and glowed with a deathly light. In a flash of movement, Cornar struck the monstrous blade with his short-sword, and it too began absorbing the Darkness magic.

"Clever…" Kaescis growled, retracting his blade while stepping back over the dead.

"Slay the Praetorians," Cornar shouted, dropping into a wide stance, his weapons spread to shield his men. "Once they are dealt with, secure the vault."

—◦•◦—

Igan heard Cornar's command to the brash warriors. They had instinctively engaged Kaescis. With their plan in shambles, and all the Praetorians engaged, there was no reason for them *not* to attack the prince. Igan was grateful for their intervention, as Kaescis would have undoubtedly come after the party's other mages.

This was not the last place Igan wanted to see.

Shifting his focus, Igan gazed at a Praetorian fighting Hemrin and Cordel. Though the warriors' barsions had vanished, both were holding their own against the armored Mindolarnian. Igan's eyes fell upon the Praetorian's breastplate, and he willed a volley of arcane orbs toward the armored man.

The Praetorian started at the magical assault. He tried to evade, but Igan manipulated the orbs to strike the breastplate. The two warriors leapt back, barely evading the eruptions. Igan, however, manipulated the explosion, forcing the blast toward the Praetorian. Soon, a crack appeared in the crimson armor. Igan redirected the orbs meant for the Praetorian, sending them circling throughout the room near the ceiling.

Hemrin forced the Praetorian to parry blows from his sword. Cordel moved in, stabbing through the crack in the armor. Within seconds, the warriors disarmed their foe and forced the Praetorian to the ground.

With one Praetorian subdued, Igan scanned the battle for his next foe, but noticed Nordal running back to the vault.

"Cover me!" Nordal shouted to Igan. Nodding, Igan stepped backward toward the hole leading to the vault. However, there wasn't any danger of a Praetorian breaking past the warriors.

As Igan searched for another Praetorian to weaken his eyes fell upon Kamdir. The young warrior was struggling for breath, but there was nothing Igan could do about it. *If only Iltar were here...* he groaned inwardly. Poor Kamdir's wounds looked severe. Kaescis's devouring magic had torn through Kamdir's ribs and dissolved part of the warrior's lung. Igan could see Kamdir's heart beating.

It was an inhuman sight.

Repeated pounding echoed from the vault. What was Nordal doing? Igan peered through the hole, but Nordal was around the corner. No matter, there were more important things to deal with.

Whirling back to the battle, Igan eyed the two Praetorians fighting Kalder, Midar, Kren, and Drenor. Both Praetorians struggled against their foes.

Igan wasted no time, raining the orbs down upon both Praetorians. Amid the assault, he heard Nordal cursing profusely.

What's Nordal doing? Igan wondered, his magic cracking the armor of Kalder's foe. The Praetorian was bleeding within seconds, the warriors taking advantage of the opening.

With only a few arcane orbs left, Igan hurried through the hole to the vault. But to his surprise, the remaining orbs vanished, and Igan could feel his spell no longer. It was as if the orbs were dispelled.

"By all that's magical," Igan murmured.

A slew of curses resounded through the vault, and Igan turned to see Nordal hacking at one of the large orange shards protruding from the wall.

"I can't get this damn thing loose!" the warrior shouted, growling and grunting as he struck the pommel of his sword against the strange rock.

Igan looked back to his hands. Why had the magic vanished?

"Too bad you can't help me," Nordal snarled, his anger directed at the rock. "If you could only blow apart the wall."

"What are you doing?" Igan demanded.

"Trying to get one of these shards," Nordal said. "What else does it look like I'm doing?"

Igan shook his head. "This stuff prevents magic from forming," Nordal said, grunting as he strained to free the orange rock. "I happened to turn when Cor shouted for us to attack. The prince was trying to summon his blade, but he couldn't. We can use this—turn the tide against Kaescis and the Praetorians."

That intrigued Igan. He crept through the vault, searching for any loose fragments. *So, this can nullify magic,* he thought, eyeing the orange rocks impaled in the walls. Could this negate the effects of the storm beyond the island? If so, they wouldn't need to gamble on the elves granting them mercy.

Igan assumed they could evade the Mindolarnians until Solidin arrived to attack. The elf *would* come to Dalgilur. Igan was sure of it. But with this—if it did as Nordal supposed—they could flee to the *Promised Maiden* and set sail before word of Kaescis's death reached the Mindolarnians.

Nordal continued to curse and strain against the large shard as Igan reached the opened end of the pedestal. Another tome—like the one Cor had been reading—was standing on end. Five red porous rectangular cases were neatly stacked beside the tome, their length the same as the tomes' width. But something orange caught his eye.

Might as well take these out, Igan thought, removing the cases. Once he removed two, an orange shard—about the length of his hand—slid from the opening.

"This must have penetrated this… box," Igan muttered, pulling the shard close to his face to examine it.

A light flickered within the hollowed pillar.

Surprised, Igan pulled out the other tome and the three remaining cases—one of which was cracked—and set them on the floor.

Is this pedestal some kind of tevisral? Igan wondered, glancing to the shard in his hand. Intrigued, Igan moved the shard farther away, stretching his arm as far as he could.

More light filled the hollowed pedestal.

"It is," Igan whispered.

"What are you muttering about?" Nordal demanded between curses.

Igan didn't answer. He stepped back, moving almost to the hole leading to the cratered mountainside.

The pedestal's interior became brighter. Soon, it was more luminous than the sun's light at noon. The light then turned red, and a deafening screech resounded throughout the vault and seemed to permeate the entire mountainside—no, the entire island.

The screech soon ceased.

"What on Kalda was that?!" Nordal demanded, turning from his vain attempt. The warrior raised an eyebrow at Igan. "Where did you get that?"

"It was inside," Igan said warily, looking at the shard in his hand. *Was that an alarm?* he wondered.

Luring Kaescis into their trap should have made Ordreth apprehensive. Instead, he felt rather calm about it. Uncle Cor had made his opinion of the prince quite clear. Kaescis must die. He was a threat to all Kalda. And that was good enough for Ordreth.

"Oh, I wish we could stay longer," Hem said, his wide-eyed wonder apparent in his voice.

"Why?" Demsal asked tersely. "How I see it, our stay here has been totally fruitless."

Hem shot Demsal an appalled glance. The two of them continued bantering as they crossed the hall leading to the enormous chamber and the war camp.

Ordreth kept his gaze forward. He had to be calm. He couldn't let the prince see anything other than an eager explorer ready to make a report. In order to make the ruse believable, Ordreth turned his mind to other adventures, where grand discoveries *were* made. Nothing but elation accompanied those memories.

"You're grinning…" Sharon said, her hand brushing against his.

"Just reminiscing," Ordreth replied, taking Sharon's hand in his. He squeezed reassuringly.

Sharon looked tense. "It'll be fine," Ordreth said.

"And what if it's not?" she asked, frowning.

Ordreth took a deep breath and opened his mouth but a deafening screech resounded through the corridor. They all clapped their hands over their ears, and Ordreth heard Demsal shouting, "What on Kalda is that?!"

The sound soon ceased, and Ordreth's elation faded. Grim-faced, he dashed through the corridor, coming to the balcony on the western side of the enormous Hall of the Guardians.

And then, he saw the unfathomable. The enormous statue depicting a dragon was shifting. Its wings fluttered while its tail slithered across the stone floor.

"By all that's magical!" Hem said with a gasp. "Am I *really* seeing this?!" Both Sharon and Demsal gawked with slack jaws.

The dragon-statue *flapped* its stone wings, then lifted itself into the air. It *flew* through the enormous chamber, climbing nearly to the towering ceiling.

With the dragon-statue moved out of its place, the three smaller statues—still twice as large as any man—were *walking* from their pedestals. The weapons they held turned from stone to other substances—by some sort of transmutation, Ordreth assumed. The sword held by the center statue turned to glistening metal while the staffs held by the other two began glowing with what Ordreth could only assume was magic.

The three statues lumbered across the enormous space, following the path the dragon-statue took through the air.

How are they moving…? Ordreth wondered. He looked to his friends, who gazed at the unbelievable sight with amazement.

"Come on," Ordreth urged. "Let's get to Kaescis. Hopefully we can still persuade him to go to Uncle Cor."

<hr>

The reports from Crenai and her scouts of the last two days were quite interesting. Krindal was particularly fascinated by their finds to the north—a whole naval yard concealed within the mountain. Entire ships hung from mounts on the walls. Crenai explained it as "an armada suspended in the air."

Oh, I must see that, Krindal thought, flipping the page of scribed reports. He sat at a table within the Royal ring of the war camp. His eyes went to Bratan, who was at a nearby table examining the weapons found the previous day three levels below the war camp. The weapons were right out of a fairy tale.

Smiling, Krindal returned to the report, but as his eyes fell upon the words, a deafening screech filled the enormous chamber. Krindal fell out of his chair, clutching his ears. Then the noise ceased. Soldiers rushed about, as did Crimson Praetorians. Bratan called for soldiers to investigate the sound. An uproar echoed throughout the entire war camp.

Krindal sat up, but remained on the ground. He had never heard such a noise.

"Are you all right?" Bratan asked, looming over Krindal.

"I... believe so."

"Here," Bratan said, offering his freehand to Krindal. In his other hand, Bratan held a staff. The weapon was divided into thirds by narrow grooves. Long slits ran the length of the end sections. It seemed familiar to Krindal. Reluctantly, Krindal took the Praetorian's hand. Bratan grunted as he helped Krindal, then stomped off with annoyance.

A shadow suddenly veiled the Royal ring. But it vanished as quickly as it had appeared. Bratan tensed, then shouted commands for the nearby soldiers to prepare for combat. The order soon left the Royal ring, and Krindal heard the orders noised throughout the war camp.

"Bratan, what is happening?" Krindal called after the Praetorian, but Bratan didn't answer. "What aren't you telling me?" Bratan disappeared within the Imperial Tent, still clutching that staff.

Unsettled by the lack of answers, Krindal hurried through the war camp. Pandemonium reigned. Squads mobilized. Mages enhanced nearby soldiers. Praetorians hustled to the entrances. Wildmen milled about, awaiting orders from Mindolarnian squad leaders.

That shadow passed again.

Krindal looked up, then started in horror. He cursed under his breath and his eyes widened. One of the white statues—the one representing a dragon—was *flying* through the Hall of the Guardians. He had heard tales of statues coming to life, but he had thought they were just that—tales. Krindal had never considered they were real—but then again, this was the home of the ancients.

The dragon flapped its wings, and the stone of the massive span seemed to ripple—but how could stone *ripple?*

A Wildman bumped into Krindal, nearly knocking him off balance, and the dragon-statue soared overhead once again, casting another shadow.

That noise... Was it an alarm? Had someone intruded on something forbidden within Dalgilur?

The dragon-statue swooped by again. It was studying them... the Mindolarnians, the war camp. Was it sensing whether they were intruders? No one beside Krindal was attuned to Dalgilur. Surely, they *would* be seen as intruders.

Panic struck Krindal. He ran, pushing his way past soldiers and Wildmen. He wound through the war camp, making his way to the entrance aligned with the massive twenty-story doors.

I need to distance myself, he thought. *I can hide in one of the buildings outside.* Krindal dashed out of the war camp, passing a group of mobilizing soldiers and Wildmen. As he neared the massive doors, they swung open. *But I'm not close enough…* Krindal thought, then his panic turned to dread.

Krindal abruptly stopped as the massive portico became visible through the doorway. Dozens—no hundreds—of figures in white armor marched through the portico and toward the opening doors. They gleamed with bluish tints—undoubtedly barsion barriers—their weapons also shining with auras of destructive magics.

Not them! Krindal froze. Though he couldn't see their pointed ears, Krindal *knew* they were those relentless elves.

Behind the armored elves marched colossal conjurations towering almost five times the height of a man. They were elementals of fire, ice, and stone. Gray skinned horrors were mingled in the ranks of the invaders—creatures that *consumed* magic. When enthralled, these nightmarish monsters were a mage's bane. It was no wonder they were called mages' parasites.

But the most horrifying sight marched at the head of this invading army. He was the one responsible for the massacre resulting in the deaths of Krindal's friends and scholarly cohorts—Solidin, the Swift-Dagger. Clad in his white plate armor with a blue emblem emblazoned across his breastplate, the notorious elf twirled his two short daggers.

Oh no… not him! Krindal wanted to scream, but no sound left his lips. He tried to retreat, but stumbled, landing on the cold stone floor.

The Sapphire Guard had arrived, and Krindal was doomed.

Despite his efforts, several more of Cornar's warriors had succumbed to Kaescis's deadly blade. Naelis and Corbai were sprawled upon the floor, their bodies nearly mangled beyond recognition. Three others lay in pieces, cut down by the vile prince: Rediban, Durdar, and Yenal.

His blades glowing with stolen power, Cornar lunged toward Kaescis. He landed a blow against the prince's breastplate, but instead of eroding the armor the black mist wisped into the gems inlaid in Kaescis's suit. The gems immediately reformed the magic into a type of damaging shield, but Cornar's weapons simply reabsorbed the shield. Kaescis spun, yelling with such rage that his mouth frothed.

The two men clashed, unleashing blow after blow against each other. Cornar parried the blows, getting in an occasional swing that nicked Kaescis's armor. The prince, however, was not as fortunate.

It's working, Cornar thought, blocking a blow from that monstrous sword. A total blackness veiled both his serrated dagger and short-sword. The weapons had absorbed so much of the Darkness magic that they could probably cut through solid stone as if it were wet parchment.

Cornar got in another glancing blow against Kaescis's arm. Despite the armor siphoning the magic persisting around his blades, Cornar's weapons remained sufficiently enhanced.

"You can't do this forever!" Kaescis growled, swinging at Cornar in a flurry of blows. Cornar blocked each perfectly. The prince yelled with rage, undoubtedly infuriated at Cornar's skill. Kaescis took one step back, moving beyond the range of Cornar's sword.

The battle continued between Cornar's men and the Praetorians. Only a few were left. A few of his warriors had fallen to the Praetorians: Hemir and Morgad were among them. Cornar counted the casualties. *Eleven,* he thought in despair. He had let eleven of his companions fall. The very thought of their deaths sickened him. If only they had been able to implement their plan, things would have been different.

Kaescis steadied himself, then dashed toward the fray.

Oh no you don't! Cornar thought, running parallel to Kaescis.

The prince ran straight to Aron and Shen. But before Kaescis reached them, Cornar tackled the prince. They fell to the floor, and Cornar reared back, slamming his weapons point down into Kaescis's breastplate.

"You're a persistent bastard!" Kaescis shouted. "Just like your father!" The mention of Melthas Dol'shir struck Cornar with realization. Everything he had dreamed was true. Kaescis *was* the man who had murdered his father.

"And you'll die just like him!" the prince shouted. Kaescis grabbed Cornar by his mail shirt and threw him aside—Kaescis's additional strength from his armor enabled him to hurl Cornar like a rag doll. Cornar hit stone and slumped to the ground. His vision spun, and he staggered to his feet.

Kaescis, however, was already bolting toward Monaris—another of Cornar's warriors. The man met the prince's blade with a blood-curling scream. Yelling, Kaescis spun around the falling warrior and cut down another of Cornar's men.

"No…" Cornar stumbled forward.

Kaescis advanced upon Jorkal and Rinder, but as he lifted his black sword it puffed to mist, then vanished. Even the gems in Kaescis's armor—which were clouded in blackness—became transparent. Magic all throughout the room disappeared in like manner. Light that shone from all sides of the room—walls and ceiling—flickered and dimmed.

The prince started with horror, then turned toward the hole leading to the vault. Cornar continued forward, still staggering, but glanced in the direction of Kaescis's gaze.

Igan emerged from the crude doorway, holding an orange shard above his head. "You will not slay our men any longer, Kaescis!" the wizard shouted, stepping farther into the room.

Nordal moved through the crude opening. He too held an orange rock, but Nordal's was much larger than Igan's. The warrior cradled it under one arm while wielding his sword with the other. As Nordal came beside the wizard the room was plunged into darkness.

"There were some men of the Cheserithean Empire who saw the deceit of their so-called God. Those men found their way to Aridia. Over the years, others fled to Aridia, the birthplace of ancient humanity on Kalda. It was a beautiful place, until the onset of the war."

- From *The Thousand Years War, Part I*, page 46

Cornar blinked as his eyes adjusted to the sudden darkness. The lack of light, however, didn't stop the conflict. Sparks flew as metal clanged against metal. The brief flickers flashed images of the combatants.

Still slightly disoriented, Cornar searched for Kaescis. The prince was struggling against Jorkal, defending himself with his gauntleted hands. Amid Jorkal's assault, Kaescis grabbed the warrior's sword, then kicked Jorkal in the stomach. The jolt sent the warrior backward, separating him from his sword.

Kaescis twirled his newly seized weapon, turning to face Cornar. "Using that tazerin will only put you at a disadvantage," the prince said, and shook his head. Kaescis noticed Jorkal rebounding, and the prince executed a flurry of swings that forced the warrior to evade.

Tazerin? Cornar wondered. Was the prince referring to the orange rocks? Those rocks seemed to snuff out magic. That gave Cornar an idea. Cornar and his band could use the rocks to escape Dalgilur. If the so-called tazerin dispelled magic, it would dispel the storm, enabling the *Promised Maiden* to sail unmolested.

Invigorated by the thought, Cornar burst toward Kaescis. He clashed with the prince, then sliced his short-sword at Kaescis's face, barely cutting the prince's chin. Cornar couldn't quite tell, but he thought he saw blood dripping down the prince's armor.

Kaescis cursed and jolted backward. In near frantic haste, the prince pushed through the battle and fled. *You're not getting away that easily,* Cornar vowed, turning toward Kalder. "Get everyone to the *Promised Maiden!*" he yelled and then dashed after Kaescis. "I'll join you!" As Cornar ran, he heard several of his men—including Igan and Nordal—shouting after him.

The hallway outside was dim. The walls and ceiling near the sitting room were darkened, but light spilled into the darkness farther down the hall. Kaescis was in the lit part of the corridor, dashing away while mustering white enhancing magic. The prince glanced over his shoulder, smiling sinisterly as his violet eyes fell upon Cornar.

A surge of exhilaration filled Solidin. He had led the Sapphire Guard into this place hewn out of the mountain. His eyes fell upon the aged necromancer from Soroth, who gazed at him and the Sapphire Guard in utter fright.

You brought them here, Solidin thought. *I will not permit you to infect this place any longer.*

Noises of war carried from beyond the coward. Soldiers poured out of the war camp. Their ranks were mingled with the primitives of Klindala—though these did not look exactly like the Wildmen Solidin and the others had seen. They were more human. Solidin noted that there were nearly as many Wildmen as there were Mindolarnians.

Outnumbered nearly five to one, Solidin thought, twirling his blades as he continued his march.

A Praetorian caught Solidin's eye, pushing through the ranks of the army. It was that brutish man who had helped the half-breed prince lead the assault on the Keepers' Temple. *Bratan was it?* Bratan was part of the half-breed prince's powerful triad—the so-called Decimators of Angolith. But instead of wielding a fanisar—the typical Praetorian weapon—Bratan held a staff of intricate design.

Isn't that odd—

Bratan twirled the weapon, holding it near its ends. The staff glowed a vibrant green, then axe-blades formed upon its ends. The transformation was unlike anything Solidin had ever witnessed—magic became matter. Both metal axe-blades of Bratan's staff-turned-fanisar glowed with a green aura.

Most would have paled at the sight of such a weapon, but Solidin relished its existence. Bratan's double-bladed fanisar was obviously of ancient origin. Its presence was a testament that Dalgilur held secrets well beyond the wildest dreams of the Elven Aristocracy of Merdan.

Fueled with exhilaration, Solidin shouted in Elvish, "Let the cleansing begin!" He raised a dagger into the air, signaling the charge. The roaring thunder of footfalls echoed around him, and Solidin dashed straight for the cowering scholar.

Bratan, however, moved straight for Solidin. The brutish Praetorian dashed past the petrified scholar, swinging that glorious fanisar at Solidin. Parrying the blow, Solidin maneuvered closer to Bratan and struck at the seam between breastplate and pauldron. He struck again, and again, before Bratan retaliated. Solidin dodged the blow, then landed three more strikes.

Out of the corner of his eye, Solidin noticed the aged scholar stumbling to his feet. At that moment, the ranks of the Sapphire Guard flooded around Solidin and Bratan. The Mindolarnians were also charging, and both forces clashed.

Solidin lunged again at Bratan, but the Praetorian intercepted the piercing daggers. The acidic aura of Bratan's fanisar clashed with the imbued dispel around the dagger, but didn't reach the blade. Solidin's dagger was still sharp. Bratan yelled as he swung blow after blow. Solidin defended himself, but managed several piercing strikes against that same spot on Bratan's armor.

A shadow veiled Solidin and Bratan for a moment, but Solidin didn't dare avert his gaze. He parried, blocked, and landed an occasional blow. Solidin's barsion flickered under the acid of Bratan's fanisar. Amid their intense duel, Solidin was thrown sideways. The force felt like a blast from a kineticist. He landed on the floor, then skidded back up onto his feet.

Bratan charged, twirling his fanisar.

Another combatant was close to where Solidin had been repulsed, her hand outstretched. It was that woman, the same who was hurled into the chasm around the Keepers' Temple, Laeyit—the third member of the half-breed prince's deadly trio. *She survived,* Solidin mused, dashing to intercept Bratan.

Laeyit was right beside the hulking Praetorian. She reached to an empty sheath on her back and a haviklur materialized through transmutative means. Laeyit drew the single-sided straight sword from its sheath, and the weapon burst with a shimmering disintegrating aura.

Bratan and Solidin met once again. They exchanged blows in a rapidly moving melee. Laeyit, however, uttered an enhancing incantation. White light surrounded both her and Bratan. Both Bratan and Laeyit moved to flank Solidin, but they obviously underestimated him. Solidin evaded and parried both their blows, then pierced Bratan once, and slashed Laeyit's garb. It surprised Solidin that neither had yet mustered barsion.

Laeyit leapt away, glancing at the cut on her clothing. Her lips twisted with wrath. "You insolent elf!" she barked. Solidin smirked, then resumed his bout with Bratan, landing another blow. The joint in the armor was weakening.

"Today you die, Swift-Dagger!" Laeyit shouted. "And we'll deliver your head to our beloved prince!"

Solidin landed a few more blows, then tripped Bratan. *You'll have to do better than this if you want my head,* he thought, landing a flurry of blows against the weakened joint.

On the fifth strike Solidin drew blood.

━━●━

Run! Krindal told himself. *Hide!*

Panic overwhelmed Krindal. He stumbled past soldiers and Wildmen advancing to the battle. He couldn't go to the war camp. No. *They* would find him there.

The shadow passed briefly, and Krindal glanced to the flying dragon-statue. *I have to get out of here,* he thought, frantically looking past the army. Many were charging. Most avoided him.

Soon, Krindal was near the edge of the war camp, but he dashed around it. More squads were filing out of the side entrance, but not so many that would require dodging.

Heart pounding thunderously, Krindal ran faster than ever before. The sounds of battle faded behind him. But Krindal was not far enough away. He kept running, nearing the western end of the hall. He was almost a grand phineal away from the battle. Krindal glanced over his shoulder, looking back across the enormous room. Eruptions of magic sounded, their light filling the air above the war camp. Those colossal conjurations were amid the Mindolarnian ranks, wreaking havoc—one rampaged through the war camp. Tents flew through the air, thrown by the conjuration.

They're looking for me! Krindal gasped, averting his gaze from the destruction. He kept running toward the western end of the Hall of the Guardians, toward those three statues. *They weren't this close before, were they?* Krindal squinted. He cocked his head. Their feet were *moving*.

Krindal started, halting. Horrified, he froze once again, watching the statues approach. *Are they coming for me?* Krindal shuddered. Soon, those three towering statues were upon him. Each stood over twice Krindal's height. The statue carrying the sword—clad in that scaled formfitting armor—looked down at Krindal. There was something serene about the statue's gaze. Its eyes were soft, even gentle. That settled Krindal's nerves.

"You are an oddity," the statue remarked. "Branded a Keeper, but to no Order."

An oddity? Hadn't those illusions in Klindil said the same?

"An oddity he is," said the statue with elven features.

Krindal started, but the elven statue had the same gentle expression across its stony face. The elf's chiseled armor was unlike anything Krindal had ever seen—congruent angles forming diamond-shaped plating. Why would someone make armor such as that?

"Indeed an oddity," the third statue said, the one wearing the flowing robe. Despite being made of stone, the robe fluttered with each of the statue's movements. That statue looked familiar.

He resembles the Losians' first king.

"Tell us," the sword-bearing statue said, "why is there war on Dalgilur?"

War?

"Who are the vying factions?" the robed statue asked.

Factions?

"And to which are you allied?" the sword-bearing statue asked.

"He is in a state of shock," the elven statue observed.

Krindal stared at the three statues, but glimpsed movement behind them. *Some of Cornar's band?*

"Come, let us discern the combatants," the sword-bearing statue said, stepping past Krindal. It lumbered with a slow, even, deliberate gait.

The other two statues followed, leaving Krindal alone. Still perplexed, Krindal turned and watched the statues move away.

"Master Krindal!" He knew that voice… it belonged to Cornar's nephew.

Four youthful members of Cornar's band were sneaking toward Krindal—Ordreth, Demsal, a mage, and that thieving woman. The thief was about to pull her cloak about her, ready to disappear, while the warriors were brandishing their weapons. The young mage, however, was gawking.

"What's happening out there?" Ordreth asked.

"*They've* come…"

"Who?" Demsal demanded.

"Oh!" the young mage exclaimed, snapping his fingers. "It's Solidin, and the Sapphire Guard." He seemed excited about their presence. How could anyone be excited about *them?*

"Is it Solidin?" Ordreth asked. Krindal nodded. "Where's the prince?"

Krindal hadn't seen Prince Kaescis during the battle. In fact, he hadn't seen the prince for hours. "I don't know where His Imperial Grace is…" Krindal muttered.

Ordreth paled.

Does he fear the same as I? Krindal wondered. Without Prince Kaescis they wouldn't survive those merciless elves.

The need to run returned. Krindal pushed past the young mage, Hem, and darted westward. He had to hide. *That naval yard,* Krindal thought. Yes, he could hide there.

⤙•⤚

"What are we going to do?" Sharon asked warily. Ordreth furrowed his brow, gazing across the massive chamber. The battle looked intense.

"I don't want to get close to that," Demsal said flatly.

"The carnage is probably horrible," Hem frowned. "I bet our tents are torn to shreds, too."

Demsal gave Hem a sideways glance. As he bantered with the illusionist, Ordreth ignored them.

What *were* they to do? If Kaescis were there in the war camp, he wouldn't just leave. The prince would be in the midst of the fighting. They would have to wait until the battle ended to lure Kaescis back to their feigned discovery. But then they wouldn't be able to use the Sapphire Guard as a diversion for their escape…

But again, it was possible that Kaescis wasn't at the battle. The prince could be anywhere. Ordreth groaned within himself. Despite all their efforts, Uncle Cor's plan had failed. "We need to get back," he said.

Gesturing back to the way they had come, he turned and ran.

⤙•⤚

Cornar's serrated dagger clashed with Kaescis's Darkness blade. Black particles wisped to the dagger, making it glow that deadly hue. Kaescis had fled down several flights of stairs and resumed their duel in another hallway.

Though this was not how Cornar had planned the conflict, it was exactly what he wanted.

Just him and Kaescis.

"I don't know if you're brave," Kaescis said, as he lunged backward, "or stupid." The prince's massive blade required great distance to be effective. Cornar grinned at the insult and held his ground. His blades needed more of the Darkness magic if he were to breech Kaescis's armor.

"I know what you're trying to do," the prince said, chuckling. "You think you can use my magic against me."

Clever, Cornar thought.

"You're using the same strategy your father used at Laelin Lake," Kaescis said, taking another step back. "Dueling you like this is risky. I know the capabilities of your weapons."

Kaescis then uttered an incantation, and gray magic clustered in his hands.

The incantation was so swift Cornar didn't recognize it. He recognized most spells when they were cast, and that gave him an advantage on the battlefield. Luckily, Cornar also knew the colors associated with the various types of magic. Manipulation spells were gray.

What's he doing? Cornar wondered. He hadn't seen Kaescis use many spells, other than to summon that blade of his.

The prince finished his incantation, and a gray cloud zipped toward Cornar.

Cornar threw himself out of the way, swatting at the cloud with his weapons. The blades drew some of the gray magic, but most wisped to Cornar's nostrils.

An enthralling— Cornar couldn't move. Limp, he fell facedown on the ground, his head turned awkwardly toward the prince and his eyes as immobile as the rest of his body.

"This isn't how I envisioned killing you," Kaescis said, slowly closing the gap between them. "This isn't how *they* want me to kill you."

They?

"*They* want a glorious battle, rife with perils. *They* thrive on that." The prince continued to advance, his Darkness blade held out.

"I could use you as a puppet," Kaescis continued, "But I don't think *they* would approve. Even now *they* want me to relinquish my hold on you."

The prince continued explaining himself, but Cornar ignored Kaescis. This couldn't be the end, could it? Feelings of melancholy washed over him. He yearned for Karenna. He missed his children. *I've failed them*, Cornar thought. Kaescis would triumph. Even after Cornar's inevitable death, the chances of his men finding the prince were slim. They could search this labyrinth for days. Kaescis would undoubtedly make his retreat to his war camp and bring the full might of his forces upon Cornar's band.

"… even if I did release you, and we had this monumental battle, I don't think *they* will leave me alone. *They* just want death." The prince sounded like a madman. But then, most tyrants were mad.

With the wonders of Dalgilur, Kalda would be subject to another crazed oppressor. Nations would suffer. The dead would litter the streets of countless cities. The Mainland would bleed with the blood of any who resisted the Mindolarn Empire. That scene of sorrow was more than Cornar could bear, and the agonizing moment seemed to last forever.

Then, Cornar remembered.

Can't you do anything? he directed his thoughts toward that strange being from his dreams. It claimed Heleron was a petty creature. *Your words imply you're greater than a god. If so, I implore you, reach out and free me!*

Movement down the hall caught Cornar's eye. He couldn't hear anything above Kaescis's reasoning, nor could he redirect his gaze to see who was there. Reddish boots and the skirts of a dark-red robe came into Cornar's vision, and then an aged hand touched the ground. Had his plea been answered?

Off-white light gathered between the stranger's aged fingers and the ground, but again, Cornar couldn't hear anything above the prince. He watched as the magic formed. Was it a dispel?

Through unblinking eyes, Cornar noticed something different about the stranger's clothing—what he had thought was red, was actually a tint of pink against black. *An arcane barsion?*

"… unfortunately, you won't be able to see it," Kaescis said, his blade rising out of Cornar's field of vision.

The off-white light shot across the ground, like lightning. It wove between Kaescis's sabatons and struck Cornar. The enthralling spell vanished.

In one swift motion, Cornar gripped his weapons and threw himself upright.

"What?!" the prince shouted, swinging his blade in a downward strike meant as an executioner's blow.

With lightning finesse, Cornar blocked and parried the prince's Darkness blade while grating his serrated dagger upward along Kaescis's breastplate.

Stunned, Kaescis leaned backward to evade, but Cornar rose, following the prince. He sliced his serrated dagger—still imbued with the Darkness magic—across the right side of Kaescis's face, from chin to cheek. Cornar barely grazed the prince, but the devouring particles eroded flesh, drawing an enraged scream.

Kaescis dropped his blade and threw his hands to his face, falling backward. Cornar fell with the prince, then rebounded for another attack. But his blades met only armor, and the gemstones in Kaescis's suit absorbed the dark mist around Cornar's weapons.

At that moment, Cornar saw his benefactor—Jahevial. The necromancer-scholar rose from his crouched position, clothed in a veil of arcane-infused barsion.

Returning his attention to Kaescis, Cornar struck again, attempting to reach the prince's bare face, but was barred by thrashing arms.

Still screaming, Kaescis grabbed Cornar with one hand and *threw* him against the wall. The prince was still enhanced, and thus able to manage the feat. Now freed from Cornar, Kaescis scurried away, shielding his face.

An incantation sounded in the direction of Jahevial, and more white magic gathered in front of the necromancer-scholar. Jahevial's gaze was focused on Cornar.

Not the first person I expected to come to my aid, Cornar thought, recovering from the repulsion. Jahevial's spell zipped through the air, surging around Cornar— enhancing magic.

The screaming ceased, and Kaescis staggered to his feet, gazing down the hall. Kaescis lowered his gauntleted hand, revealing grotesque scarring. The right corner of his lips was gone, exposing his teeth. The wound lacked blood, as the Darkness magic cauterized the gash.

"You…" Kaescis slurred, his tone mingled with pain and anger, "you betray me too?!"

Jahevial grunted with amusement. "You're the betrayer, Kaescis," he said, moving down the hall toward Cornar. The prince growled.

"First you lie to us about Klindil," Jahevial said, "then you deprive us of our discoveries, and now you attack us!" Jahevial uttered another incantation. It was a type of barsion—arcane, from what Cornar could tell.

"You're barsion won't save you," Kaescis slurred, then uttered that incantation to summon his blade. It had since puffed away.

Jahevial finished his spell and a pinkish tint veiled Cornar's vision. Although the barsion wouldn't protect Cornar from Kaescis's blade, it would prevent the prince from placing another enthralling spell upon him.

Now, Cornar could finish what he'd started. He would be a *shield* against Kaescis's maniacal ambitions. With Jahevial's aid, Cornar would slay Kaescis and bring an end to the threat of this madman.

Amid the thought, a sudden surge swelled through Cornar. He felt renewed, even empowered. But no spell was cast upon him.

You… Cornar glanced to the ceiling. *Are you helping me?* There was no response, but Cornar felt his muscles quicken. His mind sharpened, and the fuzziness from the various blows he had sustained during the fight vanished. The clarity ignited a burning zeal within him, and he dashed toward the prince.

⎯⎯⎯⎯◗●◖⎯⎯⎯⎯

The last of the Praetorians fell in the darkness.

Nordal drew his blade from the dead man's neck, cursing as his foe fell to the ground. Several more of his fellow warriors had fallen, but he couldn't tell if their wounds were life-threatening. The only one totally unharmed was Hemrin.

Lucky bastard… Nordal shook his head. "How many did we lose?"

"Thirteen," Kalder replied. "Kamdir just stopped breathing." Kalder picked his way across the sitting room-turned-battlefield. "And four are severely wounded."

Nordal cursed again.

"Midar, start bandaging the wounded," Kalder commanded.

"What are we going to do about the dead?" Tinal asked.

Nordal shook his head. They didn't have time to bury them.

"We leave them," Kalder said solemnly, making his way toward Nordal.

The wounded were soon tended to, and Nordal eyed the giant orange shard, about the length of his forearm, in his hands. Nordal was still amazed at how it snuffed out magic.

We could make a killing selling this, Nordal thought. He envisioned nations vying for such a powerful tool. These shards could turn the tide of skirmishes, disrupt battle strategies, and negate tevisrals... *Oh, the possibilities—*

A hand clasped Nordal's shoulder. Kalder leaned close. Though it was dark, the sternness in Kalder's face was visible. "What are you thinking?" Kalder whispered.

"How lucrative this could be," Nordal answered, grinning. "We should go break off more pieces." Kalder narrowed his eyes at the rock.

"Igan thinks we should use this in our escape," Nordal said. "He believes it'll negate the storm." Kalder seemed intrigued.

"I don't see any other way to leave the island," Nordal said, shaking his head. "It's not like we can drag Krindal back to the *Promised Maiden.*"

"Fetching him would be unwise," Kalder said, his tone still stern. "Let's get more of that rock. There's no telling how much we'll need to survive that storm."

❖

Where is that half-breed prince? Solidin wondered, swiftly landing another blow against Bratan's wounded shoulder. Solidin was close to severing it. Both Bratan and Laeyit had mustered barsion, but Solidin had dispelled each.

Bratan yelled while swinging his ancient fanisar at Solidin. Effortlessly, Solidin parried the blow. Solidin created another opening and rapidly struck at the bloodied joint. On the third strike, Bratan's arm fell, painting the ground red.

The sound of a singing blade filled the air, and Solidin whirled to meet Laeyit, who screamed with unquenchable wrath. They exchanged rapid blows, blocking and parrying each other's flurry of swings and jabs. Laeyit's weapon exhausted the dispel on Solidin's daggers. She struck again, cutting Solidin's left dagger in two.

Solidin started, evading by throwing himself back toward the massive doors and rolling over one shoulder. He recovered from his evasion, turning so both his foes faced him: Bratan rose from the ground, seeming unaffected by the loss of his arm. Laeyit, however, swiftly closed the gap.

That shadow rushed toward the three combatants, and Solidin finally allowed his gaze to wander.

A dragon? His eyes widened. *Here?*

Laeyit was upon him, but Solidin evaded her advance. *No, it's too small to be a dragon,* Solidin noted, observing the white winged creature soaring toward him. The scales were wrong too—no, those were not scales. *Stone?* Solidin wondered, dodging another blow from Laeyit.

Bratan was also upon Solidin, swinging his fanisar. Undaunted, Solidin kept evading his foes. He needed another weapon if he were to overpower them. There were plenty of dead around, both elf and Mindolarnian. Unfortunately, no weapon nearby was short enough.

Evading another blow from Bratan, Solidin moved closer to the battle. His forces had since pushed the Mindolarnians back toward their war camp, a good hundred or so phineals from the towering doors.

Still. there was nothing on the ground short enough.

Blast! Solidin sighed, then his eyes fell on Laeyit's haviklur. *Perhaps—*

That shadow passed over once again. *It is stone!* Solidin grinned as he advanced on Laeyit, narrowly ducking under her haviklur. He closed the gap between them, then grabbed Laeyit's sword arm, pushing it aside while knocking her off balance. In one swift motion, Solidin threw Laeyit to the ground and wrested the blade from her.

The haviklur was now his. Laeyit cursed, and the shadow passed over once again.

Impressive. Solidin's grin widened. The shadow was cast by a statue of a dragon. In the draconic tongue such statues were called mis'thralim, but the elves called them gholistra—statues imbued with the minds and memories of the beings they represented. A gholistra could withstand an onslaught of magic greater than the strongest barsions. And a dragon as a gholistra… it would be nigh indestructible.

The draconic gholistra soared through the opened doors, landing in the portico to block any from escaping. It spread its wings wide while whipping its tail.

Laeyit began uttering an incantation, but Solidin ignored her. With his stolen weapon, Solidin unleashed a flurry of blows against Bratan. The haviklur was larger than the weapons he was accustomed to wielding, but it would do. Magic crackled as haviklur and magical axe-blade clashed.

After a moment, purple light caught Solidin's eye. Laeyit was mustering disintegrating magic. A ball nearly the size of her torso was forming.

That looks like a hefty beam… Solidin mused, landing a blow that cracked Bratan's breastplate. He spun, positioning Bratan between himself and Laeyit—her disintegrating blast was building.

"A Keeper of Truth and Might," a deep voice bellowed from behind Solidin. "A Bladesinger, no less."

Bratan started, apprehensively glancing beyond Solidin.

What's he looking—?

Bratan staggered, retreating from Solidin. "Laeyit…" he murmured.

Laeyit's attention was no longer on Solidin. She gazed over his shoulder, her expression aghast.

Solidin decided to chance a glance. Behind him were three more gholistras, each advancing slowly and brandishing glistening weapons. One was an elf whose likeness resembled Ilnari, Kardorth's Supreme Commander from a thousand years ago. Another was a mage-looking fellow. The last was clad in armor akin to that worn by the ancient heroes of the Kaldean Alliance. The sword it wielded resembled a sword of legend, one said to amplify the soul of its wielder. The last person to wield that weapon was the man who led the revolt against the Karthar Empire, General Lith Luzdom.

These can't be who I think they are, can they? Solidin wondered, his eyes narrowing. If the elven gholistra was Ilnari, and the sword bearer Lith, then the mage must be none other than the Losians' first ruler—Dorin, the Mage-King.

But how…? Solidin wondered. The Keepers of Truth and Might had disappeared before the rise of the Karthar Empire. Why would gholistras of these three—those who toppled the Karthar Empire—be here on Dalgilur? There was a two-hundred-year difference between the disappearance of the Keepers and the rise of Lith's rebellion.

Suddenly, Laeyit unleashed her attack upon the Lith gholistra. The gholistra stood its ground, swiftly extending its freehand to the beam. Laeyit's magic was as nothing against that stony hand. The figure simply swatted Laeyit's magic.

"Whatever faction vies against a Keeper is an enemy to Dalgilur," the Lith gholistra said. "So, you and your forces must die," it added flatly, then stepped forward, raising its blade to strike.

Solidin backed away. If the gholistras were going to deal with Laeyit and Bratan, then he could focus his attention elsewhere. He turned to the battle raging near the war camp—many of the Sapphire Guard had fallen, and the situation looked grim.

Laeyit ran, leaving Bratan to stand alone against the three unstoppable beings.

"Laeyit!" Bratan shouted, his face twisting with anger.

The flapping of wings filled the enormous space, and the dragon gholistra zipped from the entrance, flying straight for Laeyit. With incredible swiftness, the stony claws snatched Laeyit from the ground. The draconic gholistra soared with its prey toward the war camp.

Soon, the other three gholistra were upon Bratan. The elf and the mage twirled their staffs, which suddenly burst with light—the elf's red and the mage's blue. They became double-bladed fanisars, like Bratan's, then separated into three sections—connected by flowing chains of pure magic.

Bratan stumbled backward, tripping over a lifeless Wildman. He looked frantic, and rightly so. The slow movements of the three gholistra changed as quickly as a flash of lightning. The three of them moved so fast that Solidin barely caught it. In unison, they cut down Bratan. The hulking Praetorian was dead in less than a second.

Solidin stared in amazement. He knew the stories of gholistra, but seeing them in action conjured a sense of wonder.

"We will destroy your enemies," the Lith gholistra said. "Dalgilur's invaders must be eliminated."

"Spare the elves," Solidin pleaded.

With that, Solidin and the three gholistras marched toward the raging battle. Solidin twirled his dagger and stolen haviklur. Today he would reclaim this place lost to the ages.

The shadow passed by once again, and Solidin watched the draconic gholistra soar through the massive doors, carrying more victims in its stony claws. The dragon disappeared, flying far above Dalgilur.

⋯⋯⋯

Chilling wind whipped against Laeyit's face as she struggled to break free from her captor's grip. Panicked cries from the others clutched by the draconic mis'thralim reached her ears.

Kaescis, you fool, Laeyit thought as she struggled. *We should have destroyed those mis'thralim when we had the chance!* For as much as she loved Kaescis, Laeyit hated him in that moment.

The air became foggy. They were in the clouds now.

What is this—? Laeyit felt herself falling. The clouds disappeared, and she saw the island far below her. She wasted no time and uttered an incantation, mustering pure barsion magic. Blue light gathered in front of her.

Shrill screams pierced the air, coming from a falling Wildman. The fool, grabbed at empty air.

Idiot... She shook her head, finishing her incantation, enclosing herself in a protective sphere. The Wildman's screams became muffled as the barsion formed.

She wouldn't have time to cast another incantation. The mountaintops of Dalgilur were speedily approaching.

Soon, Laeyit and the others snatched by the draconic mis'thralim hit the tops of the mountain range. Laeyit left a tiny crater, an effect caused by her barsion absorbing the impact.

She recovered from the otherwise fatal drop and took in her surroundings. The others, however, lay still on the peak—their bodies broken from the fall.

Laeyit squinted, studying a flat structure just to the north. It was a sprawling balcony carved from the peaks.

Leaving the dead behind her, Laeyit hurried to the balcony. It was as large as the chamber where they had erected the war camp. *Was this a landing platform for the sha'kalda?* she wondered, walking to the western side of the balcony, the side overlooking the ocean.

There was no apparent way down from this mountaintop roost. Perhaps she would have to scale the mountain... Laeyit started as she reached the edge of the balcony. A massive crater marred the western side of the mountain. So much of the mountainside was gone that parts of the Hall of the Guardians were exposed. As she scanned the crater a shimmering glint caught her eye.

What is that?

A rushing of wind pushed against Laeyit. She turned as the draconic mis'thralim soared past Dalgilur's buildings and toward the pier.

It's going to destroy the ships! Her lips twisted into a snarl. What were they going to do now? There was no way for them to escape the island without—

Her expression lightened, remembering the vessels found to the north. *That might do,* she thought. They could use one of the ancient vessels once the fighting was finished.

Laeyit turned back to that shimmering light, drawn to it by curiosity. She removed a shallow domed tevisral from her tunic. It was a type of monocle. Laeyit placed it over her left eye and closed her right, touching the dome in angular patterns. Soon, she saw *through* the tevisral.

While refocusing her gaze to find the light in the crater, Laeyit slid her hand along the tevisral's edge, magnifying her vision.

Her curiosity, however, turned to horrified perplexity. "Kaescis!" she cursed, seeing the helmet of her beloved prince wedged against the rock, its polished gold reflecting sunlight.

How? *No…* Kaescis couldn't be somewhere down there? Could he? She remembered him speaking of going to confront the Butcher of Tor's accursed son, somewhere within the upper reaches of the Hall of the Guardians. She imagined Kaescis falling from a great height…

No, she told herself, *he would have been able to prevent such a fall.* Dozens of tragic scenarios ran through her head, and a tear trickled down her cheek. Then her greatest fear confronted her. *No*—she shook her head—*he's not dead. He was* chosen *by the Messenger.*

After quelling her fears, Laeyit uttered an incantation, mustering enthralling tentacles. They shot across the crater, zooming toward Kaescis's helmet. Once the helmet was in her grasp, Laeyit pulled it up the mountainside. She opened her barsion sphere and took the helmet into her hands.

"Where are you, Kaescis?"

✦

Kaescis staggered against another blow from Mister Dol'shir. How was the man able to land so many hits? Dol'shir wasn't even enhanced, yet he countered every blow Kaescis attempted to land. Somehow, Mister Dol'shir was empowered. And to make matters worse, the voices were a blaring mess that was near distracting.

Suddenly, that serrated dagger swung toward Kaescis's face once again, but he swatted the weapon with his left gauntlet. Blade and armor met amid a veil of blackness persistent around the gauntlet. Kaescis's Triaindium Suit had repurposed the stolen Ko'delish, emitting a damaging veil. It would have proved devastating against most opponents' weapons, but this was not the case with Mister Dol'shir. The man's weapons simply reabsorbed the damaging veil, then used the reabsorbed magic.

It was an endless cycle that wreaked havoc on Kaescis's armor.

Though he lacked his helmet, Kaescis could tell his Triaindium Suit was reaching its capacity for absorption. Black light filled the gemstones, with occasional streaks of green and pink—spells cast from the treacherous scholar, Jahevial.

Mister Dol'shir lunged again; his serrated dagger scraped against the golden plating of Kaescis's left gauntlet—blackness wisped from the blade to a gemstone along his forearm.

And then the gem cracked.

No… Shocked, Kaescis retreated, warding off his foe with his Ko'delish blade. *Aunok'sha!* Kaescis pleaded. *Lend me strength against my foe!*

Mister Dol'shir advanced, closing the gap quickly. He struck with both weapons: his short-sword sliced across Kaescis's breastplate while the serrated dagger grated along Kaescis's gauntleted forearm.

And then the impossible happened—the cracked gemstone shattered.

61

FLIGHT

"The elven races also saw through Cheserith's deceit. None of them worshiped the abominable creature. They kept to themselves on Tagal'shilm, the northwestern continent of the world."

- From *The Thousand Years War, Part I*, page 48

Cornar repulsed Kaescis, forcing the prince down another corridor. Since Jahevial had joined the fight, they had pushed Kaescis through several halls. The prince's armor seemed weakened by Cornar's onslaught of blows. Several of the gemstones on the armor had cracked or shattered, and the persistent mist around parts of the plate had dissipated.

The prince staggered, then turned, dashing down the corridor.

"What a coward!" Jahevial shouted, then uttered an incantation. Several acidic orbs appeared, floating around the scholar.

Cornar didn't skip a beat. He chased after Kaescis with Jahevial in tow. The prince ran full tilt down a long corridor, glowing a faint green hue.

He's healing himself, Cornar thought, watching as arpran magic surged from Kaescis's hands. Seeing the arpran spell made Cornar revise his estimate of the prince's abilities. How adept in the magical arts *was* Kaescis?

Kaescis abruptly turned into an adjoining corridor, briefly disappearing from view.

"We can't let him get back to the war camp!" Jahevial shouted to Cornar. Cornar didn't reply. He just kept running. They turned the corner, finding a stairwell that led down two floors, separated by a landing. A hallway continued from the bottom step, but Cornar couldn't see how far it went. Kaescis, however, was nowhere to be found.

"Wait…" Cornar stopped abruptly. *He must have shrouded himself in invisibility.*

Jahevial halted, breathing heavily beside Cornar. Cornar calmed his breathing, listening for any trace of the prince. The necromancer-scholar shifted uneasily. "Where did he go?" Jahevial asked warily.

"How proficient are you at casting dispels?" Cornar asked.

Jahevial answered by uttering an incantation. Within seconds, off-white light surged down the stairs and into the hall below them.

"Good, keep that up," Cornar said, hurrying down the steps.

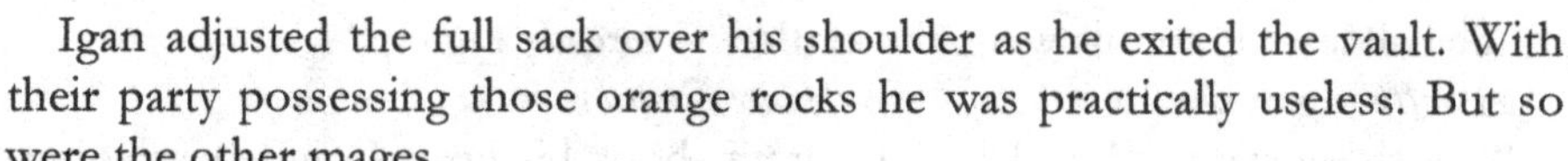

Igan adjusted the full sack over his shoulder as he exited the vault. With their party possessing those orange rocks he was practically useless. But so were the other mages.

There was light in the sitting room. Shadows cast by torchlight danced throughout the space. Nordal had suggested the idea of traveling by torchlight, since the wizards wouldn't be able to muster their globes of light. It was quite ingenious, actually.

Most of the warriors wore bandages. But Igan's gaze was drawn to those more severely wounded. Brendar's arms and left leg were bound in several places and Jorkal helped the man to stand. Both of Kren's legs were wrapped tight, and he lay on a makeshift litter of fanisar shafts and sloglien sacks. Luckily, the sacks were so strong that not even the weight of a man could tear them. Vaemar wasn't as fortunate as Kren. Poor Vaemar had lost his left hand. Midar had managed to stop the bleeding, but there was no way to save the hand. Another warrior—Laerin—also lay on a litter. His abdomen was bandaged, and his left arm was wrapped from wrist to shoulder.

"Are you ready to go, Master Igan?" Kalder asked, holding a torch. Igan nodded.

Nordal took the lead of the party with Midar and Cordel. They filed out of the room-turned-battlefield and soon everyone was traveling down the darkened corridors.

The crystals extinguished the light from the walls and ceiling for quite a distance, but the torchlight managed to make the halls visible.

Their plan was quite simple, especially after Cornar's last command: Get everyone back to the *Promised Maiden* without the Mindolarnians noticing them. It would be the safest place. Many of the warriors wanted to go after Cornar, but Igan hadn't the faintest idea of where he had chased Kaescis. Besides, Cornar didn't want them following him. Igan too wanted to aid Cornar, but this is what their leader wanted—to face Kaescis alone.

Cornar was confident he could defeat the prince. That was implied in his last words—"I'll join you." But what perils would Cornar face after slaying the prince? Igan worried for his friend as he and the others descended to the lower levels.

They were partway down the stairs leading to the twenty-third floor when hurried footfalls echoed beneath them. Nordal signaled for a halt, and everyone stilled, their hands on their weapons. The footsteps grew louder.

Sounds like a small group, Igan thought.

A gasp echoed up into the stairwell. Igan heard someone whisper, but he couldn't identify the voice. There was another reply, but it was faint. Nordal immediately whistled the party's signal, and it was returned in kind.

Ordreth, Igan thought.

Nordal resumed his descent with the others in tow. Igan heard a brief reunion between the main party and Ordreth's group, followed by a hasty report. Igan pushed his way through the crowd, straining to hear Ordreth. It sounded as if Cornar's nephew was talking about living statues and elves.

"… and that's when we decided to turn back," Ordreth said. "When we got to the hall leading to this wing, the battle was already raging."

A battle? Igan wondered. *So, the Sapphire Guard is here.*

"But those statues, Nordal…" Ordreth shook his head. "There was something terrifying about them."

"Well you don't need to fret," Midar said. "Your uncle's plan hasn't failed." Ordreth cocked his head in surprise.

"Yeah," Nordal chimed, "Kaescis and a bunch of his Praetorians attacked us not long after you left."

Cornar's nephew looked shocked. "But how did he know where—?"

"Don't know," Nordal interrupted. "Cor is fighting him now. We need to hurry to the *Promised Maiden.*"

"But Uncle Cor—"

"I'm sorry, Ordreth," Nordal said, pushing past the younger warrior. "Cor ordered us not to follow him. None of us like it."

Ordreth looked defeated, overcome with dismay. Nordal, however, continued down the stairs while the rest of the party filed past Ordreth. Hem and Demsal joined the main group, but Sharon lingered with Cornar's nephew—her hand gently resting on Ordreth's arm. Sharon was shrouded in her cloak but was completely visible.

The rocks are stopping her cloak from working, Igan thought.

"Oh, Igan!" Ordreth turned, looking frantic. "I can't abandon my uncle." The outburst was heart-wrenching. Igan stared at Ordreth as the last of the party descended the stairs. Soon, only the three of them remained. "I know how you feel, Ordreth," Igan said, "but there's no way to know where Cor went. We could spend days searching this labyrinth for him…"

"I can't lose him, Igan!"

With tears welling in his eyes, Igan looked at Ordreth. He too yearned to reunite with Cornar, but Igan saw no feasible way.

Sharon tugged at her lover's arm. "Ordreth…" she urged, "we're getting behind."

"Trust in your uncle, Ordreth," Igan said, stepping past the couple. "He's escaped perilous circumstances before. Have faith that he will find a way back to the ship."

Igan turned and continued down the stairs. As he rejoined the party, reluctant footsteps echoed behind him.

❧

There was nothing in the hall beyond the stairs.

Cornar ran through each of Jahevial's dispels, and the necromancer-scholar managed to keep pace with his dash. Jahevial was almost as proficient with his dispels as Iltar or Hagen.

They hurried down the hall, toward an archway leading to another room several hundred phineals away. No other corridors or doors branched from this hall. Kaescis could have only gone one way.

Our brief halt must have bought him enough time to get ahead of the dispels, Cornar thought.

Faint sounds of battle reached Cornar's ears, coming from the archway. *What's that?* They soon approached the archway, and Jahevial's dispel washed through the opening. Cornar stopped short of entering and examined the space beyond the archway.

This looks familiar, Cornar thought. The space beyond the archway was roofed by a giant shallow dome, about the size of a city block. A gigantic polished crystal hung in the center of the space, with a walkway running from the archway to the crystal. Four other archways branched off from the crystal, connecting to a balcony that ran the dome's entire circumference.

"I know this place," Jahevial said. "We're above the main room, near the war camp."

Cornar nodded. His men had reported finding the entrances to these domes while exploring the enormous pillars in the main room. He glanced beyond the walkways. It was a long drop to the bottom.

Don't look down, Cornar told himself, averting his gaze and fighting off a spell of dizziness. He briefly glimpsed one of the enormous pillars while refocusing his vision.

Jahevial uttered another dispel, and it washed across only a quarter of the domed space. "He could be anywhere," the scholar cursed. "Let's go!"

Together, they hurried onto the walkway leading to the crystal. Cornar kept his focus on the giant crystal while Jahevial mustered another dispel.

Amid their dash, Cornar heard that booming voice. *STOP!* it commanded.

As Cornar obeyed, a streak of blackness zipped between him and Jahevial. It was Kaescis's blade, flying like a javelin. If Cornar hadn't stopped, the sword would have impaled him.

An enraged yell echoed throughout the dome. Jahevial finished his incantation, turning toward the yell. He hurled his magic, and it washed across another walkway leading to the crystal.

Kaescis appeared, running toward the crystal, his hand outstretched, with blackness gathering around his gauntlet. The wounds on Kaescis's face were gone—a result of his arpran spell.

Cornar resumed his dash, passing Jahevial. Both he and Kaescis reached the balcony wrapping around the crystalline structure.

Kaescis disappeared for a moment, but Cornar could hear the prince's heavy footfalls growing louder. As Cornar rounded the crystal Kaescis reappeared, his blade forming as he ran.

The prince lunged, raising his Darkness blade. Kaescis swung, but Cornar leaned backward, sliding beneath the prince. Cornar managed to land several blows against Kaescis's sabaton as the prince sailed through the air. The blows overloaded another gemstone near the prince's knee, cracking it. Recovering from the slide, Cornar flipped onto his stomach and pushed himself upright, watching as Kaescis rebounded.

They clashed once again, struggling against each other. Neither landed blows. All the while, Jahevial hurled his acidic orbs at the prince. Several orbs flew toward the back of the prince's head. Kaescis, however, heard the whizzing acid and twisted with unnatural speed to counter them with his monstrous weapon. The blade's misting blackness *consumed* the orbs. However, nearly a dozen of the other acidic projectiles struck the prince's armor.

Cornar glimpsed a gemstone shattering along the prince's back, and more of the damaging veil around the armor vanished. The veil persisted only around parts of the prince's breastplate and left arm.

We almost have him, Cornar thought. He took advantage of the opening, striking several blows against Kaescis's armored ribs.

The prince whirled, lowering his Darkness blade, but Cornar intercepted it with his serrated dagger.

⎯⎯◆◆⎯⎯

Kaescis recoiled, furious at the stalemate between him and the accursed Dol'shir.

Why can't I hit him?! The thought evoked further fury. The voices were a thunderous rumble in Kaescis's mind, indistinguishable. Nothing but insatiable hate raged within him, fueling him.

The zipping sounds of magic reached Kaescis's ears, and he twirled, kicking his adversary, then turned in time to deflect more acidic orbs from reaching his face.

"You…" he growled at Jahevial. Kaescis could hear Dol'shir rebounding, but that didn't matter. Enraged, Kaescis ran toward his enemy's would-be protector. Jahevial retreated, mustering more magic. Lime-green light gathered around his arcane barsion. Yelling, Kaescis swung his blade, aimed to cut the fool in half. Jahevial, however, threw himself backward.

Kaescis's weapon met Jahevial's barsion, shattering it. The tip of his Ko'delish blade narrowly sliced across the scholar's arms and chest, dissolving cloth and flesh. The blow, however, was not enough to kill the traitor.

Jahevial screamed as he fell to the walkway. Misting particles left in the wake of Kaescis's blow eroded the sinews of Jahevial's arm, revealing bone. Kaescis swept his weapon, but he wouldn't have time to strike again. He spun just as Mister Dol'shir lunged at him, weapons extended.

They collided, and Kaescis fell backward. Dol'shir's short-sword flew past his face. The dagger, however, struck repeatedly against Kaescis's breastplate.

Another gemstone cracked, falling out of its mounting. *No!* Kaescis growled.

As they fell onto the walkway, Mister Dol'shir reared up, slamming his weapons toward Kaescis's face. With lightning speed, Kaescis threw his left gauntleted hand to shield himself. Both his foe's weapons struck the gauntlet.

Gemstones shattered.

Plating cracked.

And then anguish. Coldness surged through his forearm. The tip of his foe's short-sword protruded near the crook of his elbow. The pain was excruciating, and Kaescis screamed a hate-filled yell. Then he felt his forearm no longer. And that was worse than all the pain in the world.

⟢•⟢

Cornar's short-sword jerked free of the prince's gauntlet. His serrated dagger, however, still pierced the now dismembered limb.

The prince wailed, gazing horrifically at what Cornar had done.

Now's my chance, Cornar thought, swinging his serrated dagger aside. He brought his short-sword close to defend himself while Kaescis's severed gauntlet flew over the walkway's rail.

Kaescis yelled, swinging his monstrous weapon, but Cornar intercepted the blade with his short-sword. Now twisted over the prince, Cornar slammed his newly freed dagger toward Kaescis. The dagger struck the upper-right part of the breastplate, eroding the golden-red plating.

Cornar jolted, a result of his serrated dagger piercing the prince's armor.

Kaescis wailed again.

The pressure against Cornar's short-sword lessened. Cornar glimpsed the prince's black weapon fall onto the walkway. Jahevial was also nearby, straining against pain. It sounded as if the scholar was uttering an incantation, but it was almost indistinguishable amid his groans and grunts.

Cornar jolted again, his serrated dagger sinking deep into the prince's chest.

"Aunok'sha!" the prince screamed, "why have you forsaken me?!"

Ignoring the mad would-be tyrant, Cornar reared back, slamming his short-sword into the hydra emblem on the prince's armor. A *tang* resounded as sword and armor met. Blackness eroded the crimson gilding and soon pierced the prince's chest.

A wailing howl echoed throughout the domed space, accented by the sounds of battle somewhere below the walkways.

"For my father," Cornar shouted. "And for all of Kalda." The words were laced with protective fury.

Kaescis's violet eyes met Cornar's, his gaze filled with unquenchable malice. The prince's face twisted in rage and anguish. Never had Cornar felt such violent hate. The prince's lips twisted, and he began uttering sharp sounds.

"No…" Cornar shook his head, drawing his short-sword from Kaescis's chest. The prince jolted, but his speech was uninterrupted.

Cornar aimed his short-sword toward Kaescis's throat, but before he could strike, a burst of orange light raced toward them. Cornar stopped the blade short of the prince's neck, seeing a slithering streak of orange racing from Jahevial to Kaescis.

A life-draining—

The orange magic swiftly wrapped around Kaescis's neck, interrupting that strange incantation of his. Kaescis writhed in pain. Cornar stabbed another part of the prince's breastplate, further anchoring him in place.

The orange magic—a life-draining cord—pulsed rapidly.

Soon, Jahevial was on his feet. Cornar looked to the scholar, whose clothes were tattered. The wounds caused by the Darkness magic, however, were regenerating.

Suddenly, the writhing prince fell still. The life-draining cord pulsed several more times, then slithered back to Jahevial.

"He's dead," the scholar said.

Cornar looked at Jahevial for a moment, then back to Kaescis. A twisted expression marred the lifeless face. Cornar knew that a necromancer could sense the death of any bound by such a cord. And, Kaescis had stopped breathing.

Reluctantly, Cornar removed his weapons from the prince's breastplate. Blackness festered around the wounds, devouring flesh. Cornar waited for a moment, watching for any signs of life.

Jahevial, however, stepped away, moving to the rail of this walkway around the giant crystal.

"Cornar, I see your men."

My men? Cornar thought, abruptly looking up from the lifeless prince. He hurried to the railing, bracing himself for the dizziness that would accompany his gazing.

On the ground floor, far below the walkway, a large group was moving as one. Cornar quickly counted them. *Twenty-nine,* he thought, furrowing his brow. Two of the men were on litters. Some of the men were snuffing out torches and discarding them. *Clever,* Cornar smiled, admiring his men's ingenuity.

"Kalder!" Cornar shouted. "Nordal! Igan!"

The shout echoed in the dome, but didn't seem to draw the attention of the group.

"Where are they going?" Jahevial asked.

"To the *Promised Maiden,*" Cornar replied. "We're leaving Dalgilur."

"Do you have a way through the storm?" Jahevial asked incredulously.

"We do," Cornar said. "Some orange rocks that seem to negate magic."

Jahevial gasped. "Tazerin? Here, on Dalgilur?" The scholar looked confused.

Kaescis called it that, Cornar thought, turning back to his men.

"I might as well join you," Jahevial said. "I smuggled some tevisrals aboard the *Maiden,* for the Order." Cornar eyed the scholar as he continued his confession. "After the prince's announcement I figured he would not honor his agreement with Grandmaster Alacor."

Cornar nodded, remembering Aron's report. He turned back to his men. They were almost out of sight. "We need to get down from here," Cornar pushed away from the rail, blinking several times to vanquish the dizziness.

"Come, this way," Jahevial said, tugging on Cornar's arm. "We can access those pillars from these walkways."

Jahevial hurried away, but Cornar turned, glancing once more at his fallen foe. The prince didn't move. He didn't breathe. An eerie stillness rested upon him.

Kaescis *was* dead.

⟢•⟣

The war camp was in shambles.

Nordal watched warily as colossal conjurations and those tall statues destroyed the Imperial Tent. *What a sight…* he thought. Nordal didn't feel an ounce of pity for the damned Tilters. They were getting what they deserved.

"I don't think we want to get any closer…" Midar cautioned.

Nordal raised an eyebrow at the warrior. "Oh, really?" he asked sarcastically. Those behind the leading trio laughed. "Let's veer to the left," Nordal suggested. "If we stay between the wall and that pillar, hopefully they won't notice us."

"And if they *do* notice us?" Cordel asked, his tone serious.

Nordal hoped the Tilters and the pointed ears would be too engrossed in their mutually shared bloodshed to notice the group. If either faction diverged from the battle, Nordal and the others would be safe from all but arrows, at least initially.

"Then we kill them," Nordal answered. "We cut our way to the pier, even if we have to trudge through a river of blood."

"Typical Nordal," Midar said, snickering. Nordal grunted.

They veered to the left, passing behind the pillars on that side of the enormous chamber. Horrified screams echoed through the space, undoubtedly a result of those statues—the stony things were relentless.

Ever cautious, Nordal led the band between the wall and the pillars, careful not to get too close to either in case the orange rocks snuffed out the lights within them. Nordal had discovered the rocks' dispelling effect spread nearly a hundred phineals in each direction. The effects seemed greater than when they first pried them from the vault, as if touching them had increased their potency. But that couldn't be possible…

As they passed the pillar nearest to the war camp, Hem cried emphatically, "Look!"

Nordal—and the others not beleaguered by the wounded—spun with their weapons drawn. Frightful possibilities flashed through Nordal's mind. He expected to see Prince Kaescis darting toward them with that misting black sword. Once he turned, however, the fear vanished.

Hushed gasps and the sounds of restrained cheers washed all around the battered warriors and mages. Nordal too smothered a whoop.

He survived! Nordal cheered inwardly. Many of the warriors raised their weapons high, saluting their leader, their mentor, and their friend. *You really are a legend,* Nordal grinned. He thought of what it must have taken to slay that bastard prince. *If only I could have witnessed it.*

Cornar ran with weapons drawn, his blades glowing with that deadly black light. He ran ahead of another, a man in a black robe. The very sight was akin to many a charge Nordal had witnessed—Master Iltar and Cornar dashing headlong into danger ahead of the rest of the party.

But it was not Master Iltar who ran with Cornar—it was Jahevial.

"Uncle!" Ordreth cried, pushing his way toward the party's rear. The young warrior looked frantic.

As Cornar and Jahevial reached the effects of the orange rocks, the blackness around both the serrated dagger and short-sword disappeared. Cornar sheathed his weapons just in time to embrace Ordreth. The two hugged tightly, and Nordal barely heard the young warrior exclaiming heartfelt gratitude for his uncle's safety.

Cornar patted his nephew on the back, then gestured to the others. Together, they ran to the head of the party.

"You're one tough bastard," Nordal said with a sly grin. "First you defy earthquakes and now diabolical princes. What's next?"

Cornar chuckled, grinning widely. He turned back to the others and his expression darkened. "Kamdir…?" Cornar asked, allowing his emotions to seep through the question.

"He didn't make it," Midar answered solemnly. "His lung was eroded, as was part of his heart."

Tears welled in Cornar's eyes, but he managed to hold them back. "We need to hurry before the fighting stops," Cornar said, glancing to the war camp.

Marching with determination, Cornar took the lead of the party.

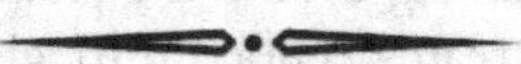

Solidin stabbed a Wildman through the stomach, then whirled to meet his next foe. In Solidin's other hand he wielded a broken sword. Most of the blade was sheared, forming a jagged slant. Though the handle was too large, the broken blade was just the right size.

The weapon Solidin had stolen from Laeyit had since vanished. It crumbled in his grasp not long after she disappeared with the draconic gholistra. He supposed she had deactivated the weapon—it was a result of a tevisral, after all.

Both dagger and broken sword clashed with a fanisar, wielded by a Crimson Praetorian. Solidin rebounded, and both he and the Praetorian clashed in another deadlock.

The Praetorian had a notch in his breastplate. *Oh, you,* he thought, remembering this particular Praetorian from the Keeper's Shrine in the Igeacean Sea. Solidin and the Praetorian fought wildly as the battle raged around them. They dueled over the dead, elf and Mindolarnian alike. Several half-breeds lay about, too.

Amid one of their deadlocks, Solidin glimpsed a familiar face on the ground. Kaldarin. Solidin's lieutenant was maimed, his torso partially eroded—disintegrated, by the looks of it. A leg was also missing.

Oh, my friend, Solidin mourned. But there was no time to grieve.

Relentlessly, Solidin pressed his foe, forcing him toward the main battle. They neared a small group of the Sapphire Guard leveling a squad of Mindolarnians. Gladis was among them.

The transmuter noticed the duel, and Solidin knew what he must do. He carefully maneuvered himself so that the Praetorian's back was turned toward Gladis. He roared continuously, using his voice to flood the Praetorian's hearing. All the while, brown magic formed around Gladis's hands—transmutative magic.

A sudden blast of brown light shot to the ground behind the Praetorian. Some of the corpses—and the floor—liquefied. The now liquid matter rose from the ground in a curving arc, solidifying as it moved.

Solidin charged, evading the sweeping fanisar. He rammed the Praetorian with his shoulder, forcing him toward the transmutation. Solidin briefly glimpsed Gladis's creation—it was a metal stalagmite, curved so its tip pointed horizontally at chest height.

Ingenious, Solidin thought as a resounding crack reached his ears.

The Praetorian gasped, struggling to free himself from both Solidin and the transmutation. Solidin, however, spun around his foe. He grappled the Praetorian, using his weight to hold his foe in place upon Gladis's deadly transmutation.

As the Praetorian struggled, Solidin noticed movement to his right, to the northern side of this place cut out of the mountain.

A small group—perhaps thirty—was moving between the pillars and the wall. Many looked wounded, and two were carried upon something Solidin couldn't quite discern. At their head, however, was a man Solidin could recognize at any distance.

Cornar Dol'shir.

Where are you going? Solidin thought, *And why are your men wounded?* Solidin buckled amid the thought, but regained his hold upon the Praetorian.

More transmutative magic struck the ground in front of both Solidin and his foe; all the while, the Praetorian began uttering his own incantation. Violet light shone around the crimson armor.

Solidin warily eyed the liquefying ground. *Hurry, Gladis!* More violet light shone around the Praetorians hands as he continued uttering the disintegrating incantation.

Two more transmuted stalagmites shot from the ground, arcing toward the Praetorian's chest.

Solidin relinquished his grip, and the Praetorian lurched forward, attempting to free himself, but he was too late. All three of Gladis's transmutations pierced the Praetorian's breastplate, holding him in place.

The violet light flickered as the Praetorian slurred the incantation, but exhaled in a way that held the spell.

No you don't. Solidin rebounded. He weaved between the curving stalagmites and stabbed his broken sword through the crack between breastplate and helmet, piercing the Praetorian's neck.

The humming ceased.

"That'll interrupt you," Solidin said, turning from his dying foe. He returned his gaze to Cornar Dol'shir. The man was passing the pillar nearest the towering doors.

You're escaping, Solidin thought. Their flight gave him pause.

"More Mindolarnians?" Gladis asked, coming beside Solidin.

"No." Solidin shook his head. "Cornar Dol'shir."

"I will take my squad," Gladis said, hastily turning, but Solidin caught his arm.

"Don't pursue him," Solidin said sternly.

"Why?" Gladis asked tersely.

Honorable in all things, the words echoed in Solidin's mind. They were part of the Keepers' vow, a vow he had taken while succumbing to the attunement process. Pursuing Cornar and his men—especially in their current state—would be dishonorable. They weren't the Sapphire Guard's foes, though they were trespassing on Dalgilur.

"It doesn't feel right," Solidin finally answered. "Besides, he didn't stand in the way of our escape from Klindil. Think of it as returning a favor."

Gladis remained silent, but Solidin could tell he disapproved.

"And the Mindolarnians?" the transmuter asked, sounding annoyed.

Solidin gave his friend a sidelong glance. "We give them battle until they capitulate. Until then, we slay them."

——◦•◦——

Cornar thought he saw a couple elves eyeing him and his men as they escaped the Hall of the Guardians. But none diverged from the battle within the Mindolarnian war camp. The trek through Dalgilur was also uneventful. Faint sounds of battle reached the party, coming from both the east and west.

Once they cleared the outer ring of Dalgilur's buildings they continued down the road leading to the pier. Cornar could see a battle, but it was nearly four grand phineals away, so nothing was discernible.

A shadow suddenly passed over them. Startled, Cornar gazed skyward and saw what he thought was the impossible. That statue—the one resembling a dragon—swooped toward the pier.

How... Cornar shook his head, dumbfounded at the sight. The dragon-statue soared straight for one of the ships anchored to the north, probably the *Executor's Breath.* The statue *ripped* the foremast from the decking, soared over the pier, circled once, and then hurled the mast like a javelin, impaling the ship.

"By Heleron's Trident..." Cornar cursed. He abruptly scanned the rest of the pier. One of the Mindolarnian warships was tilting, its stern rising out of the water. *It's sinking...* he thought. Cornar searched for the *Promised Maiden,* but didn't see it.

"Where is the *Promised Maiden?*" Cornar muttered under his breath.

"Farther down the pier," Kalder said, pointing.

Nordal cursed, and rightly so. The pier was eight grand phineals long. If they started running now, it would take them half an hour to reach the *Promised Maiden*.

"We need to get to the *Promised Maiden* before that *thing* sinks it," Cornar said, glancing over his shoulder. Several of the wounded were walking only by the aid of another. There was no way they could run.

Blast, Cornar cursed. He feared they wouldn't make it, not with that flying statue wreaking havoc. The situation seemed hopeless, but Cornar pushed ahead anyway. He hadn't brought his men this far only to fail. They *had* to make it.

Cornar led them toward the pier, warily watching the dragon-statue continue its assault. The statue would swoop toward the sinking vessels or the pier, then take to the skies, briefly disappearing within the clouds before attacking again. As they neared the battle, the dragon-statue snatched the combatants, taking them to staggering heights and then dropping them.

How horrific...

Soon, they neared the battle.

Mindolarnians and Wildmen clashed with a small group of the Sapphire Guard. The dragon-statue ignored the elves, focusing on the Mindolarnians and Wildmen. Occasionally, armored men fell from the sky, crashing into the plains around the battle.

"Veer right!" Cornar commanded through clenched teeth. He did not want to get mixed up in that battle. Perhaps if they stayed aloof, the statue would ignore them.

Cornar kept his band a few hundred phineals away, skirting around the southern part of the battle. He watched the skies, wary of being struck by the statue's victims. Once they were halfway to the pier, the dragon-statue noticed Cornar and his men.

"It's looking at us..." Midar muttered.

"We'll be fine," Nordal said reassuringly, his tone confident.

The dragon-statue hovered. *How can it do that?* Cornar furrowed his brow. *It defies all logic!* The statue bellowed sharp words and bared its teeth. It swooped toward Cornar and the others, exhaling brilliant blue flame. The fire raced above the battle, approaching faster than an arrow.

There was no time to flee.

Nordal defiantly stepped forward, raising his shard of tazerin. "You cannot burn us!" the warrior shouted. Cornar could see the fury on Nordal's face.

The unnatural fire engulfed the sky as it approached, but dissipated a hundred phineals away.

"It worked!" Aron shouted.

"Of course it did," Nordal remarked smugly.

Cornar wasn't as convinced. Sure, they were protected from any of the dragon-statue's magic—and the fire was surely magical—but the tazerin couldn't stop the thing from squashing them.

"Keep moving!" Cornar shouted.

As the last of the blue flame dissipated, the dragon-statue appeared, banking immediately. Was it attempting to evade the tazerin's effects? The dragon-statue arced in the air, but its wings stiffened.

Intrigued, Cornar watched as the dragon-statue plummeted uncontrollably. It crashed into the grassy plain, spewing earthen debris as it skidded to a halt over two hundred phineals away.

"Wow!" Cordel exclaimed, "that worked, too!"

That gave Cornar an idea. "Igan, get me your largest shard!" Cornar shouted, pushing his way through his men.

The wizard didn't hesitate. Igan undoubtedly understood Cornar's plan. When Cornar reached the wizard, Igan tossed him a long shard of tazerin.

Cornar caught it and dashed away. "Hold here," he shouted. The dust settled as Cornar darted toward the dragon-statue, bounding across the carved ground. The dragon-statue struggled to stand, tail pushing against the dirt. Amid its struggling, the statue turned its stony head, eyeing Cornar. The dragon-statue spun, rising on its foreclaws.

"Oh no you don't!" Cornar shouted, his advance causing the dragon-statue to stagger. The stony behemoth became rigid. The expression on its chiseled snout was that of perplexity. Did it comprehend what was happening to it?

Cornar neared the dragon-statue and hurled the shard at it. The stony figure froze, its stony eyes fixed on Cornar. *There,* he thought as the shard struck the dirt beside the stony tail.

With the dragon-statue debilitated, Cornar shouted for his men to continue to the pier, and then dashed toward the party's head once again. Each of the men was beaming.

"Well, I suppose we can add Dragonslayer to the list," Nordal quipped. Cornar gave him a sidelong glance, but continued leading the men around the battle. The elves paid little attention to Cornar and his men. The Mindolarnians, however, shouted for them to join the fray.

Odd... Cornar thought, *why would they want us to join them?* Wouldn't Kaescis have ordered his soldiers to attack? Perhaps the prince had acted without informing his forces.

Either way, Cornar didn't dare stop. They had to make it to the *Promised Maiden.*

"Be ready," Cornar commanded. "Keep the injured on the right." There was a shuffle among the party as the uninjured warriors formed a line of defense. Nordal took up the lead on the left, followed by Midar. Aron and Cordel were there as well, followed by Kalder and Hemrin. Ordreth and Demsal moved toward the rear with Grensil.

As they stepped onto the pier, the Mindolarnians shouted at Cornar and his men, infuriated. Shouts of "cowards" and "traitors" resounded behind them. A few cursed furiously.

Cornar passed what remained of the *Helidar.* The vessel had sunk, and only its broken masts and tattered sails rose above the water. The *Ulicin* was also in disarray, but it wasn't in as bad a shape as the *Executor's Breath.* Kaescis's warship was taking on water, tilting to one side. The mast thrown by the dragon-statue protruded from the portside hull.

Cornar heard his name shouted from the *Executor's Breath*. Admiral Kaetet waved his arms, pleading for assistance.

"Come on," Cornar urged his men, ignoring the admiral. Under any other circumstance, Cornar would have gone to the admiral's aid. He would have gone to fight alongside the Mindolarnians, too. But not today. Not after what had transpired with Kaescis.

Once they were beyond the ships, Cornar gave more orders to his men. "Nordal, run ahead and inform Captain Salisar that we will embark immediately. Kalder, hold the rear, in case any of the Mindolarnians decide to come after us."

Both warriors obeyed, and Nordal dashed ahead of the others.

It took over a quarter of an hour to reach the end of the pier. Nordal hadn't returned yet, and Cornar feared that Captain Salisar would refuse to leave without Krindal. After all, what Cornar was asking would be tantamount to suicide. Cornar found Nordal on the pier, arguing with the captain. The rest of Salisar's crew was also on the pier. It was a safe choice.

"... if you just listen," Nordal's voice carried across the pier, "this *thing* will protect us."

"You can't expect me to accept only your word," Captain Salisar retorted.

"Look, woman," Nordal nearly shouted, "this stuff works. Ready your ship, because we need to leave, now!" Nordal and the captain continued arguing as Cornar approached.

"Rein in your man!" Salisar shouted to Cornar. "Or I'll put him in his place."

"Oh really?" Nordal asked, laughing. "C'mon woman, hit me. I dare you." Salisar's face flushed. She formed a fist and reeled back.

"Wait!" Cornar held out his hand, attempting to defuse the hostilities. "There's no need to fight."

"Well," Nordal put his hands on his hips, "if she doesn't comply, we'll just have to commandeer the ship." Salisar swung at Nordal, but the warrior evaded swiftly. "Watch your follow-through," Nordal said, snickering as he dodged another swing.

The captain must have sensed the futility of her actions, for she stopped her advance. Her face, however, was still flushed.

"Thank you," Cornar said, his hand still extended. "We need to leave Dalgilur. The tazerin"—he gestured to the shard in Nordal's hand—"will negate the magic causing the storm in the World's Frown. And I can prove it. All of you mages, cast spells. Now."

A roar of incantations rumbled around Cornar. One by one, the mages finished casting their spells, but no magic manifested.

Every crewmember of the *Promised Maiden*—including Captain Salisar—gawked at the mages, dumbfounded. Amid her astonishment, the captain relaxed, dropping her fist.

"The Sapphire Guard is here slaying the Mindolarnians," Cornar added. "They have Dalgilur's defenses at their disposal—things we can't hope to defeat."

Salisar looked beyond Cornar. "Are you sure this is going to work?" she asked, her tone tinged with bewilderment.

Igan stepped forward. "It's stopped every other form of magic."

"If you will not believe the laymen," Jahevial said, pushing his way through the warriors, "then hearken to a scholar. Tazerin will negate the storm. The storm is produced by tevisrals. These shards negate all magic, even that produced by tevisrals. See her cloak," he gestured to Sharon.

The captain sucked in her breath, eyeing the group. She then turned, looking to her first mate, then to her mother—the chef.

"Trust them, darling," Salisar's mother said.

Emila—the captain's first mate—shrugged. "I don't want to be around when that flying thing comes back," she said.

Captain Salisar spun back to Cornar. "Get aboard!"

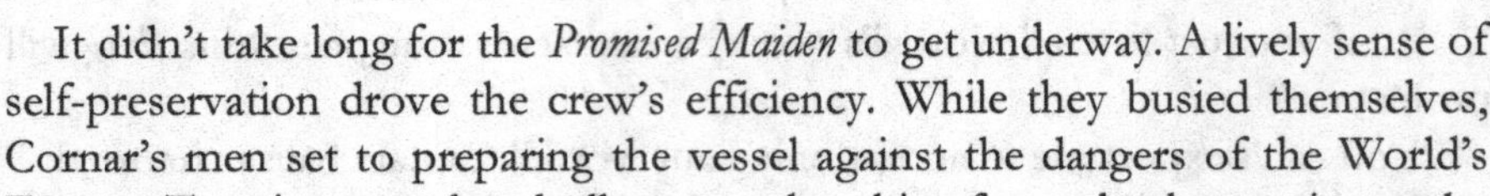

It didn't take long for the *Promised Maiden* to get underway. A lively sense of self-preservation drove the crew's efficiency. While they busied themselves, Cornar's men set to preparing the vessel against the dangers of the World's Frown. Tazerin was placed all across the ship, from the bowsprit, to the crow's nest, to the aft cabins.

The wounded were also tended to with greater care. Midar was busy inspecting each of the men. They were organized on the main deck according to the severity of their wounds.

Once the vessel sailed away from the pier, Cornar made his way to the bow. Though he knew the effects of the tazerin, he was still nervous about traversing the World's Frown. What kind of man wouldn't be nervous?

He looked to the timepiece tevisral, but the spindles were motionless. In fact, they showed a time before noon.

"Are you ready for this?" Igan asked, coming beside Cornar.

"As ready as I'll ever be," Cornar said, propping a boot against the bowsprit. He grabbed a nearby line while gazing at the distant horizon—a picturesque illusion masking the raging storm.

After sailing for several minutes, part of the pretty picture distorted, then vanished. A hole, nearly two hundred phineals in diameter, tore through the illusion. It revealed that odd white space with distorted sound. But even that white void fled in response to the tazerin's presence.

Waves crashed into the burrowed opening, and the *Promised Maiden* tipped forward. Jolted by the turbulence, Cornar braced himself against the waves.

As the *Promised Maiden* reached the hole, Cornar glanced back to Dalgilur. He could no longer see the pier, or the wrecked ships. Dalgilur's buildings and its mountain range were barely visible above the *Promised Maiden's* stern.

We made it, Cornar thought. He felt a burden lift from his shoulders, but there was still the storm.

Turning back to what lay ahead, Cornar watched as the tazerin burrowed through that white void and revealed the raging torrent.

Soon, they were beyond the white void and at the mercy of the World's Frown. Lightning surged across the sky, racing toward the *Promised Maiden*. Cornar gritted his teeth, but relaxed as the lightning dissipated. Even the waters—as turbulent as they were—became calm around the *Promised Maiden*.

Cheers resounded across the main deck.

"It worked, Cor!" Igan exclaimed, grabbing Cornar by the arm. "We did it!"

Cornar smiled, sighing with relief. Lightning continued surging across the sky and rain fell from abysmal clouds, but neither reached the *Promised Maiden*. The tazerin—similar to Krindal's gem—burrowed a tunnel for the ship to sail through. It was an astounding sight.

62

VOWS

"Tension rose all across Aridia. Those who believed in Cheserith fought against the Channelers of Aridia in a devastating civil war. The Channelers were forced to flee to the heart of the continent, and sought refuge in a remote mountain range."

- From *The Thousand Years War, Part I*, page 49

Two days had passed since Pagus had gone missing. No one had seen the boy. It was as if Pagus had just vanished. Iltar inquired of the attendants at the Royal Archive, but they hadn't seen Pagus. The librarian, Vaegris, had not dealt with Pagus either.

Alanya's guards kept watch for the boy, but Pagus never returned to the mansion. Bilda and Agen took it upon themselves to search Vabenack, but the Translucent Fields were empty.

Pagus's disappearance angered Iltar, but there was nothing he could do about it. So, Iltar returned to his research, alone. The women were busy helping prepare the palace, since it was the day before the Imperial Ball.

Iltar strolled into the Royal Archive near the crack of dawn, hoping to have a day of uninterrupted study. He had finished most of the volumes Vaegris had delivered to him in the last week. Today, Iltar would require more material to read.

The Royal Archive was oddly quiet. Usually, the old librarian could be heard shuffling about, but there were no signs of his stirring. Iltar sauntered through the archive, searching the aisles as he passed. He walked from one side of the archive to the other and even glimpsed a desk at the far end of the archive—it too was empty.

Well this is odd, Iltar thought, furrowing his brow. "Vaegris!" he called, walking back across the archive. "Vaegris, are you here?"

As Iltar passed the entrance, one of the Crimson Praetorians turned around. "We haven't seen Master Vaegris today," the Praetorian said coldly.

Iltar spun, shocked that the man was speaking to him—no Praetorian had as much as flinched since he began visiting the archive. "And when was he seen last?" Iltar asked. The Praetorian shrugged and returned to his post.

Great, Iltar sighed. He glanced at the Praetorians, wondering if he could peruse the archive without them interfering. That was a risk Iltar was willing to take. Acting nonchalant, Iltar returned to his alcove in the corner of the underground library. He read through the rest of the tome he was studying. Then he left his alcove in search for other texts.

I wonder if I can find something about this Crimson Eye, he thought. Iltar didn't know where to start looking. Hopefully, one of the titles would have that name in it.

One book caught his eye: *The Fall of the Cheserithean Empire.* Iltar started upon reading the title. He grabbed the book, but his hand went *through* the spine.

"An illusion," Iltar whispered, pulling his hand back. *Why would they have an illusion of a book?* Mindolarnians were odd, but putting an illusion of a book in a secret archive? Preposterous...

Iltar continued scanning the shelves. He came to another interesting volume, *The Prophets of the Trifica.* This too was an illusion.

What on Kalda?! Iltar cursed. A second illusion? *What was this*—he suddenly came to a realization.

"Oh, you stupid boy..." Iltar shook his head. He leaned toward the illusionary book, a scowl forming upon his face. "Pagus, I know you can hear me. Stop this charade at once."

He waited for a moment, hoping the illusion might *do* something to indicate that Pagus was listening. A mage could hear through the illusions they created, regardless of its form. It was an excellent way to spy on someone.

The illusion didn't *do* anything.

Foolish boy, Iltar thought. *You have no idea what you're doing. This is not Soroth.* Taking a deep breath, Iltar spoke to the illusion once again. "This isn't Soroth, Pagus. Your father's influence cannot save you here."

Again, there was no change.

Iltar grumbled, then continued his search for something to read. Finally— after finding three more illusionary books—he found a text called the *Legacy of Ku'tharn.* Iltar remembered hearing that name while at the palace. The book shared the name with the palace's southern temple.

Interesting... he thought, eyeing the book—it wasn't that big. He could easily read the entire text within a few hours. Iltar took note of its position on the shelf and tucked the tome under his arm. He continued searching the rows of shelves, but he couldn't tell much from the titles.

I probably should have found an appendix or something, Iltar sighed. His eyes then fell upon another tome, *Basics of the Keadal Tongue.*

Iltar grinned and took the book, tucking it under his arm beside the other one. He finished winding his way through the various rows, but didn't find anything else. Iltar did, however, come across another illusionary tome.

With only two books in hand, Iltar returned to his alcove. He set aside the primer for the Keadal language and began with the *Legacy of Ku'tharn.*

Iltar flipped through the first few pages, coming to the preface. "*She is the mother of us all, the eternal goddess, daughter of Cheserith. After the Crimson Eye devastated our world, she led three others of our Father's children into safety, guided by the Grand Oracle. Through her the Lish'sha roam Kalda once again, and the line of Cheserith is preserved. It is she who birthed the first qui'sha in this new era of desolation. Praise be her name—Ku'tharn the Eternal—for all time."*

He then flipped the page, seeing a depiction of a beautiful woman—tall and slender—standing atop a jagged cliff. Her left hand was raised high, clutching a translucent yellow orb. She wore a flowing crimson dress, with woven symbols similar to the robe Reflection wore in Vabenack. Silky black hair hung almost to her waist, and her turquoise eyes gazed skyward.

There was something oddly alluring about that picture. Iltar found himself gazing at it—for how long he couldn't tell.

Research, Iltar, research! he chided himself, flipping the page.

"Long ago, when the Crimson Eye decimated the world of the gods, Ku'tharn survived. She took her sister—the goddess Es'bereth—and the gods Zal'usnyl and Yarthar'sthul— and fled to the Heart of the World. They slumbered for centuries, watched over by the Grand Oracle..."

The text continued with myth-like narration that sounded borderline scriptural.

Finally, Iltar came to a passage that shed some light on the Crimson Eye. It was a quotation from this goddess, Ku'tharn, as she taught her followers about the past. *"The traitorous metallic beast came, wearing the Crimson Eye upon his chest. The Eye shone with a luster that debilitated the gods. They became vulnerable, even pliable, under its influence. None could resist its gaze, except my Father. The Crimson Eye bound any whose veins ran with divine blood..."* The passage continued citing the horrors one experienced when subjected to the Crimson Eye's influence. Iltar found it similar to emotionally charged rhetoric.

"And once the gods were bound, the bearer of the Eye purged the gods from Kalda, hurling them to other worlds, the realms of exile."

Iltar paused, sitting back on his bench. *Other worlds?* he mused, shaking his head in disbelief. *Like in The* Myth of Morgrid. A boyish smile formed on Iltar's face. Could there really be other worlds? Iltar had seen Vabenack, but that was like a different reality. This text, however, claimed there were worlds *other* than Kalda. Iltar's mind spun with possibilities.

He soon regained his composure and continued reading. *"After the dismal tale was recited, a vow went abroad through the Heart of the World: 'May the Crimson Eye remain hidden for all time.' Since then, the followers of Ku'tharn use this vow to identify a brother or sister, as all who know it would zealously fight to defend their gods from exile."*

Iltar continued reading for several hours. The book only mentioned the Crimson Eye several times more. He couldn't deduce much else about it, but Iltar assumed the Crimson Eye might be a tevisral of some kind. *What would it be like,* he wondered, *to control a god...*

The rest of the book proved intriguing. Some of the topics sounded similar to things he had read in *The Codices of Soron Thahan.* One such topic, however, he had never come across elsewhere. Supposedly, Ku'tharn chose a pious man to revive a long extinct race—part god and part man. She bade him mate with her and eventually presented him with a child who would live far longer than any man. His mind would be far superior, able to fathom the mysteries of divinity.

Iltar wondered about that passage. His mind was taken back to his conversation with Raedina four days ago. The princess had mentioned that the Keadal tongue was spoken by her ancestors—the true rulers of Kalda.

From what Iltar could tell, this Ku'tharn and her offspring fit Raedina's cryptic description.

Though the text did not expressly say it, Iltar supposed the Mindolarnians must be part of this race, whatever they were.

After putting *Legacy of Ku'tharn* aside, Iltar picked up the primer of the Keadal tongue. He flipped through several pages explaining the purpose of the book and how to most efficiently use it. The text was straightforward. Iltar then came to a table spanning several pages, filled with the Keadal alphabet and its Common equivalents.

Iltar felt a sense of victory. He *would* unravel the secrets of this language, and then the Translucent Fields of Vabenack would finally obey him.

⁓•⊂

The sun was setting as Lirathay'lu finished planting the last bush in the upper gardens around the Mindolarn Palace. He wiped the sweat from his brow and sighed heavily.

"Tired, Sakal?" Gersu asked. He was a middle-aged gardener who had worked in the palace most of his life, a decent man. But the poor fool actually believed all the Mindolarnian religious rhetoric. Lirathay'lu had gazed into Gersu's mind as soon as they met—of course, Gersu had no clue it had happened. Lirathay'lu made him just as oblivious as Constable Hashar and the other watchmen.

Lirathay'lu gave the man a hard look. "That's a stupid question," he said sardonically, sighing once again.

Gersu laughed, wiping the dirt from his hands. He was careful not to get it on the path. The Royals were picky about getting dirt on their precious stone.

"Why don't you head back, I can take care of the rest of this," Gersu said.

Lirathay'lu nodded. He sauntered back through the gardens and came to the path leading to the palace. He was about to descend the steps when a Crimson Praetorian approached with his hand extended.

"Stay where you are," the Praetorian said.

Great… Lirathay'lu drew his lips to a line. He had been careful to blend in with the other servants. He loathed saying that pitiful vow. Had someone picked up on that?

"Just wait until the procession passes," the Praetorian said.

Procession? Lirathay'lu peered around the trees. Soldiers were marching, surrounding servants carrying a covered palanquin of intricate design. The palanquin exuded everything Mindolarnian.

Must be a member of the Royal Family, he mused.

The Praetorian turned from Lirathay'lu, taking up a sentinel position where the paths to the garden and the palace met.

Others were gathered along the palace's grand stairs. They lined the path from the courtyard to the palace.

Soon, a proclamation reached Lirathay'lu's ears. "… to commemorate this monumental event. Tomorrow will be a day recorded in the annals of history, as Our Imperial Grace will unveil the advancements of the Hilinard…"

Our Imperial Grace? Lirathay'lu wondered, and then he heard *it.*

"Citizens of Mindolarn, all make way before our beloved emperor, His Imperial Majesty Marden Midivar, son of Madars, descendant of Cheserith through the loins of Ku'tharn. His Imperial Majesty has returned to the seat of the empire to honor the great men and women who have labored without rest to advance our empire. He graces us with his presence to commemorate this monumental event…"

Lirathay'lu tuned out the crier, gazing sternly at the palanquin now crossing the path through the Middle Gardens.

A few royal attendants gathered behind Lirathay'lu, muttering about the Praetorian barring their path, and then they heard the crier announcing the emperor's presence.

"Oh my, Meralda, can you believe this?" an attendant asked with a gasp, her voice high pitched.

"Perhaps we can glimpse him," Meralda said, and giggled giddily.

They pushed past Lirathay'lu, peering around the Praetorian. Both women were beaming with excitement.

Lirathay'lu fought the urge to roll his eyes. He focused on the approaching procession, eyeing the palanquin. *I wonder if he's really in there?* Lirathay'lu wondered. Of all Mindolarn's brothers, Marden was the most reclusive.

Soon, the emperor's forward guard passed. There were at least thirty soldiers ahead of the palanquin. Mages were interspersed among the soldiers, carrying channeling staffs. And then the palanquin passed.

The women sighed with disappointment, as the windows of the palanquin were closed. Lirathay'lu had expected that.

Another thirty or so soldiers passed with a second attachment of mages. The emperor's rear guard forced the followers trailing behind the procession to keep back a good twenty phineals.

Soon, the forward guard entered the palace, followed by the palanquin.

Once the last of the procession was inside the palace, the Praetorian moved from the gardens, allowing Lirathay'lu entrance onto the palace's main path. The women followed the crowd into the palace while Lirathay'lu headed down the stairs.

Odd that they would announce his arrival, Lirathay'lu thought. *I would have expected Medis to do something like that, but not Marden.*

Lirathay'lu passed other servants, all chattering about the unexpected arrival of their monarch. They too found it out of character. As Lirathay'lu made his way to the servants' quarters, a conflict began swelling within him. He had vowed to watch and observe—like the other usa'zin'sha—but a deep yearning compelled him to commit an act so treacherous that it might brand him vik'sha. *No, it's too perfect an opportunity,* he thought. Yes, the emperor would be vulnerable. But Lirathay'lu wasn't an assassin—he was no Zanxsthy'll.

Struggling with the growing conflict, Lirathay'lu turned back to the palace. *There will be too many guards,* he argued with himself. But he *could* bypass that. The thought of feeling the winds beneath him flooded his mind, and for a moment that distracted him from the conflict.

But right now he had to concentrate. *He's the last of Mindolarn's brothers,* Lirathay'lu thought. *If he were to die, the empire would never be the same. In fact, it might be better off...* The fat prince was next in line to inherit the throne. *Jeridi, isn't it?* Lirathay'lu squinted thoughtfully. *If he were in charge, the Mindolarn Empire would change. Kalda could benefit from that.* Jeridi wanted peace. But how long before one of his brothers slayed him and claimed the throne for himself? That would create a power struggle, ignite a civil war.

Lirathay'lu liked that notion, but then the unified voice of the Ril'Sha came to his mind. *You are to watch and observe—nothing more. Do not dare to meddle in the affairs of men.*

The conflict inside him was raging now, like a great storm. Ideas attacked each other like bolts of lightning; their thunder pierced his heart.

He looked to Kistern, which hung in the twilight of the western horizon; the white moon was nearly at full phase. *I have to make a choice,* Lirathay'lu thought. But this was not a choice to be made lightly. If he stayed aloof, the world would keep going as it was, but if he acted he could create turmoil. And that turmoil might benefit mankind.

Do you think you can take on an entire garrison? Lirathay'lu asked himself. There was a faint "yes" lingering in the back of his mind.

Lirathay'lu contemplated attacking the palace, striking during the ball. A sense of serenity came over him, and he *knew* that was what he must do.

Instead of continuing to the servants' quarters, Lirathay'lu strode toward the bridge leading to the palace gates. Tomorrow he would slay an emperor, but more importantly he would once again feel the winds rushing beneath him. He basked in that realization, relishing his future embrace with his greatest loves.

Darkness had long since veiled Mindolarn when Iltar returned to Alanya's mansion. A note was left for him at the gates, informing him that the acolytes were going to enter Vabenack once more to search for Pagus.

"He still hasn't shown?" Iltar asked one of the guards. The man shook his head. Grumbling, Iltar stomped across the mansion's grounds. He entered the house through the main foyer and noticed Elsia sitting in the parlor.

The countess looked worried. "You didn't find him?" she asked.

"No," Iltar said, quickly crossing the foyer.

"Iltar, please..." Elsia pleaded, her voice trembling.

Elsia hurried to him. She looked desperate. "Please find my nephew."

Her pleading gave him pause. Did he dare tell her what he assumed? Iltar had found another illusory tome after finishing the primer and the *Legacy of Ku'tharn*. His hypothesis was that Pagus had pilfered tomes, replacing them with illusionary ones, and was hiding somewhere—or so he hoped.

"I should have been more concerned three days ago." Elsia shook her head, her lips quivering. "I guess I don't know him as well as I thought."

"I don't think Pagus is in any danger of being harmed," Iltar said, then added the next with reluctance. "He's probably hiding somewhere, reading some old tome." For as much a pain as Pagus could be, the boy had a definite thirst for knowledge. *If he were only more disciplined,* Iltar thought.

"Let's hope you're right," Elsia said, then somberly walked to the door.

"I'll look for him tomorrow," Iltar said, "even if I have to miss the ball. I'm sure Alanya will understand." At least, he *hoped* she would understand. Iltar liked the idea of not dressing up again.

"Thank you," Elsia said, pulling the large door open.

After Elsia left, Iltar hurried to the kitchen and grabbed a goblet of the dream elixir. They had since brought Pagus's batch to rest with the original brew—it too was separated into bottles to more easily track consumption.

Six bottles had been taken: Agen, Bilda, Tigan, Kaelar, Petral, and Alanya. Iltar took one for himself and drank a bit of it once inside Alanya's bedchamber.

The high duchess lay on her bed, wrapped up in the blankets. *She didn't leave any blankets for me,* Iltar pouted. He undressed and put on a pair of light pajamas. Though it was fall in the northern hemisphere, Mindolarn rarely got cold at night.

Iltar swallowed the last of the elixir and began to feel its effects. *Potent… does it get stronger with age?*

— ◆ —

Iltar found himself in a twisted version of the Mindolarn Palace. The First Emblem—the symbol needed to bring one to Vabenack—was everywhere. The emblem's jagged sword, its accompanying spikes, and its eight-sided stars marred every surface, wherever he looked.

How strange. Iltar narrowed his eyes.

People appeared from out of nowhere. Their clothes were covered in the emblem, as were their faces—some had the emblem tattooed while others were branded with it.

"Just bizarre." Iltar shook his head. He needed to find something flat that could accommodate a door.

He came to a section of the palace wall and constructed the doorway, speaking the Keadal phrase, "Alza Cho'k sa'maz nira." The keystones glowed their yellow light, and the doorway erupted in a brilliant flash. Iltar had come to understand what that phrase meant in Common, loosely translated: "In the name of the Immortal Triumvirate, I command thee open."

Soon, Iltar was back in Vabenack.

The three acolytes were bouncing around, playing the game they had invented—Last Barsion Standing.

"Hey!" Iltar shouted, and the boys froze. "Aren't you supposed to be looking for Pagus?"

"We looked, Master," Bilda answered. "He's not around." Iltar frowned, but started as an eruption of light burst beside him. Another portal open, the scene beyond the opening resembled a lavish dining hall.

And then, Alanya entered Vabenack. The high duchess looked stunned. Her eyes were wide, and her mouth hung open. "Am I..." she muttered, glancing to Iltar, "really here?"

"Yup," Iltar answered succinctly. He was still frustrated about not finding Pagus here in Vabenack.

Alanya's surprised expression turned to jubilation. She fell upon the ground, shouting praises. "It's so beautiful!" she exclaimed, running her hands across the translucent ground. The shifting landscape beneath tantalized her.

Iltar let Alanya relish the experience and stepped toward the boys. They had since resumed their game, wildly flinging destructive magics at each other. The acolytes were *actually* quite skilled. Bilda had the best coordination by far.

That boy will be an astounding mage. Iltar smiled. He had grown fond of Bilda these last few months. In some ways, Bilda reminded Iltar of himself at that age. Those were good times, before the pain...

And then, Iltar was overcome. His mother's screams echoed in his mind. *No!*

Smoke filled his nostrils.

Not here!

Eruptions of magic filled the air—both from Iltar's memory and from the boys playing their game.

Stop! Iltar clutched his ears, dropping to his knees. It didn't help. The noises plagued his mind. They seemed amplified somehow. *Stop! Stop it now!*

He hadn't had one of his fits since leaving Soroth. Iltar hadn't told Alanya of his fits, either—how could he? She would probably think him mad, deranged even.

This is not real, Iltar told himself. *Your screams are not real. This smoke is not—*

Cool fingers on his arms drew him from his dreadful reverie. Iltar opened his eyes, as Alanya's elegant hands slid around his shoulders.

"Are you okay?" she whispered, her lips close to his ear. Her sweet scent calmed him. "You were having one of your fits, weren't you?"

Iltar's eyes widened. He pulled away, spinning to face her.

Alanya clasped her hands gently, still kneeling. "Don't be upset," she said. "Bilda told me."

Bilda? Iltar raised an eyebrow, glancing at the boy. The youth was bouncing like a ball on the ground—his reckless movements were growing graceful.

"Bilda came to me one night last month," Alanya said. "He said, 'If you plan to be with Master Iltar, you have to know how to take care of him.' The boy really likes you," she said with a chuckle. "He insisted that if I was going to be *with* you that I should be prepared."

Alanya paused for a moment, smiling. "Bilda told me that one day you were going to start panicking, and instead of panicking myself, I should go touch you, because that draws you out of whatever you're experiencing."

Iltar's expression softened.

"He didn't say more, but I understood what the boy was telling me."

Alanya's words surprised Iltar. Not even Anela—with her near obsession with Iltar—was this understanding of his fits.

"Aren't you curious about what I see?" Iltar asked.

The high duchess shook her head. "We all have our secrets, Iltar. I figured if you wanted to tell me you would, when you were ready."

Surprised, Iltar moved toward her, but was drawn by the shrilling cry of, "Master!" echoing from behind him.

Both Iltar and Alanya looked to the noise. That pained beckon echoed once again as a darkened figure approached from across the horizon.

"Is that Pagus?" Alanya asked.

Iltar didn't answer. He burst toward the figure, sprinting across the translucent ground. The acolytes noticed Iltar and stopped their game, dashing behind their master.

"Master!" the word wailed.

That sounds like Pagus, Iltar thought.

The word was repeated again and again, and Iltar *knew* that it was Pagus.

Pagus staggered, then fell to the Translucent Fields. *What happened?* Iltar gritted his teeth.

Soon, Iltar and the others were upon Pagus. The boy looked ragged, though his clothes were intact. It didn't matter what you were wearing when falling asleep, one would appear in Vabenack wearing whatever clothing one *thought* one should wear. For Iltar, it was his black tunic and pants, along with his matching boots. For Pagus, it was a mage's robe.

Pagus's hair was disheveled and cuts marred his face. The wounds looked fresh.

"Pagus!" Iltar shouted, kneeling beside the youth. A groan left Pagus's lips as Iltar sat him upright, taking the boy in his arms.

"Master..." Pagus groaned. "I... I found you."

"Pagus, what happened?" Iltar demanded. The boy's robe was wet. Iltar shot a glance to his hand, which was damp and reddened. *Blood?* His eyes widened.

"I'm sorry... Master," Pagus groaned, sounding delirious.

"What's wrong with him?" Agen asked.

"He's bleeding!" Bilda blurted, pointing at Iltar's hand.

"Master Iltar, do something!" Tigan shouted.

Iltar shot a hand to the boys, gesturing for them to be quiet.

"Pagus," Iltar said sternly, "tell me what happened."

His apprentice looked ashamed. "Th-they caught me... yesterday. That old codger of a librarian, he saw me putting back one of the tomes. I... I guess he stumbled across my illusions."

"So that *was* you!" Iltar shouted, but then bit his tongue. This was no time to scold Pagus.

"They have me in the dungeon," Pagus muttered, his eyes struggling to focus. "In the palace. Please, Master… free me." A tear trickled down Pagus's cheek. "I hurt…" the boy wept, moaning softly.

Iltar sucked in a deep breath. He hoped Pagus had learned his lesson. The boy's imprisonment was probably the most severe punishment he had ever experienced.

"I will talk with Prince Jeridi," Iltar said. "We met him at the palace a few days ago. He seemed the most merciful of all the princes."

"And I'll speak with Raedina," Alanya knelt beside Iltar, stroking Pagus's hair. "I'm sure we can rectify the situation."

"No…" Pagus cried. "You can't talk to them…"

Alanya looked confused.

"What do you mean, Pagus?" Iltar demanded. Pagus coughed, and his eyes struggled to focus once again.

"Enough of this," Iltar grumbled, then uttered an incantation. Green light formed in Iltar's hand and wisped to Pagus's unseen wounds. The boy's robe glowed a vibrant emerald hue.

"I didn't know necromancers could use arpran magic," Alanya said.

"My prowess in the magical arts exceeds the typical necromancer or illusionist," Iltar said, watching the magic repair Pagus's body.

Pagus took a deep breath and blinked several times, focusing on Iltar. "Why didn't you do that sooner?" Pagus demanded.

Typical Pagus. Iltar drew his lips to a line. "Are you going to answer me?"

The youth grinned slyly, then his face turned somber. "You can't talk to them, Master, because they're the ones who put me here." Alanya gasped.

"Not the nice emperor-man!" Bilda blurted.

Pagus turned to Bilda and nodded dreadfully. He then looked to Iltar. "They want you dead, Master. They want us all dead."

The acolytes tensed, and Alanya's face flushed with anger. "Why?!" the high duchess demanded. "What has Iltar done?"

"They believe he killed their beloved uncle, the late emperor," Pagus answered. "Because Master Iltar looks like the killer."

Alanya gasped incredulously. "But that was an Alathian! A grand mage!"

Iltar raised an eyebrow. *So, Almar killed the emperor,* he mused. *My, my, what have you gotten me into, brother?* That realization brought a flood of understanding to Iltar. It explained why his encounters with the Royals had been so intense. Raedina's restrained hostility came from a belief that Iltar was his brother. Both Iltar and his older brother—Almar—were the spitting image of their father, Adrin. Iltar imagined that if all three of them were together, one would have a hard time telling them apart.

Wait, Iltar started. *If the Mindolarnians believed me to be the murderer of the late emperor, why would they grant me access to the Royal Archive?* That question gave Iltar pause.

"The ball is a trap," Pagus said. "I… I overheard them. They were talking after they beat me. I didn't hear much, except that they hope to draw you to them, where they can strike in full force."

"That's why the emperor arrived," Alanya muttered, slumping on the translucent ground.

"I don't get it," Bilda scratched his head.

"Because they assume I want to kill him," Iltar said flatly. "They're using the emperor as bait."

Pagus nodded. "They think we're Alathians… that's why they're torturing me. They want to know how many more Agents of the Order are here in the capital. I don't even know what those are…"

Iltar considered the predicament. He could avoid this mess entirely if they fled Mindolarn at once. But Pagus would still be doomed.

"Please, Master," Pagus's voice was shaky. "Don't forsake me!" More tears trickled down the youth's face. "Have pity…" *How odd.* Never had Iltar seen Pagus beg… but the boy had never experienced such peril.

"Iltar, we can't just leave him," Alanya said, her voice panicked.

Iltar, however, studied Pagus fiercely. "Reflection?" Iltar asked, "is that you?"

"What?" Pagus gasped, mortified by the accusation. "You… you think me that—that thing who speaks to you?" His face twisted with horror. "No, Master! Please—"

A sense of dread—far beyond what Pagus had already expressed—smeared across the youth's face. "I hear them," Pagus wailed. "They're coming again!" The boy shook uncontrollably. "They're waking me! Please, Master, don't let them kill—"

Pagus vanished.

"What happened?" Alanya demanded.

"He was pulled from Vabenack," Iltar answered somberly. Iltar had never seen it happen from this end. Each time *he* was the one pulled from this realm.

"We… we can't just leave him in there," Agen muttered, pacing back and forth.

"We'll free him," Bilda said stoically. "No one takes my friend and hurts him."

"No…" Iltar muttered. "You're not going to the palace," he said sternly.

Pagus's blood—still on his hand—conjured a fury buried deep within him; a burning sensation that Iltar thought had been lost ages ago. Though Pagus had been a nuisance, he was still *Iltar's* apprentice. And Iltar was *not* going to allow *another* apprentice to be subject to the horrors of a tyrant. He would rescue Pagus, no matter what odds awaited him.

With his eyes still on the blood, Iltar declared, "If anyone is going to rescue Pagus, it is going to be me and me alone."

> *"The Channelers of Aridia decided upon a course of action that would safeguard themselves against their enemies. It would, however, come at a great cost. Nevertheless, they were united in their decision. The men of Aridia who pledged allegiance to Cheserith must be eradicated. Their ideals were a danger to all Kalda."*

> \- From *The Thousand Years War, Part I,* page 50

The plan Iltar had concocted to rescue Pagus was flawless. But the women didn't see it that way. They obviously didn't understand the laws of magic, else they would have immediately consented to Iltar's plan. Both Elsia and Alanya, however, fought him on the matter.

"No, I won't let you!" Elsia shouted. "He's my nephew. *My* nephew!" The countess's rage permeated her every word. Elsia's maternal instincts had kicked in the moment Iltar divulged Pagus's predicament. Growling, Elsia paced back and forth within the guesthouse's solarium. The sun had not risen yet, but the horizon was a warm orange.

"The palace is too dangerous," Iltar said sternly. "It'll be easier for me if I go in alone."

"And if you get caught?" Elsia asked incredulously.

Iltar sat back in his chair, folding his arms. Did he need to say it? Elsia knew he would stop anyone who stood in his way, with lethal force if necessary. No one would bar Iltar from rescuing Pagus.

"The Royals are probably expecting someone to go in after him," Alanya said somberly.

"That's why I'll make it seem like we're attending the ball," Iltar said. "My illusions will be flawless." Those illusions would run their course as Iltar made his way to the dungeon.

"And what happens when someone bumps into one of your illusions?" Alanya asked frankly. "You might be the best puppet master to walk Kalda but you can't control the actions of everyone around you."

Iltar had taken that problem into consideration. His illusions wouldn't be ordinary. They would have substance to them. Iltar considered strategically placing other illusions throughout the ball to watch every angle, but that seemed too tedious.

"I have that covered," he insisted. "Remember how I said they would have substance to them? They will be transmutations covered in illusions."

Elsia growled again. "You can be so arrogant!" she yelled, slamming her fists on the glass table. Iltar half-expected it to crack. "This is no time for one of your ego-trips, Iltar. My nephew is in danger."

You don't think I know that? Iltar thought, raising an eyebrow at Elsia.

"Iltar," Alanya said gently, then reached across the table and touched his arm. "I don't say this lightly, but I hate your plan. What if you run into more resistance than you can handle? What if Pagus has been moved? Not to mention, how do you plan on fooling Raedina when she talks to me—or rather, my illusion? The princess might not be able to walk through the illusion, but she'll *see* through the ruse at the first wrong answer. And, honestly my dear, you don't know *everything* about me."

Iltar felt stung by that last remark. But it was the truth.

"I don't think they're going to keep Pagus in the dungeon, Iltar," Alanya continued firmly. "I'm positive they will move him to the ball." She chose her next words carefully. "He will be of use to them."

Iltar could only imagine what she implied. Alanya probably assumed the Mindolarnians would use Pagus to demonstrate the capabilities of the new weaponized tevisrals. Of course, Alanya couldn't say that in front of Elsia.

"And back to Raedina," Alanya said. "She is a shrewd woman. My role will be of the utmost importance. Elsia's role, however, could easily be played by anyone—no offense, my dear." Alanya gestured apologetically to the countess.

"None taken," Elsia said with a quick smile. Her fury abated for a moment.

"And because she wouldn't need to be present," Alanya added, "she can go with you down to the dungeon."

They're thinking about this all wrong, Iltar sighed. The illusions didn't have to last long. Even if he had to fight his way into the dungeon, Iltar could still reach Pagus before any reinforcements would arrive. And that's all that he needed to do.

"You don't look convinced," Alanya observed, her lips drawn to a line.

Iltar shook his head. "If Elsia comes with me, then I have to protect someone other than myself. We are sticking with my plan. I go to the dungeon alone."

Elsia threw up her hands, shaking her head furiously. Then as she regained her composure, Elsia glanced to Iltar's closed fist resting on the table. Her expression said she knew he was holding something.

Not yet, he thought. Iltar always had a flair for the dramatic. It was one of the chief reasons he began studying as an illusionist. When Iltar was a young boy, he wanted to be part of a performing-mage troupe.

Once Elsia calmed herself, she spoke to Iltar. "You know, I can handle a sword. My father taught me." Iltar grunted, not amused. "I won the Women's Sorothian Swordsmanship Competition," Elsia said, "twice."

They have such an event? Iltar wondered. He had never heard of the competition, not even for men. Perhaps Cornar never participated. And if he did, the competition obviously wasn't prestigious.

"You know, you haven't even said how *you* intend to escape," Elsia said petulantly. The countess put her hands on her hips, demanding an answer. Iltar looked at her for a moment and then glanced to his hand. *I guess this is as good a time as any…*

"This," he said, relaxing his fist. The object inside dropped onto the table. The women's eyes widened as Iltar revealed the genius of his plan. This was why he needed to go into the dungeon alone.

Alanya sighed, shaking her head. She knew all too well what lay on the table—after all, it was one of the chief ingredients of the dream elixir.

"A rogulin crystal," Elsia muttered.

Iltar ignored her. "This is why I must go in alone. If we're all scattered across the palace, there's no way to regroup safely to teleport out of there." He sucked in his breath. "I don't know how *your* plans end, but were you thinking we just stroll out of the palace?" His question was rhetorical. "Once you leave the ball," he pointed to Alanya, "they'll grow suspicious. We could get out," he looked to Elsia, "but then we doom Alanya. And I don't want that. Your plan requires us to all meet somewhere and further complicate our escape."

The women were silent for a while, and then Alanya spoke. "I'm not leaving with you, Iltar." Her voice was stern. "If I abscond, I'll be branded a traitor to the empire. But if I attend the ball, I have a chance to rectify the entire situation. After you flee Mindolarn—and not attack the emperor—that will be proof enough that you were not the Alathian who slew Emperor Monddar. I may face other consequences, but it will pale in comparison to treason."

Iltar had not considered the motives behind Alanya's decision. He had assumed she would follow him back to Soroth. Perhaps he was wrong about her…

"What about the acolytes?" Elsia asked, sounding concerned. "How are they going to get to safety?"

"When they awake I'm sending them to the *Yaelinum*," Iltar answered. "I wanted the two of you to go with them…" He studied Alanya.

The high duchess sat straight-backed, looking dispassionate. Alanya didn't look like the woman he had come to know. "Don't expect me to pack up my mansion," she said. "I'm not going with you. And if you try forcing me to—"

"I won't force you," Iltar interrupted, turning away. He gazed at the palace rising across the city's northern skyline.

Silence hung in the solarium for a moment.

"Are we in agreement?" Alanya asked.

Iltar turned to the high duchess. He could see sadness beneath her stern façade. "Yes," he answered succinctly.

"Okay," Alanya pursed her lips and rose from her seat. She left the room without saying anything else.

Once the high duchess was gone, Elsia leaned over the table. "If she's going, so am I."

Iltar just stared at Elsia. "I suppose the only way to stop you would be to restrain you with a mind-control spell."

The countess nodded. "And that would be an unnecessary taxation of your concentration," she said flatly.

Elsia had a point. Arguing about her joining him was futile. "Have you ever fought while enhanced with magic?" Iltar asked.

"Never."

"Then we'd better get you some practice."

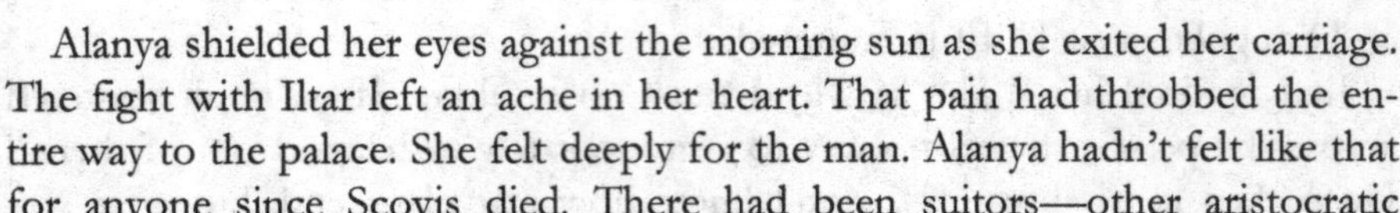

Alanya shielded her eyes against the morning sun as she exited her carriage. The fight with Iltar left an ache in her heart. That pain had throbbed the entire way to the palace. She felt deeply for the man. Alanya hadn't felt like that for anyone since Scovis died. There had been suitors—other aristocratic men—but none of them made her *feel* the way Iltar made her feel. There was something extraordinary about Iltar, though he could be rather oblivious.

Alanya pushed aside her hurt as she approached the palace gates. "I am High Duchess Alanya Tasivir," she said to the guards. "I'm here to help with the finishing touches for the ball."

The guards signaled for the gate to be opened, and soon Alanya was within the palace grounds. She hurriedly made her way to the palace proper. The last touches had been made to the gardens—the plants seemed more alive than usual.

Oh, Iltar, I hope you can accept my decision… she thought in despair. *My place is here. How could I leave everything behind?* And what of her servants and her guards? If she fled with Iltar, her entire household would suffer. Those men and women had been loyal for decades.

This is the best choice, she thought as she entered the palace. Alanya slowed her pace and glanced at the mural on the ceiling. Her eyes were drawn to the center, toward that figure in red standing behind what she now recognized as the doorway to Vabenack.

And you'll never be too far away. She thought of Iltar, tears forming in her eyes. *I can always reach you in Vabenack. No matter what happens to me I can always find escape there.*

Alanya sucked in her breath to regain her composure. She had to be calm now, acting as if nothing had changed. She couldn't think of Pagus suffering in the bowels of the palace. Nor could Alanya think of what would happen to Iltar if he were caught.

Amid her dismay, Alanya heard a greeting from Raedina. The princess was crossing the foyer. A growing animosity swelled within Alanya. She hadn't expected to hate the princess for what was happening to poor Pagus.

Suppressing her feelings, Alanya forced a smile. "Good morning."

"Where's your friend?" Raedina asked, settling into a posture that accentuated her hips.

"Elsia decided to search for her nephew," Alanya said with a sigh. "He still hasn't come back. She's going to the City Watch today with Iltar."

"Oh." Raedina looked surprised. "I hope he turns up soon."

She's an incredible liar, Alanya thought. The princess seemed so genuine.

"What else needs to be done?" Alanya asked, stepping across the foyer.

The princess joined her and they walked side by side. "I was just about to check on their progress," Raedina said.

⊸•⊂

Iltar watched his acolytes climb into the wagon Alanya had provided. They had packed their things while Iltar made one last trip to the Hilinard to recover the research notes they had left in their alcoves. Iltar didn't close out the alcoves though, so as to not arouse suspicion from anyone who might report the change to the Mindolarn Royalty. Empty alcoves wouldn't be all that conspicuous.

All twelve boys took their seats, looking somber. Bilda had shared the news about Pagus while Iltar was discussing his rescue plan with the women.

"We'll see you in two-and-a-half–to–three weeks," Iltar told them. "I've written instructions for the captain." He looked to Agen, the oldest of the lot. "Make sure he gets them." Agen nodded.

"Now make sure this stays safe," Iltar said, lifting his trunk and heaving it onto the back of the wagon. "This has all of my research in it. And a few *other things.*"

He stepped back and examined the boys. Iltar had expected them to resist being sent away. But perhaps they—unlike the women—had realized the severity of the situation.

"Enjoy yourselves on your return trip to Soroth," Iltar said, coming beside Elsia. "Consider it a reward for all your hard work. Driver, you can go." The driver urged the horse forward, and the wagon moved across the stone path toward the gates.

"You gathered all the research, I presume?" Elsia asked, watching the wagon pull through the mansion's gates.

Iltar nodded. "And a little more."

Elsia cocked her head, looking quizzically at Iltar. "What?" she asked.

"Just following the example of my rebellious apprentice," he smiled wryly.

"Oh, you're a devious man, Iltar," Elsia grinned. "I like that." The countess took up her sword—commandeered from one of Alanya's guards—and rested the flat side against her shoulder. "Why don't we go over the rest of our plan while I adjust to the feel of this magic?"

⊸•⊂

Jeridi couldn't help but feel unnerved about killing Iltar. Raedina and the others were convinced—through their various methods of investigation—that Iltar was the Liberator of Klis. Jeridi, however, was not convinced. He kept coming back to his conversation with Iltar in the palace. There was palpable anger when Iltar mentioned Alacor—it permeated his every word. Iltar *knew* the grandmaster.

Troubled, Jeridi walked the Middle Gardens of the palace. They had been made over and decorated by the servants. Lightstones hung from the trees, along with strands of diaphanous red silk. Jeridi had hoped the garden's beauty would calm him.

His hopes were in vain. *They're making a mistake,* Jeridi sighed, stopping beside a stone bench. "There's no way I can stop them…" he muttered. Once the Midivars made a decision, it was nigh impossible to dissuade them. Trying to do so would be akin to attempting to dam a tidal wave. If a tidal wave was coming, you wouldn't try to stop it, you would run from it—

That's it! Jeridi's eyes widened with enlightenment. *I don't have to stop them…*

Renewed with stoic resolve, Jeridi dashed through the gardens. He came to the path leading to the palace. Guests had already arrived and were walking up the grand stairs. They hailed him as he passed, but Jeridi ignored them.

Petty small talk could wait—it *had* to wait. There was no time to waste if he was going to find Iltar and convince him *not* to attend the ball.

⸻◦⸺

Pagus was exhausted.

The last few days had been grueling. He couldn't recall when he had slept last. But his insomniac scramble for knowledge had been worthwhile. He sighed, closing *The Fall of the Cheserithean Empire*—a tome chronicling the history of a tumultuous war. But not just any war. It was the Dragon Wars, the war everyone thought to be myth, the war that had a thousand iterations.

Pagus had probably found the only definitive volume on the subject. And the damned Mindolarnians were keeping it all to themselves.

What selfish bastards, Pagus thought, gathering the books he had *borrowed* from the Royal Archive. *But what else would you expect from a bunch of half-breed beasts?*

Pagus had stumbled across some unnerving discoveries during his furtive studies. Things he wished he had never read, or *seen.* Those discoveries turned his world upside down. Shaking off those thoughts, Pagus returned to the Royal Archive cloaked in invisibility. He couldn't let the Praetorians see him—or anyone else for that matter.

Pagus returned to each of the illusionary books he had made and replaced the corresponding tome. He then went to the alcoves here in the archive, but to his surprise both alcoves were empty. His notes—along with those made by Aunty Elsia, the high duchess, and Master Iltar—were gone.

What on Kalda? Pagus shook his head, confused. He had heard Master Iltar's voice yesterday, speaking through one of the illusionary books.

They wouldn't have left, would they? he wondered. For a moment, Pagus feared he was stranded. But Aunty Elsia wouldn't have left him behind. *Maybe they're done,* he thought, making his way to the entrance to this secret section.

Pagus hadn't been out of the Hilinard in a few days. After making the decision to conduct his own research, he had sneaked out and returned with enough food to last a week. He found a secluded spot and made camp, so to speak.

Once he was away from the Royal Archive—and of course completely alone—Pagus shed his invisibility. The attendants let him pass without question, and Pagus made his way back to Alanya's mansion.

The sun was already setting when Pagus reached the gates of Alanya's home. Petral—the gate guard who had joined the quest to unravel the mysteries of Vabenack—gasped upon seeing Pagus. The man blinked with disbelief.

What's his problem? Pagus raised an eyebrow at the guard. "You look like you've seen a ghost, Petral," Pagus said, smirking. "Say, did the chef make dinner yet? I'm starving."

"H-h-how did you es-escape?" Petral stammered.

Now things are getting weird, Pagus thought. "Uh, what do you mean, Petral?"

"From the princes," Petral spoke, as if Pagus should know what he meant. "They took you two days ago."

"Huh?" Pagus furrowed his brow. Petral glanced uneasily to his fellow guardsman. The other guard looked just as confused.

Pagus was about to speak but heard heavy footfalls and labored breathing drawing near. He turned to see a plump man in grossly formal clothing running toward him and the guards. By the way the plump man was dressed, Pagus assumed him to be someone of importance. The man, however, looked a little too fat to be running.

As the man drew near, Petral and his fellow guard snapped to attention then addressed him in unison, "Your Imperial Grace!"

Taken aback, Pagus studied the plump man. Was this one of the princes? That thought made Pagus's blood boil. What he had learned beneath the Hilinard had made him biased against the Mindolarnian Royalty.

Abruptly stopping, the plump man bent over, bracing his hands on his knees. "Aren't you a little too fat to be running?" Pagus asked. The guards gasped, sounding appalled.

"I mean, you can run all you want…" Pagus shrugged, "I just wouldn't do it wearing such fancy clothing."

The plump man chuckled between breaths. "Good… wit…" he said, and then straightened. He continued breathing heavily as he turned to the guards. "Is this the residence of High Duchess Alanya Tasivir?"

"Yes, Your Imperial Grace," Petral answered shakily.

Cowardly much, Petral? Pagus glanced to the guard. Something had Petral spooked. The other guard looked just as nervous.

"Has Master Iltar left for the ball yet?" the plump man asked, dropping back to brace his hands on his knees.

Oh yeah, I forgot about that, Pagus thought. Perhaps that's why they packed up their things.

"Yes, he has," Petral answered, uneasily hovering his hand at his waist, above the hilt of his sheathed sword.

"Great…" the plump man groaned between heaves; he didn't seem to notice Petral's gesture. "Who are you?" he asked Pagus.

"I could ask the same thing." Pagus folded his arms.

"I like you, kid," the plump man said, chuckling. "Allow me to introduce myself. I am Jeridi Midivar, eldest son of Mindolarn the First."

Pagus drew his lips to a line.

"And you are?" Prince Jeridi asked.

"The name's Pagus."

"Oh, Master Iltar's missing apprentice." Jeridi nodded, taking in a deep breath. "Well, I have some grave news," he huffed. "My brothers and my cousins… plan on murdering your master tonight."

The guards didn't seem surprised at the atrocious accusation.

"Why…?" Pagus asked, looking about nervously.

"They think he's a grand mage from Alath… the one who slew my uncle, Monddar."

Pagus laughed, albeit nervously.

"They're blinded by vengeance," Jeridi continued, "and deceived by your grandmaster. I don't know what is going on between Alacor and Iltar, but I've thought about it on my way here, and I believe Alacor wants to be rid of your master. That's why he lied to us about all of you."

"Grandmaster Alacor?" Pagus asked with derision.

"There's contempt in your voice," Jeridi said. "Just like your master's. I know Iltar is not my uncle's murderer, though he does look like him." The prince turned to leave. "I'm the only one that believes otherwise. And by your demeanor, I can tell you're no Alathian. Now, if you'll excuse me, I must find your master and stop him from attending the ball." Jeridi took in a deep breath then jogged away.

"Wait!" Pagus shouted. Jeridi stopped, glancing back to Pagus.

"Why are you doing this?" Pagus demanded of the prince.

"Because I am tired of death," Jeridi said. "I've seen too much blood spilt in my lifetime." The plump prince continued down the road.

After the prince was out of earshot, Petral began muttering. "He didn't know who you were…" Petral looked to Pagus.

"Of course not." Pagus contorted his face with confusion, "I've never met the man. Now, where's Master Iltar?"

"On his way to the palace to rescue you," Petral said.

"Rescue me?" Pagus laughed. "Why, whatever for? I've never been to the palace." Petral stared at Pagus with disbelief.

"Well?" Pagus demanded.

"You came to him last night, in Vabenack. You said the princes captured you, claiming you all are Alathian spies, as His Imperial Grace said," Petral answered. "Master Iltar already sent the acolytes to your ship. They should be leaving port by now." Pagus's eyes went wide.

"You got to get to the palace," the other guard interjected, "else you're going to be stranded here."

"What do you mean?" Pagus asked warily—this whole situation grew stranger every passing moment. And it wasn't making sense.

"They plan to teleport out of the palace," Petral said.

Pagus bolted from the mansion's gates. He was not going to be trapped in Mindolarn—not with those *monsters* lurking about. Soon, Pagus caught up with the plump prince who was struggling to maintain his flighty pace.

"You look like you could use some help," Pagus said, then uttered an incantation. White enhancing particles gathered in his hands, then shot to the prince. The magic surged across Jeridi's body, enhancing his legs. Jeridi's jog turned into a steady sprint.

"Thank you," the prince said. "Now where are you going?"

"To the palace, of course," Pagus answered. "But I doubt I can just stroll through the gates, not with your kin wanting my master dead. They probably want to kill me, too!"

Jeridi looked grave. "Let's hope we can get to him first," the prince said. "I doubt they'll strike until the ceremony. Malvonican loves a captive audience."

"Since the Channelers' numbers were few, they had to turn to an alternative method to achieve victory—tevisrals that caused destruction on a colossal scale."

- From *The Thousand Years War, Part I,* page 50

The carriage was cramped. Iltar and Elsia had to stand—invisible of course. The carriage slowed, and Iltar knew they were pulling up to the palace. His eyes, however, were on Alanya. She sat pensively. The high duchess had been like that the entire ride. Iltar didn't know what to say to her. He was never good at talking to women. Elsia had stayed silent as well. Iltar couldn't see her face, but he supposed Elsia was just as apprehensive as Alanya.

The carriage rolled forward and Iltar heard the coachman speaking with the guards. They quickly permitted them entrance.

"I'll exit the carriage first," Alanya said, staring blankly across the cabin.

"Alanya," Iltar said, reaching his invisible hand toward her.

The high duchess flinched at his touch, but then searched for him, patting his arm until she found his face. Alanya touched his invisible cheek, smiling. Tears welled in her eyes. "Save that boy, Iltar."

The carriage came to a halt. Alanya searched the area by her hand, trying to find Iltar's eyes. "Kiss me…" she murmured. "I need you to kiss me."

Iltar hesitated, and the door opened. Did he dare kiss her?

Yes.

Still invisible, Iltar leaned forward, pressing his lips against hers. Alanya embraced him passionately. It was a kiss unlike any they had shared. Alanya gazed directly into his invisible eyes as she pulled away. "I love you," she whispered. "When this is over, find me in Vabenack."

The high duchess then hurried out of the carriage.

Iltar felt Elsia move next, then he commanded the illusionary-transmutation of the countess to follow. He was right behind the magical recreation of himself and stepped out onto the bridge. Luckily, no one else was around—his and Alanya's embrace had gone unnoticed.

A hand brushed against Iltar's arm and he looked down, seeing nothing. That was undoubtedly Elsia.

"Let's go," the countess whispered.

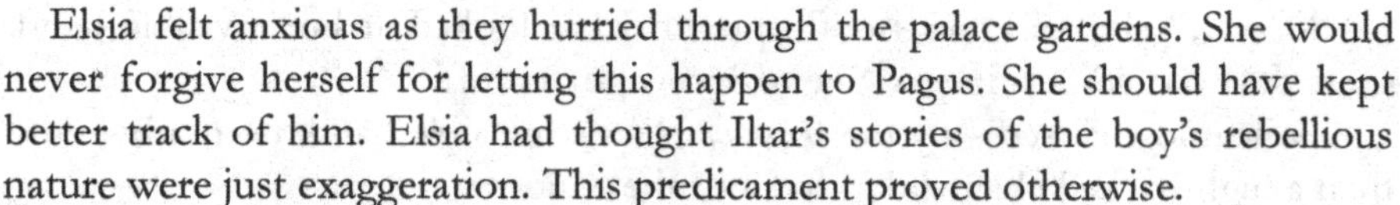

Elsia felt anxious as they hurried through the palace gardens. She would never forgive herself for letting this happen to Pagus. She should have kept better track of him. Elsia had thought Iltar's stories of the boy's rebellious nature were just exaggeration. This predicament proved otherwise.

They climbed the palace's tiers with a rope Elsia couldn't see. Iltar had claimed it was composed of magic and could adhere to anything. For being a scholar and a respectable mage, Iltar seemed to know a great deal about sneaking into places that shouldn't be sneaked into. It made her realize that she didn't truly *know* this man. Sure, she knew his character. But Elsia didn't know Iltar's past, nor what motivated him. That was something Iltar kept secret.

Soon, they were in the Palace Tier of the gardens. Though it was past sunset, the gardens were lit as brightly as noonday. The gardeners had done an exquisite job of transforming the grounds.

A patrol approached, and Iltar grabbed Elsia's arm, pulling her close to one of the stone benches. Elsia held her breath as the guards passed. She started to move, but Iltar held her back.

"Wait…" he whispered.

They stood there against the bench—still invisible. Another set of footsteps sounded not long after the first patrol disappeared. It was another patrol. It seemed that not even a minute had passed between them.

Once the second patrol was gone, Iltar pulled her close. "All right, now that I have it timed, we need to get to our entry point."

Elsia had been privy to many details about the state of the palace, due to her involvement in preparing for the ball. This turned out to be a great advantage. The northern side of the palace would be mostly unoccupied, as all the guests were to be ushered to the south stairwell.

So, Iltar chose the northern end as his point of entry. He wanted to break in through one of the windows, but Elsia thought that absurd. Someone would hear them. But Iltar reassured her that he could get in without a sound.

It wasn't long before they reached the part of the gardens where Iltar intended to enter the palace. The spot was beside one of the buildings connected to the palace by a glassy corridor. A domed pavilion sat beside the building, forcing the garden's path to wind away.

"Here," Iltar whispered. "We'll use the pavilion for cover as we climb." Elsia thought that funny. They were invisible…

Iltar waited for another patrol to pass, then he threw his rope. "It's attached," Iltar whispered, grabbing her arm. "Take it slow and stop moving if you hear anyone."

The climb up to the third story didn't take long, but a patrol arrived just as Iltar reached the window. Not long after the guards passed, Elsia heard the faint creaking of a hinge.

"Hurry," Iltar whispered, his voice coming from inside the building.

Elsia climbed through the window, reaching toward the floor to brace herself. Her hand slipped on some dust or powder, and Iltar pulled her through.

"Careful…" He gritted his teeth.

"Sorry…" she said and stood upright. Elsia looked at her invisible hand. Gray dust coated her fingers. She had to wipe that off.

The window closed—by the force of Iltar's invisible hand, no doubt—and then a high-backed chair slid in front of the window.

"How did you do that?" she asked, "open the window I mean. Wasn't it locked?"

"It was," Iltar replied. "I just got rid of the lock."

"How?"

"Magic…" he trailed off. "Now let's hurry."

Elsia felt puzzled. He hadn't used an incantation, had he?

⟡

The palace was crowded. Though Alanya knew how many people were invited, she hadn't expected to see this many attendees. There were so many guests that a line formed from the palace's entrance down to the Middle Gardens. Alanya consciously controlled her breathing, suppressing the anxiety stirring within her. The reality of the situation had struck her once she exited the carriage.

Light flickered near the ceiling. A lightstone-powered lantern—suspended in the air by a tevisral—blinked several times and then winked out. Alanya had never seen a lightstone lose its illumination. The sight of the dun stone struck her with sudden fear. In that moment, that lightless stone was a foreboding omen of their task to rescue poor Pagus. Alanya closed her eyes, tightly gripping the illusory arm that belonged to Iltar's transmuted manifestation. She felt the cold touch of the transmutation stroking her hand.

That drew Alanya from her reverie. Alanya looked to the image of the man beside her. For a moment, she thought it truly was Iltar. Her fear fled like a sunrise vanquishing the night.

The illusion smiled at her, and the cold hand patted her once again. Though it was made from dirt, the hand *felt* like flesh. "Don't worry, everything will turn out just fine," the Iltar illusion said. "This event was planned perfectly."

Those words were so vague, anyone overhearing them would think they were in relation to the ball—but Alanya knew their true meaning. Alanya breathed a sigh of relief and rested her head against Iltar's shoulder.

Soon, they were inside the palace. The transmuted illusions of Elsia and Hazais came beside Alanya as she crossed the foyer. Alanya wondered why

Iltar chose Hazais to accompany Elsia. They were an odd pair.

The throng of guests shuffled their way to the south. They passed the dining hall where Alanya and the others had shared that meal with the royalty. The southern stairs leading to the upper levels of the palace were not too far from the dining chamber.

Crimson Praetorians guarded the stairs, eyeing each of the guests as they ascended to the upper floors. The Praetorians' gazes lingered on her and the illusions.

Her heart began to race, but the Praetorians didn't do anything. Once Alanya passed the Praetorians they didn't turn. If she hadn't been paying attention, she probably wouldn't have noticed their lingering eyes.

The stairs were quite wide, roomy enough for ten people to walk abreast. They rose to a landing, where more Praetorians stood guard. The Praetorians watched the crowd file past, and like the others, their eyes lingered on Alanya and the illusions.

This really is a trap, she thought. Alanya averted her gaze as she rounded the landing, coming to another flight of stairs that rose to the second floor. The second floor of the palace was roped off, and the crowd continued to the third floor, passing more Praetorians. Alanya shouldn't have been surprised at the number of Crimson Praetorians present. After all, the emperor would be in attendance.

On the third floor, a line of soldiers stood by the stairs, barring access to the eastern parts of the third floor. The soldiers seemed to watch everyone with equal wariness. They didn't linger on Alanya as the Crimson Praetorians had. Alanya and her illusory escorts followed the crowd, winding to the western end of the palace, toward the throne room where the ball was being held.

Soft music and light chatter reached her ears as they neared the entrance to the throne room. Above them, the hallway was vaulted, its ceiling rising two stories. Pillars came into view along the interior side of the hallway, and beyond it the massive throne room packed with hundreds of guests.

The throne room hadn't actually been used as a throne room since the reign of Emperor Mindolarn some seventy years before. Now it was mostly used for events like this ball. The throne room took up nearly half of the third floor. It was an odd shape, like an oval almost—roughly measuring a hundred and fifty phineals long by eighty phineals wide—and rose four stories tall. Its ceiling was barreled, but the pitch matched the rest of the palace's dome. Railings lined the upper parts of the longer walls, on the fifth and sixth floors of the palace. Soldiers stood along the rails, gazing down into the throne room.

Towering windows lined the western wall, rising from floor to ceiling. Seven pairs of glass doors were also along that wall, leading to a balcony that overlooked the expanse of grass where the Feast of Sorrows was held. The royal orchestra sat on the balcony, their music wafting into the throne room through the open doors.

Lightstone lanterns floated throughout the throne room. Crimson globes hung from the bottom of those floating lanterns—each was transparent and glistened from the light of other nearby lanterns. Diaphanous silks hung from the barrel ceiling in seven rows, accompanied by streamers of golden leafy vines. Alanya had been in charge of creating all of that. She was so proud of them and longed for Iltar to see what she had devised. Perhaps he could see them through the illusions… but would Iltar pay attention to the décor?

Alanya sauntered behind the crowd which was being directed to the raised throne at the east end of the room.

The oversized throne sat atop a seven-sided dais elevated seven steps above the rest of the room. It was an oval seat carved from crimson-colored stone—it looked like galstra, as the stone had veins and flecks all across its surface. Seven serpentine heads rose from the back of the throne, arrayed exactly like the Mindolarn flag. Those heads too were carved from the same crimson galstra.

There was enough room on the dais for six other seats. Alanya had heard that Emperor Mindolarn had held court here with his six brothers. But today, the princes and princesses of Mindolarn occupied those seats.

Emperor Marden sat casually in his throne, leaning against one armrest and slumping a little. He didn't look like an emperor. Guests were ushered toward the dais and introduced to the emperor by the palace's chamberlain. Emperor Marden simply nodded in response.

A palace servant was moving down the line, asking for the names of each guest. The servant filled up a sheet and ran it back to Chamberlain Caedaric, but soon returned to collect more names.

Alanya's heart began to race again. *Would they strike now?* she wondered. More Crimson Praetorians stood against the wall beside the dais. There looked to be forty—no, fifty of them. Alanya's eyes were drawn back to the dais. Raedina sat with her cousins, Laedar and Negaris, to the right of the throne. On the other side of the emperor sat Princess Ilnea, the daughter of Medis, with her brother, Prince Radigar. Princess Cedara, the daughter of the late emperor, occupied the last seat.

Where is Malvonican? Alanya wondered. *And Jeridi?* She glanced around the throne room, but neither prince was present. Their absence made her stomach knot. Alanya glanced again at the soldiers standing along the upper levels of the throne room. The soldiers looked fierce, and Alanya thought she saw men holding channeling staffs.

Mages? Alanya held back a gasp. The reality of the situation was becoming grimmer by the second. Amid her horror, Alanya heard the image of Iltar speaking. Why, why was he—?

"This is High Duchess Alanya Tasivir," the Iltar illusion said. It sounded exactly like Iltar. The servant who was taking names was beside the illusion. Iltar's image then proceeded to give the names for the other magical creations. The servant took down the names and continued through the line.

"Take a deep breath," the Iltar illusion whispered. Alanya complied, staring at the illusion.

"If you don't calm down, I'm going to have to do all the work," the illusion said with a smirk.

"You really are an arrogant man." Alanya shook her head.

"Just stay calm," the illusion said, "we're almost there… I think."

———————◊•◊———————

Iltar and Elsia encountered no resistance as they descended to the lower reaches of the palace. They passed a few guards stationed by the entrance to the lower levels, but the guards didn't hear him or Elsia.

"I thought you said you knew where the dungeon was located…" Elsia said through clenched teeth.

"Well, I don't have a map," Iltar whispered.

They had already descended three floors below ground. Each floor was bigger than the last, and Iltar assumed that the palace spread *beneath* the various gardens. When Iltar first visited the palace, he thought it was small compared to everything else Mindolarnian. The Castle of Laelin Lake—which Iltar had seen in that experience with Cornar—was far bigger than the palace proper. But now Iltar began to doubt his assumption.

"We could have missed it," Elsia complained.

Faint footsteps approached from an adjoining hall. Iltar grabbed Elsia and whispered for her to stay put, then sneaked toward the footsteps.

Iltar rounded a corner, and the footsteps grew louder. It sounded like three or four people marching in unison.

A patrol, he thought.

Four soldiers marched past Iltar, clad in silvery ceremonial armor with the emblem of the Mindolarn Empire emblazoned across their breastplates. The soldiers were unaware of his presence and continued down the corridor.

I could use them, Iltar thought, raising an eyebrow. With the guards under his control, Iltar could literally deliver him and Elsia to the dungeon. No one would suspect two people in custody to actually be infiltrators.

The patrol turned another corner and Iltar whispered a mind-controlling incantation. He would have to enthrall each of them at once, but that wouldn't prove to be much of a problem.

With his magic forming beneath his veil of invisibility, Iltar crept behind the guards. Iltar was finishing the incantation as he turned the corner.

The patrol was nearly fifty phineals away, but their footsteps were jumbled with another set.

Iltar cursed and held back his spell, softly exhaling to maintain it.

The footsteps grew louder, and the patrol disappeared down another corridor.

Oh well, he thought, waiting for the source of the footsteps to enter the hall.

A man in a white robe turned the corner, his head bowed beneath a cowl. The robed man was muttering to himself in a strange language. It sounded like the Keadal tongue. He was no guard, but perhaps he knew the dungeon's location

NOT HIM, a booming voice rumbled through Iltar's mind. *CHOOSE ANOTHER.*

Iltar froze, watching as the robed man passed. The stranger's eyes were closed, and his face was painted pale. His white hair peaked from his cowl, but Iltar couldn't make out his features. The robe he was wearing bore the First Emblem on the back, but the symbol was upside down. There was also a thin crescent above the upside-down symbol.

Still muttering, the stranger turned the corner from which Iltar had come. Iltar let his magic fade, and then he crept back toward Elsia. The white-robed man moved right past her, making his way toward the stairs leading to the upper levels.

Once the robed man was gone, Iltar felt Elsia's grip against his arm. "Who was that?" she whispered.

"No clue," Iltar said. "Now let's find another patrol. I have a plan to get into the dungeon."

◆•◆

Raedina watched as the disguised Alathians made their way toward the throne to be presented. She suppressed her hatred and attempted to feign a friendly demeanor. But all she could do was act stern. It was better than hostility, but not by much.

Alanya—or at least someone who looked like Alanya—stepped forward with her three guests. Chamberlain Caedaric cleared his throat and read from the list. "High Duchess Alanya Tasivir of Mindolarn, and her esteemed guests, Master Iltar of the Soroth Necrotic Order, Countess Elsia Scurn of Sarn, and Lady Alanya's steward, Hazais Naurm."

The four of them bowed, then hurried away, mingling with the rest of the guests.

Finally, we will have vengeance, Raedina vowed.

Caedaric announced more guests, but Raedina couldn't pull her eyes away from that vile Alathian. Justice would finally be dealt this night. The deceitful son of Adrin would harm the empire no longer.

◆•◆

Fortunately, Iltar found another patrol. He enthralled them as he had intended with the first batch. Once they were under his control, Iltar inquired after the dungeon's location. To his surprise, the dungeon was actually two more floors below them.

To make their ruse believable, Iltar cast his own illusions on him and Elsia. He gave them the appearance of a young couple who was attempting to pillage the palace during the ball. They were bruised and beaten, with a few cuts on their faces. Iltar also fashioned illusionary shackles. He had thought about using actual shackles, but that would make things difficult. He also concealed Elsia's sword sheathed at her waist.

Two of the guards marched ahead of Iltar and Elsia. The other two were behind Iltar. Those guards in the rear had the tips of their fanisars at the backs of the pretend prisoners.

They reached the entrance of the dungeon, situated near the heart of the fifth below-ground floor. Only two guards were stationed outside its entrance, and Iltar learned that the patrols passed by every half hour.

One of the dungeon guards cocked his head toward Iltar and Elsia, a twisted grin forming upon his face. "What do we have here?" he asked with a crackle in his voice.

"Some thieves," said the enthralled leader of the patrol. Iltar had already told them what to say, otherwise he would have had to use his mental focus to direct their words or use his own voice. "We caught them snooping about." The lead guard gestured to Elsia. "After we roughed them up, she confessed to trying to find a treasury."

The dungeon's guard frowned. "Tumaris won't be pleased, will he Fazis?" he said, looking to the other man guarding the dungeon.

The enthralled patrol leader ignored them and reached for the dungeon's door.

"We can handle this from here," Fazis said, stepping in front of the door. "Just return to your posts."

The enthralled guards didn't move, and Iltar—through his mental link to them—commanded them to step aside.

"This one looks nice," Fazis said, grabbing Elsia by the arm. He immediately groped her chest, and Elsia slapped the man, breaking through her illusionary shackles.

Damn it, Iltar cursed.

Fazis was stunned, both by the slap and the seemingly unnatural feat Elsia had just performed.

"An illusion!?" blurted the other guard.

Elsia reached for her invisible sword as Fazis recovered. Iltar sighed, cursing inwardly. This was another reason he had wanted to come alone. Elsia had just destroyed their ruse. The other guard spun on Iltar and readied his weapon. Iltar, however, remained still, mentally commanding his enthralled guards to attack.

Both dungeon guards yelled for help. Their cries, however, were cut short. Elsia stabbed Fazis through the chin while the patrol captain slit the other man's throat. The dungeon's door flew open, and four other guards poured into the hall.

Great… Iltar thought in exasperation. He swiftly uttered a telekinetic incantation while Elsia and the enthralled guards advanced on the reinforcements. Pale-gray magic coalesced in Iltar's palm and then shot between his allies, striking one of the reinforcing guards. The blast threw the guard back through the door, where he collided with another man who Iltar assumed was the jailor. Both men were thrown into a wall with a resounding crack, followed by pained screams.

Iltar pushed through the melee, mustering more enthralling magic. He dashed into the dungeon's anteroom expecting to find more guards, but there were no others. The guard Iltar had repulsed, however, was recovering from the telekinetic blast.

Not so fast, Iltar grinned as he finished his spell. The enthralling magic shot in five directions, stilling the guards and the wailing jailor.

The commotion in the hallway quieted, and Elsia hurried into the dungeon. The anteroom wasn't large—only enough space for a desk and a few chairs.

"Perhaps I should have used real shackles," Iltar said with annoyance, dismissing the illusions he had cast upon them.

Elsia gave Iltar a sidelong glance, then ran across the room, shouting for Pagus.

"She's being foolish," Iltar grumbled, and then turned to his enthralled minions. "Pull those corpses in here and take up their posts."

The enthralled guards complied and Iltar turned to the jailor now under his control. Iltar could sense the jailor's severe situation through his spell. The jailor's back had been broken and some of his ribs had punctured his lungs. He would be dead soon.

"You have a prisoner named Pagus," Iltar said, kneeling beside the paralyzed jailor. "Where is he?"

"We have no prisoner named Pagus," the jailor spat, blood dripping from his mouth.

"What?" Iltar blurted, furrowing his brow. "He's a young man, the princes brought him."

"We have no—" the jailor cut off, his glazed eyes staring lifelessly at Iltar.

No prisoner named Pagus? Iltar rose to his feet. Perhaps they didn't tell the jailor his name. Or called him by something else. If only the jailor had lived a little longer.

Perhaps one of the guards would know. "Is there a boy in the dungeon?" Iltar demanded of his enthralled minions.

"We only watch the entrance," one of the guards replied, the same who Iltar had repelled. "But there are ledgers with current inmates."

Iltar spun, dashing to the desk. All the while, Elsia continued shouting for her nephew. Iltar rummaged through several drawers, finding the most recent ledger. He noted several prisoners, but they had all been booked and released weeks ago.

Perhaps they didn't document it, Iltar thought. It would make sense not to keep Pagus's imprisonment on record.

Elsia's cries grew frantic, drawing Iltar from his thoughts. Grumbling, he ran after her.

⚊◄●►⚊

Pagus dashed across the palace's bridge with the plump prince. It was a good thing that he was with Prince Jeridi, otherwise entering the palace would have been impossible. The guards were only permitting passage to people with invitations to the ball. The prince, however, could bypass that requirement.

"We're too late," the prince groaned. "The ball has already begun."

"I don't think Master Iltar is at the ball," Pagus said. "If you people captured me, where would you take me?"

"To the dungeon, of course," Jeridi replied. His exhaustion was returning.

"Do you need another enhancement?" Pagus asked.

"No," Jeridi shook his head. "I will be fine. I can cast it myself if need be."

Pagus raised an eyebrow at the prince. Well, if Jeridi was one of those *things*, it would make sense that magic would come naturally to him.

"But I doubt your master will be able to make it to the dungeon," Jeridi said. "It's deep beneath the palace and there are many patrols. And its location isn't well known."

"You underestimate Master Iltar," Pagus said with a chuckle.

They were across the bridge in seconds. Jeridi shouted to the guards manning the palace's inner gates, hailing them with a series of phrases, the last of which was, "May the Crimson Eye remain hidden for all time."

Pagus had read about that phrase in the Royal Archive. He didn't understand *what* the Eye was, but he knew it was something powerful.

Upon hearing the prince, the guards opened the gate. The gate's door-like slabs compressed in an unnatural fashion, but Pagus didn't have time to admire the mystery of it. He had to focus on getting to Iltar and escaping this dreadful place.

"We should check the ball first," Jeridi said. "If he's there, I can escort him away, and hopefully that will buy you enough time to escape."

"If you find Iltar at the ball, it's probably a decoy," Pagus retorted. This plump prince obviously didn't understand who he was dealing with.

Jeridi hummed between breaths. "Well, then we can show him you're safe and meet somewhere secluded."

Pagus grunted, and they dashed up the deep steps toward the palace.

"I assume you are versed in the illusionary arts," the prince panted. "I suggest making yourself more presentable so as to blend into the crowd."

That was probably a wise suggestion. As they continued up the steps, Pagus uttered an incantation, veiling his clothes with the guise of affluent attire.

⟞•⟝

"Pagus!" Elsia shouted, "Pagus, where are you?!"

Iltar finally caught up to Elsia. The cells were empty and according to the ledger they should be. No one was held captive in the dungeon.

Elsia stopped, turning about with a panicked expression on her face. "Where is he?" Elsia asked, her lips quivering and tears welling in her eyes.

"Your nephew is not here."

Iltar knew that voice. It was his... but he hadn't spoken.

Elsia looked at Iltar with confusion, then glanced back toward the dungeon's entrance, gasping abruptly.

Iltar followed her gaze. Reflection stood in the hall between the cells, smiling with a twisted sense of paternal devotion.

"You," Iltar barked, stepping away from Elsia. "What are *you* doing here?"

"Ensuring the River of Kalda runs true," Reflection said, grinning. "It is time for the Unspoken One to reveal himself to the Children of Cheserith."

"What…?" Elsia muttered, looking back and forth between Iltar and Reflection.

"Where is Pagus?" Iltar demanded.

"He is with Prince Jeridi, on his way to the throne room."

"We were too late," Elsia cried, drawing a hand to her lips. "Iltar, please, we have to save him!"

Iltar looked at her uneasily. Something didn't feel right about this situation.

"*A boy shall suffer,*" Reflection said, quoting one of Soron Thahan's prophecies. "*His anguish will unleash the Harbinger's fury.*"

"A boy…?" Elsia muttered. She looked to Iltar with confusion, but her expression became enlightened. "Pagus!"

"*Apostates will not believe the Unspoken One's advent,*" Reflection continued. "*They will fight against him, but he will prevail. None can stand against the Unspoken One and live, for Hemran'na upholds him.* Go to the throne room, Iltar," Reflection urged, "and reveal yourself."

Elsia's expression turned ghastly. "That… that's why you sought this research." She backed away uneasily. "*You're* the Unspoken One… Why-why didn't you tell me?"

Iltar just glanced to her. Elsia's face twisted with disgusted abhorrence. She looked betrayed.

"You need to hurry to the throne room if you wish to reunite with Pagus," Reflection said, then vanished.

"Come on!" Elsia shouted, dashing across the dungeon, her sword still drawn. "We have to hurry!"

Obstinate woman. Iltar shook his head, and then darted after Elsia.

In that moment, Iltar felt a total lack of control. Everything was pushing or pulling him to an inevitable confrontation with the Mindolarn Royalty. Of course, Iltar could flee like a coward with his rogulin crystal and escape the palace. But he couldn't forsake Pagus. No matter how difficult a student, Iltar would not lose another apprentice.

They dashed out of the dungeon and back the way they had come, with Iltar's enthralled guards trailing behind them. If they were to storm the throne room and rescue Pagus, they were going to need an escort.

❦

The music from the royal orchestra was serene, but the beautiful tones couldn't calm Alanya's nerves. The illusory transmutation of Iltar had whispered that Pagus was on his way to the ball, in the custody of Prince Jeridi.

It would all fall apart. Soon, Iltar would storm the throne room to free his apprentice. The Royals would see that as verification of their assumptions. To them, he *would* be the Alathian. And Alanya would be doomed.

She started when a hand touched her shoulder. She spun hastily, but breathed a sigh of relief upon seeing Lady Taeveya, the Duchess of Arido—a small duchy between Mindolarn and Ulvilo.

"Oh, Alanya, everything looks so beautiful!" Taeveya said with excessive enthusiasm. "I hear you were in charge of most of the decorations?"

Alanya nodded but didn't engage the woman any further. Lady Taeveya had a tendency to give so much flattery that she was known throughout the empire's aristocracy as a promiscuous sycophant.

"Are you all right?" Taeveya asked, coming beside Alanya. "You don't look well."

A gong rang from near the throne before Alanya could answer. *Oh no…* Alanya groaned inwardly. The gong signaled that the ball had officially begun. Raedina would speak, introducing all of their achievements at the Hilinard. After that, the emperor would give a short dedication and then the festivities would begin.

After the ringing subsided, Chamberlain Caedaric climbed partway up the dais toward the throne. "Ladies and Gentlemen of the Empire," the chamberlain said with a booming voice, "it is my pleasure to present to you the achievements of our esteemed men and women of the Hilinard."

Applause erupted throughout the throne room. Alanya, however, didn't join in. *Why isn't Raedina speaking?* Alanya wondered, looking to the princess. Raedina sat beside the throne, her eyes fixed on the image of Iltar. Alanya could *feel* the hostility in her gaze.

"You need to hurry, Iltar," Alanya whispered to the illusory transmutation.

The image of Iltar grinned. "Just watch for Pagus," he whispered back. "We're almost to the first floor."

"The elves had watched warily as dragons were hunted and the men of Aridia fought against each other. They knew war would sweep across Kalda. And so, they prepared. Their Gholirisulem Kalidrums—*the minds who controlled the elven cities—created weapons that had been lost to time."*

- From *The Thousand Years War, Part I*, page 53

Iltar dashed toward the stairs leading to the palace's main level, following his enthralled guards. Fortunately, they had encountered no resistance during their hasty flight. But if they had, Iltar would have subjugated those guards to his purpose.

"How do you plan to bypass the sentries at the stairs?" the countess asked between breaths.

The only answer Iltar gave her was the uttering of an incantation. Orange light gathered in his hands, forming a ball of life-draining magic. He held the spell in place as they climbed the northern stairwell.

His enthralled minions bounded across the landing and up the stairs, drawing the attention of the guards stationed on the first floor. Those atop the stairs started upon seeing their comrades' hasty advance.

"What—"

Iltar unleashed his spell. Orange light surged up the stairs in a flash. The life-draining wave became tentacles gripping each of the men—including those enthralled by Iltar.

The soldiers struggled against the deadly magic, but couldn't utter more than a gasp. Each was dead within seconds.

"That was stupid…" Elsia complained, eyeing the dead soldiers.

Iltar gave her a sidelong glance. The woman really didn't comprehend the laws of magic. Why would he run into the throne room with enthralled men that could easily be turned on him with a dispel?

"Go scout to the third floor," Iltar whispered, casting his concealing magic on Elsia. "I need time to reanimate these," he gestured to the lifeless guards.

"Okay..." Elsia whispered, her light footfalls disappearing as she climbed the staircase.

Iltar cast his concealing magic once again. Now invisible, Iltar uttered a necrotic spell he hadn't used in ages. Dark-purple light flowed from his invisible hands and wisped into the corpses. The reanimating spell permeated every part of each guard—it had to, otherwise the spell's effect would be less than perfect.

"It's clear," Elsia whispered from the stairs. Her footsteps slowed, indicating a halt. "Oh my..." She gasped, as the first of the reanimated guards rose from the floor, standing as naturally as if the man were still alive. Soon, all six were upright and hefting their fanisars.

"That's... disturbing," Elsia muttered.

Iltar grunted. "Let's go," he said grimly.

◆━●━◆

"Her Imperial Highness, Princess Raedina Midivar, has asked me to present the following tevisrals," Caedaric said, gesturing to the left side of the throne room.

Men marched to the throne carrying a variety of tevisrals.

"Each of these has military application," the chamberlain said, gesturing to the men now gathered beneath the dais.

Alanya watched with horror. Her eyes were drawn to an enormous sheathed sword held by two men. The blade was as long as a man was tall and had a slight curve to it. Its black scabbard was thick, adorned with red symbols that looked like the language from *Dreamwalker*. The sword's handle was a vibrant red adorned with a golden guard. A black gem rested within the pommel *glowing* a black light.

"... and this here is a miniaturized version of our current communication rods," Caedaric said. The chamberlain lifted a small shaft that fit within his palm.

Applause filled the throne room.

"Where are you, Iltar...?" Alanya murmured nervously. She scanned the throne room, looking for any sign of the captive Pagus. But there was no sign of the boy.

More tevisrals were introduced, but Alanya's focus was elsewhere. Her fears were being realized. She would lose everything—including Iltar. For how could one man stand against the might of Mindolarn?

Caedaric ceased speaking and gestured to Emperor Marden. "His Imperial Majesty will present the last and final achievement of the Hilinard." The chamberlain stepped aside.

The men carrying the sword delivered it to the emperor. He took the massive weapon by the hilt with one hand while grabbing the scabbard with the other. And then the unthinkable happened.

Crimson light burst from the symbols, and the scabbard *liquefied,* running up the emperor's hand to his elbow. The liquid hardened, forming a gauntlet with glowing symbols identical to the scabbard.

Now exposed, the sword's black blade glistened, misting blackness. Its edge was a deep red.

"Behold, citizens of Mindolarn," the emperor bellowed, "Shal'mirak, the Deathcleaver. Its blade—forged by infusing the essence of the gods—harnesses the power of the Ko'delish. The weapon's edge—imbued with ever-persistent annihilation particles—will disintegrate anything it touches. This magnificent weapon is the first of many blades that will be crafted for our brave soldiers."

Cheers and applause resounded.

"Deathcleaver's light weight makes it a formidable weapon, allowing grace and finesse in combat. And now to demonstrate Deathcleaver's majesty."

Alanya was pushed forward, but grabbed from behind. *No!* she gasped as her hands were pulled tight behind her back. Green light flashed before her eyes and then her mouth was bound.

Another flash of green passed beside Alanya.

A glistening cord appeared around the mouth of Iltar's illusory transmutation. An invisible force tightened around the transmutation's head, making it impossible for him to speak.

Elsewhere in the throne room, Iltar's other illusions were bound.

Gasps resounded throughout the chamber as Alanya and the others were dragged to the dais.

"Citizens of Mindolarn," the emperor declared, "today I deliver to you the murderer of my beloved brothers. The notorious grand mage of the Alathian cult, the accursed son of Adrin, the so-called Liberator of Klis."

Alanya and the illusions were forced to their knees. Men behind them cast spells. Something reached up behind Alanya, grabbing her ankles and pulling her arms back, forcing her chest to arc. The others were also bound, shackled to the floor with some kind of transmutation.

"Today, justice prevails!" the emperor shouted.

Raedina rose from her chair, her eyes fixed on Alanya. The princess strode down the dais, her face contorted with suppressed fury. "Give her to me," Raedina commanded. "I want her to watch."

The transmutative shackles broke, and Alanya was pulled from the ground. Raedina took the cord binding Alanya and dragged her up the dais. Many of the guests gasped, and Alanya heard her named muttered among the crowd. Before reaching the top of the dais, Raedina spun Alanya to face the attendees. The princess forced Alanya to the step. Alanya fell, struggling to stay upright. Everyone looked at her with disbelief. Many were appalled. Some were disgusted.

Those gazes pierced her heart like a thousand daggers. Tears filled Alanya's eyes. Her only escape was to gaze out the throne room's towering windows. A burst of brilliant light caught her eye across the horizon—like lightning. But there were no clouds in the night sky.

"Today you die, son of Adrin!" Emperor Marden shouted. He twirled

Deathcleaver, so the blade pointed toward Iltar's illusion. The emperor reared back and hurled it like a javelin.

Deathcleaver struck the image of Iltar through the chest, tearing through flesh and fabric. The blade struck the floor behind the illusion, lodging so deep that the sword's guard was shoved into the illusions chest.

Iltar's image gasped and its eyes bulged. But there was no outcry.

"That was too easy," Laedar said skeptically, leaning forward from his chair.

Though Alanya knew it was not Iltar, she couldn't help but *feel* excruciating anguish. Seeing that monstrous blade piercing the image of her lover was too much to bear.

Despite the gag, Alanya screamed.

⬥•⬥

That horrific wail debilitated Iltar. He staggered, feeling weak.

No, he groaned. *Not now!* The smell of smoke filled his nostrils.

Eruptions of magic rang in his ears. And the world became a blur. No longer was he in the palace at Mindolarn. Tree branches swayed against strong erratic gusts. Explosions were crisp, booming through the forest.

Why… Iltar wondered. "Why am I here?" Alanya's scream must have triggered one of his fits. But this was beyond what he typically experienced… Iltar felt the wind against his face, and the smells of the forest—and the battle—struck him.

It all felt so real… Was he in Vabenack? No, the sky was blue. A pained cry echoed through the forest and smoke rose nearby.

"This isn't real," Iltar growled. "I'm in the palace at Mindolarn, not in the forests of Soroth."

More eruptions filled the air, and strong gusts blew the trees. It was as if they challenged his statements. A sudden surge of anger welled within Iltar. At what, he did not know. But that rage compelled him forward. Iltar dashed through the trees, coming to the battle-riddled yard of his family's woodland estate. Men in black robes stood to the north, hurling deadly orbs of magic past the homestead. Armored men—who he recognized as Crimson Praetorians—charged with fanisars drawn, mustering their own magic.

They were all focused at the center of the yard behind the homestead. Iltar hurried around his family's home, finding the guesthouse aflame. Beyond the burning rubble, a lone man encased in barsion danced acrobatically, hurling a rainbow array of orbs against his foes. It was Iltar's father. Adrin, the Hero of the West.

"Iltar, no!" his mother screamed.

Gwenyth lay on the ground between Iltar and the burning guesthouse. Her brown hair was matted with blood. Ash covered her face. Her clothes were ragged. His mother looked directly at him. "Go, Iltar!" she screamed frantically. "Run!"

Years ago, Iltar had obeyed—to a point. He hid in the trees, watching the battle.

"No…"

Arcane bolts whizzed past Iltar, striking his mother. She wailed horrifically. A Praetorian charged at Iltar, knocking him to the ground. Iltar recovered, rolling sideways and coming back onto his feet. The repulsion felt so real… The Praetorian ignored Iltar and ran straight for Gwenyth, stabbing her in the back with his fanisar. Iltar watched his mother die for the second time in his life.

A second surge of fury swelled within him.

The murderous Praetorian ripped his fanisar from Gwenyth's back. Gwenyth's corpse turned and her lifeless eyes gazed skyward. The Praetorian ran off, joining the tumultuous battle.

The guesthouse collapsed, but the flames continued to burn. Fiery magic shot from the yard, striking the trees. Leaves ignited, and smoke veiled the northern skies. The remaining Praetorians and mages were flushed from the trees, all focused on their lone foe. Amid their advance, Iltar noticed a hulking figure standing within the burning woodland.

The stranger wore black armor beneath dark robes, his head hidden beneath a cowl and his face covered with a mask. His gauntleted hands crossed his chest. The figure exuded arrogance.

Had there been a man like that all those years ago? Iltar couldn't remember. And then, black mist appeared beside the hulking figure. Two others emerged from those mists, assuming the same arrogant demeanor as the first. One wore formfitting plate armor the likes of which Iltar had never seen. The other wore a black robe, his head covered with a blackened helmet.

Together the three of them gazed across the yard, standing within the flames. Eruptions grew louder, and strong gusts blew through the air. Iltar's fury swelled upon seeing the battle. Though hundreds of men and women littered the ground, Adrin struggled to hold his own. He had slain more than any one man should. It was no wonder he was a legend.

Dozens of Adrin's disintegrating orbs volleyed through the air, striking the advancing mages and Crimson Praetorians. Adrin's magic tore through their armor, evaporating their flesh. Wails resounded as a dozen mages and Praetorians collapsed before reaching the fray.

Adrin leapt unnaturally into the air, glowing a vibrant violet. He hovered for a moment, then a beam of disintegrating magic shot to his foes beneath him. The attackers scattered, but some could not escape. The disintegrating blast eliminated six men while maiming a dozen others. Adrin landed among the decimation, casting another spell. A plethora of orbs gathered about him, arrayed in a myriad colors.

Black blades sung through the air, thrown like javelins. They hit Adrin's barsion, shattering it. All but one blade erupted, exploding with a shower of blackness that rained destruction upon friend and foe alike. The lone blade, however, pierced Adrin above the elbow. That blow maimed him. Fighting through apparent anguish, Adrin finished his spell.

A rain of orbs—composed of arcane, acidic, flaming, icy, and disintegrating magics—struck the regrouping army. Dozens more fell to his spell, but more soldiers and mages advanced. Iltar started upon recognizing many of his father's assailants.

Prince Kaescis Midivar charged at Adrin, wielding a blade composed of pure blackness, about the size of a long-sword. Prince Laedar was right beside Kaescis, wielding an identical blade. The five brothers of Mindolarn—Medis, Mendal, Magdolin, Monddar, and Marden—each advanced in their own unique way, wielding a variety of tevisral-type weapons. Among the mages was Prince Negaris, casting his own necrotic spells to reanimate his fallen comrades. That woman—Laeyit—was also among the Royal ranks, charging beside a burly Praetorian.

They all converged on Adrin.

Iltar's father held his own, keeping some at bay. Adrin deflected weapons and dodged blows, but struggled to resume his barsion.

Kaescis lunged, stabbing Adrin through the stomach. The prince yelled a cry of vengeance. That caused a fourth surge of fury within Iltar.

Adrin brought the brunt of his orbs upon the prince, stalling his advance. Wounded, Iltar's father leapt backward unnaturally. Adrin staggered as he landed, violet magic surging around him. And then, Adrin *exploded* with energy. A violet burst washed from him, streaming off his body. Amid that disintegrating aura, Adrin glowed a brilliant green hue—undoubtedly the result of some arpran spell.

Iltar could see the pain in his father's face, but that didn't stop Adrin. Only death could do that. Kaescis lunged to attack, but Adrin leapt, striking the prince with his lone fist. The violet aura disintegrated Kaescis's armor and dropped him to the ground. Adrin moved through his foes, slaying or wounding each enemy he touched. He fought his way across the yard, leaving no one standing. In that moment, Iltar realized what drove his father—Adrin was fueled with a righteous fury, a fiery imperative to protect his son.

The resentment Iltar once had for his father was washed away in that moment.

Adrin's violet aura lessened, and then completely dissipated. Iltar's father was vulnerable. And then Rovin emerged onto the battlefield. He stepped from the flaming forest with his brother, Cordis. Each had acidic javelins hovering about them. Weakened from his rampage, Adrin turned to see the men who would be his killers. The brothers struck, one after the other. Adrin fell to the ground, an acidic javelin protruding from his chest. The Hero of the West had been slain.

A fifth surge of fury swelled within Iltar.

Armored footfalls sounded from the burning woodland, and those three arrogant men approached the battlefield. Rovin and Cordis abruptly bowed with awed reverence. The armored trio walked through the corpse-ridden field, waving their hands while uttering sharp words. Those words sounded as if they were part of an incantation, but they were too sharp, too guttural.

Some of Adrin's foes stirred, including the Mindolarnian Royalty. But before anyone rose from the ground, the three mysterious men vanished, disappearing within mists of blackness. The benefactors of his father's enemies were gone.

Kaescis was the first to rise, followed by Laedar, and then the rest of the royalty. Adrin's valiant last stand had been undone. The renewed survivors made their way to Iltar's fallen father.

A sixth surge of fury burned within Iltar. He felt as if his soul were about to burst.

"Our pact has been fulfilled," Medis—the then-emperor—declared. "My brother's killer is no more."

Now Iltar knew *why* his parent's had died. Vengeance. That realization ignited an unquenchable fury.

Iltar blinked and staggered forward. He was no longer at his family's homestead. He was back within the three-story hallway of the palace.

Appalled gasps sounded from down the hall.

"Are you all right?" Elsia demanded. "You looked like you were about to collapse."

Had he relived that entire battle in a single moment? That question was fleeting amidst the fury burning within him.

The Mindolarnians *had* killed his parents. They had destroyed his life. And Iltar would not let that go unpunished. The image of Adrin—erupting in a glorious blaze of magic—persisted in Iltar's mind.

Iltar *knew* what he must do. He dashed ahead of Elsia, running down the hall to the throne room. Raw power surged from his core. Iltar focused on those latent energies buried deep inside him. He dug deep, pulling that power to the surface. He *commanded* it to manifest. It was akin to mustering magic, but *this* could be accessed *without* incantation. And it would *devour* all it touched.

Blackness misted from his clothes. It came from his pores and gathered around him.

His fury peaked.

Iltar screamed, reaching the end of the hall. He turned, launching himself into the chamber filled with the highest echelon of Mindolarn society.

All eyes were on him. Soldiers spun, twirling their weapons. Praetorians dashed to protect the Royals atop the dais. Incantations rang above him. Panicked screams echoed all around.

It was pandemonium.

An eruption—like a repulsing wind—shot from Iltar and rippled through the throne room. The hovering lightstones shifted. The hanging silks wafted. A tint of blackness covered Iltar's vision. He smiled, relishing the raw power surging through him. It invigorated him. Renewed him. A thrill for battle pulsed through his veins. He *yearned* for conflict.

Iltar was himself again.

⬥

Alanya was crying.

Defeated, she slumped against her captor's grip.

And then *he* appeared. An enraged battle cry—from a man burdened with glorious purpose—rippled across the throne room. It was followed by a burst of wind that left the ears buzzing. Alanya started and found herself gaping with the rest of the ball's attendees.

Iltar dashed into the throne room and *exploded* with a colossal energy. A burst of blackness washed from him, waves of black mist seething from his every pore—the unbridled power of the Unspoken One. It was the power of a god—the Ko'delish. Its erupting force eroded the polished ground.

"No…" Negaris gasped. "It can't be!"

Iltar rebounded and continued running. His hand raised, fingers splayed. The horrifying darkness condensed into spheres all around him. But the mist continued to flow. It turned to a steady glow that persisted around his body— a deadly aura that would protect him but devour all it touched.

Nearby, guests fled, though many turned toward Iltar, revealing weapons previously concealed by illusionary magic. They were an army disguised. Iltar dashed into them, a destructive force that dissolved all *he* touched.

"Weighed down with sorrow, the Channelers of Aridia enacted their plan. They sent some of their members across their beautiful continent with the tevisrals that would ensure peace. Once at the edges of Aridia, those in their mountain sanctuary performed that cruel and unforgivable act. The tevisrals that were sent out—along with those around the mountain refuge—turned solid ground into an ocean of despair."

- From *The Thousand Years War, Part I,* page 55

Pagus darted up the steps to the palace's third floor. Jeridi huffed beside him, barely keeping pace. The plump prince looked exhausted. The palace's guards stared at Jeridi quizzically, but didn't bar him or Pagus passage.

"To… the left." Jeridi struggled between breaths. Gasps resounded from that direction. "It's… happening," the prince groaned.

Pagus dashed ahead of the prince, running toward the entrance of the throne room. Many of the wealthy guests stared across the room, appalled.

A resounding battle cry echoed from the throne room, reverberating into the hall. An eruption followed, akin to explosive magic.

Master Iltar? Pagus wondered, reaching the entrance to the throne room.

Panicked screams followed, and those near the entrance fled into the hallway. They nearly trampled Pagus, but he pushed his way toward a pillar, taking refuge behind it.

Dying wails pierced the air. Incantations sounded throughout the throne room. Armor clanged. Weapons sang.

As the stampede lessened, Pagus inched around the pillar, seeing a figure alight with black flame. Dozens upon dozens of orbs formed around him, zipping into a small army. The black magic *tore* through the armor and turned flesh to dust—not like disintegrating magic. Whatever the magic touched was *eroded.*

The man aflame turned briefly and Pagus *saw* him.

Master Iltar.

Pagus gawked. How had Master Iltar learned to harness *that* power? Pagus had suspected—Iltar *was* the Unspoken One. Why else had he been so engrossed in the subject? Iltar didn't research things because he was curious. Master Iltar always had a purpose behind his studies.

"What…?" Jeridi gasped, coming beside Pagus. "Why?!"

"Haven't you read the prophecies of Soron Thahan?" Pagus asked smugly, glancing at the prince. Jeridi panted, but didn't reply.

Pagus turned back toward the battle, but a thunderous crash resounded from his left.

The throne room's towering windows shattered, and the wall crumbled. Glass, metal, and stone sprayed across the throne room. The debris, however, formed the outline of something enormous. What exactly Pagus couldn't tell—as it was invisible—but it was something with wings. The hanging silks were torn from their ceiling mounts or pushed upward. The floating lanterns flew across the room, crashing into the wall. Soldiers fell to the ground. It was as if something had *pushed* everything.

And then a brilliant flash, like lightning, surged across the throne room, zipping to the floor in front of the dais.

Pagus squinted against the light. The brilliance persisted, but Pagus saw the outline of a kneeling man glowing with a splendor that exceeded the combined luster of every light on Kalda.

* * *

Lirathay'lu had *embraced* the winds.

And now it was time for battle. Today he would slay an emperor. The light of his glorious transformation subsided. Those around him were still dazed. Some blinked with disbelief. Others cried out his identity with vehemence. Praetorians gathered in front of Lirathay'lu, barring his way to the throne and the accursed emperor of Mindolarn.

Rising from the throne room's stone floor, Lirathay'lu uttered a swift incantation in the *true* magical tongue. "Rina'milista ul'irg shail…" Brilliant blue barsion shone from Lirathay'lu's hands, surging along his arms and spreading across his body. Unlike the spell he had cast within his shop, this barsion would protect him.

The barsion completely veiled Lirathay'lu as his nearest foe—a Crimson Praetorian—swung his fanisar. The Praetorian wasn't slow by any means—he had reacted as soon as Lirathay'lu appeared. But Lirathay'lu was just *that* fast.

Lirathay'lu blocked the blow and then spoke another incantation. "Xu'tak ilmis'ra." Vibrant red light burst from his hand, instantly forming a sharp shaft the length of a long-sword. It was a blade composed of condensed annihilation particles—a powerful variant of the disintegration line within the Xu or Destruction Channel of magic.

Once the blade formed, Lirathay'lu forced his eyes to return to their *natural* state. With his irises swirling around his pupils, Lirathay'lu locked a brief gaze with the advancing Praetorian. Lirathay'lu didn't want to *freeze* this foe as he had with Constable Hashar and his watchman. No, he only had to know one thing: was his foe human or qui'sha?

That answer came quicker than a heartbeat. *Human.* Lirathay'lu kicked the man away, propelling him with what many would deem unnatural strength.

Another Praetorian advanced. Again, Lirathay'lu probed his foe's mind. *Qui'sha.* Lirathay'lu lunged toward the Praetorian, stabbing his annihilation blade through the *abomination's* chest. The Praetorian gasped and fell backward.

Before the Praetorian fell, Lirathay'lu spun to meet another foe. He didn't have time to watch his enemies die. More were upon him. At every clash, Lirathay'lu probed his foes, determining wither they were human or qui'sha.

The humans he repelled or wounded. The qui'sha he killed.

Glorious! Lirathay'lu rejoiced, repelling a Praetorian. He hadn't had this much fun since helping Zulsthy'l capture the Vik'sha—what a treacherous endeavor that had been.

Six Praetorians had fallen, but there were still thirty more. And then there were the Royals. The ruling qui'sha remained upon their dais, gazing contemptuously at Lirathay'lu.

—◦◦◦—

Alanya's tears subsided. Awestruck adoration replaced her sorrow. She gawked as Iltar tore through the ranks of soldiers, relentlessly killing all who stood in his way. He was a man possessed.

Raedina tugged on Alanya's bonds, forcing her to stand. Something cold pressed against Alanya's neck, about the size of a fingertip. "If you mutter as much as one word of an incantation, I *will* kill you," the princess threatened.

"I'm not an Alathian…" Alanya muttered.

"Then you are a traitor," Raedina growled.

Alanya tensed. She glimpsed what Raedina had pressed against her neck. It was a wand. Sharp words left Raedina's lips, and a blue hue shone from the princess's forearm, followed by a constant hum. Suddenly, a wave of blue light rippled around Alanya and the princess. It was barsion, mustered by some kind of tevisral. Amid the forming of Raedina's shield, the emperor said something, and then Deathcleaver—the blade that had pierced Iltar's illusory transmutation—*flew* back to his gauntleted hand.

"I take it that's the herbalist?" the emperor asked. He pointed the tip of his sword toward the short man slaying the Crimson Praetorians.

"I assume so," Raedina said contemptuously.

The herbalist? Alanya wondered. They weren't talking about that hostile little woman from the market, were they? Iltar had insisted she was a man, but she had *definitely* been a woman.

"I'll kill him," Prince Laedar snarled, thrusting his hand to his side and mustering a blade composed of black magic—it looked like the Ko'delish.

"And I'll deal with this so-called Iltar," Prince Negaris said. His anger tinged his strange incantations—the likes of which Alanya had never heard. The robed prince descended the dais with magic forming about him.

⎯⎯⎯⎯⎯•⎯⎯⎯⎯⎯

Iltar created a front for himself, his reanimated soldiers, and Elsia. He kept the Mindolarnians at bay with his deadly projectiles—what he referred to as "globes of darkness." Prior to his discoveries in Mindolarn, Iltar had always referred to this power of his as simply "the Darkness" or "the Darkness magic." But now he knew its true name—Ko'delish.

The globes of darkness continually formed, coalescing from the streaming blackness seething from his pores. Elsia dashed beside Iltar, running to engage a soldier dodging a zipping globe of darkness. Settling into a wide stance, Iltar focused his mind on Elsia's blade. What would have normally been an enhancing incantation was merely thought. He *willed* her blade to burst with a flame of Ko'delish, and the power obeyed.

Black particles shot from his hands and wisped around Elsia's sword, imbuing it with a deadly power. That enhancement was like any other spell. It could be countered by a dispel, and Iltar would have to command the power to resume. But the process wouldn't take long. In fact, it would be much quicker than any incantation.

This power of his was based completely on his mental state. The keener his mind, the faster it manifested. And today his mind was sharp, honed by his fury.

While Elsia cut down her foe, Iltar uttered an incantation. Green magic—acid mixed with barsion—shot from his hands and surrounded Elsia. As the spell formed, Iltar commanded the Ko'delish to mingle with the acidic barsion. It formed a deadly shield that would send bursts of acid and darkness at anyone who struck the barsion. Now fully enhanced, the countess engaged another foe. Elsia dueled with the man for a moment, then ran him through. Her blade tore through his armor like wet parchment.

Incantations finished above Iltar, and a rain of magic plummeted from the upper floors of the throne room. A flood of bolts and orbs—consisting of a variety of magics—struck Iltar, his reanimated minions, and Elsia. Elsia's barsion flickered but persisted.

The Mindolarnian mages blew holes through the reanimated soldiers, but Iltar's minions continued fighting—the necrotic magic bound them together, keeping their moldering bodies whole. And when Iltar was struck, the Ko'delish streaming from his body *consumed* the deadly orbs.

That was a surprise; usually, the Ko'delish acted like barsion. Sure, it would consume whatever physical matter came in contact with it—but it never swallowed up magic.

An odd steam rose all around him—a result of the consumption.

Panicked commands resounded above Iltar, and the mages frantically uttered more incantations. Archers readied their bows, and soldiers tossed ropes over the railing. Were they actually going to rappel into the throne room? *How foolish.*

Iltar turned his focus to his reanimated minions, commanding the Ko'delish to enhance their fanisars. The bladed staffs glowed black within seconds. He enshrouded them with barsion next, but not like Elsia's. Their barsion consisted only of the Ko'delish. It was more of a countermeasure against a dispel rather than a protection.

With his tiny force enhanced, Iltar returned his attention to his foes.

Soldiers were rappelling from the fifth floor. Those in the throne room were dodging his globes of darkness—but nearly fifty had already fallen, mostly wounded. That did not include any of the Praetorians.

Eight Praetorians had fallen, slain by that mysterious combatant who had joined the fray against the Mindolarnians. Iltar didn't recognize him. He was short—almost to an extreme—and wore a black garb. The man mustered magic at an incredible, unnatural speed.

When the mysterious stranger had suddenly appeared, it was as if he had *shot* through the western wall of the throne room by some magical means. Iltar had only heard the crash and seen the eruption of light zipping to the dais. After determining the stranger was not another foe, Iltar had turned his attention to more pressing matters.

Iltar's gaze fell upon the dais. Alanya was bound beside Princess Raedina, a wand held to her throat. A perfect ovoid of barsion surrounded them both.

Pagus, however, was nowhere to be found... Hadn't Reflection said Pagus was on his way to the throne room with that fat prince?

Another wave of fury rose within Iltar, and he dashed into the enemy ranks. More globes of darkness formed about him, and Iltar *hurled* them across the throne room, striking the soldiers who were rappelling. Iltar lunged toward a distracted soldier, punching the man's helmet. The streaming Ko'delish instantly eroded the helmet before the blow connected. Iltar's fist went right through the man's head—the Ko'delish devoured everything above the man's shoulders.

Nearby soldiers cringed. Some gasped. Iltar could *feel* their dread. Their fear further fueled his fury. He lunged toward another soldier, nearly flying into him. The soldier withered in Iltar's presence, turning to a pile of ash. Another soldier—an officer denoted by the crimson plume atop his helmet—called for the soldiers to strike. The soldiers swung their fanisars with trepidation, but Iltar's streaming Ko'delish dissolved the weapons' blades *and* shafts.

"You throw away your lives so recklessly," Iltar growled, then lunged toward the nearest man. The soldier was gone within seconds.

Iltar fought his way through the throne room—as Adrin had fought through the homestead's yard years ago. Iltar's aura dissolved all he came across. None could withstand his presence. More soldiers were rappelling into the throne room, but Iltar's prolific globes of darkness felled them.

Iltar was nearly to the far side of the dais when a ball of vibrant green arced across the throne room. It was too big to be an offensive spell—although he had heard of mages mustering orbs that were larger around than a man was tall.

Iltar recoiled from his latest foe, ready to attack, but started. A person was within the green magic. Someone familiar… Gasping, Iltar clearly saw who was within that acidic barsion.

It was Pagus.

The boy landed, looking smug. "Fancy meeting you here," Pagus said with a smirk, rebounding from his magically assisted vault. He came beside Iltar, standing just out of range of the streaming Ko'delish. Pagus wore affluent attire, as if he were dressed to attend the ball.

"How?" Iltar demanded. "How were you freed?"

Pagus grinned slyly.

Never mind that, Iltar chided himself. "Get to your aunt," he commanded his apprentice. "I'm fetching Alanya. Then we're getting out of here."

"You mean you don't want to kill every last one of them first?" Pagus asked.

That question stoked another wave of fury. Iltar *felt* compelled to kill every last Mindolarnian in the room. *No,* Iltar fought the urge. That was not why he was here.

But, *they* had killed his parents.

Iltar spun back to the battle. Officers called for more soldiers to reinforce the line between Iltar and the throne. They were determined to protect their monarch, even in the face of inevitable death.

⟐•⟐

Pagus bounded across the throne room, dashing through piles of ash—the remains of soldiers who had foolishly stood against Master Iltar. He mustered a life-draining incantation as he neared his aunt.

Aunty Elsia was struggling to keep several soldiers at bay. They sliced at her barsion, their fanisars bathed with violet disintegration particles. Pagus finished his spell as he neared the fray, flinging two life-draining tentacles toward a pair of soldiers. The tentacles shot through the air, wrapping around the soldiers' necks. Both soldiers struggled, but succumbed to the magic, collapsing on the floor.

That gave Aunty Elsia an advantage. She parried a blow, then sliced across one man's arm. Her enhanced weapon left the man's arm hanging by a few sinews.

Still focused on his life-draining magic, Pagus hurled the two tentacles— with his mind—toward two more soldiers dueling with his aunt. He sapped their strength, and they dropped to the floor like their comrades. Their deaths, however, expended the spell.

Aunty Elsia killed the rest of her foes and turned to Pagus. Bolts of deadly magic zipped from above them, all focused across the throne room— undoubtedly intended for Master Iltar.

"Pagus?!" she blurted. Her face was a mixture of emotions: panic, anger, and disbelief.

"At your service, Aunty Elsia." Pagus smirked. He settled into a stance beside her and surveyed the battle. Soldiers were jumping from the upper stories—shielded by barsion—and running toward Iltar and that incredibly short man. "I guess we're not important…" Pagus frowned.

"Oh, Pagus…" Aunty Elsia groaned. She looked beyond the battle to the throne. "How-how did you escape?"

Pagus gave his aunt a quizzical gaze. "They never captured me. I don't know who Master Iltar saw in Vabenack, but it wasn't me."

Aunty Elsia looked aghast. Her perplexity didn't last long. "We can't leave Alanya…" she said, her face contorting. Aunty Elsia was formulating a plan—or trying to at least.

"Do you think you can break through their ranks?" she asked.

"To the throne?" Pagus asked. "Of course! I got all the way over here, didn't I?"

Aunty Elsia rolled her eyes at Pagus. "Iltar was right," she grumbled. "You really are an arrogant ass."

Pagus chuckled. "Just give me a moment." He uttered an incantation. Illusionary magic formed, creating a replica of himself veiled in acidic barsion. Pagus cast another spell, making a replica of Aunty Elsia. And then Pagus created a third illusion. This one would evoke fear. It was an illusion of Master Iltar—in all his dark splendor. Pagus hoped this final illusion would cause the soldiers to disperse.

"All right, let me send these—"

"Oh no!" Aunty Elsia interrupted. "Those stupid boys!"

"What?" Pagus spun.

Aunty Elsia shook her head, staring at the broken wall of the throne room.

Eleven short figures—all shrouded in green barsion—climbed across the rubble. They were dressed in black robes, the common attire of a necromancer acolyte. Though their faces were partially concealed behind their barsions, Pagus knew who they were—his fellow pupils.

Wait! Pagus started. Why were there only eleven? He counted the boys, noting all but Kaelar was present.

"I should have known better!" Aunty Elsia shouted, her face flaring with maternal rage. Pagus had never seen her that way. "This is all your fault!" she shouted at Pagus.

Pagus was flabbergasted. How could he be held responsible for all of *this?*

"This is getting worse each passing moment," Aunty Elsia complained.

Once all the acolytes were inside the throne room they began hurling magic at the enemy ranks.

"It'll be fine," Pagus said reassuringly. He eyed the acolytes while sending the illusions of Master Iltar and Aunty Elsia into the soldiers barring the throne.

◆━●━◆

Agen was nervous. This was an actual battle. An *actual* battle. It wasn't some drill Master Iltar had concocted. People were trying to kill them. Of course, he knew that. They all did. Agen and the other acolytes hadn't come to this decision lightly. But they knew they couldn't let Master Iltar go to the palace all alone.

Agen's fellow acolytes hurled acidic orbs into the fray where Master Iltar was *dissolving* people. The people just turned to ash. It was actually quite amazing to watch. Agen never knew Master Iltar could do such things. And there was someone else fighting…

He was a short man in black, wielding some kind of red sword. The Shorty was fighting those red-armored guys. The princes were eyeing the Shorty, as well as some other guy with a really, *really* big sword. Agen didn't recognize him.

"Bilda, Tigan, begin your layers now!" Agen commanded. "Silmar, Waedan, you're next."

The young acolytes began casting their spells—barsion barriers.

Agen didn't think their individual barsions would be enough to protect them. During their recent studies, Agen had found a story with a strategy in it that he thought worth trying. The mages in the tale moved as a single unit through a battle, and instead of using individual barsions they made one collective barrier with multiple layers.

Bilda finished his spell first, and a big dome of acidic barsion surrounded all eleven acolytes. Tigan's barsion formed just outside Bilda's spell. The whole thought process behind the strategy was that if someone dispelled one layer, another would be cast. It would work as long as there weren't more dispels than there were layers.

Agen counted the mages on the upper floors. There were at least a hundred… probably. And the mages were all focused on Master Iltar. If only a fraction of the mages turned on the acolytes, the boys would be rendered defenseless.

That was something Agen hadn't considered…

"Who's next?" someone shouted.

Agen came to his senses. "Callon and Dreymon." The boys began casting their layers as a figure in green barsion approached.

It was Pagus.

"What are you idiots doing here?" Pagus demanded.

"We're here to save you," Bilda said, sounding tough.

"Do I look like I need saving?" Pagus demanded. That gave Bilda pause.

"Look, make your way to the north side," Pagus said. "Follow this illusion. I'm going to need your help to punch a hole through the soldiers so we can get to the throne."

⇥•⇤

Another Praetorian fell before Lirathay'lu. The battle was glorious! And the Praetorians weren't half bad. They were decent opponents. Lirathay'lu had to recast his barsion several times. He locked gazes with a Praetorian—the forty-fifth one.

Human.

Lirathay'lu broke his gaze, cutting off the man's lead arm. He leapt into the air, kicking the maimed Praetorian across the throne room. As Lirathay'lu landed, one of the princes advanced. *Laedar, isn't it?* He evaded a swing from the prince's black Ko'delish blade. It wasn't that big a weapon, about the size of a long-sword. Lirathay'lu had heard of the Mindolarnians summoning much bigger blades of that accursed magic.

"Are you judging me by my size?" Lirathay'lu asked, glancing at Prince Laedar's sword. "I know I'm short, but I'm not *that* short…" The snarky comment was rewarded with an enraged yell and a swift combination of swings that struck Lirathay'lu's barsion several times. Laedar was quite skilled.

A few other hits landed against Lirathay'lu's back—blows from more Praetorians. He still had to disable eight. While keeping Laedar at bay, Lirathay'lu uttered more incantations in the *true* magical tongue. Purple magic immediately clustered in his hands.

He parried a blow from Laedar, and spun, launching a side-kick into the prince's chest that repulsed Laedar. While spinning, Lirathay'lu probed three other Praetorians. They were all qui'sha. *What luck,* he thought, landing gracefully and releasing his clustered magic in three disintegrating beams. The magic broke through the barsions of each, burning holes in the Praetorians' chests.

Five more, he thought, spinning back toward Laedar. The prince hadn't advanced. Laedar stood, glowing a black hue, whispering an incantation.

Lirathay'lu took a moment to take in his surroundings. Each of the other five Praetorians were edging around him. However, there was movement on the dais. Emperor Marden—son of the accursed qui'sha Madars—stepped onto the battlefield, wielding a gigantic black blade that misted pure evil.

Finally, Lirathay'lu grinned, turning toward the emperor. All seven of Lirathay'lu's surviving foes gathered in a circle around him.

"A fitting test," Marden declared sardonically. "This blade was designed to kill your *kind.*" The emperor settled into a wide stance, taking that gigantic sword in both hands. He raised the sword, tip toward the ceiling.

Still grinning, Lirathay'lu lunged at the emperor.

FOOLS' GAMBIT

Iltar broke through the last line of defense between him and the throne. He fixed his eyes on Alanya, who was held captive by the treacherous princess.

"Let her go!" he bellowed. Raedina just stared at Iltar. She looked horrified.

Another wave of fury pulsed through Iltar. He angrily scooped his hand through a stream of Ko'delish while commanding it to form in his hand. If the princess wouldn't let Alanya go, then Iltar would take Alanya by force. He would break Raedina's barsion using a steady beam of Ko'delish.

Iltar extended his hand to hurl the beam, but a brilliant explosion of off-white light raced toward him from his right. Hundreds—perhaps thousands—of dispelling orbs struck Iltar's streaming Ko'delish. The orbs did nothing at first, but they lessened the streaming power and then snuffed it out entirely.

No! Iltar growled, turning toward the source of the massive dispel.

Prince Negaris stood at the southern end of the throne room, enveloped in a protective sphere of blackness—obviously composed of the Ko'delish. A plethora of spells hovered about the prince.

Though Negaris's dispels had extinguished Iltar's streams, they had not quelled their source. Iltar began glowing again just as Negaris launched a beam of crimson annihilation magic.

The streaming Ko'delish consumed part of the crimson beam, narrowing it to a finger-size point. Iltar's magic, however, couldn't prevent the beam from reaching him. Negaris's blast pierced Iltar's abdomen, shooting out the small of his back.

He felt his stomach shriveling, and the sinews around it turning to dried husks. Parts of his torso went numb—the beam having severed part of his spine. There was no blood, as annihilation particles *dried* everything they touched.

Another wave of dispelling orbs struck Iltar's streaming Ko'delish. It quelled the dark power, briefly creating an opening.

No... Iltar struggled against the pain. He *commanded* his surging power to surround him.

The Ko'delish took the shape of a spherical barrier as orbs of various destructive magics flew from the balconies. Most of the deadly projectiles were consumed by Iltar's forming barrier, but a few were reduced to raindrop-sized bolts that struck his face, arms, and chest.

Acid burned holes through his tunic while the flaming magic ignited his clothes—the fire, however, didn't last long, as the streaming Ko'delish consumed the flames. A few disintegrating bolts pierced his shoulder—they blasted through his flesh with the sensation of a thousand piercing needles.

Pained, Iltar fell forward, collapsing on the floor as his protection took shape. Though it was composed entirely of Ko'delish magic, the sphere of protection resembled a barsion bubble. Years ago—when Iltar lacked an understanding of the Ko'delish—he had dubbed this barrier as his "necrotic sphere of protection."

More soldiers surrounded him, but they kept their distance. The soldiers were probably waiting for the mages to weaken Iltar's barrier. But Iltar wouldn't allow that again. He focused his streaming power to reinforce the barrier.

"You are outnumbered and surrounded," Negaris shouted. "Give up!"

Iltar cursed at the prince inwardly. He would not give in to this fool. The pain escalated his rage. Perhaps Iltar *would* kill everyone in the throne room. Still lying on the ground, Iltar brought a hand under his chest and uttered an incantation, mustering orange life-draining magic. Both the position of his hand and the streaming Ko'delish concealed the orange light from his foes.

"How pitiful," Negaris said, mustering more dispelling orbs. "You cannot survive this."

Watch me... Iltar gritted his teeth. He finished the life-draining incantation, slamming his hand into the floor. He pushed against the stone, awkwardly bracing himself.

Negaris cocked his head at Iltar, as did the rest of the soldiers.

Iltar, however, focused on Negaris. He didn't want to give away his intended targets.

A sudden surge of orange erupted amongst the soldiers. The enemy ranks attempted to disperse, but it was too late. Tree-trunk sized tentacles rose from the stone floor, gripping five of the soldiers and sapping the life from them. Each of the tentacles pulsed, transferring arpran-type energy back to Iltar.

The cuts on his face—caused by the acid—began to close. The husks that were once flesh became renewed. His stomach regenerated. The holes in his shoulder also closed. Feeling throughout his torso returned. The rejuvenating effect didn't last long, however.

Negaris hurled several of his dispelling orbs at the life-draining tentacles. The dispelling orbs vanquished the tentacles, freeing the soldiers.

Iltar cursed at the prince again. Yet, Iltar's spell had healed him enough to resume the fight.

Soldiers tensed uneasily. Incantations resounded from the upper railings of the throne room. Negaris mustered more dispelling orbs.

At that moment, Iltar realized he had to remain on the defensive. He could deal with Negaris alone, but combined aid from the Mindolarnian mages was enough to weaken his protection. That left him with only one tactic.

While still focused on fortifying the Ko'delish barrier, Iltar uttered an incantation, mustering his ensnaring tentacles. Green magic clustered in his right hand. As the spell grew to fruition, Iltar thrust his hand toward the upper railing.

A dozen ensnaring tentacles shot from Iltar's palm with incredible speed. They raced over the heads of the soldiers and slithered across the railings. Iltar could *see* the mages through his magic. The mages were gripped within seconds, and Iltar pulled them through the stone railing.

A tumultuous crash resounded as twelve mages—still uttering their incantations—were whipped across the throne room toward Iltar. Horror smeared across their faces as they struck the Ko'delish barrier. They had no time to scream, as their bodies were instantly turned to dust.

"Clever…" Negaris said, the word oozing from his lips. "But that tactic will not work a second time."

Iltar ignored the prince. He flung the tentacles again, but as they reached the broken rail dispelling magic struck each of them.

Damn it, Iltar cursed. He cast the ensnaring spell again. As the magic formed, Iltar willed a few-dozen globes of darkness to form from his streaming magic. The tentacles flew from his palm again, along with the black balls.

Dispelling magic raced from Negaris and a few of the remaining mages, but Iltar intercepted most of the dispels with his globes of darkness. Only half of the tentacles survived and six mages were pulled into his Ko'delish barrier.

He tried the tactic again, but slew fewer mages. But even if he could only ensnare one at a time, Iltar *would* whittle their ranks.

⟣•⟢

Raedina was angry. Angry at herself. Angry at her family. And angry at her God.

This man—this so-called Iltar of Soroth—was not the vile Alathian. But he was just like him—murdering any Mindolarnian who stood in his way. Raedina watched in confusion as Iltar decimated more of their forces. Men were pulled from their hiding places and slammed into his barrier of Ko'delish. That power was so grand, so majestic. None of her family had ever manifested the Ko'delish with such grandeur. The magnificence of his mani-festation rivaled even God, her Divine Father, Aunok'sha. Raedina shuddered at that implication.

This Iltar couldn't be the Unspoken One—the Harbinger of Cheserith—could he? No, he couldn't. Her family had watched over the hiss'thraks for centuries. They were all accounted for, weren't they?

Nevertheless, this man was wielding the power of the gods, and it mani-fested so quickly—faster than any incantations in any of the magical tongues. Perhaps he was the Unspoken One… but that implied she and her family had somehow evoked the displeasure of their God. Had Lord Cheserith bestowed his power on someone not of their lineage?

That notion was blasphemous.

He can't be the Harbinger… she thought. Raedina would prove he wasn't. In that moment, her hatred for Iltar swelled. This was a man who had invaded their home, stolen their family's birthright, and mocked their God.

She would deal with him. Raedina deliberately pulled on the cord binding Alanya, escorting the traitor down the stairs.

"What are you doing?" Alanya demanded.

"Ending this…"

Elsia felt manipulated. By whom she didn't know. And their reasons were even more elusive. But someone or *something* wanted this battle to happen. She kept coming back to the prophecies of Soron Thahan, trying to piece together any possible reason as to *why* this battle was happening. Elsia dwelt on that vague passage about apostates fighting the Unspoken One. Is that conflict the fulfillment of that prophecy?

With her nephew and Iltar's acolytes, Elsia broke through the soldiers. Pagus wasn't a half-bad mage. But if Elsia had her way, Pagus wouldn't be seeing battle for quite some time, if ever.

They charged near the battle with the emperor and that short man in black. The Praetorians who had stood guard were either dead or wounded. As Elsia neared one of the corpses, she started with fear. "What on Kalda?!" She gasped. That was no man lying before her.

The Praetorian's helmet had been knocked off, revealing an elongated face that resembled a snout. Crimson scales covered the Praetorian's head. Violet eyes were stark against the scales. The Praetorian's maw was ajar, his sharp teeth exposed as was his forked tongue.

Confused, Elsia turned to another dead Praetorian. That man—no that *crea-ture*—still wore his helmet. A crimson-covered snout was pressed against the helm, looking smashed.

"What are these things…" Elsia muttered.

"Oh…" Pagus groaned, "You don't want to know, Aunty. You don't want to know…"

"Wow, that's a creepy monster," Bilda blurted. He was encased in a thick bubble of acidic barsion magic with the rest of the acolytes. Elsia was impressed that the boys had come up with that strategy.

Several of the other boys quizzically muttered to each other about the monstrous corpses. The acolytes too were perplexed. Pagus seemed to be the only one *not* confused. What had Pagus learned in his absence?

Elsia turned from the corpse to see Raedina descending the dais with Alanya. The princess tugged the high duchess along like a dog.

How dare she...? Elsia growled inwardly, then dashed toward Raedina. The princess spun, gripping Alanya tightly while extending her wand. Raedina said something in a strange language, and then a flurry of arcane bolts shot from the wand.

Elsia tried to dodge, but one of the bolts struck her shoulder with a violent eruption. She flipped through the air, landing on her stomach. Elsia expected the blow to hurt, but neither the magic nor the harsh landing fazed her.

Rebounding, Elsia dashed again to Raedina. She *would* free her friend. Elsia would not allow Alanya to suffer because of this manipulation. Raedina fired several more bolts. Elsia couldn't dodge them and was thrust onto her back. Pagus leapt over her, clutching three shimmering orbs of acidic magic. He hurled the corrosive balls at the barsion surrounding Raedina and Alanya, but it had no effect.

"You cannot break this barsion, boy!" Raedina spat. "No matter how hard you try, you can never breech it."

The acolytes joined Pagus in his attempts; they perched on the stairs, shrouded in their unified barsion. Their magic—a jumble of arcane orbs and acidic bolts—crashed into Raedina's barsion, but none of the spells took effect.

In retaliation, Raedina fired a volley of arcane bolts from her wand. Pagus dodged gracefully. The acolytes, however, held their ground. The outer layer of their barsion shattered. Acid spilled down the dais's steps.

Elsia resumed her dash, finally reaching Raedina. "Let her go!" Elsia shouted, readying her sword.

Raedina's eyes flashed with fury, and she turned the wand back to Alanya. The princess pressed the tip of her wand into her captive's neck. "Call them off or she dies!" the princess spat.

"Boys..." Elsia called, not taking her eyes off Raedina. Incantations ceased behind her—the acolytes didn't *hold* their magic like other mages. Perhaps they weren't adept enough. "Your Imperial Highness, please let Alanya go," Elsia pleaded. "This entire thing is a misunderstanding. We've both been manipulated—"

"Silence!" Raedina shouted, burying her wand deeper into Alanya's neck.

Elsia sucked in a breath. The battle continued raging around Elsia. More men were pulled into Iltar's devouring magic. The sight was sickening. "If you let Alanya go, we will leave. We are not Alathians."

Raedina cackled dryly. "You don't think I *know* that," the princess retorted. "You are far worse!" Elsia started at the accusation.

"This is not how it's supposed to be!" Raedina spat vehemently. "*He* cannot be the Unspoken One…" Her words trailed off, sounding as if she were in denial. The princess's eyes wandered.

"Just let Alanya go," Elsia said, forcing a calm tone. Raedina snapped a fierce glance at Elsia.

"We will leave once she is safely with me," Elsia said, her tone slow and deliberate. "We didn't come here to kill anyone. We came to free my nephew. But now things have gotten out of hand." Elsia studied the princess, but Raedina's eyes were filled with animalistic rage. Raedina regarded Elsia briefly, then hauled Alanya toward Iltar.

"Now what?" Pagus demanded, coming beside Elsia.

A knot formed in Elsia's stomach. "I don't know…"

———◆·◆———

Lirathay'lu contended with only *two* foes now. He dueled wildly with Emperor Marden and Prince Laedar, swiftly casting destructive spells amid his swings.

Marden's barsion weakened, and Lirathay'lu repulsed Laedar with a telekinetic spell—the prince landed among the soldiers warily eyeing Iltar.

For a moment, Marden was Lirathay'lu's only opponent. Both began casting their own spells while executing a flurry of blows. Their blades crackled as they met. Lirathay'lu finished first, relentlessly hurling a disintegration beam at Marden, further weakening his foe's protective magic.

The emperor's barsion shattered. Marden abruptly ceased his offensive spell. Amid a swing with his monstrous sword, Marden attempted to recast his barsion. Lirathay'lu, however, deflected Deathcleaver. *Now!* he told himself, swiftly lunging at Marden. The emperor attempted to evade, but Lirathay'lu swiftly stabbed Marden through the chest.

Blue barsion dissipated as Marden gasped, gawking at the magically composed blade. Regal clothing dried and cracked. Flesh turned to dried husks.

"Finally!" Lirathay'lu cheered, violently slicing upward. His blade cut effortlessly. Annihilation particles dried flesh, sinew, and bone as the blade raced through the emperor. The blade's tip reached the crown of Marden's skull, and Lirathay'lu drew it from the emperor's forehead.

Lirathay'lu leapt, spinning and kicking the lifeless emperor away. He recoiled, landing in a crouch. Lirathay'lu eyed Laedar, who was closing in on him. The prince's eyes were ablaze with fury.

Good, Lirathay'lu grinned. *One down, one to go…*

———◆·◆———

Iltar had eliminated most of the mages. Negaris had resumed assailing Iltar's Ko'delish barrier with blasts of dispelling magic, but no matter how hard the prince tried, Negaris failed to breech Iltar's protection.

That surprised Iltar. He had never mustered this much of the Darkness—rather the Ko'delish—in any instance. Amid Negaris's assault, Raedina approached, coming within arm's reach of Iltar's Ko'delish barrier.

"You…" the princess growled. "You intrude upon our home, you kill our people, and you blaspheme our God!"

Now's my chance, Iltar thought. He would have to sacrifice maintaining his barrier against Negaris. He hoped it would last long enough for him to free Alanya. Iltar resumed mustering the Ko'delish in his hand, watching the princess's face contort with rage.

Snarling, Raedina jabbed at a bracelet on her forearm. An opening appeared in the barsion and Raedina shoved Alanya toward Iltar's devouring barrier.

Alanya screamed, falling forward.

No! Iltar gasped. *Move!* he commanded, willing his Ko'delish barrier to spread away from Alanya.

The magic *flew* sideways, completely exposing Iltar to Raedina. A few of the devouring particles, however, wafted in the air, eroding holes in Alanya's gown. The rest of the black magic washed across the room, forming a wall that devoured some of the soldiers. Several were maimed, and their cries echoed throughout the throne room.

Alanya landed near Iltar's feet, groaning.

Raedina's barrier closed as she pointed her wand at Iltar. She said a word in the Keadal tongue that launched a volley of arcane orbs.

Infuriated, Iltar flung his hand toward the princess, unleashing a blast of the Ko'delish. He glimpsed Alanya stirring, but she didn't push herself up.

The magics clashed—Iltar's beam devoured all but two of the arcane orbs. The beaming blast of Ko'delish struck Raedina's barsion, instantly cracking the barrier.

Raedina's two remaining orbs struck Iltar's chest, erupting in a blinding flash that hurled him backward.

His skin *burned* from the explosive magic—though it was not on fire. The bolts should have killed him, but the Ko'delish streaming from his body had absorbed some of the explosion.

Gasping, Iltar hit the floor and struggled to maintain focus on the beam. He pushed himself upright, refocusing his blast of Ko'delish; it was a column of blackness ramming Raedina's barsion. The cracks widened rapidly.

"No!" Raedina exclaimed, gasping. "This is impossible!"

Pain surged across Iltar's chest and he struggled to breathe, but he forced the Ko'delish beam farther into the princess's barsion.

A resounding shatter echoed throughout the throne room. Raedina wailed. Iltar felt the Ko'delish beam burrowing through the princess's chest. She shrieked a dying howl that ceased abruptly. Raedina fell backward, passing from life to death before hitting the floor.

Iltar groaned, feeling his wall of Ko'delish weakening. Negaris had almost broken through.

I'll kill him—no! Iltar cut himself short. He wasn't here to lay waste to the Mindolarnians. His purpose here at the palace had been accomplished. Pagus was freed and Alanya was safe—*Alanya!*

The high duchess lay near where she had first fallen. But she wasn't moving. Iltar staggered toward her, but started upon seeing a giant dome of acidic barsion. Inside it were eleven short figures. Though their faces were partially obscured, he recognized them.

They were his acolytes.

What?! Iltar started. What were *they* doing here? And why were there only eleven? Had one of them—

The Ko'delish wall shattered. Iltar instinctively threw his hand toward Negaris, willing his streaming Ko'delish to form another barrier. Out of the corner of his eye, Iltar saw his acolytes advancing on Negaris. Pagus was with them as well. They flung acidic magics at the prince, drawing his attention.

"No, you fools!" Iltar shouted. "Come to me!"

The acolytes obeyed their master's cry, but still hurled their magics at the prince.

Iltar's skin burned as he continued toward Alanya. Elsia was already there, kneeling beside the high duchess.

"Alanya!" Elsia shook the woman. "Alanya!"

Had Alanya been too close to the blast? The back of Alanya's gown was tattered, ripped apart by the explosion of Raedina's arcane orbs. Her dress also showed signs of erosion from the Ko'delish. The skin on her back was charred. She couldn't be dead, could she?

"Alanya!" Elsia shook the woman again.

No… Iltar shook his head. *No, she can't—*

Iltar was no longer in the throne room. A yellow sky stretched above him, a blue sun hanging above the horizon. Translucent ground spread beneath his feet. Iltar was in Vabenack.

Anger flooded his veins. "Reflection!" Iltar cried, searching the Translucent Fields. "Reflection, where are you?!" He looked down at his hands, noticing the Ko'delish no longer streamed from his pores. *What on Kalda—?*

A snickering cackle sounded from behind Iltar. "What an odd name," a deep voice bellowed.

Iltar spun, seeing a man in a white robe—wait… this was no man.

This thing—whatever it was—looked humanoid, but was covered in crimson scales instead of skin. The creature's face was elongated, like a snout, and vibrant yellow eyes glared with thrilled passion.

"A man should always know his killer," the thing said with a grin that revealed sharp teeth. "I am Xalutir, son of Mindolarn the First."

◆◦◆

"Oh great…" Pagus groaned, watching as that wall of black magic just *fell* to the ground.

What had happened? Master Iltar lay beside Alanya, face against the floor. Pagus hadn't seen anything hit his master. It was as if Master Iltar suddenly collapsed.

"Iltar!" Aunty Elsia shouted, shaking the necromancer. Master Iltar didn't move.

"Boys!" Pagus shouted, hurrying toward Iltar. "I need help!" He then uttered an incantation, a variation of the acidic barsion Iltar had taught him and the other acolytes. Green magic swirled around his hands.

As the magic took shape, that mage-prince turned his attention to Pagus and the acolytes. *Damn it!* Pagus cursed.

The mage-prince hurled several dispelling orbs, along with some flaming spheres. He dispelled half their multi-layered barsion with a resounding clatter. The flames erupted, weakening the remaining layers.

Pagus finished his spell, and yellow-green magic sped in front of the acolytes, forming a towering wall.

"Do the same as that!" Pagus shouted the command as he reached Master Iltar. "And don't encase us, otherwise we can't escape!" Pagus knelt swiftly, propping Iltar on his side. "Wrong time to take a nap, old man," he said, frisking Iltar's tunic.

"What are you doing?" Aunty Elsia demanded.

"Getting us out of here…" Pagus grumbled. "If I can find the damned thing!"

More acidic magic washed around them, bathing the air in a semi-protective shield.

"Keep those barriers up," Pagus shouted, and felt something hard—like a rock. Without any consideration, Pagus *ripped* the tunic. A coin-sized blue gem with golden flecks fell from the hidden pocket—a rogulin crystal.

"Do you even know how to use that thing?" Aunty Elsia barked. She turned back to Iltar, shaking him further.

Pagus didn't answer his aunt. He didn't have time for that. "Everyone grab onto me!" Pagus shouted, then uttered an incantation. He hoped it was the right incantation…

Lady Alanya gasped and then groaned. "She's alive!" Aunty Elsia cheered, gripping the high duchess.

Amid her outburst, the acolytes gathered in a ring around Pagus, all holding hands. Bilda grabbed Alanya's limp hand, thus connecting Aunty Elsia and Master Iltar to the rest of them.

"The barsions aren't holding!" Bilda cried. "He's too fast!"

None of the other acolytes bothered to reply—they were all too busy recasting their barsions.

Pagus finished, but nothing happened. *Damn it,* he cursed again.

"What's wrong?!" Aunty Elsia shouted.

Pagus ignored her again. Perhaps he had the words wrong. After all, Pagus hadn't *actually* used a teleporting incantation.

Aunty Elsia resumed shouting at Master Iltar, but her cries didn't jar the necromancer.

⋄•⊂

Iltar started.

This *thing* was one of the Mindolarn princes? But… this was no man. This was… a monster.

Bewildered, Iltar glanced about, searching perchance for anyone else here in Vabenack. But the Translucent Fields were empty.

"They call me the Master of Dreams," Xalutir said haughtily. "Do you know why I am called that?" A twisted grin crawled across his scaled snout. "Because you are in a world of dreams." The monster cackled. "Whatever I do to you in here will happen out there," he gestured across the horizon.

"Here, let me demonstrate," Xalutir said, then spoke a harsh guttural language—the same that Raedina had spoken to Iltar while in the Royal Archive—the Keadal tongue.

A sudden pang of pressure and pain struck Iltar's belly. He looked down to see the banister of a railing running through him.

How… Iltar gasped. He didn't even see the railing form. The railing just *appeared.*

"So out there, you've just started to bleed out," Xalutir sneered. "I could leave you like this, pinned in place. I've done it before," the monster mused. "But you're a mage, so you'd probably just break it down. I expect you would cast some arpran spell, and then we'd be back where we started."

Xalutir waved his hand in a dismissal and the railing vanished. Iltar collapsed, and his blood gushed onto the translucent ground.

"There are so many ways I could kill you," Xalutir said, reveling in the thought. "I could keep you here until you starved. It's an excellent way to interrogate someone." The monster continued ranting as Iltar uttered an arpran incantation. A wave of rejuvenating magic washed from Iltar's hands to his fist-sized wound.

"So predictable," Xalutir smiled. Iltar glared at the creature as his magic regenerated his flesh.

"I am nigh unstoppable in here," Xalutir gloated. "Whatever you attempt is ultimately futile. You *will* die here." Xalutir waved his hand again, speaking that same guttural tongue.

The translucent ground shifted, growing walls that spread to a ceiling. Soon, Iltar and the monster were in a large room made of polished stone. It was filled with furniture. Paintings hung on the wall. A table was to the left. Torture tools lay atop the table, along with a variety of other things—some Iltar didn't recognize but supposed to be tevisrals.

"Welcome to my *favorite* place," Xalutir grinned, walking to the table. Iltar's eyes widened. *Impossible!* The back of the monster's white robe bore the upside-down First Emblem with that crescent atop it.

That man… Iltar furrowed his brow. Was this Xalutir the same white-robed man he had passed within the bowels of the palace? The one the voice forbade him to enthrall. But Xalutir wasn't a man…

I hate you, Reflection, Iltar growled, feeling a swelling surge building within him. If this Xalutir was that man, then Iltar could have avoided this predicament. Iltar would have enthralled the beast and slain him as he had the patrol.

Renewed flesh sealed Iltar's wound as Xalutir reached the table.

"So many people try to escape," Xalutir said, picking up a serrated knife. He gleefully tested its sharpness against his thumb. "But they can't. There's nowhere for them to go. They could wander the Translucent Fields but never find their way back to Kalda. Only a Dreamwalker could accomplish that."

Dreamwalker...

That's it! Iltar thought. He slammed his fist to the floor, uttering the words, "Alza Cho'k sa'maz nira."

The portal to his subconscious opened beneath him, and Iltar fell into a brilliant void.

Iltar started, finding himself upon the floor of the throne room with blood pooling around him. Eruptions of magic resounded. Barsion shattered with that unmistakable crash. A feminine voice groaned.

"He's alive!" Elsia shouted. The countess was holding his hand.

Why—?

Golden light caught Iltar's eye, coming from Pagus kneeling beside him. The boy was uttering an incantation—a teleportation spell.

"Oh no!" Bilda cried.

Iltar glanced over his shoulder, watching a wall of acidic barsion shatter. Pieces of the acidic barsion fell as Negaris hurled an array of deadly orbs, aimed at the acolytes.

The golden light grew brighter as the magic approached.

And then, in a crystallized moment, Iltar noticed a figure wearing a white robe along the fifth story railing. His pale-painted face and white hair were unmistakable. He was that same man Iltar had encountered on his way to the dungeon. He looked directly at Iltar with vibrant yellow eyes. Those eyes stared at Iltar with the hatred of a hunter whose prey had escaped his clutches.

Xalutir...

That moment faded as golden light erupted from Pagus's hands. Amid the blinding flash, Negaris's magic struck little Bilda.

"No!" Iltar screamed as a brilliant light engulfed his vision.

"The Channelers called their island refuge, Dalgilur. They locked them-selves away, sealing off their island by their powerful tevisrals. There, they built a utopian civilization that lasted for several centuries, until their descendants could no longer watch the world suffer."

- From *The Thousand Years War, Part I*, page 56

The eruption of golden light faded as Lirathay'lu drew his blade of an-nihilation magic from Laedar's torso.

The prince groaned, dropping to the rubble littered floor of the throne room.

"Good riddance," Lirathay'lu spat, twirling his magically composed blade. He watched as Laedar's form shifted, reverting to his *true* nature—it was like the dismissal of a transmutation.

Though his clothing remained, Laedar's skin rippled from flesh to crimson scales. His hair—both on his face and atop his head—faded as his features stretched, elongating into a snout.

The emperor, however, remained human. His death had not returned him to his qui'sha form.

Impossible, Lirathay'lu muttered, edging toward Marden's corpse. *Does he possess a ring of longevity?* he wondered, studying the emperor's lifeless fingers. It would make sense. A ring of longevity would prevent a qui'sha from returning to their *natural* form, as it would preserve their life. Qui'sha would only revert when they were dead.

An orange band on Marden's middle finger caught Lirathay'lu's eye. Curious, Lirathay'lu knelt to inspect it. *This is not a ring of longevity…* he thought.

The ring looked akin to an elven creation crafted long ago, before the Thousand Years War. Such rings altered the shape of its bearer—elven children often used them as toys.

Curious, Lirathay'lu twirled his blade, guiding its tip to the knuckle behind the ring. With excellent precision he stabbed the knuckle, severing the finger.

Marden's pale hand rippled, turning from flesh to crimson scales. The change was more like a dismissing illusion than a fading transmutation.

There you are, Lirathay'lu mused, watching Marden's lifeless human form vanish, revealing a dead qui'sha. But was this even the emperor? Why would Marden want to mask his true form?

Those questions gave him pause.

Perhaps I acted too hastily, Lirathay'lu thought, taking the ring from the severed finger. He felt foolish. Had he been duped into exposing himself?

Shouted commands resounded from his right, and Lirathay'lu turned to see the survivors of Iltar's onslaught readying to attack. Prince Negaris was busily enhancing each of the surviving soldiers.

Suddenly, everything changed. Lirathay'lu was no longer in the throne room at Mindolarn. Instead, he stood within a cavernous room that lacked any windows or doors.

"I expected you to be bigger," a wry voice said disappointedly.

Lirathay'lu turned, seeing a qui'sha wearing a white robe. The crimson scales along the qui'sha's snout twisted into a sinister grin.

"You must really believe you are human," the qui'sha said, sounding amused with his observation. "We masquerade as men, but we retain our true identity. Here in Vabenack, one is revealed as one's *true* self."

Vabenack?

Lirathay'lu glanced down, examining his hands.

How had he come to this place… this realm of a mad god? His clothes were different. Instead of his black garb he wore a brown smock stained with traces of herbs. How had that happened? And where was his Annihilation Blade?

"You look so confused," the qui'sha said, snickering. "And here I thought your *kind* was the most intelligent of the sha'kalda breeds."

Lirathay'lu shot a glance into the qui'sha's yellow eyes, but nothing happened.

"Are you trying to probe me?" the qui'sha stepped forward. "Oh, let me get closer. Do you think that will help?" he said mockingly. Lirathay'lu continued staring into the qui'sha's yellow eyes, but nothing happened.

The qui'sha grinned. "Cast a spell, I dare you…" A sudden pang of fear struck Lirathay'lu. He uttered an incantation in the *true* magical tongue, but nothing happened. What was wrong with this accursed place? Couldn't magic be manifest here?

"It's because you see yourself as human!" the qui'sha exclaimed with triumphant laughter tinged with condescension. Still laughing, the qui'sha clasped Lirathay'lu's shoulders. "Your mind here is human," he cackled. "Now, you are nothing! Nothing! And you're going to die…"

The qui'sha continued laughing like a madman. Defiantly, Lirathay'lu punched the qui'sha's stomach, knocking him backward. Even if he couldn't use magic, he could still beat his foe to a pulp.

"Oh my," the qui'sha grinned. "You'll be fun. I've never had one of your *kind* in my clutches. I almost didn't think I could do it—bring you here to

Vabenack, I mean." Suddenly, excruciating pain surged through Lirathay'lu, but abruptly stopped. The room seemed to tip and spin. He was falling though it didn't feel that way. In fact, he felt nothing.

And then, everything went black.

⋘•⋙

Jeridi was still exhausted. He leaned against a pillar between the throne room and the third floor's southern hallway. He had taken shelter there amidst the tumultuous battle.

The violence had finally ceased. Ashes and rubble, as well as mangled bodies, were scattered across the throne room. The wounded were mingled with the dead, especially among the ranks of the Praetorians. Jeridi was numb after gazing at the destruction.

The devastation was worse than the Feast of Sorrows… But this rampage wasn't a continuation of that massacre.

"I knew you weren't the Alathian," Jeridi whispered to himself. He sucked in his breath and averted his gaze. His family had been foolish. Not only had they attacked the wrong man, they had attacked the Unspoken One. There was irony in that. Their hastiness had been punished by divine retribution.

Regaining his composure, Jeridi gazed across the throne room, his eyes settling on his brother's corpse. *Laedar, you fool,* he thought, bemused. *If only you had listened to me, we could have avoided this—*

Footsteps drew Jeridi's attention, and he turned to see his brother approaching—Xalutir, second in line to the throne. As usual, Xalutir wore a white robe bearing the twisted depiction of the First Emblem of Cherisium. His face was painted pale to look like one of the Chosen, his blond hair dyed to match. Xalutir's delusions of grandeur had driven him mad. His pride came from his accomplishments in unlocking the forbidden secrets of Vabenack— knowledge prohibited to all but the Chosen.

Over the last few decades, Xalutir had become a near recluse, communicating only by messengers until a few years ago. The Losians' attack at the Feast of Sorrows had drawn him out, and Xalutir returned to Mindolarn for a time, but soon left. Of all the sons of Mindolarn, Xalutir was the strangest. Jeridi didn't really know his brother.

The estrangement suited Jeridi just fine. Xalutir was disturbing.

A sneer crossed Xalutir's pale face as he looked to Jeridi. "Someone decapitated my prey," the pale-painted prince complained. "Did you see who, Jeridi?" Jeridi didn't answer. He turned back to the throne room, watching as Negaris removed that giant sword—Deathcleaver—from the stone floor. A small decapitated body lay before him, clothed in black.

"Figures he would do it," Xalutir spat, stomping into the throne room.

Sighing, Jeridi closed his eyes. *You poor fools…* Raedina had fallen, as had Malvonican—who had worn the illusion of Uncle Marden. Jeridi mourned their deaths. Their efforts were akin to a roaring tidal wave crashing against a towering cliff. They had attacked Iltar, but shared the fate of the dissipating waves.

Jeridi swallowed hard, sorrow welling within him. He embraced his grief, but was drawn by his arguing brothers.

"Will you wear it, Xalutir?" Negaris asked.

"I will not do such a thing," Xalutir murmured, his tone wry. "Find someone else!"

Negaris looked disappointed. He was holding out the ring Raedina had crafted.

Xalutir turned, looking at the opening where the western wall once stood. "Twice my prey has been taken from me this day," he groaned. "One I can no longer hunt, but the other…" His words trailed off, and his pale face twisted with enlightenment.

"The plan was for you to draw them into the Translucent Fields so we could kill them," Negaris said sternly. "I wasn't about to risk *this* one escaping." He gestured to the small headless body.

"You confuse the details of our arrangement," Xalutir murmured. "But that doesn't matter now. I can still hunt the other." With a last disgusted glare, Xalutir turned and stormed away. He seemed determined to slay Iltar.

Negaris watched as Xalutir left, but his eyes were drawn to Jeridi. "And what were you doing this entire time?" Negaris shouted. Jeridi took courage and moved away from the pillar. "I was trying to avert this madness," He gestured to the destruction in the throne room. Jeridi didn't dare say exactly what he had intended, lest Negaris retaliate.

Negaris shook his head, still holding the ring that had granted Uncle Marden's likeness. "I don't see how…" he muttered, then took one last glance across the throne room. After a moment, Negaris gave a command for the survivors to secure the palace.

"I will not let that man go unpunished," Negaris said as he neared Jeridi. "One way or another, I will find him and kill him."

"Do you still believe he is the Alathian?" Jeridi asked warily, hoping to probe his brother's grasp of the situation.

Negaris paused. "He is not… but his identity doesn't change the fact that I will exact vengeance upon him. He stormed the palace, butchered our soldiers, murdered our family, and desecrated the Royal Archive. This Iltar is an enemy to the empire, and I will see to it that he is punished as such."

Jeridi watched his brother leave. The rest of the soldiers followed Negaris, and soon only Jeridi remained. He lingered in the throne room, gazing at the starlit sky.

Even with the truth staring his family in the face, they refused to accept it. Negaris had battled with Iltar and experienced his glorious power. Yet he refused to acknowledge Iltar's divine mantle. Negaris would stubbornly face Iltar and die. Eventually, the rest of his family would suffer that same fate. And then, Jeridi would be alone.

Despair came over Jeridi. It formed an unsettling knot in his stomach, and he *knew* his family would only bring folly to the empire. He alone would be the voice of reason, but would undoubtedly be ignored.

Resigning himself to that fate, Jeridi left the throne room.

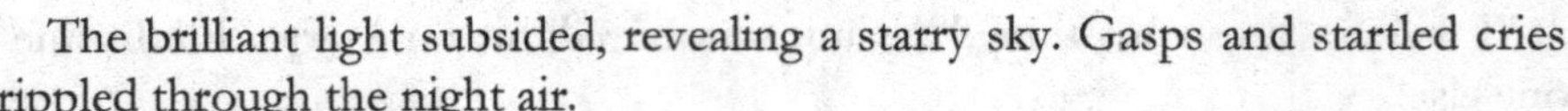

The brilliant light subsided, revealing a starry sky. Gasps and startled cries rippled through the night air.

Iltar leapt over Alanya, bounding across gray galstra tiles. He ran toward the falling Bilda, uttering an arpran incantation. Of all his acolytes, why was *this* boy struck? Agony and wrath vexed Iltar's heart as he caught the boy. His emotions escalated as green magic appeared in his hands, lighting the surrounding area.

Bilda's eyes darted erratically, and he convulsed. The boy's robe showed signs of acidic erosion, and his chest was burned and bubbling. Droplets of acid dribbled from the wound. The acid, however, soon vanished, since its caster was thousands of grand phineals away, unable to maintain the spell from such a distance.

Iltar's eyes welled with tears as he finished the incantation. Healing light seeped into the boy, and Iltar held Bilda tight.

"Is he going to be okay?" Agen asked.

"Bilda!" Tigan shouted.

A clatter of footfalls washed around Iltar, but he didn't pay attention. He had to focus on saving Bilda. "Oh, Bilda," Iltar whispered, his voice shaky. He focused his mind on spreading the arpran particles across the boy's entire body. Bilda was near death; the acid had reached the boy's veins and spread through him like a wildfire. Though the acid had dissipated, its destructive rampage remained.

Bilda continued convulsing. He gasped horridly, heaved violently, then abruptly stilled. *No!* Iltar gritted his teeth. He would not let this boy die. Iltar stared wide-eyed at Bilda as the boy glowed with vibrant arpran light.

The arpran aura brightened, then faded. After a moment, Bilda jolted, gasping for air as if he had been underwater. He coughed several times and then slumped against Iltar.

"You did it!" one of the boys cheered.

"He's alive!" Tigan shouted.

Several of the acolytes whooped, celebrating Iltar's intervention.

Bilda turned, looking at Iltar with a weakened grin. "Thank you, Master Iltar." Iltar pursed his lips to a line, fighting back the whirlwind of emotions raging within him. He was both angry at the acolytes but thankful none of them had perished. Yet, there was still one missing. Kaelar was absent.

"Kaelar!" Iltar started, relinquishing his grip on Bilda.

"He's fine," Agen said. "Kaelar is on Pagus's ship."

"Where are we?" an acolyte asked quickly, glancing at a darkened parapet.

"Atop my tower," Iltar answered, "in Soroth." He looked to Agen with confusion and was about to press him further when Elsia screamed.

"Iltar, she's bleeding badly!" the countess shouted.

Iltar spun. He could barely see the darkened outline of the women—Elsia was kneeling and holding Alanya. Heart thumping, Iltar cast the arpran incantation once again. He dropped to his knees beside Alanya as the magic formed. Green light illuminated the surrounding area, revealing Elsia's tearstained face. Alanya was gasping for breath; her face was strained and partially covered in blood. A large gash marred her forehead—she must have hit her head when Raedina's arcane orbs erupted. The high duchess's eyes fell upon Iltar, and she smiled at him amid her anguish.

"Why didn't I see this sooner?" Elsia demanded shakily. Iltar ignored the countess, extending one hand toward Alanya's face and the other toward her chest.

Alanya's eyes—still fixated on Iltar—widened, and her expression *froze*.

Arpran light blasted from Iltar's hands, enveloping Alanya in a green hue. The healing magic surged across her body, regenerating her forehead. Fresh skin covered the wound. Iltar could *feel* the magic flowing through her, repairing the damage inflicted on her body… but something was wrong.

Alanya's heart wasn't beating. The green arpran hue faded, but the high duchess remained still. Her wounds had healed, but it was too late.

Alanya had died.

The realization hit Iltar like a stunning blow. It debilitated him, shackling him with grief.

"Alanya?" Elsia demanded. Though it was dark, Iltar could see the countess's face twisting in disbelief. "Why is she so heavy?" Iltar sank, weighed down by that incapacitating sorrow.

"Why isn't she moving?!" Elsia cried. Iltar didn't answer. He *couldn't* answer.

Elsia continued shouting a torrent of questions. The acolytes gathered around, each anxious. Pagus knelt beside his aunt, wrapping his arms around her shoulders. He whispered for Elsia to let go of her lifeless friend. Pagus's urging sent Elsia into a wailing frenzy. She beat a fist upon her nephew's chest as she sobbed uncontrollably.

Amid Elsia's sobbing, light shone from a stairwell leading to the lower levels of Iltar's tower, accompanied by demands from Delrin.

The limping guardsman hobbled up a staircase and onto the tower's roof, carrying a lightstone lantern. Delrin looked stunned upon seeing Iltar and the others. He asked a flurry of questions, but Iltar couldn't answer him. Though Iltar was physically atop the tower, his mind felt so far away.

Pagus was quick to answer Delrin's questions. He then pulled his aunt toward the staircase and descended into Iltar's tower. The acolytes followed Pagus, but Delrin remained, hurrying to Iltar. Once near, Delrin knelt, warily gazing into Iltar's eyes. He spoke, but Iltar didn't understand what he was saying. All he could do was stare at Alanya's lifeless body. Her eyes were frozen in that final glance they had exchanged.

Eventually, Delrin left.

Now alone, Iltar struggled to move toward Alanya. It was an excruciating moment before he reached her, taking her cold body into a tight embrace. And then, Iltar cried. His tears flowed until the western horizon became alight with a warm-orange hue. That night of mourning felt like an eternity.

How he had loved her!

The realization almost broke him. Overwhelming anguish filled him. Though Iltar had experienced much pain in his life, this was far beyond anything he had ever felt.

The sun was rising in the west as Belsina—Iltar's maid—ascended the stairs to the tower's rooftop. Belsina shook her head as she crossed the roof. She took a deep breath before kneeling beside Iltar. After a moment, Belsina wrapped one arm around Iltar and rested the other upon the lifeless Alanya.

"Give her to me," Belsina urged gently.

Iltar turned to her as Hegdil—the groom—stepped onto the tower's rooftop with Delrin and Jalim.

"Go with Hegdil," Belsina suggested in a calm tone. "We'll take care of her." With a gentle touch, Belsina ran a hand through Iltar's hair. Iltar struggled to relinquish his grip. If he let go, he would lose her, forever.

"Iltar," Belsina urged. They exchanged pained gazes, then Iltar reluctantly complied. Belsina gently took hold of Alanya, closing her eyes. She heaved the high duchess's rigid body with a groan.

Weakened from his sorrow, Iltar struggled to stand, and Hegdil dashed across the tower's rooftop. Pained by his master's loss, Hegdil wrapped an arm around Iltar and helped him walk.

"She's gone, Hegdil…" Iltar muttered. "And I never told her." His own words struck his heart, and he suddenly felt numb. Hegdil looked at him quizzically, but didn't respond. His demeanor was somber as he guided Iltar to the stairs.

"You need to rest, Master Iltar," Hegdil said, intending to usher his master down the steps, but Iltar grabbed hold of the nearby parapet. His grip abruptly stopped them both.

Iltar's sorrow had bored a hole in his soul. But that hole was filling with an inferno of rage. An unquenchable fury contorted Iltar's face as he glanced back to Alanya's corpse. The woman he loved was dead. His quest for knowledge had brought nothing but folly. Though he had gained much, he had lost something far greater. What could have been something beautiful was now exquisitely bitter. Alanya—and her love—had been taken from him by the very people who had taken everything else he had cherished.

Iltar would not let them go unpunished.

Still gripping the tower's parapet, Iltar gazed to the northeast, toward Mindolarn. "I will topple your empire," he vowed, his tone filled with wrath. "Your cities will crumble, and your people will turn to dust. When I am through, Mindolarn will only be a memory."

THE END OF

Part Three

GREATER KALDA

VII-IX

Kenard · Brandir · Almar

Sea breezes always felt glorious, even in the most precarious times. Sure, if you were on land you could feel similar gusts blowing in from the sea, but there was something lacking about those winds. Perhaps it was the rocking of a vessel, or the mists that accompanied the waves as they broke against a hull. Whatever it was, Captain Joselin Kenard *knew* he could only experience true magnificence at sea, and there was nothing quite like sailing the oceans of Kalda.

Taking a deep breath, Captain Kenard reveled in that breeze washing across his ship, the *White Duchess*. He stood at the portside rail, running his hand through his thick shoulder-length blond hair. He often tied it back, letting only his gray lock hang down beside his face, but today all his hair hung loose. There was something relaxing about free-flowing hair, and he *needed* to relax.

Kenard surveyed the horizon, his hand clasping the portside rail, which was made of a material that would neither rot nor rust. Despite this being *his* ship, Kenard had never known what the *White Duchess* was made from. The ship had been in his family for nearly a hundred years. Ole Pappy inherited the ship from his captain, who suddenly passed away without any warning. Since then, Kenard's family had passed the *White Duchess* from father to son.

The *White Duchess* was also the fastest ship in the known world. The ship made the Isles Run—a popular trading route in the Kalishir Ocean—in twenty-one days. Most ships would require a month and a half or more to complete the route, depending on weather conditions. For a time, the *White Duchess*'s speed had given Kenard a favorable reputation. Merchants requiring speedy delivery of their goods often hired him—whenever he was in port, of course. Kenard was quite prosperous for a while, but he had since fallen upon hard times.

His current circumstances weren't entirely his fault, though. Like other sailors, Kenard always enjoyed a tankard or two of strong drink—maybe even a barrel's worth. That wasn't the problem though…

It wasn't his fault that someone would start a brawl. It wasn't his fault either that his crew would get swallowed up in the violence. And a captain couldn't just let anything happen to his crewmen. He was the captain, after all, and a captain *had* to look out for his crew. Most City Watchmen, however, didn't accept that reasoning.

No matter where Kenard moored, the watchmen were always unreasonable. He didn't start the brawls. It was as if the brawls were *seeking* him out, and a man couldn't be held responsible for that.

Paying for fines and bails began to add up, but that wasn't the worst of it. Port officials all across the Kalishir Ocean began noticing the *White Duchess.* Kenard was making more runs between the various nations than any other shipping captain. A few places, Nemdar and Damnir, imposed an expedited shipping tax. Merchants didn't want to pay the tax, of course, so they passed it on to their suppliers, who in turn passed it to the shipper. In order to combat that madness, Kenard upped his rate.

That was probably the worst mistake he could have made. More places began enforcing the new tax; Soroth, Keth, Gredas, and even some cities on the Mainland. Kenard's business had dwindled from then on.

Several deckhands left to work on other ships. Few merchants were accepting his contracts. He tried accepting charters for passengers, but those ventures barely covered expenses. After almost a year, Kenard's fortune disappeared completely.

So, Kenard resorted to other methods.

The *White Duchess* was well suited for the art of smuggling. On the second deck below the main—within the aft cabins—were hidden compartments. The compartments were practically invisible, making them perfect for smuggling unsanctioned goods. Most places in the Kalishir Ocean were not tolerant of smugglers, except Soroth. Well, to a point. Sorothians had laws against smuggling, but they were rarely enforced, and port officials were easily bribed. After all, Soroth had a prominent and well established black market.

Since falling upon hard times, Kenard dealt quite frequently with merchants peddling on the black market of the Principality. He ran routes between Soroth and the Mainland, smuggling goods for various merchants. Kenard had even smuggled a tevisral. That shipment alone paid a quarter of the year's expenses. But then business slowed again.

Hopefully this run will be as lucrative, Kenard thought, playing with his gray lock. Kenard often twirled it when nervous. His current shipment was a little out of the ordinary. Harvil Grave, a merchant Kenard often worked with, wanted a large shipment of roloush, a hearty elven grain. That wasn't out of the ordinary. Roloush was a rare enough import on Soroth that transporting it paid well.

The roloush, however, covered up something else. Harvil had made a deal with a member of the Elven Aristocracy of Merdan who was willing to sell him some elven-made scarves and ropes—objects with magical properties. Kenard didn't know *exactly* what they did, nor did he care to broaden his understanding on the matter. Kenard was a sailor, not a mage.

The scarves and ropes weren't illegal to possess—at least in Soroth. Harvil just didn't want to pay the additional tax. That was typical of Harvil.

Kenard took in another deep breath as he gazed across the bow. The Isle of Soroth was spreading across the horizon.

Commotion from the rigging drew Kenard's attention. Several of the crewmen struggled to adjust the lines and yardarms. The *White Duchess* was running on a near skeleton crew, after all. Turning from the rail, Kenard shouted to the sailors, "Throw me a line!" Kenard stayed with the rigging as they continued toward Soroth.

The *White Duchess* soon moored along Pier Twelve, one of the southern piers. Kenard helped to anchor the ship and furl the sails—he often performed those duties, as they evoked nostalgic memories from his youth. Once the *White Duchess* was anchored and its gangway lowered, a burly port official came aboard.

"That was quick," Kenard remarked sardonically, then noted the port official's stern demeanor. The man looked stuffy, like a Losian. *That doesn't bode well,* he thought, grabbing one of the lines and swinging down to the main deck.

"Ho there!" Kenard said, swaggering to the man, "What's your—?" Then, Kenard held his tongue as his first mate—Cadru—met the official, greeting him emphatically. Cadru looked tiny beside the Sorothian official. The first mate wasn't that tall a man. Cadru ran a hand through his wavy light-brown hair as he handed the port official their charter and manifest.

"… from Keth, I see," the port official said, eyeing the manifest.

"Yes, sir." Cadru glanced to Kenard, his sea-gray eyes looking wry. "And this is our captain," Cadru said, and gestured to Kenard.

The burly Sorothian gave a sideways glance to Kenard, then returned to the charter. "Where is your hold?" he asked.

"This way," Cadru said, gesturing toward the stairs leading to the lower decks.

The no-name Sorothian official was quite thorough. Not only did he search to the bottom of *every* barrel of roloush, he even painstakingly inspected the engine room on the third deck below the main. The engine room intrigued most officials; no other ship on Kalda had one. It was the engine—which Kenard believed to be powered by tevisrals—that granted the *White Duchess* such incredible speed.

After the inspection was finished, Kenard and Cadru warily watched the official disembark from the *White Duchess*.

"That was… unusual," Cadru whispered. "I thought for a moment there that he would want to pry the bulkheads open." Kenard nodded with a frown. Most Sorothian port officials were lax in their duties. Some were downright corrupt. But this burly no-name man was quite the opposite.

The port official had come close to discovering the smuggling compartments. After inspecting the engine room, the official had wanted to see the aft quarters on the second deck below the main. Those particular quarters were situated directly above the engine room. It was there that the hatches for the smuggling compartments were located. The compartments themselves were secreted behind the engine room's bulkheads.

Luckily for Kenard, there was more to the *White Duchess* than met the eye. The official had them remove the furniture and expose the decking in the cabins. To the official's disappointment, he found nothing.

Once the port official was out of sight, Kenard turned to Cadru. "C'mon," he whispered, "let's get the shipment ready." They hurried to the second deck below the main, where the cabins were still in disarray from the inspection.

"At least we don't have to move the furniture again," Cadru said, winking at his captain. Kenard chuckled and turned toward decorative domes on the wall. He touched one at eye level, swiping his finger to his right, then diagonally to the top of the dome, and lastly to the bottom. A glimmer of blue light reflected through the room, and Kenard turned. Grooves appeared in the decking, as well as a handle carved into the floor. The whole process was far beyond Kenard's comprehension, but he knew it had something to do with tevisrals and transmut-a-something.

Cadru swiftly opened the newly formed hatch, revealing one of the hidden compartments. The first mate then removed a brown sack that glowed a pale-green—a result of the elven scarves and ropes within it.

"Bury it in one of the barrels," Kenard said.

"Aye, Joselin," Cadru nodded, hurrying out of the cabin.

Kenard then turned back to the decorative dome and touched it, moving his finger in the same pattern. The hatch disappeared, and the decking looked like one solid mass.

Kenard waited until nightfall before making the delivery to Harvil. Cadru and two of his more loyal crewmen—Vedwin and Alban—drove filled carts toward the shady merchant's shop.

"Why don't y'all make your way to the Lovely Lady," Kenard suggested, referring to a tavern they frequented often.

"You sure, Joselin?" Cadru asked, sounding nervous. The inspection probably still bothered him.

"Yeah." Kenard waved his hand dismissively. "I got this handled. I'll meet you there once I get the payment."

"If you don't get distracted by a pretty face on your way," Alban said, chuckling. Kenard laughed. There were some attractive women on this street, two of whom he had enjoyed in the past. Memories of their lush bodies drew a smile.

At Harvil's shop, Kenard knocked on the shop's back door while Cadru and the others unloaded the barrels. Harvil soon emerged with his hired guards, who also acted as grunts for receiving large deliveries. The guards hurried to the carts, helping unload the barrels.

"Ahoy there, Kenard," Harvil cackled. He stood a head length shorter than Kenard and was a portly fellow.

Kenard raised an eyebrow at the merchant. "I'm standing right in front of you," he said flatly.

"Isn't that how you sailors greet each other?"

From afar… Kenard thought, but bit his tongue.

Harvil engaged Kenard in small talk about the voyage from Keth, but there wasn't much to say. The winds were fair, and the waters calm. The hirelings finished unloading the barrels—forty in all—and began moving them through another entrance.

"Why don't we go inside," Harvil suggested. Kenard nodded, waving to dismiss Cadru and the others before joining Harvil. The sound of horse hoofs and wheels faded into the night as Kenard made his way through Harvil's shop.

"They're in the barrel with the scratches on the top," Kenard said.

"You mean they didn't search the barrels?" Harvil asked incredulously. Kenard gave the merchant a sidelong glance. He wanted to set the short man straight, but doing so would only expose his secrets. So, Kenard bit his tongue again.

They made their way to the shop's storeroom where the guards were securing the barrels. Harvil wound his way around the shipment, looking for the scratched top. He giddily opened the barrel and rummaged through the round grain. The bag containing the elven scarves and ropes made the storeroom brighter, veiling the room with a greenish tint.

"Ah, magnificent!" Harvil exclaimed, opening the bag. "Exactly as promised."

"You didn't think an elf would go back on his word, did you?" Kenard asked, his hands on his hips.

Harvil grinned. "I wasn't concerned about the elf," he commented.

Was that a jab at me? Kenard felt a tad insulted.

"They will get to measuring the roloush," Harvil said, picking his way through the barrels. "You and I will sit down and talk payment."

There was a fixed price on the roloush, but their agreement for the elven fabrics was open to debate. For the next half an hour—as the roloush was weighed—Kenard haggled with Harvil in the merchant's private office. Amid their negotiations, one of the guards entered with a tiny piece of parchment.

Harvil took the sheet and squinted. "Looks to be more than I ordered," he said, sighing. "I'll pay the difference, I suppose. One can't go wrong selling roloush."

Kenard nodded and was about to open his mouth when rapid pounding echoed into the room—a harsh knock against the shop's main entrance. *Oh no…* His eyes widened in horror.

"Go check on that," Harvil snapped, but the guard was already away before the merchant finished the command.

Both Kenard and Harvil held their breaths. Kenard *knew* what often accompanied that type of knocking. The very sound knotted his stomach. He frantically searched the office, but there was no way out besides the door where the guard had left.

A sudden commotion rang through the shop: clanging armor was followed by hurried footfalls and accompanied by declared threats from city officials for anyone who resisted.

"What have you done?" Harvil snapped at Kenard.

"Me?" Kenard asked, insulted at the accusation. He felt the urge to run.

"They must have glimpsed the sack in the barrel!" Harvil cried. "You fool!"

Kenard tensed as the commotion grew louder. A scuffle reached his ears— undoubtedly the hired guards engaging the authorities raiding Harvil's shop. A man in armored livery of Soroth's Port Authority barred the office's doorway, holding a decorative fanisar. "Two more back here," he said from behind his visor.

Kenard's heart accelerated. He *had* to run. Harvil shouted curses. Panic overwhelmed Kenard, and he ran.

He attempted to push past the armored man, but was stopped by the blunt end of the fanisar striking his gut. Gasping, Kenard fell to the floor.

"Not so fast," the armored man said, his voice muffled behind his visor.

It wasn't long before the scuffles throughout the shop ceased, and Kenard was lifted off the floor by a gauntleted hand and dragged through the shop. He could see Harvil attempting to break free from another armored fellow. The merchant, however, wasn't successful.

"Well, well, I *am* fortunate tonight," a familiar voice said. "Two ruffians for the price of one."

The gauntleted hand dropped Kenard, and he fell to the floor. Kenard looked up, seeing Soroth's port magistrate standing above him, Magistrate Rosten.

A broad smile spread across Rosten's face. "You know, I didn't expect to find *you* here, Joselin." Kenard staggered to his feet, meeting Rosten eye to eye. Like Kenard, Rosten had long hair, but the magistrate's was a dark brown. He had an olive complexion, like a typical Sorothian. "I do hope you were conducting *legal* business," Rosten said mockingly.

The armored authorities hauled Harvil's hired men beside Kenard, each in shackles. One of the hirelings was unconscious, and another was bleeding from his nose.

"You can't just barge in here!" Harvil shouted, struggling against the armored man holding him in place. Harvil's captor also carried the glowing bag with the elven scarves and ropes.

Rosten turned toward the shady merchant. "In fact I can," he said, removing a piece of parchment from a black case. "This warrant grants me every right to search your shop."

Harvil gasped.

The magistrate continued recounting the legality of his actions as more armored men brought him various boxes and bags—undoubtedly more smuggled goods. Rosten ordered the men to open the containers.

"Oh my," Rosten said in feigned surprise. "I don't recall seeing *any* of this on your previous import forms." He then picked his way toward Harvil. "And what's in here?" he asked, taking the bag from Harvil's captor.

Green light shone into the room as Rosten removed one of the elven scarves. The fabric was *glowing* as if filled with magic. "I take it you were discussing payment for this?" The port magistrate glanced to Harvil, then to Kenard. "You have the proper import forms, don't you?"

Kenard didn't speak. He *couldn't* speak. Of all things that could happen, this was the worst. The fines and bail fees were nothing compared to what Rosten would level against Kenard. One might think the magistrate was a paragon of justice, but Rosten was one of the most corrupt men Kenard had ever met.

"Of course I do," Harvil lied quickly.

Rosten narrowed his eyes at the merchant, then turned and paced between Kenard and Harvil. "And I'm sure you'll have this recorded on your mooring papers?" he held up the scarf.

Kenard didn't answer.

"Search that office," Rosten ordered, and several armored men hurried off. The port magistrate then walked to Kenard, grinning in a gloating manner. Kenard could almost read Rosten's mind. The magistrate *knew* he wouldn't find the documents.

Before long, one of the armored officials returned. "We found documents for the roloush, magistrate," the man said. "But nothing on the elven fabrics."

Rosten's smile turned to a wide grin. He shook his head at Kenard. "I have you now…" He smirked.

"But I have an invoice for scarves and ropes," Harvil shouted. "He must—"

"I advise you to hold your tongue," Rosten said. "Anything you say can and will be held against you in a court of law. I can levy enough fines against you, Harvil Grave, to drive you out of business." Harvil's eyes bulged.

"And you, Kenard," Rosten smiled. "I assume you can pay the fine for smuggling?" Kenard swallowed hard.

"If not," Rosten continued, "I suppose I will have to impound your ship."

No! Kenard gasped. *Not the* Duchess!

Rosten had coveted the *White Duchess* for years, ever since his first dealings with Kenard. At one time, Rosten had offered to buy the ship, but no man in his right mind would sell a ship as magnificent as the *White Duchess*.

"You do realize Sorothian impound fees have changed recently, don't you?" Rosten asked mockingly. "They are based on material value of the ship. And seeing as your vessel is quite rare, I suppose the fee is quite high. Not to mention, interest on impound fees were reorganized to compound daily."

Kenard froze in horror. This was his worst nightmare realized. In all his hardships, Kenard never thought he would actually lose the *White Duchess*.

Rosten continued gloating, but his words only stoked a hidden anger welling within Kenard. "… you would need the wealth of nations to—" Kenard leapt to Rosten, punching the magistrate's jaw. The blow knocked Rosten to the ground. Armored officials were all over Kenard, then something hard struck his head, and everything went black.

———❖———

"Joselin," Cadru said, though he sounded so far away. "Joselin, wake up."

Kenard felt himself spinning. What happened? He struggled to open his eyes. Everything was gray. Gray floor, gray walls, and gray ceiling. And it was cold.

"Joselin!"

Creaking metal sounded above Kenard, but that wasn't the direction of the ceiling. Kenard looked up, seeing black metal bars and City Watchmen. Was he in a cell? Cadru was by the bars too, as were Alban and Vedwin. They looked terrified.

Do I look that bad? Kenard wondered. *It's not like they haven't seen me in a cell before...*

"Oh, Joselin," Cadru said, hurrying into the cold jail cell. "Are you all right?"

Kenard groaned. "I feel like I drank several barrels of brandy," he said, and rubbed his head.

"Come on. We paid your bail," he said, helping Kenard to his feet.

"Bail?" Kenard asked as he stood, confused. He hadn't been to a tavern. In fact, he hadn't even left Harvil's—

Kenard's eyes widened with horrified realization. "The *Duchess!*" he shouted, breaking free from Cadru.

"Joselin!" Cadru's tone was firm. "They took her, Joselin. She's gone."

The *Duchess?* Gone?

"We'll get her back, Captain," Vedwin said. "I don't know how, but we'll get her back." Kenard staggered, bewildered at his crewmen's words.

"We will find a way," Alban affirmed.

Heartache—unlike any Kenard had ever felt—tore through him. He slumped, then collapsed to the ground. Tears fell from his eyes, and the tears turned to sobbing, then the sobbing turned to an anguished wail. The only home Kenard had ever known was gone.

There was no blood surrounding Lady Ralisu Davig's body. That ruled out quite a few modes and methods as a cause for her demise. There was also no sign of a struggle. The lady lay on her side as if she had simply collapsed.

Chief Discerner Coridas Brandir sighed as he eyed Lady Ralisu's corpse. Many of Sarn's Royals suspected foul play and insisted that Brandir come from Soroth to investigate the matter. He was, after all, the premier discerner in the entire Principality.

Luckily for the Royals, Brandir was in Serinta—on the northwest coast of the Isle of Soroth—so his trip to Sarn was rather speedy. Lady Ralisu's body had not fallen completely into the death stiffness, but reddening marks had appeared on her face and exposed arms.

The usual clues that pointed to murder were also missing. Besides the lack of struggle, there was no sign of forced entry at her door. The discerners from Sarn's City Watch thought the cause of her death resulted from drugging or poisoning, perhaps perpetrated by a member of her household. But the lady lacked any signs of either. If her death *was* an act of murder, her killer had simply appeared and disappeared without a trace.

That narrowed potential suspects to the worst kind of murderers—*mages*. Brandir grumbled to himself, shaking his head in annoyance. He narrowed his eyes scornfully, carefully examining Lady Ralisu for signs of destructive magic. Her clothing, however, was unmarred.

Elemental magics always left a trace; fiery magic would scorch clothing and flesh, acidic spells would leave burns, as would electrical attacks. If a mage tried using water, there would be signs of dampness and asphyxiation akin to drowning. Any wind or telekinetic spell would leave bruises so severe that they would make physical assault look like a playful touch. And then there were the myriad of arcane attacks… those wounds were so unique any fool could tell what killed the victim.

Murderers who used magic thought themselves clever, as they believed their modes of murder were untraceable. But there were means for sniffing out a murderous mage. Over the years, Brandir had learned that most criminal mages were stupid. Of course, the same could be said of all criminals, but mages were exceptionally sloppy. There were, however, a few exceptions…

A wise murderous mage would often mask the mode of death in an environment that *might* produce those effects naturally. Brandir once found a burned body in the remains of a home destroyed by arson. The scene was a smart choice until further investigation revealed burn marks on the victim that lacked the typical residue left behind by such intense heat.

And now, a similar incident had occurred with Lady Ralisu. On the surface, her death appeared natural. But if it was murder, there was only one type of magic that would steal her life without a trace. Brandir's lips curled into a snarl. "Necromancy…" The word left his lips with a weight of vehemence. The very thought of a necromancer committing murder made his blood boil.

Calm yourself, Brandir thought. There was no concrete evidence that this *was* a murder. *In all likelihood, the lady—*

A sudden commotion started near the entrance of Lady Ralisu's private quarters. Behind red cords indicating a quarantined scene under investigation, gray-clad watchmen prevented several regal-looking men from entering the scene. They were obviously members of Sarn's aristocracy.

"Chief Discerner!" one of the regal men shouted, his face barely visible. Brandir recognized the man, though—High Duke Finlar Aliteran. "Have you found anything?!" the high duke almost barked.

"Move aside," Brandir commanded the watchmen, gesturing with his hand. He pulled aside the red cords, then slipped through the doorway.

"Well?" another Royal demanded.

There were now seven of Sarn's aristocracy outside the lady's chambers, each dressed in regal attire. When Brandir had first arrived at the Davig estate, only three Sarn Royals were present—including the high duke. News of Lady Ralisu's death had spread quickly, as Brandir was only an hour and a half into the investigation.

"A possibility," Brandir said, "if she did not die of natural causes."

One of the Royals growled in frustration.

"We've already said she was murdered!" A newcomer shook his fist at Brandir. "And we know who to blame. There is only one man who—"

"Conjecture isn't proof," Brandir interrupted. Prior to investigating the lady's chambers, Brandir had been barraged by hasty accusations against the Baron of Sereth. He was also aware of the feud for the barony between Cilgan and the late lady.

Brandir didn't dismiss the accusations, but keeping them at the forefront of his mind would only cloud his judgment. A skilled discerner could set aside such accusations until the proper time when considering the motives behind a death.

High Duke Aliteran abruptly held out his hand to his fellow Royals. "Let the discerner speak," he commanded. The other Royals obeyed and their eyes fell upon Brandir.

"The only possibility I can discern would be death by necromancy," Brandir said. "Particularly, a life-draining spell. There are no signs of forced entry or struggle. She appears to have collapsed upon spontaneous death. That in and of itself would be enough to sway my opinion to natural causes. But there are the accusations," he said as he studied the Royals. "If she *was* murdered, then whoever committed the act must have hid in her chambers for a considerable length of time, and then waited until they could escape undetected."

Such assassins were not unheard of, especially on the Mainland. Brandir, however, doubted Cilgan had access to such an assassin.

"What about poisoning?" a Royal asked.

Brandir shook his head. "She shows no signs of any fast-acting poisons. Besides, someone would have needed to administer it to her, and we have questioned and thoroughly searched everyone in this household. I can say with all confidence that she was not poisoned."

"Then *he* sent a necromancer," a Royal murmured. "We know he has many of those in his employ."

Brandir raised an eyebrow at the man. "More investigation will need to occur before I can determine the cause of death. If she did indeed die from natural causes, a necropsy will reveal that. It would also verify the alternative."

"How?" a Royal asked incredulously.

"Life-draining magic will instantly sap the life out of an individual," Brandir answered. "A necropsy on such victims will reveal a completely healthy body that suddenly stopped working."

"What are you waiting for, then?" another Royal snarled. "On with it!"

Brandir tensed, pursing his lips and narrowing his eyes. These men were eager for even a sliver of proof that they could use against Baron Cilgan. Even if a necromancer were responsible, it didn't automatically mean the baron was to blame.

The situation was precarious.

The Royals ranted to each other, each incensed that Cilgan would "get away" with Lady Ralisu's murder. In that moment, Brandir feared that whatever the outcome of his investigation, these men would twist it to their advantage. The tension between Sarn and Sereth had grown uneasy these last few months. Lady Ralisu's death would only complicate the matter. Brandir knew all too well that emotionally charged conjecture in the hands of powerful men was a recipe for disaster. Not even the truth—in all its plainness—could dissuade those infected by such propaganda.

This investigation was a delicate matter, and one misstep might plunge the Principality into civil war. "There are legal formalities I must observe," Brandir said. "Then I will announce my findings, in a public setting." He hoped that would deter any sedition these Sarn Royals would brew.

With resolute steps, Brandir turned back to the late lady's chambers. He had an important duty to perform. One misstep and he would doom Soroth to folly.

Determined zeal often accompanied Almar when he visited his father's memorial. But today was different. A sense of anger and sorrow weighed him down. He was melancholy, even lonely.

The alabaster statue of his father—Adrin, the Hero of the West—stood in the western park of Alath's Inner City. After Adrin's untimely death some forty years ago, the citizens of Alath erected this memorial. It was akin to the statues found in the Estate of Concorious Knowledge: standing twice as high as an average man, constructed from fine alabaster, and infused with magic.

Adrin's likeness was carved so that Almar's father stood stoically. The hawk-like features were chiseled with such fine precision that the statue looked a near-perfect copy. Adrin's statue held a long channeling staff and wore a robe that looked as if it were rippling in the wind. People often remarked that Adrin had the makings of a king, and this statue captured that trait perfectly.

It was that trait that Almar had hoped to draw upon. But his hopes were in vain.

Though Almar often came to this memorial to ponder or seek inspiration, today he felt empty. His soul yearned for fulfillment, but no matter what he did Almar couldn't fill the despairing void in his heart.

Oh, father… Almar thought, gazing at the stony face with his sapphire eyes. Almar stepped toward the foot of his father's memorial, his gaze falling to the chiseled words engraved on the pedestal upon which the statue stood.

Tears welled in Almar's eyes as he read the words he had read so many times throughout his life. *"In memory of Adrin, a beloved father, a trusted general, and a powerful grand mage of the Order. May the Hero of the West always be remembered for his sacrifices. Without him, the tyranny of the Mindolarn Empire would not have been suppressed. The free citizens of Kalda owe him their gratitude. May all who come to this memorial pay homage to this esteemed hero."*

Almar's heart wrenched as he read the next line. *"Adrin was slain in 6,455 C.D. on the Isle of Soroth, along with his second wife, Gwenyth, and their son, Iltar."*

Almar lingered on his brother's name. That undertone of anger suddenly turned to fiery indignation, and Almar was incensed at what Iltar had been deprived of. His brother would never grow to maturity. He would never know love. But most importantly, Iltar would never realize his dreams and ambitions.

Why… why did they have to kill you too? Almar lamented, thinking of young Iltar—then only fourteen years old. *You were just a boy…* tears fell from Almar's eyes. The memory of his brother's corpse haunted him even to this day.

Almar could never forget that sight.

After word of Adrin's death had reached Alath, Almar rushed to Soroth. He was permitted to see what remained of his family. Others had already identified Adrin, Gwenyth, and Iltar. Their exhuming was only for Almar's benefit. They were near unrecognizable, and Almar could only tell his father and stepmother apart from their rings.

Almar could never forget those rings.

The Sorothian officials never concluded who committed the atrocious acts. Arrests were never made. Justice's hand was shackled. But the Order of the Mages of Alath knew the culprits.

Emperor Medis and his brothers had sought to slay Adrin after the death of Emperor Mindolarn. Their desires for vengeance grew after Adrin—with the help of a group of rebels—killed Mentas, the empire's second emperor. It took them nearly a decade to strike a devastating blow against Adrin.

Almar lingered on the chiseled name of his brother. *Perhaps I am not as different from them as I'd like to believe…* No. That was despair talking. Though Almar did embrace killing each of the subsequent emperors, he did not seek them out.

Once Almar became a well-regarded Agent of the Order, he followed in his father's footsteps. But this time, a rebellion was forged in the nation of Gastrim, and eventually Almar confronted Emperor Medis. An undying fury of retribution empowered Almar that day.

Those same feelings accompanied Almar as he assailed the Mindolarn Palace some ten months ago, when he clashed with Emperor Monddar.

"There's only one of them left," Almar whispered, still staring at the name of his brother. In that moment, Almar felt a temptation that he had grappled with for years.

Hunt them, a faint voice whispered in his mind. Averting his gaze, Almar took a deep breath, attempting to quell his stoked emotions. It was futile. His anger raged like an unquenchable inferno.

I would be no different from them! Almar argued with himself. His fury began to abate. If he were allowed to follow that temptation he would become a monster. *The last of my family's murderers will most likely fall at another's hands,* he thought. That notion quelled the indignation further.

It had taken years to find the perfect opportunity to slay Monddar. Marden was even more paranoid than his brother. In all likelihood, it might take several decades to slay the last founder of the empire. By that time, Almar would be nothing but a memory.

"Master Almar," an urgent voice called,

A young page from the Estate of Concorious Knowledge—the headquarters of the Mages of Alath—was running toward the memorial. The youth looked flushed. "Master Almar," the page panted, "Grandmaster Dorith wishes to speak with you immediately. It's a matter of great importance."

—•—

Storm clouds were approaching from the east when Almar reached the Estate of Concorious Knowledge. Almar made it to the Main Hall just as the rain began to fall.

The page who had summoned him gave little more information. The secrecy didn't bode well. Worrisome possibilities raced through Almar's mind as he hurried to the grandmaster's office, not far from the Main Hall's oversized foyer.

Almar reached the office door, but hesitated for a moment. His wrinkled hand rested upon the handle and he took a deep calming breath before turning the knob.

To Almar's surprise, most of the Order's council—a body of twelve of Alath's most powerful mages—was gathered in the large office. Several stood by the floor-to-ceiling windows in the far corner. Others leaned against the bookshelves beside the door. Each was somber.

"Come in, my friend," Grandmaster Dorith said from his opulent desk. Though the grandmaster looked tense, Dorith's thin lips relaxed into a genuine smile. He rubbed his long forehead and sighed. His hazel eyes calmly scanned the others standing in the room.

"That leaves only Nemmerin," Thranar said from the foot of a long white lounge chair by the bookshelves. Rildan sat beside him, hands clasped.

The grandmaster nodded, rubbing his square jaw. He stood and took one step toward Almar. Dorith was a man of average height, standing shorter than Almar

"Why the solemnity?" Almar asked, shutting the door behind him.

Rinden was the first to speak. "Oh, Almar, we finally have an opportunity to bring peace to the world."

Almar started. If this was such a momentous occasion, why were they so solemn?

"I suppose we can tell you while we wait for Nemmerin," Grandmaster Dorith said. His tone was hesitant. "One of our agents contacted us with information about Emperor Marden of Mindolarn. He was spotted at the Hilinard four days ago. Our agent followed him to the city of Rinolas, where Marden then retreated into the mountains along the borders of the Mindolarn Empire. He has since sequestered himself within a stronghold on the edge of a high valley."

Almar's eyes widened at the report. Had they *actually* located the last of Mindolarn's brothers?

"I knew he couldn't resist," Mathal said from beside Dorith.

The grandmaster nodded. "We are waiting for Nemmerin to take a vote on this information."

Almar looked at the other council-mages in the room. None looked opposed to the unspoken proposal.

If Marden were deposed, Prince Jeridi would be appointed emperor in his stead. They all knew of the prince. His pacifistic reputation preceded him. He was probably the only Mindolarnian prince that Almar would *not* be willing to slay; after all, Almar *had* spared Jeridi on the battlefield years ago. With Jeridi in power there was potential for peace between the empire and the Kingdom of Los.

Almar felt that temptation welling within him again. *Only if we agree,* he told himself. *Then I will gladly lead the assault.*

When Nemmerin joined the rest of the council in the grandmaster's office, they discussed the news in lengthy detail, then voted on the matter. The votes were unanimous.

"I will go," Almar said, stepping forward. He stood in the middle of the room, assuming a bold demeanor. His despair plagued him no longer. "I will lead the assault to slay Marden. We will put an end to this conflict which has lasted over a century."

"I support the motion," Thranar said.

"And I second it," Mathal said.

Each of the others gave their votes on Almar's proposal.

"So let it be done," Dorith said.

Without hesitation, Almar turned to leave the office. Much had to be done in preparation for Marden's demise.

At last, Almar would avenge his father, stepmother, and brother.

PART

FOUR

A Homecoming

Iltar · Cornar · Kaescis · Solidin

69

RECLAMATION

Perilous times are upon us, even more so than what befell our ancestors during the ancient days.

Solidin breathed heavily, dropping his broken weapons. He and the others of the Sapphire Guard had defeated the Mindolarnians and the Wildmen. But the Sapphire Guard hadn't escaped without heavy losses.

At first glance, Solidin supposed the Mindolarnians had slain nearly a hundred of the Sapphire Guard, and perhaps another thirty were severely wounded. Not even Solidin had escaped unmarred—his armor was cracked and his left arm was bleeding.

"You," Solidin called to one of the uninjured mages, "go send Silrian the signal." The elf hurried across the rubble without question.

Solidin turned back to the other survivors, those whose wounds weren't too severe. "These aren't the only Mindolarnians we must dispatch." He paused, searching the survivors for an arpranist or a barsionist, but found none. "Leave the wounded as they are. We will come back for them once the rest of our foes are defeated."

Quickly, Solidin scanned the ground for some suitable weapons. His daggers and his stolen weapons had since broken beyond use.

"Solidin," Gladis said, then uttered an incantation.

Solidin watched as the transmuter formed two daggers from the rubble. "Thank you, my friend," Solidin said, taking the transmuted weapons.

Now armed, Solidin marched at the head of his ragtag force. The three gholistras—which were unscathed—dashed through the enormous doors of this place cut out of the mountain. The gholistras ran at incredible speed and quickly vanished amid Dalgilur's towering buildings. Soon, the elves made their way into the open air, passing the statues that stood as sentinels—the Ancient Keepers, Solidin supposed.

Solidin had seen this place in his mind as they traveled the seas. He had sensed Dalgilur's grandeur. This was a place that rivaled the ancient cities of the elves.

They were soon on a road leading to the isle's eastern shores. Eruptions of magic flashed across the horizon. As they neared the shoreline, Solidin noticed the draconic gholistra frozen within a shallow crater. It stood motionless, a perplexed expression across its stony snout. *What happened to you?* Solidin wondered. He knew of nothing that could disable a gholistra. Had the Mindolarnians something *that* powerful? No, else they would have used it on the three gholistras assailing the war camp.

Three capsized vessels caught Solidin's eye. Two had their masts ripped from them. Another was on fire. These three were the Mindolarnians' warships, but the Sorothian vessel was nowhere to be found.

"Cornar Dol'shir escaped," Solidin whispered. *He must have taken that scholar with him.* The old scholar would have been Cornar's only means of escape. Solidin didn't recall seeing the coward's body among the dead. The other Sorothian scholars were there—he had slain two.

Solidin and the remaining Sapphire Guard came within a hundred phineals of Dalgilur's western shores as the last of the Mindolarnians were defeated. They had succumbed to the three gholistras, and what few elves remained of Fingas's force.

One of the survivors shouted to Solidin, informing him of their losses. Fingas had fallen, as had their arpranist and barsionist.

Solidin eyed the dead, searching the wounded Mindolarnians. He had not found the half-breed prince among the dead at the war camp. *Where is he?* Solidin wondered. His eyes fell upon a short Mindolarnian wearing a charcoal naval uniform. His golden tassels and buttons indicated that he was a highranking officer. Solidin picked his way to the man, then kicked him.

A sudden groan left the officer's lips. "This one is alive," Solidin said, gesturing for two of his soldiers to grab the man. The elves hefted the officer onto his feet, his head hung low. By the looks of his uniform Solidin assumed the man was an admiral.

"Where's your prince?" Solidin asked in Common.

The admiral looked up, an expression of defiance on his face. "I won't… betray… His… Imperial… Grace."

"We've conquered your forces," Solidin said. "But your prince is not among the dead."

The admiral grinned. "Then… he will… come for you." He coughed, spitting blood.

Solidin averted his gaze for a moment. There were some still living among the Mindolarnians. "Kill the mages," he shouted, "but keep the others alive."

"You won't… get anything out… of me," the admiral said.

"Perhaps not willingly," Solidin said.

At that moment, the three gholistras approached. "Bladesinger," the Lith gholistra called to Solidin. "There is something that prevents Zu'mal'thisr'nsar from moving." Solidin started. *That is a Draconic name,* he thought, then glanced to the draconic gholistra, still frozen. "Please investigate it," the gholistra said, "we would go to his aid, but we fear that whatever ails him will undoubtedly ail us."

"Gladis," Solidin turned to his friend, "go inspect the draconic gholistra."

The transmuter hurried off without a word.

More of the surviving Mindolarnians were brought beside the admiral, all wounded and weary.

"Surely, one of you knows where your prince is hiding," Solidin said, pacing along the survivors.

"His Imperial Grace is not a coward!" one of the soldiers spat.

"Of course he's not," Solidin said. "But I have a score to settle with him." None of the Mindolarnians spoke. Solidin shook his head, sighing. "Your survivability depends upon your cooperation."

"Admiral Kaetet, surely you know from your meetings in the war camp," said another naval officer.

"Silence!" the admiral slurred.

Solidin studied the admiral and bent forward, gazing into the man's eyes. "Tell me, admiral, where is your prince?"

"I… don't know," the admiral said, groaning. "And even if… I did… I would not tell… you."

Solidin nodded. "I see," he twirled his transmuted dagger, resting its tip against the admiral's throat. "Then you've outlived your usefulness." He thrust the dagger, but instead of piercing the admiral it crumbled to dirt. *What…?*

Solidin looked to his other transmuted weapon. It too lost cohesion.

Each of the gholistras staggered, their movements becoming rigid.

"Blade… singer…" the Lith gholistra muttered, "some… thing… prevents—"

The gholistra froze. Their weapons reverted to stone—the fanisars dropping to the ground in pieces.

Confused, Solidin turned from the Mindolarnians, seeing Gladis approaching with a large orange shard. The draconic gholistra was also moving. It took to flight, flying toward the towering structures. Solidin's eyes, however, were drawn to that shard. He had heard stories of a substance that could render magic inert. The Cess'nal warriors of old wore rings that were composed of such substances, though their rings were designed to negate only certain effects. But this shard seemed different.

Returning to the Mindolarnians, Solidin pointed to Gladis. "What is that?" he asked.

"I don't know…" the admiral said tersely.

Solidin wasn't convinced. "You disabled a powerful creature with that. Surely you *know* what it is."

"They did not overcome the gholistra," an elf interjected. "The Sorothians did."

Cornar disabled a gholistra? Solidin wondered. That gave him pause.

"They had several of those shards," a Mindolarnian said. "When the cowardly Sorothians fled past us they destroyed our magic."

"This is impressive, Solidin," Gladis called in Elvish. "I cannot feel my transmutations anymore. It is as if they were dispelled." Gladis sounded intrigued, even amused.

Solidin glanced to Gladis, then to the three frozen gholistras. "Get rid of that shard, Gladis," Solidin commanded in Elvish. "The gholistras cannot move."

Gladis nodded, then hurried off. Soon, the three gholistras began moving again. They picked up their weapons, their touch transforming the deadly tools of war.

"Tazerin," the Lith gholistra said. "In its raw form it negates our functions."

"We will keep it away," Solidin said.

Each of the gholistras nodded with gratitude, then moved toward the surviving Mindolarnians. The gholistras readied their weapons, poised to strike swiftly.

"It seems your time is at an end," Solidin said. He turned as the statues executed the admiral and the others. "Let's return to the place cut out of the mountain," he shouted to the rest of the Sapphire Guard. "We have a half-breed prince to slay."

⟶•⟶

Solidin and the rest of the Sapphire Guard were once again inside the place cut out of the mountain. Silrian and those with him had since joined them. The arpranist under Silrian's command immediately healed the wounded.

Together with Gladis, Solidin picked through the dead Mindolarnians.

"We would have noticed the prince," Gladis said. "Especially with that vile blade of his."

Where could he be? Solidin wondered. He recalled seeing Cornar Dol'shir fleeing with his men, some wounded. *Perhaps Cornar heeded my warning...* Had Cornar clashed with the prince? With those weapons of his, Cornar would have had a chance. But Solidin doubted Cornar could have defeated the half-breed prince on his own.

Solidin crossed the ruined war camp, gazing to the far end of this enormous space—a space that could house a dragon. He marveled at the grandeur as the rest of the Sapphire Guard was renewed. It didn't take long to heal the wounded, even the most severe.

Eighty-seven of the Sapphire Guard had survived the assault. That was better than Solidin had hoped. But they hadn't faced that abominable prince.

Incantations sounded behind Solidin. The mages cast enhancements and barsions. Weapons were imbued with destructive power.

"Here," Gladis said, handing two daggers to Solidin. Undoubtedly more transmutations.

"Thank you, old friend," Solidin said.

With weapons in hand, Solidin turned back to face the rest of the Sapphire Guard. "We have a prince to slay. He cowers somewhere in this mountain, desecrating this sacred place. We will hunt this half-breed abomination, and exact vengeance upon him!" Battle cries echoed through the enormous chamber. "We move as one," Solidin shouted, "and we will slay him as one!"

Solidin spun, marching across the enormous space. After they were several hundred phineals from the ruined war camp, Solidin noticed movement at the far end of the room. *Another Mindolarnian?* Solidin thought.

All was still until a feminine figure, shrouded in tan, darted toward one of the enormous pillars and disappeared within it. Intrigued, Solidin led the Sapphire Guard toward that pillar.

70

REBIRTH

And when I say "us" I include men and elves. They too are a part of this world.

Kaescis opened his eyes. He gasped for breath, but could not breathe. *I survived?* No… he had died, and he remembered the pain so vividly. Kaescis tried to move, but there was no strength in him. Pain surged through his body, near unbearable pain. He opened his mouth to scream, but he made no sound. The pain swelled, becoming excruciating.

Voices shouted in Kaescis's mind, craving death and destruction. They roared like thunder.

And then, blackness.

Kaescis opened his eyes again. He was adrift within an endless white void. The pain was gone. Kaescis opened his mouth to breathe, but it wasn't necessary. And his thoughts were quiet.

"I know this place…" he muttered, looking around. He floated in an endless expanse. Kaescis tried to turn, but couldn't *feel* the movement.

"Why am I not dead?"

"You are."

Kaescis turned again. A man in a crimson robe stood within the white void. His hawk-like features were stern, even disapproving. Brilliant sapphire eyes glared with restrained anger. Kaescis *knew* this man… but the memory was out of reach.

"You are a fool," the man said petulantly.

Why? Kaescis wondered, confused.

"Because of your disobedience I will have to recalibrate everything," the man said, fury tainting his voice. "Now, events will transpire differently. Eons of careful planning now rendered useless because *you* wouldn't listen!"

The anger was baffling.

White light blurred the man, and he kept talking, but Kaescis couldn't understand him. The words became mumbled and then ceased.

Kaescis opened his eyes. He gasped for breath, but he could not breathe. Malicious voices rumbled in his mind. Kaescis glanced about, taking in his surroundings. He was still on the walkways where he had… died.

Pain surged through his body and he heard… footfalls. A feminine voice shouted Kaescis's name in a panicked frenzy just as death overtook him once again.

And then, blackness.

Once again Kaescis found himself in that white void.

"… perhaps I should have commanded you to forsake your armor."

Kaescis blinked, looking for the voice. A man stood in front of him, dressed in a red robe. He knew that man, he thought… but Kaescis couldn't place him. The robed man droned on, talking nonsense.

White light filled Kaescis's vision, washing out the robed man and his voice.

Kaescis opened his eyes. He gasped for breath, but could not breathe.

Death… voices rumbled in his mind, *give us death—*

"… on. You just need to hang on," a feminine voice said, quelling the others. Was that… Laeyit?

Pain surged through Kaescis's body. He took in a sweeping glance as white-gray particles of light—a telekinetic spell—surrounded him. More pain filled him as he suddenly became weightless.

And then, blackness.

Again, Kaescis was in the white void.

"… that tedious suit of yours is getting on my nerves."

Kaescis looked up, findng a crimson robed man. There was something familiar about him.

"I could reach out and kill you, but then it would just revive you again. Over, and over."

Rebirth? Kaescis wondered.

The white light returned, engulfing everything.

Kaescis opened his eyes. He gasped for breath, struggling to breathe.

Eruptions resounded around him—explosions of magic. Those eruptions spurned the voices demanding death. A shield of barsion hovered at his feet. Flashes burst against the barrier. Walls whizzed past him, and Kaescis felt weightless.

Muttered curses reached Kaescis's ears. Was that Laeyit?

The pain grew more intense. Suddenly, Kaescis couldn't breathe. It was as if he were drowning.

And then, blackness.

Once again, Kaescis was in the white void. A man in a crimson robe shook his head disapprovingly.

Why does he not like me? Kaescis wondered. He thought he knew that man.

White light blurred his vision.

Kaescis opened his eyes. He gasped for breath and struggled to breathe.

The malicious voices returned, but were soon silenced.

"… lost them. I hope we can stay ahead."

Amid his pain, Kaescis noticed Laeyit above him. She was pulling him through the air. *A telekinetic spell...?* Kaescis wondered. Walls raced past him, and barsion was at his feet.

"It shouldn't be far," she said.

Burning filled Kaescis's lungs. He gasped a muttered cry.

Laeyit glanced over her shoulder. "Oh, it's working!" she exclaimed.

Pain surged through Kaescis, excruciating pain.

And then, blackness.

Kaescis blinked, finding himself in that white void.

"... either way, I will make this work." The words came from a man in a crimson robe. Kaescis recognized symbols woven into that robe. He *knew* they were important.

"You present a unique divergence," the robed man said. "I always thought your death was necessary, but I now see that I was wrong. I rarely admit that..." he said with a chuckle.

White light obscured the man, and his words.

Kaescis opened his eyes. He gasped, but only sucked in a shallow breath. Pain surged across his body. Pain meant that he was alive.

Give us death... the voices echoed. They continued chanting, but were quelled when he heard *her.*

"... around this corner," Laeyit said. "We're going to make it, Kaescis!"

Kaescis sucked in another shallow breath. "Laey—"

Laeyit spun, her face beaming exuberantly. "Oh, Kaescis!" she cried, "it's working." He wheezed and felt faint. "We're almost to that naval yard," Laeyit said. She then resumed pulling him.

Kaescis continued wheezing, watching the hall become an expansive cavern. All the while, he itched. Vessels—large and small—hung on the walls, suspended by beams filled with coursing light—magic. Laeyit's footsteps echoed loudly.

Breathing gradually became easier. "Laeyit..." Kaescis groaned.

A sudden burst of laughter resounded. "Oh, Kaescis!" she exclaimed triumphantly, still laughing.

Although the pain lingered, Kaescis grinned. He uttered an incantation to muster arpran magic, but he gasped too many times and the spell fizzled. Kaescis wheezed. His lungs burned.

I'm still alive, he thought, closing his eyes in an attempt to vanquish some of the pain. It was in vain.

"Your Imperial Highness!" Kaescis knew that voice...

"Your Imperial Highness!" Faint footfalls echoed toward Kaescis and Laeyit.

Kaescis struggled to open his eyes. The old Sorothian scholar was running toward them. "Krindal..." he wheezed.

"Oh, Your Imperial Highness!" Krindal said with a shudder. "What happened to you?"

Still amused, Laeyit remarked, "Aunok'sha smiles upon us today. We shall escape."

Kaescis eyed the scholar and Krindal paled.

Suddenly, incantations sounded from beyond Kaescis's feet. He looked *down* and figures in white armor dashed from a corridor. Blue emblems caught his eye.

The Sapphire Guard. At their head dashed the Swift-Dagger. The accursed elf charged with unconquerable fury.

"Come on!" Laeyit shouted, dragging Kaescis—still suspended by telekinetic magic. "We can't stay here any longer."

Krindal dashed beside her, frazzled and wide-eyed. "Did *they* defeat us?" the scholar asked in a shaky tone.

"Yes," Laeyit murmured. "They destroyed the war camp, and the mis'thralim destroyed our vessels."

"The what…?"

Laeyit explained as Kaescis uttered the arpran incantation once again. Green light gathered in his only hand. Kaescis smiled as the spell neared completion. The arpran light washed over Kaescis's armor, seeping through cracks and holes. Bone reformed, sinews grew, and flesh spread.

The pain subsided, and Kaescis felt renewed—except for his missing forearm. Anger accompanied flashes of memory—his defeat at the hands of Mister Dol'shir.

Kill Dol'shir! the voices cried, *hunt him!*

Ignoring the voices, Kaescis bellowed, "Laeyit, let me down!"

She relinquished her spell, gently settling him on his feet. "Here," she came beside Kaescis. Laeyit held his severed gauntlet in one hand and his helmet in the other. "Hurry, we need to escape."

Magic shot from the accursed elves, explosively striking Laeyit's barsion. Nearly a dozen elves charged behind the Swift-Dagger. Dozens more were pouring into the cavernous naval yard.

Kaescis took his severed forearm, casting another arpran spell. He held his severed limb to the stub below his elbow, green light surging between them.

Laeyit reinforced her barsion, casting another spell as more magic from the elves assailed them.

Fibers of bone, muscle, and flesh re-knit from both limb and stub. The feeling in his hand soon returned, and Kaescis flexed the fingers of his once severed arm.

The elven mages unleashed another onslaught against Laeyit's barsion.

"Done!" Kaescis shouted, grabbing his helmet.

Laeyit spun. "This way!" she shouted. Kaescis hurried behind her, as did Krindal.

They dashed farther down the pier, crossing the naval yard with Laeyit's barsion trailing behind them. Magic erupted against the barrier, but the barsion held.

"We can take one of those!" Laeyit pointed to a section of the wall which held dozens of tiny ships. Kaescis had only glimpsed them on his first visit to this hidden naval yard.

Each tiny sea craft was sleek in design, ovoid shaped, and made of a material that would neither rot nor rust. A single window spanned its enclosed forward section, allowing a glimpse into a cabin twice as large as a typical carriage.

Laeyit hurried down a nearby wharf to the nearest vessel. She touched its exterior and an oval outline formed along its hull—a doorway. All the while, destructive magic erupted against Laeyit's barsion.

Kaescis spun, eyeing the accursed Swift-Dagger and his elves bounding across the pier, their weapons gleaming with imbued auras of arcane, elemental, and acidic magics. There were nearly a hundred of them now. But the mis'thralims Laeyit mentioned weren't around.

Death… the voices whispered, crying for destruction.

I could kill them, Kaescis thought, eyeing the elves. He held out his hand to summon his Ko'delish blade, but was jarred by Laeyit's call.

"Hurry, Kaescis!"

Furrowing his brow, Kaescis spun back to the tiny ship. Both Krindal and Laeyit were already inside the vessel. He dashed just as Laeyit's barsion shattered.

Once Kaescis was aboard, Laeyit touched the interior hull and the doorway closed, compressing like the gates of the Mindolarn Palace. She lunged to a seat near the window, touching a slanted console that spanned the breadth of the cabin. Light shone from the console, and Laeyit touched the lit surfaces in sweeping patterns. All the while, the vessel shook and explosions flashed across the window.

"Do you know what you're doing?" Krindal demanded shakily, standing behind her seat.

"Yes!" Laeyit barked.

All the while, Kaescis watched as the elves approached. More arcane orbs flew past the Swift-Dagger, striking the window. Explosions blocked their view, but Laeyit continued operating the vessel. A blue tint covered the window. *Barsion?* He wondered. This vessel was a wondrous thing.

The eruptions dispersed, and the vessel was now in the water.

Laeyit swiftly piloted the small craft. It zipped through the naval yard and through an illusionary barrier of rock. Soon, they were in open waters, racing toward Dalgilur's defenses.

"We're doomed…" Krindal muttered. "The storm…"

Kaescis started. "You don't have your gem?" he demanded warily.

Krindal shook his head, trembling.

"Don't worry about the storm," Laeyit said reassuringly, glancing wryly to Kaescis. "I'm sure this vessel can withstand it. Or, outrun it," she said.

Krindal paled.

Outrun the storm? Kaescis thought, moving through the cabin. He took the seat beside Laeyit, marveling at the vessel's nature. Could it really withstand the storm? Laeyit seemed confident it could.

They hit the barrier a second later, passing through that strange void. They didn't remain there for long. Soon, they were within the storm.

Bolts of lightning streaked toward them, but they seemed to miss.

"See," Laeyit grinned, "we're moving too fast."

More lightning shot from the clouds, zipping toward the vessel. The bolts, however, disappeared above them.

Laeyit relaxed, touching the console again. Illusionary light appeared—much like Krindal's mapping tevisral—forming a localized topography. A golden speck pulsed, moving through the map.

"What is that?" Krindal asked, leaning over Laeyit's chair.

"This vessel," Laeyit said, sticking her fingers into the map. She reduced the map's magnification, revealing the entirety of the World's Frown.

Interesting, Kaescis thought, narrowing his eyes at the map. They had traveled a considerable distance in only a matter of minutes. At this rate, they would soon be out of the treacherous Frown.

More lightning flashed outside. Kaescis turned just in time to see a bolt strike the window. The force jolted the vessel. Another bolt hit, knocking Krindal to the decking.

Both Laeyit and Kaescis grabbed the console, watching as more lightning assailed their ship.

The map flickered.

"I knew we were doomed!" Krindal moaned.

"By the Crimson Eye!" Laeyit cursed, fiddling with the vessel's controls. Kaescis, however, held on tight. More lightning struck the vessel and parts of the console flickered. Suddenly, the map disappeared.

"I've lost control!" Laeyit screamed.

The vessel reeled back and forth, and Kaescis fell from his chair. Krindal was also on the decking, huddled and muttering. They continued barreling through the storm. Light within the cabin flickered. The console went dark. Kaescis struggled to get back into his chair, but Laeyit fell, knocking him back to the decking.

Laeyit looked into his eyes, frightened. She had made a gross miscalculation, and it showed on her face. Laeyit wrapped her arms around Kaescis's broken armor, trembling. The lightning persisted, bolts building upon each other. Krindal wailed again, but Kaescis ignored him.

After several more bolts, the window cracked. Laeyit winced, gripping Kaescis tighter.

We won't make it, Kaescis thought. They would succumb to the storm. Both Krindal and Laeyit would die… But Kaescis—he would be doomed to perpetual death and rebirth within the World's Frown. It would become his prison… The thought enraged him.

Lightning constantly assailed them, and Laeyit began weeping. Kaescis held her close and gazed at the breaking window. The window shattered. Thunder erupted. Lightning flashed. Rain and wind gushed into the cabin.

Kaescis closed his eyes, gripping Laeyit tightly. And then, the tumultuous storm ceased. Only the wind remained.

Kaescis squinted, shielding his face with a gauntleted hand. Blue skies hung above the speeding vessel.

"We made it!" Laeyit laughed. She pushed herself up and struggled against the wind, climbing into her seat. Her laughter, however, died.

"What's wrong?" Kaescis gritted his teeth.

"The storm damaged the controls," Laeyit shouted over the wind. "But we're still being propelled."

"What does that mean?" Krindal muttered.

"We'll keep going until we crash," Laeyit barked over the wind.

Kaescis furrowed his brow. He noted an island off the portside bow, but it soon passed. *We* are *moving fast,* Kaescis thought. *Too fast.* Based on the wind and the speed at which they passed the island, they were most likely traveling twenty or thirty times faster than any ship in the Mindolarnian Navy. At that speed, crashing would be beyond fatal—unless barsion protected them.

"If we are still on our previous heading, we'll most assuredly hit the Aegalian Peninsula," Laeyit added.

"In the Forbidden Lands?!" Krindal blurted.

"At this rate we'll probably be there in less than an hour," Laeyit shouted, looking to Kaescis.

"When we spot land, we need to cast our barsions," Kaescis said, then turned to the broken window. Crashing would be the least of their concerns. Surviving the Forbidden Lands, that was another matter entirely.

I know you will say these perils are a by-product of the degeneracy left over from the Karthar incident. Oh, how wrong are you!

Cheers erupted as the *Promised Maiden* cleared the storm of the World's Frown.

We made it! Cornar breathed a sigh of relief.

A hand gripped Cornar's shoulder, and he turned to see Igan. The wizard clutched a sloglien sack. Igan didn't speak, but the expression on his face asked, "What shall we do with this?"

The tomes, Cornar thought, recalling the sack's contents. He had nearly forgotten about them in their hasty flight. But now Cornar felt drawn to those tomes—it was the same irresistible pull he felt when gazing at the crater on Dalgilur. He remembered the words, "THIS IS YOUR DESTINY, CORNAR DOL'SHIR…" spoken by that booming voice in his mind—the voice of that being from his dreams.

Cornar suddenly knew that those texts were more important than anything else he or his men had uncovered on this expedition. It was his *fate* to claim them.

But why me? Cornar wondered. From what he had gleaned from the tome, the texts would better suit a Keeper of Truth and Might.

But the Keepers had vanished. Solidin had claimed as much.

"Cor…" Igan whispered, bringing Cornar back to reality.

Cornar blinked once, then scanned the main deck. His eyes fell upon Jahevial at the portside rail, talking with Aron. Though Jahevial had helped defeat Kaescis, Cornar felt he should keep this find from the scholar. After all, Jahevial was loyal to Grandmaster Alacor and would claim the discovery for the Necrotic Order.

Cornar could not allow that. "We need to get *that* to my cabin," Cornar whispered. "And we can't let Jahevial see it." Igan nodded.

Kalder approached quietly. The brawny warrior must have eyed the subtle exchange. "Do you need help?" Kalder whispered.

Cornar scanned the main deck once again before answering. "I think we'll be fine. Just keep an eye on the others. I'll be in my cabin, if you need me." Kalder nodded silently.

"Too bad I can't conceal this," Igan whispered. With the tazerin around he wouldn't be able to muster any magic.

"We'll be fine," Cornar said, stepping away from the bowsprit.

Together, they wove around the starboard side of the ship, unnoticed. The wounded were resting, and the crew was busy adjusting the rigging. Cornar heard commands from Emila—Salisar's first mate—to adjust for a northwest heading, indicating that the vessel would sail around the World's Frown.

The stairs leading below deck were darker than usual. Igan glanced to Cornar. "I hadn't considered the lightstones wouldn't work," the wizard said with a sigh.

"Let's hope they have something else aboard to light the ship…"

Faint candlelight flickered along the main corridor of the lower deck. Two of the crewmen were busy replacing the lightstones in the wall sconces with thick candles. The candles were wider than they were tall.

As they approached the crewmen, Igan stepped ahead of Cornar, moving the sack between them.

"I do hope you have enough candles for the cabins," Igan said.

"Oh… uh," a crewman muttered. "I don't know."

"You can't expect us to be stuck in the dark," Igan retorted. The crewman looked sheepish, then handed the wizard several candles.

Igan tipped his head appreciatively. "Thank you," he said. They continued toward Cornar's cabin, and Igan handed the sloglien sack to Cornar.

"See if you can round up some more candles," Cornar said, opening the door to his cabin.

"I will," Igan said with a nod, looking back down the dim corridor. "We'll need plenty. You're not the only one who wants to read." The wizard glanced to the sack, indicating his interest in the tomes.

Cornar grinned. "I'll let you start once I'm finished with the first one."

"Much appreciated," Igan said with a wink. "Now I'm going to have a word with the captain. Hopefully, she'll honor Krindal's charter. I'd hate to arrive back home with a surprise bill." The wizard hurried back down the dim corridor, leaving Cornar alone.

Cornar entered his cabin, set the sloglien sack on the bed, and then went to work lighting a candle. The sconce on the wall wasn't suited for anything but lightstones. It was a tight enough fit, and the candles were squat enough so they wouldn't tilt. But there was no basin to catch the wax, which would undoubtedly drip onto the decking. Unfortunately, it was the only suitable place for the candle.

With his cabin lit, Cornar shut the door and locked it. He moved to the bed, emptying the sack. He laid the tomes by his pillow. Then he removed the cases, one by one. Each was rectangular, with a porous texture—almost like a scroll case. One of the cases, however, was cracked.

Ignoring the damaged case, Cornar inspected the one nearest the tomes. The case was sealed shut, with a shallow groove near one end. *How do I open this?* Cornar wondered, then fingered a tiny lever by the groove. A click accompanied the lever's movement, and Cornar twisted the case's end, opening it.

To his surprise, the case contained several rolls of parchment. The case's interior, however, was rectangular—definitely not suited for a scroll or rolled sheets.

Odd, Cornar thought, removing the parchments. There was *something* on the top parchment, but nothing Cornar could decipher. The marks looked like the scribbles Solidin had shown him on the walls of the Keepers' Temple at Klindil—the Draconic language, the elf had claimed.

Cornar thumbed through the parchments, finding a sheet with Elvish upon its surface. *Perhaps there's something in Common?* he hoped, continuing to thumb through the parchments.

Then, he saw familiar writing.

"Men and elves of Kalda, hearken to my words and open your minds to the truths that have lain hidden for generations; the beings ascribed to legend and myth do, in reality, exist. Creatures far more intelligent and powerful than you or I, have claimed this world their own for thousands of generations. These extolled and exalted beings are called in their own tongue, 'sha'kalda,' but we know them in our languages as 'draco' and 'dragon.' Much of their origin is uncertain, for as long as men and elves have lived, the sha'kalda have dominated our world.

"For tens of millennia, the sha'kalda roamed across our world. Countless numbers of these majestic beings soared through the skies unmolested and nested upon the mountaintops without disturbance…"

Cornar paused, simply blinking at the parchment in disbelief. He flipped through the remaining pages, skimming their contents. The pages recounted a brief history of draconic breeds, gave a primer on the Channels of Magic, and spoke of a *true* magical tongue. It recounted the beginnings of a war—the *Dragon Wars*—and how a faction called the Kaldean Alliance was nearly defeated. It spoke of powerful tevisrals—a stone capable of tethering worlds and an amulet to control dragons.

That amulet, Cornar thought, recalling the diagram in the tome.

He returned to skimming the sheets. The last few pages described the events leading to the eventual victory of the Kaldean Alliance, and how their enemies were exiled to a world called Kalish.

"Five millennia have passed since the end of that dreadful war," Cornar read. *"Peace filled much of that time, but as of late the world has gradually become tainted with ways that once abounded in Cheserith's empire. In the last two hundred-and-some-odd years I have seen the hearts of men change; slowly turning to base desires of lust, greed, and malice. Men have become degenerate, killing their own brothers for the sake of gain. They treat life as if it is an autumn leaf in the wind. It is this growing evil among humanity that has me concerned."*

Cornar paused. *He's describing a world not unlike this day and age*, he thought.

The text concluded with a warning. *"I fear that not all the Lish'sha were exiled to*

Kalish. I believe some survived and are furtively influencing the humans of our day.

"If a remnant of Cheserith's seed exists upon Kalda, then I implore you, believe my words and seek the Au'misha'k. It is our only hope for peace.

"I am Ilnari, a Cess'nal and the former supreme commander of the elven armies of Kardorth. I have told you of the Au'misha'k and its power, and now I will tell you how to retrieve it so it may be re-forged."

The rest of the sheet was blank.

Intrigued, Cornar flipped through the parchments again, but found nothing more than he had already read. Cornar secured the sheets and moved on to the next case. Two small objects were inside: an oval-shaped silver rod the length of a finger and a polished ball of glistening white metal. Tevisrals, Cornar supposed, but with the tazerin nearby, they would be inert.

He secured the objects again and opened another case. This third case contained more rolled parchments. As with the first case, the parchments were divided into three sets: the strange symbols, Elvish, and Common. These parchments, however, were not penned by the elf, Ilnari. The writing had a different tone and was an amendment to the text Cornar had not found.

I'll read that later, he thought, putting away the parchment.

Cornar grabbed the last intact case, but found another object—probably a dormant tevisral—instead of parchment.

That left only the damaged case. Cornar warily eyed the crack. It wasn't large, but it exposed the case's interior. *Perhaps I should wait,* he thought. If the contents were damaged, opening the case now would not be a wise choice. He gently set the cracked case back within the sack.

I suppose you're next. He eyed the two red tomes. Cornar cleared a spot on his bed and opened the first volume of *The Thousand Years War.*

Dusel Nadim's narrative was enthralling. Cornar devoured the tome's contents like a starving man. The account was far more detailed than any narrative of the Dragon Wars he had ever heard or read. The tome spoke of terms and places unfamiliar to Cornar. Though one place in particular, Aridia, he recognized. It was a continent destroyed by tevisrals at the outset of the war. Raging waters and a terrible storm had replaced its lands.

The World's Frown, he thought. That realization gave Cornar pause. The *Promised Maiden* was sailing through waters that had once been land. Cornar marveled that the ancient Kaldeans had had the power to destroy a continent. They had been far more sophisticated than Krindal supposed.

But tevisrals were not the only wondrous things prevalent in the text. Dragons made their appearance quite often. Dusel referred to them as if they were commonplace. Each time Cornar read the word "dragon" or saw one of their strange names, he felt his disbelief in their existence wane.

Cornar was nearly halfway through the tome when a knock rapped on his cabin door. A whistle followed the knock, signaling it was his men. Still, cautious, Cornar tucked the tome under his pillow—the sack with the other texts was concealed elsewhere in the cabin.

He strode to the door, finding Igan, Kalder, and Nordal standing outside.

"We have reports," Nordal said. "May we enter?"

"Of course," Cornar stepped aside, gesturing with an open hand. Once they were inside, Cornar locked the door behind them. "How is everyone?" he asked.

"Most seem to be in good spirits," Nordal answered. "They're all talking about our escape. I imagine they will be spreading quite the tale once we return home."

"And the wounded?" Cornar asked, his tone carrying a weight of concern.

"Vaemar isn't doing any better," Nordal answered. "Midar is trying everything, but I don't know if he'll recover. Vaemar might lose one if not both his legs." Cornar sighed, making his way back to his bed.

"Brendar is improving though," Nordal said. "The others are about the same. Hopefully we'll see progress in a few days. I just wish we were closer to a port. An arpranist would be nice…" Cornar nodded.

Nordal continued reporting on each of the wounded warriors, sharing Midar's thoughts on their recovery.

Once Nordal was finished, Kalder spoke. "Aron said Jahevial will consult with Grandmaster Alacor about our share in the tevisrals he smuggled aboard. Once the Necrotic Order decides what they'll do with them, we'll be paid a fee or a portion of the sale."

"That's fine," Cornar said. "But make sure Aron negotiates for more than they offer. I don't want them suspecting—let alone discovering—we have our own cache."

"It would be wise to see what Jahevial smuggled aboard," Igan suggested. "This way we can compare his finds against our own."

"Nordal, will you be in charge of that?" Cornar asked.

"Gladly," the warrior grinned.

"Where are the tevisrals we found?" Cornar asked.

"In Ordreth's cabin," Kalder answered. "Do you want them moved?"

Cornar shook his head. "They should be fine where they are. Just ensure someone is in that cabin at all times." Kalder nodded and folded his arms. The gesture indicated Kalder had finished his report.

Cornar then turned to the wizard.

"We're rounding the World's Frown at the moment," Igan said. "Salisar intends to moor on an island called Galium, a small port along the fringes of the Isles Run."

"Where is that?" Nordal asked.

"A few thousand grand phineals southeast of Merdan," Igan answered. "She thinks we'll reach it in about two weeks. It's the closest port."

"Soroth will be a month away from there," Kalder observed.

Igan nodded. "Or more. She wants to make a stop in Damnir, so we will be taking the southern route of the Isles Run back to Soroth."

"Great…" Nordal grunted. Igan raised an eyebrow at the warrior, obviously expecting some snide remark. But Nordal said nothing. The southern route along the Isles Run was a longer return trip to Soroth. It would be faster to sail north of Merdan and follow the Coastal Current back to Soroth, despite the greater distance.

"How are your studies?" Kalder asked.

Cornar sucked in his breath. "It's definitely interesting… There are many references to dragons and tevisrals. But it is a history of the Dragon Wars, after all."

"Really?" Nordal said, frowning.

"I'm through the first few hundred years of the war," Cornar continued. "The Cheserithean Empire has driven the Kaldean Alliance to the borders of the Elven Realm. The Kaldean Alliance is losing, badly. They're desperate."

Cornar paused, his thoughts turning to Ilnari's warning. The elf's words conjured the image of that amulet within Cornar's mind. He closed his eyes and shook his head, but he couldn't shake the image of the amulet.

"You all right, Cor?" Kalder asked.

Was he? Cornar looked to Kalder. "I'm just consumed with this, that's all."

"Well, don't become too obsessed," Nordal quipped. "I'd hate for you to turn into Krindal."

Laughter filled the cabin. Cornar grinned, settling back on his bed. Small talk filled the cabin as the men discussed their plans for the next few days. It would be a long trip back to Soroth.

One by one, the men left and Cornar was once again alone. He retrieved the book from under his pillow and continued reading. But he couldn't shake the image of that amulet. Page after page, Ilnari's warning and the amulet lingered at the back of his mind.

If you would but examine the sacred texts of our Enemy's *followers, you would understand my urgency.*

Laeyit was wrong. They had not crashed into the Aegalian Peninsula as she had supposed. Their broken vessel chased the setting sun, and Kaescis knew they were headed east.

"We're doomed!" Krindal moaned, crouched against a bench at the back of the cabin.

"Quit your sniffling!" Laeyit shouted, still sitting in her chair. The old scholar continued muttering, but Laeyit chided him. She was a remarkable woman—firm and indomitable.

Why didn't I notice her sooner? Kaescis thought, feeling regretful. He huddled behind his chair, exhausted from the ordeals of the day. His rebirth had been rejuvenating, but after hours on the waters, exhaustion had overtaken him.

Kaescis closed his eyes, remembering odd images after his defeat at the hands of Mister Dol'shir and that traitorous scholar, Jahevial. *The Messenger of the Promise. Was he really there?* Kaescis recalled images of a man in red within an endless white void. His memory was a blur, jumbled with flashes of unyielding pain. But one sentence seemed to stand out against the confusion, "*… I always thought your death was necessary, but I now see that I was wrong…*"

My death, a necessity? Memories from his first experience in Vabenack came to him, as well as that behest from the Messenger: "*One wrong step, and you could doom your God.*"

Kaescis played through the events in his mind, simultaneously comparing his vision to reality.

And then, a dreadful notion hit him. *I was meant to die in that vault.* In the vision, Kaescis had gone to the vault without his armor, and without his Crimson Praetorians. He vaguely remembered Mister Dol'shir mentioning a summons. The man *wanted* Kaescis there. And then there was Dol'shir's order for his men to attack.

So, they were laying a trap for me. Kaescis shuddered. Without his armor, Kaescis would have fallen. The tazerin would have kept him weaponless.

Dol'shir would have killed me, Kaescis thought. If he had adhered with exact obedience, Kaescis *should* have died. Was he intended as a sacrifice? But why hadn't the Messenger told him? That question gave him pause.

Had Kaescis not enough faith in the *Will* to accept such a task? *Perhaps I am not as devout as I thought…* Kaescis sighed.

"Land!" Laeyit shouted. "I see mountaintops on the horizon."

Krindal groaned uneasily, staggering to his feet. The old scholar moved past Kaescis, standing behind Laeyit. "Is that… the Desolate Lands?"

Laeyit ignored the question. "Hurry, cast your barsions," she said to Krindal and Kaescis. The old scholar complied, muttering an incantation.

Kaescis, however, didn't move. Why was his death necessary to usher the return of Lord Cheserith? Was he not *chosen* as His champion? Sorrow flooded his mind.

"… Kaescis!"

Laeyit moved in front of Kaescis, grabbing him by his pauldrons. "Cast your barsion!"

"Oh… Laeyit," Kaescis muttered, removing his helmet. "I've failed." He then unlatched both gauntlets. They broke into pieces and fell to the decking.

"He won the first round," she said, "But you can beat him. You'll come back stronger, Kaescis!" Laeyit flicked her gaze to the broken window, and her mouth dropped open in horror.

"There's no time, Kaescis!" Laeyit shouted, and uttered an incantation. As her magic formed she grabbed Kaescis, pulling him tight.

"No!" Kaescis kicked Laeyit, sending her across the cabin as her barsion formed, encasing her. Kaescis unlatched his breastplate. His pauldrons were next.

Laeyit's face twisted with abhorrence. Krindal's protection formed at that moment—an acidic barsion bubble.

Kaescis's leggings fell to the decking, followed by his sabatons.

Laeyit recovered, her lips moving—undoubtedly casting another incantation.

Don't do it, Laeyit, Kaescis thought, gritting his teeth. Now without his armor, Kaescis braced for the inevitable.

Her second spell coalesced, but it was too late.

A resounding crash echoed all around Kaescis. The world spun. Pieces of the hull broke apart, flying wildly. Krindal followed the wreckage, tumbling away. Laeyit vanished also, and then Kaescis felt himself hurled through the air. Land and sky flashed before him. The wind whipped around him violently.

He glimpsed rock approaching.

In that moment, Kaescis hoped he could right his mistakes. He prayed a final prayer to his God. "Aunok'sha, receive me!"

And then, blackness.

Death, however, did not persist.

Kaescis opened his eyes.

He gasped, sucking in a deep breath. Pain shot through his entire body—no part was unscathed. But how had he survived? Kaescis had shed his armor—the tevisral which would preserve him was gone, lost in the crash.

"A noble move, but I have work for you yet, Kaescis Midivar."

Struggling against the pain, Kaescis saw the skirts of a crimson robe. That robe bore the emblems of Cherisium—the robe of the Messenger of the Promise.

"He who has lost his life seven times over shall be greatly esteemed," the Messenger said, kneeling close to Kaescis's face. He stroked his white beard as he eyed Kaescis, grinning—his sapphire eyes striking. "Here, why don't I fix that," the Messenger said, touching Kaescis's bleeding forehead.

73

THE KEEPERS' LEGACY

Those accursed scriptures point to a terrible event occurring in this day and age. What we thought impossible will come to pass.

Since the abominable half-breed prince and the cowardly scholar had fled, there wasn't any danger left in Dalgilur. The four gholistras were actively searching the island. If there were any stragglers, the gholistras would deal with them.

With the Mindolarnians defeated, Solidin and the survivors returned to the ruined war camp to retrieve their fallen comrades.

The foul stench of death met Solidin's nostrils as he picked his way through the rubble. All around him, the members of the Sapphire Guard carried the dead to a place beyond the war camp.

Soon, Solidin came to Kaldarin's corpse.

"You will not be forgotten, my friend," Solidin said in Elvish, tears welling in his eyes. "I will ensure that your name is remembered in the annals of the Aristocracy."

Still empowered by enhancing magic, Solidin sorrowfully picked up Kaldarin and carried his fallen lieutenant to lie among the dead.

It wasn't long before they cleared the lifeless elves from the rubble.

At Solidin's command, the survivors picked through the war camp, retrieving tevisrals and relics. At the heart of the war camp, the so-called Royal ring, they found most of the tevisrals.

They also found strange and ancient weapons—tools of war from Kalda's past—amid the rubble. Few Mindolarnians had come against the Sapphire Guard with these weapons—only Bratan and a handful of Crimson Praetorians. The weapons burst alight when touched—blades of fanisar and sword alike formed as if transmuted, despite the lack of matter. Destructive auras ignited around the weapons, immune to dispelling effects.

As the elves collected the weapons, Solidin held one of the long-swords. The blade glowed a vibrant orange, with shifting hues of red and yellow—

fiery magic. *Was this a Keepers' weapon?* Solidin wondered. The blade and its hilt looked elven. Solidin had heard stories of weapons that burst into existence. They were often described in the erroneous tales about the Thousand Years War, said to have been wielded by footmen and common soldiers.

But the Keepers' weapons were said to be greater than those wielded by the Kaldean Alliance—or so it was claimed in the texts found by High Lord Medrayn.

A sudden commotion drew his attention. With the flaming sword still in hand, Solidin turned toward the rear of the war camp. Two members of the Sapphire Guard held a brown-haired man captive. The man wore red-and-gold regal clothing—the kind a Mindolarnian Royal might wear.

"Solidin," shouted one of the captors, "we found him attempting to cross between the pillars."

The man looked terrified. "P-pl-please," he stammered, "spare me. I beg of you!"

Solidin picked his way through the rubble, coming to the captive man. Normally, Solidin would have ordered the man executed… but the supplanted honor within him compelled an act of mercy.

The outcry drew the attention of those around Solidin, and they came beside their leader.

"Who are you?" Solidin asked in Common. *This man is not a Sorothian,* he thought. *Not one of Cornar's men.*

"My name is… P-Practil," the brown-haired man answered. "A servant."

Practil's captors looked to Solidin inquisitively. Their gazes anticipated Solidin's order of execution.

But Solidin gave no such order. "Tell me more about yourself, Practil," Solidin asked. He glanced to the blazing weapon in his hand. *I wish I could dismiss this…*

"I… I belong to the Royal retinue of Prince Kaescis Midivar," Practil answered.

Intrigued, Solidin searched the man's eyes. They were a pale brown—a normal color for a man. *Not a half-breed abomination,* he mused.

"This coward must have fled the battle," an elf commented in Elvish.

Practil shot a frantic glance to the elf, but then returned his gaze to Solidin. "Will you spare me?" the servant asked, his voice trembling.

Solidin considered the request. *This man might serve a purpose…* He grinned. "Our reputation for relentlessness can only be maintained if a survivor is left, now and again," Solidin said. "It has been some time since we intentionally left a straggler to tell the tale of their comrades' defeat." The fear on Practil's face dissipated.

"Though a discovery such as Dalgilur *should* warrant secrecy, your return to Mindolarn will send a powerful message," Solidin continued, eyeing the servant. Practil tensed. "We will keep you captive until we return to Keth. Once there, we will see to your return to Mindolarn, where I expect you to inform your emperor of your prince's failure."

Practil swallowed hard.

Solidin opened his mouth to continue, but was interrupted by a shout. He turned to see one of the female scouts hurrying toward him, carrying a silvery oval disk, domed on one side.

Could it be? Solidin wondered, his eyes wide. The disk looked akin to the mapping tevisral he had lost during the earthquake on Klindala. But then, Solidin's eyes were drawn to the scout's clenched fist. Did he dare hope that she held the other component? The thought of it made him feel exuberant.

"Solidin!" the elven maid cried triumphantly. "The qui'sha is dead!" She neared Solidin and opened her hand, revealing a tiny twenty-one sided gem.

Gasps of surprise and intrigue filled the air.

Solidin beamed with elation. "It seems you have another matter to relay." Solidin turned to Practil, his tone jubilant. "Your half-breed prince is dead."

Practil paled.

The elven maid came within arm's reach and handed Solidin both the mapping tevisral and the gem. Solidin activated the tevisral, and then it projected the map of Kalda. Its appearance pleased him, but then he wondered about Kaescis's hasty flight. Had the prince entered that vessel knowing that his cowardly ally was without his means to negate the storm? Solidin had witnessed their sea craft disappear within Dalgilur's defenses.

Perhaps he thought the ancient vessel was enough to withstand the storm, Solidin mused. But no vessel had ever survived the tempests of the Anomalous Corridor.

"Oh, my prince!" Practil wailed.

Solidin waved his hand, dismissing the elves holding Practil. "Secure these," he handed the mapping tevisral and gem back to the scout. Solidin then turned to the crowd now gathered around him. "Continue clearing the war camp. I want this filth transmuted and cleared before sunset."

⟞•⟝

When darkness settled on Dalgilur, Solidin was drawn to the upper reaches of this place cut out of the mountain. Solidin *knew* the route he must take as if he were walking through his own home.

After climbing forty stories, Solidin wound through corridors until he came to a set of doors unlike any other in Dalgilur. It bore the Keepers' emblems of each Order, and writing in Common, Elvish, and Draconic.

At his approach, white light shot from beneath his armor and illuminated the details on the door. A faint hum resonated throughout the corridor, then the doors *slid* apart—much like those found in the headquarters of the Elven Aristocracy of Merdan.

The space beyond the doors was akin to the attunement chamber in the Keepers' Temple at Klindil. Twenty-one thrones lined curving walls, with a lit emblem above each—the symbols of the various Keepers' Orders.

Solidin moved to the center of the room, knowing that his presence would summon a kolphigrym. Once at the room's heart, Solidin stopped, waiting in anticipation. But nothing happened.

Where are you? he wondered, scanning the chamber. "Dusel Nadim," Solidin shouted, "show yourself!" Nothing happened.

Solidin sighed, his irritation forming a scowl upon his face. He waited for another moment. *There's nothing here,* he thought. Was he wasting his time? No… he had felt compelled to come here. It was the same sensation that drew him to Dalgilur.

He took another step into the room. Nothing changed.

"I am a Keeper of Truth and Might!" Solidin shouted. "A Bladesinger!" He removed the necklace housing his gem, holding it aloft. "Can't you see this? Can't you sense me?"

There was no reply.

Solidin growled with frustration. "Why will you not show yourselves?!" His cry echoed, but when it faded an eerie silence lingered in the chamber.

Suddenly, Solidin felt alone.

No… He shook his head. There *had* to be something here. Why else was he compelled?

Solidin spun, dashing to one of the thrones. He touched it, but nothing happened. He then moved to each of the other thrones, but none reacted to his presence. The walls were next, and he touched every square phineal of their surface.

Again, nothing. After a long time of searching, Solidin returned to the center of the room. A sad realization came over him. This was a place where *other* Keepers greeted the newly initiated.

But there were no other Keepers on Dalgilur. And there were no other Keepers in the shrines or the temple. They were gone.

Overcome, Solidin fell to his knees, despairing the fate of this long-lost Order.

74

MOURNING

Our Enemy will *return. And there is only one way to prevent his advent. But I doubt you will consent to destroying the symbol of our ancestors' victory.*

Sorrow once again consumed Iltar's soul. He had experienced cycles of wrath and weeping since leaving the top of his tower. This was grief unlike any other he had experienced. *Oh, Alanya…*

His heart swelled with anguish as he knelt upon the grass within the manicured grounds of his tower, watching Delrin and Jalim. The two guards were waist deep within a hole, shoveling dirt for Alanya's grave. Delrin took a deep breath, resting on his shovel. The hobbling guard noticed Iltar and gave him a smile, but Delrin's expression soon saddened. Iltar's anguish was infectious.

With red-rimmed eyes, Iltar watched his guards. He *should* have transmuted the ground and reformed the raw matter into a pile beside the grave. But Iltar could not find the will to break the bonds of his despair.

The guards were finished before long and climbed out of the hole. They left Iltar alone to gaze at the pit that would hold his beloved. *My beloved?* Iltar wondered. He had long given up hope that he would ever refer to a woman as such. The thought left a wrenching pang.

Faint footsteps crunched the grass behind him, then Iltar felt a gentle touch against his shoulder. "Do you want to sit, Master Iltar?" Belsina asked.

Completely numb, Iltar stared blankly at her. Belsina gestured to a chair from the dining room. The acolytes were carrying more chairs, setting them beside the one mentioned by Belsina. Iltar, however, simply stared at the chairs. Belsina said something to him, but Iltar didn't quite hear it. He was drowning in his emotions. Belsina left after a while, and Iltar was once again alone.

It wasn't long before the guards returned with the acolytes, carrying an elaborate casket. The wood was exquisite, ornamented with gold embellishments and brilliant jewels.

Iltar marveled at the sight. They had no such things here at his family's homestead. He gazed at the casket quizzically as Bilda and Tigan hurried around the procession. They stopped beside Iltar, looking excited.

"Doesn't it look great, Master Iltar?" Bilda asked.

"Pagus changed it, sir," Tigan interjected. "Hegdil only made a crude box, but Pagus put an illusion on it."

Iltar didn't reply.

A moment later, Elsia entered the grounds of Iltar's tower. The countess walked somberly, following the procession. She had since cleaned up from the battle, wearing one of Belsina's dresses. Her face was plain, as when they first arrived in Mindolarn—after all, Belsina wouldn't have any makeup for her to wear. The countess took a seat behind Iltar. She simply gazed at him with a blank expression. She too was grieving.

As the procession crossed the grounds of Iltar's tower, Belsina and Hegdil hurried through the gates, carrying sawhorses. Both maid and groom moved passed the pallbearers, placing the sawhorses in front of the open grave.

Delrin and Jalim guided the boys toward the grave, where they set the casket atop the sawhorses. Each of the pallbearers stepped away, except for Pagus.

The youth uttered an incantation, dressing the sawhorses and the air between them in an illusion befitting royalty. Pagus then took his seat beside his aunt. He studied Elsia for a moment, then cast another incantation, veiling her face with an illusion. Elsia forced a smile and muttered what Iltar could only assume was a "thank-you."

"Master"—Bilda clasped Iltar's shoulder—"do you want to sit?"

The boy's touch jarred Iltar from his reverie, and he found the strength to move into the chair.

Soon, Hegdil and Belsina stood between the grave and the tiny assembly. The groom stepped forward, clearing his throat. "With the countess's permission, I have volunteered to conduct this burial ceremony for the High Duchess, Lady Alanya Tasivir," He droned on, keeping with traditional Sorothian customs. After he was finished, Hegdil invited those in the assembly to step forward and speak.

One by one, the acolytes stood and spoke about Alanya. Each shared fond experiences with her during their time in Mindolarn. Hearing the boys only evoked more sorrow. Elsia was the last to speak. She was brief, and Iltar barely comprehended her words. She mourned for the loss of her friend. There was an undertone of anger as Elsia spoke. Iltar did hear her mention something of manipulation. There was a moment of silence after the countess was finished, then Hegdil arose and instructed the pallbearers to put Alanya to rest.

Bilda and Tigan also stood, standing on either side of the grave. The younger boys uttered incantations, mustering green magic. Soon, both wielded a mass of ensnaring tentacles. The pallbearers heaved the casket, moving to the open grave. Once there, the tentacles under the two acolytes' control grabbed the casket, gently setting it in the ground.

One by one, the boys left, following Belsina. Elsia stood at the grave, gazing at the casket, then she too departed. Only Hegdil and the guards remained. The three men shoveled the dirt, concealing Alanya's casket. They were nearly finished when Hegdil stopped to study Iltar.

"You know, it's customary for the spouse to lay the final shovel of dirt," the groom said. He took a full shovel and walked to Iltar. Hegdil held the shovel out, gesturing for Iltar to take it.

Iltar furrowed his brow. "I know you were not married," Hegdil said, "but I'm sure you would have been, eventually. Here, Master Iltar." Iltar stared at the shovel for a long while and then stood. He eventually complied and dumped the last of the dirt onto the mound. Hegdil patted Iltar on the shoulder, then took the shovel. The groom walked across the manicured lawn with Delrin and Jalim. Soon, the three of them disappeared through the wrought-iron gate.

Once again alone, Iltar stared at his lover's grave. He thought this final action would grant a sense of finality, but it hadn't. Iltar remembered Alanya's last words to him: "Come find me in Vabenack."

Suddenly, sorrow was replaced with a faint glimmer of hope. Though Alanya was dead, Iltar *could* find her in Vabenack—he would manipulate the Translucent Fields to manifest Alanya in all her splendor. Still staring at the grave, Iltar smiled, feeling a measure of peace.

As Iltar's spirit lifted, a displeased rumble echoed on the wind. He looked around, searching for its source, but found nothing. *Reflection...* Iltar squinted at the sky.

⸺•⸺

Iltar stepped onto the covered porch leading to the side entrance of his family's home. Hearty aromas—mingled with the sweet smell of baked furnapel—greeted him as he entered the homestead. The scents were comforting, evoking fond memories from his youth. He basked in the momentary recollection before striding down the corridor. The mirror by the door caught his eye. There was a steady calmness on his face. His sapphire eyes reminded him of his father—firm and resolute. The sight solidified that sense of peace he had felt.

He continued down the hall, nearing the kitchen. Hegdil's voice came from the front of the home, retelling a fanciful story.

"Iltar," Belsina called. Iltar turned toward the kitchen. His maid was handling a metal baking sheet full of fresh furnapel tangrils. "Come here," Belsina said, setting the sheet down on a wire rack. Iltar complied, picking his way across the kitchen.

"You look better," Belsina noted, eyeing him up and down. "Dinner should be ready in a few hours. But you need to eat," she said in a motherly tone, handing him one of the pastries. The tangril was a little too hot, but its sweetness prevailed.

As he ate, a sudden calmness washed over Iltar—like the effect of a spell. Though the loss of Alanya was fresh in his mind, the bitterness associated with her death was swallowed up in that moment.

Belsina's cooking lifted everyone's spirits. The conversation at the dining table was quite lively. Even Elsia smiled. After dinner, the countess retired to one of the upper bedrooms, leaving Iltar and the acolytes to converse. Hegdil and Belsina cleaned up the table as the boys uneasily eyed each other.

"So, can we talk about what happened?" Agen asked. Iltar raised an eyebrow.

"Aunty didn't want us speaking of Mindolarn," Pagus said. "Probably too tender of a subject, I assume."

"That's oddly sensitive of you, Pagus," Iltar remarked. Pagus shrugged, sitting back in his chair.

"I just want to know what those *things* were," Bilda said. "They were creepy!"

"Hush, Bilda," Pagus chided. "We don't want her to hear us." He gestured to the ceiling. Bilda frowned.

A few of the other boys voiced questions and opinions about Bilda's comment. They claimed some of the dead Crimson Praetorians had red scales instead of skin, and long snouts. *Like that Xalutir I encountered in Vabenack,* Iltar thought.

"They're called qui'sha," Pagus answered, looking at the table. His demeanor was oddly reluctant.

Qui'sha? Iltar thought, recalling the name from the *Legacy of Ku'tharn*—the supposed race birthed by the book's titular deity.

"They are part human, part dragon," Pagus said. "They're human-like, but covered in scales instead of skin. They have tails, but not wings. And their eyes… their eyes are the strangest of colors. Unnatural colors. They can change their shape, too. Only when they die do they reveal their *true* form." Pagus's words rang with dreadful recollection.

"How do you know that, Pagus?" Iltar asked.

Pagus started. He swallowed hard. "Because I killed one…"

"You killed one of the Praetorians?" Tigan asked with wide eyes. Pagus didn't answer, averting his gaze to the table.

"Vaegris," Iltar whispered the name, and his apprentice started again. "Vaegris had yellow eyes with orange flecks—that's an unnatural color." Pagus remained silent. "Vaegris went missing the day before the ball. The attendants said they never saw him leave, and the Praetorians hadn't seen him in the Royal Archive, either." Iltar chuckled, amused by his deductions.

"Why are you laughing, Master Iltar?" Agen asked.

"Because Pagus *killed* Vaegris," Iltar said. "He *saw* the old librarian change from human to qui'sha. I imagine that was quite the surprise." Pagus slowly turned to Iltar, but didn't speak.

"Don't worry, Pagus," Iltar grinned. "Your crime will go unpunished. Let me guess, he caught you pilfering one of the tomes? You must have been holding a spell in order to strike fast enough to prevent an outcry. I assume you had several of your illusionary books persisting as well, and most likely a veil of invisibility." Iltar felt a sense of pride for his apprentice as he voiced his speculation. "That's quite the feat," he grinned. Pagus looked unsure of what to say.

"You know, I encountered one as well," Iltar said. "In Vabenack. It was one of the princes."

"What?!" Bilda blurted, but abruptly covered his mouth, his eyes going wide. The rest of the acolytes looked surprised, except Pagus.

"You knew about that, too?" Iltar asked. "The princes, I mean."

Pagus nodded. "I read about it in one of the books. All the Mindolarnian Royals are those monsters. Half their empire is probably like them, but maybe not as pureblooded." Pagus summarized some of what he found during his furtive studies. He had read from a tome entitled *The Fall of the Cheserithean Empire* that chronicled the ancient Dragon Wars. Iltar remembered that was one of the illusions he had encountered in the Royal Archive.

The rebellious apprentice had delved into greater detail about the qui'shas and their heritage. During Pagus's discourse, Hegdil returned to the dining hall, looking intrigued. "Are you talking about the dragonmen?" Hegdil asked. His eyes flashed with wonder.

"You know about them, Master Hegdil?" Bilda asked.

"Why of course!" Hegdil exclaimed. "The dreadful foot soldiers of the *Enemy*, the Dark One, the self-proclaimed God of—"

"Cheserith, you mean?" Pagus interrupted.

Hegdil laughed. "No… I am talking about Cheserith's master." Iltar found himself leaning forward, intrigued by Hegdil's words. "Sure, Cheserith proclaimed himself as a god, but he wasn't the architect of the ancient conflict that sundered dragonkind," Hegdil said, chuckling. "Cheserith was merely the figurehead. No, I am talking about Hemran'na."

Iltar's eyes widened. He *knew* that name. It had been spoken to him by Reflection, mentioned in *The Codices of Soron Thahan*, and the writings of Algas Marn. *The Unspoken One, the Harbinger of Hemran'na,* Iltar recalled the synonymous titles.

"That name sounds familiar," Agen said.

"It's in the *Codices* tome," Pagus interjected, turning toward Iltar. His face paled and his eyes widened. The connection obviously came to him as well.

"The dragonmen are dreadful creatures," Hegdil continued. "Their minds are keener than men or elves, and they are devious. They have quite the lifespan, too. A dragonman can live for over a thousand years, or so the legends claim. You haven't seen one, have you?" the groom asked, looking around the table.

Bilda nodded.

"In Mindolarn," Tigan said.

The groom hummed. "If you have seen dragonmen, then the Enemy's return is soon upon us," Hegdil said. "There are dark times to come, I fear." The boys looked uneasily at each other.

Iltar eyed his groom, studying him closely. Hegdil casually spoke about things Iltar had fought hard to uncover. Where had Hegdil come across this knowledge?

Footsteps interrupted Iltar's reflection, and Belsina entered the dining room. "Are you spreading doom and gloom, Hegdil?" Belsina asked, her face stern, her expression almost chiding. "The boys are tired, and you shouldn't be scaring them with fictitious horrors."

"No!" Bilda blurted. "The dragonmen are real, we saw them!"

"Bilda…" Pagus gritted his teeth.

"Sorry," the boy said, slumping in his chair.

Belsina scanned the table, but her eyes lingered on Iltar. "I think you should all hurry off to bed," she suggested. "None of you have slept." The younger acolytes groaned.

"Do we have to, Master Iltar?" Tigan asked.

As much as Iltar enjoyed the conversation, he knew Belsina had a valid point. "We can continue this insightful discussion tomorrow," he said. "This has been quite the day—two, actually. Besides, we have plenty of time to kill." The boys looked confused. "We need to wait for the *Yaelinum*," Iltar said matter-of-factly. "None of us are leaving this homestead until it arrives. We must maintain our ruse."

Each of the acolytes pondered their master's words. They obviously hadn't considered the implications of their return to Soroth without Pagus's vessel. Iltar was grateful none of them had left without consulting him. That could have ended in disaster.

"You better have a talk with Aunty Elsia," Pagus said, sighing. "She wants to return to Sarn in the morning. She's planning on riding to Serinta to catch a ferry. And, she wants me to go with her."

"You're leaving?" one of the acolytes asked.

Pagus gave the boy a sidelong glance, then turned back to Iltar. "She is worried about those dreams she's had when trying to access Vabenack. She kept seeing my death at the hands of Grandmaster Alacor."

"They're just dreams…" Bilda interjected. "They're not real."

"Not how she sees it," Pagus said. "Aunty claims the dreams one experiences when accessing Vabenack are glimpses of the future—frightful glimpses. They're meant to deter the faint of heart."

Iltar thoughtfully scratched his goatee, ignoring the additional insight about Vabenack. "You going to Sarn wouldn't be a problem. In fact, it might be wise for all of us to go. But we do it my way.

"Hegdil, fetch Delrin and Jalim," Iltar commanded. "We need to pry my conjuration anchor from the top of my tower."

The groom nodded, then hurried out of the dining room.

Belsina raised an eyebrow at Hegdil, then studied Iltar. "What are you planning now?" she asked, not amused.

A sly grin formed upon Iltar's face. "Traveling to Sarn unnoticed with this many people will be much easier by way of rogulin crystal. Once the anchor is moved, we will simply teleport to Elsia's mountain villa. And when Kaelar arrives on the *Yaelinum*, Hegdil will meet him and redirect the vessel to pick us up on Sarn. We will return to Soroth aboard the *Yaelinum* and no one will be the wiser."

Belsina drew her lips to a line. "You've entrenched yourself in a difficult position, Master Iltar," she scolded. "Be wary."

Iltar grinned. His maid obviously underestimated his clever abilities. After all, Iltar had accomplished many things by furtive means. Elsia was a kindred spirit in that regard. The countess had a perfectly planned explanation for the entire ruse—a lie within a lie. Her contrived plot would answer many questions, especially if Alacor had sent someone to inquire after Pagus's inheritance and the acolytes' training.

But if perchance Elsia's careful planning failed, Iltar would deal with the consequences—even if that meant confronting Alacor once and for all.

And the Messenger of the Promise shall prepare the way before him, purifying the Children of Cheserith.

- Prophecy of the Unspoken One

Yes, this *is* the right course," Reflection mused aloud—he had taken a liking to the nickname. And a fitting name it was. He stood alone within the newly rebuilt throne room at Mindolarn. Not even the Praetorians were present. But that was common for days such as this, because today was a day of commiseration. The day of the Feast of Sorrows.

Anger boiled within Reflection as he recalled the reasons behind the feast. But he put the fury aside. "I don't know why I hadn't considered this path before," he mused, turning to the rebuilt wall. "It even allows the Unspoken One a bit of morality—and the powers *know* he has an odd streak of it."

Though events had transpired as Reflection wanted, Iltar still maintained a measure of his humanity. That was worrisome.

Reflection sauntered to the rebuilt wall, carefully examining it. "Whoever performed the melding did a poor job," he murmured, noting the apparent seams where the old and new wall met. The seam was most assuredly unseen to the natural eye, but not to him. After all, he was more than *natural*. The glass doors leading to the balcony were shut, but Reflection had passed *through* them without resistance.

Reflection eyed the wall. "That was a bold move, I must say. Crashing into the throne room—what a spectacle! Normally you platinum beasts aren't so overt," he said, chuckling. Reflection gazed across the sky, retracing the path Lirathay'lu had taken through the air. It was a considerable distance, nearly the entire length of the city. But such distances were a mere stride for a dragon.

Now at the railing, Reflection gazed down into the palace's western gardens. Elegant round tables and chairs were arranged around a series of long tables spanning the length of the banquet yard. All were empty. The royal orchestra was preparing themselves at the far end of the banquet yard, behind the stand used by the Presider of the Feast.

"I suppose this is as good a spot as any," Reflection said, hefting himself onto the railing, feet dangling over the edge. Oh, what a sight it would be for someone to see *him* perched atop the balcony. "I wonder, what would that be like?" Reflection mused.

A sudden wave of prescience filled him. His vision was multifold—based in reality and possibility. They overlapped each other, but Reflection *knew* the difference between them. In possibility, he saw servants and aristocrat alike gawking at him, pointing with hasty fingers and shouting jubilant cries. They broke into singing praises that became a joyous celebration.

That evoked a wry smile. "Perhaps for the final feast," he considered. Reflection dismissed the prescience and simply observed.

Commiserating aristocrats entered the banquet yard, somberly moving toward the tables. Reflection noted each as he saw them. Their disfigured countenances amused him. "Oh, to mourn a god," he said with a laugh.

Amid the throng, Reflection directed his gaze to the heir of the Mindolarn throne—Jeridi Midivar. "You play an important role here," he said. "Before, you were nothing, but now you are essential."

Jeridi moved around the throng, distinguished by his stride—he did not commiserate. Other things were on the fat prince's mind. His thoughts were directed to Iltar, and his glorious appearance as the Harbinger of Hemran'na. The prince took his seat near the Presider's stand, watching the Partakers of the Feast but thinking of his brothers—Xalutir and Negaris.

"That will be quite the rematch." Reflection chuckled, instantaneously moving from his perch and appearing in front of Jeridi's table. "Yes, you will be well suited as emperor," Reflection nodded, turning to the north. "You will create a suitable dam. A dam your brother will break."

Through omnipresent vision, Reflection saw Almar furtively guiding a small army through the mountains. "How fitting that you kill two emperors on this most sorrowful of holidays. Oh, Almar... they will curse your name for generations." Reflection laughed. Amid his mirth, Reflection moved *through* the table, sliding into the chair beside Jeridi. Of course, he wasn't actually sitting on the chair. He could not react to matter, not in his present state.

"Oh, I long for the days of freedom," he smiled, glancing to Jeridi. The fat prince stared blankly across the now bustling banquet yard, oblivious to the remark.

"You know, I thought you people useless," Reflection said, leaning back. "Well, you had your purposes leading up to now. I could have taken myriad paths without you. There are really only two people that *truly* matter," he said frankly. "Them, and the Au'misha'k. I can interchange all the other players.

"But these two... they are men of destiny. Their very existence is woven into the fabric of the universe—tied to Fate itself. Them I *must* protect—even against my own creations. For if they die, all will be in ruin."

Princess Ilnea approached the table and quietly took her seat beside Reflection. "Has there been any word from your brothers?" she asked Jeridi.

"No," the prince replied. He was trying not to think of what his brothers were plotting. The princess nodded, closing her eyes and silently praying. Jeridi, however, remained troubled.

Reflection raised an eyebrow, then another wave of prescience filled his vision. No longer was he in the banquet yard at Mindolarn. He stood within the vastness of Vabenack with myriad possibilities arrayed around him—like tiny bubbles clustered tightly in the air. They hinged upon a simple decision, but each diverged into countless futures.

He examined each possibility in an instant, seeing them to a distinct point in time. "Ah, that one," Reflection grinned, touching the possibility. Events flashed before him and he *breathed* the possibility into himself.

Reflection returned to the banquet yard—not even a second having passed. He turned to Jeridi, his hand flashing the symbols to enable him to speak beyond the veil barring him from reality. Then, Reflection whispered into the prince's ear. "Fear not for the Unspoken One, for he is upheld and sustained."

Jeridi started. Reflection burst into laughter. The startled reactions never ceased to amuse him. Even throughout all the eons, it was still humorous.

"Are you all right, Jeridi?" Ilnea asked, having seen the fat prince startling.

"I heard something," Jeridi said, "like a whisper on the wind."

Ilnea's eyes widened with wonder. "The *Will?*" she asked. Jeridi nodded tersely. "Praise Aunok'sha!" she exclaimed in a whisper.

The fat prince didn't share her enthusiasm. Jeridi worried about what he deemed revelation. The prince's thoughts turned to sorrow for his brothers, and Reflection heard the prince's internal voice: *Oh, you poor fools!*

"Poor fools indeed," Reflection mused, watching the rest of the Partakers taking their seats.

The new Steward of the Empire—Admiral Vedigar—arose to begin the Feast of Sorrows. But as Vedigar moved to the Presider's stand the servant Practil emerged from the palace.

"Ah, right on time!" Reflection beamed.

There were enthralling particles within the servant. "A wise choice, Solidin. But I expected nothing less from you."

Practil staggered down the steps, his brown hair disheveled and his clothing dirty and tattered. He stumbled awkwardly, an enforced drunkenness the elf controlling him intended to use to grab attention.

And attention it grabbed. Hushed gasped filled the banquet yard as Practil neared.

"Isn't that Kaescis's servant?" Ilnea warily asked Jeridi. The fat prince answered only in his mind.

"We have failed!" Practil screamed, bumping into one of the long tables. Reflection could sense the Partakers' utter disgust at the outcry. Practil staggered, stumbling through the banquet yard. "Our prince is dead! And all hope for the empire lost with him!" The servant jolted, a result of the elf relinquishing his enthralling spell.

"Oh no!" Practil cried with utter horror, "What have I done?!" The servant fell to his knees, sobbing at what he considered a disgraceful act.

"Don't be too hard on yourself, Practil," Reflection said, rising out of his chair and passing through it. "You've initiated the beginning of the end. And that is to be commended."

THE END OF

Book One of
TALES OF THE AMULET

TO BE CONTINUED IN…
THE DARK NECROMANCER

GLOSSARY

For a complete glossary of names, people, places, objects, and terms found in *A Prince's Errand*, visit our website at www.legendsofkalda.com/glossary.html. Pronunciations and brief descriptions or definitions included.

CONNECT WITH THE AUTHORS

Stay up to date on future releases, upcoming Kickstarter campaigns, booksignings, and author appearances by signing up for Dan Zangari & Robert Zangari's mailing list at http://www.legendsofkalda.com/newsletter.html

Official Facebook Page https://www.facebook.com/legendsofkalda

AUTHOR'S AFTERWORD

ROBERT ZANGARI

The idea for *A Prince's Errand* came about while I was working on what is now going to be the fourth novel in this series, *The Mages' Agenda*. It first came about as a prequel novella idea. I was starting to write the short stories for our series and I thought it might be fun to write a larger work, just not something the size of a novel. It would be something along the lines of Robert Jordan's *A New Spring*.

Several of my readers had questions about our main characters, Iltar and Cornar, and they wanted to know more about their past. How did Cornar become such a great fighter? Where did he get his weapons? Why is Iltar 'broken'? Those questions sparked ideas that eventually made it into this book, particularly the dream-realm, Vabenack. I had wondered for years how I was going to tell the story of Iltar and Cornar's pasts, but those most critical moments happened thirty plus years before Tales of the Amulet.

Those ideas floated around for awhile, but nothing happened.

I was working on Treachery in the Kingdom, which will be the fifth installment in the series, when my wife, Tamila, urged me to do a rewrite. Back then our novels were published in the present tense, with a third person perspective. I liked it, but a decent chunk of our readers found the pacing distracting. So, that birthed the idea for *A Prince's Errand*. She had read the first book, then titled *The Dragons' Legacy*, while we were dating. She hated it. And she ***loves*** fantasy fiction.

I decided to stop working on Treachery in the Kingdom and start the series over. People had liked our books. We sold out at book signings. But we weren't seeing the success we wanted. So, enter *A Prince's Errand*.

This novel, well epic really, marks a new era for mine and my dad's book series. My dad's been working on these stories since 1991. We first published in 2013, but since then we've learned a lot about the publishing world. *A Prince's Errand* is a manifestation of all of our lessons learned.

I hope you enjoyed it. There are more to come, hopefully a total of twelve novels and twelve short stories. Nearly half of those are already written, but they need to be rewritten and changed to match the caliber of *A Prince's Errand*.

I wish to thank all of our readers for all their feedback and questions. You have helped us shape the Kalda Universe. Thank you for your support.

–Robert Zangari
Salt Lake City, 2019

ACKNOWLEDGEMENTS

Though we only started working on *A Prince's Errand* in 2018, the groundwork for the novel stretches back several decades. There have been many people along the way that have helped us refine our craft and hone this story that is TALES OF THE AMULET.

First and foremost, we want to thank the wonderful team that has helped us create such a fabulous book. Kerem Beyit is such a wonderful artist who has captured our imagination and brought it to life, visually. We are in awe over his talents and abilities to create stunning pieces of art. Whether it's our pieces or others he has produced, we find ourselves staring for hours at the meticulous detail he puts into every scene. Suleyman Temiz is another wonderful artist that has helped us bring our ideas to life. He has refined the details of various pieces of art relevant to our works. Linda Branam, our editor. Linda has refined our words in such a way that has left us stunned. She has brought a professional polish to the novel that was beyond our expectations.

We would like to thank our wives, Belinda and Tamila for supporting us in our writing career. Belinda has been an encouraging wife and mother through various seasons of life. She has been there from the beginning and supported us from the earliest day when the Legends of Kalda were merely an idea.

Tamila needs a special acknowledgement of her own. If it were not for her, *A Prince's Errand* wouldn't exist. As an avid reader and devotee of the fantasy genre, her opinion has helped us shape a story that has been the best thing we've ever written.

We wish to thank all of our Beta-Readers who have helped us refine our craft over the years. Your questions and feedback have been invaluable. And a special thank you to one Beta-Reader in particular, Ginger Heuer, who has voraciously read all of our works—your opinion has been greatly influential.

And now a heartfelt thank you to all our fellow authors that we have crossed paths and who have shared their knowledge and experience with us. We've learned much for each of you and we wouldn't be here today if it were not for you.

Kickstarter Backers

And now we would like to acknowledge and give thanks to the following people who helped bring *A Prince's Errand* to life by contributing to our Kickstarter campaign. First and foremost we want to give a special thanks to those contributors who backed the project at the "Patron-for-Life" tier: Patricia Johnson, John Johnson, Devon Nelson, Becca Summers. We also want to make a special dedicatory note to Ben Perkins who loved the fantasy genre.

Abdul Hadi Sid Ahmed • Adam Donovan • Adam T. Billups • A. Gadd •

Alex Hanold • Ser Alexander of House Ourique • Anthony (Tony) Hernandez • Barde Press • Belinda D. • Benjy Milder • Beth Ferris • BobaFettish • Bradon Barfuss • Brian Griffin • Cameron Day • Christopher J. Smith • Christian Meyer • Christopher Heuer • Clifton Roberts • Cory Finch • Craig Hatch • Dale A. Russell • Dalton Rodriguez • Aunt Debbie • Denali Hatch • Dennis Romback • Don Ferris • Elijah "Wolfie" Dennis • Emily Wagner • Eoin Burke • Eric Nielsen • Eric Travoli • Eugéne Roux • Ezra Choudhury • Franklin E. Powers, Jr. • Gary • Bruno Geraldes • Ginger Heuer • Gordon Milligan • Gordon D. Sturgeon • Hilary Anderson • Ivan Torres • Jade L. Johnson • James Hammond • James Heuer • Jay Cone • Jimmy Lopez • Jeff Heuer • Jeffrey "Jeff Bob" Combs • Jennifer Kinne • Jennifer Priester • Jenny Sullivan • Joel Baumgart • John Chattaway • Josh D. • Joshua Preece • Katherine Thomas • L. Shawn Lindsey • Lady Wild Rain • Lily Heuer • Luceil Heuer • Mark C. • Marvin W. Weddle • Matt Armstrong • Matt Heuer • Meghan Ferris • Mikael Monnier • Mollie Openshaw • Morgan Ewers • Nathan Memmott • Nick Goertzen • P. Morin • Pedro Silva • Phil Johnson • Richard Radgoski • Rico • Russell Ventimeglia • Ryan Pearmain • Scott Maynard • SkEyesOGrey • Shawn Hanna • Spencer Thurman • Steffen Nyeland • Stephen Hughes •Tim • Tellgryn • Travis Miller • Tristan Retzlaff • William Stewart Armstrong • Zach Jackson.

ABOUT THE AUTHORS

Dan Zangari is the creator of the Legends of Kalda fantasy universe, a work-in-development since the early 1990's. He received a Bachelor's of Science in Aerospace Engineering from the University of Southern California and a Masters Degree in Systems Management. His love for science fiction and fantasy prompted the creation of this fantasy universe. When he's not writing he enjoys reading, watching movies, spending quality time with family and serving in his local church congregation.

Robert Zangari is the co-author of the various books which belong to the Legends of Kalda universe. He studied Bio-Medical Engineering at the University of Utah; however, his love for stories and storytelling took him down a different career path. When he's not writing he enjoys spending time with his wife and daughters, playing video games, practicing martial arts and immersing himself in a good story.

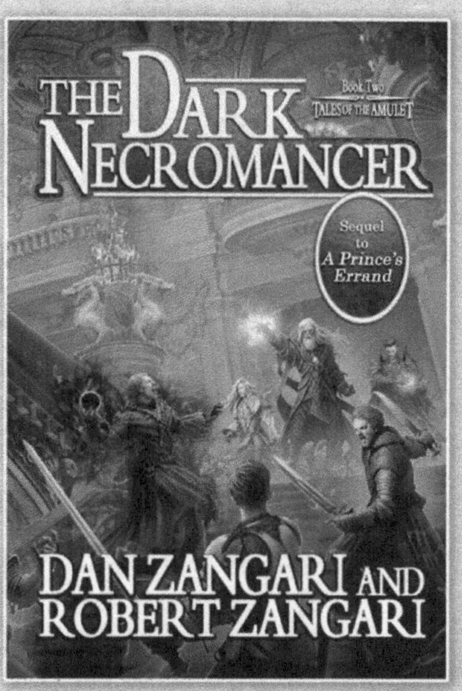

THE DARK NECROMANCER
Book Two
TALES OF THE AMULET
Sequel to A Prince's Errand
DAN ZANGARI AND ROBERT ZANGARI